THE WAY OF ALL FLESH

THE WAY OF
ALL FLESH

AMBROSE
PARRY

CANONGATE

First published in Great Britain and the USA in 2018 by Canongate Books Ltd,
14 High Street, Edinburgh EH1 1TE

canongate.co.uk

Distributed in the USA by Publishers Group West

1

British Library Cataloguing-in-Publication Data
A catalogue record for this book is available on
request from the British Library

ISBN 978 1 78689 378 9
EXPORT ISBN 978 1 78689 379 6

Typeset in Van Dijck by Palimpsest Book Production Ltd,
Falkirk, Stirlingshire

Printed and bound in Great Britain by Clays Ltd, Elcograf S.p.A.

MIX
Paper from
responsible sources
FSC® C018072

For Natalie

ONE

No decent story ought to begin with a dead prostitute, and for that, apologies, for it is not something upon which respectable persons would desire to dwell. However, it was the very assumption that the gentle folk of Edinburgh would shy from such a thing that set Will Raven upon his fateful path during the winter of 1847. Raven would not have wished anyone to consider the discovery of poor Evie Lawson as the beginning of his own story, but what truly motivated him was the determination that neither would it be the end of hers.

He found her four flights up on the Canongate, in a cold and crooked wee garret. The place was reeking of drink and sweat, barely tempered by a merciful note of something more perfumed: a womanly musk to be sure, if cheap and redolent only of a woman who sold herself. With these scents in his nostrils, if he closed his eyes he could imagine she was still there, about to haul herself down to the street for maybe the third or fourth time in as many hours. But his eyes were open, and he didn't have to feel for the absence of a pulse to know otherwise.

Raven had seen enough death to understand that her passing from this life into the next had not been an easy one. The sheets on the bed were swirled up around her, testament to more writhing than she ever feigned in her counterfeit passion, and he feared it lasted longer than any of her customers ever did. Her body, far from lying in repose, was in a state of contortion, as though the pain that had carried her off was still with her and there had been no release in death. Her brows remained contracted, her lips drawn apart. There were collections of froth at the corners of her mouth.

Raven laid a hand on her arm and quickly withdrew it. The cold was a shock, though it shouldn't have been. He was no stranger to handling a corpse, but seldom one whose touch he had known when warm. In this moment of contact, something ancient in him was moved by how she had gone from a person to a thing.

Many before him had seen her transformed in this room: from the sum of their desires to a wretched vessel for their unwanted seed, adored and then despised in the moment they spilled it.

Not him, though. Whenever they had lain together, the only transformation he contemplated was the desire to elevate her above this. He was not merely another customer. They were friends. Weren't they? That was why she shared with him her hopes that she might find a position as a maid in a respectable house, and why he had promised to make enquiries on her behalf, once he began to move in the right circles.

That was why she came to him for help.

She wouldn't tell him what the money was for, only that it was urgent. Raven guessed she owed somebody, but it was pointless trying to prevail upon her to reveal who. Evie was too practised a deceiver for that. She had seemed mightily relieved and tearfully grateful that he had got it, though. He didn't tell her from where, concealing a concern that he might have put himself in hock to the self-same money-lender, effectively transferring Evie's debt to him.

It was two guineas, as much as he might expect to live on for several weeks, and thus a sum he had no immediate means of paying back. He hadn't cared, though. He wanted to help. Raven knew there were those who would scoff at the notion, but if Evie believed she could reinvent herself as a housemaid, then he had been prepared to believe it twice as hard on her behalf.

The money had not saved her, however, and now there would be no escape.

He looked around the room. The stumps of two candles were guttering in the necks of gin bottles, a third long ago melted down to nothing. In the tiny grate, the embers were barely glowing in a fire she would otherwise have sparingly replenished hours ago from the coals in a nearby scuttle. By the bed was a shallow basin of water, wet rags draped over its rim and a ewer alongside. It was what she used to clean herself afterwards. Close by it on the floor lay an upended gin bottle, a modest puddle testifying to there being little left inside when it tumbled.

There was no label on the bottle, its provenance unknown and therefore suspect. It would not be the first time some back-alley gut-rot distiller had inadvertently brewed up a lethal draught. Complicating this thesis was the sight of a bottle of brandy on the windowsill, still half full. It must have been a client who brought it.

Raven wondered if the same individual witnessed Evie's throes and left it behind in his hurry to escape the aftermath. If so, why didn't he call for help? Possibly because to some, being found with a sick hoor was no better than being found with a dead one, so why draw attention to yourself? That was Edinburgh for you: public decorum and private sin, city of a thousand secret selves.

Aye. Sometimes they didn't even need to spill their seed for the vessel to be transformed.

He looked once more upon the glassy hollowness in her eyes, the contorted mask that was a mockery of her face. He had to swallow back the lump in his throat. Raven had first set eyes upon her four years ago when he was but a schoolboy, boarding at George Heriot's. He recalled the whispers behind hands of the older boys who knew the truth of what they were looking at when they spied her walking along the Cowgate. They were full of that curious mix of lustful fascination and fearful scorn, wary of what their own instincts were making them feel. They wanted her as they hated her, even then. Nothing changed.

At that age, the future seemed unattainable even as he was hurtling towards it. To Raven, she appeared an emissary of a world he was not yet permitted to inhabit. For that reason, he regarded her as someone above him, even after he discovered that the future was unavoidably here, and learned how easily certain things *were* attainable.

She seemed so much older, so much more worldly, until he came to understand that she had seen only a small, grim part of the world, and far more of that than any woman should. Woman? Girl. He later learned that she was younger than him by almost a year. She must have been fourteen when he saw her on the Cowgate. How she had grown in his mind between that moment and the first time he had her: a promise of true womanhood and all he dreamed it had to offer.

Her world had been small and squalid. She deserved to see a wider one, a better one. That was why he gave her the money. Now it was gone and so was she, and Raven was none the wiser as to what his debt had paid for.

For a moment he felt as though tears were about to come, but a vigilant instinct cautioned him that he must get out of this place before he was seen.

He left the room on quiet feet, closing the door softly. He felt like a thief and a coward as he crept down the stairs, abandoning her to preserve his own reputation. From elsewhere in the close he could hear the sounds of copulation, the exaggerated cries of a young woman feigning her ecstasy to hasten the end.

Raven wondered who would find Evie now. Her landlady most likely: the redoubtably sleekit Effie Peake. Though she preferred to pretend ignorance when it suited her, she missed little that went on under her roof unless she had already succumbed to the gin for the night. Raven felt sure the hour was yet too early for that, hence the softness of his tread.

He left out the back way and through the middens, emerging from an alleyway onto the Canongate a good forty yards west of Evie's close. Beneath the black sky, the air felt cold but far from fresh. The smells of ordure were inescapable around here, so many lives piled one upon the other in the foetid labyrinth that was the Old Town, like Bruegel's *Tower of Babel* or Botticelli's *Map of Hell*.

Raven knew he should repair to his cold and joyless wee room in Bakehouse Close for one last night. He had a whole new beginning ahead of him the next day, and he ought to rest himself ahead of it. But he also knew sleep was unlikely to come after what he had just witnessed. It was not a night for solitude, or for sobriety.

The only antidote to being confronted with death was the hearty embrace of life, even if that embrace was smelly, sweaty and rough.

TWO

itken's tavern was a morass of bodies, a thunderous noise of male voices ever rising to be heard over each other, and all enveloped in a thick fog of pipe smoke. Raven did not partake of it himself but enjoyed its sweetness in his nose, all the more in an establishment such as this for what it covered up.

He stood at the gantry sipping ale, talking to nobody in particular, alone but not lonely. It was a warm place to lose oneself, the greater cacophony better than silence as a backdrop for his thoughts, but he also enjoyed the diversions afforded by homing in on individual conversations, as if each of them were tiny vignettes playing out for his entertainment. There was talk of the new Caledonian Railway Station being built at the end of Princes Street, fears expressed about the possibility of hordes of starving Irishmen finding their way along the track from Glasgow.

Any time he turned his head he saw faces he recognised, some from long before he was permitted inside an establishment such as this. The Old Town teemed with thousands of people, glimpsed upon the street and never seen again, and yet at the same time it could feel like a village. There were always familiar faces anywhere you looked – and always familiar eyes upon you.

He noticed a man in a tattered and ancient hat glance his way more than once. Raven didn't recognise him, but he seemed to recognise Raven, and there was little affection in his gaze. Someone he had gotten into a brawl with, no doubt, though the same draught that precipitated the fight had also blurred the memory. From the sour look on his face, Tattered-hat must have taken second prize.

In truth, mere drink might not have been the cause, on Raven's part at least. There was a dark want in him sometimes, one he was learning to be wary of, though not enough to be the master of it. He felt a stirring of it tonight inside that gloomy garret, and could not in honesty say whether he had come here to drown it or to feed it.

He met Tattered-hat's gaze once more, whereupon the man scurried towards the door. He moved more purposefully than most men might exit a tavern, casting a final glance Raven's way before disappearing into the night.

Raven returned to his ale and put him from his mind.

As he raised the tankard again, he felt a slap on his back, the hand remaining to grip his shoulder. Instinctively he pivoted on a heel, fist formed tight and his elbow drawn back to strike.

'Hold, Raven. That's no way to treat a colleague. At least not one who still has coins in his pocket to match his drouth.'

It was his friend Henry, whom he must have missed in the throng.

'My apologies,' he replied. 'One cannot be too careful in Aitken's these days, for standards have slipped and I'm told they're even letting surgeons in.'

'I didn't think to see a man of your prospects still patronising an Old Town hostelry. Aren't you moving on to fresh pastures? It won't make for the perfect start should you present yourself to your new employer having had a bellyful of ale the night before.'

Raven knew Henry wasn't serious, but it was nonetheless a timely reminder not to push things too far. One or two would be adequate to help him sleep, but now that he had company, one or two was unlikely to be the whole of it.

'And what of you?' Raven batted back. 'Have you not duties of your own in the morning?'

'Indeed, but as I expected my old friend Will Raven to be indisposed, I sought the ministrations of another associate, Mr John Barleycorn, to soothe the woes cast by my duties today.'

Henry handed over some coins and their tankards were refreshed. Raven thanked him and watched Henry take a long pull at the beer.

'A taxing shift, was it?' Raven asked.

'Bashed-in heads, broken bones and another death from peritonitis. Another young woman, poor thing. Nothing we could do for her. Professor Syme could not discern the cause, which drove him to a state of high dudgeon, and which of course was everyone else's fault.'

'There'll be a post-mortem, then.'

'Yes. A pity you are not free to attend. I'm sure you could offer greater insight than our current pathologist. Half the time he's as pickled as the specimens in his laboratory.'

'A young woman, you say?' Raven asked, thinking of the one he just left. Evie would be afforded no such attention once she was found.

'Yes, why?'

'No reason.'

Henry took a long swallow and eyed Raven thoughtfully. He knew he was under exacting scrutiny. Henry was quite the diagnostician, and not merely of what ailed the body.

'Are you well enough, Raven?' he asked, his tone sincere.

'I'll be better once I've got this down me,' he replied, making an effort to sound cheerier. Henry was not so easily fooled, though.

'It's just that . . . you have a look about you, of which I have long since learned to be wary. I don't share your perverse appetite for mayhem and nor do I wish to find myself treating your wounds when I ought to be resting.'

Raven knew he had no grounds for protest. All charges were true, including the glimmer of that dark want he feared was in him tonight. Fortunately, given Henry's company, on this occasion he felt sure the ale would quench it.

You've the devil in you, his mother used to tell him when he was a child. Sometimes it was meant in humour, but sometimes it was not.

'I am a man of prospects now, Henry,' he assured him, proffering payment and gesturing for two refills, 'and have no wish to jeopardise them.'

'A man of prospects indeed,' Henry replied. 'Though why the esteemed Professor of Midwifery should award such a coveted position to a reprobate such as yourself remains a mystery to me.'

Reluctant as he was to admit it, it was a question that gave Raven pause too. He had worked hard to win the professor's approval, but there had been several equally diligent and committed candidates for the apprenticeship. He had no solid notion of why he had been given the nod ahead of the rest, and did not like to dwell upon the precariousness of such caprice.

'The professor hails from humble stock,' was as much as he could offer, an answer unlikely to satisfy Henry any more than it satisfied Raven. 'Perhaps he believes that such opportunities should not be the sole preserve of the high-born.'

'Or perhaps he lost a wager, and you are the forfeit.'

The drink flowed, and with it old tales. It helped. The image of Evie flickered in and out of his vision like the guttering candles in her room. But listening to Henry, Raven was reminded of the world Evie did not get to see, reminded of the opportunity waiting for him across the North Bridge. A little of his love for this place and for the Old Town in general had died tonight. It was time to leave it all behind, and if anyone was a believer in new beginnings, it was Will Raven. He had reinvented himself once before and was about to do so again.

Several tankards later they stood outside Aitken's watching their breath turn to steam in the chill of the night air.

'It's been good to see you,' Henry said. 'But I'd best be getting my head down. Syme's operating tomorrow, and he's all the pricklier when he can smell last night's tobacco and beer on his assistants.'

'Aye, "prickly" is the word for Syme,' Raven replied. 'With emphasis on the first part. Meanwhile I'm back to Mrs Cherry's for one last night.'

'Bet you'll miss her and her lumpy porridge,' Henry called out as he turned onto South Bridge in the direction of the Infirmary. 'Not to mention her effervescent personality.'

'For sure, she and Syme would make a fine match,' Raven called back, crossing the road and heading east in the direction of his lodgings.

Raven knew there were elements of his time here that he might one day regard with nostalgic fondness or regret, but his accommodations were not among them. Ma Cherry was a cantankerous old crone who resembled her name only in that she was round and reddened, for there was certainly nothing sweet about her. She was as sour as earwax and as desiccated as a corpse in the desert, but she kept a lodging house that was among the cheapest in the town; just above the workhouse in terms of comfort and cleanliness.

A smir of cold rain blew about him as he headed down the High Street towards Netherbow. Clouds had gathered and the moonlight disappeared since he made his way to Aitken's. He noticed that some of the street lights remained unlit, making it almost impossible to avoid the piles of muck on the pavement. He inwardly cursed the lamplighter who had failed to do what Raven considered to be a straightforward job. If he himself was as incompetent, lives would be lost.

Lighting fell within the responsibility of the police office, as did keeping the gutters clear. Their main priority, however, was the investigation and recovery of stolen property. If they observed that as well as their other duties, Raven thought, then every thief in the Lothians could sleep easy.

As he approached Bakehouse Close he stepped on something soft and his left shoe began to fill with water; at least he hoped it was water. He hopped for a couple of yards, trying to shake off whatever was clinging to his sole. Then he became aware that a figure had emerged from a doorway and was loitering in front of him. He wondered what the fellow was waiting for, and why he would be lingering with the rain becoming heavier. Then Raven drew close enough to see his face, which in the gathering darkness was also close enough to smell the rancid decay from his carious teeth.

Raven did not know his name, but he had seen him before: one of Flint's men. Raven had christened him the Weasel, after his furtive manner and rodent-like features. The Weasel did not strike him as the type to chance confronting Raven alone, which meant he was bound to have an accomplice nearby. Probably that slow-witted fellow he was with the last time: Peg, Raven had named him, for the sole tooth standing amid his ruin of a mouth. Raven had probably passed him without realising a few moments ago. He would be hiding in another doorway ready to cut him off if he ran.

This encounter was not mere happenstance, he realised. He remembered the man who had been staring at him and then departed so purposefully from the tavern.

'Mr Raven, you're not trying to avoid me, are you?'

'As I can think of nothing that would commend your company, then my general intention *would* be to avoid you, but I was not aware I was being sought.'

'Anyone who owes Mr Flint will always be sought. But you can guarantee my absence just as soon as you make good on your debt.'

'Make good on it? I have barely owed it a fortnight. So how about you sub me an advance on that absence and get out of my way.'

Raven brushed past him and resumed walking. The Weasel did not seek to apprehend him, and nor did he immediately follow. He would be waiting for his accomplice to catch up. He and Peg were used to breaking the bones of already broken men, and some craven instinct perhaps detected that Raven had a greater stomach for the fight. The ale might have doused what burned in him before, but the sight of this sphincter-blossom was reigniting it.

Raven walked slowly, aware of the footsteps behind him. He was searching in the gloom for a weapon. Anything could be turned to such a purpose: you simply needed to know how best to use it. His foot happened upon something wooden and he bent to lift it. It was a splintered length, but solid enough.

Raven turned around and rose in one movement, the stick drawn back in his right hand, then something exploded inside his head. There was light everywhere and a whiplash movement, as though his inert body was being hauled like a dead weight by the momentum of his head. He hit the wet cobbles with a rattle of bones, too fast to make any attempt to cushion his fall.

He opened his dazed eyes and looked up. The blow had rendered him insensible, he reasoned, for he was having visions. There was a monster above him. A giant.

Raven was dragged from the street into the dark of an alley by a creature that had to be seven feet tall. His head alone was twice the size of any man's, his forehead impossibly overgrown like an outcrop of rocks at a cliff-edge. Raven was paralysed by pain and shock, unable to react as he saw this Gargantua rear up before him and bring down a heel. The sound of his own cry echoed off the walls as pain erupted inside him. He flailed in response, curling his limbs tight about him, then felt another post-holer of a blow drive down through the huge trunk of his assailant's leg.

Gargantua crouched to sit astride him, pinning his arms to the floor with the sheer weight of his thighs. Everything about this brute seemed stretched and disproportionate, as though certain parts of him had just kept growing and left the rest behind. When he opened his mouth, there were even gaps between his teeth indicating that his gums had kept spreading out around them.

The pain was indescribable, worsened by the knowledge that Gargantua's fists were free to rain down more damage. No amount of alcohol would have been sufficient to dull his senses through this, else the operating theatres would be going through more whisky than Aitken's.

His mind was a storm, coherent thought nigh impossible amidst such agony and confusion, but one thing seemed clear: there was no prospect of putting up any kind of fight. If this monster wished to kill him, then he was going to die here in this alley.

Gargantua's face was a compellingly grotesque vision, more fierce and distorted than any gargoyle clinging to the walls of a church, but it was his thick, sausage-like fingers that drew Raven's gaze in the gloom. With his own hands helplessly restrained, he was entirely at the mercy of whatever these outsize pommels might wreak.

Raven felt relief when they were directed to rifling through his pockets, but this was short-lived as he remembered that there was little to be found there. Gargantua held what few coins Raven had left in the palm of his hand, which was when the Weasel emerged from the shadows, pocketing the money and crouching down alongside the monster.

'Aye, not so free with your mouth now, are you, Mr Raven?'

The Weasel produced a knife from his pocket and held it up in what little light was to be found in the alley, making sure Raven could see it. It was about four inches long, the blade thin, a bloodstained rag wrapped around the wooden handle for a surer grip.

Raven silently prayed for a quick end to his ordeal. Perhaps a stab upwards under his ribs. His pericardium would fill with blood, his heart would stop beating and it would all be over.

'So now that I have your attention, let us properly address the issue of your debt to Mr Flint.'

Raven could barely find the breath to speak, with the weight of the monster crushing him and the pain still gripping his trunk. The Weasel seemed to notice and ordered the hulk to raise himself just enough for Raven to be able to issue a whisper.

'See, it seems you were keeping your light under a bushel. Since lending you the sum, we have learned that you are the son of a well-to-do lawyer in St Andrews. So having re-evaluated your status, Mr Flint has brought forward the expected date of redemption.'

Raven felt a new weight upon him, though Gargantua had eased himself off. It was the burden of a lie returned to its teller, in accordance with the law of unforeseen consequences.

'My father is long dead,' he wheezed out. 'Do you think if I could have borrowed from him, I would be seeking out cut-throat usurers?'

'That's as may be, but the son of a lawyer must have other connections, in time of need.'

'I don't. But as I told Flint when he lent me, I have prospects. When I begin to earn, I will be able to pay, with interest.'

The Weasel leaned closer, the stink from his mouth worse than anything in the gutter.

'Oh, there will be interest. But for an educated man, you don't seem to understand this very well. Mr Flint doesn't wait for prospects. When you owe him money, you find a way to get it.'

The Weasel pressed the knife against Raven's left cheek.

'And just so you know, us usurers don't only cut throats.'

He drew the blade across, slow and deep, all the time looking Raven in the eye.

'A wee something to remind you of your new priorities,' he said.

The Weasel slapped Gargantua on the shoulder by way of telling him they were done. He climbed to his feet, freeing Raven to put a hand to his face. Blood was welling through his fingers as they tenderly probed the wound.

The Weasel then pivoted on a heel and kicked Raven in the stomach where he lay.

'You find the money,' he said. 'Or next time it's an eye.'

THREE

aven lay in the dark for a while and concentrated solely on breathing. With his assailants gone, he felt relief flood through him, an uncontainable elation that he was not dead. Unfortunately this manifested itself in an unexpected urge to laugh, which proved far more containable under protest from his ribs. Were they broken, he wondered. How much damage had been done? Were any of his organs contused? He could imagine blood dribbling between the layers of the pleura, putting pressure on his bruised lung, constricting its expansion even now that the brute had removed himself.

He put the image from his mind. All that mattered was that he was still breathing, for now, and while that remained true, his prospects were good.

He put his hand to his cheek again. It was wet with blood and mushy, like a bruised peach. The wound was deep and wide. There was no option to return to Mrs Cherry's without this being seen to.

Raven dragged himself to Infirmary Street, where he decided it would be best to avoid the porter's lodge and the stern questions his appearance would surely prompt. Instead he made his way along the wall to the section most favoured by the house surgeons for climbing over. Henry and his peers used this means of ingress when they did not wish to draw attention to late-night excursions, as such behaviour might see them called in front of the hospital board. It took several attempts in his enfeebled state, but Raven eventually hauled himself over the wall before climbing in through a low window that was always left unlatched for this specific purpose.

He shambled along the corridor, leaning against the wall when his breathing became too laboured and painful. He crept past the surgical ward without incident, hearing loud snoring emanating from just behind the door. The noise was likely coming from the night nurses, who frequently imbibed the wines and spirits supplied for the benefit of the patients in order to ensure for themselves a good night's sleep.

Raven made it to Henry's door and knocked repeatedly on it, every second it remained unanswered adding to the fear that his friend was in a post-tavern stupor. Eventually, the door swung inward and Henry's bleary and tousled visage appeared around it. His initial response was one of horror at what creature had visited him in the night, then came recognition.

'Gods, Raven. What the bloody hell has happened to you?'

'Someone took exception to the fact that I had nothing worth stealing.'

'We'd better get you downstairs. That's going to need stitching.'

'I diagnosed that much myself,' Raven said. 'Do you know a competent surgeon?'

Henry fixed him with a look. 'Don't test me.'

Raven lay back on the bed and attempted to relax, but this was not easy given that Henry was approaching his lacerated face with a large suture needle. He was trying to recount just how many times Henry's tankard had been refilled, calculating the implications for how neatly he would be capable of stitching. Drunk or sober, no quality of needlework was going to spare him a scar, which would be the first thing anyone noticed about him in the future. This was likely to have ramifications for his career, but he could not afford to think about that right then. Most immediately his priority was to remain still, but the pains racking him and the prospect of Henry's needle were militating against that.

'I realise that it's difficult, but I must ask you to refrain from writhing, and when I commence, from flinching. Part of the wound is close to your eye and if I get the stitching wrong it will droop.'

'Then I will have to be rechristened Isaiah,' he replied.

'Why?' Henry asked; then it came to him. 'Mother of God, Raven.'

Henry's expression was funnier than the joke, but any relief it gave Raven came at a sharp cost to his ribs.

Raven lay still and attempted to transport himself from the here and now, so that he was less conscious of the procedure. Unfortunately, his first destination, quite involuntarily, was Evie's room, the sight of her twisted body appearing in his mind just as Henry's needle first penetrated his cheek. He felt it push through the skin and into the soft layer below, could not but picture the curve of it bridging the sides of the wound before re-emerging, which was when he felt the tug of the cat-gut through his already ravaged face. It hurt far more than the Weasel's knife, that being over in a couple of seconds.

He put up a hand as Henry was about to commence the second stitch.

'Have you any ether?' he asked.

Henry looked at him disapprovingly. 'No. You'll just need to tolerate it. It's not as though you're having a leg off.'

'That's easy for you to say. Have you ever had your face stitched?'

'No, and that good fortune might be related to the fact that nor do I have an inclination to bark at the moon and pick fights with Old Town ne'er-do-wells.'

'I did not pick any— ow!'

'Stop talking,' Henry warned, having recommenced. 'I can't do this if your cheek is not still.'

Raven fixed him with an ungrateful glare.

'The ether doesn't always seem to work anyway,' Henry told him, tugging the cat-gut tight on the second loop. 'Syme has just about given up on it, and with someone dying of the stuff recently, I think that will nail down the lid.'

'Someone died of it?'

'Yes. Down in England somewhere. Coroner said it was a direct result of the ether but Simpson continues to champion it.' Henry paused in what he was doing. 'You can ask the man about it yourself when you start your apprenticeship with him in the morning.'

Henry continued with his needlework, his head bent low over Raven's face. He was close enough that Raven could smell the beer on his breath. Nonetheless, his hand was steady, and Raven got used to a rhythm of penetration and tug. No stitch was any less painful than its predecessor, but nor were any of them more painful than the ache in his ribs.

Henry stepped back to examine his handiwork. 'Not bad,' he declared. 'Maybe I should conduct all my surgery after a bellyful at Aitken's.'

Henry soaked a piece of lint in cold water and applied it to the wound. The coolness of the material was surprisingly soothing, the only pleasant sensation Raven had felt since his last swallow of ale.

'I can't send you back into the arms of Mrs Cherry looking like that,' Henry said. 'I'll give you a dose of laudanum and put you in my bed. I'll sleep on the floor for what's left of the night.'

'I'm indebted, Henry, truly. But please don't allude to Mrs Cherry's arms again. In my current state, the image is liable to make me spew.'

Henry fixed him with one of his scrutinising stares, but there was mischief in his tone.

'You know she provides extra services for a small additional fee, don't you?' he said. 'I gather many of her young lodgers have sought comfort in those arms. She's a widow and needs the money. There's no shame in it. I mean, between the scar and the droopy eye, you may have to begin revising your standards.'

Henry led Raven to his bed, where he lay down delicately. He hurt in more places simultaneously than he had ever hurt in individually. His face was full of cat-gut and, joking aside, he really might have to alter his expectations with regard to his marriage prospects. But it could all have been so much worse. He was still alive, and tomorrow was a new beginning.

'Right,' said Henry, 'let's get you that laudanum. And if you are going to be sick, please remember that I'm on the floor beside you and aim for my feet rather than my head.'

FOUR

arah was tarrying in the professor's study when the
bell rang, an unwelcome but inevitable interruption
to a moment of tranquillity. She was taking time and
care about her duties as she loved being in this room.
It was a sanctuary of calm insulated from the chaos in the rest
of the house, but her opportunities for asylum were infrequent
and usually short-lived.

She had taken some trouble over the laying of the fire, ensuring
that there was a plentiful mound of coal piled in the grate. The
fire was lit winter and summer to ensure the comfort of the
patients the doctor saw here, but it was a particularly cold day
and it was taking some time for the air in the room to thaw. A
small amount of ice had formed on the inside of the window
beside the doctor's desk, a delicate pattern of fern-like fronds
that disappeared when she breathed on it. She wiped the resulting
moisture away with a cloth and took a moment to admire the
view. On a clear day such as this you could see all the way to
Fife. At least that is what she had been told. She had never
ventured much beyond the outskirts of Edinburgh herself.

The desk beside the window was piled high with books and
manuscripts that Sarah had to clean around without disturbing.
She had over time perfected her technique, a skill acquired through

painful trial and error and the rescuing of errant scraps of paper from the fireplace.

The room had not always seemed so welcoming. When she first came into Dr Simpson's service, she had been quite terrified by what confronted her in here. Against one wall stood a tall cabinet upon several shelves of which sat jars of anatomical specimens: all manner of human organs immersed in yellowing fluid. More troubling still was that many of them were damaged, diseased or malformed, as though their very presence was not unsettling enough.

In time she had come to be fascinated by all of it, even the jar that contained two tiny babes, face-to-face, joined together along the length of the breastbone. When she had first seen it, Sarah had been gripped by questions regarding where such a thing had come from and how it had been procured. She also wondered about the propriety of keeping such a specimen, preserving what was quite clearly human remains instead of burying them. Was it right that such a thing be displayed? Was it somehow wrong to look at it?

Beneath the shelves was a cupboard housing the doctor's teaching materials for his midwifery class. Sarah was unsure whether exploration of the cupboard's contents was permitted, but as it had not been specifically prohibited she had indulged her curiosity on the few occasions when time allowed. It contained an odd collection of pelvic bones and obstetric instruments, the use of which she could only guess at. There were forceps, of course, with which Sarah was familiar, but there were other more mysterious implements, labelled as cephalotribes, cranioclasts and perforators. Their names alone suggested something brutal and Sarah could not imagine what place they had in the delivery of a child.

In keeping with its curator, there was a distinct want of method in the organisation of the study in general and of the library in particular, which Sarah would have remedied had she the time to do so. Books seemed to be randomly allocated a position on the shelf. For instance, there was a red-leather-bound compendium of Shakespeare sandwiched between the family Bible and the *Edinburgh Pharmacopoeia*, and she recalled how a list of the family's pets had for some reason been inscribed within the cover.

Her finger reverentially touched each spine in turn as she read the titles: Paley's *Natural Theology*, *The Anatomy and Physiology of the Human Body*, Adam's *Antiquities*, Syme's *Principles of Surgery*. Then Jarvis popped his head round the door.

'Miss Grindlay is calling for you,' he said, rolling his eyes as he withdrew.

Sarah allowed the tips of her fingers to linger for a few more moments on the spines of the leather-bound volumes. It was one of the great frustrations of her position: ready access to an eclectic collection of books but very limited opportunities to read them. Her hand came to rest on a book she had not seen before. She removed it from the shelf and slipped it into her pocket.

As she left the room and headed for the stairs she became caught up in a storm of newsprint precipitating from the upper floors. The doctor was evidently on his way down. He liked to read the daily papers – the *Scotsman* and the *Caledonian Mercury* – in their entirety before getting out of bed, and thought it entertaining to drop them over the banister on his way down the stairs. This was much appreciated by the two elder children, David and Walter, who liked to ball up the paper and throw it at each other and the staff; less so by Jarvis who had to clear it all away. Sarah manoeuvred her way around falling newspaper, excitable children and grumbling butler and ascended the stairs.

She entered Aunt Mina's room on the third floor and was confronted by the usual chaos. The entire contents of Miss Mina Grindlay's wardrobe appeared to have been scattered about the room, dresses and petticoats strewn over every available surface, bed, chair and floor. Mina herself was still in her nightclothes, holding up a dress in front of the mirror before discarding it with all the others.

'There you are, Sarah. Where on earth have you been?'

Sarah assumed the question to be rhetorical and so remained silent. Mina seemed to be continually frustrated at Sarah having to perform other duties around the house, oblivious to the fact that, being the only housemaid, if she didn't lay the fires, bring the tea, clean the rooms and serve the meals there was no one else who would do so. Mrs Lyndsay seldom left the kitchen and Jarvis, butler, valet and general factotum, had his hands full tending to the doctor.

'How many times have I said,' Mina continued, 'that a woman in my position should have a lady's maid?'

Almost every time I come in here, thought Sarah.

'I can't be expected to dress myself.'

'Mrs Simpson seems to manage it,' Sarah suggested.

Mina's eyes flashed and Sarah immediately knew she had spoken out of turn. She was about to apologise, but Mina had begun to speak and it would compound her transgression to interrupt.

'My sister is a married woman and in mourning to boot. Her choice of attire is an entirely straightforward matter.'

Sarah thought of Mrs Simpson in the heavy black bombazine she had been wearing for months, pale and wan from prolonged time spent indoors.

'But Sarah, you really must refrain from giving voice to your every thought. Your opinions, unless specifically requested, should be kept to yourself. I was indulgent of this when you were new to the position, but I might have done you a disservice by not reining you in. I fear you will misspeak before someone less understanding and find you have talked yourself onto the street.'

'Yes, ma'am,' Sarah replied, casting her eyes down in contrition.

'There is much to commend the simple discipline of holding one's tongue. I have to do so often enough when I disagree with how my sister wishes to run her household. I am merely a guest here, and grateful for that, as you should be grateful for your position. We each have our duties, and dressing well is an essential one for a woman of my station.'

Mina gestured towards the mountain of clothes on the bed, indicating that she required Sarah to help her choose what she should wear.

'What about this?' Sarah held up a modest grey silk dress with a lace collar which she had starched and pressed only the day before.

Mina looked at it for a few minutes, assessing its suitability.

'Oh, it will have to do,' she said, 'although I fear it is a little too plain to have men reaching for their pens in order to write me a sonnet.'

Sarah glanced in response towards Mina's writing table. As always there was a letter in progress, and beside it a novel.

'What are you reading?' Sarah asked, knowing the subject of literature would reliably serve to put her recent impertinence from her mistress's mind.

'A novel called *Jane Eyre*, by Currer Bell. I have just finished it. I was not previously familiar with the writer.'

'Did you enjoy it?'

'That is a complex question in this case. I would prefer to discuss it with an informed party, so please feel free to take it for yourself.'

'Thank you, ma'am.'

Sarah slipped the book into her pocket alongside the other slim volume she had just procured from the library.

Now that an acceptable gown had been selected, Mina stepped into her corset and stood with her hands on her hips as Sarah grabbed the laces and pulled.

'Tighter,' Mina demanded.

'You'll be unable to breathe,' Sarah said as she hauled on the laces again.

'Nonsense,' said Mina. 'I haven't fainted yet, despite the fact that all the ladies of my acquaintance swoon with great regularity. Sometimes with an element of stagecraft,' she added, a hint of a smile playing upon her lips.

Once Mina was suitably clothed Sarah then had to style her hair. This took considerably longer than tying a corset. A starch bandoline had to be applied to ensure that the hair, once wrestled into place, would remain there throughout the course of the day. The hair was then parted in the centre at the front, braided and looped round the ears. A second parting was made across the top of the head, from ear to ear, and the hair swept up in a tight bun at the back. The task required patience and precision, two qualities when it came to styling hair that Sarah seemed to lack.

'This is why I need a lady's maid,' Mina said to her reflection, her lips pursing at Sarah's efforts. 'I know that you do your best, Sarah, but I will never attract a husband without the right kind of help.'

'I could not agree more, Miss Grindlay,' Sarah replied, gratefully laying down brush, comb and hair pins.

'The problem is that good, reliable help is so hard to come by. Look at the difficulties Mrs Simpson has had trying to find a suitable nurse for the children.'

The rapid turnover of nursery nurses was no mystery to Sarah. The Simpsons had three children: David, Walter and baby James. David and Walter were rarely confined to the nursery at the top of the house, their natural curiosity at all times indulged, and previous incumbents had baulked at the behaviour that was not just permitted but encouraged. Another factor was that Mrs Simpson seemed reluctant to fully hand over responsibility for her children to anyone else, presumably as a consequence of having already lost two at a young age.

'The Sheldrakes have just lost one of their housemaids,' Mina continued, turning in her chair to address Sarah directly.

'Which one?'

'I think her name was Rose. Do you know her?'

'Only in passing. I know the other housemaid, Milly, a little better. What happened?'

'Absconded. Just like that. Though there are rumours that she was seeing a young man. Actually the rumours are that she was seeing several.'

Mina turned back to the mirror and applied a little rouge to her cheeks. Sarah made it for her using rectified spirit, water and cochineal powder. She wondered why it should be considered so wrong for a housemaid to court male attention when it seemed to be Mina's predominant purpose.

'I met her just last week,' Sarah said. 'Outside Kennington and Jenner's.'

'How did she seem?' Mina asked, turning in her chair again.

'Fine,' Sarah replied, ever aware that duty obliged her to give a neutral answer.

In truth Rose would have seemed fine to anyone who had never met her before, but Sarah had been struck by the sullenness of her demeanour. She had come upon Rose and her mistress as they were exiting the shop on Princes Street. Mrs Sheldrake stopped to exchange pleasantries with an acquaintance, allowing Sarah and Rose to do the same, albeit more awkwardly. As Sarah had told Mina, she was more familiar with Rose's colleague Milly, and was easier in her company. Rose was 'vivacious', according to Milly, a politer way of describing a girl Sarah regarded as flighty and full of herself, and of whom she was instinctively wary.

Rose had seemed uncharacteristically reserved that day, as though weighed down by a heavier burden than the packages she was carrying. She was pale, her eyes puffy, and she said little in response to Sarah's gentle enquiries as to her health.

Sarah had glanced across at Rose's mistress, a heavy-set woman around the same age as Mrs Simpson but who seemed considerably older. This was partly due to her physical appearance, about which she did not seem to take the greatest care, and partly because of her austere countenance. Sarah wondered uncharitably what her husband must look like, never having seen Mr Sheldrake.

It was well known that Mrs Sheldrake had a temper, of which the young women in her employ frequently bore the brunt. Rose was doubtless on the receiving end more than most, but this lifeless despondency seemed more than the result of a hearty dressing down. Perhaps it was cumulative, Sarah had thought gloomily, worrying for her own future. If life in service could dull the light in someone like Rose, what might it do to her?

'Well, don't just stand there, Sarah,' Mina said, the subject of Rose's disappearance quickly forgotten. 'I'm sure you must have other things to attend to.'

Thus dismissed, Sarah left the room and made her way downstairs, thinking about the many duties she could have completed in the time it took to squeeze Mina into a dress and subdue her hair. As usual there were more things to be done than hours in which they could be accomplished, and today there was the additional task of airing one of the spare bedrooms for the arrival of the doctor's new apprentice.

Sarah wondered if he could be prevailed upon to take an interest in Mina. At least that would make the extra work his presence generated worthwhile.

FIVE

gust of wind whipped about Raven as he crossed the North Bridge, causing him to reach up with one hand to secure his hat. Its sting made the warmth of August seem a memory of a forgotten age, and within it he felt the harsh and certain promise of winter. There were other promises in that wind, however. The blast was cold but fresh, blowing away the pervasive reek that had surrounded him these past years. Here on the other side of the bridge lay quite another Edinburgh.

He turned onto Princes Street and passed Duncan and Flockhart's, where he caught sight of himself in the druggist's window. In the glass he was reminded that though the Old Town's stink could be blown away, its mark would be upon him for life. The left side of his face was swollen and bruised, the stitches sitting up prominently along the contused curve of his cheek. Beneath his hat his hair was sticking out at odd angles, matted together in places with dried blood. When he arrived at Queen Street, Dr Simpson was as likely to send him abed as a patient as to welcome him into his practice.

The pavement was broader here, the crowds thinner. The people he passed were straight-backed and assured in their gait, strolling in a manner that was purposeful and yet unhurried as they browsed the shopfronts. By contrast, the Old Town was a hill of ants, its inhabitants bowed and scuttling as they hastened about its twisted byways. Even the road seemed to lack the mud and ordure that piled up relentlessly within the narrow alleyways of the Canongate.

As he turned onto Queen Street, a brougham carriage drawn by two lively steeds pulled to a halt just ahead, prompting Raven to wonder absently if the coachman had trained his beasts to void themselves only in the poorer parts of town.

No. 52 was one of the largest houses in that part of the street, spread out over five levels if the basement was included. Broad steps, clean and recently swept, led up from the pavement to a large front entrance framed by two pillars on each side. Even the railings appeared to have been freshly painted, giving the impression that cleanliness and order would be found inside. This caused him to think of how late he was, due to Henry's laudanum. He considered what he might say by way of explaining himself. Perhaps his face would be excuse enough. And perhaps he would be told the offer of apprenticeship was void given that he had not shown sufficient decorum as to at least be prompt on his first day.

Raven straightened his hat and tried not to contemplate the condition of his clothes as he reached for the brass knocker. Before he could grasp it, the door began to open and a great beast of a dog bounded through the gap, almost bowling him to the floor. It continued towards the waiting brougham, where the coachman held open the door as though the hound itself had summoned the carriage.

The dog was followed by a figure clad in a voluminous black coat and top hat. Professor James Simpson seemed equally intent upon the carriage until his attention was taken by the waif reeling on his threshold.

Raven's new employer stopped and looked him up and down. He seemed momentarily confused before one eyebrow shot up, signalling that some form of deduction had taken place.

'Mr Raven. Not a moment too soon, yet within a moment of being too late.'

Simpson indicated with a sweeping gesture that his new apprentice should follow the dog into the carriage.

'We have an urgent case to attend – if you feel you are able,' he added archly.

Raven smiled, or at least attempted to. It was hard to know exactly what his damaged face was doing. He hauled himself aboard the carriage and attempted to squeeze in beside the dog, which seemed reluctant to surrender any part of his position on the seat to the newcomer.

No sooner had he gained a small piece of the upholstery for himself than Dr Simpson took his position opposite and called to the driver to proceed. The carriage took off at impressive speed and the dog immediately hung its head over the edge of the window, tongue lolling as it panted with delight.

Raven did not share its joy. He winced as they rattled over the cobbles, pain shooting through him as though the wheels were running over his ribs. The doctor did not fail to notice, and was intently scrutinising his damaged face. He wondered if he should try to concoct some more palatable explanation for his injuries, or whether he would be storing up greater trouble by lying to his employer on his first day.

'I should perhaps have left you in the care of our housemaid, Sarah,' Simpson said reflectively.

'Your housemaid?' Raven asked, his discomfort rendering him unable to moderate an ungracious tone. He wondered if this was Simpson's subtle way of conveying displeasure at his tardiness, downplaying his afflictions by implying that they required no greater ministration than a hot cup of tea.

'She is rather more than that,' Simpson replied. 'She helps out with the patients: dressings, bandages and so on. Quite a capable young woman.'

'I'm sure I'll manage,' Raven said, though his ribs were telling him otherwise. He hoped that the patient they were going to see could be dealt with quickly.

'What happened to you?'

'If you don't mind, I'd rather not revisit the subject,' he replied, which was honest at least. 'Suffice it to say I am glad to have left the Old Town behind me.'

The brougham turned left onto Castle Street, prompting Raven to wonder where their destination might lie: Charlotte Square, perhaps, or one of the fine townhouses on Randolph Crescent. On the bench opposite, Dr Simpson was looking through his bag, an expression upon his face indicating concern that he may have forgotten some vital piece of equipment in his hurried departure.

'To where might we be bound, professor?'

'To assist a Mrs Fraser. Elspeth, if I recall her name correctly. I haven't had the pleasure of a formal introduction.'

'A fine lady?' Raven ventured, the promise of moving in more rarefied circles like a balm to his wounds.

'No doubt, though we are unlikely to find her at her best.'

At the foot of the hill, the carriage turned left again, proceeding east away from the castle. Raven speculated that perhaps Mrs Fraser was staying at one of the impressive hotels along Princes Street. He had heard tell that wealthy ladies would often travel from the country so that physicians of Simpson's calibre might attend them.

The brougham did not stop at any of them, however, instead continuing the very length of Princes Street before turning right onto the North Bridge and taking him straight back to the very place he thought he had left behind.

The carriage drew to a stop outside a shabby building only yards from where he had found Evie last night, and just around the corner from his own lodgings. As he climbed down from the brougham he wondered if Mrs Cherry might be in the process of tossing all his belongings into the street, as he was moving out today and should already have been back to collect them this morning. He wondered too if Evie had been found yet. If not, she would be before long. The smell would become obvious soon enough, even in that squalid close.

Simpson stepped from the carriage followed by the dog. He searched the doorways and shopfronts momentarily, then set off up a narrow and dimly lit close, the dog scampering after him.

Confusion reigned in Raven's aching head. What was a man of Dr Simpson's stature and reputation doing in the Canongate? Where were the rich ladies of the New Town that he had been led to expect? What of the grand houses wherein lay the sweet-smelling wives and daughters of the quality?

Raven followed his new chief into the passageway and was confronted by a familiar ammoniacal aroma, like cabbage boiled in urine. Clearly Mrs Cherry had been sharing recipes around the neighbourhood. They climbed three storeys up a dark staircase, Simpson's pace remaining steady throughout the ascent even as Raven felt the strain grow in his thighs and an ache pound in his battered chest.

'It's always the top,' the professor observed, with gratingly good cheer.

The door was opened by a typical male inhabitant of these parts, unshaven and missing his front teeth. It always amazed Raven that he could live so close to people and yet never have seen them before, or at least not noticed them any more than the cursory assessment of whether they might be a threat. The sight of this one would ordinarily be enough for Raven to check his pockets were secure, but there was no need, they having already been emptied by the Weasel and Gargantua.

Despite his unkempt appearance, the man did not smell too bad, which came as a small relief. The same could not be said for the chamber they were shown into. The stench hit him full in the face, an ungodly combination of blood, sweat and faecal matter. He observed the merest wave of discomfort on Simpson's visage, before the doctor masked his response behind a calm veil of politeness.

The man of the house hovered at the threshold a mere moment before absenting himself with visible relief.

Mrs Fraser was lying within a tangle of visibly soiled sheets, her face contorted with pain. Raven banished an image of Evie in the throes she endured alone and confined himself to the here and now, though this was scarcely more pleasant. The patient was evidently in labour and making heavy weather of it, drenched in sweat with her face an unnaturally purple colour. She was scrawny and malnourished, similar to many of his erstwhile neighbours and almost all of the patients he had encountered both in his dispensary work and in walking the wards of the Royal Infirmary.

Simpson seemed unfazed by his surroundings, which did not bode well as far as Raven was concerned. He really did not wish to spend his time ministering to the poor when there was money to be made among the wealthy, particularly with his eye under threat should he not soon make good on what he owed.

Simpson whipped off his great black coat and rolled up his sleeves.

'Let's see what's what, then,' he said, as he made his initial examination.

A few moments later he reported that the cervix had not yet fully dilated and declared himself content to await events. He installed himself on a chair beside the only window, where he began to read his book. The dog curled itself up beside him on the floor, indicating that the beast was sufficiently versed in its master's habits to know they were in for a long haul.

'I like to make use of bits and pieces of time,' Simpson said, indicating the volume on his lap. 'Some of my best papers have been written at the bedside of my patients.'

Raven took in the only other seat in the room, a three-legged stool, liable to put skelfs in his arse. He lowered himself reluctantly onto it, thinking he would have ideally preferred to wait out the time in a nearby hostelry, which prompted him to remember that he had no money on him, and precious little back at Mrs Cherry's either. He would have little option but to develop more abstemious habits. Would that he had done so one day sooner.

Lacking any reading material by way of diversion, time seemed to slow. Raven reached instinctively for his watch and remembered that it was gone. Gargantua had been through his pockets and found the one thing of value that Raven possessed. In truth, the old timepiece was of modest monetary worth and would do little to reduce the sum that he owed even if it was passed on to Flint, which he doubted. But its absence was felt keenly, because his father had given him that watch. It was thus a valuable keepsake inasmuch as it was a constant reminder that the old wretch had given him nothing else worth having.

With some difficulty he got up and moved the stool into a corner of the room, hoping that by doing so he might rest his head on the wall and perhaps sleep for a while. He changed his mind when he saw the damp and peeling plaster, seemingly held together by clumps of black mould. He had to make do with sitting upright and letting his head fall forward onto his chest.

He must have drifted off at some point because he was suddenly hauled from oblivion's gentle respite by a scream from the patient. The laudanum which had been liberally applied to Mrs Fraser by a local midwife prior to their arrival had evidently worn off. There was a young, worried-looking girl – when did she arrive? he wondered – filling a bowl with water from a jug.

Simpson looked over at his new apprentice as he washed his hands.

'Ah, Mr Raven. You are awake. It is time to re-examine the patient and decide upon the best course of action.'

Raven rinsed his own hands in the bowl and watched as Simpson performed the examination, but there was little he could see. A blanket had been draped across the woman's knees, obscuring the view. The doctor then turned to face him.

'Would you care to make an examination yourself?'

Raven could think of little he would like less right then, but it was not an invitation. He steeled himself and took a moment to remember how hard he had worked to put himself in this position.

He reached beneath the blanket, closing his eyes as he attempted to work out the position of the infant's head relative to the maternal pelvis. With only touch to guide him, his inexperienced hands were not so gentle as the doctor's, and the woman grunted in her discomfort, occasionally eyeing him with a resentment bordering on violence. He was increasingly tempted to toss the blanket aside. If he was to learn anything from these encounters, it would be better, would it not, if he could at least see a little of what he was doing.

'What are your findings?' Simpson asked, his voice calm and quiet. Raven was uncertain whether this tone was intended to reassure him or the patient, but it served to remind him that he was not the one who ought to be feeling the greater stress.

'The infant's head is sitting at the pelvic brim,' he stated, surprised at his own conviction. 'It has not descended as it should have done.'

Simpson nodded, eyeing him thoughtfully. 'How should we proceed?'

'Forceps?' Raven ventured, a question rather than a statement of fact.

The mere mention of the dreaded instrument drew a loud moan from Mrs Fraser, while the young girl diligently mopping her brow stopped what she was doing and began to weep.

'Fear not,' the doctor told her, his tone still as measured. 'Bear with us just a bit longer and we shall have the little one delivered safe.'

Simpson then turned to Raven, his voice deliberately quieter, inaudible to the others above the cries and moans.

'The head has not yet entered the brim of the pelvis, so it is too high even for the long forceps. In this case I think turning would be the better option.'

The doctor picked up his bag and rooted around in it, eventually removing a piece of paper and a stubby pencil. Leaning on the wax-spattered table, he drew a cone shape and pointed at it as though it explained everything. Raven's incomprehension proved legible enough upon his expression for Simpson to add some arrows as he attempted to clarify what his diagram represented.

'The whole child can be considered cone-shaped, the apex or narrowest part being the feet. The skull can also be thought of as a cone, the narrowest part of which is the base. By turning the child in the womb, the feet can be pulled through the pelvis first, distending the maternal passages for the transit of the larger part. The feet are first brought down then used to pull through the body and the partially compressible head.'

Raven grasped the notion only vaguely but nodded vigorously to forestall any further explanation. The screams were rattling his aching head and he wanted the whole thing to be over almost as much as Mrs Fraser.

Simpson then removed an amber-coloured bottle from his bag.

'This is an ideal case for ether,' he said, holding up the vessel as evidence of his intentions.

Raven had seen ether used before in the operating theatre. The patient had complained vigorously about its lack of effect while oblivious to the fact that his gangrenous foot was being removed even as he spoke. Raven was amazed, but there were those who argued it had only been partially successful, inasmuch as they thought the very purpose of the anaesthetic was to render the patient insensible and therefore altogether less troublesome.

He had inhaled it himself at a meeting of the Edinburgh Medico-Chirurgical Society, shortly after its anaesthetic effects had been discovered. It produced an unpleasant dizziness resulting in much staggering about. This caused some short-lived hilarity but he had not fallen asleep as others had done. He had wondered if perhaps he was resistant to its effects in some way.

Raven watched as Simpson poured some of the fluid onto a

piece of sponge. The air was immediately filled with a pungent aroma, which was welcome in that it partially masked the other odours still permeating the place. The sponge was then held over the patient's nose and mouth. She recoiled initially at the fumes, before the young girl said gently: 'It's the ether, Ellie, like Moira had.'

The agent's reputation evidently preceding it, she breathed in the vapour eagerly now, before passing quickly and easily into sleep.

'It is important to administer a narcotising dose,' the doctor said, 'thereby avoiding the potentially troublesome primary stage of exhilaration.'

He spoke of ether with knowledge and enthusiasm, just as Henry had implied. There were those who were already dismissing it as a passing novelty, but clearly Simpson was not among them.

He indicated that Raven should take command of the soporific sponge while he busied himself at the other end.

'Ether is most helpful when turning or using instruments,' he said as he reached his hand into the patient's uterus. The lack of response from Mrs Fraser, in contrast to her previous tortured writhing, convincingly bore this out.

'I've found a knee,' the professor reported, smiling.

With Simpson's activities largely obscured by the blanket, Raven looked down at the sleeping woman; except she wasn't sleeping. She lay completely still, almost as though she was suspended in some realm between life and death. She had become an effigy of herself, a figure cast in wax. Raven found it hard to believe that she would ever wake up, and with alarm recalled Henry's mention of a recent death from the stuff.

A few minutes later Simpson announced that the feet and legs had been delivered. The body and head soon followed in a gush of blood and amniotic fluid which formed a puddle at the doctor's feet.

Simpson produced the infant from beneath the blanket, rather like a stage magician revealing a dove from an upturned hat. It was a boy. The child began to cry, lustily. The ether evidently had little effect on him.

The baby was swaddled and handed to the young girl, who had been standing statuesque and wide-eyed while the delivery was in progress. She stirred herself now and began singing softly to the child, seeking to soothe its angry bawling.

The mother slept on while the placenta was removed and the baby cleaned and dried. Then she woke as if from a natural sleep and seemed surprised to the point of confusion to find that her ordeal was over.

As the child was placed in the delighted mother's arms, the young girl went to summon the new father. Mr Fraser stepped tentatively into the room at first, almost in a state of disbelief. He looked to Simpson as though for permission, before approaching closer and placing a hand gently onto the head of his newborn son.

Raven was surprised to see tears welling in Mr Fraser's eyes. He hadn't thought him the sort. That said, there had to be a great well of relief gushing through him, as the outcome in cases of obstructed labour was always far from certain. Raven was more surprised to feel tears well up in his own eyes. Maybe it was an effect of all that had happened last night, but he felt this dank and squalid place transformed briefly into one of hope and happiness.

Mr Fraser wiped his eyes on his grubby sleeve then turned to shake the doctor's hand while fumbling in his pocket for the fee that was due. Raven caught a glimpse of the modest specie in the man's dirt-smeared palm. It seemed a paltry sum to offer a man of Dr Simpson's reputation, particularly as he had performed the delivery himself.

Simpson also appeared to be examining the proffered coins. Clearly it wasn't enough, and Raven was bracing himself for an awkward exchange. Instead the doctor reached out and gently closed Mr Fraser's fingers around the money.

'Naw, naw. Away with ye,' he said, smiling.

He picked up his bag, waving to Mrs Fraser who was now nursing her infant son, and led Raven from the room.

They stepped out into the Canongate, Raven enjoying the feel of a cool breeze upon his face. He imagined it blowing away all that had adhered to him in the preceding hours, feeling as though he had been confined inside Mrs Fraser's womb itself.

Simpson was looking about for his carriage, which was not where they left it, the coachman having perhaps decided to take a turn to relieve the monotony during the many hours they were inside. Raven cast an eye about the street also, which was when he noticed a small gathering outside a close across the road. Evie's close.

He drifted nearer, as though conveyed there by an involuntary compulsion. There were two men carrying out a body swathed in a shroud, a cart waiting by the roadside. The shroud was grey and tattered at the edges, one that had been used many times before. Nothing fine, nothing new to clothe poor Evie, even in death.

There were several familiar faces standing on the pavement, other prostitutes. Some he had known through Evie, and some he had merely known. Evie's landlady was there too, Effie Peake. Raven kept his head down. He did not wish to be recognised, and even less to be hailed.

There was an officer of the police standing at the mouth of the close, watching the corpse being loaded onto the cart. Raven overheard someone ask him what had happened. 'Just another deid hoor,' the officer replied neutrally, not even a note of regret in his voice. 'Killed herself with the drink, looks like.'

The words echoed and echoed around Raven's head. He felt a hollow open up inside him, something deeper than shame.

Just another deid hoor.

That was not the woman he knew. Evie deserved to be more than that.

SIX

arah surveyed the waiting room and observed with a frown that there were a good many patients still to be seen. Dr Simpson's sudden departure had resulted in an inevitable delay as Dr George Keith, his assistant, was left to deal alone with all those who remained. Sarah liked George, but he was slow and had a tendency to lecture the patients, which she didn't care for. She wondered if she should request that Dr Duncan come and help but decided it was unlikely he would. He was always too busy with his experiments, though this was perhaps no bad thing. He had the coldest of manner and seemed better suited to dealing with chemicals than with people.

She much preferred watching Dr Simpson work, but that was a relatively rare occurrence. He mostly saw the well-to-do patients upstairs, where Jarvis had the equivalent to Sarah's role. To be fair, Jarvis was better equipped to deal with the clientele up above, being seldom cowed by their complaints. He exhibited a healthy disregard for their position in society and as a result was seldom intimidated, browbeaten or lost for words.

Jarvis was a tall man, which made it difficult for others to physically look down on him. He was also very particular about his appearance, carrying himself with great elegance and dignity, and was confidently articulate. Sarah often thought that with a different set of clothes Jarvis could easily pass for a member of the upper orders himself. On one occasion she had seen a gentleman approach the butler, waving a rolled-up newspaper in a rather threatening manner. 'I have been waiting to see Dr Simpson for more than an hour,' he had said, 'which I find to be quite unacceptable. I have come all the way from Jedburgh.'

'Is that so?' Jarvis had replied witheringly. 'The last patient was from Japan.'

Sarah looked again at the sorry assembly littering the downstairs waiting room that was her domain. They were poor-looking souls suffering a variety of maladies that Sarah could often diagnose merely by looking at them. Scrofula, consumption, ringworm and scabies were all frequently in evidence. The sound of coughing and expectoration was so commonplace that she was no longer aware of it, although it was always there.

She sighed as she noticed the time on the clock above the fireplace. There was always so much work to be done and so little time for the pleasures that others took for granted. She patted the books still weighing down her pocket and wondered if she would have the opportunity to open them today.

She was shaken from her musings by the sound of someone coming down the stairs. She looked up, expecting to see Jarvis, but it was Mina.

'Sarah, I have been ringing the bell in the drawing room repeatedly and no one has answered.'

'Mrs Lyndsay doesn't always hear the bell when she's in the scullery, ma'am.'

That was certainly what Mrs Lyndsay claimed to be the case. The cook insisted that she was deaf in one ear, which was why the bell sometimes went unanswered, but Sarah suspected otherwise. Mrs Lyndsay resented being interrupted when she was cooking.

'I am in need of tea. I have been struggling with the same piece of embroidery for the past hour. Such a difficult pattern.'

'Wouldn't it calm your spirits to be reading a book instead?' Sarah suggested.

Mina's expression indicated that this was a notion so self-evident as to be stupid, and was about to explain why.

'Of course I would rather be reading. I would spend all my days reading if I could. But for reasons passing understanding, embroidery is considered a desirable accomplishment in a prospective wife, and therefore it is incumbent upon me to master it, such is my lot. So for pity's sake, bring tea or I shall run mad.'

Sarah looked again at the waiting patients. She was unlikely to be called upon to escort any of them to the consulting room soon, as a dependably garrulous old woman had only recently been shown in.

'I shall bring up some tea directly,' Sarah said as Mina retreated swiftly back up the stairs with her handkerchief at her nose, evidently having caught a whiff of the waiting room.

Sarah plodded down to the kitchen, wondering if she should ask Mrs Lyndsay about Rose, the Sheldrakes' missing housemaid. In her time at Queen Street, Sarah had developed a degree of scepticism about the veracity of Mina's accounts of things. Her stories always contained a kernel of truth but this was frequently obscured by the embellishments she so liberally applied.

The cook was bent over a large pot on the range. The kitchen was filled with a rich, meaty aroma and Sarah's stomach rumbled in response to it.

'Game pie, is it, Mrs Lyndsay?'

Sarah liked to guess what was on the menu by the smell of it. She had a good nose and was usually correct in interpreting what it told her.

'The doctor delivered the heir to a great estate last week and received a brace of pheasants and some rabbits for his efforts. Is her ladyship wanting tea?' Mrs Lyndsay looked towards the ceiling as she said this, indicating that she had indeed heard the bell.

'Yes. She's doing battle with a troublesome bit of sewing,' Sarah said as she filled the kettle.

Mrs Lyndsay chortled, the laughter rippling through her large frame. 'Still busy upstairs?'

'There seems to be no end to it today.'

'Having the new apprentice should help. And then perhaps you will be able to concentrate upon the job you're actually employed to do.'

'But I like helping out with the patients,' Sarah said. 'It's the best part of my duties.'

'That's as may be, Sarah, but the floors won't wash themselves. The medical work should be left to those who have been trained to do it. Don't you think?'

Sarah could see no point in arguing. 'Yes, Mrs Lyndsay,' she said with a sigh.

As she placed the teapot and cups on a tray she thought she might risk bringing up the subject of Rose Campbell. As a general rule Mrs Lyndsay disliked gossip, but would often divulge small pieces of information if asked directly.

'Miss Grindlay says that the Sheldrakes' housemaid has run away.'

'Apparently so.'

'Why would she do such a thing? The Sheldrakes are good people, are they not?'

'Who is to say what happens when the doors are closed and the world's not watching.'

Sarah waited for elaboration but there was none. Mrs Lyndsay's aversion to gossip often meant things were referred to rather elliptically.

Any request for further information was curtailed by a very insistent ringing of the drawing-room bell.

'Best take that up,' the cook said, indicating the tea tray.

Sarah lifted it and left the kitchen before anything further could be ascertained.

She entered the drawing room, happy that she had managed

to navigate stairs and door without any spillage. Mina was propped up on a chaise-longue reading a book, her embroidery discarded on the floor beside her. Mrs Simpson was in an armchair by the window staring at the view outside. She looked pale and tired, her fatigue exacerbated by the black she was obliged to wear.

'Are there any ginger biscuits?' Mrs Simpson asked.

'Yes,' said Sarah. She was happy that she had anticipated this need – Mrs Simpson frequently suffered with her digestion – though she began to fear she hadn't brought enough as Mina was already hovering above the tray.

'Sarah, I wish to go shopping tomorrow,' Mina said, biting into a biscuit before her tea was even poured.

Sarah groaned inwardly at the prospect. Shopping with Mina was usually a prolonged affair. There was likely to be no time for books today and there certainly would be no time tomorrow.

She had just finished pouring when another bell sounded, the front door this time. She excused herself and exited in time to see Jarvis escorting one of the upstairs ladies into the consulting room.

Sarah trudged down the stairs feeling increasingly irritated. On her way through the hall she passed the lower waiting room, where the same patients (to her mind suffering from more pressing complaints than the ones upstairs) sat listlessly, staring at their shoes.

Sarah opened the door and what little patience she still possessed drained from her. She was confronted by two women who were, without doubt, of the upstairs variety. They were extravagantly dressed in what Sarah assumed to be the latest fashion: ermine-trimmed coats, kid gloves, boots with no mud on them (how did they manage that?), and elaborate hats perched precariously upon their coiffured heads. Compared to those already waiting they seemed to be in robust good health, though one kept dipping her head as if attempting to hide her face beneath her hat. Large, perfectly formed ringlets dipped down below the border of her bonnet. Her hair was the most remarkable shade of red.

'Is the doctor at home? We should like to consult him,' said the one with the bigger hat, the less retiring of the two. Her companion's gloved hand was resting in the crook of her arm and she gave it a reassuring pat as she spoke. Sarah was momentarily distracted by the huge piece of millinery balanced at an improbable angle on her head. There was a profusion of feathers, brightly coloured ribbon and lace. Sarah could imagine magpies nesting in it.

The lady looked at Sarah with disdain, as though she had expected the doctor to answer the door himself and was disgruntled at having to deal with an intermediary. Her gaze was so disapproving that Sarah initially thought she must have something unseemly on her apron to cause such offence. But there had been no contact with pus or blood that morning and a quick look confirmed that her apron was in fact quite clean.

'I'm afraid the doctor is from home. An urgent visit,' she said, hoping that this explanation would suffice.

The lady in the bigger hat sighed and turned to her companion. 'Shall we wait, dear? I think that we shall wait.'

Her companion did not respond.

Sarah took a deep breath and explained that there were already more patients waiting than could reasonably be seen upon Dr Simpson's return, thinking while she did so that she might have been better fetching Jarvis to deal with this.

Both ladies now looked at her as though she was being deliberately obstructive. Did they think she was lying about the doctor's absence and the waiting patients?

The lady with the large hat looked down her aquiline nose and spoke firmly. 'My dear girl, I am sure we can be admitted. Take my name. Dr Simpson knows me!'

Sarah looked back at the accumulated mass of human misery already installed in the waiting room. There were almost as many upstairs too.

'Madam, Dr Simpson knows the Queen,' she said, then closed the door.

SEVEN

r Simpson's coachman had brought the brougham around after only a few minutes, the dog taking its preferred seat with proprietorial speed before Raven could climb aboard. Raven settled himself back against the red leather upholstery and closed his eyes. He hoped Dr Simpson would return to the book he had been reading all afternoon, but he was to be disappointed.

'Where do you hail from, Mr Raven?' the doctor said as the coach set off.

Raven tried to sit up more erectly in his seat.

'I was born in Edinburgh, sir.'

'And what does your father do?'

'He is no longer with us,' he replied. 'But he was a lawyer.'

Rehearsing this lie brought him back to last night in that alley not a hundred yards from here. It would have to serve once again, however. The truth was for another time, once Raven had enjoyed the chance to cultivate a reputation based upon his deeds rather than his provenance.

'In Edinburgh?'

'Originally. But lately in St Andrews.'

This at least had a modicum of truth to it. His mother lived there now, reliant upon the generosity of her brother. He truly was a lawyer, and a miserable, pious and self-righteous one at that.

'I once contemplated studying the law,' Simpson mused wistfully.

'Really? For how long?' Raven asked, wondering how the man could possibly have accommodated more than one field of study given his relative youth and famously prodigious career.

'Oh, at least the length of a day. An early encounter with the operating theatre had me racing off to Parliament House to seek employment as a clerk.'

Raven responded with a smile, no doubt a lopsided one given the burden on his cheek. He too had little love of the operating theatre. Much as he had admiration for the swift and steady hand of the surgeon, he had no wish to spend his time excising tumours and hacking off limbs. The barbarity of it appalled him, for no surgeon was as steady and swift as to spare the patient unimaginable torment.

'What brought you back?' Raven asked with genuine curiosity.

'The desire to alleviate pain and suffering, and the belief that one day we will find a means of achieving it.'

'And are you of the belief that ether has done that?'

'It is a step in the right direction but I believe we can do more. Now we understand that the inhaling of certain chemical compounds can produce a reversible insensibility, I am sure that if we experiment we will find something better than ether. It was one of the reasons I decided to take on an apprentice again this year. I need as many hands as possible to assist me in my search.'

This was not Raven's primary interest in working with the professor but he quickly warmed to the idea. If he was involved in the discovery of a new anaesthetic agent, his success in the profession would be assured. A share in the patent, aye, that would be the keys to a fortune.

'And do you believe you can succeed?' Raven asked, the prospect of such riches prompting a cautious scepticism.

The professor leaned forward in his seat. 'I believe that with a passionate desire and an unwearied will, we can achieve impossibilities.'

The door to 52 Queen Street opened the moment the doctor's carriage pulled up outside the house. A young woman in a starched cap stood in the doorway adjusting her apron as Raven stepped down onto the pavement. She recoiled momentarily at the sight of him and a sadness fell upon Raven as he realised that this was something he would have to get used to.

The dog ran into the house first, followed by the professor, who shrugged off his coat and handed it to a male servant who had materialised behind the young woman as though from thin air. He was tall, clean-shaven and immaculately dressed, which only served to emphasise Raven's state of dishevelment. The man stared down at this unkempt new arrival with unguarded disapproval.

'Jarvis, I'll take tea in my study,' Simpson said.

'Very good, sir,' he replied, before nodding at Raven, who was still loitering on the threshold. 'And what would you like me to do with that?'

The doctor laughed. 'This is Mr Raven, my new apprentice. He won't be joining us for dinner as I believe he's in need of his bed.'

Simpson met Raven's eye with a knowing look. Raven endured a moment of concern regarding just *what* the doctor knew, but mainly what he felt was relief.

'Show him up please, Sarah.'

The doctor proceeded along the corridor towards the back of the house. 'Jarvis will arrange to have your belongings collected,' he said over his shoulder.

'That is assuming you have any belongings worth collecting,' the butler said, closing the door.

Raven followed the housemaid up the stairs to a bedroom on

the third floor, the ascent sapping the last of his energy so much that he feared she might have to grab his lapels and drag him up the final flight. She breezed fussily ahead of him into the room and placed a towel onto a chair before he could sit on it, any concerns about offending him apparently trumped by the state of his clothes.

'We'll need to draw you a bath,' she said, evidently deeming his current condition an affront to the crisp white sheets adorning the bed. Raven hadn't seen linen so clean in a long time. He could think of little he wanted more right then than to crawl underneath it, but was too weak to argue. He sat holding his head in his hands, only vaguely aware of the bustle around him.

When he raised his head once more, he saw that a hip bath had been placed before the fire and filled with warm water. The butler helped him off with his clothes and offered an arm to steady himself as Raven climbed over the side. There appeared to be petals and twigs floating in the water, which caused him to pause with one foot in.

'Camomile, rosemary and lavender,' Jarvis offered by way of explanation. 'Sarah says it will help with the bruising. And the smell.'

Raven sat down in the warm, fragrant water and felt his aching muscles begin to relax. He could not remember having a bath quite like this. At Ma Cherry's, an old tin tub would be grudgingly filled with tepid water, just enough to cover the buttocks and feet. He could still hear the old sow's sighing and tutting as she hauled in the cans, as though bathing was some strange and alien practice he was inexplicably insisting upon. From the smell of her, it was certainly strange and alien to Mrs Cherry.

A sponge and a bar of soap had been left just within reach, but Raven felt disinclined to move. He allowed his good eye to close and time to drift. He heard the tread of footsteps in and out of the room a couple of times but he chose to ignore them. He then felt the sponge move across the tops of his shoulders.

He knew there was further insult implicit in Jarvis letting him know he did not trust Raven to clean himself properly, but he was too exhausted to object. He kept his eyes closed, however, as he had no desire to see the distasteful look on the butler's face while he performed this task.

'You'll have to lean forward so I can rinse your hair.'

It was a female voice that spoke. Raven lurched upright and opened his good eye. The housemaid Sarah was standing in front of him, holding a large ewer in both hands.

'What do you think you're doing?' he asked, thrusting his hands down to cover himself.

She smirked. 'Helping you get cleaned up,' she said. 'No need to be bashful. I'm as much nurse as housemaid in this place, so whatever you've got, I've seen it before.'

Raven hadn't the will to do anything but submit, though he kept one hand in place.

Sarah was very gentle, perhaps because of his obvious injuries – he seemed to have bruising from sternum to pubic bone. She smelled of tea and lavender and freshly laundered linen. Clean smells, healthy smells. New Town smells.

His hair was duly rinsed, after which Sarah offered to help him get out of the tub.

'I'm not an invalid,' he objected, a little more harshly than the girl deserved.

She gathered up his clothes. 'I've left a nightshirt on the bed for you,' she said, leaving him to perform the last of his ablutions alone.

When he did attempt to stand, he was almost toppled by a sudden onset of vertigo. He sat down again and waited for the spinning to stop. Given the impression he had made on the household staff thus far, he did not wish to be found prostrate on the floor with his arse in the air.

Rising more cautiously, he managed to get himself dried and into bed before Sarah entered again, this time carrying a tray.

'Beef tea, bread and butter.'

She put the tray down and took a small tin from her pocket.

'I'm going to put some salve on your wound. It's looking a bit red.'

Without waiting for his consent, she began applying some strange-smelling ointment to his cheek. With her eyes intent upon the work of her hands, he allowed himself to gaze upon her face: the freckles on her nose, the curl of her lashes.

For a moment he pictured Evie before him, dressed like that, a housemaid in the New Town. He could not sustain the image, though, and it was rapidly replaced by his memory of her contorted body.

Another deid hoor.

As Sarah put the liniment tin back in her pocket and bent to pick up his wet towel, Raven hoped she appreciated how fortunate she was.

EIGHT

onsciousness came at Raven like an ambush, sudden and without mercy. For the second successive morning he had woken in an unfamiliar bed, but on this occasion it was not his new surroundings that disoriented him so much as what he had left behind in sleep. He had been with Evie, the essence of her suffusing a dream so vivid that upon waking he felt the enormity of her loss all over again. How could she be gone when she still felt so real to him? It seemed as though he could walk to her lodging this very morning and find that it was her death that was the dream.

Raven looked at frost on the room's tiny window and was instantly transported to a freezing cold day they had spent together in her room, sharing a dry loaf and washing it down with wine, only leaving her bed to use the privy. It was not the physical intimacies that echoed now, but the warmth of friendship, of being in the company of someone with whom he could let the hours drift. He recalled how he had talked about his ambitions, and his promises to help her as soon as he was in a position of any influence.

He had caught her staring at him, that inscrutable look upon her face. It felt good to be stared at by her, to be the subject of her fascination, though he had no notion what she was thinking, what observations and secrets she was keeping to herself. Perhaps she heard such promises all the time. When he spoke this way, Evie seemed to accept that he was sincere, but that wasn't the same as believing him.

'You're always looking to take up cudgels for a noble cause, aren't you, Will?' she had said, lying with her head propped up on one hand, gently stroking his back with the other. She sounded amused but sympathetic. 'Always in search of a battle to fight.'

His instinct was to deny it, as people always do when someone has shown that they know them better than they find comfortable. However, to Evie such a denial would be as good as an admission, so he said nothing.

'Was there a particular one you lost, that you're ever after trying to make up for?'

'No,' he had replied, grateful he had his back to her. His answer was the truth, yet nonetheless a deliberate deceit.

Sometimes it was a fight you won that proved hardest to bear.

Raven got out of bed and examined his face in the mirror above the washstand. He was pleased to discover that he could open both eyes. He gently prodded along his cheek, which was coloured by purple bruising that extended almost to his chin. The wound remained tender but looked clean, without any signs of impending infection around the stitches. The salve that Sarah applied appeared to have been quite effective. If it was a remedy of her own making, she should patent it, he thought. Or perhaps *he* could, once he had qualified and could put his imprimatur upon the product as an Edinburgh doctor. He would ask her about it later. Obtaining the patent on a popular new medicine could prove highly lucrative, especially if it actually worked.

He recalled his conversation with Simpson the day before regarding the search for an alternative to ether. The alleviation of all pain and suffering was certainly a lofty ambition, but Raven doubted if such a thing was possible, even with an unwearied will and a passionate desire or whatever pieties Simpson had been spouting. However, anything that offered a way out of his chronic penury was worth pursuing, particularly with Flint's debt to be considered. Simpson would find him a willing participant in whatever experiments he proposed.

His bags had arrived from Mrs Cherry's, a clean shirt and trousers making him look and feel instantly more respectable. His clothes from yesterday seemed to have disappeared. He wondered if the butler had burned them.

Raven rubbed a hand across his chin. At nineteen years old, his face was not quick to bristle, but stubble was beginning to form a shadow as he hadn't shaved in two days. He had never pictured himself with a beard, but looking at Henry's needlework, it struck him that growing whiskers may prove a necessity, as they would cover up the scar.

He descended to the dining room, finding it empty, though the fire had been lit and the table laid, suggesting he would not have long to wait for breakfast. It was a large room dominated by an expansive table and a mahogany sideboard. A richly patterned paper decorated the walls and a pair of heavy brocade curtains in a complementary colour hung either side of the windows. A cage containing a large grey parrot was situated before the glass, presumably so that the bird could enjoy a view of the street and the gardens beyond. The parrot's interest was primarily taken right then by a Raven, which it was eyeing with the same mixture of curiosity and distrust as its housemate Jarvis.

On top of the sideboard a selection of serving dishes were waiting to be filled. Raven picked up a pepper shaker, turning it upside down to look for a hallmark. This resulted in a streak of pepper spilling onto the sideboard which he hurriedly swept up in his hand and then sprinkled onto the carpet. The parrot squawked loudly, as though in rebuke.

Placing the shaker carefully back down, he noticed that one of the sideboard doors was ajar, and he bent to satisfy his curiosity. As well as a stack of crockery and a large soup tureen, he spied several piles of papers with barely legible notes scribbled upon them, as though scrawled in a hurry. More intriguingly he also observed a selection of glass bottles containing a variety of clear liquids. These were labelled in a contrastingly precise hand, though some of them were smudged, presumably from repeated handling. Nitric ether, benzine, chloride of hydrocarbon. To Raven, who had been a middling chemistry student at best, the names didn't mean much. He removed the stopper from the bottle of benzine and took a sniff. It had a pungent aroma and caused a slight dizziness. Given his recent infirmity, he decided that further investigation was best avoided at present.

He had just returned the bottle to the cupboard when the dining-room door opened and the entire household seemed to pour through it.

'Mr Raven. What a pleasure it is to meet you.'

The woman who greeted him had a pleasant, open countenance but appeared exceedingly pale, as though she hadn't been outdoors for some time. She was dressed in black, evidently in mourning. Raven wondered for whom.

'I am Mrs Simpson and this is my sister, Miss Wilhelmina Grindlay.'

'Delighted to make your acquaintance,' Raven replied.

Miss Grindlay looked momentarily taken aback by his appearance but regained her composure to offer him a smile.

'You may call me Mina,' she said.

Mina was slightly taller and thinner than her sister, making her features seem pinched in comparison. She was beyond the first flush of youth but still pleasing to the eye. Raven wondered why she was not yet married.

The ladies were followed by the domestic staff, who lined up along one wall. Raven allowed himself a glance at Sarah, but averted his gaze as a matter of reflex when she met his eye. It was his understanding that servants were specifically not supposed to do this. He wondered whether the Simpson household afforded greater leeway to those below stairs or whether this meant that his status was not considered to be above.

His attention was taken by the arrival of a fellow surely not much older than him, but who carried himself with a great deal more certainty and poise (not to mention within a suit of far finer tailoring). He had the gait of someone comfortable in his surroundings and enjoying great confidence in his purpose. He did not introduce himself, instead taking position behind a chair as they awaited the master of the house.

Dr Simpson entered last of all, bade everyone good morning and took his seat at the head of the table. He opened a grand leather-bound Bible and read something from Psalms. Everyone then bowed their heads for a few minutes of silent prayer. To Raven's empty stomach, this represented an unwelcome delay, rendered all the more frustrating by his never having been much inclined towards the church. He was not even sure whether he believed in God. (The devil was quite another matter.)

Eventually the doctor said amen and the domestic staff left the room, Raven hoped as a prelude to their imminent return bearing food. When the door opened once more, however, it was the dog that entered, followed by two small boys who proceeded to chase it round the table, and from whose giggling entreaties he learned that its name was Glen.

He heard an approaching thump of hurried footsteps and had to suppress a smile at the harassed appearance of their nanny, who looked mortified that they had escaped her charge. Raven felt guilty for his amusement as he braced himself for the rebuke that would surely be handed down, reckoning that whether the boys or the nanny got the worst of it would be a revealing detail. However, Simpson responded instead with raucous laughter, to which almost everyone reacted with similar mirth, prompting the dog to bark with excitement before even the bloody parrot joined in.

Almost everyone, mark you. There was an exception. The

smartly dressed young man merely issued a tired sigh, while presenting a token smile as thin as Ma Cherry's porridge.

Simpson quieted the dog with an affectionate hand upon its head, the tail wagging like a metronome. Then the squealing boys were similarly calmed by the tender ministrations of their father's hands before being led away meekly by their grateful governess. The sight piqued something bittersweet in Raven, but before he could dwell upon it, his senses were busied with the arrival of platters piled high with sausages, eggs, kippers and freshly baked bread.

Raven eyed it all longingly, awaiting Simpson tucking in as his cue to commence. The doctor was reaching for a sausage with a fork when he suddenly paused and put it down again.

'But I am forgetting myself. Introductions! James, this is my new apprentice, Will Raven. Will, this is Dr James Duncan, recently arrived from Paris.'

Raven was about to extend a hand but noticed that Duncan's remained fixed by his side. He wasn't sure he was on the right side of the etiquette, but he was quite sure Dr James Duncan saw him as an inferior, and by 'saw him', he meant much as in the way one sees a fellow by using a telescope.

If Raven was the type to feel slighted, then the sting would have been drawn by Simpson finally signalling that everyone should eat. For appearance's sake, he did not pile his plate conspicuously, but even then it was probably more food than he had faced at a sitting since last he visited his mother, and he was sure it would taste so much the better without his uncle reminding everyone who had paid for it.

'Dr Duncan, I meant to ask but I kept forgetting,' ventured Miss Grindlay, peering across the table. 'Are you any relation to Mr Duncan of Duncan and Flockhart on Princes Street?'

Duncan gave her a look indicating that he considered this a self-evidently stupid question.

'No. Though I understand they're doing a fairly brisk trade

in ether since its discovery.' This latter he addressed towards Simpson, by way of moving the subject on.

Raven decided to move it right back again.

'Any relation to Mr Duncan the surgeon at the Infirmary, then?'

For this he earned a sour look, one of which Raven was sure Duncan had a varied repertoire.

'Again, no. There appears to be a surfeit of Duncans in Edinburgh at the moment. I am considering adding my mother's maiden name to mine to distinguish myself.'

'And what will your name become?' asked Mina.

'James Matthews Duncan.'

'That does sound most distinguished,' said Mrs Simpson. 'You'll have to make some notable contribution to medicine now, in order to be worthy of it.'

'I intend to,' he replied flatly.

Raven thought this was another pass at shutting down irrelevant contributions from the distaff side, but it was in fact merely an overture. Once Duncan had gobbled down the solitary boiled egg he had abstemiously selected from the cornucopia before him, he proceeded to lay down his credentials, at the end of which Raven had a stark perspective upon just how powerful that telescope would have to be.

Duncan had studied medicine in Aberdeen and Edinburgh, gaining his MD last year at the tender age of twenty, which required some form of special dispensation. He had travelled to Paris to further his studies, and while there had made extensive pathological examinations of women who had died in childbirth, considering himself to be something of an expert upon inflammatory conditions of the female pelvis. He spoke fluent German and French, and had translated Dr Simpson's 'Notes on the Inhalation of Sulphuric Ether' into the latter, which had naturally flattered their host and no doubt played a part in his being offered a position as an assistant to the professor.

'I have come here to find a better drowsy syrup than ether,' he declared, which put a stopper in it as far as Raven was concerned, as he had only just begun entertaining the notion that this might be his own route to success.

James Matthews Duncan, he decided, was going to be insufferable. He had the bearing of a young man who had never been punched full in the face for an unguarded remark, and Raven instinctively felt he might be the one to remedy that.

The gathering was soon joined by another gentleman, who apologised for being late (having come on foot from his home on Howe Street) and insisted nobody should rise. He looked a few years older than Raven, tall and neatly dressed, with a receding hairline and a full beard. He was evidently well known to the family, as he sat down at the table without waiting for an invitation and was promptly served a cup of tea by Sarah.

'This is my associate, Dr George Keith,' Simpson explained, before completing the introduction.

Dr Keith reached across the table to shake Raven's hand, pausing momentarily as he took in his appearance.

'What the devil has happened to you?' Keith asked, not restrained by the same delicacy as the ladies around the table.

'I was set upon by thieves in the Old Town,' Raven said. 'They came at me late at night and dragged me into an alley. I tried to fight them off, but that proved a mistake. They took every penny I had on me, which was quite a sum, as well as my watch. So as well as being battered and bruised, I am out of pocket and out of time.'

He laughed a little at his own polite joke, as though trivialising his condition. Nobody joined in.

'How awful for you,' Mina said, looking genuinely distraught at his misfortune.

'Are you quite out of funds, then?' Simpson asked. 'I'm sure that I could assist.'

'Oh, not at all. I couldn't possibly,' he replied.

The words spilled from his lips before Raven was aware of

saying them. He knew immediately that his refusal of Simpson's offer would come at a cost. Living here he would have bed and board, but beyond that he had only a small sum of money left among the belongings delivered from Mrs Cherry's. Certainly not enough to keep Flint and his creatures at bay.

However, having turned up bloodied and bruised, he did not wish his hosts to know also that he was impoverished. If you wished to be accorded respect by those who had money, it was imperative that they believed you had money too. It was a deception at which he had become practised, but it was easy to disguise your penury when you were a student living among your peers.

'Well, at the very least allow me to lend you a spare timepiece until you can replace your own,' Simpson insisted.

'You are most kind, sir. I thank you.'

Raven was contemplating a second serving of everything and wondering how much he could make selling stolen sausages when George Keith placed a hand upon his shoulder.

'I think it's about time we got started, don't you? They were spilling out of the waiting room already as I came through.'

'Who were?' Raven asked.

'The patients,' Keith replied, holding open the door. 'Our consulting rooms are this way.'

Raven obediently took his cue, though not without noticing that Duncan remained where he sat, the remains of his miserably ascetic breakfast still in front of him as he continued to converse with Simpson.

'Dr Duncan's duties are confined to the area of research,' Keith explained. 'You will be required to assist him, but mornings are for clinics.'

Raven followed Keith out and past the stairs, where a woman wrapped in a dirty shawl was sitting nursing a grubby infant.

'Dr Simpson sees the patients here, in his home?' he asked.

'Yes. They turn up every morning and draw lots to determine who is seen first. That is unless a case is conspicuously urgent.'

'There is no appointment book?'

Keith pointed to his temple. 'Dr Simpson insists that he can retain all important appointments and visits in his head.'

'And can he?'

Keith smiled. '*Most* of the time,' he replied. 'And when he forgets, the patients usually forgive him.'

'But why see them here?' Raven thought that if he were ever to own a house such as this he would not permit the great unwashed to parade through his downstairs hallway.

'Convenience, I suppose. The professor is not unique in having consulting rooms where he resides, although many of his colleagues choose to keep their patients at a distance. Professor Syme, for one, lives out at Morningside, far away from the patients that he sees.'

Raven was shown into a small room containing a desk and a couple of chairs.

'When you're ready, call for a patient and Sarah will show them in. I'm just next door. If you see anything strange or unusual let me know. Dr Simpson likes to see the rare stuff himself. He'll be seeing the upstairs patients. The ones who pay the large fees.'

'So what kind of fees do the ones we'll be seeing pay?' Raven asked, reckoning it would at least be better than nothing.

'The invisible kind.'

Raven saw a variety of complaints, mainly in women and children: sore throats, painful ears, coughs, sprains and skin diseases. He had hoped that Dr Keith would be on-hand to supervise his diagnoses and prescribed remedies, but it quickly became apparent that there was no time for such doubling of duties. He was unsure just what Sarah's contribution in all this was supposed to be, particularly given that each time he emerged, he found her perched on a chair outside the door reading a book.

'What are you doing?' he asked.

She looked up from the volume, her expression suggesting she was suppressing any number of impertinent replies.

'Reading a novel.' She flicked back to the title page. 'By someone named Currer Bell.'

'A novel?'

'Yes. It's called *Jane Eyre*. Have you read it?'

Raven was exasperated. 'Do you think a man has time to read fiction when he is training to be a doctor?'

'I'm rather sure Dr Simpson did.'

She put the book in her pocket and got up from her chair.

'I'll bring the next patient, shall I?'

Raven was speechless as she summoned a bald-headed man suffering from the most distressingly livid rash. This was not how he imagined household staff ought to behave. His uncle certainly wouldn't tolerate it, but this thought gave him pause. If he was using Miserly Malcolm as the compass for his behaviour, then he would soon be lost.

He returned to his consulting room and sat down with the next patient, the poor fellow concerned that his rash might soon be the death of him. Raven diagnosed it as a psoriatic eruption and dispensed a soothing ointment to calm its angry heat. Without even having applied it, the man appeared to experience some relief, merely at his suffering having been given a name. Raven suspected this effect might not be so efficacious if the man knew how little experience his 'doctor' had, but was satisfied to be of assistance.

He showed the man from his consulting room and stepped back into the waiting area, where the numbers appeared to have grown. So, quite considerably, had the volume of noise. Alerted by his appearance, he was dismayed to spot Sarah slipping the novel into her pocket again as she got to her feet. If she wasn't even paying attention, he didn't see what need there was for her to select the next patient when he was perfectly capable of assessing such things for himself.

To wit, his attention was immediately drawn to a shabbily dressed man convulsed by bouts of coughing, a rattletrap undertaking which he was directing into a singularly gruesome handkerchief. This bark might ordinarily have shaken the room, but at that moment it was all but drowned out by the sounds of three nearby children, two of whom were bawling while a third shrieked in on-going delight merely at the volume she had discovered her voice might achieve.

Mindful of the possibility of consumption, and keen to put at least a door between his ears and these intolerable howls, Raven bid the man follow.

Sarah stepped between them, signalling to the man to remain seated.

'Mr Raven, this woman here ought to be your next patient,' she told him, while to Raven's growing chagrin, the coughing man retreated in obedience.

'What is your name?' he asked, almost breathless in his incredulity.

'It is Sarah,' she replied, her words barely discernible over the sound of the screaming children.

'Yes, I know that part. Your surname.'

'Fisher.'

'And you are a housemaid, Miss Fisher, are you not?'

'Yes, sir.'

'Then by what rationale do you see fit to gainsay my instruction as to which patient should be seen next?'

'It is my duty to assess those waiting and to recommend the order of urgency by which they ought to be admitted.'

She had to raise her voice to be heard, which Raven was aware did not make for a fitting spectacle in front of the patients. Nonetheless, some lessons were best learned in public.

'You may *recommend* an order, but if I call for a particular patient, then you ought to remember that my knowledge of such matters considerably trumps your own.'

Summoned by the altercation, Dr Keith appeared in the waiting area and stepped closer to enquire after the dispute.

'I wish to attend to this man suffering from what may prove to be a serious ailment of the chest,' Raven explained, almost shouting over the clamour of tiny but disproportionately loud voices that was filling the hallway. 'However, the housemaid evidently believes she has a sharper diagnostic eye than mine and is insisting I prioritise that woman there, who appears to be suffering from nothing more troubling than having too many children in her care.'

Dr Keith turned to look at Sarah, then back at Raven.

'Do you mean the woman accompanied by her three bairns over whom we are fighting to make ourselves heard?'

'Indeed.'

'And whose subsequent absence would make the waiting areas considerably quieter and more agreeable?'

Raven felt a sudden heat in his cheeks as the manifold elements of his humiliation compounded. He looked like a fool, an arrogant fool at that, and had been made so foolish by a household servant in front of Dr Keith. It could only have been worse had it been the professor himself.

NINE

arah tramped along Princes Street several paces behind Mina, giving her an uninterrupted view of the dirt that was becoming attached to Mina's skirt. She was effectively sweeping the pavement with her numerous petticoats. Sarah added the cleaning of these to the perpetually lengthening list of chores that she would be expected to complete by the end of the day. She thought of Sisyphus and his giant boulder, condemned for all eternity to engage in an ultimately pointless task.

Mina had dressed with particular care that morning, most likely for the benefit of the doctor's new apprentice, but was perhaps now regretting her efforts given that the man in question bore a closer resemblance to a street urchin than a practitioner of the healing arts. Mina was no doubt disappointed, seeing another opportunity to escape her suffocating spinsterhood evaporate into the ether.

Mina had questioned Sarah about Raven that morning before breakfast, and she had been tempted to give her a detailed physical appraisal, afforded by having helped him bathe. Having studied Dr Simpson's anatomy textbooks, Sarah could have traced out various muscle groups on Raven's lean frame: pectoralis major, latissimus dorsi, gluteus maximus. He was a fine specimen of a man in the anatomical sense. His personality was another matter.

The short time she had known him had been enough to identify Raven as typical of his kind: self-regarding and prone to pomposity, believing his education elevated him above those who had been more limited in their opportunities. She thought of his arrogant dismissal of her advice at the clinic. He would soon learn that she made a better friend than an adversary, but she was prepared to be either – it all depended on him.

His behaviour may have been typical, but his appearance had definitely fallen short of expectations. When he arrived on the doorstep it looked as though he had been mauled by a rabid dog. Mrs Lyndsay and Jarvis could offer no explanations as to why the professor would employ such a man, let alone allow him to live with them. Sarah imagined that, whether she knew the reason or not, Mina would likely have an opinion on the matter, and so ventured a question.

'Is it usual for the professor to take on an apprentice like Mr Raven?'

Mina stopped walking. 'To take on an apprentice, yes. Like Mr Raven, no.'

'Why do you think he has done so?' she asked as Mina resumed her progress. 'Mr Raven seems rather . . .' Sarah paused for a moment searching for an appropriate word. 'Disreputable.'

'Rather a strong sentiment to be voiced by a housemaid, Sarah. But on this occasion, I find that I am in agreement. It may be that my brother-in-law has taken it upon himself to save this young man, rescue him from his circumstances. It is perhaps an expression of grief.'

'Grief? How so?'

'One of the greatest physicians in Edinburgh has lost two of his children, powerless in the face of infectious fevers. If he could not save them, with all his knowledge and accomplishments, perhaps there is some solace to be found in the salvation of someone else.'

Sarah paused for a moment to rearrange some of the packages she was carrying. Mina's explanation certainly seemed plausible enough, though it was not one she had considered herself. Had the doctor seen something in Raven worthy of salvation? If that was the case, she would perhaps be forced to search for the attributes that commended him to the professor but had so far been hidden from her.

Sarah shifted some of her load from one arm to the other. None of the parcels was particularly heavy but together they were cumbersome. She was weighed down with life's necessities wrapped in brown paper: reams of fabric, lace and embroidery thread. Sarah vastly preferred shopping trips in the company of Mrs Simpson. They occurred infrequently and were limited to a few establishments as Mrs Simpson was an efficient shopper with little time for dallying over ribbons and frills.

They had already been to the dressmaker, the milliner, and of course Gianetti and Son on George Street, perfumers to the Queen. Mina rarely purchased anything there but was a frequent visitor, trying scents and exchanging gossip with Mr Gianetti. Today's conversation had centred upon a murder and scandal reported in that day's newspaper. 'A gentleman in Glasgow has been found guilty of killing his wife,' Mina said. 'And what drove him, it turns out, was that he had entered into a relationship with one of the servants. Further, it is speculated the gentleman had previously murdered a housemaid because she bore his child. It seems the girl died in a fire, her room locked from the outside.'

Sarah did not think the word 'gentle' ought to be appended to such a creature, but from her tone, it appeared Mina regarded his consorting with the help to be the real affront to decent values.

Mina spent her usual half an hour trying various scents before deciding against such an expensive purchase because her allowance would not stretch to such luxuries. She would have to make do, she complained to Sarah as they left the shop, with her usual brand of eau de cologne and handkerchief water from Duncan and Flockhart's, where Dr Simpson had an account.

'I long for the day when I have control of my own household,' Mina said. 'In my present state I am but a burden to my relatives.'

As they resumed their progress along Princes Street, Mina beckoned Sarah walk alongside for a spell, which meant there was something she wished to discuss.

'Have you finished reading *Jane Eyre*?' she asked.

'No, ma'am,' Sarah replied, bracing herself for Mina's disappointment. There was so little time, particularly during daylight, and she was still annoyed by Raven's response to finding her reading between cases.

'But you have made some progress?'

'Yes. About half.'

This seemed satisfactory enough, and her mistress proceeded to probe her for her impressions. Sarah liked this about Mina. She was extraordinarily well-read and had a keen mind for analysis of books and poetry, yet she was always hungry for Sarah's perspective. Sarah suspected this was because she lacked a suitable companion with whom to discuss such things. Mina socialised a great deal, but understandably considered many of the women she visited to be intellectually inferior, concerned only with talk of husbands and children – in each case both real and prospective.

'I find the heroine courageous and impressively strong in her will,' Sarah said.

From her expression she could tell Mina did not share this opinion.

'I found her rather frustrating,' Mina observed. 'But upon reflection I realise that this frustration was born of recognising that I share certain of her traits. And what might seem strong-willed decisions to a younger woman appear more like follies with the wisdom of experience.'

'What do you consider follies, ma'am?'

'I feared she was being too exacting in what she sought in a husband, with the consequential danger that she may end up with no one. It ends well enough for her, as it only can in the realm of novels, but the real world is usually less forgiving.'

Sarah knew that Mina had been romantically disappointed on more than one occasion; promises made and then broken. She knew also that there had been suitors Mina considered beneath her expectations, something Sarah admired in her.

'I have not finished the story, but is it not better for a woman to remain alone than to be married to someone unsuitable? Someone who does not meet whatever standards she sets?'

'That is a question I ask myself ever more frequently as the years pile one upon the other. I would not consider an unsuitable man, but I would admit that what I consider suitable has changed. I have long since discarded the foolish notions of my youth. I think there is much to commend a companionate marriage: a man I respect, whose work I admire and whose household I would be proud to run. I confess that in this I am envious towards my sister. She has all of this with a man she truly loves, and who truly loves her.'

Sarah was always flattered to be the recipient of such candour, but the feeling only ever lasted until she remembered that Mina felt free to be so open with her because she didn't count. She would never be so candid with anyone of status.

Following a detour into Kennington and Jenner's to examine their silks, they arrived outside the druggist's. It was a premises with which Sarah was very familiar and more than a little fond. She was frequently sent there on errands, Dr Simpson's practice always having a need for items such as dressings, plasters, ointments and unguents.

Mr Flockhart was a surgeon as well as a druggist, and both he and his partner Mr Duncan had many friends among the medical practitioners of the city. They were intelligent and innovative gentlemen: excellent practical chemists who could turn their hand to the production of any medicinal product, and according to Dr Simpson, the results were always of the highest standard. Sarah was in no position to judge such matters, but she had found Mr Duncan to be a kindly man, always willing to share his expertise regarding the healing properties of certain medicinal plants which he grew in his herb garden, just outside the city.

As she pushed open the door the little bell above it tinkled and she smiled to herself. This was one of her favourite places in Edinburgh.

The shop was dominated by a marble-topped counter, behind which shelves containing rows of glass bottles stretched all the way to the ceiling. The bottles held powders, liquids and oils with exotic-sounding names. Some she was familiar with – ipecac, glycerine, camphor – while others were labelled with abbreviated Latin terms she could not decipher.

When they entered, the druggist's assistant was carefully weighing out a powder on a set of brass scales. He looked up and winked at Sarah, his expression at once lecherous and self-satisfied. Sarah hated having to deal with this one. His lasciviousness was matched only by his stupidity. She wasn't sure what effect he believed his wink to have: whether she was supposed to be intimidated by his worldliness or weak-kneed in delight.

'Good afternoon, Master Ingram,' she said, flashing him a smile that was as broad and confident as it was insincere.

Master Ingram rapidly lost his concentration and the powder he was measuring spilled across the counter. He stopped what he was doing and rushed through to the dispensing room at the back of the shop, presumably to find someone more competent to help him. Mr Flockhart duly emerged.

'Ladies,' he said, opening his arms as if he was planning to embrace them. 'How may I be of assistance?'

Mr Flockhart was a tall man, as effervescent as the stomach powders he sold. He was a great enthusiast for social gatherings and functions, and as such he always had stories to tell and gossip to impart. Mina made straight for him.

Meanwhile, Mr Duncan emerged from the back, presumably to tidy up the mess left by his assistant.

'Are you in need of anything today, Sarah?' he asked as she approached the counter.

'Not today, thank you.'

Mr Duncan took in her weary face and suggested she place her parcels upon a chair in the corner of the shop. He glanced over at Mina, who was enthusiastically engaged in conversation with Mr Flockhart.

'You could be here for some time.'

Once she had divested herself of her packages, Mr Duncan told her: 'I have something for you to try. I have been experimenting with a new confection made with icing sugar and flavoured with lemon and rosewater.'

He held out a piece of wax paper bearing two round comfits, one pink and one yellow, each with a little heart-shaped pattern imprinted on one side. Sarah tasted each in turn. They fizzed on her tongue and flooded her mouth with sweetness. She closed her eyes briefly. When she opened them, Mr Duncan was smiling at her.

'They're wonderful!' she said. 'What are they called?'

'Haven't decided yet,' he said, wrapping a few more for her to take home.

Sarah took the proffered paper parcel and quickly put it in her pocket, reasoning that if Mina saw it, she might object. She had rules of etiquette which defied any rational explanation and which she applied with equal measures of vigour and caprice. The only consistent element appeared to be that they interfered with whatever Sarah happened to be doing or saying at any given time.

The junior assistant had still to reappear and Sarah wondered if he was being punished somewhere – perhaps being forced to make a large batch of a particularly pungent and malodorous ointment. She hoped so. She watched as Mr Duncan cleaned up the mess on the counter. He transferred a quantity of the powder from the scales to a mortar and began to grind it.

'What do you look for when taking on a new assistant?' she asked, thinking about the daft lad who had already gained a position there.

Mr Duncan paused before answering and looked towards the back of the shop as though trying to remind himself.

'We require someone who can read and write well,' he said, continuing to pound away with his pestle. 'They must have a good grasp of mathematics in order to accurately calculate totals on bills of sale. They must be industrious and well presented.'

He paused again and smiled.

'An ability to decipher hieroglyphics is also useful. Some of our customers write their requirements on slips of paper and their command of the written word is not always their greatest strength.'

He pushed a soot-soiled scrap of paper towards Sarah. On it was written in childish script: 'Dull water for eye cups'.

Sarah could make nothing of it. She looked at Mr Duncan and shrugged.

'Dill water for hiccups,' he said, laughing. 'Why do you ask about the job of assistant? Do you know someone who might be interested in a position here? A brother or a cousin perhaps?'

Sarah thought for a minute about her own abilities. She had a neat hand, a good head for numbers (she always checked Mrs Lyndsay's account books before they were presented to Mrs Simpson and they were seldom in error) and was already familiar with a host of herbal remedies. She looked over at Mina, who was testing out a hand cream and was oblivious to Sarah's conversation. She thought about the drudgery of much of the work at Queen Street and Mrs Lyndsay's determination to limit her involvement with the more interesting parts of her job.

'I was thinking about myself,' she said.

'You?'

Sarah straightened her back and lifted her chin.

'Yes, me. Why not?'

Mr Duncan gave her an apologetic look.

'Sarah,' he said, 'our assistants must inspire confidence in our customers. For that, only a man will do.'

TEN

n a few short days, Raven had become accustomed to journeying to the Old Town in Dr Simpson's carriage, a luxury which spared him from (or perhaps merely deferred) the anxiety besetting him now. His duties as Simpson's apprentice also involved assisting with the professor's lectures at the university, and on this occasion he was having to make his way there in advance, in order to prepare a practical demonstration while the doctor attended a case out in Balerno.

His fear was all the more unsettling for being an unfamiliar sensation in entirely familiar surroundings. These streets had been his home for almost seven years: he well knew their dangers but that was not the same as being afraid. He had never felt scared here before.

Raven had first come here at the age of thirteen, when he was enrolled in George Heriot's, a school 'for poor fatherless boys'. It was an educational opportunity that would previously have been far beyond his means, an unforeseen consolation accruing from the tragedy that had otherwise so reduced his family's circumstances. The significance was not lost on Raven that dying was the most substantial contribution his father ever made towards providing him with a future.

He recalled how tentative his early ventures out to the surrounding neighbourhood had been, haunted by the stories the older boys told to frighten their juniors. But Raven had always been drawn to explore that which he feared, not to mention that which might seem forbidden. By the time he was a student at the university (the requisite fees extracted with difficulty from and following prolonged negotiation with his parsimonious uncle) he felt like a native of the Old Town, if not entirely at home there.

Up ahead, the sanctuary of the university's courtyard beckoned him in the murk. He felt he would be safe within its walls, particularly as it was daylight; or daytime, at least. The whole city remained shrouded in a choking fog that refused to lift though it was already after noon.

From the moment he crossed the North Bridge, he had been looking over his shoulder for the Weasel and Gargantua, though together with Peg, these were the only associates of Flint that he even knew to be on the lookout for. Gargantua at least he should be able to see coming, perhaps the most conspicuous creature in Edinburgh. What gruesome disorder had blighted the fellow? Given the nature of their only encounter, Raven was disinclined to be sympathetic towards the monster's plight, but as a medical man he recognised that the man was surely afflicted. He wasn't merely large: parts of him had kept growing when they ought to have stopped, and that didn't augur well for his prospects. Unfortunately he was unlikely to die soon enough to save Raven, and even then Flint would not be short of a replacement.

He had tried to steady himself by considering his situation rationally. It had only been a matter of days since the Weasel braced him: surely they wouldn't expect his financial situation to have sufficiently improved as to be able to redeem the debt? But then he realised that making rational assumptions was a dangerous mistake. He had to stop thinking of them as reasonable people. They were demanding he got them their money by any means necessary, under the threat of mutilation. It wouldn't stop with an eye, either.

Meanwhile, the longer he went without seeing them, the more they would expect him to pay when they caught up to him again.

The archway to the courtyard was mere yards away, and Raven's stride grew apace the closer he got. His view was fixed upon it, eyes dead ahead, when he heard someone call his name.

A shudder ran through him. More than a shudder, for a shudder passes quickly. It was a tremor, accompanied by the threat of tears and a sharp twinge in his cheek as though he could feel the slice of Weasel's blade again. It happened every time he was startled, whether by a sudden noise or a phantom in the dark as he waited for sleep. It had even happened at dinner two nights ago, when Simpson raised a carving knife and the gleam of the blade caught his eye.

He came close to breaking into a sprint, before the voice resumed and he was able to recognise it.

'Slow down, man. You're walking like the wolves are at your back.'

It was Henry, jogging to catch up, and Raven was able to disguise his relief as pleasure.

'We New Town residents walk as quickly as we can through the poorer districts, don't you know.'

'I don't doubt it. How are you finding the estimable Professor Simpson and his household?'

'I'm not sure what I expected, but I can say that it wasn't what I found. It's a menagerie, Henry. Dogs, children, chaotic clinics. I may need some time to adjust.'

'And what of colleagues?'

'There is a Dr George Keith, who lives nearby. He is a decent sort. And there is a James Duncan, who if he was made of chocolate would surely eat himself, were his appetites not so abstemious.'

'James Duncan? I think I may have encountered him. Studied here, and at Aberdeen before that? An uncommonly young graduate?'

'That's right.'

'Yes. Gifted of mind but an altogether odd creature. Set upon an ostensibly humanitarian undertaking and yet giving off as much warmth as a dying penguin's last fart.'

'Sadly not unique among our peers. Impeccable in his conduct but a singularly joyless soul.'

'Never trust a man who has no apparent vices. The concealed ones are apt to be disgusting. And what of the staff at Queen Street? Any pretty housemaids to delight your eye?'

The image of Sarah leapt unbidden into his head, but whether she delighted his eye was moot, because he could not picture her without reliving the incident at his first clinic. The very thought of her made Raven feel awkward and embarrassed. For all his years of diligent study, a mere girl had been able to make him feel like he had learned nothing of practical worth. That she was worldly and he a schoolboy.

'Unfortunately not,' he said, hoping that Henry read nothing in his expression that encouraged him to press the subject.

Henry's scrutinising eye was upon him, but fortunately focused on something more superficial.

'Your swelling is going down nicely,' he remarked, words that put Sarah right back into Raven's mind. He had to get off the subject.

'Evidence of a deft hand,' he said. 'So what business occupies those deft hands today?'

Henry's gaze returned to the courtyard widening before them, students traversing the flagstones in all directions, flitting in and out of vision like ghosts in this stubborn fog.

'I am in search of a butcher,' he replied.

'Then I may be able to assist, now that I am widening my circle of acquaintance. Mrs Lyndsay, the Simpsons' cook, buys her meat from Hardie's, on Cockburn Street. He would have to be a fine butcher, as her standards are exacting.'

'I am not looking for a fine butcher. I am looking for an unconscionable one.'

Henry had a singularity about his expression, his thoughts finely focused.

'You recall that death from peritonitis that was so vexing Professor Syme? When we carried out the post-mortem we discovered that her uterus had been perforated, as had a loop of small intestine.'

'A butcher indeed,' Raven said.

'She wasn't the last, either. We've had another case since, also fatal. Similar injuries.'

'Have the authorities been informed?'

'Yes, but they won't act. No one is going to admit that they know anything about it, and more importantly it hasn't affected the right class of people. You know how it is. There's no way of knowing for sure it's the same culprit, but I fear somebody has set up to trade.'

'An amateur?' Raven asked.

'Impossible to be sure. It's certainly not the worst I've seen in my time.'

'When it comes to this, nobody truly knows what they're doing,' Raven stated. 'But nonetheless, a level of medical knowledge is necessary to even know where to begin.'

'I wouldn't speak those words too loudly, my friend, and nor would I wish to be the first to suggest adding it to the curriculum. But you speak the truth. It is disappointing to think of someone offering what they know to be literally a stab in the dark, butchering women in their greed for fast cash.'

Raven thought of Weasel's blade and understood how quickly one's ethics might be abandoned given a powerful enough motivation.

'We can only hope that his technique improves quickly,' he suggested. 'Else these two won't be his last victims.'

'Can we say for certain it is a he?' Henry asked.

'I suppose not,' Raven admitted. 'There are always unscrupulous midwives ready with a sharp knitting needle if the price is right, and I have heard it suggested that women feel easier about approaching someone of their own sex when soliciting such illicit services.'

'Not merely for illicit services,' Henry replied. 'I have heard tell that there is a French midwife working in the city, eagerly sought after by ladies who would rather not be treated by a man.'

Raven thought of the needless encumbrance of the bedsheets that prevented him and Dr Simpson seeing what they were doing. He wondered if the preservation of modesty was less of an issue when the practitioner was female.

'French, you say?'

'A graduate of the Hôtel Dieu, no less, if the accounts are to be believed.'

'Then you don't need to worry about her being this butcher,' Raven said. 'A graduate of the Hôtel Dieu would know well enough what she was about.'

'Then perhaps it's not I who ought to worry about her. You're the one she's competing with.'

'I'll start worrying when they start training women to be doctors.'

Henry laughed.

'So who were they?' Raven asked. 'The victims?'

'One of them was a tavern maid, the other a prostitute.'

Another deid hoor, Raven thought.

'We don't get fine ladies washing up at the Infirmary,' Henry went on. 'The quality can afford a home visit from the likes of Dr Simpson.'

'I don't believe this is a service that he offers,' Raven said, though it struck him that he had no means of knowing.

'No, and nor was that what I was suggesting. Though I

sometimes wonder what they do over in the New Town when there is an inconvenient issue.'

'They simply have the babies,' Raven supposed, thinking of the household staff commanded by Mrs Simpson, reputedly modest by some standards. 'Then pass them off to nurses and nannies. It is always different when there is money. These young women must resort to desperate measures because they feel they have no alternative.'

Henry nodded solemnly, slowing his stride as they reached the entrance where their routes would diverge.

'More desperate than anyone might believe,' he said ruefully. 'I'm told an infant's leg was found in a gutter by a scavenger rooting in an alley near the Royal Exchange. The authorities are looking into that one, at least.'

As they parted ways, Raven was left with a profound sense of sadness over the fates of these women, though he had not known them, nor even seen them. He knew that it was down to a sense of guilt over Evie, whose death scene he had run from like he had something to hide.

Raven wondered what he might have missed. Had he been so startled by the discovery that she was dead and the danger of being found in there with the body that he hadn't looked properly – hadn't seen things he might otherwise have noticed?

Though Flint's men were on the prowl, he knew he had no choice. He would have to go back.

ELEVEN

The waiting rooms always filled up quickest on a Monday morning, there being no clinic on the Sabbath. Sarah took a moment to catch her breath and rapidly assessed the assembly: old and young, male and female; a chest infection here, a fever there; swellings, rashes, sweats, shivers. There was a general, low hubbub of muted conversation, punctuated at irregular intervals by spluttering coughs and ill-contained sneezes.

One young woman sat with a small child on her knee, his cheeks lividly flushed and two rivulets of greenish mucus escaping from his nostrils to form a small lake on his top lip. He appeared far from content with his circumstances and Sarah knew the threat of voluble crying was never far away. However, his mother proved herself resourceful in having come equipped with a means of soothing her fractious charge. Every now and then her hand would disappear into a pocket and then emerge with a small piece of confectionary, which would be popped between his lips to buy a few more minutes of silence.

Sarah watched this from her position at the door and groaned inwardly at the thought of the threads of stickiness his little fingers were likely to leave behind. There was also a trail of muddy footprints leading from the door to the fireplace. As much as she enjoyed helping out at the doctor's clinic, the daily congregation of patients fairly added to her workload.

She noticed that the fire was beginning to die down, so she crossed the room, knelt down at the grate and shovelled in some more coal. As she poked at the fire, Will Raven emerged from his consulting room. He took a moment to spot her, crouched by the hearth, but she knew he would not proceed until he had her attention. She stood up and indicated a man cradling his right hand, which was wrapped in a particularly grotty cloth. Sarah had no inkling what was beneath it, but the smell had made it a priority, and not merely because the source might prove serious.

Sarah watched Raven lead the man away, still holding his forearm as though bearing a dead weight. She remained unsure quite what to make of the professor's new student apprentice. He lacked the confidence and self-assurance she was used to in the gentlemen who called to the house, and even allowing for his comparative youth, Raven's manner was in marked contrast to that of his predecessor, Thomas Keith. Dr Keith's younger brother had seemed altogether more comfortable in his position, although she ought to consider that when Thomas first arrived, Sarah was new too, and not merely to the household, but to her job.

She had the impression Raven was out of practice in dealing with domestic staff, most likely resultant of his time spent in lodgings whilst attending the university. This perhaps also accounted for the fact that he seemed rather thin and not nearly as well-nourished as she would have expected. Sarah had heard tell of how driven young men could become obsessive in the pursuit of their studies, and consequently neglectful of their worldly needs. This struck her as ironic in one studying medicine, training to look after bodily health, but for Raven to have secured such a coveted position with the professor, she supposed he might have been just so single-minded.

If there was one thing she had to give him credit for, it was that he was always kind and solicitous towards the patients, listening attentively and never talking down to them. Once again, it might seem ironic that such a trait should be remarkable in a supposedly caring profession, but Sarah had come to recognise a particular haughtiness common among medical men. Perhaps Raven hadn't yet acquired it, or perhaps it was this aspect of his manner that had won him Dr Simpson's approval.

Sarah occasionally amused herself by dwelling on the notion of herself as a student: what her days would have been like and which subjects she might have liked to study. She had an interest in botany and horticulture, as well as in the traditional healing arts, inherited from her family background. Any time spent in the professor's study caused her to marvel at all of the myriad disciplines and fields of knowledge one might explore, and the idea of spending whole years doing precisely that seemed heavenly. However, this was a distraction that came at a price, for although it was pleasant to indulge such fantasies, they also forced her to confront the harsh truth. She had not the means to attend university nor any prospect of ever acquiring them. Being female was also an obstacle that she could not easily overcome.

Mrs Lyndsay told her she would only enjoy contentment once she came to accept her station, but Sarah could not imagine anything quelling this restless want, and nor could she imagine ever feeling a genuine desire to do so. To numb her curiosity would be to cut off a part of herself.

Sarah did not consider it a coincidence that since that conversation, she had been permitted to assist at the morning clinic on fewer occasions. Mrs Lyndsay would assign her extra chores, or find fault with the tasks she had already carried out, and as a result declare she could not be spared. Nor did she consider it a coincidence that the clinics she missed appeared to be even more noisy and disorderly than usual.

From behind her, Sarah heard an explosive bout of coughing, ending in a loud and voluminous expectoration which prompted her to hope this individual was in possession of a handkerchief, as those without had been known to spit upon the floor. As she resumed poking at the fire she noticed how red and sore her hands looked, the skin beginning to split across the knuckles. This was a result of the recent cold weather and she hoped that she still had enough of her oatmeal ointment left to treat them, as she had not the time to make another batch.

Climbing once more to her feet, she heard a panic-stricken voice call out: 'Jamie! What on earth is the matter with you?'

Sarah turned to see the young woman with the catarrhal child grip her son by the arms, shaking him as though he was refusing to heed her instructions. Drawing closer, Sarah could see that the child was frantically struggling against her grasp, his eyes wide with fright. The boy's growing terror was mirrored in the face of his mother, who began loudly appealing to the room for assistance.

'I don't know what's wrong with him,' she squealed, shrill in her desperation. 'For the love of God, please, someone help him!'

The boy seemed unable to draw breath, his lips turning blue. Sarah could tell that the fight was beginning to drain from him, his movements becoming languid. She looked at his helpless, flailing arm and recalled the sticky fingers that had so recently concerned her. Suddenly, she knew what was wrong.

Sarah grabbed the child from the woman and bent him over her forearm. With her other hand she slapped his back sharply between the shoulder blades: once, twice. On the third attempt, something hit the carpet at her feet, whereupon the boy drew in an enormous breath and then began to cry.

The child's mother took him back onto her knee to comfort him as Sarah stood motionless, staring at the small, orange, sticky lump that was now firmly imbedded in the pile of the carpet.

The commotion had alerted the rest of the house. Dr Keith and Will Raven were quickly in the room, Dr Simpson arriving at the door moments later.

'Whatever is the cause of this?' Raven demanded.

Sarah pointed at the floor.

'Barley sugar,' she answered.

Whatever fortitude had guided Sarah's vital intervention quickly deserted her once the danger had passed, and she found herself suddenly tremulous and unsteady on her feet in the aftermath. At the professor's bidding, she was escorted to his study, where she was furnished with a strong cup of tea. Mrs Lyndsay had great faith in its restorative powers, but as Sarah sat on the couch and slowly sipped, she reflected that perhaps simply enjoying the peace and time to drink it was the brew's most efficacious property. The pounding in her chest gradually subsided and her breathing, which had been for a while rapid and shallow, returned to its usual rate and depth.

There was a gentle rap at the door and Dr Simpson entered.

'How are you feeling now, Sarah?' he asked.

'Much better, thank you, sir.'

'I must congratulate you. You showed great presence of mind in dealing with that situation. You saved that wee fellow's life, and no mistake. I am immensely proud of you. But I am also most curious as to just how you knew what to do.'

Sarah cleared her throat. '*Buchan's Domestic Medicine*, sir. We didn't have a great many books at home, only that one and the Bible. As a result, I must have read it through a number of times.'

'Indeed?' asked Dr Simpson, smiling. Something about her answer appeared to have amused him. She felt that she ought to explain further.

'My grandmother was the village howdie. A midwife and a healer. That is probably why I developed an interest in such matters. I know a little about herbal remedies. What she taught me.'

Dr Simpson smiled again. 'Hence your efforts in cultivating a little herb garden at the back of the house. I hope you're not planning to go into competition with me as a healer.'

'No, sir,' she answered bashfully.

'My grandfather too was a healer of some repute,' Dr Simpson told her. 'Mainly of livestock but he set a few bones in his time. He was, however, prone to indulging in country superstitions. He once buried a cow alive in an attempt to halt the progression of cattle plague, the image of which stayed with my father and haunted him to his dying day.

'Fortunately, there is no place in modern medicine for such nonsense. Health and disease is not a straightforward business. It would seem that the more we know, the more there is to know. Always be suspicious of those who claim to have simple answers to complex problems. Beware the foul waters of quackery.'

Sarah had heard similar speeches before and was well aware of the less-than-scrupulous travelling salesmen with their cure-all mixtures. While it was certainly true that country folk could still be a little credulous, being far removed as they were from great seats of learning, Sarah understood that when there was a dearth of knowledge and education, people – no matter their origins – were inclined to believe just about anything communicated to them with sufficient confidence and authority. However, Sarah also knew from personal experience that when all hope was lost, when all else had failed, people were willing to try almost anything to save those that they loved.

'Surely botanicals cannot be considered quackery?'

'Most definitely not,' the doctor replied. 'Nature has provided us with many useful remedies, but it is chemistry that will unlock her secrets. As a result of chemistry, we now know that it is quinine in Jesuit's bark that makes it useful in tertian fever and morphine that gives the opium poppy its power.'

Dr Simpson went to his bookcase and began searching the spines.

'I have the most informative book on the subject: *Outlines of Chemistry, for the Use of Students*, by my colleague Professor William Gregory. Would you be interested in learning more about it?'

Sarah smiled, put down her teacup and held out her hand.

TWELVE

aven entered the lecture theatre alongside the professor, loaded down by a stack of notes which Simpson typically ignored. The lecture room was full and the students unusually attentive. Raven had been on those same benches in the preceding two years, and it had been Simpson's passion and clarity on his subject that had drawn him towards the field of midwifery.

On this occasion the lecture was about the parturient with a contracted pelvis. As always the professor was a warm and engaging speaker, seldom taking his audience's attention for granted, and illustrating his points through reference to relevant clinical examples. These were detailed in the case notes Raven had looked out and hefted into the room at Simpson's request, but he never had need to refer to them.

Looking at the packed theatre and comparing it to some of the sparsely attended meanderings he had sat through in the same venue, Raven considered how much the professor would make from the fees of this class alone. By his calculations it was a significant amount. Perhaps one day he might lecture here himself, or in the short term at least, now that he had been over the course, he could offer personal tuition to some of the rich students lining the benches. These were pleasant enough daydreams, but even if they were to come to fruition, it would not be soon enough for Flint.

Towards the end of the lecture a messenger appeared at the door, sweaty and breathless from running, and clutching a soiled piece of paper. Raven intercepted him in the corridor outside before he could disrupt the doctor's concluding remarks.

'The professor is urgently requested to attend at a house in the Grassmarket, sir,' he panted, thrusting the paper into Raven's hand.

'By whom?' Raven asked, opening the note, the penmanship of which was illegible.

'By the doctor who is already there.'

'And did he write this with his feet?'

'No, his left hand. He was using his right to stop the bleeding.'

The doctor's carriage sped them through the narrow streets, avoiding carts, barrows and the odd heedless pedestrian seemingly intent upon self-murder. The dog would have loved this, thought Raven, though he was not sorry that on this occasion the beast had been left at home.

They pulled up outside a building on the south side of the Grassmarket and were directed by the messenger to an upper apartment. Simpson for once was panting due to the urgency of his ascent, unable to spare the breath to again observe 'always the top'.

Inside they found a young woman in labour, deathly pale and covered in a sheen of perspiration. Standing useless against the wall was a terrified-looking midwife who had some hours ago realised she was out of her depth.

In this, she was not alone.

The young doctor who had written the left-handed note looked besieged by his circumstances, crouching at the foot of the bed, blood spattering his face and his clothes. He had clearly been there for some time, and looked up with a bright expression of relief upon seeing Simpson, betraying that he had not been sure the professor would respond.

Raven took hold of the woman's wrist while Simpson shed his coat. Her pulse was rapid and thready. With the professor stepping in to intervene, the young doctor moved aside and climbed to his feet. He was shorter than Raven and slight of build, with something boyish about his countenance. He was expensively tailored, however, the clothes sitting elegantly upon his neat frame even as blood and sweat stuck the shirt to his chest.

'Tell me what we have here,' Simpson bade him.

Raven had expected an anxious voice befitting the circumstances and his physical stature, but the young doctor explained the details of the case in a calm, clear register, his account as lucid as his note had been illegible.

'Liquor amnii discharged early, ineffectual pains, two doses of ergot of rye given. There was considerable vomiting after the first dose, and after the second the patient said that she felt "something give" inside. The infant's head remained high, and so I employed long forceps but to no avail. Considerable haemorrhage followed the attempt at delivery, whereupon I dispatched my urgent note requesting your assistance.'

Raven was impressed as much by this display of professional detachment as by the contents of his description. He knew well enough how flustered one could become in the face of mounting trauma, sufficient that the maelstrom inside his head could pour out as babble from his mouth.

'Name?' Simpson asked.

'Beattie, sir. Dr John Beattie.'

'Of the patient,' he clarified.

'Oh. Williams, I think. Or was it Williamson. I can't quite recall. It has been a long day.'

Dr Simpson examined the patient, looked at Raven and beckoned him closer. His face was grim.

'The infant's head is at the upper aperture of the pelvis and is fairly wedged there,' he whispered. 'It is not sufficiently far down in the pelvis for a forceps delivery to have any chance of success and I am worried that the uterus itself might have ruptured. We must deliver the infant without delay – it is the mother's only chance of survival.'

As Simpson began fishing about inside his bag, Raven wondered what implement might be in there that could succeed where the forceps had failed. Simpson withdrew what Raven recognised as a perforator, and immediately he understood what was about to happen. He should have known already, but his faith in the professor as some kind of miracle-worker had caused him to misread the possibilities. He was going to perform a procedure known as a craniotomy.

Simpson took the bottle of ether from his bag. At least she wouldn't have to be awake during this.

'She shouldn't need much,' he said, looking at Raven.

'Mrs Williamson won't be having any of that,' the midwife objected. 'We're of the same church and the minister says it's not right to use it.'

Raven looked at her in confusion and disbelief.

She responded by thrusting a pamphlet at him, a diatribe penned by one Reverend Malachy Grissom.

Raven glanced at it and then looked to Simpson, who responded with a weary expression. He had clearly encountered this form of resistance before.

'The primeval curse,' he said by way of explanation. 'Genesis. "In sorrow thou shalt bring forth children." Some consider it to be anti-scriptural to remove the pain associated with labour.'

Raven thought that this sounded like needless stupidity, a description that fitted many words and deeds he had witnessed on the part of churchmen. Why a so-called man of God would deny a woman pain relief, especially given what was about to happen, made no sense to him.

'Perhaps Mrs Williamson should be permitted to make that decision for herself,' Raven suggested, earning himself a scolding look from the midwife.

The woman herself could not be persuaded, however.

'I'll not risk eternal damnation for the sake of delivering a child,' she replied weakly.

The midwife nodded with undisguised satisfaction, her eyes fixed on Raven, and so Dr Simpson proceeded without the aid of a soporific.

For once Raven was grateful for the sheet that was shrouding the woman's legs and genital area. He knew what was happening, he had seen it before and he had no desire to see it again today. He could more or less recite Dr Simpson's lecture on the subject anyway:

Many children can be brought into the world by the use of forceps and turning, but there are cases where the infant's head is too large and the maternal passages too small to admit the delivery of the child alive without bringing the life of the mother into the most imminent danger. In such circumstances, we can save the life of the mother by sacrificing that of her pregnancy. By opening the head of the infant by means of perforating instruments, we can remove the contents of the cranium and then break down the vault of the skull, bringing away the fragments until only the base of the cranium and the bones of the face remain to be extracted by means of the crochet.

Even in her weakened state, Mrs Williamson writhed a great deal as the various instruments were inserted to break down the infant's head and haul it out. Raven felt turmoil watching her and thinking of the tiny life that was being snuffed out before it had a chance to take a single breath. This was the thing that most caused him to fear he was not made of the right stuff to be a doctor. He knew for sure it was why he couldn't be a surgeon.

His mother always said he had the devil in him, but she simply meant he had a keen sense of mischief, the imp of the perverse. The human in him had a tendency to feel other people's pain too keenly.

After the infant was delivered – what was left of it – the placenta followed without delay, but the uterus would not contract. The patient continued to bleed despite the binder tightly wound round her abdomen. Raven knew this was a serious complication. He also knew there was nothing more they could do.

The cleaning and tidying away of instruments was performed in near silence. Dr Simpson spoke to the midwife, giving instructions that she should see to her patient's every comfort, vowing to return later in the day to check on her progress.

He shook his head as he left the room.

THIRTEEN

he medical men, all of them now dishevelled and blood-spattered, emerged onto the Grassmarket, which was busy with carters and street-traders going about their business. It seemed incredible that the rest of the world could carry on as if nothing had happened: small-scale horror and tragedy swallowed up by the day-to-day affairs of the city.

Simpson suggested that they repair to a local hostelry for a restorative to raise their spirits, nominating an establishment he had frequented as a medical student.

Baxter's tavern sat rather incongruously beside Cranston's Teetotal Coffee House, which Raven noted with some satisfaction had little in the way of customers. Given the nature of the afternoon's proceedings, he had no doubt which he would rather patronise but did have his concerns regarding who he might see in the alehouse, or more pertinently who might see him.

Entering at the professor's back, he scanned the room from the doorway, ready for a sharp departure. Simpson seemed to be on friendly terms with both proprietor and clientele. He ordered a round of Edinburgh ales, which he took an age to bring across due to how many conversations he struck up between the gantry and their table. Raven drank deeply, thirstier than he realised and in need of the comforts alcohol could offer.

Beattie seemed altogether less traumatised by the outcome of the case. Perhaps this was because he had been a participant throughout rather than merely an impotent witness, and perhaps his greater experience of such things had inured him to the emotional effluent. He seemed unperturbed by the spit and sawdust of the pub, despite his expensive outfit suggesting he might be used to more salubrious surroundings. There was an awkwardness about his gait in keeping with a pronounced quickness to all his physical movements that reminded Raven of a small bird: fleet but restless, as though wary of predators.

Up close and in clearer light, Raven enjoyed a closer appreciation of his boyish visage, which revealed the man to be not so youthful as he first appeared. Initially he believed he had encountered another prodigy like James Duncan (though hopefully not such an obnoxious one), but he could now see the lines around his eyes, suggesting Beattie might be in his late twenties.

Simpson asked Beattie a little about his background, beginning with the seemingly inevitable question regarding his father's occupation.

'My father is dead, sir,' Beattie replied. 'Indeed, I lost both my parents when I was twelve. However, I am fortunate in having a benefactor in the form of my uncle, a Mr Charles Latimer, who is a man of some property in Canaan Lands on the Morningside.'

Raven hoped Beattie's uncle wore his largesse more lightly than Miserly Malcolm, who turned every penny spent on his nephew into a token of his sister's failure and poor judgment in her choice of matrimonial partner.

'You don't sound as though you hail from these parts,' Simpson suggested.

'No. I was schooled in the south of England, but my mother grew up here. I attended university in Edinburgh to be closer to my uncle, who has become frailer over the years.'

In the manner peculiar to all medical men, Simpson ignored all reference to finance and property and asked for details regarding the uncle's debility.

'He suffers from a severe form of rheumatism which causes him much pain. He has tried all manner of therapies in his attempts to find relief. He most recently embarked upon a trip to Austria to try a water treatment promoted by a fellow named Priessnitz. Runs a therapeutic establishment somewhere in the mountains.'

'Did your uncle find any of this helpful?'

'He found his pain to be somewhat improved but his spirits more so. It makes me think that there may be something in it – cold baths, simple diet and the withdrawal of all internal medicines. His response to these therapies – and more pertinently the sum he paid for them – leads me to envisage that there might be a lucrative market for hydropathic treatments.'

Simpson rubbed his chin, fixing Beattie with a thoughtful gaze.

'It could perhaps be argued that it was the withdrawal of his usual medicaments which resulted in his improvement, and not the regular soaking with cold water. We are perhaps too ready to dose our patients with powerful purges and bleed them to the point of depletion, don't you think? My friend and colleague Dr George Keith is a great believer in Nature's Method and the idea of masterly inactivity on the part of the physician.'

'*Primum non nocere*,' nodded Beattie in agreement.

Do no harm: the Hippocratic injunction.

Simpson took a gulp from his ale by way of toasting the sentiment, draining the last of it.

'Forgive me, Dr Beattie, I have just spied a good friend at another table. But before I go, let me say I have very much enjoyed meeting you this afternoon. You must come to dinner at Queen Street.'

'I would be honoured,' Beattie replied with a quiet grace.

Raven could only imagine how he might have spluttered his

response had someone so feted extended such an offer. This together with his fine garb suggested it was not the first time Beattie had been invited to dine in estimable company.

They watched the professor stride across the tavern and loudly hail a fellow on the other side of the room.

'The professor is a man of broad acquaintance,' Beattie said, as though this was in some way amusing. 'I wouldn't have thought him comfortable in a place like this these days. He is reputedly much in demand among the ladies of the aristocracy.'

Though I am yet to see much evidence of it, Raven thought.

'He is of humble origins, though,' Raven said. This was another of the factors that had drawn him to the professor. If Simpson could rise to such stature and wealth from ordinary beginnings, he had reasoned, then perhaps a keen apprentice might learn to follow his path.

'The son of a village baker,' Beattie stated. 'A seventh son and the last of eight.'

This was more than Raven knew, and it showed.

Beattie flashed him a self-conscious smile. 'It is always wise to learn as much as you can about the great names in your field, in case fate should throw you into their company. Though being found blood-spattered and helpless at the foot of a patient's bed – a patient I failed – is not the best first impression I could have hoped to make upon the man.'

'Well, it can't have been so bad if he invited you to Queen Street. And frankly, I was amazed at how calm you seemed amidst it all. I can't keep my mind from returning to that room and of thinking about how it is likely to go for Mrs Williamson.'

Beattie supped from his beer, an equanimity about him that further belied Raven's early impression of his youth.

'I very much doubt she will live,' he said. 'Even despite the attentions of Dr Simpson.' His tone was even, as though discussing something third-hand rather than a woman whose blood even now daubed his shirt.

'Does it get easier, then?' Raven asked.

'Does what?'

'Dealing with such suffering. When I witness a case such as we just left, it holds me in its grip long after, and I fear the cumulative burden. Yet you were reasoned amidst it all and seem unaffected now.'

Beattie regarded Raven for a moment, giving some thought to his answer.

'Each man only has so much pity to give, and in our profession we encounter every day some tragedy upon which one might spend a large portion of it.'

'Are you saying that in time I will become numb to this? For I am not sure I would wish that either.'

'It is not so much a process of becoming numb, but of a perspective that is harshly learned through your own wounds rather than those you might treat. When you have known true sorrow, the plight of a patient, no matter how pitiful, will not hurt you like you have felt hurt before.'

Raven thought he had known sorrow enough, but if he was still so vulnerable to the sufferings of others, then perhaps he had not known as much as Beattie. He said he had lost both his parents at the age of twelve, but something about the man suggested there was more than that. He was curious to know, but did not feel it his place to press.

'And if I have not yet felt true sorrow?' Raven asked.

'Be grateful, and do not wallow in the misery of others. I am sincere in this. The patients require a distance from you, that you may exercise your judgment and skill undistracted by your emotions.'

Raven knew this was right, though it was not easy to hear. He knew there was much he could learn from a doctor such as Beattie, but equally, seeing how he conducted himself was a stark reminder of how far he had to go.

'So you're set on a career in midwifery yourself?' Beattie asked, this change of subject accompanied by a lightening in the tone of his voice.

'Yes. I had thought of surgery, but it is decidedly not for me.'

'Good choice. There is a brighter future in this profession than among the sawbones. Financially speaking, I mean.'

Raven took in Beattie's expensive garments and wondered whether these had been paid for by his uncle or by his earnings.

'I have not seen much evidence of that so far,' he confessed. 'Unless some day I can be the one delivering those aristocratic ladies, but that seems likely to be a long way off.'

Beattie had an impish grin, the lines around his eyes more distinct as he smiled.

'This is a wider field than you understand, one that is even now opening up to new and lucrative possibilities. You need to think beyond babies and more about the women who bear them. There are all manner of new and exotic treatments for the various maladies the fairer sex seem prone to. Galvanism, uterine manipulation – scientific treatments for that perennial female affliction, hysteria. There is much money to be made from unhappy women and their exasperated husbands.'

Raven made no reply, causing Beattie to continue in a similar vein.

'Success is all about identifying opportunity,' Beattie told him. 'Talking of which, this ether stuff is promising, is it not? Think of what a price patients would put upon the oblivion you can provide during a procedure.'

'Those who don't have a religious objection,' Raven muttered.

'It's potentially a gold mine,' Beattie went on, paying no heed. 'I gather the dentists in this town can't get enough of it. You must be getting rather adept at its administration, working with Simpson.'

'He has been training me in its use, yes. When it's a complicated case, that is often the only thing he lets me do myself.'

'Don't complain. I'm sure it will prove a valuable skill.'

'Though maybe not as valuable as dousing rich people in cold water,' Raven replied.

Beattie laughed, and suggested they have another ale. Raven would have dearly loved to. This was an acquaintance he would do well to cultivate, but he had other business to attend, and he would need all his wits about him for it.

FOURTEEN

t was dark as Raven made his way down the Canongate, bound for Evie's lodgings. The lamps seemed almost futile in their efforts to penetrate the blackness and the fog, but he quietened his fear with the knowledge that if he could not make out his enemies amidst such gloom, then neither could they.

He entered Evie's close with a soft tread, but did not make it as far as the stairs before a familiar figure blocked his path. She had emerged from her lair on the ground floor, beyond which a mouse could seldom pass unnoticed unless this fearsome sentinel was already well in her cups.

Evie always described Effie Peake as her landlady, but she didn't own the place. She merely collected rent and kept a close eye on behalf of whoever did, for which she presumably got her own lodgings at a short rate. The woman was the nature of Edinburgh in microcosm, adept to the point of self-deception at compartmentalising her public and private faces. She insisted on being addressed as Mrs Peake, but this was rumoured to be an affectation, as according to Evie there had never been a Mr Peake. She reacted with outrage at any suggestion she was aware immoral conduct might be taking place upon her premises. But in truth, very little business escaped her notice: 'Not when she's taking a slice of every

storm of heaves that happens beneath her roof,' as Evie had put
it.

So she knew who came here, and who they saw. Raven had
no doubt that as well as the local clientele, those visitors included
men of high standing, of impeccable moral repute, of power and
of influence. He also had no doubt that neither Effie's word nor
the word of any woman here would be worth a fig against such
men should an accusation be made. Nonetheless, Raven suspected
Mrs Peake might prove a rich fount of information, if anyone
could find the right means of tapping it.

She was short and stout, as though having developed her shape
specifically to block this passageway. Despite her girth there was
something narrow about her features, pale and pinched, suggesting
that should she ever smile it would unravel the tight bun her hair
was scraped into at the back. 'If you're looking for Evie, she's not
here,' she said. An interesting choice of words, not least because
it reassured him that she did not know he had been in the building
that night.

Raven opted therefore to play along.

'Where is she?'

'Gone.'

'Gone where? Will she be back soon?'

Effie sighed, a weary look coming over her. 'I'm only telling
you this because I recognise your face and I know Evie had a
fondness for you. Evie is dead.'

Raven feigned shock and hurt, a task assisted by what Effie had
just said about Evie having a fondness for him. It was also the first
time he had heard anyone talk about her death beyond those callous
words that had spilled from the mouth of that policeman.

'What happened?'

'Found her that way. Four, no five days ago.'

'Where is she now?'

She looked at him as though he was a simpleton. 'Buried.
Where else would she be?'

'I merely wondered, given that her death had been so sudden, whether it might have prompted an investigation of some kind. A post-mortem perhaps?'

'A post what?'

'An examination of the body, to determine the cause of death.'

'Doctor from the dispensary determined it simply enough. Said it was the drink. Signed the certificate to that effect. Didn't need much time to work that out.'

Raven pictured the body being carried out to the cart in that tattered and filthy shroud. Never mind a post-mortem, the doctor from the dispensary would have barely looked at her. Sometimes they didn't even enter the house.

'Where was she taken?'

'How should I know? Some pauper's grave, as there was no one to pay for anything else. Anyway, that's all I can tell you, so you ought to be on your way.'

She folded her arms, her posture unmistakably defensive. She wanted him gone.

'Could I see her room?'

'Why? Are you some kind of ghoul?'

'No, I'm a man of medicine.'

Effie allowed herself a scornful smirk. 'You don't look like a *man* of anything to me.'

Raven ignored this. 'I would like to see if there is anything there that might help me deduce what became of her.'

'I've already rented it. Can't afford to keep good lodgings empty.'

'Was there anyone with her before she died?'

'I wouldn't know. I respect my tenants' privacy.'

Like her folded arms, this mutually understood lie was an indication that she was putting up the shutters. She would tell him nothing more, which served only to make him wonder what she wished to conceal.

Raven heard a door open above, saw a female face peering over the stairwell to investigate what she had overheard. The face disappeared again following a sharp look from Effie.

'And what of Evie's possessions?' Raven enquired.

'Sold. To cover expenses. Not that you get much for a couple of dresses and a pair of jet earrings.'

'What about the brandy?' he asked, wondering whether it and not the gut-rot might have proven toxic.

'What brandy?' she asked, but she had betrayed herself with her transparent surprise that he should know about it.

'The bottle I saw in her room when last I visited.'

Effie's face took on a defiant expression. 'That's long gone too,' she said. 'I drank it.'

'In that case, I have reason to thank you.'

This truly confused her. 'Thank me?'

'For performing the most basic but reliable form of toxicological analysis. I had a concern that Evie's death might have been attributable to drinking something that proved poisonous. By virtue of the fact that you are standing in front of me, I can deduce that it could not have been the brandy.'

With that, Raven departed back into the gloom.

He had barely traversed the breadth of the building when he heard footsteps at his back, approaching at speed. He turned, bracing himself to attack or to flee, but found himself confronted by the young woman who had been peering down the stairs some moments ago. It was difficult to be sure in the paltry light that fell here between two street lamps, but he thought she seemed familiar.

'It's Will, isn't it?' she asked.

'Yes.'

'Aye. I saw you with Evie sometimes. She talked about you. I'm Peggy.'

'I recognise you. Can I help?'

'I overheard. You were asking if Evie had anyone with her the night she died. She did. I'm in the next room.'

'You saw who came and went?' he asked, suddenly fearing where this might be going.

'I never saw. I heard them, though.'

This came both as relief and disappointment. She hadn't seen Raven, but nor would she be able to identify the visitor.

'I don't suppose his voice was familiar to you?'

'No, but see, that's the thing. It was a woman's voice I heard.'

FIFTEEN

or all Raven had told Henry that it would take some adjustment in getting used to his new accommodations, he could not deny he felt a sense of sanctuary as he crossed the threshold. He hoped the Simpson family appreciated how privileged they were to live in this place, safe not only from cold and hunger, but from the world of danger, anxiety and suspicion that he had grown used to. Here on Queen Street, he no longer had to be in a state of constant alertness, concerned for his possessions, his safety, or, in the cramped confines of Ma Cherry's, his privacy.

He remained conscious of being a guest in another family's home, but equally he was aware of their efforts to make him feel welcome. It was true Jarvis still regarded him with less respect than Glen the dog, and of course there was Sarah, who did not accord him as much as that, but on the whole, he was beginning to feel comfortable at No. 52.

He walked quickly towards the stairs with the intention of warming himself before he got cleaned up for dinner. A fire was always lit in one of the large public rooms on the first floor at this time of day, particularly welcome after the cold breeze that had chilled him on his walk back from Effie Peake's place.

As he began to ascend, something shot past his head, an

improvised missile that served as warning that Walter and David were on the loose. Raven heard the roar of a war cry as David chased his younger brother down the stairs, excited giggles and screams accompanying their progress as usual. They disappeared into a room below with the inevitable slam of a door, after which the ensuing moment of silence seemed all the more pronounced by contrast.

It was broken by voices from his intended destination, Mrs Simpson and Mina continuing what sounded like a fraught conversation. The door was ajar and from the unguarded nature of their discussion, he deduced they were heedless of his approach because his tread upon the stairs had been masked by the noise of the children.

It was Mina he heard first, her tone soft but adamant, as though concerned about being overheard. He felt trapped, conscious that were he to continue his progress, he would be heard and his eavesdropping discovered. Even if it was by accident, people did not readily forgive it when they knew you had happened upon their secrets.

'I think you have become so used to the status Dr Simpson's good name confers, that you forget how precarious reputations can be when there is scandal in the offing.'

'It is blethers, Mina. Nothing more.'

'You should consider that it's not just his reputation that is at stake. It's yours too. He is paying out twelve pounds a year to another woman. Isn't the obvious question: why?'

'It is an act of charity. Surely no one can cast aspersions over something so noble.'

'In my experience people are happy to cast aspersions over anything when the morality of an action can be called into question. You would be naive if you didn't anticipate the conclusions that are likely to be drawn. In your interpretation, it is an act of charity. To someone else, it might imply a guilty conscience.'

'That is absurd, Mina. There is nothing of any substance for rumours to attach to.'

'Jessie, James is a man much admired by the ladies of this town, and you shut away in mourning all this time. They rain upon him compliments and affection. Is it so difficult to imagine where that might lead?'

'I have no control over gossip. What is important is that I know the truth of it.'

'Do you?'

'I would warn you, Mina, to remember beneath whose roof you reside.'

A door flew open downstairs and the boys exploded from it once again. Raven seized the opportunity to proceed unnoticed to his bedroom. They were joyfully oblivious of the complex ways of adults, and he had been almost as naive. Cut beneath the epidermis in any household and you would surely find that life there was not as harmonious as it appeared on the surface.

He had only heard a brief exchange, but he recognised what was going on. Mina was trying to gently coax her sister into seeing what was obvious to her and therefore to others. Raven was only too familiar with the spectacle of a wife seeking every possible interpretation that might allow her to escape the most painful of conclusions. He recalled his own mother, a bright and intelligent woman, making herself seem foolish in her desperation to elude the inevitable truth. Her husband had been a drunk and a philanderer. She couldn't deny the former, for she was confronted with the fact of it in her household almost every night. But it was the nights on which she was spared by his absence about which she had persistently deluded herself.

Could Raven believe this of Dr Simpson? Unlike his own father, he seemed the perfectly contented family man, available and affectionate around his children where so many others were aloof and distant. But Raven had always to remember that this was Edinburgh, the city whose crest ought to be the head of the Janus: one face for polite society, another behind closed doors.

SIXTEEN

arah picked up the shirt, pinching a small amount of the filthy material between the tip of her index finger and thumb. She wished she had a pair of tongs for the job. It looked like Raven had been washing floors or cleaning the grate with it.

As if.

The thin cotton, which she presumed had at one point been white, was now grey in colour and streaked with dirt. There were dark splotches on both sleeves that she recognised as blood. One of the sleeves was attempting to part company from the rest of the garment, a tear at the seam having been ineptly repaired at some point.

'I hope he can stitch wounds better than that,' she mused as she dropped the offensive item into a basket by the door. The notion brought to mind the nasty cut on Raven's cheek, about which she suspected he was being less than truthful. He claimed he had been randomly set upon, but her instinct was that he must have played some part in precipitating the attack. She recognised something restless in him. Ambitious and driven, yes, but not at peace with himself.

He struck her as impetuous, desperate to prove himself, though to whom would be an interesting question. Since he got here, he had been trying too hard to look like he was in control, over-compensating for the fear that he was in over his head. Recalling her own first steps and missteps as a housemaid, Sarah well understood how difficult it could be when you were new to a situation. However, her sympathy was limited by the fact that his was a privileged problem to have. She would have loved to be negotiating his new situation rather than that of a domestic servant, who could be cast out onto the street for speaking out of turn.

Sarah had come into service here at Queen Street following the deaths of her parents, the local minister finding this position for her as he was an old friend of Dr Simpson. Her premature departure from the parish school had no doubt been a relief to her schoolmaster, who was becoming increasingly wearied by her arguments regarding her exclusion from subjects deemed suited only to boys, such as Classics and mathematics. He was convinced that her grasp of reading, writing and arithmetic was sufficient for a girl of her station, insisting that knitting and sewing would be of more use to her and would open up the possibility of industrial work in the future. As though a factory job or work in a mill should be the culmination of all her ambition. If one was capable of carrying out a task or learning a body of knowledge, then why should it matter whether one be male or female? Her fury at this injustice had cooled little since.

She turned to take in the rest of the room, wondering what other horrors might be lurking there. To be fair it was not as messy as Mina's chaotic fiefdom but it was far from tidy. Open books and papers were scattered across the small writing desk in one corner, spilling onto the floor in a wide circle. A black coat – mucky cuffs, threadbare around the collar – was hanging from the back of a chair and muddy boots had trailed clumps of dirt across the carpet from doorway to fireplace. Sarah sighed. This was going to take a bit of time to sort out.

In order to see more of the carpet so that she could put some tea leaves down and sweep it, she decided to start at the desk, or at least the floor surrounding the desk. As she stooped to pick up some of the discarded papers she found herself next to the battered trunk that had followed Raven from his previous accommodation. It was open, some of the papers having landed inside. The trunk mostly contained books, presumably not deemed of immediate necessity, as there were plenty of those piled elsewhere.

She recalled his high-handed conduct on the morning of his first clinic.

Do you think a man has time to read fiction when he is training to be a doctor?

Evidently, he had time to read fiction once, for there were several piled up inside the box. She picked up the topmost one, *The Luck of Barry Lyndon* by William Makepeace Thackeray. Beneath it was *The Last of the Mohicans* by James Fenimore Cooper, and below that three works by Walter Scott.

Sarah turned the Thackeray book in her hand. She was sure Mina had a copy. She opened it, noting that the inside of the cover had been proprietorially inscribed with a handwritten name: Thomas Cunningham. A gift? A theft? Sarah examined the Cooper, noting the same name inside. Second-hand, then. A job lot, purchased from a fellow student.

She gathered up the papers and attempted to order them. Some dealt with what looked like injuries sustained during childbirth, others concerning a procedure known as a craniotomy, the illustrations for which she was sure she must be misreading. Sarah winced and picked up another, which turned out to be a letter. Upon discovering this, she turned it over and put it back down, but not without observing that it was from Raven's mother, and more intriguingly that she had addressed him neither as Will nor William.

She smiled at this discovery, moving the letter to one side so that it did not get lost among the piles of notes. That was when she encountered an open journal, her eyes drawn by the contrast between two pages. On one side were dense paragraphs of Raven's neat handwriting, a cursory glance at which revealed them to be detailing the procedure for administering ether. On the opposite folio, there were but two words in impatiently scrawled capitals:

EVIE POISONED?

Sarah heard the tread of footsteps too late. She had been seen.

'What the devil do you think you're doing?' Raven asked. He snatched the journal from where it lay upon the desk, slamming it closed with a force that caused several of the papers she had gathered to drift from their piles. He seemed disproportionate in his vehemence, making her wonder at the significance of whatever he feared she might have read.

'There is no need for temper,' she responded, keeping her voice even in the hope that it would calm his ire. A complaint from the professor's apprentice would give Mrs Lyndsay all the reason she needed to curtail Sarah's clinic duties. 'I am merely attempting to tidy up.'

'You were not merely tidying up, you were going through my private things, which I will not tolerate. There is nothing among these papers that concerns you, and still less that you would even understand.'

Despite the precariousness of her situation, Sarah could not prevent Raven's words from raising her hackles. She knew she should retreat, but an uncontainable instinct urged her to advance instead. She could just about tolerate bowing and scraping to the upstairs patients, but not to this scruffy youth.

'Who is Evie?' she asked.

He seemed flabbergasted, which had the unintended effect of spiking his bluster by putting him on the back foot.

'She is . . . no business of yours.'

Sarah decided to press her advantage. 'How did you really get that cut on your face, *Wilberforce*?'

His eyes flashed, but she could see a hint of anxiety beneath the outrage. Raven had secrets, and that was the real reason for this display of indignation.

'You read a letter from my *mother*?'

'I would not so intrude. I merely saw the addressee. I have heard Mrs Simpson address you as William several times and you've never corrected her. Why would that be? Does Dr Simpson know your real name is Wilberforce?'

Raven's face flushed. 'You would do well to remember your position. You seem to forget that you are a servant. What kind of house is this where such behaviour is not reined in?'

Sarah gazed down at the trunk and then to her basket. 'Are you used to greater deference from those below stairs, *sir*?' she enquired.

He did not answer. He looked worried now more than angry. He was afraid of what she might know, and he was right to be. It appeared there was someone in the household with an even more tenuous grip upon his position than she had.

'Who is Thomas Cunningham?'

'I don't know.'

'Yes, you do. He was the previous owner of the second-hand books in your trunk. Mrs Simpson said your late father was a lawyer in St Andrews, but I'd wager you're no higher born than I am.'

She lifted up the soiled and threadbare shirt from the laundry basket.

'There is little you can conceal from the woman who does your laundry.'

Raven looked at the shirt, his indignation spent, his demeanour meek, even vulnerable. It was as though her seeing the state of the garment was a greater trespass than the reading of his notes.

'What are you doing with that?' he asked meekly.

'Your shirt is soiled. It needs to be cleaned and is in sorry need of repair. I was going to soak the stains out of it and stitch the hole in the shoulder seam.'

Raven took a step towards her, fire returning to his eyes.

'I will thank you not to touch my things,' he said.

Sarah held his gaze.

'As you wish.'

She dropped the shirt onto the floor, turned on her heel and left the room.

SEVENTEEN

he brougham was fairly bouncing on its springs as it raced down the hill past Gayfield Square. The day was young but not bright, relentless fine drizzle falling from low skies. Raven was grateful for the early hour and the shelter of the carriage. From his schooldays he recalled a classmate remarking that the further one traversed down Leith Walk on foot after dark, the more likely one was to end up with, as this boy had put it, 'a burst mooth'.

'I used to have this two-wheeled claret curricle,' Simpson told him. 'If you think this swift, you ought to have seen how that contraption clattered over the cobbles. Mrs Simpson insisted that I change it for something more weatherproof.'

There was a joyous twinkle in his eye as he spoke, but the professor's enthusiasm proved less infectious than usual because Raven could not help recalling Mina's conversation with Jessie the night before. Who was this woman Simpson was paying money to, and for what? Raven knew that Mina could be wrong, and equally that without the full context he might have misunderstood the brief exchange he had overheard. Nonetheless, the scars left by his father ran deeper than the one upon his cheek, and therefore he could not look upon the professor without suspicion.

He attempted to put it from his thoughts, but the other

matters he turned to offered little respite. The sad fate of Evie
was seldom far from his mind, but was all the more prominent
since his conversation with the evasive Mrs Peake. And then there
was his most recent encounter with Sarah.

The girl had seen through him, her gifts of deduction as sharp
as her inquisitiveness was impertinent. And though nobody else
in the house was likely to reach the same conclusions, it was in
her power to help them see the truth too. He just hoped that her
appetite for novels had not led her to read the Thackeray she had
spied, for it was about someone from a fallen family attempting
to pass as a member of the upper orders.

He had felt such a stab of fear when she asked him about Thomas
Cunningham. Fortunately she had wrongly inferred the significance
of finding his name written inside Raven's books, so she maybe
wasn't quite as clever as she imagined. Nonetheless, clever she
undoubtedly was, and he appeared to have made an enemy of her.

Why did she despise him so? He hadn't done anything to harm
her. Obviously there had been that incident at the first clinic,
but she had shown disdain for him before that – almost from the
moment he walked in the door.

He would simply have to endure it. His time at Heriot's had
taught him that sometimes people could take an instinctive or
irrational dislike to you, as you could to them. In such instances,
there was nothing you could do to change that, and it proved a
fool's errand to try.

Similar difficulty attended his relationship with James Duncan,
although in that case the cause of dislike wasn't instinctive or irrational. Duncan seemed to regard him not so much as a subordinate
as an affront, a burden Dr Simpson had foisted upon him rather
than a potentially valuable assistant. Although Duncan was content
enough to assign him menial and unpleasant tasks, he behaved as
though he resented Raven working alongside him even in the capacity
of dogsbody. Raven suspected that this was because he did not wish
anyone to have even a partial claim of contribution to anything that

he was to discover. The young doctor was brilliant no doubt, but at the same time lacking in any grace, humour or humility.

The carriage swung around, Raven sliding in his seat as it turned at speed onto Great Junction Street, heading for the port. The professor had not said what it was they were rushing to attend. Someone had come to the house, as was often the case, requesting his urgent presence. As always, a part of Raven was surprised and admiring that someone of Simpson's stature should answer these calls with no promise of a commensurate payment, far less a guarantee that it was worth the time of one so eminent. He suspected the professor enjoyed the thrill of the urgency, and of being needed. For who would not?

Raven became conscious of a growing hubbub beneath the constant ululation of seagulls, the sound increasing as they drew nearer its source. He leaned out of the window to see a crowd gathered at the edge of the Water of Leith, the numbers thick enough that should someone trip, he might send a dozen of them tumbling over the edge. Over their heads he could see a forest of masts stretching into the middle distance, as though the ships in the dock were also craning to see whatever had attracted this gathering.

A cry went up as soon as Simpson stuck his head out of the carriage.

'It is Dr Simpson. Clear a way, clear a way.'

The sea of people parted before him as Simpson stepped down into the street, Raven tight in his wake lest the crowd close before him again. At the end of this human channel there were three policemen, two standing to the left of a smartly dressed fellow Raven took to be their superior. This was confirmed when Simpson hailed him.

'Mr McLevy, sir. May I be of assistance?'

Raven felt an involuntary tightening in his chest, reminiscent of those times at George Heriot's when the headmaster would enter his classroom unannounced. The policeman in charge was no less than the famous James McLevy. Raven had never seen the man in person but knew him by his reputation – the nature of which tended to alter depending on which side of Princes Street you stood. Among the respectable citizens of the New Town, he was a dogged and resourceful detective, peerless in his recovery of stolen property and indefatigable in the lengths to which he would go to get his man. Over in the Old Town, however, he was feared for the brutality and ruthlessness of his methods, and while legendary for always closing his cases, rumour was that this didn't necessarily mean the true perpetrator was the one brought to justice.

He did not look so fearsome right then, for there was a look of sorrow and regret upon his face.

'It's too late for even your skilled hands, Dr Simpson,' he replied, his accent pegging him from the north of Ireland.

At McLevy's prompting, the other officers stood aside and Raven was able to see a sheet upon the flagstones, damp soaking through it from the rain.

'Drowned?' Simpson asked.

'I suspect so. But I think she may have had some kind of seizure that caused her to fall in.'

McLevy briefly tugged the sheet back and a chill engulfed Raven as though he had been plunged into the cold, black waters below. Beneath the sheet was a young woman, blue-lipped and grey of skin. She had been dead in the water for some time. But what gripped Raven was her twisted expression and the contorted posture of her body.

He only glimpsed her for a moment, and then the sheet was replaced.

'May I see?' Raven asked.

Simpson put an arm on his shoulder. 'No, we must away. This is not what we were summoned for and time is of the essence. There is another young woman whose life we may yet be able to save.'

The patient turned out to be the labouring wife of a mariner, her husband having recently left the port of Leith on a voyage to

Stromness. She was in a state of visible distress and exhaustion, to Raven's eyes resembling a wrung-out cloth as she lay almost lifeless upon the bed.

'Mrs Alford has an extremely contracted pelvis,' said the worried-looking gentleman who was her usual medical attendant, a Mr Angus Figg. He was a grey-whiskered and fidgety old soul who introduced himself with great deference to Dr Simpson. He spoke to them in hushed tones, away from the bed.

'This led to a previous confinement lasting four days. In that instance, delivery by forceps was unsuccessful and eventually the infant had to be drawn out in pieces.'

He glanced back at the patient.

'She was advised about the hazards of risking another pregnancy,' he went on. 'I was not made aware of her condition until earlier today when she was already at full term and in labour.'

Raven looked to Mrs Alford and found her gazing back, weak but anxiously awaiting the results of their council. He understood that her torment was not merely from the pain she was experiencing but in anticipation of what was to come.

Simpson examined her, Mrs Alford's eyes permanently upon him.

'Am I going to die?' she asked rather matter-of-factly, as though she had been preparing herself for such an outcome.

'Not if I can help it,' Simpson replied.

He announced that he would attempt podalic version, or turning, and instructed Raven to administer ether.

'That is if you have no objection to it?' Raven asked her, dousing the sponge in readiness.

Mrs Alford looked at him as though she didn't understand the question, which struck him as the correct answer.

She breathed in the vapour with some alacrity and soon slipped into a state of unconsciousness. Raven found the rapidity of the transition somewhat alarming but her breathing remained regular and her pulse rate, which had been elevated, began to decline to a more acceptable level.

With the patient in this relaxed state, the child was turned easily, the feet, legs and trunk pulled down without much effort. The extraction of the head proved to be more difficult. Simpson applied the forceps and some considerable exertion was required on his part before the infant's head would pass through the woman's misshapen pelvis. Difficult as it was, the delivery was completed in less than twenty minutes.

The infant was handed to Raven while the afterbirth was delivered. It gasped several times but would not breathe, its head having been flattened and compressed, the parietal bone indented on one side. He wrapped the child in the blanket which had been laid out for this purpose and looked around the small room for a place to put it. There were several tallow candles lit around the bed and Mr Figg held an oil lamp, but the corners of the room remained in darkness. As no appropriate receptacle presented itself, he placed the small, pale, lifeless bundle beside the still sleeping mother. The child was pale, tinged with blue.

At this point Raven realised that he hadn't noticed the sex of the baby; he wouldn't be able to tell the mother when she woke up whether the child was a boy or a girl. He hoped that she wouldn't ask.

When the patient did come around, she seemed to be primarily concerned that her ordeal was over. She had evidently not expected a live child to result from this confinement. She showed no emotion when the infant was presented to her, but expressed relief that she had not suffered this time as she had before.

Simpson promised to return in a day or two to see how she was.

'You would do well to heed Mr Figg's advice and take pains to avoid another pregnancy,' he told her softly.

'Best tell that to my husband,' she said in reply.

EIGHTEEN

The sounds of disputation once again greeted Raven's approach to the drawing room as he ascended the stairs, though on this occasion the voices were male. He paused on the threshold, keen to gather what was being discussed by way of forearming himself. He could make out Duncan's assured tones, sounding as always like he was carrying the Ten Commandments. Raven was in no mood to be lectured to and was thinking about beating a retreat when he heard someone clear their throat behind him. He turned to see Sarah carrying a tray bearing a decanter and glasses.

'Open the door, if you please, Mr Raven,' she said, smiling, evidently amused at catching him eavesdropping.

She haunts my very shadow, he thought.

Raven did as he was bid, allowing her to proceed into the room before him. Mrs Simpson and Mina were sitting beside each other on a sofa while the men, Drs Simpson, Duncan and Keith, were gathered round the fireplace.

'Raven!' said Duncan, with unaccustomed brightness. 'Come and join the fray.'

'What is the subject?' he replied, wary that Duncan was about to seize an opportunity to make him look uninformed.

'We are discussing Hahnemann's theories of *similia similibus curantur* and infinitesimal doses,' Duncan chimed.

Like cures like. Duncan would have to try harder than that to catch him out.

'Homeopathy,' he replied.

He looked over to where Sarah was pouring out measures of sherry into glasses, hoping that she had witnessed this small triumph. She seemed intent on her task and failed to raise her eyes from the decanter.

'And what is your impression of it?' Duncan pressed him, this time with one eyebrow raised, as though waiting for Raven to position himself squarely on the wrong side of this debate.

'The doctrine that like cures like makes little sense to me,' Raven said. 'And as for the notion that repeated dilutions paradoxically increase the efficacy of a solution, I believe my former landlady Mrs Cherry must have been a firm advocate. Her soup often contained only an infinitesimal trace of meat, which according to Hahnemann would provide greater nourishment than a juicy steak.'

Simpson laughed and thumped Raven heartily on the back. He was never at risk of being on the wrong side of this argument, as the professor had made his views clear to his class on many occasions. He liked to recount the story of receiving a box of homeopathic remedies from a friend and giving them to his sons to play with, which of course had led to the medicines being mixed up. The same box had then been passed on to an enthusiastic practitioner, who later reported that he employed them with great success.

'Some homeopathic remedies are not even taken internally but applied using the technique of olfaction,' Simpson said, demonstrating by taking a theatrical sniff from his sherry glass. 'I heard tell of a lady who was subjected to the process,' he went on. 'When it came time to settle the bill with her practitioner, she passed the fee before his nose and then put it back into her pocket.'

The professor's joke was greeted with laughter by everyone,

with the familiar exception of Duncan. He looked thin-lipped and impatient for the moment to pass, which was his response to every interruption for laughter. It was as though his mind did not understand the very mechanism of humour, or perhaps saw no need for it.

'Though at least the consolation of a medicine without effect is that it has no ill effects either,' suggested George Keith. 'For there are some utterly abhorrent concoctions foisted upon unwary patients every day. Mercury, for one, is a pestilent and entirely pernicious drug. And Syme is sceptical about almost every internal medicine with the exception of rhubarb and soda.'

At that moment, the door opened and John Beattie strode into the room with his over-eager birdlike gait, bringing with him a scent of tobacco and a far stronger smell of cologne.

'Gregory's powders,' he said, responding to Keith's last remark as though he had been present the whole time. 'I prescribe it frequently. But then I hardly ever leave the bedside of a patient without providing a new bottle or prescription of some sort. Dr Simpson, good evening.'

Simpson got to his feet and introduced his guest, who shook each offered hand with accustomed grace.

Raven was impressed with the assuredness of Beattie's manner. Though he was not the tallest of fellows, he thrust himself into company in contrast to Raven's instinct, which was to shrink against the side-lines. Raven noted the curiosity and instinctive suspicion in Duncan's expression at this unheralded interloper and felt all the warmer towards Beattie as a result. The man had looked smart enough even spattered with blood and in his day clothes, but dressed for dinner, Beattie in his dandified pomp was a sight to behold. As Raven's mother might have put it, he was wearing the clothes; the clothes weren't wearing him.

The effect was not lost on Mina, who rose from the sofa and approached him, her hand extended. Beattie bowed and kissed the offered fingers.

'I find the scent of your cologne to be quite divine,' Mina said. 'Did you purchase it from Gianetti's? In George Street?'

'I did not. This scent is Farina's original eau de cologne, imported from Europe. Bergamot and sandalwood with top notes of citrus.'

'How exotic,' said Mina, clearly impressed.

'The sense of smell is the one most closely related to memory,' he added with a smile. 'One always hopes to be remembered.'

Raven cast another glance at Duncan, who looked unsettled, as though the new arrival represented a threat to his supremacy. His brow furrowed as Beattie accepted a glass of sherry from Sarah.

'I *intend* to be remembered,' Duncan said, raising his glass in a toast, 'for something more significant and more popular than even Gregory's powders. To memorable contributions.'

'To being remembered,' Beattie replied, raising his own glass and draining it. He turned to face Mina again, denying Duncan the opportunity to elaborate on his grand plans. 'I cannot recall the last time I encountered so many beautiful women in one room,' he said, taking in all of the ladies present.

Mrs Simpson smiled, Sarah snorted and Mina demurely lowered her eyes to the hem of her dress, etiquette precluding any direct acknowledgement of the compliment.

Raven watched their charmed reactions and realised with a certain sadness that though he might learn much from Beattie as a doctor, there were certain talents that simply could not be taught.

Beattie sat beside Mina at dinner, which surprised Raven. He had thought their new guest might wish to seize the opportunity to make a direct impression upon Dr Simpson. It had not occurred to him that Beattie might take a genuine interest in the professor's sister-in-law, who was on the edge of spinsterhood, but perhaps her age liberated Beattie from concerns that his attention might be misconstrued. They spoke freely and at length, Beattie seeking her opinions on everything from women's fashions to literature and poetry.

He had perhaps sought to impress her with his wide-ranging knowledge of the latter only to find that Mina had a familiarity with Byron and Shelley which easily surpassed his own. And rather than withdraw from the conversation now that his superiority had been challenged, Beattie seemed to relish it all the more, and the two discussed the relative merits of the romantic poets as though they were alone at the table and had been intimates for some time.

Beattie interrupted their conversation only briefly to express his admiration for the Simpsons' cook. 'Sublime!' he pronounced as he cleared his plate.

Raven did not feel he was in a position to make an informed contribution, given the measly portion he had been served. He could identify but two chunks of mutton amongst the carrots on his plate. This amount of food would be insufficient for the parrot, never mind a fully grown man. Raven noticed that everyone else had received a more generous portion than he, and tried to catch Sarah's eye as she passed between sideboard and table with various dishes, but she seemed intent on ignoring him.

During the serving of dessert (of which again Raven received a homeopathic helping), Mina continued to hold Beattie's attention until his host intervened and dragged him back into the general conversation.

'Dr Beattie here was previously availing me of his ambitions for opening a hydropathic spa,' Simpson announced, a familiar spark of mischief in his eye. 'Before you arrived, we were deep in discussion about unregulated practices and I was wondering where you might draw the line between physic and quackery.'

'I remain unconvinced about the benefits of homeopathy,' Beattie replied, which made Raven wonder if he too had paused outside to eavesdrop before making his entrance. 'It seems to be based upon a somewhat flimsy premise and yet it has proven to be quite popular.'

'I know many who swear by it,' said Mina, in support of this last statement.

'Indeed,' Beattie said, turning back to her. 'And that is why it would be premature to dismiss it entirely, Miss Grindlay.'

'Professor Christison refers to homeopathic remedies as "drops of nothingness, powders of nonentity",' Duncan added, his tone as tactlessly dismissive as Beattie's had been polite.

Mina looked at him as though he had just blasphemed in some way. Raven could imagine Dr Duncan being struck off Mina's mental list of potential suitors, Beattie's name being added instead, and perhaps underlined. Several times.

'What about phrenology?' Simpson asked.

'That the shape of the skull can provide information regarding the personality? I think that there may be something to it,' Beattie replied. 'There are many medical men who support it, Professor Gregory among them.'

'I'm not sure that the belief of others makes for a convincing argument,' Simpson chided gently. 'While it is true that many eminent medical men are members of the phrenological society, that in itself does not convince me.'

'Quite so,' said Duncan. 'No absurdity is ever too groundless to find supporters.'

Beattie looked momentarily at a loss, as though slighted by the harshness of Duncan's rebuttal. Then his countenance cleared and his smile returned, his equanimity restored.

'Whoever determines to deceive the world may be sure of finding people to be deceived,' he said.

Duncan smiled thinly in reply, satisfied that this served as some form of surrender.

Raven drank more of his wine. He had consumed several glasses of the doctor's claret by this point (and not that much to eat) and was beginning to enjoy himself.

'The waters of quackery may be foul,' he said, 'but there's money to be made if you're prepared to swim.'

His contribution was not so much in support of Beattie as in solidarity against a common foe.

'You would risk drowning, my boy,' said Simpson. 'A reputation thus tarnished could never be recovered.'

At this point Sarah entered the room with a pot of coffee and bent slightly to pour. Raven found that his eye was drawn to her head, although any detail of its shape was hidden by her white cap. What would an examination of her skull reveal? Combativeness? Lack of propriety?

As she turned to leave the room, he noticed that a small ringlet of honey-coloured hair had escaped the confines of her cap and was delicately hovering at the nape of her neck. He wondered absently what her hair would smell like, and realised, perhaps for the first time, how young she must be.

Raven took his coffee and stood by the window, mindful of the parrot, which was eyeing him suspiciously from its perch. Beattie appeared at his side, ostensibly examining the flamboyant but cantankerous bird, clearly wishing to talk away from the rest of the room.

'It's easy for him to say,' Beattie stated quietly.

'What is?'

'Pontificating about how a doctor might make money. There is little sacrifice in taking the moral high ground when your coffers are overflowing.'

Raven wondered if Beattie had guessed about the parlous state of his own finances.

'I admit,' Raven replied, 'I might find it difficult to remain noble to my principles should some rich and credulous lady offer to reward me for harmless but useless therapy. And if it made her feel better purely because she believed it efficacious, then was the therapy truly useless? Perhaps that question would be enough to salve my conscience.'

'I have a proposition that would require you to broach no such ethical dilemmas,' Beattie stated. 'A patient who requires a certain procedure but is reluctant to submit without the benefit of ether. I told her I had found someone who could administer it.'

'Me?' Raven asked, barely daring to believe it.

'Of course. As an associate of the great Dr Simpson, your services would attract a handsome fee.'

'A junior associate and hardly an expert.'

'I'm sure you are proficient enough. What is there to lose?'

Raven caught sight of his reflection in the black of the window. The wound on his cheek tingled as if to remind him what indeed he had to lose.

'How handsome?' he asked.

NINETEEN

he following day Raven was granted respite from the chaos of the morning clinic, as part of his apprenticeship was to include regular duties at the Royal Maternity Hospital. Unfortunately, it would have taken a higher power than Dr Simpson to offer him respite from the piercing headache that was plaguing his every step. He would admit he had drunk of the professor's claret with uncommon gusto in celebration of Beattie's offer and the imminent prospect of making back the money he owed to Flint. However, the tolerable ill effects of this indulgence had been brutally compounded after breakfast, when Duncan compelled Raven's assistance in his researches.

Raven was initially curious about Duncan shedding his reluctance to involve him directly in his work, and wondered whether his contributions the previous night had raised him in the young prodigy's estimations. Then he discovered that Duncan had assembled a fresh batch of potential anaesthetic agents, and Raven's role was little above that of poison taster; or poison sniffer, to be strictly accurate. Duncan had wafted various vapours beneath his nose, none of which precipitated any effect greater than mild dizziness and a cumulative pounding in his brain.

The Maternity Hospital was situated within Milton House

on the Canongate, a Georgian mansion that had either seen better days or had been built with the intention of warning off unwanted visitors with the threat of impending collapse. He was due to meet Dr Ziegler, the hospital's surgeon, and given the pounding in Raven's head, he hoped the man was more a Simpson than a Syme.

The door was answered by a tall woman in a starched cap, who, on looking him up and down, gave the impression she was about to fetch a stick with which to chase him off. Clearly his beard was not growing thick or fast enough to effect the transformation he had hoped for.

'Mr Will Raven. For Dr Ziegler. I'm Dr Simpson's apprentice. I believe I am expected.'

Raven hoped that the mention of his employer would smooth his passage into the hospital, past its sullen gatekeeper. The woman made no reply but let her eyes drift downwards, where her gaze remained. Raven felt compelled to do the same and found himself examining his own footwear. His boots looked as they usually did, a thin layer of mud clinging to the sides: unsurprising as he had made the journey from Queen Street on foot.

'Mrs Stevenson. Matron,' she said. 'I'll thank you to wipe your feet before you come in.'

Raven wagered that she wasn't the type to thank anyone for much else. She stood with her arms folded, watching as he applied his feet to the boot scraper at the door. Once satisfied with his efforts, she stood aside and let him enter.

'Dr Ziegler is in the ward, making his rounds.'

She indicated a door to the left, then disappeared into a room on the right, closing the door to leave Raven alone in the hallway. He proceeded as directed, becoming aware of the faint aroma of lemons mixed with something earthier. It was a considerable improvement upon the foetid stink he associated with the wards of the Royal Infirmary.

A strong breeze was gusting through as all of the windows

were open – an attempt to blow away the spectre of puerperal fever perhaps, the scourge of any such institution – and consequently the fireplace at the end of the room had a good fire going, helping to take the chill out of the wind. There was a row of beds against one wall and a large table in the centre of the room where a small, dark, spectacled man was writing in a ledger. Without lifting his eyes from the volume, he raised a palm as he heard Raven approach, by way of telling him to wait.

Raven complied silently, the question of a Simpson or a Syme now tipping towards the latter.

Ziegler finished what he was writing and looked up, a brightness about his features. 'Keeping the casebook up to date,' he said, closing the ledger and placing his hand reverentially upon it. 'Every delivery must be entered. Accurate information is the key to unlocking many a mystery. Now, would you care to take a tour, Mr Raven?'

Ziegler proceeded to show Raven around, evidently proud of the small hospital and its collection of expectant or recently delivered mothers. To a woman they were poor souls whose personal circumstances made a home confinement impossible.

'We do good work here,' Ziegler said as he showed Raven into the empty delivery room, 'but our funding is precarious. Charitable giving is frequently inhibited by moral concerns.'

'Moral concerns?'

Raven was reminded of the pamphlet penned by the Reverend Grissom denouncing the use of ether in labour, but Ziegler was referring to a more general anxiety regarding the hospital's attendees.

'Our policy of admitting unmarried mothers provokes a deep discomfort in many a Christian breast. Some believe that it encourages immoral behaviour.'

'What is the alternative?' Raven asked.

'A worthy question, young sir. In my opinion it is illogical to withhold care from someone who needs it merely because you disagree with the manner in which they conduct themselves. Judge not lest ye be judged.'

'Quite so,' Raven agreed, thinking again about Evie and the manner in which her death had been dismissed.

Another deid hoor.

'I believe it is important to provide the best possible care for patients regardless of the manner in which they got themselves into their present predicament,' Ziegler continued. 'Desperate people are often driven to do desperate things. I have known young women to take their own lives because they could not face the consequences of being with child; and some because they could not face their families discovering it. Sometimes one has to contemplate which is the lesser of two evils.'

Ziegler fixed Raven with a piercing look. Raven sensed that he would be evaluated according to his response, beginning with whether he even understood what Ziegler was talking about.

'You mean abortion?'

Ziegler nodded solemnly. Raven hoped he had passed.

'Abortion, infanticide. These things happen more frequently than we would like to admit. When no records are kept, there is no way of knowing with any degree of certainty.'

'There have been two cases recently at the Infirmary. Perforated uterus and peritonitis in each instance.'

'Fatal?'

'Yes. Tantamount to murder.'

'When you deliberately inflict such damage and are only interested in the fee, then it *is* murder, plain and simple. And the culprit?'

'Hasn't been identified.'

'That doesn't surprise me. It is a relatively easy thing, getting away with murder, especially when the victims are deemed to be of no consequence.'

'Do you know anything about it?' Raven asked.

'Me?' Ziegler replied, his curious look making Raven fear for a moment that the man thought he was being impugned.

'I only mean that the women must talk about such things. Perhaps you have heard something.'

'I can't say that I have. The women don't tend to confide in me and I disregard anything I hear from them during labour. Perhaps matron might have heard something, though. Women seem to be more at ease discussing such things with each other.'

Ziegler led the way back to the small room Mrs Stevenson had retreated to after letting Raven in. Given his introduction to the woman, he was sceptical as to whether an interview with the gatekeeper would yield much. The matron was seated behind a desk, totting up a column of figures in an account book when they entered.

'Dr Ziegler,' she said, smiling as she looked up from her calculations, her affection for the little man quite evident.

'Mr Raven tells me that someone's practising the dark arts again,' Ziegler said, sitting on the edge of her desk.

Mrs Stevenson sighed and put down her pen.

'Heard any tales?' he asked.

Raven was surprised at the ease with which such a delicate subject was raised.

'About the dark arts, no,' she said. 'Though I have heard talk about some new secret remedy to "restore regularity".'

Raven did not follow. 'A laxative?'

'To the monthly cycle,' Ziegler explained.

Raven smiled at his own misapprehension, but the grave expression on Ziegler's face told him he was still missing something.

'A euphemism,' Raven acknowledged.

'Indeed. Sometimes such remedies are advertised as "for the relief of obstruction", but it is the same thing.'

'And is this new secret remedy reputed to be successful?'

'As successful as any before it,' Mrs Stevenson said, by which she meant not at all. 'We deliver the obstructions here all the time, whereupon the monthly cycle is restored to regularity.'

'There has long been a trade in such quackery,' Ziegler explained. 'Pills and potions with no effect. Cheap tricks and empty promises.'

'Oh, they're never cheap,' the matron stated, 'for that's the hook. The more expensive the remedy, the more a desperate woman is likely to believe the rumours of its efficacy and part with her coin.'

'Rumours no doubt sown by the same rogue who is rolling the pills,' Ziegler added.

Raven thought of the discussions the previous evening. The principle was the same, but there was a greater dishonesty here, for the patient's belief that the medicine was working would make no difference in this case.

'Charlatanry,' he observed.

'Aye, though there is worse,' said Mrs Stevenson. 'More dangerous than the mere charlatans are those attempting to concoct genuine medicines. I've seen girls become horribly sick after taking such remedies, without any relief of the "obstruction" they were intended to remove. Racked with pain, they were. God only knows what they ingested, believing it would lift their burdens.'

Her words called up Evie's contorted posture, her agonised expression, as well as the brief glimpse he had been afforded of the woman pulled from the water yesterday. But there was more than the usual regret and anxiety attending his memory of finding Evie. Her urgent need of money and her reluctance to say what for might finally have an explanation.

For the first time, it struck him that she might have been pregnant.

Raven was turning this new possibility over in his mind as he made his way back along the Canongate in the gathering darkness, trying to calculate the implications and reliving some of the last conversations he had had with Evie. Belatedly he realised that if she had been pregnant, then she must have known there was no future for her in a job as a maid, even if there was a house that would have her. She had been stringing him along, knowing it couldn't happen. Raven had always been a little blind when it came to her, willingly so. This dream of her raising herself up had been no more than that: a dream, a fantasy. And he understood now that it had been a fantasy to entertain him rather than one genuinely held by her.

So lost was he in this reverie that he failed to notice a distinctive shape approaching him until it was almost too late. The unmistakable silhouette of Gargantua was emerging through the fog, lumbering down the hill from the High Street.

At this distance, in the gloom of the narrow channel, Raven could not be sure whether he had been seen. There was little chance of passing Gargantua unnoticed, however. Raven had no option but to duck through the doors of the nearest tavern and hope for the best.

The place was crowded, which was a blessing, its warmth welcome on a chill evening. The fug of smoke and the smell of spilled ale instantly wrapped around him like an old friend's embrace. He only wished his pockets were not so empty.

Raven made his way towards a dark corner to wait it out. He had barely pulled up a stool when he saw the doors swing and the giant thrust himself through them, bowing down so that his head would not strike the lintel.

Raven pressed himself against the wall as Gargantua approached, the monster's gaze fixed intently upon him. Raven looked about the room but saw no faces he recognised, no stalwarts who might come to his aid. He had no friends here, but realised strangers might still be his salvation, for surely the man would not carry out an attack in front of so many witnesses.

The comfort of this thought lasted as long as it took to wonder how many men might be prepared to stand and testify against this creature in court.

'I will have money for you soon,' Raven pleaded, feeling the scar upon his cheek tingle afresh as the giant drew within feet of where he stood.

'Sit,' Gargantua ordered.

Raven complied, though it pinned him in a corner with Gargantua blocking the route to the door. He was a conspicuous sight, and yet he drew few direct looks, Raven noticed: only stolen glances. They wanted to gawp at him, but not to meet his gaze.

'I will be carrying out well-paid medical work in a few days with a wealthy patient of the New Town,' Raven told him, quickly and quietly. 'I am apprentice to Professor Simpson, training to be a doctor, and—'

Gargantua held up a huge hand by way of silencing him. His face was all the more disturbing now that Raven could see it in indoor light. Its proportions were wrong, the flesh loose in places, stretched in others. He was sweaty despite the cold outside, a sickly pallor about his skin.

'I know what you are training to be. That's why I followed you in here.'

Raven saw a glimmer of hope and struck out for it. 'Is there something I can assist you with?' he asked as brightly as his fear would allow.

Gargantua's expression darkened. 'You misunderstand. I wanted you to know that I despise your profession.'

Raven could barely find the breath, but somehow managed to reply, as he felt the question was being invited.

'Why?'

'Because of your attitude to people like me. Freaks of nature.'

'I assure you, we only wish to understand any unusual medical condition, and by that understanding to assist those afflicted.'

'Tell that to Charles Byrne,' Gargantua said, the words grumbling across the table like thunder at the head of a storm. 'Have you heard of him?'

Raven nodded. Much had just become clear, none of it good.

'A man like me. Even bigger, though. The Irish Giant, they called him. He came here to Edinburgh once. Lit his pipe from one of the lamps on the North Bridge without even standing on his toes. Aye, you medical men all wanted him, but not to "understand", or to "assist". The shameless maggots were offering him money for his corpse while he was still alive.'

Raven knew the story, as any medical man would. Byrne had refused their advances, no matter how much coin was offered. He believed in the resurrection, that the Lord was going to raise him up when Judgment Day came, and for that he would need his body. But the anatomists had plans for their own resurrection, and when Byrne died in June of 1783, they were fighting each other for the spoils, heedless of the man's own wishes.

Byrne's friends rallied to protect his corpse. They exhibited his outsize coffin to help raise funds to charter a boat and saw that he was buried at sea in accordance with his will. But with a vast bounty being offered for the body, there was always a danger of treachery, and unbeknownst to the burial party, it was a coffin full of stones that they tipped into the water. Somewhere on the way to Margate, a switch had been made and the body stolen. Inevitably, it found its way into the possession of the man who had prized it most, the esteemed surgeon and anatomist John Hunter.

News of the theft made the papers and raised a scandal, which was why Hunter never dissected the body as he planned, instead swiftly chopping it up and boiling it down to bones. He kept his possession of the remains secret for several years, but in time reassembled the skeleton and put it on display. Perhaps the worst of it was that Hunter thus learned nothing from the corpse. He spent a great sum to acquire not a crucial specimen but a mere trophy, like an organ in a jar.

Gargantua's eyes flashed and he leaned forward, gripping Raven's neck and pulling their foreheads together, the giant's foul breath engulfing his face.

'Eight hundred guineas, Hunter paid. Do you think Charles Byrne earned a fraction of that his whole life? Men like you see men like me as worth more dead than alive. And that is why, should Mr Flint give the command, it will not merely be my duty to rip you apart, but my pleasure.'

Gargantua let go and stood up, the throng parting before him as he walked to the door.

Raven sat there trembling, his mouth as dry as he could ever remember, his drouth all the more a mockery for him sitting here in a tavern.

Charles Byrne died at the age of twenty-two. Raven wondered if Gargantua understood the implications for himself. He had not seemed well, and was unlikely to live long, but he might yet outlast Raven.

Beattie's commission was now a matter of life and death.

TWENTY

arah was sweeping out the downstairs hall, pondering just how many pairs of feet had tramped through it during that morning's clinic, when Jarvis materialised silently at her side and placed a hand upon her broom.

'You are to report to the kitchen. Mrs Lyndsay would like to speak to you.'

Sarah's insides turned to stone. She knew from the wording and the tone – as well as the fact that Mrs Lyndsay had not summoned her directly by a shout or a bell – that she was in trouble. There was a degree of theatre to it that she had learned to recognise, and she knew what it was about too. She had seen the woman head up the stairs earlier that morning, shooting her a scowl as she passed. It took her but a moment to deduce why her sour face seemed familiar.

Sarah walked down the stairs slowly, dreading what might await her at the bottom. She tried to convince herself that it was not what she assumed: perhaps merely another harangue about her duties at the clinic interfering with the rest of her workload. Mrs Lyndsay had always been opposed to this secondary draw upon her labour, but from Jarvis's summons she knew this must be regarding a matter as serious as it was specific, and there was only one thing it could be.

Mrs Lyndsay was standing with her back to the range, gripping a wooden spoon tightly in both hands. It being some time since she last provoked this formal level of ire, Sarah had thought that she was no longer afraid of the cook. One look at her stern expression told her otherwise, bringing back all the fear she had felt every time she faced Mrs Lyndsay's wrath.

When she first started working here, she had to be thoroughly trained in her tasks, in the rules of the house and in all manner of arcane etiquette. Any lapse, misstep or failure to meet the required standards would lead to a dressing down in the kitchen and often some form of disciplinary measure. Sarah was always diligent and didn't find any of her duties difficult to master, so it was seldom the quality of her work that was at issue. Rather, it was the way she comported herself that most frequently provoked the cook's disapproval. 'Overstepping the mark' was the most common citation, a phrase she had learned to both dread and detest, along with 'you have ideas above your station, girl'. This one stung the more because it was true, and Mrs Lyndsay's job was to hammer home what Sarah's station was.

'There has been a complaint of quite disgraceful conduct towards one of Dr Simpson's patients,' Mrs Lyndsay said. Her tone was even but spoke of a controlled anger she could unleash at will.

Sarah's reaction was one of cold fear. Deep down, she had known these consequences would find her. Even as she closed the door that day, she knew it was the beginning rather than the end of the matter. The sour-faced woman on the stairs was one of the pair for whom she had refused to make special accommodations on a day when the clinic was particularly busy and Dr Simpson was from home.

'A Mrs Noble, who had travelled here from Trinity, said that not only were you unspeakably rude and disrespectful, but that you refused to admit her and then slammed the front door in her face.'

Sarah gaped. 'I did not slam the—'

'Are you compounding this by calling Mrs Noble a liar?'

Sarah averted her gaze, staring at the floor and feeling her cheeks begin to burn. She knew from experience that further explanation would not assist her case. A housemaid's account of such an exchange did not matter. And besides, the force with which she closed the door was not the issue, but that Mrs Noble was on the wrong side of it at the time.

It was the remark about the Queen that had really torn it. It had felt satisfying in the moment, but her satisfaction had turned almost instantly to regret. She had wounded the woman's pride, and that would never go unanswered.

'No, ma'am. But the clinic was especially busy that morning and I merely—'

Mrs Lyndsay silenced her by simply raising the spoon.

'The details are immaterial, and I doubt this woman is in the habit of making up complaints to amuse herself. Your conduct caused her gross offence and this in turn has caused embarrassment for the entire household. Mrs Noble has demanded your dismissal.'

Mrs Lyndsay let her words hang there, allowing Sarah time to contemplate what this would mean. She felt tears well up and was a moment from begging.

'If you ask me, it is only because Mrs Simpson does not take well to being told how to run her own house that you are to be retained. Nonetheless, she has asked that I deal with it. I think this business of assisting at the morning clinics has been giving you ideas above your station.'

There it was, and what hurt the most was that she had brought it upon herself. Again. Why could she not learn to control her mouth? Master, as Mina had recently told her, the commendable art of holding her tongue?

'You will not be spared to assist any more, at least until you have better learned your place.'

'But I am needed at clinic,' she protested, thinking not so much of what she was losing but of the chaos in the hall every morning, and her role in managing the crowds.

Mrs Lyndsay scoffed at this. 'Needed? Do you know how easy it is to replace a housemaid? That's what you have to understand. I don't want to see you on the street. Do you know what it is to be dismissed without character?'

Sarah nodded silently. It meant being dismissed without letters of reference vouching for one's worthiness to a prospective employer. Without those, it would be impossible to find a position in another house.

'Because that is the danger for a girl who is disrespectful, who brings disgrace upon her place of employment. I have worked in many houses and I have seen it happen many a time. But what is worse is I have seen what became of those girls, when they had no other means to make a living.'

Mrs Lyndsay prodded Sarah in the chest with the spoon, lifting her chin with it so that she met her eye.

'Selling themselves: that's how they ended up. Didn't know they had a good life until it was gone, same as will happen to that one who ran off from the Sheldrake house. I wouldn't want that happening to you. Is this not a good house to work in?'

'Yes, ma'am.'

'Are you not grateful for your position here?'

'Yes, ma'am.'

'Then remember that, for you are on your final warning. Keep your head down and think only of your duties, nothing else. Otherwise you will *have* no duties to keep you under this roof.'

TWENTY-ONE

Nobody knew her name.

This was the third tavern Raven had visited in Leith, insinuating himself into company and conversation so that he might turn the subject to the young woman whose body he so briefly glimpsed on the quayside. A few people had heard about the discovery, but that was as far as it went.

He thought of James Duncan, so quick to state his ambitions when he sensed a rival in Beattie. It was in the gift of caprice to decide whom history would remember, but it struck Raven as a particularly sad fate to die unknown, nobody to miss you, to remember you.

'I'll tell you what I did hear,' said a ruddy-faced docker with salt-blasted skin and the roughest hands Raven had ever seen. 'That she was twisted up and tied in knots.'

Raven was in an ancient establishment called the King's Wark, close to where the girl had been recovered the day before, and was seated at the gantry, where he thought himself best positioned to pick up on what was being said. The landlord had noticed this and regarded him with a modicum of suspicion, but as long as he was buying ale, Raven knew he would be tolerated.

Raven had not learned what he came for, but he was enjoying

the opportunity to sit in a tavern without fear of who he might run into, emboldened by the promise of Beattie's paying work. If he encountered the Weasel, he would be able to tell him that his debt would be redeemed very soon, but only if he remained corporeally intact to carry out work for which he would be handsomely rewarded. His men might be vicious, but Raven was confident that a man such as Flint would not wish to dole out punishment that reduced his chances of being paid.

'That's the devil's work,' said another, a wiry fellow with eyes so narrow it was a wonder he could see out of them.

'A bad business, for sure,' said the docker.

'No, I mean the work of Satan and his worshippers. That's a sign of possession, when a body is all twisted like that.'

'Or a seizure,' Raven suggested.

'If that were the case, the body would straighten again in the water,' Gimlet-eyes insisted, which Raven would have to concede was a fair point. He didn't know how long she had been floating. 'She was bewitched, I'm telling you. Could be she flung herself to her death because it was the only way to be rid of the demon inside her.'

'There are Satanists abroad,' another man agreed, nodding sagely as though no reasonable fellow might dispute it. 'I've heard they gather on Calton Hill.'

'There's no end of strange and godless types come off the ships down here,' the docker said. 'From all manner of dark and far-flung lands.'

'There are devils enough come over from Ireland,' another drinker averred, drawing murmurs of agreement from all around. 'Glasgow is over-run with them, and soon Edinburgh will be too.'

'They eat their babies,' said a yellow-skinned old goat, clinging on to a table as though he would otherwise be spun off. 'So who knows what other abominations they commit.'

'Aye, when Ireland sends its people, they're not sending their best.'

'There was a bairn's leg found in a gutter last week.'

'The savage Erse bastards.'

'I don't imagine an Irishman was responsible for that,' Raven argued.

'And why not?' demanded Yellow Skin.

'Well, if what you say is true, he would hardly waste good eating.'

This drew a gale of laughter, but Raven knew there was nothing to be learned from this gathering. He took in the room to estimate whether anyone else might be worth talking to. This was when he appreciated how profoundly his medical studies had changed him. No longer could he enter a place without assessing the pathology presented there, of which there was usually a plentiful supply. The wheezily obese barmaid currently pouring whisky at the end of the gantry sported a sizable goitre; a fellow headed for the door was demonstrating the wide-based, stamping gait of *tabes dorsalis*, an advanced stage of syphilis; and a man in the corner was exhibiting great difficulty in getting his glass to his mouth without considerable spillage as a result of a shaking palsy. It seemed that once such knowledge had been acquired there was no respite from it.

A sudden shout from the corner of the room caused Raven to look up just as a tankard sailed over his head and hit the soot-blackened wall behind him. A scuffle broke out but the combatants were too far gone to land many punches on one another. The landlord ejected the pair without difficulty. He was a tall, muscular specimen with a domed, bald head, no hair upon his brow either. Upon disposing of his unruly customers, he bent down to retrieve the discarded tankard, which had landed close to Raven's feet.

'You're not from round here, are you,' he said, a statement rather than an enquiry. Evidently Raven's scar did not have the same impact upon everybody.

'No, I live in the town.'

'I heard you talking about that lassie they found. How come you know about that?'

There was an unmistakable note of suspicion in his voice.

'I happened to be passing yesterday when she was laid out on the quayside. Did you see it?'

'Too busy in here. I've heard all the blethers, though. Eejits. If you ask me, she probably fell from a ship – or was tossed from it. In which case the poor soul could have come from anywhere.'

'From her clothes, she didn't look at all far-travelled. Too pale of skin also.'

The landlord trained a scrutinising gaze upon him. Raven guessed that in his line of work he was an accomplished reader of men, and wondered what he saw in the one before him. Someone out of his element, for sure, and quite possibly out of his depth. But maybe, if he could truly peer beneath the surface, he saw something darker.

'So what do *you* reckon happened to her?' the landlord asked.

'I have a medical background,' Raven said, by way of establishing some measure of credentials. 'I have a suspicion she may have been poisoned before she went into the water.'

'Why would someone poison her and *then* throw her into the drink? Surely the villain who murders with poison wishes to disguise his intentions, so that it may look like she died in her sleep?'

'I don't know,' Raven conceded. 'Maybe it didn't work as swiftly as intended. It makes more sense than the notion that it was the work of Satan.'

'Don't you believe in the devil?' the landlord asked, his countenance darkening. 'You would if you lived round here.'

Raven didn't answer. He looked down into the last of his drink. He heard his mother's voice. *You've the devil in you.* Said in humour, said in reproach.

Many was the time Raven had witnessed demons seize a man and transform him. They had seized him too, as Henry could

attest. It usually began with a mischievous tongue when he knew
the wiser path lay in remaining circumspect. But he chose the
reckless path because something in him sought 'mayhem', as
Henry described it: inner torments demanding their external
manifestation.

And then there was the night that Thomas Cunningham died.

Raven was condemned for ever to see himself standing over
the body of the man he had just killed, while his wife cowered
on the floor beside him, weeping.

Yes, he believed in the devil.

Raven felt altogether less emboldened about who he might
encounter as he made his way home in the blackness of the night.
His eyes searched beyond the shallow pools of light beneath the
lamps, probing into the shadows for shapes and movement that
might signal danger.

He made it past Great Junction Street without having to
negotiate anything more hazardous than a few drunks and beggars,
but as he began his ascent towards the town, he soon became
convinced there were footsteps behind him. When he stopped so
did they. And when he turned, there was nobody to be seen.

He felt reassured when a coach passed upon the road, for it
meant potential witnesses and people he could call out to for help.
But when the clip of hooves faded, he was even more conscious
of his isolation. There was greater light where buildings stood,
particularly at the junctions, but between these were stretches
of foreboding gloom, hedgerows bordering fields shrouded in utter
blackness. If he wished to do a man harm unseen by any witness,
this would be where to strike.

He hurried his pace towards Pilrig Street. Still he heard the
footsteps, and again they stopped when he did. He glanced back,
and this time spied a darting movement on the edge of the light.

He was not deluding himself. He truly was being followed.

Should he run? He thought of how he had been blindsided

by Gargantua when his attention was fixed upon the Weasel. He had no way of knowing what he might be running into.

Raven slowed beneath the lamps where Pilrig Street met Leith Walk. Buildings stood upon each corner of the crossroads, gaslight and shadows flickering behind the windows. There was comparative safety here, but Raven could hardly loiter all night. He looked at the climb still ahead, the New Town a dim glow in the distance. That was when he realised that the darkness was his ally.

He passed into the space between two lamps, softening his tread. Then he veered sharply from the path and hopped over a hedgerow, where he concealed himself behind the dual trunks of a great tree in the field beyond. There he waited, drawing shallow breaths and listening for his pursuer. Sure enough, he soon heard footsteps, quickening presumably for fear that they had lost their quarry.

Raven watched him pass beneath the next lamp, approaching Haddington Place. With his back to Raven there was no way to see his face, not that he would have been able to see much at this distance. However, even in the gloom he could make out a domed, bald head atop a tall, powerful frame.

It was the landlord from the King's Wark.

TWENTY-TWO

Raven shifted in his seat, putting down his finished cup of tea upon the silver tray with a loud finality that he hoped would be the cue to move things along. Beattie did not seem to notice, but his patient started a little at the sound, and from that Raven suspected she was as nervous about the planned procedure's commencement as he was about further procrastination. Only Beattie seemed relaxed, though on this occasion his confident manner was not proving as infectious as usual.

They sat in a drawing room on Danube Street. It was Raven's first venture behind the grand doors of the New Town in any kind of a professional capacity. Everywhere wealth was ostentatiously displayed. A gilt-edged mirror spanned the width of the fireplace, emphasising the height of the ceiling, while vast landscape paintings lined the walls. From the ceiling hung two matching glass chandeliers, each large enough to kill a man should they fall, and Raven gauged that if the furniture was pushed back there would be enough room to perform an eightsome reel.

Raven told himself he was anxious to get started, but in truth he was just anxious. This in itself was annoying him, as such anxiety was needless. He had administered ether at least a dozen times now, with no ill effects, and though Henry's report of a death in England preyed on his mind, Simpson was adamant that the case had been mismanaged and the agent itself was safe.

Nonetheless, a nagging voice kept asking why, if there was no risk attached, he had not told Simpson he was doing this. The stark answer was that he needed the money more than he needed the professor's permission. Perhaps if there had been a salary attached to his position he might have felt differently, but right now he feared Flint's ire more than that of his employer.

The maid who answered the door to them had given Raven a disdainful look when she saw him. He had felt the sting of the slight, thinking that his problems with housemaids were becoming more general – did they communicate with each other? Was Sarah part of a coven of like-minded insurgents? – until he remembered that his face was still conspicuously bruised. The swelling had gone and his features had regained their usual symmetry but the purple on his cheek had transmuted into an array of yellow, green and brown which he had to admit was far from attractive. His nascent beard could only be expected to cover so much.

Beattie greeted the mistress of the house, Mrs Caroline Graseby, with an easy familiarity more akin to friend than physician and Raven wondered how long he had known her. She gazed upon the man as though eager for his approval, which seemed odd for a woman of her stature and wealth.

Raven had heard Mina talk about how certain women would fuss over Simpson, hungry for his attention. Beattie could not boast Simpson's accomplishments, but given his fine dress and youthful countenance, it was possible to imagine rich and bored ladies manufacturing complaints in order that he might minister to them – with their husbands footing the bill.

Beattie had warned Raven that she was extremely nervous about medical matters, and to this end asked him to call him only by his first name. 'A certain informality puts her at ease, as would the avoidance of the word "doctor".'

They had all sat down and taken tea together, which Raven

thought an odd prelude to any form of surgical procedure. Mrs Graseby sat by the fire sipping her Darjeeling. Beattie, Raven noticed, sat in close proximity to his patient and touched her hand frequently when speaking. He enquired after her health and made conversation about the weather and acquaintances they had in common. She did not address him as Dr Beattie, rather as 'Johnnie', which sounded not merely informal but a pet name. Given the nature of what Beattie was about to do, Raven wondered how this sat with the professional detachment Beattie had previously espoused. Perhaps how Beattie behaved and what he genuinely felt were two different matters; certainly there was little doubt the man knew how to present a version of himself appropriate to the company before him.

Raven was beginning to wonder whether this visit would turn out to be a mere prelude to carrying out the procedure at a later date, when Beattie put down his cup and declared: 'I think we had best be about our business.'

At this point Mrs Graseby visibly paled and dabbed her lips repeatedly with her handkerchief. 'I suppose we must,' she said, rising from her chair. She looked to Raven with apprehension, as though he might step in and call a halt. 'The room has been prepared,' she added quietly.

She led them from the drawing room towards the back of the house, past a portrait of an austere-looking individual with an ostentatious moustache. She noticed Raven studying it.

'My husband,' she said. Raven had assumed it was her father, given their respective ages.

They entered a smaller chamber at the back of the house which appeared to have been cleared of all furniture with the exception of a daybed and a small side table. Beattie asked for a larger one to be brought in so that he could lay out his instruments, and there ensued a degree of fuss as a servant searched upstairs for a table of suitable size before manoeuvring it into the room.

Raven was still unclear as to the precise nature of the procedure that Beattie intended to perform, and had initially been told
little about the patient herself apart from the fact that she was
young and in good health. He had pressed Beattie for more details
as they made their way to the house, but the only thing he had
been forthcoming about was the reason for his reticence.

'If this procedure is successful – and I have every confidence
that it will be – then there will be demand for it, and I will only
profit fully from my innovation if I am the sole doctor who can
offer it.'

'I am not going to be able to replicate your technique if I
can't see it,' Raven had argued. 'All my business is at the other
end, so you could at least tell me the generalities of what you
are attempting.'

'A fair point,' he conceded with a sigh. 'I will be performing
a manipulation to correct a retroverted uterus, which I have
assured Mrs Graseby will increase her chances of conception. Her
husband is keen for a son and heir, and is frankly becoming impatient with what he considers a failing on his wife's part.'

'And will Mr Graseby be present?' Raven had asked, thinking
he could do without the pressure.

'Gods, no. He is overseas. America, I think.'

Raven watched as Beattie laid out a selection of probes and
a uterine sound. How this manipulation was supposed to assist
with conception he wasn't entirely sure, but whatever was
intended did not seem unduly complicated and was therefore
likely to be achieved quickly.

Raven removed a bottle of ether and a sponge from his bag,
Simpson's voice sounding in his head as he did so. *The only difference between a medicine and a poison is the dosage.*

Mrs Graseby lay down on the daybed and placed her handkerchief across her eyes. Her respiration was shallow and rapid
and Raven could see small beads of perspiration on her top lip.
He realised, perhaps a little belatedly, that she was unlike

anyone he had anaesthetised before. For one thing, she had not been in labour for several hours and she was considerably more nervous than her predecessors. In many cases they had been so desperate for oblivion that they had forcibly pulled Raven's hand towards their own faces. Mrs Graseby, by contrast, initially turned away as the sponge was brought near, whimpering into her pillow.

'Now, Caroline,' Beattie said in a firm tone. 'You know this must be done.'

Mrs Graseby swallowed then nodded. She took a couple of breaths of the ether but then attempted to move Raven's hand away. Speaking to her in a calm tone, as he had seen Simpson do, he brought the sponge in closer to her nose and mouth, and within a few minutes she appeared to succumb.

Beattie began the procedure and Raven felt for the pulse at the wrist. All was well.

'I notice there is no painting of her,' Raven said quietly.

'No,' Beattie replied. 'It's an expensive business, so they often don't commission one of the wife until she has brought forth an heir. And survived it.'

'Unless it's a love match,' Raven suggested, deducing that this was most probably not.

'One should never assume in such matters,' Beattie replied. 'But no, I suspect not in this case.'

'She certainly seems taken with you,' Raven ventured, injecting a note of humour into his tone.

Beattie seemed bemused in his response. 'It is a double-edged sword,' he said. 'Women tend to think my appearance boyish and their maternal instinct draws them to me. It is therefore easy to strike up a rapport but there is a danger they may misinterpret my intentions.'

'And is such attention so unwelcome?' Raven asked, curious at Beattie's thin-lipped expression and, he would admit, a little envious.

'When a woman is attracted to my boyishness, that often goes with a tendency to regard me as junior, as trivial. Even worse is when the woman is young and trivial herself and thinks me an ideal match. You might imagine such attentions flattering, but I have quite had my fill of flirtations.'

Raven thought of how Beattie had talked so long with Mina at dinner, and suddenly saw their conversation in a different light.

His reverie was interrupted as Mrs Graseby uttered a moan and her hand shot up in apparent response to something Beattie was doing. It caught Raven on the left side of his face and he shouted out, more in surprise than pain, the noise causing Beattie to drop the instrument he was holding.

'For God's sake, Raven. Keep her still, will you.'

Raven quickly poured more of the ether onto the sponge and pushed it roughly onto the writhing woman's face. Within a few breaths she had quietened again. Beattie looked up at Raven as though he would like to stab him with the implement he had retrieved from the floor.

'I shouldn't be much longer here but I am at a critical point in the procedure. Please ensure that she does not move again.'

Beattie's face was flushed and Raven decided not to argue with him. He merely nodded and continued to feel for the pulse. He noticed that it had become quite rapid, much as his own in the last few minutes, but even as his calmed, Mrs Graseby's continued to increase.

'Is everything all right down there?' Raven asked. 'There isn't any bleeding, is there?'

'There is but a little,' Beattie replied, a little testily.

A few minutes later he threw his instruments down on the table and wiped his brow.

'I am done,' he declared.

'I am worried about the pulse rate,' Raven told him. 'It is very high.'

'It is the ether. You must have given her too much.'

'I don't think so,' he argued, though in truth he knew he couldn't be sure.

They looked at each other as Beattie wiped his hands. 'There is no bleeding,' Beattie said again. 'We must simply wait for her to recover.'

The next few hours were among the worst that Raven had ever known. Mrs Graseby remained drowsy, never fully regaining her senses. Her pulse rate remained high and her pallor corpse-like.

'All will be well,' Beattie assured him, no more flustered than had she been suffering a nosebleed. 'Time and patience are all that is required. You should leave her in my care and get yourself home.'

Raven had no intention of abandoning her in this condition, and steadfastly refused to move from her bed. Finally, however, her pulse began to slow, which he reported to Beattie with some relief.

'She will rally now,' Beattie insisted. 'Go back to Queen Street and get yourself some rest. You look quite spent.'

'I would rather wait until she is fully awake.'

'Your work is done, Will. But I will send for you as soon as she opens her eyes.'

Raven did as he was bid, feeling the burden begin to lift as he made the short walk back to Queen Street. He suspected that his anxiety had been magnified because he was working for the first time without Simpson's supervision, but perhaps taking difficult steps on your own was the only way to learn. Nonetheless, he knew he would not feel entirely secure about it until he had returned to Danube Street and seen Mrs Graseby fully conscious again.

He ate little at dinner, which piqued the unwanted interest of Mina.

'Are you troubled by indigestion? You might care to try one of my stomach powders. I got them from Duncan and Flockhart and they work very efficiently indeed.'

Raven respectfully declined and excused himself as soon as he deemed polite, unable to concentrate on the conversation. He retreated to his room, waiting impatiently for word and emerging to disappointment twice when the doorbell rang with messages for the professor.

The longer he waited, the more he began to fear, as it did not augur well if it was taking this long for Mrs Graseby to recover. That said, it was possible Beattie had been tardy about remembering his promise, and was engaged in further flirty conversation with his patient.

Finally, at about ten o'clock, there was a third ring on the doorbell. A few moments later Jarvis knocked on Raven's door.

'Dr Beattie is here to see you,' he said quietly. Raven wondered anxiously what he might infer from the butler's soft tone, but told himself his quiet delivery was more a reflection of the hour. Nonetheless, he hurried down the stairs and found Beattie awaiting him in the half light of the hallway.

He was clutching his hat. Raven's stomach turned instantly to lead.

Beattie waited until they were alone, and when he spoke, his words were barely above a whisper.

'She did not recover.'

'Dear God. How?'

'I fear it was the ether.'

Raven felt himself shrink, the darkness around threatening to swallow him. 'I am finished. I will have to tell Dr Simpson.'

Beattie gripped his arm and whispered into his ear. 'You will tell no one. I brought you into this. I will see you are not blamed.'

With this, Beattie walked to the door and closed it quietly behind him. As Raven watched him withdraw, he felt an undeserving gratitude, but no relief and absolutely no comfort.

TWENTY-THREE

aven was engulfed by the bleakest misery, confined within a prison of his own making, and what made it harder still was that he had to conceal his pain from everyone around him. He had to conduct himself as though nothing was amiss, there being no option to withdraw and hide away, as the following day had been hectically busy.

It had begun with a typically rumbustious morning clinic, at which he was besieged by unwary souls to whom he felt he ought to admit to being a dangerous fraud. He felt nervous and under-confident in his diagnoses and the advice he dispensed. Consequently, several patients left him with the impression that they were not convinced by what he told them, and therefore less likely to take the steps he recommended.

He thought of the homeopaths and the benefits their patients experienced due solely to the confidence they had in their doctors. If there was an opposite effect, then he was surely generating it.

Nonetheless, there was one case in which he had no doubt regarding his diagnosis, though his confidence did not provide for any better an outcome. The patient was a Mrs Gallagher, who had presented with what she initially described as a stomach complaint. Raven had palpated her stomach to little response, but when he put the merest pressure against her ribs, she winced and withdrew. He instantly recognised what he was looking at, just as he recognised her reluctance to lift her chemise and show him her sides.

'I need to check for a particular kind of rash that may be infectious,' he lied, by way of convincing her to cooperate.

He found the bruising where he expected, extensive but easily concealed.

'Your husband did this,' he stated.

She looked hunted, afraid even that Raven had said this aloud.

'It was my ain fault. I burnt the scones and there was nae mair flour. He had a tiring day and I should have been paying mair heed.'

'Where might I speak with Mr Gallagher?' Raven asked, but she was already on her way to the door.

She departed rapidly, leaving him with the impression that he had made matters worse, or at least frightened her into leaving before he was able to do anything for her.

This miserable morning had been followed by the usual diet of assisting at lectures and home visits. Adding insult to injury, one of the latter marked the first time he had accompanied Simpson to a rich client in the New Town, where inevitably he had been required to administer ether. When Simpson suggested it, Raven had looked around in the hope that he might see one of the Reverend Grissom's pamphlets, but he was not so blessed.

How his hands had shaken as he fumbled for the bottle, Simpson asking with a mixture of concern and irritation if he was all right.

The final trial was dinner, when once again he had to conceal his torment lest someone enquire as to what was troubling him. The hardest thing about this burden was that he absolutely could not share it with anybody.

Raven had seldom felt so isolated, so lonely, but at least his efforts at such concealment appeared to be successful. Following last night's solicitations and attendant offer of stomach powders, Mina's attention was notably not upon him this evening. She seemed distracted by some hidden excitation. She had news she was impatient to share, but had to await her moment.

Raven suspected Simpson had divined this, as he seemed to draw out saying grace as though intent upon frustrating her. Ordinarily this would have frustrated Raven also, with his meal having been placed before him, but he was lacking in appetite.

His head bowed, Raven observed that he had been given a larger portion than anyone else. He glanced up, caught Sarah's eye, and saw a conciliatory expression upon her face which told him his true condition had not gone entirely unnoticed. She could have no idea what was wrong, only that he was suffering.

He offered her a tiny nod of acknowledgment. He just hoped she wouldn't misinterpret if he failed to clear his plate.

The formalities concluded, Mina did not pause to eat before making her contribution.

'I learned the most dreadful news today,' she said. 'Truly dreadful and most tragic.'

Raven felt his insides turn to ice as it struck him that she was about to reveal the death of Mrs Graseby, right here before Dr Simpson.

'You will remember the Sheldrake family's housemaid, the one who had run away?'

'Sheldrake?' asked James Duncan with a sour curiosity, by way of emphasising that he had not been party to the previous discussion to which Mina was alluding.

'Mr Sheldrake is a dentist,' Mrs Simpson informed him, 'with a very successful practice. One of his housemaids absconded recently.'

'Rose Campbell,' said Mina. 'She was found dead, and there is a rumour that it was murder. Pulled from the dockside down in Leith. It's thought the man she ran off with must have done for her.'

'How awful for the Sheldrakes,' said Mrs Simpson. 'And for the staff who knew her.'

'It is thought that her own behaviour might have contributed to her demise,' Mina went on. 'She was reputedly free with her favours.'

Mina shook her head as though the relevance of this last statement was self-evident. Raven wondered at this sense of natural justice people seemed to draw from such judgments, as though any carnal knowledge of which they did not approve must inevitably lead to the direst of consequences. Perhaps they embraced this by way of reassurance that they could never meet a similar fate because of the morality they observed.

He sometimes felt sorry for Mina in that she appeared to have no greater purpose in life than to get herself married off, and was making scant progress in this endeavour. Vicarious excitement and scandal were therefore of disproportionate significance to her, and she was a busy conduit for all manner of gossip. Mina spoke with ill-disguised fascination about this poor girl's gruesome fate, as though she were reading from a penny dreadful.

Raven's eyes lit briefly upon Sarah. She was upset and attempting to conceal it. Her efforts were precisely as successful as his had been, in that only one person had seen through to the truth.

Sarah knew the girl.

Mina's reverie was cut off by the professor, who had heard enough.

'This kind of speculation is not appropriate for the dinner table, Mina,' he stated firmly. 'And it is no more than blethers. I happened to run into McLevy the police detective today, and he said nothing about murder.'

'What did he tell you?' Mina asked.

'The details are not for sharing in gentle company,' Simpson replied, which closed the matter for the duration of the meal.

Raven made a point of seeking out the professor on his own

once dinner was concluded. He intercepted him on his way to the stairs, before he could disappear into his study.

'What did McLevy tell you, sir?'

Simpson looked at him as though surprised at his interest, then a dawning passed over his expression as he remembered that Raven had been there at the quayside.

'He is awaiting the results of a post-mortem by the police surgeon,' Simpson said, his voice low. There was nobody in earshot, but he was perhaps concerned that a door might open nearby at any moment. 'I implied to Mina that there was no murder, but the truth is McLevy has not ruled anything out until he knows more.'

'So was there anything specific to suggest foul play?'

'He was very guarded. Between you and me, McLevy sometimes says more than his prayers. He likes to exaggerate the enormity of what he is up against so that it reflects the greater upon his achievement when he gets his man. But on this occasion, I do not believe that to be the case. He asked for my discretion, which you understand I would therefore expect of you also.'

'Unquestioningly, sir.'

'With a young woman found dead like that, he does not want word to spread that there may be some monster at large.'

Raven recalled the absurd talk of devils and Satanists that he had overheard. He well understood the hysteria that might ensue, not to mention the accusations. He recalled also the landlord, who had been keen to know the nature of Raven's interest, and who had followed him later. He might even have discovered where Raven lived, had he not managed to give him the slip.

'Had McLevy any suspicion as to what might have happened?'

'As Mina has said, Rose Campbell was rumoured to have been seeing a number of men, and possibly to have run away with one of them.'

'When we saw her by the quay, her posture was strangely contorted. What of that?'

'McLevy made no mention of it. But as we have no notion how long she was in the water, that might have been the result of rigor mortis. Why do you ask?'

What could Raven tell him? *Because a whore of my acquaintance, and of whom I have occasionally had knowledge, died in a similarly twisted posture and I crept away like a coward in order to protect my own reputation.*

'I am simply curious as to what might have caused it.'

He watched the doctor slip away quietly into his study. There was nothing further to be learned from him, but there was one person in the house who might know more.

Raven waited until he knew her duties were complete and she would have retired to her quarters. He ascended the stairs to the topmost floor and knocked softly upon the door.

'Yes, come in?'

Despite the invitation, Raven opened the door but remained in place, not considering it appropriate to proceed fully inside. He knew that he was not who Sarah was expecting when she called out her reply. She was sitting upon the bed, a book open on her lap.

She wore a familiarly implacable expression: a mixture of defiance and disapproval, though on this occasion missing the usual note of amusement bordering on scorn. Her face nonetheless failed to conceal that she was surprised to see him.

She closed the book and got to her feet.

The room smelled like fresh linen: clean and crisp. Sarah herself had a scent of cooked meat, smells that had adhered to her clothes from working in Mrs Lyndsay's kitchen.

'How may I help you, Mr Raven?'

So, not Wilberforce today. She was caught off-guard and using formality to shore up a barrier. There was a redness about her eyes to indicate that she had recently wept.

Raven was struck by how small and bare her room was. He had imagined it must be at least the same size as his, his position being temporary while hers was long-term. He realised with private embarrassment that this had been a baseless and indeed foolish assumption. It seemed so drab, so inadequate, and yet this was her lot.

The furnishings consisted of a small bed, a trestle table, and a chest of drawers atop which sat a sewing basket and a washing bowl. There were no pictures on the narrow walls, no shelves full of books. He had imagined she would have a collection of novels at least, but understood now that she must borrow them from Dr Simpson's library.

Behind her on the bed was the volume she had just closed, an illustrated work concerning the cultivation of herbs and other plants. He recalled seeing her tending a particular patch of garden at the back of the house. On the trestle table sat *Outlines of Chemistry, for the Use of Students*, by Professor William Gregory, who taught at the university. Raven was intrigued as to what she could possibly be wanting with that. He had found it challenging enough, so what chance did she have of comprehending anything from it?

'What are you reading?' he asked.

'I am interested in the healing properties of herbs,' she replied, an impatience to her tone clearly not welcoming further discussion.

'And what about the Gregory?'

She glanced towards the volume that had once so tormented him.

'Chemistry is the key to identifying the properties of individual plants which provoke specific effects. But as you had no way of knowing these books were here, I can deduce that this is not what you have come to enquire about.'

'No, it is not,' he admitted. 'May I come inside?'

Sarah nodded, though she folded her arms and took a step back — not that there was much space to put between them in this small chamber.

'Rose Campbell, the young lady who was found. You knew her, didn't you?'

Sarah glanced down for a moment, a darkening in her expression.

'Only a little. I knew her mainly through a mutual friend, Milly Conville. We sometimes meet when we are out in the town on errands.'

'She and this Milly were maids in the same house?'

'Yes. I believe Mr Sheldrake has the richest dental practice in the city, his clientele drawn primarily from here in the New Town. He has a household staff to match. What of it?'

'It was rumoured that Rose had run away with someone. Had you heard anything about this?'

Sarah's eyes narrowed. 'Why do you wish to know?'

'I am simply curious.'

'Enough to venture forth into the uncharted territory of the top landing and knock on this door. That is not an idle curiosity, Mr Raven. Something else must be driving it, so you ought to do me the courtesy of disclosing what.'

Raven had no such intention, but he had to step lightly. If she knew nothing, she would have simply told him that.

'When Miss Grindlay said that she was dead, I observed that you appeared distressed by the news. I was concerned that you might be upset.'

Sarah looked him in the eye, nodding to herself. 'That would be most solicitous of you, Mr Raven, if it were the truth.'

'It is the truth,' he insisted. 'I was aware you may not have anybody you could talk to about it, so I sought you out.'

'I mean the whole of the truth. You have described a mere pretext. What is the real nature of your interest?'

Raven searched for somewhere else to cast his gaze. There was but one small window, and nothing to be seen through it at night time.

'It concerns matters that would not be appropriate to share with someone of your standing.'

Sarah's eyes flashed with anger. 'My standing? Do you mean as a housemaid or as a woman? How little you must think of me that you would come here seeking information, but with no intention of reciprocating even if it might assist in what I could tell you.'

Raven withstood her ire, for in it she had betrayed what he suspected.

'So you do know more?'

'I am answering no more questions until you answer some of mine. Such as why you have seemed so burdened these past couple of days. Is that related to your interest in poor Rose?'

'No. I have merely been suffering the trials of my apprenticeship and of being new to certain duties.'

Sarah scoffed, that scornful look putting in its first appearance. 'I don't believe you. If you were struggling with your duties, I would discern it in Dr Simpson's manner. Something more specific is troubling you. Is it to do with this Evie, whose name you wrote down in your journal? Who is she?'

Raven felt something tighten inside him, an instinct drawing him to fold his arms too.

'That is absolutely no business of yours.'

'Indeed it is not,' she replied. 'And as I have absolutely no interest in your business, I will bid you goodnight.' She stepped past him to hold open the door. 'Though before you go, Mr Raven, I would suggest that you might seek out my friend Milly at the Sheldrakes' house. See if she wants to speak frankly and openly about this raw and painful loss. I can imagine no impediment. After all, you have already established such great rapport with me, so I see no reason why that should not be reprised with a complete stranger.'

Raven got the message. He could vividly imagine how such an approach was likely to go.

'Very well,' he said. 'Evie was a friend who lived in the Canongate, close to my former lodgings.'

'Was? Lived? So she is no more?'

He spent a moment calculating what he could disclose, attempting to anticipate the ramifications within ramifications. It was impossible. He could not tell her anything without telling her everything. If he really wanted to find out more, he would have to commit, holding nothing back.

'If I am to tell you this, I must have your absolute confidence. I need to know I can trust you.'

Sarah seemed momentarily taken aback. 'I guarantee my discretion. Your words will not pass these walls.'

'They will not have to. Your hearing it will be enough. Once I have told you what I must, you are not going to like me, Miss Fisher. That is, you are going to like me even less than you do already.'

Sarah looked at him almost pityingly. 'I do not dislike you, Mr Raven. You have misinterpreted. You see, I am in the household to serve, but that does not mean you may automatically command my respect or my affection; or even, though many would be satisfied with it, a pretence of either. But you can have my trust.'

Raven saw a sincerity in her face that he had not observed before, having seldom witnessed anything other than studied neutrality, practised detachment and outright hostility.

'Evie was a prostitute,' he said quietly.

Sarah considered this a moment. 'One you used?'

He sighed, battling his own resistance. 'I had . . . knowledge of her, yes. But it was what she did, how she made her money. I did not judge her for—'

'One you used,' she repeated. Her tone was not bitter, but it was insistent and inescapable.

Raven felt the shame of it now, of what he had done, of the vulnerability he had exploited. The lies he once told himself about the nature of it were now crumbling.

'Yes,' he admitted. 'I was younger then, curious. Tempted. She seemed far above me, something unknowable and forbidden

– and yet attainable. I was troubled then, given to bouts of . . . abandon. But yes, I used her. At first. Then we became friends.'

'Close friends? Or merely a prostitute and a former client who might yet be a client again?'

'I thought we were close friends, but I accept now that I will never know. When you lead a life such as Evie did, you cannot afford the luxury of trust, or of becoming close to anybody, though you may become adept at feigning it.'

Raven paused, picturing Evie how she once was, wondering whether her friendship was as illusory as her bedroom intimacies.

'She asked me for money,' he said. 'She wouldn't say why, only that her need was urgent. I gave her it. Then I visited her on the night before I came to live here, hoping to hear that her troubles were dealt with. Instead I found her . . . no more, her body twisted in agonised contortions. When I glimpsed Rose Campbell lying upon the quayside, she was in a similar condition.'

'Did you tell anyone what you had found? Or about this similarity?'

'I could not. On the night I found Evie, I had to leave unseen, lest anyone thought I was responsible for what happened to her.'

Sarah's reaction mirrored everything he felt about it himself.

'Oh, I think it would only be fair to conclude that you were not *responsible*.'

'I am not proud of what I did, but I panicked. What if I was thought a murderer?'

'So you believe she was killed?'

'I suspect she was poisoned, yes. And it is possible Rose was too, by the same means if not by the same hand.'

'Was any investigation prompted by Evie's discovery?'

'No. It was assumed she had died from alcohol.'

'Even though she was found as you describe?'

'Nobody looks closely when it's "another deid hoor", as I heard a policeman call her.'

'Rose was no hoor. They will investigate her, surely. You must tell McLevy what you know.'

As soon as the words had fallen from her mouth, it was clear Sarah understood how this could not be so.

'Except that you cannot, in case he thinks you were involved,' she stated.

'They say McLevy always gets his man, but living in the Old Town, I heard it different. Over there, they say he gets *a* man, then doesn't worry so much about whether it is the right one as long as the story fits and the jury convicts.'

Raven swallowed, looking her in the eye. 'I want to find out what happened to Evie, which is why I want to know more about Rose. Will you help me?'

Sarah returned his look, contemplating, evaluating. She appeared to arrive at a verdict.

'My assistance comes at a price, Mr Raven.'

'As you so accurately deduced, I have very little money.'

'Not that kind of price. I would ask the same thing you asked of me. Trust. You will keep nothing from me, and in this endeavour you will at all times treat me as your equal.'

'I give you my word. It is agreed then?'

'Not yet. Those were merely my conditions. The price I will tell you when I am good and ready.'

TWENTY-FOUR

arah found herself repeatedly falling into step a few paces behind Raven as they made their way along the Cowgate. A pattern had emerged whereby Raven would slow down in response, only for her to drift into the rear again soon after. Eventually he stopped dead and turned to her with a querulous expression.

'Why are you dawdling? Are you trying to make us late?'

It took his saying this for her to understand what she was doing. She had an impulse to apologise but she swallowed it.

'I was not dawdling,' she replied. 'I am more used to accompanying Miss Grindlay or occasionally Mrs Simpson, servants not being expected or indeed permitted to walk alongside their employers. It is a matter of habit rather than a reflection of your perceived status,' she added.

Raven's ignorance of the everyday practicalities of her station was proving a source of frustration to himself and of teeth-grating irritation to Sarah. In the ensuing couple of days following their late-night discussion, he kept appearing in the kitchen or intercepting her in hallways with the same question.

'Have you had opportunity?' he would ask.

After a good half-dozen replies in the negative, she laid it out for him.

'My duties do not allow much time for social visits; certainly not during hours that are safe or appropriate for a young woman to be out upon the streets. Besides, it is not as though I can simply knock upon the Sheldrakes' kitchen door and start asking questions. It would be best if it appeared a casual encounter.'

'You said you know this girl. When do you normally see her?'

'My opportunities to converse with Milly in the past have generally been in the gift of happenstance. As I said before, we would sometimes meet when we were both on errands, such as to the haberdasher's or occasionally Duncan and Flockhart.'

'You were out in the town only today,' he pointed out.

'I was with Miss Grindlay,' she responded.

Raven looked exasperated. 'Then the Lord knows how long I might be waiting.'

Sarah was about to give him a broadside by explaining that the only free time she got was on Sundays, when she realised that she knew precisely where and when she would find Milly and indeed the entire Sheldrake household.

'You will be waiting until the Lord's day,' she said. 'I can speak to Milly after Sunday worship.'

'The Sheldrakes attend the same church as we do?'

'No,' she confessed, immediately seeing where her plan would fall down. The Simpson household all had to attend Sunday worship together at St John's, Dr Simpson favouring Thomas Guthrie's sermons above all others. Milly would be in attendance elsewhere. 'Though perhaps you could suggest to Dr Simpson you have heard that the minister in a particular church is an interesting speaker and that we are both curious to find out his perspective upon certain matters.'

Raven had looked less than hopeful in response to this notion. They both knew it would sound an odd and unlikely thing to suggest to the professor.

'Do you even know the name of this minister whose church the Sheldrakes attend?'

'I *only* know his name,' Sarah admitted. 'Not where his church is. He is the Reverend Malachy Grissom.'

At this, Raven's eyes bulged. 'You know, I think we just might be able to convince Dr Simpson of my curiosity after all.'

It was for this reason that they were now walking along the Cowgate, Raven having discovered the location they sought. It was a bright, if cold, Sunday morning and yet he seemed to be permanently looking about himself, as though wandering here in the dead of night. This state of anxious vigilance was perhaps why he was so irritated at having to slow down for her.

'What are you looking for?' she asked. 'Anyone would think you were avoiding someone.'

'I am. Some former acquaintances with whom I'd rather not be reunited.'

'Why not? Who are they?'

'They don't concern you, for which you ought to be grateful.'

'I thought we agreed you would keep nothing from me.'

'Only in matters pertaining to this endeavour.'

'And how am I to know you are telling the truth regarding what matters do or don't pertain to it?'

'I was attacked and I had my face slashed, remember? I am apprehensive of running into the culprits again.'

'But why did they do it? Don't say you were robbed at random, because I don't believe you.'

Raven sighed. 'Because I owe them money, and I don't have it. Is that clear enough for you?'

It was not. Sarah had plenty more she might ask, not least *why* he owed them money, but she knew when to leave well alone.

Sarah had been speaking the truth when she said she didn't dislike him, but she did dislike his presumption of superiority over her, as she disliked it in all young men. Given the same chance, she was confident she would excel over any of them, so it stung when all they saw was a housemaid. Out of necessity,

Raven was looking beyond that. Or at least she was offering him the occasion to. She hoped he didn't disappoint.

'Why were you so confident that Dr Simpson would sanction this absence from our normal Sunday worship?' she asked as they passed beneath George IV Bridge.

'The Reverend Grissom has been campaigning against the use of ether in childbirth. He has been distributing pamphlets about it all over the city.'

'Why on earth would he want to do that?'

'Not why on earth. Why in heaven. There is a Bible verse stating that "in sorrow thou shalt bring forth children". He believes that the pain of childbirth is in some way sacred.'

'What arrant stupidity. And we are to listen to this man?'

'I anticipated that Dr Simpson would be curious — or at least amused — to know what else he might have to say. The Bible also states that when you are committing a charitable act, the right hand should not know what the left hand is doing. Given that surgery could be described as a charitable act, perhaps the Reverend might suggest the surgeon be blindfolded, or have one hand tied behind his back out of sight.'

Raven found this notion more amusing than Sarah, but that was because he was missing something rather obvious.

'He would suggest no such thing, for I doubt it a coincidence that he has chosen to object to the relief of a pain he is certain never to endure. If Grissom had a dose of the toothache, I can't imagine him finding a theological justification why Mr Sheldrake should not use ether in his dental extractions.'

Raven indicated that the place they sought was just ahead, its congregation already filing through a set of doors on the south side of the Cowgate. It appeared to be a modest meeting hall, and not a church as anyone might ordinarily recognise one.

'I expected somewhere grander,' Sarah admitted.

'Not all ministers of the Free Church were as fortunate as

the Reverend Guthrie in retaining their premises following the Disruption,' Raven told her. 'Many have had to make do with whatever halls and meeting places can be found.'

Sarah had heard mention of the Disruption, but paid little attention to matters involving pious old men bickering with each other. As she understood it, the schism had come down to the right of patronage, which allowed the state and wealthy land-owners to appoint a minister to a parish over and above the wishes of the parishioners. Those who broke with the main Church four years ago had consequently needed to form their own ministries, with the support of those in the laity who wished to follow them. Hence the ad-hoc nature of this place of worship.

She and Raven slipped inside, taking their seats towards the back. Sarah had seldom found churches to be joyful or inspiring places, but this one seemed particularly drab, and yet very well attended. A few minutes later, she watched the Sheldrake house-hold file in close to the front, their position perhaps reflecting the dentist's contributions to the new parish's coffers. Mr Sheldrake walked in at the head of the line, his wife, son and two daughters taking their seats alongside him as Milly and the rest of the household staff slipped into the row behind.

Sheldrake struck Sarah as an unlikely match for his dowdy and grim-faced wife. He was a tall, smartly dressed fellow, slim of build and clean-shaven. In the same way that it was said of certain women that they were handsome, Sheldrake could be said to be pretty: a feminine quality not only to his features, but also in the way he carried himself. His clothes were modern and fash-ionable to the point that there seemed something incongruously rakish about him, though perhaps any note of finery seemed out of place in this dour setting.

She glimpsed Milly momentarily between the rows of heads. She looked numb and shocked, trying to suppress tears. Milly would have known for some days about Rose's death, but Sarah understood from experience that being back in a familiar place for the first time could serve to bring it all home, another reminder of death's finality.

The room fell silent as the Reverend Grissom entered and took his place behind the lectern that served as his pulpit. He was a small man with the proud gait of one who believed himself to be at least a foot taller. Fine grey hair hung lank around his crown as though draped from a circular pelmet, his pate bald but for a few wispy tufts that Sarah felt the constant urge to ascend the stage and shave. Beneath it his face was dominated by a nose so large and pointed that when he turned his head it was as though he were indicating the direction in which he imminently intended to leave.

Unfortunately, he did not leave for quite some time. He preached at considerable length, though had nothing to say about ether. He talked much of humility whilst his tone, demeanour and indeed every physical gesture emanated self-importance, his permanently serious expression admitting no hint of levity.

Sarah thought it must be exhausting to be constantly dismayed by so many things.

'Pride makes men fools,' he said, his voice surprisingly loud for a small man. 'Vanity makes them seek glory in their own reflection, and they do not seek that reflection merely in the looking glass, but in the admiration of others. How they wish to see it in the faces of their peers, but worst is how they crave to see it in the faces of *women*.'

His voice dropped as he said this, as though the word itself were obscene.

'And in this, the worst of women are complicit, for they are the tauntresses. *Their* pride is served by this. *Their* pride escalates that of men. They paint themselves, they dress themselves, these jezebels. Not only the fallen ones upon the night-time streets, but in their husbands' homes too. The proud man seeks their approval. And he seeks that approval manifest in physical knowledge. That is why the greatest sin of a woman is to feed this pride in men, to encourage it. For to do so is to be the occasion of another's sin, to lead another into temptation.

'The good wife is modest. The good woman is modest in her appearance and in her manner. It is modesty that I commend, modesty to which I entreat you. As the Lord's mother was modest.'

Raven leaned towards Sarah and spoke softly as the service ended and the congregation began to disperse.

'And yet Jesus chose the company of prostitutes over that of preachers.'

Sarah had to stifle a gasp, concerned that his remark might be overheard. However, she suspected that to shock her had been his intention, so she decided to respond in kind, albeit more quietly.

'I don't believe your own such dalliances put you closer to the Lord. Was it the sin of pride that made you seek out a woman of the night?'

'As I recall, the sin of lust was adequate to the task. I cannot pretend to the Reverend Grissom's modesty, but perhaps he has greater reason to be modest than I.'

Sarah made her way smartly out onto the Cowgate, where worshippers were gathering to trade their Sunday greetings. She and Raven stood close to the doors, the ideal vantage point for interception.

'You had best keep your distance,' Sarah told him, watching Mr Sheldrake lead his family down the aisle towards the vestibule. 'Milly is not going to be very candid with a stranger in our company.'

Raven's attention appeared to have been taken by something else in any case.

'Yes, certainly. I'll meet you back here,' he said, swiftly departing through the crowd.

Sarah saw Mr and Mrs Sheldrake stop in the vestibule to talk to Reverend Grissom, Milly continuing towards the exit. She stepped into her path and offered a conciliatory smile.

'Sarah!' Milly said, surprise in her voice. She sounded meeker than usual, her tones more nasal. Sarah could tell she had cried a great deal in recent days. 'What are you doing here?'

'I got permission from Dr Simpson to worship here today. I wanted to see you and to tell you how sorry I was to hear about Rose.'

Milly swallowed, looking as though her eyes might fill again. She nodded. 'Thank you. It has been difficult.'

'I can't begin to imagine. I felt so guilty.'

'Guilty? Why?'

'Because when I was told she had absconded, I was envious, imagining some exciting life she might have escaped to. I had heard rumours she was seeing someone and had run away with him. Was this true?'

Milly cast an eye to the side, towards the Sheldrakes. It was innocent enough for her to be talking to Sarah, a fellow housemaid, but she was clearly concerned not to be overheard. For the moment, they were not in earshot.

'I couldn't say,' Milly replied. 'Rose had secrets, and there was a man involved. That much was inescapable.'

Sarah thought this an odd choice of word.

'Inescapable how?'

Milly glanced again at her employers. She looked afraid she had given something away.

'I shouldn't speak further. I've said too much as it is.'

'You can trust me, Milly,' Sarah implored.

'I do. But it's not you I've said too much to.'

Sarah placed a hand on her shoulder. The poor girl looked like a hollowed-out shell where once there had been so much more.

'You must let me know about the funeral,' Sarah said, trying to keep her talking.

This seemed to burden her even more, tears threatening again.

'I do not know that there will even be a funeral. And it is my fault.'

'How can that be?'

'A policeman came to the house to ask us questions. An Irishman, McLevy. I was only trying to be honest, but because of what I told him, he is of a mind that Rose killed herself.'

'For what reason would Rose possibly take her own life?'

Milly's eyes swept to the side again. The Sheldrakes had finished speaking with the Reverend Grissom and were moving towards the door.

'She was sure she would be dismissed, and she did not know what else she could do.'

Sarah gripped Milly's arm in case she should walk away.

'Dismissed for what reason?'

With Mr Sheldrake imminently in earshot, Milly's last words were but a breath.

'She was with child.'

TWENTY-FIVE

aven had just been told to keep his distance when his eye was drawn to something on the other side of the Cowgate. At first he couldn't be sure because he only glimpsed them through the departing congregation, but as he moved beyond the crowd and the pair drew close, there could be no mistake. Walking westward towards the Grassmarket was the woman who had recently come to him with such horrific bruising, accompanied by a scowling and ruddy-faced man.

They were both dressed for church, heading home from worship. Her head was bowed low, as though reluctant to meet anyone's eye, while he walked with his chin thrust forward, his peering eyes seeming to challenge the world around him to explain itself. It was Sunday morning, but Saturday night was still etched across his visage, a drinker's face with pudgy pink skin and a bulbous nose. These were the only parts of him that appeared soft. The rest of the man resembled a coiled spring.

They had passed by the time Raven made it across the road. 'Mr Gallagher!' Raven hailed him, making sure he had the right person.

The man turned around, his expression conveying irritated curiosity when he failed to recognise who had called him. His

wife, by contrast, had a look of fear as she immediately identified the man approaching them. She was evidently terrified of
the repercussions should her husband learn what Raven had
deduced, or maybe even the mere fact that she had visited a
doctor.

'What do you want?' he asked, looking Raven up and down.
There was evident disdain at being summarily apprehended by
some young upstart, though Raven noted that his eye lingered a
moment upon the scar.

'I need to speak to you.'

'Then speak.'

Mrs Gallagher's head remained down. Raven was sure she was
trembling.

'It concerns a delicate matter, inappropriate for discussion in
front of your good lady wife.'

Mr Gallagher looked confused and dismissive, instantly rele-
gating anything Raven might say in terms of its potential
relevance.

'Please, I'm sure what I have to impart will be greatly to your
benefit. Let us step somewhere close by where we might enjoy
some privacy.'

Raven led him off the Cowgate into a narrow close between
two buildings, the hubbub from the Free Church congregation
immediately softer.

'Well,' Gallagher said impatiently, 'out with it.'

'I am your wife's medical practitioner. I thought we ought to
discuss a chronic condition that has been afflicting her.'

His suspicious eyes narrowed further. 'What condition is that?'

'Please do me the courtesy of not thinking me a fool. She
endeavoured to conceal the source of her injuries for fear of more.
But I understood what I was looking at all too well.'

Gallagher looked outraged at Raven's impertinence. 'She
doesn't pay attention. She gets distracted. A man works all day,
then comes home to find the last of the flour's been ruined. What

business is it of yours how a man runs his house or disciplines his wife?'

'Oh, we're talking about discipline? Is that the same mettle you require to say no to another whisky when you've already drunk your fill and spent the wages your wife needs to live on?'

'Who the hell do you think you're addressing, boy?'

'I am acting in my patient's interest.'

'No, you're sticking your neb where it ill belongs. So you should mind it doesn't come to some harm.'

Raven noticed Gallagher ball his right hand into a fist. It hadn't taken much. He knew a thing or two about men like this.

Raven put up his palms in a placatory gesture. 'Very well, Mr Gallagher. It is your business how you discipline your wife. Just as it is my business how I treat her affliction. And having identified that affliction as the lump of shite standing in front of me, I hereby prescribe a remedy. I am going to ask her to come and see me regularly, and if I see further evidence of your hands upon her, I will find you and I will knock seven bells out of you. That way you get to handle your business and I get to handle mine.'

Rage built up in Gallagher, but he did not move. Yet.

'I'll do what I will with these hands, son, including beating you to a pulp if you ever cross me again.' Gallagher made another fist. He was getting there, but something was holding him back: the very fact that Raven was not afraid.

'Why wait? I'm in front of you right now. Come now, you've shown great vigour in hitting a woman. Why don't you show me how you hit a man?'

'I won't do this on the Sabbath.'

Raven put his hands by his sides, leaving himself open. 'Does that mean your wife can burn the scones with impunity today?'

That was the tipping point, the moment Gallagher's rage overcame his cowardice. He swung for all he was worth, launching his fist towards Raven's face. But Raven was quick; quick enough for a drunk like him. He moved his head in a twinkling and Gallagher punched the wall, with all his weight behind the blow.

Gallagher dropped to his knees, letting out a guttural moan as he looked in horror at the mangled fingers, broken, bloody and raw. The only thing he had beaten to a pulp was his own hand.

Raven stood over him and held his chin, forcing him to look up.

'Remember I did this without even touching you. Strike her again and that will change.'

TWENTY-SIX

arah looked about for Raven, unable to find him in the throng that had spilled out of the Reverend Grissom's service. The Sheldrakes had gathered their staff and were proceeding in the direction of Blair Street, Milly walking with her head bowed. She did not glance back.

Sarah located him emerging from a close across the street, his countenance a grim contrast to the departing worshippers'. Their expressions befitted those who believed they had just communed with the Lord, while Raven's intimated dealings altogether less holy.

Sarah felt vindicated in her instinctive impression that there was something restless and impetuous in Raven. She estimated that both of these traits had played their part in whatever had led to his face being wounded, but she also doubted he would tell her the truth about it. There was a swirling fog of dark secrets behind his hazel eyes.

She would admit that there was undoubtedly something kinder in there too, though at Queen Street anyone might seem warm next to Dr James Duncan – or Dr James Matthews Duncan as he was now insisting upon. That one was restless and impetuous also, but driven entirely by ambition and the desire to make a name for himself, as evidenced by his concern that his name itself should be distinct.

Raven, by contrast, was striving on behalf of a woman who was too dead to thank him for it. Perhaps he was trying to atone for not having helped enough to keep her alive. Sarah knew to be wary of such motives, noble as they may seem. They said the road to Hell was paved with good intentions, and she suspected Raven had the recklessness to take her there with him if she did not step carefully.

'Did you speak with her?' he asked.

'Rose was pregnant,' Sarah told him. 'She feared she would be dismissed as soon as it was discovered. Milly told McLevy as much, and now he is apt to conclude she drowned herself.'

Raven took a moment to absorb this.

'I have a suspicion Evie might have been pregnant too.'

'How do you know?' Sarah asked, before realising what the question might imply.

'It would not have been mine,' he answered evenly. 'I told you, I was no longer using her in that way.'

'Then what makes you think . . .?'

'I don't know. It just fits. But what does not is the idea that Rose drowned herself. That would not explain the contortions, similar to Evie's.'

'You said you suspected they both might have been poisoned. Is it not possible that they took a poison to kill themselves?'

Raven considered it. 'Theoretically, yes. But the same one? And one that appears to have racked them with pain? Why choose to die in such a horrible manner?'

'Perhaps they were misled into believing it would ease their passing, like opium.'

'I find it too hard to accept that Evie would end her own life. Why would she need money so urgently if she planned to kill herself?'

'I find it difficult to believe the same of Rose, but how can anyone know what they might do in a position of utter desperation?

To be with child but having no means of supporting it or herself once she was dismissed.'

'Professor Ziegler at the Maternity Hospital did say he had known young women to kill themselves,' Raven admitted, his voice taking on an apologetic tone. 'In some cases they could not even face the prospect of their families discovering their condition. It seems such a resort of final despair, though.'

'What other resort would be open to a girl like Rose?'

Raven gave her a look that said she already knew the answer to that question; and knew also that it could not be spoken aloud in the hearing of strangers.

They increased their pace, putting some distance between themselves and the departing worshippers.

'Desperate women explore all manner of options before self-murder,' he said. 'There was a newborn's leg found recently in a gutter near the Royal Exchange. I suspect the poor mite was done away with by its mother.'

It was not the first time Sarah had heard of such a thing.

'The mother must have been able to keep her condition secret, though,' she said. 'I doubt that would have been an option for Rose. She feared she would be dismissed long before such a horrible course would even have been open to her.'

'There are other desperate measures,' Raven said. His voice was low even though there was no one close by. It was an invitation to complicity.

'Indeed,' Sarah replied, by way of accepting.

'Though if they had chosen to go down that route, it might have ended just the same for them. My friend Henry recently encountered two cases of young women who died from attempted abortions.'

Sarah was trying to imagine the fear and hopelessness Rose must have felt, asking herself what she might do in the same situation. She suspected there was nothing she would not consider. That was when an idea struck her.

'What if they took a poison not in order to kill themselves, but believing it would purge the burden they carried?'

Raven turned in response. She could tell the notion was not outlandish.

'Women have taken all manner of concoctions in the hope that they might induce a premature labour,' he agreed. 'Thus far they have either been utterly without effect or harmful only to the mother.'

'Nonetheless, one could charge a great deal for a pill or a draught that promised to solve such a problem, as long as the buyer believed in it. Could this have been what Evie needed the money for?'

'Evie was no gullible fool. But desperation is often the mother of misplaced faith. I think you could be right.'

Raven gazed up towards the grey skies, as though answers might be hidden behind the canopy of clouds.

'I just wish we knew what manner of poison she might have taken.'

TWENTY-SEVEN

aven came to in the darkness, his half-waking dis-orientation suddenly sharpened into alert conscious-ness as he observed that there was a figure standing at the end of his bed holding a lamp. In his startled state and in the poor light, it took him a moment to recognise the intruder as Jarvis, the butler.

'What the devil are you doing?'

'I came to rouse you, Mr Raven.'

'Then why are you looming there like a bloody phantom? Why didn't you call my name?'

'I have called your name three times, and before that spent some time knocking upon your door, all to no avail. My next resort would have been to fetch a cup of water to throw over you, but happily we have not reached such an eventuality.'

As always, Jarvis's voice was calm and implacable, answering questions with patience and yet nonetheless conveying the impression that merely speaking to Raven was somehow beneath him. He hoped he was making some headway in breaking down Sarah's antipathy, but suspected Jarvis's disdain would remain a permanent fixture.

'What is the hour?'

'It is a quarter after four. Dr Simpson has been summoned to an urgent case and wishes you to ready yourself and accompany him forthwith.'

'Do you know where we are bound?' he asked, reckoning a carriage journey would give him time to fully wake up and gather his wits.

'Nearby, I gather. Albyn Place.'

'Not two hundred yards away,' Raven observed. 'At least for once the patient should be able to properly compensate Dr Simpson for coming forth at such an hour.'

Jarvis audibly scoffed. It was hard to see his expression in the half-light but Raven could vividly imagine it.

'What?'

'You have been studying under the professor but you have observed so little about him.'

'I have observed him refusing payment from the poor, but surely he would not need to extend such exceptions to the rich.'

'Mr Raven, there is not the time to discuss this at length, but may it suffice for me to tell you that I have on occasion found Dr Simpson to be using rolled-up five-pound banknotes in order to stop the rattling of a window.'

Raven and Jarvis made it to the foot of the stairs as Simpson emerged from his office on the floor above, grasping his bag. Jarvis held out his hat and coat in readiness, sweeping the latter about the professor and placing the former upon him in a practised motion before opening the door.

The cold hit Raven like the cup of water Jarvis had threatened and he eyed the professor's sealskin overcoat enviously as they swept westward along Queen Street.

'An early start to a Monday morning, but an exciting one, no doubt,' Simpson said, a croak in his voice betraying how he had been recently hauled from sleep.

'You were late to bed, were you not?' Raven asked, knowing Simpson had still been out when he turned in for the night.

'I had dinner at Professor Gregory's house. We talked a very long time.'

'Have you bumped into McLevy again on your travels? I was wondering what emerged from the post-mortem on Rose Campbell.'

'I have not heard anything, no. What specifically is your interest?'

'I remain curious as to what might have caused the body to be so contorted. Is it possible that this was evidence of poison?'

'I wouldn't know,' Simpson replied. 'If it's poisons you're interested in, then Christison is your man.'

Raven felt his pulse race. This could make being dragged out of bed into the darkness worthwhile.

'Professor Christison? You would make an introduction?'

'Introduce you to his work, for sure. I have his treatise in my office. You would have much to learn from studying it.'

'Thank you,' Raven said, though gratitude was not what he felt.

Simpson had no curiosity over the fate of Rose Campbell, beyond perhaps a physiological explanation for what had happened to her corpse. The greater drama around her did not seem visible to the man. Perhaps he only saw such things in abstract, and that was why he was able to distance himself from the horrors and tragedies that he dealt with in his job.

He thought about Jarvis's story of Simpson fixing a rattling window with a banknote. Money meant nothing to him. He inhabited a realm of books and theory.

If Mrs Gallagher had come to Simpson instead of Raven, he would have treated her injuries, but it would not have occurred to the professor how he might address the cause. When he went to dangerous parts of town, the crowds parted for him. They all knew his name, looked up to him, wished him well. He was like a god who did not inhabit the same plane as mere mortals, and though he would help them, he was not affected by their plights.

'Now, let us test how your faculties serve you at this ungodly hour,' Simpson said as they approached Albyn Place. 'The patient we are about to treat is a young woman in her eighth month of pregnancy, who suddenly started bleeding, painlessly but heavily. Diagnosis?'

Raven searched his tired brain for the answer. A number of possibilities presented themselves, but he dismissed those that would not justify their hurrying to her aid at this hour.

'*Placenta praevia*,' he said.

Simpson nodded sagely as a door opened ahead of them.

A maid stepped forth to greet them, anguished and on the verge of hysteria. She babbled indecipherably, tripping over her own incoherent words as she pointed to the stairs inside. All Raven caught was the name: Mrs Considine. The maid's hand, he noticed, was smeared with red, and a livid crimson streak extended from the waist of her skirt to its hem.

Simpson took the stairs two at a time. Raven was a little slower, his climb burdened by memories of what had happened by his hand at another New Town address not two weeks ago. It was ever-present in his mind that someone had died as a result of his actions, yet he was equally consumed by the question of how this had happened. Had he been incompetent? Was ether itself dangerous?

He had attempted to discuss the issue in a general way with Dr Simpson, in the hope of salving his conscience.

'Do you have any concerns about the safety of ether, given that a small number of deaths have been attributed to its administration?' he had asked one morning after breakfast.

'The deaths that you refer to occurred two or three days after severe operations, and should not be attributed to the inhalation of ether itself. Many of the alleged failures and misadventures ascribed to it are to my mind the result of errors in its administration,' Simpson said, a reply that did not allow Raven much comfort. 'Successful etherisation requires a full and narcotising dose be administered by impregnating the respired air as fully with the vapour as the patient can bear, and the surgeon's knife should never be applied until the patient is thoroughly and indubitably soporised.'

Raven thought of Mrs Graseby's initial reluctance to inhale the ether and her sudden movement in response to Beattie's manipulation.

'Have you ever experienced any difficulties?' he asked.

'For the past nine months I have employed it in almost every case of labour that I have attended, without any adverse consequences. I have no doubt that in some years hence the practice will be general whatever the small theologians of the kirk might say.'

Simpson had laughed then, incognisant of Raven's growing unease.

But what was a soporising dose? How could such a thing be measured? What was the difference between Simpson using ether for the first time and Raven using it unsupervised on Mrs Graseby? It occurred to Raven that it was as much an art as it was a science, and that his own efforts had surely not deviated so far from what was required as to have caused a death. Yet he had no other explanation for what had occurred. Without that he was still inclined to blame himself.

They found the patient in a bedroom on the second floor, the door thrown wide to the wall. Lamps and candles had been placed upon every available surface, the flickering play of light picking out a dark glistening seemingly everywhere, a gory spectacle that made Raven grateful he had not breakfasted. Mrs Considine was supine upon the canopied bed, her nightclothes a red-soaked mass of material hauled up around her knees. There was blood over the bed, upon the carpet and on every item of furniture that had been touched by the patient or her maid.

Mrs Considine appeared to have lapsed into unconsciousness, which was a source of some mercy to Raven, in that there would be no need for him to administer ether.

Simpson had his coat off and his sleeves rolled up by the time Raven had closed the bedroom door. He performed a rapid examination in order to ascertain the cause of the haemorrhage.

'Prepare a dose of ergot, Will,' he stated without looking up. 'Hurry, man. I must deliver the child without delay. It is the only way to arrest the bleeding.'

The doctor all but shouted his instructions. Raven had never heard him raise his voice before, which was almost as disturbing as the blood. His anticipated diagnosis had been correct: a low-lying placenta, the afterbirth, situated at the opening of the womb so that it had presented before the child. Raven remembered the description word for word from the textbook, principally because of the lines that followed: *In such circumstances, catastrophic haemorrhage is inevitable, with one in three mothers dying as a result.*

With fumbling hands, Raven did as he was instructed. He was still measuring out the required dose as Simpson brought down the breech and delivered the infant, who remarkably was found to be alive. The troublesome placenta was then removed, the ergot given and pressure applied to the flaccid but now empty uterus.

The bleeding slowed to a trickle and the patient roused a little, but Raven was reluctant to feel any relief while Caroline Graseby remained fresh in his memory. She had shown signs of recovery too, only to succumb hours later while he waited anxiously for news.

A small army of housemaids appeared, armed with hot water and towels. The infant was wrapped up and placed in a corner while the worst of the mess was cleaned.

Mrs Considine attempted to sit, but found this more than she could manage and sank back onto her pillows, exhausted. She cast a tired but fond eye towards the newborn, and only then did Raven feel he could breathe free.

Then Mrs Considine began clutching at the front of her nightgown, a look of fear upon her face. Raven tried to assist by loosening the fastenings at her throat. She was breathing rapidly, gasping, her eyes wide with panic. It was as though she was struggling to find enough air in the room to sustain her.

Raven looked to the professor, who stood at the other side of the bed, wearing an unusually stricken expression.

'Dr Simpson, what should we do?' he asked.

Simpson swallowed, and when he replied, it was in a quiet, hollow voice.

'Speak to her.'

Three words that told him it was hopeless.

Raven held her hands and tried to say reassuring things, his own voice distant as though he was witnessing himself from without. Mrs Considine continued to stare at him, her gaping eyes and terrified expression reminding him of the look on Evie's face when he had found her. He willed her to keep breathing, hoping that she had retained just enough blood to remain alive.

Her breathing slowed and then ceased.

Raven looked to Simpson, hoping for some words of wisdom, some consoling thought to help make sense of what had just happened. Instead Simpson turned and made his way to a chair in the corner of the room, heedlessly spreading gore over an ever-increasing area. The professor sat down heavily and placed his head in his hands.

An eerie silence settled upon the room, broken only by the disconcerting sound of dripping. Then the baby began to cry.

TWENTY-EIGHT

No. 52 Queen Street was in a strange state of suspension. Raven sat by a window in the drawing room, Professor Christison's *Treatise on Poisons* weighing heavily upon his lap, while George Keith and James Duncan were perched either side of the fireplace, also poring over papers and books. The house was unsettlingly quiet and still for this time of the morning, nothing functioning according to normal manner. For the second day, the morning clinic had been cancelled, and everyone was quite at a loss as to how they ought to occupy themselves.

Breakfast had been served without Dr Simpson arriving to say grace, which indicated that the staff knew not to expect him. Upon returning from Albyn Place the previous morning, he had taken to his bed and had not emerged since. Mrs Simpson had joined them but briefly today in the dining room, eating a few mouthfuls of toast before withdrawing again without speaking a word.

All was silent but for the crackling of the fire and the occasional shriek from the parrot. Nonetheless, despite the absence of distraction, Raven was not making any headway in finding a possible cause of Evie and Rose's apparent agonies.

Raven became aware that Duncan had closed the volume before

him and was gazing thoughtfully in his direction. This was seldom the overture to anything good.

'Tackling Christison, eh?' he said. 'An excellent resource, incontestably, but as physicians we must all take care not to be throwing the baby out with the bathwater.'

Ordinarily Raven would not have encouraged him to expand, but right then he was content to be drawn away from the labour of his fruitless search.

'What do you mean?'

'One could argue that all poison is essentially an overdose. For surely there are properties in everything mentioned in Christison that may be beneficial in the right measure, or that may induce an effect we can harness in the patient's interest.'

'Yes, but establishing the relationship between dose and effect is fraught with difficulty. Speaking as one who has been exposed to all manner of foul vapours after dinner most evenings.'

'Yes, but through such endeavours, posterity might at least find a footnote for you in medical history,' Duncan replied.

Keith smirked at this, which provoked a smile from Duncan. Raven strongly suspected the latter did not appreciate which of the pair the former had been amused by.

Raven was less inclined towards levity; he regarded the on-going testing model as a catastrophe in the making. Simpson had every professor and chemist of his acquaintance on the lookout for prospective compounds that might exhibit anaesthetic properties. Any time one of them identified a new one, they would bring a sample to the house and it would be tested after dinner by all of the medical men present. Professor Miller, the surgeon who lived next door at No. 51, had taken to dropping in most mornings on his way to the Infirmary just to make sure everyone had survived the night. So far, nothing they tested had provoked anything more dramatic than dizziness, nausea and blinding headaches, but Raven couldn't help thinking this was down to good fortune rather than sound judgment. It was not difficult to imagine

Professor Miller arriving too late and discovering the entire gathering fatally poisoned.

'I would rather my honour not be posthumous before I even qualify to practise,' Raven said.

'Oh, don't be melodramatic. Though you are right in that testing remains the great challenge, not helped by the vocal opposition abroad these days to using animals as subjects. How else are we to establish lethal doses, and how else to determine effects if we cannot dissect the creatures afterwards?'

'I am of the mind that anyone opposed to a dog testing poison should volunteer himself in its stead,' Raven suggested. He was not serious but it amused him that Duncan would not realise this.

'Indeed. The problem is that canine physiology is insufficiently similar to our own for us to draw accurate conclusions. I only wish we had such a supply of disposable human subjects.'

'How about prisoners?' Keith suggested.

Raven glanced across and caught the gleam in his eye. For pity's sake, don't give him ideas, he thought.

Too late.

'Indeed,' Duncan mused. 'It would be a means by which murderers and thieves could contribute something to the overall good of humanity.'

'Why not whores?' Raven asked, his tone more aggressive and forceful than he intended.

Duncan responded with a strange look, as though weighing up what might be behind this interjection. The ensuing tension was accentuated by the house's unaccustomed silence, until it was dispelled by Keith diverting the subject.

'At any dose, there are some poisons that have no effect but harm, and yet they continue to be prescribed. Mercury, for goodness' sake. Apart from causing ulceration of the mouth, the loss of both teeth and hair, its only effect is to precipitate salivation, which flimsy wisdom interprets as the body purging itself in order to balance the humours. Such thinking is positively medieval.'

'This is why homeopaths continue to prosper,' Raven offered. 'So much allopathic medicine is toxic, so the benefit of homeopathy is that you don't get sicker other than from the natural progression of your disease.'

'And as you will learn, Will, patients demand pills, and doctors are only too willing to supply them while there is money in it. Polypharmacy is as much the resort of greedy charlatans as homeopathy: doctors selling complex combinations of remedies, then still more to offset the side effects of those. I feel I am shouting into the wind telling patients that the surest route to health is good diet and regular exercise. They feel they have not had their money's worth if they do not leave with a prescription, and in their minds, the more complex the physic, the more impressive the physician.'

'Nonetheless,' Duncan argued, 'we have established the efficacy of some truly remarkable medicines, so there are surely more to be discovered. And I don't mean some nebulous tonic such as Gregory's powder. Who knows what conditions might be improved or actually cured by some natural derivative or by simply the right compound? I have made it my purpose to find out.'

'Though until you can solve the aforementioned problems of testing them,' Raven said, 'it will be your destiny to fail.'

Duncan got to his feet and regarded Raven for a moment, much as an owl might regard a field mouse.

'We shall see,' he said quietly, then walked from the room.

Raven returned to the Christison, though his commitment was hardly redoubled by having had a break. He pored over another few pages and issued the deepest of sighs. It would have been simple enough if he knew the name of a poison and wished to learn more about its catalogued effects, but he was attempting the very opposite.

Keith put down the journal he was reading and glanced across.

'Is everything all right with you, Will? You seem profoundly restive.'

'I think the mood of the house is infecting me.'

Keith nodded, sitting back and contemplating for a moment.

'The majority of cases that you will see with the professor will be difficult ones. You must prepare yourself for that.'

Raven offered a weak smile in response, thinking that the true reason for his having witnessed so few normal deliveries since he began his apprenticeship was that he was not permitted to accompany the professor to see his more aristocratic clients. The obstructed labours of the poor – that's what he was left with.

'You would benefit from a diversion,' Keith continued. 'A non-medical pursuit that would provide you some fresh air and a new perspective.'

Keith was trying to sound like he was mulling over the possibilities, but Raven could tell he already had something specific in mind. Raven also suspected he had an agenda.

'If it will deliver me from Christison, I am open to any suggestion.'

'Have you heard of photography?'

Raven perked up. This was the remarkable means of capturing reflected light upon treated paper, creating images far more accurate than the hand of the finest painter.

'I have heard of it, but I confess I have never seen an example. Do you know someone who has a camera?'

'I know two people who are among the most renowned exponents of the art. You may remember my friend David Hill: he visited the house a few days ago.'

Raven nodded. He vaguely recalled Keith introducing an acquaintance to Simpson, but he had not heard the details as he was on his way out, having been dispatched to pick up some chemicals for Dr Duncan.

'He and his partner Robert Adamson have their studio on Calton Hill, where they are utilising a new process, the calotype. They have requested Dr Simpson sit for a photographic portrait, but I doubt he could be imposed upon to remain still for the length of time required. The man is never at peace.'

Raven smiled at the thought of the professor attempting to hold a pose for more than thirty seconds.

'You on the other hand would be ideal. They are looking for subjects with interesting faces. Would you sit for them?'

Raven didn't like to think of his face as 'interesting'. Among the medical fraternity this was seldom a complimentary adjective. He wondered if Keith was referring to his features in general or to his scar, which although healing still tended to draw unwanted attention.

'As a subject?'

Keith nodded. 'I am seeing Mr Hill later today. I will suggest we visit tomorrow, first thing. It has to be when the light is brightest.'

'I should be honoured,' Raven said.

Keith gave him an odd smile; approving and yet calculating.

'You were out on Sunday with the maid, Sarah, were you not?'

Raven felt rather exposed. He had not thought of the repercussions of their excursion, beyond reporting back to Simpson about Grissom's oratorical expertise in turning humility into self-aggrandisement.

'What of it?'

'If you have a certain rapport with her, then you might ask her to join us too. They are particularly interested in working women. I think she would make a splendid subject.'

Raven realised this was the agenda he had suspected. Hill must have caught a glimpse of Sarah during his visit, and it was she he was truly interested in. Keith was engineering a pretext to deliver her there, with Raven as his instrument.

He didn't mind. He would rather be Keith and Hill's instrument than be Duncan's, and if it got him out from beneath the shroud of despond blanketing the house, he would welcome the chance.

TWENTY-NINE

Sarah was walking into the teeth of a chill and blustery wind, but she was relieved to be outside. Even opening the front door to commence her journey had felt like lifting the lid on a boiling pot, venting the pressure that was building up within. An atmosphere of gloom had descended upon No. 52, and from experience Sarah knew it was destined to continue for at least another day or so.

Dr Simpson had a tendency to retreat to his room from time to time, when his reserves of energy and enthusiasm had been drained to the very dregs by what he was forced to confront on a daily basis. She understood there had been a case that had gone badly and for which he blamed himself. In the year or so she had been working at Queen Street, she had learned that Simpson was generous in spreading the happiness of his successes, but the corollary was that his failures he took very much to heart.

So when this outing was suggested, Sarah had seized the opportunity, despite Mrs Lyndsay's reservations about the propriety of it.

'Whoever heard of such a thing?' she had said, kneading dough with a degree of violence provoked by having had her well-developed sense of decorum thus offended. 'A housemaid accompanying the gentlemen of the house on a walking tour of the city? No good will come of it, you know.'

She would have forbidden it altogether, Sarah had no doubt, but that it was Dr Keith who had requested Sarah's presence and secured Mrs Lyndsay's agreement before telling her why he required her. The cook was already simmering that her suspension of Sarah's clinic duties had been cut short at Dr Keith's insistence, so Sarah knew she would be made to pay for this later in extra chores and Mrs Lyndsay's glowering disapproval. Nonetheless, she was determined to enjoy her excursion in the meantime.

Sarah had thought that the walk might provide an opportunity for sharing any new intelligence on the matter of Evie and Rose. She had been attempting to make her way through Christison's *Treatise on Poisons* (the book having been surrendered by Raven, who had entirely given up on it) but it was an imposingly weighty volume and her time was limited. She was finding the book fascinating, but her reading so far had failed to shed any light on their particular area of interest. She wished she had all day to study it. How blessed was the lot of a student, she thought.

Raven was unusually quiet, as if the pervading melancholy of the house was proving contagious. He was often sullen, but he usually had something to say for himself, even when it seemed inappropriate; in fact, especially when it seemed inappropriate. He walked beside her in silence, hands in his pockets, kicking at loose stones on the cobbles.

'How did he talk you into this?' Sarah asked. She nodded towards George Keith, who was striding on ahead, muttering excitedly about the clear conditions and the implications this had for the morning's events.

'He thought I was in need of distraction.'

'Are you?'

'I suppose I am. I'm beginning to feel that I am in over my head, entering into a profession that is doomed to be forever fighting a losing battle.'

Sarah felt her hackles rise at this pompous perspective, putting himself at the centre of an almighty drama. He was exhibiting the male trait of believing the world revolved around them, usually because it did.

'That seems a rather self-indulgent interpretation,' she told him, attempting to keep the annoyance out of her voice, though it was evident enough in her words.

'What would you know about it?'

'You forget that some would be happy to have your problems. To be learning a profession,' she added pointedly.

Raven took on an unusually sheepish demeanour. Unlike some men, at least this indicated he had understood her point.

'Nonetheless, that doesn't make it any easier to be every day confronted with suffering and death.'

Sarah looked at his face, the dark circles around his eyes, the scar still livid on his cheek, and felt her anger subside.

'My grandmother once told me about a king who sought a single thought that would raise his spirits when they were low, but keep him vigilant when he was happy.'

Raven lifted his head, curious if not optimistic about what she might be able to offer.

'A wise man told the king but four words: "This too will pass." Dr Simpson won't remain cloistered in his room for long, and things have been worse than this before now.'

'In what way?'

'You'll have noticed Mrs Simpson is in mourning?'

'I had not thought black to be the new fashion.'

'They lost their daughter in February. Mary Catherine. Just before her second birthday. They had already lost their first daughter, Maggie, at the age of four.'

'What did they die of?'

In other company Sarah would have considered this to be a heartless and insensitive enquiry, but she was sufficiently used to medical men by now that it came as no surprise. It would have been unusual if he had not sought clarification upon this point.

'Maggie was before my time,' she replied. 'Mary Catherine died of scarlet fever. It was awful. She kept crying out for water but couldn't drink it.'

'I'm sorry,' he said. 'It's difficult watching a child die.'

'It's difficult watching anyone die, is it not?'

Raven looked pensive. 'Some deaths are easier than others.'

'I suppose you're in a better position to judge, though I have seen my fair share.'

'Have you, now,' he said. His tone was distinctly sceptical.

Sarah stopped walking.

'My mother died in childbirth and my father followed shortly after. Of a broken heart, the doctor said. That is how I came to be working here. I had no one, and our minister knew Dr Simpson.'

Raven had the decency to look contrite.

'I'm sorry if I seemed insensitive. Hazard of the job.'

They walked on again in silence for a few yards, George Keith pressing on ahead of them up the slope. Despite the cold it was a fine day to be out, as the wind had blown away the fog and the sun was shining from a clear sky. As they ascended Calton Hill, Edinburgh fell away beneath them in all directions. To the north Sarah could see all the way to the Forth and beyond, sails dotted along the water in a procession in and out of Leith. The geometry of the New Town was strikingly vivid from up here too, its layout so precise and uniform in contrast to all the districts that surrounded it. It spoke of order and elegance, but also of rigidity and unbending rules.

When Raven spoke again, his tone was pitched a little brighter.

'Miss Grindlay seems remarkably unaffected by the prevailing gloom, don't you think?'

It was true that Mina had been in unusually high spirits for the best part of a week.

'Why do you think that is?' he continued.

'I imagine we have your acquaintance Dr Beattie to thank.'

'Beattie?'

She could be wrong, but Raven seemed oddly uncomfortable at the mention of his name. She had assumed they were friends, but she knew how medical men were in the habit of falling out.

'Yes. They have been seeing a great deal of each other.'

Raven nodded to himself. 'Now that you mention it, I was sure I had smelt his cologne on occasion when I returned from my duties.'

'I would have thought you more surprised,' she confessed.

'Why?'

'I had not thought Mina the type to take Beattie's interest. She is older than him and I cannot think that he would want for younger ladies' affections.'

Raven snorted. 'Jealous, are you?'

'Don't be ridiculous. What interest would I have in such a man?'

'The same interest that a great many women seem to have. As you say, he does not want for younger ladies' affections.'

'Jealous, are you?' Sarah batted back.

Raven ignored this. 'Beattie is older than he appears, and he told me he has come to find such flirtatious attentions trivial and tiresome. I got the impression that he might have found something in Mina that these other women lack.'

'Yes,' she replied, 'her brother-in-law's name and the connections attached to it.'

Raven seemed shocked at her bluntness, enough to make her fear she had overstepped the mark.

'I only say this because I would hate to see Miss Grindlay deceived.'

'It is not an outlandish suggestion,' Raven conceded. 'But equally, though Mina may be in want of a husband, she does not strike me as naive in such matters. What they see in each other may not be what the rest of us assume. She may be aware that the Simpson connection confers certain advantages, but that does not preclude a companionship.'

Sarah frowned. 'You make it seem like a business transaction. It makes sense but it sounds terribly bloodless.'

'In marriage, there are worse things to be than bloodless,' Raven replied.

'How do you mean?'

She could tell from his eyes that he was not going to elaborate.

'Let's just say that while you lost your father too soon, I did not lose mine soon enough.'

As they skirted the Royal Observatory, hurrying to catch up with Dr Keith, Sarah tripped on a loose cobblestone. Raven grabbed her arm to prevent her from falling, keeping hold of it thereafter. His grip was strong and she found she had no objection to it.

'Do you have an interest in photography?' he asked.

'I can't say that I know much about it, but Dr Keith has been kind enough to show me his daguerreotypes. From his travels in Palestine and Syria.'

'Lucky you,' said Raven, smiling for the first time that day.

THIRTY

aven felt himself already in better spirits by the time they arrived at Rock House, the walk having the effect Keith so faithfully promised. He would have to admit that the chance to talk with Sarah had done him good too. Perhaps it was merely relief at the contrast to how badly their early encounters had gone, but he derived a degree of satisfaction from merely conversing with her without rancour.

He had even found himself smiling for the first time in days, and was pleased that he could do so without producing any sense of pain or tightness in the left side of his face.

Rock House was a two-storey building with a courtyard to the front of it boasting a small fountain with a Grecian urn in its centre. It was only a stone's throw from Princes Street and yet seemed to be held in an arboreal cocoon, sheltered from the noise and smog of the city. It was surprising then that Keith had to knock several times before the door was answered.

'They'll be in the garden, I should imagine,' he said as they waited. 'They generally take their photographs outdoors.' He pointed at the sky. 'For the light.'

When the door opened it was a woman who greeted them. She wore an apron but no cap, and had a black stain on the back of one hand, visible when she tucked a stray curl of greying hair behind her ear.

'Good day to you, Miss Mann. We are expected.'

'Of course, Dr Keith. Come in. We are all out at the back.'

She turned and led the way through the house to the garden. Raven followed Keith, leaving Sarah to close the door.

'Miss Mann is the indispensable assistant of Mr Hill and Mr Adamson,' Keith explained as they marched in procession through the narrow hallway.

They emerged into the garden, where it appeared that the house had extruded most of its furniture. There were chairs, a table, wall hangings and a birdcage all arranged as if it were the corner of a well-appointed drawing room. Two men were busy manoeuvring the camera into position. They were so absorbed in their task that they were initially unaware of the arrival of their visitors. Miss Mann loudly cleared her throat and the pair of them looked up in unison.

'Ah, George. You have brought us some willing subjects, I see,' said one, as though this had not all been carefully arranged. The speaker was lively in his features, a great mane of hair spilling about his face. He strode forth and enthusiastically shook their hands, including the surprised-looking Sarah.

'David Octavius Hill at your service. And this,' he said, waving his hand in the direction of the other man, 'is my good friend and colleague Mr Robert Adamson.'

Mr Adamson was the younger of the two, thin and frail-looking. He merely nodded in acknowledgment and resumed his work.

'Mr Adamson is the technical genius within this partnership,' Hill continued. 'He has mastered the method of creating the calotype. I know not the process though it is under my nose continuously, and I believe that I never will. I for my part organise the subject. Together we make art.'

Raven considered this a rather grandiloquent claim to make

until he was shown some of the fruits of their labour. A picture of the Scott Monument before its completion made a particular impression upon him. The clarity of the image and the detail that could be discerned in it were remarkable, a moment frozen in time.

'We had to climb onto the roof of the Royal Institution with the camera to get that one,' Hill said.

The rest of the album of prints consisted principally of sombre men in dark suits. Before he could ask about these uniformly severe-looking sitters, the doorbell rang out and Mr Hill rushed off to answer it.

He returned with another visitor, a tall woman towering a full head above him.

'Here is Miss Rigby,' he explained. 'Writer, patron of the arts and a great supporter of our endeavours here.'

'Not to mention occasional sitter,' said Miss Rigby, removing her hat. 'When you can be forced to drag your attention away from the fat martyrs of the Free Kirk,' she added, indicating the prints Raven was looking at. 'Mr Hill has spent an inordinate amount of time procuring the images of all these ministers for his great Disruption painting. But between you and me, I can't see it ever being finished. He has fortunately begun to cast his artistic net a little wider.'

She regarded Raven with an intensity that he found disconcerting, as though he were being physically assessed. He looked instinctively for Sarah, uncomfortable beneath this woman's forthright scrutiny, though he could not rightly say what succour he thought she might offer. In any case, she had wandered off to the other end of the garden, watching Mr Adamson and Miss Mann as they made various adjustments to the camera.

'I think you will find that the Newhaven photographs are far more interesting,' Miss Rigby said as Raven continued to turn the pages of the book, an on-going catalogue of grim-faced clergymen.

He stopped suddenly, recognising the face that presently glowered at him from the open page.

'Here's one I am familiar with,' he stated. 'The Reverend Malachy Grissom.'

'You're not of his congregation, are you?'

The manner of Miss Rigby's asking indicated that an affirmative answer would be met with disapproval.

'No, though I have heard him preach. He was blaming immodest women for male lust and railing against prostitutes.'

Miss Rigby wore a slyly amused smile. 'Railing against them? That's a term for it I haven't heard before.'

Raven looked up at her. 'I'm sorry, I don't understand.'

Rigby was remarkably tall and thin, her hair clamped in tight coils at the side of her head. She spoke with authority and candour, which was surprising in that she was undeniably a lady and yet seemingly prepared to discuss all manner of subjects with a man to whom she had only just been introduced. Raven suddenly had an image of her picking up the miserable Reverend Grissom bodily and breaking him over her knee.

'From what I am told, the Reverend Grissom knows of what he speaks. Strident denunciations most often hide a secret shame,' she continued, entirely unabashed by the direction she was taking the conversation.

Raven could not envisage her being abashed by much. He preferred this manner of dialogue to the empty pleasantries that one was normally forced to endure in such circumstances.

'Are you saying he has been consorting with prostitutes?'

'Not *consorting* with them, Mr Raven. Using them. Exploiting them.'

The word fell from Miss Rigby's lips so matter-of-factly, and yet as it lit upon his ears it echoed like thunder.

Raven was simultaneously in awe of this woman and terrified of her. She seemed to grow even taller before him, or perhaps it was that he felt like he was shrinking as he considered what she might think of him if she knew that he had thus used Evie.

'But how could a fellow in his position expect to get away with such behaviour?'

'It is the downfall of many a proud man to imagine everyone around him stupid. He frequents places where he thinks he is unknown, although perhaps the good Reverend should have travelled a little beyond Leith and Newhaven. He forgets that even prostitutes will sometimes attend church.'

Further conversation was interrupted by Mr Hill deciding that Raven should now be positioned for his portrait.

He was placed in an upholstered chair beside the birdcage, his face examined from every angle. The position of his arms was arranged and rearranged several times before Hill was satisfied.

Miss Mann handed Mr Adamson a wooden box that was slid into position at the back of the camera. Adamson buried his head under a piece of cloth and removed a cap from the front of the machine while Miss Mann counted off the seconds with a pocket watch.

Raven thought he had remained still, but he noticed Adamson shake his head.

'You moved your arm,' Hill stated wearily.

'A full minute is required for the exposure,' Miss Mann reproached him with a sigh. 'I'll get some more paper.'

Raven was posed a second time, on this occasion with the aid of a box to rest his arm upon, assured its black colour would render it invisible in the finished picture. He felt he was entirely still throughout the ensuing minute, but neither Hill nor Adamson looked particularly pleased.

'We usually pose children as though asleep,' Miss Mann muttered. 'Perhaps we could try that.'

This suggestion turned out not to be in earnest but by way of reproach, and Raven was relieved of his role as sitter. A short time later, he was warming himself with a cup of tea while watching Hill position Sarah. She was seated in a chair, her head turned to the side and resting gracefully on one hand. She had a purple shawl wrapped around her shoulders and her hair was loosely tied at the nape. Hill stepped back and examined her from several angles before announcing that he was content. He implored her to remain as still as possible, looking pointedly at Raven.

Sarah exhibited no similar difficulty, remaining entirely immobile as though she had fallen into an open-eyed trance.

She was not the only one. Raven found himself gazing rapt at her face, the paleness of her skin, the golden highlights in her hair. A sense of tranquillity settled upon him, as though the serenity of her stillness had somehow been transferred to him.

'You seem transfixed,' observed Hill quietly, walking past. 'A pity you could not have held such a pose earlier.'

THIRTY-ONE

arah watched Miss Mann carefully remove the plate from the camera, handling it like a newborn. Her gaze was trained intently upon what she was about, but she still noticed Sarah's attention.

'You made an excellent subject, Miss Fisher. You could sit for a painter with such poise.'

It was a pleasant thought, but Sarah could not imagine ever having such a luxury of time.

'I would be most interested to know what happens next,' she observed. 'The calotype process is a matter of chemistry, is it not?'

Miss Mann looked at her with a degree of consternation that made Sarah fear she had misspoken.

'Or am I mistaken?'

'No, you are quite correct. I was simply taken aback. Most of our subjects are more apt to believe it the work of fairies and angels. And that's just the clergymen. Do you have an interest in chemistry?'

'I have read Professor Gregory's work, but I have not had the opportunity to practise experiments.'

Miss Mann seemed pleased with her answer, which in turn pleased Sarah.

'Would you care to accompany me? I can show you how it's done.'

'I'd like that,' she replied.

They strode towards the house together, the plate still clutched possessively in Miss Mann's hands.

'You took Mr Hill's instruction very well,' she said.

'I am a housemaid. I am used to doing as I am told.'

'You would be surprised. The most subservient of people can nonetheless struggle to follow instructions, while the mighty are prepared to humble themselves when a portrait is at stake. I once photographed the King of Saxony, and had you been there that day, you might have believed I was the monarch and he my subject.'

'You photographed a king?'

'Yes. He turned up at Rock House unannounced, Mr Hill and Mr Adamson's reputation having reached him abroad. Unfortunately, neither of the gentlemen were at home. I told him I could carry out the procedure and he gladly acquiesced.'

Sarah was agog. She thought of the leering squirt rolling pills behind the druggist's counter not a mile from here. Clearly there were some customers who did not always believe that 'only a man will do'.

'And was he pleased with the result?'

'Enchanted. He said it would have pride of place in his palace. Though as the name Jessie Mann is of less renown than Hill and Adamson, I suspect it will be theirs and not mine attached to it.'

'That is unjust,' Sarah stated.

Miss Mann did not reply, for what else could be said?

She led them into a room in which newspaper had been affixed to the window to block out the light.

'We need relative darkness for the preparation of the calotype paper,' she explained.

Sarah went to close the door, out of habit.

'Leave it for now, otherwise I won't be able to show you anything.'

'Of course.'

Miss Mann indicated a table laden with bottles and shallow trays. 'A piece of good-quality paper is first washed in a solution of silver nitrate then a solution of iodine. Once dry, this iodised paper is dipped in a mixture of gallic acid and silver nitrate, and it is this which is placed in the frame that is slid into the back of the camera.'

Miss Mann held up her right hand, which was streaked with black. 'It is a dark art,' she said. 'The silver nitrate stains the skin.'

'How did you come to be involved with Mr Hill and Mr Adamson?' Sarah asked, watching as Miss Mann pinned a piece of prepared calotype paper to a wooden frame.

'My brother Alexander and Mr Hill are friends,' she replied. 'I am a supporter of the Free Church, and have been helping him with the photographs for his Disruption painting. His interests have extended beyond that now, of course, which makes me wonder sometimes if the painting will ever be done.'

'What exactly will the painting depict?'

'It will be a representation of the meeting at Tanfield Hall that followed the mass walkout from the General Assembly by two hundred ministers and elders. As Mr Hill wishes to depict all who were present, he is using calotype to record their faces, that he may work from the photographs.'

Sarah thought of her grandmother, who dispensed wise words as well as herbal remedies. *Where there are men, there will be dispute,* she once said. *Put ten of them in a room and soon enough you'll have two groups of five.*

Sarah watched Miss Mann carefully prepare the next plate.

'You must have a remarkable knowledge of chemistry to be able to do all of this.'

'Only as it pertains to the photographic process. Mr Adamson is a patient teacher. Why do you ask?'

Sarah paused for a second. She felt oddly dishonest to be speaking about this, though she was bearing no false witness.

'An acquaintance of mine died recently, and when she was found, her body was contorted as though she had suffered a fit of some kind. There seems a possibility that she took a poison, though unless I can discern what, I will never know whether she died accidentally or . . .'

Sarah let the other possibility remain unspoken.

Miss Mann put down the framed sheet she was holding. 'I am most sorry to hear that.' She placed the stained hand on Sarah's arm and spoke softly. 'Was it likely that your friend meant herself harm? I mean, did she have reason?'

'I believe she was most troubled. But it makes no sense that she should choose a means whose effects would be so unpleasant.'

'Your description does remind me of something,' Miss Mann said. 'A relative of mine was suffering from a neurological palsy. She was given a tonic medicine which helped for a while, but she kept increasing the dose. It brought on increasingly severe convulsions and eventually killed her. Her body remained in a contorted pose for a long time after. It made it impossible to lay her out properly, which caused a deal of additional distress for the mourners. There was some concern that they wouldn't be able to chest her. You know, fit her into a casket.'

'Do you know what was in the tonic?' Sarah asked.

'Yes. It contained strychnine.'

THIRTY-TWO

The pavements seemed busier as they made their way back down Calton Hill towards Princes Street. Sarah heard a whistle carried on the wind, and in the middle distance she could see steam rising from the new North Bridge station. The sight of clouds rising from below rather than floating up above was one she might be a long time in getting used to. She had only once travelled on a train and had found the experience noisy and frightening.

Dr Keith was not with them, having remained at Rock House taking lunch with his friends. Sarah had explained that she needed to return to Queen Street and her duties, and expected to be walking back alone, but Raven had announced that he also had matters to attend. Sarah was not sure whether this was true, given Dr Simpson's on-going self-confinement, and allowed herself a moment of pleasure that Raven had chosen accompanying her over the prospect of what would undoubtedly have been a sumptuous meal in the company of Messrs Hill and Adamson, as well as the remarkable Miss Mann and the formidable Miss Rigby.

However, once they began talking, she realised that perhaps his principal motive was his impatience to impart Miss Rigby's revelation.

'The Reverend Grissom using prostitutes?' Sarah asked. She

kept her voice low, wary as much of passing pedestrians as of being overheard by someone at an open window. 'Surely she must have been mistaken?'

'She was adamant that he is well known to the pinch-cocks of Newhaven and Leith. Is it so hard to believe?'

Sarah was conscious of an innate sense of duty driving her to question it, and she wondered why this should be so. What made a minister's word or reputation seem beyond question? It was possible that Miss Rigby might be mistaken or even motivated by malice (she certainly had not spoken with much reverence for the 'fat martyrs', as she described them), but Sarah could not envisage the woman making such a serious accusation without having a profound conviction that it was true.

'I suppose such a thing is easier for you to believe,' she replied, which made Raven's cheeks burn a little.

'I sorely doubt I was the only student to do so, as much as I doubt Grissom to be the only minister. And as he is connected to the Sheldrake household, I have to ask myself where else he might have spilled his seed.'

Sarah's voice dropped to barely more than a whisper. 'Are you suggesting . . .?'

She stopped there, unprepared to even voice the words.

'When we heard him preach, he seemed intent on blaming women for the temptations to which men succumb. Miss Rigby suggests he has often fallen to such temptations. Grissom is the Sheldrakes' minister. Rose would have attended his services and I am sure he must have visited the Sheldrakes' house, as I believe Mr Sheldrake is a benefactor of his new ministry.'

Sarah recalled her impression of an awkward and self-regarding little imp. She would admit that she could imagine him using prostitutes to slake his lust, but housemaids were another matter.

'What would make Rose want anything to do with him?' she asked.

'He is an important man. Status, influence and respect might exert an intoxicating influence on a young woman who has none of those things. And if she found herself pregnant by him, he might find himself in a difficult spot.'

Sarah felt a shudder run through her, as though she might face a terrible reckoning for even entertaining these notions. It was one thing to claim that the Reverend Grissom was a hypocrite, but quite another to suggest him capable of murder.

'We are looking for a common cause for Rose and Evie's deaths,' she reminded him. 'My conversation with Miss Mann leads me to believe that strychnine might have been responsible for their contorted conditions. She knew someone who died of it and was left similarly twisted. There is nothing that connects Grissom to Evie.'

'Is it unreasonable to speculate that his appetites took him to the Canongate as well as to Newhaven?'

'I can accept that complacency might make him think he would not be recognised further afield, but surely he would not go whoring half a mile from his own church?'

'Such a man might believe himself beyond suspicion. If he was seen entering or leaving a bawdy house, he could claim he was interested in their souls, not their bodies, trying to convince them away from their lives of sin. Nobody would believe the word of a whore over that of a minister.'

Sarah had to concede this point, but in it also lay the reason Grissom would have had nothing to fear from Rose.

'Nor would they believe the word of a housemaid claiming a man of the Church had got her pregnant.'

'Unless Grissom feared Rose's employer might believe her. Why would she lie about something so heinous?'

Sarah failed to suppress a scornful look. 'Speaking as a housemaid, I find that extraordinarily unlikely. The family would not entertain the scandal. A pregnant housemaid would be embarrassing enough, but an accusation against their reverend minister would be intolerable. No, I consider your hypothesis hopelessly flawed, Mr Raven. Nor have you offered any reason why he would wish to harm Evie.'

Sarah turned to him for a response, but his eyes were looking down Leith Street.

'Do you ever recollect seeing him around Evie's lodgings?' she asked.

'I vaguely recognised his face when we went to the church, but no, I don't recall seeing him down at that end of the Canongate. I certainly don't remember seeing him the night I found Evie dead. One of her friends said the only person who visited that night was a woman.'

'Who was this friend?'

Raven did not answer. Instead he put a hand around Sarah's waist and pulled her bodily into the darkness of a narrow close. In the work of a second she found herself plucked from the brightness of the street and thrust against the wall in a cramped and dank passage, just beyond where the light spilled in.

'What on earth do you think you're doing?' she tried to ask but Raven had already clamped a hand across her mouth. She grabbed his arm with one hand, her other pushing his chest, but he was strong and lithe. Physically she was no match for him.

Shock and anger quickly gave in to dread and fear as she wondered what outrage might be inflicted upon her. Was this the real reason he had opted to leave Rock House and accompany her alone? She tried to wriggle free, but Raven's grip only tightened. She looked desperately into his eyes, which stared back manically, pupils ever widening. Loosening his hold of her with one hand, he put his index finger to his lips. He gestured with his eyes towards the mouth of the close.

Sarah heard male voices approach, one of them rumbling and gruff, the other reedy and nasal. She saw two fellows briefly pass: a rodent-like specimen who looked all the smaller next to the freakish creature alongside. She was allowed only the briefest glimpse as he strode past, due to the speed of his lolloping and awkward gait. He was an ugly and overgrown individual, benighted by some hideous condition that had inconsistently enlarged certain parts of him in the most grotesque manner.

She looked back at Raven as the voices receded, saw the tension in his face lest they turn around again.

She realised that these were the people Raven had been so vigilantly looking out for. Also in that moment, it struck her why he was in their debt, and she felt a little ashamed for not having worked it out before.

Evie had asked him for money, in urgent need. Raven had borrowed it from them though he had no swift means of paying it back; had put himself in danger to help her.

She hardly dared breathe now, her eyes drawn to the scar barely hidden by Raven's developing beard. She recalled the mess of his face when he first arrived at Queen Street, the deep slash upon a cheek held together by cat-gut, and the bruising upon his body. The men who had inflicted it were mere yards away, still in earshot. She stood perfectly still, perfectly silent, not daring to make a sound until they were sure the danger was truly past.

Long after the footsteps and voices had receded, she and Raven remained motionless, their faces barely inches apart, hardly breathing. The intent look in Raven's eyes became something else, their gazes locked upon one another. With her hand still pressed upon his chest, Sarah could feel his heartbeat and thought he must be able to hear her own.

She felt unaccustomed stirrings in unaccustomed places. She wanted to feel his lips upon hers, wanted him to pull her closer.

Raven backed away, though. Edging to the mouth of the passage, he risked a look along the street. The moment had passed. With the spell broken, Sarah felt a flush of relief that nothing had happened. Nonetheless, as she stepped back into the light, she was trembling from head to toe, and not from fright.

THIRTY-THREE

here was frost on the ground as Raven accompanied Simpson along Princes Street, the paving stones slippery underfoot, a glowering sky above promising snow. Adding a further element of hazard was Glen the hound, which seemed determined to entangle him in the coils of its lead as it looped and slalomed before its master.

They were late, or in growing jeopardy of being so, and what was particularly annoying was that Raven had no enthusiasm for reaching his destination. He was being excused from assisting at this afternoon's lectures because Professor Syme was carrying out surgical procedures and Simpson felt Raven should take the opportunity to observe. Having once studied under Syme, Raven had not wanted for such opportunities and lacked any desire to seize another, but he knew not to question the professor's will in such matters.

They were proceeding on foot rather than enjoying the speed and comfort of the brougham because, since Simpson's emergence from his great depression, George Keith had been prevailing upon him with typical evangelism regarding the benefits of simple diet, fresh air and exercise. Simpson had listened with much patience and consideration before ultimately deciding that two out of three would have to suffice. 'I agree with much of George's thinking,' he had told Raven, 'but I draw the line at there being any benefit to culinary asceticism sufficient to offset the impact on one's soul. I am of the opinion that we should live to eat, not merely eat to live.'

Spoken like one used to Mrs Lyndsay's cooking rather than Mrs Cherry's, Raven mused.

Simpson walked for the most part at a brisk pace, barrelling along the pavement with a redoubtable energy that Raven was relieved to see fully restored. However, their progress was slower than it ought to have been due to the fact that Simpson knew simply everybody. With most people there was time for merely a nod and a greeting, but with others there were longer courtesies to be observed, particularly as Simpson had been in confinement and there was catching up to do.

As they passed Kennington and Jenner's store, the professor stopped once more, he and a fellow pedestrian having recognised one another with mutual surprise and delight.

'I would not have known you, sir,' Simpson told him. 'You are considerably changed since our student days.'

'I will take that as a compliment,' the man replied.

'Will Raven, this is Mr David Waldie,' Simpson said warmly, and they shook hands, Waldie's encased in fine leather gloves against the cold. He was a slight man about the same age as the professor, mid-thirties, and peering through spectacles as though Raven was under his microscope.

'Are you currently residing in Edinburgh?' Simpson asked. 'I had thought that you moved away some time ago.'

'I am visiting relatives. I live and work in Liverpool these days, as a chemist for the Liverpool Apothecaries Company.'

'I know the city well,' the professor replied. 'My wife hails from there.'

Having heard that Waldie worked as a chemist, Simpson was not long in turning the conversation to his great quest, explaining the work that had been done with ether and his search for an improved alternative.

'In all your chemical endeavours, have you encountered anything that might exhibit comparable properties?'

Simpson was truly indefatigable in the search for his Holy Grail, but Raven feared his efforts were ultimately going to prove as fruitless as every knight before him. He was beginning to think that ether might prove as good as it got, and far from being the first in a series of ever-improving anaesthetic agents, it would turn out to be an anomaly, the mirage promising water in the desert.

'There is something called perchloride of formyle,' Waldie said.

'The name is not familiar. What is it?'

'A component of chloric ether cordial, a popular remedy in Liverpool for the management of asthma and the relief of chronic cough. The vapour of this cordial has been tried as an anaesthetic on several occasions but was unsuccessful. Nonetheless, I think it may have potential.'

Simpson's features were alert, and Glen, sensing his master's interest, was looking up at Waldie with eagerness as though he might throw the dog some meat.

'Why?'

'The lack of success with the cordial is unsurprising as the amount of the perchloride in it is small – the patients would have been in effect breathing only the vapour of alcohol. I have devised a method of manufacture that produces a pure form of the chemical, which is then dissolved in rectified spirit. It is this pure form that I think may be of interest to you. On my return to Liverpool I would be more than happy to send you a sample.'

'I would be much obliged to you, sir.'

One more thing to sniff after a future dinner, Raven thought.

'A serendipitous encounter?' he asked as they resumed their progress.

'Och, you never know,' Simpson replied, sounding less enthusiastic than he had during the conversation. 'I have to investigate every avenue, but if I remember Waldie, he is as apt to blow up his own laboratory as to come up with something ingenious.'

They did not make it as far as West Register Street before Simpson encountered another acquaintance, this time Professor Alison. At this point, Raven was compelled to make his apologies. 'I will need to take my leave and walk on, sir. Professor Syme deplores late-comers.'

As he deplores most things, Raven thought, hurrying towards the North Bridge.

Raven broke into a run to make up time, though he was conscious this might make him conspicuous. It spoke of his enduring terror of Syme that he was more afraid of incurring his wrath than of increasing the risk of being spotted by Flint's men.

His thoughts turned to his most recent sighting of them, on his way back from Rock House. In truth, his thoughts had turned to it frequently in the days since, but only because of what his evasive action had precipitated. That briefest frisson between him and Sarah, a glimpse of tantalising possibilities. Raven's instincts warned him that less trouble awaited down the path leading to the Weasel and Gargantua. Nonetheless, his mind kept returning to the moment, and wondering whether hers did too.

As he walked past the courtyard at the university, Raven became aware of an unmistakable smell of oranges – or bergamot, as Beattie had corrected him – and a moment later the man himself fell into step alongside. A cold breeze was blowing in from the east, from which Raven's care-worn jacket was offering scant protection. His companion, by contrast, was swathed in a flowing greatcoat that made him appear to glide along the cobbles. It made him appear taller too, while Raven's lack of a similar garment caused him to shrink into himself.

Though Beattie had visited Queen Street a number of times since the death of Mrs Graseby, Raven had not found himself alone with him and had therefore enjoyed no opportunity to discuss it – or indeed anything else. The estrangement saddened him. He had felt they were on the verge of a valuable friendship, but knew now that this dreadful thing would always be between them – unless this was another lesson he needed to learn: that such professional tragedies were part of the job. He therefore wasted no time in broaching the subject.

'I have been meaning to enquire, was there any manner of investigation following what happened at Danube Street?'

Beattie wore a burdened expression as he replied: 'She died under her doctor, so I was able to handle the formalities. However, the smell of ether hung about the place for a long time afterwards, raising curiosity among the staff. They were too ignorant to ask the right questions, but one's concern is always who they might have mentioned it to.'

This was not the stuff of Raven's dread fears, but nor was it entirely reassuring.

'I am sure I didn't overdose her. She must have had an unforeseen reaction.'

'Possibly. What is without doubt is that my patient died as a result of your anaesthetic, though why that was, we may never know. Which is why I have endeavoured to ensure that you do not find yourself accused.'

'And thus I am indebted to you, John. Whatever I can do to repay you, please let me know.'

Beattie gave him a sincere nod. 'I will hold you to that. In the meantime, I am sure you must be aware of my interest in Miss Grindlay, so if Dr Simpson or anyone else in the household should ask about my character, I assume I can rely upon you to speak generously?'

Raven stopped his tongue before offering the assurance Beattie sought, recalling his discussion with Sarah. He owed Beattie a debt, but felt compelled by an instinctive loyalty towards the household that had taken him in.

'If you can guarantee that your affections are genuine and that Miss Grindlay is the sole object of them.'

Beattie stopped and shot him a piercing look, a volatile mixture of shock, dismay, insult and outrage. Raven had never seen such fury in his face before, which was usually a picture of concentration or composure.

'I do not mean to offend,' he attempted to explain. 'It is merely that—'

'You have such a low opinion of Miss Grindlay that you cannot believe I would be drawn to her?'

'Quite the opposite. We are all of us at Queen Street protective of Mina, so the household would not forgive it if I were party to an advance that proved –' he sought for the word '– insincere.'

Beattie opened his mouth to retort, then appeared to think better of what he was going to say. That familiar composure fell over his face like a mask covering his anger.

'Do you recall how I told you that true sorrow would grant you perspective?'

'Indeed,' Raven answered humbly.

'It does not merely apply to medicine. I was once betrothed, to a young woman who lit up the world like the morning sun. You would have no difficulty in imagining my intentions towards her sincere. She was the love of my life, as she would have been the love of anyone's. But she died the day before we were to be married. She was thrown from her horse.'

Raven felt half Beattie's height. The man's life had been ripped apart, not once, with the deaths of his parents, but twice, and here he was, questioning his motives.

'I am so terribly sorry. What was her name?'

Beattie took a while to answer, as though he had to think about it. Clearly he was bracing himself for the pain of saying the word.

'Julia. Her name was Julia. After her death, I could not imagine a future with anyone else. I saw small aspects of her in every woman who ever showed an interest in me, and that brought me only pain. That was until Mina. Mina is the first woman I have truly seen for herself, because when I look at her I am not searching for Julia.'

Raven and Beattie resumed their march past the main Infirmary building towards the new surgical hospital in High School Yards, where they followed a large group of gentlemen making their way towards the operating theatre. It seemed half the doctors in the city would be present to observe. Syme would love that.

'I imagine it will be full today,' said a familiar and unwelcome voice. 'Novel operations always draw a crowd.'

Raven turned to see James Duncan inviting himself into their company. Perfect.

'Have you seen Syme operate before?' Duncan asked.

'Indeed,' Beattie replied.

Raven said nothing. He had seen Syme operate many times, but had no desire to share this information with either of this pair, for fear of where the conversation might lead.

'One could argue that he is the best surgeon in the country,' Duncan ventured.

Raven certainly had little doubt that Syme himself would agree.

'Did you know that he was the first in Scotland to perform an amputation through the hip joint?'

'I did,' Raven replied, suppressing a note of irritation. He disliked the way Duncan presumed upon his ignorance. As though one could be a medical student in Edinburgh and be unaware of such a thing. 'The patient died, though,' he added.

'Not for several weeks after the operation, which matters little enough.'

'I'd wager it mattered to the patient. Anyway, I don't think Dr Simpson would agree with you regarding Syme's pre-eminence.'

'Probably not,' Duncan admitted. 'I gather there is a considerable degree of animosity between them. I am told they nearly came to blows on the stairs outside a patient's bedroom.'

'Why?' asked Beattie, his face lit up with delighted curiosity.

'I believe Syme wrote an article in a professional journal in which he criticised Dr Simpson's management of a case.'

'I see,' said Raven, though he truly didn't. The senior men of medicine all seemed to indulge in this sort of behaviour. Criticising one's colleagues in the pages of a publication was not generally regarded as grounds for fisticuffs, so there had to be more to it.

The operating theatre was indeed already packed by the time they made their way inside. They found some seats at the back, where the view of the operating table was obscured by an undulating sea of headwear, a situation Raven was not inclined to complain about. Then above the low murmur of the crowd, someone shouted 'Hats! Hats!' and in a seemingly synchronous movement, all obstructing millinery was removed. Duncan leaned forward eagerly, while Beattie settled back into his seat and folded his arms in a relaxed attitude, as though it were a playhouse they were attending. Alongside them Raven felt stiff with a growing unease about what was to come.

A few minutes later the door at the back of the theatre opened and all conversation ceased. The first to enter was the instrument clerk, a small man in a large apron, who made a final check of the well-stocked table under the window. The door then opened again and Professor Syme entered, followed by Henry, who was his house surgeon.

Raven was always a little surprised by the professor's meek appearance. This leviathan of surgical practice was a small, thin man with a severe, unsmiling face. He was rather grey — eyes, hair and clothing — and his voice was muffled and lacking in power. He had neither the energy and flamboyance attributed to Liston nor the reputed oratory talents of Knox. In fact, there was something altogether miserable about Professor Syme, and Raven would have doubted the many stories of his voluble ill temper had he not experienced such displays first-hand. Despite this, he was reputed to induce a profound loyalty in those who worked closely with him. Perhaps beneath his sullen exterior lurked a magnanimous and caring individual, but Raven had encountered no evidence to support this notion and plenty to refute it.

Syme had demonstrated an open disdain towards Raven during the brief period he studied surgery under him, the roots of which he attributed to one unfortunate incident in this very theatre. It happened during a warm afternoon in August, shortly after Raven began attending the university. The room had been as crowded as it was today, but also stiflingly hot, and Raven was feeling light-headed even before the operation began. He recalled how the smell of putrefaction from the patient's diseased limb filled his nose and his throat, as though he might choke on it, then the grinding of the knife cutting through bone, combined with the horrifying screams of the patient, caused him to feel sick. He had tried to rush from the room, but his way was barred by spectators, too intent upon the spectacle to notice his urgent need to get past. Thus delayed, he had vomited as he neared the door, in full view of Syme, thereby marking him in the Professor of Surgery's sharp and unforgiving eyes. Syme had thereafter treated him like a cur, singling him out for ridicule any time he needed to make a point to Raven's peers.

He particularly recalled the laughter and mockery of Syme's surgical dressers. Raven recognised some of the same men standing in the theatre now, lengths of cat-gut spilling from their pockets in readiness to be handed to the surgeon. Before that, they would be required for more brutal purpose.

Syme took a seat on a plain chair to the left of the operating table, bobbed his head to the assembled dignitaries in the front row and then signalled for the first case to be brought in.

'It has been said that he wastes not a word, nor a drop of blood,' Duncan whispered in admiration.

The four dressers carried in the patient upon a wicker basket, a rough red blanket pulled about him and his face buried in its folds. When he raised his head, Raven was appalled to recognise the man he had confronted over beating his wife.

Gallagher looked about himself apprehensively, taking in the large congregation of strangers who had gathered to witness his operation. He was initially reluctant to let go of the blanket, gripping it in his good hand and causing a ripple of laughter amongst the audience. This was quickly silenced by a reproving look from the still-seated professor.

Raven too could find no levity in the situation. The mirth from the gallery called to mind the words of Simpson regarding this tendency among medical men to make light of suffering: *They jest of scars only because they never felt a wound.*

Raven's hand went automatically to his cheek. He had felt that wound all right, but he was feeling something deeper now: guilt and shame.

Syme rose, and with his back to the patient addressed the room.

'This man has a putrid inflammation of the right hand,' he said, pulling back the blanket to reveal the offending appendage, which was grossly swollen and horribly discoloured. The smell of rotting flesh, synonymous with the surgical wards of the hospital, wafted all the way to the back row. Those in the audience less inured to the odour quickly sought out handkerchiefs in an attempt to blot out the olfactory assault. To Raven's nostrils it smelled all the worse for his part in it.

'It is obvious,' continued the professor, 'that amputation is required.'

Gallagher gestured at Syme with his good hand. 'I beg you, sir, is there no other way? For I am a joiner, and without my hand, my wife and I shall be for the poorhouse.'

'If I do not amputate, you will be for the grave, and what of your poor wife then?'

Gallagher offered no response other than a look of fear and confusion. The man was right, though. He would lose his livelihood:

had done the moment Raven goaded him into punching that wall. Through his vainglorious actions, Raven had condemned Mrs Gallagher to penury, driven more by his need to punish her husband than to offer her genuine help.

Syme continued to describe the procedure to the audience, oblivious to the anxiety of the patient who was being roughly coaxed from his basket. Raven had more than once witnessed those in Gallagher's position yelling and sobbing in a panic of fear, trying to escape the hefty assistants as they were hauled to the operating theatre like it was the gallows. Gallagher said nothing as one of the dressers held up the diseased limb.

'The forearm ought to be amputated by making two equal flaps from before and behind,' said Syme, pointing out to the audience where he intended to make his incisions. 'The arm should be held in the middle state of pronation and supination in order to relax the muscles equally and facilitate the operation. The hand may be removed at the wrist joint but the larger stump thus obtained is not found to facilitate the adaptation or increase the utility of an artificial hand, and the large articular surface which remains, though it may not materially delay a cure, must always cause a deformity.'

Raven wondered at the professor's insensitivity. Without doubt the patient was fortunate such an eminent surgeon was to perform his operation and thereby save his life, but surely it was a form of torture to describe within his hearing the mutilation that was about to occur. His mind was taken back to George Heriot's school, where a singularly vicious mathematics master administered the strap if one's marks did not meet his standards. Raven was a dedicated and eager pupil, but he unavoidably fell short on occasion and condemned himself to be beaten. What he recalled more than the pain was the ritual with which it was delivered. The master produced the dreaded tawse and laid it on Raven's desk, forcing him to contemplate it for the duration of the lesson, before finally delivering his thrashing at the end. To this day, Raven still harboured murderous thoughts towards the man.

While the professor was speaking, the patient had been strapped down to the table and the four surgical dressers had positioned themselves around him to provide additional physical restraint if required. It was at this point that Raven remembered Henry saying that Syme had given up on ether, finding it unreliable, not fit for purpose. This operation would be performed without it.

Raven felt suddenly sick, his guilt compounded further by his knowledge of the horror that was about to unfold. It was impossible to predict which patients would submit to their fate meekly and which would struggle; sometimes the frailest-looking specimen would find remarkable strength and attempt to withdraw the limb just as the surgeon's blade descended for the first cut. Gallagher seemed of the more submissive sort, weeping quietly and then whimpering when the professor was handed his knife.

An assistant grabbed the patient's arm just above the elbow, holding it steady. Syme began immediately, cutting through flesh with absolute certainty and precision, undistracted by Gallagher's screams. Raven was both awed and horrified by this, for he felt the anguish of every cry, and had he been holding the knife, such screams would surely have stayed his hand. He failed to understand how surgeons could work as they did, insensitive to the pain that they inflicted, speed their only clemency. It was this more than anything that had told Raven he had no future in it, and which led him to seek another field.

The professor himself was silent in his task, gesturing to the instrument clerk for what he required. Raven felt sweat run down between his shoulder blades and realised he was holding his breath. Alongside him, Beattie and Duncan watched with detached fascination, evidently troubled by no such emotional responses. They might as well have been watching Mrs Lyndsay carve a joint of ham.

Within minutes the gangrenous hand was slung into a sawdust-filled box at the end of the table, spurting vessels were quickly tied, the edges of the wound stitched together and a dressing applied to the stump.

An animalistic keening emanated from Gallagher, his eyes shuttling incredulously between the box of sawdust and the stump where his hand used to be.

One of the surgical assistants quickly wiped the blood that had collected on the operating table. Another threw fresh sawdust onto the floor, covering the majority of the blood spatter and lumps of tissue as though hiding the evidence of what had just occurred.

Raven understood now why Simpson had all but insisted he attend, why his mentor was relentless in his quest for that Holy Grail, and why he would never again complain about sniffing strange potions.

There had to be a better way than this.

THIRTY-FOUR

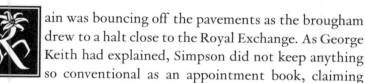ain was bouncing off the pavements as the brougham drew to a halt close to the Royal Exchange. As George Keith had explained, Simpson did not keep anything so conventional as an appointment book, claiming all such relevant information to be locked safe in his head. Consequently Raven seldom knew their destination much in advance, or what the next case might involve.

He did know there had been a messenger to the house this morning during clinic, resulting in their first stop being an address in Canonmills, where Simpson had delivered a baby using his forceps. It had been an unnecessarily traumatic affair, the household being another contaminated by the Reverend Grissom's leaflets and therefore ether had not been permitted. Raven's lingering anger had occupied his mind on the subsequent journey, and he had not thought to enquire as to what was next on Simpson's mental list.

He looked up at the grimy windows looming above the pavement, wondering what sights and smells awaited inside the ramshackle tenement before him. There was a lodging inn on the ground floor, an establishment he had passed many times, but the unfamiliarity of the building itself made him realise how seldom his gaze was drawn above street level. Gazing up for too long in the Old Town was merely an invitation to pickpockets.

Simpson looked out into the driving rain and waved acknowledgement to a fellow hailing them from a doorway. Raven quickly
recognised him as McLevy, the police detective, accompanied by
one of his burly assistants.

Simpson turned briefly to Raven, an odd look upon his face.
'We are here to assist with a police inquiry,' he said. He seemed
rather bemused by this notion, but offered no further detail as
to why. 'It is always advantageous to have the constabulary owing
one favours,' he added.

Raven wondered whether Simpson was waiting for a break in
the rain, then observed that McLevy was coming to join them
inside the carriage. He clambered in, water running around the
brim of his hat even from the journey of a short few yards.

Simpson made introductions. At such moments, most men of
station inferred that they could now safely ignore the apprentice,
but McLevy looked Raven up and down carefully, as though taking
the measure of him.

'May I pick your brains before we proceed?' McLevy asked.
Though he was looking directly at him, it still took Raven a
moment to realise that McLevy meant him and not the professor.

'By all means,' Raven replied.

'You may have heard tell of a scavenger discovering a bairn's
leg in a gutter pipe, not far from here?'

Of course. It had been near the Royal Exchange.

'I have indeed. And I have heard all manner of gruesome
explanations for it. From devil-worshipping child sacrifice to
cannibalistic Irish immigrants.'

'And what do you think to it yourself, Mr Raven?'

'I would expect the cause to be more prosaic. An unwanted
baby, disposed of in a hurried manner suggesting desperation and
panic. The act of a person not thinking clearly.'

'Aye,' McLevy said with a nod, causing more rain to run from
his hat. 'The leg was found inside a main pipe, into which pipes
from all the nearby dwellings feed as well as Mr White's inn,

wherein several females dwell. There are many females of a higher grade resident hereby, thus I have had to be most delicate in my investigations; perhaps too delicate, hence my lack of success up until now. This inquiry contains an imputation wont to stain a woman's name forever after.'

Raven noted that such delicacy was only to be extended when the subjects laid claim to a certain level of respectability. He could not imagine the policeman treading so lightly around Evie's lodgings. Nor did he care for how McLevy used the term 'females'. He made it sound as though he were talking about some other manner of species; exotic and of interest, no doubt, but somehow beyond the human. Or beneath it.

He wondered how McLevy would get on against Miss Rigby. She was a species apart, for sure, but one beneath nobody.

'My enquiries have so far borne little fruit, but I recently heard it said that Mr White, the landlord, has been known to impose himself upon some of the young ladies in his employ. There are staff who have bed and board in part lieu of a wage, and that can bring its complications.'

Impose.

Complications.

Raven thought there an obscenity about this politesse.

McLevy led them from the carriage and into the inn. They gathered at the foot of a staircase leading up to the lodging rooms; to their right, next to the kitchen, was a common area in which several young women were about their duties.

White was ill-named for such a red-faced individual. He did not look pleased to see McLevy, but quickly concealed this behind an oily display of obsequiousness.

'How may I help you on this occasion, Mr McLevy? Did you ever get to the bottom of that unpleasant matter that brought you here before?'

'That is indeed what brings me back, sir. I need to speak to the female domestics once again.'

White's eyes narrowed. 'As I assured you before, it would not have escaped me had one of them been in such a condition. And I would have surely acted upon it, as my house has its pride and reputation to uphold.'

As he spoke, McLevy turned his gaze to the young women, picking out one in particular for his piercing stare. She was sweeping the floor near the back door, keeping her head down just a little too keenly.

'That one there,' McLevy announced. 'I don't recall seeing her the last time.'

Raven was beginning to suspect he knew why, though he remained unsure what Simpson's role in all this might be.

'What is her name?'

'Mary Brennan,' White replied.

The girl started at the mere mention. She looked to her land-lord in pale fright, though Raven was not sure whether it was him or McLevy she was more afraid of.

'We would speak with her alone.'

White issued a sigh, then told the other girls to leave the common area.

'I said we would speak with Mary alone,' McLevy reiterated with a firm tone, his eyes fixed on White.

The landlord retreated with hesitancy, sending one last look to Mary before the door closed. Raven did not imagine it escaped McLevy's notice.

Mary Brennan stood before the four of them, clutching a broom as though she might fall down without it. She was trembling.

'We are investigating the discovery of a bairn's leg, wrapped in cloth and flushed down a pipe. Do you know anything about this?'

Her eyes searched back and forth along the line, as though seeking an ally.

'No, sir,' she replied, her voice feeble. There was a determina-tion there, however: an awareness of the stakes should she crumble.

'Do you know who this gentleman is?' McLevy asked.

'No, sir.'

'His name is Professor James Young Simpson. Does that name mean anything to you, Mary?'

Her expression was blank, but all the more worried for not knowing the potential significance of this esteemed gentleman's presence.

'He is one of the foremost medical men in the city, specialising in the care of pregnant women, and assisting them in their time of labour.'

McLevy then turned to address the professor.

'Dr Simpson, if you were to examine a young woman such as Mary here, would you be able to ascertain whether she had recently given birth?'

'Most certainly and unmistakably,' Simpson replied.

That was all it took. The girl dropped to her knees and broke down in tears, spilling forth a confession there on the floor as though relieved to be finally shedding her burden.

'God forgive me, I confess that I bore that child, but it was dead when it came into the world. Wild with sorrow and pain, I cut it into pieces and put it into the soil pipe so that nobody would know my shame.'

'Did anybody know of your condition?'

'No, sir. I kept it secret for fear I would be cast out onto the street. Mr White insists he keeps a respectable house.'

She looked to the door as she said this. A greater threat lay beyond it than anything she faced inside this room.

'Whose child was it?' McLevy asked, though the question struck Raven as redundant.

She hung her head, her hair all but sweeping the floorboards.

'A wicked man seduced me,' she answered, not looking one of them in the eye.

McLevy pressed her, but she would not name him.

She did not have to.

McLevy's assistant helped her to her feet and led her away. She looked hollow-eyed, as though entranced, then a panic enlivened her face. 'Am I to hang?' she asked McLevy, terrified.

'Not if what you told us was true, about the child being stillborn. You will only be confined a short while.'

Simpson shook his head sadly as she was led away.

'It is a tragedy that this young woman should be facing any greater punishment than that which she has already endured,' he stated.

'And it sorely compounds the injustice that there should be no consequence for the landlord,' ventured Raven, struggling to keep bitterness from his voice.

'I'll have a stern word,' McLevy assured him. 'He'll understand I have my eye on him, but what more can I do?'

Raven thought of what more he would like to do, then remembered the fate of Mrs Gallagher, in danger of the poorhouse as a consequence of his previous thirst for justice.

McLevy thanked Simpson for his assistance, which had amounted to little more than his august presence, but Raven had to commend the policeman's cunning in knowing this alone would do the trick.

'You are most welcome, as always,' Simpson replied.

'If I may ever be of assistance, just say the word.'

'Certainly. But in the meantime, I believe Mr Raven was curious about another case you were looking into.'

Raven looked at him in some surprise, and wondered how conspicuous his interest might have been.

'Which case would that be?'

'Rose Campbell,' Raven replied. 'She was a housemaid of Mr Sheldrake, the dentist. Her body was pulled from the water at Leith.'

'Oh, yes. Dr Renfrew, our police surgeon, carried out a full examination of her remains. He concluded that she had drowned.'

'So he found no trace of poison?'

'Why would he?'

'The agonised posture of her body. It is my understanding that it can be a symptom of strychnine.'

Raven was aware of Simpson regarding him with some scrutiny, but had to press on while he had McLevy here before him.

'As I say,' continued McLevy, 'no evidence of poison was found. When the bodies of the drowned are removed from the water their limbs may be contorted, indicating their final struggles, contortions which persist because of the rigidity that follows on after death.'

That may well be true, thought Raven. But Evie did not drown.

'This was a case of accidental death,' said McLevy, with a finality that suggested further questions were superfluous. Raven ignored this.

'Didn't you previously entertain the notion that she had done away with herself?'

McLevy looked at him with wariness and some surprise.

'I did indeed, as I was informed she was pregnant, as much as five or six months. But here's the strangest thing: when the post-mortem was carried out, she did not appear to be with child after all.'

Raven reeled from this, as though the walls around him had moved. 'Are you sure?'

McLevy allowed himself a grin. 'Speaking candidly, Dr Renfrew is not the greatest medical mind I have ever encountered, even on the rare occasions he is sober, but I am confident that even he would not have made a mistake about something like that.'

Raven felt numb in his confusion, the world swirling around him as the brougham pulled away, rain hammering upon its roof.

'You did not hear the answers you were hoping for,' Simpson observed.

This was to say the least. His belief in a connection between

Rose and Evie, about which he had been so certain, now appeared to be groundless. He had no real evidence that either of them had been poisoned, McLevy having provided an adequate explanation for the condition of Rose's body when he suggested rigor had set in while she was still in the water. Now it transpired that Rose had not been pregnant, and he was forced to own that it had been mere speculation on his part that Evie was with child.

'I will not intrude to ask why you were so exercised by Miss Campbell's death, but I will impart a lesson that will serve you well in all your dealings as a doctor.'

Raven looked up, eager for the comfort wisdom might bring.

'Always remember that the patient is the one with the disease.'

Raven's expression betrayed that he did not understand.

'It is easy to become burdened by responsibilities, to become so obsessed with a problem that you lose perspective. Evidence can be confounding, unlikely coincidences do happen, and an over-wrought mind can leap to wrong conclusions. Remember your own good judgment when McLevy asked how you would explain the dead baby's leg. In that instance, your detachment served you well. People often hypothesise the sensational, and become inexplicably blind to the obvious that is before their very eyes.'

THIRTY-FIVE

he rain let up as the carriage took them down the Mound and north again into the New Town. Simpson occupied himself with a book, while Raven was left to mull over what the professor had told him. He began asking himself whether he had concocted some greater malfeasance on the part of an imaginary villain as a means of dealing with his own guilt over Evie. In his need to do something for her after her death, he feared he had constructed a fantasy, pulling elements in from around him to support it, tilting at windmills like Don Quixote. Worse still, he had drawn Sarah into it too.

The brougham began to slow after turning a corner into a street that was familiar to Raven in the most uncomfortable way. With a horrible inevitability, the coachman drew his horses to a stop outside a handsome enough building, but one that he could no longer lay eyes upon without a stomach-churning guilt.

The Graseby residence.

Raven endeavoured to keep the alarm from his expression, already worried enough about how transparent Simpson found the inner workings of his mind. The professor looked up from his book as the carriage halted. His expression was briefly curious, as was often the case as he sought the item on his mental list that had brought him here. Then his visage darkened.

'Here, Mr Raven, I'm afraid I must insist we part ways. I have been called to this address on a very sensitive matter, under condition of such strict confidentiality that I am not permitted to discuss with anyone the reason for my visit.'

Raven experienced a sickening dread. It was as Beattie had feared. Someone had mentioned the lingering smell of ether in the aftermath of Mrs Graseby's death, and this had led to the summoning of the man regarded as the city's primary expert on the stuff. If there was one stroke of fortune, it was that this need for confidentiality spared Raven having to walk in there right now, to be recognised.

It would only be a matter of time, however.

'I should stay here in the meantime?' he asked.

'No, I need you to busy yourself with an errand. You recall my encounter with Mr Waldie, who told us of a cordial containing perchloride of formyle and promised to send me some?'

'I recall you said he was as likely to blow up his own laboratory as to come up with something ingenious.'

'Proving that many a prescient word is spoken in jest, his sample was never dispatched on account of a fire at the Liverpool Apothecaries Hall. It remains unclear whether Waldie was personally responsible for it, but I was intrigued by his suggestion, and as he is unlikely to make good on his promise any time soon, I asked Duncan and Flockhart to prepare a batch for trial. I need it collected.'

'Very good, sir.'

Raven hastened from the carriage, keeping his head down though the rain had stopped. He did not want to risk being seen by one of the staff at a time when they were casting their minds back to the night the mistress of their house died.

He was grateful for the walk in the fresh air, the carriage having begun to close in on him like a cell as soon as Simpson announced his reason for being there. His legs felt heavy, though. Simpson's enquiries would now surely lead to Beattie, and there would be no reason for Beattie to protect him. As he strode east along George Street, he was conscious that at that very moment, the mechanism was being set in motion whereby his medical career might soon be ended.

As he approached the druggist's, his nose was assailed by a variety of medicinal scents. Through the glass of the door, he could see a young assistant rolling pills on the marble counter and the well-dressed, bespectacled Mr Flockhart pouring a clear liquid into a number of small glass bottles. All his senses seemed enhanced right then, as though drinking in all they could because this might be the last time.

These premises had always held a fascination for him, more so than any baker's or confectioner's in his youth. The cabinets accommodated neatly ordered rows of soaps, tooth powders, lotions and liniments, while upon the shelves a hundred bottles and jars glinted in a play of colours. The floor was always swept and polished, a place where neither dirt nor disorder would be tolerated. Its greatest pull upon Raven, though, was the knowledge that within these premises they made medicines. Here they powdered, mixed, brewed and diluted, creating tinctures, pills and potions from roots, herbs, minerals and sundry other substances. Here, they experimented, developing remedies for all manner of ailments. Here, progress was made.

He had always wanted a part of this, and had relished each visit, even upon errands for Dr Duncan. He had begun to believe it a part of his world, a part of his future, but now he feared it was all about to be taken away.

Flockhart looked up from what he was doing.

'Mr Raven. You'll be here for *this*,' he said with pointed emphasis, and picked up a bottle that was sitting to his left upon the counter. It contained a fluid so viscous you could have stood up a spoon in it.

'Yes, sir. For Dr Simpson. I believe he asked you to reproduce a formula suggested by a Mr Waldie of Liverpool.'

Flockhart issued a stern sigh. 'That we did. Resulting in a small explosion which scorched our walls and ceiling and could have resulted in irreparable ocular damage had we not been wearing our spectacles at the time. I trust we can add the repainting cost to Dr Simpson's account?'

Raven did not reply, unsure whether he had the authority to approve this or even whether Flockhart was joking. He took the bottle and departed.

When he reached Queen Street, he made straight for the dining room, where he intended to leave the bottle, ready for trial after that night's dinner. He found James Duncan knelt by the open doors of the sideboard, all the previous samples and a dozen other vials laid out on the top.

'I'm attempting to rationalise this mess and dispose of a few things,' he said, his tone indicating irritation at Raven's interruption, or maybe his mere presence. 'What do you have there?'

'Something Dr Simpson requested from Duncan and Flockhart. I imagine he wants to test it after dinner.'

'Let me have a look.'

Duncan took the bottle, tilting it on its side, and frowned in disapproval at the dense liquid. He unstopped it and held the open neck to his nose, which he wrinkled, though not in reflexive response. He sniffed deeper, then shook his head, handing it back.

'Most unlikely to serve,' he predicted.

Raven had a sniff too. He thought he felt a hint of light-headedness, but this might have been resultant of having just hurried to get there.

'Perhaps if it was warmed to make it more volatile,' Raven suggested, conscious that the bottle was chilled from being outside. 'The heat of the room will render it so by the time dinner is concluded.'

'*Peut-être*,' Duncan replied, in a tone that did not sound hopeful. He had an irritating habit of slipping into French, an affectation no doubt intended to remind everyone of his having recently arrived here from his prodigious studies in Paris.

Raven felt reluctant to dismiss the bottle so quickly, then remembered Dr Simpson's entreaty not to make it about oneself when dealing with matters of evidence. He was attributing the stuff significance due to the fire it might have caused in Liverpool and the subsequent explosion in the druggist's lab, not to mention the distance he had walked in retrieving it.

'I have higher hopes for this, though,' Duncan said, holding up another bottle. He took out the stopper and held it beneath Raven's nose. There was something sharp and acrid about it, causing him to recoil. He felt an immediate sense of dizziness too. Raven could understand Duncan's optimism, but equally could already anticipate tomorrow's resultant headache.

Duncan observed him with a wolfish grin.

'What is this stuff?'

'I suggested a formula to Professor Gregory.'

'So this is of your own devising?' Raven asked. That would certainly account for Duncan's enthusiasm.

'Indeed, though this is merely a preliminary distillation. He assured me a refined batch will be ready tonight. Now that you are here, you can go and retrieve it.'

'I have to get back to Dr Simpson,' Raven protested. 'His visits are not complete.'

'Don't you have duties at the Maternity Hospital later?'

'Yes.'

'Then you can go once those are concluded. Professor Gregory works late at his laboratory. In fact, I suspect he sleeps there.'

It was not strictly true that Raven had to return to Dr Simpson, as the professor had made no direct instruction regarding the matter. It was more the case that Raven felt an urgent compulsion to report back to him, due to a combination of guilt and anxiety and his resultant impatience for this uncertainty to be at an end.

If there was a reckoning, he wanted to face it sooner rather than later, though not so much that he was prepared to expedite this himself by coming clean. While there was still hope that his role in Mrs Graseby's death might never emerge, he would cling on, though it become ever more agonising.

He set off towards Danube Street, striding briskly north along Gloucester Lane. He had no guarantee Simpson would still be at the Graseby house, but little over an hour had passed since they parted. It was as he crossed the junction at Doune Terrace that he spied a brougham and its pair, halted not fifty yards away. He saw Simpson emerge and quickly cross the pavement towards the door of a terraced townhouse.

Raven hastened to catch up with him, but as he did, Angus the coachman stepped into his path to arrest his progress.

'The professor is not to be disturbed,' he said.

'What, here too?' Raven asked.

'Here too,' the coachman confirmed with a solemn nod.

Raven glanced towards the house, where the door was closing behind Simpson. Perhaps it was his imagination, but he thought he detected an anxiety about Angus, a degree of alarm at Raven having come so unexpectedly upon them.

Raven was about to turn towards the carriage when he saw movement through the window of the large front room. He watched an elegantly dressed young woman rise to her feet and greet Simpson as he strode into the room. They embraced warmly, exchanging words Raven could not hear.

The professor bent briefly out of sight, and when he stood up again, he was holding an infant: a baby of perhaps eighteen months, swaddled in a pink dress. Simpson hugged the child to him while the woman looked on, smiling with the most tender affection.

There did not appear to be any medical matters to attend, far less an emergency.

'What is Dr Simpson's business here?' Raven asked. He did

not expect a straight answer, but sought to measure subtleties in how Angus evaded it.

'I know only that it is a private matter, and I know not to ask further detail. You would be wise to follow suit, unless you would rather Dr Simpson was made aware of your curiosity.'

'May I wait in the carriage?'

Angus gestured him welcome. Raven wondered at his loyalty: what secrets he might know; what further secrets he did not *know* he knew.

His thoughts were called back to the fraught conversation he had overheard between Mina and Jessie: '*He is paying out twelve pounds a year to another woman. Isn't the obvious question: why?*'

'*It is an act of charity. Surely no one can cast aspersions over something so noble.*'

'*In my experience people are happy to cast aspersions over anything when the morality of an action can be called into question.*'

Raven recalled Simpson's own advice to him this morning regarding sensational hypotheses. Nonetheless, this woman was in no need of charity, and here was Simpson visiting her alone, knowing Raven had been sent elsewhere, his coachman acting to protect his privacy. Had Mina been trying to make Jessie see what should be obvious before her eyes?

Simpson was not there long, perhaps half an hour. He strode back out to his carriage, a look of surprise lighting upon him at the sight of Raven waiting there. If it was accompanied by alarm, he concealed it swiftly. Nonetheless, there ensued a moment of silence once they were both seated, an uncomfortable intermission during which it was evident that Raven's presence was as unwelcome as it was unexpected.

'I was making my way back to Danube Street when I saw your carriage,' Raven ventured by way of explanation. He swallowed, the better to keep his voice steady and bright during his next words. 'What of your visit there? I appreciate it was confidential, but went everything well?'

Simpson's countenance became regretful, like clouds gathering. He let out a deep sigh. 'A bad business,' he said, gazing through the window. Then he turned to look at Raven. 'And one not yet concluded to my satisfaction.'

THIRTY-SIX

Sarah elbowed her way into the room, balancing the tea tray on one arm. She manoeuvred carefully around the mess on the floor, trying not to stand on any remnants of material or any part of the seamstress who was lying prostrate at Mina's feet, making adjustments to the hem of her new dress. The tray contained but one cup, Miss Tweedie the seamstress considered too lowly a person to merit refreshment.

Sarah placed the tray on a small table in the corner.

'Shall I pour, ma'am?'

'In a minute, Sarah. I think we're almost finished here.'

Mina swung around to face Sarah, ignoring the fact that Miss Tweedie was still in the process of pinning the hem.

'What do you think?'

Sarah stood with her arms folded, making a convincing pretence of considered study. She knew from experience that it did not do to answer too quickly. The dress was a damson silk satin, wide at the neckline, narrow at the waist, with a full skirt.

'It's beautiful, Miss Grindlay.'

As indeed it was, but Mina was looking good in whatever she wore these days simply because of the glow of contentment she was giving off.

'As you know, Sarah, I was in desperate need of a new evening gown.'

A slight emphasis was added to the penultimate word to remind Sarah, lest she had forgotten, that Mina was now being escorted with some regularity to evening functions.

'Plain is the fashion now,' piped up Miss Tweedie, kneeling on the floor and speaking through two pins gripped between her lips. 'No applied decoration.' She groaned a little as she stood up. 'Now, we'll get that off you and I shall make the adjustments we discussed.'

Sarah helped the seamstress wrestle Mina out of the dress and into her old one.

'When will it be ready?' Mina asked. 'I have a number of important engagements in the near future.'

The word *engagement* was also given extra stress, Sarah noticed, though not so much that Miss Tweedie would surely infer its significance.

'End of the week, I should imagine,' Miss Tweedie said, collecting up her pins.

'I think Dr Beattie will like it,' Sarah said, offering Mina the opportunity to talk about him, though she seldom needed prompting.

'Yes, I do believe that he will.'

'Is he your intended?' asked Miss Tweedie, gathering up the garment under discussion.

'Nothing has been made formal,' replied Mina, although the implication was that it would be soon.

This gave Sarah pause, prompting an involuntary tightness in her chest. Happy as she was for Mina, Sarah retained an instinctive suspicion about Beattie's intentions. Perhaps it was a natural caution born of concern that Mina should not get hurt. Mina was a sensible and strong-minded woman, but if there was one area where she might be vulnerable to deception – and most dangerously self-deception – it was in the matter of finding a husband.

When she had first mentioned her reservations to Raven, he had told her how Beattie insisted that he was not interested in trivial flirtations. This sounded well and good, but did not entirely tally with how she often felt Beattie's eyes lingering upon her as she went about her business. Men deluded themselves that you didn't know they were staring – or *where* they were staring.

Looking and desiring were different things, however, and she would admit to being moved when she learned from Raven how Beattie had lost his bride-to-be on the day before their planned wedding. It was truly tragic, like something from a novel. Nonetheless, she was not convinced that his previous loss meant his feelings for Mina were everything Mina would like to believe. Simply not reminding him of the woman he lost did not strike Sarah as a strong foundation upon which to build true feelings. In fact, it seemed the opposite of true feelings: a bulwark against genuine emotion.

'Do you believe an announcement is imminent?' Sarah asked.

She realised her question might be considered impertinent, but she was confident that this would be overlooked in Mina's desire to share her news.

'I believe so.'

Mina had a flush of colour rising from her neck to her face.

'How wonderful,' said Miss Tweedie, sounding like she meant it.

'Yes,' agreed Mina. 'I was beginning to think that it might never happen.'

Sarah noticed that she spoke this more quietly, as though to herself.

'Is remaining unmarried such a disaster?' Sarah asked. She knew that Mina was in love with Beattie; she was less sure that these feelings were being genuinely reciprocated. Sarah thought about Rose Campbell, perhaps similarly afflicted by an all-consuming passion that left no space for doubt. Look where that had led.

Mina looked at her as though she might have lost her mind.

'To be a spinster aunt reliant on the generosity of family? What kind of life would that be?'

'Can't a woman have aspirations for herself beyond marriage?' Sarah responded.

'"Aspirations"? What on earth can you mean?'

Sarah thought of Miss Mann and Miss Rigby, and of Mina's love for the written word. Nobody she had met knew more about novels and poetry. It seemed a shame that there was no means of harnessing this.

'A profession of some kind. I mean, do you not wish there was a worthwhile way to use your intellect and knowledge?'

'Sarah, a woman's God-given role is to be a wife and mother. Any profession is a poor substitute for that. And what sort of profession would be suitable for a lady? Governess? I shudder at the very thought.'

Mina turned back to the mirror and adjusted her hair, pinning a loose strand back into position.

Sarah poured the tea, thinking how narrow Mina's assessment of a woman's role was, how restrictive. Why couldn't a woman aspire to more? Why shouldn't she? Why did Raven get to do whatever he wanted? She was convinced that they were of similar backgrounds and she was damn sure they were of similar intellect, yet he had opportunities that were denied to her, and seemed not always to appreciate his privilege.

Sarah bent down to retrieve a stray pin from the carpet. As she did so her hand brushed against the new dress. She wondered if she would ever wear a garment made from such fine material. She was surely not destined to remain as she was, the hired help, condemned to domestic servitude for the rest of her life. Yet how was she to escape? If a man of means offered to take her away from all of this, would she not leap at the chance? Or would that merely represent the exchange of one form of servitude for another, albeit one with greater comfort and fewer chilblains?

Would it be possible to meet a man who would accept her ambitions to educate herself and be of use? Did such a man exist? If he did, she was sure she hadn't met him yet.

She also thought of Mrs Lyndsay's admonitions about seeking to better herself. Should she just be grateful for what she had, accept her position in society that God had seen fit to give her and avoid the trouble that would inevitably come her way should she try to change things?

She handed the stray pins to Miss Tweedie, who, having wrapped the new dress in a protective layer of brown paper, made her farewells and left the room.

Sarah decided to turn the conversation back to Beattie, a sure way to restore Mina's good humour.

'It is a blessing that you should both have found each other, is it not?'

'Truly. I shudder to think how capricious fate can be.'

'You both deserve such happiness. It warms the heart to know that Dr Beattie should be able to put such painful tragedy behind him.'

Mina gave her a quizzical look. 'What tragedy?'

Sarah froze for a moment as it dawned that Beattie had not told Mina about his previous engagement. She cursed her own foolishness: she could suddenly see all of the reasons he might choose to keep it from her. Why he had chosen to confide in Raven was a more curious question, but no matter.

'That he lost his parents so young,' she said, by way of covering her misstep.

'Yes. His life has not been easy. But I am sure that it is about to improve.'

As she left the room and made her way downstairs, Sarah thought about how Mina had looked in her new dress. She radiated the joy of being admired, esteemed, raised above her peers. If love was a potion that could be bottled and sold, it really would be the cure for many a drawing-room malady.

She tried to assuage her doubts about Beattie. It was a good match in many ways, after all, and perhaps he did love Mina in a way he could love no other after losing his first intended wife.

Unlike Raven, Sarah was prepared to accept that her instincts were not infallible. But they were seldom completely wrong.

THIRTY-SEVEN

The girl on the table in front of Raven looked fourteen at the most, and plainly terrified.

'Lynsey Clegg. Been living on the streets for months,' Mrs Stevenson had told him earlier. 'Thrown out by her father when it was discovered she was pregnant, and I wouldn't be surprised if he was responsible for her condition too.'

Mrs Stevenson did not say what her grounds were for believing this. She didn't make such accusations lightly, however, and Raven had come to learn that she made it her business to find out as much as possible about the women who passed under her roof.

Lynsey was slight, about four and a half feet tall with a skinny frame that spoke of years of malnourishment. It would have been impossible for her to disguise her condition long past the quickening.

'The child is breech,' Ziegler observed quietly. 'I anticipate problems delivering the head.'

He kept his words out of the girl's hearing, but Raven did not imagine she would have picked up much anyway. She was nearly hysterical from the pain and her growing panic.

'She is not built for this. She has such a narrow pelvis. She is but a child.'

'Ether?' Raven suggested, the word emerging before he could question himself.

Ziegler merely nodded.

The contrast was, as always, astonishing. The girl went from torment to easeful sleep in a matter of minutes, and remained oblivious of the violent manoeuvres Ziegler was necessarily inflicting upon her. Despite all of this Raven could not help but think about Mrs Graseby. He remained ignorant as to what had gone wrong, what had caused her adverse reaction and why it had proven fatal after she appeared to rally. But then, such ignorance was the very reason he should not have been administering ether unsupervised.

Ziegler brought forth a baby girl and handed her to a nurse while he delivered the placenta. Raven hoped the infant would see more than fourteen years before she was giving birth too. The mother started to come around, her oblivion one last sleep before waking up in a new world.

Having swaddled the child, the nurse held her out towards her mother. The girl simply looked afraid of it.

At that point, they were interrupted by Mrs Stevenson, hastening towards them down a corridor and calling out as she ran: 'Dr Ziegler! You are needed urgently. You too, Mr Raven.'

In the lobby of Milton House, just inside the door, a young woman lay writhing upon a cot, while alongside her stood a burly fellow, clutching his hat nervously.

'He carried her here,' Mrs Stevenson informed them.

'They wanted to call for a doctor,' the man said, 'but I suggested I fetch her here, as that would be quicker. We came from just along the street.'

'Who is she?' Ziegler asked.

'Her name is Kitty. That's all I know.'

There was a smell of brick dust about the man, and he had the rough hands of a labourer.

'And who are you?'

The man paused, mulling it over before venturing his name. 'Mitchell, sir. Donald Mitchell.'

Ziegler examined the woman, as much as she would allow. She was squirming in pain, sweating and incoherent. He asked her some questions, but it was as though she was not in control of her faculties. Ziegler looked again at the man who brought her in.

'What can you tell us? What did you see? What do you know of her?'

Again, he seemed reluctant to answer. Raven reckoned he knew why.

'Were you *with* her, sir?' he asked pointedly, so that the man could make no mistake as to his meaning.

He eyed Raven with surprise, but the surprise of one who has been caught out.

'I was with another,' he admitted. 'Across the landing. We heard her cry out like the very devil was about her. I kicked in the door because I feared she was being attacked, then when we discovered her ill, as I say, I opted to bring her here directly.'

Raven contrasted this with his own conduct, sneaking away so that he was not seen. He liked to think it would have been different had Evie not already been dead, but had no doubt that Mitchell was a stronger man than he, in many ways.

They wheeled Kitty to a room where they had better light, though at this hour that was not saying much. She seemed to pass out momentarily, which allowed Ziegler an opportunity to put his hands about her.

'She's pregnant. Past the quickening.'

The calm did not last. As soon as her eyes opened again, her body buckled and twisted on the bed as though indeed the devil was not merely about her, but inside her. Raven watched her contort herself and felt sure he was witnessing what had happened to Evie before he got there that night.

'Did you take a draught or a pill?' he asked her. 'Did you seek to rid yourself of what grows in your womb?'

Her eyes fixed on his long enough for him to believe she had heard the question, but she offered no word of answer.

'She wouldn't tell you if she had,' said Mrs Stevenson. 'For fear.'

'We are here only to help you, Kitty,' he insisted. 'Please, if you took something, let us know.'

At that point, the convulsions worsened as though Raven's words had angered the demon that possessed her. Her limbs became rigid, her head thrown back.

Ziegler tried to dose her with some laudanum but her jaw was clamped shut. Her convulsions continued unabated and it was clear they were powerless to intervene.

'There is nothing we can do,' he said quietly. 'You should leave now, Raven. Go home and rest, for this all begins again tomorrow.'

'I would stay,' Raven replied. 'If there is nothing else anyone can do, then this much I can offer.'

Ziegler looked upon him curiously for a moment, then nodded by way of acquiescence.

Raven sat with her for the next few hours, watching her tormented mercilessly, her body pulled around as if she was trying to escape her very being. Though she barely seemed aware he was there, he would not let her endure these throes alone as Evie had.

Even the end was not a gentle fading, but a final, brutal jolt.

Raven remained still alongside her, his heart anxious that she might resume her agonies. After a short time, he tested for a pulse and found none.

'She has passed?' Ziegler said, appearing in the doorway. He had absented himself upon Raven's insistence, but Raven wondered whether he had ever been far.

'Indeed. I will tell Mitchell.'

Ziegler looked apologetic. 'He left some time ago. It was mercy enough for him to bring her here.'

'Did he tell you anything else? From where he brought her, at least?'

'No. He did not wait long. I don't think he knew her.'

'Then have we any means of knowing who she was?'

'Not unless someone comes to claim her remains.'

Raven thought of Evie, hauled down the stairs wrapped in a soiled shroud and slung onto a cart.

No funeral, no mourners, no headstone.

'I never knew her surname,' he said.

'Mitchell didn't give us it.'

But Raven wasn't talking about Kitty.

THIRTY-EIGHT

The hour was getting late by the time Raven left the Maternity Hospital, sharp pangs of hunger bringing him back to more immediate concerns. Dinner would be over by the time he returned to Queen Street, but Mrs Lyndsay should be able to offer him something, he was sure. Perhaps Sarah might even keep some leftovers aside for him, though he knew not what he would tell her about today's contradictory discoveries.

What made it worse was that though he would be too late for the meal, he would most likely return in time for the testing afterwards. His brief exposure to the nasty stuff Duncan had concocted was sufficient to suggest that all his previous headaches would prove joyous memories compared to the after-effects of that.

With this thought, he realised he had a means of avoiding it. Duncan had exposed him to a preliminary distillation, and Raven had been instructed to pick up a more refined sample. Professor Gregory might well have gone home by this hour, but he would take a walk up past the college building anyway. Either way, it would provide a plausible reason to delay his return until the testing was over and everyone had removed to the drawing room to smoke pipes and sip whisky.

Professor Gregory's laboratory was housed in a far corner of the university buildings, Raven attributing its remote location to the potentially explosive nature of his work. It was not easily found, Raven traversing a labyrinth of passages and stairs, though it was possible to discern that he was drawing nearer because the smells became stronger.

The laboratory was the very antithesis of Duncan and Flockhart's pristine premises: a claustrophobic and permanently cluttered chamber lined from floor to ceiling with bookcases and shelves, its floor an evolving hazard of boxes, crates and discarded equipment. The bookcases housed an extensive collection of ancient and in some instances dusty tomes, some of which Raven suspected had not been disturbed since being placed there, not by the incumbent, but by his predecessor.

In the centre of the room was a large wooden table etched with stains and scorch marks. A stooped figure was holding a flask above a spirit lamp, the purplish flame licking the underside of the glass, which caused the liquid inside to bubble furiously as though incensed by the application of such heat. Raven waited in the doorway so as not to interrupt, but without looking up the professor beckoned him with a wave of his hand before brushing a long strand of black hair from his forehead.

William Gregory was a thin man who appeared older than he was. He hobbled when he walked, the result of a childhood illness from which he had never entirely recovered, but he had a lively energy about him when his enthusiasm was piqued – usually by his work. His father James Gregory had been the renowned formulator of Gregory's powder, the most prescribed medicine in the *Edinburgh Pharmacopoeia* and thus the standard by which James Duncan intended to measure his own success.

According to Simpson, Gregory Sr had been by nature a belligerent man, prone to feuding with individuals and institutions alike. He had carried a cane and on one notorious occasion used it to attack the then Professor of Midwifery, James Hamilton, following a dispute. This resulted in a court hearing at which Gregory was ordered to pay Hamilton £100 in damages, which he said he 'would pay all over again for another opportunity of thrashing the little obstetrician'.

By contrast, William Gregory was known for his calmness and self-possession, having inherited only his father's academic brilliance. Simpson told Raven that early in his career, he had developed a process to produce morphine in a high state of purity. However, Dr Simpson could not help but also impart that Gregory was an enthusiast for phrenology and hypnotism, and it was said that his choice of wife had been made only after phrenological examination.

Raven approached, stepping around a three-legged stool upon which sat a beaker with a long retort just asking to be knocked over and smashed. Next to that was a pile of leather-bound volumes and what appeared to be two dead rabbits in a wooden crate. Raven wondered if they had been delivered thus on order, though he did not wish to dwell upon what purpose they were about to serve.

Gregory removed the flask from the flame and held it up, swirling the contents under the dim light of a gas lamp, a look of dissatisfaction upon his face at the results.

Raven took in the ramshackle chaos of bottles, jars and vials arrayed close to the professor. His eye was also drawn to several jars of a bright red powder, one he did not recognise.

'Mr Raven,' Gregory said. 'Here at Dr Duncan's request, I assume?'

'Indeed.'

'He's fairly got you people fetching and carrying for him. The initial distillation of this stuff was collected by some young girl. Gave me quite the interrogation, too. Would you know who that might be?'

Raven could not help but smile. 'She is Dr Simpson's house-maid.'

'Really?' Gregory replied, given pause. 'His housemaid. I wish my students were half so inquisitive. Or as informed. Now, where did I . . .'

Gregory turned to the array of glass containers before him, reaching towards the vial Duncan was waiting for, but then his attention suddenly diverted to the red powder.

'I forgot to say to the young girl when she was here. You must take this to Dr Simpson as a gift. I was sent a batch of the stuff by Professor Joao Parreira of the University of Coimbra in Portugal. We met in Paris over the summer.'

'Is he a chemist?'

'Yes, and an esteemed one, but this is not a chemical compound. It is a powder ground from dried capsicums: a powerful strain originally deriving from Africa, I believe. They call it *peri-peri.*'

'What does it do?'

Gregory became animated, his face charged with enthusiasm.

'It adds the most enlivening flavour to food. It is the stuff of miracles, believe me. It can transform the most miserable and mundane of stews into something that will delight your palate.'

Having had his scale of miserable cuisine calibrated by life at Ma Cherry's, Raven looked sceptically upon the jar Gregory was proffering.

'Try some,' he said, unscrewing the lid. 'Just take a pinch.'

Raven dipped three fingers into the neck of the jar and scooped out the equivalent of a teaspoon, transferring it swiftly between his lips.

Gregory's admonition – 'I said just a pinch!' – hit his ears at the same moment the powder had its seemingly incendiary effect inside his mouth. His tongue felt aflame and his eyes began to stream. He spat it out, but the burning continued.

'Water,' he coughed, to which an amused Gregory held out a cup. Raven poured it into his maw, but this only seemed to exacerbate the intensity, like pouring water upon burning oil.

He would have to admit that there was an intriguingly smoky

flavour about it, but worried that he was tasting his own burnt flesh.

Gregory's eyes were moist too, but merely from mirth at Raven's affliction.

'I won't have to warn you to tell Dr Simpson's cook she should use it sparingly.'

Raven was sceptical as to whether Mrs Lyndsay could be prevailed upon to use it at all. She was a fine cook, but according to Sarah, extremely set in her ways. Nonetheless, Raven looked forward to offering a taste to Jarvis, and to Duncan. He would recommend a generously heaped spoonful to each of them.

He replaced the lid and placed the jar in the pocket of his jacket so that his hands were free to carry the vial for which Gregory was now reaching.

'I thought I could improve the distillation process, but in truth it is all but identical to the first attempt. I wasn't so sure about some of the ingredients Duncan suggested. The combination struck me as potentially lethal, a danger he seemed to be blithely ambivalent towards.'

Yes, that sounded like Duncan, Raven thought. He couldn't imagine the man shedding many tears if his experimentation happened to kill somebody. He'd probably view it as a necessary sacrifice on the altar of progress. With that thought, he resolved to walk home slowly despite his rumbling stomach.

'That said, I think he may be onto something,' Gregory added. 'I was reluctant to test the formula on myself, so I experimented on some animal subjects a short while ago. They became quickly unresponsive, proving impervious to painful stimuli. I was intending to check on them again, but your arrival distracted me.'

'What manner of animals?' Raven asked.

'A couple of conies.'

'Do you have a lot of rabbits that you experiment on?'

'No, just the two over there.'

Raven felt something solidify within him, like mercury in the chill. He reached into the crate, placing a hand on each of the rabbits in case he had misapprehended their condition.

He had not.

'These rabbits are quite dead. How much did you give them?'

'It was but the slightest dose of vapour. A single drop upon the muslin.'

A single drop.

Raven bolted from the lab, clattering his way down the staircases and halls. In keeping with the normal testing practice, Simpson and the others would be gathered around the dining table, dispensing ever more liberal quantities, sniffing it deeper and deeper until it had an effect or was declared useless. He had to get back to Queen Street, though it may already be too late.

Raven barrelled out of the college and onto rain-swept Nicholson Street, where he looked about for a hansom cab. He didn't have the funds for such a journey but he would borrow the fare from the professor, and if he got there too late, payment would be the least of his worries.

The streets were all but empty: a few damp souls wending their way home upon the pavements, and not a carriage to be seen. Ruefully he recalled guests to Queen Street complaining that there was never a cab to be had in Edinburgh, particularly when it rained. The hour was late too: most respectable people would be digesting their dinner or preparing for their beds. The only people on the street were drunks. One of them swayed into his path, suddenly enraged and irrationally regarding Raven as his enemy. He screamed out an oath and challenged him to fight. Raven checked his stride and harmlessly passed around him.

Then up ahead he saw a carriage approach the junction with Infirmary Street. The gentleman inside was bound to have heard of the professor. Surely he would assist when he heard how he was imperilled.

Raven ran towards it, waving his arms and beseeching the

coachman to stop. He heard an urgent voice from within as the coachman urged his steeds to hurry, cracking his whip at the approaching Raven to warn him off. He was not surprised. He must have looked like a madman trying to attack them.

He had no option but to run. And though it burn his muscles and crush his lungs, he would drive himself without rest until he reached Queen Street.

He calculated the most direct route as he ran, his splashing footsteps echoing off the buildings. The rhythm of his lengthening stride was soon accompanied by another beat in his chest, though he felt a welcome easing as his route took him steeply downhill on Cockburn Street, where he was able to run faster with less cost to legs and lungs. As he picked up momentum, he skidded on something – he didn't stop to consider what – and almost tumbled. It was a near thing: a twisted ankle would have ended his mercy dash right then and there.

Righting himself, he stepped up the pace again, his eyes trained upon the flagstone and cobbles, straining to pick out potential hazards in the gloom. Then he felt an impact that shuddered every bone, and almost bit through his tongue as his teeth clattered together. It felt as though he had run into a wall, except walls weren't usually warm and clad in cloth. He rebounded and tumbled to the ground, feeling a blow against his thigh and a crack as the jar in his pocket smashed between his falling weight and the hard stone beneath. As he tried to focus in his daze, two horribly familiar faces loomed over him beneath the glow of a street lamp.

He had run straight into the Weasel and Gargantua.

THIRTY-NINE

aven felt Gargantua's huge hands about his shoulders, gripping him and hauling him upright like he was a carcass in a slaughterhouse.

'Mr Raven,' the Weasel said, a vicious delight dripping from his voice. 'What a lovely surprise to run into you. Now, do you know what time it is?'

He theatrically produced Raven's father's pocket watch and dangled it from its chain.

'Well past time you paid up – either in coin or in kind. I think I said an eye, didn't I?'

The Weasel put the watch back in his pocket and took out the same blade that had ripped Raven's face the last time they met.

Raven started at the sight of it, but Gargantua's hands held him firm.

He felt sick with fear. He was barely able to think of anything other than the pain he would endure, but some part of him was thinking of the consequences beyond. Could he still have a career with one eye? It was a moot question, he realised. Being held here and mutilated meant his mission tonight was at an end. With Simpson dead, he would have no apprenticeship anyway. It was all about to be lost, for the price of trying to help Evie.

To add insult to imminent injury, he hadn't even helped her. In fact, it was quite possible he had merely borrowed the means by which she purchased her own death.

Fear caused his mind to race, revisiting the events of the evening like he was experiencing them all simultaneously. Every sight, every smell, every sensation and emotion flashed before him, and amidst it all, something stuck.

Raven's shoulders remained gripped, but his hands were free and he could bend his elbow.

'No, I have it,' he implored. 'I have Mr Flint's money upon me. Please, I beg you. I have just sold a treasured heirloom and I have it here in my pocket.'

Mindful of the broken glass, he dipped his fingers carefully and scooped up a quantity of the red powder. Then he closed his eyes and tossed it backwards into his captor's face.

Gargantua let go immediately and spun away, bending over and howling as he put his hands to his eyes. Even as he did so, Raven was scooping another handful, which he cupped in his outraised palm and blew, sending a red cloud to engulf the Weasel's eyes, nose and mouth.

The Weasel fell, his screams echoing about the walls, while behind him Gargantua remained bent, emitting a low moan and muttering about being blinded by hot coals.

Raven crouched over the Weasel and swiftly retrieved his stolen pocket watch. Would that time itself could be recovered so easily.

Raven resumed his running, powering down the grass of the Mound in darkness, his eyes fixed on the lights of Princes Street ahead. His heart was fluttering both from his fear and from his exertion, but he felt as though some analgesic draught was surging through him, dulling the pains in his legs and in his chest.

The draught had worn off by the time he was careering down Frederick Street, but by that time gravity was assisting his flight. He almost flattened a gentleman alighting from a carriage as he turned the last corner, the front door of No. 52 in sight ahead of him. He barely dared to consider what awaited him behind it.

Raven burst into the hall past a startled Jarvis, his thighs screaming from his efforts. His breath was so short he feared he would not have enough left to speak, but as he bowled through the door into the dining room, he discovered that it didn't matter.

He was too late.

The room was in disarray. The lace tablecloth was hanging askew, a number of glass tumblers lay smashed upon the wooden floor and several of the dining-room chairs were on their sides. Amongst the detritus on the floor, beneath the mahogany table, were the lifeless bodies of three men: Simpson, Keith, and one he did not recognise. A fourth, James Duncan, was slumped face-down on the table, a single bottle open in front of him next to a folded cloth.

Raven cursed the man. In his blasted quest for a place in history, he had killed them all.

FORTY

arah carried a tray into the drawing room bearing a pot of tea, three cups and a tray of fancies. She did not think that anyone could still be hungry after the bounteous meal she had watched them consume, but she was aware of Agnes Petrie's eyes tracing the progress of the little cakes from door to table. Mina often claimed to have 'a second compartment for sweet things' to excuse how she fell upon such treats after a generous dinner, though Sarah had noticed that her habits had been more abstemious in recent times: specifically since Dr Beattie started showing an interest in her.

The ladies had retired upstairs to the drawing room while the gentlemen remained around the dining table to commence the professor's preferred after-dinner pursuit: that of testing new candidates to improve upon ether as a drowsy syrup. Drs Simpson, Keith and Duncan were joined by a layperson, Captain James Petrie, but as he described himself as 'a man of intrepid spirit', he had had no qualms about throwing his weight behind the medical men's pioneering quest.

Captain Petrie was Mrs Simpson and Mina's brother-in-law, the widower of their late sister. He was a voluble personality, a man who looked like he did not quite belong amidst domestic gentility. He had been friendly and polite to the staff, however.

Indeed, while Sarah waited at the table, he had asked her to pass on his compliments to Mrs Lyndsey for a remarkable meal, though it became retrospectively clear that this was merely a pretext for him to hold forth on the subject of 'the only meal I might be permitted to consider more remarkable'.

He proceeded to talk at length of his exploits defending Britain's interests in the American War, telling of how in 1814, following victory in the Battle of Bladensburg, his company had marched on Washington. 'We took the city with such swiftness and audacity that James Madison's dinner was still warm upon the table when we stormed his house and set it ablaze. I fetched a leather-bound book of poetry from the library shelves and briefly sat down to finish the abandoned meal before the flames took over, for it is a sin to waste good food.'

Sarah was most impressed with this tale, thinking Captain Petrie sounded gallant and colourful; certainly a good deal less dusty than most of the grey-faced medical men who had dined there. It was only as they ascended the staircase that she overheard Mrs Simpson say to Mina: 'I wonder how many times we have sat through him telling that story.'

'Almost as many as the number of soldiers who claim to have eaten of that meal,' Mina replied. 'Truly, it must have been quite a plateful.'

This exchange had, of course, taken place out of earshot of Agnes Petrie, the captain's daughter and Mrs Simpson's niece. Agnes was a plump and rather giddy creature who did not strike Sarah as blessed with the highest level of intelligence, though at least this did not mean another fine female mind condemned to atrophy through disuse. Neither had she inherited her father's easy grace in dealing with the staff, and came across as a rather spoiled and self-regarding young woman.

Sarah was pouring the tea when the entire house was shaken by the crash of the front door being thrown open against the wall. It was followed by a sound like rumbling thunder, the shuddering thump of someone rushing down the hall with such haste and force of weight that she could feel it vibrate through the boards beneath her feet.

'What on earth is that?' asked Mrs Simpson.

Sarah hastened to investigate, the ladies rising to their feet at her back. She looked over the banister and observed Jarvis standing against the wall with an affronted expression upon his face.

'What occurs?'

'Mr Raven just came charging through here like he had the devil at his heels,' he said.

Sarah hastened downstairs into the dining room. She found Raven crouched over Dr Simpson, who lay face-down upon the floor, the bodies of Dr Keith and Captain Petrie motionless alongside. Raven rolled Dr Simpson over and placed his ear to his chest.

'He breathes,' he announced, panting heavily, a near-tearful anxiety in his voice. He was soaking wet, his hair plastered to his face, which was red with exertion.

'You've been running.'

'I rushed here from Gregory's lab,' Raven said, still struggling to catch his breath. 'The formula Duncan ordered is poisonous. It rendered two rabbits unconscious before killing them shortly after. I fear it may yet do the same here.'

Sarah noticed a bottle sitting on the table where Dr Duncan sat slumped, his arms sprawled before him as though reaching for it. She recognised the handwriting on the label.

'But this bottle isn't from Professor Gregory. It came from Duncan and Flockhart. "Perchloride of formyle",' she read.

She handed it to him, Raven's hand outstretched impatiently. He read the label, a look of confusion upon his face, and as he did so, Dr Simpson's eyes opened.

Sarah thought back to earlier in the day, when she had come here to prepare the dining room and lay the table for dinner. She had found easily a dozen bottles untidily ranged on top of the sideboard, still others seemingly abandoned on the floor. As she endeavoured to tidy the former away, she had knocked one onto its side, causing it to roll to the back where it dropped into the gap between the wall and the cabinet.

She didn't have the strength to move the sideboard on her own, and besides, at that moment, Dr Duncan had come in and begun chastising her for interfering. She therefore decided it best not to mention how she had just mislaid one of his bottles.

Dr Simpson tried to sit up then lay back again, blinking several times and looking at his surroundings as though they did not make sense. Sarah fetched a cushion to help support his head as Mrs Simpson and Mina appeared in the doorway.

'Oh, dear heavens, what has happened?' Mina asked.

Mrs Simpson rolled her eyes. Clearly it was not the first time she had witnessed such a sight.

The professor focused upon his wife and propped himself up with his elbow. He looked at the concerned faces crowded above him and smiled.

'This is far stronger and better than ether,' he said.

Dr Keith was next to stir, but there was no gentle waking for him. Instead he began to thrash about, kicking at the table as though trying to overturn the few items that had thus far managed to remain upright upon it. This was accompanied by loud snoring on the part of Dr Duncan.

After several minutes of this, Dr Duncan began to rouse and George Keith, having ceased his semi-conscious violence, raised himself to his knees. He gripped the table, only his eyes visible above the edge, and stared in an unfocused way, with a hauntingly vacant expression on his face, as though his human spirit had abandoned him. For some reason he directed this ghastly gaze at Mina, who looked reciprocally transfixed, horrified by what she was seeing. Thus, just as everyone else was regaining either consciousness or composure, Mina threatened to faint. An upturned chair was righted for her, and Sarah was dispatched to find her fan and fetch her a glass of water.

Dr Simpson climbed to his feet, assisted by his wife.

'Waldie was right,' he declared, delight in his voice. 'This is by far the most promising of all our experiments.' He looked about himself eagerly. 'Where has it gone? Is there any left?'

The sopping Raven held out the bottle to him, but Mrs Simpson gestured him away.

'I think perhaps we have all had enough excitement for one evening.'

The professor would not be denied. 'But this is just the beginning. We may well have found what we have been searching for. Who else would like to try?'

Mina was first to find her voice. But not in the affirmative. 'I for one will not be making such an exhibition of myself. The look on Dr Keith's face just now will haunt me for the rest of my days.'

'Oh, come away now, Mina. It may be your chance to form part of history.'

Dr Simpson grabbed the bottle from Raven, removed the stopper and waved it in Mina's direction. Looking suddenly alarmed, Mina got out of her chair and backed away from him. The professor then began to chase her round the table as she shrieked her objection.

The pursuit was short-lived as Dr Simpson subsided into laughter and had to give up. Raven rescued the bottle before its contents were inadvertently poured onto the carpet.

'I'll try it,' said a voice, which turned out to belong to Agnes Petrie. She had been standing in the doorway and now pushed forward into the room. 'Oh, do let me have some.'

Dr Simpson looked to her father, who nodded assent. Sarah suspected he had said no to few requests where his daughter was appellant.

Agnes squeezed herself into a dining-room chair and began to inhale the saucer of liquid that had been poured for her. Within a matter of moments, her eyelids fluttered and she declared herself to be lighter than air, which seemed all the more remarkable given her size. She then began shouting 'I'm an angel, I'm an angel,' before sliding to the floor in a manner far removed from the seraphic. She remained there, peacefully unconscious, for a full five minutes.

Dr Simpson decided he would try it upon himself again, ignoring the concerned looks of his wife. Dr Duncan joined him and Dr Keith took out his pocket watch to time the duration of the drug's effect.

'Perchloride of formyle,' Keith stated, taking a note. 'Somewhat more of a mouthful than "ether". Can we give it a shortened name?'

As Dr Simpson raised the glass to his nose, he paused momentarily. 'I believe Waldie said it was also known as "chloroform".'

FORTY-ONE

arah watched Raven quietly withdraw from the dining room, suspecting she was the only one who noticed. Everyone else remained fixated upon the experiments, though in Mrs Simpson and Mina's cases this seemed more an act of vigilance than enthusiasm.

Raven had observed the recent activities wordlessly, and declined the offer of partaking in subsequent experiments. The man looked drained. He had turned up looking like he'd been pulled from the river, and if anything for a while he had become wetter. The warmth of the room made him sweat all the more following what appeared to have been considerable exertions. It had been half an hour before his face returned to a normal colour.

None of the people he had exhausted himself to protect were even aware of his efforts. That they had never truly been in danger because of Sarah's earlier mishap was something she decided she should not immediately share with him, though he would have to be told.

With the hour drawing on and her own services seeming superfluous in the face of this new distraction, she followed him out a few moments later, ascending the stairs at his back. He heard her and stopped just before reaching his room, turning to see who was there.

'Would you like some supper, Mr Raven?' she asked. 'You didn't eat yet.'

He managed a weak smile. 'That would be most welcome.'

His voice had a tremor to it. She realised he must be cold now, and would get colder.

'You need to get out of those clothes at once. You'll catch a fever. Come on,' she said, following him into his room, where she lit a gas lamp. She turned to help him remove his jacket, which felt twice its normal weight.

'I'm perfectly capable . . .' he began, then seemed to surrender to her assistance, lacking the strength or the will to resist.

'You really need to get yourself a proper coat, Mr Raven. Before winter truly bites.'

'I know.'

She lifted the damp garment from his shoulders, her gaze drawn by how his hair was stuck flat about his face.

'You ran all the way from the college?'

'Yes, but that was not even the worst part of my evening. I watched a young woman die in agony before me at the Maternity Hospital. And I am certain she died the same way as Evie: racked with spasms, and pregnant too.'

'"Racked with spasms": the way Miss Mann described one who had taken strychnine?'

'Precisely. But what is confounding is that earlier today, I met McLevy, and he said that there was no trace of poison in Rose Campbell's remains. More confounding still, that neither was she found to be pregnant.'

Sarah could well understand Raven's consternation. One part of this made sense to her, however.

'I have been reading about strychnine in Christison's *Treatise*. An added boon to any malefactor is that there *is* no test for it. It would not be traceable in any post-mortem examination. So it remains entirely possible that strychnine was responsible for Rose's death.'

'Yes, but there is an irrefutable post-mortem test for pregnancy, and McLevy insisted no baby was found.'

This part, Sarah had to concede, truly was confounding.

'Milly was not mistaken about this,' she argued. 'It is the very reason Rose feared she would be dismissed.'

'McLevy insists otherwise, and they cannot both be right.'

But as Raven spoke, Sarah realised there existed a reason that they could.

'Perhaps she was not pregnant by the time she went into the water. What if she successfully rid herself of her unwanted burden? Strychnine brings on spasms. Could it have been used in a medicine to bring on the contractions of premature labour, which in Rose's case it succeeded, only for her to die later?'

Raven's eyes widened. 'It is my suspicion that the girl who died tonight took something to get rid of her child. Perhaps Evie did too, but in each of their cases, it killed them before it could have any other effect.'

'Who was this girl? Could she have any connection to the Reverend Grissom?'

Raven wore a look of regret. 'I know nothing about her. Not even her full name, only that she was known as Kitty. I know not where she lived, other than that it was near enough for a man to have carried her there. But in the Old Town, that radius might include a thousand dwellings.'

His voice wavered again, shivers taking him. Even his shirt was wet through. Without asking, she began to unbutton it for him.

Sarah had seen Raven fully naked when he first arrived and was in need of a bath. This felt different, now that she knew something of him. She recalled her words – *whatever you've got, I've seen it before* – and though she had now indeed seen him before, this time her eyes wished to dwell.

Her hand brushed his chest as she tugged at his wet shirt, the cloth sticking to skin. She felt something surge inside herself, and the insistence of it unnerved her.

As she undid the final button, she sensed a stirring close to where she touched him, and belatedly understood what was meant by the expression 'proud below the navel'.

Raven flinched away from her in response, presumably because he could not flinch away from himself.

Sarah stepped back from him, looking to the floor.

'You must be starving,' she said quietly. 'I'd best get down to the kitchen and fetch you something to eat.'

He said nothing as she departed. She waited a moment outside his door, as she felt so light-headed as to fear she might trip on her descent.

Upon reaching the kitchen, Sarah took a plate and gathered some leftover pie, a slice of ham and a hunk of bread. She held it in her left hand, grabbed a bottle of ale with her right, then made for the stairs once again.

When she reached the top landing, she found Raven deeply unconscious, and no chemical agent had been necessary to produce the effect.

FORTY-TWO

arah entered Kennington and Jenner's on Princes Street and was immediately grateful to be out of the cold. Her callused hands were cracked and sore, the result of washing household linens the day before. Her hands were always bad in the winter. The cold made everything worse.

The shop was warm and inviting, a place she had always enjoyed spending time, fancying what she might buy if she only had the money. It was always brightly lit either by daylight streaming in through the windows that lined the front of the shop or from the large gas chandeliers that hung from the ceiling. Bolts of cloth in every conceivable colour were stacked on shelves, smaller samples of fabric arrayed across the counters.

The shop had been established by two draper's assistants who had found themselves out of work following an unauthorised leave of absence to attend the races at Musselburgh. In opening their own store they had been determined to provide the ladies of Edinburgh with the finest silks and linens, previously only available in London. They had thus far been successful in their endeavours, having recently acquired the neighbouring premises to expand their textile emporium.

Sarah liked this story; ordinary people making their own way in the world. It gave her hope. Or at least it used to. Now

Kennington and Jenner's would always remind her of the last time she saw Rose Campbell, a young woman cut down in her prime, all her potential lost. It would make her think of the husk Rose had become even before she died: ground down by a life of servitude, a dead-eyed and depleted version of the girl whose confidence and energy Sarah once found intimidating.

She gazed at the fabrics that were, as always, elaborately displayed. Today yards of expensive material in a variety of vibrant hues had been pinned to a high point on one wall and allowed to cascade down onto one of the counters as though a flood had occurred. She used to daydream about the goods on offer in this place. Now they seemed an affront, and not merely because the limitations placed upon her meant she would never own such luxuries. They served to remind her that it wasn't only those women below stairs who would never be permitted to realise their potential. Those above could aspire to no more than marriage and motherhood, and thus were encouraged to fuss over fripperies as they concerned themselves with how they might adorn themselves the better to please men.

Sarah would have turned and departed from the place if she could, its previous pleasant associations tarnished, but her time was not her own to command and she was obliged to go wherever she was sent. She had been dispatched by Mina to collect a length of black velvet, ordered the week before, which was to be made into a cape to go with her new evening gown.

She proceeded towards the main counter, but as she approached it she became aware of a familiar smell, of citrus and sandalwood, though it was a fragrance that seemed incongruous here among women's finery. This, she realised, was because she associated it with a man, and there indeed he stood at a sales counter, in conversation with the assistant.

Sarah loitered behind a pillar, reluctant to be seen and perhaps recognised. Beattie never struck her as the type to notice much about servants beyond the pair of hands that was handing him something, but having accompanied Mina so often, if he was going to remember any housemaid, it would be her. His attention was upon the counter, however, so she felt emboldened to peer around the pillar, which was close enough for her to overhear the exchange taking place.

Beattie was turning a pair of gloves over in his hands upon the counter top.

'These are the very best that we have, sir. Kid, although we have silk and cotton too if you would prefer to see those.'

'It has to be kid. Silk and cotton are a little vulgar, don't you think?'

Sarah watched the assistant nodding in agreement, beaming pleasantly, flattered by Beattie's easy charm.

She looked again at her own hands, turning from white to red in the warmth of the shop. She knew that she ought to be reassured by what she was witnessing. Buying expensive gifts was, after all, the way a man was expected to show his affection, and Mina would be delighted with such a token. Yet Sarah felt a persistent unease. On paper, when all was totted up, he seemed eminently suitable, but she couldn't help thinking there was something beneath the veneer that was not as it appeared.

Whenever she raised her concerns about how sketchy their knowledge of him was, Mina was ready with excuses. Little could be known as to his background, as both his parents were dead. Beattie's father had been a merchant, his unfortunate early demise much lamented. His mother hailed from just outside Edinburgh, on the Morningside. She was survived by her brother, one Charles Latimer, who still lived in the family home he had inherited in Canaan Lands. He was a frail man, more or less confined to his house these days, but it was furnished with large gardens and had views to the surrounding countryside, which made it an agreeable confinement. 'The uncle has a large hothouse,' Mina had said, 'wherein he grows exotic fruit and flowers. I have been promised orchids and pineapples.'

Such treasures, Sarah noted, had so far not been forthcoming.

Mr Latimer's home sounded very much like Millbank, where Professor Syme lived, half an hour's walk from Princes Street but far removed from the smoke and bustle of the city (and more significantly from his patients). It had extensive gardens and beautiful views towards Blackford Hill. Sarah knew this because Mrs Lyndsay had a relative who worked there.

Mrs Lyndsay often made comparisons between the regime at Millbank and that of Queen Street, trying to inculcate a sense of gratitude in Sarah about her place of work. She was conscious of Sarah's restlessness and talk of wanting more than she had. To Mrs Lyndsay's mind, this lack of appreciation was likely to provoke some form of divine intervention that would see Sarah much reduced in circumstances by way of punishment.

Sarah remained unconcerned about providential retribution, being more troubled by Mina's mention of the debt currently being accrued by Beattie as he struggled to establish himself in medical practice in Edinburgh.

'Don't look so alarmed,' Mina had said. 'It is often how things are in the beginning. Dr Simpson himself owed a considerable sum of money at the time he married my sister.'

Perhaps, Sarah had thought, but Beattie is no Simpson.

Sarah watched him as the assistant wrapped his purchase. Oblivious of any onlooker, his gaze lingered upon the girl's behind as she bent to retrieve paper and string from a drawer beneath the counter. Sarah had never seen him look at Mina that way, but it was Mina he was buying gloves for, so perhaps she should be assured that it was this way round.

When the assistant presented the bill, Beattie told her to add it to his account. He then picked up his package and made for the door with an unhurried gait, the smell of his cologne lingering long after his departure.

FORTY-THREE

aven doubted there had been a more crowded meeting of the Medico-Chirurgical Society. News of chloroform had already begun to spread throughout the city's medical men, though the knowledge that Simpson and Syme were both to be present no doubt played a part too. The prospect of an argument between these two known adversaries would often draw a crowd.

Though this was to be the first formal announcement of his discovery, Simpson was making no secret of his new anaesthetic agent, and had used it in an obstetric case a mere four days after the experiments at Queen Street. He was called to see a Mrs Jane Carstairs in Albany Street, the wife of a physician recently retired from the Indian Medical Service. A difficult labour was anticipated due to a previous confinement having lasted three days and ending with the baby's head having to be broken up to permit extraction. (Raven frequently had to remind himself that many infants did in fact make it into the world alive and fully intact.)

Mrs Carstairs was persuaded to try the chloroform when her pains became severe.

'I've taken it myself,' Simpson assured her. 'It is really quite pleasant.'

Half a teaspoon of liquid was poured onto a pocket handkerchief, which he rolled into a funnel shape and held over her nose and mouth. She quickly drifted off into what appeared to be a comfortable sleep, and the child was born without difficulty some twenty-five minutes later.

The crying of the newborn had failed to rouse the sleeping mother, which caused Raven to feel a pang of anxiety at the memory of Caroline Graseby. His hands became sweaty, his mouth dry and he found himself offering a silent prayer to a God he was convinced had no interest in helping him. Punishing him, yes. Helping him, no.

The placenta was expelled and the child removed by the nurse to another room before the mother began to waken. But waken she did, to Raven's profound relief. When she had returned to full consciousness she expressed her gratitude at having been provided with such a restful sleep. 'I now feel quite restored and better able to deal with the trial ahead of me,' she said, which to Raven did not sound like the most optimistic view of motherhood. Then he noticed the look of concern spreading upon her face.

'I fear that my sleeping has somehow stopped the pains.'

Simpson smiled and patted her hand. 'Your trial is at an end,' he said.

He called to the nurse in the next room, who appeared with the newly bathed and swaddled child, to the mother's astonishment.

'I cannot believe it,' she said. 'It is a miracle. She is here and I have suffered hardly at all.'

'Perhaps you should name her Anaesthesia,' Simpson suggested.

At that juncture, she had discovered a limit to her gratitude.

The meeting was called to order by the society's president, Professor William Pulteney Alison, and the audience began to settle themselves into their seats. Raven noticed Henry in the crowd and quickly beckoned his friend sit with him. He had spotted Beattie also but failed to catch his eye in the throng.

'Is this new discovery truly better than ether?' Henry asked as he sat down.

'So much so that even Syme might be convinced to use it.'

Henry looked sceptical, as Raven knew he might. This was a long-standing source of frustration. 'Then may he set the rest of the dominoes to fall,' he replied. 'There are still surgeons who believe that the patient's pain serves as a useful guide to their endeavours. In my opinion, this merely demonstrates that they lack a sound knowledge of anatomy and the appropriate skill.'

'Simpson receives letters from the outraged on a regular basis.'

'Yes, you told me about the Reverend Grissom and his leaflets. The primeval curse and all that.'

'In fact, the religious types tend not to write. The most vociferous correspondents are other obstetricians. Barnes, Lee and Gream in London; Meigs in Philadelphia.'

'And what is their objection?'

'God, nature and bad language.'

Henry looked at him askance. 'Please explain.'

'Pain in labour is natural, a manifestation of the life force, an ordinance from the Almighty and therefore painless childbirth is unnatural and improper. Under the influence of anaesthesia, some women have been heard to use obscene and disgusting language – words that they should never have had the opportunity to hear – which of course means that it is wrong ever to employ it.'

Henry began to laugh. 'I can't imagine any of the women of my acquaintance sharing such concerns. What does Simpson say about it?'

'That the same logic would suggest it is unnatural to wear clothes, to use condiments in aid of digestion, and the stagecoach to relieve ourselves of the fatigue induced by walking.'

Dr Simpson stood and walked to the podium. Silence descended upon the crowded hall.

'I wish to direct the attention of the members of the society

to a new respirable anaesthetic agent which I have discovered,'
he began.

Simpson proceeded to outline the events which had led to the
successful trial of chloroform and stressed the many advantages
it had over ether: the relatively small dose required; a more rapid
and persistent action; a more agreeable smell; and that no special
equipment was necessary for its administration.

When he concluded his presentation, there was much discussion amongst the assembled throng, many of those present asking
if they could try it for themselves. A bottle of the stuff appeared
and chloroform was liberally applied to several handkerchiefs,
which were then passed round. One arrived in Henry's hand and
he put it to his nose.

'Don't let it touch your skin,' Raven warned him, indicating
a tender spot beneath the bridge of his own nose. 'Direct contact
results in irritation, like a burn. I learned that the hard way.'

Henry inhaled but there was an insufficient dose on the handkerchief to produce anything more than a pleasant feeling of
intoxication. The effect was nonetheless enough that Henry took
a seat, which cleared a line of sight between Raven and Beattie.
He began striding across the room, intent upon sampling the
stuff himself. James Duncan made his way over also, no doubt
keen to claim his role in the new agent's discovery.

'May I?' Beattie asked, though his hand was already gripping
the bottle.

'By all means,' Raven replied, watching him pour an injudicious dose onto the cloth.

He considered warning them about direct contact, but held
his tongue, some bitter instinct eager to inflict damage upon
Duncan for a change. More surprising was an ambivalence about
Beattie inflicting a mark upon his otherwise unblemished face.
Raven was not sure where this unpleasant sentiment came from;
perhaps a lingering anger over his scar, or a latent resentment at
Beattie having dragged him into the Graseby incident. (That was

how he thought of it – the Graseby incident. He was unable even within the confines of his own head to label it for what it was: a death for which he was responsible.)

Beattie having over-soaked the handkerchief, the vapours hit him before he might press it to his face. He lay himself down on a bench as around him others staggered and fell over. Beattie slept peacefully for several minutes, during which time Raven found himself making a careful study of his deceptively youthful features, contemplating how old he truly was, and what events had shaped him. Raven wondered also at his greater ability to deal with their shared disaster. Granted, the larger part of the blame lay upon Raven for attempting something beyond his experience, but Beattie seemed untroubled by remorse while Raven was incessantly tortured by what had occurred that day. Was he really as unperturbed as he appeared? Was such detachment a good thing in a doctor? A necessity for self-preservation? Perhaps it was.

He knew it was unworthy, given all Beattie had done for him, but again he felt a sting of envy towards the man: of what he had and of all he was going to have. No doubt he would soon marry Mina, which as Sarah noted, would instantly confer a considerable advantage in his field. That was how it went: a doctor from a wealthy background would swoop in, trade on his association with the great Dr Simpson and accumulate a wealthy client list on the back of it. Raven, by comparison, would merely pass through the house and be gone, replaced by another apprentice once he had served his time, then promptly forgotten.

Henry got to his feet, regarding the host of sleeping doctors around him with some amusement. 'I do hope I can come to Queen Street some evening and participate in the experiments there,' he said.

'Be careful what you wish for,' Raven replied, thinking about the prostrate forms lying under the dining-room table.

'Why?'

'There is a want of caution which at times disturbs me. I have no wish to sacrifice myself at the altar of scientific progress.'

Duncan scoffed. 'Boldness and a certain want of caution are necessary for scientific progress to be made,' he said.

'I'm not convinced lives should be put at risk,' Raven replied.

'We should certainly be endeavouring to make our methods more scientific,' Henry suggested. 'With the use of statistics and experimentation, we would soon get rid of the quacks, charlatans and snake-oil salesmen once and for all.'

'But there must always be room for a certain degree of resourcefulness, inventiveness, ingenuity,' Duncan argued. 'And the march of progress should not be restrained by faint hearts.'

Raven looked at him, wondering if this statement was general or making reference to particular circumstances.

'Simpson likes to think of medicine as more than pure science,' he countered. 'There must also be empathy, concern, a human connection.'

'I suggest that both elements are required,' offered Henry. 'Scientific principles married to creativity. Science and art.'

If it is an art, it is at times a dark one, Raven thought, though he chose to keep this observation to himself.

FORTY-FOUR

ohn Beattie was in Dr Simpson's study, an unusually sincere expression upon his face as he sat opposite the professor. Sarah had brought in a pot of tea and was prolonging the pouring of it in order to ascertain what was being discussed, as the mood suggested something of great import.

She often thought that the household's preoccupation with tea-drinking provided her with untrammelled access to important conversations: hers was such a familiar presence that it was sometimes as though they all ceased to see her. However, there was only so much time to be taken in the pouring of tea without breaking this spell, and Sarah was forced to leave just as Dr Simpson tantalisingly stated: 'You will of course have to write to her father in Liverpool, but in truth I can foresee no objection.'

Sarah had to stifle a gasp as she left the room. This could mean only one thing. She hovered just outside the door in her determination to hear what else was being said.

'What of Mr Latimer?' Dr Simpson continued. 'Is he happy with the arrangement?'

'My uncle is terribly frail at the moment and his physician has proscribed excitement of any kind. A visit is therefore out of the question, but a carefully worded letter has been written and sent. I expect a reply imminently. I have no doubt he will be entirely in agreement with the match. It will do much for his morale, in fact.'

Sarah's joy on Mina's behalf was short-lived, giving way instantly to suspicion. How convenient that the old man could receive no visitors. She was also annoyed at these discussions taking place in the absence of Mina herself. It was as though she was the inanimate part of a business transaction, a consignment of whale oil or shares in a coal mine – profits could not be guaranteed but the prospects were good.

Sarah was so intent upon hearing what was being said on the other side of the door that she did not hear an approach from behind her, and consequently jumped at the sound of someone clearing his throat.

'What are you doing, Miss Fisher?' Raven said with open amusement, though from the merciful quietness of his tone it was clear he knew precisely what she was doing.

Sarah scowled at him and put her finger to her lips. She turned back to the door to listen again but the sound of footsteps on the stairs put a definitive end to her eavesdropping.

She pulled Raven into an adjoining room to avoid them being seen. They stood in silence, waiting for whoever ascended the staircase to pass, her hands on his lapels. She was sharply aware of his proximity. His breathing seemed loud in her ears and she sensed the heat coming from him. He smelled clean, of soap, and his clothes had benefited from being properly laundered and mended. His overall appearance had improved considerably in his time at Queen Street, in fact. His face had lost its gauntness, having filled out from regular food. An image of him naked in his bath on that first day came to mind, and Sarah felt her cheeks flush at the memory. She was glad that he was unlikely to notice: as the room was unoccupied, the lamps had not been lit.

She realised she was clinging on to him and let go, embarrassed.

'Care to tell me what is so compelling?' Raven asked.

'It's Beattie. He has asked for Mina's hand.'

'Well, we all knew that was coming.'

He seemed oddly regretful about this, and yet resigned to it.

'I don't like it,' she stated.

'It is hardly a matter for you or me whether we like it or not.'

'I have my concerns. There is a whiff of deceit about that man. I can sense it.'

'Are you still suspicious that he did not tell Mina about this Julia? Because it is hardly a damning omission. What woman would wish the ghost of another haunting her marriage?'

Sarah felt a surge of irritation. 'He hasn't given her the gloves,' she said.

'What gloves? What are you talking about?'

Sarah tutted at her own impatience. She had sought to clarify things for him, but only succeeded in confusing him further.

'I saw him buying ladies' gloves and assumed they were a gift for Mina, but he has not given them to her.'

'Perhaps he intends to give them to her at a later date.'

'Perhaps he intends to give them to someone else. And there have been no orchids. Or pineapples for that matter.'

'Sarah, you are making little sense.'

'He promised gifts from his uncle's hothouse and they too have failed to arrive.'

'What is it exactly that you suspect?'

Sarah had no ready answer for him. There was something about Beattie that troubled her, but she could not put it into words.

'And anyway, what can you do about it?' he asked.

Looking back, Sarah might have left it at that, but the assumption that she was powerless lit a fire under her.

Why it burned the hotter for coming from Raven was a question she did not wish to dwell upon.

FORTY-FIVE

he final outcome of any sequence of events can turn on many pivots: there is always a multiplicity of nodes, intersections in a fragile system of happenstance whereby the slightest divergence at one would have altered all. The fate of chloroform and the mystery of Evie's death were intertwined in just such a system, and either could have easily been diverted down a path to a dead end by the slightest whim of chance.

For instance, Professor Miller was equally enthusiastic about his Queen Street neighbour's discovery and was keen to be among the first to use it in a surgical case. A messenger had arrived at No. 52 the day after the Carstairs case, looking for Simpson to administer chloroform to a patient suffering from a strangulated hernia at the Infirmary. Unfortunately, the doctor was not at home and his whereabouts unknown, prompting Raven to once more lament the lack of an appointment book, as well as to wonder if the refusal to keep one was a deliberate tactic to hide the doctor's more clandestine calls. Several students, including Raven, were dispatched to find him, but to no avail. Sarah even suggested Raven stand in for the professor. He scoffed at this proposal but was secretly pleased that she thought him capable of such a thing.

Professor Miller was forced to proceed without any anaesthesia, as the surgery could not wait. Upon the first incision, the
patient fainted and could not be revived. He died with the operation unfinished. If chloroform had been administered, it would
have been blamed. If Raven had administered it, so would he.

Dr Simpson posited that it was fortunate he could not be
found on this particular occasion. The damage to chloroform's
reputation at this early juncture could have been irreparable.
Raven felt obliged to comment that this was surely no justification for not keeping an appointment book.

Though it was not ultimately crucial in terms of the information it imparted, Raven would have reason of his own to thank
serendipity, given how easily a particular encounter that occurred
shortly after this might never have taken place.

It was amidst the chaos of the morning clinic, such sessions
becoming steadily more crowded as the weather grew colder.
Raven emerged from his consulting room to summon his next
patient and found himself confronted by Mitchell, the burly
individual who had conveyed poor Kitty in his arms but left
without conveying much else. Had Raven been delayed a little
longer by the previous patient, or had George Keith finished with
his but ten seconds sooner, Mitchell might have passed through
and been gone again without Raven seeing him.

It had been a hectic – if exciting – time since the night their
paths last crossed, given it had been the same night Simpson
discovered the effects of chloroform. The matter of Kitty's death
was seldom far from Raven's mind, but opportunities to investigate further had been limited. Not only was he hard-pressed to
find time away from his duties, but a greater factor was his
reluctance to traverse the Old Town other than via the safety of
Simpson's carriage. He knew that Flint's men would be looking
for him with redoubled interest now, and in certain cases with
vengeance on their minds. It seemed reasonable to fear that Flint
might even wish to make an example of him.

Raven had briefly happened upon Peggy, who had shared lodgings with Evie at Mrs Peake's house. He asked if she had heard of a girl named Kitty, but was sent away with a flea in his ear when he further explained that they shared a profession. 'We don't all know each other,' she scolded him. 'We're not all friends, or some sisterhood of hoors.'

Mitchell stood clutching his cap in much the same posture he had done before. When he looked up, his expression betrayed that he recognised Raven, though a degree of puzzlement indicated further that he did not remember from where.

Raven showed him into the seclusion of his consulting room and let him outline his complaint, his uncomfortable hobbling gait providing an overture.

He rolled up his trouser leg and showed Raven a long cut, slightly swollen and weeping pus. 'I cut it upon a splintered board about a week ago. I thought it just needed time to heal, but what started as a scab has turned into this.'

Raven immediately thought of the preparation Sarah had given him for his face when first he arrived at Queen Street. He said nothing of that quite yet, however.

'Mr Mitchell, I work also at the Maternity Hospital. You were the gentleman who so kindly carried a stricken woman to us recently, weren't you? Kitty, you said her name was.'

He looked on his guard. 'Yes. I gather it did not go well.'

'No, sadly we were unable to do anything for her. I need to know who she was, where she lived. Can you tell me from where you carried her? Or the name of the girl you were with, that I might find her?'

Mitchell sat back in his seat, folding his arms. Raven had anticipated this. It was one thing to act upon the spur of the moment, quite another to speak of one's dealings with whores.

'I am not sure I recall the details of that night,' Mitchell said, 'and nor do I particularly wish to.'

Raven nodded, as though understanding. 'A pity. Just as I am not sure I recall the formula for the ointment that would surely cure your wound.'

A few hours later, Raven was standing inside a ramshackle building on Calton Road being confronted by a woman about whom he had been warned by Mitchell. He had come here on his way to the Maternity Hospital, reasoning that not only would it be easier to spot the Weasel and Gargantua in daylight, but also less likely they would attempt to assail him in full view of a busy thorough-fare.

The madam of the bawdy house to which he had been directed was a corpulent and intimidatingly ugly woman by the name of Miss Nadia. Raven could not imagine her ever having worked on her back, but reckoned she was particularly suited to her role in that by the time the customers got past her, any girl they were presented with would look like Venus by comparison.

'I wish to see a woman by the name of Mairi,' he stated. 'I am informed she works here.'

Miss Nadia gave him a cold smile. 'She does indeed. I can enquire if she is available, but I'll be wanting to see the colour of your money first.'

If Raven's finances had a colour, it would be deathly pale. His mother had sent the regular allowance permitted by his miserable uncle, but that had been almost three weeks ago. How he envied the likes of Beattie, typical of those he had studied with whose family riches comfortably financed their living while they learned their profession. His uncle had plenty more to give, and his mother would go to any lengths to secure it if he asked, but Raven would not have her further humbled before him. Once he began to make money in earnest, he would free her from ever having to ask Malcolm for another penny. For now, however, he had to find another currency.

'I am a doctor at Milton House. I recently treated a girl named Kitty, late of this establishment.'

'Didn't treat her very well, did you? She never came back from Milton House. Are you after payment in kind for services rendered? Because it doesn't work like that.'

Raven fixed her with the same look he had given Mr Gallagher. His dealings with Effie Peake had let him know it was best not to show any weakness. Such women dealt in counterfeit emotions, and in this place there was no reward for honesty.

'There is growing police interest in what might have brought on Kitty's condition. So unless you would prefer James McLevy and his men knocking on your door instead of me, I would suggest you do me a courtesy.'

Miss Nadia considered this for a moment, then bid him follow, leading him to a room on the second floor. Mairi was tall, appearing all the more so for being undernourished. Her olive skin suggested a more exotic provenance than was usual in these parts, though sadly it most likely derived from a father who briefly put to shore some twenty years previous on a ship from Spain or Italy.

'Give him what he wants,' Nadia instructed her. 'And by that I mean answer his questions. Anything else comes at the usual rates.'

Raven closed the door. Mairi was sitting on the bed with an anxious look, detecting that the circumstances were out of the ordinary.

'I treated Kitty at Milton House,' he explained. 'Your client brought her to us. There was nothing we could do to save her, so I sat by her until the end.'

Mairi bit her lip, sadness immediate upon her face. 'Thank you for that,' she said.

'I would know what caused her agonies. She was with child, wasn't she?'

Her expression betrayed that Mairi knew this and more.

'I believe she took measures to get rid of it, and I believe you know that too.'

'I know nothing about that,' she answered, a little too fast.

'Then let's talk about what I think you do know. If you were to find yourself with child, you would have a notion who to speak to about dealing with it, would you not? Who did Kitty speak to?'

Mairi said nothing, but from the widening of her eyes, it was clear that there was a specific something she was not saying.

'Have no fear. I am not looking to get anyone into trouble. But I am a man of medicine and I need to know how this happened. Kitty was not the first to die in this manner and I would ensure a similar fate does not befall any other women.'

She swallowed, looking about herself as though afraid someone might overhear.

'There is a French midwife,' she answered quietly. 'Worked in the service of queens and contessas, Kitty reckoned. She had special training. Knows how to do things that doctors won't, if you know what I mean.'

'Well enough. Do you know her name?'

Mairi answered in a whisper, 'Kitty called her Madame Anchou. Said she wore a hooded cape of the finest cloth and spoke with a strong accent.'

'How did Kitty get in touch with this woman?'

'She has rooms at a tavern. You have to speak to the landlord, though. He makes the arrangements.'

'For a slice, no doubt.'

Mairi nodded. 'It cost a lot of money, I know that. Kitty had this locket her mother gave her that she had to pawn. Broke her heart to part with it, but she had no option.'

'What exactly did her money buy her?'

'That's the thing: only pills. I told Kitty she was robbed if she handed over all her money just for that, but she said there was an agreement. Madame Anchou assured her the pills would deal with the problem: you know, make the baby come right soon. But as a guarantee, if that didn't happen, Kitty should come back and she would perform her service in respect of the fee. Kitty reasoned she would rather take the pills and see how that worked out if it spared her knives and knitting needles.'

Raven recalled his discussion with Ziegler and Mrs Stevenson. Desperate women would pay handsomely for a 'secret remedy', especially if it was dispensed by a midwife from Paris, trained at the famous Hôtel Dieu, and formerly in the service of French aristocracy. But as Mrs Stevenson warned, it was not always harmless pills their money bought them.

'And where is this tavern she works out of?' Raven asked.

'It's down in Leith. It's called the King's Wark.'

FORTY-SIX

arah sat at a table by the window, chosen for the view it afforded of Leith Shore stretching southwards towards Tolbooth Wynd. On Sunday morning, she could have accurately stated that she had never been inside a tavern in her life, and now she found herself patronising such an establishment for the second time in three days.

She was nursing a glass of gin, purchased primarily for appearance's sake. It was her first taste of the stuff, and she had resolved that it would also be the last, until she discovered the ameliorating effect it had upon her anxiety. She could not imagine why anyone would choose to drink it for pleasure, but under needful circumstances, the flavour was to be tolerated like that of any other medicine.

'It is the only way to draw out this Madame Anchou,' Raven had insisted. 'I can't go myself, for what reason would a man have to be seeking her services?'

'You could be seeking them on behalf of your lover.'

'Yes, but this landlord would recognise me. He followed me after I went to the King's Wark asking questions about Rose's body.'

The landlord's name was Spiers, according to a plate above the door. He was exactly as Raven described: bald-headed, tall and burly, an intimidating presence fit for rousting drunks. He had come over to her table unbidden, seeing her sitting there alone. Sarah guessed he already knew what she was there for.

Sarah had never considered herself to have any kind of gift for the dramatic. Her sole experience had been staging scenes from Shakespeare at school, where she had distinguished herself only by her recall for the lines, an ability entirely down to hours of rote learning. However, as Spiers approached her, she had realised she would need no talent for acting in order to deceive him. She was there to play the part of a frightened housemaid, and that required no pretence.

'Are you quite sure you are in the right place, miss?' he had asked.

'I am not sure. I have been told you have a tenant, a French-woman by the name of Madame Anchou. Is she present? I would speak with her, if you please.'

'And what would you speak with her about?'

'That is a personal matter, between ladies.'

'Madame Anchou is not present. She does not reside here, but keeps a room for consultations. However, I can arrange an introduction.'

'I would be most grateful.'

'Your gratitude will suffice for that, but should you require her services –' Spiers paused, casting an eye towards her middle '– and if you've come here, I wager you do – then the fee is two guineas.'

Though Raven had warned her about the likely cost, Sarah's eyes still bulged. This was more than two months' wages. It was the cruellest extortion of the desperate.

Spiers had noted her reaction. 'If you cannot meet the price, you and Madame Anchou should not waste each other's time.'

'I can . . . obtain it.'

'Good. For though her services are expensive, they are worth it. She was trained in Paris and retained by French aristocracy.'

Sarah had already heard about her reputation. 'Such are her reputed abilities,' Raven had said, 'it is a pity she was not around during the Revolution, for she surely would have had a balm fit to reattach Marie Antoinette's head. All of which begs the question of what happened to her that she's plying her trade here.'

Spiers had offered to arrange an introduction the very next day, but Sarah knew that Monday's duties allowed no opportunity to absent herself. She had therefore agreed to return on Tuesday, when she always had errands to run during the afternoon, giving her dispensation to be out of the house. Procuring two guineas in such a time frame was mercifully not a task upon which the success of their plan was predicated.

Even within the bounds of such dispensation, she knew she was still risking her position by partaking in these activities. It had preyed upon her mind from the moment Raven asked her to come to Leith, and yet it had not occurred to her to say no. Though it set her trembling from her gut to her fingertips, pursuing these investigations gave her a sense of freedom and usefulness far greater than anything she felt assisting at clinic.

Sarah glanced out of the window, checking that she could still see Raven on the dockside. He had chosen a discreet vantage point where he was unlikely to be noticed by the landlord, but close enough to move in and join them once Madame Anchou was settled at Sarah's table.

A twelfth glance at the clock told her the appointed time had come and gone. Spiers had warned her not to expect sharp punctuality, but Sarah was more concerned about completing the errands she still had to run before returning in time for her pre-dinner duties.

Then, as she gazed into the ever-shifting traffic upon the quayside, she noticed a distinctive figure approaching from the south. She wore a flowing black cloak with a capacious hood, and though her head was slightly bowed, there was an upright confidence about her as she walked. Sarah had no question but that this was her, as described in the albeit second-hand accounts Raven had relayed. She was tall and graceful, gliding through the crowd as though she was not of them.

Sarah downed the rest of the gin, wincing against the taste. She needed something to steady her, already feeling intimidated by this woman before she had even reached the tavern. She felt the liquid burn all the way to her stomach.

Sarah looked along Leith Shore once again, hoping to glimpse the face beneath that hood, but Madame Anchou was no longer in sight. She surveyed the crowds upon the dock, expecting the hooded figure to re-emerge, but the woman was not to be seen.

What she did see was Raven charging past the window, taking off in urgent pursuit.

FORTY-SEVEN

s always in Leith, Raven felt surrounded by bustling movement in every direction; even above, where seagulls wheeled amidst rising clouds sent up by a departing packet steamer. He could barely see the water for sails, and upon the shore there was the liveliest throng and babble, everywhere teeming with activity and busy purpose. Raven heard half a dozen languages spoken in the space of a few minutes, noticed a boundless variety of features, skin colours and clothing upon men toting crates, bales and trunks.

Smells of coffee and spices hung upon the air. Raven breathed them in gratefully, aware the shore was not always so blessed. Simpson had told him about an altogether less fragrant cargo that landed here once, both of them taking pleasure in a tale that reflected poorly upon Professor Syme. In the days before the Anatomy Act, when bodies for dissection were in short supply, Syme had acquired cadavers from Dublin and London, transporting them to Edinburgh via the docks at Leith. During the summer of 1826, the stench coming from a shipment resulted in Syme's crates being opened and their unauthorised contents discovered, generating much outrage and scandal. 'Syme's cargo was marked "perishable goods",' Simpson told him, wheezing with laughter.

Raven thought he had chosen his position well. It was a spot where he would remain largely invisible should the landlord happen to look out of the window, but affording a clear view north and south along the shore, for he didn't know from which direction Madame Anchou would approach. As he had explained to Sarah, his concern was that, should Spiers see him, he might suspect something was afoot and take steps to warn off the midwife. The unspoken further implication was that the landlord might simply move against Raven directly, or God forbid even Sarah.

In order to reduce her exposure to danger, Sarah was under instruction to conduct her conversation only in the tavern and not to agree to a consultation upstairs in the midwife's rooms. She was to discuss the services the Frenchwoman might offer, but then admit she did not have the money yet. This would give Raven the opportunity to follow Madame Anchou and confront her on neutral ground, or even to find out where she lived so that he could choose his moment judiciously.

What he hadn't anticipated was that she would see him first.

He was hopping from foot to foot as he waited, in an effort to fend off shivers. It was a cold day, an unforgiving wind blowing in off the water. Sarah was right: he urgently needed to get a heavier coat.

He ceased his hopping and stood rigid when he saw his quarry moving through the crowd, striding down the incline from Tolbooth Wynd. The moment he saw that hood, he had no question that this was the woman he had heard described. The black cloth was swaying back and forth with each step so that he could only glimpse fragments of her face, never the entirety. The view was further obscured by people moving in and out of her path, sometimes causing her to disappear from view altogether. He thought she might have looked at him, but with her eyes in shadow beneath the hood, it was impossible to be sure. She was getting steadily nearer, though, so he would get a close-up view soon enough.

Again she vanished from view behind a shore porter pushing

a cart, and when next he spied her, she had turned and was running. Raven watched her part the crowd, hurrying back in the direction from which she had just come.

She knew something was wrong.

He took off, signalling through the window for Sarah to follow. There was going to be no meeting. They had to catch her now, or they might never track her down.

Weaving between the people milling along the dockside, Raven quickly began to gain ground. He had always been swift on his feet, and it was easier to run in gentleman's clothing. For that reason, he knew that he would be leaving Sarah far behind, but the important thing was that the midwife did not get away.

She was easier to keep in sight now that she was moving faster, as he could see the movement ahead of her as people stepped out of her way. However, when she reached the first side street, she took a hard turn and was gone from view. Raven stepped up his pace, and to his relief she was back in his sight when he reached the corner, both of them now hurrying along a narrower but altogether quieter thoroughfare.

Anchou glanced back upon hearing his footfalls, then diverted to speak briefly to three stevedores who had just emerged from a doorway. Raven was out of earshot, but as he watched her point towards him, it was not difficult to deduce the crux of their conversation.

She resumed her flight as the three stevedores began marching on Raven, one hefting a heavy stick. He reckoned he could possibly take one of these men on his own, or at least be swift enough to evade him, but not all three at once. He had to back away for his own safety, and in his retreat he did not see where the midwife went. In order to resume his pursuit, he would have to double back and loop around, by which time she would be long away, or at least have plenty of time to hide.

As he turned the corner back onto the dockside, he saw Sarah hurrying towards him.

'She got away,' he confessed. 'She set some dockers to block my path. Must have told them I meant her harm.'

'Why did she run, though?' Sarah asked.

'It is my assumption that she recognised me, enough to know what I was about.'

'And therefore she feared you would recognise her also. But from where?'

'I can't imagine. I don't know any Frenchwomen.'

'Then perhaps she is not French,' Sarah suggested, 'but rather a woman pretending to be something she is not.'

Raven suddenly saw how Madame Anchou's exoticness was part of her attraction to prospective patients. It might be as false as the medicines she was hawking.

Raven waited until he saw the three stevedores pass, then slipped along the side street again. He and Sarah reached a thoroughfare that ran parallel to the dockside, but there was no sign of her. He knew it was hopeless.

'She could have gone anywhere,' he admitted.

'At some point she will have to go back to the King's Wark, surely,' Sarah reminded him.

They had no notion when that might be, nor the option to keep vigil for its happening. However, there was reason enough for them to visit the place.

'We have some questions we ought to ask Mr Spiers,' he said.

'And what if he has a strong will not to answer them? A violent will, even?'

Raven had considered this, but he had his leverage now. 'He has seen you too. I will tell him that you wait for me, and should I fail to return or come to any harm, you will be going straight to McLevy to tell him everything we know.'

'We don't know much.'

'Nonetheless, it is what he fears we know that will restrain him.'

They made their way back towards the King's Wark, approaching from the rear having come around in a circle.

Raven's plan to keep Sarah out of the landlord's sight was immediately dashed as they saw Spiers emerge into a courtyard at the back of the tavern. He pitched forward as though about to sprint towards them, but as Raven altered his stance and put out an arm to warn off Sarah, it became clear that the landlord was in fact staggering. He fell against a stack of beer barrels, gripping one to prop himself upright. As he turned, Raven was able to see a patch of dark red staining his grubby shirt around his middle.

Spiers noticed them and reached out an imploring hand before dropping to his knees.

They hurried into the courtyard.

'She stuck me,' he said, clutching his hand to his side. 'The French bitch. So quick. I didn't even see a blade.'

'Why?'

'I don't know. She didn't stop to explain.'

Raven helped Spiers take his rest against a barrel. The patch of red was widening by the second. He and Sarah shared a look. Spiers was bleeding badly and they both knew he had little time left.

'What was your arrangement with this woman?'

'I will not condemn myself with my own testimony,' he replied, grimacing against the pain.

'Your wound is grave, sir. Without help you will die within the hour. I am a doctor. I can keep you alive long enough for us to get you to Professor Syme, the best surgeon in the city. But only if you answer our questions.'

'Do not take me for a fool, son. There's not a surgeon in the world who can mend this. She has done for me.'

'Then you owe her no loyalty. Speak, man.'

'She is a French midwife who rents rooms. That is all I know.'

'You must know more than that. She carries out abortions on your premises and she pays you a percentage. Who is she really? What more do you know about her?'

'Nothing. She told me if I didn't ask questions, it would protect us both.'

'Well, your silence has not served you well today, has it? What more do you know?'

Spiers considered it, a bitter look on his face, from which colour was visibly draining.

'She has a partner,' he said, swallowing.

'Who?'

'I never knew his name and I saw him but once. I tried to enter her room when I thought her not home and found him there.'

'What did he look like?'

'I saw him but for a few seconds, and even then only from the back. I had barely opened the door when he pushed me out and slammed it shut. He was standing by a table with instruments and potions ranged upon it. A medical man, like yourself. Older, though.'

'And what of Rose Campbell?' Sarah asked.

'Who?'

'She was a housemaid. The one who was pulled from the water.'

'I know nothing about that.'

'You followed me after I asked about her,' Raven reminded him. 'Come on, would you not make your confession that you may face death without fear?'

Spiers winced, the blood oozing between his fingers where he clutched them to the soaking cloth. He looked afraid now.

'She came here, paid the money. The procedure was successful but she was ill afterwards. They often were . . . and we turned them out, though they were barely fit to walk. We let them stay a couple of days, and if it appeared they would not recover, we put them out because we did not want any bodies to dispose of or deaths to explain. God forgive me,' he said, his voice faltering.

Sarah had found a wooden tankard upon a bench and pulled

out the stop from a barrel to fill it. She offered it to Spiers, who sipped it gratefully.

'Your one, Rose . . . she was recovering. She was here a few days, but she was on the mend. I brought her water, meals. Then I was woken by her screaming in the night. When I went to her room, she was in her final throes. She died all twisted and agonised.'

Sarah offered another sip, though he barely had the strength to take it in. Most of it dribbled down his chin, and when he spoke again, his voice was dry and faint.

'I was sore afraid. I feared it would bring all hell crashing down upon me if it was found out what was being done here. I had to get rid of her, so I took her to the water and dropped her in. But I didn't kill her. God as my witness, I didn't . . . kill her . . .'

With these words, his voice became a pitiable whisper and his head rolled forward onto his chest.

'He is gone,' Raven said.

Sarah looked ashen, but it was not merely the sight of a dead man that was troubling her.

'What do we do now?'

'Leave. Quickly.'

'Just abandon him here? Shouldn't we alert the police?'

'Only if you feel confident about explaining your role in all of this to McLevy.'

This silenced any moral qualms Sarah might have about his suggested course of action. They looked left and right out of the back court to ensure nobody had seen them, then slipped quietly down the same narrow lane by which they had approached.

'Why would Anchou kill him?' Sarah asked as they walked briskly but not in a conspicuous hurry back towards the anonymity of the busy dockside.

'I know not, but I fear it was our actions that brought her knife down upon him. She knew we were investigating her, and there was something she feared Spiers might tell us.'

'Then why didn't he? He gave us nothing of any great import.'

'Perhaps there was something she merely feared he knew, and could not take the risk.'

Sarah suddenly pushed Raven against a wall, her hands upon his chest. He could feel his heart thump against her fingers, his whole body still trembling from what he had just witnessed.

'What is—?' he began.

'I cannot be seen,' she said urgently. 'I am supposed to be in the town on errands. I could be dismissed.'

'Seen by whom?'

'Do not look,' she insisted. 'Keep your head down.'

But by that time he had already spotted the problem. Walking south along Leith Shore was the man who was these days affecting to call himself James Matthews Duncan.

'What is he doing down here?' Raven wondered aloud.

'I don't know. Just take care he doesn't see you.'

As though to ensure this, she pulled his head down nearer to hers. She was close enough that he could smell that familiar aroma, like fresh linen. His thoughts returned to their encounter the night he had run home in the rain. Many times since, he had revisited the memory of her hands against him as she helped take off his shirt.

They stayed like that a while. Raven saw Duncan pass from view, but was long in saying so, for he did not wish the moment to end so soon. In time, it had to though.

They broke apart, an awkwardness between them as though they did not know how to acknowledge what had just happened. Fortunately, there was plenty to talk about.

'You were vindicated in your thinking about Rose,' he said. 'What Spiers told us would explain why the police surgeon found her not to be pregnant.'

'Yet clearly, she died in the same way as Kitty and your Evie. If she had successfully rid herself of the baby, why would she take the same pills?'

Raven had been asking himself this question too.

'Perhaps she did not take them voluntarily,' he suggested. 'It might be that she had discovered something about Madame Anchou that the midwife wished to keep hidden.'

'Or about her partner. Could it be that he is the one who actually carries out the procedures, while she brings in the business with the allure of having trained in Paris and worked for the French aristocracy?'

This was an astute supposition, in keeping with the mystique that allowed her to charge exorbitantly.

'Not to mention of being a woman and therefore earning their trust,' Raven added. 'Such an arrangement would allow a doctor to practise this dark art without the risk that would attend advertising such services.'

They strode south in the direction of the city, the crowd thinning as they moved further from the water. Raven could not help but search ahead in case he spied that black hood, while he suspected Sarah's eyes were still concerned with the whereabouts of Dr Duncan.

'In recent months there have been several cases of young women dying following abortions,' Raven said.

'So they might all have been the work of Madame Anchou and her partner?'

'Spiers admitted they turned out the sick ones so that they did not die at the tavern. And if Rose was deliberately poisoned, it could have been either of them who killed her. We came here seeking one anonymous malefactor and depart in search of two: Madam Anchou, who may or may not be the Frenchwoman she pretends, and a doctor of little conscience or humanity.'

FORTY-EIGHT

arah maintained a respectful distance while the parish clerk dealt with the fellow who had arrived at St Cuthbert's just ahead of her. He was a young man but looked as though he carried the weight of the world upon his sloping shoulders. He was attempting to hire the parish mortcloth for the burial of his mother, but there appeared to be some issue over the fee.

The clerk examined the pile of pennies that the man had deposited upon his ledger. He separated them with the end of his pen as though reluctant to sully his fingers with the contents of the young man's pockets. He sighed and then frowned.

'This is insufficient. I suggest that you return with the fee already stipulated or your mother must be buried without the parish cloth.'

Then he smiled at the bereaved man with a chilly politeness and dismissed him as though they had been discussing a frippery of no earthly significance. The man said nothing, rendered mute by the clerk's unbending adherence to his ecclesiastical price-list. Christian charity evidently did not extend to the parish's funeral shroud. He turned and shuffled out of the clerk's office, back into the body of the church.

The clerk watched him leave with a tiny shake of the head,

as though other people's poverty was an affront, then turned his attention to Sarah, peering over the top of his spectacles.

And anyway, what can you do about it? Raven had asked when she told him about her suspicions regarding Beattie. It had been a rhetorical question, to his mind. She would show him otherwise by answering it.

'How may I help you?' the clerk asked, in a tone that suggested he had little intention of doing so.

'I come at the behest of Dr James Young Simpson,' Sarah replied, hoping that the mention of the professor's name would oil the wheels of cooperation.

It seemed to have some effect, as the clerk stood a little more upright and pushed his glasses back up to the bridge of his nose. His tone became oleaginous and a ghost of a smile appeared upon his thin lips.

'How may I be of assistance to the professor?'

'A woman has died at the Maternity Hospital,' Sarah said. 'Her child lives. The woman's name is known but not that of her nearest relative. There is a need to find someone to care for the baby, to see it baptised and properly raised. The professor requested that I consult the local parish registers to see if she was married, and who her parents are, if they are still alive.'

The clerk briefly brightened at the mention of baptism but snorted at the suggestion of a marriage. It was well known that many of the women treated at the Maternity Hospital were not in possession of a spouse. He wrinkled his nose as though assailed by an unwelcome smell.

'I am surprised such an important task has fallen to you. Has the professor not an apprentice or some other suitable person to do it?'

'Indeed he has,' she replied. 'But they are all so busy, what with the recent outbreak of typhus.'

The man immediately sought out his handkerchief and held it to his nose as though the mere mention of the disease would cause it to arrive. He looked at her for a while, weighing up her request. She perhaps should not have mentioned the Maternity Hospital. Or typhus.

'The information you request will take some time to find,' he said at last. 'And I should point out to you that our records are far from comprehensive: those who are not prepared to part with the necessary fee often do not bother with registration at all.'

'I understand,' said Sarah. 'I can see you are a very busy man and I have no wish to impose upon you. Perhaps you would permit me to look through the book myself.'

He looked at his pristine ledger and then down at her hands.

'My hands are clean, sir,' she replied. 'Dr Simpson insists upon it.'

The mention of the professor's name again seemed to tip the balance in her favour.

'You'll have to look through several of the registers. The current one only goes back to 1840.'

Her search did indeed take some time, and bore no fruit. As the vestry began to darken, she tried not to think of what Mrs Lyndsay would say upon her return, what punishment she would have to endure as a result of her tardiness. A suitable excuse would have to be found or her clinic duties would be severely curtailed.

Sarah had always considered herself an honest person, and was feeling increasingly uncomfortable about the lies she now found herself having to tell on a regular basis. She felt that her concern for Mina justified her current endeavours, but she would have to make sure that this propensity for subterfuge came to an end once everything was resolved.

Yet even as she thought this, she considered what she was about and contrasted it with the person she used to be, only a few weeks ago. That meek housemaid would not have dared to deceive anyone, far less embark upon clandestine investigations in the realms of abortionists and murderers. There was a comfort and security in knowing one's place and asking no questions. But she had never felt that a role of meekness and acceptance *was* her place.

Sarah was fastidious in her search, but she could find no record of Charles Latimer or of Beattie's mother. The name 'John Beattie' was cited, but the dates did not tally up unless the apparently sprightly young doctor was in fact approaching his eightieth birthday.

Sarah slumped in her chair, unsure as to what this lack of information represented. She had to admit that it was hardly conclusive evidence that Beattie was a fraud of some kind. Could she be entirely on the wrong track? Were her emotions clouding her judgment, her disapproval of Mina's choices colouring her view?

She regarded the stack of dusty registers piled in front of her and wondered if she was wasting her time. Perhaps in a desire to gain something from her afternoon's efforts, it occurred to her that Raven's family might be listed among them. He was someone else whose account of his own background rang false.

Sarah checked for the clerk but he had disappeared. It seemed he was content to leave her to her own devices as soon as he was sure she had no intention of amending entries, ripping out pages or drooling on the paper.

She estimated Raven's age to be twenty and so looked at the records for the years 1825 to 1830. She found no entry for the birth of Wilberforce Raven, but she did find a record of the marriage of a Margaret Raven to an Andrew Cunningham in 1826. The surname was familiar but for a moment she couldn't think why. Then she remembered: it was the name inscribed inside some of Raven's books.

Sarah looked at the births registered in the following year and found him: Thomas Wilberforce Cunningham.

Raven had changed his name. But for what purpose? She tried to think what else she knew about him, what she had been told regarding his background. His mother lived in St Andrews with her brother, Raven receiving letters from there on a regular basis. She knew his father was dead, hence the removal of his mother to Fife.

Sarah wondered when this tragedy had occurred, from what age Raven had been raised without a father. She turned to the registers again, searching for burials. She looked from the present day all the way back to the year of Raven's birth. There was no entry for the interment of Andrew Cunningham.

According to the records of St Cuthbert's parish, which covered all of Edinburgh and some way beyond, Raven's father was not dead at all.

FORTY-NINE

itken's tavern was crowded, a thick pall of pipe smoke coiling up to the rafters. It was warm, almost uncomfortably so, the press of bodies elevating the temperature and causing the windows to run with condensation. As Raven returned from the bar, it took him a few seconds to locate Henry, who had managed to find a table in a corner, where he was chatting to a man Raven failed to recognise.

He wondered again why he had been summoned here. Henry had accosted him as he stood by Simpson's carriage, waiting to accompany the professor home. Raven had confided in his friend about the French midwife and her medical accomplice, whereupon Henry told him he had news that might be of interest.

'What news?' he had replied, but Henry wagged a finger by way of denying him.

'This is information I will only share with a tankard in my hand, for it has been too long since we supped together.'

Raven feared he was being sold a bill of goods, as he would have much preferred to know the value of this information before he traded it for a safe means of conveyance home.

The man sitting with Henry looked young but exceedingly weary, sporting dark circles beneath eyes that betrayed a profound want of sleep. Raven was unsurprised when Henry introduced him as a doctor at the Royal Infirmary.

'This is Fleming,' he said. 'Replaced McKellar, Christison's resident clerk who died of fever last month.'

Raven sat down and took a long pull of his beer, involuntarily calculating what fraction of Flint's debt the price of a round would have redeemed. '"The poisoned breath of infection",' he said, wiping froth from his beard.

'"A young and early sacrifice at the shrine of professional duty",' replied Henry archly. It was a well-worn phrase trotted out by the medical professors when such an incident occurred, which was a little too often in Raven's opinion. Not for the first time, he felt relief that his present duties seldom required his attendance at the Infirmary.

'We imperil our own health working in that place,' said Henry's lugubrious companion, staring disconsolately into his beer.

Raven wondered why Henry had seen fit to bring him along.

'So what is the news?' asked Raven, feeling disinclined to tarry. He had grown his beard since last he was in Aitken's, but the very reason he needed it had stemmed from being recognised in this place on the night he was attacked. Flint had eyes in here, he had little doubt.

'There's been another one,' Henry said.

'Another what?'

'Another death. Young woman.' Henry nodded at his drowsy companion, who was still staring into his beer. 'Fleming dealt with the case.' He kicked the young man under the table, which caused him to rouse himself.

'Yes,' Fleming said, rubbing his eyes. 'Moribund when admitted. Didn't wake up.'

'What was the cause of death?' Raven asked.

'Peritonitis. All the signs of puerperal sepsis but no sign of a baby.'

Raven could feel his anxiety grow. He had a fear that if he

was going to be caught by Flint's men, it would be due to an avoidable lack of vigilance in the service of an ironically pointless risk. Diverting here merely to learn about yet another victim of their anonymous abortionist definitely came into that category.

As if sensing his friend's deteriorating mood, Henry nudged Fleming again. 'Tell him what you told me.'

'Oh, yes,' he responded, as though in his fatigue his brain needed a shunt. 'She had an unusual smell about her. It was on her clothes when she first came in: a sweet smell. Like over-ripe fruit. And she had unusual marks around her mouth.'

'Abrasions?'

'No, not abrasions.'

'Bruising, then?' Raven suggested impatiently.

'No, it looked like—'

'Ligature marks, as though she had been gagged?'

'For pity's sake, let him speak, Raven.'

'What, then? Why did you drag me here?'

'These looked more like a burn,' Fleming stated.

Raven understood. 'Chloroform.'

'You see?' said Henry, with a flourish of his hand. 'This individual you seek has been keeping up to date with new developments.'

Beyond proving how quickly the new anaesthetic was being adopted, Raven did not see how this assisted in his quest. He took a glum gulp of his beer by way of consolation.

'You seem less than elated,' Henry observed.

'Why should I be other? This does not bring me any nearer to knowing his identity.'

The young surgeon's familiar wily grin informed him there was something he had missed.

'Not at this moment,' Henry said. 'But I can tell you where you will find it written down.'

FIFTY

arah stood on Princes Street, peering through the window into Duncan and Flockhart's. She was choosing her moment carefully, and as she waited for the opportunity she required, she worked on composing herself, because for the first time in her life, she was about to commit a crime.

She was not going to steal anything, merely borrow without leave, but by the borrowing she intended to facilitate a trespass upon this property. Technically, this would be a burglary, albeit one in which, again, nothing would be taken save information. Nonetheless, though there would be no theft and no damage, she would not wish to find herself explaining it to anyone, least of all McLevy. It might be enough to see her in jail, and would be more than enough to see her dismissed.

Duncan and Flockhart were the primary manufacturers of chloroform throughout Edinburgh. Every doctor using it was buying their supplies from here, where their purchases were recorded in the druggist's ledger. Raven had enquired of Mr Flockhart whether he might see who had been ordering the stuff, feigning a curiosity regarding the uptake of the new anaesthetic agent, but Flockhart had told him the ledger had to remain confidential. When it came to the purchase of drugs, customers needed to be able to rely upon their suppliers' discretion. Yet one of those customers was Madame Anchou's mysterious confederate, and very possibly the man who had murdered Rose Campbell.

'I need to see that list,' Raven told Sarah, almost uncontainable in his frustration. 'But how can I do so if it is locked safe in their keeping?'

'Every lock has a key,' Sarah had replied. 'It is simply a matter of acquiring it.'

'I would not be able to locate it, far less procure such a thing unnoticed.'

'A set of keys hangs from a hook on the wall behind the counter, just to the right of the cash register. They are in the charge of Ingram, the assistant. I have heard him talk of how he opens the shop and prepares the premises before the Misters Duncan and Flockhart arrive.'

'And how do you propose that I lay my hands on them unseen?'

'I do not propose that you lay your hands on them at all. For such a task you require a person to whom nobody pays any notice. Such as a housemaid.'

Watching through the window, she observed what she expected: Mr Flockhart tending to some matter at the counter, assisted by the smug and dim young runt whose suitability for employment here was considered greater than hers by virtue of what dangled between his legs. Mr Duncan was, as usual, not to be seen, busying himself in the laboratory towards the rear of the building. Mr Flockhart was the more garrulous of the pair, and therefore more frequently the public face of the partnership.

In time, she saw Mr Flockhart slip out of sight too, either to the lab or one of the storerooms. She knew from experience that he was happy to let Ingram deal with customers of lesser standing, such as a maid running an errand. If someone important came in, the lad would fetch his boss.

This was her moment.

As she stepped through the door and the bell rang, Sarah felt it trilling right through her. She was jangling with tension. She didn't only feel it in a quickened heartbeat and a tightness in her gut; her fingers tingled, her elbows, her knees. It was manifest in a heightened state of perception affecting all sensations. The colours in the room seemed brighter, the smells more distinct, the sounds sharper.

She wondered if this was down to a pronounced awareness of all that she stood to lose should she be caught. Never would she be allowed in this shop again. She would be thrown out of the household, in fact, and what future would be open to her then? Sarah became privately angry whenever someone suggested she should be grateful for her job as a housemaid, but she knew there were worse fates. Nonetheless, there was someone in this city who saw housemaids and other young women as disposable, and she was resolved to see their wickedness unmasked.

'Can I help you, young lady?' the assistant asked.

She wanted to swat him for that. She estimated she was at least a year older than him, possibly two.

'I require some items for Dr Simpson.'

'Dr Simpson of Queen Street?'

This annoyed her too. He was verifying whose account should be billed, even though he saw her at least twice a week. Either he was acting as though he didn't recognise her or he genuinely didn't recognise her, and she wasn't sure which one was the greater insult.

'Indeed.'

'And what does Dr Simpson require?'

Sarah rhymed off a short list and cast an eye upon the high shelves while Ingram retrieved her requests, all of which were within easy reach.

'Oh, and he also wished a quantity of carbonic acid.'

Ingram frowned and turned to search the nearby cabinets. He did not see what he was looking for. This was because she had asked him to supply a quantity of fixed air, the transparent and colourless gas that, according to Gregory's *Outlines of Chemistry*, he was currently exhaling and he hadn't the knowledge to realise it.

'I'll just go and ask Mr—'

'It's right up there,' Sarah interrupted, stepping behind the counter and pointing to a high shelf.

'I don't see it.'

'Then let me fetch it,' she said, reaching for the ladder.

Ingram blocked her way. 'That is not permitted,' he told her in a scolding tone.

'For only a man will do,' Sarah muttered, stepping away from the ladder but closer to the cash register.

As Ingram climbed, his attention firmly upon each spar, Sarah lifted the keys from their hook and slipped them into her pocket.

'I still don't see it,' he reported.

'My apologies. I just remembered that Dr Simpson merely mentioned it. He didn't mean for me to buy some, otherwise he'd have told me a quantity, wouldn't he?'

Ingram sighed with irritation at this stupid woman.

As he began descending, Sarah was already heading for the door, as though some force was pushing her out of the shop before she could be apprehended. She felt heat in her cheeks and it was all she could do not to break into a run once she was back on Princes Street.

She had travelled only a few yards when she heard the voice.

'Young woman! Stop!'

Sarah felt time suspended as the recklessness of her actions came crashing in upon her. She saw McLevy hauling her away, the stern face of a judge, rats and chains in a jail cell.

When she turned to face this grim future, she saw Ingram striding towards her, holding a brown paper bag.

'You forgot to lift what Dr Simpson *did* order,' he said, his tone patronising and heavy with scorn. 'That would have earned you a dressing down when you got back, wouldn't it?'

'Thank you,' she said, relief lending her tone sincerity. 'Indeed it would.'

Much like one might receive for misplacing one's keys.

FIFTY-ONE

aven tried turning another key without success, huddled in the darkness at the back door to the building. Though few people were likely to be passing at this hour, he had opted to approach from the rear as it was secluded from view. Unfortunately it was also secluded from the illumination of the nearest street lamp. Sarah had tried lighting a candle, but the breeze was too strong even back here, whipping through any gap it could find.

His hands were cold and he was shivering. Neither of these things were helping either.

'Are you sure you lifted the right keys?' he asked.

She did not respond to this, but he could imagine her expression. Sarah had only surrendered the keys on the walk here, once everyone at Queen Street had gone to bed. It had been her way of ensuring that he could not go without her. He did not understand why she would wish to, but he was learning that it was usually futile to argue.

'We are equals in this enterprise,' was all she told him.

Raven tried the first key again, and this time it turned. In his trembling anxiety, his fumbling fingers had not inserted it properly before.

The door opened with rather more of a creak than was

comfortable. With the wind blowing so hard, the sound would not carry more than a few feet, but to Raven's ears it sounded like the wail of a banshee calling attention to their crime.

Sarah lit the candle now that she had some shelter. By its meagre light, they found their way into the laboratory, where Raven located an oil lamp. As he turned up the flame, he saw dozens of leather-bound volumes lining a bookcase, amidst shelves upon shelves of powders and liquids. Bottles, beakers and flasks reflected the light. Raven was wary of the many retorts jutting out, inviting accident, which would preclude their intention to pass here without leaving any record.

He held the lamp to the spines. None of them was what he sought.

'I have often seen Mr Flockhart write in his ledger upon the counter,' Sarah told him. 'I imagine it is kept close by.'

They crept through to the front of the shop on quiet feet, though Raven did wonder why he felt an instinct to tread so softly. The glow of the lamp through the window was more likely to be noticed than any footfall.

He turned down the lamp accordingly and they waited for their eyes to grow more accustomed to the dark, alleviated only sparingly by the street lamps on Princes Street.

Sarah went to the back of the long sales counter and rolled out a shallow drawer from beneath. There indeed was the sales ledger.

'Let us take it where we can turn up the lamp,' Raven said.

They withdrew into the laboratory, where they placed the ledger upon a table. Raven turned the pages carefully as Sarah held the lamp close. It was not difficult to find what they were looking for. Sales of chloroform had only commenced in the past month.

Raven ran a finger down the column on the far right, where it stated what had been purchased, and each time he encountered the word chloroform, he traced his finger left, to the name of the customer.

The first few instances were no surprise.

Simpson.

Simpson.

Simpson.

Then other names started to appear: Professor Miller, Professor Syme, Dr Ziegler, Dr Moir. Surgeons, obstetricians. There was Dr J.M. Duncan, insisting upon the extra letter, Raven observed. Mostly they were names he recognised, and it gave him pause to ask whether he was truly considering them to be his abortionist.

He saw a couple of names unfamiliar to him: a Dr John Mors, a Dr Edgar Klein. He was about to bid Sarah fetch some paper to write these down when the next purchaser stopped him with a jolt. Sarah's eyes were quicker than his finger, and she spoke the name aloud even as he read it.

'Adam Sheldrake. Rose's employer.'

Raven gaped, feeling like a fool. He recalled Simpson's lesson outside the inn near the Royal Exchange: *People often hypothesise the sensational, and become inexplicably blind to the obvious that is before their very eyes.*

It had been in front of him all along. He and Sarah attended the Sheldrakes' church in order to talk to Milly, and that led them to suspect Grissom. It had never occurred to him that Sheldrake himself was the obvious suspect.

'Not a doctor, but a medical man, of sorts,' Raven said. 'A dentist. Perhaps the wealthiest in the city. He might even have been responsible for Rose's condition. She was scared she would be dismissed if he found out.'

'I heard Mina make mention of a man in Glasgow believed to have murdered his housemaid because she was pregnant by him. But why would a wealthy dentist risk his reputation to carry out abortions?'

'Perhaps dentistry is not his most profitable practice. And you forget he has an ingenious means of protecting his reputation. Madame Anchou is the public face of the business, while he remains in shadow. Besides, his clients are young women from the lower orders, unlikely to be familiar with him as a dentist.'

'Until one of them turns out to be his own employee.'

Raven opened his mouth to speculate further, but no word issued from it, for at that moment they heard a key in the front door. He looked down the passage and saw the silhouette of a man in a top hat behind the glass.

Though the hour was past midnight, Mr Flockhart had returned to his shop.

FIFTY-TWO

arah had seldom moved so fast in her life. The state of heightened alertness she had experienced in these same premises several hours previously restored itself in an instant and drove her to action. In a quarter of a second, she recognised Mr Flockhart at the door and understood all possible implications as they applied to her circumstances. She also understood that the doom she envisaged earlier, when she heard a voice call 'Stop!', might merely have been postponed, not avoided.

She turned off the lamp as Raven lifted the ledger from the table, and led him swiftly to the storeroom. If Mr Flockhart was visiting at such an hour, it was either to retrieve something or because some idea had come upon him, and both were likely to bring him to the laboratory. The storeroom was off the passageway between it and the shop. There was no reason Flockhart would not need to visit it also, but it was the best chance they had to avoid detection.

Sarah ushered Raven inside and pulled the door to, but not fully closed. She could hear approaching footsteps and knew the sound of it meeting the frame would be too loud. It was not so much a room as a cupboard, a tiny space within intended for one person to reach the shelves on three sides.

They were pressed tight against each other, lest they nudge the door open. Sarah could feel the warmth of Raven against her chest, his scent in her nostrils, her nose almost touching his chin.

She tried not to breathe as she heard footsteps nearing. Through the crack in the door, she saw a dance of shadows, the aura of a lamp as Mr Flockhart made his way through the building.

She heard a cough, a clank of glass upon wood, a bottle or flask being placed on a table. Laughter, a tipsy giggle. Mr Flockhart was a noted socialite. He had stopped off after a night of revelry, but for what?

A few moments later, footsteps approached again. Did he need something from the store?

Once more the shadows flickered, the dancing aura visible through the crack. Sarah felt her heart thump against Raven as the footsteps grew closer.

Then they grew fainter. She heard the front door open. Flockhart was leaving.

Sarah breathed again, then the feeling of relief gave way to something more powerful, as though the lifting of fear had broken a dam within her. Even as the sound of the bolt reverberated from the front door, she pulled Raven closer, though that felt barely possible. She lifted her head in the darkness and found his lips. It felt as though this cramped little space was the whole world, and that world was filled with light.

FIFTY-THREE

aven extinguished his lamp and lay down, though he knew he would not sleep. The events of the past hour felt like they might take days to absorb. He could not even settle his mind to focus upon a single component of it, tossed amidst a storm of information, revelation and emotion. He did not lie alone in the dark as long as he feared, however.

He had barely settled into the pillow when he heard his door open and the sound of dainty feet upon the floor. Sarah stood before him clutching a candle, by the flickering light of which he could see that she was dressed only in her nightgown.

'What are you doing here?' he asked, his voice a whisper. He could not disguise how pleased he was to receive her, but was mindful of the consequences should they be discovered.

'I would hold you just a little longer,' she replied.

She slipped beneath the blankets alongside him, her arms tangling around him and pulling him close. There were but two thin layers of cloth between them as she pressed herself against him.

Raven recalled his youthful excitement when first he saw Evie unclothed, and of all that followed. This felt more powerful, though they merely lay together in silence, unmoving, the darkness enveloping them as though banishing the world outside. There was a rushing in his ears, soothing for being a sound without meaning. Sleep might come yet, though not with Sarah here. Much as he enjoyed the warmth of her against him, for them both to fall asleep would be to court disaster.

In time Sarah spoke softly, but one word.

'Thomas?'

'Yes?'

Raven's response was instinctive, too fast to avert.

He endured a moment of shock, but no fear and no threat. It felt like an intimacy, almost as much as the one that had preceded it.

'How do you know?'

'From parish records. I went in search of knowledge about Beattie, and in particular his family background. While I was there, I confess I indulged my curiosity. I smelled secrets upon you from the moment you entered this house.'

'And what do you smell upon Beattie, beyond oranges and sandalwood?'

Sarah paused.

'Hidden purpose. A man whose true intentions are always occluded.'

'What did you learn of him?'

'There is no record of Beattie's uncle or his mother ever having lived in Edinburgh. Nor is there record of his uncle living here now. I consulted the Post Office directory too.'

'Have you told Mina this?'

'Certainly not, for fear she shoots the messenger. She has an understandable faith in him, and would see it as inexcusable impertinence were I to reveal what I have found or even that I went looking for it. Nonetheless, I will not let her be deceived and walk blindly into a marriage that is not all she believes. There may yet be an innocent explanation, but I suspect Dr Beattie is not all that he pretends, and it is my intention to have answers from him.'

'He will not answer to a housemaid.'

'He will if she might otherwise reveal what she knows to her employer, Dr Simpson. I am tenacious, Mr Raven. And I would have answers from you also.'

She prodded him in the chest accusingly.

'Do not think I failed to notice that you changed the subject. How did Thomas Cunningham become Will Raven?'

Raven had indeed hoped she would forget. It would not do to deny her satisfaction, or some honesty.

'I changed my name when I enrolled at the university,' he said. 'I took my mother's surname and the middle name she chose for me. I wished to be entirely her son and not my father's.'

'Dr Simpson said you attended Heriot's school for fatherless boys. Yet the parish holds no record of your father's death.'

Raven lay quiet a moment, considering how he might best explain.

'I told Dr Simpson my father was a lawyer in St Andrews. That was not true. My father was a philanderer and a drunk, one prone to violent rage. A vintner whose business faltered because he was too fond of his own goods, and who took out his anger at his failings on us. My mother and I lived in permanent fear, never knowing what demeanour would be upon him when he came home.

'Then one night he beat my mother so viciously I feared he would kill her. After that, he walked out and left us. Perhaps when he saw what he had wrought, he finally felt shame, or perhaps he merely sought to escape the debts of his collapsing business.'

'He left and did not return?'

'Days passed, then weeks, then months, until it became clear he had abandoned us. My mother's brother, a lawyer, had some influence with George Heriot's school, and a special accommodation was made, as I was to all intents and purposes a fatherless boy. He took in my mother, as she was left mired in my father's debts.'

'You must feel a great fondness for an uncle who would be so generous. And yet I have never heard you speak of him.'

'I despise the man. His apparent generosity is in fact a cheap bargain for possessing and controlling my mother. He disapproved of her marrying my father and enjoys every opportunity to demonstrate how his judgment was vindicated while hers was responsible for her shameful plight. It is as though every penny he gives her further elevates him and further diminishes her. Thus it is my ambition to make a success of myself and buy back her dignity.'

'Did you ever hear word of what became of your father? Might he one day return? What would your mother do then?'

These were three questions for which Raven was prepared to offer but one answer.

'We are no longer afraid,' he told her.

FIFTY-FOUR

arvis was lighting lamps as Raven descended the stairs from his room, darkness already falling in the late afternoon. He encountered Sarah almost sprinting along the second-floor landing, laundered sheets piled so high in her arms he wondered how she could see where she was going. Raven halted her course before she could trip over David and Walter, who were huddled in her path as they waged an imaginary war down upon the carpet.

'What is your rush?' he asked.

'I am trying to discharge my duties swiftly so that I have a little extra time on the errands I must run before dinner. I wish to factor in an errand of my own while I am out.'

'You mean Beattie. You may not find him at home,' Raven warned. 'I am unsure of the hours he keeps.'

'Then I will make time to return each day until I have the truth from him.'

'After which you will have another problem – that of what to tell Mina.'

'Let us cross that bridge when we come to it,' she said, brushing past him to resume her work. 'I cannot tarry.'

Raven was full of admiration for Sarah's loyalty and sensitivity. He knew she often found Mina a trial and at times rather demanding, but nonetheless, she was prepared to go to great lengths to prevent any harm coming to the woman. The pity was that if Sarah unmasked Beattie as a fraud and a rogue out to take advantage of her, Mina might never forgive her for it.

Nonetheless, he was relieved that Sarah was busying herself with this quest right now. She had frequently insisted upon being involved first-hand in his investigations, but his mission today was taking him into more hazardous territory, and was best carried out alone.

Since their discovery at Duncan and Flockhart, Raven had asked himself how he might best investigate Adam Sheldrake, and the principal answer he had come up with was this: very carefully. He was a man with a great deal to lose, and that made him dangerous. It was possible he had already murdered Rose because of what she might reveal about him. Even if he had not, then his confederate surely had, and with Spiers's killing Raven had witnessed what she was prepared to do, without hesitation, in order to protect herself.

Since the encounter at the dockside, he had worried over how quickly the midwife had recognised him. He searched every face in his memory but still could not think of where they must have seen each other before. This was inclining him further towards the belief that Madame Anchou was an alias for someone else. Did Sheldrake know her real identity, he wondered? Had Spiers? She had murdered him as soon as she calculated he was a liability. Was her true name the thing she feared he might reveal?

Raven and Sarah had speculated that Rose might have been poisoned because she had discovered this forbidden knowledge too. However, if Sheldrake was secretly working as an abortionist, then the dentist had reason of his own to silence his housemaid after her plight led her to the King's Wark.

Perhaps they were both capable of murder: each as ruthless and deadly as the other.

Raven had enquired as to the location of Sheldrake's dental

surgery. Though he also did home visits, he spent several hours each day offering a clinic wherein patients might attend. Raven's intention was to follow him unseen to discover where else he went once these clinics were over, because at some juncture he would have to resume meeting his partner in these dark arts.

The surgery was on the edge of the New Town, on London Street, not half an hour's walk to the Leith tavern. The clinic was likely to finish within the hour, so like Sarah, Raven had no time to tarry.

Raven opened the front door and promptly felt the ice-cold wind sting his cheeks. He closed it again and looked covetously at Dr Simpson's coat, hanging up just inside the hall. The professor was home for the evening now, busy upstairs in his study. He surely wouldn't miss it for a couple of hours.

Raven looked around for Jarvis, who had disappeared into the drawing room. He slung the coat about his shoulders, its weight pleasingly heavy. He felt transformed, like a knight in armour better equipped to face his foe, even if his foe was merely the weather. He only wished that he could take on the professor's mantle so easily as donning his sealskin.

As he stepped through the front door, the coat swirling about him like a cloak, a number of disparate fragments swirling at the forefront of his thoughts coalesced at once into a visible whole.

He saw the figure in the cape, walking towards him on Leith Shore.

Someone pretending to be what they are not.

Each as ruthless and deadly as the other.

A French midwife who may not be French.

A person transformed by a single garment.

'*Such an arrangement would allow a doctor to practise this dark art without the risk that would attend advertising such services.*'

Sheldrake was not in league with Madame Anchou. Sheldrake *was* Madame Anchou.

He saw it all now. Sheldrake's already feminine face, disguised beneath powder, peering out from the shadows of a hood. And how much easier to hide your true voice when speaking in another language or accent. It was the perfect way to protect his reputation while carrying out his illegal but lucrative sideline.

Raven's head spun with it as he stepped onto Queen Street, which was why he failed to notice the three men rapidly approaching, their eyes fixed upon him. In this moment of revelation, he was heedless of the danger until it was too late.

Two of them grabbed him from either side and bundled him into Dr Simpson's carriage, the third knocking the protesting coachman to the ground and seizing the reins.

Raven did not recognise them, but it took only one name to tell him all he needed to know.

'A Mr Flint humbly requests your attendance, sir.'

FIFTY-FIVE

arah felt a familiar unease about walking the streets after dark, particularly as her journey had just taken her beyond the bounds of the New Town. In her growing fear, she could not help but ask herself what she hoped might come of this. If there was an innocent explanation for Beattie's apparent dishonesty, then she would surely be dismissed once he reported her impudence and accusations to Mina and to Dr Simpson. However, until she had such an explanation, she could not in good conscience allow her employer to be deceived like this, and for Mina to be so ill-used.

There was only one house on the narrow lane, a good thirty yards along Shrub Hill from Leith Walk and the comparative reassurance of its street lights. Beattie's address was a solitary cottage, a glow from the windows enough to guide her path. She recalled Raven saying he might not be at home, but clearly someone was. Sarah didn't know if Beattie kept a housemaid like herself. Perhaps if he did, and he was indeed from home, she might prove someone from whom Sarah could discreetly solicit some information.

She approached the front door on quiet tread, fearful of the sound of her own footfalls. From what she could make out in the dark, it was a neat little cottage, a dwelling she could imagine being maintained with the same attention Beattie afforded his own appearance.

She rang the bell and heard footsteps in response, which she confidently predicted to be male. It was indeed Beattie who opened the door. He looked most surprised to find her there, and not pleasantly so.

'I am sorry to trouble you at home, Dr Beattie, but I have difficult news concerning your uncle, Mr Latimer.'

Beattie was taken aback, though whether his expression reflected concern for the welfare of his uncle or suspicion over the potential unravelling of his deceit remained to be seen.

'You must come in,' he said.

There was a sternness to his tone, at once commanding and yet eager. He bade her follow him into the house. It was brighter than she anticipated. There appeared to be lamps lit in several rooms, as well as the hall itself.

There was no maid in evidence, and Sarah wondered whether the expense of having one would prove an economy over the wasteful burning of so much oil and gas. Perhaps he was busy with activities that required him to flit from room to room, though such matters would surely be simpler to deal with by day.

He ushered her to the drawing room, where he took the time to light still more lamps. An uncharitable part of her wondered if it was so that he might better stare at her bosom. On her way down the hall, she had noticed another open door and caught a glimpse of Beattie's study, which, from the equipment she spied, appeared to function also as a laboratory.

He gestured her to a chair. Beattie sat down opposite, a low table between them at their knees. Sarah was unused to being seated at such a fixture, more accustomed to serving tea upon it.

'So, what news is it that you have for me?'

Sarah swallowed. She hoped that the anxiety she might be displaying would be read by him as evidence of her apprehension at sharing difficult tidings.

'Your uncle's house is in Canaan Lands, is it not? On the Morningside?'

Beattie paused a moment before responding. It struck her that one should not be so wary of a question to which the answer is a simple yes or no. Did he suspect she was testing him? Probably not. Men such as him did not believe the lower orders to have the audacity or imagination to so deceive.

'It is.'

'Miss Grindlay told me how you described it, with its views and fine gardens and even a large hothouse. She said your mother was born and raised there, which makes this all the more difficult.'

He regarded her with piercing eyes, his expression impatient.

'What of it? Come to the point, Miss . . .?'

'Fisher,' she reminded him, though she was unsure he had ever heard her surname before. 'I met a friend today, in the service of a family in Canaan. She was talking about what sounded like the very same house, which was occupied by an elderly gentleman who lives alone. Canaan Bank, I think she said the house was called. Is that your uncle's? Or did she say Canaan Lodge?'

'What of it?' he demanded, his irritation growing. Sarah noted that he had not answered the question.

'The most dreadful calamity. The reason she mentioned it was that there was a terrible fire overnight. They woke to the sight of smoke. The house is ruined. I had hoped word might already have reached you, so that I would not be the one to bring such news, but alas it does not appear to be the case.'

'I had heard no word.'

She noted that he did not ask after the welfare of his uncle.

'I realise this must be particularly distressing as you were to inherit this house, were you not? Though Miss Grindlay said it was in a state of some disrepair and would not be all you once hoped.'

She could see cogs whirring behind his eyes. Raven had warned her that Beattie would not answer questions of a housemaid, so she had considered her strategy accordingly. The bait in her trap was to offer Beattie a lie that would extricate him from a previous deceit, one she believed he was already laying the groundwork to escape. Tales of the house's disrepair and his uncle's illness were a means of preparing the path to tell Mina there would be no house to inherit, from an uncle who would die before she could meet him. If it turned out there was indeed a house in the area that had been so devastated, inhabited by a single elderly gentleman to boot, then this would solve the problem for him.

'Indeed. This is distressing news. You describe the place I know so well. Canaan Bank is lost.'

Sarah suppressed a smile of satisfaction. By naming the house, he had committed himself. She had him.

'I must say, Dr Beattie, I am troubled that you have not enquired as to the welfare of your uncle.'

Beattie was unfazed in his response. His answer was calmly logical, and for that, betrayed him all the more.

'I assume he was not a casualty, otherwise you would have led with his demise.'

'Or is it not that you have no such concerns because you have no such uncle? There was no house named Canaan Bank, and no fire either. I made it up — as did you. I would know why.'

Beattie appeared frozen for a moment, his expression fixed like one of Miss Mann's calotypes. He blinked once then gave his answer, his nose wrinkling in distaste.

'I cannot think what possessed you to undertake this charade, Miss Fisher, but I knew you were making it up from the moment you walked in here. Which is why I indulged your silly parlour games in order to see where this impertinence might lead. And the answer is that it will lead to the street. I will see you dismissed without character.'

As a threat Sarah had lived under for some time, it held far less fear than Beattie intended. Sarah met his eye brazenly.

'I suspect Dr Simpson might take a different view, unless you can produce this uncle of yours and the house he lives in. I have consulted the parish register and there is no record of a Charles Latimer. I have been also to the Post Office, where I verified that nobody by that name lives in the city even now. Why are you deceiving Miss Grindlay, Dr Beattie?'

FIFTY-SIX

The carriage bucked and rattled, travelling faster than it ever had before, faster than it was designed for, in fact. Raven heard crack after crack of the reins, Flint's man showing no restraint as he urged on the horses, giving little consideration to the growing dark and fog. Many an unwary pedestrian had found themselves in need of Syme's ministrations after straying into the path of a carriage when visibility was this bad, but at such speed it was unlikely any unfortunates would survive long enough to face the further ordeal of surgery.

Each corner threatened to tip the brougham, though it never quite came to that; more's the pity, Raven thought, as it might have offered the opportunity to crawl from the wreckage and flee. He tried to estimate the damage should he throw himself from the carriage in order to escape, but it was as though his captors had anticipated such a manoeuvre. They were seated tight on either side of him, wedging him in place. One of them bore a scar from his forehead to his chin, as from a sword blow. The other was distinguished by a goitre so pronounced that he looked like a toad. They had said little, and Raven less.

He saw his foolishness now. He had come to believe he merely had to keep evading Gargantua and the Weasel, and had reserved

his vigilance for his ventures south of Princes Street, as though
the New Town was some protected kingdom beyond Flint's reach.
They had been lying in wait, apprehending him as soon as he
stepped outside the door to 52 Queen Street. They had asked
questions and tracked him down, and now he was being taken to
his doom, a fate he had long tempted.

You have the devil in you.

He thought of the recklessness with which he had regarded
his debt. He feared men such as Flint, but that did not leaven
the contempt in which he held them, and sometimes the former
was over-ruled by the latter. It satisfied that perverse and angry
part of himself to defy them. Thus he had not merely evaded
making repayment, but had insulted Flint in the way he resisted,
and even injured his men.

As though mocking him, Dr Simpson's bag sat upon the bench
opposite, a totem of the future he dreamed for himself and which
he would not live to see. It had been at the coachman's behest
that he leave it in the brougham between trips, Angus having too
frequently been forced to double back mid-journey because
Simpson had forgotten it in his haste to reach an urgent case.

Raven found it difficult to make out the buildings clearly in
the gloom, but his sense of direction told him they were in
Fountainbridge, on the outskirts of the Old Town. Tellingly, the
carriage pulled up not in front of a building, but at the rear,
where he was bundled out of the coach and marched into a back
court, gripped either side by Scar and Toad.

The Weasel came scurrying from the close at the back of the
building in response to the coach's arrival. He gazed upon Raven
with an ugly mix of anger and confusion at him being delivered
thus. Raven wondered why he would seem surprised.

The Weasel was followed by a frightened young woman
sporting the beginnings of a black eye, the skin around her right
orbit red and swollen with a small amount of conjunctival haemorrhage. She looked drained and pale, with blood smeared about

her clothes. Raven could barely guess at her role here, and wondered at the whereabouts of Gargantua.

The Weasel strode across and punched Raven hard in the stomach but was pushed back by Toad.

'What the devil are you doing? This is Dr Simpson, whom Flint bid us fetch.'

'No, it isn't,' Weasel replied. 'This is Will Raven, the whelp who near blinded me and who yet owes Flint two guineas.'

'I assure you it is Simpson. Flint told us he lives at 52 Queen Street and is to be recognised by his black sealskin coat. We saw him leaving that very house dressed thus.'

'And I'm telling you this one might be wearing his coat, but that's as close as he will ever get to being Dr Simpson.'

At that moment, out strode the man to whom Raven owed the debt: Callum Flint himself. He was as Raven remembered: not the biggest of men, but lean and wiry, quick of mind and quick of movement. The build of a pugilist and the brain of a schemer.

He looked unlikely to be in a forgiving mood, as rather improbably, his nose was bleeding, the blood still dripping onto an already damp shirt. Some altercation had recently taken place. Raven could hear screaming from somewhere within, no doubt retribution being meted out to whomever had dealt the blow.

'What in the name of God is this wee streak of piss doing here?' he demanded. 'Where is Simpson?'

The Weasel wore a look of satisfaction, enjoying the moment his colleagues had their mistake confirmed. It was like an overture for the symphony of vengeance with which he was about to indulge himself.

Flint wiped the blood from his nose with his sleeve. He had an overwrought look about him, a man at the end of his tether. A man in need of an outlet for his frustrations.

'They lifted this skitter by mistake,' Weasel said. 'He owes you two guineas and me a debt of another kind.'

Flint looked at Raven with sparing regard, as though his true thoughts were somewhere else.

'Do you have the two guineas?' he asked.

Raven could not speak to answer, such was his fear.

He heard another scream, thinking for a moment it was a foretaste of his own. Then he realised it was a woman's scream, and deduced what was going on.

'Mr Flint, you sent for Dr Simpson. Is your wife in labour?'

'Aye,' said the young girl with the black eye, hurried and imploring. 'She is, these fourteen hours. Blind and insane in her agonies. Lashing out at those who would try to assist her.'

'I can help.'

'What know you of such things?' Flint demanded.

'I am Dr Simpson's assistant. A man midwife.'

'I want the professor, not his student.'

'But I am here now, and Dr Simpson yet at Queen Street.'

At that moment, there came another scream from inside the building.

'Bring him forth,' Flint decided.

'I need the bag that sits inside the carriage,' Raven said.

'Fetch it,' Flint commanded Scar. 'And see to it that this time you don't bring a hat or a horse-turd by mistake.'

Raven was escorted into the building and led to a room on the first floor, where he was confronted by a scene that immediately brought to mind the Simpsons' dining room on the night of the chloroform discovery. Several pieces of furniture were upturned and a ewer and basin were in pieces upon the floor. The smell was reminiscent of a tavern at the end of a busy night, a noxious mix of stale alcohol fumes combined with various bodily odours and the very distinct tang of blood.

Flint's wife was being forcibly held in the bed by a number of persons including Peg and Gargantua. They were all in a state of dishevelment and perspiring almost as much as the patient herself. Gargantua looked at Raven with confusion and growing rage, but did not abandon his post.

Among those around the bed was a midwife, sporting a bruise to her cheek. She looked upon Raven with almost as much disdain as the giant. Midwives had little love for their male competitors, and that she was being asked to defer to one as young as him would be all the more galling. That said, like everyone else present herein, she looked desperate. This was one occasion where Raven felt sure he couldn't make the situation any worse. However, his only chance to avoid being murdered was if he could make it better.

'Tell me what has gone on and make it quick,' he said, his commanding tone a means of disguising his fear.

'The membranes ruptured in the early hours of this morning and I have been dosing Mrs Flint regularly with brandy and water,' the midwife said.

The woman was writhing and thrashing, trying to free the arm the midwife clutched.

'However, she became delirious and increasingly restless. I administered several doses of laudanum but to no avail; her delirium only worsened, and as you can see, she became most violent in her agonies. If you believe *you* can restrain her where all of us have failed, then I would welcome the chance to watch you attempt it.'

With that she let go of the arm she was holding, all the better for Mrs Flint to lash out at Raven with it, and stepped clear of the bed.

Raven delved into Dr Simpson's bag, struggling initially to see into it in the dim gaslight. For a heart-stopping moment he could not find the bottle he sought, but then there it was.

Raven put about twenty drops of the chloroform onto a pocket handkerchief, which he rolled into a cone shape as he had been taught. Mrs Flint bucked and screamed, swiping an arm at him as he approached. Raven blocked the blow with his forearm and held the moistened handkerchief about an inch from her face before bringing it closer until it covered her nose and mouth. Within about a minute, her writhing ceased and her attendants were able to release their hold of her, though they appeared wary that she might resume.

'He has poisoned her!' the midwife cried. 'Mr Flint, this man has murdered your wife!'

'This is chloroform, a new drug,' Raven retorted, looking Flint in the eye. 'She will sleep and feel no pain until I revive her.'

With the patient now at rest, Raven was able to perform an examination, upon which he ascertained the position of the infant and the reason for the lack of progress. He felt a knot tighten inside him. He had been wrong in his impression when he first entered the room: there was a way he could make the situation worse, if only for himself.

His examination had identified not the head of the infant in the birth canal but its arm. The mother and baby could both die here. He had administered chloroform, and though it would not be what killed her, if Mrs Flint never regained consciousness, he would be blamed. The midwife would make sure if it.

Raven could not afford to think what would happen after that.

He would have to turn the child in the womb before he could attempt to deliver it, a manoeuvre he had never performed. If he failed, he would certainly be killed. Even if he succeeded, his fate was far from certain.

Raven closed his eyes a moment and took himself from this place. Not far, perhaps a little more than a mile, to a room above the Canongate: the first case he had visited in the company of Dr Simpson. He pictured the diagram the professor had sketched on a sheet of paper upon a wax-spattered table in that hot and foetid room. *The whole child can be considered to be cone-shaped, the apex or narrowest part being the feet. The skull can also be thought of as a cone, the narrowest part of which is the base.*

Raven took a breath and began. His hand passed easily into the uterus and found the infant's knee without difficulty. From there he found both feet and pulled them down, firmly but gently. The chloroform had relaxed the maternal muscles and the delivery was completed some five minutes later; a male child, born alive, although the arm which had been residing in the birth canal for some considerable time was almost black in colour.

The placenta followed shortly after the child, and there was little bleeding. The child was swaddled by the girl with the black eye, whose name turned out to be Morag.

Flint took the baby from her, holding his son in his arms quite jealously.

His wife awoke shortly after, her face a study in disorientation and confusion, as though rousing from a dream. Flint offered her the child, which she regarded with disbelief for a moment before hugging it to her breast.

'I thought myself in the throes of death,' she said. 'Yet here is the bonniest wee thing. How can this be so?'

'It was the young doctor, ma'am,' said Morag.

Flint walked Raven out to the back court, Peg and Gargantua at their backs. The Weasel, the Toad and Scar awaited, accompanied by the man who had so terrifyingly driven the horses. He was a gaunt and ancient thing, looking like his bones ought to have crumbled from the shaking. Evidently he was made of sterner stuff than he appeared, inside and out.

The Weasel was sharpening his knife by dragging it across the stone of the building, eyeing Raven with a purposeful stare. They were all five at their boss's command, which Raven was also waiting for, upon tenterhooks.

'I remember you now,' Flint said. 'When you came to me for money, you said you might not be able to pay it back swiftly, but that you were a man of some prospects. I can see that to be true. That stuff you used was quite miraculous. What was it called again?'

'Chloroform,' Raven replied.

'Where might a man procure this wondrous liquid?'

'From Duncan and Flockhart, on Princes Street.'

'Hmm,' Flint mused. 'A business such as that is liable to take note of who is purchasing their wares. Might one acquire it otherwise? Through an intermediary, perhaps?'

Raven could see where this might lead, but was in no position to refuse.

'Perhaps.'

The Weasel continued to scrape his blade, impatience writ upon his face as he became concerned that the evening might not reach the conclusion for which he hoped.

'Put that damned knife away,' Flint commanded, as though irritated by the sound.

The Weasel complied with a sigh.

'Mr Raven here is to go about his business unmolested from here on,' Flint announced to the ragged assembly. 'I am the one in *his* debt tonight.'

'He's still in mine,' the Weasel protested. 'He near took my sight.'

'You seem able to see well enough,' Raven retorted.

'Aye,' Flint mused. 'I gather you bested this pair single-handed a wee while back.'

'He blinded me with a powder,' Gargantua grumbled.

'Exactly,' said Flint. 'You strike me as a man of some resource and gumption. I wonder if in lieu of your debt, you and I might reach an understanding.'

Flint looked him in the eye. Raven knew he was doing a deal with the devil, but it was better than having the devil on his back.

'We might.'

'And is there something I can offer you, by way of thanks?'

Raven was about to politely refuse, not wishing to delay his departure, when it occurred to him that this was a man with an ear to the underbelly of the city, and many eyes reporting back to him.

'Only information. There is someone I seek. Perhaps you might get word to me if you or your men should encounter her.'

'A woman? Who?'

'She is a French midwife who goes by the name of—'

'Madame Anchou,' said the Toad. 'Sells pills and potions, at quite a cost.'

'Aye,' said Scar with a chuckle. 'He bought one from her that was supposed to help him stand proud, if you take my meaning. Suffers from brewer's droop.'

'Didn't bloody work, did it?' the Toad moaned bitterly.

'What did you expect?' asked Scar. 'There isn't a potion known to Merlin could make a man's cock stand tall at the prospect of any woman who would have you.'

'Where did you see her?' Raven demanded, his urgency cutting through the growing levity.

'In a tavern off the Canongate. I was given her name by a Mrs Peake, runs a whorehouse nearby.'

'What do you remember of her?'

'Not much. It was dark and she had on a cape and a hood. I recall that she had a smell about her, an exotic scent. So strong it would have choked you.'

Raven felt his skin prickle, cold even beneath Dr Simpson's troublesome coat.

'What was it like, this scent?'

'Oranges.'

FIFTY-SEVEN

eattie now had a thunderous look on his face. This was when Sarah expected to be shown the door, amidst a pompous tirade about impropriety and further insistence that he would see her sacked.

Instead, a sudden calmness seemed to come upon him. A transformation. He sat back in his chair, holding open his hands in a placatory gesture.

'Miss Fisher, I owe you an apology. You are correct. All is indeed not as it would appear.' He got to his feet, his expression sincere. 'I would ask of you the courtesy of allowing me to explain. And by way of contrition, let me offer you some tea, that we might take it together while you hear me out.'

Sarah stood up too, almost by reflex. 'Allow me to assist you then, sir.'

'No, please. The kettle is not long boiled in the grate, and you have served me often enough. It is right and fitting that I should reciprocate for once.'

Sarah knew not to push the issue. She watched him leave the room, then made use of the brief time he was absent to step quietly across the hall and take a closer look at his study.

She saw anatomy specimens arrayed in jars upon shelves against the wall, reflected gaslight glinting in the glass. There were examples of every organ preserved in clear fluid: hearts, lungs, kidneys, even a brain. Sarah could well imagine how this sight might unnerve many an unwary visitor, but as someone used to the ways of medical men, she did not regard it as out of the ordinary. That said, something struck her as unusual about the specimens, though she could not from such a brief glimpse discern what it was. It gave her a vague sense of unease, but that was as nothing compared to the shock of seeing the pair of kid gloves that were lying upon his desk.

Sarah returned to the drawing room in time for Beattie's reappearance bearing the promised tea on a tray. He placed it down on the low table, whereupon it was made clear that he was unused to serving anyone. She noticed that the cups were not matching and that the tea was already poured.

'Thank you,' she said. 'It is such an unaccustomed honour to be waited upon by a gentleman. Might I then be so bold as to trouble you for a fancy or even a biscuit?'

Beattie looked annoyed with himself at this oversight.

'Of course. I bought scones this morning, if that would suffice.'

He returned presently with a solitary scone on a plate. He had forgotten to bring a knife or butter, but she was content with what was offered.

'How did you come to be in Dr Simpson's service?' he asked.

Sarah answered briefly, sipping from her cup. The tea was passable, but far from the finest.

'It is a most unusual household, is it not?' Beattie went on. 'What strange sights you must have seen there.'

For a man who normally talked exclusively about himself and his ambitions, this was a remarkable level of interest to be showing in anyone else, far less a housemaid. It was almost as though he was waiting for something. Perhaps he thought that if he stalled her long enough, she would forget about her own questions. She would put him straight on that.

'Dr Beattie, you promised me an explanation. I wish to know

why you lied to Miss Grindlay and to Dr Simpson about having this uncle. Because if you are prepared to lie about that, one must wonder what else you might be lying about.'

With that, she drained her cup, thus underlining that the niceties were over.

Beattie watched her place it down upon the saucer, at which point she was sure she detected another transformation. He seemed more himself again, confident and haughty.

'I asked about your service, Miss Fisher, because I hoped you would understand that opportunities are not always easy to come by. Sometimes they must be manufactured. People can be encouraged to believe in something, that they may have confidence in it. I wished them to have confidence in me.'

He took a drink from his own cup.

'You are correct. I have no uncle and no house to inherit. All that I have, I have made for myself. My background is of no real relevance. It is my prospects and my future that are important, and I will have a great future. Mina is very lucky that she will share it.'

'You are only interested in her for the connection to Dr Simpson such a marriage would afford, are you not?'

'Let us be realistic. Mina's only hope of a husband was someone seeking association with Dr Simpson. She is fortunate that it should be me. In the field of my profession, my gifts are only matched by my ambitions.'

He was finally showing the true face she suspected, and he clearly knew that he had nothing to fear from such candour. Not from this housemaid before him.

'On the subject of gifts, Dr Beattie, I saw you purchase a pair of kid gloves at Kennington and Jenner's. I assumed them wrapped as a present intended for Miss Grindlay, and yet I spied them open and worn in your study. Do you have another woman?'

'I have many women. One would imagine Mina ought to be realistic enough to understand the nature of the match. But I will own that those gloves do belong to one who is particularly dear to me.'

He wore an odd smile, one that Sarah found unsettling.

'You were prying around my study, then,' he went on, standing up once more. 'Perhaps you should come and pry a little closer. For I have something there that I would like you to see.'

Beattie took hold of her arm and pulled her roughly to her feet, leading her from the room with a tight grip. He hauled her into the study, where he stood her next to the table upon which the gloves lay.

'I am not the only one disguising their true intentions. You and young Raven are secretly in league, are you not?'

Sarah said nothing. She was looking for how she might flee, but Beattie stood in the doorway.

'Have a look in that press, there by the window.'

Sarah approached it, her heart beating a tattoo. Even before opening the door, she knew what she would find inside.

Hanging before her in the cupboard was the French midwife's robe.

'Have you answers enough now?' Beattie asked, his tone distressingly calm.

She stared at the garment, contemplating all of its implications.

'The gloves were for you. You are Madame Anchou. You murdered Rose Campbell because she discovered this.'

'Like you, she saw things she should not have. At least in her case, she was not spying. I thought her asleep and she witnessed me take on my disguise.'

Sarah turned to face him. 'Why are you telling me such things? Why would you show me this?'

'I'm sure even a housemaid must have the wit to work that out.'

Sarah swallowed, her mouth dry and her voice failing. 'Do you intend to kill me, Dr Beattie?'

'No, Miss Fisher, I do not *intend* to kill you. I killed you two minutes ago, when you drank your tea.'

FIFTY-EIGHT

aven clung to the inside of the door as the brougham took another tight corner. His heart leapt as he felt the wheels on one side actually leave the ground, but he suppressed the urge to tell the skeletal coachman to slow down. Shorn of the weight of two passengers, he was driving the horses even faster upon the return journey, and Raven had no wish to interfere with that.

Sarah's instincts had been right all along. She had talked of a whiff of deceit, but it was a stench, covered up by bergamot and sandalwood. It was not Sheldrake, but Beattie who was the French midwife, Beattie who had recognised Raven from a distance as he waited on the dockside, Beattie who had killed Spiers for fear that the landlord might spill his secret. And Beattie to whom Sarah was headed to confront this night, alone and with no notion of just how dangerous he was.

Raven had deduced all of this in a twinkling the moment that overpowering scent was described. He saw beneath the veil Beattie had cast about himself and understood what had been before him since the beginning. That calm he exhibited in the face of suffering was not due to knowing true sorrow. It was because he genuinely felt nothing. He did not care about the patients. He did not care about anyone. That equanimity, that assuredness, it was a detachment from human emotion.

Raven thought back to when Beattie told him about his lamented Julia, his one true love who died the day before their wedding. What a look of anger had preceded this revelation, an outraged fury that briefly surfaced at having been challenged. Beattie had then composed himself and responded with a tale so tragic, so poignant, and so tailored to assuage Raven's suspicions.

Raven recalled the pause after he asked for her name. Beattie had needed a moment to make one up.

Suddenly every remembered conversation seemed to reveal a hidden truth.

It is always wise to learn as much as you can about the great names in your field, in case fate should throw you into their company.

Beattie boasted how he had researched Simpson's background in depth. Did he know all along about the unmarried sister-in-law who might provide a route into Simpson's family and his name? Was this in his plans even as he sent that blood-smeared note calling for Simpson's assistance?

Raven understood now how adept Beattie was at playing a part. He could pretend to be genuinely interested in Mina, just as he could pretend to be protecting Raven from the consequences of Caroline Graseby's death. Raven had been unable to see how she could have died from the ether. It was clear now that it was likely something Beattie did that killed her. He had killed Graseby and he had killed so many others: some he perhaps hadn't meant to and some he certainly did – those whose on-going existence threatened to expose him.

Raven had raced without hesitation from Flint's yard to the brougham, urging they proceed with all haste, until the coachman asked where they were bound. That was when he realised he did not know where Beattie lived.

He leapt from the carriage even before it had come to a halt outside No. 52, racing across the pavement and throwing open the door. He found Jarvis in the hallway, Mrs Lyndsay standing beside him. Her face was ruddy, and not merely from the heat of the stove. She looked furious.

'Where is Dr Simpson?' Raven demanded.

'He is gone with Angus to fetch McLevy,' Jarvis answered. 'His coach and horses were stolen – with you in it, I believe. They hailed a hansom and set off for the High Street and the police office. Where have you been? Why are you wearing Dr Simpson's coat? And do you know what is become of Miss Fisher? She has not returned for dinner duties.'

'Nor ought she to return now,' Mrs Lyndsay added, 'for if she does, she will find no tasks awaiting her. She is gone without leave and it is the last I will tolerate. The girl can consider herself dismissed.'

He took the stairs three at a time in a rapid ascent towards Dr Simpson's study. He knew there had been correspondence between Beattie and the professor, from which his place of residence might be ascertained. He knew also that Mina's own letters had been Sarah's source, but there were any number of subjects he did not wish to broach with Miss Grindlay in order to procure this information.

Simpson's desk was in its usual state of chaos, covered in so many sheets of paper that it resembled the floor of a white-treed forest in late autumn. Raven rifled through it, separating technical notes from correspondence and discarding items he had checked by dropping them to the floor. He soon happened upon what he required: a letter from Beattie formally proposing his marriage to Mina. There it was: Shrub Hill, just beyond the edges of the New Town.

Raven's eyes had no sooner lifted the letter than he noticed Simpson's case journal beneath it. It was open at a recent entry concerning a visit to a house on Fettes Row, the chloroform-assisted birth of a daughter to a Mrs Fiona McDonald. Simpson kept detailed notes of all his visits in this volume, and that would include the case at Danube Street about which he was sworn to secrecy.

He was aware time was wasting but he had to know, especially in light of what he had now discovered about Beattie. He flipped the pages frantically until he found the entry, made only hours before that fateful gathering in the room downstairs.

Raven felt a lurching in his gut as he confirmed that the procedure at which he assisted had in fact been an attempted abortion. But that was nothing compared to what he felt as he read on. Rather than having difficulty in becoming pregnant, Caroline Graseby's problem had been quite the opposite. She *was* pregnant, but the dates of an extended business trip to America quite conspicuously precluded her husband being the father. 'Inconvenient evidence of indiscretions' was how Simpson delicately put it. Terrified of the consequences, Mrs Graseby had sought the means to correct her condition.

According to Simpson's notes − which mercifully did not mention Raven's name − the individual who carried out the procedure was a Dr John Mors. It was an alias, and one of the unfamiliar names that had appeared in Duncan and Flockhart's ledger. Graseby had called him Johnnie, and Beattie had instructed Raven similarly to call him only John. He had claimed this informality put the nervous Graseby at ease, but now Raven understood that it was to prevent them each learning that the other knew him by a different surname.

Raven recalled the easy manner with which Beattie and Graseby had sat together, and the pressure he was putting on her to submit to the procedure. He suddenly had a notion that Beattie had been attempting to abort his own child.

However, none of these things was yet the most shocking. Simpson had been able to discover all this from the patient herself, for Caroline Graseby was not dead.

FIFTY-NINE

aven ran out onto the pavement, where he found that his ancient coachman had vanished. Perhaps they had passed a comfortable-looking cemetery on the return journey and he had gone there to take up residence. Raven looked left and right in the hope that he might find Dr Simpson and Angus hurrying back. Instead he merely saw darkness and fog.

Having no notion of how to drive horses or to ride one, he had little option but to run. He took off along Queen Street, heading east at a pace he estimated he could maintain for the entire journey. Shrub Hill was almost the distance he had run from Professor Gregory's lab after discovering the dead rabbits. Recalling that occasion, he wondered whether once again he might be wrong about the danger, just as it transpired that Sarah had mislaid the deadly vial. Beattie would have no reason to suspect Sarah's queries on Mina's behalf indicated any inkling of his greater secret, so perhaps at most he would send her away with a scolding for doubting his word, and for her insolence in pursuing those doubts.

After all, Sarah *had* no inkling. If she did, she would never have gone there.

But as he ran, he saw how Beattie might indeed suspect. He

had recognised Raven on the dock outside the King's Wark and understood that Raven was looking into these matters. Beattie had fled, and then doubled back to kill Spiers. Had he also seen Sarah, and deduced she was the housemaid who sought Madame Anchou's services in order to draw her out?

Raven cut around the back of Hope Crescent, sacrificing street light for the ability to approach Beattie's cottage from the rear. It would not do to present himself at the front door, as Beattie already knew Raven was a threat. He would have to take him by surprise.

He crept quietly into the grounds, picking his path carefully in the sparing glow of light from a rear window. He saw no shadow, no flicker of movement from within, and heard no voices. The sound of argument would have been a welcome one.

Raven drew closer, crouched beneath the sill, then slowly raised himself up to look inside. All thoughts of stealth and strategy flew from his mind as he peered through the glass and saw Sarah's body lying on the floor.

He ran directly to the back door, ready to break it down if he had to. It was not locked. He charged inside with no thought for quiet, passing through a kitchen where he caught a glimpse of a mortar and pestle next to the kettle, fine powder dusting the marble's rim.

From the hall he could see Sarah's arm outstretched where she lay on the floor of Beattie's study. Raven felt propelled towards her as though driven by a hand at his back. As he neared the doorway, he was felled by an explosion of light and pain. Something solid and heavy struck him across the face, the full force of its swing added to the weight of his own momentum.

He reeled from the impact, blind and dazed, his legs weakened beneath him. Raven caught a flashing glimpse of Beattie clutching a poker or a stave. Further blows rained without mercy, one to the base of the spine, another to the back of his legs, another smashing down upon his head. He collapsed face-first to the floor, where still another strike to his side left him barely able to breathe. He was helpless.

Beattie knelt on his back and began securing his wrists with twine. He did so tightly and expertly, in a way that told Raven he was not the first person to be bound by this man.

He tried to raise his head, but as he did so, blood ran from his scalp into his right eye. Through his left he could see Sarah lying on the carpet a few feet across the room. She was utterly still. No twine had been necessary for her.

He would have cried then, but he did not have the breath.

Above her body, he saw shelves upon shelves of anatomy specimens ranged in jars, dominating the room. Even in his damaged state, something about the collection struck Raven as strange, though it took him a moment to grasp what was wrong with them.

The answer was: nothing.

Most medical men kept specimens of diseased organs as well as healthy ones, illustrative of unusual and damaging conditions. Beattie's were all perfectly healthy, utterly normal.

'You killed them,' Raven said, finding a voice.

'Killed who?' Beattie asked, as though irritated by the query.

'So many. The women who took your pills. You gave them a slow and painful death, and you cared not. The women you operated on for abortions died just as slowly. You killed them too.'

Raven glanced across the room once more, some part of him still hoping he would see the movement that would prove him wrong. It did not come.

'And you killed Sarah.'

'Quite,' Beattie replied, as though it were a mere detail.

Raven struggled to find his voice through anger and grief. 'My God, man. The only woman you *didn't* kill was Graseby, yet you told me I had. Did you think I would never find out?'

'As you suggest, I cared not. But I knew that believing it

would make you most obedient, almost as obsequious as you are towards that bombastic and self-regarding prig you work for.'

'Self-regarding? You murdered Sarah, Rose Campbell and Spiers, merely to silence them.'

'Their sacrifice is unfortunate, but they forced my hand. I am on the cusp of remarkable things that will bring untold benefits. For a housemaid or a publican to have stopped my work would have been a disaster.'

Beattie satisfied himself that the bonds around Raven's wrists were tight and began binding his ankles.

'You, by contrast, will not be a great loss. You would not have made a good doctor, Raven. You let sentiment hold you back: sentiment and sympathy. To truly succeed, you must set the patients apart from yourself, and I saw no evidence you could do that, which is why you would never have been anything more than a nurse.'

'Set them apart? You use them as subjects for experiment. You poisoned those women. Was it not enough to profit from their desperation by selling them a useless pill at exorbitant cost? Did you have to give them a painful death so that they did not come looking for their money back?'

'That was not my intention. Again, you do not have any understanding. These were necessary sacrifices on the path to progress. I sought to get the measure right so that it might bring on premature labour without harming the mother. Imagine what a boon it will be when I perfect a safe and effective means to deal with the unwanted fruits of passion, to say nothing of a preventative check on the relentless spawning of the poor.'

Beattie stood up straight, standing over Raven as he lectured him. He always did love the sound of his own voice. Raven was keen to keep him talking, as his only hope of salvation lay in Simpson and McLevy getting his message via Jarvis and hurrying here in response.

'I sold my remedy in good faith, Raven. If the pills did not get the desired result, I offered the operation. There were many who took formulations of my drug and, though it did not have the desired effect, they did survive to request the procedure.'

'Which was when you killed them with your ham-fisted butchery.'

'How else is one to learn but practise? And it is vital to perfect a technique before offering it to the wealthy ladies of the New Town. So who better to learn on than whores and housemaids, as the former will be buried unmarked and the latter buried unmourned?'

'What about Graseby? Your technique was not perfected when you operated on her, for I know you have killed others since.'

'That was something of an emergency. Her husband was apt to cause trouble so I had to act, and I knew that if she died, then either way it solved my problem.'

'So the child was yours. You are an abomination, Beattie. *Primum non nocere.* Do you remember quoting those words to me? You say I am held back by sentiment and sympathy, but what is our purpose if not to alleviate suffering? To lengthen out human existence, not to curtail it? And to do those things, a doctor must not be apart from his patients, but one with them.'

Beattie sneered, ugly and yet amused. 'You sound like your mentor: encumbered by emotion to the point of being unmanned. Do you think posterity will remember him just because he spared a few women an everyday and natural pain? I will grant you his chloroform has proven useful, but in the grander scheme, suffering has an important purpose, Raven. It is necessary. As is sacrifice.'

Raven swallowed, the fear gripping him as surely as the bonds. Beattie had said all he wished to, and was preparing for action.

'What do you mean to do?'

'Young Dr Duncan was right, though he spoke in jest. A footnote might yet be made of you in medical history. You will not be a doctor, but you will make a contribution as the subject of experiment.'

Raven's eye was immediately drawn to the jars. He felt a growing panic, manifest in a struggle against his bonds, but his hands and feet were securely tied.

'No, no, you misunderstand,' Beattie told him. 'The late Miss Fisher will fulfil that purpose adequately, for which I am grateful to her. Even with the Anatomy Act, cadavers for dissection are not so easy to come by. Whereas you, Raven, will provide me with something far more valuable: the opportunity to practise multiple surgical techniques on a live patient.'

He felt rough hands around his shoulders as Beattie began to drag him from the study.

'I warn you,' Raven said breathlessly. 'You are already undone. When I left, Simpson had gone to fetch the policeman McLevy. I have left word for them to come to this address.'

'Yet they do not arrive. But thank you for the warning: I shall extinguish the lights, so that if they do visit this house, they shall find me not at home. For the only lamps I burn will be down in my cellar, illuminating our work together.'

Raven saw the inescapable truth of it, and had no play left but to cry 'Murder!'

Even as he shouted, he could tell his voice would not carry beyond the house. Nonetheless, Beattie stopped and crouched over him once again in order to stuff a handkerchief into his mouth.

This is how it ends, Raven thought. This is how it ends, as it was always destined to do. It was where his path began: with two bodies lying on a floor, one man and one woman. In the beginning, the man was dead, the woman alive, though scared and bleeding. At the end, it was the woman who was slain and the man bloodied but breathing – though only for now.

Where it began: in his mother's kitchen, watching his father beat and kick her, oblivious of the blood and the screams, too drunk and blind in his rage to see that he would soon kill her.

Too drunk and blind to see his son approach from behind, clutching a candlestick, its round, heavy base to the top.

He had swung it only once, to the back of his father's head. He meant only to stop him, but his blow was truer than intended.

You have the devil in you, she always said.

And in that moment, the devil claimed him.

Raven set out upon a mission to redeem himself, to become a doctor: to heal, to save, to atone. It was one of many fool's errands in his life, for there was no redemption: only the twisting path that inevitably led him here to his final damnation.

He heard a whipping sound, something cutting through the air.

Beattie stopped. He let go of Raven, his eyes bulging as he clutched between his legs, a crippling, uncomprehending agony on his face.

He dropped to his knees, revealing Sarah behind him. She stood with a poker gripped in both hands, fire in her eyes.

'I also have the wit to know that a preening onanist who regards himself a god does not gladly wait upon a housemaid,' she said.

As these words met Beattie's ears, the poker whipped through the air again, this time connecting with his skull.

SIXTY

It was tea that proved her salvation.

This most mundane of tasks had insultingly come to define her everyday life: an endless ritual of making and serving hot refreshments, but loath as Sarah might be to admit it, it had also saved her life.

Miss Fisher, I owe you an apology.

Beattie's manner had changed so suddenly. His look of gathering anger had vanished in an instant, replaced by a solicitude that was supposed to reassure her, but which in fact provoked an impulse to flee. She felt an acute sense of impending peril, an instinct of fear more profound than she had ever known.

She might have dismissed this as merely an accumulation of her anxiety in confronting Beattie about his lies, but that he meant her harm was in no doubt when a moment later he offered to make her tea. A man of his character did not make tea for anyone, least of all a housemaid.

In that moment Sarah understood that he meant to poison her, and from such a horrific realisation she began to understand far more than that. But to be absolutely sure, she offered to join him in the kitchen. She knew not to push the issue, for if she did not make it easy for him to carry out his plan, he would surely improvise another.

Though her instinct was to run, she feared she would be caught, and at that point her only advantage would be gone: that he did not realise she knew what he was about. Had he locked the front door? She could not remember. Even if it was open, he would be faster, and he would certainly be more powerful. She would have to choose her moment, when he believed he had already dealt with her.

While Beattie busied himself preparing her death, she seized the opportunity to search his study. Something unsettled her about his anatomy specimens, but the thing that most set her mind racing was the sight of the black gloves. It all fell into place when she saw those. She knew who had been wearing them and why. She knew that Beattie was Madame Anchou.

He brought the tea in already poured, which was quite wrong. This was because there was something slipped into one of the cups: cups that did not match – also quite wrong – so that he knew which one to offer her, and also an insurance against her having guessed his intention and swapping them around amidst distraction.

Steeling herself to hide her fear, she had asked him for a biscuit. As soon as he left the room, she emptied her tea into an earthenware vase, replenishing it from the pot before Beattie returned.

His conduct had been utterly transparent after that. He was stalling for time, avoiding giving anything away until he was certain of her fate. As anticipated, his manner changed again as soon as she had drained her cup.

After that, it was a question of choosing her moment to feign the effects. To assist with this, she had to know what he thought he had given her.

She clutched her stomach in reflexive response. 'Strychnine?'

Beattie wore a patronising smile. 'Yes, I gather you have been reading Christison. Not, I imagine, that you have understood much of it, but be reassured that no, I have not used *nux vomica*. It is my intention to dissect you, and I don't wish to have to wait so long for the rigid contortions to loosen. No, I have given you prussic acid. It is a narcotic poison, swift and painless. Believe me, I would have done the same for Rose had it been to hand. I do not believe in unnecessary cruelty, Miss Fisher. I am not a monster.'

Prussic acid. She knew it from her reading. Symptoms commenced within two minutes and it caused death within ten. She also knew that unlike strychnine, prussic acid was detectable after death, but this would be of significance only if a body was found.

Sarah looked at the jars and understood Beattie's full intentions.

Her legs had gone from under her shortly after that. She fell to the floor, breathing slowly at first, then gasping deeply for a while before lying absolutely still. Beattie did not check her pulse, which would have easily betrayed her, for it was pounding. He seemed absolutely confident about the poison, which made her wonder whether it wasn't the first time he had done this.

Shortly after, she heard the back door open followed by footsteps from the kitchen. She dared open her eyes just a little, and almost cried out in warning to whoever approached when she saw Beattie swing back with a wooden stave, but it was already too late. She would only get one chance to act, and she had to make it count.

Sarah untied Raven and together they fastened the twine around Beattie, who was beginning to rouse. He and Raven were both bleeding, but her healing instinct only applied to one of them. In the case of Beattie, she merely wished she had hit him more than twice.

From outside, she heard the sound of horseshoes on cobbles. 'Simpson,' said Raven.

So he had not been lying in desperation when he told Beattie he had left word for the professor to come here.

Dr Simpson swept in through the front door. His expression of irritation and curiosity turned to one of confusion and dismay as he took in the scene that greeted him: his housemaid in another man's home after dark, his apprentice bruised and bleeding, and both of them standing over the trussed-up figure of his sister-in-law's betrothed.

'I have one or two wee questions, laddie,' he said quietly.

Raven told Simpson all.

Sarah had seldom seen the professor angry. It was a slow process, like clouds rolling over the Pentlands, thickening and darkening, gradually portending the storm to come. He looked down with fury and disgust upon Beattie, who was in turn eyeing the group standing over him with a calm that unnerved Sarah.

'Where is McLevy?' Raven asked.

'He went away as soon as we returned and found my brougham back in its right place. I offered him a drink for his trouble, but he had a matter to return to. I entered the house to find Jarvis beside himself, and that is not a sight one sees every day.'

'We must fetch him back again,' Raven insisted. 'Tell him what has transpired. And then this diabolical specimen will surely hang.'

Beattie snorted. 'This gentleman and physician surely will not,' he said, an arrogant confidence about him despite his predicament. 'For you have proof of nothing. What can you present? A robe that you claim I wore in order to disguise myself as a French midwife? How preposterous do you think that will sound?'

'You murdered Spiers and Rose Campbell,' Raven retorted. 'You dealt in poison. You killed we know not how many women.'

Beattie shrugged, as though this were all a trying inconvenience for him. 'Again, you have no proof.'

Sarah wanted to hit him with the poker again, but there was something worse than his manner. He might be right. Strychnine could not be tested for. It left no detectable trace. There was no evidence Beattie carried out the fatal abortions, as the only witnesses were dead, and those who survived would not come forward to admit their own crimes.

'We will search this place and find your pills,' Raven told him.

'And how would you prove my intention in concocting them was other than noble? How would you even prove what the pills might do? Or perhaps you could volunteer to take one in court, Mr Raven, in order to demonstrate your hypothesis. That is a trial I would be happy to attend.'

Sarah felt like the solid ground beneath her was turning into mud. Raven sensed it too. They both looked to the professor, who always had wisdom, always had answers.

Dr Simpson led them from the study and into the hall, away from where Beattie might hear.

'This is unthinkable,' Raven said. 'Surely he will not walk away from this, and escape justice as he describes?'

'I cannot say for sure,' the professor replied. 'It is the case that what you know and what you can prove are often two entirely different matters, and the court of law can be a harsh place to see that difference demonstrated. But there is another consideration.'

Sarah noted the unusually troubled expression upon Dr Simpson's features, and she guessed what it was before he could voice it himself.

'Such a trial would crush Miss Grindlay,' she said.

'Indeed, Sarah. Imagine Mina's anguish should all of this be made a public spectacle. Not merely for the world to know how she was used and deceived, but to think that she set her heart at this vile creature.'

Raven looked withered and pale in his incredulity, as though the last of his hope was draining from him.

'You cannot be suggesting we ignore what we know simply in order to spare Mina.'

'I could not spare Mina such hurt were it to stand in the way of justice, but nor would I put her through it when the risk is that a murderer will walk free at the end of it anyway. But you are right: we cannot ignore what we know, for a man such as Beattie will surely repeat his crimes. That would be, as you say, unthinkable.'

'So what should we do?'

The professor looked at the wretched figure lying upon the floor of the study, gazing at him a long time. He then glanced at the array of jars, containing so many specimens of untold provenance. There was a look of resolve upon his face, an expression of stony determination.

'The course we must take is also unthinkable,' he said. 'And as such its sin will bind we three, a burden we each will have to carry for the rest of our days. Nonetheless, this duty has fallen to us and we are left with no other choice.'

Dr Simpson put a hand on Sarah's shoulder, his voice low. 'Go to the carriage,' he instructed. 'Fetch me my bag. Raven, you will help me carry him to the cellar.'

SIXTY-ONE

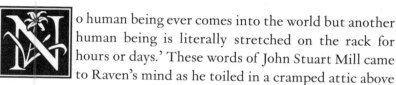'o human being ever comes into the world but another human being is literally stretched on the rack for hours or days.' These words of John Stuart Mill came to Raven's mind as he toiled in a cramped attic above the Lawnmarket. He was no great reader of philosophical tracts, not having the time, so presumably he had heard the quote cited by the professor, or by one of the visiting dignitaries at Queen Street. Raven might be sweating from his efforts, though the room was cold, but he knew the woman lying before him had already given so much more before he arrived to assist.

His perspiration was not entirely down to his physical exertions, but as much from his anxiety that there should be no mishap. Simpson had entrusted him to deal with the case on his own, not deeming it sufficiently challenging to haul himself away from a particularly busy morning clinic. Raven was dispatched in his stead, having been told: 'You felt able enough to administer ether unsupervised.' How typical of Simpson that his words should be simultaneously a reassurance and an admonishment.

Raven pulled down hard on the forceps as the uterus contracted again. He almost laughed with relief as he felt movement of the infant's head in response to his efforts, while before him the patient slept on despite his less than tender manipulations. In addition to relieving her pain, which had been considerable, the chloroform had worked its usual magic in relaxing the maternal passages, allowing Raven to apply the forceps blades with ease. The insensibility of the patient also allowed him to dispense with the modesty blanket that pointlessly impeded his view. Draping such a thing was akin to asking a surgeon to operate in the dark. He wondered what Syme would make of such a request.

Another contraction and the head emerged, followed by the trunk and possibly a gallon of amniotic fluid, which rapidly filled his shoes. Raven cared not at all, as he had just performed his first forceps delivery – with a pair of Simpson's forceps, of course – and it appeared as though both mother and child were going to survive it.

'A wee lassie,' the mother said upon waking shortly after, tearful in her gratitude as the baby was placed in her waiting arms. 'Dear heavens, you're so bonny,' she told her daughter.

A little later, having packed away his instruments, Raven bade his patient farewell and made for the door, his feet squelching quietly in his sodden shoes. His exit was impeded by the arrival of the patient's husband, who shook Raven's hand vigorously before reaching into his pocket.

Raven's financial situation had improved of late, sufficient that he would not need to borrow from his mother for a while, and therefore she would not need to humble herself before his miserable uncle. In order to conceal what they had done with John Beattie, it had been necessary to give the impression that he had fled his home. This they had achieved by packing up certain of his clothes and belongings in a trunk and quietly disposing of them. Though he did not say as much to Simpson, Raven had privately decided that it would create a more convincing picture if it appeared such a fugitive had not left any cash behind.

It was just a pity this windfall had not come a day sooner, as he could have comfortably paid off Flint even after giving half to Sarah. Flint had, of course, forgiven Raven's debt, but he feared the new terms he was on with the man might prove far more onerous in the long run.

The smiling new father pressed a clutch of coins into his palm. It was the first money he had earned as a medical practitioner, and he thought with some pride that he had earned it well.

Raven looked around the attic room in which he had spent the last couple of hours – a few bits of furniture, no coal for the fire – and came to a remarkably easy decision, one that would have been unthinkable a few weeks before.

'Naw, naw,' he said. 'Away with ye.'

SIXTY-TWO

arah was tarrying in the professor's study when the bell rang, an unwelcome but inevitable interruption to a moment of tranquillity. It reverberated all the louder because the house was unusually quiet, the insistent peals rattling back and forth off the walls of empty hallways. The morning clinic was over, all of the visitors dispatched with poultices and prescriptions. Dr Simpson was on his way to Musselburgh to see a patient, Raven was out on a house call, Mrs Simpson had taken the children to visit a friend in Trinity, and of course Miss Grindlay remained confined in her room.

Poor Mina had not emerged in days. She was distraught and inconsolable over the news that her intended husband had absconded, having been unmasked as a fraud. She was told that he lied about his uncle and the fine house in Canaan Lands, that his intentions towards her were insincere and that his name was probably not even John Beattie.

'We may never know who he truly was,' Dr Simpson had informed his weeping sister-in-law, but it was the knowledge of *what* he truly was that she had to be protected from. Sarah did not like to think what it would do to Mina if she were to learn this, and still less what had really happened to him at the hands of three people who lived with her under the same roof.

The bell sounded a second time. Sarah sighed and was about to head for the door when she remembered that she didn't have to respond. Though she knew Jarvis was out on an errand, the new girl had started yesterday, so she could let her jump to it instead.

With a smile she resumed the task of restocking the medicine cabinet, arranging the bottles in neat rows, labels to the front. She took a satisfaction from their careful organisation and from her understanding of their names, regarding the medicines as tokens of her new responsibilities.

Dr Simpson had taken on a second housemaid in order to free more of Sarah's time for assisting with clinics and other related matters. This had come about as a result of her informing the professor that she intended to hand in her notice so that she might seek her living as a nurse at the Royal Infirmary.

'Why ever would you want to do that, Sarah?' he asked, looking not merely surprised but, she would have to admit, a little hurt.

'Through my duties here, I have felt privileged to assist in the care of patients and would prefer a position that allowed me to dedicate more of my time to that.'

'That strikes me as a terrible waste. As a nurse at the Infirmary, you will spend most of your time washing floors and emptying bedpans. A bright girl like you will learn a great deal more if you simply remain here.'

'But what is the point of learning that which I cannot put into practice? I could accumulate more knowledge than any man in Edinburgh, but my status would be that of the best-read housemaid in the city.'

Passion drove her words, but she feared she had been injudicious in venting her frustrations to Dr Simpson in such an unguarded manner. The professor had merely nodded, however.

'It may not always be thus,' he said softly. 'And if things are ever to be different, it will take women like you to change them.'

SIXTY-THREE

He feels the lurching again as he lies in the dark, a sensation he cannot make sense of. It is dizziness, perhaps, like when he has drunk too much wine. There are cries from without, shouts of men, like labourers working a job. They are oddly muted, though, no sense of echo from the walls of buildings.

He can open his eyes now, he discovers. He has memory of being unable to before. He thinks he was blindfolded. He can see little nonetheless. The room is almost completely in darkness. His hands remain bound together, but his feet are free.

There is a dreadful smell, sharp and choking, and he is aware of a dampness next to his cheek. It is vomit, his own. He remembers nausea, but not the action of being sick. Consciousness has been an occasional visitor of late but not a fast friend. He recalls a blurry semi-waking state, feelings of disorientation, not assisted by his being able to see nothing. Exhaustion despite never being fully awake. Sleep coming as a mercy.

He does not know how long he has lain here. He puts his bound hands to his face and feels the growth. He estimates it has been at least three days since last he shaved.

Slowly come the memories, incrementally into focus like he is minutely twisting the lens on a microscope.

Being dragged to the cellar. Lying there on his own operating table, bound and strapped to it, unable to move. Lacking any sense of time, long fearful seconds turning into minutes turning into hours. Wetting his trousers for there was no option to relieve himself any other way.

Raven and Simpson returning. Neither of them speaking. Raven forming the cone of a handkerchief, dripping the chloroform. Then oblivion. Then this dark chamber, its whereabouts unknown.

He sits up and promptly cracks his head on something. At first he thinks the ceiling must be low, but his hands discern there is a bunk above. There is no window, no lamp, and he cannot see to find a door.

Tentatively he puts his feet over the side and slowly stands up straight. He hits his head again, for the ceiling is indeed low.

He advances, hands extended until they meet a surface. He is lucky, he thinks, for his fingers are touching wood. It is the door. Now he must find its handle.

He cannot. He searches with his hands, and discovers that all around him is wood. What manner of chamber is this? Is he in the country, the forest?

He balls his fists and begins to pound on the wall, shouting to be let out.

Shortly after that, he hears footsteps. Light spills in, dazzling his unaccustomed eyes as a door is pulled open perpendicular to where he had sought it. There are strong hands about him and he is hauled down a corridor. Even here, all around him is wood. The men hauling him along are in uniform. Soldiers. Has he been taken to Edinburgh Castle?

As he ascends a narrow staircase, he hears more shouts of men and once more feels the lurching sensation. With a burning fury, he understands.

He hears the slap of the waves against a hull, feels the stinging cold as he steps onto the deck.

All around is water, horizon to horizon.

He is presented to a bearded gentleman, by his uniform clearly a man of some rank.

'Good morning,' he says. 'I am Captain Douglas Strang.'

'Where am I?'

'You are aboard the Royal Navy survey vessel HMS *Fearless*, bound for South America on an extended mission of coastline cartography.'

'How long are we from Leith? You must turn around at once!'

Strang laughs. 'We will not be turning around for some time. Perhaps never, in fact, as we may be circumnavigating dependent upon further orders. Our commission is for three years, initially.'

Beattie feels his legs weaken, and not from the sea.

'Captain James Petrie volunteered your services as ship's surgeon. His brother-in-law, Dr Simpson, intimated that you had problems regarding your conduct with women, so I am sure it will come as some relief to know that you will not be in the company of one so long as you remain under my command.'

'This is illegal. This is press-ganging!'

'Captain Petrie did forewarn that you may not be satisfied with the arrangement, so we came to an understanding. I am obliged to offer an alternative should you decide you do not wish to take up the post.'

'And what is this alternative?'

'We drop you over the side. Your choice, Dr Beattie.'

ACKNOWLEDGEMENTS

Warmest thanks to:

Sophie Scard, Caroline Dawnay and Charles Walker at United Agents.

Francis Bickmore, Jamie Byng, Jenny Fry, Andrea Joyce, Becca Nice, Vicki Watson and all at Canongate. Their passion and enthusiasm for this book has been overwhelming.

Professor Malcolm Nicolson at the Centre for the History of Medicine, University of Glasgow, whose MSc course led to the material upon which this book is based.

Moniack Mhor, Scotland's Creative Writing Centre. Their course on historical fiction was an inspiration.

The National Library of Scotland, whose digitised town plans and Post Office directories provided an invaluable resource.

And of course to Jack, for listening without complaint to long-winded tales of the nineteenth century; and to Natalie for her indefatigable enthusiasm for this project from its inception.

Imprimé en France

To all my librarian friends, champions of books, true magicians in the House of Life. Without you, this writer would be lost in the Duat.

Jules Roy

MÉMOIRES BARBARES

Albin Michel

ISBN 2-226-03531-1

à mes pères,
à ma mère
et à tous les miens,
Dieu sait où

Dans l'ordre des Mémoires, je crois que la chronologie n'est pas la vérité. Si je veux faire un récit de ma vie, ce qui est essentiel échappera absolument.

André Malraux,
Entretien avec Pierre de Boisdeffre, 1967,
La Manufacture, 1987.

J'ÉTAIS figé devant lui, et il me faisait face debout, nu-tête, le dos à la fenêtre, à contre-jour avec sa haute taille, sa carrure, une ombre immense, imposante, gigantesque, inquiétante : de Gaulle, le général de Gaulle, l'homme qui avait dit non au moment où la nation écrasée demandait grâce, le seul qui avait osé se rebeller, lui, un militaire passé à l'étranger, qui avait lutté des années avant de gagner, était rentré victorieux et arrogant à la tête du gouvernement puis s'en était allé sur un mouvement d'orgueil et attendait qu'on vînt le rechercher. Nous étions le 6 juillet 1955, un mercredi, j'ai retrouvé la date dans mes carnets.

Il passait tous les quinze jours à Paris, voyait les uns, les autres, quelques fidèles. Aucune raison d'en être, je ne l'avais jamais rencontré. Ouvrier de la dernière heure ou presque, je m'étais rangé sous ses ordres en 1943, et il ne nous avait jamais adressé le moindre signe. Douze ans après, j'étais convoqué par son aide de camp, tiens, pourquoi ? Parce que j'écrivais des livres, *la Vallée heureuse* pour commencer, en 1946, que je lui envoyais parce que je l'admirais et que j'aurais voulu l'aimer, eh ! oui, on a de ces illusions. Il me répondait, nous étions presque en relations suivies. A chaque livre un mot de lui, deux pages, dix lignes par page, de sa fine écriture couchée, moulée, coulée, sans rature. Et pas des banalités. Ah ! ah ! lui qui n'était pas prodigue de compliments me disait que j'avais du talent. Tout de même, semblait-il, on devinait chez lui une tendance gendelettre, hôtel de Massa ou Académie : il avait écrit lui aussi avant la guerre. Des livres que personne n'achetait, surtout pas les militaires, et qu'on venait de rééditer, des livres pas drôles du tout, il me sentait peut-être

proche de lui parce que j'étais un ancien officier, le clan, la famille, la tribu, l'épée, le confrère de plume. Là, devant lui, comme tant de fois j'aurais voulu être, il m'avait lancé de sa voix rude et sourde : « Je vous écoute… » Et avait reculé. Lui qui parlait tout le temps, cette fois ne disait rien. Et moi rien à lui dire, désarçonné. J'y avais bien pensé, ça ne venait pas, je croyais qu'il m'aurait interrogé. La hiérarchie de l'armée s'adoucit parfois, se fane, s'efface mais ne s'éteint jamais : il était général, et quel général, quel homme ! moi simple colonel en congé. Allez, gros malin, il t'a appelé, vas-y, n'importe quoi comme les autres, il veut savoir ce que tu as sur le cœur, qui sait ? Qu'est-ce que tu risques ? Suppose qu'il revienne au pouvoir, on ne peut jurer de rien, imbécile ! Flatte-le.

L'ombre démesurée me fixait derrière des verres ronds brouillés, opaques, comme ceux qu'avec une monture de cauchemar l'ophtalmo vous colle sur le nez, et semblait m'examiner sans ciller, impitoyablement, dans la pièce nue ou presque où nous étions : un bureau de fonctionnaire sans rien, une lampe et un téléphone, un siège ou deux, peut-être quelques gravures aux murs. Plus tard, j'apprendrai qu'il venait d'être opéré de la cataracte. Pour lui aussi j'étais une ombre.

Dix ans s'étaient écoulés depuis la fin de la guerre, on commençait à l'oublier, il n'intéressait déjà plus grand monde, combien de Français croyaient encore en lui ? J'avais écrit un nouveau livre qui allait paraître chez Gallimard, il faisait beau, c'était l'été, un vent de bonheur soufflait. J'habitais un hameau non loin de Versailles, une bicoque retapée grâce à l'argent économisé sur ma solde d'Indochine, j'avais de la chance d'avoir eu une pièce jouée par Pierre Fresnay à la Michodière pendant trois mois, je venais d'acheter une garçonnière à Paris dans un immeuble neuf au-dessus de la villa Montmorency, en plein ciel, et puis, sacré gaillard, j'avais passé l'hiver dans une sorte de folie et d'agitation. J'avais traversé le Sahara d'Ouargla à Djanet pour *Paris-Match* avec la Légion, un général était venu me chercher à Tamanrasset pour me conduire à Gao, à Bamako et à Dakar, après quoi j'avais couru à Rome derrière une femme et je me trouvais devant de Gaulle immense et glorieux. A contre-jour. Allons-y.

Puisque nous étions entre soldats, je choisis de lui dire pourquoi je n'étais pas comme les autres et donc, me

rapprochais de lui. Officier d'une armée dont on se méfiait, l'armée d'Afrique qui avait servi Pétain, j'avais, en Indochine, après la guerre, quitté un corps expéditionnaire qu'il avait lui-même envoyé là-bas, et, du coup, l'armée de la nation. Je n'étais plus d'accord. Il le savait puisqu'il avait lu le livre que j'avais consacré à mon séjour en Extrême-Orient. Il m'avait écrit : « ... *cela se passe où tout se décide, sur les champs de bataille d'Asie.* » Ça m'avait rappelé quelque chose. Mon Malraux. Il avait aussi ajouté que mon livre l'avait ému, qu'il me remerciait de « *l'avoir écrit* ». Oh ! Oh !...

Là, je plongeai. Il me semblait que le problème d'un officier de carrière qui, après avoir combattu, quittait les rangs pour des raisons comme les miennes, ne pouvait pas le laisser indifférent. A la colonie, on torturait systématiquement les suspects, on grillait les villages au napalm, on zigouillait tout ce qui bougeait, paysans, femmes, enfants, buffles, on disait à ceux qui étaient chargés de la besogne : « Vous allez me traiter ça... » On traitait. L'Indochine n'était pas une colonie comme les autres parce qu'elle touchait à l'empire communiste et qu'on y avait des intérêts. Dans quelle colonie n'a-t-on pas d'intérêts ? Ces gens-là ne voulaient pas de nous, sauf ceux qu'on payait pour nous servir, et les prévaricateurs ne manquaient pas.

Je dis à de Gaulle qu'après avoir combattu les nazis, je n'avais pas supporté que nous nous conduisions comme eux. Là, j'avoue que j'y allais un peu fort. Un officier n'était-il pas dans l'armée pour obéir ? Pouvait-il se poser des questions de ce genre-là ? Je laissai entendre que, sous ses ordres à lui, de Gaulle, de telles erreurs ne se seraient pas produites, pas de cette façon-là en tout cas. Tout juste si je n'accablai pas l'amiral Thierry d'Argenlieu, son homme lige, qu'il avait nommé à la tête de l'Indochine. Dans l'armée, comme tout était question de caractère et d'humeur, il le savait mieux que moi. Pas un instant je ne pensai qu'un rebelle n'aimait probablement pas les rebelles, voulait être seul et obéi. Surtout obéi. Je lui dis aussi qu'en Grande-Bretagne où nous l'avions rejoint, nous avions subi de dures pertes, cruelles même, dans nos bombardements de nuit sur l'Allemagne, on aurait été heureux qu'il vienne nous saluer parce qu'on se sentait par moments orphelins et que Pétain nous avait fait avaler trop de couleuvres. Je disais ça comme en rêve, comme dans le vide, à

13

une ombre dardant sur moi des yeux mécaniques, aveugles. Et pourquoi, à quel titre ? Né illégitime, descendant de petits colons d'Algérie, ancien séminariste, ancien officier de tirailleurs avant l'aviation, même pas saint-cyrien, divorcé (ce qui était mal vu chez les de Gaulle) et cherchant désespérément une compagne pour la vie, une reine Guenièvre, une amoureuse (ce qui ne l'intéressait pas), autrement dit, je n'étais rien, moins que rien. Peut-être un chevalier errant à son commencement.

L'esprit ailleurs, je me demandai ce que je faisais là et marquai un temps d'arrêt. Ah ! si, encore quelque chose : l'Algérie. Sur ce qui se passait en Algérie où, depuis près d'un an, la rébellion d'Indochine avait gagné, j'aurais pu parler puisque j'étais de là-bas et que j'y avais les miens et beaucoup de tombes. Sur ce point-là, je m'en rapportais à Camus, de là-bas comme moi, fils d'un commis de ferme du Constantinois tué en Quatorze et d'une mère espagnole qui ne savait ni lire ni écrire, lui, c'était l'auteur de *l'Etranger* et de *la Peste*, gourou, frère, maître bien-aimé, directeur de conscience. Et là, soudain, je fis silence, et ne prononçai plus un mot. Et sans doute n'attendait-il rien de plus, sinon peut-être un compliment majeur, l'expression d'un attachement définitif, une obédience absolue, que j'aurais dû formuler et qui ne vint pas.

Quand, le menton levé, il conclut que j'en avais fini, de Gaulle me tendit une main d'évêque, une main de cardinal en congé, et son ombre parut se rapprocher : « Il faut que vous voyiez Malrôôô... » « Malraux ? » dis-je, croyant avoir mal entendu. Il hocha la tête, répéta : « Malrôôô. » Je m'inclinai, tournai les talons et m'en fus. A Bonneval, l'aide de camp, je lançai en sortant, avec un geste incertain : « Le Général m'a dit : " Il faut que vous voyiez Malraux." » Bonneval ne répondit rien. Il sourit. Nous nous quittâmes. Je m'en allai reprendre ma 2 CV quelque part. En 1955, on n'avait pas encore de peine à se ranger. Tout cela ne me disait plus grand-chose. Sur le moment, j'étais resté pensif, un peu décontenancé. On m'aurait dit que, plus tard, je m'en souviendrais, cela m'eût étonné, tout cela me paraissait bizarre, sans grande conséquence.

*
**

A Camus je n'ai jamais parlé de cette rencontre. Pour l'homme de Londres, pour le sauveur de la patrie il avait beaucoup d'admiration, mais marquait une certaine réserve pour le militaire. Si je lui avais raconté mon entrevue, il aurait simplement dit : « Ah ! Comment est-il ? Qu'est-ce qu'il t'a dit ? » J'aurais dû parler de sa référence à Malraux. Camus était un fan de *l'Espoir*. Malraux l'épatait. Il l'avait vu, Malraux était allé le saluer. On avait tiré pour la postérité une photo du commandant de la brigade Alsace-Lorraine en canadienne et en calot à cinq galons, face à face avec l'auteur de *l'Etranger*, au marbre de *Combat*. Camus faisait du bruit à l'époque mais ne s'habillait pas chez Lanvin.

Je ne sais pourquoi je me méfiai. Je ne lui dis rien. Je gardai mon Malraux pour moi. Façon de parler. Il y avait vingt-cinq ans qu'on me promettait Malraux et que je le ratais. « Il faut que vous voyiez Malrôôô... » Le Général avait bien noté tout de suite que l'Indochine avait été pour Malraux et pour moi le contraire de la Terre sainte mais bien un lieu de pourriture où nous avions, lui, Malraux, provoqué le colonialisme omnipotent, et moi rompu avec l'armée, bras du colonialisme. Tous les deux, nous nous étions battus pour une certaine justice, pour le roi de Prusse ou pour la Chine ? Tous les deux, nous avions pris là (lui très tôt, moi très tard) conscience de notre condition. Verdict pour lui : de la prison avec sursis puis la gloire. Pour moi, le mépris des militaires assurément, et une cassure avec eux. Donc pour la peau.

Sortons du chapeau une marionnette : René Louis Doyon, mandarin à la noix, qui se prétendait mon père putatif, m'appelait « mon filsque » et avait guidé les premiers pas de Malraux. Doyon, nous sommes bien d'accord, est oublié, englouti, et personne ne sait plus qui c'est. N'empêche qu'en 1932 déjà, il n'arrêtait pas lui aussi de me parler de Malraux, mais voilà, il était où, en 1932, Malraux ? Il s'échinait sur *la Condition humaine* après avoir donné à Grasset *la Tentation de l'Occident, les Conquérants, la Voie royale*. « Les champs de bataille d'Asie », comme m'écrivait le Général. Barricadé quelque part, Malraux pondait, il fallait que son séjour en Indochine (il disait en « Extrême-Orient », ça sonnait mieux) lui serve. A quoi ? Tout au début des *Conquérants*, il faut entendre le jeune Malraux : « Je veux — tu entends ? — une certaine forme de puissance, ou je l'obtiendrai, ou tant pis

pour moi. » Et si c'était manqué ? « Si c'est manqué je recommencerai, là ou ailleurs. Et si je suis tué, la question sera résolue. »

Doyon annonce des banquets en l'honneur de Malraux, des banquets où Malraux sera là, Doyon rameute de partout des copains, des ratés comme lui, Turpin, Pillement, Talvart, Bollery. Il m'extirpe de Versailles où je suis en garnison comme lieutenant au 24e régiment, il m'excite avec la promesse qu'un de mes flirts, Rita, sera là aussi. Doyon fricasse des dindons, des boudins d'Auvergne, invite des cocottes de la Galerie de la Madeleine où il tient ses assises, et pas de Malraux. Monsieur n'a pas daigné se déranger, je n'aurai jamais vu chez Doyon ce familier de la maison. Doyon, Simon Kra, Max Jacob et les autres premiers inspirateurs du génie de Malraux, Lacouture les appelle « les boucaniers ». Malraux les évitait, les fuyait, les laissait à leurs fantasmes et à leurs mirages. Moins cultivé et tellement moins intelligent que lui, attaché à l'armée, peu ambitieux ou ne sachant pas comment le devenir, je me contenterai de rester à bonne distance de Doyon sans pour autant me rapprocher de Malraux. D'ailleurs, que lui aurais-je dit à ce moment-là ? Et en 1955, à l'invite du général de Gaulle ? Personne n'était de taille à soutenir une conversation avec lui, sinon Camus, et encore par sous-entendus. Je rencontrerai Malraux plus tard, quand il ne sera plus ministre, et que j'oserai lui adresser la parole, moi, poussière.

Cependant, du temps de Doyon, normalement j'aurais dû. L'éviter a tenu de l'exploit. A la longue, Doyon avait fini par m'exaspérer aussi. Sa jalousie, sa tyrannie avaient réussi à m'éloigner. Nous étions même fâchés. J'allais et venais sans plus lui rendre compte, j'écrivais ce qui me plaisait, je fuyais ses commentaires acides. Quand le prix des Bouquinistes, peu connu, lui fut décerné au printemps 1956, un an après ma convocation par le Général, Doyon invita encore Malraux qui, cette fois, accepta parce qu'il savait que Doyon était dans la mouise, et lui remit l'écrin qui contenait un franc en argent, symbole du prix. Je n'en sus rien, je descendais le Niger pour *Paris-Match* en pirogue avec Pierre Moinot et un photographe. A mon retour, ce fut Camus qui m'apprit l'événement et me dit : « Tu devrais lui téléphoner. Doyon, c'est ton père, quand même. » Camus se fichait de moi mais j'aurais dû

encore, je ne le fis pas. J'appris par la suite qu'il avait eu dans *le Figaro littéraire* deux colonnes et une photo où Malraux apparaît la cigarette au bec, très chic, très vedette avec son regard orageux, et lui, Doyon, confit en dévotion, la bouche en cul de poule, l'appelant d'une voix fondante : « Mon cher André... » et l'enduisant à tour de bras de pommade. Dans *la Saison des Za*, j'ai raconté ce déjeuner chez Georges, 34, rue Mazarine, à deux pas de la Coupole sous laquelle Malraux refusait de s'asseoir avant qu'on lui ait attribué le Nobel. Devant Doyon, Malraux évoqua le paradis des bouquinistes où ils se retrouveraient tous plus tard avec Barbey d'Aurevilly, Villiers de L'Isle-Adam, Jehan Rictus, Fontenelle et Diderot, puis chacun s'en alla de son côté, Malraux à sa nouvelle femme pianiste et aux voix du silence, Doyon à ses puces. Je n'entendrai plus jamais le Général me parler de Malrôôô, et Malraux, plus tard, ne fera pas la moindre allusion à nos relations communes, presque une parenté, avec Doyon, au point que je me demande quelquefois si je n'ai pas raté ma vie parce que je n'ai pas rencontré Malraux quand il le fallait.

Imaginons que Malraux m'ait pris comme collaborateur, ou que le Général — car il m'avait dit aussi : « Il faut venir me voir à Colombey » — m'ait confié par la suite un rôle quelconque auprès de lui, eh bien ? Hypothèse ridicule. J'ai longtemps considéré comme une sottise et un manque d'ambition de n'être pas allé à Colombey, et ensuite les événements ont marché trop vite, j'aurais cru passer pour un flatteur comme je m'y invitais moi-même avant l'entretien, puisque les puissants ne supportent que la flatterie. Eh bien, je n'aurais pas non plus rompu avec Gallimard à la mort de Camus, pas écrit *la Guerre d'Algérie*, pas écrit *les Chevaux du Soleil*, puisque j'aurais suivi le Général et Malraux. Autrement dit, à la remorque de Malraux, je n'aurais rien fait et ne serais rien. Si je vaux quelque chose, c'est parce que, vrai sauvage, vrai contempteur des valeurs admises, j'ai osé, à l'écart de Malraux, défier les militaires mes camarades, soulever la fureur de mes compatriotes pieds-noirs, et même traiter de Gaulle de procureur impitoyable, ce qu'il ne me pardonna jamais.

Laissons les morts enterrer les morts, venons-en au tout

début de la barbarie, à ma mère, à mes vrais pères, à tous les miens, et poussons un triple hourra en leur honneur. Tout me surgit à la mémoire. Je sens même déjà quelque chose qui me monte à la gorge et m'étouffe.

I

L'oncle Jules

J'AI QUATRE ANS. Je marche d'un pas décidé, les cheveux sur l'épaule, derrière mon oncle Jules qui a son fusil à la bretelle. Quelquefois je suis enfermé entre les rangs de vigne tracés au cordeau, sur fil de fer, plus hauts que moi, entre des allées de feuilles bleues et de grappes de raisin en train de mûrir. Déjà l'été. La terre est plate, chaude, avec des touffes de roseaux et d'anciennes plaques de vase craquelée par le soleil. C'est la terre où je suis, la terre où je vis. Sur des routes droites roulent des chars à bancs, des voitures de maître et de lourds charrois avec des attelages de chevaux. Parfois, précédée de ses coups de trompe, une automobile file en soulevant un nuage de poussière derrière elle. On se gare, on admire, nous avons déjà dépassé 1910, le progrès se précipite. Le ciel s'étend des montagnes de l'Atlas blidéen aux collines qui cachent la mer. Et quelle lumière éblouissante ! Le vent souffle tantôt du nord, tantôt du sud. C'est la riche plaine derrière Alger, avec ses villages, ses petites villes, ses fermes, ses douars, l'odeur des eucalyptus et du sulfate de cuivre, ses chemins bordés d'asphodèles, ses parfums féroces que je hume goulûment.

L'oncle Jules est un homme grand à la puissante musculature, au visage régulier barré d'une moustache rousse qui cache ses lèvres. Il a le corps serré dans des fringues étriquées, il est chaussé de vieilles bottines à boutons et, pour cacher sa calvitie précoce, coiffé d'un canotier défoncé qu'il n'enlève même pas les jours de pluie. Sous ce galurin un peu rabattu sur le front, un air fouineur, calculateur, rusé. Il a trente ans, il fait marcher la ferme, commande tout, sauf sa mère. La mère règne sur tout, mais lui c'est un dieu, c'est le seigneur de la plaine,

19

des machines, de l'eau, du vin, des moissons, des fêtes ; il voit tout, il sait tout, il parle arabe, il menace, il rit, il a toujours au coin des lèvres, à la plissure du nez un mot piquant, une allusion qui pétille, on le devine plein de secrets, de malice et, pour moi, d'indulgence. C'est l'homme dans sa splendeur et son isolement, tel que je veux être plus tard, l'homme comparable à rien, l'unique, le seul que j'aie devant moi au moment où tout commence à m'apparaître, l'homme dans son empire, tel que je suis déjà, tel que je me comporterai en tout. Tout dépend de son humeur, nous sourions quand il sourit, nous tremblons quand la colère le hérisse et que son regard étincelle. Si fort, si généreux de clins d'œil, il se retourne vers moi et me hisse à califourchon sur ses épaules. Là, je domine jusqu'au bout de l'horizon la plaine couverte de vignobles et de blés. Nous allons tuer des lièvres à la fourrure fauve palpitante et pleine de sang. Je tangue comme un navire, je respire des odeurs de miel, des odeurs de feu de bois, de semoule, des odeurs salées, la mer peut-être ?

Nous rentrons, j'avance entre les cyprès puis dans l'orangerie, comme on dit toujours en Algérie, les semelles de l'oncle Jules crissent sur les galets. Voilà les larges toits de la maison, du hangar, de l'étable et de l'écurie, j'entends le mugissement des bœufs et le hennissement des chevaux qui saluent notre retour. L'oncle Jules me remet aux femmes comme s'il leur tendait une part de sa vie, un trésor, et rentre chez lui, où tout est vide et nu. Il n'est avec nous qu'au moment des repas et dans les grandes circonstances. Le reste du temps, il travaille dans les vignes ou sur les machines, ou encore, le soir, il file au village, à l'Espérance, où il a ses habitudes. Alors, on l'attend, on écoute, on regarde le ciel devenir rouge puis sombre, puis tout brillant d'étoiles.

Si belle qu'elle fût, si élégante, ma mère était tout le contraire d'une femme légère. Je la revois toujours, jupe jusqu'au sol, corsage de satin, broche sur le cœur, ceinture à boucle de porphyre. Tout en noir, comme sa propre mère, comme la plupart des femmes de là-bas, toujours en deuil. Des veuves antiques.

Là, déjà, sur moi qu'elle retient contre elle comme si je devais lui échapper, ou qu'elle agrippe par les épaules, pèse le destin qu'elle nous a fabriqué. Après quinze ans de mariage, n'en pouvant plus de dormir chaque soir près d'un mari

qu'elle ne supportait plus, elle l'a trompé dans un miroitement d'illusions pour un homme venu d'ailleurs, qui portait fièrement le chapeau melon, savait parler et enseignait. Cela n'aurait sans doute provoqué aucun grabuge à Paris ou à Lyon ni même à Auxerre ou à La Rochelle, encore que nos provinces soient plus qu'on ne croit respectueuses des convenances et révérencieuses en réputations.

Mais à Rovigo où nous vivions, un village rigide et bienpensant de colonisation où, d'une rue à l'autre, tout se savait, il en allait autrement. Chaque matin à sept heures, le curé sonnait la messe, le berger municipal soufflait dans sa trompe pour rassembler ses troupeaux près de la fontaine et le garde champêtre partait en tournée le fusil à la bretelle comme l'oncle Jules. Quand je lis les romans de Gabriel Garcia Marquez, il me semble que je suis là où j'ai vu le jour, à Rovigo, canton de L'Arba, arrondissement de Boufarik, à trente kilomètres au sud d'Alger. On colle des affiches toutes les nuits aux portes des maisons, j'entends le maire parler au coiffeur et au forgeron ; des gendarmes emmènent, enchaîné entre eux, un Arabe à la prison de Maison-Carrée. Je n'imagine pas comment le pauvre, l'infortuné mari de ma mère aurait pu résister à l'idée qui lui vint, un jour de colère et de malheur, de nous flanquer à la porte, elle et moi. A sa place, j'aurais probablement été encore plus violent. Ma mère prit ses cliques et ses claques, attela le break avec lequel elle allait à Alger faire ses courses et retrouver son amant le jeudi. Je la vois dans *les Chevaux du Soleil* tournés à la télévision par François Villiers, incarnée par une Catherine Rouvel décidée, droite, superbe, conduisant son cheval, mon berceau à côté d'elle sur la banquette, fouette cocher ! Sans un regard vers ce qu'elle quitte, elle file se réfugier chez sa propre mère, veuve depuis sept ans d'un mari mort des fièvres, au-delà d'un autre patelin du même genre, Sidi-Moussa, plus au nord. La route ne tourne que pour enjamber le pont de fer sur l'oued Djemaa : l'été, un filet d'eau dans un large lit vide, avec des lauriers-roses ; l'hiver, parfois, ça déborde. Ma grand-mère, c'est la tendresse et la miséricorde sous une multitude de jupons, de jupes et de tabliers qui font d'elle une matrone un peu austère et lente à se mouvoir. Quand elle sourit, c'est à peine si son visage s'éclaire. Elle a subi tant d'épreuves, elle ne sait ni lire ni écrire, elle a si peu confiance dans l'avenir. Il me

semble que je l'ai toujours vue assise à sa place, dans la salle à manger, ou donnant du grain à ses poules dans la cour. La plupart du temps, je suis dans ses bras, au plus doux, ou à côté d'elle toujours prête à me protéger. Elle a un visage immobile de vieille reine, sent l'huile d'olive mêlée d'ail, le benjoin et la rose.

Ce jour-là, il y a une autre femme, ma tante Marie, épicerie fine, 95, rue Michelet à Alger, appelée par télégramme, méfiante, jalouse, jouisseuse, friande de nouveautés, d'inédits un peu olé olé, belle brune aux plantureux appas, qui s'ennuie depuis qu'elle est veuve elle aussi et s'est acoquinée avec Hayek, un Libanais gentil, artiste, premier coupeur chez Larade, le tailleur chic d'Alger. Hayek donne à ma tante tout ce qu'il gagne et se fait traiter de métèque. Ma grand-mère, déesse imperturbable, visage douloureux et impassible, approuvant ? désapprouvant ? Muette. La journée passe, on parle devant moi comme s'il y avait un mystère. Dans le silence du soir qui tombe, la pendule bat dans son coffre, son balancier jette un pâle éclair, la plainte des chacals commence à grelotter, quelque chose embaume dans la cuisine. L'oncle Jules, qui n'a pas été au village, attend que la mère lui demande d'allumer la lampe à pétrole suspendue à son globe au-dessus de la table. Un événement vient d'avoir lieu, il s'est passé quelque chose. Quoi ? Je suis heureux, on va sortir en voiture, voir des gens, assister à des cérémonies. Meftah, le serviteur arabe, apparaît, disparaît, glisse pieds nus, l'oreille aux aguets, va, vient, et après être allé chercher à la pompe du puits un dernier arrosoir d'eau, s'en retourne au gourbi où il vit avec sa femme et ses enfants dans un coin du jardin potager, près d'une haie de roseaux. Il m'aime bien, je l'aime bien, je suis souvent avec lui, ma mère ne voit pas cela d'un bon œil ; elle sort, elle crie : « Zizi, où es-tu ? » Quand je ne suis pas à la maison, je suis avec Meftah ou avec l'oncle Jules. J'apprends la vie, je règne aussi, non sans une certaine arrogance naturelle. D'un geste de petit seigneur comblé, je rejette en arrière mes cheveux longs et bouclés avec une frange sur le front, « comme Bonaparte », dit ma grand-mère qui regarde en fondant d'amour l'enfant sans père que je suis. Ah ! mon Dieu, je vois à peu près ce qu'elle veut dire, mais Bonaparte avait les cheveux plats et bruns, et qu'est-ce qu'un père ?

Je sais, je sais. Où est le père de ma grand-mère ? Où est le

père de ma mère ? Tous morts, tous disparus. Le père est celui qui sème en nous la vie ou une chose essentielle. Quelquefois le père donne tout. Souvent rien, ou des tares ? A-t-on besoin d'un père ? Qui est mon père ? L'oncle Jules ? Sûrement pas Meftah, qui n'est ni de ma race ni de mon rang. Une interrogation pèse soudain dans mon âme d'enfant. Je ne connaîtrai la réponse que plus tard. Devant moi, jamais une allusion. Le silence. Des regards quelquefois qui me paraîtront bizarres, parfois une sorte de commisération : « Pauvre petit... » Pourquoi ? Pauvre petit sans père. Mon frère René plus âgé que moi de quinze ans a un père dont on ne parle jamais non plus. Alors, où est la différence ? J'en aurai des pères, à ne pas savoir qu'en faire. Qui sera le vrai ? Quel est le bon ? J'ai raconté tout cela en détail, comme si j'avais tout vu moi-même et tout compris, dans *les Chevaux du Soleil*. J'y suis encore. L'oncle Jules, l'œil à tout, se pourlèche déjà les babines des conversations au village. Ce jour-là, mon fameux père inconnu est mort et ma mère déclare qu'elle n'assistera pas à l'enterrement, à Rovigo. Tout le monde essaie de la dissuader d'une pareille décision. Avec sa sœur de l'épicerie fine, elle passera une nuit semée d'éclairs et de coups de feu. Elle ne cédera pas. Le scandale sera énorme. On me le cachera jusqu'au jour où, cinquante ans plus tard, j'apprendrai tout de la bouche de ma belle-sœur Louise, témoin incorruptible, infaillible mémoire de la famille.

Ma mère a mené quinze ans la vie d'une femme de gendarme et quarante ans la vie d'une femme puis d'une veuve d'instituteur, et quelle sainte femme alors ! Pourquoi Dieu lui fit-il expier par une si longue souffrance la passion de son unique adultère ? « Ah ! elle l'a payé cher, ta mère, mon pauvre », m'a toujours répété Louise qui a tout vu, tout retenu. Sans Louise, je n'aurais rien su en détail. Quoi donc ? Tant d'histoires pour un enfant qui est, comme on dit, « de l'autre côté du polochon ». Et après ? Ça arrive, ces choses-là, même à des gens qui ne s'en doutent pas. Oui, mais, à Rovigo, à Sidi-Moussa, on se méfie, on est à l'affût de tout, on se régale. Par bonheur, l'œil aigu, la langue bien pendue, parfois trop pour certains, le cœur toujours prêt à saigner, Louise a vécu dans la vie comme au théâtre : elle riait ou pleurait sans cesse, mais n'a rien perdu du spectacle.

Dieu sait ce qui se passait au début de ce siècle dans ces trois villages de la Mitidja, Sidi-Moussa, L'Arba, Rovigo, créés par l'armée vers 1844, triangle sacré et secret, au pied de l'Atlas qui borde la plaine au sud d'Alger ! On se déplace en voitures à chevaux, les premières autos commencent à rouler, les routes sont toutes droites, on peut surveiller de loin les Arabes en guenilles qui les empruntent à pied, parfois en carrioles dont les roues oscillent parce que leurs moyeux ne sont jamais graissés. Il y a depuis peu un chemin de fer à voie étroite qui longe les routes pour gagner Alger, un tortillard dont la machine à vapeur tire quatre ou cinq wagons derrière elle avec des voyageurs et quelquefois des marchandises. D'Alger, il halète aussi le long de la côte, vers l'est jusqu'à Aïn-Taya, et vers l'ouest jusqu'à Guyotville. Dans chaque village dessiné au carré comme un camp militaire, l'église, la mairie et les écoles au centre, autour de la place. A Rovigo, toutes les maisons sont de même type ou presque, couvertes de tuiles romaines. Ça sent la semoule, le piment, le feu de bois, le pain chaud, le crottin de cheval, l'eucalyptus. L'enclume du forgeron sonne joyeusement dans le matin, et quand le vent souffle de la mer, il charrie l'odeur des géraniums rosats qu'on cultive sur des dizaines et des centaines d'hectares. L'essence de géranium est l'élément de base de la parfumerie. Rovigo, c'est le paradis. Un café ou deux, le curé, les commères, le médecin, les maîtres d'école, le boulanger. Ce serait le paradis s'il n'y avait pas les Arabes, c'est ce que j'ai toujours entendu dire autour de moi, souvent avec humour, parce que si on les craint, on les aime ussi.

Les Arabes, terme générique sous lequel on groupe ces indigènes à qui il a fallu enlever leurs terres, ce sont aussi, ailleurs, des Kabyles, des Chaouïas, d'anciens esclaves noirs du Sud, des Berbères dont on dit qu'ils descendent de Jugurtha, un mélange incroyable, avec des traces de Phéniciens, de Grecs, de Romains, depuis les premières invasions d'Arabie se bousculant vers l'Espagne et en lutte avec les Berbères mais laissant sur place les vraies dominantes : la langue arabe et l'islam. Dans la plaine, les Arabes métissés de tout, bâtardisés de tout, avec des noms de partout, vivent en tribus, en groupes de gourbis, de tentes ou de masures, avec de

pauvres troupeaux de moutons ou de bœufs sur des champs mal travaillés, couverts de broussailles et d'épines. Ils sont partout, on les repousse comme on peut vers la montagne, comme les chacals, on les emploie comme serviteurs, ou bien ils sont petits commerçants, petits exploitants et se débrouillent comme ils peuvent. On leur a laissé leurs chefs administratifs, les caïds, eux-mêmes serviteurs de l'administration, souvent propriétaires avec un semblant de puissance, insensibles à tout sauf à l'argent, habiles à pressurer leurs coreligionnaires et à soutirer l'impôt vers les caisses du Trésor français après le Trésor turc. Les premiers colons ne s'y sont pas trompés. Ils ont vu tout de suite qu'ils avaient affaire à des gens qui n'avaient rien de commun avec eux, à qui les armées des croisades avaient déjà arraché le tombeau du Christ, à des fanatiques. Des mosquées monte le vibrant, le mystérieux, le modulant, l'angoissant appel du muezzin. Tout ce qui porte burnous, tout ce qui vit et parle autrement, tout ce qui fait carême, tout ce qui mange différemment que nous est arabe.

Les Arabes occupent une partie du monde et de l'Afrique, le sud de la Méditerranée depuis qu'on les a chassés du nord. Pour les miens, c'est un danger. Pas de compromission avec eux, on les soumet ou ils vous tuent. « Ce sont des gens qui ne connaissent que la force et qui ont tous les vices, fainéants, menteurs, pédérastes et voleurs. Partout où ils sont passés, ils ont semé misère et désolation », j'entendrai cela toute mon enfance. « Attention aux Arabes. Ne va pas avec les Arabes, Meftah comme les autres, ne va pas plus loin que les roseaux. » Pourquoi ? Parce qu'il y a les Arabes. Dans mon enfance, quatre-vingts ans après la conquête, on commence cependant à voir des instituteurs arabes, des sous-officiers et même de rares fficiers arabes. Les colons se souviennent en se touchant la tête qu'à son passage en Algérie en 1865, l'empereur Napoléon III a prononcé ce mot inouï : « Nos frères les Arabes. » Une guerre est passée là-dessus, l'empereur a été balayé. Ma mère est née en février 1871, au moment où éclatait la dure insurrection de Mokrani en Kabylie : sur la colonie, un vent de panique. La révolte brisée, on les a soumis, écrasés, dépossédés, le bachaga Mokrani fut tué, ses terres rasées, les notables kabyles déportés en Nouvelle-Calédonie. La colonisation a triomphé, l'ordre règne, chacun est à sa place, personne ne songe à mettre notre présence en question,

l'Algérie est divisée en départements français, les Arabes eux-mêmes sont enrôlés dans l'armée, mais la peur est restée.

Derrière la montagne, on dit qu'il y a de hautes plaines à blé, puis des étendues immenses de cailloux et de roches, des dunes de sable, le désert, des oasis, l'Afrique soumise par d'autres conquérants français après les conquérants arabes, notre drapeau flotte là et sème peu à peu à travers le monde des notions de civilisation. Dans la Mitidja, les colons font fructifier la terre avec l'aide des indigènes, des artisans et de l'administration. Ces colons sont pour la plupart d'origine très modeste. En France, ils vivaient mal, ils ont cédé à la tentation de l'Eldorado, ils sont venus comme mes arrière-grands-parents, avec femmes et enfants, ou célibataires. A L'Arba, chef-lieu de canton, en plus des écoles, de l'église et d'une fontaine, on a bâti une perception, un tribunal, une gendarmerie. Au nouveau village de Rovigo établi entre Sidi-Moussa et L'Arba aux noms arabes, certains croient qu'on a prêté le nom d'une petite ville vénitienne. En vérité, c'est le titre que portait le commandant en chef des troupes à ce moment-là, un ancien ministre de la Police fait duc de Rovigo par Napoléon Ier dont il avait été aide de camp. Si féroce au moment où il avait repris du service en Algérie en 1813, que les Arabes l'avaient surnommé « l'égorgeur ». Les Arabes ne l'oublieront pas. A l'indépendance, ils se hâteront de débaptiser Rovigo qui s'appelle maintenant Bougara.

De Rovigo dont je suis parti si tôt, il ne me reste aucun souvenir. Dans *les Chevaux du Soleil,* j'ai tout reconstitué comme un décor. Je n'y suis retourné que très tard, il n'y avait plus que des Arabes qui m'ont reçu avec gentillesse et curiosité. L'ancien hôtel des Eaux-Thermales de mes parents, converti en épicerie, n'était qu'une maison à tuiles rondes surélevée d'un étage : des chambres avec carrelage à damier noir et bleu ou rosaces à fleurs de lis comme dans toute l'Algérie et une vague terrasse sous une treille où l'on devait mettre des tables à la belle saison, mais tout avait changé. On ne cultivait plus le géranium rosat. De la fabrique il restait encore des citernes et des conduits dont on disait qu'ils avaient gardé l'odeur merveilleuse. Rovigo, hélas, ne sentait plus que le mouton, le suint. J'ai cherché en vain la villa de l'ancien médecin dont j'avais une photo prise un jour de fête, avec des gandins acrobates et des élégantes à tailles de guêpe et gros

chignon. Pour la demeure de mon oncle Désiré, ce fut plus facile : il y avait encore, devant, une vieille machine pour les battages, toute rouillée. L'église, bâtie en pierres de la montagne à l'aspect tigré, était devenue mosquée avec une cloche qu'on ne sonnait plus, dans un campanile. De l'autre côté de la place et de la fontaine, j'ai revu l'école de garçons et l'ancien logement de mon père, la fenêtre d'où il guettait ma mère derrière les persiennes, et, en face, l'école des filles. A l'heure de la récréation, un immense cri s'éleva, et un grouillement formidable d'enfants, pareil à une mer agitée, m submergea un moment. Nous n'en étions plus au peuplemen de 1900 : au lieu de quatre cents Européens, il n'y en avait plu un seul, et au lieu de cinq mille Arabes, il y en avait quinze mille.

Rovigo ne m'inspirait rien que mélancolie. Je n'y ai pa vécu, et au cimetière où reposent quelques-uns des miens, je ne trouvai aucune trace de mon père légal le gendarme. Lui, avant l'heure, il était devenu poussière.

Ma mère et moi, c'est dix kilomètres au nord après Sidi-Moussa. La route est encore toute droite ou presque. Pas la moindre côte. Quand il m'arrive encore d'y revenir en pensée, je me sens chez nous, chez moi, je suis bien. Dans la buée de l'air qui danse au plus chaud de la journée, mes souvenirs se brouillent, je me perds dans les noms et les visages, je ne sais plus où j'en suis des autres et de moi-même. L'air que je respire là est chargé d'une odeur d'asphodèle avec un infime soupçon d'absinthe ou de fenouil peut-être, une puissante vague de vignes et d'eucalyptus roule sur la plaine selon l'heure, selon que le vent souffle de la mer ou des terres. De l'autre côté de la montagne, vers le sud, c'est le désert qui nous a toujours fait rêver, mais quand le vent vient de là, c'est le sirocco, la désolation, et parfois les sauterelles. Pour le reste, personne ne savait très bien où ça allait. Par l'est, vers la Kabylie, par l'ouest, c'était la plaine encore, la plaine sans fin. Je m'y serais bien risqué par curiosité, mais ma grand-mère — la reine — ne voulait pas. Ma mère non plus. Les femmes ne se sentent en sécurité que chez elles, sous les toits d'une ferme qui me paraîtra à l'époque si vaste. En vérité, perdue parmi

d'autres fermes puissantes et prospères. Nous n'aurons qu'une dizaine de bœufs, trois ou quatre chevaux, une noria avec machine à vapeur et une trentaine d'hectares de vignes, céréales et primeurs. Une misère. L'oncle Jules conduisait les travaux avec Meftah, modeste factotum et éducateur. Quand il le fallait, des ouvriers saisonniers descendaient de la montagne, des moissonneurs, des vendangeurs. C'était le Far West, la riche Mitidja odorante et encore insalubre, le jour sous le soleil dominateur et, le soir, sous une immense plainte qui faisait vibrer les étoiles.

Les fusils étaient toujours pendus dans la salle à manger, on ne s'éloignait jamais sans une arme à côté de soi : les Arabes, toujours. Ma mère m'inculqua pour eux des sentiments que nous étions nombreux à partager, encore que son départ de Rovigo restait pour elle l'épreuve la plus terrible. Ma mémoire des hommes à la ferme, c'est l'odeur des fusils ; ma mémoire des femmes, un parfum d'œillet et de benjoin ; ma mémoire de la maison, un signe de croix sur le pain, des croûtons frottés d'ail, ou encore le froissement des feuilles de maïs et le goût des caroubes. Il n'est pas sûr qu'à un âge si tendre, je ne me sois pas déjà senti illégitime. Une tare ? Une honte ? Je n'explique pas autrement l'insolence dont j'ai fait preuve. Je disais non à tout ce qui ne me plaisait pas, je tapais du pied, j'exigeais, je boudais si on me résistait car je devinais que j'avais toutes raisons pour qu'on me cède. « Sale caractère », disait l'oncle Jules en reniflant. Il me soupçonnait de tenir de l'instituteur dont personne ne parlait. Pas du gendarme, bon bougre à ses yeux, ni de ma mère, une Paris : les Paris étaient des natures placides avec de terribles colères mais sans caprices d'enfant gâté.

L'une des premières images que je garde du monde est une immense table paysanne que préside à un bout ma grand-mère, un fichu noir sur les épaules, les mains posées devant elle, digne, impassible, ses cheveux gris presque blancs partagés par une raie au milieu, avec un chignon plat. Son regard tourné vers l'intérieur observe le petit bâtard que je suis. Elle fond d'amour pour lui. Une pendule comtoise bat dans son coffre et sonne les heures ; une cheminée assez haute, toute simple, sans ornement, sert plus à exposer des bibelots ou la publicité des machines agricoles McCormick qu'à faire du

feu : il faudrait qu'il fasse très froid et avoir du bois sous la main. Pour la cuisine, on n'use que de charbon en briquettes, le même qui sert aux machines qui font tourner la noria, la batteuse ou la défonceuse. Je me jette souvent dans les bras des deux femmes qui sont là, je me serre contre elles, je m'enroule dans leurs robes, je noie mon cœur dans le leur : elles sont pour moi la miséricorde, comme si je savais ce que c'est ! Leur beauté me charme, leur bonté me comble. J'ai la bouche gourmande et le menton obstiné des Paris ; l'hiver je porte un chandail bleu marine à col haut qui se boutonne sur l'épaule. Ma grand-mère est fière de ma hardiesse : « Au moins celui-là ne se laissera pas faire… » Personne n'ose se moquer de moi. A peine des silences quand nous avons des visites, des regards appuyés, à quoi je réponds, sans savoir pourquoi, par des attitudes de défi. A lire dans les yeux de ma grand-mère la faiblesse qu'elle a pour moi, peut-être parce que je suis l'enfant du péché ou le dernier venu, j'en profite pour devenir un potentat. Je le suis resté. Au fur et à mesure que je grandirai, je considérerai comme des prérogatives ma condition à la ferme. Je m'arrogerai tous les droits : c'était un peu la coutume reconnue, transmise et voulue par les femmes. Un enfant mâle qui n'aurait pas leurs faiblesses était une gloire qu'elles revendiquent moins de nos jours. De mon temps, elles célébraient l'homme à sa naissance par des réjouissances appuyées : un héritier que ces esclaves élèveraient à leur guise et qui les protégerait. Dans le matriarcat en honneur chez les barbares, les femmes commandaient par les hommes.

La ferme de Sidi-Moussa, c'était hier et j'y suis encore. Les montagnes loin au sud, un grand frêne près d'un hangar, des noyers, des orangers, quelques grenadiers, des néfliers bordés par une haie de cyprès et des touffes de roseaux. Au-delà, des chemins de terre et de galets, d'autres fermes, des éoliennes, des toits rouges, de hauts murs blancs. Au nord, des collines grenat couvertes de vignes, le Sahel, un mouvement qui se perd à l'horizon. Derrière, c'est la ville d'Alger et la mer. Invisibles.

Avec l'oncle Jules parfois, je vais à Sidi-Moussa, à l'Espérance où il joue aux cartes espagnoles. Nous nous coulons d'abord dans la route, nous longeons d'énormes propriétés avec un luxe et des richesses qu'on ne trouve pas

chez nous, des allées de palmiers au fût surmonté d'un panache, des colonnades qui mènent à des demeures de maître. Puis nous nous engageons dans une avenue d'eucalyptus géants dont l'odeur éloigne les moustiques. Deux kilomètres. Une nef sans fin, une voûte parfumée, bruissante, pleine d'oiseaux, une ombre sous laquelle je glisse avec un frémissement. Un monde secret, l'approche du saint des saints. Le sabot des chevaux et le fer des roues de la voiture sonnent, la lumière est moins vive. Après un coup de vent ou une tempête, des branches cassées barrent la chaussée. Au bout, les maisons basses du village apparaissent, à tuiles rondes comme à Rovigo, comme partout en Algérie, puis la mignonne église, puis la place avec de rares magasins, le café de l'Espérance, plus loin la mairie et l'école vers le cimetière. Au café, je respire l'odeur lourde de l'absinthe et du tabac. L'oncle Jules est heureux, il salue les amis, il s'installe, je me colle contre lui, je m'ennuie, parfois je m'endors pendant qu'il joue à la *ronda*. Quand nous revenons, la nuit est tombée, l'allée des eucalyptus est terrifiante, une bougie dans une lanterne éclaire la croupe du cheval qui trotte allégrement vers l'écurie. Des étoiles nous accompagnent.

Chaque matin sauf le dimanche, annoncé par les aboiements de César, vers midi, à bicyclette, le facteur apporte le courrier. S'il y a une enveloppe de Rovigo, ma mère la glisse dans son corsage. Silence. Est-ce qu'elle avait dû avoir si mal ? Est-ce qu'elle était dégoûtée des hommes ? Elle ne disait plus rien. Parfois des signes, des regards. Ou des demi-mots. Ou alors des crises, quand elle s'apercevait que je n'étais pas là depuis un moment. Des cris : « Zizi, où es-tu ? » Elle courait jusqu'à ce qu'elle me ramène et me plaque à côté d'elle, sur un banc.

La bande d'abonnement de *la Dépêche algérienne* indique encore le nom du grand-père : « M. Paris Jean-Pierre, propriétaire, Sidi-Moussa. » Le soir avant le dîner, l'oncle Jules lira les titres à voix haute, pour sa mère, quelquefois tout un article. Du café il ramène d'autres nouvelles et des cancans. Il sait tout, va partout, à pied, à bicyclette ou avec son deux-roues, parle arabe dans les douars, visite les voisins, parfois s'habille en milord avec un canotier neuf, des bottines jaunes à boutons, et hop ! file à Alger. Avant d'entrer dans la ville, il met la voiture et le cheval en fourrière. Là, mystère. L'oncle

Jules revient plein de rencontres, de choses qu'on dit de la ville et de la politique, des vues sur l'avenir, et le prix du vin, de l'huile, du blé qu'à cette époque on paie en pièces de bronze, d'argent, parfois d'or. Les billets de cent et de mille francs sont rares. Il parle des navires qu'il a vu accoster ou appareiller. Parfois il sifflote ce qu'on chante là-bas. Ma grand-mère dresse l'oreille. Il fredonne d'une voix un peu nasillarde :

L'youpin nous dégoûte
avec son lorgnon...

Ma mère poursuit :

Va-t'en d'là, sal'youtre
Avec ton sal' pognon...

C'est vrai, c'est ce qu'on entend partout. En ce temps-là, Drumont, le fameux antisémite, était député d'Alger. Comme les Arabes n'aimaient pas les juifs, les colons croyaient trouver là un moyen de se rapprocher des Arabes. Etait-on chez nous plus antijuifs qu'ailleurs ? Pas moins en tout cas. Les manifestations d'Alger, ce seront surtout des mots, des menaces, le moyen de se libérer de quelques dettes, on incendiera quelques magasins et la synagogue de la rue de Chartres, il y aura des troubles à Blida, on chantera longtemps « la Marseillaise antijuive » comme on chantera « Viens, Poupoule... ». L'air m'en est resté dans la mémoire, le refrain aussi. L'oncle Jules et ma mère continueront d'admirer les juifs pour leur sens des affaires et leur intelligence. Pour enfoncer dans la caboche de ses élèves que les juifs sont des hommes comme les autres et que, pour lui, le capitaine Dreyfus n'est pas coupable, l'instituteur laïc de Rovigo, mon père, fera mieux : il en accueillera un chez lui, et ce sera un drame, mais ce drame-là, c'est moi qui l'ai inventé.

A travers les voyages de l'oncle Jules, Alger prenait pour moi des allures féeriques. Quant à la France, c'était la patrie secrète de l'autre côté des mers, où cela ? La première fois que j'irai à Alger, ce sera l'émerveillement des multitudes, des navires, de l'inconnu, de l'invisible au-delà de cette France chérie et lointaine, inaccessible, que l'on désirait par bouffées brûlantes, comme un destin au-dessus de la terre barricadée d'interdits. L'oncle Jules était tout imprégné de l'odeur de péché que ma grand-mère respirait sur lui avec une moue ; elle

31

sentait des traces de femme étrangère, un danger de ruine. Pour moi, l'oncle Jules revenu, c'était le retour du héros.

Le soir, après le souper, après la partie de dominos, le marchand de sable m'incline la tête dans les bras, ma mère m'emporte dans ma chambre, derrière la cuisine. Là, j'ai mon lit avec, l'été, un matelas de feuilles de maïs qui craquent et protègent de la chaleur. La pièce, toujours sombre, a sa fenêtre souvent ouverte sur l'écurie-étable. On y entend le piétinement des sabots, la sourde rumination des bœufs, le bruit de leur chaîne contre la mangeoire, leurs mugissements parfois, parfois aussi quelque hennissement d'étalon. Meftah vient changer les litières ou emplir les râteliers, il parle aux bêtes, il les appelle par leur nom. L'odeur chaude de la paille, l'odeur lourde du fumier, l'odeur du foin et de la luzerne se mêlent à l'odeur entêtante des caroubes. Il y en a un sac dans lequel l'oncle Jules puise pour en distribuer une poignée aux chevaux les jours de fête, comme une friandise. Ce sont de grands haricots secs à longue cosse épaisse et savoureuse, très sucrée, un peu alcoolisée, semble-t-il. Les chevaux en sont gourmands, moi aussi. Eux, ça leur flanque comme un coup d'éperon, ça les excite, ça les saoule. En revanche, les noyaux des caroubes, petits et ronds, durs et lisses, je les crache. Les chevaux les mangent.

A table, l'oncle Jules parle d'une lettre reçue, car une lettre, surtout si elle annonce une visite, est un événement, ou d'une balade dans les vignes, ou du temps qu'il prévoit, puis décroche son fusil et disparaît. Où va-t-il dans la nuit d'étoiles ? Le chien César, à peine détaché, court au maître . « Ah ! te voilà, toi... » Est-ce qu'on peut avoir confiance dans ces chiens-là ? Est-ce que ces chiens qu'on appelle des chiens kabyles, ne sont pas, quoi qu'ils montrent, obscurément fidèles à leur race ? Celui-là, de taille moyenne, jaune et blanc, feint de détester les Arabes, il se déchaîne avec des aboiements rauques quand l'un d'eux approche, on le lâcherait qu'il mordrait peut-être, mais n'est-ce pas de la frime ? Ces chiens hargneux et sournois nés dans les douars attaquent par-derrière et par surprise, jamais par-devant, ils ont trop peur, ce sont des descendants de chacals. La nuit, César est supposé garder la ferme : les murs, les récoltes, les machines, les outils, le bétail. Un chien de France conviendrait peut-être mieux, gendarme solide, costaud et avec consigne, il en existe, certains

colons en ont, mais il faut les acheter. L'oncle Jules fait le tour de la ferme à pas tranquilles, ses yeux se sont accommodés à l'ombre, la lune est dans le ciel, les fenêtres de la salle à manger ressemblent à des lanternes vénitiennes blondes, il n'est pas tard, il y a peu de lumière dans la plaine, davantage du côté d'Alger qu'on devine par une lueur derrière les collines : les réverbères au gaz allumés le long des boulevards et sur les places, les lampes des cafés, des restaurants, des maisons à étages, des voitures, et les calèches, les trams ! C'est une nuit calme, douce, tiède, une odeur de feu de bois et de piment s'échappe du douar, mêlée à une senteur d'eucalyptus quand le vent porte de ce côté-là ; les étoiles brillent à peine, à demi cachées par de hauts nuages qui annoncent peut-être la pluie. Oui, où allait-il, l'oncle Jules, quand il nous quittait le soir après la partie de dominos, son fusil sous le bras, en pleine force comme il était, revenant du café de Sidi-Moussa et de la partie de cartes avec les amis dans une chaude rumeur de voix et de rires, et dans le parfum de l'anis ?

Je me souviens du logis de l'oncle Jules dans les communs, entre l'écurie et le hangar de la machine de la noria : deux pièces pleines de sacs de grains, d'appareils à phosphater et de tapettes à souris. Un lit de camp, un seau et une cuvette, des serviettes sur le dos d'une chaise, une glace pour se raser, des frusques dans une armoire en bois blanc, pas une image, pas une douceur, pas un livre, sans doute un carnet de comptes, un verre, une lampe Pigeon avec une boîte d'allumettes soufrées sur la cheminée. Spartiate. On pourrait se demander quel genre d'homme il est, on ne sait pas. Il vit là, l'esprit ailleurs. Où ça ? L'oncle Jules est demeuré avec son mystère jusqu'au moment où il a épousé une de ses cousines germaines, une fille Bouychou, petite-nièce de la mère, mais qu'on ne voyait plus, charmante, qui s'appelait Marie comme la mère et avait une sœur, Manon, belle aussi, d'une beauté un peu piquante et qui ne manquait pas d'esprit, ce qui tout à coup, comme les deux sœurs étaient quasiment inséparables, mit deux jeunes femmes dans la maison. C'était beaucoup plus tard, quand nous n'étions plus là, ma mère et moi. Avant ou après la mort de ma grand-mère ? Après, probablement.

En moi les souvenirs se télescopent, se chevauchent, des étalons se battent pour une jument. Les questions à propos de l'oncle Jules, cet homme plein d'ardeur qui veille sur la ferme

en compagnie de César, m'amènent à ne rien savoir de lui. Il mourra jeune, à cinquante ans à peine, d'un coup de sang, et laissera trois enfants. Tout se dispersera sous les coups du sort, la ferme suivra le destin de l'Algérie. Un moment, en pleine débâcle, je songerai à l'acheter pour qu'elle ne tombe pas dans les mains des Arabes.

C'était de la folie. Ça ne se fera pas.

*
**

« Je crois que cela a été pour moi un bien grand malheur que de grandir au sein de ma famille, du milieu et de la conception de vie qui m'ont vu naître et qui ont été les miens », écrit Karen Blixen, longtemps après avoir publié son fameux livre *la Ferme africaine*. Pour moi, ce serait tout le contraire. Née en 1885 près de Copenhague, Karen Blixen était partie en 1914 pour le Kenya où, avec un mari, elle dirigea une plantation de café, divorça, vécut dix ans là-bas seule, puis revenue au Danemark, se consacra à la littérature avec une gloire qui, tout à la fin de sa vie, éclata.

Nairobi n'est pas Alger, et les populations indigènes du Kenya n'ont rien de commun avec les Arabes. Quelle chance j'ai eue de naître en 1907 dans le village de Rovigo, là où la plaine de la Mitidja bute contre un redan de l'Atlas tellien ! Quelle chance pour moi que ma mère chassée ait dû se réfugier dans sa famille ! Quelle chance d'avoir vécu mes premières années parmi des femmes et des hommes simples, presque frustes, pour qui l'existence consistait à résister aux fléaux naturels, au milieu dans lequel ils se trouvaient, à la solitude, aux maladies, et à produire de bonnes récoltes pour s'enrichir raisonnablement ! Quelle chance d'être, dès le plus jeune âge, face à face avec les réalités de la vie : les drames entre époux, la crainte du présent et l'incertitude de l'avenir, la splendeur du ciel et la simplicité des mœurs, quelle chance qu'un pays neuf où tout était à inventer, avec des gens à l'état brut : ceux qui travaillaient sur un sol à défricher, ceux qui les aidaient avec le sentiment d'être dépossédés, ceux qui veillaient à la sécurité publique, l'armée qui tenait l'ensemble du pays, le curé qui était le ministre d'une religion pratiquée par une minorité face à l'islam, religion de la multitude qui nous cernait. Presque à vue d'œil, tout changeait par le peuplement, les routes, les

transports, les écoles, l'accélération des relations, l'organisation de la santé, de la justice et de la répression, l'établissement d'un mode de vie sur le modèle métropolitain et tout ce qu'on inventait : l'automobile, l'aéroplane, le téléphone, l'électricité. Il n'empêche qu'au début du siècle, l'Algérie était encore loin de posséder l'équipement du territoire métropolitain. Ce qui frappait surtout, c'était le contraste entre colonisateurs et colonisés, les uns soulevés par une sorte de frénésie de puissance, les autres écrasés par une civilisation déjà mécanique, d'où une différence de taille dans les niveaux de vie : les uns près d'un mode pastoral et patriarcal, les autres décidés à imposer une sorte d'impérialisme souvent naïf et bon enfant.

Trop modeste, éprouvée par la mort prématurée de ses fondateurs, la famille Paris ne figurait pas parmi la fine fleur. On ne comptait pas les Paris parmi les princes du pinard, de l'alfa, du blé, de l'espadrille, de l'huile, de l'anisette ou des transports sur route. Encore moins parmi ceux qui dirigeaient l'administration et la politique. Les Paris n'appartenaient pas à l'aristocratie du Tout-Alger, la nomenklatura du moment. Les banques ne les rangeaient pas parmi les puissances. Cette famille qui ne faisait parler d'elle en rien, peut-être avait-elle des principes trop rigoureux. J'ai vu ma grand-mère, inquiète des écarts de conduite des uns et des autres, généreuse avec les siens et avec les *meskines*. Elle ne savait ni lire ni écrire mais elle savait compter. Je l'ai vue intraitable quand il s'agissait d'argent qu'il ne fallait pas gagner sur le dos de n'importe qui. Avec elle on ne volait pas leurs terres aux Arabes, on ne spoliait pas ceux qui ne pouvaient pas se défendre. Les frères Paris essayaient parfois de se rouler eux-mêmes, je ne vais pas en faire des saints, mais personne ne les accusa jamais de fraude ou d'exactions. Honnêtes, ils sont restés pauvres. D'autres Paris ont gagné la petite noblesse de l'enseignement, certaines filles, grâce à leur beauté et à leur esprit, ont épousé des avocats, des officiers, des ambassadeurs, l'une d'elles osa même épouser un étudiant arabe, problème auquel personne ne s'attendait.

Pour moi, enfant, l'adoration de ma grand-mère m'aida à croire que j'avais tous les dons, ce qui me conduisit souvent à me juger à tort au-dessus des autres et ma mère ne facilitera pas les choses. En même temps, elle justifiera sa faute par une surabondance de grâces et je m'habituerai à ce que tout me soit

dû. Quand il m'arrivera d'être humilié, je le supporterai mal. Ai-je jamais « senti le souffle derrière moi dès l'enfance », comme Romain Rolland le dit pour lui dans *le Royaume du T.* ? Il ne m'en souvient pas, de si loin. Je ne me souviens que de mon désir d'aller au-delà d'où j'étais, de savoir ce qui était derrière ce qui m'était caché. Souvent j'ai été tenté de me dire que ma carrière dans les lettres eût été plus facile si j'étais né au milieu des bibliothèques et des salons et si, dès mon jeune âge, j'avais pu lire les *Mémoires d'outre-tombe* plutôt que *le Chasseur français*. Fils de consul ou de riche colon, j'aurais appris à dissimuler ma pensée et à m'exprimer avec discernement. La fréquentation des beaux esprits aurait favorisé mes rencontres avec les entremetteurs de la culture.

Eh bien, il n'est pas de jour où je ne rende grâce au ciel de sortir d'un milieu d'hommes et de femmes intègres, de caractères entiers et passionnés, parmi les violents et les injustes, sous un ciel de bonheur et de cruauté, et fils d'une femme qui préféra l'amour au désamour et la vérité au mensonge. Je lui dois l'essentiel d'un caractère dont je n'ai pas toujours eu à me féliciter.

D'apparence frêle, pas grand, maigre, vêtu de choses indistinctes : un saroual, une sorte de chemise, plutôt un sac ; l'hiver, une sorte de cachabia, c'est-à-dire une enveloppe de laine grossière percée de trous pour la tête et les bras, le serviteur arabe, Meftah, portait une sorte de chéchia sans couleur et allait nu-pieds, quelquefois avec, pour semelles, une feuille de cuir retenue par des lanières. Si, dans mon enfance, je l'ai tant et tant de fois vu, l'ai-je jamais regardé ? Il était là et ne comptait pas. Sa condition était tellement inférieure que le meilleur, pour lui, était d'être comme s'il n'existait pas, sauf pour chercher de l'eau, des briquettes de charbon et du bois, allumer la cuisinière, atteler le cheval, mettre les bœufs au joug. De petites choses. Il panse les chevaux, change les litières, lave les voitures, fauche l'herbe pour les mangeoires, se livre à tous les travaux qu'exigent le bétail et la terre. A la maison, s'il n'est pas là et qu'on ait besoin de lui, quelqu'un l'appelle. « *Ya Meftahooôh...* » C'est l'homme de rien sans qui rien ne se ferait, de qui nul ne peut se passer et qui doit être là.

Il boit de l'eau. Jamais de vin. Du café, ça arrive. Nous allons rarement chez le boucher, on a des poules et des lapins, des pigeons, souvent des lièvres, des perdrix, des cailles, on tue le cochon l'hiver : il dure toute l'année dans le saloir et en saucisses, boudins espagnols et saucissons suspendus au plafond de la cuisine en chapelets à des roseaux. Meftah ne touche pas à la vaisselle, il se contente de ramener les arrosoirs pleins du puits, car il n'y a pas l'eau courante à la ferme, ce n'est pas encore inventé. Dans la maison, il passe et ne reste pas, ou alors, dans les grandes circonstances, quand il y a de la famille, il est de la *gens romana,* salue tout le monde, touche les mains, mais lui est d'ailleurs, c'est un Arabe du pays, c'est Meftah (nom qui signifie la clef), nous sommes souvent ensemble, ma mère n'aime pas ça puisque, pour elle, les Arabes ont des poux. Du moins les pauvres.

Il y a chez nous quelqu'un de moins considéré que Meftah : César, attaché toute la journée sous le hangar qui touche la maison, à côté d'une gamelle d'eau. Le soir, Meftah lui porte une casserole de soupe avec de gros morceaux de pain trempé, des os, des débris, César frétille d'abord de plaisir puis avale à grosses goulées et broie les os dans ses mâchoires. Il n'entre jamais à la maison. Il est plein de puces. On ne le nettoie jamais, personne n'y pense. Jamais de coup de brosse, jamais de bain, rien ne l'empêche la nuit de plonger dans le bassin de la noria comme font les renards ou de se gratter l'échine sur le sol. Je ne le découvrirai qu'après Meftah, à cause de ses aboiements furieux et du raclement de sa chaîne dans la niche aux approches d'un rôdeur, d'un étranger. A distance, il me semble qu'il existait une sorte de complicité entre César et Meftah. César avait de l'affection et de la considération pour Meftah. Meftah parlait à César.

Quand Meftah nous quittait, la nuit tombait vite. Je percevais alors comme un phénomène d'un autre monde, un cri multiple et haletant, d'abord incertain, vague, confus, comme se cherchant lui-même et peu à peu se renforçant à son propre écho : les chacals. Quelques-uns d'abord — les plus jeunes ou les plus inquiets ? puis s'étendant vite, se multipliant, couvrant toute la terre et la criblant de leur plainte. On aurait pu croire qu'ils s'interrogeaient et, ne recevant pas de réponse, qu'ils s'effrayaient. Tous, à l'envi, poussaient alors

une sorte de jappement de douleur ou de plaisir, avec des moments de silence et d'interrogation puis des reprises folles. Le nombre, la multitude s'y ajoutait, la crainte chez eux prenait corps, devenait terreur panique. Ces gémissements hachés et tremblants étaient-ils l'effet de leur épouvante devant l'ombre de plus en plus profonde où ils s'enfonçaient ou, au contraire, le contentement de voir s'ouvrir des espaces qui leur étaient interdits pendant le jour ? Les chacals descendaient de la montagne, sortaient de tous les fourrés, de tous les ravins, se répandaient en bandes furtives et affamées à travers les vignes, les récoltes, les abords des poulaillers ; déjà glapissant et se mordillant, frénétiques, pathétiques, délirants, ils tournoyaient comme des meutes sans chefs et sans courage, car c'étaient des poltrons, un rien leur faisait peur et suffisait à les chasser. Cette immense extravagance que personne d'autre que moi ne semblait entendre remuait mon âme. Le balancier de la pendule allait et venait dans son coffre avec chaque fois un pâle éclair et un toc minuscule ; à la cuisine ma mère préparait le repas à la lueur de la lampe Pigeon. Assis sur un banc face à la fenêtre qui ouvrait sur le nord, je regardais les premières étoiles trembler à la cadence de la mélopée lugubre, au-dessus du chemin par où l'oncle Jules allait revenir. Très loin grinçait enfin le mince bruit aigrelet du fer des roues sur les galets et sonnait le claquement des sabots du cheval. Alors ma grand-mère se levait, prenait une boîte sur l'étagère de la cheminée, venait sous le globe au milieu de la table, levait un bras puis le rabaissait en posant le tube de verre, grattait une allumette, attendait que le soufre qui renforçait la petite flamme ait promené sa langue vert et or. Soudain une lueur jaune nous inondait. L'ombre était lentement repoussée, les visages apparaissaient, mes mains, la table, la bouteille de vin rosé, la gargoulette, les murs blanchis à la chaux avec les gravures de Jean-qui-pleure et Jean-qui-rit, le calendrier des machines McCormick, le secrétaire où l'oncle enfermait ses papiers, le cadran de la pendule, un fusil accroché derrière la porte. Le soir profond se refermait sur nous comme une mer. Au tournant de l'allée qui menait à la ferme, la voiture de l'oncle ralentissait puis c'était l'éclat de l'arrivée dans la cour sous le gros figuier. Avec des « O ô ô... », l'oncle Jules retenait le cheval que Meftah attrapait par la bride. Les deux hommes se parlaient, l'oncle Jules sautait à terre, sa voix, comme

cuivrée par l'anis qu'il avait bu, sonnait plus clair, Meftah répondait d'un ton neutre et rapide, puis tandis que Meftah dételait, l'oncle Jules grimpait les marches du perron, poussait la porte, sa haute et large silhouette surgissait dans la lumière. Le visage encore palpitant de la conversation au café, il accrochait son fusil derrière la porte, souriait, nous regardait. « Ah !... » Un cri de plaisir à nous revoir, à s'attabler sous la fenêtre en face de moi, sur l'autre banc, à droite de la grand-mère. Grâce au globe translucide pareil à une grosse lune opalescente et douce, si attirante, nous résistions victorieuse-ment à la vibration de la nuit. Dans les ténèbres qui descendaient sur la planète, nous devenions brillants, le palpitement de la plainte des chacals était moins strident. L'oncle Jules resplendissait. Derrière lui, sur le rebord de la fenêtre, j'apercevais le gobe-mouches en verre. Ma mère posait la soupière devant nous, les chacals disparaissaient, rejetés hors de tout, infiniment loin, par le ton de la conversation qui s'amorçait et les premières lichées.

Etait-ce le meilleur moment de la journée ? Le soir avait son mystère, ébauche de tous les mystères à venir. Le soir, c'était la descente de l'ombre, le rassemblement familial devant les dangers inconnus, la prise de possession du silence par l'immense lamentation des chacals, puis le repas, la plage dorée de la lumière au pétrole, la partie de dominos interrompue par le passage ponctuel du marchand de sable. Ma mère m'empor-tait vers mon lit. Les feuilles de maïs du matelas craquaient sous moi, la douleur des chacals me berçait. Elle atteignait sa culminance à la pleine lune. Parfois, avant de sombrer dans le sommeil, tandis que ma mère me faisait réciter mes prières, je percevais de vagues clameurs, leurs brisements, leurs embruns leur écume sale. C'était le bonheur. Je ne me souviens pas que ma grand-mère ou ma mère m'aient jamais murmuré des contes de fées. De quoi me parlait-on pour m'effrayer ou pour m'émerveiller ? Des Arabes, des gendarmes ? Des cigognes peut-être, qui venaient de France et repartiraient au printemps avec leurs petits...

Karen Blixen avoue qu'elle a eu l'occasion de rencontrer le regard de ses indigènes avec le sentiment qu'elle était loin d'eux et qu'ils étaient découragés par les idées qu'elle pouvait avoir, elle. Elle avait admis une fois pour toutes qu'elle

n'arriverait jamais à les connaître alors qu'ils n'ignoraient rien de ses pensées. Il en était de même en Algérie, et pourtant les Arabes étaient de la même couleur que nous. Evidemment, on avait conquis leur pays, on les avait soumis. On pouvait se demander si, à la longue, au fait qu'ils ne pouvaient rien changer à l'ordre voulu par Dieu, les relations ne deviendraient pas franchement amicales. Elles l'étaient par moments. Il semblait admis, comme une loi naturelle, que les Arabes étaient des serviteurs, les Français des maîtres, et que tout était bien ainsi parce que les Français appartenaient à une race entreprenante mais généreuse et que les Arabes dépendaient toujours de quelqu'un. Les Français possédaient tout, comme les Turcs avant eux, mais d'autres — les Anglais ou les Espagnols — eussent été plus impérialistes. A la lecture des journaux locaux de l'époque, la différence entre Algériens et Indigènes (car le titre d'Algériens était réservé aux colonisateurs, les colonisés n'étant que des sidis) semblait plus marquée dans les principes que dans les relations courantes : les choses allaient de soi sans qu'il fût nécessaire d'insister comme dans les journaux, peut-être parce que les journaux étaient la propriété de la classe au pouvoir et qu'il fallait répéter sans cesse qu'il y avait en Algérie deux poids et deux mesures, deux modes de vie, deux civilisations, encore que ce terme-là ne convînt qu'à l'une des deux espèces d'hommes, l'autre se contentant plutôt du terme « mœurs », et que cela était ainsi : les hommes de ce pays ne pouvaient pas avoir des droits égaux. Pas étonnant que, plus tard, j'aie adhéré à la convention que les Arabes n'avaient pas d'âme. Meftah aurait-il pu avoir une âme ? Meftah était-il un homme ? Cela ne pouvait pas ne pas marquer l'enfant que j'étais. J'appartenais à la race des seigneurs.

Quand je le surprenais posé sur moi et vite se détournant, le regard de Meftah me paraissait un oiseau qui allait et venait, rapide, agile, leste, flou ? Terriblement indiscret mais ne le montrant pas, fureteur et scrutateur comme tous les faibles. Je possède une photo de famille où figurent tous les personnages de la ferme, sauf Meftah. J'ai donc besoin de le réinventer. Je suis sûr que Meftah n'aurait pas refusé d'être photographié avec nous. Il aurait peut-être fait des manières, la première fois, pour la forme ; son sens religieux était si faible qu'il n'aurait pas refusé qu'on prenne une image de lui. On aurait

insisté, il aurait cédé. Comme il ne manquait pas d'humour, cela l'aurait amusé de se voir ensuite sur du papier. Le photographe n'a pas pris non plus les bœufs. Le cheval seulement, quand il était attelé aux deux-roues avec l'oncle Jules sur le siège. Dans l'esprit du photographe, ni les bœufs ni Meftah, encore moins le chien, ne valaient la dépense d'un cliché, et cette vérité n'a rien d'offensant. A l'époque, on ne photographiait les Arabes qu'au marché ou dans les rassemblements. Avec toutes les questions qu'il se posait sans doute sur moi (« qu'est-ce qu'ils vont faire de ce fruit du péché, qu'est-ce que cet enfant a dans la tête ? »), le regard de Meftah aurait été de trop. Sur la photo de famille dont j'ai parlé, personne n'aurait eu l'idée d'appeler Meftah pour poser avec nous. Même l'oncle Jules aurait jugé cela inconvenant. Meftah faisait sans doute partie de la *gens* au travail, mais là, c'était vraiment la vraie famille, entre soi, les intimes, les descendants de l'Ariège et de la Franche-Comté, la race des conquérants et pas celle des vaincus.

J'examine bien cette photo. A la droite de ma mère, mon frère René va partir sous les drapeaux comme artilleur. Il ressemble à son père jeune, au gendarme qui a séduit ma mère. L'a-t-il séduite, en vérité ? Visage pur, moustache peu fournie et forte chevelure à crans. Il porte un costume de toile fripé, avec gilet, sans cravate, un brassard de crêpe au bras gauche car il est en deuil récent de son père, nous sommes en 1911 et à la fin de l'année, le sol est couvert des feuilles mortes du noyer à l'entrée de la cave. Les hommes encadrent les femmes, ma grand-mère dans sa robe noire à fronces, col montant et tablier en satinette à poches, ma mère dans une robe noire aussi, du taffetas ? tombant jusqu'au sol et lui couvrant les pieds, avec ceinture de soie à boucle.

Cette image que j'ai toujours eue devant moi, comme celle de mon père et de ma mère, est l'œuvre de mon frère René. Très ingénieux en mécanique, féru de tout ce qui est nouveau, il se sert d'un Kodak de poche avec déclencheur automatique qu'il fixe sur un trépied. Il nous prend, et lui en même temps. Je lui dois des documents sans prix — les traits des êtres chers et leur parfait naturel, car l'objectif tenu par lui ne gêne personne. Moi, j'ai quatre ans, je suis un petit merdeux, j'ai une culotte avec gros boutons sur la cuisse, des chaussettes blanches au-dessus des bottines lacées, je suis là

contraint parce qu'on m'a demandé de **venir** et que je dis
toujours non. Ma mère me tient solidement devant elle par les
épaules, je baisse la tête, bouge la main droite, lance ma jambe
gauche de travers comme si je ruais, secoue ma chevelure et
fais la moue, le poing droit au côté, le coude en aileron, avec
un regard qui fuit dans une attitude de défense, ah ! le sale
gosse ! L'oncle Jules qui nous domine tous de la tête est
drôlement fringué : paletot étriqué, pantalon rapiécé aux
genoux, escarpins, pas de cravate, et avec son canotier défoncé,
posé droit pour la circonstance, quelle envie de se foutre du
monde ! Quant à Meftah, ombre fidèle, témoin discret et
attentif, peut-être un peu hypocrite, un peu sournois et très
subtil de ce qui apparaît et encore plus de ce qui se cache, j'ai
dit qu'on n'ose pas le montrer à côté de l'oncle Jules au falzar
de clown. D'ailleurs, où l'aurait-on mis ? Un peu en retrait,
pensez, avec ce colosse ! ou accroupi devant lui ? Bref, pas de
Meftah. Dommage. Son image ne flottera que dans un
brouillard. Meftah sur la fameuse photo, j'aurais sa tête, son
œil malin, son apparence de serviteur arabe conduit par la
nécessité à s'attacher à des colons français et finalement ne le
regrettant pas. Mais peut-être est-ce lui qui ne veut pas se
montrer. Evidemment, il n'est pas bien payé, mais quel Arabe
est bien payé ? Il a à peine de quoi empêcher sa famille de
mourir de faim, il pleure misère, sa femme Zohra est malade, il
loge dans le gourbi qu'il s'est construit, où il abrite aussi
quelques poules et deux moutons qu'il élève sur la ferme ; de
temps en temps, il réussit à soutirer quelques piécettes à ma
grand-mère, d'autres que lui sont dans la mouise, et les Arabes
d'à côté encore plus, dans leur promiscuité sordide et vivant de
quoi ? Donc, pas de Meftah. Et cependant je me revois
toujours à califourchon sur son cou au milieu des vignes, à peu
près à hauteur de l'oncle Jules marchant le fusil à la bretelle
prêt à tirer dans le cas où le lièvre apparaîtrait, un capucin
comme on disait. Etrange trio, étrange compagnie perdue dans
l'immense plaine avec toutes ses fermes orgueilleuses et, à
perte de vue, ses vignobles en damier, ses éoliennes, ses
palmiers, ses douars disséminés, ses routes grinçantes d'équipages et de charrois escortés d'une nuée de claquements de
fouets. Rien de tout cela ne m'appartient et ne m'appartiendra
jamais, sauf peut-être le vent chargé d'odeurs de vinaigrette
sauvage et d'eucalyptus, sauf le ciel, sauf le soleil roi, ce

seigneur tout-puissant. Ai-je la moindre idée que je vis dans un paradis terrestre ? Je ne sais pas que je suis innocent, gâté, préservé, né à quoi, pour quoi ? Plus tard, la découverte de notre présence à nous, mortels, me surprendra au-dessus d'un gouffre. A ce moment de mon enfance, je vis dans un songe, il ne m'arrive que des merveilles.

Sur les épaules, tantôt de Meftah, tantôt de l'oncle Jules, je me crois au centre de l'univers. Le soir, quand ma mère me prend par la main pour me montrer les étoiles, me dit-elle qu'elles sont d'autres mondes à travers lesquels nous voguons, y cherche-t-elle son destin ou pense-t-elle qu'il s'agit là d'un mystère sans commencement ni fin ? Pour moi, ces points d'or piqués dans le velours de la nuit sont comme les grenouilles et les têtards dans le bassin de la noria. Tout s'agite dans une simplicité sans vertige, dans les proches comme dans les lointains. Je ne sais pas que je vis sur un globe tourbillonnant sur sa trajectoire d'éternité, au rythme des saisons, et condamné à ne jamais dévier. Ma mère m'entraîne vite. « A la maison. »

La suspension est allumée, l'oncle Jules rentre du village avec le bruit des sabots du cheval, dans le roulement rassurant et doux de son tilbury. « Oh là, ôôô... » Meftah surgit, tout est dans l'ordre. On va dîner, on jouera aux dominos pendant que ma mère débarrasse, puis elle ira me coucher et l'oncle partira avec son fusil.

Au point où me voici déjà, il va m'être difficile, comme l'avoue Clamence dans *la Chute* de Camus, de « démêler le vrai du faux ». Clamence est avocat, chacun de nous est son propre avocat. On plaide pour soi, pour se défendre des méchants, des envieux, des méprisants, des indifférents, de nos contemporains comme de ceux qui viendront après nous, et pour les gagner à notre cause, pour attirer à nous ceux de qui on voudrait être aimé, pour retenir ceux qui s'éloignent. Dieu, en voilà un difficile à séduire ! Alors, qu'il soit miséricordieux. On plaide pour l'implorer. Pas un jour où je ne lui dise : « Ayez pitié de votre pauvre imbécile, est-ce ma faute si je suis comme vous m'avez fait ? » Mon malheur, c'est que je n'ai pas changé. Je retrouverai bientôt mon père et ma mère comme ils

m'ont fabriqué, pareil à eux, pas plus malin, à peine moins dans la gêne, sans autre fortune qu'une maison, encore que la mienne soit plus grande et plus plaisante que la leur. Là où nous nous retrouverons, nous serons à l'aise, la terre est vaste. Certains d'entre nous dorment dans les environs de Bar-sur-Aube, mon frère René et Louise à Argelès-sur-Mer, presque tous les autres dans la terre d'Algérie, ma mère aussi, mais Dieu sait où et en quel état de délaissement ou de profanation, je le dirai plus loin ; un de mes pères dans la banlieue parisienne au cimetière de Pantin dont le nom convient bien à ce qu'il était. Je quitterai ma femme qui m'est plus chère que moi, notre chienne, notre chat Staline, peut-être une page inachevée. On me déposera pas loin d'ici.

Quand on se met à des Mémoires, d'habitude on est au bout du rouleau. Voilà des années que je résiste et que j'écris des livres « intercalaires » en les glissant dans la rangée des autres. Est-ce que s'éteindre avec des Mémoires, surtout si c'était comme une nova, serait déchoir ? N'est-ce pas plutôt qu'il faudrait se résigner à s'arrêter bientôt ? Comme cette idée me faisait horreur, ainsi me suis-je hâté d'écrire un *Guynemer,* comme si j'avais vingt ans, dans la fièvre et la joyeuse ardeur de célébrer un héros, prédateur de génie, et courageux presque jusqu'à la démence, avant d'entreprendre ce travail qui soudain me paraît utile : je vais encore tirer quelque chose de moi, me battre avec notre plus mortel ennemi, le temps, et faire de l'avenir avec le passé. Regardons-nous avec un peu d'humour.

A Vézelay, c'est le pire moment de l'année, le fond pourri de l'hiver, la course des nuages de pluie, le balayage des dépressions atlantiques. L'aube émerge sinistrement des ténèbres, le jour se traîne pour sombrer de nouveau dans la nuit. Quand, avant midi, je sors la chienne, le vent se jette sur moi, m'assaille et me force à lutter tête baissée contre des tourbillons qui rebondissent au bas des tours.

Sur la terrasse de l'ancien château, je me retourne un instant. D'habitude, c'est ma récompense de la matinée. D'habitude, la basilique se montre douce et altière, souveraine, quelquefois elle ressemble à une femme d'Abyssinie, grise de peau, quelquefois elle a des frisures blanches sur le front,

quelquefois elle est blonde comme l'étaient mes cousines, et je la vois toute noire, sombre vaisseau naviguant à travers les embruns. C'est ce moment-là que j'ai choisi pour me mettre à ces Mémoires, barbares comme moi, comme le temps et les guerres traversées. Quatre-vingts virages autour du soleil me pèsent sur les épaules et dans les jambes. Du haut de la falaise, je tente d'ouvrir mes poumons devant la vallée gorgée d'eau et les forêts qui grondent comme des armées de chars ; je n'aspire qu'un air flasque, imbibé de ténèbres, de vase, de doute. Cette fameuse terre de légende est un royaume de chouettes qui se poursuivent en ricanant. Elles se perceraient le crâne les unes des autres si elles pouvaient, condamnées qu'elle sont à vivre et à gémir.

La chienne et moi, nous rentrons ruisselants, nous nous séchons devant le poêle, je m'aperçois dans une glace au milieu des bibliothèques. A quoi servira un livre de plus ? A présent, vieux cheval fourbu, je m'arrête et je souffle. La tempête nous vient d'Irlande et je l'entends siffler. Elle a chassé les choucas dans les anfractuosités des tours. J'en ai assez. De tout, de moi-même et même d'écrire. Grand Dieu ! Je m'aperçois avec horreur que je nourris le dessein de m'en aller. Où cela ? On verra bien. Ma femme aussi en a assez. Elle est venue ici parce que depuis trente ans je tournais autour de Vézelay avec le fantôme de Louise de Vilmorin et de Balthus, et que Marie-Madeleine, l'annonciatrice de la Résurrection, la courtisane amoureuse du Christ, m'a enchanté et enchaîné. Depuis que Maurice Clavel et Max-Pol Fouchet nous ont quittés, il n'y a plus qu'elle ici, il n'y a jamais eu qu'elle, on peut continuer à l'aimer et dire cependant qu'on en a assez des lieux, quand le pèlerinage dure trop longtemps. Pour elle, Henri Petit, né près d'ici, a écrit, quand il était scribouillard de l'administration de France à Damas, vers 1926, un hymne merveilleux que les Cahiers Verts ont publié à l'époque et que personne ne connaîtrait plus si je ne m'étais mis en dessein de le rappeler. Henri Petit avait une maison ici, comme Romain Rolland, comme Georges Bataille, ils y ont invité des amis : Jean Grenier, Louis Guilloux, tant d'autres. Claudel y a passé quelques jours avec Ysé au moment de la débâcle, en 1940, chez Romain Rolland. Il y a écrit dix pages sublimes ; et la vieille Ysé s'est prise là de tant d'amour qu'elle y est encore, sous un rosier qui fleurit longtemps et une phrase du poète qui

l'aima : *Seule la rose est assez fragile pour exprimer l'éternité.* Vézelay est un lieu qu'on désire et qui dévore. J'écoute les vieilles chouettes hoqueter de plaisir. Qui sait ? Le printemps reviendra. Il y aura des rossignols.

Quelquefois, le médecin de Sidi-Moussa envoyait ma grand-mère consulter pour son diabète à vingt kilomètres de Sidi-Moussa, à Boufarik. C'est là que ma grand-mère avait rencontré le jeune homme qui était devenu son mari. C'est là que ses parents, paysans de Montségur en Ariège, avaient abordé dans leur quête du pactole. C'est là que, dans *les Chevaux du Soleil,* j'ai imaginé que le nom de sa propre mère, Aldabram, était un nom d'étoile, et que sa sœur aînée, Marguerite, s'était toquée d'un fringant officier de zouaves. Ma grand-mère y avait encore sa sœur cadette, Laetitia.

Meftah attelait deux chevaux au break. Je montais devant, à gauche de l'oncle qui conduisait ; les femmes se serraient derrière, à l'abri des vues, du vent, de la poussière, comme des Mauresques. Après la longue nef d'eucalyptus, la plaine frémissait, s'étalait. Ce qui me frappait toujours c'était la différence entre l'œuvre des colons — les fermes, les récoltes, les vignobles — et celle des indigènes : des gourbis, des troupeaux de moutons broutant le sol, les chaumes, l'herbe sèche des talus. On se saluait, on échangeait en arabe des formules de politesse. Par amusement, l'oncle Jules faisait claquer son fouet avec chic sur la route encombrée de lourds charrois de futailles ou de blé. On traversait Chébli, connu par son tabac à cheveux blonds. Boufarik apparaissait enfin avec ses murailles, ses alignements de rues bordées de platanes, des boutiques pimpantes, on entendait des fanfares de cavalerie. « Ah ! on voit que c'est une ville », disait ma mère. Devant la villa du médecin, les femmes descendaient, l'oncle confiait l'attelage à un gardien et je l'accompagnais à la découverte. Pour lui, Boufarik c'était la légende : le camp d'Erlon, les chasseurs d'Afrique, le sergent Blandan qui résistait seul à une armée de troncs de figuiers. A la terrasse des cafés, à l'ombre des platanes, il y avait des officiers en sabre, des colons à chaîne de montre en or, des femmes en chapeau de paille à fleurs. Plus loin, de faramineuses pâtisseries, des magasins.

46

Après la consultation et un passage à la pharmacie, nous allions déjeuner chez la grand-tante Laetitia, une personne fluette et stricte, toujours seule, veuve de vocation en quelque sorte, soucieuse de sa mise, toujours élégante et nette. Elle avait le visage des Bouychou, un petit nez, une bouche assez forte, un front têtu, un maintien légèrement distant et autoritaire. Elle habitait un minuscule appartement merveilleusement lustré et plein de plantes vertes. Les femmes se comprenaient à demi-mot et parlaient de Marguerite, veuve de son colonel et isolée dans son orgueil, qui n'apparaissait qu'à l'occasion d'un enterrement, pour l'ouverture du testament, et filait de nouveau s'enfermer à Alger en jetant des baisers d'oiseau. Cette part de la famille nous échappait à nous, les hommes. Ma mère s'enfonçait dans ses propres rêves, elle serrait mes épaules, approchait mon front du sien, je respirais l'huile d'œillet et de benjoin qu'elle s'était généreusement répandue sur les cheveux. « Et toi, Mathilde ? » demandait ma grand-tante Laetitia avec un regard piquant. « Rien, ma tante, tout va bien… » Laetitia n'avait pas d'enfants, pas d'argent non plus, mais savait par ses talents de couturière mettre en valeur les robes démodées de quelques dames de Boufarik. Elle sentait le beurre un peu rance, et sa bouche exhalait une haleine aigrelette. Esprit critique mais pas acerbe, elle nous considérait avec un brin de commisération : elle n'habitait pas la cambrousse, nous étions des barbares. Elle ira un jour en pèlerinage à Lourdes, en rapportera un lourd chapelet à gros grains dont ma mère héritera et que j'ai encore sur une étagère de ma bibliothèque. Sur un cœur de bois, on peut lire une parole de la Vierge : « Allez boire à la fontaine… » Cela ressemble au vers d'un poème. Ce chapelet, j'ai vu souvent ma grand-mère l'égrener, songeuse, le regard perdu au-delà des orangers et des cyprès, vers le nord, vers Montségur où elle n'est jamais retournée.

Moi, oui. Cinquante ans plus tard, sur leurs traces à eux tous, j'ai vu, au sommet d'un piton, le château aux pierres brûlées, entouré de montagnes aux arêtes aiguës. A Montségur, il y a toujours des Bouychou, de vieux hommes secs qui me ressemblent comme des éperviers se ressemblent, eux méfiants, assis sur une chaise devant leur porte et ricanant Personne ne m'a offert un verre d'eau. J'ai compris pourquoi mon aïeul les avait quittés pour s'engager dans l'expéditior

d'Alger, puis toujours fou d'amour pour sa Marie Aldabram, pour s'installer à Boufarik comme colon.

Ma grand-mère ne savait pas exactement pourquoi son père s'était lancé dans cette aventure-là. J'en ai inventé le détail et personne parmi les miens n'a protesté. Eh quoi, il nous fallait bien une dynastie et, à son sommet, un homme de qui nous pouvions être fiers. Au bout d'un siècle, son tombeau a été entièrement rongé par le soleil, les pluies et les saisons. Je serais incapable de le retrouver, mais pour lui, ça ne me gêne pas : dans *les Chevaux du Soleil,* il est mort noblement, il a eu des obsèques sublimes, avec des cavaliers aux bottes bien cirées et des marquises.

Comme Marie Aldabram, comme ma grand-mère, ma grand-tante Laetitia n'a aimé qu'un seul homme dans sa vie, un certain Rayret, qu'elle a perdu très vite, mais l'a-t-elle vraiment aimé ? Il me semble que ce mariage avait dû se faire par convenance, un peu au hasard, et que cet homme était aussi transparent qu'elle. La preuve, après lui, plus rien, pas ça. La tante Laetitia a alors décroché de son armoire à glace un visage de vieille demoiselle, lisse, sans émotion, sans douleur non plus, impassible et inaltérable, que je lui ai toujours connu. Pas comme pour ma grand-mère. Si ma grand-mère ne riait jamais, c'est qu'elle n'avait jamais eu aussi qu'un homme dans sa vie, qu'elle l'aimait, qu'elle n'avait pas pu le guérir des fièvres. Les filles Bouychou étaient des femmes à un seul homme, donc des terribles, des intraitables. Après quoi elles se desséchaient comme de vieilles nonnes jansénistes. Pas ma mère, heureusement.

Nous ne faisions jamais long feu à Boufarik. L'oncle Jules avait hâte de retrouver la ferme, il n'était pas tranquille, et ma grand-mère craignait que Meftah ait oublié de donner à manger aux poules et aux lapins. De la langue, l'oncle Jules excitait les chevaux. J'essayais moi aussi, je n'y arrivais pas, je me contentais de toucher les guides que l'oncle Jules m'abandonnait un instant, et alors je me prenais pour un empereur romain conduisant son char. Les chevaux sentaient l'écurie, nous rentrions comme l'éclair, tout le monde était de bonne humeur. Moi, parce que je m'étais promené, ma grand-mère parce qu'elle avait vu sa sœur Laetitia, ma mère parce qu'elle avait repris contact avec la ville, et l'oncle Jules parce que le vin rosé de la tante Rayret était frais et délicieux. Il relevait son

fusil resté pendant le voyage sous la banquette et le replaçait entre ses jambes. Je ne sais pourquoi, à cause de son nom peut-être ? je comparerai toujours la tante Rayret à une rainette grise. Elle viendra quelquefois à la ferme et couchera avec ma grand-mère dans le même lit, sous le crucifix orné d'un rameau d'olivier, toutes deux papoteront sans bouger de place, presque sans bouger les lèvres, en citant des noms inconnus de moi, et tourneront lentement les feuillets de l'album où maintenant j'ai une photo d'elles : en robe de brocart boutonnée du col aux talons, un peu en retrait, la tante Rayret se tient debout derrière sa sœur, un éventail à la main. De Marguerite la superbe, je n'ai rien. Aucune image, aucune photo. Elle ne se montrait pas. N'aurait-elle existé que dans mon imagination, pour les besoins de la cause ? Il fallait à la famille une lignée d'officiers, et où aurais-je trouvé le premier lieutenant si Marguerite n'avait pas commencé par le séduire dès leur première rencontre dans une ferme de la Mitidja en plein été, et, avec les mœurs de ce temps-là, où donc, sinon dans une écurie ? Je n'ai pas dû me tromper, car c'est sûrement à cause de cela que ma grand-mère et Laetitia n'ont pas pardonné à leur sœur Marguerite, c'est pour cela qu'elles ont toujours eu de la jalousie pour ses élégances qu'elles jugeaient excessives. Il faudra leur rappeler que le Christ est né dans une étable. Pourtant, si je ne suis jamais allé chez Marguerite, j'ai su où elle habitait et je saurais retrouver la maison, une villa de corsaire barbaresque sur l'ancien boulevard des Palmiers qui n'existe plus, entre l'esplanade Bab el-Oued et l'Amirauté, en plein sur la mer, j'ai même un tableau du lieu. Cette maison existe toujours, mais c'est comme si je retournais à la ferme à présent. D'avance, j'en frémis. A la ferme, il y a peut-être encore quelques murs, des toits en loques, des bouts de ferraille, un figuier. Les vignes ont été arrachées, le village de Sidi-Moussa s'étend jusque-là et les masures en carton-pâte de la banlieue d'Alger dégringolent des collines du Sahel, avec les églises transformées en mosquées.

Ce n'est plus ma plaine à moi, ma plaine immense et bleue. Je ne respire plus de la même façon.

*
**

L'aîné des fils Paris, Hippolyte, était boucher, comme un des oncles de Camus, comme le père de Marcel Jouhandeau. Il habitait L'Arba, on se voyait peu, je ne sais pourquoi. Il semblait d'une autre famille. Le deuxième fils, Désiré, était à Rovigo. A la mort du père, mon oncle Jules, amoureux de la terre et aimé d'elle, prit la ferme en charge. Il avait de l'ambition. Lui, un petit colon, il ne voulait pas se laisser dévorer par les gros. Peu à peu il arrondit le domaine de son père et de sa mère et s'en bâtit un autre, à côté, modeste aussi, qu'il exploitait en même temps avec le même outillage, les mêmes bœufs, le même Meftah, et sa sueur à lui, Jules. Grâce à ses économies, son courage, sa ruse et son obstination, il acheta des machines américaines pour labourer la terre, d'autres pour battre les moissons, et s'associa avec son frère Désiré, mécanicien de vocation.

Parfois, l'été, on m'emmenait aux battages ; l'hiver, aux défonçages. Je goûtais une sorte d'envoûtement à voir des machines transmettre leur force par des volants, des courroies, des treuils et des câbles, et transformer ainsi les montagnes de moissons en montagnes de grains, ou les misérables pacages achetés aux Arabes en profonds et gras labours. Comme un cirque, l'usine arrivait par la route, tirée par la machine à vapeur tel un petit train. Pour les battages, on s'installait autour des meules, et tout se mettait à tourner dans un nuage suffocant de poussière d'épis broyés et dans un sourd ronflement avec chutes et reprises harmonieuses du son. Des nuées de Kabyles à chapeaux de paille tressée se jetaient les gerbes de l'un à l'autre, à la fourche, puis un dernier les enfournait dans le broyeur, le grain coulait dans des sacs, la paille montait sur une autre meule dans un bruit de toupies géantes. Les Kabyles chantaient, le mécanicien criait pour régler le rythme de l'ensemble. Il fallait une organisation, du matériel, un plan. Tout n'allait pas toujours sans heurt dans cet agencement qui était signe de puissance sous les yeux des Arabes pastoraux. Ce qui me grisait, c'était le soleil de plomb, la fumée, l'odeur du charbon, l'odeur du blé, l'odeur de l'huile chaude des graisseurs, l'odeur de la sueur. J'étais ivre de l'été que j'aime si peu maintenant, de ses merveilles, des trombes de poussière qui s'élevaient dans la plaine en colonnes tourbillonnantes, en torsades folles. Dépoitraillé au milieu des poulies, des régulateurs, des fumées, des vibrations, des luisances de métal, du

claquement des courroies, du halètement de la vapeur, du grondement énorme et majestueux de la batteuse, déchaîné, l'oncle Jules vérifiait tout, commandait tout, régnait.

Quand des querelles éclataient, il les apaisait, distribuait éloges et blâmes. Sur l'appareillage, sur le travail qui s'amoncelait, sur la plaine qui dansait dans l'air brûlant, il laissait errer un regard souverain tandis que, aux commandes de la machine, une courte calotte de mécano sur son crâne déplumé tout maculé de cambouis, l'œil inquiet, la moustache tombante, l'oncle Désiré fignolait la pression de la chaudière, le régulateur des bielles et la tension des entraînements. Au bout d'une longue journée étouffante, Désiré actionnait longuement le sifflet de la machine, les volants tournaient encore un temps à vide, le ronflement diminuait et s'éteignait dans un râle tandis que des appels joyeux montaient de partout. Le soir tombait, les oncles sirotaient une anisette, les Kabyles allumaient des feux de brindilles entre des pierres, le parfum des épices et de la galette d'orge se répandait dans les lueurs du couchant, une flûte de roseau enrouée accompagnait des chants mélancoliques, parfois sauvages, surgis d'un ailleurs lointain et menaçant, lourd aussi d'un mystère que je ressentais avec délices. Parfois je goûtais à la soupe rouge des moissonneurs, je m'asseyais au milieu d'eux, on m'offrait un lambeau de galette salée toute chaude encore, puis l'oncle Jules m'arrachait à la barbarie, me lançait sur le deux-roues et nous rentrions à la ferme où ma mère s'inquiétait des coups de soleil et de la vermine que j'avais pu attraper. « Tu as bien surveillé Zizi ? » demandait-elle à son frère avec un fond d'appréhension. Zizi, c'était toujours moi, c'était le surnom un peu ridicule dont on m'avait affublé. Tout le monde, même Meftah, m'appelait Zizi. Cela signifiait « chéri, aimé, mignon ». On aurait dû me le dire, j'en aurais été flatté, alors que je trouvais ce nom indigne de moi. C'est pour cela que je mettais du temps à répondre. Au retour des battages, je tombais de la lune avec le calme de la maison, la douceur féminine, la pénombre, les lumières qu'on commençait à allumer, les nouvelles que l'oncle Jules lançait en lisant le journal à voix haute : un incendie de meules dans la région de Batna, de nouveaux horaires de trains, on mettrait bientôt par l'express moins d'une heure pour aller d'Alger à Blida, de grandes manœuvres allaient avoir lieu en Champagne, qu'était-

ce que la Champagne ? Tout me semblait étranger, insolite et à des distances incommensurables. C'est vrai. J'avais vu que la différence entre habitants de la plaine n'était pas seulement entre Meftah et nous. Elle s'étendait, il y avait des races diverses, des langues diverses, des espaces inconnus, des couleurs d'au-delà des mers, des musiques, des odeurs surtout qui pénétraient l'âme et la changeaient. Il y avait ces Kabyles qui descendaient de leurs montagnes pour travailler dans la plaine. J'étais troublé.

L'oncle Désiré, comme responsable, couchait dans sa roulotte. Il aimait les Kabyles. Il partageait facilement tout avec eux, peut-être même les femmes s'il y en avait. A peine après dîner, ma tête tombait dans mes bras, je m'endormais, la conversation me berçait un peu avant que ma mère m'emporte dans ma chambre.

Parfois, l'oncle Jules m'emmenait aux labours. C'était l'automne. Le cirque ne comprenait plus de batteuse ni de monte-paille, mais une charrue géante, sorte d'insecte à longues pattes articulées avec deux énormes socs luisants, un pour chaque sens, qui éventraient la terre à des profondeurs inouïes. On appelait ça le défonçage. Un homme perché tout en haut de l'appareil ajustait l'inclinaison du soc, et deux machines, une à chaque bout du champ, actionnaient à tour de rôle sous leur ventre le treuil qui tirait. Pour les défonçages, trois ou quatre ouvriers suffisaient. L'ensemble et les enroule-ments du câble en filins d'acier constituaient un système délicat, souvent en panne, mais quel beau travail ! La charrue déchirait et retournait l'épaisse couche de terre végétale. Je n'étais pas fasciné comme par le monde jovien des battages. Je m'amusais à découvrir les lombrics, les oignons et les bulbes de plantes vénéneuses que ramenait le versant de l'acier, les mulots et les musaraignes qui s'enfuyaient sur les couches de limon. Après ça, les colons pouvaient semer ou planter n'importe quoi. La terre devenue meuble s'asséchait, les anciennes racines des palmiers nains périssaient, les richesses enfouies dans le sol fertilisaient la surface.

Un jour, le sirocco apporta les sauterelles, je l'ai raconté dans *les Chevaux du Soleil*. J'ai assisté au cataclysme du brillant nuage métallique tournoyant au-dessus de la plaine, accompagné d'appels angoissés, de coups de fusil, de tambours nègres, qui s'abattait n'importe où et détruisait tout. J'ai vu la

ruée compacte et fluide des insectes pèlerins recouvrant les troncs d'arbres, les rameaux, les feuilles, dévorant tout, se dévorant eux-mêmes parfois par mégarde, huitième plaie d'Egypte expédiée aux hommes pour les punir de quoi ? Les chevaux glissaient sur cette couche gluante, cette grêle lourde aux pattes coupantes, et qui craquait sous les semelles quand on marchait dessus. L'oncle Jules était fou de rage, la grand-mère hagarde de désespoir, ma mère et Meftah s'acharnaient à défendre la maison à coups de balai, je poussais des cris d'horreur en découvrant des sauterelles dans mon lit.

A l'aube il n'y avait plus rien. Plus d'orangers, plus de vignes, plus de jardins, rien que les carcasses funèbres des cyprès et la puanteur des feux allumés partout. Nous étions nus, sans défense, devant le Créateur suprême que ma mère me faisait prier avant de m'endormir. Les sauterelles pondirent des œufs dans le sol et moururent, mais, deux semaines plus tard, naquirent les criquets qui dévorèrent à leur tour ce qui restait. Les colons qu'une force surhumaine paraissait pousser hors d'eux-mêmes et comme broyer, labourèrent la terre pour essayer de détruire les nouveaux œufs. Les criquets naissaient quand même. Les colons semèrent de nouveau.

Tout finit, même le malheur. Le fléau cessa par épuisement, la dévastation céda comme un incendie qui a tout brûlé ; la famine s'étendit chez les Arabes, des troupes misérables parcoururent la plaine, le gouvernement distribua de la semoule, les gendarmes rétablirent l'ordre, la terre réensemencée redonna du blé et de l'orge, la vigne se recouvrit de bourgeons, la métropole intervint par une loi, les mairies allouèrent quelques dédommagements, l'espoir brilla de nouveau. A présent, les sauterelles ont atteint les Antilles et la Sicile.

Une autre année, une inondation, provoquée par une crue soudaine de l'oued Djemaa, dévasta une partie de la plaine et fit croire à la vanité de tant d'efforts. Les anciens marécages su⁻ lesquels nous vivions reprenaient possession de leur empire, l'eau noyait tout, puis le mildiou, l'oïdium et le phylloxéra détruisirent les vignes, ah ! il était beau le paradis, il était riche le pactole qui devait rouler des paillettes d'or ! La plaine fut recouverte d'une couche de vase, l'oncle Jules se crut ruiné, j'éprouvai avec lui l'accablement du malheur enduré. Cette terre, je l'aimais, c'était la mienne, c'était la nôtre. Plus,

nous semblait-il, que celle des Arabes, qui subissaient les coups du ciel sans se révolter, peut-être parce qu'ils avaient peu de biens ou qu'ils étaient habitués au pire. Leur pauvreté s'accroissait, le rien qui leur restait devenait bénédiction. A la longue, la vase que les herses firent éclater dans les rangs des vignes fertilisa le sol et on se félicita que le fondateur des Paris ait un peu surélevé sa maison avec double escalier à l'entrée. Il y eut de nouveau des récoltes, des battages, l'oncle Jules retourna au café, à Alger, à ses amours secrètes, j'appartenais au rythme des saisons, à tout ce qui faisait travailler et vivre, et quand il arrivait que le groupe des cousins et surtout des cousines vint nous surprendre à Pâques ou pendant la moisson ou, mieux encore, aux vendanges, quelle fête ! Nous suivions les Kabyles dans les rangs de vigne, nous nous soûlions de raisins de cinsault, d'aramon, de chasselas, de muscat parfois, nous revenions grimpés sur les chariots au milieu des comportes débordantes. Avec nos visages barbouillés, nous étions les enfants de Dionysos et de jeunes bacchantes, nous assistions au pressage dans le fouloir, le flot odorant coulait, nous respirions l'alcool du moût. A la tablée du soir, dans la lumière blonde du pétrole et des bougies, tout le monde était un peu paf, des vapeurs inhabituelles d'adoration flottaient, des voix plus gaies et des rires éclataient, on s'endormait dans les bras les uns des autres et dans une innocence de création du monde. Le vin bouillonnait déjà dans les cuves et dans les cœurs. Sur les murs et au plafond zigzaguaient en éclairs sombres les tarentes, ces lézards plats qu'on ne chassait pas parce qu'ils gobaient les moustiques.

Le lendemain, tout recommençait. Le soleil se levait comme une gloire. Toute la plaine vibrait.

Au début du siècle, les voitures automobiles surgissaient parmi nous comme des apparitions. Quand l'une d'elles cornait dans l'allée, toute la ferme accourait. Meftah appelait les siens. Qui était-ce ? Quelque chose allait changer dans l'ordre de la vie, et quand l'automobile partait, elle nous arrachait un peu à nous-mêmes. Nous restions un moment à rêver.

Quand c'était le docteur, la surprise était moins forte. Il

visitait régulièrement ma grand-mère. On l'attendait, on savait qui venait. Il avait une Bébé Peugeot basse, peinte en gris avec, tout à l'avant, comme des yeux de crapaud, deux gros phares qui s'éclairaient à l'acétylène. Il sortait de son habitacle, prenait sa trousse et montait dans la salle à manger, accompagné pour nous comme un dieu. Là, je quittais ma mère, me glissais dehors et m'approchais de la machine, toute petite à vrai dire, à peine deux places, je grimpais sur le marchepied, j'enjambais le garde-boue. Ça sentait le pétrole, l'huile, la peinture, le métal chaud, le cuir, tout luisait, je caressais le bois précieux du tableau de bord où des instruments étaient fixés. En plus des phares, il y avait des lanternes, tellement plus belles et brillantes que celles du deux-roues, une capote qu'on pouvait rabattre, un pneu de secours derrière. J'ouvrais la légère portière, je me faufilais avec une certaine appréhension sous le volant derrière le pare-brise, touchais les leviers de changement de vitesse et du frein. J'appuyais sur les pédales, j'étudiais les cadrans, je caressais le klaxon, la poire en caoutchouc de la trompe, je me regardais dans un miroir rond : le rétroviseur. Immobile dans cette machine, je me voyais filant à toute allure sur la route d'Alger, avalant les poteaux télégraphiques et les carrefours, frôlant les chars à banc aux roues oscillantes des Arabes, épouvantant les troupeaux de moutons, puis ralentissant, tournant près de la ferme : ponh ponh ! quand ma mère surgissait en haut du perron. « Veux-tu descendre de là !... » L'oncle Jules venait à moi, m'aidait à m'extirper puis, à son tour curieux, muet d'admiration, se penchait sur le siège du conducteur et dessous, reniflait, tapotait le volant, hochait la tête. Evidemment, lui aussi il aurait aimé rouler là-dedans, quel triomphe s'il avait débarqué ainsi à l'Espérance ! Oui, mais était-il bon d'exciter la jalousie, ne valait-il pas mieux placer l'argent dans la terre ? Sur la route, quand une automobile s'annonçait, l'oncle ralentissait et garait presque le deux-roues dans le fossé pour laisser passer ce qu'on appelait alors un bolide, puis il se répandait en cris d'exclamation et d'envie. Quelle merveille ! C'était le progrès, les hommes iraient bientôt à cent kilomètres à l'heure, les guerres deviendraient impossibles parce qu'elles seraient trop rapides, le commerce allait être complètement bouleversé, mais il faudrait revoir le revêtement des routes et cet engin coûtait si cher ! La mécanique, il le savait aussi, se

dépréciait. « Tu nous vois là-dedans, Zizi ? » me demandait-il, les lèvres mouillées de désir.

Je m'y voyais. En imagination, nous conduisions tour à tour, ponh, ponh, nous allions d'abord à Alger : la ville, le port, les navires, puis en sens inverse, ce qui m'intriguait autant que la mer, ce qu'il y avait derrière les montagnes. « Le désert », disait toujours l'oncle Jules. C'était quoi, le désert ? « Ce n'est rien. Oh ! là là... » Bien au-delà de Rovigo, après les crêtes dont le sommet parfois, en hiver, était tout blanc, on débouchait sur de hauts plateaux. L'oncle Jules y était allé quand il avait servi dans l'artillerie, à Batna, mais personne d'autre que lui dans la famille ne connaissait ces étendues où ne poussaient, à l'infini, que des moissons — l'ancien grenier de Rome — et de l'alfa. L'été, d'innombrables troupeaux de moutons y paissaient, gardés par des bédouins à lourd chapeau de paille aux rubans de toutes les couleurs. Ces gens-là vivaient sous des tentes en peaux de chèvre et se nourrissaient de semoule, de lait de chamelle. Ils allaient de pâturage en pâturage, avec des ânes pour les fardeaux domestiques. Plus loin, après une région asséchée et de sel gris, s'élevait l'autre chaîne de l'Atlas, l'Atlas saharien, ras, pelé, tondu où les hommes ressemblaient à des pierres et habitaient des cavernes pour s'abriter du vent sec et coupant, tantôt brûlant, tantôt glacial. Après, le vrai désert commençait : des dunes, des cailloux noirs, des tempêtes de sable, un océan de sable, des oasis aussi, des palmiers comme à Biskra ou Ouargla d'où venaient les dattes les plus succulentes. Là, les automobiles devaient filer comme l'éclair. L'oncle Jules parlait parfois du Sud. Ce qui l'avait troublé, là-bas, c'était les mirages. Il expliquait qu'en plein cœur du néant, là où il n'y avait pas une goutte d'eau, on voyait briller des lacs avec des roseaux agités par le vent, des villes étincelaient, on avançait, ça s'éloignait puis ça se dissipait sans qu'on pût jamais toucher quoi que ce soit, sinon le sable, le roc : rien. L'oncle balayait l'espace de sa main calleuse. Quoi, rien ? Un leurre, une apparence. Des eaux qui ne désaltéraient pas, des roseaux qui ondulaient, des remparts qui n'existaient pas. Par moments, on aurait cru qu'il en voyait encore. Je voulais approcher, je voulais toucher cela. « Est-ce qu'on touche le vide ? » disait l'oncle Jules d'une voix rêveuse. Je ne me laissais pas convaincre, je foncerais avec mon automobile ou autre chose, on parlait déjà d'aéroplane, je

crèverais cet imaginaire. S'il le fallait, je reviendrais avec des débris d'apparences fracassées.

Peu à peu nous nous écartions de la Bébé Peugeot, le petit docteur descendait du perron, jetait sa trousse sur un siège, se penchait sur le capot, tripotait quelque chose, tournait la manivelle et lâchait une exclamation de plaisir. « Au quart de tour », s'écriait l'oncle. Le docteur s'asseyait derrière le volant, embrayait avec un doux craquement des engrenages, manœuvrait, nous lançait un geste d'adieu et s'en allait dans l'allée de gravier en pétaradant. Longtemps après j'aspirais avec délices l'odeur du pétrole brûlé.

Dans la famille, l'oncle Désiré fut le premier à avoir une auto. D'abord une de Dion ou une Léon Bollée d'occasion, ce qu'il y avait de mieux et qui vous classait. Sa femme, la tante Henriette, prétendait que c'était nécessaire pour son travail. En vérité, l'oncle Désiré avait des goûts de milord. Chez Baranès, le tailleur à la mode, il se commandait des complets qu'il était incapable de payer. Son avoir se composait surtout de dettes : celles de ses clients envers lui, et celles qu'il avait contractées lui-même. Il vivait dans un rêve qu'il prenait pour la réalité et allait de déception en déception, attribuant ses déboires financiers à la mauvaise foi universelle. Il devait paraître, ne rien laisser percer de ses soucis, il roulait donc en carrosse. Sa femme l'aimait et l'admirait trop pour lui laisser entendre qu'il aurait pu mener un train plus modeste.

Trop de complaisance pour l'oncle Jules m'empêche souvent d'accorder à l'oncle Désiré ce qui lui revient. De belle taille, bien bâti, avec la même tendance à une calvitie précoce, signe trompeur de réflexion, l'oncle Désiré avait surtout un regard pervenche à quoi on ne résistait pas. A sa femme il avait donné coup sur coup quatre filles (sauf un garçon qui n'avait pas vécu), toutes plus séduisantes les unes que les autres et dont j'ai été tour à tour amoureux. Elles n'avaient pas ses yeux mais, chacune à sa façon, un charme incomparable. Chez lui, si pauvre que ce fût, on respirait une atmosphère de grâce. On poussait un portail, on entrait dans la cour, au fond étaient la forge et le hangar, à gauche un jardin avec un gros figuier, à droite la maison sans étage : une immense cuisine, une table

avec des bancs, une véranda, une chambre où tout le monde dormait, où les parents avaient leur lit à boules de cuivre. Avec ces filles miraculeuses qui adoraient leur père, l'oncle Désiré aurait pu, par des mariages dans la plaine où les fortunes ne manquaient pas, couler une existence protégée. Il voulait réussir par son travail, c'est pourquoi chez lui il y avait partout des machines à vapeur, des batteuses, des treuils, des monte-charge, des défonceuses, des carcasses d'automobiles, des tracteurs qui n'avaient jamais tourné, des outils et des roues de toutes sortes. On savait où il habitait à cause du hangar qui dépassait les toits et de la fameuse machine dont j'ai déjà parlé, qui avait rendu l'âme depuis longtemps et qui était là, devant le portail, à jamais immobile, à jamais inutile, et si lourde qu'on ne pouvait la déplacer. Rien n'a pu la détruire, même pas une révolution, même pas le passage de l'Algérie à l'indépendance. Elle doit être encore là, pareille à un squelette de dinosaure à quoi personne n'ose toucher.

Dans les affaires de l'oncle Désiré, l'association avec son frères Jules ne fut pas la plus mauvaise, mais il finit par s'y enferrer et traversa des moments difficiles. Ses filles, qui avaient pris goût à la mécanique, savaient conduire et réparer. Pour les automobiles, elles étaient parfois réduites, faute de pouvoir acheter de nouvelles chambres à air, à bourrer de paille ou de crin les enveloppes des roues. On n'en était plus aux de Dion, aux Delage ou aux Panhard, mais à des bagnoles de série, les premières des grands constructeurs, des Renault, des Citroën. Désiré empruntait souvent un gros billet ou deux à ma mère. On ne pouvait pas lui résister : il allait rembourser le lendemain, une semaine après au plus tard. Il ne remboursait jamais. Les dettes se surajoutaient, mais si la fortune frappait à la porte, il fallait lui ouvrir, et, en attendant, se montrer et rouler. Chez lui, une mélancolie douce et lointaine remplaçait la dure passion de l'oncle Jules pour la terre et l'argent. Pour l'oncle Désiré, la terre ne servait qu'à fournir du travail à ses équipes toujours impayées, et l'argent qu'à éduquer ses filles. Leur père était trop souvent en bleu de chauffe et les mains noires de cambouis. Sa femme le poussait à aller à Alger, à se montrer à l'apéritif-concert du Tantonville, et après, à dîner à la brasserie Grüber, rendez-vous des colons chic. Pour cela, il fallait des vêtements de chez le bon faiseur et une automobile.

C'était l'avenir, c'était le progrès, on ne pouvait pas réussir sans cela.

*
**

Chaque hiver, à la ferme, on tuait le cochon. La veille, le charcutier venait visiter les lieux et installer son atelier. Le lendemain matin, avec ses aides, le cérémonial se déroulait. Les femmes se préparaient à recueillir le sang pour le boudin et les énormes *boutifaros* bourrés d'ail et d'oignon ; les hommes à flamber l'animal puis à l'ébouillanter avant de racler sa peau. On allumait des feux, des baquets d'eau chauffaient sur des trépieds, on aiguisait les couteaux, on vissait les hachoirs sur des tréteaux, on se bardait de tabliers, puis l'heure venait et, dans l'aube radieuse, les exécuteurs allaient chercher le condamné. Pour m'épargner les horreurs du supplice, on essayait de me tenir à l'écart. J'observais cependant, de loin d'abord, puis saisi d'une curiosité cruelle et, peut-être même, d'une horrible délectation, je m'approchais. Le cochon sentait la mort. D'abord il renâclait, résistait tant qu'il pouvait aux invites et aux poussées, grognait puis, quand on lui avait lié les pattes et qu'on le couchait sur la planche de l'exécution, comprenant alors qu'il n'échapperait plus au sort, poussait des hurlement déchirants qui ne cessaient même pas, le coutelas plongé dans sa gorge. Puissant moment, terrifiante agonie. Le sang coulait à bouillons vermeils dans les bassines, tandis que les cris se prolongeaient. Tout le monde était soulagé quand ils cessaient. Enfin le cochon n'était plus un être vivant refusant le supplice, il devenait le bonheur des hommes. C'était d'une façon joyeuse qu'on lui grillait le poil sur la paille enflammée. Ensuite on le rasait, on le vidait, on le fendait en deux, on transformait peu à peu cette masse de chair rose et grasse, comme immatérielle, en pièces à rôtis, en jambons, en lard, en chapelets de saucisses et de soubressades, cette saucisse espagnole rouge épicée qui nous venait des Baléares, en fromage de tête, en lardons grillés dont j'étais friand.

Au premier repas partagé avec le charcutier et ses aides, la tante Henriette de Rovigo était là, mais pas la tante de L'Arba qui, femme de boucher, répugnait à des besognes de ce genre. Le vin rosé égayait les propos. Au repas du soir avec boudin grillé craquant, le charcutier partait avec son équipe, ma

grand-mère rayonnait d'une sorte de gloire : la nourriture abondait, il y avait à manger pour longtemps, nous étions des gens honorables et solidement installés. En même temps, comme Meftah veillait à ne se souiller de rien d'impur, nous étions entre nous, le cochon nous séparait des Arabes.

On avait beau se méfier de moi, je touchais à tout, je mettais mon nez partout. Un jour où j'avais vu l'oncle Jules allumer une mèche dans des bonbonnes de vin, j'avais voulu en faire autant. Je soufrai une bonbonne d'acide sulfurique qui éclata. Un hiver où l'on tuait le cochon, je me renversai un baquet d'eau bouillante sur les pieds. Meftah courut atteler le deux-roues, ma mère m'emporta au village où je reçus des soins. Comme je me sentais coupable, je souffris en silence. Ce que j'endurai et la façon dont je l'endurai firent taire les reproches qu'on était tenté d'adresser au garnement. Ce fut longtemps un jeu pour moi d'offrir mes pieds, le plus meurtri à ma grand-mère, l'autre à ma mère, pour des caresses et des baisers qu'elles ne marchandaient pas. Ce fut là ma vraie guérison. J'ai boité pendant des mois. On dut m'acheter des chaussures spéciales et j'en profitai pour choisir les plus chères. Après quoi, presque en même temps, j'eus les jambes dévorées de furoncles, et il fallait y vider de la teinture d'iode. Quand l'automobile du docteur surgissait, je me cachais, on envoyait Meftah à ma recherche et il multipliait les bonnes paroles qu'il déguisait parfois dans son langage à lui : la rébellion me servirait à quoi puisqu'on était plus fort que moi ? Qui sait ? Peut-être parlait-il en son nom, peut-être vidait-il son cœur encore soumis ? Je feignais de céder, je me rendais avec hauteur : je n'étais pas un serviteur, moi. On me saisissait malgré mes pleurs, on m'immobilisait comme le cochon, on inondait mes plaies de teinture d'iode. L'opération achevée, je m'enfuyais, éperonné par la brûlure. Comme soulevé de terre, je galopais avec des jambes de feu, je ruais, je hennissais, puis, quand la douleur s'apaisait, je revenais en affichant, en guise de défi, une sorte d'indifférence.

Il m'arrive encore à mon âge d'apercevoir ces vieilles cicatrices et de me demander si ce ne sont pas là les stigmates qu'a laissés en moi la perte de ce paradis, dans les bras des femmes qui m'aimaient. Ces traces brillantes, je ne les aperçois jamais non plus sans entendre la longue plainte du cochon et un élancement me laboure un instant.

II

Les mystères et les splendeurs

J'AI CRU longtemps que j'étais né sans père. A-t-on besoin d'un père ? Un soutien, un modèle, l'arbre de qui on sort, l'homme qu'on peut regarder avec tranquillité, peut-être avec admiration. A la ferme où j'étais en plein dans la vie, mon père, s'il avait absolument fallu que j'en aie un, aurait été l'oncle Jules. Pas Meftah naturellement, j'avais vite discerné que nous n'étions pas du même bord. Il y avait les Paris, puis les Français d'ici, puis les autres. L'oncle Jules m'enseignait à conduire les chevaux et les machines, à cultiver la vigne, à élever le vin, à chasser. Meftah aussi, mais sur la banquette du break ou du deux-roues que les Anglais appellent plutôt un buggy, les Français de France un boguet, j'étais assis à côté de l'oncle. Jamais à côté de Meftah.

Des pères, j'en ai eu au moins deux : le gendarme qui m'a donné son nom, mon père légal, et, nous y voilà, l'instituteur de Rovigo, département d'Alger, mon vrai père. Ensuite, il y a ceux à qui je dois des choses essentielles : Doyon, que je partage un peu avec Malraux comme je l'ai dit au début de cette confession, Camus et enfin Amrouche. Sans compter les autres. J'en ai beaucoup, tant mieux. Bâtard ou pas. je suis fier d'eux, ils m'ont tous légué quelque chose. Je n'ai pas honte, comme les Arabes qui s'accusent parfois d'être le fils de trente-six pères. Et Abraham ? Et Dieu ? ne sont-ils pas nos pères aussi ?

La mort du gendarme que je soupçonnais d'abord d'être mon père semblait avoir tout arrangé. Nous étions heureux. Moi d'un bonheur d'innocence, ma grand-mère de me voir, ma mère... Par moments, des nuages passaient sur son front. Elle guettait le facteur, des silences tombaient, que l'oncle

Jules rompait en faisant claquer sa langue comme s'il avait des chevaux à exciter. Il se levait, décrochait son fusil, partait.

Le temps passait, je grandissais. Une fois par semaine, ma mère peignait longuement les cheveux de ma grand-mère, les lissait, les oignait d'huile à la rose, au benjoin et à l'œillet, la maison en était embaumée. On ne m'enseignait rien que la vie, j'étais trop petit pour aller à l'école de Sidi-Moussa, il aurait fallu, et cela posait un problème, que Meftah m'y conduise tous les matins avec le deux-roues et que l'oncle Jules vienne me chercher l'après-midi ; j'apprenais vaguement à lire avec ma mère dans *le Chasseur français,* j'apprenais la terre avec l'oncle Jules et, tout seul, avec l'énorme catalogue à couverture grise de la Manufacture d'armes et cycles de Saint-Etienne (Loire), j'apprenais le monde. Là je passais des heures de délectation : les armes, les machines, les lampes, les vêtements, les meubles, l'outillage, l'horlogerie. Il y avait aussi des presses à imprimer, des appareils de photographie, des articles de toilette et de voyage, des jouets perfectionnés, de la sellerie, des accessoires pour automobiles, des articles pour chiens. La machine à coudre Singer dont ma mère se servait à la ferme venait de là, comme la bicyclette de l'oncle. Je rêvais devant les seize drapeaux des plus grandes nations du globe représentés en couleurs ; même le drapeau chinois : des bandes horizontales rouge, jaune, bleu, blanc, noir ; le drapeau russe : trois bandes horizontales blanc, bleu, rouge. Un bon fusil à canon acier coûtait de 50 à 100 F, des armes à quadruple verrou et à clé invisible valaient jusqu'à 500 et 1 200 F (à multiplier par 10 ou 20 aujourd'hui) avec crosse de luxe en noyer, agrémentée de stries en festons et de fleurs. Je méditais devant des fusils à répétition, des Winchester, des fusils Gras avec cartouches Lebel pour la guerre, des canons à tir rapide sur roues ou sur affût. Un chasseur brandissait un lièvre sous le nez d'une cuisinière émerveillée, un autre s'accroupissait derrière un écran de feuillage, un autre tirait un perdreau, cassait la croûte avec son chien ou se voyait dresser procès-verbal devant un panneau « chasse interdite » ; des Dianes en chapeau tyrolien abattaient des canards ; des éléphants à qui j'avais envie de crier : « Attention ! » avançaient dans la savane tandis que des explorateurs les visaient en appuyant le canon de leur fusil sur une épaule noire ou posaient le pied sur la dépouille d'un tigre, des cavaliers galopaient derrière des buffles. A certains

moments, je trouvais cela horrible. A d'autres il me tardait d'en faire autant. Je voulais foudroyer les lièvres à longues oreilles, je guignais le Flobert dont ma mère se servait parfois devant l'écurie : un bruit sec, un pigeon tombait, je le palpais, chaud comme un pain sortant du four, j'avais les mains gluantes de sang. Hors de portée dans la chambre de ma grand-mère, au-dessus de l'armoire, le Flobert s'appelait dans le catalogue « carabine de précision Buffalo-Lebel » ou encore « carabine de précision populaire-scolaire » ; il tirait des cartouches minuscules, un instituteur exerçait ses élèves à son maniement dans la cour de l'école. Mon désir se voyait. « Patience », disait l'oncle Jules en souriant. Je le regardais droit dans les yeux en secouant ma crinière. Pourquoi, puisque je savais tirer ? « Pas n'importe où, pas sur n'importe quoi. » Des marais où il ne m'emmenait jamais, l'oncle rapportait des perdrix, parfois des canards bleu et or dont je caressais longuement les plumes. « Des migrateurs », disait-il. Le mot me laissait songeur : des oiseaux qui traversaient les mers. Le soir l'oncle s'en prenait aux chouettes parce qu'il croyait, comme des générations de paysans avant lui, que le cri de la chouette porte malheur.

Comme tout chasseur bien né, l'oncle faisait lui-même ses munitions. Il achetait les étuis amorcés et les transformait en cartouches. Pour cela il se servait d'une chargette à poudre et à plombs, d'une balance de précision, d'un bourroir de buis et enfin d'une petite machine qu'il fixait à la table de la salle à manger par une pince à vis. Il utilisait différents plombs selon le gibier : plombs pour lièvres ou perdreaux, chevrotines pour le cas où il s'en prendrait à des sangliers ou, qui sait ? à des hommes. Je le regardais puiser dans des sacs minuscules, garnir les étuis, séparer poudre et plombs par des bourres, sertir enfin les cartouches, les caresser avant de les glisser dans la ceinture, puis ranger son attirail dans un tiroir.

De temps en temps les fièvres s'abattaient sur nous. Les cachets de quinine ne servaient qu'à espacer les crises. Bien que la maladie — la malaria — fût connue, presque personne à cette époque ne se protégeait de la piqûre des moustiques par des moustiquaires ou des fenêtres grillagées. Mon grand-père était mort à soixante ans. Rares étaient les colons qui atteignaient cet âge-là. Tout à coup des tremblements vous

secouaient, le froid vous pénétrait jusque dans les os, on grelottait. Quand elle sentait venir l'accès, ma grand-mère se couchait. Sa chambre donnait dans la salle à manger, elle ne nous quittait donc pas. Quant à l'oncle Jules, il disait à ma mère : « Fais-moi une bouillotte, Mathilde. Brûlante, hein ? » Et il partait chez lui, un arrosoir plein d'eau à la main, sa bouteille de grès sous le bras, sans rien demander à personne. Avec un bol de bouillon, ma mère passait, le soir, voir où il en était. Après les vagues glacées, des vagues de chaleur, des vagues d'enfer incendiaient les moelles et le cerveau. Alors l'oncle Jules buvait au tuyau de l'arrosoir. Moi aussi, à celui de la cuisine. Un répit, puis ça recommençait comme une roue, banquise et feu. Dans les bras de ma mère, je souffrais moins qu'en apparence, une sorte de volupté sauvage m'anéantissait sur sa gorge. Je ne détestais pas me sentir devenu proie.

On ne mourait plus du paludisme, le mal était presque vaincu mais on en souffrait encore. Il m'arrive parfois de ressentir une brusque lame de fond qui me rappelle mes origines en se glissant dans ma carcasse. Je me remets à claquer des dents puis à brûler. Les Arabes, on prétendait qu'ils étaient immunisés. On leur distribuait de la quinine qu'ils hésitaient à avaler parce que ce qui venait de nous leur était suspect. Ils mouraient comme nous, plus facilement même. On y faisait moins attention. Après sa crise, l'oncle Jules réapparaissait comme si de rien n'était. Quant à ma mère, je ne l'ai jamais vue couchée.

Rencontrait-elle l'instituteur ? Ce ne sont pas des choses qu'on apprend cinquante ans après, quand les derniers témoins ont oublié ces détails. Ma mère serait bien restée près de moi à attendre sans jamais rien demander. Par moments, je ne suis pas tellement sûr que ce soit par amour qu'elle ait cédé à l'instituteur ; elle en avait peut-être assez de son gendarme, de sa vie à Rovigo, elle est allée à un de ces mirages dont l'oncle Jules parlait, mais son mirage à elle ne s'est pas dérobé ; il y avait là un homme qui se disait fou d'elle, des roseaux agités par le vent, une ville, un enfant. C'était peut-être l'enfant qu'elle voulait. Ainsi, avec moi, ma mère n'aurait peut-être rien fait pour revoir son séducteur, le père de son enfant. Oh ! le père : l'intermédiaire, plutôt, le prétexte. Si elle avait pu avoir un enfant sans père, elle aurait peut-être préféré. Pour moi, je me trouvais bien comme j'étais, je ne manquais de

rien, je ne vois pas quel besoin j'aurais pu avoir d'un père. J'explique encore ainsi ma méfiance à l'égard des hommes et la leur à mon égard. Je ne sais pourquoi, je les ai toujours agacés. Mais finissons-en avec les amours de ma mère.

Au cours d'une tournée, l'homme de qui je porte le nom, le gendarme Louis Alfred Roy, était tombé amoureux d'elle. Elle avait vingt ans. Il avait dû l'éblouir avec une photo de lui en cuirassier avec cuirasse et casque à queue de cheval. Là où elle vivait, qui pouvait-elle espérer d'autre ? D'ailleurs, il avait une sacrée allure sur cette photo. Le mariage eut lieu à Sidi-Moussa en 1891. Mon frère René naquit. Dix ans de caserne dans la maréchaussée à L'Arba puis à Aumale, elle en eut assez. Elle pensa se rapprocher des siens en gérant un petit hôtel à Rovigo, un caboulot. Le gendarme obtint sa mise en congé, ils déménagèrent. Hélas pour elle, heureusement pour moi, il y eut l'instituteur.

Il avait quarante ans, il s'appelait **Dematons**, Marie Léon Henri, c'était un barbare de l'Est, un mâle à fort tempérament. Redoutant de se laisser piéger une fois de plus, tout flambant, flambard aussi, il se jeta tête baissée dans une nouvelle aventure. Faux col raide en cellulo, cravate plate à perle, joues rebondies sous une barbe peu fournie tournant au roux, crâne dégarni, mais le regard, la bouche ! ça brûlait, ça cachait son désarroi, sa tristesse et son avidité de Scorpion anxieux et passionné, en perpétuel conflit avec lui-même et avec tout le monde. D'abord, dès sa naissance, dans un village de rien, non loin de Bar-sur-Aube, où son propre père, intelligent et despotique, brisait tous les siens. Chez les Dematons, garçons et filles devenaient instituteurs, il semblait n'y avoir rien d'autre pour eux. A peine instituteur à son tour, il se maria pour fuir son père, eut un fils, Robert, un rouquin, puis ne pouvant plus supporter sa femme, divorça, se colla avec une donzelle, une certaine Eugénie qu'il appellera « la Sarraute ». Elle le poussa à des dépenses, et comme elle avait le feu quelque part, le trompa et le rendit enragé jusqu'au jour où, n'en pouvant plus, profitant d'une fournée de recrutement pour l'Algérie, il décampa, passa deux années dans un bled infernal de la vallée du Chélif, mit son gamin au collège, puis ce fut Rovigo, le parfum des géraniums rosats et nous. Plus tard il disait qu'il tenait son journal, qu'il l'avait donné à lire, qu'on lui avait dit que c'était l'œuvre d'un fou et qu'il l'avait

65

jeté au feu. Ce journal, je l'ai fait renaître de ses cendres. Le Prussien, comme l'appelait ma tante l'épicière, m'a légué une part de lui-même. En Algérie il travailla à l'éducation des peuples colonisés, se frotta à l'avant-garde de ceux qui croyaient à l'enrichissement de la nation par ses nouvelles conquêtes, enseigna aux enfants la Déclaration des Droits de l'homme et du citoyen, protégea les juifs, recueillit un petit Arabe dans sa classe et devint par hasard ami d'un cinglé de son genre, le mari de la fameuse Marguerite, la sœur un peu snob de la tante de Boufarik et de ma grand-mère. Ainsi traversa-t-il la société d'Alger au moment de l'affaire Dreyfus et de Drumont.

Où est le vrai, où est le faux dans le portrait que j'ai brossé de lui dans *les Chevaux du Soleil*? En ce temps-là, chaque jeudi, il sautait dans le tortillard d'Alger et filait à l'hôtel du Chien qui fume, près de l'Opéra, et voilà ma mère enceinte de moi. Pour elle, drame et catastrophe; pour lui, nouveaux ennuis. Après le repas de fête de mon baptême, à Noël 1907, le gendarme se mit enfin en colère, chassa ma mère et son bâtard, et me voilà à la ferme de l'oncle Jules, mon parrain. J'ai raconté cela en détail, je n'y reviens qu'en passant. Bien qu'on ait ajouté à mon premier prénom celui de Désiré, je doute fort que ma naissance, qui provoquait scandale, ait été espérée.

Ce qui me passionnait, c'était le phonographe.

Le dimanche au début de l'après-midi, comme l'oncle n'allait à l'Espérance qu'à cinq heures, c'était devenu un rite qu'il feignait d'oublier. J'insistais un moment puis je me mettais à bouder. « Jules, tu vois bien que le petit attend », disait ma grand-mère. Il me taquinait encore en regardant l'heure à la montre plate qu'il tirait d'une poche de son pantalon, puis à la pendule, comme s'il hésitait, et enfin ouvrait le secrétaire et posait l'appareil sur la table. Alors, je trépignais de joie. Grimpé sur une chaise, je lui passais le « pavillon volubilis » si léger, si délicat, qu'il fixait. J'aurais su, je savais, mais on n'avait pas confiance en moi, on ne me permettait pas. Notre Pathéphone, ce qu'il y avait de mieux au catalogue de la manufacture de Saint-Etienne, avait coûté 70 F,

un prix déjà. Ce n'était pas un appareil à « saphir inusable », mais un appareil à aiguille. L'aiguille rendait mieux la voix, paraît-il.

Un plateau de fonte recouvert d'un drap de billard entraînait le disque. L'oncle ajustait le diaphragme, cette petite boîte magique où se formait le son, y serrait l'aiguille puis remontait le mécanisme. « Qu'est-ce que tu veux ? » demandait-il en brandissant la peau de chamois dont il allait essuyer amoureusement un disque. Notre répertoire était succinct : « Madame Angot », « la Marseillaise », « Sambre-et-Meuse » et « le Chant du départ ». D'autres titres peut-être, dont je ne me souviens pas. Les chants patriotiques, l'oncle aimait bien, ça lui rappelait son service et l'artillerie. D'habitude, je me décidais pour « Madame Angot ». Les airs sautillants, gracieux et vifs de Charles Lecocq avaient valu à cette opérette un prodigieux succès. Cela me changeait de l'austérité de notre vie. Quand le disque se mettait à tourner, il y avait d'abord un chuintement, un raclement, puis tout à coup une harmonie et des voix. Avec « le Chant du départ », l'oncle battait la mesure. L'œil vague dans un visage de sphinx, il soupesait la discipline, le poids des canons de montagne chargés à dos de mulet. Notre civilisation épatait tout le monde, surtout Meftah. Pour lui, cela n'aurait pas agi pour des mots arabes et de la musique arabe. « Mais si, répliquait l'oncle. S'il n'y a rien d'arabe là-dedans, c'est que vous n'avez pas été assez malins pour inventer ça avant nous. Est-ce qu'il y a des automobiles arabes ? *Trabadja la mouquère, trabadja bono*, c'est bien à vous, ça ? Un jour, grâce à nous, tu verras des Arabes monter dans les automobiles. » Meftah hochait la tête. « Pas moi, disait-il. Des caïds. Peut-être dans la tienne... »

Là tout le monde riait, même moi, car l'oncle Jules ne rêvait que de ça, une automobile. S'il admirait ouvertement la Bébé Peugeot du docteur, il parlait des automobiles de nos voisins avec une hauteur qui cachait mal sa jalousie. Pour rouler dans une Panhard et Levassor, une de Dion-Bouton ou une Léon Bollée, la Rolls de l'époque, il fallait être un seigneur de la plaine. Comment ? Pourquoi ? C'était comme ça, il y a beaucoup de poissons dans la mer, beaucoup de petits, mais aussi des gros qui mangent les petits et deviennent de plus en plus gros. « Au lieu d'envier les autres, disait ma mère, tu ferais mieux de te marier. » Il reniflait, se grattait la gorge.

« Tu entends, Jules ! » reprenait ma mère. « J'entends, j'entends, je ne suis pas sourd. Ça te va bien, à toi, de dire ça. Je ne peux pas avoir une femme et une automobile. C'est l'un ou l'autre. » Et il frottait deux doigts de sa main droite contre le pouce en clignant de l'œil. « Tu préfères l'automobile ? » demandait ma mère.

Il reniflait encore, réfléchissait, pesait en lui le pour et le contre tandis que ma grand-mère le regardait d'un œil sévère. « On verra après les battages. » C'était la formule consacrée. Si, après avoir vendu leurs récoltes, les colons payaient le travail fait chez eux, si Désiré n'avait pas trop dépensé pour le charbon et les machines, si la main-d'œuvre n'avait pas coûté trop cher... Désiré pleurait toujours misère, Jules le soupçonnait de le tromper, et puis il y avait déjà des sommes engagées pour les défonçages de l'hiver. L'oncle Jules avait surtout peur qu'on le croie devenu riche. Par quel miracle ? Il fallait du temps, beaucoup de calculs, beaucoup d'économies et puis aussi de la chance, de bonnes affaires. Et qui faisait les bonnes affaires ? Là on entendait souvent, je ne sais pourquoi, le cri lamentable du paon que nous avions et dont je n'ai pas parlé. L'oncle levait le doigt : « Hein ? Il te répond : les bonnes affaires, c'est pour ceux qui ont de l'argent. » Les minables comme lui, pensait-il, en étaient réduits à ramasser les miettes. Il regardait encore l'heure à la pendule et à sa montre : « Tu rangeras tout comme il faut », me recommandait-il, et il filait au village.

Du paon, puisque j'en parle, on sait que c'est une pintade qui vole. Oh ! pas beaucoup, de pignon à pignon, dans la cour, si beau avec sa crête et sa longue queue lorsqu'à certains moments, il fait la roue et déploie des plumes vert et bleu à reflets brillants. Personne chez nous n'aurait osé tuer pour le manger un si admirable oiseau, au cri pourtant si peu harmonieux. Parfois, il perdait quelques-unes de ses plumes. Je les cachais dans mon réduit, à côté de mon lit, je contemplais, émerveillé, l'œil d'or qu'il y avait en chacune d'elles.

De temps en temps aussi, l'hiver, on entendait sur le toit comme un craquement prolongé qui ressemblait à un rire acerbe : les cigognes. C'était la mère ou le père qui portait quelque chose aux petits, et tous se mettaient à claquer du bec. Tout le monde se réjouissait quand les cigognes arrivaient à la

fin de l'automne, fuyant les glaces de l'Europe. On disait qu'elles apportaient la paix, quelque chose d'heureux dans la marche du monde. Les nôtres venaient d'Alsace, l'oncle Jules prétendait qu'elles avaient les couleurs allemandes : noir, blanc, rouge, le rouge de leur long bec et de leurs pattes, le noir et le blanc de leurs ailes. Un jour, avant le printemps, elles disparaissaient, on s'en apercevait aux nids vides. On disait : « Les cigognes sont parties. » La plaine semblait déserte, elle avait perdu un peu de son âme, il y avait comme une tristesse chez nous et le paon poussait des cris encore plus grotesques. « Elles reviendront », disait ma grand-mère.

Chaque matin, je me levais dans la splendeur. La salle à manger était déjà fracassée par le soleil et cet éblouissement me paraissait naturel comme le monde où je me trouvais, les odeurs de la plaine, les vagues de vent, la vie douce, immense. Le jour éclatait, atteindrait son plus haut, puis retomberait vers quoi ? La terre tournait, me disait l'oncle Jules, et quand nous avions le dos au soleil, c'était la nuit. Le matin, je courais vers les cyprès et les roseaux à travers l'orangerie, j'entendais des chants de coq, des bruissements dans les herbes et, dans les poteaux de bois du téléphone, des bourdonnements d'abeilles. La ligne de téléphone marquait encore la civilisation française, est-ce que les Arabes connaissaient le téléphone et le télégraphe ? Prêtant l'oreille, j'entendais aussi des halètements de machines, des chants de flûte, des craquements d'essieux, des crissements de roues, j'entendais des claquements de sabots de chevaux, ça c'étaient les gros colons, les roues de leurs voitures étaient bandées de caoutchouc, ils avançaient sans bruit, j'entendais la trompe de l'automobile du petit docteur. La journée montait. A midi, on déjeunait puis c'était la sieste. Après quoi, la journée très chaude, souvent étouffante, descendait avec des bruits plus sourds. Je la voyais, je ne sais pourquoi, pareille à la mer, et je voyais le soir comme le commencement d'autre chose. Parfois un voile s'étendait sur le ciel avec une sorte de tristesse ; on aurait dit que s'arrêtait la machinerie du cosmos. Pour moi, la vie n'était que déclenchements et apparitions. Toute la différence d'à présent où tout est calme.

L'enfance elle-même est mystère et je devinais qu'on me cachait des choses. D'où venais-je, où allions-nous ? J'aurai vécu mes premières années dans un monde d'illusions.

Croyant me garder de l'illégitimité et de la honte, on me condamnait à chercher. Il est vrai qu'on ne pouvait pas me dire, comme à un individu raisonnable, que ma condition d'illégitime n'avait rien d'infamant. On a préféré ne pas me troubler, ne pas déballer devant moi des erreurs de parcours, des fautes, des péchés dont ma mère ne pouvait pas se reconnaître coupable. Pouvait-on m'expliquer comment naissent les hommes ? A l'époque, on ne parlait de cela qu'à demi-mot entre grandes personnes, ce qui m'a valu de me faire à moi-même du cinéma et de m'en faire peut-être encore. Par tant de précautions et de sous-entendus, on a fabriqué un individu tourné sur lui-même, trop sensible, exagérément en état de déséquilibre et d'interrogation. Serais-je devenu un écrivain sans cela ? A des origines qu'on a voulues obscures et qui ne le sont pas, je dois d'avoir été une sorte de hors-la-loi, têtu, gâté, curieux, profitant de toutes les faiblesses, dans les mains d'une grand-mère confite dans l'admiration et dans celles de l'oncle Jules au canotier défoncé. Sur ma naissance tout servait à m'éclairer dans ce que je surprenais.

Le train des journées courait : nouvelle aube, parfois troublée d'orages et de coups de tonnerre qui nous rassemblaient près de la flamme d'une bougie tandis que ma grand-mère égrenait le chapelet de la tante Rayret, puis retour des chevauchées de nuages jusqu'au soir. Soudain, les chauves-souris titubaient, les montagnes semblaient se rapprocher de nous. Dans ce ramassis d'éternité, de feux couchants, d'étoiles piquées dans les dernières écharpes de l'orage par-dessus la plainte des chacals, une voix traînante, une voix lointaine, pareille au hululement d'un chat-huant ou à un cri confus poussé par quelles gorges ? s'étendait sur toute la plaine, comme un autre appel du crépuscule. « Les Arabes », disait l'oncle. Et il ajoutait en regardant ailleurs, dans le noir : « Les Zouaouis... » Les Zouaouis, c'étaient les gens de la tribu à un kilomètre de la ferme, des gourbis dans des bouquets d'arbres, après les vignes, là où la terre n'était plus que mauvais labours, maigres moissons, chaumes rongés, chardons, chevaux efflanqués, troupeaux de moutons dévastateurs, et tout à coup, il y avait une enceinte de figuiers de barbarie, gardée par des chiens au poil hérissé et à la voix rauque. Nous avions débouché là un jour avec l'oncle, mon esclave Meftah me

70

portant. L'oncle avait son fusil à la main, il avait tiré sur un capucin qu'il avait raté. « Il n'a pas dû venir par ici, avait dit l'oncle, à cause des chiens… » Soudain, ça s'était mis à aboyer de partout. Après les chiens, des femmes habillées de rose ou de vert étaient sorties que les hommes avaient repoussées à l'intérieur avant de parler à l'oncle Jules et à Meftah en arabe et avec beaucoup de gestes.

Les Zouaouis chantaient donc le soir ? « Quatre ou cinq fois par jour, dit ma mère. Pour la prière. Je les entends… »

Les Arabes étaient une menace vague, à la fois lointaine et proche, une sorte de nuée d'orage ou de sauterelles à l'horizon, qui pouvait soudain fondre sur nous. Pas une fois ne s'est posée à moi la question de savoir comment et pourquoi ils étaient là. Jamais. C'était un problème mineur. Tout simplement, ils occupaient l'Algérie avant nous, et nous étions là parce que leur gouvernement avait insulté la France : le fameux coup d'éventail que le dey d'Alger avait flanqué à notre consul. L'affront avait été vengé, l'expédition avait suivi, nous étions chez nous, comme partout où flottait le drapeau français. Vers 1854, mes aïeux avaient reçu une concession, bâti leur maison, cultivé la terre qu'on leur avait désignée. Ils apportaient la civilisation. « Qu'est-ce que tu avais avant nous ? disait l'oncle Jules à Meftah. Les Turcs vous prenaient tout. Et puis ? Les fièvres, les bêtes sauvages, c'est vrai, oui ou non ? » « *Ci vri* », disait Meftah avec un geste fataliste. « Vous creviez de faim avant nous », ajoutait la grand-mère d'une voix neutre. Elle avait vu les Arabes du Sud déferler en troupeau sur la plaine et mendier. Pour elle, leur patrie, c'était la misère.

A cette époque, personne ne pouvait être plus déshérité qu'eux. A la distance où j'écris, j'oserai dire que la façon dont je les vois enfant est encore douce et tendre : mon cœur n'était pas féroce, j'avais des attentions pour Meftah. S'il était d'une position inférieure à la mienne, il méritait des faveurs. Nous étions forts de notre bon droit, de notre puissance et d'un état de fait universellement reconnu. L'Europe entreprenante, l'Europe audacieuse, l'Europe débordante avait colonisé l'Algérie, une partie de l'Afrique et de l'Asie, puis des îles et des archipels dans les océans. L'Algérie avait, sur le Maroc et la Tunisie, la chance d'être la chérie, la préférée, le prolongement

71

même de la patrie, quelles questions aurait-on pu se poser quand on y était né français ?

La vérité profonde de tout cela, ma grand-mère la possédait. Dans *les Chevaux du Soleil,* en réplique à une de ses filles qui s'inquiétait de l'insécurité : « Ma fille, dit-elle, on ne travaille pas quand on a peur. Ton père n'avait peur de rien. Moi non plus. Nous avons des armes et on le sait. Si on nous attaque nous nous défendrons. Et on nous attaquerait pourquoi ? Nous ne faisons de tort à personne, nous ne prenons le bien de personne. Personne ne pourrait nous prendre ce qui ne devrait pas nous appartenir, nous ne l'avons pas. Ce qui est dans nos mains est à nous. Alors, nous n'avons rien à craindre... » Elle ne savait ni lire ni écrire mais elle savait parler, elle était ma conscience. Elle tirait la substantifique moelle de tout. Elle résumait la situation en un mot tellement spontané, tellement naturel : « A la ferme, il n'y a pas une miette de terre qui soit injuste. »

Une seule question, à l'époque : les Arabes ne nous acceptaient-ils pas qu'à demi ? Ne nous reprochaient-ils pas d'avoir transformé leur pays en un fabuleux jardin, un paradis qui ne serait qu'à nous ? Ne préféraient-ils pas vivre chez eux, même si c'était dans la pouillerie ? Certains d'entre nous le croyaient. Nous n'avions dérobé le bien de personne, mais peut-être la langue, la mémoire, l'Histoire... D'autres parmi nous, très rares, pensaient vaguement que les meilleurs des Arabes s'apprivoiseraient, que le progrès les rapprocherait de nous. Pour épargner l'enfant que j'étais, ma mère, si elle avait pu, aurait effacé les Arabes, mais le moyen ? Ils couvraient la terre où nous étions, ils servaient partout de main-d'œuvre, ils descendaient en masse des montagnes pour les moissons, les vendanges, les battages, les labours, et quels regards lançaient-ils sur tout ! C'est pour cela que les femmes craignaient les Arabes : les anciennes captives des Barbaresques s'étaient-elles plaintes des mauvais traitements subis dans les harems ? Le sentiment à l'égard des Arabes restait trouble.

En parlant d'eux, l'oncle Jules les désignait sous le terme de « troncs de figuier », une expression admise, courante, que tout le monde employait. Cela signifiait que les Arabes, souvent assis au pied des figuiers, contre le tronc des arbres, n'étaient pas des bourreaux de travail. Il en venait parfois jusqu'à la ferme. Des apparences hâves, chétives, souvent

pieds nus, une grisaille de vêtements en loques. César s'étranglait de fureur. « Et tous ces poux », disait ma mère à voix basse en me serrant contre elle. Avec l'oncle Jules, ça ne traînait pas. Il allait à eux en leur montrant la direction d'où ils venaient et dans leur langue : « *La, la, la,* non, non, non, dommage, ô hommes, dommage, nous n'avons pas besoin de vous... » Meftah apparaissait derrière lui, vaguement inquiet. Ce n'était pas la saison, ils devaient aller s'informer au douar à côté. « Pas très loin, c'est ça, et que la bénédiction soit sur vous, *baraka laoufikoum...* » Ils n'insistaient pas, s'en retournaient, le bâton à la main, vermine grouillante qu'on distinguait à peine de la terre. Quand l'oncle Jules n'était pas là, alors Meftah accourait. Plein de terreur qu'on essaye de lui voler sa place, plein de colère, comme César, à l'égard de cette racaille de gens sans emploi qui erraient sur les routes comme au temps des Turcs pour manger, en dérobant tout ce qu'ils pouvaient sans qu'on s'en aperçoive sur le moment. De vrais escamoteurs. Quelquefois ils avaient avec eux, si maigre, si mal nourrie, une poule déplumée que l'un d'eux tenait par les pattes, la tête en bas, pour faire croire qu'ils pouvaient la vendre, avec des œufs qu'ils faisaient le geste de chercher au fond d'un capuchon de burnous. Quand il les apercevait de loin, Meftah s'installait au milieu du chemin et là, d'une main qu'il agitait comme aujourd'hui les agents de la circulation quand ils excitent les automobilistes à rouler : « Allez, allez... » Il parlait en même temps qu'eux, plus vite et fort, ah ! il avait du gosier à ce moment-là, pas comme dans une conversation avec nous, dans un échange entre gens de bonne compagnie, il couvrait leurs paroles, il ne voulait rien entendre de ce qu'ils disaient : « *La, la, la...* » Comme l'oncle : non, non, non. Puis il ouvrait les deux mains avec le geste de les repousser, comme on repousse un troupeau gênant, des individus de trop. Si elle ne me voyait pas, ma mère sortait sur ce qu'on appelait du mot pompeux de perron ou de marquise, qui n'était qu'un très modeste emplacement couvert par une avancée de tôle entre le toit et la cour, une sorte d'auvent au-dessus de la porte, et là, lançait un cri strident : « Zizi !... » A quoi parfois répondait le paon. D'habitude, je n'étais pas loin. J'apparaissais avec plus ou moins de rapidité selon l'intonation. « A la maison... » Je rentrais. Meftah imposait silence à César mais ne cessait pas de parler tant que la misérable

troupe, d'abord figée sur place par son verbe, puis oscillante, n'avait pas rebroussé chemin, découragée. « Qu'est-ce que c'est que ça... » disait Meftah à l'adresse de ma mère quand il repassait devant la maison, encore tout courroucé et avec un certain contentement dans son âme inquiète pour cette race maudite à l'affût de ses pauvres biens à quoi il était si attaché. Comme César.

Là furent à peu près les seules relations que j'eus avec les Arabes. Ils existaient, et on faisait tout pour me les cacher. Quant à ceux qu'on connaissait, la famille de Meftah, celui qui lavait les verres au café de l'Espérance, ceux qui traînaient sur la place du village, ceux qu'on emmenait entre deux gendarmes à cheval, ceux qu'on dépassait ou ceux qu'on croisait, non sans méfiance, sur les routes, et à propos de qui l'oncle Jules disait toujours, quand il ne les connaissait pas, après les saluts d'usage : « D'où ils viennent, ceux-là ?... » A première vue, ils semblaient des hommes, mais si différents de nous, ne buvant pas ce que nous buvions, ne mangeant pas ce que nous mangions, ne parlant pas la même langue, n'adorant pas le même Dieu, ne considérant pas les choses et les gens de la même manière. Nous les Paris, les Français, nous possédions à peu près tout : les maisons, les vraies terres, les vrais troupeaux, les machines, la maréchaussée, les églises, les villes, les arbres, les voitures, les chevaux, les charrois, les facteurs, les bicyclettes, les automobiles. Eux rien, ou si peu que rien : des bœufs pas plus gros que des veaux, des moutons souffreteux. Et les femmes, ils les cachaient. Ils n'avaient sûrement pas d'âme.

Je ne savais pas qu'à cette époque-là, on croyait aussi que les Chinois n'en avaient pas non plus.

A peine avais-je ouvert les yeux que, par le muezzin, le Dieu d'un Meftah plein de poux s'imposait à moi plus que le Dieu des Paris, le mien, par le signe de croix sur le pain avant de l'entamer et par le Notre-Père que ma mère m'obligeait à réciter, le soir, quand je ne dormais pas déjà. A l'enfant de la ferme, une première approche mystique était fournie par les Arabes, dans un décor cosmique qui n'inspirait pas tellement les Paris sinon, peut-être, pour les effrayer. Le chapelet de la

tante Rayret était le signe d'une prière silencieuse, secrète, vers qui ? Les étoiles, les mondes lointains de ma mère, c'était Dieu, le régulateur qui les avait lancés dans l'univers. Quand Chateaubriand parle de la chambre où il naquit à Saint-Malo, dans une rue étroite et sombre qui s'appelait la rue des Juifs et d'où l'on dominait la mer qui se brisait sur des écueils, il écrit : « C'est là où ma mère m'infligea la vie. » Pour moi qui n'oserais accuser personne de quoi que ce soit, je m'en tiens à la formule de Calderón : « Le plus grand crime de l'homme est d'être né », ce qui rejette encore plus les responsabilités sur Dieu.

Il arrivait qu'on aille à la messe. Pour les Rameaux, Pâques et la Pentecôte, pour Noël aussi, peut-être à cause de Meftah, sinon la grand-mère se serait crue déshonorée. Ses prières, Meftah les faisait seul, sans ostentation, souvent même il ne les faisait pas, pour ne pas interrompre son travail ou pour ne pas subir les reproches ou les taquineries de l'oncle Jules. Chez lui, il n'y avait étalage de religion qu'aux fêtes musulmanes où l'on tuait le mouton ; pour ma grand-mère, les Paris devaient montrer qu'ils ne vivaient pas comme des chiens, ce qu'on entendait dire par les Arabes de beaucoup de colons. La veille de la messe, ma mère et ma grand-mère lissaient l'une l'autre longuement leur chevelure, répandaient sur leur tête des flots d'huile de rose, d'œillet et de benjoin que je respire encore, et se coiffaient. Le lendemain, très tôt, ma mère me lavait, me peignait et me revêtait de ce que j'avais de plus beau. A leur tour, les femmes s'habillaient. Elles y passaient beaucoup de temps. Ma grand-mère se parait de quelques bijoux et en parait ma mère. Meftah attelait deux chevaux au break, l'oncle Jules et moi montions devant, les femmes derrière à l'abri des toiles gommées rabattues, et nous rejoignions la route de Sidi-Moussa. Au carrefour où l'on apercevait les hauts bâtiments de la cave des Manint, cela donnait une idée de ce qui séparait les Paris des autres, l'oncle Jules haussait les épaules et on s'enfonçait sous l'ombre bleue des eucalyptus, une navigation sur un fleuve bruissant et odorant. Notre canot, c'était le break ; le bruit des rames, le sabot des chevaux ; le glissement de l'eau sur la coque, c'était le vent dans les branches aux longues feuilles effilées. Sur la chaussée, les roues craquaient et heurtaient du fer les fon-

drières. De leur allure pépère, nos chevaux, que l'oncle essayait vainement de ravigoter, mettaient dix minutes pour traverser ce long chenal étroit et couvert, je guettais le moment où brillerait à l'autre bout ce que je croyais être une apparition.

Les cloches sonnaient déjà, l'église Saint-Charles se dressait comme une poule d'Inde tout de suite après les premières maisons et la poste. Nous descendions du break en même temps que d'autres familles, les femmes se saluaient tandis que ce mécréant d'oncle Jules continuait à pied vers le café. Nous prenions place sur les bancs, la messe commençait, célébrée par le curé à longue barbe grise, M. Jousserand. En ornements verts, dorés ou rouges, flanqué d'enfants de chœur rutilants, il surveillait ses ouailles avec autorité dans l'espoir qu'elles méritaient ce que Dieu leur avait prodigué, comme aux fils d'Israël à la sortie d'Egypte, les meilleures terres, les meilleurs pâturages. L'harmonium soutenait des cantiques, parfois du latin que personne ne comprenait mais qui nous rattachait à l'universalité de l'Eglise romaine. Ma grand-mère priait sincèrement, pieusement, ses yeux brillaient, elle respirait, elle renaissait. Mélancolique, ma mère me serrait contre elle. Je n'étais pas son péché comme on pouvait le croire, j'étais son orgueil, je devais oublier qu'avec la plupart des hommes, à l'Espérance, l'oncle sirotait son anis et riait. L'encens embaumait, une sonnette tintinnabulait, je regardais ébloui la profusion de cierges, le lourd missel qu'on portait de part et d'autre de l'autel. Le vieux prêtre montait en chaire et parlait de Dieu, j'entrais dans un mystère de plus, un cérémonial m'introduisait dans une communauté de gens dignes, bien habillés, je devenais l'un des leurs, ils avaient besoin de se réunir en nombre pour établir la différence avec les autres, souvent errants, miséreux et couleur de poussière dont je n'entendais la voix que le soir.

Soulevés par l'onde joyeuse des cloches, nous sortions, les familles se dispersaient avec des sourires, des inclinaisons de tête, parfois des embrassades ; les femmes faisaient étalage de leurs équipages, parfois de leurs limousines automobiles, ma mère nous emmenait avec le break à deux pas de là, au cimetière où, avec ma grand-mère, elle se recueillait devant le tombeau des Paris. Pas de chapelle comme pour beaucoup d'autres, quatre degrés de marbre blanc et une large forme de

granit surmontée d'une croix, avec en lettres d'or FAMILLE PARIS, presque en face des noms rutilants de la plaine, des Pélégri, des Schembri, des Ronda. Ma grand-mère versait une larme, se signait. C'était là qu'à son tour, un peu à l'écart du village, après la mairie et l'école, dans un enclos plein de cyprès et d'arbres exotiques à chevelure argentée, elle reposerait. Ma mère s'emparait de nouveau des guides et s'arrêtait devant l'Espérance. Je descendais chercher l'oncle. « Envoyer cet enfant dans un endroit pareil », disait ma grand-mère comme à elle-même. L'oncle me hissait un instant sur ses genoux, je respirais l'odeur des cigarettes et de l'anis, les voix m'étourdissaient, les hommes me regardaient en souriant. Il y avait les fortes personnalités du village, une partie du conseil municipal, les grandes gueules, le forgeron qui faisait griller les poils de ses avant-bras au feu de sa forge et ne pouvait sentir les curés, ni les gendarmes, ni les Arabes. Et peut-être M. Kradt, un petit colon que tout le monde appelait M. Crotte, et qui dressait ses chiens, des bergers allemands, à mordre tous les Arabes qui approchaient de chez lui. « On m'attend », disait enfin l'oncle Jules en se levant. Il serrait les mains, semblait s'arracher à cette autre église colorée plus animée, bruyante et enfumée où des rites se célébraient aussi. Ma mère cédait les guides à l'oncle, puis descendait et m'asseyait contre elle, à l'intérieur du break. « C'est lui donner de mauvaises habitudes », disait ma grand-mère, qui reniflait un peu. « Ça sent l'absinthe... » « Mais non, mais non », répliquait ma mère. L'oncle secouait les guides et faisait claquer sa langue : « Allez, allez !... » Je demandais à ma mère ce que c'était que les péchés dont le curé avait parlé. « Les fautes qu'on commet, répondait ma mère. Laisse, ce n'est pas de ton âge. » Il y avait un âge pour ça ? « Oui, il y a un âge. » C'était la vie.

Ma mère pensait sûrement à son péché à elle. Tout le monde y pensait sauf moi. Elle s'interrogeait. Aurait-elle dû ne pas céder, rester fidèle à la parole donnée, ne pas verser dans un moment de folie qui pouvait se changer en désespoir et en désolation ? Je ne comprenais pas le regard si doux, si dévorant, que ma grand-mère et elle avaient alors pour moi. Ma mère aurait résisté à l'instituteur, elle jouirait des sèches et tristes récompenses de la vertu, elle servirait des clients à l'hôtel des Eaux-Thermales de Rovigo sous l'œil oblique de son mari derrière le comptoir, ils attendraient l'un et l'autre le

passage des voyageurs et des saisons dans un village de colonisation où l'on vivait, paraît-il, plus à l'aise qu'en France. Que pouvait-on espérer d'autre qu'une réputation de fricassée de veau aux olives et une bonne entente avec le serveur arabe ? Mon frère René suivait des cours d'apprentissage chez un garagiste de Mustapha, il était doué pour la mécanique, il aimait ses parents. Après son service militaire, ils se marierait à Sidi-Moussa avec Louise, une des filles du charpentier Berthaut, déjà allié aux Paris par sa propre femme, sœur de la tante Henriette. Ne pas pécher, c'était pour ma mère se dire, devant son miroir qui était un peu le regard de Dieu, qu'elle renonçait aux tentations de l'instituteur, à sa bille de Prussien dominateur, à sa moustache conquérante, à l'allure qu'il avait, avec sa canne à pommeau d'argent, quand il l'emmenait sous les arcades d'Alger devant les terrasses des brasseries où ma mère refusait de s'asseoir. Ils se promenaient un moment sur le boulevard, devant le port plein de mugissements de navires. « Voyons, voyons, et rien de tout ça à cause des joies futures ? Ne me dites pas qu'une femme comme vous a peur. De quoi ? » Je suppose qu'un jour l'instituteur lui avait dit quelque chose comme ça. Lui n'avait rien à craindre, mais elle, face au scandale des imbéciles et des timorés ? Elle avait dû longtemps se répéter le mot : « Une femme comme vous... » Une femme comme elle. C'est vrai, elle était belle, elle pouvait braver la société, que pouvait-il se passer ? Délices coupables, douleurs, larmes. Devait-elle renoncer aux flammes du Prussien et se garder pour ce qu'était devenu, hélas, le gendarme son mari : un homme ordinaire, soumis, insignifiant ? A trente-cinq ans, elle lui avait donné quinze ans de paix, de bonheur conjugal, il lui restait combien de temps avant les flétrissures et la résignation ?

Au retour de la messe et au bout de l'allée d'eucalyptus, le break débouchait sur la plaine dans un brasillement. Face aux collines d'Alger, face au nord, il me semblait que nous allions vers l'inconnu, tandis que pour les émoustiller un peu, l'oncle Jules caressait la croupe des chevaux de la mèche de son fouet. Ils sentaient l'écurie, ils allongeaient le trot, l'air de la mer invisible nous frappait. La vie s'ouvrait. Un jour de fête s'étalait lisse et pur.

***
****

A Pâques, la fête se prolongeait par la visite de l'oncle Désiré avec sa femme, la tante Henriette, et leurs filles, de mon âge ou presque. De Rovigo ils arrivaient, ô merveille ! dans une nouvelle automobile que l'oncle Jules considérait avec ombrage. Toujours en quête d'argent, pleurant misère, Désiré s'excusait presque d'avoir sauté sur une occasion. Cette automobile, une sans-soupapes toute neuve, avait eu des malheurs, son propriétaire qui conduisait mal l'avait endommagée. Désiré l'avait-il seulement payée ? Il l'avait retapée et elle roulait. « Nous sommes venus comme ça », disait-il de sa voix traînante en étendant une main à plat devant lui. « Sans bouger, on se serait cru la reine d'Angleterre... » Mes cousines et moi, nous n'arrêtions pas d'inspecter cette merveille, d'ouvrir et refermer le capot, de descendre, de remonter, de sonner à la trompe ponh, ponh, de toucher à tout jusqu'à ce que ma mère intervienne. Les filles de l'oncle Désiré, mon Dieu, comme je les trouvais jolies, comme j'essayais de les épater ! Je les promenais à travers la ferme, je leur montrais les fleurs, les arums surtout, les chevaux et les bœufs que j'appelais par leurs noms, les cochons à l'engrais, la machine de la noria que je savais mettre en route, le bassin gorgé de têtards et de grenouilles et couvert d'araignées d'eau, le jardin avec ses belles-de-nuit et ses buissons de menthe et d'héliotrope, la cave où le vin regorgeait dans les cuves, le logis de l'oncle Jules, le plaqueminier, la passiflore que j'inventerai plus tard, le gourbi de Meftah défendu par des figuiers de barbarie aux raquettes hérissées d'aiguillons. Là, je cueillais une corolle jaune, je la collais au lobe d'une oreille. Puis c'était l'orangerie et les cyprès, les oiseaux qui nichaient dans les arbres, César devant sa niche. Nous rentrions pour la mouna, ce gâteau d'origine espagnole en forme de miche. Dans chaque famille on travaillait la pâte longtemps d'avance, on la mettait à lever dans des corbeilles sous des édredons, et enfin au four. On y goûtait déjà le dimanche de Pâques, mais surtout le lundi. Le lundi de Pâques, toute l'Algérie allait en promenade « faire la mouna ». C'était une fête sans pareille, une communion avec la nature, une fraternisation immense. Sans les Arabes évidemment. La tante Henriette nous portait quelques-unes de ses mounas, on comparait avec les nôtres, on s'extasiait sur les dons des pâtissières. Chacune était jalouse du secret, des

parfums. J'aimais beaucoup la mouna, j'en aurais toute la semaine avec mon café au lait. Enfin l'oncle Jules montait le phonographe, ah !... Ça n'était pas encore arrivé à Rovigo. Les cousines écoutaient, le menton dans la main, j'étais fier d'assister l'oncle, tous les disques y passaient.

La conversation revenait sur la mécanique, la tante Henriette disait que son mari s'y ruinait mais que c'était sa passion. « Ah ! il aime ça », répétait-elle. Il rougissait, il souriait en lissant sa moustache blonde. Déjà déplumé, Désiré portait les cheveux plutôt longs par-derrière, il avait les yeux pervenche, limpides, des Paris, alors que Jules avait les yeux couleur de châtaigne des Bouychou, comme ma grand-mère, couleur queue de renard, ma mère avait les mêmes. « Non, prétendait ma grand-mère. Dans tes yeux à toi, Mathilde, il y a du vert comme dans les miens. Jules, c'est les yeux de Marjol qu'il a... » Elle ne disait pas Marjol, mais Jean-Pierre. Marjol, c'est moi qui l'invente. Marjol, c'était le nom du mythe que je me suis fabriqué pour l'histoire et aussi pour avoir des raisons de me montrer digne de lui, un peu brigand. L'oncle Jules se rengorgeait. Les esprits s'échauffaient. L'oncle Désiré bâtissait de nouveaux rêves : ces machines battraient toutes les récoltes et défonceraient toutes les friches de la plaine, son auto servirait à voler d'un chantier à l'autre. Qui pourrait lutter avec une entreprise aussi moderne ? L'oncle Jules affichait un air sceptique. « Et si tu crèves ? » Il voulait parler d'un pneumatique. « Je répare, répondait Désiré, j'ai tout ce qu'il faut. » « Et si tu ne peux pas payer tes ouvriers parce que tu n'as pas d'argent ? » « Eh bien, tu m'en prêteras », répliquait Désiré. « N'y compte pas », concluait Jules en refermant son visage.

Sans doute restait-il entre eux un litige de la campagne précédente, Désiré devait toujours à son frère l'argent qu'il avait encaissé et roulait carrosse avec des dettes tandis que lui, Jules, hésitait à se payer une automobile. Pour lui, Désiré avec ses airs bonasses était un esbroufeur, la conversation prenait un ton aigre. « Si vous saviez combien il travaille, disait tante Henriette, comment il compte, comment j'économise, moi. Il devrait avoir plus de chance qu'il en a... » « La chance, ça se mérite », disait Jules. « Ah ! je ne la mérite pas ? » répliquait Désiré. Ma mère changeait le cours des propos et demandait des nouvelles du berger municipal, des moutons rassemblés à

son de trompe, des matins de Rovigo, et du petit train qui allait à Alger le long de la route, ah ! s'il avait pu parler, ce petit train... A Sidi-Moussa, il fallait aller le chercher à la gare des Eucalyptus, du côté de Rivet, au diable. « Est-ce que ça sent toujours les géraniums rosats ?... » demandait ma mère. Cette merveilleuse odeur la poursuivait, elle en était inconsolable. « Oui, ma pauvre, répondait tante Henriette, ça embaume. Nous n'avons pas beaucoup d'argent, mais ça au moins... » Ma mère respirait fort comme si l'amour lui revenait.

Un silence tombait, les regards se fixaient un instant sur moi. Ça me flattait et m'inquiétait. Quelle liaison avec les géraniums, Rovigo et moi ? La tante Henriette se levait pour m'embrasser, ma mère essuyait furtivement une larme, eh bien, eh bien... D'un geste un peu nerveux, l'oncle Jules empoignait son fusil et nous quittait.

On dînait tôt. Avant la tombée de la nuit, s'ils s'en allaient avec la fameuse automobile, j'étais tout triste. Mon Dieu, comme je les ai aimées, ces cousines-là... Quelquefois, d'autres cousins venaient, les enfants de l'épicerie fine ou de l'autre veuve, ou ceux du boucher. On mettait des matelas par terre dans un bonheur fou, on se gavait de mouna. Nous écoutions la sarabande des rats au grenier, les chacals. Brisé de fatigue et de je ne sais quoi qui me gonflait le cœur, je sombrais aussitôt dans le sommeil. Je n'entendais même pas la chouette. Encore moins la prière des Arabes. Si un orage éclatait, je me réveillais, je hurlais de joie au déchirement de la foudre tandis que les filles enfouissaient leur tête sous les oreillers.

Debout dans la salle à manger, un bougeoir allumé à la main, ma mère regardait la pluie flageller les vitres.

Une nuit, la ferme fut en révolution. César aboya férocement, ma mère se leva, observa des ombres sous les noyers. C'était après minuit. Des voleurs ? Ma mère consulta ma grand-mère, saisit un fusil, le chargea de deux cartouches à chevrotines, se posta derrière les persiennes de la salle à manger, tira. Le bruit parut terrifiant, puis il y eut un vaste silence, l'oncle Jules appela de loin et arriva avec Meftah. Personne ne dormit plus, on attendit le matin dans les allées et venues. Quand je me réveillai, ignorant tout, les gendarmes étaient là. L'oncle avait trouvé sous un noyer une chéchia

tachée de sang que les gendarmes tripotèrent longuement, puis emportèrent.

L'incident fit le tour de la plaine, les journaux en parlèrent, on regarda désormais ma mère avec admiration, sa faute presque effacée. Moi aussi j'étais fier. On soupçonna un moment Meftah de complicité avec des gens des Zouaouis, mais pourquoi Meftah nous en aurait-il voulu ? La tante d'Alger, l'épicière, dit : « Ces gens sont capables de tout. Dommage que tu ne l'aies pas tué, Mathilde. » L'enquête ne mena nulle part, on ne sut jamais rien. Sauf que ma mère était devenue presque une héroïne.

Des coups de fusil de chasseurs, il en partait beaucoup. Le gibier abondait. Rarement autre chose. Les coups de fusil de la révolte de Mokrani ou de la rébellion de Margueritte, au moment où mon père l'instituteur arrivait à Rovigo, étaient depuis longtemps étouffés. Parfois des coups de fusil de fantasia sur le champ de manœuvre d'Alger quand un grand personnage nous visitait. Evidemment, il y avait parfois des crimes ; on se tuait entre Européens et Arabes à coups de fusil, mais la sécurité s'installait. Nous vivions en paix. N'empêche. Par habitude, l'oncle Jules gardait son fusil à la bretelle.

L'instituteur Dematons fut muté à Staouéli, là même où l'armée de M. de Bourmont avait remporté sa première victoire sur les Turcs en juin 1830. De là, il écrivit avec un peu de forfanterie à un de ses cousins, un certain Honoré Virgile Dematons, tailleur de pierre à Arsonval (Aube), qu'il avait « une superbe situation ». Il nous sortit de la ferme, se maria à Alger avec ma mère et me confia à un instituteur indigène qui m'apprit à lire et à écrire convenablement. Nous ne restâmes pas longtemps à Staouéli. Vers 1912 nous étions à Aïn-Taya, où mon père avait sous ses ordres son propre fils Robert, une demoiselle Louise Guédant âgée de vingt ans, et encore deux instituteurs indigènes. Je me vois photographié sur trois rangs avec ma classe dirigée par cette demoiselle Guédant, une nonne laïque à bandeaux de chocolat brun qui menait ses élèves à la baguette. Je suis tout en haut et à gauche, à côté du directeur à grosse moustache et à casquette. Dans ma classe,

une dizaine de petits bicots, comme on les appelait à l'époque, récitaient avec moi Victor Hugo :

Gloire à notre France éternelle,
Gloire à ceux qui sont morts pour elle...

Aïn-Taya était un gros village accroché au-dessus d'une falaise escarpée, à trente kilomètres à l'est d'Alger, de l'autre côté du cap Matifou. J'allais avoir cinq ans, j'étais considéré par tous comme le fils du directeur d'école, à qui je disais papa. Je ne portais pas le même nom que lui mais c'était mon père. Vrai ou pas, je ne me posais pas la question. D'Aïn-Taya, on avait accès à la mer par une plage étroite, couverte de galets. L'hiver, des tempêtes secouaient les arbres, les embruns brouillaient les vitres des maisons ; l'été, la mer était toujours agitée, seuls y allaient les pêcheurs et les petits Arabes qui nageaient comme des tritons. Quand nous nous aventurions à la plage, mon père m'attachait à une longue corde pour qu'une vague ne m'enlève pas. C'était ça, la mer dont je rêvais, la mer immobile, la mer toute bleue ? Je disparaissais souvent avec des vauriens dans les vignobles proches et dans les roseaux. Nous guettions le gibier, nous comparions nos anatomies, intense curiosité de notre vie ; ivres de vent, nous courions sur les rochers avec les mouettes, prêts à nous envoler avec elles par-dessus l'écume. Pour me punir, mon père m'attachait encore, dans ma chambre, au lit, et tirait les persiennes. Une discipline de fer régnait chez nous, ma mère terrorisée se soumit : après tout, elle était devenue la femme du directeur d'école, je n'étais plus un enfant perdu.

Par réaction avec la liberté dont j'étais, à la ferme, comblé, je devins de plus en plus indocile. A la moindre incartade ou insolence, Mlle Guédant, qui m'adorait cependant, me collait au piquet. Mon frère Robert, superbe rouquin sapé et chapeauté comme un gandin, snobait ma mère et me considérait avec condescendance. Pour lui, j'étais le vil bâtard de son père et un garnement trop gâté. A dresser. Je me souviens d'Aïn-Taya comme d'une géhenne : n'affrontant la mer qu'au bout d'une corde, souvent bouclé la journée dans ma chambre et, en classe, debout, la tête dans les bras, flanquant des ruades dans le bas d'un placard. De rage.

Dieu sait si, à cette époque, on voulait venger les hontes

de 1870 et reconquérir l'Alsace et la Lorraine. En classe, Mlle Guédant ne nous parlait que de la patrie : tout le monde attendait la guerre. Quand elle éclata, la joie et l'enthousiasme débordèrent. Sous mes yeux, mon frère se transforma en sergent de zouaves, ceinture rouge, flottard rouge, boléro bleu foncé, chéchia à gros gland sur le cou et large chevron d'or sur les manches. Il nous quitta, soulagé. Mon père ne partait pas à cause de son âge, mais, avec Robert, il se sentait le géniteur d'un futur héros. Il me hissa sur ses épaules, m'emmena sonner le tocsin, harangua les indigènes qui se précipitaient en foule, ces imbéciles, vers le bureau de recrutement et leur extorqua des paroles historiques. Ma mère pleurait. Son fils René achevait son service militaire en France dans l'artillerie lourde, il était déjà en ligne. Je profitai de l'émotion générale et, avec mes camarades de vadrouille, je me faufilai derrière des soldats et un drapeau. En route, à pied, pour Alger, nous voulions devenir zouaves avec un falzar écarlate, et libres de tout zigouiller. On nous arrêta à mi-chemin. Nous rentrâmes. On m'attacha de nouveau. Tout se calma.

Probablement pour boucher des trous, mon père fut muté à Alger. Décoré des palmes académiques, il enseignait dans une école en haut de la Casbah, rue Marengo. Dans sa classe grouillait une horde piaillante et déferlante de cinquante chiards de bicots. Lui marchait dans les rues en distribuant des coups de canne à ce qu'il appelait « cette racaille » : pas seulement les Arabes, tous ceux qui parlaient mal le français. Parfois il sombrait dans des angoisses noires. Capable de rester huit jours enfoncé dans le silence, il allait, venait, sortait, se couchait et repartait sans un mot, avec l'impression d'avoir tout raté dans sa vie. Nous habitions à Bab el-Oued, 16, rue Montaigne, un quartier neuf plein de petits-bourgeois et de voyous. Je m'en donnais à cœur joie, nous formions une bande et fréquentions rarement l'école où les coups de règle étaient notre pitance. On chipait de l'argent pour acheter ce qu'on trouvait dans la rue : des bliblis, des parts de *calentita*, des tramouss, des beignets, des gâteaux au gingembre, des *mantecaos*, et de quoi nous payer le cinéma qui commençait. De l'autre côté de la mer, très loin, en France, c'était la tuerie, les tranchées ; à Alger, en 1915, dans les quartiers chic, des cocottes laissaient des traînées de patchouli derrière elles, les soldats retour du front menaient la vie à grandes guides, les

officiers occupaient la terrasse du Tantonville où, à présent, il y avait un orchestre, les femmes se donnaient à qui les voulait, les gendarmes s'affichaient pour un semblant de discipline. La photographie des permissionnaires appuyés sur le bastingage des navires devint une affaire : ça se vendait. Quand un de mes frères revenait, c'était la nouba.

Une fois, tous deux furent là, par miracle. Robert, déjà sous-lieutenant, en kaki avec croix de guerre, un as avec un sabre ; l'autre, René, maréchal des logis d'artillerie lourde, en bleu horizon avec des houseaux. Robert avait levé une fille qu'il amena chez nous, et comme mon père feignait de se scandaliser, il le rabroua. C'est vrai qu'on engageait les zouaves dans des affaires terribles et c'est vrai que Robert n'avait peur de rien. Il resplendissait dans sa tenue. Mon père lui parlait d'une voisine d'en face au premier, où les persiennes n'étaient jamais ouvertes, Mme Trouette, une vieille dame à la chevelure rouge flamboyant dont le fils venait d'être tué sur la Somme. Elle était déjà la veuve d'un officier du Tonkin, il y avait beaucoup de chinoiseries chez elle. Ma mère allait en visite quelquefois chez elle, qui ne sortait plus, ne voulait plus voir la lumière du jour ni personne. Robert répondit en bougonnant : « Qu'est-ce que tu veux que je foute de cette vieille folle ?... » Je le regardais, ébahi, fiévreux, je voulais de la gloire. L'amour, je ne sais pas. Mes frères avaient ramené aussi un parabellum, un fusil Mauser, un mousqueton de cavalerie, des cartouches, on alla tout expérimenter à la ferme où l'oncle Jules, un moment mobilisé à Batna, avait repris les travaux. Il n'y en avait que pour les héros que ma grand-mère contemplait avec des yeux mouillés. On tira beaucoup de coups de fusil, ça fit du bruit, on fit ripaille, on but beaucoup, je tirai aussi, le recul de l'arme m'impressionna, la plaine pétait de tous les côtés. De retour à Alger, le verbe haut, rigolard et insolent, orgueilleux lion roux en rut, Robert courut de gueuleton en gueuleton, de fête en fête, de fille en fille, la guerre l'avait changé, il se livrait avec fureur à la chasse aux embusqués, aux nantis et aux salauds ; dans les rues, les injures pleuvaient, on s'engueulait, parfois on cognait, et quand je l'accompagnais, je cognais aussi. Robert ne s'en laissait imposer par personne, il avait tué, demain il serait peut-être tué, les jours passaient vite, il repartit et dit à ma mère : « Pas de larmes, pas de simagrées. » Cette fois, sur le bateau, il eut

droit à une cabine de première. Il passa deux jours à Paris à ribouldinguer et ne s'en cacha pas, je l'enviai. Mon frère René, bon garçon, n'avait pas quitté d'une semelle sa fiancée, Louise Berthaut, une des filles du charpentier de Sidi-Moussa et la jeune sœur de tante Henriette, et ne revint que pour s'embarquer. Il y eut un grand vide dans la maison. Mon frère Robert avait laissé une drôle d'odeur derrière lui, et des armes que je caressais.

Avec la bande de voyous de l'école, nous nous mîmes à montrer plus d'audace. Au cinéma, quand le shérif sautait dans sa Ford haute sur pattes, on criait. Les zéros pleuvaient sur moi. Raison : mauvaises fréquentations. Mon père me fit quitter l'école publique et j'entrai en sixième A2 au lycée Bugeaud, face à la caserne Pélissier, au pied du jardin Marengo et de la Casbah, tout près du quartier de la Marine et des bordels de la rue des Consuls. Toute l'élite d'Alger passera par là : je précède de sept, de dix ans, Camus, Fréminville, Max-Pol Fouchet, Jean Daniel, Jean Pélégri, tant d'autres qui auront nom plus tard dans les lettres ou dans la politique. Le proviseur et le censeur inspiraient de la terreur, le tambour battait pour l'entrée des classes, notre professeur de latin-grec, M. Sarret, portait une lavallière gris perle saupoudrée de tabac à priser, nous le mettions en boîte et nous séchions ses cours : petite guerre dans les massifs du jardin Marengo, timides incursions autour des bouges de la Casbah qui sentaient le péché, la mouquère, le stupre, la soldatesque, la canaille. Nous en venions aux mains pour un mot ou une insulte. Pour un « sale juif » ou un « sale Français », on « se donnait ». Un cercle de spectateurs se formait autour des adversaires jusqu'à ce qu'un juge arbitre accordât la victoire à l'un de nous. Au lycée, il n'y avait pas encore d'Arabes. Ça viendra. Pour le moment, les élèves étaient des fils de famille. Je me liai à quelques camarades, à ceux qu'on ne venait pas chercher en calèche ou en bagnole. Nous sautions en marche dans les trams sans payer, nous nous accrochions aux tampons, nous courions après Galoufa, l'équipe municipale qui attrapait les chiens errants au lasso et les mettait en cage dans une voiture à bras. Mon père qui n'avait pas fait de service militaire parce que, de son temps, les élèves instituteurs en étaient exempts, ne voulut pas être en reste avec son fils Robert et s'engagea comme secrétaire à l'état-major du XIXe corps. Il eut une

tenue, porta un képi, un écusson, mais revenait coucher à la maison.

Ma mère et moi allions passer les vacances à la ferme. Nous prenions l'autobus rouge des frères Monico qui stationnait place Mahon, près de la mosquée de la Marine et des caboulots qui sentaient l'anis, au milieu des vendeurs de beignets et de créponnés, ces sorbets de neige au citron dont je n'ai déniché le nom dans aucun dictionnaire. Après Alger, jusqu'en Turquie et en Indochine j'en chercherai et n'en trouverai jamais. Jamais je n'aurai mangé de glaces plus délicieuses que là, au soleil de la place du Gouvernement, parmi les vendeurs de cartes postales obscènes, les entremetteurs de toute sorte que mon innocence ne discernait pas. L'autobus aura des bandages en caoutchouc pendant la guerre et, après, des pneus. Il longeait les boulevards, le champ de manœuvre, grimpait vers Kouba, descendait les collines du Sahel par Baraki où parfois, comme une baleine dans le ciel, naviguait le dirigeable qui surveillait les sous-marins et parfois appareillait ou s'amarrait. Deux kilomètres avant Sidi-Moussa, le conducteur nous arrêtait devant le chemin de terre de la ferme. Ma grand-mère pleurait, Meftah touchait ma main puis sa bouche et son cœur, César mort avait été remplacé par un autre César, le paon criait toujours, j'avais grandi, tout avait rapetissé, seul l'oncle Jules n'avait pas changé. Les filles de l'oncle Désiré étaient de plus en plus belles. De l'une je ferai plus tard une héroïne des *Chevaux du Soleil*.

Ai-je eu pour celle que j'appellerai Marguerite des sentiments qui iront presque jusqu'à vouloir mourir de désespoir ? Ce n'est pas impossible. Là intervient la liberté du romancier qui n'est forcé de respecter ni la vérité ni l'exactitude des faits, et même son devoir est d'en prendre à l'aise avec elles. Tout a été dit sur ce thème, je n'ai pas dérogé aux usages. Dans la fresque consacrée aux miens et à ma patrie perdue, j'ai décrit le cadre et les personnages tels qu'ils étaient. Hector Koenig, c'est moi, je le tuerai sans qu'on connaisse son meurtrier, le romancier aura survécu à son personnage. Mais quand il s'agit de Mémoires, je me sers d'une autre plume. Je cerne la vérité d'aussi près que je peux.

De retour à la ferme, je retrouvais mon lit dans le réduit sur l'écurie, j'écoutais les bœufs ruminer, je respirais l'odeur

mêlée du fumier et des caroubes. Vite le phonographe, vite les machines, vite les fusils. Maintenant je savais me servir du Flobert et tirer, c'était la guerre. Un jour, je tuerai un rouge-gorge. J'aurai du sang plein les mains et soudain honte de moi. Ma mère était triste parce que je n'étais pas un bon élève. Je ne fréquentais que des cancres, j'employais des gros mots, je n'écoutais rien. « Et que fait ton mari » ? demandait ma grand-mère, soudain inquiète. L'oncle Jules appellera mon père « Henri » mais ma grand-mère ne dira jamais que « ton mari ». Elle ajoutera parfois : « M. Dematons ». Elle apprenait qu'habillé en militaire, il servait au Palais d'Hiver, près de la cathédrale. Elle haussait les épaules.

Au bout de quelques jours, je m'ennuyais. Rien n'était plus comme avant, la ville me manquait, mes copains aussi. Non sans plaisir, je regagnais a Alger.

Le jeudi, avec ma mère, nous allions à l'épicerie fine, en haut de la rue Michelet. Ma tante Marie bavardait beaucoup avec les clients, sa fille, une Marie aussi, servait la semoule, les conserves, la confiture. Je grignotais du chocolat, des biscuits. Je n'ai jamais entendu les tramways chanter qu'à Alger dans les tournants : une longue note puissante, qui variait de ton. Parfois, quand le convoi descendait, le wattman freinait et lâchait du sable sur les rails, les roues de la motrice grondaient, le sable écrasé fumait. Un illustré faisait fureur en 1916, *les Pieds nickelés* : je dévorais leurs aventures et m'en inspirais. Le quartier du plateau Saulière était bien fréquenté, on ne criait pas dans les cinémas. Nous passions l'après-midi dans l'odeur des pruneaux et du pétrole dont on se servait pour les lampes, bien qu'on commençât à s'éclairer au gaz de ville, comme nous, rue Montaigne. La lumière du gaz était blanche, un peu bleue, mais ses manchons délicats s'usaient vite. Certains magasins de la rue Michelet avaient déjà l'électricité.

Nous reprenions le tram jusqu'à Bab el-Oued avec un ticket de dix centimes. Nous montions dans ce qu'on appelait une jardinière pour mieux voir. Alger défilait ; bientôt les Facultés, la Grande Poste qui ressemblait à une mosquée, puis la rue d'Isly où, quand il était là, mon frère Robert déambulait dans la foule en lançant des œillades aux filles ; le convoi contournait la statue de Bugeaud, passait devant le square Bresson et l'Opéra où était rappelée la mort du poète Regnard, captif des Barbaresques, puis devant le Tantonville où, quand

il était là, mon frère Robert emmenait des femmes au café-concert. De là, on avait un aperçu du port, on entendait des sirènes de navires, puis c'était l'étroite rue Bab-Azoun et la porte où le chevalier Pons de Balaguer avait, en 1541, planté sa dague en s'écriant : « Nous reviendrons. » Puis les arcades avec le côté des riches et le côté des pauvres, le Petit-Duc et les Deux-Magots, la merveilleuse pâtisserie Fille devant laquelle le tram changeait de câble et d'aiguillage, puis la place du Gouvernement où l'on vendait le *Papa Louette,* la rue Bab el-Oued et ses arcades puantes, et enfin mon lycée. Nous descendions avenue Durando, nous habitions près de la fabrique de cigarettes Bastos. D'une joyeuse voix modulée, des vendeurs de légumes vantaient leurs belles carottes, leurs patates douces, leurs haricots mange-tout.

Où était la guerre ? Il y avait des cartes de rationnement pour le pain, mais on ne manquait de rien. Les deuils ne se remarquaient que par les femmes en noir et les persiennes tirées de Mme Trouette. Les nouvelles circulaient, des multitudes de soldats traversaient la mer. La guerre commençait sur notre cheminée avec les débris de shrapnell, les douilles d'obus à fleurs d'iris et les photographies : mon frère Robert nu-tête en sous-lieutenant, gaillard, provocateur ; mon frère René en barbu devant sa cagna, méconnaissable, à côté d'un canon en batterie. Ici, le soleil entrait à flot, la mer n'était pas loin. Les petits télégraphistes se faufilaient pour porter aux familles les fatales nouvelles. Dans les douars aussi. A la Casbah aussi. Là, on ne les voyait pas.

Le dimanche, parfois, pour nous distraire, après déjeuner, mon père nous emmenait chez les Clauze. Les Clauze avaient déjà perdu un fils à la guerre et ne sortaient jamais. Nous prenions l'autre ligne de tramway, la ligne grenat des CFRA plus proche du rivage. Après le Champ de manœuvre, juste avant le Jardin d'Essai, la voie longeait une plage de galets où la mer était toujours agitée. C'est là que, plus tard, le jeune Albert Camus encore inconnu qui viendra de publier *l'Envers et l'Endroit,* annoncera à son ami Max-Pol Fouchet qu'il lui a pris la fille qu'ils aimaient tous deux et qu'il va épouser, lui, Camus. Max-Pol répondra : « Eh bien soyez heureux », et Camus conclura : « Tu es encore plus grand que je ne pensais. »

Là étaient les quartiers populaires de Belcourt, une zone

noire que je trouvais nauséabonde, où était jadis le palais de l'agha, chef des troupes de l'ancienne Régence de 1830. On descendait du tram, les Clauze habitaient dans un immeuble morne, il y avait des barrières partout. On aurait cru que la mer n'était pas la même. Le vent lui-même semblait pourri.

Les Clauze étaient des Champenois, des « pays » de mon père. Au deuxième étage, leur appartement étroit faisait face à l'énorme cylindre peint en gris, emberlificoté de tuyauteries d'une usine à gaz qui empuantissait. « C'est calme », disaient-ils. Ancien employé à l'administration des chemins de fer, M. Clauze était minuscule, tondu de près, mince de ceinture et humble de sa personne. Il veillait à ce que Mme Clauze fût pour nous en grand soin : le café au lait prêt en un clin d'œil, la boîte de biscuits sur la table. M. Clauze, triste et réservé, ravivait chez mon père des souvenirs de Bar-sur-Aube et de Brienne-le-Château, leur paradis perdu ; Mme Clauze écoutait, le visage illuminé. Les Clauze demandaient des nouvelles de mes frères qu'ils avaient aperçus pendant leur permission. Mon père s'alourdissait de gloire. Ma mère, toujours un peu pincée quand elle venait là, et moi semblions de trop. Pour elle, on sentait que les Clauze n'étaient pas de notre condition sociale. Sur la cheminée des Clauze, il y avait les mêmes douilles d'obus à fleurs d'iris ciselées et des photos encadrées : leur autre fils était zouave aussi, mais pas officier comme Robert. La guerre revenait, déesse lointaine, mystérieuse et aveugle, distribuant trophées ou mort. Le nez sur la grille d'une courte balustrade devant la fenêtre, je regardais, après la masse de l'usine à gaz, les terrains vagues qui descendaient jusqu'à la mer livide, j'attendais que la conversation tarisse. Il n'y avait chez les Clauze ni phonographe, ni livre d'images, ni appareil de TSF. Chez nous la TSF n'apparaîtra qu'après la guerre. Ce qui se passait, on ne le savait que par les lettres et les journaux. Quand les Clauze nous rendaient notre visite, ma mère les recevait avec une tarte et des œufs à la neige, l'air pur entrait à flots par le balcon, mon père offrait un petit cigare. Plus tard, une certaine égalité s'établira entre les Clauze et nous, quand mon père, en retraite, réduira aussi ce qu'il appelait, comme l'oncle Désiré, son « train de vie » et que je serai au séminaire. « Nous avons vu les Clauze », me dira encore ma mère un temps, puis les Clauze s'engloutiront dans l'oubli. Toute ma vie, chaque fois que je viendrai à Alger, je

penserai à Camus qui habita par là, un peu plus haut, rue de Lyon, avec sa mère, veuve de guerre ; je me souviendrai du temps qui durait tellement chez les Clauze et de la barre de chocolat qu'ils me glissaient dans une poche quand nous partions. Le quartier n'est pas mieux aujourd'hui avec les HLM et les réservoirs de pétrole. Les quais d'Alger s'étendent jusque-là, souvent vides.

Nous reprenions le tram rouge. Aux arrêts, le receveur lançait le signal du départ avec une trompette ridicule au son aigre. Ça faisait quand même une promenade. L'après-midi du dimanche était moins désolé.

A ce moment de mon enfance, j'ai hâte de rejoindre mes frères. J'aurai toute ma vie hâte de ce qui me manque. Le désir de devenir un autre me brûlera et une bête féroce dévorera tout ce que j'atteindrai. La sagesse, je l'attends encore.

La guerre, nous, les mauvais élèves de 1917, nous ne la faisions pas au Chemin des Dames, mais à notre professeur de latin et à son gilet semé de petites fleurs. Nous provoquions de beaux chahuts. Nous discutions sans fin des galons, des décorations et des insignes des uniformes comme des caractéristiques des navires qui mouillaient dans le port, nous nous frôlions avec une sourde volupté à l'atmosphère de luxe, nous nous roulions dans les vapeurs que certaines femmes tiraient derrière elles. A l'idée de compter pour si peu en face des héros, je rejetais toute contrainte. Pour essayer de me dompter, mes parents me conduisirent un jour au Palais de justice. Là, dans une salle d'audience vide, un huissier en robe — un de leurs amis sans doute — me parla de prison. « C'est plein de rats. Que feras-tu quand ils viendront te boulotter ? » Je regardai l'homme avec mépris : « Je leur ficherai des coups de pied. Je les écraserai. »

De cette parodie de jugement il me resta une impression d'humiliation et de révolte quand soudain, un matin de novembre, un bruit de cloches, de foule et de sirènes emplit la ville. Dans les rues grouillantes de monde, les trams avancèrent lentement dans le grelottement de leur timbre avec des grappes de yaouleds accrochés aux marchepieds, des musiques déferlèrent, le désordre éclata en fanfare. C'était l'armistice. Je

crus à une fantasia qui ne finirait pas. Je me trompai. On sonna. C'était Mme Trouette, en chapeau et en robe chic, avec sa chevelure brique. Ma mère lui offrit du café. Elle admira les douilles des obus à fleurs de lis. C'était chaque fois la même chose, elle voulut voir de près les photographies de mes frères, se pâma sur Robert, ma mère en était toute triste à cause de René. Mon père dit à Mme Trouette : « Il a les mêmes cheveux que vous. Tout rouges... » Elle sourit : « Mais lui, il est vivant, et moi... » Mon père craignait qu'elle ne s'incrustât, mais non, elle s'en alla presque tout de suite.

L'ordre se rétablit, la discipline aussi, mon père fut démobilisé, mes mauvaises notes l'accablèrent. « Elève intelligent mais dissipé et qui ne se donne aucun mal. » Le proviseur décidait de me maintenir en sixième. Mon père crut que je devenais un voyou. Mon ancienne institutrice, Mlle Guédant, qui venait nous visiter de temps en temps se désolait. Comme ma mère fréquentait beaucoup les églises et que, ramené à Dieu par elle, mon père assistait à la messe des hommes à la cathédrale, l'idée d'aller plus loin, pour moi, leur vint peut-être, ou peut-être voulurent-ils remercier le ciel d'avoir épargné mes frères dans la tuerie la plus dévastatrice que l'Europe eût connu, ou plutôt cédèrent-ils au zèle que déployait l'administration diocésaine à recruter. On me parla du séminaire comme d'un idéal d'instruction et d'élévation. A la fin de la guerre, l'Eglise d'Afrique resplendissait. Un orateur de talent et de belle prestance, Mgr Bollon, rassemblait des foules. Entre cancres, les propos que nous échangions étaient autres : il nous venait à l'esprit que le caporalisme qui sévissait au lycée pouvait faire place à de la douceur et de la câlinerie, nous étions tentés de suivre des cours et de gagner des diplômes par d'autres moyens que les punitions, ce que l'éducation religieuse laissait miroiter à nos yeux. Ne confondîmes-nous pas le séminaire qui renaissait de ses cendres à Saint-Eugène avec le collège des jésuites de Notre-Dame d'Afrique qui couverait bientôt dans ses classes les rejetons de toute la nomenklatura algéroise ? Le bruit courut parmi nous que les élèves du séminaire avaient du café au lait tous les matins et, le dimanche, du chocolat. Etions-nous si maltraités chez nous et au lycée ? Toujours est-il que la chaude exhalaison des croissants eut un effet qu'on n'attendait pas. Tous en bloc, nous nous déclarâmes pour les séductions, nous vou-

lûmes faire échec aux méthodes de prytanée militaire qu'employait le lycée Bugeaud. Ce jour-là, en arrivant à l'heure du déjeuner, je déclarai à mes parents éberlués : « Je veux entrer au séminaire. » Ma mère fondit en larmes.

Ce fut impressionnant. On me céda. Je ne me demandai pas si c'était là pour eux le rachat d'une faute lointaine. Je n'en savais rien. Ils ne s'entendaient plus. Ma mère souffrait. Pour moi, c'était le moyen d'échapper à tout, et, en plus, l'eldorado. Trois mois plus tard, à l'automne, j'y étais.

III

Les caroubes de Dieu

L A VEILLE, une voiture était passée prendre la cantine en bois où mes affaires étaient serrées. Ce jour-là, au début de l'après-midi, ma mère, chapeautée et vêtue de noir, me conduisit en tram à Saint-Eugène, banlieue résidentielle de la bonne société d'Alger, sur la côte ouest. Dans la calme rue Salvandy bordée de grilles, au 55, nous grimpâmes timidement, par le jardin, vers une villa que l'autorité ecclésiastique avait louée en attendant que fût prêt le vrai séminaire, l'antique, celui d'avant la confiscation des biens du clergé, et que le gouvernement général venait de restituer à l'archevêché.

Un chemin en gradins conduisait, entre des orangers, à une bâtisse en équerre dont je ne vis d'abord que la cour de graviers, encombrée de parents et d'élèves ébahis parmi lesquels je cherchais les joyeux cancres, mes anciens camarades. Avaient-ils confondu, eux aussi, avec le riche collège des jésuites ? Avaient-ils changé d'avis ? Il n'y avait autour de moi que des inconnus. Un prêtre massif en soutane se présenta comme le Supérieur, nous tendit une main grasse et molle et, d'un geste vague : « Voyez comme il sera bien »..., il montra le réfectoire, les études, les classe, la chapelle. Un autre lazariste, plus jeune et souriant, nous mena à un pavillon devant lequel je reconnus ma cantine : le dortoir, divisé en chambres sans portes, avec des lits qui n'étaient pas faits. Ma mère tâta avec inquiétude la sangle métallique du mien, le matelas de crin plié en deux, le boudin du polochon, les draps rugueux. Sous les couvertures rêches, elle cacha un gros paquet de gâteaux de patates douces à la cannelle dont j'étais friand, puis nous gagnâmes le parloir où un crucifix dominait une confusion de chuchotements, de valises et de couffins.

J'entendis que, dans un an, **nous** serions installés tout en haut, sur un éperon voisin de la basilique Notre-Dame d'Afrique. De là, parmi les oliviers de la vallée des Consuls, la vue sur la mer était, paraît-il, prodigieuse. Tout le monde levait la tête vers l'avancée d'un mur ocre qui, sans que je le sache encore, allait devenir pour moi, plus tard, comme une citadelle et la terrasse des contemplations.

Ma mère et moi n'avions plus grand-chose à nous dire. Le pas décisif franchi, il fallait se quitter. Ma mère m'embrassa en cachant ses larmes et s'éloigna d'une démarche un peu cassée comme si elle portait le poids d'une rançon à verser. Tout à coup, je me rappelai l'orphelinat Saint-Vincent-de-Paul, à Mustapha, où je l'accompagnais certains dimanches, en alternance avec les Clauze et l'épicerie fine, embrasser deux cousines de mon âge, d'une troisième tante qui était veuve, des filles en tablier gris et au visage triste, avec des tresses dans le dos. Il y avait le même soleil, les mêmes jardins, le même ciel lessivé. Simplement, ici, la barrette noire à pompon de ces messieurs les lazaristes remplaçait les ailes de la cornette des sœurs.

J'eus conscience qu'il m'était arrivé quelque chose, je ne savais quoi d'implacable. J'avais perdu la rue, le timbre des tramways, les cris de Bab el-Oued, la liberté. Retrouverais-je jamais, entre les vignes et les haies de cyprès, la ferme de ma grand-mère et de mon oncle Jules, et les odeurs du fourrage, du fumier et des bœufs? L'étrangeté du monde me frappa. J'avais un costume bleu marine à veston croisé. Les anciens arboraient une casquette à visière courte et à torsade avec une croix dorée dans des lauriers. Une cloche fêlée sonna. Je fis quelques pas dans la cour, ramassai sur le gravier la gousse longue, épaisse, un peu arquée et tordue d'une caroube tombée d'un arbre, et me mis à en grignoter la pulpe sucrée. A la ferme, je l'ai dit, on distribuait parfois une ration de caroubes broyées aux chevaux pour leur flanquer du nerf. Moi aussi j'aimais ce goût de miel, je recrachai rêveusement les noyaux durs et lisses comme des galets minuscules. Qui sait? Je deviendrais peut-être un cheval, je galoperais, on me bouchonnerait pour essuyer ma sueur et activer la circulation de mon sang. Je pensais qu'un cheval pouvait s'échapper quand l'ombre épaisse du Supérieur, qui s'appelait M. Payen, pesa sur moi. « Que mangez-vous là? » demanda-t-il sur un

ton d'étonnement. Sa face lunaire s'inquiéta. Une large barbe s'étalait sur ses joues, son regard divergent semblait me fouiller. Quel œil dirigeait-il sur moi et quel œil devais-je fixer pour lui répondre ? « Une caroube, monsieur.

— Allons, dit-il en me prenant la gousse poisseuse qu'il jeta avec répugnance, ce n'est pas propre. Qu'avez-vous ? Vous n'êtes pas bien ? Nous allons prier à la chapelle. Voyez : c'est là-bas. »

Il me montra, au deuxième étage, des fenêtres sur les vitres desquelles était collé du papier gommé à fleurs de lis. Je récitai déjà les premiers mots du Notre-Père. L'homme qui était mon père était si dur, si replié sur lui-même, si étranger. Ma mère était si douloureuse. Ainsi Dieu avait remplacé pour moi ma famille, la ville et les chevaux, des camarades m'avaient trahi, je me sentis à mon tour orphelin de tout.

Le Supérieur tapa dans ses mains, et avec l'aide de quelques-uns de ces messieurs qu'on appelait « les directeurs », nous fit mettre en rangs. Un silence tomba. M. Payen nous invita à nous recueillir, à chasser les idées du monde que nous avions quitté et à tout ramener au Seigneur. D'une voix qu'il voulait joyeuse il nous annonça qu'après la chapelle nous irions faire nos lits, que nous dînerions et que, le lendemain matin, à cinq heures, nous serions réveillés par une exhortation à élever nos âmes : *Benedicamus Domino.* Nous devrions répondre : *Deo gratias.* Plus tard, je pensai qu'il aurait plutôt dû nous dire : « Vous ne serez pas malheureux avec nous. Vous irez deux fois par semaine en promenade à la mer. » Cela m'aurait consolé puisque mes parents ne me menaient jamais plus sur les plages, et même me les interdisaient. Je ne m'aventurais aux bains Matarès ou Padovani, à Bab el-Oued, qu'avec les garnements qui m'avaient décidé à entrer au séminaire et qui n'étaient pas là, justement. La voix du Supérieur était la voix même du devoir, la voix du censeur du lycée, ennuyeuse, fatale, monotone, inexorable. Du coup, je me mis à douter de tout, même du café au lait, des brioches et du chocolat, et je regrettai l'aimable discipline du lycée Bugeaud, mes mauvaises notes, les colles, les classes insipides, la mine sévère du surveillant général et mes retours à la maison par l'avenue fabuleuse de la Bouzaréa. Tout se brouilla soudain à ma vue : la cour, la terrasse, la mer entre les orangers plus bas, et jusqu'à la lumière. Dans le sentiment que je vivais

un moment important comme j'en avais déjà connu quelques-uns, il y eut cet espoir fragile que Dieu avait placé ici pour moi un arbre avec des caroubes, comme pour un cheval.

J'étais pris au piège tellement mieux qu'au Palais de justice d'où j'étais revenu. Là, je me sentis coincé dans l'implacable. Est-ce à partir de ce moment-là que, par la suite, j'ai su encaisser en silence quand je me reconnaissais responsable de ce qui m'arrivait ?

Mes parents pouvaient croire que je l'avais voulu, puisque pendant les grandes vacances je n'en avais pas démordu, que j'avais commencé à fréquenter la nouvelle église Saint-Vincent-de-Paul du quartier de l'Esplanade : un vaste hangar avec des chaises, un autel, une chaire, un bon curé au visage fripé qui venait de Lyon. Je regrettais l'église Saint-Joseph sur son tertre au-dessus du marché de Bab el-Oued, au pied de la colline de Notre-Dame d'Afrique, tout près de l'hôpital Maillot. C'était plein de vie, de cris, d'odeurs fortes. Là, non. C'était plat, ça ressemblait plutôt à un temple protestant.

Plus intime, le séminaire était un lieu clos où la règle était le silence. Des élèves plus jeunes que moi, soudain chamboulés, pleuraient. Ceux-là, je les méprisai, il fallait se montrer à la hauteur. Avec quelques camarades de mon âge, il nous parut amusant de déballer nos affaires. Il faisait doux. Nous n'osions pas chiper des oranges sur les orangers du jardin. C'était la première fois que je couchais dans un dortoir, avec une veilleuse dans chaque chambre. Je m'endormis avec un parfum de patates douces et de cannelle dans la bouche. Faisait-il jour quand on nous réveilla ? Après la prière, la méditation et la messe, on nous conduisit au réfectoire. Naturellement il n'y eut pas de café au lait mais de la soupe. Elle était bonne. Nous avions faim. J'avais douze ans. Il y avait l'électricité partout pour éclairer, au lieu du gaz comme chez nous.

J'ai toujours hésité à parler de cela. Par pudeur ? Par honte ou crainte de quoi ? A cause des regards qui se posaient sur moi jadis quand on apprenait que j'avais passé huit ans de ma jeunesse au séminaire. Etais-je un animal sacré ? Un

renégat ? Un défroqué ? Ah ! voilà le mot terrible ! Combien d'hommes politiques puissants, combien d'illustres écrivains ont eu le séminaire pour formation ! Combien même ont reçu les ordres mineurs ! Moi pas. On ne les conférait plus avant le service militaire, il y avait trop de « déchet ».

Au fond de moi, dans le doute qu'une période aussi longue et aussi importante de ma vie, où la glaise molle que j'étais a pris forme définitive, je n'ai presque jamais parlé de ce temps-là. Au fond de moi, si étonnant que cela paraisse, je ne suis pas encore sûr de porter un jugement clair.

De ces huit années à la fois obscures et lumineuses, il ne me reste qu'une félicité spartiate. Le séminaire a fait de moi l'homme que je suis. Il m'a séparé des miens pour m'introduire dans la maison du père ; il m'a cruellement imposé une autre famille que la mienne, j'y ai été heureux et je ne serai heureux ensuite que lorsque je passerai de ce séminaire-là, provincial et campagnard, à un autre séminaire armé : l'école militaire, le régiment de tirailleurs, l'escadrille des Alpes, l'école de pilotage, l'escadrille de Sétif, le camp de terreur dans la RAF en Grande-Bretagne pendant la guerre. Le séminaire m'a sauvé de la médiocrité, puisque j'étais déjà un mauvais élève. Sans le séminaire je serais peut-être devenu un chenapan, un vaurien. Mais un enfant entre là pour devenir prêtre. Dans *le Rouge et le Noir,* il s'agit beaucoup aussi pour le héros d'une double trahison : s'il cède à l'amour de Mme de Rênal, Julien Sorel trahit sa vocation et il pousse Mme de Rênal à rompre des serments qu'elle a prêtés. Quand on quitte le séminaire, on est ce héros-là, condamné aux exigences les plus hautes, poursuivi toute une vie par la question de savoir si on est digne ou non de l'appel qu'on a cru entendre, où Dieu culmine et parfois fulmine.

Il me semble que, de séminariste, je suis devenu le chevalier errant ou le templier que j'aurais aimé être et que peut-être je suis toujours. Jeune barbare enfermé au séminaire, je ne me sentis pas malheureux. Sinon je me serais jeté dans les bras de ma mère quand elle venait me voir le dimanche et je l'aurais suppliée de me ramener à la maison. Au contraire ! J'étais reconnaissant de ce que ma mère m'apportait : les mêmes gâteaux de patates douces, des oranges, du chocolat. Les vacances m'apparaissaient toujours désirables parce qu'elles rompaient le rythme de la discipline et que je

pouvais dormir plus longtemps, mais tout me manquait de ce que j'avais quitté. A l'église de ma paroisse, je critiquais le déroulement des cérémonies auxquelles je participais déjà en surplis ; je critiquais les chants surtout, quand ce n'était pas les prônes du bon curé si paternel. Faut-il l'avouer ? J'avais rompu avec le désordre de ma vie d'élève dissipé et je ne tendais plus qu'à une conduite inflexible. L'idée de célébrer le culte en chasuble ou en chape m'aidait déjà à me déguiser en officiant, comme, pendant la guerre, je me déguisais en officier avec les tenues de mon frère Robert, son baudrier, le sabre qu'il avait laissé chez nous. Loin de m'accabler, le terrible emploi du temps du séminaire, lever parfois dans la nuit, débarbouillage à l'eau froide sous des robinets récalcitrants, prière, méditation, examen d'une conscience déjà compliquée à souhait, après quoi ces messieurs disaient chacun leur messe à des autels différents, et nous assistions à la nôtre, servie, à tour de rôle, par deux d'entre nous, coucher à neuf heures, ce sévère emploi du temps me manquait. Les camarades me manquaient aussi et c'était avec une joie sauvage que je retrouvais mon lit au dortoir, ma place dans les rangs et mon banc à l'étude, à la chapelle et au réfectoire.

Une mystique nous avait labourés, ensemencés et vite recouverts, nous n'étions pas comme les autres, Dieu nous avait choisis et nous conduisait à travers les vicissitudes et les iniquités du monde. Nous nous sentions élus. Quand nous allions, deux fois par semaine, en début d'après-midi, en promenade, en rang, à travers les rues de Saint-Eugène et par le boulevard qui longeait la mer, à la pointe Pescade ou dans les collines, une ivresse me gagnait : écouter mourir ou gronder les vagues, contempler les navires qui sortaient du port d'Alger ou y entraient, c'étaient aussi des appels. De quoi ? Vers qui ? Ce romantisme échevelé, le lycée ne l'aurait jamais inspiré. Je me souviens que la première année, toute de bonne soupe, de haricots charançonnés, de bœuf bouilli et d'omelettes aux pommes de terre, nous la passâmes, comme les Hébreux en Égypte, en attente. Notre Terre promise c'était, à hauteur du dôme de la basilique de Notre-Dame d'Afrique mais sur la colline voisine, plus à l'ouest, d'où l'on surplombait la mer de haut, le bâtiment superbe du séminaire, la royale chapelle au clocher en forme de minaret. C'est là que nous grimpâmes l'année d'après. D'une villa banale et sans

âme, nous passions à un château de la chrétienté qu'avec le temps je vois, les fortifications en moins, semblable au Krak des Chevaliers dans le désert de Syrie. Le nôtre était bâti de pierre rose, ses austères façades cachaient les bâtiments mauresques de l'archevêché, des jardins et presque une forêt d'eucalyptus : le cardinal Lavigerie n'avait pas vu petit. Là serpentait la route de la célèbre vallée des Consuls, où résidaient la plupart de ces messieurs les diplomates au temps du dey d'Alger : des palais mystérieux, comme la résidence des Polignac où devaient se cacher tant de secrets , tant de richesses. Il y avait aussi un asile de fous, un carmel, et un ancien fort turc auquel on avait donné le nom de l'amiral Duperré qui commandait l'armada de 1830. Plus haut, dans la colline couverte de lentisques, de chênes verts, d'arbousiers et de cyclamens sauvages, un sémaphore guidait les navires et surveillait la navigation ; au-delà on découvrait le village de la Bouzaréa, où le jeune Camus et le jeune Max-Pol Fouchet, élèves de philosophie des facultés d'Alger, viendront après moi dans un cimetière de terre rouge méditer sur la fragilité des sentiments humains. Là, le ciel est vide. On ne voit pas Alger. On voit la mer, brumeuse dans ses lointains, la baie de soie bleue, l'avancée du cap Matifou, l'immensité.

Je vivrai là sept ans. En sortant de classe ou d'étude, nous débouchions en hurlant sur la cour, vaste terre-plein ocre qui se perdait dans l'azur. Notre dortoir s'ouvrait à l'est. Les chambres de ces messieurs les directeurs et celles du grand séminaire qu'on n'avait pas pu complètement séparer de nous étaient tout en haut. Le vent de la mer soufflait. Il y avait de quoi rêver, mais nous n'avions pas une minute à nous, du matin au soir, sauf pendant les récréations. Quand notre supérieur, M. Payen, se laissa enfin convaincre de mauvais gré qu'il pouvait nous accorder de jouer au football, ce fut pour nous un triomphe dans la furie.

M. Payen n'avait qu'un bon œil, je l'ai dit. Le cher homme suivait avec suspiscion nos allées et venues, nos assises, nos cours et notre participation aux offices. Son inquiétude était permanente. On lui avait confié un troupeau indiscipliné, inculte et populaire. Nous étions, avec les ensoutanés du grand séminaire, une cinquantaine d'élèves. M. Payen enseignait la théologie, il en était docteur. Aux cinq, six ou

sept messieurs de la congrégation de Saint-Vincent-de-Paul, il distribuait notre instruction : français, latin, grec, histoire et géographie, mathématiques et devait nous conduire les uns à la prêtrise, les autres jusqu'à l'orée de la philosophie. Pas de langues étrangères. Pour quoi faire ? Nous n'aurions à parler qu'aux fidèles de la chrétienté, des Européens mélangés d'un peu de toute la Méditerranée. Nous étions dans un pays d'Arabes, mais personne ne songera jamais que l'arabe pouvait nous servir. Un demi-siècle plus tard, mon ancien professeur de grec et de mathématiques, M. Baligand, avec qui je renouerai à Paris, me dira que les professeurs avaient pour directive de ne jamais aborder la question indigène. Pour M. Payen, conscience intègre, magister austère, la population d'Algérie avait le verbe coloré et s'exprimait avec trop de gestes. Il fallait se méfier de ses rejetons, injecter du plomb dans nos cervelles de petits voyous et nous convertir en aspirants au sacerdoce. Quant à l'archevêque, il voulait éviter tout conflit et mériter le soutien du pouvoir établi. Donc les musulmans, dont cependant quelques mosquées avaient été converties en églises, n'existaient qu'à peine. L'archevêque avait pour ambition de succéder au cardinal Lavigerie qui, s'il avait converti les parents d'Amrouche à coups de goupillon, portait aussi des toasts à la République, mais notre archevêque avait aussi pour guides, vers la vie éternelle, saint Augustin, et dans la vie temporelle, M. Louis Bertrand, amouraché de l'Afrique, qui avait écrit une vie de l'évêque d'Hippone puis célébré les premiers colons, le sang des races et les Arabes soumis. Notre bon archevêque présidait ses conférences et frappait la table en s'écriant : « Cet admirable chrétien n'est pas encore de l'Académie !... »

Messieurs les directeurs assistaient à la prière en commun, célébraient leur messe, participaient, les plus jeunes d'entre eux tout au moins, à nos récréations, allant et venant en avant puis en arrière, mains glissées dans les manches, barrette à pompon sur le crâne, ceinture noire et soutane au vent, sans jamais la moindre allusion aux Arabes. En plus de M. Baligand, barbe blonde tirant sur le roux, il y avait M. Anselme, censeur sévère, barbe châtain en houppe renversée, M. Lesage, aux joues et à la lèvre supérieure rasées avec une sorte d'impériale carrée au menton, enfin le professeur de latin aux yeux de biche et à large barbe noire. Etalage de barbes,

exposition de barbes de tous types auxquelles il fallait ajouter les fraîches pilosités des grands séminaristes et le fleuve gris de l'archevêque, le bouc blanc de l'évêque coadjuteur, les pinceaux, blaireaux, colliers, éventails, barbiches, brosses ou queues-de-morue de ces messieurs les curés, vicaires, chanoines, protonotaires ou vicaires généraux qu'il nous arrivait d'approcher dans les cérémonies à la cathédrale ou à Notre-Dame d'Afrique, galerie de faces patibulaires dans les stalles comme dans un funèbre tableau du Greco. Il y en avait une assyrienne, qu'on prétendait parfumée et qui appartenait à un curé mondain. On ne pouvait pas ne pas songer à une suite tragique ou cocasse de condamnés à la prière, offrant un poil élégant et soigné ou à la va-comme-je-te-pousse, sans soin, sans rien. J'en étais hanté. Devrais-je porter la barbe à mon tour ? J'en frémissais déjà, je me sentais farfouillant les tendres joues de ma mère, de ma grand-mère et de la tante Laetitia, la bouche de mes cousines bien-aimées, *horresco referens,* je parlais déjà latin, j'étais en quatrième, lisais *l'Enéide* dans le texte et traduisais Cicéron, belle face rasée. On disait que la barbe était le signe de la virilité, de la sagesse, de l'âge. On nous montrait saint Augustin barbu, et notre archevêque rêvait d'ériger par souscription sur le parvis de Notre-Dame d'Afrique une statue du cardinal Lavigerie barbe au vent. On n'imaginait pas en Algérie de prêtre imberbe, pouvant être confondu avec une femme. Une femme ? Les représentants de la religion catholique devaient rester sans commerce avec les personnes du sexe. La vérité ne pouvait sortir que d'une bouche barbue. La foi elle-même devait l'être.

Pour imiter les musulmans qui n'accordaient de place aux femmes dans les mosquées qu'à l'écart (on n'imaginait pas les femmes se prosternant au milieu des hommes et leur présentant leurs reins), il y avait le dimanche, à la cathédrale, une messe où les femmes, si elles voulaient y assister, devaient se tenir dans les nefs latérales, séparées par des grilles symboliques, ne voyant rien de l'office et entendant mal le prêche. La formule née du tragique de la guerre avait moins de succès, on voulait la redorer. Oui, mais qui allait monter en chaire ? Qui serait digne ? Les sermons que nous subissions au séminaire, car chacun de ces messieurs s'y escrimait le dimanche à tour de rôle, étaient d'un ennui profond. Le Supérieur était le champion : des mots pieux, du déjà entendu, du vent. On

n'écoutait pas. L'archevêque endormait pontificalement, mitre en tête et crosse en main. Ah ! Mgr Bollon ! Seul de tous les orateurs sacrés, Mgr Bollon, dont personne ne savait d'où il venait, avait su emplir, pendant la guerre, la nef au point qu'on se poussait jusque sur les marches de la chaire, l'ancien minbar de la mosquée. Il ne disait pas « mes frères », il ne s'adressait pas au troupeau bêlant des fidèles, il disait « messieurs ». On s'étouffait, on applaudissait à la péroraison, ce dont certains feignaient de s'offusquer. Prétexte de médiocres, car on applaudissait dans les églises au Moyen Age, on riait, on allaitait les nourrissons à la mamelle. Les applaudissements s'étaient éteints depuis que ce qui coulait des tribunes ne méritait pas d'être applaudi. Aucun dignitaire de l'église algérienne ne pardonnera à Mgr Bollon ses succès, son aura, son élégance mâle, sa voix de violoncelle, ses joues rasées sur un court plumet poivre et sel au menton, son front altier, ses gestes sobres, ses allusions à la vie et à la politique enfin, qui sortaient le texte de la banalité et le haussaient à une actualité brûlante. L'auditoire en avait le souffle coupé. J'ai appris là qu'on obtenait l'adhésion populaire en rompant avec le ronronnement, en bousculant les coutumes au besoin, si peu que ce soit, en choquant les bonnes âmes somnolentes qui s'offusquent de rien. Il me semble aussi que le succès obtenu (et pourquoi un séminariste n'aurait-il pas songé à devenir disciple de Mgr Bollon ?) devenait gage de durée et force de loi. Je me trompais.

Sous prétexte de ne pas l'épuiser, on écarta Mgr Bollon. La messe des hommes à la cathédrale se décomposa, la niaiserie triompha, Mgr Bollon se retira dans une villa d'El Biar que de saintes âmes (de saintes femmes, disait-on) lui avaient offerte. Mgr Bollon devint pour nous, si jeunes et tout brûlants de mystique, une figure allégorique. Pour nous, il n'était de fête que si Mgr Bollon y parlait. Vers nous il avait un regard fulgurant. Les vérités qui tombaient de sa bouche n'étaient peut-être pas bénignes pour tout le monde. Pas d'*amen* non plus. Il achevait brusquement et se détournait et nous applaudissions aussi. Nous étions ses fans. Peu à peu, cependant, avec le temps, on l'oublia. Pas moi.

**

Notre professeur de latin participait à nos jeux et au football. Il devait manquer d'affections temporelles car je ne pus pas ne pas remarquer qu'il était amoureux de moi. Econome de la communauté, il me comblait de gâteries, car j'étais gourmand, et m'attirait dans sa chambre. Un jour, je sentis sur mes lèvres ses lèvres à lui, humides dans un frisottis de barbe. Je le repoussai avec horreur et désormais l'évitai. A ce moment-là, un autre de ces messieurs, chauve au regard perçant et à l'esprit pédant, qui professait les sciences, m'adressa des épigrammes à double sens auxquelles j'eus la faiblesse de répondre. A cet âge, je devais être séduisant. N'aurais-je pas été tenté aussi par hasard, par le danger de la provocation ? N'aurais-je pas joué, par sadisme, ma petite putain ? Les billets se montraient terriblement pressants, je n'étais pas naïf au point de ne pas comprendre. J'étais aussi amoureux, mais pas des professeurs. D'un condisciple puis d'un autre, plus jeunes que moi d'un an ou deux, parce qu'ils avaient de beaux yeux. Par quoi est-on séduit ? Soupirs à la promenade, brûlantes pressions des mains, baisers ? Le souvenir de l'économe m'épouvante encore. Que voulais-je alors ? D'impossibles étreintes, des rapprochements de corps nus ? La puberté précoce qui me tourmentait allumait en moi des embrasements qui ne menaient à rien qu'à exciter davantage nos deux bons pères dont le manège n'échappait à personne, sauf peut-être à M. Payen. L'atmosphère du séminaire était-elle, à cause des interdits, sulfureuse ? Il me semble que pendant les vacances, à Alger, j'étais moins troublé, ou alors c'est que je ne savais plus de quel côté lorgner ou que l'ambiance de secret ou d'empêchement du séminaire manquait. En ville, tout était imagination et donc hors d'atteinte, tandis qu'au séminaire la tendresse n'était qu'un désir déguisé, et son objet, à ma portée, flambait et me déchirait. Que de regards amoureux échangés, que de frôlements, que d'adorations se détournaient de Dieu pour ses créatures ! De quoi m'accusais-je désespérément, à genoux, devant M. Baligand, mon confesseur régulier, choisi par moi parce qu'il était de tous ces messieurs le plus convenable, le plus rigide, peut-être pas le plus bienveillant mais le plus insensible à la fièvre qui frémissait partout, palpitante, et parfois franchissait les étages quand elle ne s'égarait pas à l'abri des autels et des jardins ? A M. Baligand, je m'accusais de mauvaises pensées, de désirs

impurs. Impurs de quoi ? Le savais-je ? Saurai-je seulement, plus tard, plus tard ? Que faire ? Où aller ? Que dire après la pénitence rituelle de deux *pater* et de deux *ave* ? Baisser les yeux, se remettre à l'étude, éviter l'œil soupçonneux de M. Payen encoigné, immobile et silencieux, sous une arcade du cloître comme une chouette borgne ? Echapper à l'inflexible rival de l'économe qui, sous prétexte de censure morale, épiait tous les gestes, tous les déplacements, toutes les visites aux confesseurs chez qui n'importe qui pouvait, à tout moment, être autorisé à se rendre ?

On croirait que c'est une part d'enfer que je traverse, que le séminaire de Saint-Eugène, près de la colline sacrée où sonnent les cloches de Notre-Dame d'Afrique est le vestibule de Sodome et de Gomorrhe. J'entends déjà des amicales d'anciens élèves, qui en savent et en ont fait bien plus que moi, condamner avec indignation ce que j'ose suggérer et se scandalisant, naturellement. Arrière, fils de pharisiens, hypocrites fripouilles ! Je ne suggère rien. Je ne dénonce rien. J'ai trop d'admiration pour M. Baligand et trop de dévotion pour mes chers lazaristes, moins habiles que les jésuites. Je suis passé par leurs mains vénérables, je sais de quelles frustrations ils souffraient tous : non des biens de ce monde dont ils se moquaient, mais de chaleur et d'amitié. M. Payen, cerbère soupçonneux, croyait que la sévérité était la clef du système, de la discipline et de la piété. Son échec m'a enseigné que ce n'est pas la hargne qui doit régir une communauté et que le gros œil bigle qui nous effrayait un moment ne nous inspirait que le souci de le prendre en défaut. Enfer ? Non. Paradis. Tout était merveille dans ce minuscule univers et dans nos consciences qui s'ouvraient au monde. Si, trop souvent dans ce que je prenais pour une atteinte à la sainte règle, j'ai vu ou aperçu du mystère interdit ou des flammes, ce fut par ignorance, dans la fraîcheur et la candeur de nos âmes. Il ne se passait rien. La plus énorme de nos fautes n'était qu'une mince curiosité, un élan ou un débordement de nos cœurs, rien qui pût à jamais nous marquer. Seuls des prédestinés que je rencontrerai plus tard, pourquoi les nommer ? chercheront l'enfer en eux-mêmes. Je me suis demandé si je pouvais citer un nom sans nuire à la mémoire de qui aurait quatre-vingt-quinze ans s'il vivait. Il a dû rejoindre ses frères au cimetière des lazaristes, après avoir vécu un temps à la maison mère,

95, rue de Sèvres à Paris où j'ai vu M. Baligand, tout menu tant il était vieux, et que je ne reconnus pas tout d'abord parce qu'il était rasé. Qui survit des maîtres de ma jeunesse ? Je me sens mystérieusement, mystiquement uni à eux par un réseau de racines emmêlées, et nous formons un vraie communauté, nous sommes en route vers ce qui nous comblera dans l'infini et, surtout, conscients des interdits dans quoi ils nous ligotaient, ils approuvent l'audace que j'ai dû avoir pour me délivrer.

Quand nous sortions en troupe dans la vallée des Consuls, nous courions d'un bout à l'autre de la promenade, nous contemplions en silence le gouffre béant de la mer et du ciel, nous ne fuyions pas les lèvres barbues d'un serviteur de Dieu un instant dévoyé, nous dévalions à la poursuite de notre âme. Ressemblions-nous à des anges de la Mitidja ou à des anges de péché ? Moi, peut-être, né d'une pauvre faute dont je commençais à me douter, de mon père et de ma mère. Je ne savais pas qui j'étais, d'où je venais ni où j'allais. Plus tard, bientôt, Camus et Max-Pol Fouchet viendront aussi interroger sur la vie et sur la mort le même maquis de lentisques, d'arbouses et d'absinthe sauvage.

J'y suis encore. J'ai un autre regard pour la colline du sémaphore couverte d'écailles de grès et de silex, notre promenade de prédilection : à l'est les crêtes bleues de Kabylie, la mer en demi-lune semblait monter vers moi et battre au pied des rochers. De là on apercevait les avancées du port d'Alger, la digue qui menait à l'Amirauté, l'ancien nid de pirates, nous entendions la rumeur de la ville, les cris d'enfants et les chants de coqs des maisons d'en bas, plus proches. Je ne savais pas encore qu'il y avait presque un siècle, écrasées de beauté, de chaleur, d'odeurs, assourdies, les troupes de M. de Bourmont s'étaient emmêlées dans les ravins où nous jouions à nous perdre. Nous nous cherchions, nous nous appelions nous-mêmes et qui encore, et quoi ? Les astres invisibles sous la force du soleil ? Les navires au large ? Il n'y a rien de pervers ni de corrompu chez l'ange qui grandit de jour en jour. Il n'a même pas été effleuré autrefois par les allées et venues de l'oncle Jules à l'aube, du côté du douar, le fusil sous le bras ; ni contaminé par la louche et sournoise multitude que l'oncle Jules appelait les bicots. Sans qu'il le sache, il est déjà à cause

de la lumière sur les collines d'Alger, moins fils de la chrétienté que fils du vent ou fils de chacal.

*

Le dimanche après-midi, à deux heures, ma mère se présentait au parloir avec un lourd couffin. Le trolley ne menait qu'à Notre-Dame d'Afrique. Après, chargée comme elle était, elle continuait à pied. Elle me demandait si j'étais heureux, si je n'avais besoin de rien. Elle sentait que je lui échappais et en même temps voulait se montrer digne servante du Seigneur et de ses desseins. Avare de baisers et de nouvelles, je gardais mon mystère pour moi. Elle n'osait pas me forcer : je ne lui appartenais plus, on nous le laissait entendre, je voyais là un signe qui m'emplissait d'orgueil, je me taisais. Elle me parlait des uns, des autres, des voisins, d'une famille qu'elle ne fréquentait plus, de Mme Trouette qui était morte, des Clauze qui ne venaient plus parce qu'ils se faisaient vieux. Et puis, à présent, on s'éclairait aussi à l'électricité. Sauf dans les rues, où l'allumeur de becs de gaz passait toujours.

Mon père l'accompagnait parfois. Rarement. La curiosité le poussait à interroger un de ces messieurs pour savoir où j'en étais, il aurait bien voulu visiter le réfectoire, les dortoirs, il n'avait droit qu'à la chapelle, vaste comme une église, sonore et vide. Il appréciait la cour, le panorama, et, vite, s'embêtait. Il entraînait ma mère, ils repartaient, je courais cacher mes gâteries sous mon lit et retournais vite jouer au foot, de plus en plus égoïste et cruel. L'oncle Jules ne venait jamais, il ne pouvait pas, de si loin, et aurait-il osé ? Et Meftah ? Je les voyais quand nous retournions à la ferme, ma mère et moi, aux vacances, de moins en moins souvent. Et mes cousines ? Je n'osais plus parler d'elles, on me laissait entendre qu'il fallait éviter la compagnie des femmes, sauf notre mère, nos tantes. Mes cousines, à qui je pensais parfois, devenaient un interdit. Même en vacances, j'étais comme dans un couvent, je devais renoncer au monde, mes cousines étaient le monde. A elles seules ? C'était peut-être à cause d'elles que ma mère n'osait plus rester longtemps à la ferme.

Ça devait se savoir, ma naissance irrégulière. Tout se sait

dans les milieux d'Eglise. On sait mais on se tait. D'où peut-être le regard indulgent, parfois souriant de M. Baligand. « *O felix culpa* », me disait-il parfois tout bas, en confidence, presque en complicité. Je ne mis pas longtemps à comprendre où il voulait en venir avec cette « heureuse faute ». A présent, comment le revoir, de si loin, dans ce linceul noir de la soutane qui les enveloppait tous ? Son visage doux respire la finesse, il parle peu, sait écouter, fait ses cours de grec et de mathématiques avec délices. Sa piété est sûre, tranquille, sans excès, un tantinet savante, sans écarts démonstratifs. Il bricole dans ses batteries et ses appareils de TSF, écoute les ondes, se perd dans ce qu'on n'appelle pas encore le cosmos, mais l'éther, domaine mystérieux qui n'est pas celui de M. Payen ni d'aucun autre de ces messieurs. Réservé à M. Baligand, à sa barbe blonde tirant sur le roux, à son regard qui flotte, à son pince-nez qui laisse, quand il l'enlève, une trace rouge à la base du nez. Sa chambre a par deux fenêtres étroites vue sur la mer. Elle est encombrée d'un bric-à-brac de bobines, de variomètres et de condensateurs qu'il repousse pour loger une chaise et un prie-Dieu quand il confesse. Sa table déborde de toutes sortes de trucs. Un long fil d'antenne court sur la terrasse, s'accroche au clocher : la TSF menait déjà les nations, et il écoutait dans la nuit ce qui bougeait, ce qui parlait de l'autre côté de l'espace. Pas du nôtre : l'Afrique était muette. Ou alors, il entendait le vent de sable au-dessus du désert. Déjà il expérimentait des lampes à électrodes, pareilles à des insectes dans des ampoules, mais c'était la galène, ce brin de minerai de plomb bleuâtre qui détectait les courants de haute fréquence à faible densité. On piquait une pointe de cristal et tout à coup... M. Baligand savait aussi partager. Parfois, en récompense de quelque chose, il nous tendait un casque à écouteurs et la musique emplissait nos oreilles : des chants célestes, des courants de mystère. Où était Dieu là-dedans ? « Dieu est partout », répondait M. Baligand. « Dieu est tout, nous ne sommes rien... » Tout à coup, il se repentait d'avoir pu me laisser croire que nous n'étions rien. « Enfin ce rien pour lequel le Christ est venu. Vous voyez ?... » Non, je ne voyais pas. Je me demandais souvent si j'avais la vocation. Nous nous le demandions tous : la question majeure était ce vœu de chasteté qui nous séparait des femmes. Le reste, la foi, la prière, ne posait pas de problème. Pour M. Baligand, la vocation était une grâce. Elle m'avait été

109

accordée, je l'avais, je pouvais la perdre, tout dépendait de moi. Auprès de lui, représentant du savoir et de la raison, je me sentais assuré, il veillait sur moi, mais lui sans aucune idée biscornue derrière la tête, il avait dû une bonne fois briser les reins à tous ces machins-là, pas le moindre désir chez lui de me serrer sur son cœur ou d'effleurer mon front de ses lèvres. C'était un pur, un homme de Dieu, et qui savait rire.

Les années passaient. Les jours où nous allions à la cathédrale, aux fêtes carillonnées, pour chanter, presque toute la semaine pascale, nous descendions de la colline à pied, nous traversions Bab el-Oued, nous entendions parfois d'horribles couacs sonores à cause des soutanes qui nous accompagnaient. Pour nous c'était une récréation, nous perforions le monde impur de notre pureté. Après la cérémonie, ma mère venait à la sacristie m'embrasser puis s'en allait tristement tandis que notre mince file d'uniformes bleus à boutons d'or et à casquettes à lauriers repartait en babillant et en reluquant les mouquères à jambes nues, les putains bariolées des bordels proches. Nous étions un peu ivres, nous avions banqueté chez les petites sœurs des pauvres qui nous gâtaient, nous remontions comme des aiglons sur leur rocher, nous nous glissions en frissonnant sous les plumes d'une chouette qui nous gardait d'un bec acéré.

Notre professeur de français, M. Lesage, ne vivait que dans les livres, avec ce qu'il aimait, et ce qu'il aimait, c'était Chateaubriand, Victor Hugo, Musset, Lamartine, il nous les lisait en extase, le front dans les nues, transporté ailleurs, transfiguré, et d'une voix de fausset désincarné qui montait peu à peu jusqu'à éclater. Nous le regardions bouche bée. Déjà, il sortait de l'ordinaire avec sa lèvre supérieure et ses joues rasées, et un mince collier de barbe de frère de la côte. Avec lui, il fallait s'attendre à tout. Il aimait tellement la littérature qu'il était prêt à nous la livrer comme un diamant, parfois comme une prostituée. Baudelaire, il n'osera pas. Pourtant, il aurait pu :

> Soyez béni, mon Dieu, qui donnez la souffrance
> Comme un divin remède à nos impuretés...

De Verlaine, que je prendrai longtemps pour un saint homme, nous apprendrons *O mon Dieu, vous m'avez blessé d'amour*. Il ne nous disait pas que c'était à cause de Rimbaud.

Il n'osera pas non plus, Rimbaud. Les poèmes renfermaient de la magie, et pour qui savait écrire pareille langue s'ouvrait un univers que je trouvai soudain vertigineux. Quand M. Lesage avait fini, il reposait son livre, et son visage d'astrologue reprenait ses traits familiers. Je m'interrogeais. Quelque chose m'avait transpercé l'âme, j'étais transi, haletant, bouleversé, j'allais me mettre à écrire de la poésie comme tous les potaches. Je le dois à M. Lesage que j'imagine toujours comme si nous étions sur le mont Sinaï, je l'entendrai toujours nous dire comme Simon Pierre à Jésus : « Il fait bon ici. Dressons-y trois tentes : une pour vous, une pour Moïse, une pour Elie... »

*
**

Un matin d'hiver, M. Payen entra dans l'étude en m'appelant d'un doigt crochu et de son œil incertain. Je sortis avec lui en tremblant. Qu'avait-il découvert ? Il me dit d'un ton affectueux, inhabituel de sa part, que Dieu avait rappelé à lui ma grand-mère, que je pouvais mettre mon uniforme et descendre chez moi, rue Montaigne, où l'on m'attendait. Ma mère avait déjà rejoint Sidi-Moussa, mon père ne pouvait s'absenter, et c'était Hayek, l'amant libanais de ma tante Marie, qui était premier coupeur chez Larade et gagnait tant d'argent, qu'on avait chargé de m'emmener.

Emu et fier, se sachant pas très bien comment se comporter avec moi, il avait loué une automobile, une torpédo Citroën découverte, presque comme pour une noce. Naturellement, il ne conduisait pas, il avait aussi un chauffeur, nous étions à l'arrière tous les deux. Il parlait avec un accent doux, gris, pareil à son visage bien rasé. Il s'intéressa beaucoup à moi, me demanda si je comptais continuer, et, comme charmé par tant d'attentions, je lui répondais « oui », il me dit : « Seulement voilà, il y a les femmes. Saurez-vous vous passer des femmes ?... » Sa question me surprit. Je pensais qu'il aurait été plus heureux en s'en passant, lui, des femmes. La sienne, ma tante Marie, lui en faisait voir de toutes les couleurs et le traitait comme un chien, un peu comme on traitait ici les indigènes. Ma mère disait qu'il couchait souvent dans son atelier parce que ma tante lui refusait sa chambre. Les femmes avaient-elles un tel attrait, ce qu'elles livraient d'elles-mêmes

111

était-il si fantastique pour qu'on ne pût vivre sans elles et que lui, que tout le monde appelait simplement Hayek, acceptât si docilement, comme avec délices, les humiliations que ma tante lui infligeait ? Je ne sais comment il interpréta mon silence, mais pendant tout le parcours, qui me parut rapide, pensez : une auto particulière ! il répéta : « Les femmes, quel problème... » On sentait qu'à mon âge il me considérait comme un ange, j'avais quatorze ans. Il ajouta : « C'est vrai, vous aimiez beaucoup votre grand-mère. Elle, c'était une sainte... »

Il faisait beau, à la ferme j'embrassai toute la famille, mon frère René et sa femme Louise étaient là, ma mère en larmes me couvrit de baisers et m'emmena doucement dans la chambre où ma grand-mère, le visage diaphane, était figée dans ce qui me parut l'acceptation d'une fatalité. J'étais tellement ébahi, tellement frappé que je n'éprouvai pas de douleur, seulement cette stupeur qui rend muet. Puis je fus dans la salle à manger où l'on s'extasia sur ma casquette. Je cherchai en vain mes cousines, elles n'étaient pas là, il y en avait d'autres qui me laissaient de marbre, et aussi des cousins. L'oncle Jules m'attira près de lui et j'eus une tasse de café. J'ai raconté l'enterrement dans *les Chevaux du Soleil*, j'ai parlé du partage qui suivit, des billets de banque sur le lit de mort. Nous étions encore dans la salle à manger, mon frère René et Louise m'encadraient, quand ma mère sortit blême de la chambre et m'entraîna dehors. Je compris que l'oncle Jules aurait voulu que son frère Désiré lui rendît aussitôt l'argent qu'il lui devait, mais l'oncle Désiré était trop heureux d'avoir une belle somme à lui. L'oncle Hippolyte s'en alla en silence, mais l'oncle Désiré rouge de colère menaça son frère Jules : « Je lui ferai la peau », grondait-il tandis que sa femme Henriette répétait : « Calme-toi, Désiré. Un jour pareil... » Nous étions tous muets d'épouvante. « Oui, un jour pareil, reprenait-il, me réclamer une chose pareille... » Du haut du perron, l'oncle Jules, blême, les regarda filer.

Hayek nous raccompagna. Ma mère et moi nous nous serrâmes à l'arrière avec lui. La tante Marie calée à l'avant se retourna : « Si le sale métèque espère en avoir la queue d'un, il se fourre le doigt dans l'œil... » Il sourit, soupira, un peu excédé, vers moi : « Voyez comme elle me parle... » Il avait l'habitude.

Ce soir-là, je couchai rue Montaigne. L'électricité était un

vrai changement. Du lit on pouvait, avec une poire, éteindre la lampe de chevet. Au réveil, j'eus mon café au lait avec des gâteaux à la patate douce et de la confiture, je paressai, je me lavai dans la cuisine avec des bassines d'eau chaude, grâce au tub, car il n'y avait pas de douches au séminaire, c'eût été trop indécent. Je sortis peut-être, j'allai peut-être à l'église Saint-Vincent-de-Paul saluer le curé, puis nous déjeunâmes. Ma mère me supplia de rester et tenta de m'allécher par un riz à l'espagnole que j'aimais tant, avec de la soubressade, pour dîner.

Je remontai au séminaire tôt dans l'après-midi. J'avais de la peine pour ma grand-mère, je ne me résignais pas à l'idée que je ne la verrais plus, j'entendais encore les menaces de l'oncle Désiré, mais surtout c'était le mot de Hayek : « Les femmes, quel problème... » qui me hantait. Je traversai Bab el-Oued sans m'arrêter à l'église Saint-Joseph, je gagnai l'arrêt du trolley pour Notre-Dame d'Afrique et, de là, m'engageai dans la vallée des Consuls d'un pas décidé, comme si je défiais la mort entraperçue. J'avais déjà quitté ma grand-mère, je la quittais encore plus. Avec elle s'en allait la tendresse de ma vie.

Une fois par an, nous partions pour une grande promenade, les deux séminaires : le grand et le petit. Le grand comptait une quinzaine d'élèves. Son recrutement provenait surtout de l'Ardèche dont l'archevêque était originaire, en attendant que ce fût, avec nous, d'Algérie. De rhétorique nous monterions en philosophie et revêtirions la soutane, mot terrible, mot effrayant qui représentait l'engagement de notre vie. Bref, un jour de juin, les deux séminaires, toujours séparés, même aux récréations, et qui ne se rapprochaient qu'à la chorale ou quand nous chantions à la cathédrale, se mêlaient dans le divertissement et les jeux.

On parlait longtemps d'avance de cette promenade, on comptait les jours, on espérait qu'il ferait beau, que ce serait réussi. Le jour venu, on se levait comme d'habitude, puis c'était la prière coupée par l'interminable silence de la méditation et de l'examen de conscience. Après la messe, on descendait en rangs au réfectoire avaler notre soupe d'un trait. Vite dehors, nous dévalions, toujours en rangs, vers Saint-

Eugène. Affrété pour la circonstance, un autobus nous attendait. D'ordinaire, seuls les Arabes — les indigènes — se hissaient à l'impériale où on les entassait. Nous qui n'avions pas peur du vent, de la vitesse, du vertige, nous nous y serrions sous la surveillance de M. l'économe et du maître de chorale, un solide Hollandais en soutane déjà, à la réputation d'autorité. Nous chantions des cantiques, nous élevions notre âme à Dieu, à la vie, au bonheur. Partagé entre l'inquiétude, la responsabilité et ce qu'on pouvait autoriser de distraction, M. Payen s'installait à l'intérieur avec ces messieurs, l'ensemble du grand séminaire et le reste du petit. Le conducteur démarrait prudemment, puis empruntait, à l'aller, la route du littoral et, au retour, celle qui passait par les terres. Une heure de trajet ou presque. Après Guyotville et la Madrague, nous arrivions au village de Staouéli et à son église minuscule, et nous débouchions sur une longue rive plate, toute blanche, éblouissante, qui s'avançait en pleine mer : Sidi-Ferruch. J'aurais dû me trouver chez moi, puisque ma mère et moi avions vécu dix ans plus tôt à Staouéli où mon père dirigeait l'école. J'aurais dû en tirer avantage. Je ne disais rien. Je me laissais aller à l'émerveillement de cette presqu'île qui partageait la mer en deux : du côté où nous étions, la mer était calme, immobile ; de l'autre, des courants l'agitaient. Il faisait un temps éclatant. Dégringolant de notre perchoir, nous étions pareils à des prisonniers libres au bout d'une longue année d'internement, médusés, stupéfiés, muets, les pieds dans le sable déjà chaud. Frappé aussi par une intimité proche de la promiscuité, et qui explosait soudain entre les élèves et lui, M. Payen ne savait quelle attitude adopter. Nous ne lui connaissions pas cette mine débonnaire qui ressemblait à un commencement de mollesse. On se déshabillait, on se mettait en maillot. M. l'économe et M. Baligand eux-mêmes, les plus jeunes de ces messieurs, les plus à la page, s'extirpaient de leur soutane comme d'une gaine d'insecte et apparaissaient en long costume de bain devant la mer plate. A cinq cents mètres du rivage, on avait encore pied, et nous les suivions, déchaînés, barbotant, patouillant dans des vaguelettes tièdes, voluptueuses, enlaçantes. Quelque chose nous grisait, la liberté seulement ? l'immensité ? l'azur opaque ? Nous nous assourdissions de cris, nous nous aspergions, nous culbutions sur la plage, personne ne nous disait que c'était là même qu'un

siècle plus tôt ou presque, l'armée française avait débarqué en pantalons rouges trempés, personne n'ajoutait que la mer efface toutes les traces comme elle effacerait les nôtres.

Cette folle journée durait plus que d'habitude, au comble de nous-mêmes et d'une sorte de folie païenne. Nous découvrions à nos professeurs des visages inconnus, même chez ceux qui n'avaient pas osé quitter leur sombre étui à boutons et qui, assis sur le rivage, souriants comme malgré eux, nous regardaient nous ébattre. A l'époque, personne ne songeait à se protéger des coups de soleil dont nous étions tout rouges. Et quel pique-nique ! Nous nous disputions les œufs durs, le jambon, les tomates crues, sans bénédictions ni grâces, quel événement ! Nous entonnions de la limonade, et ces messieurs les directeurs se passaient une bouteille de vin de messe, enveloppée dans des serviettes avec de la glace. Certains d'entre eux, refusant le verre en carton de l'économe, poussaient l'audace jusqu'à boire au goulot. Une orgie dionysiaque, une bacchanale sans bacchantes.

Etait-ce là l'esprit du lac de Tibériade avec les apôtres et les pêcheurs quand le Christ multipliait les pains et les poissons ? Etait-ce une sainte joie ? Plus loin, au pied de la montagne du Chenoua, brillait Tipasa que nous ne connaissions pas. Camus, à l'époque élève de l'école publique de Belcourt, n'était pas encore allé s'étendre sur les mosaïques chaudes, au milieu des sarcophages et des absinthes sauvages. La mer n'avait pas encore, dans notre littérature africaine où, à peu près seul, M. Louis Bertrand officiait, ce caractère sacré que des mortels pouvaient lui vouer. Gabriel Audisio ne publiera *Sel de la mer* qu'en 1936. *Noces* paraîtra en 1938 et je n'en saurai rien. Peu à peu cependant, Sidi-Ferruch, que l'architecte Pouillon transformera plus tard en superbe marina pour congés payés, deviendra pour moi mon cap Canaveral, un lieu mythique. Le premier sang entre la France et l'Algérie avait été versé là, un jour de juin semblable au nôtre, et je ramenais des images de bonheur. Au fur et à mesure des années, c'est un dieu couronné de pampres, dispensateur d'extases, qui mêlera sur la plage de Sidi-Ferruch notre petite troupe à d'autres enfants arabes presque noirs. Malgré la présence de notre supérieur, notre sombre et incorruptible vigile, nous célébrerons avec le soleil des noces inattendues, brutales et à jamais fatales.

115

Encore à l'impériale, cramoisis, brûlés de partout, enfiévrés, nous rentrions. L'autobus nous déposait au pied de Saint-Eugène. La grimpette nous dégrisait, une visite à la chapelle aussi. Nous avions de la peine à ne pas dormir à la prière du soir. Nos lits étaient pleins de sable. Nos corps flambaient. Nos âmes aussi.

*
**

La salle du réfectoire était soutenue par des colonnes. D'un côté, la longue table du petit séminaire ; en face, loin, celle du grand, recouverte comme la nôtre d'une toile cirée ; au milieu, en équerre, celle de ces messieurs, avec une nappe blanche resplendissante, et de face, comme le Christ et les apôtres dans la Cène. Dans le fond, une sorte de tonneau surélevé qui servait de chaire au lecteur.

Après le *Benedicite* dit par lui, le bruit des chaises et des bancs épuisé, M. Payen frappait sur un timbre. Le lecteur commençait à lire *recto tono*, d'un ton égal et sans expression, le texte, d'ordinaire fort ennuyeux, d'une vie de saint, de savant pieux ou d'homme illustre. Dans mes débuts au séminaire, il me parut bizarre qu'on pût traiter ainsi le combat d'une existence, même vénérable, sans y mettre la moindre expression. Ainsi le voulait le règlement. Plus tard, je compris que c'était le style de l'église, que tout y était effacé, écrasé et damé comme nous : unis, sans nuances, neutres et gris, nous ne devions pas réagir, détruits pour mieux constituer par inertie une force capable de résister à tout. A moins qu'on ne voulût justement dépouiller le texte de toute réflexion pour nous laisser libres de mieux l'assimiler. Si le lecteur commettait une faute, M. Payen frappait sur son timbre, le lecteur s'arrêtait et reprenait en se corrigeant. S'il ne se corrigeait pas, M. Payen l'interrompait encore et corrigeait alors à haute voix, ce qui provoquait de légers rires.

Le menu était, pour nous, toujours le même : de la soupe, un plat de bouilli ou de poisson, des pâtes, des légumes secs ou des pommes de terre, souvent des haricots. Pour dessert, une orange, deux figues sèches ou trois dattes. Le tout dans la même assiette, que nous nous contentions d'essuyer avec beaucoup de pain. Le menu était-il amélioré pour le grand séminaire par de la salade ou de la confiture ? Et bien que les

116

lazaristes eussent pour patron saint Vincent de Paul, incarnation de la charité pour les humbles et les déshérités, seuls ces messieurs les directeurs avaient droit à une chère délicate, un mets de plus, du vin et deux changements de couverts.

A tour de rôle pendant une semaine, trois d'entre nous servaient. C'était une fonction dont nous attendions avec impatience qu'elle nous échoie. Les serveurs prenaient les plats que les sœurs laies posaient sur le guichet de la cuisine. Ils les portaient sur les tables sans jamais d'erreur. Le serveur de ces messieurs était choisi pour l'art avec lequel il savait glisser les assiettes et présenter les plats. Je le fus souvent, par faveur. Il fallait rester debout face à ces messieurs, attentif au moindre signe. Le repas fini, M. Payen donnait deux coups de timbre. Certains jours de fête, ou parce qu'il recevait un hôte, M. Payen, après le *Benedicite*, lançait à voix haute *Deo gratias*. C'était l'autorisation de parler. Les voix explosaient alors. Qu'avait-on à se dire depuis la veille ? On avait dormi, il y avait eu classe, étude, prière. Notre vie si bien réglée, si monotone en apparence, était fertile en événements minuscules qui avaient leur importance. Les détails infimes du service, les moindres variations dans l'attitude de ces messieurs, le temps qu'il faisait, les cours, tout devenait bavardage et caquetage sans fin. Ce que nous mangions, une subsistance de bahut, nous semblait délicieux parce que nous parlions. Quand le timbre rétablissait le silence, le lecteur débitait alors, en latin, dans le *Martyrologium romanum,* la page consacrée aux martyrs du jour, à la longue suite des supplices qu'ils avaient endurés pour la gloire de Dieu, puis tout le monde se levait, M. Payen récitait les grâces et c'était le départ en rang pour la récréation. Les serveurs mangeaient après les autres, près du guichet, et avaient droit au menu de ces messieurs, à une goutte de vin de messe et à du dessert. Des cuisines, devant leurs fourneaux et leurs bassines, les sœurs mineures nous observaient, avec une joie naïve, nous en fourrer jusque-là.

Aux grandes vacances, mon père nous emmenait à Lévigny, son village natal, à une douzaine de kilomètres de Bar-sur-Aube sur un plateau nu, au nord, en pleine Cham-

pagne pouilleuse, là où les vignes ne laissent couler que de la piquette.

Au bout d'un jardin clos de grilles, étroit et avançant entre deux rues, la maison ressemblait à une cabane à lapins. Avec elle, mon père avait acheté un lopin de terre, quelques rangées de vigne et des ruches sur un coteau. Presque sur la place, traversée matin et soir par quelques troupeaux, un peu en dessous et en retrait, c'était la mairie-école. En face, derrière des murs et de hauts marronniers, le presbytère flanquait l'église et le cimetière. Pendant l'été, tout se passait dans les champs, les moissonneuses cliquetaient, de lourds charrois aux essieux grinçants rentraient la récolte dans les fermes. Il n'y avait de vie que le dimanche, à l'heure de la messe, quand les cloches sonnaient.

Nous vînmes là trois ou quatre années de suite. On nous appelait « les Africains ». C'était un voyage héroïque. Nous faisions la traversée sur le pont ou en troisième classe, la mer était toujours agitée dans le golfe du Lion, on vomissait beaucoup. Avant de débarquer, ma mère cachait dans un sac sous ses jupes le tabac pour la pipe de mon père et cousait la poche où était l'argent. Pour mon père, les dockers de Marseille étaient des Apaches, et les gabelous haïssaient tout ce qui venait d'Algérie, il fallait se méfier. La ville me semblait fiévreuse et sensuelle. A cause des bagages, nous prenions un taxi pour la gare Saint-Charles. Là, nous dînions sur un banc en attendant le train du soir. Nos places en troisième étaient réservées, mais la cohue était féroce. On changeait à Dijon, à Culmont-Chalindrey, et encore à Chaumont. Un omnibus nous laissait à Bar-sur-Aube au petit matin, brisés, fourbus. Encore fallait-il atteindre Lévigny par le courrier postal. Ma mère avait un accès de paludisme, mon père était furieux. Je me répétais : « Voici la France, voici la France. »

La sœur de mon père, ancienne institutrice aussi, nous attendait, vaguement goguenarde. Peut-être voulait-elle montrer qu'elle ne serait pas dupe de ce que son frère raconterait. Elle habitait à l'écart, près d'une ferme qui sentait le lait et le purin. Cette autre tante Marie, déjà âgée, moustachue et peu alerte, se déplaçait avec une canne à bout de caoutchouc. Mon père l'appelait la Bleuche, je n'ai jamais su pourquoi. Il ne l'aimait pas. Qu'aimait-il en vérité ? Moi, peut-être. Les soirs d'été où il n'y avait dans la rue que de rares

lampes électriques, ils se parlaient de loin, assez haut. Mon père lui racontait l'Afrique en abrégé. Elle, sa vie, plutôt morne depuis qu'elle était veuve et à la retraite. Parfois, elle écartait les jambes et pissait, comme une vache, comme toutes les vieilles femmes du village. Au début, je trouvais cela répugnant, puis je m'en amusai. En ce temps-là encore, dans les maisons, on s'éclairait au pétrole et à la bougie, et ce qu'on appelait les commodités étaient dans la grange attenante. Encore, à cause de ma mère, les avait-on mises, par des planches, à l'abri des vues. Deux fois par mois, mon père transportait la tinette à la vigne ou au potager. Je l'aidais. Dans le village que de terribles odeurs traversaient, tout le monde agissait de même. Le vidangeur avec sa pompe était un luxe.

J'occupais au grenier la chambre du grand-père. Elle avait un plancher en sapin, une alcôve, un bureau à tiroirs et une bibliothèque fabuleuse : tout Chateaubriand, tout Victor Hugo, tout Musset, tout Molière, des dictionnaires, des livres d'histoire, des atlas. Au-dessus, dans un cadre, trônait le portrait de l'ancêtre, Louis Nicolas Léon Dematons, qui avait terrorisé les siens et, à la mort de sa femme, s'était remarié à une jeunesse : un front large et dégarni, un regard froid, un nez court et massif sur de grosses moustaches et une barbiche. Mon père lui ressemblait, à part cet éclat qui lui manquait dans l'œil. Je me jetais sur le *Génie du christianisme* et *les Martyrs*, et tombai aussitôt amoureux d'Atala.

On ne nettoyait jamais les rues après le passage des troupeaux. Les gens ramassaient bouses et crottin à la brouette, près de chez eux. Pour ça, mon père, coiffé d'un vieux casque colonial comme s'il allait au combat, était un champion. Il s'arrêtait partout, discourait avec les gens. Lui qui détestait tant l'Algérie, il la célébrait et, lâchant de grands pets sonores, vantait ce qu'il appelait « les pays neufs ». Une fois, j'osai lui exprimer mon écœurement. Il répondit que son père à lui, quand il recevait des amis, montait au grenier où était sa chambre, grimpait sur une chaise et pissait dans son vase de nuit. Ça s'entendait, les amis se tordaient, c'était le fin du fin. Une année où il passa quelques jours à Lévigny, mon frère Robert qui se disait honteux des incongruités de son père, lui répliquait en lui lâchant au nez d'autres pets protestataires. Sa femme Marie-Louise, une belle brune délicate et élancée, était horrifiée. Ma mère avait un sourire désolé

119

Chez les Paris, ces choses-là ne se faisaient pas. Mais quoi, les Dematons étaient nés dans un bled que les invasions balayaient régulièrement, on se montrait les portes d'armoires entaillées par le sabre des uhlans qui y découpaient leur viande, on savait aussi quels étaient les bâtards de Prussiens et de cosaques, tout se mélangeait dans l'atroce.

Le dimanche de son unique séjour, mon frère Robert se mit en tenue de capitaine à képi bleu ciel pour aller à la messe. Il n'était pas croyant, mais il jugeait qu'il devait s'afficher catholique pratiquant pour faire échec aux radicaux-socialistes qu'il détestait. Comme « rouge », il n'y avait que le facteur, rond comme une boule et très curieux. Ce jour-là, après la messe et l'arrêt au cimetière devant la tombe des Dematons, tous avec un Léon dans leurs prénoms, Robert eut une conversation sur les affaires du monde avec un professeur agrégé de lettres de Paris, Pierre Messiaen, qui enseignait au lycée Charlemagne et avait une sœur mariée au propriétaire d'une grosse ferme dans le bas du village. Je liai timidement amitié avec son fils Olivier, de mon âge. Il étudiait la musique, jouait du piano et venait de recevoir le premier prix du Conservatoire, ce qui m'impressionna. Je lui promis une visite. J'étais soudain heureux : j'avais peut-être un compagnon de vacances. Je ne voyais personne que le curé, un solide gaillard au nez saillant et aux cheveux rebelles en brosse.

Un peu bourru, bâti de bric et de broc, taillé à coups de hache, l'abbé Martin flottait dans sa soutane. Heureux de la présence d'un séminariste, il m'apprit à sonner les cloches, ce qui demandait de la force physique : à la volée pour la messe, en tintement pour l'angélus et le glas, tout un art. Il connaissait les choses de la terre et avait une foi naïve et forte. Dieu existait, le Christ avait sauvé le monde, le péché était l'ennemi de Dieu, Dieu réglait tout, il fallait se soumettre et l'adorer. Comme M. Payen, mais avec quelque chose de loufoque, il avait un œil qui ne savait où se poser et lançait des éclairs, alors que celui de M. Payen semblait sournois. À la grand-messe du dimanche, sa voix montait, descendait, changeait de ton, devenait bêlement, cri plaintif ou perçant pour finir gargouillement ou miaulement de chat sauvage. Un vieux chantre lui répondait comme un terrible tonnerre. Mon grand-père Louis Nicolas Léon avait été chantre aussi, paraît-il, au lutrin. Je connaissais le solfège, le curé me nomma en quelque sorte

maître de chapelle et demanda à ses paroissiens de se mettre à l'écoute de l'Eglise nouvelle. J'avais une voix de baryton et l'instinct de la musique, je chantais en grégorien antiennes, psaumes, hymnes et motets. Comme, avec l'harmonium, je me débrouillais, l'assistance fit des compliments au curé. Je crus, de mon côté, surprendre des regards qui me troublèrent.

Le dimanche, s'il ne devait pas grimper sur son vélo de dame pour aller célébrer une autre messe dans un village voisin, l'abbé Martin m'invitait à sa table. Sa servante effacée, dévouée à son maître et à Dieu, était une fine cuisinière. Les curés de ce temps-là avaient au moins ça. Toutes les fois où j'allais avec le mien en visite chez un confrère, la table était merveilleuse. Les bibliothèques aussi. Celle de l'abbé Martin, bien fournie en ouvrages apologétiques, était assez audacieuse : il avait Barbusse, il avait Victor Margueritte qu'il hésita à me donner à lire puis qu'il cacha. En revanche, il me chargea de tout Henry Bordeaux, de tout Paul Bourget. Il avait peu de poètes, sauf Adolphe Retté, à cause de son récit édifiant, *Du diable à Dieu*, et Francis Jammes. Pas Rimbaud. D'ailleurs je ne connaissais pas encore le nom de Rimbaud. Avec le Chateaubriand de ma mansarde, j'abusai peut-être de la lecture, mais je n'avais de distraction qu'aux champs, à la moisson, chez le cultivateur qui avait épousé une des tantes d'Olivier Messiaen. Lui, Olivier, ne se mêlait pas à ces distractions-là. Derrière la faucheuse-lieuse mécanique et son moulinet, on dressait les gerbes en tas coniques, puis on les hissait sur des chariots attelés à des percherons. On suait beaucoup, on mangeait du saucisson et du fromage blanc, on buvait de l'eau rougie. Je m'instruisis des mœurs et de la vie en écoutant le parler, assez cru. J'en entendais de vertes et de pas mûres. Derrière nous, comme dans les tableaux de Millet, les croupes des glaneuses ondulaient et, à l'angélus, personne ne priait. Je rentrais le cou piquant de barbes d'épis et parfois de baisers.

Enfin, j'osai aller à Fuligny, un village voisin, où la famille d'Olivier Messiaen possédait une belle demeure. Olivier travaillait le piano et une cantate pour le théâtre. Il avait un visage doux, réfléchi, lumineux en dedans et pourtant effacé ; il semblait mal à l'aise en société. Cependant il fascinait. Sa mère était poète. En mauvaise santé, elle n'apparut jamais. Son mari le professeur la décrivait menue, avec des yeux d'un brun doré,

des cheveux noirs aux reflets bleuâtres et un large front bombé. Olivier écoutait en silence son père parler d'elle. Elle publiait des poèmes sous son nom de Cécile Sauvage. Son mari la comparait à Louise Labé qu'on ne nous laissait pas lire au séminaire parce que, je le sus plus tard, c'était une âme trop éprise d'amour temporel. Aux mains d'Olivier, j'écrivis un poème que je n'osai montrer à personne et surtout pas à lui.

> *Les touches vibrent, les notes tombent*
> *parfois comme des larmes*
> *comme des gouttes d'eau qu'un brillant ricochet*
> *soulève à peine*
> *comme un vol d'alouettes ivres*
> *et que je n'aperçois plus.*

Chateaubriand m'avait cligné de l'œil, en quelque sorte. Mon vrai ami, mon héros, mon dieu, c'était lui qui, jusqu'à dix-sept ans, s'était cru aussi destiné à entrer dans les ordres Ça me rassurait.

J'étais abonné à une revue pour séminaristes qui s'appelait *le Lien*. Elle lança un concours sur le thème « Un saint de chez nous ». Je racontai ma visite à une chapelle sur une colline voisine et j'eus la surprise de recevoir le premier prix avec la publication de mon texte. J'en eus de l'orgueil. Mes parents et mon curé aussi. Je montrai ce numéro du *Lien* à Olivier qui en parla à son père. Je sentis dès lors comme une certaine attention.

Une autre fois, ce fut *la Semaine religieuse d'Alger* qui nous demanda une sorte de devoir de vacances. Le mien parut sous le titre « Visite à la cathédrale de Troyes », avec mon nom au sommaire. J'en éprouvai un frémissement qui dura longtemps. Comme Olivier exprimait son regret de ne pouvoir jouer de l'orgue, je courus à Bar-sur-Aube et obtins pour lui une autorisation du curé de l'église Saint-Maclou. Nous y allâmes à bicyclette, nous grimpâmes à la tribune. A cette époque, les souffleries électriques n'étaient pas inventées, il fallait de l'aide pour manœuvrer des pédales ou un levier. Je me jetai sur la besogne. Olivier, j'en étais sûr, allait devenir un grand compositeur. Je me considérais comme un séminariste de province, peu apte à partager quoi que ce fût avec un astre à côté de moi. Peut-être était-il moins doué sur le plan de la

camaraderie ? Nous revînmes à Saint-Maclou, puis nous allâmes essayer l'orgue de Ville-sur-Terre, chef-lieu de canton voisin, et ce fut fini. Sa mère dut rentrer à Paris. La rencontre d'Olivier Messiaen ressembla pour moi à la rencontre d'une comète, si haut dans le ciel, si loin que je la voyais à peine. Il est grand à présent, il ne se discute plus, sa gloire est immense. Je n'ai échangé avec lui que des signaux d'abîme ou des cris d'épervier.

Les regards que je sentais sur moi le dimanche quand, en surplis, je tenais l'harmonium, je me mis à les accepter, puis à les désirer quand ils manquaient. Comme ils ne me suffisaient pas, je me mis à tourner, à bicyclette, autour de la ferme d'où ils venaient. On me rejoignit. La fille était appétissante, pulpeuse, ardente. Elle s'appelait Hélène. Nous nous parlâmes, nous allâmes ensemble dans les bois, nous échangeâmes des baisers maladroits. De ma main sur ses seins et sur ses cuisses, je gardai une brûlure ; j'errai en pleine extravagance à la vue de tout le village, en plein délire, et m'exhibai sans que personne ose seulement m'interroger. Tout le monde jouait à ne s'apercevoir de rien. L'abbé Martin consterné craignait de surprendre des allusions sur son séminariste, mon père ne quittait plus sa vigne et ses abeilles, ma mère se taisait. Je rêvais d'étangs nostalgiques et des yeux d'Hélène, j'étais René soutenant le beau corps d'Atala. J'avais détaché la gravure où, à demi nue, ses longs cheveux sur les reins, elle se laisse adorer par les sauvages. Comme René, j'avais la gorge serrée, je marchais un peu égaré, une voix semblait me dire : « La saison de ta migration n'est pas encore venue, attends que le vent de la mort se lève, alors tu déploieras ton vol vers ces régions inconnues... » Comme j'étais exalté en ce temps-là ! J'avais connu une passion. *Les Martyrs* avaient triomphé du *Martyrologium romanum*. Le vent de la mort ? Peut-être celui de la mer. Celui du désert que je sentais, déjà enfant, me brûler. Si cette belle Hélène qui doit être une vieille dame indulgente me lit, elle se reconnaîtra et sourira.

Par chance, c'était la fin des vacances, on fit les malles. Avant mon départ, le curé me dit que, par devoir, il écrirait au séminaire mais qu'il ne dirait mot de mon écart de conduite. Il avait du mérite car il était à cheval sur les principes. Mon père

se plaisait dans ses cambrousses mais ma mère commençait à en avoir assez. Nous regagnâmes Alger.

Chaque rentrée au séminaire s'ouvrait par une retraite. J'avais approché le monde, j'avais péché, je me repentais, je me replongeai dans la règle, la discipline, la prière, j'étais de nouveau sur la sainte colline, en rhétorique déjà, face à face avec la mer infinie et soumis au même emploi du temps : lever comme les poules, vague débarbouillage, prière, méditation, examen de conscience, messe avec communion, soupe, étude, classe, réfectoire, récréation, étude, classe, récréation, étude, réfectoire, prière du soir et coucher. La vie de couvent me ressaisit avec ses rivalités mesquines, ses amitiés équivoques, *numquam duo semper tres,* sous l'œil oblique de M. Payen et le pince-nez de M. Baligand. Le problème de la vocation devenait de plus en plus pressant, bientôt il serait trop tard. M'étais-je jamais posé des questions sur Dieu ? On ne s'interrogeait pas sur Dieu, il existait, un point c'est tout. « Dieu est un pur esprit infiniment bon. » Comment un pur esprit pouvait-il agir sur la matière ? Sujet tabou. Dieu est Dieu.

Les questions, c'est aujourd'hui que je me les pose. Alors, tournant autour de la basilique de Vézelay, je chante à mi-voix le *Credo* en latin et descends vers le cimetière. Quand je l'atteins, j'en suis à la résurrection des morts et à la vie des siècles à venir... *Et expecto resurrectionem mortuorum,* je crie ces mots dans les grandes oreilles d'Ulysse, enfermé là dans son enclos, et qui vient à moi dans l'espérance, non pas de l'éternité, mais de carottes et de tranches de pain. S'il est content de me voir, il brait et ses longs cris de basse d'orgue désaccordée peuvent faire croire à ceux qui dorment là que c'est la trompette de Josaphat et qu'il est temps de se réveiller. S'il est d'humeur moins gaie, il se contente de flairer ce que je verse dans sa mangeoire. Venu ici tout jeune avec une troupe de cinéastes américains qui voulaient du médiéval, il fut mis en vente après le tournage et le brocanteur qui l'acheta crut qu'il saurait promener les enfants à la belle saison. Il s'appelait Ulysse, du nom qu'on donne encore dans nos campagnes aux chevaux et aux ânes qui, autrefois, voyageaient. Dans son

nouvel office, Ulysse prit trop de liberté, on dut le châtrer, il refusa dès lors le bât ou la selle. Cependant on le garda et il échoua dans un enclos d'orties, entre des murs de pierraille, devant le cimetière, où il s'ennuie. Il a peut-être cinq ans à présent. Il est de couleur brune à rayures fauves. On chercherait en vain sur ses épaules la croix blanche qu'aurait dû lui léguer l'illustre ancêtre, mais cet âne-là était gris, paraît-il, que monta le Christ le jour de son entrée triomphale à Jérusalem. Ulysse serait-il un païen ? Comme les morts ont peu de conversation, ma femme et moi allons, avec la chienne, le visiter.

« Saurez-vous vous passer de ces dames ? » Au séminaire, le mot d'Hayek me laminait. Ainsi la vie coulait. Il existait rue des Consuls, dans le quartier de la Marine et de la prostitution, un journal peu affiné, bien qu'il fût inspiré par les jésuites, qui s'appelait *la Jeunesse catholique* et dont la direction littéraire relevait d'un intellectuel d'avant-garde et plein d'audace, Robert Dournon. Je me présentai, on m'offrit d'y écrire. Je me risquai à toutes sortes de balbutiements qu'on accueillit avec empressement et qu'on publia. Depuis mon aventure amoureuse, mon père commençait à s'inquiéter de mon avenir et demanda par lettre à M. Payen si on ne songeait pas à me présenter au baccalauréat. Pour l'archevêque, le baccalauréat offrait trop de facilités de départ aux séminaristes : on aurait dépensé en vain de longues années d'études. Mieux valait des prêtres sans baccalauréat que, dans le monde, des jeunes gens issus du séminaire avec baccalauréat. M. Payen répondit qu'il aurait fallu penser plus tôt à une langue étrangère. De mon côté, je renâclai devant l'effort d'apprendre l'anglais et de travailler mon faible, les maths. A quoi servent les maths quand on songe à servir Dieu ? Mon père se résigna. Désœuvré depuis sa mise à la retraite, s'échinant à de misérables besognes alimentaires, il n'était pas heureux et ne le cachait pas, son seul plaisir était de retrouver ses compagnons, place du Gouvernement.

Assis sur des bancs, à l'ombre ou au soleil suivant l'heure, au pied du minaret de la mosquée de la Pêcherie avec son horloge bleue et sous l'épée de bronze du duc d'Orléans à cheval, chassant les yaouleds qui insistaient pour leur cirer les souliers, ils parlaient politique, commentaient le satirique et

ordurier *Papa Louette* et se laissaient aller à dauber sur les scandales du moment, les pouilleux qui passaient, les curés, les militaires, les bourgeois. Les femmes surtout excitaient leur verve. Après la rigolade et les imprécations, mon père rentrait, à pied toujours, par les arcades de la rue Bal bel-Oued. Enjambant parfois des ruisseaux de fange, il marchait tout droit, sans se détourner de sa trajectoire, et se servait de sa canne comme d'une arme, enfonçant comme un tank tout ce qui ne s'effaçait pas assez vite devant lui et qu'il appelait toujours « cette racaille ». Il était ailleurs, et moi, loin de lui, aussi. Les petits articles de moi qui paraissaient dans *la Jeunesse catholique* flattaient ma vanité. J'appris là que M. Louis Bertrand n'était pas le maître de la littérature algérienne. Robert Randau était plus grand que lui. Louis Lecoq, Charles Hagel, le poète Jean Pomier, Ferdinand Duchêne constituaient un groupe qu'on appelait les Algérianistes. D'autres romanciers, d'autres poètes publiaient à Alger leurs œuvres. Des femmes avaient un nom : Elissa Rhaïs, Lucienne Favre, Marie Bugéja, d'autres. Elles comptaient. On parlait aussi d'Isabelle Eberhardt. Gabriel Audisio, de sept ans mon aîné et qui allait devenir notre père à nous tous qui arrivions, chantait la mer, le soleil, l'amour. J'aurais été heureux de le rencontrer, mais comment ? Par moments, c'était moins la soutane proche qui m'épouvantait que la menace de recevoir, dès que je rentrerais au grand séminaire, les ordres mineurs : portier, lecteur, exorciste, acolyte, et d'abord l'imposition de la tonsure. Le coiffeur qui passait régulièrement nous couper les cheveux rafraîchissait en même temps, au rasoir, le cuir de ces messieurs. Que diraient mes cousines quand elles me reverraient avec une petite lune sur le crâne ? Et Hélène ? Et les voisins de mes parents ? Et Hayek ?

Ainsi peut arriver l'événement le plus lointain quand, à force de le repousser, on travaille obscurément à ce qu'il ait lieu. L'enfant qui entre au séminaire en suçant une caroube se découvre tout à coup en soutane, devant le sacerdoce. Ainsi Julien Sorel aura la tête tranchée.

Je ne sais pourquoi il me semble que cette année de rhétorique fila plus vite que les autres qui m'avaient paru interminables. A tant prier, nous avions des bourrelets aux genoux ; à tant méditer, nous ne pensions plus à rien, surtout

pas à la mort. Nous en avions soupé de Bossuet, de Lamennais, de Fénelon, et même de Victor Hugo. Nous savions qui était Flaubert, mais M. Lesage n'osa jamais nous lire des pages de *Madame Bovary,* seulement de *Salammbô,* et encore pas les affriolantes. J'essayais de m'aveugler. Si l'on m'avait demandé : « Pourquoi êtes-vous là ? », j'aurais peut-être répondu : « Par erreur. Parce que j'ai confondu mes intentions. Parce que j'ai cru à une vie plus facile et plus douce. » Qui avait montré sa voie à M. Payen ? La grâce de Dieu ? L'envie qu'avait pu avoir Dieu de le placer parmi ses serviteurs à cause de ses disgrâces physiques ? Et pour M. Baligand ? Selon M. Baligand, personne n'imaginait les détours que Dieu prenait pour piéger ceux qu'il avait choisis. Qu'importaient les raisons ? Quand il s'agissait de grâce, il n'y avait pas de raison. La pauvreté non plus n'entrait pas en compte. Si aucun de nous ne sortait de famille riche, c'est qu'il était plus facile aux pauvres d'être appelés. Oui, j'avais la vocation. « Saurez-vous vous passer des femmes ? » susurrait Hayek. Les femmes tenaient-elles donc une telle place ? Le besoin qu'on avait de les aimer était-il si nécessaire ? J'errais, pourquoi le cacher ? en quête et en désir de la femme, j'appelais peut-être le double de mon âme à qui j'aurais pu m'exprimer sans même lui parler. C'est cela, la femme deviendrait pour moi la sœur que je n'avais pas eue, incestueuse, qu'importe ! En serrant Hélène contre moi, je me serrais contre moi-même, j'avais quelqu'un de très proche qui pourrait partager mon sort comme je partagerais le sien, le sort des créatures qui étaient, sans savoir pourquoi, sur terre, une planète parmi les autres, et qui allait vers quoi ? N'était-ce pas pour cela que j'éprouvais tant de sentiments pour les femmes ? N'en avais-je pas fait l'expérience pendant les vacances ? Naturellement, j'étais hanté par l'image de la femme, je me demandais comment la femme était fabriquée, j'éprouvais le besoin de le découvrir moi-même. A la ferme, dans les premières années de ma vie, j'avais cru que le corps féminin, tout de chair, se terminait par des pieds. Moins favorisé qu'aujourd'hui où, avec la publicité de la télévision, le corps des femmes n'a plus de secret, je ne savais rien d'elles. Les femmes avaient des cuisses, des reins, des seins, et nous avions pour elles ce goût étrange, cette inclination qui devenait convoitise, irrésistible passion, violence parfois.

Naïvetés qui de nos jours font sourire. Ce que je lisais

dans la Bible me ramenait à cette réalité que l'homme et la femme ne font qu'un, destinés qu'ils sont à vivre ensemble, fondus l'un dans l'autre dans une union presque divine. La littérature n'était-elle pas la relation de cette poursuite pathétique ? L'idée du vœu de chasteté que, plus tard, je devrais prononcer me mettrait obligatoirement à l'écart des femmes, ce qui me ramenait en esprit à Hayek, humilié et pourtant tellement attaché que j'en demeurais confondu.

J'avançais à tâtons dans une nuit profonde. Ainsi, nous considérions avec une sorte d'admiration jalouse le curé d'une grosse paroisse de banlieue, le seul prêtre mondain qu'il y eût dans l'Église d'Alger. Parmi ses confrères si négligés dans leur mise et leur personne, ce prêtre-là cultivait une réputation d'élégance. Il sentait bon, portait du linge fin et des soutanes bien coupées, parlait avec distinction, certains disaient « aussi bien que Mgr Bollon », de qui on se souvenait et qu'il espérait remplacer un jour. Le bruit courait qu'il avait une cour, que beaucoup de jolies femmes l'admiraient et qu'il n'était pas insensible à leur charme. On pouvait donc briguer l'état sacerdotal sans renoncer au sortilège des femmes et à leur séduction ? De mauvaises langues racontaient encore que la prestance et le talent de Mgr Bollon lui avaient valu bien des ravissements. Que ne disait-on pas dans les couloirs entre élèves du grand séminaire et élèves de rhétorique qu'un seul étage séparait dans notre château caserne ? La vie au grand séminaire nous apparaissait déjà comme une promotion fantastique. Chacun y avait sa chambre ; déjà, je pourrais écrire. Il arrivait aussi comme par hasard, à nos promenades, de se rencontrer et de se mêler. Sur la colline du sémaphore, des regards se fondaient, des familiarités se nouaient. Je n'étais curieux que des femmes, mais je restais en quête d'amitié, j'ai pu en provoquer, je leur ai répondu. J'avais le goût, que j'ai toujours, de compagnons avec qui il est bon de partager. Rien de commun, je l'ai su plus tard, avec Maurice Sachs qui, du même âge et au même moment que moi, entrait dans un séminaire de Paris et se fourrait dans une soutane sous l'influence de Maritain et de Cocteau. C'était un intellectuel, un juif frais converti, je n'étais qu'un enfant du péché né parmi les barbares dans la plaine de la Mitidja, entre Meftah et l'oncle Jules. Je n'en étais pas non plus à me demander si, par hasard, je ne serais pas placé sur la voie de la sainteté. Terrible

question que Bernanos nous posait. D'abord il fallait la foi qui déplace les montagnes. Ce n'était pas la mienne.

Un jour, ma mère me dit que mon père était parti. Après un moment de stupeur, cela ne m'étonna pas. Sa terre natale lui manquait, il se répétait qu'il avait trahi en épousant la fille d'un colon et en ayant poussé au séminaire un bâtard qui allait devenir prêtre à cause de lui, jadis antiratichon. Il avait hâte de renouer avec son propre père avec qui il n'avait jamais pu s'entendre de son vivant. Il voulait lui ressembler, qui sait ? Devenir un notable du lieu après sa vie aventureuse ? Oui, qu'était-il venu faire dans cette Algérie où il se sentait de plus en plus étranger ? Subitement, d'un coup de tête, comme il avait fait à l'inverse vingt-cinq ans plus tôt, il lança une demande pour reprendre du service comme instituteur dans l'Aube. La guerre avait creusé des vides qui n'étaient pas comblés, on le rembaucha, il fit sa malle et partit, seul. Ma mère me dit qu'il enseignait dans un village proche de Lévigny, fricotait sa tambouille dans l'âtre, couchait dans une chambre sans feu et sans jamais retaper son lit, sauvage, silencieux, buté, obstiné, tel que je l'imagine maintenant que je le connais, amoureux de la pluie, du vent, de ses forêts à sangliers, de ses horizons de champs catalauniques et des femmes à grosses jupes lourdes et en sabots. Je restai songeur, vaguement inquiet.

Si chargée de nuées qu'elle fût, la classe rhétorique passa. Nous vivions dans la lumière du monde, nos maîtres s'efforçaient de poser peu de problèmes à nos esprits, j'avais tort de me torturer, M. Baligand me rassura, j'avais la vocation. Mais alors, si je m'en allais, sans diplôme, que deviendrais-je ?

Etroite, glissante, puante et sombre, la rue des Consuls existe-t-elle encore ? N'a-t-elle pas disparu en même temps que le quartier quand on a réduit cet amas de cafés turcs, de bordels, de commerces louches et de bâtisses d'avant la Conquête qui étaient devenus un repaire de terroristes ?

Longtemps après, au bout d'une vie de combat, je souris au jeune homme que grise déjà l'odeur d'encre d'imprimerie.

Grâce à la bibliothèque du curé de Lévigny, j'avais découvert Adolphe Retté et Francis Jammes, des poètes. Je leur écrivis, ils me répondirent. Au séminaire, on accepta que l'autorité militaire recrutât, comme au lycée Bugeaud et au collège des jésuites, des candidats pour l'école des officiers de réserve. Ainsi, pensait-on, les séminaristes éviteraient l'atmosphère délétère de la caserne, ce fut l'argument décisif. S'ils réussissaient aux examens, ils serviraient comme officiers, donc parmi l'élite. L'autorité diocésaine décida que ces séminaristes-là ne recevraient pas la tonsure ni les ordres mineurs avant leur départ pour l'armée. A leur retour, ils entreraient en théologie, et tout leur serait conféré en deux ans. Du coup, le port de la soutane que je venais, presque en catimini, d'endosser, ne m'inquiéta plus, et cependant le jeune homme que traversaient tant de désirs n'avait pas fini de se tourmenter : il vivait dans un étourdissement de sensualité qui le faisait par moments tituber. N'était-il pas un autre avec cette robe noire ? N'avait-il pas tout à coup changé de nature avec cette façon de glisser dans les rues sans trop se montrer, pour ne pas provoquer les imbéciles que la vue d'un « corbeau » rendait soudain furieux ? Oui, mais il y avait, chez les catholiques fervents, chez les dames d'œuvres comme chez les enfants du catéchisme, des regards qui compensaient. On m'appelait « monsieur l'abbé ». J'étais déjà quelqu'un, l'archevêque m'avait distingué. Plusieurs fois, il m'avait appelé dans son cabinet de travail, un oratoire de sa villa mauresque au milieu de jardins délicieux, et m'avait relevé de ma prosternation devant lui. C'était un prélat imposant, au visage grêlé de petite vérole mal guérie, pareil à de la terre glaise. Il se pencha sur moi et, chuchotant presque, me laissa entendre qu'à mon retour du service militaire, il m'enverrait deux ans à Paris au séminaire de Saint-Sulpice, puis me prendrait comme secrétaire. Qu'importait alors le baccalauréat ?

L'expérience de mon père fut courte. Vaincu par la solitude et par l'hiver, il vendit la maison de Lévigny et s'en vint renouer avec ses amis de la place du Gouvernement, les retraités, les fervents du *Papa Louette*. Il marchait toujours d'un pas rude en écartant la canaille à coups de canne. Rue Montaigne, il bricolait, farfouillait dans les tiroirs de son

bureau ou dans sa mâchoire qui se débinait : il perdait ses dents et s'en arrangeait. Pour ne pas dépenser son argent chez un dentiste, il attendait que ses molaires se déchaussent et se dessèchent d'elles-mêmes, étayait les autres, les remplaçait avec de la colle solide et du mastic, il était son propre prothésiste. A plus de soixante ans, il trouvait que, de son côté, ma mère avait bien décliné et, vieux bouc, il lançait des regards vers les créatures. Certaines, ici, avaient des croupes de jument comme les aimait Apollinaire. Quand il passait devant les bordels de Bab el-Oued, il pensait à son bâtard, en soutane maintenant, comme Julien Sorel l'avait été, ce qu'on pouvait dire aussi de Staline maréchal de la Russie des Soviets, et aussi de tant d'hommes illustres ou de simples ministres de la culture. Maurice Sachs n'avait porté la soutane que six mois. Aux vacances de Juan-les-Pins de 1926, il jettera tout aux orties, même son cilice, et partira pour l'armée.

A part quelques jours de sirocco où le ciel est obscurci, à Alger, le vent de la mer souffle, délicieusement doux, pendant l'été. Mon père traînassait entre les conférences de Saint-Vincent-de-Paul et ses papas louettes encanaillés de la place du Gouvernement. Pour moi, évidemment, pas de plage, pas de baignades, rien que de la piété. Chaque défunt de la paroisse me rapportait cinq francs au sercice funèbre où je servais de chantre ou d'organiste. Je me constituai une cassette, j'achetai des livres à la librairie « Nostre-Dame », rue Michelet, qui recevait les nouveautés de la NRF. Pendant ma traversée de Bab el-Oued, je feignais de ne pas entendre les cris de corbeaux, pour moi des crachats. A *la Jeunesse catholique*, je ne tarderai pas à faire scandale en écrivant l'éloge de la *Jeanne d'Arc* de Joseph Delteil que les bien-pensants considéraient comme une offense à Dieu et à la sainte. Il faudra encore dix ans pour que Camus, qui est à peine au lycée Bugeaud, publie *l'Envers et l'Endroit* et joue *le Temps du mépris* avec son équipe de théâtre. Loin d'ici, hélas, je n'en saurai rien. Avec Dieu, que je me suis ennuyé pendant ces étés d'Alger ! Ma mère s'inquiétait parfois de me voir poursuivre d'assiduités inconvenantes une de nos voisines qui habitait sur le même palier que nous, une Espagnole aux yeux de feu, que depuis

des années j'essayais de toucher et qui m'échappait toujours. J'avais été longtemps un gamin. A présent, elle évitait comme la peste, comme le péché, le jeune ensoutané qui n'arrêtait pas de la guetter.

Notre député socialiste avait une trogne d'ivrogne, on l'appelait Fiori l'Anisette, il avait été élu grâce aux innombrables tournées qu'il payait. L'autre député, Raymond Laquière, était l'élu des gens d'ordre ; notre sénateur Duroux possédait toutes les minoteries et le journal *l'Echo d'Alger*. La société ne courait pas de risques avec eux, le capital triomphait, la magistrature protégeait les bons citoyens, l'armée défendait le territoire national. L'Algérie, c'était la France, on commençait déjà à préparer la célébration du centenaire de la Conquête. Ce seraient, paraît-il, des fêtes fantastiques. Dans la rue, passaient des chanteurs ambulants qui chantaient les airs à la mode : *Ferme tes jolis yeux, Ramona*. Des balcons, on leur lançait des piécettes. Ou alors une troupe de nègres dansait en agitant des castagnettes de fer, pareilles à des poissons métalliques cliquetant de toutes leurs écailles. L'Afrique noire battait à nos portes. L'oncle Jules s'était marié, nous n'allions plus à la ferme, je ne rencontrais plus mes cousines.

Il m'arriva une fois de prendre un autobus plein d'Arabes pour gagner un presbytère perdu derrière l'Atlas blidéen au milieu d'étendues sans fin de blé déjà moissonné et d'alfa. Les hivers y étaient rudes, les étés torrides, mais quelle beauté ! D'innombrables troupeaux de moutons broutaient les chaumes. Après les montagnes, la vue s'étendait sur le désert, la terre nue se colorait de violet, de vert tendre, d'ocre. Dans les vallées brillait le sel des chotts. Là s'élevait Tiaret, un bourg de western, au milieu de fermes puissantes et de gourbis de torchis, là se carrait une pauvre église. Son curé portait le nom ridicule de Cas, c'était l'abbé Cas ! Il avait une réputation de don Quichotte au langage fort et sans détour. Sa légende m'avait attiré. Long, décharné, sec, le visage taillé à coups de serpe et semé d'une barbe incertaine, il haranguait, le dimanche, quelques fidèles sur le ton d'un prophète qui ne craignait que la colère de Dieu. Sous son toit, c'était le dénuement. A la cuisine, un réchaud, des pâtes et des tomates. Dans une autre pièce, une table sur des tréteaux, des bancs, un crucifix, quelques caisses d'oignons. Lui couchait sur des nattes. Il me céda un coin dans l'entrée vide, et comme les

nuits étaient fraîches, j'eus pour me couvrir le drap des enterrements. « Avec ça, vous n'aurez pas froid. » Ça pesait, les broderies en fils d'argent me râpaient les joues, c'était rugueux et d'un lugubre au-dessus de mes forces. Je m'en retournai en hâte répandre la louange héroïque de l'abbé Cas. Je ne me sentais pas du tout destiné à la barbarie des hauts plateaux, là où dans quelques années, Max-Pol Fouchet, jeune apôtre rouge de l'université d'Alger, viendra prêcher la doctrine socialiste à de maigres auditoires incrédules pendant que Camus le trahira.

Ainsi resterai-je presque deux ans sous l'habit ecclésiastique. Au séminaire, dans ma cellule, je traficotai l'installation électrique pour avoir du courant après l'extinction des feux et lire sous les couvertures. Parfois, avec un camarade qui, à présent, célèbre la messe intégriste à Saint-Nicolas-du-Chardonnet, nous nous étendions, la face au ciel, sur la terrasse. Où étions-nous ? Où était Sirius ? Où était Mars ? Et Bételgeuse, et Véga ? Je m'habituerai à ma robe comme les notables d'autrefois, j'aurai le réflexe de la remonter légèrement pour grimper les escaliers. Ce qui m'étonne aujourd'hui, c'est mon extraordinaire indifférence d'alors devant ce qu'on appelle les traverses de la vie. Etait-ce de l'inconscience, une absence de toute peur ou la conviction que rien de fâcheux ne pouvait m'échoir ? Parfois, ma conduite frisera l'indiscipline, je ne saurai pas composer avec la foi et l'opportunisme politique. Par *l'Action française* j'eus la révélation de Bernanos et du *Soleil de Satan,* je devins comme beaucoup un fidèle de Léon Daudet et de Charles Maurras. Quand le journal fut condamné à Rome, je courus le risque d'une menace de schisme et continuai de l'acheter. Royaliste, je portais une fleur de lis d'argent sous ma soutane, sur mon cœur. J'écrivis à Bernanos qui me conseilla de me soumettre, quand soudain nous changeâmes de supérieur : M. Payen fut remplacé par un vieux lazariste, épais de taille mais vif dans sa démarche et si bon, si plein d'affection et d'indulgence pour nous que nous eûmes l'impression d'être aimés comme des fils et non plus seulement comme des moinillons soumis à la règle. Notre attachement à *l'Action française* ne provoqua chez lui qu'un sourire.

J'allais avoir vingt ans. Le 9 novembre 1927, je quittai ma colline sacrée, mes maîtres et mes condisciples. J'allai chez

moi, repris mes effets civils et, ma feuille d'incorporation à la main, un peu fiévreux et inquiet, je montai à pied vers la caserne d'Orléans, au-dessus de la Casbah, sur le glacis de l'ancien bastion où Charles Quint avait campé en 1541 et que, depuis, les Français appelaient Fort-l'Empereur. Je me présentai au bureau d'incorporation des élèves officiers de réserve du 9e zouaves.

Seul séminariste en face d'une horde d'instituteurs qui vivaient dans le classique troupier et employaient son vocabulaire, blancs-becs qui jouaient aux débauchés, je devins leur cible. J'ai oublié ce que fut notre voyage de deux jours en bateau puis en train pour la France, leurs allusions, les conversations obscènes. Mon frère Robert avait dû être comme eux. Je les traitai par le mépris.

Je sentais qu'une autre vie commençait.

IV

Le sabre et le mandarin

A SAINT-MAIXENT-L'ÉCOLE, dans les Deux-Sèvres, où nous débarquâmes dans le brouillard, des officiers nous attendaient. L'atmosphère rigide qui datait du siècle dernier ne me changeait guère. Un adjudant nous conduisit au pas dans une ancienne abbaye transformée en caserne : Canclaux, où on nous distribua notre fourniment. Avec bonheur je découvris que je n'étais plus seul à subir le déferlement des ordures et des hurlements ; dans ma section commandée par un sous-lieutenant de la promotion précédente, un pète-sec à l'accent rocailleux de Perpignan, nous étions trois séminaristes. Dans la compagnie, une dizaine. Nous nous serrâmes vite, d'instinct, les uns contre les autres, puis nous fîmes front et relevâmes le défi. Sous la voûte humide de ce qui avait été jadis un cloître, une vingtaine de lits de fer étaient alignés au cordeau sur deux rangées. Au milieu un grand poêle. A l'appel du soir, au moment de se déshabiller et de se coucher dans une explosion de plaisanteries éculées, nos lascars un peu éméchés (on buvait beaucoup de pinard à la cantine) regardèrent leurs trois « curés » s'agenouiller au pied de leur pieu. Après un moment de stupéfaction, quelques quolibets et quelques exclamations, ça se tassa, ils n'osèrent plus, et nous, tels des exhibitionnistes transis de foi, nous nous fourrâmes dans nos lits. Les matelas étaient des galettes de crin, et sous les couvertures rêches et pesantes, les draps raides et glacés me rappelaient la tenture funèbre de l'abbé Cas.

Le métier militaire m'apparut comme un bagne. On se rassemblait en courant sous les insultes des chefs de section, on marchait en ordre serré et en cadence, l'arme sur l'épaule, on se couchait sur la terre mouillée. Il pleuvait beaucoup et

135

nous n'avions qu'une capote pour nous protéger, comme si la toile imperméable n'avait pas encore été inventée ou qu'elle eût été indigne du soldat : le soldat devait souffrir. On nous apprit à manier fusils et mitrailleuses et à manœuvrer au combat, on nous brisait comme nous devrions briser à notre tour les recrues. Les instituteurs faisaient des étincelles et, quand la fin de la semaine arrivait, sans doute par vantardise et pour nous choquer, ils ne parlaient que de prendre une cuite et de passer la nuit au bordel. A leur avis, il n'y avait que ça. Pour des incroyants, ils avaient raison, saint Paul l'avait dit avant eux. C'était des jeunes loups, il suffisait de leur tenir tête. Ni plus bêtes ni moins vigoureux qu'eux, nous devînmes avec entrain des aspirants modèles, notre retenue morale nous valut d'être appréciés. Au bout de six mois de crapahutage, j'étais un élève officier convenable. En fin de stage, entre les instituteurs et nous, il n'y avait plus qu'une camaraderie râpeuse et franche. Je profitai de quelques jours de permission pour aller voir Adolphe Retté sur qui je me proposais d'écrire un essai. Jadis compagnon d'hommes politiques et d'écrivains célèbres, devenu poète symboliste ennemi des rimes riches, il avait conquis au Mercure de France une certaine gloire, et l'enthousiasme de nombreux adolescents qui récitaient ses vers au charme mélancolique :

> O vent hagard, chevauche à travers les taillis,
> Froisse et disperse au loin les fleurs de l'anémone,
> Ravage la futaie et jonche de débris
> Le sentier sinueux où ne passe personne.

Puis subitement, tournant casaque, il avait lancé un livre retentissant, *Du diable à Dieu*, et, tour à tour désespéré et illuminé, avait décidé de se retirer du monde. Il n'écrivait plus que pour combattre l'athéisme et vivait reclus à Beaune en Côte-d'Or. Revenu de beaucoup de vanités, tout frémissant de piété, il m'encouragea fort à persévérer vers le sacerdoce. Il avait un visage doux à petit bouc blanc, gardait encore beaucoup de fougue à soixante-dix ans, mais la maladie avait ruiné sa santé, il ne pouvait plus se déplacer et subsistait de quelques misérables droits d'auteur au milieu d'une bibliothèque débordante de livres. Je ne savais pas que la plupart des écrivains finissaient ainsi. Je passai une journée avec lui et le quittai.

A l'amphi des garnisons, je choisis, à cause du képi bleu ciel plus élégant que le bandeau noir des zouaves, le 1er régiment de tirailleurs à Blida, et regagnai Alger avec un galon d'or sur les manches, fou d'orgueil : j'appartenais à une classe honorée de la nation, mon père et ma mère me regardèrent avec fierté. L'exercice physique, les fatigues endurées et l'habitude des armes m'avaient durci, on me fêta, au séminaire on m'admira comme un bel oiseau. Grâce à une indemnité de première mise d'équipement et une avance de solde, j'avais un peu d'argent. Je n'en avais jamais eu, je crus que j'en avais beaucoup. Ce qui me frappa surtout, ce fut rue Bab el-Oued : on ne me couacquait plus, on me saluait. Le regard des femmes sur moi avait aussi changé.« Les femmes, a écrit Labiche dans *le Plus heureux des trois* aiment s'appuyer sur un bras qui porte une épée à sa ceinture. »

Nous étions trois élèves de Saint-Maixent à avoir choisi le 1er tirailleurs. Nous nous rendîmes ensemble à Blida où le régiment avait son état-major. En ce temps-là, les officiers portaient le sabre. Nous étions dispensés d'en acheter un, en raison de notre très court passage dans l'armée, ce qui marquait que nous n'étions pas de vrais officiers de carrière mais seulement des apprentis. Le colonel, court de taille et hérissé comme un coq, nous rappela les faits d'armes et la gloire du drapeau dont les dorures luisaient dans une armoire vitrée. Blida était sans doute jugée une garnison trop facile pour nous. On expédia deux d'entre nous au bataillon de Médéa, le troisième à Djelfa, triste bourgade perdue dans des plateaux désolés. A Blida, nous eûmes à peine le temps d'apercevoir la place d'armes entourée d'arcades avec son célèbre kiosque à musique percé d'un palmier, l'hôtel de France où siégeait le cercle des officiers, les rues animées et les boulevards plantés d'orangers. Le club de football, le Football-Club blidéen, le FCB, avait une grosse réputation. Nous étions en mai, tout resplendissait sous un soleil vif, j'étais subjugué, je vivais un rêve, je me demandai si Gide ne hantait pas encore le Bois sacré des *Nourritures terrestres,* ce livre voluptueux dont on osait à peine parler entre nous et que j'avais lu en cachette. Le surnom de Blida, « la petite rose », inventé par Gide ? était merveilleux. Il y en avait partout, des roses, la montagne de Chréa où les gens chic allaient faire du ski l'hiver dominait la ville qui sentait la farine, le jasmin, la

semoule, la femme. Je n'arrêtais pas de saluer ou d'être salué, j'avais constamment la main au képi. La garnison comptait aussi des spahis, des artilleurs et des tringlots. Il y avait beaucoup d'Arabes. Comme figurants, « pour la couleur locale », me dis-je. Rovigo n'était qu'à une vingtaine de kilomètres, je me souvenais que mes cousines allaient chaque année à la fête de Blida, le lundi de Pentecôte : on y dansait autour du kiosque à musique et, ce jour-là, éclatait toujours un orage. A Bou-Sbir, le quartier des bordels, des tambours nègres battaient le soir dans le ciel d'étoiles.

Hélas, le lendemain, mes deux camarades et moi prîmes le train à voie étroite qui s'engageait vers le sud. Dans les gorges de la Chiffa, il traversait beaucoup de tunnels puis escaladait les pentes de l'Atlas et atteignait Médéa, où nous descendîmes. Notre camarade de Djelfa continuait vers le désert dont je rêvais.

A près de mille mètres d'altitude, Médéa avait la réputation de jardins publics enchanteurs. On disait que des eaux vives y coulaient comme en Provence. La garnison comprenait un régiment de spahis et notre bataillon. L'église, dans laquelle je n'entrai pas, me parut toute pimpante. Dans cette sous-préfecture cernée de remparts où l'on commerçait beaucoup avec le Sud, les spahis à burnous rouges tenaient le haut du pavé, des trompettes de cavalerie retentissaient. Par chance, j'aimais bien, depuis mon enfance, l'odeur du crottin de cheval. Sur la ville, toute mignonne, l'horloge de la mairie égrenait les heures. Il y avait une place plantée de platanes, des terrasses de café et un kiosque à musique mais sans plumet de palmier. Je m'installai dans un modeste hôtel, dans ma chambre, je sortis de ma cantine l'*Imitation de Jésus-Christ* que je plaçai sur ma table avec un recueil de poèmes d'Adolphe Retté. Le curé, que j'aperçus de loin, portait le titre de chanoine et une barbe poivre et sel en éventail. C'était là, dans ce cadre désuet, que j'avais, sans le savoir, rendez-vous avec l'amour.

Un poète y était né, Jean Richepin, mais c'est surtout au romancier Pierre Benoit que je pensai quelques mois plus tard, quand je lus *l'Atlantide*. Ses héros avaient dû partir de là, à la rencontre d'Antinéa. Au moment où je m'y retrouve en esprit cinquante ans après, l'émotion fait un peu trembler ma plume : les spahis sont partout, leurs éperons tintent, je me

sens gêné de n'être qu'un modeste biffin à leggings, les officiers de cavalerie ne fraient pas, ou alors à leur cercle, à leur quartier aux sonneries argentines ; peut-être se croient-ils d'une essence supérieure comme beaucoup de snobs en ce temps-là. A Médéa, on vous jugeait à vos bottes et à votre façon de monter.

Notre caserne à nous était une sorte de bastion sur les hauts, près de l'hôpital, où des pans de remparts dataient de la conquête. Notre chef de bataillon portait des lorgnons. Avec son air débonnaire et une tête de rat musqué, il me rappelait mon premier professeur de latin du lycée Bugeaud. Il nous reçut gentiment, mon camarade et moi, et nous envoya chacun à une compagnie. Je tombai sur la neuvième. Mon capitaine faisait très officier subalterne qui n'irait pas plus loin. Bas sur pattes, méfiant, grognant, il me parut peu enclin aux choses de l'esprit et rebelle à tout ce qui pouvait n'être pas la tradition. Il arborait la Légion d'honneur et une croix de guerre, mais n'avait pour lui que cela et le règlement. L'officier en second, un lieutenant saint-maixentais très à la hauteur, se montra un peu condescendant. Il abandonnait beaucoup de contingences à l'adjudant, un indigène francisé, bouillant, flatteur, avec de la gueule, et qui cachait ce qu'il pouvait avoir d'humour sous une autorité débordante. C'était la terreur des tirailleurs et des sous-officiers de la compagnie, sauf du sergent fourrier, un indigène encore, intelligent, délicat, qui me prit vite en dilection et s'appelait Boualem. De lui, je tirerai un personnage des *Chevaux du Soleil*. Le lieutenant me conduisit à ma section : une trentaine de tirailleurs, tous de la région. Certains étaient engagés, la plupart faisaient deux ans de service. Soumis, gentils, ils subissaient leur sort avec résignation comme l'islam le leur ordonnait. On ne leur passait pourtant rien. La discipline était de fer. Sur eux les punitions pleuvaient au moindre prétexte : de la salle de police, de la prison, des coups. Sur le moment, je fus un peu choqué, mais le lieutenant me dit que, là où j'étais, nous devions nous plier à des usages immémoriaux car la chance des unités d'élite était à ce prix. Que savais-je des Arabes ? Pas grand-chose : qu'il fallait se méfier d'eux. Je songeais à Meftah, à ma mère. Comme la question indigène n'avait jamais été abordée au séminaire, j'avais tout à apprendre. Je n'étais qu'un sous-lieutenant de réserve, je devais me montrer respectueux des

anciens et zélé au service de la patrie. Cette épreuve ne durerait d'ailleurs que six mois. Ce n'était pas la mer à boire.

Au bataillon, on nous offrit un pot dans une ambiance chaleureuse, avec farces et attrapes de coutume, puis on nous jeta dans le service comme on jette dans un court-bouillon de petits homards vivants. Il n'y avait pas de popote ni de mess. Chaque officier vivait à l'hôtel. Après mon enthousiasme du début, je m'aperçus que je ne mènerais pas grand train avec ma solde, mais désirais-je mener grand train ? L'uniforme m'allait, la vie militaire me plaisait, un autre monde s'ouvrait à moi, je me mis à inscrire sur un carnet, pour les apprendre par cœur, le nom des officiers du bataillon puis des sous-officiers et des soldats de ma section. Beaucoup de ceux-là avaient des surnoms ou des sobriquets que l'adjudant me dicta. Je devais prendre soin de mes hommes et d'abord les connaître, ce qui ne fut pas facile.

Le lendemain matin, je me levai à cinq heures pour me présenter avant six heures à la compagnie rassemblée. Le soleil était déjà haut, nous étions presque au début de l'été. On me serina le vieux principe : « Le militaire ne fait rien mais il le fait tôt. » Je reçus l'appel du sergent de semaine, j'inspectai ma troupe en essayant de me montrer sévère et je me mis à sa tête. La cour de la caserne résonnait de sonneries et de commandements que les murs des bâtiments répercutaient. Le lieutenant en premier arriva, je lui rendis les honneurs, puis ce fut le tour du capitaine à qui le lieutenant en premier offrit la compagnie comme sur un plateau, et alors tout s'ébranla vers la ville puis vers le terrain de manœuvre. J'étais heureux. La cadence du pas, l'odeur du cuir astiqué et de l'acier graissé, les aboiements de l'adjudant, tout me semblait bizarre et exaltant. Cette colonne de soldats en tenue kaki, ceinture rouge et chéchia qui s'en allaient allègrement, emmenés par ses cadres et par moi-même, séminariste en armes, n'était-ce pas ce que j'avais désiré sans le savoir ? A l'époque, j'aurais dû connaître Psichari. On aurait dû, au séminaire, me conseiller de lire *le Voyage du Centurion*. J'éprouvais, à un échelon très modeste, ce que le neveu de Renan avait connu à la tête de ses méharistes dans le désert de Mauritanie. Evidemment, mon lot était plus humble. La même foi nous éclairait, je n'avais encore ni son style ni sa race, je ne humais pas la poésie qui se levait de son décor de roches et de sables, j'étais tout au début de ma vie, je me

sentais emprunté, et cependant je frémissais comme si quelque chose allait se produire.

Les officiers du bataillon ne manquaient jamais une occasion de se moquer des spahis, de leur morgue, de l'odeur d'écume de cheval en sueur qu'ils traînaient avec eux, de leur front court, de leurs bottes à éperons. Nous n'avions à rougir de rien. Chez nous, seuls les capitaines et notre chef de bataillon en portaient, des bottes : ils avaient droit à un canasson qu'ils montaient parfois, en tête de la troupe, timidement. Notre brave capitaine prêtait volontiers le sien à ses lieutenants. Je n'osai pas m'y risquer.

Nos casernes dataient. C'étaient d'immenses bâtiments : des bureaux et des magasins au rez-de-chaussée avec grilles aux fenêtres et, sur deux étages, d'immenses chambres qu'on nettoyait chaque mois au crésyl et qu'on grillait deux fois par an à la lampe à souder tant elles étaient infestées de punaises. Je compris pourquoi Lyautey détestait la caserne. La nôtre, où l'adjudant inventait chaque jour une inspection de paquetage, d'armes ou de tenue de campagne, retentissait de ses hurlements et de ses menaces de schlague. Le soir pourtant, lorsque, officier de semaine, je couchais au quartier, j'entendais monter de ce décor des chants arabes accompagnés d'une flûte de roseau, comme pendant les moissons et les vendanges à la ferme. Ce n'était pas Biribi mais presque. Le capitaine qui commandait la compagnie de mitrailleuses, un homme puissant à la face cramoisie, qu'on appelait le capitaine Boum-Boum, demeurait impassible quand de mauvais traitements s'exerçaient sous nos yeux, et, prévenant mes objections : « Vous avez une âme sensible, mon petit, une âme religieuse ? Vous êtes à l'armée d'Afrique et des Indes où l'on a aussi des mœurs spéciales. Pas vous ?... » Les officiers éclataient de rire. Je me souvenais qu'après la résurrection du Christ, Pierre discutait parfois de religion et du messie avec les centurions de Césarée. Les miens, qui sait ? étaient donc des hommes de bonne volonté. Le capitaine Boum-Boum s'étonnait qu'un garçon né en Algérie comme moi fût si ignorant des usages. C'est vrai, j'avais tout à apprendre des mœurs de la soldatesque, je manquais de naturel, de classe, je ne pratiquais pas non plus le baisemain avec ces dames, en ville. D'après lui, j'aurais dû, parce que j'étais séminariste, en connaître un brin, un peu comme du temps des Templiers, ces moines soldats. Pour lui,

141

l'armée d'Afrique se suffisait à elle-même, les bordels n'étaient là que pour sauver les apparences. On le craignait. Il buvait beaucoup de bière et de pernod et entrait parfois dans des colères terribles. Sur sa face rouge, l'énorme cicatrice qui lui fendait le front en deux et qu'il tenait, disait-on, d'un coup de sabre de Chinois devenait alors toute blanche.

Mon capitaine à moi était, hélas, considéré par tous comme un pauvre type. J'en étais gêné pour lui. Pourquoi ne m'avait-on pas affecté à Boum-Boum ou à une autre compagnie de voltigeurs que commandait un capitaine que j'admirais à la folie pour ses décorations, son allure et son nom ? A mes yeux, il incarnait le panache, la valeur, c'était un chevalier. Il montait à cheval avec élégance, avait baroudé au Tonkin comme Boum-Boum et en avait ramené l'opium. Il fumait. Ça se savait. Pour moi, c'était une magie de plus. Comme il était souvent malade, je me demandais si c'était pour cela qu'il fumait, ou si c'était de fumer qui le rendait malade. Les autres officiers ne m'emballaient pas. Le chef de bataillon essayait de ménager les tempéraments. Les lieutenants jouaient les seigneurs et le prenaient de haut avec les sous-lieutenants. Nous étions assez étrangers les uns aux autres, ce qui augmentait ma gaucherie. Dans *les Chevaux du Soleil*, j'ai brossé des portraits de cette galerie, surtout du sous-lieutenant indigène qui ne me parla jamais que des femmes et de la façon de coucher avec elles, ce qui paraissait la seule préoccupation de son existence. Le service fini, les officiers dînaient les uns chez les autres ou buvaient des anisettes au cercle. On n'invitait pas un godiche comme moi et, à Médéa, il n'y avait à voir, à part les ruines romaines, que la maison où était né Jean Richepin, et à entendre que le tintement des éperons des cavaliers et la cloche des heures. Le cinéma n'ouvrait que le samedi et le dimanche. Je prenais mes repas souvent seul, au restaurant de l'hôtel où je finis pas m'apercevoir que la fille des gérants ressemblait à une vierge de Giotto. J'essayai un temps de me garder de la tentation qu'elle représentait. Ma curiosité des femmes et mon faible pour elles eurent vite raison de moi. La Vierge de Giotto promenait son chien, le soir au clair de lune, dans les jardins près des remparts. C'est là que nous nous donnâmes rendez-vous. Elle me résista tant qu'elle put. Moi aussi, à elle. Puis je me laissai couler au fond de la félicité.

Dès que j'allai à Alger en permission, ma mère s'en aperçut mais n'osa m'en parler. D'un autre côté, je ne sus pas mieux me comporter avec une de mes cousines. Elle passait chez ma mère par hasard et me trouva là. Nous sortîmes ensemble. Il me sembla que c'était Dieu qui me l'envoyait. A quel titre ? Ma foi était moins ferme qu'on aurait pu le croire, comment n'aurais-je pas encore succombé ? Depuis le grand séminaire, je tenais un journal succinct que je n'ai pas perdu. J'y ai écrit à la date du 5 juillet 1928 : « Je ne rentrerai pas au séminaire en novembre. » J'ai encore noté, sans plus, que je connus à cette époque des heures importantes, qu'en octobre j'étais autorisé à servir dans l'armée en situation d'activité et qu'en décembre, Francis Jammes m'écrivait : « Vous avez toute la belle et pure vie chrétienne devant vous. » Je ne savais plus où j'allais ni qui j'aimais et, en même temps, je sentais le besoin d'un ordre dans ma vie, et de valeurs, si démodées fussent-elles. Deux années vont passer dans le dérèglement, presque dans l'inconscience, à moins que ce ne soit une ivresse de jeunesse. Affaire de cœur, affaire d'âme, je n'ai pas fini de m'interroger. Est-ce de l'amour, et qu'est-ce que l'amour ? Dois-je briser mon penchant pour les femmes au profit de ma vocation en danger ? Ne suis-je pas infidèle à moi-même et à l'appel de Dieu ? Dieu ne m'a-t-il pas envoyé lui-même ce moment d'égarement ? Voilà ce que je me dis. Par acquit de conscience, je ferai retraite sur retraite. Chez les Pères blancs. Dans un couvent. J'en sortirai gros-jean comme devant, et personne ne me dira rien, même pas le cher Retté à qui j'écrivais toujours et qui avait vu clair en moi : j'avais trop d'appétit pour la vie, je manquais trop de charité et d'humilité, j'étais trop occupé de moi-même, trop avide. A Médéa, où, pour plus de liberté, je louai une chambre en ville, je connus un instant de nuit profonde ou d'illumination et la tentation du suicide. Je pris mon pistolet d'officier dans le tiroir de ma table de travail, manœuvrai la culasse et n'osai pas appuyer sur la détente. Personne n'en saura rien, sauf le brillant capitaine à qui je me confiais. Un jour, il tentera de m'initier à l'opium, chez lui. Pénombre, lits bas, longue pipe, cérémonial, boulette qui brille pendant qu'on aspire. Longtemps après un long silence, il me demandera où j'en suis. Nulle part. Sur terre. Rebelle à toute illusion, je m'étais plutôt embêté.

Quelque temps après, à la mairie d'Alger, fringué d'un

complet bleu et chapeauté d'un feutre d'artiste, j'entendais un officier d'état civil me demander si je voulais prendre la Vierge de Giotto pour épouse. Nous déjeunâmes à la Pêcherie, mon père pensa que j'étais dans de beaux draps, ma mère essaya de cacher ses larmes. Ma jeune femme et moi avions une chambre près de l'Opéra à l'hôtel de l'Oasis. Peut-être allâmes-nous le lendemain assister à la représentation de *Faust*, puis je repris mon service. A ce moment-là, j'écrivais des articles de choses vues dans un nouveau quotidien d'Alger, *la Presse libre*, qu'un homme de courage et de culture, André Servier, venait de lancer. Mes articles n'étaient pas payés, mais avais-je jamais eu déjà des articles payés ? J'écrivis sur la première neige qui tombait à Médéa, sur le soleil de la place du Gouvernement et je signai d'un pseudonyme pour éviter les difficultés. La question se posa de savoir si je deviendrais journaliste ou si je resterais dans l'armée. Mon père craignait que *la Presse libre* ne pût tenir en face de *la Dépêche algérienne* et de *l'Echo d'Alger* aux mains des colons. Il avait raison, il me répétait que le métier de journaliste était un métier de crève-la-faim, mais j'aurais débuté. Pourquoi n'ai-je pas persévéré ? Six ans plus tard, après l'échec d'*Alger républicain*, Camus partira pour la France rejoindre Pascal Pia, son soutien, mais en ce temps-là, qui lisait *Alger républicain*, considéré par tous comme un organe communiste ? Qui savait que Camus avait publié là une suite d'articles sur la misère en Kabylie ?

Un moment, Francis Jammes, par lettre, me suggéra de m'exiler en Argentine et d'y fonder ma famille et une exploitation agricole. D'après lui, on faisait vite fortune là-bas. Je ne concevais pas de vivre ailleurs qu'en Algérie. Je sortais à peine du séminaire, j'allais avoir un enfant, je n'étais sûr de rien, on réussit à m'impressionner. J'écrivis d'autres papiers sur des élections qui venaient d'avoir lieu et avaient vu triompher les puissances d'argent. La seule politique qui m'intéressait était celle de *l'Action française*, et je dénonçai d'une plume acérée et sous un autre pseudonyme les combines et les faiblesses de la démocratie. Selon mon père, militariste dans l'âme depuis que mon frère Robert avait réussi par la guerre, il ne me restait qu'un seul atout : l'armée.

A présent, parfois je m'en veux de n'avoir pas été plus tenace. Les journalistes sont une force. Ils se soutiennent, bâtissent toutes les réputations, celles des hommes politiques

comme celles des écrivains, et souvent les leurs, à charge de réciprocité. Même de bords opposés, ils ne se combattent qu'à fleurets mouchetés, leurs coups de feu entre eux ne sont que des tirs à blanc. On courtise leur plume plus redoutable qu'une épée, plus valeureuse qu'une armée. Je n'aurai été journaliste qu'à deux moments de ma vie et de ce siècle : en Indochine et pendant la guerre d'Algérie, mais en Indochine je n'étais pas libre, et on se souvient plus des positions que j'ai prises que de ce que j'ai écrit. A quoi bon remâcher des regrets ?

Si ardue et ingrate qu'eût été alors ma position, je m'y fis, je l'aimai. Pour rivaliser avec les cavaliers de la garnison et tromper ma petite vanité, je commandai chez le maître bottier des spahis une paire de bottes blondes et m'inscrivis à l'école du manège. Nous étions souvent en manœuvre, nous marchions beaucoup, cette vie me plaisait. Elle m'épargnait de me poser des questions. Même quand on m'imposait la charge de la popote des officiers, j'avais souci de me distinguer. Là c'était facile. Je n'avais qu'à choisir les cuistots, surveiller l'achat des produits et faire régner qualité et abondance au moindre prix. A certains rares moments, je pouvais me croire le maître. L'exercice terminé, le lieutenant en premier me chargeait de ramener la compagnie au quartier. Quand la nouba répétait dans le voisinage, je la retenais et nous rentrions derrière elle en défilant tambours battant, clairons sonnant, raïtas miaulant, moi seul en tête devant la troupe, fier comme Artaban. Le roi n'était pas mon cousin, j'appartenais à l'armée d'Afrique, des Indes et de Boum-Boum, je voulais que mes tirailleurs n'aient rien à envier aux cavaliers dans l'admiration des pékins. Chose étrange : alors que j'accorderai par la suite tant de place à l'amitié, je ne me souviens pas d'un seul ami parmi mes camarades d'alors, à part le capitaine fumeur d'opium, trop au-dessus de moi pour être un confident. Peut-être me sentais-je, avec les sous-lieutenants indigènes, relégué au degré le plus bas de l'échelle ? Peut-être, trop déchiré entre l'amour des femmes et l'appel d'En-haut que je croyais avoir entendu, essayais-je de résister à Dieu qui aurait dû être mon meilleur

ami ? Personne ne me l'avait montré tel et personne n'avait su me dire non plus que je devais aimer Dieu.

Je reportai mon dévouement sur mes hommes. D'eux j'exigeais beaucoup. Nous n'étions jamais fatigués, nous n'arrêtons pas de chanter en marchant des sortes de complaintes poétiques en arabe, sur des kilomètres et des kilomètres : *La nuit tombe où nous nous arrêtons... Attends-moi ma belle, j'arrive...* Frappé par les paraboles évangéliques sur les militaires, par la parole du centurion qui ne disait que l'essentiel : « *Je dis à un soldat va, et il va* » ou encore se montrait si humble devant un prophète, j'essayai de me mettre à l'unisson. Entre officiers, nous parlions avec ardeur du service, avec prudence les uns des autres, avec admiration de ceux qui avaient des pouvoirs supérieurs aux nôtres et en toute liberté, enfin, des femmes. De la pratique de l'amour brut. Nos propos se limitaient à cela. A chaque passage à Blida où nous allions parfois à pied, avec une étape parmi les singes à Sidi-Madani, là où, plus tard, le tourisme littéraire rassemblera Camus, Guilloux, Francis Ponge, Roblès et Mohammed Dib, nous n'avions pas la conversation sublime de ces messieurs les écrivains mais celle du capitaine Boum-Boum en route pour le bordel. Je m'esquivais. Boum-Boum insistait lourdement alors sur ma délicatesse d'âme d'ancien séminariste. J'avais vaguement honte. Je ne devais pas être encore dans la vraie vie des armes.

Jamais de politique chez nous. Sinon par des allusions à la gueuse, la République. On savait ce que nous voulions. Clemenceau venait de mourir. Tardieu était président du Conseil, on construisait la ligne Maginot et Lindbergh avait franchi l'Atlantique. Aurions-nous prêté attention à d'autres événements ? Sous ma vareuse, je portais toujours la fleur de lis épinglée sur mon cœur. Que la France fût en Algérie pour toujours, la question ne se posait même pas. La France était la force, la justice, la civilisation. Elle accorderait sans doute des réformes, modestes et prudentes. Boum-Boum lançait sa formule sur les Arabes du même ton définitif : « Tous voleurs, tous menteurs, tous pédérastes » ; le sergent Boualem se le tenait pour dit. Il deviendrait peut-être adjudant, peut-être sous-lieutenant. Il ne serait jamais admis dans une école militaire où la présence d'un indigène eût provoqué trop de dégâts. « Restons entre nous, laissons les indigènes où ils

sont », telle était notre morale. En avril 1930, l'armée d'Afrique tout entière défila à l'hippodrome du Caroubier devant le président de la République, M. Doumergue, et sur le boulevard de la République devant le maréchal Franchet d'Esperey. Grand moment où je me découvris patriote et lyrique. A la cathédrale, ce ne fut pas Mgr Bollon qui harangua les autorités, mais le prédicateur de Notre-Dame de Paris, le père Janvier. Cependant, l'horizon se chargeait. La France évacuait le Rhin. En Italie, le Duce portait son populo à haute température. Nous continuâmes notre train-train de marches et de manœuvres, je devenais peu à peu un vieux routier de la routine. Je passai l'écrit de l'examen d'élève officier d'active à Alger et l'oral à Marseille ou j'agrémentai mon séjour, rue Paradis, d'une aventure amoureuse. Sans plus. L'amour avait toujours pour moi les délices du fruit défendu. En réponse à Lindbergh, Costes et Bellonte traversèrent l'Atlantique à bord du *Point d'interrogation* dans le sens Paris-New York. Le 1er octobre 1932, je repartis pour Saint-Maixent-l'Ecole avec ma Vierge de Giotto et une petite fille qui nous était née. Cette fois, élève officier marié, j'eus droit à un logement en ville. J'avais un métier, mais étais-je fait pour lui ? J'aimais la gloriole, l'ordre, la discipline chez les autres. Je me montrais autoritaire et assez fat. J'étais toujours l'enfant de la ferme : trop gâté et ne supportant rien que les compliments.

Avant de quitter Alger, j'osai aller saluer Mgr Bollon, qui me reçut dans sa villa d'El Biar et m'offrit le thé. Il souffrait de la gorge qui avait fait sa gloire et je crus discerner chez lui une certaine tristesse. Avec insistance, il me demanda, quand j'irais à Paris, de téléphoner à un éditeur de ses amis né à Blida, un ancien élève des jésuites qui avait réussi et occupait, disait-on, une belle place : René Louis Doyon. J'entendais prononcer ce nom pour la première fois : « Il vous recevra avec affection, j'en suis sûr. » En me quittant : « Ecrivez-moi », ajouta-t-il avec un peu d'émotion.

Je ne sus pourquoi, je fus à la fois fier et troublé. C'était la seule personnalité du diocèse que j'admirais avec des sentiments confus : un peu distant, il aimait les poètes, les aventuriers de l'esprit, on le sentait vulnérable aux attachements de la terre, il parlait trop bien et sa voix, quand il la maîtrisait, éveillait des vibrations secrètes. Il y avait en lui un je-ne-sais-quoi de rare dans le commerce des hommes, le

comportement, la pensée, le mépris de la laideur. C'est à quelqu'un comme lui que j'aurais voulu ressembler si j'étais resté au séminaire. Conquérir des foules, affronter des dangers et vivre dans une solitude choisie, était-ce très catholique ? Loin de Bernanos en tout cas. Chez Bernanos, j'étais touché par la pauvreté des prêtres, leur cœur qu'on ne trompait pas, leur fermeté devant les méchantes langues, leur condition terrifiante et désarmante. Mgr Bollon semblait moins un homme de Dieu qu'un homme par qui Dieu indiquait la voie à suivre. Le métier des armes ne manquait pas de noblesse. L'auteur des *Sept piliers de la sagesse*, qui avait tellement souffert de sa propre naissance illégitime, voyait là comme une messe célébrée par une multitude, une prière. Pour lui, on entrait dans un monastère.

A peine à Saint-Maixent, j'écrivis donc à ce fameux Doyon. Il me répondit aussitôt, m'envoya des livres superbes et promit de venir me voir. A son style comme à sa générosité, je sentis qu'il était un phénomène. L'hiver et le printemps passèrent, puis soudain il s'annonça par un télégramme et débarqua à la gare avec un feutre à la mousquetaire sous un soleil d'été. C'était presque un gnome à côté du grand échalas de Bollery, directeur des *Cahiers Léon Bloy*, qu'il était allé cueillir à La Rochelle. Coup d'œil sur moi : il me jugeait un Eliacin ou presque. D'emblée, il m'offrit de me servir de père : je deviendrais son fils bien-aimé. J'étais à la fois suffoqué et flatté. « Vous n'allez tout de même pas passer votre vie avec ces imbéciles-là ? » s'écria-t-il devant le premier officier que nous croisâmes et que je saluai la main au képi. Submergé sous le flot d'une parole savante, alambiquée, piquante, cocasse, frôlant parfois le vulgaire, je me demandais un peu comment il avait pu séduire Mgr Bollon, si éminent, si réservé.

Fils d'un boucher de Blida qui vendait de la viande casher, Doyon ressemblait à un commerçant de la rue Bab-Azoun. Il se mit sans raison à taper sur les juifs, puis s'acharna sur Bloy dont Joseph Bollery était l'écuyer spirituel. Bollery prit d'abord cela pour une plaisanterie puis finit par se fâcher. Son Léon Bloy n'était pas le misérable cagot que Doyon attaquait. Alors, Doyon passa à Malraux. Je commençais à savoir qui

était Bloy mais j'ignorais tout de Malraux. J'appris qu'entre 1919 et 1921, Doyon avait reçu, aidé, exploité peut-être, un jeune homme qui allait, si les petits cochons ne le mangeaient pas, devenir quelqu'un.

Ce jour-là, à peine expédié le déjeuner que ma femme lui avait fricoté, Doyon la pelota un brin, lui baisotta un long moment le cou, puis nous entraîna Bollery et moi dans la vieille rue où j'habitais. Un peu éméché, il s'assit sur le poussoir de la borne-fontaine qui était là, nous empoigna par le bras et demanda à quelqu'un de nous photographier. A qui ? Mystère. Depuis belle lurette, j'ai sous les yeux cette photo agrandie en poster : entre les cuisses de mon père en goguette coule un gros jet d'eau tandis qu'à sa gauche, Bollery, fonctionnaire de l'administration des domaines, rigole vaguement et qu'à sa droite, en tenue d'aspirant, je souris car je n'ai pas d'instructeurs à saluer. Je me dis avec un brin d'inquiétude : « Quel gaillard, ce Doyon ! Quel sacré luron ! Comme ça nous change !... »

Et, en effet, ça me changea. J'entamerai avec Doyon une correspondance sans fin, et, aux vacances, je me précipiterai à Paris chez lui, 2, impasse Guéménée, dans le quatrième arrondissement et au quatrième étage où il m'hébergera. Il avait la terreur du chiffre 2. Tous les ennuis lui tombaient un 2. Le 2 du mois, il ne sortait jamais. Il m'exhibera comme un singe savant montre son brave couillon de singillon. On ne sait jamais. J'apprendrai la vie. Ce sera en effet mon nouveau père. Tout de même, mon troisième.

Il n'était pas tout à fait tel que m'avait dit Mgr Bollon. C'était Pic de La Mirandole. Il savait tout. Court de taille, presque chauve, la main leste, fureteur, éclabousseur, indiscret, jeteur de poudre aux yeux, il faisait tourner les assiettes au bout d'une baguette, tirait des lapins et des colombes de son gibus, c'était l'as de pique. Il parlait sans arrêt de tout, de rien, de Blida, des bons pères, de Galtier-Boissière, de Jean-Jacques Brousson, d'Anouilh, de Jouvet, lançait des vacheries à propos des uns, des autres, de leurs femmes ou de leurs anciennes maîtresses, vous quittait un instant pour retourner une viande ou épucer son chien, allait ouvrir à une sommation d'huissier, téléphonait pour annoncer un gueuleton en mon honneur tandis que Mme D., sa femme, en voiles mauves, désabusée, revenue de tout et surtout de lui, nourrissait ses chats en

minaudant. Perpétuel agité, il se couchait tard, se levait tôt. Les yeux écarquillés, il ressemblait à un oiseau de nuit. Pourquoi m'aimait-il ? Parce que j'étais né près de Blida, d'extraction populaire et, en quelque sorte, illégitime ? Parce que j'avais traversé des années de séminaire comme lui ? Il me comblera d'éditions rares qu'il me reprendra plus tard, quand il sera dans la débine. J'écrirai dans *la Presse libre* sur lui. Très vite je me brouillerai avec les *Amitiés foréziennes et vellaves*, une revue de Saint-Etienne où je commençais à signer des notes critiques, parce que j'emboîterai le pas à Doyon, considéré là comme critique méchant, sophiste, maniaque, redoutable contempteur des valeurs les plus nobles : la religion, la patrie, Léon Bloy. Drôle de pater que j'accepterai en sa personne, moi, un élève officier de l'armée française ! Drôle de lascar de qui j'épouserai toutes les querelles, sauf à propos de l'écriture, parce qu'il était brouillon et ne se relisait jamais dans la conviction que son premier jet était superbe. Peu importaient les bavures et les erreurs, il rectifierait par la suite. Pour lui, la vérité et le talent ne se charcutaient pas. Là, je n'étais pas dupe. Il m'entraînait à des générales, à des concerts, à des expositions où il s'exprimait à haute voix sur tout. On était gêné. A toute pompe, il m'enseignait Paris, la littérature, le théâtre, la peinture.

Au dîner en mon honneur, il pinçait des jarrets, soulevait des jupes, se livrait à des agaceries, piquait parfois. Il comblait de compliments et d'adoration toutes les femmes qui étaient là. Sa femme à lui, Mme D., ne comptait plus. Il l'avait enlevée à un photographe pendant une tournée de conférences, l'avait séduite et aussitôt délestée de son argent pour acheter une librairie, galerie de la Madeleine. Quand elle se plaignait encore : « Eh bien quoi, Malraux a-t-il agi autrement avec Clara ? » Nous y étions enfin. Malraux dont on parlait si souvent ne s'était pas dérangé pour lui. Doyon se vengeait comme il pouvait. Malraux n'avait-il pas joué à la bourse avec le fric de Clara ? Ne l'avait-il pas ruinée pour l'associer à la véreuse affaire du Cambodge ? Et si on reprochait à Doyon les bienfaiteurs qu'il plumait : « Est-ce qu'un mécène n'a pas le devoir d'aider un artiste à inventer des formes qui vaudront demain des fortunes ? » Il avait réponse à tout, se lançait dans un nouveau monologue, essuyait ses lunettes, allait, venait,

postillonnait ou se mettait à déclamer du Verlaine ou du Victor Hugo.

« Il te donne une belle éducation »... Quand, de retour à Saint-Maixent, je lui brossais le tableau de mon nouveau père, mon ex-vierge de Giotto devinait que je ne lui disais pas tout. Je ne lui parlais pas des femmes que je voyais et qui m'éblouissaient. J'ai tout raconté dans *la Saison des Za,* j'étais fou, et, c'est vrai, Doyon était un drôle de pistolet. N'empêche. Peu de mes valeurs anciennes résistèrent à cette tornade. A part Retté et Jammes, tabernacle sacré, mes autres amitiés littéraires s'effondrèrent : Jean Tenant, rédacteur en chef des *Amitiés foréziennes et velaves,* Louis Lecoq, romancier algérois qui s'était montré si bon pour moi, Claude-Maurice Robert, poète du Sud, Jean Pomier, poète encore, président de l'Association des écrivains algériens et directeur d'*Afrique,* et même Jean de Fabrègues, directeur de *la Revue du Siècle,* Doyon les balaya tous. Pour lui, à part Mgr Bollon, la plupart des gens d'Eglise étaient des hypocrites, la plupart des écrivains à succès des affairistes ou des arrivistes et très peu avaient du talent. Si, Céline, qu'il couvrait de cris d'admiration où l'antisémitisme n'était pas pour rien, et Anouilh, qu'il plaçait au-dessus de tous les auteurs dramatiques contemporains. Doyon, quand il admirait, claironnait son admiration, et si les voisins feignaient de ne pas l'approuver : « Encore des imbéciles !... » s'écriait-il. Lui, il était le Mandarin. Il publiait *les Livrets du Mandarin.* A cause de moi, il épargnait un peu l'armée et les traîneurs de sabre. Une belle éducation, c'est vrai. Au temps où, tout englué de religiosité, il se cherchait, il avait pondu une plaquette, *Un passé mort,* et raconté un pèlerinage à Lourdes en trempant sa plume dans le vinaigre. Pour lui l'Algérie ? Un ramassis de crétins et de fripouilles. Les Arabes ? Les victimes de la colonisation, sauf les caïds et les bachaghas, rangés du côté de la puissance et de l'argent. Lorsque le jeune Malraux en Extrême-Orient avait été appréhendé et traduit en jugement pour avoir emprunté quelques têtes de dieux khmers dans la forêt, pensez, des pierres qui n'appartenaient à personne ! Doyon avait couru avec des pétitions, publié des plaidoyers dans *Comoedia* et remué tout Paris. Ensuite, que le mari de Clara Goldsmith ait lutté un temps à Saigon comme directeur de *l'Indochine enchaînée* l'avait comblé de joie. Il avait cru y reconnaître son influence à

151

lui. Là, il se trompait. Il n'en eut jamais aucune sur l'auteur de
la Condition humaine.

*
**

J'abusai de la générosité de mon nouveau père. Je
profitais de tout pour me libérer des servitudes militaires.
Entre Paris et Saint-Maixent, je n'arrêtais plus. Aux vacances,
j'envoyai ma femme en Algérie accoucher d'un deuxième
enfant. Comme je traînais depuis Médéa une sinusite maligne,
Doyon m'emmena consulter une célébrité qui me convainquit
d'entrer au Val-de-Grâce. C'était le début de ma deuxième
année d'école. Mon cas exigeait presque une trépanation. Je
sortis de la salle d'opération avec la tête comme une citrouille
au point que je me crus défiguré à jamais. Doyon lui-même fut
effrayé, mais un pulpeux et délicieux bas-bleu à la cuisse
chaude vint chaque jour porter des gâteries, et la première de
toutes, elle-même, au sagouin que j'étais. C'est à elle que, pour
beaucoup, je dus ma guérison.

A Saint-Maixent, je finis l'année vaille que vaille. On
travaillait beaucoup à l'école. Nous nous voulions aussi
brillants qu'à Saint-Cyr, notre glorieuse rivale. Nos origines
étaient plus humbles, nous étions surtout moins jeunes.
Malgré mes efforts, je ne pus rattraper le retard que je dus à
mes absences prolongées. J'avais de bons camarades. De l'un
d'eux je fis un ami. Il s'appelait Joseph Katz. Colosse dévoré
d'ambition, il ne supportait ni les médiocres ni les crétins. A
l'amphi des garnisons, je choisis Versailles pour y être près de
Doyon. Le bataillon du 24e régiment d'infanterie installé à
Satory avait une solide réputation. Je tombai dans un milieu
relevé. J'avais monté d'un échelon dans le métier des armes.
Satory, c'était encore la caserne mais d'un niveau supérieur.
Nous n'instruisions plus des indigènes mais de jeunes soldats
du contingent. Le chef de bataillon était breveté d'état-major,
beaucoup de lieutenants préparaient l'Ecole de guerre. Je louai
une villa à Viroflay et j'achetai un vélo, je grimpais lentement
presque toute la célèbre côte, mais je la descendais à toute
vitesse, j'étais chez moi en un quart d'heure. Et surtout, Paris
n'était pas loin. Un de mes anciens me prit sous sa protection à
la compagnie d'engins et de transmissions. Je n'ai vu sourire
que deux ou trois fois le capitaine qui la commandait. Réglo à

152

l'extrême, il voulait avoir une unité d'élite. Il nous persécutait, nous obligeait à nous astiquer et à cirer nos souliers chaque fois qu'on traversait un village ou qu'on rentrait au quartier. A la fin, je compris que ce fayotage nous contraignait à un certain chic, pas seulement pour la tenue. En 1959, il finira sa carrière comme commandant en chef en Algérie, sans accroc et sans lustre.

Quand Doyon annonçait un nouveau banquet, je me précipitais. Cette fois c'était sûr, Malraux serait là. En 1933, il avait publié *la Condition humaine* et décroché le prix Goncourt. Il était devenu un personnage de légende, et il ne venait toujours pas. Doyon en avait gros sur le cœur. Clara disait : « André est tellement pris... » Doyon avait un mouvement d'humeur : « Dites plutôt : tellement de prix ? » L'année où il était venu changer ma vie à Saint-Maixent, Doyon avait eu une voix au Goncourt, celle de Rosny aîné, pour son roman *l'Enfant prodiguée*. L'avait-il seulement eue, Malraux, cette voix qui comptait aux yeux de Doyon comme la voix du seul juré intelligent ? Clara ne savait. Malraux avait décroché la timbale. Il allait falloir m'y mettre aussi, car l'ambition pointait en moi. Je me creusais la cervelle, m'escrimais sur un vague roman de banlieue. S'entraînait-on pour le Goncourt quand on enseignait le combat du groupe, le démontage du fusil-mitrailleur 24 et le fonctionnement de l'émetteur-récepteur ER 17 ? En littérature, j'avais pour modèle le mandarin : histoires de midinettes, vagues rencontres, coucheries, j'envoyais de minces papiers ici et là, même à Jean Paulhan. Je tâterai d'un peu de tout, je lécherai le même ours pendant dix ans. L'infanterie en temps de paix à Satory incitait peu à la gouaille et *les Gaietés de l'escadron* n'étaient pas mon genre. Les illisibles *Sous-offs* non plus. Si seulement j'avais osé parler de mon métier et des militaires. Là tout était tabou. Il aurait fallu de l'esprit, j'en ai un peu à présent, je n'en avais pas le moindre à l'époque. On ne publiait qu'avec l'approbation de l'armée et l'armée n'aimait pas ces officiers-là : ils mettaient tout en question, à moins, comme Pierre Loti, de se limiter, sous un pseudonyme, aux paysages, aux petites amies exotiques, sans allusion à rien d'autre. Je n'allais pas dégorger de la bile ou réveiller des images d'épouvante et dire que le sang des fusillés de la Commune n'avait pas encore séché dans le camp

de Satory. On ne parlait jamais de ça. On s'en serait bien gardé.

Chez les officiers subalternes, la seule distraction était de nous rendre, pour l'instruction des cadres, à l'état-major du régiment, rue de la Pépinière, de boire un verre au bar du Cercle de la place Saint-Augustin, à deux pas de l'église où le lieutenant Charles de Foucauld s'était converti. En groupe, nous nous livrions à des plaisanteries, moins sinistres qu'à Médéa, sur les femmes. C'était toute la nouveauté. A sa sortie de Saint-Maixent, Katz, par amitié, m'avait suivi mais il était en garnison à Paris. Bouillant, féru de tout ce qui pouvait injecter à l'armée de la jeunesse et de l'ardeur, il enrageait car les vieilles croûtes résistaient. Il préparait déjà lui aussi l'Ecole de guerre. A cette époque, les officiers portaient le sabre. Ça ne nous gênait pas, au contraire, personne ne trouvait cela étrange. Quand il m'arrive de voir dans un film, affublé d'un sabre, un acteur qui joue les officiers de ce temps-là, j'ai de la peine pour lui. Il ne sait comment tenir son sabre, il lui arrive même de se prendre les jambes dedans. Pour que le commandement juge le port du sabre désuet, il faudra attendre une nouvelle guerre. Jusque-là je trimballerai mon sabre qu'un officier allemand a dû s'approprier comme prise de guerre à Lyon où il figurait comme ex-voto au mess, en 1940.

La vie de caserne, c'était le rata, l'école de section, les potins. J'avais un tel besoin de gratter du papier que je m'escrimai à des études sur le combat — alors que je n'y connaissais rien — pour la seule revue où il était bien noté de se voir publier, *la Revue d'infanterie*. Je gravitais toujours dans l'ombre de Léon Bloy et de Barbey d'Aurevilly, et me glissais dans toutes les querelles de Doyon. Après Bernanos, je découvris la littérature héroïque de Montherlant, *Mors et Vita, Chant funèbre pour les morts de Verdun*. Ce paganisme froid m'enthousiasma. J'écrivis à l'auteur qui me répondit en me fixant rendez-vous dans un café de Montparnasse. Sans doute me sentait-il sur le même plan civique que lui : voisin des Croix-de-feu. Sur d'autres plans, mon peu d'intuition laisse pantois. Pour moi, l'auteur de *la Petite Infante de Castille* aimait les femmes. J'ignorais qu'il courait toute la Méditerranée comme un corsaire, en quête de mignons. J'étais frappé par les beautés viriles du *Songe* et d'*Aux fontaines du désir*. Sa façon de proclamer que les morts de Verdun étaient les

victimes de la bêtise universelle et d'une fatalité grandiose m'apparut proche de ce qu'il était juste de penser. Aux obsèques nationales de Painlevé, je fis reposer les armes de mon peloton dès que les généraux furent passés, ainsi n'eus-je pas à saluer les hommes politiques. Montherlant ravi m'envoya une longue lettre pour me demander un article sur lui, grâce à quoi des hebdomadaires et *la Revue universelle* allaient s'ouvrir à moi. Une autre fois, il m'invita à déjeuner. Mon orgueil fut à son comble. Il m'apparut sec, grêle, le visage dévoré et comme sous un masque, buvant du sauternes et se goinfrant de desserts. Finalement ce fut à Mme de Fels et à la *Revue de Paris* qu'allèrent mes pages. Montherlant devint mon nouveau maître, ce qui agaça Doyon. Et lui alors ? Doyon était pour moi comme Dieu, il s'effaçait. Dieu et Doyon s'éloignaient ou peut-être était-ce moi qui m'éloignais d'eux, quand l'affaire Stavisky éclata.

Entre officiers nous parlions avec répugnance de l'ignominie politique. Nous étions le sel de la terre, nous attendions l'homme qui nous délivrerait de cette clique, de ces canailles, de ce régime de ministres véreux. On s'arrachait *l'Action française.* Le colonel de La Rocque nous paraissait frileux. C'était quelqu'un comme le général Mangin qu'il nous fallait, quelqu'un qui n'aurait peur de rien, surtout pas de massacrer. Dans la nuit qui suivit le 6 février 1934, un soldat vint m'alerter : je devais être à sept heures du matin à Satory. La radio existait à peine et on n'y entendait jamais d'informations. Pour les nouvelles, il n'y avait que les journaux. A Versailles où je filai à bicyclette, j'achetai *l'Echo de Paris.* Manchettes énormes : *Le gouvernement de M. Daladier a provoqué hier à Paris la guerre civile. M. Bonnefoy-Sibour, préfet de police, a fait tirer sur les patriotes. Il y a des morts et des blessés. Le gouvernement invente un complot contre la sûreté de l'Etat.* J'avais des jarrets en ce temps-là. Je montai la côte en danseuse. Hors d'haleine, je déboulai dans la cour du quartier où, dans le brouillard, les compagnies se rassemblaient. Mon capitaine m'accueillit le visage fermé. Je le saluai puis je lui dis ma colère. Il leva sur moi un visage étonné : quelle colère ? « On va nous employer contre les patriotes. » Il me répondit qu'il avait lu *l'Ami du peuple,* le journal de François Coty, qu'il n'y avait pas un seul ancien

combattant parmi les manifestants. « Et puis gardez cela pour vous ! » Je lui tournai le dos, courus à la rencontre de camarades bouleversés comme moi. Je n'étais plus un sous-lieutenant de réserve au bas bout de la table des officiers subalternes. J'étais un lieutenant de l'armée active, je m'appuyais sur l'armée tout entière.

On distribua vivres et munitions de guerre. Le bruit courait qu'à la Concorde, il y avait eu dix morts. Des mitrailleuses auraient tiré. A huit heures les rangs se formèrent, le jour se leva, nous nous préparâmes à défendre un régime que nous méprisions. Dans la bruine qui nous enveloppait, le commandant apparut. Il arrivait de Paris, nous l'entourâmes. C'était un homme dur et froid, intraitable et insensible en apparence, qui m'aimait bien. « Les événements sont graves, dit-il, très graves. » Je lançai une accusation que j'avais lue : « Les gardes mobiles sont des brutes. » Il me regarda et enfila ses gants avec lenteur : « Il n'y a pas que de la grandeur dans notre métier, messieurs. Regagnez vos places. Discipline d'abord, obéissance. Sinon on tire sa révérence et on s'en va. » Puis à moi : « Qu'auriez-vous fait, mon cher, à la place de l'officier qui commandait la compagnie de la Concorde ? Relisez Vigny. »

Il se fit présenter le bataillon puis rassembla les cadres. Les visages étaient anxieux. A haute voix, il lut les paragraphes du règlement qui concernaient la défense de l'ordre public, énuméra les cas où la troupe pouvait faire usage de ses armes et ajouta : « Quoi qu'il arrive, je vous demande de ne pas oublier que vous avez en face de vous, non pas des ennemis, mais des Français. »

Deux compagnies embarquèrent dans des camions et disparurent. D'autres, comme la mienne, attendirent. Des rumeurs circulaient : le président du Conseil aurait démissionné, le général Weygand aurait dit à Daladier : « Si vous faites donner la troupe, je vous préviens qu'elle ne recevra pas d'ordres de moi. » Ce qu'on apprenait par téléphone nous laissait dans le vague. Dans trente ans, le transistor sera inventé, la face du monde et des opérations militaires sera changée. Le mot du chef de bataillon m'avait impressionné. A Saint-Maixent, on m'avait enseigné le combat de l'infanterie, la vie en campagne, l'histoire militaire, les sciences appliquées. On m'avait répété que l'officier était propriétaire de son grade,

ce qui lui conférait une singulière indépendance dans les relations avec ses chefs, mais notre brillant professeur d'histoire et de littérature, le capitaine René Jeanroy, n'avait jamais, jamais prononcé devant nous le nom d'Alfred de Vigny. Du livre auquel le commandant faisait allusion, je ne connaissais que le titre : *Servitude et grandeur militaires*. Le plus ancien des lieutenants que j'interrogeai répondit avec un geste négligent : « Des histoires de guerres de l'Empire. Ce qui peut germer dans l'esprit d'un romancier. »

Le soir bascula sur Satory, un régiment de chars de la garde mobile démarra pour Paris. On m'envoya installer un poste émetteur-récepteur à la caserne de la Pépinière où des troupes en armes étaient entassées dans la cour. J'accrochai une antenne au sommet de la coupole du Cercle militaire. Ah ! si M. Baligand m'avait vu... Il m'aurait aidé, il aurait été heureux. Dans le cas où les liaisons téléphoniques seraient coupées, il fallait que nous restions en contact avec l'ensemble de postes de commandement. Chose étrange, on m'autorisa à rentrer coucher chez moi. Paris était sombre, vide, des trains de banlieue circulaient mais une grève menaçait. Le lendemain, le plan de protection appliqué, je passai la nuit à la caserne sur un banc. De rares autobus traversaient la place Saint-Augustin, la gare Saint-Lazare déversait une foule encore nombreuse. Ma liaison radio marchait, je me frottais à beaucoup d'officiers supérieurs de la division qui usaient de mes transmissions et ne manquaient pas d'humour. « Oubliez ce que vous entendez », me dit le colonel qui commandait le régiment et avait une tête de mouton malade. On disait que toute la cavalerie de France était déjà là. Paris, le soir, sembla mort. D'Amiens, de Reims, de Cherbourg, d'Orléans, de Limoges, des renforts se hâtaient vers nous. La garde mobile avait mauvaise presse et ses officiers étaient mal accueillis au mess. Finalement, il ne se passa rien, le calme se rétablit, les contre-manifestations n'eurent pas lieu. L'armée, tout entière hostile au gouvernement, regagna ses garnisons et moi Versailles, dix jours plus tard. Sans même une allusion aux événements que nous venions de traverser, Montherlant m'écrivit que mon article sur lui allait paraître dans *1934*, un hebdo.

V

Des ailes, des ailes...

OYON s'éloignait. Je devenais de plus en plus royaliste et la République passait de mauvais quarts d'heure avec nous. De leur côté, les communistes laissaient entendre qu'ils prendraient bientôt d'assaut les poudrières de Satory. Nous échangions entre officiers un bref regard : qu'ils s'y frottent, les gaillards !

Quand ai-je lu *Servitude et grandeur militaires* ? N'aurais-je pas redouté d'ouvrir le livre pour ne pas renoncer à mes idées ? En plus de l'ours mal léché que le commerce de Doyon m'avait inspiré, je pensais à un ouvrage dont le titre sentait le soufre : *la Trahison du maréchal Bazaine*. Les hurlements d'Adolf, son coup de force sur la Sarre ne nous tourmentaient pas tellement. A propos de l'Allemagne et de nous-mêmes, mes cahiers de l'époque me saisissent de vertige : juchée sur un sommet d'illusions, l'armée n'était pas que muette, elle était aussi aveugle et sourde, et elle ne lisait rien. De Gaulle avait publié *le Fil de l'épée* en 1932 et *Vers l'armée de métier* en 1934, mais personne ne connaissait cet officier d'état-major qui s'acharnait à intéresser les hommes politiques à ses idées et, par miracle, réussit à convaincre Paul Reynaud.

Nous travaillions avec acharnement à instruire en six mois le contingent des jeunes soldats. D'un camp à l'autre, de Sissonne à Mourmelon, nous menions une existence harassante sans voir plus loin que le bout de notre nez. Officier de transmissions, je sortais de la banalité quotidienne, et surtout, à chaque séjour dans les camps, je volais comme observateur en avion pour mieux assurer nos liaisons au combat. Ainsi m'étais-je déjà risqué sur un Breguet 19 d'un modèle très ancien. Dans une étude parue dans *la Revue d'infanterie*,

159

j'imaginai, pour accompagner les fantassins dans la bataille, un appareil blindé mais le blindage, c'était du poids. Alors, des moteurs plus puissants, des chevaux, des compresseurs. Il fallait aussi faciliter le travail dans l'avion. Rien ne devait échapper à l'observateur debout dans son baquet, aux prises avec le vent et les relents d'huile chaude, qui se penchait pardessus la carlingue, descendait et remontait son antenne, scrutait le sol, émettait des signaux et forçait parfois le pilote à manœuvrer. Les avions d'observation étaient les bêtes de somme de la bataille. Par chance, un capitaine de mes amis, qui commandait une escadrille, m'invita à voler avec lui au Bourget.

L'avion me fascinait en même temps qu'il m'effrayait. Je souffrais du mal de l'air mais je voulais approcher mes maîtres spirituels et les imiter. Kessel d'abord, et surtout Saint-Exupéry, tellement grands tous les deux, tellement loin, inaccessibles. Quand j'avais acheté *l'Equipage*, j'étais séminariste. Que pouvait m'apporter Kessel ? Des rêves troubles. Et quand je lirai *Vol de nuit*, je serai au 1er tirailleurs ; le livre m'ouvrira au monde sublime et scintillant. Je m'acharnai à voler, les choses se firent d'elles-mêmes. Quand en 1934, Hélène Boucher se tua dans un accident près de Satory, j'allai sur le lieu où son Caudron s'était écrasé. J'assistai à la cérémonie des Invalides où son cercueil disparaissait sous les roses blanches. J'écrivis à sa gloire un article qu'on refusa. Trop lyrique. Et, à Satory, mon chef de bataillon m'expédiait à Vigny.

Le brevet d'observateur en avion se décidait d'abord à la visite médicale du personnel navigant, au Val-de-Grâce. A peu près sourd de l'oreille gauche, je fus recalé. Furieux, un moment abattu, je demandai, comme le règlement m'y autorisait, une contre-visite et j'allai implorer le professeur qui m'avait défoncé les sinus. Est-ce qu'une oreille allait m'empêcher d'aller où je voulais ? A la nouvelle visite, quand on m'interrogea, je mentis. On feignit de me croire. Quinze jours plus tard, j'étais reçu. A l'aviation comme à Mimi Pinson, je m'écriai : « A toi pour la vie... » L'avion était le forceps qui allait m'enfanter moi-même. S'il l'avait fallu, je me serais ouvert le ventre.

En 1935, Staline et Pierre Laval signèrent à Moscou le pacte franco-russe. En avril 1936, l'armée allemande réoccupa

la Rhénanie, des divisions furent dirigées en hâte vers l'Est. Tandis qu'un terrible orage enflait aux frontières, la France se marrait à la radio avec les pitreries de Bach et Laverne. Montherlant me conseilla d'écrire quelque chose là-dessus, que Massis ne publia pas. Qu'importe ! Mes parents m'avaient acheté une moto pour m'éviter la côte de Satory ; fou de joie, je l'enfourchai vers le camp d'Avord avec les poésies d'Adolphe Retté dans ma sacoche. Commençait la vie à pleins tubes. Dans les carlingues cahotantes et puantes, je vomissais tripes et boyaux en réglant des tirs d'artillerie et en maniant un appareil photo qui pesait une tonne. Avord était proche de La Chapelle-d'Angillon, le pays d'Alain-Fournier : des étangs, des brumes, des bois enchantés. De temps en temps, un équipage tombait, on célébrait une messe à la chapelle du camp. L'aviation était encore un métier risqué à cause du vent, notre ennemi, et des nuages. J'en bavais, et d'autres que moi descendaient des carlingues, la face blême. On s'aguerrissait, on s'habituait aux abîmes, aux coups de tabac, aux temps de chien. Quelquefois, par plaisir, nos pilotes nous abrutissaient par des acrobaties : l'observateur s'écrasait alors dans sa tourelle comme un sac de farine. L'idée que j'avais dû mentir pour être là me taquinait un brin : le mensonge est un art que je ne possède pas. Si j'aimais le métier militaire, n'était-ce pas parce qu'on y disait la vérité ? Je quittai Avord sans avoir découvert le château du Grand Meaulnes, et un autre camarade se tua. Puis ce fut Cazaux et les écoles à feu au-dessus de l'étang d'Arcachon. Le paysage marin m'exalta et puis nous changeâmes d'appareils. Les Potez 25 étaient plus souples, les bimoteurs Lioré et Olivier me semblèrent des montagnes volantes. Le vent nous claquait dans les oreilles et sifflait dans les haubans, la terre était toute blonde. Maxence, le héros de Psichari, me hantait, quand je fus envoyé à Lyon.

La 35e escadre aérienne était équipée de Breguet 27 à moteur Hispano de 450 CV. La carlingue de ces avions était reliée à l'empennage par une simple poutre d'acier léger, ce qui offrait à l'observateur des vues dégagées vers l'arrière, mais cette poutrelle cassait quelquefois. Je me présentai à la base en grande tenue de fantassin : longue tunique à galons et épaulettes d'or, pantalon rouge à bande noire, et sabre. En ce temps-là, je ne passais pas inaperçu ; de nos jours, les

pantalons rouges ne sont pas rares mais tout le monde ne peut pas avoir été traîneur de sabre. Cinquante fois, je claquai des talons et saluai. Le lendemain, en tenue de tous les jours, on s'habitua à moi. Au mess des lieutenants, l'ambiance était chaleureuse, j'avais de la voix, on chantait beaucoup, la jeunesse se croit immortelle. L'escadrille était commandée par le capitaine Challe, lyonnais et saint-cyrien. Homme de prestance à la cordialité mesurée, il préparait l'école de guerre, pilotait parfois, bridgeait beaucoup. Quand, vingt-cinq ans plus tard, son nom jaillira dans la fanfare des événements, il sera, après mon capitaine de Satory, commandant en chef en Algérie. Le titre sembla lui gonfler le jabot, l'ambition le perdit. En 1961, il se lança dans le putsch des généraux. Contre de Gaulle, il ne fut pas de taille.

De la planète, j'avais connu, avec le Bordelais, des mers bleues, des dunes pareilles à des seins, des plateaux de chair blonde et les plaines boueuses de nos camps du Nord. Je passai soudain à une fantasmagorie minérale. A peine quittions-nous l'amas des brumes où se mêlaient les eaux du Rhône et de la Saône et les fumées de la ville, que nous étions propulsés en divine majesté. Un exercice avec le bataillon de chasseurs de Gap nous trimballait au-dessus d'un immense squelette neigeux. A quatre mille mètres, les pilotes rasaient des crêtes, se faufilaient entre des falaises et des gorges. Dans les remous, l'empennage du Breguet 27 vibrait. Il fallait s'y résigner, et, mieux encore, devenir soi-même prédateur. Au milieu de cette carcasse des origines du monde, au-dessus de ces rugueuses vertèbres, je n'avais pas le vertige. Nos moteurs tournaient comme des horloges, la poutre tenait, les pilotes jouaient à s'impressionner eux-mêmes. Nous étions dans un au-delà de lumière, dans un immatériel azur.

L'escadrille s'établissait parfois en plein massif, sur une pente, au milieu d'arêtes. On bâchait les moteurs pour la nuit, on les réchauffait le matin pour la mise en route. Vêtus de cuir, bardés de laine jusqu'aux yeux, nous grimpions dans nos habitacles et les pilotes décollaient face au vide. Avant le vide, ils devaient être en l'air, sinon... Dans la vallée, ils redressaient et le ciel s'emplissait d'un chant d'orgue. Je n'étais plus à gonfler les soufflets de Saint-Maclou pour Olivier Messiaen,

j'étais à cheval sur l'orgue même, je baignais dans une beauté terrifiante.

Décoller de cette rocaille coupait déjà le souffle. S'y poser, c'était autre chose. L'aire était si courte que seuls les acrobates réussissaient. Les pilotes évitaient beaucoup d'obstacles jusqu'au-dessus du dernier et, là, à la limite du décrochage, ils se laissaient tomber. Avec du vent et des freins, on s'arrêtait à temps. Sinon, il fallait remettre les gaz et recommencer. Si quelqu'un ratait son coup, c'était le cirque, quelquefois la culbute.

Je n'avais pas trahi l'infanterie pour rien : j'avais changé d'élément, j'étais promu ange des neiges, j'avais une mère nouvelle, ma souveraine ! A la ferme, je demandais ce qu'il y avait de l'autre côté de l'Atlas. « Le désert », répondait l'oncle Jules. J'y étais presque. La montagne était une monstrueuse solitude. Nous n'étions pas au milieu des astres mais au milieu des aigles que nous dérangions. Retourné, basculé, je me hasardais aussi vers des mondes nouveaux. « Surtout ne soufflons pas, me disais-je, n'arrêtons pas, laissons-nous emporter. » Catapulté hors des petites choses et des bagages, des impedimenta chers à mon vrai père, et à ma famille, j'appartenais à la garde royale. Où étaient désormais les miens ? L'ivresse des vols alpins m'infligea des nausées sidérales qui étaient le péage pour l'accès aux autoroutes de l'au-delà, tant recherchées. Nos courses à travers le fantastique faisaient de nous des hommes d'une autre espèce. Le cœur me battait, notre terrain ressemblait à un nid d'oiseaux de proie. Un jour, je n'y résistai pas. Au-dessus des glaciers de la Meije, à pleine voix, j'entonnai le *Magnificat*. Mon pilote se retourna et me cligna de l'œil. Le *Magnificat* tout entier, en latin, proche du *Te Deum* en vérité, et comme on me l'avait appris au séminaire : « Seigneur nous te louons, nous te rendons gloire au milieu des cimes. »

J'en ris encore.

Le lieutenant qui remplaça le capitaine Challe, lorsqu'il nous quitta pour l'Ecole de guerre, s'appelait Ventré. C'était le meilleur pilote de l'escadrille, il avait l'instinct de l'air, des courants, des moteurs et le don d'obtenir sans imposer. Peut-

être n'était-il pas tellement militaire ? Peut-être la discipline n'était-elle pas pour lui la force principale des armées ? Là où Challe se montrait rigide et froid, il se révéla douceur et fermeté.

L'escadrille, c'était la cavalerie de jadis. L'avion, un cheval mythique avec sa noblesse et ce rien de mystère qui m'avait attiré et que je ne sentais pas encore très bien. Griller une bielle datait de Saint-Exupéry, déjà un ancêtre, et l'avion n'avait que mon âge : vingt-huit ans. Le risque touchait surtout la navigation. L'altitude à laquelle nous voguions permettait à peine d'éviter les obstacles. On les frôlait seulement et il fallait souvent se poser au milieu d'eux. Par le danger, le métier ressemblait à la guerre : quand un avion cassait ou s'effondrait, il entraînait son cavalier avec lui.

Mon attachement pour Ventré dépassera la camaraderie. Les vols accomplis ensemble, le temps passé à s'attendre, à se retrouver, à se quitter encore, à tout mettre en commun composait une sorte de religion. Nous étions les membres d'un ordre barbare, un dieu nous dévorait sans que nous le sachions. L'amitié est-elle moins jalouse que l'amour ou tout autant ? Elle s'exalte, s'aiguise, s'éprend. Il arrive qu'on se dégage de l'amour profane comme d'une bête féroce et qu'il n'en reste même pas le souvenir. Même si je fais la part de ma jeunesse, toujours un peu grisée d'elle-même, et d'une mémoire qui parfois s'égare, je me demande si l'attachement que j'eus pour Ventré eût existé sans l'imaginaire qui nous emportait, sans la légende. Entre nous, l'avion était le plus fort, nos héros étaient les ombres de certains camarades disparus en accident. Quand nous descendions d'avion, nous passions une main amoureuse sur le fuselage comme sur une robe de cheval ; à présent je caresse les pierres de Vézelay. Sans ce mythe, tout serait tombé comme un soufflé raté. Nous étions quelques inséparables à nous saouler de remous, de nuages, d'immensités de champs de neige. Nous étions amoureux, moins les uns des autres que de cet amour-là.

De naissance et de goût paysan pyrénéen, moins exalté que nous mais de l'espèce des hommes oiseaux, Ventré ne sortait pas d'une grande école. Son ambition était de voler tant qu'il pourrait et, l'âge venu, de se retirer chez lui, face aux montagnes. Il m'aida en partie à décider de ma vie. Montherlant crut que je me perdais. Doyon pensa que nous ne

nous verrions plus. J'étais si épris de mon nouvel état que que je prêtai à peine attention à la situation internationale. Le bruit courait que M. Albert Sarraut, président du Conseil, avait demandé au général Gamelin de se préparer à occuper Milan, Turin et toute la Lombardie, que Gamelin avait exigé la mobilisation de six classes et qu'alors M. Sarraut aurait calé. On disait que Gamelin avait proposé d'occuper la rive droite du Rhin et que M. Sarraut n'avait pas osé. On s'attendait aussi à ce que des escadres aériennes allemandes bombardent Paris. Montherlant m'écrivait : « Depuis six ans je vis comme si je n'avais que quelques mois devant moi... »

Ce furent alors le Front populaire et la guerre d'Espagne. Dans les écoles, les fils des Croix-de-feu traitaient de fripouilles les fils des prolétaires. Nous n'osions plus monter dans les trams en tenue et nous recevions de nouveaux avions : des Mureaux, puissants, rapides, des chevaux de race, pensions-nous. Et sans poutre fatale en guise de fuselage. L'observateur y était mieux protégé du souffle de l'hélice, mieux assis, mieux armé. Nous allions souvent en manœuvre. Au camp de la Cavalerie, en plein causse du Larzac, la piste d'envol était couverte d'anémones sauvages. Nous frôlions des falaises, des gouffres, des cavernes, une immensité de landes, des troupeaux de moutons. Le ciel de lavande, allègre et vif, était parfois zébré par une averse. La salle de renseignement, la popote, nos lits s'abritaient sous des tentes. Un jour, Armand Guibert avec qui j'étais en relations épistolaires vint me surprendre. Je le vis tel que j'attendais un poète : grand, très mince, son bec de faucon dressé, l'œil sans cesse en éveil. Nous parlâmes de Montherlant, du Berbère Jean Amrouche que je ne connaissais pas encore et qui m'apparaîtra déjà comme un prince punique égaré dans la religion de Claudel. Ses poèmes, que Guibert savait par cœur, étaient d'un prophète brûlé par des ténèbres et du silence, peut-être par l'orgueil.

Un mal soudain s'abattit sur moi. Je n'eus plus que la peau et les os. De retour à Lyon, je fus contraint de m'aliter quand à son tour Doyon annonça son arrivée. Je n'eus pas la force d'aller l'attendre au train ; il s'enfuit sans même rester dîner, tant je l'effrayai. Il murmura à ma femme : « Mon cœur est un cimetière... » Pour lui, j'allais mourir. De son côté, Guibert accourut de nouveau avec la Quête de joie de Patrice

de La Tour du Pin, et soudain je me levai. Nous allâmes sur le Rhône, à la Croix-Rousse, aux Terreaux, nous dînâmes, nous parlâmes des *Jeunes Filles* de Montherlant. Je m'indignais non pas que Montherlant aimât les garçons, mais qu'il déguisât ses amours. Guibert tenta de me ramener en vain à la littérature. Montherlant ne s'était-il pas présenté, si jeune encore, à l'Académie ? Pour moi, l'Académie ne pouvait l'abriter : il était trop grand. Comme on se trompe !

On se battait en Espagne. Il y avait, paraît-il, quelques officiers de chez nous du côté des républicains, des hommes d'une autre race sans doute. Doyon m'écrivit qu'à l'affût de tout ce qui pouvait le mettre en vedette, Malraux s'était bombardé là-bas colonel et qu'il avait appelé son escadrille *España.* Tiens, Malraux ! Cela ne me parut pas sérieux. Brisé, j'enviais ceux qui avaient des ailes et qui volaient. Un peu au hasard, on m'opéra, je sortis de l'hôpital tel un spectre tandis qu'à Alger Montherlant publiait *Il y a encore des paradis.*

Mon stage fini, je retournai, la mort dans l'âme, à Versailles. Doyon pensait que j'aurais dû rejoindre Malraux. Il avait raison : j'aurais dû, mais comment aurais-je osé quitter l'armée pour une aventure considérée par la plupart d'entre nous comme une folie ? Doyon, qui appelait son chien Askari comme les soldats du Négus, aurait trouvé cela normal à cause du chiffre 2 : Malraux l'avait trahi et était en Espagne, je devais presque en faire autant. Mais non, c'était Malraux. Il avait du génie et pas de scrupules. Mon seul génie était dans mes scrupules, et je ne savais pas les exprimer. Et puis, comment Malraux m'aurait-il accueilli ? J'avais bien, jadis, écrit une note élogieuse sur les *Conquérants,* et l'auteur m'avait remercié, est-ce que cela comptait ? L'idée de l'Espagne ne me vint pas, et si elle m'était venue, je l'aurais repoussée car j'étais tout le contraire d'un républicain. Je croyais à la victoire de Franco.

Les événements excitaient Doyon. Presque chaque soir, il improvisait un banquet avec les habitués : Pillement à la face vaguement asiatique, doux et filiforme, qui écrivait sur Paris ; Tahon, un éditeur d'art aux cheveux en brosse et à la voix puissante, l'œil brillant dès qu'on parlait de femmes ; Turpin, qu'on appelait l'archevêque, avec sa chevelure neigeuse, qui imprimait sur beau papier ses propres pièces en un acte que personne ne jouait jamais, encore qu'il eût un certain talent, ah ! le théâtre ! Parfois apparaissait Bollery, et c'était avec

Doyon une nouvelle bagarre à cause de Bloy. Puis venait Dubois qui avait un poste à l'état-major du métro, et qui était mon ennemi intime et mon rival à cause de Rita, ah ! Rita ! Reine de nos soirées, elle sentait la poudre de riz, la violette, elle incarnait Paris, Doyon voulait qu'elle s'installe impasse Guéménée et que Dubois l'épouse ; je brûlais de passion pour elle, je lui fixais parfois des rendez-vous dans un bar des Champs-Elysées. Elle ne venait jamais. La seule fois qu'elle y consentit, Dubois surgit cinq minutes après, la vache, alerté par Doyon : « Attention, mon fils est en train de te la soulever... »

On fêtait parfois d'autres beautés. C'était des cris, des chants, le vin coulait à flots. Doyon déchirait à belles dents Malraux en Espagne avec sa casquette de chez Lanvin. Quand le rôti était servi, il se collait sur les épaules une cape doublée de violet épiscopal, prenait Askari sur les genoux et l'épuçait en lui arrachant des touffes de poils. Dans ses voiles mauves, comme loin de tout, Mme D. savait qu'il la trompait sans arrêt, qu'elle avait tout perdu le jour où il l'avait enlevée et qu'elle ne verrait plus jamais les cinquante mille francs or qu'il lui avait escamotés, comme Malraux avait ruiné Clara, mais Clara possédait une vraie fortune. Mme D. se consolait avec ses chats, tolérait la donzelle qu'on appelait la cheffesse, qui disparaîtrait comme elle était venue. Léonie la servante au grand cœur changeait les assiettes en se déhanchant. Elle relevait d'une poliomyélite, boitait effroyablement, traînait la savate, échangeait des injures et des baisers avec Doyon qu'elle appelait « sa » père. Elle faisait partie de la maison au point que, si elle manquait, tout allait à vau-l'eau. Elle avait un visage de femme du peuple dans la suite du Christ portant la croix. C'est dans *la Saison des Za* que j'ai le mieux parlé de Doyon, de nos frasques et des institutrices qu'il ramenait de ses tournées de Haute-Loire, qui sentaient la framboise et me mettaient dans tous mes états.

Quand il lui tombait un peu d'argent, Doyon publiait un autre de ses *Livrets du Mandarin*, qui avaient remplacé *la Connaissance*, la revue où Malraux avait écrit son premier article. Il traitait de tout ce qui lui passait par la tête, distribuait louanges et diatribes, expédiait son factum à une centaine d'abonnés, aux journaux, aux éditeurs et envoyait les relevés de l'imprimeur à des mécènes qui lui auront été fidèles jusqu'à

leur mort pour tout, pour le loyer, pour les impôts : sans Marteau, par exemple, comment aurait-il vécu ? Depuis 1930, il n'avait plus le sou.

Quand il était trop tard, je couchais sur un matelas au milieu des chats qui me piétinaient toute la nuit. Bollery et moi, nous nous demandions ce que nous faisions là. Le Mandarin était-il seulement quelqu'un de recommandable ? S'il n'avait été que ça, il n'aurait été ni tellement admiré par nous, ni l'un de mes maîtres. Passons sur l'écrivain. Au moins devrait-il demeurer comme un éditeur des œuvres du XVIIIe siè-cle, connaissant tout, aimant ou haïssant avec passion et se ruinant pour fabriquer ce qui lui plaisait. Naturellement, après une suite d'érotiques où le jeune Malraux avait laissé son empreinte (à moins que ce ne fût le contraire), il avait réimprimé *le Cantique des Cantiques*, les *Canciones* de saint Jean de la Croix, la *Douloureuse Passion* de Catherine Emmerich, il s'était jeté avec fureur dans le *Port-Royal* de Sainte-Beuve, avait réédité Huysmans, Barbey d'Aurevilly, Octave Mirbeau, Renan, Verhaeren, et tant d'autres. Il faisait composer les textes par Coulouma à Argenteuil ou par Nyppels à Maastricht (Hollande) et demandait des dessins, des eaux-fortes, des lettrines et des culs-de-lampe à des artistes qu'il payait en monnaie de singe. Pendant dix ans, ça avait marché et il avait gagné beaucoup d'argent. De temps en temps, il glissait dans le flot de sa production une de ses découvertes, comme les *Oraisons amoureuses* de Jeanne-Aurélie Grivolin, *Commentaire* de Marcelle Sauvageot, *les Journaliers* d'Isabelle Eberhardt, *Mon oncle Benjamin* de Claude Tillier ou encore un roman à lui dont il espérait monts et merveilles. Il n'eut jamais la patience de dresser le catalogue de ses éditions ni personne après lui. Ce trésor a disparu avec sa devise « On se lasse de tout excepté de connaître », orgueilleusement érigée en tête de tous les colophons si divers, si drôles parfois. En 1930, la mode était passée de ces richesses-là, ça ne se vendait plus, d'autres temps avaient commencé, mais il ne perdait pas ses habitudes du grandiose et du magnifique, il aimait régaler, tenir table ouverte et la retrouver telle chez ses amis restaurateurs qu'il célébrait dans ses chroniques. Doyon aimait d'amour les livres, les femmes, les chats, et ceux que le hasard mettait sur sa route avec une sorte de prédestination, comme Malraux et moi, et qu'il ne

pouvait s'empêcher de détester, à la fin. Sans doute gaspillait-il tout. Il m'apprenait dans l'anarchie les vraies valeurs, se laissant aller à de nouvelles imprécations contre les imbéciles, méprisait les puissants, les ministres, les généraux, claironnait que demain ce serait la guerre et qu'on assisterait à des événements mémorables. Je ne voulais pas aller en Espagne, je ne m'intéressais qu'à l'avion, mais je me doutais que le pire approchait. L'horizon s'assombrissait. J'avais serré dans ma cantine *la Quête de joie, Mors et Vita,* j'étais tenté d'y ajouter un *Livret du Mandarin.* Ah! oui, que faisais-je là, surtout moi, jeune officier à qui il enseignait l'indiscipline, mais voilà, il était blidéen de naissance, et le Blida de ce temps-là gardait sur moi le même empire, avec ses calèches autour de la place d'armes, son fameux kiosque à musique avec palmier, l'odeur de péché que toutes les femmes répandaient derrière elles. Dès qu'on parlait de Blida, un soleil éclatait sur le boulevard planté d'orangers et j'entendais résonner la nouba de mon ancien ·égiment, avec son chapeau chinois et ses fanfreluches bleues, ou encore la fanfare des chasseurs d'Afrique sur leurs chevaux piaffants. Naturellement, à Blida comme ailleurs, il y avait des Arabes, mais on les voyait autrement, ils n'étaient pas dangereux, ceux-là, et le soir, le tambour nègre du quartier réservé battait sous les étoiles. On aurait cru qu'à Blida on ne pensait qu'à l'amour, et pourtant la ville était pleine de riches grainetiers, de marchands de vin, d'exportateurs d'agrumes, tout le trafic d'Alger avec le Sud passait par là, on disait aussi que les filles de Blida étaient les plus sensuelles de la plaine. La preuve, moi qui sortais puceau du séminaire, je n'avais pas résisté à l'une d'elles, je l'avais épousée. Fils de boucher juif sans doute, malgré son nom, Doyon avait dû, pour se tirer de là, se démener comme un singe de la Chiffa. Pour lui, Blida était la pire des putasseries et des hypocrisies. Il avait beau dire du mal de Gide qui n'aimait, comme Montherlant, que les petits garçons, Gide avait écrit *les Nourritures terrestres* à Blida et la petite rose de la Mitidja restait dans mon cœur. Mgr Bollon n'avait pas perdu son temps : Doyon devenu mon père m'enseignait le contraire de ce que j'aurais dû apprendre.

« Qu'est-ce que nous faisons là ?... » Voilà ce que nous nous disions avec Bollery dans notre soupente empoussiérée. En même temps, nous savions qu'il n'y avait que Doyon à Paris, et qu'ailleurs on s'embêtait. Bollery avait plus de mérite

que moi à rester dans le galetas : il était d'une plus grande taille, il avait du mal à marcher, il venait de loin, le voyage lui coûtait plus cher, il gagnait moins que moi, lieutenant avec des primes d'aviateur, quand j'en avais. Encore s'ingéniait-il à soutenir des créatures (une au moins) qui, selon Doyon, ne le méritaient nullement, et payait-il de ses deniers l'impression et la diffusion des *Cahiers Léon Bloy,* d'une autre tenue que les *Livrets du Mandarin,* mais voilà, tout se réalisait par passion. Ma passion à moi, ce n'était pas tellement les femmes (sauf Rita qui ne voulait pas de moi) ni même, il faut bien l'avouer, ma famille. Eh oui, j'étais marié, j'avais des enfants, et après ? Etais-je un individu indigne parce que j'étais un filsque à Doyon ? Ma vraie et unique passion, c'était l'avion, l'aéroplane comme nous disions par amusement, tragique et funeste besoin, que Doyon ne comprenait pas, de quitter le sol et de s'aventurer ailleurs. « Qu'est-ce que tu vas fabriquer dans ces nuées impalpables, crétin, à bord de machines capables de se détraquer et de s'écraser avec toi dedans ? » Je ne répondais pas. Il avait ses lubies, j'avais les miennes. Il disait assez qu'on devait agir comme on sentait.

Très tôt le matin, car il était debout avant l'aube à pondre sur Port-Royal ou sur Barbey, il nous portait à chacun un bol du café qu'il avait grillé lui-même et qu'il venait de passer dans une chaussette, et il nous demandait si nous avions bien dormi. « Oui, oui... », grognait Bollery, et ça recommençait : Doyon se mettait à débiner Léon Bloy et Bollery répliquait, nous débouchions dans la salle à manger qui sentait l'osso-buco de la veille et la compote de fruits qui baignait encore dans un jus noir parmi la vaisselle empilée dans la cuisine. Léonie arrivait quand elle pouvait ; elle allait toute la matinée laver et ranger, Léonie, avec sa patte qui se dévissait. Doyon endossait une robe de chambre rouge foncé râpée, usée, salie, déchirée, puis l'heure venait, et il jetait sur ses épaules sa cape doublée de violine, comme on pouvait le voir et l'admirer sur le tableau d'un mandarin trônant au-dessus de la cheminée de la salle à manger, après quoi il s'habillait vaguement pour sortir Askari et me raccompagner au métro. Je regagnais Versailles avec un des premiers trains et remontais la côte de Satory sur ma moto laissée dans un garage.

Chez les militaires, une autre ambiance m'accueillait. Je n'étais plus dans une escadrille avec Ventré, j'étais revenu dans

l'infanterie en attendant de regagner l'armée de l'air, fissa, vous pensez. Quand Olivier Messiaen devra accomplir son service, il me demandera d'intervenir en sa faveur. Grâce à moi, il entrera à la musique du régiment. Les archives de la Pépinière ont-elles gardé trace de lui ? Y joua-t-il jamais d'un instrument ? Déjà à la tribune de Saint-Maclou, je lui attribuais du génie. De ses claviers les harmonies s'échappaient comme les ondes d'un alléluia sans fin.

*
**

C'est une période heurtée, pareille à beaucoup d'autres de ma vie. Je savais où je voulais aller sans savoir si j'y réussirais. J'écrivais sous l'influence de Psichari quelque chose qui aurait dû ressembler au *Voyage du Centurion*, mon héros ne s'appelait pas Maxence mais Patrice, et je m'échinais aussi en vain, à l'exemple de mon fameux père, sur un roman, *Soldes après inventaire.* A la longue, je me suis résigné à le détruire parce que, ne ressemblant à rien, cela ne pouvait devenir quelque chose.

Pour retourner dans l'armée de l'air, il me fallait subir de nouveaux examens de santé. Malgré ma demi-surdité et une éventration chirurgicale, je parvins à m'introduire presque en fraude où je voulais. D'abord, je décrochai un stage dans l'escadrille que Ventré commandait toujours. Elle recevait d'énormes avions de bombardement de nuit peints en noir, des Amiot 143, quand se produisit l'écrasement de la ville espagnole d'Almeria par des croiseurs allemands. Certains camarades approuvèrent l'agression. La guerre approchait de plus en plus. Enfin, toujours en pantalon rouge et le sabre au côté, je me présentai au commandant de la 51e escadre de Tours où j'étais affecté définitivement. On me baptisa à bord d'un bimoteur Potez 540, le type d'avions tout en bois sur lesquels Malraux avait volé en Espagne. Pas en pantalon rouge comme moi, mais avec sa casquette de colonel à visière d'or.

Certains camarades prétendaient, comme Doyon, qu'il n'avait agi que par ambition. Ils ajoutaient qu'il ne savait pas commander, qu'une pagaille noire régnait chez lui et qu'il était plus souvent à discourir à Paris qu'à se battre contre Franco. Peut-être. Cependant, si des Français ont pu lâcher quelques bombes sur Franco pour aider les républicains, ce fut grâce à

171

lui, Malraux. Il ne savait sans doute ni piloter, ni naviguer, ni même mitrailler, mais il risquait sa peau, ce qui n'est pas le fait des intellectuels, il écrivait *l'Espoir,* tournait un chef-d'œuvre, et de toutes les interventions et proclamations enflammées d'alors sur l'Espagne, il ne reste que cela : de la pellicule échappée par miracle à la destruction, des images sublimes nées chez cet homme qui luttait pour les pauvres et la révolution en s'habillant rue du Faubourg-Saint-Honoré et en déjeunant chez Lucas-Carton, près de la librairie de Doyon. Ce qui me frappera en 1937 — ce qui prouve déjà que j'étais moins Croix-de-feu que je le dis — fut un reportage de Saint-Exupéry, contraire et antithèse de Malraux, sur Madrid bombardé, et la photo affichée boulevard des Capucines d'une petite fille de Bilbao dont la mère avait été tuée par des aviateurs allemands. J'essaierai en vain de me détourner de cette image et d'un article de François Mauriac dans *le Figaro* sur les malheurs du peuple basque crucifié. Je commencerai à me poser des questions.

Par lettres, mon amitié avec Guibert et Amrouche flambait. C'était la lune de miel rouge entre nous. Quand ils vinrent en France, je les rejoignis en hâte à moto, à la mi-juillet, aux Deux-Magots. Amrouche, que je ne connaissais pas encore, surgit, le front haut, l'œil dominateur, la lèvre gourmande. Dans une bamboche de poésie, nous partîmes à la recherche de Montherlant que nous trouvâmes rue de Bourgogne sur son palier, comme il sortait. Nous réussîmes à nous faire inviter par lui dans un restaurant à bosquets. Après quoi, je regagnai Tours en vitesse dans la nuit, car notre commandant d'escadre ne plaisantait pas sur l'exactitude. Là, je n'eus pas le temps d'être dressé qu'on m'expédiait de nouveau à Avord pour y devenir cette fois, en cent heures de vol, pilote. Nous décollions les Morane au milieu des prairies, avec les hurlements des moniteurs dans les oreilles. Le capitaine Chainat qui commandait notre section était un ancien as de la chasse, il avait servi dans l'escadrille des Cigognes avec Guynemer et nous parlait de lui sans admiration. Il prétendait que Guynemer lui avait volé une victoire et qu'une histoire de jupon avait causé la perte du héros légendaire.

Chainat était un maniaque de la perfection, une grande gueule ; il nous tenait pour des incapables, des bons à rien, et nous injuriait sans arrêt. Pour lui, l'avion se pilotait avec douceur, ce qui semblait le contraire de son naturel. « Comme une femme », ajoutait-il. Il n'y avait qu'à l'avion que j'étais fidèle et naïvement je mêlais Dieu à cela tandis que Chainat nous traitait de brutes. J'avais la vie qui me plaisait, je me moquais du reste. Ma mère m'annonça la mort de l'oncle Jules au moment où Chainat nous distribuait l'insigne de notre brevet. « Les ailes vous portent, une étoile vous guide. Que la couronne de lauriers ne se transforme pas pour vous en couronne d'immortelles... » Meftah aussi était mort mais on ne me l'avait pas dit. Il me sembla que j'avais définitivement quitté l'Algérie. Pétant feu et flammes sur mon avion et sur ma moto, je retournai à Tours où l'on me colla dare-dare à l'entraînement de nuit. Avant chaque décollage, le capitaine qui commandait notre escadrille se signait plusieurs fois et baisait une médaille. Cela nous paraissait ridicule. Quoi, c'était donc si dangereux, le Potez 540 ?

Je n'ai pas gardé de ce machin-là un souvenir exaltant. Malraux, oui. En photo, on ne l'a vu qu'à côté de Potez 540 ratatinés. Ce pauvre avion faisait ce qu'il pouvait. Pataud, lourd à manier, à quoi pouvait-il bien servir en guerre ? Plus tard, quand je vis l'Espoir je reconnus le siège où le pilote était juché comme sur un trône de roi nègre. On décida de former une aviation d'observation au plus près des troupes et je fus muté à Chartres avec le titre de commandant d'escadrille. Là, j'eus d'autres engins, des Potez 39 encore plus anciens que les 540 car ils n'avaient même pas de train d'atterrissage escamotable, tout comme les avions de chasse de la base, des Nieuport 62 qui dataient de la dernière guerre et sautillaient longuement à l'atterrissage. Nous demeurions les contemporains de Guillaumet et de Saint-Exupéry au moment de la traversée de la cordillère des Andes alors que les Allemands avaient expérimenté leurs Messerschmitt 109 pendant la guerre d'Espagne.

Les événements s'aggravaient. A la conférence de Prague, l'Angleterre nous obligea à céder à Hitler le territoire des Sudètes, la Tchécoslovaquie mobilisait, on rappela chez nous certaines catégories de réservistes. Nous étions résignés. Pour m'obliger à abandonner ma moto, mes parents m'offrirent de

quoi m'acheter une 7CV Citroën qu'on appelait une traction parce que les roues avant étaient motrices. Pour sept mille francs, à l'époque, on en avait une d'occasion. Le dimanche, on se baladait en Touraine ou dans la Beauce, j'allais pêcher en famille sur les bords de la Loire. A Chartres, où nous étions installés, je connus un moment heureux de ma vie. A l'escadrille nous n'étions pas si inconscients, nous espérions que la conflagration ne se produirait pas. Qu'y pouvions-nous ? Je commandais des bidules démodés, pour moi de merveilleux engins. Je n'arrêtais pas de photographier la cathédrale et je lisais Huysmans, j'apprenais que les druides avaient déjà élevé là un autel à la Vierge qui devait enfanter. Plus tard, après le déferlement de tant d'abominations, je ne passerai jamais à Chartres sans une émotion d'amour, j'essaierai même plus d'une fois d'habiter dans la plaine, en vue des flèches sacrées. Chartres restera une lumière de ma vie.

Fin août 1938, je reçus l'ordre, par chance vite annulé, d'exécuter une reconnaissance sur les axes de la ligne Siegfried, et ce fut Munich. Doyon publiait un nouveau roman, *le Baiser du retour*, et Montherlant *l'Equinoxe de septembre* où il bottait les fesses de la bourgeoisie, ce qui me fit hennir d'enthousiasme. L'armée envoya ses pilotes en stage de neige pour assouplir leurs réflexes, je lisais *Adolphe* et Barcelone était livré à Franco sans combat.

Je bouclai une fois de plus ma cantine. Les chasseurs s'entraînaient enfin avec des Morane 406 neufs et nous partîmes, on ne sut jamais pourquoi, pour le camp de Gaël, en bordure de la forêt de Brocéliande, où l'enchanteur Merlin s'était métamorphosé en sanglier. Pour sacrifier aux rites, je bus de l'eau pourrie de la fontaine de Jouvence et, un jour, sans savoir qui l'y avait mis, je trouvai un œillet blanc sur le tableau de bord de mon avion. Pas Mélusine tout de même ? Peut-être une beauté de l'hôtel à qui j'avais fait la cour. Si innocente, si fraîche, me semblait-il. Un camarade m'éclaira : elle tenait un bordel à Rennes. Peu importe. Dans mon Potez 39, je ramenai aussi des roses, de la bruyère et des lambeaux de lichen. C'était un poète que la férule de Chainat avait maté.

Mes parents arrivèrent d'Alger tandis que, dans le glorieux été, de formidables insectes mécaniques moissonnaient dans la plaine. Bernanos publiait *Scandale de la vérité* et éreintait quelques prélats espagnols et romains. Vers la fin du

mois d'août, les escadres de chasse mirent en route leurs échelons précurseurs. Chartres, que Huysmans avait traité de nécropole, devint tout bruissant de convois. A tout casser, nos misérables veaux s'essoufflaient à 180 kilomètres à l'heure. « Cela suffit pour observer », disait notre commandant. A condition de pouvoir rester en l'air. La DCA nous descendrait comme des perdreaux. Quant aux Messerschmitt, si par malchance nous en croisions, nous serions pour eux des proies faciles, et nous rejoindrions le sol plus vite que nous ne volions. Notre brave commandant croyait à la victoire. A table, nous chantions « le Forban » :

> *Je suis forban, que m'importe la gloire*
> *Enfant de roi, fils de prostituée,*
> *Vivre d'orgie, ma seule espéran-ance...*

Les paroles nous semblaient adaptées à la situation. « Le Forban », nous le chanterons toute la guerre, je le chante encore. Seulement, je n'ai plus de voix.

Un gouffre s'ouvrit devant nous. Dans le choix de Goering entre le beurre et les canons, nous étions allés au pire. Un cœur enfiévré battait en moi, il allait falloir se montrer digne de ce qui approchait. A l'idée de me laisser aspirer par les événements, j'éprouvai une sorte de volupté sauvage. La cathédrale devenait soudain une ruine debout, une grandiose madone de pierre. Mes camarades de la chasse, presque tous imberbes sous leur casque de cuir, ressemblaient aux anges des vitraux qu'on déposait. Ils brûlaient de transformer les Messerschmitt en carcasses fumantes. Nous étions plus modestes. A grands coups de badigeon, des peintres camouflaient les fuselages et les ailes de nos avions. Trois par trois, les chasseurs décollèrent, beaucoup encore avec leurs antiques Nieuport 62, d'autres avec des Morane 406 ; ils tournaient au-dessus des flèches bleues puis disparaissaient vers le nord. Nous restâmes seuls. Le 2 septembre, un samedi, mes parents se lancèrent courageusement dans le flot des voyageurs et regagnèrent Alger. Le 5, j'emmenai mon escadrille à Guise, non loin de Saint-Quentin, un peu au sud du Luxembourg. Pendant deux mois, nous vécûmes à l'écart de la réalité, en

surnombre et en survie, dans une sorte de trompe-l'œil où l'on jouait à la guerre qui ne tue pas. Notre commandant se prenait pour le Grand Turc et nous entraînait souvent boire du champagne à Reims. Le soir, avec quelques officiers désignés à tour de rôle, il couchait au Sphinx, le célèbre bordel, où les filles étaient belles. Il m'y emmena une fois. Alors il se déchaînait dans une vague noce crapuleuse qu'il prenait pour une débauche rituelle la veille d'une bataille. Il croyait grimper vers le zénith, vers la gloire.

Comme à nos yeux il ne se passait rien, et aux yeux du commandement pas grand-chose à côté de ce qu'on attendait, sinon que la Pologne avait été écrasée en trois semaines par Hitler et la Finlande par Staline, on nous retira sur la Riviera. Notre commandant parlait du front où nous avions combattu en héros. Les hôtels étaient vides, la pluie tombait. A Noël, nous nous trémoussions avec des vieilles Américaines émoustillées dont les tibias tintaient, et, par miracle, une merveilleuse danseuse russe en instance de visa pour New York dont je gardai longtemps les chaussons. Enragé, râleur, hargneux, j'exigeai ma mutation pour le centre de pilotage que commandait Ventré entre Grenoble et Lyon, où l'on transformait sur des bimoteurs flambant neuf, des Potez 63-11, les équipages qui ramaient encore sur nos anciens veaux. Avec Ventré, nous montâmes en pleine cambrousse un camp de baraquements et nous nous jetâmes d'arrache-pied dans une course contre la mort. Nous n'arrêtions que la nuit. Le 10 mai, l'enfer éclata et les premiers craquements retentirent. Moins d'un mois après, l'armée française refluait en désordre ou était prisonnière, les panzers dévalaient, irrésistibles. On annonça que des bombes étaient tombées sur Chartres. Le pays entier nous parut à feu et à sang, je sautai dans un dernier train et courus enlever ma femme et mes enfants. De retour le lendemain au camp, nous vidions les lieux et mettions le feu aux avions en panne. Nous partîmes un peu au hasard, comme un cirque, vers le sud, derrière Ventré. Un moniteur se tua au décollage. A Nîmes, nous apprîmes que Lyon était occupé. Le téléphone ne marchait plus, la radio ne servait à rien, sauf pour une voix de détresse : « Françaises, Francais, je vous le dis, il faut arrêter le combat... » D'habitude, c'était de haut que nous voyions la France. A terre, nous étions aux prises avec des fuyards, des paniquards, des femmes en larmes. Les trains étaient stoppés,

les gares envahies et fermées, les soldats débandés parmi des embouteillages de bagnoles. On n'y comprenait rien sinon que, sans avoir eu le temps de nous en apercevoir, nous étions rayés de la surface de la terre, assommés, ahuris. Je ne résume pas la débâcle du pays, mais la mienne. Le bruit circulait qu'un général de Gaulle, ancien sous-secrétaire d'Etat à la guerre, était à Londres et appelait tous ceux qui le pouvaient à le rejoindre. De Nîmes, c'était impossible. Nous n'étions plus que des poussières nous cherchant dans le désordre, flottant dans un rayon de soleil. C'était la folie et le malheur partout. Adieu ma vie, adieu mon cœur, adieu mon espérance.

Le salut était hors de France. Sans directive de personne, nous nous décidâmes pour Alger, par la seule route possible. Là, on verrait. Ce général de Gaulle y serait peut-être déjà, qui sait ? Ce n'était pas si bête, notre idée. Claudel eut la même. Ambassadeur à la retraite depuis quatre ans, espérant peut-être aussi, avec sa haute idée de la France, un autre gouvernement, et sautant sur l'occasion de se débarrasser de sa femme car il n'aimait, même à son âge, que l'aventure, il prit le bateau pour Alger à ce moment-là. Nous nous rapprochâmes de la côte pour réduire la distance à franchir et nous posâmes à Perpignan. La radiophonie de bord n'était pas encore inventée, chacun se débrouillait comme il pouvait, le contrôle de piste du terrain était une carriole qui lançait des fusées rouges ou vertes. Des camarades relâchaient de partout, des chasseurs cherchaient du carburant et repartaient au hasard ; des observateurs s'étaient battus, d'autres pas. Quant aux bombardiers, l'armée de l'air n'en possédait pas. « Qu'est-ce que tu fais, toi ? » Les uns voulaient atteindre Oran, la plupart Alger, certains Tunis. Il y avait encore de l'essence, nous échelonnâmes les départs. La météo n'était pas si bonne que ça.

VI

Les années noires

L'HORIZON était un camaïeu ocre et gris, l'île de Majorque glissait vers nous, je surveillais l'espace au-dessus de moi car l'Espagne avait menacé de lâcher des chasseurs à nos trousses. Je n'étais pas armé. A mes flancs, plus haut, plus bas, des camarades nous dépassaient. Ce jour-là, le 21 juin 1940, j'étais aux commandes d'un avion moderne, moi devant, mon passager derrière, à 3 500 mètres d'altitude.

C'était la première fois que je volais au-dessus de la mer. Ce qui paraît tellement banal aujourd'hui était encore, en 1940, réservé aux avions de ligne et à l'aéronavale. Nous étions hommes de la terre. En cas de panne, Chainat nous avait enseigné à nous poser dans une prairie. Là, où aller ? Les îles dérivaient, j'affichai le nouveau cap qui devait nous amener à Alger, trois cents kilomètres plus au sud. Les moteurs synchronisés à deux mille tours tournaient rond. Le temps était calme avec quelques cumulus vers l'est. Le Potez 63 B2 que je pilotais sortait à peine d'usine, nous l'avions reçu sans notice d'emploi, Ventré l'avait essayé, l'avait trouvé un peu nerveux au décollage, très docile ensuite. Depuis le premier vol, j'aurais dû m'inquiéter de la consommation en carburant. A quelques minutes près, il devait avoir trois heures de rayon d'action. Dès que la côte apparaîtrait, je réduirais le régime et me mettrais en léger piqué. Un sentiment bizarre, quelque chose comme une fatalité pesait sur moi : nous changions de continent, la guerre changeait d'espace, le monde changeait d'ère, je pensais à toutes les roses dont la France était fleurie. Toutes ces roses pour l'arrivée des Fritz, blonds, en command-cars, sans même un coup de fusil, que nos filles

179

regardaient passer dans le glorieux été. Les forbans, ce n'était pas nous.

Les mains gantées de cuir sur un volant en nœud papillon, j'écoutais mes moteurs, je surveillais le ciel et la mer, suspendu entre deux mondes. J'abandonnais une patrie naufragée. En état de choc, j'étais en route vers un ailleurs, une Terre promise ? Un devenir, une incertitude. Au cap 180, je n'allais pas tarder à apercevoir le Djurdjura. J'avais derrière moi un précieux mécanicien, le sergent-chef Lemoigne. Autour de moi des camarades. Ventré avait dû décoller le dernier du groupe. Au sud, des montagnes apparurent, je réduisis les moteurs à dix-huit cents tours et mis la commande de profondeur en léger piqué. Je devinai la côte que je connaissais, Bône, Dellys puis la crête du Chenoua et Tipasa, mais je ne savais pas encore qui était Camus. Alger brillait comme un mirage au pied de la colline du séminaire. Je me laissai glisser sur l'aérodrome de Maison-Blanche où je me faufilai entre les camarades de tout à l'heure à Perpignan. D'autres pleuvaient de partout, les réservoirs à sec. Il me restait combien d'essence ?

Ventré descendait prudemment de son habitacle sous un soleil radieux et innocent, comme pour une éblouissante escale. Miracle, j'étais chez moi. Il n'y avait pas de guerre, je renaissais. Un instant, j'oubliai le malheur, les roses, les morts, puis tout revint avec une majestueuse fatalité. En un éclair, tout s'était brisé, détraqué, disloqué. Les Fritz avaient dû dépasser Reims sans s'arrêter au Sphinx : réservé à ces messieurs de la super-intendance ou aux grands chefs. A présent, d'ici, où aller ? Vers qui ? Contre qui ? Ventré calcula les distances, les moyens en ravitaillement. L'Egypte était loin et on n'entrait pas à Gibraltar comme dans un moulin. Nous étions sur une autre planète, à l'écart des bouleversements. Les combats ici, c'était, à travers des étendues enchanteresses ou désolées, des rezzous, les razzias, la philosophie, l'amour, la poésie : un rêve, un mirage d'un naguère englouti.

Mes parents n'en crurent pas leurs yeux. Là, chez eux, Ventré et moi ? Personne ne mesurait l'étendue de la catastrophe. Ventré et moi reçûmes une réquisition pour un hôtel sur la mer. J'avais encore dans l'oreille la voix chevrotante de la débâcle et de l'armistice. Des trams passaient, le soir tomba, les rues s'éclairèrent, des étoiles brillèrent, rien ne semblait

atteindre la quiétude d'une ville que Montherlant avait comparée au paradis. A mille lieux de la tourmente et du cyclone qui nous avaient jetés là, à la terrasse d'un café, au milieu de camarades éberlués, nous nous regardions, assommés, sans savoir ce qui nous était arrivé. Soudain le silence pesa.

Elle avait chu, la grande Babylone. Le 23 juin, Claudel était à Alger où, hôte sans doute du gouverneur, il essaya en vain de joindre le général Noguès. Comment l'aurions-nous su ? Dans la chronologie de l'édition de la Pléiade du théâtre de Claudel, Jacques Madaule signale ce voyage. Gérald Antoine qui a épluché le journal de Claudel en cite une phrase : « *La France était vaincue, mais il lui restait une aviation, une flotte, un Empire, et je croyais impossible qu'on abandonne tout cela.* » Quant à l'Etat français qui succédait à la IIIe République, chez nous personne ne broncha. Nous n'avions rien à regretter du régime et des gouvernements précédents.

A cinquante ans de distance, j'ai du mal à mesurer les impulsions de mon cœur pendant ces deux années noires. Un enfant de septembre, comme Patrice de La Tour du Pin l'avait décrit, un migrateur égaré, tel j'étais. Nous avions cru tomber sur une plage de l'autre côté de la mer. La débâcle nous rattrapait.

Le lendemain, nous retournâmes à nos avions. Combien y en avait-il sur la base de Maison-Blanche ? Mille ? Deux mille ? Tous les jours il en arrivait. Ils étaient notre seule arme. Nous les flattions, nous leur parlions, nous sautions à notre place comme en selle, et là, nous rêvions. Je réussis à obtenir qu'on fasse les pleins du mien. C'était une règle encore respectée : ainsi je sus qu'il me restait cinquante-quatre litres à notre arrivée de Perpignan. Avec l'autorisation de personne, sans ordre de personne non plus, puisque chacun faisait ce qu'il voulait et qu'il n'y avait aucun contrôle de piste, je mis les moteurs en route, j'extirpai mon avion de la longue file où il attendait, comme un cheval dans une écurie sans lads ni palefreniers, et, avec Ventré derrière moi, je décollai sans dire où j'allais et sans que personne me le demande. A Ventré, je montrai Alger, le séminaire, Notre-Dame d'Afrique, la Bouzaréa, la plaine, Boufarik, Blida. A Ventré ou à moi-même ? Je ne les avais jamais vus de haut. Blida ressemblait à une étoile

de mer avec deux rayons sur la montagne et trois sur la plaine. Où était Rovigo ? Avec son lit où ne coulait qu'un filet d'eau, l'oued Djemaa tenait une place si large que je ne m'y reconnaissais plus. Je virai, revins à ce que je crus le village de Sidi-Moussa, descendis une allée où les eucalyptus avaient été coupés et découvris enfin la ferme minuscule, insignifiante, où ma mère et moi avions vécu. Je me rappelai alors le pont qu'on franchissait, l'année de l'inondation, les soirs où l'oncle Jules chassait dans les marais. A présent, le canard aux ailes bleues, c'était moi, avec du plomb dans l'aile. Un fils ou un petit-fils de Meftah dut voir avec effroi notre machine volante passer en trombe au-dessus des toits. Pour un serviteur arabe, ce fut peut-être un événement de plus à un moment où le ciel s'abattait de partout.

De là, pour regagner Alger, il suffisait de réduire les gaz. Au dernier virage, je n'eus plus devant moi qu'une lande vide et des hangars. Le Potez 63 B2 sautillait, il fallait pousser un peu sur le manche pour plaquer les roues au sol.

Le lendemain, les pleins refaits, je recommençai. Sur mon carnet de vol, j'ai écrit : « Entraînement. » Alors, qui nous empêchait de partir d'abord pour Oran, pour Gibraltar ensuite ? Oran n'était qu'à trois cent cinquante kilomètres d'Alger, Gibraltar à quatre cents d'Oran. A présent, je savais que nous n'avions pas sept cents kilomètres de rayon d'action. Peut-être la base d'Oran était-elle commandée par un colonel soupçonneux ? Peut-être nous demanderait-on où nous allions ? Un vol direct pour Gibraltar était hasardeux, le vent pouvait être contraire. Partir, ne pas partir, épouser ou ne pas épouser, plonger ou ne pas plonger. On est fou ou on ne l'est pas. A quoi m'aurait servi de me rappeler qu'en mars on avait demandé des volontaires pour le Levant, que j'avais donné mon nom sans aucune suite ? Si seulement j'avais été amoureux d'une femme, par hasard, en Grande-Bretagne, comme ce fut le cas pour certains héros que je connais, j'aurais filé, comme un renard après une odeur. Le croyant ne discute pas. Abraham, quand Dieu lui ordonne d'aller vers la Chaldée, ne demande rien. Il va. Encore faut-il qu'il entende Dieu.

La prudence suggéra que nous n'étions pas sûrs de l'existence de ce général de Gaulle que nous pensions trouver à Alger. Pourquoi refuser ce qui s'offrait à nous ? La guerre s'était éloignée, il y avait encore des restaurants, des hôtels, des

filles, je m'aperçus que la discipline était la facilité. Pour moi, jeune officier, l'armée, malgré les bons camarades que j'y ai connus, fut une rigide école de non-pensée. Un militaire ne pense pas, il obéit. S'il ne reçoit pas d'ordres, il ne bouge pas. C'est vrai. Je n'ai jamais été un bon militaire. La patrie ? « Où est donc la patrie sinon où tu es ? Ce n'est pas à toi de décider », conclut Ventré. Quant à la pensée, il faut relire le *Journal* de Claudel à ce moment-là : « Je dis timidement à cet amiral : " Est-ce que vous pensez... " Au mot de pensée il bondit ! " Je ne pense pas, Monsieur, j'obéis. " » Nous avions subi une défaite, mais il y avait une mer entre la défaite et nous. Bref, je connus une défaillance dont j'aurai honte longtemps. La veulerie dont j'avais accusé les autres, je m'en rendis coupable et grossis le nombre de ceux qui s'interrogeaient et avaient peur du lendemain. Alger était la terre de la douceur. On n'y courait pas de risque, on n'y devenait pas journaliste, on n'osait rien, on restait dans la gibecière de l'oncle Jules. Bref, c'était raté. J'agis selon mon cœur, et mon cœur ne savait pas ce qu'il voulait. Ma conscience non plus. « Si tu nous quittes, tu nous affaiblis », me dit Ventré pour me consoler.

D'ailleurs, il était trop tard. Quelques pilotes avaient moins réfléchi que moi et étaient partis, pas toujours parce qu'ils avaient le feu au cul. Le commandement réagit et ordonna aux mécaniciens d'encaquer nos avions les uns dans les autres et de débrancher les magnétos. Il n'y eut plus qu'à nous morfondre et qu'à manger le couscous au restaurant oriental de la rue de Chartres. Question de Ventré : « Comment va-t-on se démerder avec eux ? » Il pensait aux Arabes. J'avais oublié nos serveurs, les guenilleux qui déambulaient sur le boulevard face à la mer, les petits cireurs, l'innombrable multitude qu'on devinait sous les terrasses de la Casbah et sur la plaine où le Potez avait passé comme une flèche. Je répondis avec assurance qu'il n'y avait pas de problème. Ventré en douta. Ventré, c'était la raison.

Les sirènes retentirent, des croiseurs et des torpilleurs appareillèrent, des hydravions décollèrent, on nous rappela à la base, un général surgit au mess, les Anglais menaçaient de couler l'escadre de Mers el-Kébir : « Remettez vos avions en état, réarmez-les. » Nous y courûmes. « J'aurais eu l'air fin, pensai-je, si j'avais été à Gibraltar. » Ventré triomphait.

183

Finalement l'ordre de décoller et d'attaquer ne fut pas lancé. Qui aurait accroché des bombes sous nos plans ? Avec quoi aurait-on visé ? Pour atteindre Gibraltar, d'où aurions-nous sauté ? Comment serions-nous revenus ? Je me souvins du fameux article d'Henri Béraud, avant la guerre : « Faut-il réduire l'Angleterre en esclavage ? » Une tempête se leva dans les esprits. Les Anglais étaient toujours nos ennemis, mais pourquoi Darlan n'avait-il pas fait sécession avec la marine intacte ? Pourquoi avait-il préféré être ministre du maréchal Pétain ? Un amiral était gouverneur général de l'Algérie, un autre résident à Tunis, un dernier amiral décidait de la destruction de sa flotte à Mers el-Kébir. C'était le 3 juillet. Claudel était reparti pour la France depuis la veille, « confondu par l'étroitesse des esprits et la faiblesse des âmes », écrit Gérald Antoine.

Une tornade de désarroi passa sur nous, les jeunes officiers se distinguèrent : tapage nocturne dans les rues d'Alger, injures aux agents de la force publique. Je manquai de pondération. J'en manquerai toujours. Quarante-cinq ans plus tard, toujours indigné, me viendra l'idée de traîner en Haute Cour l'amiral vaincu qui n'avait jamais été inquiété. Tout le monde avait oublié Mers el-Kébir, l'amiral était mort de vieillesse. Eh bien, sa casquette dorée trônerait sur un fauteuil, personne ne trouva l'idée originale, on me prit pour un inconscient. Dieu sait pourtant l'ardeur et l'imagination que j'ai jetées dans *Une affaire d'honneur* ! En juillet 1940, je jugeai Ventré égoïste, vaguement profiteur de friandises qu'il me cachait parfois. C'était un paysan madré qui avait des dons de gerfaut. Pour lui j'employais trop de mots sonores, je faisais confiance à trop de gens, j'avais trop souci de perfection. Hélas, quand je fis resurgir Mers el-Kébir, Ventré n'était plus là ; dommage, il aurait bien rigolé. Est-ce que j'étais moi-même encore en vie pour faire plaisir aux amiraux ? Fallait-il rappeler pareille honte sans attenter au moral de la nation ou braver la marine ? Je n'ai rien contre la marine de guerre — une caste privilégiée — ou la marine marchande, au contraire : je suis contre le mensonge, contre les massacres imbéciles, pour l'irrespect à l'égard de toutes les non-valeurs. J'ai écrit une provocation dont personne n'eut le goût de s'occuper. Personne ne voulait de scandale dans l'armée, nous n'étions

cependant plus sous de Gaulle. « Nos victoires sont des lumières et nos défaites des énigmes. » C'est un amiral de chez nous qui a écrit cela, peut-être à propos d'Aboukir. En Egypte, encore un désastre où l'amiral qui commandait les vaisseaux ne passa pas non plus en jugement parce que Bonaparte qui commandait en chef ne voulut pas être mêlé à une sale affaire, avec Nelson encore comme trouble-fête. Mers el-Kébir fut une tragédie, je l'ai traité comme telle, j'ai fait claquer la honte dans certains carrés où l'on n'a bu, pendant la dernière guerre, à aucune victoire, et sur certaines passerelles où l'ordre de feu n'a été lâché que contre des navires britanniques. Les acteurs d'une tragédie n'expient pas leurs propres erreurs mais les péchés de la fatalité. Ce n'est pas moi qui le dis, c'est Schopenhauer, et Pierre Leiris le rappelle à propos de Billy Bud, ce beau marin anglais qui fut pendu au temps des guerres de l'Empire parce qu'il déplaisait à un officier marinier de Sa Gracieuse Majesté.

Bref, là encore, silence dans les rangs ! silence à nos généraux, silence à nos éditorialistes qui n'ont pourtant à se mettre sous la dent que bisbilles entre partis politiques, silence de nos critiques bien-pensants qui comptent leurs voix pour une élection à l'Académie. Même silence pour les mêmes raisons, la crainte d'un faux pas, en juillet 1940, à Alger.

Les semaines passèrent. Je n'étais pas le seul, tous étaient comme moi : on ne savait pas, on n'osait rien risquer, la honte et l'ennui nous recouvrirent. Nous échouâmes, Ventré et moi, à Sétif. Lui adjoint au commandant d'un groupe de reconnaissance sur Potez 63-11, moi chef d'une des deux escadrilles. Pour tout potage, une heure de vol par avion et par semaine. Eh bien quoi, étions-nous les vainqueurs ? Sétif était l'ancien grenier de Rome. Au milieu d'un plateau où l'on cultivait le blé, la ville bâtie en damier à mille mètres d'altitude, avait une grande rue à arcades, un lycée où le jeune Kateb Yacine allait bientôt entrer, un sous-préfet, un commandant d'armes, un régiment de tirailleurs, un escadron de spahis, et nous. L'une des pharmacies appartenait à M. Ferhat Abbas, conseiller financier marié à une Française et considéré comme un esprit critique, bourgeois mais subversif. Une église, un hôtel de

France vétuste, un temple protestant, une synagogue, quelques mosquées et quelques ruines romaines. Le climat était sain, l'hiver dur, l'été torride, d'habitude le vent soufflait de l'Atlas saharien dont les crêtes hérissaient l'horizon. Les colons se sentaient un peu seuls au milieu de masses d'indigènes qui ressemblaient à la terre, aux buissons, aux écorchures des ravins. De l'autre côté des montagnes, c'était l'Aurès sauvage et nu. Le champ d'aviation s'étendait vaille que vaille, avec des bosses, sur un vaste plateau moissonné qui paraissait brûlé.

Nous eûmes le droit d'aller chercher nos familles, qu'il était prudent d'arracher à la France écrasée. J'embarquai sur une espèce de casserole, le *Djebel Amour,* qui se traîna le long des côtes et nous débarqua en cachette au bout du port de Marseille, à l'Estaque, parmi les maisons de passe. Pas de voitures, sauf pour les officiers allemands. Figé, pétrifié, le cœur comme en suspens, je découvris dans les hangars d'Istres les épaves de notre échelon roulant : des caisses, des sacs, des cantines à nos noms. Après quoi, comme je pus, je rejoignis notre ancien terrain. Les paysans rentraient leurs foins, l'incendie avait dévoré nos baraquements, tout était jonché de carcasses noircies, les troupeaux de freux avaient repris possession des maïs. De retour à Sétif, je louai une villa dans l'avenue fraîchement baptisée du maréchal Pétain. Dans un avion de liaison qui se posait chez nous, je rencontrai Saint-Exupéry. Lui aussi y croyait, à Pétain. Il revenait de Paris et s'apprêtait à gagner les Etats-Unis. Je l'avais croisé, un an auparavant, dans un train sur la Riviera ; en uniforme comme moi, il portait une casquette avec une coiffe trop haute, si vaste. J'avais hésité : « Vous êtes Antoine de Saint-Exupéry... » Il m'avait regardé avec étonnement de ses yeux de nuit. Je n'avais rien osé ajouter. Il était descendu très tôt, à Agay où vivait sa mère. Cette fois, dans le Goéland qui nous emmenait à Alger, il me raconta sa traversée sur un quadrimoteur Farman de 44 places qui sortait d'usine et dont, à Bordeaux, personne n'osait prendre possession. Il n'avait jamais piloté de mastodonte pareil, il avait racolé des passagers, bourré dans le fuselage des inconnus qui cherchaient à fuir le désastre, et même une femme, et en juin, comme nous, s'était posé à Oran, au jugé, comme un pacha. Il me dit sur un ton de confidence que le moral de l'armée allemande semblait atteint. Ça me parut

bizarre. Atteint par quoi ? A Maison-Blanche, on l'attendait, il s'en alla, je me sentis seul.

A l'état-major, on me dit qu'on comptait sur moi, on avait l'impression que je savais où j'allais, que je m'accrochais à quelque chose. Moi ? A rien. Depuis Mers el-Kébir et ensuite depuis Dakar, un échec pour de Gaulle, j'étais coincé, toujours serré dans la gibecière de l'oncle Jules. Les vieilles gloires comptaient-elles encore ? Tout petit, tout gris, pareil avec son bec rongé à une ombre shakespearienne, Weygand en tournée nous exposa les trahisons anglaises, la capitulation du roi des Belges, l'impossibilité de contenir le flot adverse avec des forces indécises, la retraite. Il ne convainquit personne. Il brandissait une épée illusoire, on aurait dit qu'il sortait de la tombe. Et la Royale, coulée à Mers el-Kébir, mon général, au mouillage à Toulon et encore sous la menace des canons anglais en Egypte ? Pas un mot sur la Royale. Il se contenta de nous placer devant la vertu de l'obéissance et laissa entendre que l'avenir n'était pas si sombre. « Appelé trop tard, Weygand », disions-nous avec nostalgie. « Qui sait ? répondait Ventré. Weygand n'est peut-être plus Weygand. » Avec l'âge, les varices, la bedaine, la mémoire qui foutait le camp, l'esprit qui n'était plus clair, le moment venait où on n'était plus ce quelqu'un-là, mais quelqu'un d'autre, un peu avachi, et les gens croyaient à celui d'avant. Pétain restait Pétain alors qu'il avait quatre-vingt-quatre ans, Weygand ne restait plus Weygand alors qu'il venait de subir comme commandant en chef un désastre semblable à celui de Bazaine en 1870. N'était-il pas aussi amoureux d'une belle Libanaise, comme mon ami Georges Buis me l'affirma plus tard ? Un général amoureux n'est plus un général, à moins d'avoir l'allure et les crocs de Bonaparte. Ventré, toujours méfiant, s'interrogeait. De Gaulle que je n'avais vu qu'en photo, un képi flambant neuf sur un échalas, ne me paraissait pas tellement admirable. Je feignais de l'ignorer, peut-être parce que je n'avais pas osé le rejoindre, comme on feint de ne plus prêter attention à qui ne s'est pas laissé séduire. Quand il fut condamné à mort par Vichy, aucune réaction chez nous : il l'avait cherché, il récoltait. On se taisait. On ne prononçait jamais son nom. Dans la famille popote et pot-au-feu de l'armée où l'on est si formaliste, on le considérait comme illégitime. S'il arrivait à quelqu'un d'évoquer son nom, les regards échappaient. De Gaulle, c'était le

silence, l'inaccessible, le rebelle dont il valait mieux ne pas parler, l'inavouable péché des autres, la robe déchirée de l'unité. Des émissaires de Vichy nous glissèrent dans le creux de l'oreille : « Le Vieux trompe Adolf. » J'aurais été bien incapable de jouer le double jeu.

La garnison semblait fidèle à Pétain mais personne ne disait la vérité. Qui croire ? Tout le monde mentait. Par prudence. Par méfiance. Sauf moi. Un journal, *la Dépêche de Constantine,* diffusait des nouvelles. De Sétif, on entendait mal les radios étrangères. Les événements, quand on les connaissait, parlaient d'eux-mêmes.

J'avais acheté au marché un âne gris. Lui, il avait la croix du Sauveur sur l'épaule. Je l'avais appelé Samson, en souvenir de la mâchoire qui avait massacré mille Philistins. L'escadrille l'avait adopté, il paissait les maigres herbages du camp et, le soir, dormait sous une tente. A mon arrivée le matin, quand je l'appelais, il lançait un braiment puissant. J'ai toujours aimé les ânes qu'au Moyen Age on représentait instruisant les évêques. Je ne sais pourquoi j'ai de la tendresse pour eux. La preuve encore : Ulysse, qui garde le cimetière de Vézelay et détient du sacré en lui, sous son poil fauve de mécréant.

Le décret Crémieux qui, en 1871, avait octroyé la nationalité française en bloc aux indigènes israélites fut aboli. Cela aurait dû déjà m'alerter. En Algérie, qui n'était antijuif ? Toutes les séquelles de Drumont, député d'Alger en 1900, marinaient dans les milieux populaires, l'armée avait toujours détesté Léon Blum, embastillé par Pétain. Comment le désastre de Mers el-Kébir n'aurait-il pas contribué à l'idée qu'il y avait du juif là-dessous et qu'entre Pétain et Eden, le choix devait être facile ? Cependant, la supression des privilèges pour les juifs d'Afrique du Nord ne souleva pas chez les musulmans une explosion de joie. Beaucoup d'entre eux se méfièrent. Ferhat Abbas, plus politique que Mokrani qui avait cru, en 1870, la France hors d'état de réagir, préparait un manifeste pour obtenir des concessions en faveur de son peuple. A Sétif, où se déclencheront en 1945 les premières réactions contre la colonisation, nous ne pensions à peu près à rien. Seuls ceux qui pouvaient écouter, la nuit, la BBC, savaient quelque chose. Je n'aimais pas les juifs et personne autour de moi ne les aimait, est-ce que Barrès s'était rangé du

côté du capitaine Dreyfus ? Zola oui, mais Zola était considéré comme un néo-Français et un écrivain du déclin. La langue d'Eglise n'était pas tendre non plus pour ces « perfides » qui avaient crucifié le Christ. Nous fûmes chagrins cependant qu'on les persécutât en France et qu'on les obligeât à porter une étoile jaune. Quant aux Arabes, si j'étais un peu l'élève de Meftah, j'étais surtout disciple des lazaristes et encore sous l'influence du capitaine Boum-Boum. La même rengaine : « Tous menteurs, pédérastes et voleurs... »

Dans cette bourgade pouilleuse des hauts plateaux, personne ne savait rien, personne ne disait rien, tout le monde se méfiait de chacun et chacun se méfiait de tous. Il n'existait aucune relation entre l'armée de terre et nous. Quand Pétain rencontrera Hitler à Montoire en octobre 1940, personne n'osera le moindre commentaire. Aucun aviateur n'allait jamais au cercle de garnison, les cavaliers en bottes rouges tournaient dans leur manège, les fantassins s'abrutissaient en inspections de paquetage dans leur quartier, nos célibataires flanquaient le grabuge dans des ménages de pétainistes endurcis. Etait-ce une politique, cette inertie voulue, ce marasme ? Fallait-il mélanger des opinions plus ou moins orthodoxes aux humeurs des uns et des autres ?

Chaque matin à sept heures, en été plus tôt, l'autocar de la base ratissait le personnel de l'aviation. Le soir, dans la base déserte, nos ânes, car j'en avais acheté un second, poussaient un braiment mélancolique, l'officier de service s'installait dans une chambre du pavillon du commandement et attendait un coup de téléphone qui ne venait pas. Pour se distraire, il inspectait la garde qui veillait sur nos deux hangars clos : une sentinelle par hangar. Pendant les fortes chaleurs, le ciel aspirait des trombes de poussière dans la plaine, puis les couchait vers les montagnes où, peu à peu, elles se dissipaient. Parfois on repêchait un aviateur à la dérive dans une barque en Méditerranée. Une fois, on me confia un pilote qui avait essayé de gagner Gibraltar. Je l'accueillis dans mon escadrille, lui expliquai pourquoi je suivais le Maréchal : pour attendre. Nous prenions, en plus de la garde, quelques précautions. Les pleins des avions n'étaient faits qu'avant un départ en mission. Notre meilleure protection était le faible rayon d'action des avions. Où aller avec trois heures de vol ? En Libye ? Même pas.

Chaque matin à onze heures, je réunissais l'escadrille. J'avais parmi mes officiers un ancien petit chanteur de la Croix de bois. Nous nous partagions l'enseignement. Même avec ceux qui croyaient ne pas pouvoir tirer un son de leur gorge, en trois mois, nous abordions les vieilles chansons françaises, les plus pures, peu connues parfois, puis des chorals de Bach. Le chant nous gonflait le cœur, nous y goûtions une sorte de bonheur triste. Refusant de bramer l'imbécile « Maréchal nous voilà », je travaillerai plus tard à un texte que j'enverrai à Henri Bosco qui en écrira la musique. Un compositeur de talent, Marcelle Schveitzer, la jolie femme ardente du vice-recteur de l'académie d'Alger, en écrira l'harmonie. Ce sera un chant de gloire, de vengeance et de nuit.

La chorale me rappelait le séminaire et le chant grégorien. Nous laissions nos âmes s'exprimer, un moment de grâce nous transportait, nous chantions. Cela fit sourire certains esprits railleurs : l'armée n'était pas une école de chant, on n'enseignait pas le solfège et l'harmonie dans les écoles militaires. On n'étudiait pas non plus Vigny. L'armée ne servait donc qu'à bouffer des fayots et à tuer ? Comme pour m'éprouver moi-même, je poussai la provocation jusqu'à exhiber chez moi une affiche en couleurs de Pétain : ce front couronné d'or, cet air de franchise, toutes ces étoiles. On en déduisit que je profitais de tout pour me faire valoir, ce qui n'était pas faux : on ne commande pas sans s'imposer. Personne n'y comprendra rien. Quant à moi, pourquoi aurais-je plu à tout le monde ? J'ai toujours eu des ennemis. Certains voyaient en moi un suppôt de Satan. Certains autres, un traître. Traître à quoi ? J'étais fidèle à moi-même, je croyais qu'il fallait donner une âme à une armée qui n'en avait pas. Soudain, à la pensée de mes camarades morts pendant les semaines de la débâcle, coula de mon cœur une prière, puis d'autres, Guibert et Amrouche les aimèrent et les publièrent dans *la Tunisie française littéraire*. Edmond Charlot les édita à Alger sous le titre de *Trois prières pour des pilotes*. Dès lors, on commença à m'appeler, non sans ironie, « le poète », « le sultan ». Depuis la guerre, les cadences jaillissaient chez moi au rythme des battements du sang. Quelque chose était cassé, beaucoup de conventions tombaient. Avec Max-Pol Fouchet qui dirigeait la revue *Fontaine*, Henri Hell, Jean Roire, Roblès, et des peintres, René-Jean Clot et Sauveur Galliéro, nous parlions du jeune

prodige Albert Camus de qui *l'Envers et l'Endroit* et *Noces* avaient paru chez Charlot à tirage limité. Sa légende était déjà établie. Il vivait alors à Oran et devait aller en France car il était malade. De la poitrine, disait-on, à moins que ce ne fût de la vie, de l'écriture, de la condition humaine. Quand on empruntait la rue de Lyon, à Belcourt, on se montrait la maison où il avait vécu avec sa mère. Les Clauze, les anciens amis de mes parents, habitaient non loin, plus près de la mer. On ne parlait pas de Camus sans un certain frémissement. On disait qu'il était né en 1914 à Mondovi, près de Bône, département de Constantine, et que son père était mort à la guerre.

J'achetai *l'Etranger* à Sétif, fin juillet 1942, dans une librairie à côté de l'hôtel de France, sous les arcades, et rentrai chez moi. A la première page je lus : « Aujourd'hui maman est morte. Ou peut-être hier, je ne sais pas... » J'allai jusqu'au bout sans respirer, hors de tout, secoué, haletant et décontenancé. C'était la célébration de l'absurde dans quelle langue, avec quelle force ! Camus ne faisait aucune allusion à la guerre, son paysage était celui de *l'Envers et l'Endroit,* les odeurs, le balcon étroit sur la rue de Belcourt, les ficus en bas, les trams qui grondaient, le vieux qui battait son chien, ne pouvait pas se passer de lui et pleurait quand le chien le quittait. L'amour se présentait au narrateur sous les traits d'une fille superbe, douce, qui l'aimait et avec qui il faisait l'amour ; elle avait un visage de fleur, ils se roulaient dans les vagues, enlacés, et, le jour d'après, il tuait un Arabe. Aujourd'hui, on ne peut pas penser qu'un écrivain né en Algérie, et qui consacrera une large partie de sa vie à conférer une dignité aux Arabes, termine cette première rencontre par le meurtre de l'un d'eux. Et cependant, le premier soir où son héros était en prison, les Arabes ne le regardaient pas de travers et lui disaient même comment arranger la natte pour se coucher. Il y avait dans ce livre quelque chose d'atroce. L'indifférence d'un monde désert et hostile, où l'on pouvait vivre ou tuer, parler ou se taire par fatalité. Ce qui me bouleversait surtout, c'était d'entendre une voix nouvelle, détachée, neutre, effrayante en cela qu'elle disait les choses terribles comme si elle parlait de riens, une voix de confidence en demi-teinte et en toutes petites phrases hachées. A l'époque, le monde était en guerre, personne ne pouvait s'indigner d'un meurtre presque gratuit. On disait

qu'un de ses amis d'Oran avait servi de modèle à Camus. Le livre me parut un chef-d'œuvre, mais je ne pensais pas qu'un récit aussi simple, à propos d'événements qui ne concernaient en rien ceux que nous traversions, atteindrait la gloire universelle. Cependant, il était clair que Camus devenait un maître.

L'état-major m'envoya à deux reprises surveiller les mouvements d'une escadre britannique qu'on soupçonnait de viser Bizerte. Je ne découvris rien. Le lendemain, nous apprîmes par les journaux que cette escadre avait bombardé Gênes. Une autre fois, avec Ventré et d'autres équipages, je fus désigné pour aller à Lyon, chercher des avions neufs et les convoyer à Casablanca. Sur le navire qui nous emportait à Marseille, nous chantâmes le soir pour les passagers. Pareils à des exilés, nous nous exaltions au souvenir de la patrie perdue comme dans le psaume 137 : *Sur le bord des fleuves de Babylone, nous étions assis et nous pleurions au souvenir de Sion...* Nous n'avions pas suspendu nos luths aux branches des arbres dans un geste de découragement.

Ce voyage en zone occupée bouleversa mes idées. La veille de notre départ de Lyon, nous allâmes dîner chez la mère Blanc. Le restaurant était envahi par des officiers allemands qui se conduisaient comme en pays conquis et s'en mettaient jusque-là. En 1870, Flaubert avait retiré de sa boutonnière son ruban de la Légion d'honneur. Si j'avais été décoré, j'aurais fait comme lui. J'avais déjà souffert de voir l'herbe du terrain d'aviation de Bron foulée par les avions ennemis. Mon cœur se mit à battre avec violence, et quelque chose se brisa dans mon dévouement à Pétain. Il y a des choses qui ne se commandent pas.

La guerre continuait. L'envahissement de l'Angleterre était toujours pour le lendemain. Les journées et les bulletins d'information nous apprenaient la lutte sur les mers, les nouvelles conquêtes de l'Axe, l'attaque allemande de l'Union soviétique. Comme Amrouche devenu franchement anglophobe, je ne croyais pas à une intervention américaine. J'embrassais beaucoup d'illusions. Je n'étais pas le seul. Dans

notre armée qui rappelait celle du roi de Bourges, d'autres exaltés, d'autres cinglés s'efforçaient de croire, à défaut d'un autre, à notre pauvre roi gâtouillard gâtouillant vers qui, quand il visitait la France, montaient des acclamations dont le bruit ressemblait à un vol d'hirondelles de mer. Nous étions une dizaine d'imbéciles que l'état-major baladait d'un bout à l'autre de l'Afrique du Nord, de Casablanca à Tunis, dès qu'un événement ou qu'un pèlerin de Vichy ou d'ailleurs s'annonçait. Les centres de réflexion se multipliaient, des séminaires, souvent inspirés par les chantiers de jeunesse habillés de vert bouteille et de rouge, à côté de qui nous n'étions que des catéchumènes ; Uriage en Savoie devenait La Mecque de la religion du pétainisme. L'état-major pensait qu'il fallait absolument changer de méthodes, renoncer, comme Lyautey, aux casernes, revenir à la vie en plein air, à l'effort physique, presque à la prière et à l'oraison. Les aumôniers faisaient florès, Max-Pol Fouchet m'invita aux journées qu'il inspirait à Tipasa pour *Jeune France,* on déclamait Péguy et Eluard, l'idée de la revanche était partout, il fallait devenir forts. La marine restait confinée dans ses amirautés et ses navires au mouillage, l'armée de terre n'osait pas s'aventurer dans le domaine de l'esprit, l'armée de l'air était à l'avant-garde.

Dans un camp pour parachutistes de choc, à Relizane en Oranie, devant la tour crénelée de l'Ouarsenis, on se réveillait presque au cri de « Vive le Maréchal », on apprenait pourquoi la France avait été battue, on saluait les couleurs avec un cérémonial digne de la Royale. Le lieu était infesté de moustiques et de punaises, envahi par des nuées de mouches et dans la boue, car à la saison où nous y étions, il pleuvait beaucoup. L'eau qu'on buvait était saumâtre. L'été, la plaine du Chélif était un enfer, comme le répétait mon père l'instituteur qui avait commencé là sa carrière en Algérie.

A notre tête, l'état-major plaça un commandant piaffant qui s'appelait Murtin. Il n'avait de modeste que la taille et dressait toujours sa huppe. Sa tenue était brillante, parfois excentrique, souvent provocatrice. En juin 1940, son nom avait paru au communiqué. Il portait la rosette et trois palmes à sa croix de guerre. Son groupe de chasse s'était distingué par un grand nombre de victoires, et c'était à lui, Murtin, que ses pilotes devaient ce qu'ils étaient devenus : il les choisissait

parfois sans les voir, à cause de leurs noms. D'eux, il exigeait toujours plus. Elégant, méprisant ou cajoleur, raffiné ou ordurier, inexorable, cassant, il n'aimait que le beau et le fort : les hommes, les avions, le style, la vie. C'était un dandy. Presque parfois un muscadin. Les femmes, pour lui quantité négligeable, n'existaient que si elles avaient épousé un as ou un héros, alors il les voulait à genoux. Il n'avait pas que des défauts. Il aimait les poètes. Il aima tout de suite Patrice de La Tour du Pin, et pas seulement à cause du nom, du portrait ou de la légende. Bref, Murtin était Murtin, une sorte de Martien martial. Pour lui, la vérité était toujours ailleurs, il fallait renverser les valeurs établies, contester les arguments, haïr les habitudes et les vieilles croûtes. Il croyait à Murtin. En attendant, comme nous, à Pétain, à ses étoiles, à ses ors, à sa moustache blanche, à son front marmoréen, pourquoi pas ? à ses yeux pervenche. Le vainqueur de Verdun approchait des quatre-vingt-dix ans mais il était resté un vert-galant, le bruit courait qu'à l'hôtel du Parc il recevait encore des dames émoustillantes. On colportait avec admiration qu'il était un vieux fripon.

Le dandy chez Murtin me parut étriqué. Son besoin permanent d'étonner tournait à l'obsession. Il allait à la messe s'il y avait de la galerie, ne supportait d'être entouré que d'archanges et ne se déplaçait qu'avec des bagages impressionnants. A Rabat où il tenait garnison, il gagnait le terrain dans un tilbury. A table, il se répandait en jugements méprisants sur les généraux vaincus : des loques, des lopes. Je n'étais pas d'accord sur les méthodes qu'il voulait employer à l'égard des sous-officiers. Pour lui, ils étaient de la matière. Pour moi, non. Je répugnais à exercer contre eux des moyens de terreur comme l'expulsion de l'armée en cas de mauvaises notes, ce qui signifiait, en un tel moment, l'inaction et la pauvreté. Le mot de goulag n'était pas encore inventé, on n'en était pas loin. Précieux exagérément, susceptible, mêlant à son orgueil une vanité détestable, Murtin était aussi homme de théâtre, tirait des ficelles usées, abusait de gestes ou de silences, et montrait des faiblesses de vedette, parfois de cabot, avec une soif inextinguible d'adulation. Il feignait de douter de lui pour mieux s'obstiner dans son idée de lui-même. Il m'avait choisi pour la chorale que je lui promettais. Je mis du temps à céder à son charme, il m'en voulut, et quand je lui demandai de traiter

sans trop les humilier les officiers qui n'appartenaient pas à l'aviation de chasse ou n'avaient pas encore combattu, nous fûmes à deux doigts de rompre.

Avec ses façons de petit marquis, Murtin était vaniteux, excentrique, insupportable, mais il était aussi un homme de fer. Dans un article, Henri Massis lui avait prêté un profil de médaille. En pleine débâcle, Murtin était arrivé une fois sur un terrain avec des avions à ravitailler en carburant et en munitions, et comme, pour lui donner ce qu'il demandait, on exigeait des ordres venant de plus haut, Murtin avait répondu : « C'est moi qui commande. Obéissez ou je vous fais fusiller. » Il fallait toujours lui répliquer du tac au tac, l'épater, ce que je fis plusieurs fois car il m'agaçait. Il avait lu mes prières pour des pilotes, nous finîmes par être amis. Il me changeait de mon commandant du Sphinx, je le rangeai à côté de mon beau capitaine de Médéa, de mon chef de batailllon de Vigny et à côté de Ventré. J'avais approché trop de chefs avachis pour ne pas admirer celui-là, son souci de grandeur, de vaincre et de se vaincre. Il n'avait jamais que trois ans de plus que moi, la chance l'avait servi. Le centre de perfectionnement accentua nos travers. J'eus tort de servir Murtin avec trop de zèle. Je me reprochai souvent de trop l'admirer. Moi aussi j'aimais ceux qui sortaient du lot. Beaucoup nous reprochèrent amèrement notre dureté. Ils avaient raison. Nous nous y prenions mal. La défaite nous avait démontés, nous ne nous étions pas remis en selle. Nous manquions de réflexion et d'humanité. Peu à peu je bâtis une doctrine mystique pour temps d'humiliation nationale, que publia *la Tunisie française littéraire*.

Subitement mon père mourut et j'eus la réaction d'un fils. Je le croyais immortel et il n'était plus. Une mort douce avait été la récompense de son humble vie. Il s'était éteint le samedi saint, à l'heure où un ange dit aux disciples près du tombeau : « Vous cherchez Jésus de Nazareth ? Il n'est plus ici... » Mon frère Robert et moi resserrâmes nos liens : il nous avait légué le pire des caractères, le goût des rêves et une rare obstination. Il avait vécu pauvre, avare et besogneux au-delà de l'imaginable, un brin sadique. Il se privait au-delà du possible pour

combler son légitime et ses deux bâtards, car il en avait, en plus de moi, un deuxième, de l'époque de ses grandes passions. Mon frère Robert lui construisit un tombeau au pied du séminaire, dans le vaste cimetière de Saint-Eugène qui escaladait les collines. Quand le tombeau fut prêt, mon frère Robert mourut : le tombeau fut pour sa femme déjà disparue, mon père et lui, tout un pan de ma vie s'abattit. Je suis à peu près seul à présent à visiter ces Dematons qui auraient dû prendre place, avec leurs anciens en poussière, dans les caveaux démantibulés par les hivers de leur village natal, à Lévigny (Aube).

La vie de l'homme est si courte, la planète Terre, sa patrie, tient elle-même si peu de place dans l'univers. A nous montrer si attachés à nos provinces, nous pratiquons encore une simplicité de mœurs proche de la barbarie. Qu'en sera-t-il quand des astronautes périront dans le cosmos parce qu'un accident se sera produit ou qu'ils ne pourront plus rejoindre leurs vaisseaux ? Les marins laissent leurs morts glisser dans la mer, les astronautes seront bien obligés d'abandonner les leurs dans l'aquarium de l'infini, au milieu d'astres qui tournent sans savoir où ils vont ni ce qu'ils sont, sans pesanteur et sans vie. J'ai toujours cru que notre patrie était la Voie lactée. Je doute que ma poussière s'y mêlera jamais avec celle de tous les miens qui dorment en Algérie, les uns dans la plaine de la Mitidja, les autres dans le seul coin que les Algériens aient conservé avec soin comme preuve de leur victoire et moyen trompeur de montrer qu'ils honorent les vaincus. Peut-on dire de ces morts-là qu'ils sont en exil d'eux-mêmes ? Quand il s'agira de ma mère, ce sera pire. J'atteindrai alors le fond de l'abomination. La barbarie n'est l'apanage de personne.

Ce qui m'effraie, à près d'un demi-siècle de distance, c'est la naïveté avec laquelle soudain, sans le conseil de personne et malgré mon voyage à Lyon où la présence des officiers allemands m'avait si fortement meurtri, je me lançai dans la célébration de Pétain. J'écrivis des articles et donnai une conférence bourrée de citations et de références où je fustigeais la mollesse, le doute, et comme j'ai horreur des tièdes, je me sortis les tripes pour susciter une certaine foi. J'en tirai une

brochure que le libraire de Montherlant à Alger publia sous le titre de *la France sauvée par Pétain*. Encore heureux que l'armée ne m'ait pas autorisé à déclarer que j'en étais l'auteur. Doyon, à qui je l'envoyai en même temps qu'une carte à formulaire, me répondit dans son style à lui : il faisait la queue et le pied de grue, il espérait la lune et le messie. Je l'entendais comme si j'y étais, s'exclamer devant son chien, la cheffesse, Rita peut-être, en se tapant sur les cuisses : « Mon fils est devenu un enfant de Pétain. Il nous la baille belle ! » A quoi bon rêver ? Si quelqu'un pouvait soulager le malheur des Français et sauver ce qui restait, c'était Pétain. Dans la masse des lettres de Guibert, je tombe cependant sur une phrase révélatrice : « J'admire — et presque j'envierai — la candeur merveilleuse, mais hélas, redoutable avec laquelle tu vois, de ton altitude froide, se dérouler les événements... » J'étais un imprudent incandescent. Parfois de glace. Mon factum signé de deux étoiles, je le contemplai dans les vitrines des libraires d'Alger, fier de moi.

Le bruit courut que les Allemands avaient demandé d'utiliser Bizerte pour secourir l'Italie en difficulté en Libye et que cela leur avait été refusé. On chuchotait que l'avion du Maréchal avait, à Vichy, ses moteurs toujours chauds. A Guibert et à Amrouche qui publiaient leurs pages de littérature dans *la Tunisie française*, j'envoyai, à propos de Verdun, un texte où je célébrais Pétain et Montherlant. Ces choses-là étaient tabou. Quand on gisait au fond de l'abîme, on ne rappelait pas les victoires à des chiens battus. Dans la passion de préparer la revanche, je me jetai à l'assaut des conventions et des systèmes, et à la conquête de notre honneur perdu. Par qui avions-nous été battus ? Par des jeunes gens enthousiastes, ardents, brûlants, aigus comme des fers de lance. Nous devions leur ressembler. Ventré rigolait.

Finalement, ces deux années noires filèrent dans une sourde inquiétude mais sans ennui. La Yougoslavie fut conquise en douze jours par Hitler, l'armée grecque capitula. Comme nous, Lindbergh croyait que l'Angleterre perdrait cette guerre. Qui aurait osé penser le contraire ? Les gavages de principes pour une revanche alternaient avec mes retours à Sétif. Nous voyagions beaucoup, sous des prétextes divers, d'un bout à l'autre du Maghreb. Weygand avait été remplacé par le général Juin, chargé de rendre confiance aux troupes. De

Lattre commandait en Tunisie. Pendant des vacances que Murtin m'avait accordées, je réussis avec mon escadrille une échappée vers les oasis sahariennes et vers Tunis. Depuis que Guibert avait gagné le Portugal en quête du génie Pessoa alors inconnu, Tunis c'était Amrouche. Il incarnait pour moi la poésie, la littérature, l'amitié. Fuyant la France et le froid, Gide venait de débarquer et vivait une lune de miel à Sidi bou-Saïd. Amrouche veillait sur lui comme un garde du corps. Ce jour-là, je fus invité à partager leur déjeuner. D'un verbe sévère très articulé, Gide me réprimanda : j'usais trop de savon en me lavant les mains. En Afrique du Nord, nous n'en étions pas à ces restrictions. Je n'ouvris plus le bec, j'écoutai religieusement le dialogue sur Œdipe du maître et d'Amrouche, qui allait devenir plus tard son interviewer à la radio. Gide, c'était le dalaï-lama. Il en avait le crâne lisse et le mystère. Il m'effraya. Je n'osai même pas lui parler de Blida la petite rose.

De Tunis, nous revînmes avec nos carlingues bourrées d'huile d'olive, de savon et de sucre. Le souvenir de l'auteur des *Nourritures terrestres* me laissait songeur. A Casablanca, je rencontrai Jean Denoël, alors adjudant du service de santé à l'hôpital militaire. Il appartenait au comité de la revue *Fontaine* et correspondait régulièrement avec Claudel, Gide, Valéry, Mauriac, Supervielle, qu'il appelait « mon cher Claudel », « mon cher Valéry », « mon cher Mauriac », etc. Menu, malingre, presque chétif, chauve comme une pomme d'escalier et avec des yeux bridés perçants, c'était à Max Jacob, frère tourier, qu'on pensait d'abord. Tout ce qui tenait une plume était jugé par lui d'une façon sans appel. Les faibles étaient ramenés dans le droit chemin, non de la politique, il n'en avait cure, mais du style et de l'art. La guerre finie, je le retrouverai chez Gallimard où il donnait son avis sur les candidats aux académies et au prix Nobel. Il ne me dit rien de mon truc sur Pétain. Doux et humble de cœur en apparence, en réalité intraitable, féroce et incorruptible, il deviendra plus tard chef d'état-major majordome de Florence Gould.

Murtin avait transplanté notre école à Fès, je repartis. Le Maroc tourmenté où nous vivions était couvert d'oliviers, la

ville de Fès ressemblait à un pain de sucre d'orge rongé de galeries, de jardins secrets, de mosquées, tout était resserré, barricadé, la médina se tassait sur une immensité de petits négoces où le soleil ne pénétrait qu'à coups d'épée, un fleuve d'or et de boue coulait partout, et par-dessus le grouillement d'une population de fourmis sacrées, la voix du muezzin et l'ombre de Dieu passaient comme des vautours par-dessus les terrasses. D'innombrables faces fermées et sombres regardaient sans les voir les étrangers porteurs d'armes que nous étions, migrateurs du Nord qui allions nous envoler de nouveau.

Sur un plateau qui prolongeait les abords de la ville flottait notre drapeau. Là, nous nous agitions beaucoup, nous célébrions le culte de la patrie en douleur. Comme pour braver le mystère qui devenait notre respiration, Murtin avait exigé pour lui seul d'habiter dans l'enceinte de la résidence royale, au palais Djamaï. Enfin il pouvait vivre comme un prince. Seul à une table de satrape, il était servi par des esclaves noirs à turban et ceinture rouges. Pour gagner l'école, il montait un pur-sang arabe. Nous étions quatre capitaines à le saluer quand il mettait pied à terre, et s'il nous arrivait de sourire, c'était par affection. Moi du moins. Il conduisait parfois aussi une voiture anglaise décapotable. C'était à qui, pour lui plaire, organiserait le plus étincelant feu de camp. Un soir, Marin La Meslée, un ancien pilote de son groupe, as aux vingt-cinq victoires, nous visita. Immense, il nous parla la tête dans les étoiles, entouré de flammes, un burnous sur les épaules. C'était Galaad à la Table Ronde. Fès avec Murtin fut pour moi un haut lieu, à jamais figé, éternel.

L'esprit qui régnait dans notre camp attirait. Amrouche vint me voir. Murtin lui plut. Amrouche tenta même de l'entraîner vers Claudel. Un soir, dans les jardins de Bou Djeloud, se laissant aller devant nous à des vues lointaines, Amrouche annonça sur un ton solennel que la guerre passerait et qu'en même temps changerait le visage de la littérature. Il dévoila des ambitions que Gide ne décourageait pas : la *NRF* compromise avec les Allemands, Gide ne refuserait pas d'entrer dans le comité de rédaction d'une autre revue qui naîtrait de la victoire. Amrouche me parut faire peu de cas de *Fontaine* où Max-Pol Fouchet publiait déjà Eluard et Aragon. Tout cela était encore dans son esprit une nébuleuse, mais de

quoi naissent les astres ? Pour lui, les poèmes qu'il aimait de moi et pour lesquels il écrivit une préface étaient les premières pierres d'un édifice. Il m'annonça que je bâtirais une œuvre et m'en brossa les perspectives. Naturellement, je devrais le considérer comme mon guide. Ses visions étaient d'un prophète, mais son bâton de marche était une trique. Il serait le magister de tout ce qui allait naître. Un seul écrivain lui échappait : Camus, en France pour raison de santé. A ses yeux, *l'Etranger* était un livre considérable qu'il ne savait encore où placer car on n'avait jamais vu un Européen d'Algérie condamné à mort pour meurtre d'un Arabe. Comme on savait que Camus avait combattu pour l'indépendance de l'Algérie quelques années auparavant au sein du parti communiste, on hésitait à plaquer une signification politique sur ce texte, *l'Envers et l'Endroit* n'en avait pas, *Noces* était un cri de bonheur, un hymne païen au soleil et à la mer, *l'Etranger* allait plus loin, mais le livre n'avait eu encore qu'une diffusion limitée. François Bonjean qui était un peu notre père à tous, et Henri Bosco que nous rencontrâmes à Rabat ne l'avaient pas lu, et comme l'adjudant du service de santé Jean Denoël n'avait pu se rendre libre, ce soir-là, nous ne sûmes pas ce qu'il en pensait. Amrouche ressemblait de plus en plus à la première image que j'avais eue de lui quatre ans plus tôt, aux Deux-Magots, quand nous étions partis à la recherche de Montherlant : d'un inspiré, d'un demi-dieu. Ses origines étaient encore plus humbles que celles de Camus. Camus était le fils d'un commis de ferme et d'une Espagnole illettrée. Amrouche, le fils de Belkacem Amrouche, un des protégés des Pères blancs du cardinal Lavigerie, et d'une mère mythique, Fadhma Aït Mansour, aux chants profondément populaires, presque primitifs, des profondeurs de la Kabylie. A chacun de mes déplacements par avion entre Alger et Sétif, je survolais Ighil Ali, son village natal, un nid d'aigle dans les cimes neigeuses de Djurdjura. De là, comme au commandement d'un ange, il était parti pour le collège, l'école normale d'instituteurs à Sousse, puis pour l'école normale supérieure de Saint-Cloud, avant de revenir à Tunis. Lui et sa sœur Marguerite Taos ressusciteront le sacré.

Avec Amrouche, Bonjean et Bosco, mon séjour au Maroc à Pâques 1942 tint de la magie. Après la publication de *Trois*

prières pour des pilotes, je regagnai Sétif où nous venions de recevoir l'ordre de nous entraîner à des bombardements en semi-piqué. Le commandement avait découvert qu'une partie de la victoire allemande était due aux stukas. Chez nous, aucun appareil ne semblait approcher de celui-là dans sa conception, sauf peut-être le Potez 63-11, notre avion. Nous reçûmes donc des instructions, Ventré étudia le problème, se livra à des essais et calcula des tables de tir. A l'altitude de deux mille cinq cents mètres, on se dirigeait vers l'objectif en plaçant la commande de profondeur sur plein piqué tout en maintenant au manche, à bout de bras, l'avion en vol horizontal. Au « top » du bombardier, le pilote engageait brutalement l'avion à quarante-cinq degrés puis, la bombe lâchée, redressait. Malgré l'émulation qui régnait entre nous, nous n'obtînmes que des résultats médiocres. Ne devenait pas stuka qui voulait. J'y laissai ce qui me restait d'ouïe dans l'oreille gauche, car nous perdions deux mille mètres d'altitude, parfois plus, en quelques secondes, et la dépression se faisait ressentir comme un coup d'épingle.

L'entraînement dura tout l'été, en alternance avec des séjours dans les maigres forêts des montagnes voisines. Nos faibles moyens nous obligeaient à imiter les chantiers de jeunesse. Quinze jours par mois, nous abattions des arbres et nous vivions sous la tente. Le soir, nous chantions en contemplant les étoiles. Le bombardement m'abrutissait, les séjours en forêt m'ennuyaient. Parfois je désespérais. « Ne tardez plus, Seigneur, à nous envoyer votre ange... » Mon dernier poème dont l'encre d'imprimerie n'était pas encore sèche dégorgeait de détresse et pourtant j'avais mis aux commandes des avions les spectres de nos camarades tués en Quarante. Je demandais à Dieu, dans la stridence des cuivres, de lâcher mes bombes sur les villes allemandes et de suivre les colonnes de la déroute dans la grille d'un collimateur. L'Amérique était entrée dans la guerre. L'Europe se massacrait. Hitler et Staline se tenaient à la gorge dans les espaces de Russie. De Gaulle faisait de plus en plus parler de lui, et Pétain de moins en moins. Nous finissions par en avoir assez d'assister les bras croisés à la tuerie générale. Nous voulions y participer. De temps en temps, un équipage britannique s'écrasait dans notre zone d'inaction. Nous rendions les honneurs aux victimes, les services de renseignement exami-

naient ce que l'avion pouvait comporter d'aménagements nouveaux. Je craignais de servir dans une subdivision d'arme, la reconnaissance aérienne, ou nous n'aurions jamais qu'un emploi peu glorieux.

Nous en discutions souvent, notre humeur s'en ressentait, il y avait parfois des éclats. De jeunes officiers qui avaient été, sous un prétexte ou sous un autre, écartés par moi de la drogue du vol parce que je les considérais indignes de servir dans notre embryon d'armée, se laissaient aller à des coups de sang et tournaient en ridicule notre dévotion au Maréchal. Ecrivant cela un demi-siècle après, je me sens confondu. Comment avions-nous pu nous laisser coincer de la sorte ? A-t-on jamais reproché à Herbert von Karajan d'avoir appartenu au parti nazi dès 1933 ? Comment aurait-il pu avoir seulement une secrétaire, donner des concerts avec un orchestre ? Nous étions depuis notre jeunesse embobinés dans la discipline, au nom de quoi aurions-nous pu désobéir ? De Gaulle avait désobéi, mais il était général de brigade, avait déjà pratiqué des hautes sphères et ne courait pas à Londres après un jupon. Dans notre armée de Bourges, il fallait réprimer, et cela ne m'entourait pas de sympathie. Je le faisais avec une espèce de joie austère que m'avait enseignée Murtin. Dans la situation où nous étions, vers qui nous serions-nous tournés, à moins de déserter, et qui aurait pu nous assurer que la désertion était le salut ? J'étais l'auteur de *la France sauvée par Pétain* et plus tellement fier de l'être ; je ne pouvais pas me désavouer, et cependant de violents accès de colère contre moi-même me secouaient. Il y avait chez nous de plus en plus de grincheux. Nous étions près de nous déterminer peut-être au pire, à condition de remonter vers le nord, vers des combats qui nous aspiraient. Avec un brin de forfanterie où se mêlait de la dignité, nous commencions à ressentir une certaine gêne de notre condition d'embusqués, de favorisés, mais peut-être avions-nous la méconnaissance d'une guerre à laquelle nous ne participions pas. Personne ne savait qui allait gagner, personne n'était sûr d'être du bon côté. Parfois il nous semblait que nous aurions dû avoir presque honte d'être des soldats fidèles à quelque chose. Je transformai l'hymne au Maréchal en un chant qu'il aurait bien été étonné d'entendre. Cela devenait plus fort que nous. Il y avait entre notre attitude et ce qu'on pouvait prendre pour nos intentions une telle distance qu'on

ne s'y retrouvait plus : à la moindre nouvelle, à la moindre rencontre, les malentendus et les contradictions explosaient. Il arrivait qu'on se haïsse. Je lus à ce moment *Jardins et routes*, le journal de marche d'Ernst Jünger pendant la campagne de France, que Gallimard diffusait avec la bénédiction de l'occupant et des services d'information de Vichy. J'en souffris beaucoup. On percevait sous la noblesse de Jünger un certain mépris pour l'armée qu'il avait eue en face de lui.

Le 30 septembre de cette année 1942, nous fûmes secoués par un tremblement de terre. Je le fus aussi par la réflexion d'un camarade : « Il nous reste une grande espérance, la RAF vient de faire quatre vingt mille morts à Brême... » La nouvelle était inexacte, mais on la colportait partout et je me sentis frissonner. D'horreur à l'idée du massacre tombé du ciel ? D'indignation parce que les auteurs de ces exterminations étaient les Anglais ou parce que rien ne se passait comme nous pensions ? Parce qu'il y avait un monde d'épouvante entre cette aviation-là et nous ? Et cependant, n'était-ce pas ce dont je rêvais ? Les événements qui ne pouvaient pas ne pas se produire, Ventré les attendait où nous étions. Plein de sagesse, il se contentait de glisser entre les écueils.

Avec le recul du temps, il est aisé de s'ériger en homme de foi. De foi en quoi ? Nous n'étions pas dans le secret des dieux. Personne ne savait rien. Chacun se conduisait comme il pouvait. Du Brésil, de New York ou de Beyrouth, on pouvait avoir une perspective. Nous n'en avions aucune, sinon que cela ne durerait pas. Comme des cigales, nous chantions. A Sétif, tout le monde s'épiait, pas une fois je n'osai m'arrêter à la pharmacie de M. Ferhat Abbas car la police en aurait aussitôt avisé le commandant d'armes. A Alger, où l'atmosphère était plus lourde, Edmond Charlot fut assigné à résidence dans le Sud et en revint tondu. Entre intellectuels et artistes, il y avait des clans. Au contact de Gide, Amrouche devint soudainement gaulliste.

Le 7 novembre 1942, comme je sortais de la petite imprimerie où l'on venait de tirer un nouveau poème de moi, un ordre d'alerte m'atteignit. Quand le car s'arrêta le lendemain 8 novembre, tôt le matin, devant le pavillon de la base, une avalanche de nouvelles inouïes tomba sur nous : Alger avait été attaqué pendant la nuit par des vedettes anglo-

saxonnes, Oran avait subi un débarquement, un convoi considérable était au large du cap de Fer, c'est-à-dire devant Philippeville et Bône. Et surtout, Darlan, l'amiral Darlan, était à Alger ! Quelque chose de fantastique se déclenchait, qui semblait agencé entre les Américains et Pétain, pour moi un triomphe. Les nouvelles tombaient par téléphone : d'Alger, de l'état-major du commandement de l'air, et, de Constantine, de l'état-major de la division que nous avions pour mission d'éclairer. Ces deux états-majors eux-mêmes devaient, pour être renseignés avec certitude, recevoir des messages d'un échelon supérieur ou d'unités au contact. Comme les liaisons par radio passaient seulement pas télégraphie, on peut mesurer, de nos jours, à quelle pauvreté d'information un groupe aérien isolé pouvait être réduit. Radio-Alger ne disait rien. Dans la nuit, rien n'avait transpiré non plus sur les ondes de la BBC. J'ai raconté cela dans *le Métier des armes* qui parut six ans après, en 1948 ; le temps passé était déjà une façon de dominer ou de travestir les événements. Peut-être n'ai-je pas été avec eux aussi libre que je le crois aujourd'hui, presque un demi-siècle plus tard. Des généraux cousus d'or ne me demandent plus ce que je pensais alors ou, s'ils me le demandent, je les envoie balader. Où étaient-ils eux-mêmes ? Que faisaient-ils ? Qu'y avait-il dans leur cœur ?

VII

Le coup de Trafalgar

AU DÉBUT de mon récit, *le Métier des armes,* accompagné d'un équipier, je survole la région de Constantine, puis je me rabats vers Alger par une route en plein relief. A un certain moment, nous nous séparons, mon équipier et moi. Mon équipier se charge du nord, moi du sud. Je file sur Médéa, puis sur Blida et Rovigo, ma terre natale que certains renseignements donnaient bourrée d'automitrailleuses américaines. En rase-mottes, je me laisse couler dans un encaissement de vallées, je me vois soudain pincé dans un cul de basse-fosse et n'ai plus qu'une chose en tête : en vitesse, me tirer de là.

Dans le *Métier des armes,* ces quelques instants-là tiennent dix pages, Rovigo est derrière moi, ma mère est amoureuse de l'instituteur et lui, le Prussien, regarde parfois du côté de la montagne sans penser qu'un de ses foutus bâtards pourrait un jour surgir par là. A l'altitude où je suis, je ne peux plus faire demi-tour. Les moteurs, toute superpuissance débridée, faiblissent et, sous moi, je n'ai plus l'espace d'un renversement : nous allons nous écraser. Dans son habitacle transparent, mon navigateur, l'adjudant chef Cimino, tourne un peu la tête vers moi et me fait signe : « On ne passe pas. » A Avord, certains moniteurs de Chainat s'amusaient parfois à nous montrer de quoi le Morane 230 était capable. Ils emmagasinaient de la vitesse en poussant sur le manche, les gaz à fond, à fond, et tout à coup... Oui, mais ils avaient sous les fesses un cheval avec du nerf, pas un veau. Je mets les hélices au petit pas pour arracher aux moteurs leur dernier souffle et en ligne droite face à la paroi, dans un espace si court qu'il ne permet pas à une rosse de s'élancer, je vise vingt

mètres plus bas que le sommet. Dix secondes, peut-être quinze, pendant lesquelles mon navigateur, un ami depuis le temps que nous volons ensemble et que nous nous disons nos quatre vérités, résigné, pense que ça y est, que ça a fini par arriver, au moment même où, tout à coup, piquant des deux à quelques mètres du rocher, de toutes mes forces, je tire sur le manche et nous nous élevons en chandelle. Allez, hop, vieille carne ! Cimino dans l'électrophone : « On a touché des arbres... »

A mon retour à la base, entre chien et loup, ruminant de sombres pensées, je roulais vers les hangars, une double flamme léchant mes flancs, quand je découvris, à l'écart, l'ombre d'un avion qu'on ne voyait d'ordinaire que dans les carnets de silhouettes. Ce gros mufle, ces moteurs effilés, ces tourelles de tir haut et bas étaient d'un Heinkel 111. Heinkel 111 H2, moteurs Daimler Benz de 950 CV, autonomie de 2 050 kilomètres. Et, sur le fuselage, des croix noires. Des Fritz ici ? A peine remis du saut par-dessus la paroi, ah ! le grand jour ! je bondis de la carlingue et, sans quitter ma combinaison de vol, casque à la main, je me hâtai vers le bureau du commandant. Stupeur : deux capitaines de la Luftwaffe en bottes vernies, avec la marque de l'escadrille von Richthofen sur les manches et le ruban de la Croix de fer à la boutonnière. Ventré me souffla : « Envoyés spéciaux du Führer. Porteurs d'un message pour l'amiral Darlan. » L'approche de la nuit les avait incités à se poser chez nous. Ils avaient eu du nez. Le petit s'appelait Sturtmeyer, l'autre von Bertau, et Darlan était à Alger. C'était bien un coup monté.

J'ai écrit dans *le Métier des armes* : « Si un vieillard l'exigeait, je devais aide et protection au capitaine Sturt-meyer. » En un éclair encore, le cœur battant à coups précipités comme à Lyon devant ces messieurs, je sentis que le moment était venu. Aussitôt, Mers el-Kébir, Dakar, les Anglais, de Gaulle, Pétain, partir, rester, tout se bouscula en une seule, brûlante, violente et charnelle évidence : on allait changer de camp. De quel côté ? Pour moi, la question ne se posait même pas. Mot de centurion, pas de général ni d'amiral, encore moins de maréchal. Pour eux, oui, la question se posait. Pour eux, où était le devoir ? Où était la vérité ? A Mers el-Kébir, le devoir pour l'amiral était moins de gagner les îles d'Amérique ou de se saborder que de se soumettre ou non à

l'Anglais. Un amiral a toujours un Trafalgar en travers de la gorge, et chaque marin britannique lui pose un ultimatum, il voit Nelson et une défaite cuisante à venger. Pour Darlan à Alger, l'affaire était moins compliquée : les Anglais avaient eu la sagesse de s'effacer derrière les Américains. Son problème était donc : les Américains ou les Allemands, situation sans la moindre ambiguïté, semblait-il. Pas l'ombre d'un cas de conscience entre le Maréchal et lui. Le jour où les Américains débarquaient, l'amiral n'était certainement à Alger ni par hasard ni pour des prunes. Giraud non plus, car on apprenait que le général Giraud, évadé de sa forteresse en Prusse et interdit de séjour en Afrique du Nord, était là aussi. Depuis le temps que le Vieux roulait Adolf, les jeux faits, le Vieux avait dépêché Darlan en avant-garde et allait se poser d'un instant à l'autre à Maison-Blanche avec son fameux avion aux moteurs toujours chauds.

Je jetai un coup d'œil sur le brillant capitaine Sturtmeyer aux cheveux plaqués sur le crâne, qui attendait la communication avec Alger tandis que von Bertau, front haut, lueur sauvage dans les yeux, ahanait en français et consultait Sturtmeyer du regard. Tous deux à la fois contrariés et soulagés. Moi aussi, soudain, je l'étais, soulagé.

Je me retirai sur la pointe des pieds, rédigeai mon compte-rendu de mission et seul, à pied, remontai vers le mess miteux où nous prenions nos repas. Ombre moi-même, je passai à quelque distance de l'avion allemand et de son équipage, autres ombres dans l'ombre. Nos ânes se taisaient.

La nuit, noire et crasseuse, fut calme. Quelques ordres intempestifs que nous n'exécutâmes pas. A l'aube, les envoyés spéciaux s'envolèrent pour Tunis où un autre amiral, Esteva, les attendait. Nous étions le 9 novembre. A 8 heures, deux Léo 45 se posèrent. Ils venaient d'Istres et ramenaient le gouverneur général de l'Algérie et sa suite. Le gouverneur exprima le désir de se reposer. On lui ouvrit la chambre de l'officier de service, encore toute chaude des envoyés spéciaux du Führer. Cela nous plongea dans une situation de complot. Nous étions tout excités, Ventré ricanait. Dans l'après-midi, un autre Heinkel 111 survola à moyenne altitude la ville et le terrain. Le gouverneur émergea de sa sieste, bomba le torse et rapporta qu'à Vichy, le président — Laval, sans doute — lui

avait dit : « C'est de la folie de partir » et que lui, gouverneur, avait répondu : « Devrais-je descendre jusqu'à Tamanrasset, ils ne m'auront pas. » Une auto vint le chercher. Il nous quitta.

Nous lançâmes d'autres reconnaissances sur nos voies d'accès. En vain. De nombreux passages d'avions allemands furent signalés par les observatoires. A la fin du jour, nous envoyâmes les couleurs avec un certain déchirement. On disait que le général ministre de l'Air, le général des chantiers de jeunesse et le directeur de la SNCF étaient dans la région dans l'intention de rentrer à Vichy avec les Léo 45. Dans la soirée, la réplique du gouverneur : « Devrais-je aller jusqu'à Tamanrasset... » fut ressassée par la radio d'Alger et de Vichy. Le gouverneur ajoutait : « Le baroud est déclenché. Ce sera un baroud de vainqueurs. » Pour nous, l'état-major envisageait de nous replier sur Laghouat ou Tiaret. Je pensai à mon fameux abbé Cas du drap mortuaire : le cher homme était-il encore en vie ? Notre intendance avait déjà prévu des camions pour l'enlèvement des lits de notre personnel avec leurs pieds de châlit, mais sans matelas ni couvertures.

A 4 heures du matin, par nuit profonde, nous allumâmes la rampe pour le départ des Léo 45. Dans le premier grimpèrent de nouvelles ombres, des membres du cabinet du ministre de l'Air. Dans le deuxième, le général des chantiers de jeunesse et le directeur de la SNCF, encore des ombres. Le premier Léo décolla en grondant et disparut avec ses feux. Le deuxième s'ébranla, prit de la vitesse puis s'embarqua dans une embardée. Le pilote réduisit les gaz, revint se placer en position de départ, s'élança de nouveau sur notre terrain en creux et bosses quand, en pleine course, un de ses pneus éclata. L'avion se ratatina sur lui-même et s'enroula dans un nuage de poussière noire d'où les passagers s'échappèrent comme des rats. Nous leur proposâmes une voiture pour Constantine, ils se hâtèrent de décaniller. A l'aube, dans les débris de l'avion, je pêchai le béret vert bouteille du général des chantiers de jeunesse que j'arborai quelque temps et que je finis par perdre. Nous étions le 10 novembre. La rumeur disait que les Américains étaient solidement installés à Alger et à Blida, et qu'à Sétif, les Allemands allaient surgir d'un instant à l'autre. Enfin, nous reçûmes un ordre qui nous parut dans la logique : n'intervenir en rien contre qui que ce soit et céder la base au premier occupant. Le soir, les directives avaient encore

changé : nous devions nous laisser dépasser par les Américains et, en revanche, interdire toute tentative d'atterrissage des avions de l'Axe. Chez nous, ce fut une explosion de joie. Des compagnies de mitrailleuses et d'engins de l'armée de terre vinrent s'installer autour de nous.

Dès lors régna la plus totale incohérence. La radio de Vichy rabâchait l'ordre de résister à l'envahisseur, Tunis signalait : « nombreux avions allemands, en route vers vous », notre ministre de l'Air était à Biskra et le général Giraud à Alger, avec Juin. Le jour s'achevait, quand jaillirent soudain quatorze avions de chasse, des Dewoitine 520. Ils étaient commandés par l'ancien chef de la patrouille de France, un capitaine au bec d'oiseau de proie dont je ne citerai pas le nom. Nous crûmes qu'ils venaient assurer la défense de la base. Nous le leur demandâmes : ils n'avaient reçu aucun ordre et nous parurent bien circonspects. Des généraux passaient, parlaient pour ne rien dire, tapotaient leur badine contre leurs bottes et reniaient le soir ce qu'ils avaient affirmé le matin.

Dans *le Métier des armes,* j'ai narré, au fur et à mesure de ce qui pleuvait sur nous, le détail de nos états d'âme. Ce qui me toucha le plus fut ce groupe de chasse qui nous tombait du ciel. Le matin du 11 novembre, nous ressemblions à un rocher battu par les vagues, tantôt recouvert d'écume et tantôt lisse. De tous côtés nous flagellaient des ordres et des contrordres. On exigea de nous deux avions pour attaquer un convoi américain près de Bougie et du cap Aokas. Mission casse-pipe. Je me désignai, le chef de l'autre escadrille en fit autant : la règle. On chargea quelques bombes de trente kilos sous nos plans. Deux avions contre un convoi américain, quelle idée ! Sans doute pour qu'un général puisse prouver qu'il s'était défendu et qu'il avait, chez nous, subi des pertes. Les moteurs tournaient. Par bonheur, un nouveau contrordre nous sauva.

Des bandes de stukas couraient le long du littoral. Les sémaphores les signalaient, les messages passaient de main en main. En haut de la tour où nous étions serrés, nous regardions le capitaine des chasseurs en combinaison de vol, casqué, impassible, muet. Quel coup de Jarnac préparait-il ? Il devait calculer le nombre des stukas, leur direction, leur altitude, le temps qu'il lui faudrait pour leur couper la route. *Un groupe de chasse français de Dewoitine 520 commandé par*

le capitaine X... a abattu quinze Stukas en route vers Alger
Nous lisions déjà le communiqué. Un dernier message situa à
Souk-Ahras une dizaine de Messerschmitt 109 en route vers
l'ouest, à une centaine de kilomètres de nous, autre occasion
rêvée. Le capitaine dégringola l'escalier. « Aux avions »
s'écria-t-il. Les pilotes coururent à leurs bolides, s'attachèrent.
Presque en même temps, les moteurs toussèrent, les hélices
rejetèrent les fumées des gaz d'échappement derrière elles
comme des ruisseaux de vent dans l'herbe sèche. Déjà le
capitaine déboitait, ses équipiers l'encadraient, les autres
suivaient comme une meute de loups, gagnaient l'aire de
décollage en patrouilles de trois, rasaient le sol d'un long cri
rauque puis s'envolaient tandis que nous tendions les bras à
des héros. Pour rencontrer les Messerschmitt, ils devaient
piquer vers le sud-sud-est, ils les apercevraient cinq minutes
après, disions-nous. Ventré renifla. A quinze cents mètres
d'altitude, ils tournoyèrent un temps puis disparurent plein
ouest, à l'opposé de nos espérances. Un traînard décolla
derrière eux et, son moteur bafouillant, s'abattit. La voiture de
piste se précipita. Le pilote était mort. Dans la grande
machinerie en marche, nous ne comptions plus. Je dus avoir à
ce moment-là une pensée pour nos ânes que je n'avais pas
entendu braire. Ils ne risquaient rien. Spectateurs lucides et
avertis, les Arabes du douar voisin les recueilleraient. Je me
demandai si je ne devais pas les envier, les bourricots.

Ventré me dit que nous nous en tirions à bon compte : un
seul mort, et qui n'était pas de chez nous. Finalement on se
prépara à partir pour Laghouat, aux portes du désert. Nous
n'étions pas fiers. Nous nous en allions piteusement et quels
ordres avions-nous exécutés dont nous aurions pu tirer un
obscur contentement ? Nous avions promené en vain nos
reconnaissances et répondu chaque fois qu'il ne se passait rien.
A qui obéissions-nous ? Le général qui commandait la division
de Constantine nous voulait « dans sa main ». Il nous croyait
plus forts que nous ne l'étions. Un autre général d'Alger se
contentait de suggérer notre comportement. A qui obéissait-il
lui-même ?

Dans *le Métier des armes*, j'ai pris trop sévèrement à
partie le général commandant la division de Constantine que je
trouvais tantôt piaffant et sûr de lui, tantôt flottant. Aucun
général ne pouvait trop s'engager sans risquer d'avoir l'oreille

fendue. Qui aurait eu assez d'audace pour contrarier plus haut placé que soi ? Un seul pouvait, comme à son habitude, blâmer et dénoncer, c'était le général de Gaulle, qui paraissait hors jeu. A part lui, il eût été bien imprudent d'aventurer quelque prévision. Pour qui Darlan négociait-il ? De quel côté penchait-il ? Ne travaillait-il pas que pour Darlan lui-même ? Pourquoi Pétain s'égarait-il dans des bouillies ?

Chez nous des camarades hésitaient encore. La belle affaire ! Devant les envoyés spéciaux du Führer, je m'étais écrié en moi-même : « Fringants capitaines, il n'est rien de commun entre nous !... » Tout semblait consommé.

Le Métier des armes parut en novembre 1948 chez Gallimard où l'on avait hâte de me voir sortir un nouveau livre après *la Vallée heureuse* et *Retour de l'enfer*. *Le Métier des armes* était un livre austère, que Camus aimait bien. Il éclairait le drame que nos consciences de soldats avaient traversé. J'avais eu scrupule à situer les événements de ces journées. Certains lecteurs auraient voulu que nous recevions plus froidement ces messieurs les envoyés spéciaux du Führer. On ne reçoit pas grossièrement des porteurs de messages de chefs d'Etat. En plus il existe, entre officiers de toutes nations, même en guerre, une courtoisie de relations comme entre hobereaux. Le livre s'achevait sur un appel utopique : « Il faut confier aux armées la cause de l'homme contre les tyrans. Il faut limiter leur patrie aux seules frontières du monde. » C'était beaucoup demander.

Le terrain de Laghouat s'étranglait en bordure de la palmeraie. La première fois que nous nous y posâmes, je dépassai les balises et m'ensablai, fou de honte. Un autre pilote brisa son avion. Il pleuvait, il y avait de la boue partout, on grelottait presque. De plus, on avait fourré là tous les indésirables du Nord. Ma première nuit à l'hôtel, je fus dévoré par les punaises. Le lendemain, on m'installa au Transat où les ululements d'une folle semblaient la voix de la terre.

Depuis que Fromentin avait illustré le lieu par son livre *Un été dans le Sahara,* beaucoup de peintres s'escrimaient là et

une certaine intelligentsia y lézardait. Pour moi, Laghouat fut moins la rencontre avec le désert qu'avec un professionnel de la poésie facile, que je connaissais de nom, Claude-Maurice Robert. Il vivait en marge, habitait une maison de pisé, portait le burnous et ne fréquentait que les indigènes ; en plus il était manchot. Il en fallait moins pour être considéré comme individu original, sinon louche, et intriguer la société européenne aux conventions étriquées. J'étais curieux, j'allai le voir et me trouvai en face d'un solide rouquin au visage aigu. Nous ne parlâmes que de Montherlant. D'abord il m'apprit que l'emmerdeuse des *Jeunes Filles*, Andrée Hacquebaut, était Jeanne Sandelion, et que la plupart de ses lettres étaient transcrites intégralement dans le roman. Je ne fus qu'à demi étonné d'apprendre que Montherlant n'éprouvait de bonheur que dans le commerce des petits Arabes, chasseurs d'hôtel, mitrons, marmitons ou employés de l'office qu'il appelait les officiers. Pour les dénicher, il écumait les tramways et les cinémas de quartier de Tunis à Alger et de Tlemcen à Colomb-Béchar, mais son vrai fournisseur et pourvoyeur était lui, Claude-Maurice Robert, qui me déballa un énorme amas de correspondance dans laquelle, sous le nom de M. Millon ou de M. des Touches et avec la liberté de propos qu'on imagine, Montherlant demandait des adresses et des protections. Avec délectation, Claude-Maurice Robert me démolit mon idole de fond en comble et moi-même je découvris un plaisir malsain et presque sadique dans ma naïveté. Que Montherlant n'eût jamais touché une femme était son affaire, mais il avait aussi peur de la mer au point de gagner l'Afrique seulement par l'Espagne. Et aussi, comme Pétain, peur de l'avion. Du cheval aussi, du désert aussi. Il n'aimait que le mouvement des villes et encore sous des noms d'emprunt. Bref, c'était un monstre de mensonge, de combines et d'intérêt, qui parfois faisait paraître sous sa propre signature, et écrits par lui-même, des articles à sa louange. « Mais alors pourquoi l'aimez-vous ? » demandai-je à Claude-Maurice Robert. Il hésita un instant devant ma candeur. « Parce que je suis comme lui. » J'aurais dû en tirer la leçon. J'apprenais qu'un écrivain n'est pas forcément l'homme de son œuvre. Guibert m'avait déjà éclairé à ce propos.

Le général Giraud lança une proclamation dans laquelle il annonçait la reprise de la guerre contre les Allemands. En même

temps, un général d'aviation dont j'ai oublié le nom faisait la tournée des popotes pour s'informer de quel côté nous étions. Ce fut moins ce qu'il nous dit que la façon dont il le dit qui me blessa : sans cœur et avec une intelligence bornée. Je demandai la parole pour rappeler doucement que nous avions prêté serment au maréchal Pétain. Un serment valait-il quelque chose ? Qui pouvait nous délier ? On me répondit par des banalités. Je n'insistai pas. Et comme Vichy nous bombardait d'allocutions bredouillantes, je déclarai à mes gens que nous étions désormais en dissidence. S'agissait-il d'être fidèles à un serment de malheur ou à la patrie ? Le ton que je pris pour dénoncer ceux qui nous considéraient comme des traîtres ne plut pas. Je ne savais ménager ni les uns ni les autres. Soudain je passai pour subversif et m'aperçus que je l'étais. Je le suis resté.

Le colonel qui commandait le territoire avait bouclé dans un camp les Anglais qu'on lui avait envoyés puis les relâcha quand il en reçut l'ordre. Le souvenir de Mers el-Kébir rendait les relations plutôt grinçantes. Le camp était effroyablement sale, les prisonniers se laissaient pousser la barbe et refusaient de prendre des douches pour protester contre leur détention. Laghouat regorgeait de tout. La saison des dattes approchait, on récoltait les oranges, il y avait des légumes toute l'année et les magasins de l'intendance étaient bourrés de sucre, de céréales, de café, de chocolat, de gandouras, de burnous et de haïks de femmes. Des officiers supérieurs intriguaient pour se constituer des réserves qu'ils envoyaient chez eux en prévision des disettes futures. Je pensai à Murtin, aux colères qu'il aurait prises, à ses imprécations, à son mépris. Je tâchai de convaincre ceux de mon escadrille de rester attachés aux disciplines militaires. Les marottes de mon ancien capitaine de Satory devenaient les miennes : j'exigeais qu'on soit rasé de frais et qu'on ait le pli au pantalon.

Le Maréchal restait en France, Darlan s'entendait avec les Américains. En raison de sa grande taille et de son évasion, Giraud jouissait d'une réputation d'homme de guerre. Il avait trahi sans problème son serment de ne pas reprendre les armes contre l'Allemagne. Les serments étaient comme les bagnoles roulant au gazogène de ce temps-là : de la camelote pétara-

dante. Le général Leclerc remontait du Tchad, mais il était si loin, on parlait du danger que Rommel ferait courir à la Tunisie par la menace d'une offensive quand la nouvelle du sabordage de la flotte de Toulon explosa. Ce n'était qu'un malheur de plus. Le moral de tous faiblissait, l'inaction nous rongeait, nous n'avions plus d'essence pour voler, l'escadrille fut dissoute. Ventré, muté à un état-major, ne nous avait pas suivis. Il me manquait. Je fus désigné pour instruire des recrues dans la région de Tipasa. Encore ! J'enrageai. Je mendiai un dernier tour avec mon avion et mon équipage. On me l'accorda. Au moment d'apercevoir l'infini du désert, je songeai à l'oncle Jules. J'y étais, j'approchais cette région tant désirée, je me grisais de toutes les illusions qu'elle entretenait, des couleurs du ciel, des franges d'or qui marquaient le commencement du royaume des sables, de la terre noire et de la terre blonde. Laghouat n'était qu'une pouillerie mais plus loin, plus loin, il y avait l'Atlantide, les montagnes en buffet d'orgue du Hoggar, Djanet, Fort-Flatters, tout ce que je ne connaissais pas. Je n'étais qu'au bord de ma destinée.

Après mon départ de l'oasis, une lettre anonyme me dénonça aux autorités comme officier indigne tenant des propos outrageants sur le chef de l'Etat. Je me souvins trop tard qu'on appelait Claude-Maurice Robert le scorpion.

La veille de Noël, sous de furieuses averses, je reçus les soixante recrues qu'on m'expédiait. Drôle de petit Jésus, saumâtre festivité dans une ferme où il n'y avait pour loger que des remises. Je mettais mes gens sur la paille, comme le Seigneur Dieu fait homme, c'est ce que je leur dis, avec la voix de Mgr Bollon, dans un sermon dont ils ne goûtèrent que médiocrement l'humour. A cette époque, dans la Mitidja, l'humidité glaçait les os, je dus aller chercher moi-même à l'intendance des boules de pain et des boîtes de sardines. Le pinard ne manquait pas, mais si certains colons n'hésitaient pas à ouvrir leurs cuves, d'autres rechignaient. Il y avait comme partout ceux qui nous aimaient et les autres. J'invitai le curé de Tipasa, qui n'avait pas plus que moi lu *Noces* de Camus, à célébrer une messe parmi nous. Chose qui m'étonna : personne ne râla. Mes jeunes gens surent encaisser. A la ferme, j'avais une chambre que Murtin, à ma place, aurait refusée. A

l'aube, on frappa à ma porte. « Connaissez-vous la nouvelle ? me demanda-t-on. L'amiral Darlan a été tué. »

Là où j'étais, la réaction fut insignifiante. C'était un loup de moins dans la meute. On se moquait bien de Darlan, parvenu à force de fayotage, d'ambition et de flagornerie au plus haut échelon de la marine et presque de l'Etat. En juin 1940, il aurait pu faire sécession avec sa flotte, la première de l'époque, il avait préféré un plat de lentilles et un portefeuille de ministre. Il avait tout trahi pour arriver à devenir le dauphin du vieux maréchal. Entre-temps, il avait osé aller, en grand uniforme, saluer le Führer dans son nid d'aigle à Berchtesgaden, et il était sur le point de s'allier aux Allemands, contre les Anglais, quand la chance l'avait envoyé à Alger, la veille du débarquement américain, au chevet de son fils malade. Il était dans la place et savait que le Vieux n'aurait jamais le courage de prendre l'avion. Alors qui d'autre que lui, Darlan ? Sans vergogne, une fois de plus, il changea de camp, les Américains le reconnurent haut-commissaire, il n'avait plus qu'à s'asseoir sur le trône de France quand il fut abattu par un jeune homme exalté, un pur, un innocent. Chez nous personne ne versa une larme. Pas un regret. Pas un mot pour Darlan. Ce que j'écris là résume ce que je pense de lui actuellement. En ce temps-là, savions-nous qui il était ? On se méfiait de lui. On le craignait. Les amiraux étaient partout, ils prétendaient n'avoir pas été vaincus et en tiraient gloire. Si j'avais su qui était Darlan, aurais-je osé le dire à l'époque ? Ose-t-on, dans l'armée, dire ce qu'on pense sans risquer d'être écrasé ? Son corps fut inhumé en secret au cimetière de l'Amirauté et, des années plus tard, la marine le transporta en catimini à Mers el-Kébir, là où reposaient les restes des mille officiers et marins tués, à cause de lui, sous les obus britanniques. J'ai vu la dalle où son nom est gravé. On m'a juré que, dessous, il n'y avait rien. N'empêche. « Au diable Darlan ! » s'écria l'auteur de *la France sauvée par Pétain*. En même temps, j'écrivis un long poème — une ode claudélienne — sur le Maréchal trahi par les siens, et l'envoyai à *Fontaine* qui depuis belle lurette voguait sur un cap plus franc.

Comme on ne savait de quelle façon se débarrasser de moi, on me demanda alors d'entrer dans un encadrement d'instruction, cette fois en Amérique. Réponse : non, et la barbe ! Pas d'Amérique. Tel l'enfant grec, je voulais de la

poudre et des balles. Je le dis, je fis ricaner tout le monde. On me proposa alors le commandement d'une fournée d'élèves officiers à Marrakech. J'acceptai. Murtin s'était laissé embrigader dans le cabinet du général Giraud avec l'espoir que tout allait changer et il était consterné : pour lui la médiocrité submergeait tout, le général n'était qu'une baderne chambrée par un entourage débraillé. Dans un bureau voisin, Paul Bringuier, un journaliste de talent, me décrivit la situation : « Personne ne gouverne, me dit-il. Giraud ne veut pas, Bergeret n'ose pas, Peyrouton ne sait pas, Noguès est soudoyé par l'*Intelligence Service,* les secrétaires lisent des romans... » Parmi les papiers, j'aperçus un *état des officiers et sous-officiers désireux de recevoir du fromage et des pommes de terre,* avec les noms de colonels à servir en priorité. En évidence sur la table d'un officier d'état-major, une note semblait résumer le problème de la journée : *sergent-chef Pierra, 1 kilo de crevettes.* François Bonjean m'écrivait : « Il faudrait les yeux des anges pour voir clair... »

La vraie France, c'était nous, les subalternes ou les sans-grade, qui ne savions pas ce que nous deviendrions, naïfs qui croyions et espérions encore à quelque chose avec acharnement, comme Murtin. Nous étions comme les disciples à la mort du maître alors que circulaient les bruits d'une résurrection. D'une disparition peut-être. Ne sachant que penser, tendant l'oreille de tous côtés, interrogeant les uns, les autres, courant de-ci de-là, discernant mal les faux bruits des vrais, sourds à tout ce qui venait d'ailleurs, car la guerre continuait en Russie, dans le Pacifique, en Europe, en Grande-Bretagne où les bombardements duraient encore et d'où partaient sans cesse des raids qui frappaient l'Allemagne de jour et de nuit. De temps à autre, je retournais quelques heures à Sétif comme dans une ville étrangère où j'aurais eu les miens. J'étais conscient de vivre les derniers instants d'un certain bonheur dans un lieu où déjà tout avait changé, d'échapper quelques heures à la vaste machinerie à tuer. A Alger, j'allais aussi surprendre ma mère en douleur de moi, inquiète des tirs de DCA qu'elle entendait parfois. Elle sursautait, elle tremblait, elle survivait sans savoir comment à son enfance sauvage, à son mariage avec un gendarme, à vingt ans de caserne de maréchaussée, puis à un instituteur à demi fou par qui tout allait se consommer dans le péché que j'incarnais. Les nuages où j'étais

et où j'allais entrer de nouveau, je les devinais qui filaient dans le regard de ma mère. Se posait-elle tellement de questions sur la destinée, sur la planète qui tournait autour du soleil avec ses misérables amas d'hommes en guerre, sur ce qu'il était bon de faire ou pas ? L'âge déjà l'avait cassée. Elle subissait. Sa vie se bornait à aller à la messe du matin, à y prier pour moi et à revenir chez elle m'attendre jusqu'à la nuit tombée. Elle semblait s'habituer à vivre seule, et devenait dame d'œuvre. Elle se plaignait de ne plus trouver au marché des oignons, des courgettes et des aubergines pour ses ratatouilles. Elle me rapporta que le bruit courait que les Allemands allaient nous réduire en esclavage. Toute ridée, si menue, elle avait déjà les mains parcheminées de ma grand-mère, ne s'habillait plus que de vieilleries et se voûtait. Je la perdais chaque jour davantage, l'envie de pleurer me venait. Parfois le hurlement des sirènes et le fracas des canons la secouaient. Quand je passais, nous nous taisions, nous regardions par le balcon, elle me disait que le prix des choses augmentait, elle faisait du café et me donnait des nouvelles des voisins. Elle touchait ma plaquette de poèmes qu'elle avait mise en évidence sur le piano, sur lequel, à la guerre précédente, mon frère Robert tapait des chansons à boire. La censure avait interdit, je me suis toujours demandé pourquoi, mon poème *Maintenant que l'ange est venu* dont Charlot avait voulu tirer quelques exemplaires à part pour son plaisir.

A Alger, tout changeait aussi. Les Américains rugissaient dans la ville avec leurs jeeps et leurs camions, ils occupaient tous les hôtels et vidaient les magasins de pacotille et de bimbeloterie. Jean Denoël, promu adjudant-chef, avait été muté à l'hôpital Maillot d'Alger où j'allais le voir. Un peu mélancoliques, nous parlions assis sur un banc sous les palmiers du pavillon des officiers, il poussait parfois de sourds feulements. Je voyais de moins en moins Ventré, de qui j'étais séparé. Parfois encore, avec lui, nous nous arrêtions un instant près du square Bresson, sur le boulevard face à la mer, là où mon père jadis regardait avec effarement l'escorte de Drumont, député antijuif, dételer les chevaux de sa calèche et le hisser vers les acclamations.

En mars, à Marrakech, la chaleur était accablante. Cette fois, je n'admis plus qu'on m'obligeât à former les jeunes officiers selon des méthodes désuètes, je protestai et me fis

vider. François Bonjean occupait un atelier de peintre dans la Bahia, les anciens jardins du sultan. Sa jeune femme, la belle Touria, une Marocaine, l'aidait à s'insérer dans le monde qui grouillait entre le Maghreb et l'Iran, entre les juifs et les Arabes. Bonjean, un homme sage, citait souvent la parole derrière laquelle s'abritaient les Chinois quand ils ne voulaient pas se battre : « Le premier devoir d'un homme est de se consacrer à sa famille... » Que je veuille me battre lui semblait contre nature. Nous étions à Sodome et à Gomorrhe. La ville avec ses murailles d'une âpre grandeur pourpre n'était que lucre, plaisirs défendus, stupre, mensonge. Pour pousser les étrangers à vider leurs stocks à des prix exorbitants, les commerçants affirmaient que les Allemands seraient là avant deux mois. Tout s'achetait, surtout les consciences. Sur l'aérodrome, il y avait des avions américains, des bombardiers légers Douglas Boston. Comme il était facile de séduire quand on était officier, je me lâchai sur l'un deux. Le Douglas, d'une puissance tellement supérieure à ce que nous avions eu jusqu'alors, se pilotait comme une moto de très grosse cylindrée. Surtout, il roulait avec une roulette avant, décollait comme une fleur de flamme et se posait comme un fer à repasser, boum ! pourvu qu'on sût manœuvrer les volets supérieurs du capot. Cela ressemblait chaque fois à un viol. Simplement, il ne fallait pas avoir peur de la vitesse ni des orages qui, chaque après-midi, transformaient en cloaque la célèbre place Djemaa el Fna où les serpents crotales frémissaient violemment. De toutes les tanneries on aurait dit aussi que le sang coulait. J'étais fou de joie. D'un coup d'aile, on survolait l'Atlas bleu aux extrêmes cimes neigeuses.

Peu à peu, les portraits du Maréchal disparaissaient des bureaux et des magasins. Je m'en offusquais alors que je ne croyais plus en lui. J'étais blessé qu'on tournât casaque si facilement. Avec ce vieillard usé mais honorable et sans péché, il me semblait qu'on insultait ce qui avait été la gloire la plus funèbre et meurtrière de nos guerres. A présent, on disait qu'il n'avait été vainqueur, jadis, que parce qu'on lui bottait les fesses. De quel vainqueur ne pouvait-on dire cela ? La honte était d'être vaincu, et c'était la nôtre, c'était nous. « La vérité, disait Touria, mets-la dans une gargoulette et casse-la. » Et encore « Celui qui dit la vérité, on lui brisera la tête. »

Pendant trois mois, j'errai, un peu perdu, parmi des

militaires abrutis et souvent ivres. Je me consolais en m'arrachant de la croûte terrestre avec un Douglas, au milieu des orages : les palais et les masures se confondaient dans des étirements de grisaille et à travers un pandémonium. C'était une sorte de souk infernal que Marrakech. Des multitudes d'ânes chargés de fruits, parfois de terre, trottinaient dans la poussière soulevée par les grosses voitures des colonels américains. Où allaient-ils, les uns et les autres ? Le luxe et la misère se côtoyaient. Des poètes grattaient leur mandoline, des souteneurs racolaient la clientèle, Bonjean écrivait un nouveau livre pour aider à la connaissance de l'islam, je rêvais d'éventrer le ciel, j'étais amoureux des Douglas qui déchiraient l'immense tenture violette des nuages. Dans cette marée humaine, il y avait peu d'hommes à qui j'osais me confier. Il n'y avait plus de discipline nulle part, chacun faisait ce qu'il voulait, je m'en allai. Nous fîmes escale à l'aérodrome de la Sénia. Oran n'était pas un immense lupanar comme Marrakech mais une ville méfiante, puritaine, un amoncellement de pierre dominé par la madone de Santa Cruz où il fallait se hisser pour voir la mer. La ville était pleine de clameurs parce que les anciennes mesures contre les juifs et les sociétés secrètes venaient d'être abolies par le général Giraud. Le soir, des filles aux yeux noirs faisaient le *paseo,* et je rentrai à mon hôtel avec *Porche à la nuit des saints* de Pierre Jean Jouve et *Cent phrases pour éventail* de Claudel sous le bras, de quoi se faire lapider. Relisant Vigny et Psichari, m'interrogeant à l'infini sur les parjures, pas un instant sur la facilité avec laquelle on menait les zozos au combat, je retournai d'un coup d'ailes à Laghouat pour retrouver un médecin qui vivait de figues sèches, de fèves crues, de blé égrené, méditait sur des traités de sagesse musulmane et fréquentait les *soufis,* ces hommes qui versaient des larmes en priant. Un autre médecin, nerveux, hargneux et pourtant plein de miséricorde, m'avait aidé à tenir dans les stalags de Relizane et de Fès et se gavait de poésie. Tous deux étaient des mystiques, des inquiets. Le monde flambait d'un océan à l'autre, pendant que, désœuvrés, nous nous agitions sur une part du Maghreb en attendant, nous, des avions de guerre neufs, d'autres des chars.

Peu à peu le vent tournait. Au milieu de tant de traîneurs de sabre à vocabulaire poussiéreux, de Gaulle, que nous avions

aperçu, et surtout que nous entendions, devenait le verbe tout-puissant, le verbe de lumière. Je pus me procurer ses ouvrages, réédités en Grande-Bretagne, qu'on vendait dans les librairies. Je dévorai *le Fil de l'épée*, *Vers l'armée de métier* et une synthèse de son œuvre et de l'homme. Je fus ébloui par la force de la pensée et du lyrisme contenu. Les principales de ses études avaient paru avant la guerre, et personne ne m'en avait parlé, même pas mon chef de bataillon de Satory. Pour lui, probablement, ce n'étaient que les idées d'un camarade d'école de guerre de qui rien ne laissait prévoir le destin. Et même si j'avais lu ces livres, leur aurais-je prêté attention ?

A présent, dans les popotes, certains de nous levaient leur verre à sa santé. A la fin des repas, nous chantions. Il y avait belle lurette que j'avais lâché ma chorale. Depuis notre départ de Sétif, tout s'était décomposé, nous nous considérions un peu comme des traîtres sans très bien savoir à quoi ni à qui. A nous-mêmes ? Il aurait fallu que Murtin fût général commandant l'aviation. Il venait seulement d'être promu lieutenant-colonel, on l'utilisait à de vagues inspections et j'étais toujours capitaine. Murtin aurait su nous galvaniser. Qui sait ? Après son désenchantement de Giraud aux belles bacchantes, il nous aurait peut-être jetés dans les bras de De Gaulle. D'ordinaire, l'armée maintient sous le boisseau ceux qui veulent secouer les routines, les pratiques usées, les formules fripées, les rengaines épuisées. Où irait-on, scrogneugneu, sans discipline, sans grades impérieux, sans vieilles badernes et sans culottes de peau suintant la fatigue ? Plus de chansons pour moi, sauf « le Forban », qui datait de quand et venait d'où ? à cause de ses paroles :

> *Dans un cadavre j'ai planté ma victoire*
> *Et dans mon crâne je bois la liberté...*

Au décollage d'un Simoun que je pilotais, des battements d'ailes à fréquence rapide me firent craindre la casse. Je réduisis les gaz, mis l'avion en léger cabré, les battements diminuèrent et s'éteignirent. Le Simoun était un appareil « juste », sans réserve de puissance et qui planait mal. A quelques heures près, j'aurais manqué le passage de Saint-Exupéry qui, le 5 mai 1943, tomba du ciel à Laghouat pour mettre à jour son dossier d'avancement, repartit, et, le mercredi d'après, revint. J'ai noté ces dates. J'occupais, à

l'hôtel Transat, un petit appartement de deux pièces. La première chambre qu'il fallait traverser pour entrer dans la mienne comme pour en sortir, était vide. Un soir, la lumière électrique de la génératrice de l'oasis venait d'être coupée, j'entendis qu'on installait un camarade dans l'autre chambre. Parmi les voix, je crus en reconnaître une, sourde et brève. Le lendemain matin, je frappai à la porte de communication et j'entrai prudemment en m'excusant. C'était bien lui, interloqué de mon intrusion et assis dans son lit, la cigarette au bec, ses yeux d'oiseau de nuit écarquillés. En un éclair, je vis ses valises de cuir béantes et un réchaud de poche où il avait fait du thé. Il ne se souvenait pas que nous nous étions déjà rencontrés. Je bredouillai quelques mots et m'éclipsai. On le changea de chambre, je lui offris mes *Trois prières* et il me donna à lire son *Petit Prince* qu'il ramenait d'Amérique, puis je le perdis car il vivait avec nos camarades du groupe voisin, son ancien groupe, qui avaient encore des Bloch 175 triplaces de reconnaissance et allaient recevoir des Lightning. Quelques jours plus tard, comme je descendais de la terrasse de l'hôtel, il m'attendait au bas de l'échelle le nez en l'air, et moi je ressemblais à l'allumeur de réverbères du *Petit Prince*. Il me dit qu'il avait failli pleurer, que mes prières pesaient plus lourd qu'un kilo de papier. Il me montra près de lui une mallette de cuir qui contenait le manuscrit de *Citadelle* : mille pages qu'il comptait mettre dix ans à élaguer et à limer. Ce jour-là, dans une tabagie de cigarettes américaines, il me tint un long discours sur la France, sur nous, sur ce qui se passait. Lui aussi il avait cru à Pétain. Il se méfiait du général de Gaulle qui, on se demande pourquoi, ne le portait pas dans son cœur. Avec ses sourcils arqués, ses yeux immenses de grand-duc, sa tête ronde et la masse de son corps, il m'apparut comme un scaphandrier de l'au-delà remonté de quelles profondeurs ? Quel trésor avait-il découvert, de quelle goélette naufragée sur la face cachée de la lune s'était-il échappé ? Les combinaisons spatiales n'étaient pas encore inventées, il ne me venait pas à l'esprit de le comparer à un plongeur des altitudes ; et pourtant le Lightning sur quoi il allait voler naviguait à plus de onze mille mètres au-dessus de la surface terrestre. De là, comme d'un Everest volant, il contemplerait la France. Comme dans le train d'Agay et comme dans le Goéland de Sétif en juillet 1940, comme la semaine d'avant, je le regardais avec adoration,

je me taisais, je pensais au bagage de gloire qu'il ramenait d'Amérique : *Pilote de guerre* qu'on avait édité là-bas sous le titre *Flight to Arras, Lettre à un otage* et le *Petit Prince*. Nous n'étions de personne ou presque, nous ne savions pas où nous allions, et Saint-Exupéry nous avait rejoints. Il était heureux que son groupe ait été placé sous le commandement américain. Par moments, il semblait vieux et las. Monument de peine, de tendresse et de bonté, il incarnait la discorde dérisoire qui divisait l'armée : il y avait les irréductibles de Pétain, les admirateurs de Giraud, les nouveaux gaullistes et ceux qui, comme moi, égarés dans l'embrouillamini des influences, orphelins de leurs espérances, se tenaient debout, désœuvrés, pareils à des bestiaux qui ne trouvaient pas preneurs à la foire. Des maquignons tournaient en silence autour de nous puis s'éloignaient. La guerre continuait, Rommel avait mordu la poussière, les combattants de la France libre avaient remporté leur première victoire dans le désert, les Italiens vaincus se remettaient à gratter de la mandoline, Giraud et de Gaulle luttaient toujours entre eux pour le commandement de la France en guerre. Ce qui comptait pour moi, plus qu'appartenir aux uns et aux autres, c'était de servir à quelque chose.

Saint-Exupéry voulait aller voir Gide à Tunis qui venait d'être libéré. Il me demanda les épreuves d'un livre qui m'avait coûté tant de mal et que Charlot allait sortir sous le titre de *Ciel et Terre*. En septembre 1941, Camus avait écrit à mon insu une note de lecture dans laquelle il relevait des qualités, mais aussi des naïvetés, quelques clichés et des marques d'influences respectables. De cet essai, Amrouche avait corrigé les épreuves avec moi et s'était montré impitoyable. Il m'avait enseigné la texture d'une phrase, d'une page, d'un chapitre, il m'avait anéanti sous les lois du style. Saint-Exupéry ne m'en dit rien. Je suppose qu'il reconnut en moi un de ses premiers disciples encore tout engoncé dans des vêtements empruntés au maître. Il me manquait le compagnonnage de la mort.

Je le conduisis à son Bloch 175, sur le terrain en bordure de la palmeraie. Finalement ce n'était pas à Tunis qu'il allait mais à Alger. Il voulait, je ne sais pourquoi, piloter jusqu'à Djelfa, je l'aidai à s'enfoncer dans sa combinaison de vol et à loger la valise de *Citadelle* dans la cabine du navigateur. Au poste du pilote, avec son casque **trop** gros, il ressemblait alors,

non plus à un scaphandrier, mais à un dieu solennel, à Jupiter régnant. Il décolla, s'éleva au-dessus d'un nuage de poussière et disparut. Je me sentis tellement seul que je sautai dans un Simoun pour le rejoindre un instant à Djelfa. Quand je me posai, avec du retard sur lui, le Bloch était avachi au bout du terrain, son train fauché. Lui était déjà reparti avec une liaison. Le terrain restait vide, ras, dans la nudité des hauts plateaux. Comment pouvait-on vivre à Djelfa ? Je songeai à mes premières années dans l'armée, quand j'étais sous-lieutenant au 1er tirailleurs, au camarade qui m'avait accompagné jusqu'à Médéa et continuait sur Djelfa où notre bataillon détachait une compagnie dont on n'entendait jamais parler. Djelfa, c'était une rue principale, une caserne, une église, quelques masures du Far West, des hangars pour emmagasiner les charretées d'alfa, dans le lointain des troupes de gazelles que des imbéciles chassaient, et des vols tournoyants de migrateurs. Pouvait-on espérer quelque chose à Djelfa ? Pas un arbre. Le vent soufflait toute l'année. Est-ce que mon ancien camarade avait repris du service ? Pour qui était-il ? Je m'en revins tout triste. Pour me consoler, j'allai contempler les dégâts du Bloch 175 au train fauché dans un cheval de bois à l'atterrissage.

A mon retour à Laghouat, je n'eus plus qu'une hâte, quitter ce Sud miteux. Le destin du monde se limitait pour moi à peu de chose : figurer sur les listes des futurs pilotes avec les Américains, les Anglais ou, dans la chasse, avec les Russes, et surtout retrouver Saint-Exupéry et Amrouche à Alger. Amrouche voulait sortir la revue qui supplanterait la *NRF*, Saint-Exupéry, voler sur un Lightning, moi me glisser au plus dur, mais où ?

La Providence m'expédia d'abord dans la Mitidja, près du village de Souma, à quelques kilomètres de Rovigo. A plus de trente ans de là, tout était déjà en ruine : l'oncle Jules était mort, l'oncle Désiré habitait une maison de retraité, sa femme la tante Henriette l'asseyait sur une chaise devant la porte, une seule de leurs filles merveilleuses passait encore les voir. J'habitais à Souma une maison qui datait des débuts de la conquête, près d'une fontaine qui coulait sous des platanes. Trois vieilles dames et un ballet de chattes me gardaient. A l'heure de la sieste, quelqu'un jouait une sonate de Schubert sur un piano grelottant. Un jour, j'amenai là Saint-Exupéry

rencontré une fois de plus par hasard, et je lui demandai de me signer ses livres. Je lui montrai quatre mots latins gravés sur une plaque de la façade : *Hic longe felix fui.* J'ai été longtemps heureux ici. Il sourit, il espérait que ce ne serait pas mon cas. Moi aussi. Il s'en alla une fois de plus, pressé, à la recherche d'un général américain qui devait hâter son affectation sur Lightning. Nous, nous n'arrêtions pas d'arracher des Douglas à la poussière de la plaine. Un de nos pilotes venait de se tuer au décollage parce qu'un moteur l'avait lâché. C'était l'été, les vignes sentaient le sulfate de cuivre. J'envoyais régulièrement quelqu'un photographier la ferme où je n'allais plus. Il me semble que j'ai, dans *le Métier des armes,* analysé d'une plume peut-être trop pudique ce qui était alors notre dénuement. Dans ce livre altier que peu de militaires ont lu, je me suis montré un peu dédaigneux, comme il convient quand on se croit digne d'un sort meilleur qui échappe. La guerre tonnait à de grandes distances, au-delà des mers, la Sicile venait de tomber, nous étions dans les nuages de nos pensées et de nos ambitions. J'avais beau m'efforcer de paraître un militaire, je n'en étais pas un. J'aimais les armes et les guerriers, mais les militaires m'ennuyaient et, de leur côté, ils me détestaient. Nous ne nous comprenions pas. Je n'aimais pas non plus la guerre, mais elle m'apparaissait comme la seule aventure où se mesurer à Dieu, au diable, à la mort, et savoir ce qu'on valait.

En cet été 1943, notre désarroi était tel que nous avions hâte de trouver un camp et de nous jeter dans la bataille. Rien ne me prouvait que l'armistice m'avait trompé et que je devais avoir honte de quoi que ce fût, mais nous n'avions fait, malgré nous, que subir. A présent, ouvriers de la onzième heure peut-être, il était temps de prouver de quoi nous étions capables. Etait-ce utile de nous déchirer pour savoir qui avait eu raison de ceux qui avaient écouté un vieillard embarrassé de sa gloire ou de ceux qui avaient suivi un risque-tout embarrassé de son orgueil ? Parmi nous, il y avait ceux qui accordaient de la valeur aux mots, ceux qui, comme Saint-Exupéry, jetaient leur vie dans la balance, et il y avait ceux qui préféraient le combat des micros et des conseils ministériels.

A Alger, toute l'intelligentsia se pressait dans les brasseries à la mode. Edgar Faure parlait beaucoup, sa femme Lucie recrutait pour sa revue *la Nef* ; Charlot publiait, non sans

risque parfois, Bernanos, Philippe Soupault, des extraits du *Journal* de Gide, Pierre Emmanuel, Giono, des poèmes de Garcia Lorca et de Rilke, il devenait l'éditeur en vogue et se lançait avec un talent d'équilibriste dans des valses avec des auteurs, des droits et des à-valoir qu'il ne possédait pas toujours. Amrouche se laissait battre par Gide aux échecs et flattait son vieux maître tout-puissant. Aussi souvent que je pouvais, je tenais compagnie à Murtin. Amrouche et moi l'aidâmes à rédiger l'éloge d'un as qui venait de se tuer sur un avion américain. De son côté, il ne parvint pas à me faire figurer sur les listes de la RAF. Je sombrai dans le découragement jusqu'au moment où je compris que, si on ne voulait pas de moi comme pilote, je pouvais briguer un poste plus humble : de bombardier par exemple, qu'on m'accorda. Le bombardier était le membre de l'équipage qui avait la responsabilité du largage sur l'objectif : tâche sans gloire, mais essentielle. J'étais donc destiné à détruire ? La paix de ma conscience était à ce prix ? Je me soumis.

Je pris discrètement congé de tous, même de Saint-Exupéry que je revis. Il se battait alors contre des influences et on le sentait au bord des larmes. Il avait contre lui de Gaulle, qui ne lui pardonnait pas d'avoir servi Pétain, n'avait pas eu l'élégance de le recevoir, interdisait la vente de ses ouvrages, et même s'ingéniait à ce qu'il n'ait aucun rôle dans les combats de la Libération.

Notre convoi d'une quinzaine de navires était dans le port. Le 26 octobre 1943, avec neuf cents officiers, sous-officiers et hommes de troupe recrutés pour la RAF, j'embarquai sur un paquebot dont je me souviens seulement qu'il était hollandais et qu'une grande inscription en français dominait la salle à manger : « Repos ailleurs ». Cela devait vouloir dire quelque chose, mais quoi ? Nous n'appareillâmes que le surlendemain.

VIII

Quelque chose approche

Nous franchîmes de nuit le détroit de Gibraltar. Je ne pus contempler le rocher qui aurait pu être, en juillet 1940, un triste exploit ou notre fin. Après, nous ne vîmes rien que la mer violette, de l'écume, des dauphins, nos voisins de galère et nos escorteurs, et n'eûmes pour distraction que les exercices d'alerte, des repas mornes et des conversations mélancoliques. Mes camarades jouaient aux cartes. Je roulais sur moi-même comme le navire, j'étais déjà dans l'ombre et dans l'inexploré, il me semblait que je ne partageais rien de ce qu'éprouvaient mes camarades, sinon peut-être la peine qu'ils cachaient d'avoir dû se séparer des leurs. De Sétif restait un seul de mes compagnons, le sergent-chef mécanicien Kopp, qui s'était attaché à moi depuis Chartres et à qui je m'étais moi-même attaché. Nous nous interrogions l'un l'autre. Où allions-nous ? Il souriait. Ventré s'était jugé trop vieux pour courir comme moi au-devant des hasards et pensait que ses chefs ne méritaient pas qu'on meure pour eux. Il me manquait.

Enfin, après deux semaines d'ennui, nous nous enfonçâmes dans une montagne de brume, le convoi n'avança plus qu'à l'allure du pas. Vaguement nauséeux, traînant avec nous des relents de cale et de tabagie, frissonnants dans nos tenues défraîchies, nous débarquâmes en plein brouillard à Liverpool. La vie avait changé : plus de soleil, des fumées grises, des odeurs de port et de marée. Nous nous rassemblâmes sur les quais, continuant à critiquer en bons Français les manies et l'organisation des Britanniques dont nous étions, à notre corps défendant, les obligés. Sans eux, que nous détestions et admirions si fort depuis Mers el-Kébir, où aurions-nous été ?

Et même, puisque nous n'étions plus rien, sous quel uniforme aurions-nous servi ? Nous venions d'un continent où l'on ne se battait pas, nous nous sentions empruntés, aux prises à des vanités. On nous considéra avec une méfiance qui se justifiait et cependant nous intriguait. Ici, du moindre policier casqué au moindre porteur de bagages, des femmes en uniforme aux taxis, à tout ce qui roulait ou respirait, des maisons meurtries par les bombes à tout ce qui vivait comme à tout ce qui mourait, jusqu'aux chiens, la guerre semblait le tranquille état d'âme. Nous ne connaissions rien de cette terre, peu d'entre nous parlaient anglais, c'est peu dire que nous nous sentions dépaysés.

A West-Kirby, près de Chester, non loin de Liverpool, nous fûmes d'abord détenus dans un camp infiniment plus strict que celui où, à Laghouat, les autorités de chez nous avaient interné des sujets de S.M. Nous subîmes un long et minutieux interrogatoire d'identité presque injurieux. Ne venions-nous pas en renfort de la RAF ? N'étions-nous pas, non seulement des citoyens français mais des aviateurs confirmés, au moins égaux sur tous les points aux Britanniques ? Certes, certes. N'empêche. Nous étions d'anciens soldats de Pétain et de Darlan qui n'aimaient pas l'Angleterre. Les questions qu'on nous posa, la liberté qu'on nous mesurait alors que nous avions hâte d'éblouir, rien ne nous parut plaisant. Nous avions peine à en croire nos yeux. Des barrières se fermaient derrière nous et, à des officiers, on offrait des chambrées de troupe. On nous soupçonna de mensonge, sinon d'espionnage ou de fausses déclarations jusqu'à ce que, nos dires vérifiés, comparés aux renseignements de l'*Intelligence Service* et contrôlés à de nouvelles sources, nous fussions introduits dans la parentèle de la RAF. Alors nous eûmes droit au mess : œufs au bacon, bouilli, frites, desserts gélatineux ; et cercle : fauteuils défoncés et journaux. Nous eûmes aussi accès au bar où coulaient la bière et le whisky. A la chambrée, les plus alertes d'entre nous se déchaînèrent : bataille de polochons, humour de caserne, conversation de bordel. Je devais me tromper quand je plaçais le métier des armes si haut. La grossièreté des propos, l'imbécillité des critiques, les quolibets me rappelaient que la vie militaire n'est qu'ordure, banalité et platitude. Nous en étions aux *Sous-offs*. Indulgent maintenant, je me dis que c'était pour mes camarades une façon de bafouer

la sensibilité qui aurait pu les habiter. Peut-être sentaient-ils âprement qu'ayant choisi d'aller au casse-pipe, ils devaient, persifleurs de tout, de tous et d'eux-mêmes, ne croire à rien, bouffer, baiser et tout tourner en ridicule. Plus tard, un caricaturiste de chez nous représentera un de ces membres distingués de notre caste auréolé d'une cuvette de w.-c., tel que je le vis toujours moi-même. Je pouvais me défendre, je ne m'en privai pas. D'autres camarades se joignirent à moi, notamment un capitaine qui arrivait de France par un circuit de la Résistance, Raymond Brohon. Il n'eut pas besoin d'un long discours. Il dit ce qu'il pensait et commanda. Il était le plus ancien, on lui obéit, l'ordre régna aussitôt. Brohon avait commencé sa carrière dans une escadrille de Syrie. Admirateur passionné de Lawrence d'Arabie, il avait parcouru en Orient tous les chemins de son héros. Je poussai mon lit de camp à côté du sien.

Dès que la nuit tombait, l'Angleterre voilait ses lumières et se mettait à bourdonner comme une usine. La sombre voûte du ciel s'emplissait d'une rumeur confuse et, de partout, d'invisibles avions décollaient, cap à l'est et s'en allaient vider leurs soutes au-dessus de la Ruhr, là où se fabriquaient les armes, les munitions, les roulements à billes et l'essence synthétique du IIIe Reich.

Nous pensions que nous serions vite engagés. Nous dûmes nous plier à la règle. Pour la RAF, nous n'étions rien et ne savions rien. Nous devions être instruits, du début à la fin, des choses les plus élémentaires de notre spécialité. Cela demandait du temps. Dans le sinistre camp de West-Kirby, nous menions l'existence ennuyeuse des armées tandis qu'en Afrique les légions de Hitler s'effondraient. L'Italie était conquise, les Russes allaient de victoire en victoire, la France commençait à être libérée par le sud, nous avions peur que l'Allemagne ne soit vaincue sans même l'ouverture d'un second front.

Un autre capitaine, Gallois, arriva du Maroc. Il sortait d'une grande école civile. C'était un cœur sensible, une âme ardente, un artiste. Pour lui, notre armée était avachie et archaïque, et nous devions nous adapter aux méthodes britanniques. De partout, de Nouvelle-Zélande, d'Australie, du Canada, de toutes les possessions du Royaume-Uni, la chair à canon affluait. Notre troupeau à nous portait l'écusson

229

« France » sur l'épaule, nous n'étions pas peu fiers. Cela me rappelait les battages de l'oncle Jules. Les machines ronflaient, nous étions les gerbes. Ce ne serait pas du blé qui coulerait, ce serait du sang dans la gigantesque boucherie de la guerre. Nous qui étions là, les grandes gueules comme les autres, les imbéciles comme les autres, les simples comme les compliqués, nous avions en commun d'accepter d'être happés. Nous avions cru à Pétain, on nous considérait avec un peu de commisération. Ce séjour à West-Kirby me fut insupportable. Cependant nous assistions à des concerts, nous achetâmes des chandails et des duffle-coats de la *Navy* avec nos tickets de vêtements.

A peine fûmes-nous dédouanés que Gallois m'entraîna à Londres. J'avais lu *l'Ode à Londres bombardée* de Philippe Soupault que Charlot avait publiée à Alger. Depuis la bataille d'Angleterre où des jeunes gens, à peine sortis de l'université, s'étaient furieusement jetés avec leurs avions de chasse sur les bombardiers nazis en y laissant, pour beaucoup, la vie, Londres était devenu le symbole de l'héroïsme. Les plaies de la ville étaient pansées. Des balustrades cachaient des îlots entiers, rasés. Des salves de DCA craquaient, nul n'y prêtait attention. Les librairies accordaient une large place aux livres de guerre et des volumes entiers d'*Air Poetry* regorgeaient de poèmes écrits par des pilotes, des navigateurs ou des mitrailleurs. La RAF paraissait une formidable machine à détruire, à tuer ou à s'immoler. Tout à coup, je me sentis fier d'être aussi poète, mais je restais étranger et je me promenais comme un poisson rouge dans un aquarium ambulant : muet, écarquillant les yeux, pris de crainte de ne pas retrouver mon chemin et usant avec maladresse de la monnaie anglaise si compliquée. De Gaulle était à Alger. A Londres, aurait-il daigné venir jusqu'à nous ? La façon dont il s'était comporté avec Saint-Exupéry me laissait craindre un certain mépris à l'égard des vichystes et pétainistes indécrottables dont la réputation nous accablait. Nous n'étions que des soldats malheureux.

Gallois et moi allâmes d'abord à la revue *Horizon* dont le directeur, Cyril Conolly, se montrait inquiet de l'avenir de la France. Il avait publié des textes importants parmi lesquels une étude de Koestler, « Naissance d'un mythe », m'alerta. « Parler d'un ami mort, c'est parler contre le temps, c'est

courir après une image qui s'enfuit, c'est la saisir, l'arrêter avant que le mythe se change en pierre. Car les morts sont arrogants... » Ainsi commençaient les pages de Koestler sur Richard Hillary, un jeune pilote abattu après qu'il eut descendu cinq avions allemands, et si atrocement brûlé qu'on avait dû lui modeler un nouveau visage. A l'hôpital, Hillary avait écrit un livre, *The Last Enemy*. Retourné dans la RAF deux ans après sa chute, il s'était tué dans un accident. Ce destin me passionna, et comme Edmond Charlot était désireux d'acquérir les droits des ouvrages qui me paraîtraient dignes d'intérêt, je me lançai dans l'étude d'*Horizon*. De retour à West-Kirby, quelques jeunes officiers se groupèrent autour de moi pour la traduction. Page après page, au fur et à mesure que nous avancions, nous découvrions la brûlante complexion de la Grande-Bretagne. Mers el-Kébir s'éloignait de plus en plus.

Gallois prit contact avec la revue *la France libre*, que la RAF lançait au-dessus de Paris en format réduit et papier bible. Nous retournâmes à Londres. Cette fois, nous nous sentîmes à l'aise. André Labarthe, bouillant scientifique plein de charme, que de Gaulle avait nommé secrétaire d'Etat à la recherche, dirigeait l'équipe de la revue mais n'était là que rarement. Il recevait beaucoup, ailleurs et somptueusement. Un jour où, dans le cabinet du général, il parlait d'abondance en se promenant de long en large, il s'était permis de s'asseoir un instant sur le bureau du général. « Pas de ça chez moi », avait dit de Gaulle. Labarthe était parti furieux, et Giraud avait eu le même mot, à Alger en 1943, quand Labarthe était entré chez lui une rose à la main. Labarthe avait des ambitions politiques et soupçonnait de Gaulle de noirs desseins. On disait qu'il avait créé *la France libre* avec six mille livres de l'*Intelligence Service* pour semer la zizanie chez les Français. Il laissait la revue dans les mains de sa secrétaire, Martha Kahn, juive de Varsovie, qui avait pris le nom de Martha Lecoutre, et d'un autre Polonais, Stanislas Szymanczyk, ancien chef communiste en Allemagne qui avait écrit les proclamations de Rosa Luxemburg. A *la France libre*, il rédigeait les éditoriaux et signait Staroblinski. Tout le monde l'appelait Staro. Né aux confins de la Tchécoslovaquie et de la Hongrie, il parlait atrocement beaucoup de langues. On avait du mal à le comprendre car les mots se bousculaient dans sa bouche comme des galets. Enorme, il avait un cou de taureau, de

grosses joues, des yeux exorbités ; tirant d'une poche des saucisses et des concombres russes d'une autre, il mangeait sans arrêt. Rude et puissant esprit, il se croyait le Clausewitz de cette guerre et pétrissait chaque jour le monde à sa manière. Raymond Aron, qu'on voyait peu, corrigeait ses papiers. De son côté, Aron avait publié un fameux éditorial « A l'ombre de Bonaparte » que de Gaulle ne lui pardonna jamais.

Martha Lecoutre s'était prise d'affection pour Gallois et pour moi. Nous ne nous quittions plus. Staro écrivait ses articles dans sa langue natale, Martha les traduisait en français, Gallois rafistolait, et Raymond Aron, qui ne passait pas tous les jours, revoyait le tout. Entre eux et Staro, la discussion s'éternisait, Staro traitait Aron de « pétit' con ». Le siège de la revue, vide de meubles et où les voix résonnaient, était une merveilleuse bohème où Labarthe payait les articles cinquante livres, une fortune. Je fus aussi l'hôte de l'Institut français où, Dieu merci, il n'y avait pas que de vieilles dames. Son directeur répétait qu'il devait rassurer le général de Gaulle sur les intentions des Anglais à l'égard de la France. Est-ce à ce moment-là que je lus *le Silence de la mer* ? Dans l'immensité de Londres semé de ruines, surtout dans les quartiers du centre, on était au cœur de la guerre. Parfois, en pleine nuit, on entendait des grondements plus forts : un raid qui se rassemblait ou qui rentrait. Cela nous laissait rêveurs, vaguement envieux et pleins de sentiments troubles. En Grande-Bretagne, les hommes servaient à la défense, à la tuerie ; les femmes à la lutte contre les incendies, à la survie. Pas une famille où il n'y avait personne sous les armes. Nous qui venions de débarquer, buvions et mangions aux frais de S.M. la Reine, parfois nous nous sentions gênés.

Avant Noël, sans explication et seul, je fus expédié au sud-ouest de l'Ecosse, à Dumfries, première étape de notre entraînement. Je me hissai dans un train de nuit bondé de soldats où quelqu'un jouait de la cornemuse. A l'aube, nous longeâmes de molles ondulations, puis nous glissâmes le long de vallées encaissées où paissaient d'énormes moutons frisés, bas sur pattes. Le paysage s'élargit et ce furent de grasses prairies, puis les fumées des usines de Carlisle. Le ciel se dégagea sur une campagne semée de meules de paille à toit pointu. Dans la nouvelle base, j'eus droit à une chambre avec

un poêle à boulets d'anthracite, des avions bourdonnaient, l'air était vif, le soleil déversait sur les chaumes et les labours des brassées de lumière douce. Je me dis : « Dieu ne m'a pas oublié. » J'étais heureux. Je m'étonnai cependant qu'on ne me donnât rien à faire. Peut-être parce que Christmas approchait ? Le cercle débordait de sapins à fanfreluches. Le soir de Noël, après le *high tea,* je restai dans ma chambre, travaillant à ce que je croyais être le roman des débuts de ma vie amoureuse, ce qui n'allait pas du tout avec le cours de mes pensées, ne menait à rien et s'acheva plus tard dans un autodafé. Gallois m'écrivit qu'à West-Kirby, Noël avait été célébré dans des vociférations, un grand bruit de mâchoires et un répertoire de chansons pour mariages de banlieue.

Enfin mon entraînement de bombardier commença et je volai avec un équipage que je ne connaissais pas, sur un bimoteur léger, un Avro Anson de 375 CV d'un modèle si ancien qu'on remontait les roues à la manivelle. Nous décollions de jour, le pilote nous emmenait sur une mer d'Irlande jaune et glauque, nous revenions en pleine nuit. L'Avro peinait contre les vents tempétueux du canal du Nord et de ses îles. Il ahanait à parcourir les distances qui séparaient nos objectifs fictifs : des cornes de cap, des rochers marqués de points lumineux. L'un après l'autre, car nous étions une fournée, nous visions et lâchions nos déclenchements de photos sur des illusions. Mais enfin l'instruction avait commencé, je m'efforçais d'être bon élève et me laissais transbahuter, parfois avec des nausées, comme à Avord, d'un bout à l'autre de cette machine étroite. Quand notre groupe de West-Kirby rejoignit enfin Dumfries, on s'étonna de me voir, car le bruit avait couru que j'étais arrêté pour collaboration, ah ! par exemple ! Un moment désarçonné, je mesurai soudain les conséquences de mon misérable factum Pétain. Un soldat qui croyait à ce qu'on lui disait, voilà ce que j'étais, ficelé comme un quartier de bidoche destiné à la casserole. Ne passais-je pas aux yeux de certains pour trop entier dans mes opinions et un peu exalté ? N'avais-je pas eu l'idée de monter avec mon escadrille une chorale que j'avais même risquée dans un cinéma d'Alger pour interpréter des chansons subversives comme *Trois jeunes tambours* et *la Claire fontaine* ? N'avais-je pas écrit des prières et des poèmes ? Etait-ce normal, dans une armée, un poète pilotant des avions, après avoir servi Pétain,

s'en allait ensuite chez les Anglais dans la RAF ? Coupable, on l'était à moins, n'est-ce pas, mes pères ? J'avais, disait-on, « un dossier chargé ».

C'est vrai, j'avais cru en Pétain, je l'avais suivi et aimé, j'avais écrit à sa gloire ce malheureux opuscule. Je ne m'étais tout de même pas engagé dans la division *das Reich* comme tant de jeunes hommes risquant leur peau, par folie et pour quoi ? Qui m'avait fait comme j'étais ? Pourquoi n'étais-je pas né faubourg Saint-Germain, fils de bourgeois ou, comme le rêvait parfois Flaubert, empereur de Cochinchine ? Bonté divine, que n'avais-je connu de Gaulle officier du cabinet de Pétain, quand il servait de nègre au Maréchal ? Que n'avais-je été à mon tour son aide de camp, son vide-pot humble et dévoué, quand, devenu général et rebelle, le hasard et le courage l'avaient servi ? Pourquoi nous étions-nous posés à Alger et pas à Londres ? Pourquoi, après la débâcle, étais-je tombé sur ma terre natale, dans ma famille, et à qui ferais-je croire qu'après avoir publié une brochure à la louange de Pétain, je n'avais pas à bon escient, ô turpitude ! rallié son camp ? J'aurais avoué tout ce qu'on aurait voulu, et d'abord que j'étais un crétin. Et encore d'avoir écrit quelque chose d'aussi mal torché que j'en rougis toujours de honte. Ah ! ce n'était pas du Claudel, ce n'était pas ces *Paroles du Maréchal* qu'Eve Francis, interprète adorée du poète, déclamait au Grand Casino de Vichy, à un entracte de *l'Annonce*, en 1941 : *Monsieur le Maréchal, il y a un destin pour les morts qui est de ressusciter...*

Mais enfin ce n'est pas le seul ouvrage de moi à ne pas figurer dans ma bibliographie. D'abord elle est médiocre, cette brochure. Ensuite, c'est Pétain. Soyons sérieux ! Même médiocre, s'il s'était agi de *la France sauvée par de Gaulle*, ne l'aurais-je pas revendiquée ? Et, admirable avec Pétain, l'aurais-je gardée ? Faut-il rappeler, pour souligner le sens de l'opportunité que j'ai toujours, qu'à mon départ de Laghouat j'avais écrit le long poème dont j'ai parlé, que personne ne publia jamais, sur le Maréchal qui nous quittait ? Aujourd'hui, j'ai vu tant de pontifes et de pantins occuper de hautes fonctions et en tirer gloire et profit que je me laisse aller, d'une plume tranquille, à un brin d'ironie.

Quelqu'un prit-il ma défense ? Je ne fus pas inquiété. Nous n'étions pas des lumières, nous faisions ce que nous

pouvions. Brohon s'entraînait sur d'autres bases, Gallois qui revenait de Londres avec une règle à calcul qu'il avait achetée ne parut accorder aucun crédit aux soupçons qui pesaient sur moi. « Il faudrait arrêter la France entière », dit-il. Il avait été désigné comme navigateur et le navigateur était le membre le plus important de l'équipage. Sans repères terrestres que la nébulosité lui cachait d'ordinaire, il exigeait du pilote une discipline sévère et des changements de cap ou d'altitude à la minute. Gallois et moi ne suivions pas les mêmes cours mais nous vivions ensemble, et parfois volions sur le même avion. Pour moi, élève bombardier, il s'agissait d'afficher sur le viseur l'altitude, la vitesse, la dérive et, le moment venu, de guider le pilote sur l'objectif, puis d'appuyer sur le bouton qui déclenchait les bombes fictives et une photo témoin.

Gallois me tint au courant des dernières vues sur la planète de Staro : le règlement de la fin de la guerre se discutait dans les sphères politiques. Allemands et Américains étaient d'accord sur le principe d'empêcher les Russes d'entrer en Allemagne. Si la victoire des Russes devançait celle des Américains, l'Allemagne se retrancherait derrière la ligne Siegfried et jetterait contre les Russes la centaine de divisions qu'elle récupérerait en évacuant la France et l'Italie, les Alliés ne dépasseraient pas la ligne Siegfried, l'Allemagne ferait la paix avec eux et les laisserait précéder les Russes. Après quoi, du Reich démembré, les minorités se rattacheraient à l'URSS, la Prusse à la Pologne, un Etat tampon séparerait l'Allemagne en deux, un autre s'installerait en Rhénanie, l'influence française serait peu à peu éliminée, Bizerte irait aux Anglais, Dakar et Casablanca aux Américains. Enfin, le second front était prévu pour février ou juin, mais si, par hasard, l'Allemagne réussissait à se servir de l'arme secrète dont elle menaçait le monde libre, si elle inventait l'arme atomique avant les Américains, elle pourrait gagner la guerre. Alors nous devrions nous jeter dans les bras de Pétain, ah ! la sainte rigolade, mon père ! Pour ces retournements savants, mieux valait être du Grand-Orient, de l'archevêché de Paris, ou du grand état-major. Aujourd'hui, on dirait de l'ENA.

Il nous suffisait de deux jours de permission pour gagner Londres. Les trains britanniques n'étaient pas toujours à

l'heure mais ils existaient, ils n'étaient pas propres, mais ils roulaient. Londres était pour nous la mère de toutes les félicités, la ville martyre et la force de l'esprit. De là, on espérait toujours quelque chose, nous y courions, Gallois et moi, quand, par chance, nos dates de permission coïncidaient, Londres était alors un débordement de bonheur, une illumination. En souci de Labarthe toujours en voyage, et de Staro, Martha veillait à tout, s'occupait de tout, adoucissait les contacts, évitait les heurts, Raymond Aron me parut d'une gentillesse infinie. Il semblait moins intimidé par Staro que par Gallois et moi qui avions son âge. Dans ses Mémoires, il se jugea même « embusqué ». Nous déjeunâmes une fois ensemble. Vive intelligence dans un corps plutôt mal ficelé, chétif ou souffreteux, comparé à la stature et à la masse de Staro, Aron semblait éprouver pour nous une immense pitié et une jalousie qui perçait parfois. Nous étions en bonne santé, sous l'uniforme, et robustes dans la machine à fabriquer des combattants, des macchabées ou des héros. Lui qui ne vivait que de l'esprit aurait voulu aussi combattre, mais, pour combattre, il fallait cultiver une certaine dose de bêtise. De mon côté, je me sentais replié sur moi-même, en doute de tout, en peine d'Amrouche et de Saint-Exupéry qui ne répondaient pas à mes lettres.

Tout le monde parlait français, on nous choyait. Beaucoup d'organisations charitables s'occupaient des Français. Les châteaux et les résidences de la *gentry* s'ouvraient à nous un peu au hasard, d'après la liste établie par l'Institut français et l'état-major. En prévision de quoi, nous devions assister à des cours de maintien et de civilité. J'eus l'impression que nous, Français, appartenions à une nation plutôt fruste, grossière et balourde, dans toutes les nuances qu'il était conseillé d'employer en Grande-Bretagne pour dire que le temps s'améliorait ou que le thé des Indes devenait rare. Il ne fallait surtout jamais faire étalage de soi. Sur ce chapitre, nous devions être des curiosités.

En février, on nous expédia tout en haut de l'Ecosse, au camp de Lossiemouth. C'est là que j'appris que Murtin, accroché en vol par un équipier au large de Djidjeli, s'était, en se jetant en parachute, fracassé contre le plan fixe de son avion de chasse. Sans gilet de sauvetage, il avait lutté trois quarts

d'heure dans une mer agitée avant d'être repêché. On l'avait amputé d'une jambe au-dessus du genou. C'était bien le plus sale tour que la Providence avait pu lui jouer. Murtin avec une patte en bois ? Murtin infirme ? Murtin estropié ? Murtin aux Invalides ? Je lui télégraphiai que je l'aimais.

Il faisait si froid que nous sautions par-dessus les grilles des réserves pour dérober du charbon. A peine le *breakfast* englouti, nous filions à l'instruction. Les cours étaient donnés par des officiers qui avaient terminé leur tour d'opérations. Ils en portaient la preuve sur la poitrine : d'ordinaire la DFC, la *Distinguished Flying Cross,* un ruban blanc zébré de violet, que nous rêvions tous d'arborer un jour, mais la DFC ne se gagnait pas aisément : il fallait aller jusqu'au bout du tour, ou avoir eu un accident sérieux et beaucoup de chance. Nous volions sur des Wellington, des chaudières qui avaient fait leurs preuves au début de la guerre et dont les moteurs tournaient encore. Au moment où l'Europe roulait vers l'abîme, les Wellington avaient permis à l'Angleterre de prouver qu'elle ne cédait pas, et qu'elle détruisait les usines de la Ruhr.

Du ciel, on voyait tant de lacs, tant de défilés et tant de détroits que les Highlands apparaissaient tout en bosses et fosses, creusés et mamelonnés en prés ras et herbeux où paissaient des moutons à qui le pays semblait appartenir. Leurs troupeaux tranquilles avançaient jusqu'au bord de la mer où parfois une marée les surprenait. On disait que leurs cornes empêchaient les béliers de garder la tête hors de l'eau et qu'ils périssaient. Dans la lumière bleue qui tournait parfois au rose matin et soir, les jours étaient si longs déjà, en avril et en mai, qu'ils semblaient ne savoir comment finir. Des landes nous entouraient, la mer battait le rivage. Le dimanche, nous traînions au cercle sans même boire du whisky, nous grimpions dans un bus pour Inverness ou pour Elgin ou dans un train pour Aberdeen, car les voitures manquaient. Nous aurions pu assister à un office ou à une messe. L'idée ne nous en venait pas. Nous avions nos aumôniers et je n'étais pas de leurs fidèles. Avec Gallois nous visitions les villages proches, nous tâtions les tweeds qu'on tissait là, nous restions rêveurs devant des falaises, des châteaux vertigineux. Notre cœur était ailleurs. Nous n'étions pas loin du loch Ness, de ses eaux grises, brillantes et glacées.

Vers le nord et au-delà, l'Ecosse continuait par l'archipel des Orcades, puis s'achevait sur une côte écumeuse, hachée menu, creusée et rongée par les flots. Plus à l'est, c'était les Hébrides que nous survolions en demandant au Seigneur de ne pas laisser faiblir nos moteurs : un si lourd espace liquide et incertain, tant d'îles désertes ou tenues par d'âpres et rares populations... L'Ecosse était loin de la guerre, les avions allemands ne se risquaient pas jusque-là. Quant à la mer, elle appartenait à la *navy* et nous la lui laissions. Là où plus tard tout sera pourri par la recherche du pétrole, c'était le désert et une paix dont nous voulions à toute force sortir. J'étais devenu voleur de charbon comme j'avais été serviteur de Pétain : par la force des choses. Si l'on m'avait surpris, j'aurais pu être traduit devant un tribunal militaire pour détournement de biens appartenant à S.M. Britannique : ces boulets d'anthracite dont le commandant de la base se montrait pour nous si avare. Les Wellington soufflaient comme des locomotives à vapeur tirant des trains de marchandises. Nous appartenions au glorieux corps de la RAF et, plus encore, à cette énorme et stupide masse des armées qui occupent une partie de la terre sans savoir souvent où elles sont ni ce qu'elles font, se désintéressent de tout ce qui n'est pas elles-mêmes, roulent en elles-mêmes de vagues espoirs ou désespoirs, des pensées minuscules ou des jalousies. Nous ne savions rien des autres, pas grand-chose de nous, et cependant nous faisions un avec ce corps immense et indélimité qui répandait à travers le monde les menaces, la terreur, des troubles et parfois d'humbles choses. Le personnage le plus important de la base de Lossiemouth à l'extrémité de l'Ecosse, loin de tout, était le vaguemestre. Grâce à lui nous resserrions nos liens distendus avec ce qui restait de nous ailleurs. Pour moi, Amrouche avait disparu, Saint-Exupéry m'avait oublié, Doyon ne pouvait plus m'atteindre. Seules, ma mère, d'Alger et, de Sétif, ma famille m'envoyaient de leurs nouvelles et en attendaient de moi. La RAF, ma nouvelle mère, vêtue de gris-bleu, me tenait par la main, me guidait, me promenait sur des machines volantes prêtes à rendre l'âme. On nous promettait pour bientôt d'autres engins plus puissants et des sillages par-dessus les continents dévastés et les villes en ruine. D'où nous étions, le soleil se levait.

En Ecosse, on admirait ce qu'on pouvait : ainsi notre

chère étoile familière, les brumes délicates que ses rayons étiraient sur l'épaule de cette terre bizarre, plus montueuse que montagneuse, célèbre par la laine de ses moutons et ses alcools, accueillante cependant si l'on savait s'y prendre. A l'évidence, nous ne savions pas, nous manquions de temps pour percer la cuirasse de ses habitants. Heureusement, à travers des châteaux si altiers, il y avait une femme si belle, une reine de France et reine d'Ecosse de qui Schiller avait célébré le cruel destin. J'aurais aimé faire la cour à l'esprit de Marie Stuart qui avait préféré mourir plutôt que renoncer à elle-même. Les Ecossais ne semblaient pas avoir tellement gardé sa mémoire. Aucune rose ne portait son nom. Nous visitâmes à Edimbourg une énorme cathédrale gothique, nous vîmes des palais, des monuments hautains. Nous retournâmes entre les barbelés du camp. De temps en temps, quelque chose passait sur nous comme un oiseau : la promesse d'une rencontre, un événement de peu d'importance qui comptait, puis l'oiseau disparaissait. Le second front allait s'ouvrir, la Grande-Bretagne était envahie par l'Amérique : les avions américains, le matériel américain étaient déjà partout, sauf ici. Le communiqué parlait des raids de la RAF sur l'Allemagne comme des cours de la bourse : les valeurs, c'était le tonnage des bombes déversées et le chiffre des pertes. Je me disais qu'il fallait se préparer à entrer dans un pourcentage d'avions manquants et que là s'arrêterait notre destin. J'entendais parfois, dans mon sommeil, un pas venir vers moi, hésiter puis s'éloigner. Quelque chose approchait, mais quoi ?

Notre stage s'acheva, et de Londres où pleuvaient les bombes volantes et les bombes fusées, je revins mélancolique. Ce qui comptait, c'était l'amour et il n'y en avait plus nulle part, semblait-il. A la fin du mois de mai, nous gagnâmes un autre camp d'instruction, le dernier, Rufforth, où nos équipages se rassemblèrent. Je retrouvai Brohon, sûr de lui, rayonnant, vaguement détaché et dominateur. Avait-il pu visiter Clouds Hill, le chalet dont le colonel Lawrence avait fait son dernier gîte ? Avait-il vu, sur la route de Bovington, l'endroit où T. E. s'était tué à moto ? Dans ce camp-là sévissait comme une hâte, chacun courait à la recherche d'une chambre, d'une chaise ou d'une table, le mess ressemblait à tous ceux que nous avions connus, que rappellent à présent les gargotes

239

des autoroutes, où chacun va se servir et s'assied comme il peut. Là, tout était répugnant et on s'y battait presque. De ce long parcours dans les écoles de la RAF, presque neuf mois, c'est mon plus mauvais souvenir. Je ne vois plus que des baraquements, des huttes, des barbelés et des demi-tonneaux. La seule satisfaction que j'éprouvai fut que l'équipage dont j'avais le commandement était sous ma main. Nous volions à présent sur des Handley Page Halifax pareils à ceux que nous aurions en opérations. 7 200 CV au total et trente-deux tonnes au décollage. Je connaissais déjà mon navigateur, Ravotti, un ardent avocat de Casablanca. Le pilote, Gronier, avait trente ans, il était brun, pondéré, avec un flegme de bon augure. J'étais un peu jaloux de lui, il ne l'était pas de moi. Il aurait pu l'être, car, dans la RAF, le *captain* était toujours le pilote, et là, c'était moi. Les seules entorses à cette règle nous étaient dues, à nous, Français. Le mécanicien était mon fidèle Kopp, qui me suivait comme mon âme, le radio et les deux mitrailleurs me parurent dévoués, soumis, plutôt effacés. Je me dis qu'il faudrait les voir à l'ouvrage ; ils en disaient autant de moi. Nous étions mêlés à beaucoup d'équipages de Nouvelle-Zélande, du Canada, d'Australie. Entre nous, nous commencions à nous connaître, les grandes gueules ne s'exprimaient plus qu'en sourdine, des amitiés naissaient, Brohon et Gallois dépassaient le lot des caractères, je commençais à me fondre dans l'ensemble et je m'y sentais bien. Nos futurs *squadrons* portaient les numéros 346 et 347 et avaient leur base près de la ville d'York, presque en plein centre de la Grande-Bretagne, non loin des collines désolées où les sœurs Brontë avaient écrit *les Hauts de Hurlevent*. J'avais appris le nom des étoiles, je les visais avec un sextant. Le 6 juin, éclata la nouvelle du débarquement en Normandie. Quelques jours après, nous partions.

Notre *RAF Station* était à côté du village d'Elvington dont les jardins débordaient de roses et d'asters. Du camp, entre les barrières de barbelés, on ne pouvait sortir que par le poste en armes où flottaient deux pavillons : celui de la RAF et le nôtre. La veille de notre arrivée, un équipage s'était écrasé sur les collines à cause du mauvais temps.

Nous habitions ce qu'on appelait, comme Diogène, des tonneaux, des huttes. Le sentier longeait une haie d'églantines en fleur, traversait une ligne de chemin de fer, longeait un maigre bois de bouleaux et débouchait sur un champ de blé en épis, bordé de chênes ; ma fenêtre ouvrait sur un pré coupé de haies. Non loin de là, le cimetière s'abritait sous des pruniers pliant sous les prunes. L'église était déserte. J'eus envie de m'asseoir à l'orgue mais je n'osai pas. Les camarades et moi avions l'air emprunté des invités qui ne se connaissent pas. Gallois n'était pas encore là, je ne faisais qu'apercevoir Brohon. Mon seul copain était un capitaine qui s'appelait Marchal et que tout le monde appelait le Barbu parce qu'il portait un collier blond roux taillé court. C'était un gaillard plein d'humour, parfois fébrile d'inquiétude, soucieux de se distinguer au feu pour en finir avec ses obligations militaires et se retirer dans un coin tranquille, comme éclusier, disait-il. Justement, à Elvington, une rivière à écluse longeait le village, des camarades y pêchaient, je me dis que, les jours de congé, j'irais moi aussi.

Inspiré par le destin de Richard Hillary, le jeune pilote de la bataille d'Angleterre, j'ouvris un cahier pour y noter les détails de notre vie. Le pas, que certaines nuits j'entendais approcher, me laissait craindre de ne pas sortir vivant de cette aventure. Pourquoi avons-nous la naïveté de vouloir que nos expériences ne soient pas inutiles ? Je pensais que si on retrouvait de moi un journal où nos vols de guerre étaient consignés, ce serait pour moi l'occasion de ne pas disparaître tout à fait. Je pris la précaution d'indiquer qu'on veuille bien remettre ce cahier à Marcelle Schveitzer, l'amie d'Alger qui avait harmonisé quelques-unes de nos chansons ou, à défaut, à Henri Bosco, le seul qui répondait à mes lettres. J'étais heureux quand je reconnaissais son écriture sur une enveloppe, j'étais sûr qu'il servirait ce cahier. Des bombardiers, on ne savait rien, ou à peu près, personne jusque-là n'avait raconté leur aventure. Saint-Exupéry volait seul dans un ciel libre. Notre nom à nous était légion, un nom de démons. Au mess, depuis qu'on était en Grande-Bretagne, on ne chantait plus.

Chaque commandant d'avion, comme chaque pilote, accomplissait un vol d'accoutumance avec un équipage déjà aguerri par au moins cinq missions. J'accomplis ce vol avec des

camarades du *squadron 346*, qui portait aussi le nom de « Guyenne ». Le chef de bord était un capitaine que je ne connaissais pas, et qui s'appelait Grimaldi. Nous devions bombarder, en même temps qu'une centaine d'autres Halifax ou Lancaster, une importante régulatrice près de Lunéville, pour gêner l'arrivée des renforts allemands vers la bataille de Normandie. Je ne sais plus comment nous y allâmes : probablement par la mer du Nord, la Hollande et la Belgique, comme si nous nous dirigions sur Cologne, pour fondre ensuite sur notre proie avec un crochet ou deux sur la Lorraine. Chaque raid avait une route précise qui devait, jusqu'au dernier moment, laisser l'ennemi incertain sur nos intentions.

Sans responsabilité, j'observai l'équipage conduire l'énorme quadrimoteur dans le flot des autres, en pleine nuit. J'occupais le siège inconfortable du second pilote, j'écoutai le navigateur débiter ses chiffres au pilote impassible. Tout se déroula sans la moindre lumière, au-dessus des nuages et à une altitude voisine de 21 000 pieds, soit 7 000 mètres. Au-dessous de nous était la terre gorgée d'eau de l'Europe du Nord-Ouest. Le raid avançait, aveugle, invisible et, semblait-il, invulnérable, presque mêlé à d'autres raids visant d'autres objectifs, et dont seulement quelques minutes nous séparaient, et sans subir d'attaque de chasseurs ni de canons, la *flak*. Au bout de quatre heures coupées de sortes de frémissements, le bombardier, tout à l'avant, prit la parole pour diriger le pilote, un léger ronflement m'apprit que les soutes s'ouvraient, puis les bombes furent lâchées et nous replongeâmes, avec un autre cap, dans les profondeurs qu'éclairait derrière nous une lueur d'incendie.

Je m'étonnai que tout fût si simple. Nous avions attaqué, en France occupée, la gare de Blainville nettement séparée du bourg. Nos visées ne s'effectuaient pas au hasard. En plus, nous ne volions pas groupés à la manière des Américains, mais séparés. Nous ne lâchions pas nos salves tous ensemble. Nous n'arrosions pas. Nous n'avions labouré et retourné que la régulatrice. La conscience pure, nous nous mîmes sur les caps du retour, en zigzags au-dessus des nuages. Notre patrie était dessous, noire, sans un feu, engloutie, nous allions franchir la côte entre le Havre et Dieppe, nos pensées roulaient à travers une vague nostalgie quand, soudain, la foudre éclata, fantasti-

que, et flagella l'avion. Nous avions dû passer à la verticale d'une batterie non signalée. Le pilote manœuvra, les canons nous pourchassèrent un moment qui me parut un siècle, je me sentis inondé d'une sueur froide. Il me sembla que ma carrière dans la RAF ne serait pas longue.

Dans l'équipage, personne ne parut étonné. Ce devait être le pain de toutes les nuits. Et, en effet, ce qui me changeait du pas hésitant qui semblait approcher, je crus entendre battre en moi comme un furieux tambour nègre, le marteau d'une forge rougeoyante, toute pleine d'éclairs.

Je l'entends toujours.

IX

Pluton, dieu des enfers

QELQUES JOURS plus tard, nos noms apparurent au tableau d'affichage. Nous devions aller écraser une corne de la haute forêt d'Eu où étaient nichées des plates-formes, bien défendues disait-on, de bombes volantes. Nous nous préparâmes comme pour une première communion. Nous n'allions pas loin, l'objectif nous avait été projeté sur un écran géant, nous ne risquions pas de toucher une agglomération. La mission fut annulée, puis rétablie, puis encore annulée. Nous étions sur le point de mettre les moteurs en route quand, pour la troisième fois, ce fut reporté. Sans doute l'état-major attendait-il des conditions de visibilité favorables sur l'objectif. Après deux jours de contrordres, nous partîmes enfin vers l'autel, moins premiers communiants que fiancés. Nous attaquâmes puis nous revînmes. Quand nous fûmes de retour au-dessus de la base, il était deux heures dix du matin.

La nuit était noire avec déjà une vague lueur au nord-est. Nos feux de position allumés, nous tournions autour de l'aérodrome en liaison avec le contrôle et à notre altitude prévue. C'était le pandémonium avec des feux partout. Au pilote près de qui j'étais alors, je signalai soudain un feu rouge assez vif à quatre heures. Un feu rouge, c'est-à-dire le feu d'extrémité de l'aile gauche d'un avion. A quatre heures, par rapport à notre sens de marche pris comme axe vertical d'un cadran horaire, cela signifiait que ce feu rouge était à notre droite, un peu vers l'arrière. Le pilote pouvait ne pas l'avoir vu.

Je n'eus pas le temps d'en dire plus. Ou peut-être alertai-je encore le pilote par un cri en lui désignant de la main ce feu

245

qui grossissait, grossissait et se précipitait sur nous. Je n'ai cessé d'y penser toute ma vie. A plus de quarante ans de distance, quand j'écris cela, le cœur me bat. Le feu rouge se changea en un fracas et un choc formidables qui durèrent peut-être une seconde, après quoi l'avion parut comme suspendu, telle une flèche au sommet de sa course et qui allait retomber. Je compris que nous venions de subir une collision en vol : un des avions qui tournaient avec nous au-dessus de la base nous était rentré dedans. Il y eut un instant de silence terrifiant pendant lequel je recalculai en mètres l'altitude en pieds à laquelle nous étions : quinze cents pieds divisés par trois égalaient cinq cents mètres, le saut en parachute était possible. D'une voix calme qui m'étonna, je donnai mes ordres : « Commandant d'avion à tous : sautez, sautez ! » Le pilote me signala des flammes au moteur intérieur droit, nous manœuvrâmes tous les deux pour couper et éteindre ce moteur tandis que je voyais le volant trépider dans les mains du pilote. L'avion vibrait avec de fortes secousses comme s'il allait casser. Pour moi, je ne sautais pas, je n'abandonnais pas le pilote. D'ailleurs, pour accrocher le parachute à mon harnais, j'aurais dû descendre de l'espèce de siège repliable sur lequel j'étais perché. Le moteur intérieur droit s'éteignit, les vibrations diminuèrent. A présent le pilote tenait presque normalement le volant dans ses mains, l'avion volait, nous allions le ramener au sol. Calme, comme résigné, vaguement incrédule aussi, je lançai un nouvel ordre dans le micro : « Commandant d'avion à tous, ne sautez plus, ne sautez plus. » Rien ne vaut, pour qui vole, l'engin sur lequel il vole, de préférence à une chute dans le noir. Je dis au pilote : « Demandez la priorité à la base. On se pose. » Le pilote appela la tour : « *Mayday, mayday. Scarface two from F Fox...* ». *Scarface* était l'indicatif de la base, *F fox* la lettre de notre avion. F comme fox, renard. C'était la première fois, me semblait-il, que je rapprochais de nous ce renard qui nous accompagnera toute une saison d'enfer, et sans doute la raison pour laquelle je protégerai les renards toute ma vie. Quarante-trois ans plus tard, j'y suis encore. Dans une de mes relations à propos de cette collision, parlant de l'avion, j'ai comparé le bruit qu'il avait fait au bruit d'un arbre qui craque au moment où il s'abat. Ce bruit-là ne m'a jamais quitté. Il m'assourdit toujours avec le tambour nègre.

Brohon, qui volait ce soir-là en même temps que nous, avait senti quelque chose et demandé à son bombardier, un lieutenant qui s'appelait Perseval, de surveiller le ciel avec attention. Aussi, lorsqu'au-dessus de la lueur rose qui se formait à l'horizon, il assista à la collision et nous désigna à son bombardier, tous deux virent un avion tomber et un autre s'accrocher désespérément dans l'air, puis ils entendirent le survivant appeler la base, mais ils ne savaient pas qui était dans le F fox. L'avion tremblait moins. Je fis couper le moteur intérieur gauche pour éviter un déséquilibre. Le pilote semblait comme exalté, survolté. Peut-être se voyait-il déjà décoré de la DFC ? Il continuait de répéter la formule de détresse : « *Mayday, mayday...* Aidez-moi, aidez-moi... » et à seriner son *Scarface*, le nom de ce gangster de cinéma et de son F fox, notre renard qui virait prudemment, sortait le train d'atterrissage intact et pointait son museau pour viser de loin la piste illuminée comme un boulevard de fête. Là, le pilote se tut enfin, se posa comme si de rien n'était et gagna sa place en lisière de bois où déjà on nous attendait.

Avant de quitter l'avion, je fis l'appel de l'équipage à l'interphone. Seuls le navigateur et le mitrailleur arrière avaient sauté ; le mécanicien n'avait pas voulu me quitter, le radio et le mitrailleur central n'avaient pas obéi. Quand nous fûmes à terre, le pilote et moi constatâmes que l'avion n'avait subi que peu de dommages. Le fuselage inférieur était éraflé et un peu aplati. L'avion tamponneur était passé juste au-dessous de nous, assez pour fracasser son poste de pilotage : il était tombé presque à la verticale et brûlait encore, on voyait monter les flammes dans la nuit. A l'interrogatoire des retours de mission, le colonel me posa quelques questions et me quitta sans me serrer la main.

Je répondis à toutes les autres questions que l'officier des renseignements me posa avec beaucoup de gentillesse, j'échappai aux camarades qui me regardaient avec des sentiments mélangés car on savait maintenant que l'équipage de l'autre avion avait péri, puis je rentrai chez moi où, dans l'état qu'on imagine, je ne pus fermer l'œil. Dans *Retour de l'enfer* je lis : « ... essayé d'appliquer mon esprit à la lecture de Vauvenargues. Très difficile. J'évite de parler de cet accident et même d'y penser, tant je suis remué... » Pense-t-on à Vauvenargues quand on vient d'échapper à la mort ? Drôle de consolateur,

Vauvenargues. Gide lisait Bossuet sur le Congo pendant que le jeune et charmant Marc Allégret tirait les crocodiles. Oui, mais Gide était un esprit supérieur. Peu importe. Je refis apparition au mess à l'heure du déjeuner. Le lieutenant Ravotti, notre navigateur, sorti glorieux de son saut en parachute dans un trou noir, rayonnait : il avait chu dans un champ de pommes de terre. Le mitrailleur arrière, qui avait aussi sauté, était assombri. Je me taisais, je revoyais sans cesse le feu rouge sur nous. La conscience tritouillée, triturée, torturée, le pilote et moi répondîmes aux questions auxquelles nous fûmes soumis par des officiers de l'état-major d'un groupe voisin. Le soir, il y avait bal au village. Certains dans l'équipage y allèrent. Je n'y parus pas, on aurait pu dire de moi ce que Conrad rapporte au commandant du rafiot qui avait traversé le cyclone : qu'il était allé « jusqu'à entrevoir les côtes de l'au-delà »...

L'enquête dura cinq jours. Après quoi, je fus convoqué par le colonel pour l'entendre m'en lire les conclusions : « Irresponsabilité du chef de bord pendant la collision en vol. Louange pour sa conduite après. » Cette fois, c'est moi qui partis sans saluer. Aussitôt nous fûmes sur la liste des équipages en alerte et nous décollâmes en pleine nuit sur notre F fox révisé. Pour nous aider, il aurait fallu un tapis rouge, une haie d'honneur, un orgue tonitruant, des lustres, comme pour des noces. J'eus beaucoup de peine à remettre les pieds dans un aéroplane, même quadrimoteur. Peut-être étions-nous des fiancés, mais la belle de qui nous tenions la main était la mort.

Loin à l'intérieur de l'Angleterre, nous n'avions rien à redouter des chasseurs ennemis, nous décollions tous feux allumés. De tous les terrains du voisinage, une multitude de feux qui nous inspiraient de la terreur montaient, tournaient, se croisaient avant de se glisser dans ce que les Anglais et nous appelions le *stream*, le flot, le courant, en vérité un grand fleuve divisé en plusieurs autres, chacun avec un objectif différent, sans compter les faux *streams*, deux ou trois avions qui lâchaient des nuages de papier d'étain pour brouiller les radars ennemis par une illusion de nouveaux raids. Chaque fleuve de ferraille et de feu, divisé en vagues, étagé en altitude, espacé en distance, descendait vers le sud ou le sud-est pour franchir la Manche ou la mer du Nord. A la côte, les feux de

position coupés, nous étions soulagés. Enfin le noir, enfin seuls ! Le danger existait toujours mais on ne le voyait plus, puis on s'accoutumait à l'ombre, on apercevait de nouveau les silhouettes des voisins et l'effroi revenait. Il arrivait parfois qu'un inconscient eût tout à coup l'idée de passer sur une autre rive du fleuve. Ainsi coupait-il la route aux autres. « Avion à neuf heures, avion à deux heures... » A bord fusaient les avertissements plus nombreux et plus nerveux, presque hystériques depuis notre accident. Il fallut y mettre bon ordre. J'y parvins avec douceur, ce qui n'est pas dans ma nature.

Cette nuit-là, le compas automatique se dérégla. Il était imprudent dans ces conditions de s'engager au-dessus de l'Allemagne. Je décidai de faire demi-tour. Nous quittâmes le *stream* comme sur la pointe des pieds, je larguai inerte mon chargement de bombes dans la mer et nous rentrâmes, bredouilles et furieux. J'étais sûr que quelqu'un nous accuserait d'avoir eu la frousse. Moins par hasard qu'en vertu d'une règle de la RAF qui exigeait que tout équipage sorti indemne d'un accident fût renvoyé aussitôt en mission, nous repartîmes le même jour, en plein après-midi, attaquer la gare de Vaires.

Nous allâmes presque en ligne droite sur Paris, heureux de voler de jour, car il était facile d'éviter les voisins. De jour cependant, les pertes étaient plus lourdes, la *flak* plus précise et les chasseurs plus hargneux. Les Américains, qui ne bombardaient que de jour et en formations serrées, subissaient malgré leurs escortes des pertes doubles des nôtres.

Nous essuyâmes de forts tirs de canons sur Dieppe. Sous nos yeux, un bombardier atteint chancela et tomba en flammes. Le vol de jour avait un désagrément, on voyait trop de choses qu'il aurait mieux valu ne pas voir. Plutôt qu'à un fleuve, nous ressemblions à un troupeau de bisons courant vers de lointains pâturages, encadrés par des gauchos à la pique levée — notre escorte de chasse, pareille aussi à un essaim de mouches brillantes. Les bisons ne sont pas les plus intelligents des animaux et ne savent pas où ils vont. Ils vont. La pique des gauchos est là pour les garder. Si un bison tombe, les autres ne s'en inquiètent nullement et continuent de courir. Quand l'un de nous tombait, quelqu'un, à bord des avions, disait : « Navigateur, notez l'heure... » Le reste du troupeau continuait. Celui qui parlait ne révélait pas ce qu'il avait vu pour ne pas démolir le moral des autres. Gallois, qui avait l'humour

249

macabre, disait qu'en perdant confiance, on avait enfin conscience que notre fin était la petite boîte. C'était sa façon de montrer qu'il n'était pas dupe. Les marchands de ferraille profitaient de la guerre, pas nous.

Comme le vent nous poussait plus fort que prévu, nous dûmes ralentir pour respecter l'horaire. Nous fûmes peut-être deux à trois cents à bombarder la gare de Vaires, après Beauvais. La gare était bien dégagée et fut touchée, sans accrocs ni écorchures, par des tirs serrés. Paris, que nous contournâmes sans le survoler, était sous une capuche de brume. Nous n'aperçûmes aucun monument, même pas la colonne de la Bastille près de laquelle était mon cœur. L'alerte avait dû sonner. Mon petit père chéri, descendu à la cave, devait discourir, annoncer ce qui allait se passer et peut-être profiter de l'occasion pour lutiner une fille. Comment se débrouillait-il ? Savait-il que j'étais en Angleterre ? Je pensais aussi à Rita et plus encore à ma belle consolatrice du Val-de-Grâce avec qui je m'étais montré tellement ingrat.

Nous nous posâmes aussi de jour et tout nous parut d'une facilité dérisoire. Le lendemain se déroulèrent les obsèques des camarades dont l'avion avait heurté le nôtre. Je n'eus pas le courage d'y assister. Les copains se montrèrent sensibles et cette épreuve me rapprocha d'eux. Nous étions des funambules, notre vie tenait à un fil. Gallois nous rejoignit avec son équipage, que commandait le capitaine Thiry, un polytechnicien ferme et sobre dans ses jugements. Gallois et lui s'installèrent dans la chambre voisine de mon tonneau. Nous volions à tour de rôle, sur le même avion, le F fox. Nous partagions la même monture qui devait, selon la RAF, nous conduire vers les astres. Gallois voulut tout de suite décorer sa chambre. Il ne savait pas encore comment, mais il avait une idée, me dit-il. D'après lui, nous étions les cuirassiers de Reichshoffen. On périrait tous sans être sûrs d'entrer dans la légende. Notre temps n'en avait plus.

Notre dette à l'égard des nations alliées était réglée rigoureusement : les aviateurs de la RAF devaient accomplir un certain nombre de missions. Les chasseurs, un nombre supérieur au nôtre, les bombardiers légers aussi. Le chiffre

variait selon l'état du recrutement ou les pertes subies. Si les pertes augmentaient, le chiffre des missions augmentait aussi : il fallait compenser. Dans le *Bomber Command,* à l'époque, le chiffre minimum était de trente. Chaque mission de guerre au-delà du sixième méridien et réussie valait deux points ; en deçà, un seulement. Il arrivait qu'un raid fût décommandé en cours de route. Dans ce cas, les avions étaient contraints de larguer leurs bombes inertes dans la mer du Nord où elles dorment encore, et c'était zéro point. Et si, pour une raison ou une autre, un bombardier devait interrompre son vol et rentrer à la base : zéro toujours. Cela me faisait penser au barème du championnat de football : deux points pour un match gagné, un pour un match nul, zéro pour un match perdu. Chacun de nous tenait le compte de ses points qui figurait aussi sur la liste des équipages requis. *It's a long way...* Long chemin avant d'atteindre le casse-pipe. Il était normal de suivre son déroulement de près. Aussitôt, Gallois sut ce qu'il allait peindre sur le panneau au-dessus de son lit : une prairie verdoyante émaillée de fleurs des champs qu'un vieillard chauve serait en train de faucher. A la place de son compagnon, je lui aurais dit que je n'en voulais pas. Thiry se contenta de sourire. Déjà à huit points, nous étions presque des anciens. Par tradition, c'était vers le chiffre vingt qu'on passait *ad patres.*

A la fin de juillet, nos deux *squadrons* participèrent à un raid sur Stuttgart, dont Gallois revint avec des images d'enfer. Il y avait dans toutes les mémoires le chiffre terrifiant d'un raid sur Nuremberg dans la nuit du 29 au 30 mars : quatre-vingt-quatorze bombardiers au tapis. Nous étions alors à Lossie-mouth. Les services de l'information n'avaient pas donné le chiffre des bombardiers qui participaient au raid : cinq cents, mille, peut-être davantage. N'empêche, c'était un rude coup pour la fanfare. A l'époque, absorbés comme nous l'étions par les incidents qui se produisaient à bord de nos antiques Wellington, nous n'avions pas osé réfléchir à cette boucherie de six cent cinquante membres d'équipages chevronnés. D'ailleurs, nous avions appris cela presque par hasard, à la lecture du communiqué routinier des opérations et nos instructeurs s'étaient bien gardés d'en souffler mot. Et les autres, dira-t-on aujourd'hui, les bombardés ? Les autres, on

n'y pensait pas, c'était la guerre. Finalement, ce carnage avait été attribué au fait que le raid avait eu lieu une nuit de pleine lune : on y voyait comme en plein jour. Mais alors un grand nombre de chasseurs allemands auraient dû aussi être abattus, et la RAF n'en signalait qu'un seul, un JU 88. On laissait entendre que certains équipages étaient descendus dans la mort avec un chasseur ou deux, les uns aux autres enlacés comme dans une mythologie sacrée, ce qui avait rendu le décompte difficile. Le récit de Gallois à propos de Nuremberg me laissa rêveur quand tout à coup nous apprîmes que la prochaine sortie avait lieu sur la Ruhr.

D'après ce qui se disait, Nuremberg était de la petite bière à côté de la Ruhr. Dans le langage de la RAF, la Ruhr se désignait sous le terme de *happy Valley*, la Vallée heureuse. Depuis des années, le *Bomber Command* s'acharnait sur elle. Là était concentrée l'industrie lourde de l'armement allemand, là Krupp fabriquait des bombes, des chars, des canons, des obus, des roulements à billes, des moteurs et jusqu'à l'essence synthétique depuis que les principaux centres d'extraction de pétrole de l'Axe avaient été détruits. Depuis des années, les bombardiers britanniques vidaient leurs soutes sur Essen, sur Dortmund, sur Duisburg, sur Vanne-Eickel, sur Homberg, sur Gelsenkirchen ou sur Bochum. Ils y avaient crevé des barrages, et, au cours d'un seul raid sur Dortmund, lancé un poids de bombes supérieur à celui des Allemands sur Coventry en 1940. La vallée de la Ruhr n'était plus qu'usines en ruine, rails tordus, cheminées aplaties, et cependant elle renaissait chaque fois de ses cendres. Le surlendemain d'un raid, les usines tournaient de nouveau. Des centaines de milliers de forçats, qu'on abritait pendant les raids, se remettaient à l'ouvrage. Le chiffre du tonnage des bombes larguées sur la Ruhr était astronomique. Les pauvres vieux Wellington qui s'escrimaient à nous transbahuter de nuit au-dessus des îles d'Irlande aux îles Hébrides ou aux Orcades avaient commencé dès 1940, en réplique au *blitz* de Londres. Ça n'avait pas arrêté depuis, comme dans un combat de poids lourds, ça n'arrêtait pas de cogner, la *flak* n'arrêtait pas de tirer, les chasseurs de nuit étaient toujours à l'affût, on disait qu'il y avait un canon et un projecteur par mètre carré. Bref la vallée heureuse était un immense nid à mitraille et un immense cimetière pour le *Bomber Command*. Cette fois-ci, ce n'était plus un divertisse-

ment comme au-dessus des gares françaises ou des plates-formes de bombes volantes. Nous nous attaquions au sanctuaire, comme je l'avais espéré dans mes poèmes. C'était le casse-pipe tel que nous l'avions désiré, les vrais problèmes commençaient. Les bruits qui couraient sur la disparition de Hitler, l'avance des divisions russes sur le front de l'Est, les accrocs que subissait l'offensive de l'Ouest, le gouvernement provisoire d'Alger, les querelles Giraud-de Gaulle, tout s'effaçait devant ce qui nous attendait. La bombe la plus grosse des Anglais pesait près de quatre tonnes. Nous l'emmenions, mais nous lancions d'abord des incendiaires.

Ce qu'on craint trop finit par tuer la crainte. C'est ce qui se passa. Nous nous fabriquions un monde de cette sortie sur la Ruhr, elle eut lieu presque naturellement. Nous passâmes sans trop de casse entre les haies des projecteurs et à travers les flocons de la *flak,* nous n'eûmes pas à nous défendre des chasseurs de nuit. Sûrs de nous, le cœur léger, nous rentrâmes. Ma seule terreur restait la collision en vol dans le flot du raid : des dizaines et parfois des centaines d'avions lourds, qu'il fallait conduire en bon ordre, dans les ténèbres, en vagues séparées parfois seulement par deux minutes. Ce gros fleuve qu'au sol on entendait de loin gronder ne suivait pas un cours rectiligne. Pour laisser l'ennemi incertain de sa destination, on lui imposait une route en zigzags, et donc de nombreux changements de direction. C'était là, d'habitude, dans les virages, que cela se produisait. Il suffisait qu'un imbécile abatte trop tôt pour nous couper la route. Je me tenais d'ordinaire à mon poste de bombardier, dans le logement profilé et transparent de plexiglas, à l'extrême avant, d'où, comme d'une proue, je dominais une demi-sphère de nuit, une partie d'espace plus dangereuse que les canons. Les mitrailleurs surveillaient le reste. Quand, au moment des changements de cap, surgissant d'une rive du fleuve, un inconscient nous croisait, j'avais parfois le temps d'avertir le pilote. Parfois non. Parfois encore, au sextant, je visais une de ces étoiles si douces à voir qui nous guidaient, Véga, Altaïr, Arcturus. Il arrivait encore qu'une boule de feu éclatât soudain à notre hauteur et je demandais au navigateur de noter l'heure. Si peu élevé qu'il fût, le chiffre des collisions ne figurait dans les comptes de la RAF que parmi les *missing,* les manquants, ces inconnus, ces pudiques dont on ne savait rien. Notre route

pour attaquer l'Allemagne passait sur les Pays-Bas ou sur la France. Le bruit d'orage de notre multitude était le chant de la liberté tel que je l'avais entendu en esprit, à Sétif, quand j'écrivais mes poèmes. J'y étais. Malgré la crainte d'avant le décollage et la pitié que je ne pouvais pas ne pas éprouver au secret de moi-même pour ceux que nous devions massacrer, un bonheur barbare m'habitait, qui me possède encore. Je n'ai pas acquis la sécurité qui peut mettre les vieux écrivains à l'abri de tout, j'ai au moins l'obscure et maigre satisfaction d'avoir agi comme je voulais et en accord avec ce que je pensais. J'ai encore, dans un plumier sur mon bureau, un bout de fonte hachuré, déchiré d'un côté et lisse de l'autre, de la longueur d'une grosse sauterelle noire, qui s'était déposé presque dans ma main, un jour que notre avion était criblé d'obus et transpercé. Cela me rappelle cette période de ma vie. Cela rappelle aussi que j'ai été épargné. Je le garde pour moi, ce bonheur-là, j'en glisse quelquefois un écho dans les grandes oreilles d'Ulysse, mon frère l'âne, gardien des morts de Vézelay.

Le plus mauvais moment était l'attente. Déjà, la convocation que les haut-parleurs tonitruaient à travers tout le camp nous serrait la gorge. On rangeait ses affaires, on achevait une lettre, on enfourchait son vélo. Toute communication téléphonique avec l'extérieur était coupée. Au lunch, Gronier le pilote avait bon appétit. Ravotti le navigateur et moi mangions nos œufs au bacon du bout des dents. Nous revêtions nos vêtements chauffants, nos bottes fourrées, le gilet de sauvetage nous prêtait la plantureuse gorge de Mae West, et nous allions à la salle de réunion où chacun de nous vidait ses poches dans deux sacoches à notre nom : la blanche pour la famille, la rouge qui serait brûlée. Nous fourrions dans les glissières de notre combinaison les boîtes de survie avec des cartes et de l'argent, et l'officier de renseignements nous éclairait sur la météo et les défenses. Quelqu'un parfois se laissait aller à exprimer bonheur ou stupeur, ce qui provoquait un instant d'hilarité. Puis nous empoignions notre sac parachute et des véhicules nous conduisaient aux avions. Gronier vérifiait sa mécanique et moi le chargement de bombes. D'ordinaire,

l'attente ne durait qu'une heure avant la mise en route des moteurs ; parfois davantage. Parfois les mécaniciens nous offraient une tasse de thé dans leur baraque, et chacun de nous s'isolait avec ses pensées. L'été et l'automne avaient passé, l'hiver approchait. Sur une des rares photos que j'ai de moi à cette époque, l'opérateur nous a saisis, le navigateur Ravotti et moi, assis dans l'herbe à quelques pas du Halifax, à l'ombre d'une aile immense. En battle-dress, sans combinaison de vol et avec la seule mae-west sur la poitrine, le navigateur partait sans l'équipement qui nous alourdissait : sa loge était bien chauffée, et surtout il avait besoin d'aise pour jouer de son attirail : règle à calcul, cartes de Mercator, gommes et crayons. En tenue de ville ou presque, c'était l' « intellectuel » de l'équipage, le mathématicien qui tenait nos existences dans ses mains : deux minutes d'avance ou de retard, une erreur dans le cap, et c'était la catastrophe. Tout avait été vérifié en salle avec les vents sur l'Europe, il n'y avait pas de gaffe possible. Parfois, à la dernière minute, un officier de la navigation venait apporter de nouvelles données météorologiques et Ravotti rajustait ses chiffres en maugréant. Le jour de la photo, coiffé d'un large béret qui déguise sa calvitie naissante, il lit une lettre qu'il va déchirer avant de gagner son poste. Couché sur un coude, presque affalé, des lunettes noires sur les yeux pour m'accoutumer déjà à la vision de nuit, j'ai l'air sombre, dégoûté de la vie. Où est le flambard qui décollait pleins tubes avec son bolide des pistes empoussiérées de Marrakech et dévorait à belle gueule des tranches de quoi ? D'espérance ? de bonheur ? de vie ? Seigneur, à la binette que je fais, à la façon dont je parais me détourner de tout, je dois sombrer dans une réflexion. A propos de quoi ? Déjà, il est peu conseillé de penser quand on est militaire. Encore moins ici. Je suis où je voulais être. C'est le crépuscule et la devise de notre *squadron 346* est : *Surgite nox adhest.* Debout, voici la nuit. Que l'heure sonne et je me lèverai. N'empêche, la guerre m'a transformé en une apparence d'homme. Sur ma carte d'identité de la RAF qu'on me volera plus tard avec mon portefeuille à des courses de taureaux, la photo que j'ai sous les yeux est celle d'un homme qui n'est déjà plus d'ici-bas, d'un illuminé peut-être, d'un transfiguré de l'au-delà. Cette photo-là m'a toujours un peu effrayé. Je ne vivais plus que de l'esprit, j'étais prêt au voyage, j'avais déjà le gros orteil sur le marchepied.

L'heure venait enfin, nous grimpions dans le ventre du mastodonte, le navigateur et le radio s'asseyaient sur une banquette au milieu du fuselage, je me plantais debout à côté du pilote, en cas de panne au départ, le mécanicien Kopp derrière moi, les mitrailleurs se carraient dans leurs tourelles. Les avions qui devaient décoller avant nous mettaient leurs moteurs en route l'un après l'autre, le bruit gagnait les lisières de la base comme un feu et, de base en base, la ville d'York, puis tout le Yorkshire et toute l'Angleterre pour devenir un grondement incertain, une sourde vibration qui, de la terre, des forêts, des étangs, des pâtures, atteignait le ciel où elle s'étalait jusqu'à l'emplir tout entier, le posséder, l'étreindre, le faire trembler et presque chanceler comme s'il était devenu le centre d'un orage immense et monstrueux. A ce moment-là parfois, au mess et dans les maisons, les verres tintaient. A notre tour nous entrions dans le sabbat. Gronier commençait par le moteur extérieur gauche qui libérait comme une chute d'eau, puis l'intérieur, qui commandait le sifflement des gyroscopes, puis le second intérieur et le dernier extérieur. Alors tout le fuselage ronflait comme une basse d'orgue qui ne me rappelait pas Saint-Maclou ni Olivier Messiaen. Dans cette énorme machine alourdie de tonnes de tolite et d'incendiaires, de milliers de gallons d'essence et de quelques bouteilles de thé fade, tout se mettait à souffler et à chanter. Quand le pilote lâchait les freins, le Handley Page Halifax s'ébranlait dans les nids-de-poule de la chaussée et gémissait à cris aigus de tous ses freins et de sa membrure. *Surgite nox adhest.* La nuit venait, sournoise, insinuante, enveloppante. Silencieux, tendus, déjà secoués, serrés juste à distance les uns des autres, nous allumions les feux de position. Déjà les premiers avions décollaient et disparaissaient. Une fois, j'en ai vu un s'écraser au décollage. Il avait eu la bonne idée de sortir de la piste, rien ne nous arrêta. Nous étions bien des bisons dans leur course, quand ils croient aux pâturages de l'autre côté des collines, nous ne pensions plus à rien, sinon que c'était une guerre que nous n'avions pas prévue si atroce, et qu'il n'y avait pas à barguigner.

Au feu vert braqué sur nous, Gronier poussait lentement, en jouant un peu avec elles, les quatre manettes des gaz en avant, les étoiles de la piste filaient de plus en plus vite et le Halifax s'arrachait tout seul, comme une fleur de mort, sans

que le pilote ait vraiment besoin de tirer sur le manche, juste comme un cavalier sollicite un cheval pour lui indiquer de sauter. Une joie futile s'emparait de nous comme si le plus dur était fait. Déduction enfantine, mais tellement puissante, soudain on était presque heureux. Le pilote réduisait les gaz ; l'avion s'arrêtait de trembler, chacun de nous gagnait sa place, le mécanicien repliait mon siège, je dépassais Ravotti déjà assis entre ses rideaux noirs et je m'accroupissais dans ma loge vitrée, à genoux, comme en prières, comme suppliant la puissance tutélaire de nous guider. De ce poste-là, je découvrais tout le quart de sphère de la route avant. Il surgissait des avions de partout, du nord, du sud, de l'est, deux ou trois raids, parfois davantage, les uns par la mer du Nord, les autres par la Manche. La puissante voix de nos quatre moteurs Hercule se mêlait à toutes les autres, et c'était le grondement de toutes les nuits, l'immense trépidation d'un millier de bombardiers lourds sans compter les Mosquitoes, en réplique à tout ce que les Allemands avaient perpétré, et en route vers eux et vers les flammes.

Dans notre ferraille *utility* rien n'était prévu pour l'aise, pas une aspérité de métal n'y avait été réduite, limée ou seulement protégée. Nous nous heurtions à tout dès que nous bougions. Dans le monstrueux ensemble, les individus disparaissaient, leur vie minuscule ne comptait pas, les pensées autres que celles du vol n'existaient plus. Le seul frémissement de l'esprit révélait un attachement disproportionné à la sombre étendue au-dessous de nous, seule mère à qui nous étions attachés, plus même qu'à la nôtre. J'avais de la peine à quitter cette planète, qui peu à peu s'engloutissait sous nos yeux comme un navire naufragé. Si viscérale aussi était notre peur de nous égarer que nous étions soulagés quand nous distinguions des silhouettes à nos côtés ou seulement quand nous sautions dans des remous. Dans un système où le nombre était la force, nous tremblions à l'idée d'être seuls. Au bout d'une longue navigation, nous approchions enfin, après un dernier virage, de l'instant fatal. D'abord éclataient au sol les bombes de couleur, les « marqueurs » plantés comme des banderilles par les éclaireurs sur la bête que nous devions abattre, et tout de suite après pleuvaient les bombes des premières vagues. L'objectif ressemblait d'abord à une île d'or étoilée de rouge et de vert, puis devenait un lac immense incandescent d'où

coulaient des ruisseaux puis des rivières de feu. Je commandais l'ouverture des trappes, et il n'y avait plus qu'à aller droit dessus, viser, puis appuyer sur le bouton qui libérait la charge : une troupe de dauphins plongeant dans une mer glauque. Le ciel s'éclairait d'une lumière grise, boursouflée, sinistre, et soudain apparaissait notre troupeau de bisons, haletants à travers les explosions de *flak,* serrés au-dessus de la fournaise et dans la grêle des bombes, empoignés parfois par une voix claquante qui tonnait dans nos écouteurs. A présent que toute ruse et tout silence radio devenaient inutiles, le maître de cérémonie excitait, dirigeait, parfois félicitait ses *boys :* « *Some more on the left, boys.* » Aujourd'hui, il nous aurait appelés « mecs » : « Bravo, mecs. » Ou encore : Visez les rouges, mecs... » Arrivé avant nous, tournant autour de nous, passant dans l'averse de nos bombes, descendant examiner les dégâts, remontant, le maître des éclaireurs, en vérité maître de l'enfer, repartait après nous, et, grâce à sa vitesse, se posait encore avant nous. Il se riait des chasseurs. Nous, pour leur échapper, nous devions exécuter un tire-bouchon dans les ténèbres, un *corkscrew* : piqué brutal à droite suivi de piqué brutal à gauche en virant. A la côte seulement, on respirait, on se passait un gobelet de thé. Notre gâterie, c'était la caféine, le maxiton et revoir les feux de la base et les nôtres qui ne nous faisaient plus peur. Si quelque pensée saugrenue me venait, je me disais qu'il y avait en face de nous de vrais barbares qu'il fallait exterminer jusqu'au dernier. Je ne pensais plus à l'élégant capitaine Sturtmeyer tombé un soir à Sétif parmi nous. Il avait dû rejoindre le corps des chevaliers teutoniques. Y avait-il encore quelque part des chevaliers, teutoniques ou autres ?

La disparition de Saint-Exupéry fut annoncée et j'en éprouvai une peine immense. Hillary aussi avait été attiré par le gouffre. Tous les deux, comme nous, ils avaient choisi. Au point où il en était de sa gloire et de ses idées sur le prix dont tout se payait, Saint-Exupéry avait atteint le plus haut. Pour moi, rien ne pouvait mieux le placer dans le cœur des hommes.

Dans sa piaule, Gallois peignait toujours : il fignolait les fleurs de sa prairie que fauchait le vieillard. Quand une mission était annulée et que je revenais contrarié de ces nouveaux points qui nous échappaient, Gallois s'écriait : « Un jour de plus pour toi, imbécile. Qui sait ? Demain, la paix sera

peut-être signée. N'oublie pas cependant. Si tu as le feu à une aile, il te reste une minute pour sauter... » On était encore des forbans, mais lugubres.

A présent que nous partagions le même avion, nous ne partions plus pour Londres ensemble, Gallois et moi, la mécanique devait tourner sans cesse, elle était fabriquée pour cela. Je n'allais plus à *la France libre* qu'en passant. Labarthe était à Alger et Aron s'entendait de plus en plus mal avec Staro. Par une journée ensoleillée, une amie m'invita à déjeuner au restaurant avec Charles Morgan, célèbre auteur de *Fontaine*. Elle avait traduit de lui une autre *Ode à la France* que Charlot avait publiée. Il rentrait de Paris où le général Eisenhower l'avait expédié avec une jeep et un chauffeur américain. A peine à la cinquantaine, il avait un beau visage aux joues profondément labourées et un regard clair. D'une élégance un peu passée et comme d'un autre siècle, il remportait tous les succès auprès des femmes grâce à une courtoisie surannée. Avec humour, il avouait qu'il n'avait jamais su se refuser. De Paris il revenait extasié, il avait vu Valéry, la marquise de Vogüé avait organisé une réception pour lui, il parlait des invités qui s'écartaient devant lui comme les vagues de la mer Rouge devant Moïse. A un déjeuner chez René Lalou, il avait apporté un saucisson, une motte de beurre et du café. Lalou avait débouché une bouteille de chambertin qu'il gardait pour le premier Anglais qui reviendrait, et c'était lui. « On ne peut pas rester deux heures là-bas sans pleurer », dit-il. A des enfants rencontrés dans le parc de Saint-Cloud il avait déclamé Baudelaire :

> *A la très chère, à la très belle*
> *Qui remplit mon cœur de clarté,*
> *A France, à l'idole immortelle,*
> *Salut en l'immortalité !*

Au Bourget, au moment de repartir, il avait distribué des paroles historiques, une savonnette et le café qui lui restaient. Tout à sa joie, il ajouta qu'il espérait devenir correspondant de l'Académie. Je lui dis qu'il était un classique, qu'on l'adorait, qu'on le lisait partout. Je ne lui demandai pas s'il connaissait Doyon. Doyon et lui n'étaient pas du même monde. Je préférais le pauvre et cher Doyon, mon père chéri.

Je rencontrai aussi Bertrand d'Astorg qui venait relever à la radio la fameuse équipe « Les Français parlent aux Français ». Il m'entraîna dans les studios de la BBC et me rassura sur l'accueil que nous recevrions en France. Et comme j'ajoutais : « Même ceux qui ont servi Pétain ? », il me répondit en riant et en me montrant Claudel, notre grand poète, qui se faufilait lourdement dans un couloir et disparaissait, vieux lion un peu tassé aux rugissements vaguement sournois.

Nous n'avions pas bousillé toutes les plates-formes volantes, il tombait toujours des V2 sur Londres et sa banlieue, au hasard. Des troupes de ballons leur barraient le passage, des chasseurs en tiraient, il en passait quand même et il valait mieux être ailleurs quand leur moteur s'arrêtait et qu'ils piquaient du nez. Les autres, les fusées V1, pleuvaient sans prévenir, *mektoub,* et, au crépuscule, le grondement de tous les jours se levait. Je pensais aux camarades qui décollaient et cherchaient leur place dans le troupeau, j'imaginais Gallois dans sa loge du F fox, affinant ses crayons et sa navigation et veillant à éviter les nids de canons. Pour Brohon, sa connaissance de l'anglais lui facilitait la vie, il revenait au camp souriant, alerte, pilotant son avenir comme son Halifax, avec un art consommé. Sur la base, personne ne savait où il nichait. Je ne le croisais qu'au mess, il nous dominait de son humour glacé. C'était un chef. Il commandait à présent une escadrille et accomplissait tout ce qui était possible. Parfois même, il flirtait avec l'impossible.

Un jour, un pilote qui avait accompli sept missions craqua et eut le courage de dire qu'il ne se sentait plus la force de repartir. On le suspendit de vol et on eut la sagesse de ne pas le traduire devant un tribunal militaire. Il ne refusait pas de voler, il ne pouvait plus. Quand on sut qu'il ne reviendrait pas sur sa décision, on l'envoya au repos dans un autre camp et nous ne le vîmes plus. Il était trop sensible. Il aimait trop sa femme, il ne dormait plus. Le condamner ne serait venu à l'esprit d'aucun d'entre nous. D'autres cas avaient déjà dû se produire dans la RAF. Parmi nous ce fut le seul. Sur lui j'ai écrit une émission dramatique à la télévision, *Lieutenant Karl,* et un petit livre qui porte presque le même titre. Quelques années après la guerre, il est mort. De cela, je pense. Pour passer à travers les épées de flammes de la Ruhr, il fallait une

rude santé, et si on me reproche d'employer trop souvent le mot d'enfer, qu'on m'en trouve un autre. Pour moi, c'est le bon. Un enfer propre où l'on grillait selon les règles de l'art, dans une fournaise d'essence en flammes, une belle mort finalement, rien de commun avec ce qui se passait dans les camps d'extermination dont nous connaissions à peine et comme honteusement l'existence, sans tellement y croire. Petit enfer que le nôtre, rôtisserie de reine Pédauque, à côté de ce qui se préparait ici et là, qu'on devinait. Tout juste si, chez nous, on ne se sentait pas bien. On avait plus chaud au-dessus de Kiel ou de Hambourg que dans les camps de cette putain d'Ecosse. Nous étions dans le piège, il n'y a de quoi en tirer gloire ni pour ce temps-là ni à présent.

La guerre durait plus que nous ne l'aurions pensé. Le *Bomber Command* subissait des pertes. De trente sorties lointaines pour être libéré, le tour d'opération passa à trente-trois. Il y eut chez nous comme un instant de découragement. Pourtant la victoire avait fini par couronner le débarquement. Paris était libéré, les Américains défilaient à Reims, ces dames du Sphinx avaient dû les recevoir aussi. Comme par routine, nous bombardions Hambourg, Kiel. Entre deux missions, j'allais à la pêche. On prenait de la bouteille, on devenait de vieux briscards, on savait se faufiler entre les salves. Si l'on me demandait ce qui m'a le plus marqué là-bas, ce temps si long, je dirais peut-être : de ne pas savoir si je serais en vie le lendemain. Et cependant je ne croyais pas que je pouvais mourir, ce qui m'aidait à repartir. Nous bombardions aussi des sortes d'usines construites sur les îles lointaines de la baie d'Héligoland, au diable. On nous disait que se fabriquaient là les armes secrètes dont Hitler menaçait de se servir. Il ne s'en servait pas parce qu'elles n'étaient pas prêtes. C'était à nous d'empêcher qu'elles le soient jamais. Cela nous contraignit à une interminable navigation dans la mer du Nord, loin des Pays-Bas et au-dessus de l'archipel de la Frise où les îles sont plates, gris-bleu et à demi recouvertes de brume. Même en guerre, est-ce que ces couleurs valaient le déplacement ? Heureusement, à ce moment-là, la chasse allemande était ailleurs, nous n'avions à craindre que la terrible *flak*. Ces fameuses installations, nous les détruisîmes en partie, grâce à la ruse des prévisionnistes de la RAF, sûrs que Goering ne

pouvait plus utiliser sa chasse contre nous. Sinon, quel massacre !

Dans des notes par miracle conservées, j'ai retrouvé, de l'amie harmoniste de mon ancienne chorale, une lettre dans laquelle elle m'annonçait qu'à Alger, Gide avait été fortement inquiété. Les communistes se souvenaient de ses *Retouches au Retour d'URSS* et la revue *Fontaine* avait relevé une phrase des fragments du *Journal* de septembre 1940 : « Composer avec l'ennemi d'hier, ce n'est pas lâcheté, c'est sagesse et accepter l'inévitable. » Un délégué de la Résistance avait demandé à l'Assemblée consultative que Gide fût « mis hors d'état de nuire », au point qu'il avait fallu l'emmener au Maroc dans un coin perdu. Quel dommage que je ne l'aie pas su quand j'avais croisé Claudel !

Ces nouvelles qu'il m'arrivait de lire au retour de la Ruhr, sous la faux d'Alcide, m'inquiétaient. Et quand on saurait que j'avais écrit *la France sauvée par Pétain* ! Les tristesses de ce temps-là m'éprouvaient encore, il ne s'agissait pas de faire le malin et de dire qu'on était un soldat de la nation qui allait où on lui disait d'aller, l'art suprême était de fermer son bec et là j'avais besoin de retourner à l'école. Gallois rentrait d'une virée à Paris et me parlait de la foire d'empoigne à laquelle se livraient nos anciens généraux d'Alger et jusqu'au nôtre qui s'était hâté de quitter Londres pour les lambris des nouveaux ministères. La politique, quand on descendait de nos chevaux de feu… J'avais fini par me convaincre que le meilleur pour moi serait de me consacrer à la littérature et à la poésie, si j'en réchappais, car la guerre durait. On avait ramené Gide du Maroc, nous passâmes l'hiver au-dessus de Cologne, de Coblence, de Stuttgart, mais surtout dans la Ruhr, au-dessus de la Vallée heureuse qui était devenue notre calorifère, et quand nous y tombions, notre usine d'incinération. Dans la nuit du 13 au 14 février, nous fîmes un voyage sur Leipzig. Ce fut le plus terrible raid de terreur auquel nous participâmes. Etait-ce pour appuyer l'offensive russe, comme on nous le disait et comme on le disait à ceux qui allaient écraser Chemnitz ? Presque neuf heures de vol par une nuit sans lune. On ne sentait pas sa fatigue en rentrant, les poumons brûlés par l'oxygène, l'esprit électrisé par les dragées de caféine. Nous devenions, l'âme tranquille, les déménageurs de la mort, les massacreurs industriels, l'élite de la destruction. Nous ne

pensions plus aux carnages perpétrés, mais aux difficultés de notre route. Déjà, au-dessus de chez nous, les nuages dans lesquels nous ramions étaient si épais que les collisions s'y multipliaient : une lueur vive dans la purée, deux avions s'écrabouillaient et tombaient en flammes. Comme on nous maintenait à cinq mille pieds pour le survol de l'Angleterre, je pris un coup de colère et commandai au pilote de grimper à dix mille. Ce fut la seconde fois où je désobéis aux ordres. Le navigateur poussa des cris d'indignation, je le laissai s'époumoner, nous débouchâmes sur le ciel libre, ce fut la seule fois où je me sentis heureux d'être seul. A tort sûrement. Les radars anglais auraient pu nous localiser comme un intrus et nous abattre. Nous eûmes de la chance. A la côte, tout était rentré dans l'ordre : les bisons nous avaient rejoints, les nuages aussi, il n'y avait plus qu'à se fier à son faible destin. Imaginons le souci qu'en route pour Leipzig, dans une ferraille *utility* non pressurisée, je pouvais éprouver pour les malheurs de Gide qui, lorsque je l'avais rencontré à Tunis, m'avait reproché de ne pas savoir me laver les mains... Que pouvait bien me faire l'auteur de *Paludes,* sinon, à présent, l'idée qui me vient que j'ai raté toutes mes rencontres : Malraux jeune, puis Gide, puis Claudel à Londres, puis bientôt encore Malraux. En revanche, je n'avais pas raté Doyon, j'étais tombé droit dessus et lui sur moi, « Encore un ingrat », devait-il se dire en pensant à moi.

En route pour Leipzig ou au retour à vingt et un mille pieds, c'est-à-dire, quand on divise par trois, sept mille mètres, déjà une belle altitude qu'on ne peut supporter sans respirer de l'oxygène et où, quand on a subi une éventration chirurgicale, tout se trimballe comme ça peut. Je n'y songeais même pas, sanglé comme nous l'étions par le harnais du parachute. A quoi songeait-on en vérité, pendant des heures et des heures, sinon à notre vie qui pouvait être tranchée brutalement, et qu'espérait-on ? Le moment de méprisable soulagement où le bombardier, moi, en l'occurrence, annoncerait : « Bombes parties », parce que je les aurais vues nous lâcher, filer et se perdre, eh bien oui, vers des blocs de maisons à boutiques et à appartements, comme les bombardiers allemands sur Coventry, comté de Warwick, deux cent cinquante mille habitants, rasé en 1940, et sur Londres pendant le *blitz.* « Dieu merci, disais-je en moi-même. Ces salopes nous ont quittés. » Je

263

donnais ce qu'on appelait dans notre jargon un « coup de *jettison* » qui décrochait électriquement toute cochonnerie bourrée d'explosif ou de phosphore, Gronier secouait l'avion, histoire d'une sécurité suprême, et hop, la fuite ! Vers quoi, en vérité, piquaient-elles, ces petites chéries balancées au-dessus de Leipzig, six cent mille habitants ?

Je me souviens de l'indignation qui s'empara, deux ans plus tard, du haut commandement de l'armée de l'air et parfois même de mes meilleurs camarades, quand ils lurent dans *le Monde*, à Paris, mon livre *la Vallée heureuse* que le journal publiait en feuilleton comme un polar : on apprenait que nous avions été des massacreurs ! Et qu'étions-nous d'autre, à l'époque, par nécessité ? Les nazis avaient assez massacré, il fallait leur rendre la pareille, c'était bien ce à quoi s'était résolu l'état-major du *Bomber Command* après mûre réflexion. Dans mon livre, je ne me scandalisais pas de me ranger parmi les massacreurs, je constatais. Eh bien non. On acceptait que les nazis eussent été des salopiauds, mais pas nous. Il y allait de l'honneur de l'armée française, de la vieille chevalerie à sauver, et de cette fiction diplomatique et de cette fable que la France, mère des libertés, ne s'attaquait qu'aux armées ennemies. Peut-être, peut-être. Mais nous étions avec la RAF, sous les ordres du maréchal de l'air Harris que les Anglais appelaient le boucher, qui avait certainement obtenu l'accord de Sir Winston Churchill, chef du gouvernement. Tous ces messieurs avaient décidé de répliquer aux raids de terreur par des raids de terreur, et je ne vois pas comment nous, simples exécutants, aurions pu émettre des réserves sans être jugés pour trahison et exécutés. A chaque fois que la croix du viseur passait sur l'objectif, je criais « Bombes parties » sans dissimuler ma joie et, dans notre équipage comme chez les autres, ce mot provoquait l'allégresse. Naturellement, à ce moment-là, je ne pensais ni à mon enfance, ni à mon éducation au séminaire, ni à M. Baligand, encore moins aux lazaristes, à Mgr Bollon ou au passage de l'évangile qui me bouleversait toujours : « Heureux les pacifiques, le royaume de Dieu leur appartient. » Peut-être aurait pu me venir un éclair du jour où, à la ferme, on assassinait le cochon ? Quand nous partîmes pour Leipzig, je ne fis même pas l'effort de me souvenir de ce que les journaux de Grande-Bretagne avaient publié d'une récente adresse de Himmler à ses troupes : « Emparez-vous de tous

les tire-au-flanc, attachez-les, chargez-les sur un camion. Je vous ordonne d'arrêter tous ceux qui essaient de fuir. Haïssez tous ceux qui reculent. Quand vous aurez réuni tous les lâches, fusillez sans pitié quiconque osera protester... » Cela aurait pu me rappeler la horde de forcenés du tout jeune officier Ernst Jünger, ces guerriers diaboliques que l'odeur de la bataille enivrait. Ils avaient refusé leur défaite en 1918 et me semblaient plus conformes à l'esprit germanique que l'élégance et la pitié des *Jardins et Routes* de 1940. Pour nous, le moment était venu de nous venger de la débâcle et de la honte, et, pour Jünger démobilisé à Hanovre à la fin de 1944, de subir la dévastation qui tombait du ciel, déluge de mort et d'épouvante.

Si je pensais à quelque chose en appuyant sur le bouton de largage, c'était à nous débarrasser de notre chargement. Peu importe s'il s'abattait sur les habitants de Leipzig terrés au fond de leurs caves. Quand ils sortiraient de leurs trous à rats en nous maudissant, s'ils en sortaient, ils ne verraient que ruines et fumées d'incendies car notre chargement était composé de tolite et de phosphore, et je ne me souviens pas si les lanceurs de phosphore nous précédaient ou nous suivaient. Toujours est-il que massacre et feu étaient admirablement agencés. Mais oui, nous étions massacreurs par nécessité. N'était-ce pas vrai ? Je me demanderai alors si, par hasard, je n'étais pas allé trop loin dans les mots. J'avais bien écrit autrefois des poèmes qui ressemblaient à cela, sans savoir ce qu'était un raid de terreur sur Dresde ou sur Leipzig. Mes poèmes étaient tout autres, j'implorais la pitié de Dieu sur nous et sur ceux que nous écrasions. Je me regarderai alors dans une glace, je découvrirai une face de revenant de l'enfer, encore ce mot ! un peu éberlué, assommé, étourdi, sonné, légèrement halluciné par les kilos de maxiton ingurgités. C'est vrai, à notre tour nous étions des barbares, des criminels de guerre, mais si Hitler avait mis au point la bombe atomique avant les Américains, la Grande-Bretagne eût été détruite et nous avec.

Confessons, avouons, l'heure n'est pas à la pitié. N'employons pas là un pluriel de modestie qui pourrait réveiller de vieilles fureurs chez les uns ou les autres. De Leipzig, que retenais-je ? Un fantastique feu d'artifice, le crépitement des

canons, et, au-dessous, le lac d'or qui devenait presque une mer, pensez donc : une ville de six cent mille habitants, la patrie de Richard Wagner, la première des cités universitaires d'Allemagne, une Bourse de la librairie unique au monde, une académie des beaux-arts, tout cela en flammes, et un imbécile qui nous coupait la route et que Gronier sautait à la lumière du brasier, une explosion formidable qui illuminait le ciel quelques instants. Après quoi, nous cassions tranquillement la croûte, car la RAF, cette bonne mère, nous avait remis avant le départ un assortiment de sandwiches au jambon d'York et au fromage de Hollande, et ça, mon Dieu, même sans la délicatesse de cornichons coupés en tranches, avec un gobelet de thé de la bouteille thermos, eh bien, ça nous remontait. Après quoi encore, Ravotti le navigateur murmurait dans le micro pour que tout l'équipage entende : « Dans une heure, nous franchirons le Rhin entre Cologne et Mayence... » En moi-même, j'ajoutai : « Si Dieu veut, si Dieu veut... »

L'Allemagne était comme une terre morte.

En février 1945, le temps ne passait pas vite. Il nous restait encore sept missions à tirer, sept matches à disputer. L'équipage fourbu commençait à battre de l'aile. La radio annonça la mort de Marin La Meslée, l'as de la chasse qui avait apparu à un de nos feux de camp à Fès, du temps de Murtin. Le descendeur de Messerschmitt avait été descendu par des canons sur lesquels il s'acharnait pour la troisième fois. Je pensai moins à lui qu'à Murtin avec sa jambe de bois. Que devenait-il, maintenant qu'il ne pouvait plus faire le gandin ?

La fin approchait quand les chasseurs allemands usèrent d'une nouvelle tactique. Tandis que nous franchissions la Manche, ils nous suivirent tranquillement, puis au moment où nous rallumions nos feux de position au-dessus de cette vieille Angleterre, au moment où le *stream* ressemblait à un tranquille fleuve d'étoiles, ils se collèrent derrière nous et nous expédièrent tranquillement au tapis, zoum, zoum. Ils étaient si bas qu'un JU 88 s'écrasa sur une route après avoir accroché un arbre. A notre cimetière de Holgate où, derrière l'aumônier à étole violette, nous allions régulièrement accompagner des camarades, et où il y avait toujours une dizaine de tombes

creusées d'avance, on avait manqué de place, il avait fallu appeler des fossoyeurs en renfort.

Pour notre trente-septième mission annoncée comme la dernière, le maître de cérémonie, je n'invente rien, c'était l'humour noir de ces messieurs de la RAF, s'appelait Pluton. Lourde ambiance dans l'équipage : le colonel nous avait félicités et semblait sincère. Nous emportions des bombes de 250 livres que nous n'aimions pas, je ne me souviens plus pourquoi. Parce que parfois il en restait une ou deux obstinément accrochées dans la soute ? Nous décollâmes en fin de journée, nous n'allions pas loin, juste après le sixième méridien pour les deux points du match, juste de l'autre côté de la Moselle. Nous devions anéantir des concentrations ennemies. Nous y arrivâmes par nuit assez claire, où Jupiter et Vénus se partageaient le ciel. A l'heure pile, les marqueurs tombèrent et le protocole se déroula. Il y eut, ce soir-là, une merveilleuse fusée d'or en paillettes papillotant avec lenteur, suivie d'une grappe de marqueurs rouges, puis rouges et verts, puis verts, superbes, brillants, éclatants, et tout à coup Pluton, la voix terrible, l'archange invisible des enfers, nous appela à la curée avec des mots qui me parurent scandaleux, mais comment s'indigner quand on se trouve où on est, et qu'on est soi-même un vautour ? Pluton qui avait dû avaler un peu trop de maxiton ou souffrait peut-être d'une déception amoureuse, s'écriait : *Hello boys, to get ready to slaughter...* Oh ! pas d'une voix méchante. Un peu comme un instituteur à ses élèves : « Allez les enfants, c'est le moment de s'amuser », il disait : « Allez les gars, allez-y pour la boucherie... » Longtemps après, ce mot-là m'a scandalisé. Il m'a paru vulgaire, trop vrai. Cette nuit-là, j'avais une âme de pharisien, j'aurais aimé qu'on n'emploie pas de terme aussi cru. Nous étions là pour quoi ? Pluton appelait sa bande de tueurs, sa bande de gangsters, sa bande de malfrats, sa bande de truands. J'aurais préféré qu'il nous dore un peu la pilule, qu'il dise « Allez les enfants, courage... » Mais là, comme ça, *slaughter*, tuerie, massacre... quel manque de délicatesse, quelle sauvagerie ! Et quelle discourtoisie, n'est-ce pas ? Sur le moment, personne n'aurait songé à résister à cette irrésistible voix. J'ouvris les trappes, je fixai mon parachute au harnais par les mousquetons. Se détachant sur l'or fauve du phosphore qui cramait déjà, des avions plus bas que nous se détachaient comme des

ombres un peu en avant, nos bombes ne risquaient pas de les atteindre, elles passeraient derrière eux. Je n'avais pas non plus à rectifier le cap, nous allions droit sur les verts. Pour rassurer Gronier, je dis : « C'est bon, mon vieux, c'est bon... » et, à l'instant voulu, quand les verts glissèrent au centre de la croix du viseur, une légère pression sur le bouton et tout s'en alla. L'avion frémit à peine comme pour marquer son soulagement. Allégé de cinq tonnes et demie de saloperie, il devenait souple, manœuvrable, capable de tous les *corkscrews*. D'une voix presque joyeuse, Ravotti, le navigateur, ordonna à Gronier d'afficher son nouveau cap. Derrière nous, la fête continuait, Pluton était content, nous nous enfonçâmes dans les ténèbres de toute la vitesse de nos quatre moteurs Hercule. Vénus était à son couchant, quelqu'un bientôt n'allait pas manquer de la confondre avec le feu d'un avion. Cassiopée et Orion chaviraient derrière nous. Après notre passage, beaucoup de télégrammes partis de ce coin-là feraient des veuves, des orphelins et des mères en larmes. Après le virage, j'emplis mes yeux pour jouir du spectacle. C'est vrai que ce n'était pas chaque fois si bien réussi. Un immense bonheur m'habitait. Je ne pouvais pas me douter qu'alors Ernst Jünger, déjà l'objet de mon admiration jalouse et de qui j'allais, à mon grand étonnement, marcher sur les traces à Paris, avait rejoint son presbytère de Kirchhorst, près de Hanovre en cendres, et qu'il nous voyait tout dévaster au point que les pierres de la ville brûlaient toutes seules, sans rien. En quelque sorte, bien qu'il gardât toujours une âme impavide devant l'adversité et qu'il pensât toujours aux insectes rares et aux serpents, j'étais devenu son ennemi mortel, moi l'aviateur, moi le bombardier ; c'était le temps où, le jour de son anniversaire, fin mars naturellement, il lisait le psaume 73 : *Ils ont brûlé dans le pays tous les lieux saints, ne nous livre pas aux bêtes, lève-toi, défends ta cause, on les a vus pareils à ceux qui lèvent la cognée dans les forêts...*

Cette nuit-là, il y eut quatre manquants chez nous. Ils étaient partis avec nous, nous les avions vus bien vivants, ils avaient disparu, on pouvait tout imaginer, même qu'ils reviendraient. C'était cruel mais propre, avec un vague espoir.

tandis qu'un pilote et un navigateur que j'aimais beaucoup s'écrasaient avec leur équipage dans les collines entre Elvington et Carnaby. Au cimetière de Holgate, l'aumônier chanta le *Libera* sur une trentaine de cercueils. Sa voix, dont le vent emportait la moitié des paroles, était frêle, nue, dépouillée, mais le texte en latin est si beau, les paroles sont si poignantes quand on les comprend. Le latin laissait planer un certain mystère, mais la mort n'est-elle pas un mystère ? Quand j'assiste à présent à des obsèques religieuses, quand j'entends les pieuses platitudes qui se dévident en français pour que tout le monde comprenne qu'on demande à Dieu d'avoir pitié, j'éprouve de la gêne. L'Eglise catholique emploie désormais une langue qui me laisse dépourvu. Autrefois, on n'entendait peut-être pas tout mais on se réfugiait dans des paroles d'autant plus miséricordieuses qu'elles se disaient dans une langue sacrée, pas une langue où rien ne se cache. Je parle pour moi qui ai fait du latin au séminaire, je me trompe peut-être.

Nous étions délivrés, nous avions mené à bien nos trente-sept sorties : trente et une au-delà du sixième méridien, six en deçà comme cela était noté sur la feuille des ordres. Nous nous sentions heureux d'être saufs, et cependant nous considérions ceux qui n'avaient pas fini avec un certain respect mêlé d'envie. Désormais inutiles, nous avions hâte de nous effacer. Gallois nous avait déjà quittés, appelé à l'état-major où on le considérait comme trop précieux pour lui laisser courir des risques. Quant à Brohon, il en avait fini aussi et il avait gardé son commandement d'escadrille au point qu'il devenait presque invisible, héros établi dans les hauteurs. Pour nous, vivants ou morts, nous valions le même prix. Nous pouvions maintenant nous présenter n'importe où, nous avions la croix de guerre avec — c'était aussi de la comptabilité — une citation toutes les cinq ou six missions, sans rien de spécial pour les difficultés rencontrées. Les morts s'en allaient tous avec le ruban rouge. La DFC, je ne sais plus si les Britiches la conféraient à titre posthume.

Beaucoup plus tard, plus de trente ans après, j'écrivais cette dramatique, *Lieutenant Karl*, pour évoquer l'incident du pilote qui n'avait pas voulu repartir. Ce n'était pas encore le temps des vaches maigres à la télévision, on pouvait encore produire des choses sérieuses en français. La réalisation avait lieu en Angleterre, à Elvington même où une base militaire

existait toujours. Gallois m'y emmena. Nous prîmes un avion pour Londres, puis le train à Charing-Cross. Gallois était furax : « Il ne part toujours pas à l'heure, et quelle saleté ! » C'est vrai, le wagon n'avait pas été nettoyé depuis longtemps. Je ne sais pourquoi, je m'étais affublé d'un lourd macfarlane, qu'en Grande-Bretagne personne ne portait plus. Nous descendîmes dans le Grand Hôtel aux armes des ducs d'York, superbe, presque désert, avec des majordomes en frac, et nous empruntâmes un taxi pour Elvington. La RAF avait là un centre d'entraînement au pilotage sur avions à réaction, mais elle n'avait pas touché à notre ancien camp de baraquements et de tonneaux, peu à peu envahis par les ronces, la végétation, la moisissure et quelque chose à quoi je ne pus, d'abord, donner un nom : une sorte de pieux abandon, pas complet cependant, un certain mystère. Tout avait été pillé, il ne restait pas une vitre aux fenêtres, c'était le royaume des renards qui laissaient là des crottes effilées. Les garnements du lieu s'amusaient comme dans un village d'Indiens. Par endroits, on ne savait plus ce qui appartenait encore à l'administration de Sa Majesté, à la commune ou à des gens. Sans Gallois je m'y serais perdu. La régie avait déniché un vieux Lancaster qui tournait, une chambre dans un tonneau, un bureau de chef d'escadrille, une salle de renseignement et, pour figurants, des soldats de la nouvelle base. Ce qui manquait c'était le nombre. Le réalisateur Michel Wyn prétendit que cela ne le dérangeait pas, car le drame était tout intérieur ; le pilote qui refusait de partir était incarné par Bernard Crommbey, le chef d'escadrille par Jean-Claude Bouillon, si vrais tous les deux que je dus les toucher pour me convaincre que je ne rêvais pas, que ce n'était qu'une reconstitution.

Ma mémoire ne pouvait plus rien situer. J'avais oublié la voie ferrée à traverser pour gagner notre hutte, la tour de contrôle n'était qu'un simple bâtiment à un étage d'où l'on apercevait les tours de la cathédrale d'York, et surtout, à cent mètres de l'endroit où, sur la piste, nous faisions notre point fixe avant de décoller, je découvris une ferme dans l'état où elle devait être de notre temps, à l'abandon, les portes de l'étable battant au vent, avec encore du foin dans les râteliers. Sur le chemin de nos chambres, ce fut plus étonnant : je vis un cottage où une jeune femme qui y vivait nous dit que sa mère, une vieille dame, avait habité là pendant toute la guerre, et

nous n'avions rien remarqué. J'écrivis là-dessus quelques pages que Christian Bourgois publia sous le titre *Pour le lieutenant Karl*. Il n'en vendit pas trois cents exemplaires. Beaucoup plus tard, en Normandie, à Grandchamp-Maisy près de Bayeux, à l'endroit d'une vaste tuerie, j'assistai à l'inauguration d'un monument à la mémoire de nos propres morts. Ni les drapeaux qui claquaient dans le vent, ni la mer qui battait le rivage, encore moins les discours, rien ne me remua jusqu'à ce qu'éclatât soudain, lent, lourd, souverain, le *God save the Queen* que, jadis, l'Angleterre déroulait sur les tombes des camarades. Là, je ne pus retenir un pleur.

Le 22 avril 1945, j'étais à Paris, porte de Charenton. Un Halifax nous conduisit à Lille où Gronier nous laissa, il était chez lui. Nous vendîmes nos vélos anglais à des gamins qui s'étonnaient de nous voir descendre d'un bombardier britannique. « Ils ont fusillé dix-sept FFI avant de s'en aller... »

Je ne me souviens pas de mes derniers jours à Londres, ni comment nous quittâmes la Grande-Bretagne. Londres était toujours en guerre. Les stations de métro étaient bondées d'enfants et de vieillards couchés dans des lits de fortune. A côté d'eux, les rames roulaient en grondant et repartaient : mieux valait la fosse du métro qu'être pulvérisé par les V2 qui pleuvaient toujours. La banlieue sud avait vingt-cinq mille maisons détruites et six mille morts, Churchill avait dit quelques jours avant : « La fin de cette guerre apparaîtra plus comme une délivrance que comme un triomphe. »

De Lille nous gagnâmes Paris en train, par Arras et Le Bourget. Il faisait beau et j'étais amoureux de la plus belle des femmes que, déjà, j'attendais ici. Depuis peu à Londres, elle allait revenir à Paris. Quel jour étions-nous ? Comment étais-je là ? Suis-je arrivé par la gare du Nord ou par la porte de Charenton ? Paris était pavoisé. Dans les rues il y avait de la musique militaire, des Parisiennes incroyables, habillées comme des mameluks, avec des chapeaux hauts d'un pied (je m'exprimais comme un Britannique) et des cheveux qui soutenaient le chapeau. De temps en temps l'une d'elles, resplendissante, laissait derrière elle un sillage de folie.

Il faisait toujours beau en France, les marronniers étaient

en fleur, je me précipitai chez mon petit père, impasse Guéménée, où l'odeur de la pisse de chat suffoquait sur le palier, pire qu'autrefois. Je tirai la sonnette qui déclencha les aboiements d'Askari. Mon petit père poussa quelques exclamations, s'étonna à peine de me voir et nous échangeâmes le baiser rituel, le baiser de paix entre curés. « Ah! mon filsque », dit-il. Il portait sa vieille robe de chambre élimée, un peu déchirée, sale, de quelle couleur? la bibliothèque ne débordait plus de livres, le soleil éclaboussait le balcon, son portrait trônait encore sur la cheminée de la salle à manger, il était resté le glorieux mandarin et j'étais sorti vivant de ce micmac. Aussitôt il enchaîna sur ce qui avait dû être notre dernière conversation ou celle d'avec le Malraux d'avant l'aventure au Cambodge, d'avant la guerre d'Espagne. « Tu ne devineras jamais ce qui m'a brouillé avec Brousson... », commença-t-il. Ce devait être avec moi, le raccord, Malraux ne s'intéressait pas à Jean-Jacques Brousson, indigne de lui. « ... Je lui ai prouvé que l'andouille de Bretagne se mangeait sans moutarde. » Les chats me regardaient en lissant leur robe, même le roux à grosse tête qui ressemblait à un poney des îles Shetland.

« On descend, je te montre... » Il disparut un moment, revint habillé, il avait maigri, à peine vieilli. J'étais en battle-dress bleu marine, avec le ruban de la croix de guerre, je portais un calot, il toucha mes pattes d'épaule. « Qu'est-ce que tu es maintenant? » Je venais d'être nommé commandant, je n'avais pas à me plaindre, tandis que Malraux s'était bombardé colonel commandant la brigade Alsace-Lorraine sans se coller des étoiles de général, peut-être parce qu'il n'en avait pas trouvé ou qu'il préférait le grade de Lawrence d'Arabie. Mais moi, c'était au *Journal officiel,* pas comme Malraux. Nous descendîmes les quatre étages, nous franchîmes la porte cochère où le nom, René Louis Doyon, en émail, rayonnait et, Askari en laisse, nous allâmes tout de suite au tabac du coin de la rue des Tournelles et de la rue Saint-Antoine. Une joyeuse rumeur et une muflée de bière et de muscadet nous accueillirent : « Eh bien, c'est mon filsque. C'est à lui que vous devez de n'avoir plus les Fritz avec vous... » Les conversations s'arrêtèrent un instant. « Il arrive d'Angleterre, figurez-vous... » Le patron s'éjecta du comptoir, me serra les mains, on me regarda comme le messie, j'étais gêné. « Qu'est-ce que

vous en dites ?... » Le patron sortit une bouteille de mousseux, et comme je protestais : « Laisse donc, il faut qu'on sache. Ils te doivent bien ça... » Le bouchon sauta, le vin pétilla dans les verres, je trinquai. « Alors, comme ça... », disaient les gens. « Qu'est-ce que vous croyez ? » continuait Doyon.

Après, ce fut le Dupont de la Bastille qui existait en ce temps-là. La caissière et les garçons, la caissière surtout, embrassaient un marin à col blanc et pompon rouge. J'inspirais plus de retenue car je suis loin d'être un rigolo, sauf à certains moments, il y avait en moi un je-ne-sais-quoi de réservé, le souvenir de la pétoche qu'on avait eue de n'être pas reçus, la pensée qu'on nous demanderait des titres à la reconnaissance du pays, comment on s'était conduits et cætera. Gallois craignait même de ne pas être autorisé à poser le pied en France parce qu'il croyait à une révolution, à la mainmise des communistes sur le pouvoir, mais non, pour moi ça se passait tout seul grâce à Doyon peut-être, à mon petit père : « Tu vois, la France n'a pas été sauvée par Pétain comme tu l'as écrit mais par l'autre, le grand escogriffe... » Il n'avait pas oublié la brochure que j'avais commise, ma première œuvre, il l'aurait brandie aux yeux de tous si le sort de la guerre avait été l'inverse. Qui sait ? Il la relisait peut-être à loisir, il n'oubliait rien. Que d'eau avait coulé sous les ponts depuis cinq ans ! Et la cheffesse ? « Ce n'est pas celle que tu as connue. Les femmes, laisse donc ! Toi tu n'auras que l'embarras du choix. Tu n'es pas amoureux au moins ? Tu ne vas pas retourner à Sétif ?... » Ma tête tourbillonnait, il me traîna encore tout à côté, chez Bofinger, pour m'exhiber, puis chez son épicier. « Tu n'as pas besoin de tickets, tout le monde est à tes pieds, tu as de l'argent, je vais te tortiller une omelette au lard... » Il me reprochait de ne rien dire. « Secoue-toi, bon Dieu... » C'est vrai, j'étais ahuri, je lui avais apporté un kilo de café de Londres, j'aurais dû ramener de la marmelade d'oranges, de la farine. J'avais assez de mal à traîner ma cantine et une énorme valise en cuir, presque une malle, achetée aux puces à Londres pour cinq livres, qui avait dû appartenir à un major de l'armée des Indes, et que j'avais bourrée de mes frusques, de livres pour Charlot, de mes manuscrits et du fameux coupon de tweed acheté en Ecosse, bleu roi.

Amrouche m'avait enfin écrit une de ces lettres auxquelles rien ne résiste. Il s'accusait de sa négligence et m'assurait que

sa pensée ne m'avait pas quitté ; il s'était inquiété de moi, il
m'aimait, il en profitait pour me demander de lui rapporter,
avec mes points de textile en trop, un imperméable et du tissu.
Impossible. En Angleterre on ne trafiquait pas avec les cartes
d'habillement. Doyon ne connaissait ni Amrouche ni Charlot.
Les années avaient creusé un abîme. Je n'avais pas sur moi
mon premier livre ni ma plaquette de poèmes. Qu'il me
rappelât *la France sauvée par Pétain* me chagrinait. Pour lui, je
m'en étais bien tiré en servant à la fin sous les couleurs
gaullistes, ou les Angliches. Les choses allaient leur train, il ne
serait plus question que d'argent. « C'est le fric qui compte, tu
en as, j'espère ? » Lui, les Frisés avaient failli l'emballer comme
juif, il s'en était sorti par miracle.

Après l'omelette au lard, je m'aperçus que je m'ennuyais.
Doyon c'était le passé, je devais aller de l'avant, foncer, il
fallait que je rejoigne au plus vite Amrouche. Je dis à mon petit
père que je devais me mettre en quête d'un hôtel. « Viens près
d'ici si tu peux... » J'allai à l'adresse que m'avait indiquée
Amrouche, rue Boissy-d'Anglas. Ils étaient tous là, chez
Henri Noguères qui les avait recueillis : lui, Jean El Mouhouv,
chaleureux, irrésistible, assuré de tout, dirigeant tout, tellement soucieux des autres que leur bonheur dépendait du sien ;
Charlot déjà adapté à Paris, tellement prudent. Un siècle avait
passé, j'avais survécu, Amrouche préparait le retour de Gide,
Charlot avait trouvé rue de Verneuil un local pour les éditions,
et habitait hôtel de la Petite-Chaise, à Sèvres-Babylone. Ils
étaient ma vraie famille, il ne manquait que Guibert. Il arrivait
du Portugal, me dit-on. Ensemble, nous allions conquérir
Paris. Pourquoi pas ? Staro et Martha y étaient déjà, comme
Labarthe, mais avec de l'argent. « Ce sera dur, dit Amrouche,
mais on y arrivera... » Charlot dit que Bosco avait écrit un
roman superbe. « Camus nous aidera », ajouta-t-il. « L'Algérie, dit Amrouche avec un geste lointain. Pour le moment c'est
ici que ça se passe. Avec de Gaulle. »

J'approuvai. A Sétif il y avait un bon lycée et moins de
restrictions qu'ici, ma famille attendrait. Camus dirigeait le
journal *Combat* que tout le monde lisait. *L'Etranger* était le
livre dont on parlait partout.

J'obtins une réquisition pour l'hôtel Montpensier, rue de
Richelieu, près de la Comédie-Française. Il suffisait de traver-

ser le Louvre et la Seine pour être rue de Verneuil. Je m'installai le soir même. C'était un hôtel modeste et vieillot sans ascenseur. Ma chambre donnait sur la cour, il n'y avait d'eau chaude nulle part et de téléphone que dans l'entrée. Comme j'attendais déjà la femme que j'aimais, je me demandai si ce décor serait digne d'elle.

Les journées étaient longues, je sortis. On faisait la queue devant les guichets de la Comédie-Française, des fontaines de la place l'eau ne jaillissait plus. Dans les rues sans voitures, il y avait du monde, beaucoup de filles à bicyclette avec des coiffures comme des tours dorées. J'entrai dans un café, dînai, grâce à un ticket, d'un sandwich au fromage et d'une bière. Les gens semblaient pleins d'un bonheur tranquille ; j'avais « drôlement trinqué » pour être là, avait dit Amrouche. Moins que ceux qui étaient morts, j'avais dû avoir beaucoup de chance. Doyon avait essayé de me faire raconter ce que nous faisions là-bas, je lui avais simplement dit que notre base était près d'York. « Si loin que ça ? Presque au milieu de l'Angleterre ? » Il connaissait sa géographie, il connaissait tout. Je lui avais répondu que c'était pour que nos bases soient hors d'atteinte des chasseurs allemands, il fallait une bonne heure de vol pour gagner la côte sud, mais nous pouvions voler dix heures. Et comme il s'étonnait encore, je lui dis que c'était presque le temps d'aller à Leipzig et d'en revenir, quand on revenait, et il avait paru songeur. Je ne lui avais rien demandé de l'Occupation. Dans ce bistrot du Louvre, je m'aperçus tout à coup que les camarades et moi avions formé une sorte de communauté religieuse, nous nous étions mal compris, parfois détestés, nous nous étions pliés à une discipline sévère, et après les premières pertes, nos rangs s'étaient soudés. Au bout de six mois de casse-pipe, une espèce de fraternité s'était même forgée entre nous, il y avait encore des jalousies mais plus d'inimitiés comme au début. Tous ne s'aimaient pas, mais nous avions l'orgueil de nos manquants dont on ne savait rien, et de tous nos convois funèbres aussi. Notre petite armée de Pétain d'Afrique du Nord s'était bien comportée. L'autre aussi, qui avait reconquis la Tunisie et l'Italie avec les Amerloques ; mais le plus dur avait été les longues heures de vol de guerre et d'attente qui nous amenaient à des réflexions qu'il aurait mieux valu ne pas avoir. Avec un peu de mélancolie, je me dis que ce côté de notre vie était achevé et

que chacun de nous allait mener son existence comme il pourrait. Y avait-il de la religion là-dedans ? Peut-être celle de la patrie. Ç'avait été notre façon à nous de payer le prix de la vie, à la manière dont Saint-Exupéry et Hillary avaient payé leur gloire. On pouvait appeler religion une telle fatalité ou une certaine fraternité, encore qu'on s'entendît parfois si mal entre frères, dans les familles, ou simplement, c'était de l'amitié. Mon amitié pour Brohon, malgré les airs qu'il prenait parfois, mon amitié pour Gallois et pour d'autres atteignait presque la rive de la religion.

Je mâchouillai mon maigre sandwich au fromage et commandai un autre demi. Autour de moi, il y avait comme une atmosphère de vacances et je pensai encore à la femme dont j'étais amoureux. Malgré la curiosité de Doyon, je m'étais bien gardé de lui parler d'elle. J'allai me coucher.

J'eus du mal à m'endormir. Je me tournais et retournais dans mon lit, je revoyais encore l'avion se fracassant sur nous, et mon imagination fit encore surgir le visage de la femme que j'aimais. Comme elle me manquait ! Comme elle avait raison aussi d'hésiter à se lier à un homme si tranchant dans ses jugements, parfois si amer, si... Elle n'était pas prude mais elle avait des principes, elle ne se commettait pas. Elle tenait à rester maîtresse d'elle-même alors que, pour moi, la guerre avait accéléré le mouvement du monde et tout saccagé. Je ne me précipitais pas sur n'importe quel jupon comme beaucoup. La guerre durait encore, mais nous touchions à la fin. L'Axe s'effondrait. Les armes secrètes avaient, en partie grâce à nous, perdu leurs usines et leurs rampes de lancement, l'offensive des Ardennes avait été un échec pour Hitler pendant que nous bombardions Leipzig et Dresde, les avions à réaction Messerschmitt 262 et Heinkel He 162 A2 n'avait plus d'aérodromes, les armées américaines avançaient en Allemagne, les Français vers l'Autriche, les Anglais vers la Baltique, les Russes allaient atteindre Berlin, la fin approchait, je devrais m'ingénier à établir ma famille à Paris dès que les circonstances s'y prêteraient. Comment allais-je me dépatouiller ? La femme que j'aimais, et l'Algérie de l'autre côté du monde. Je fus muté à l'état-major de l'armée de l'air, au bureau Etudes et Plans, que dirigeait un polytechnicien de vaste culture, le colonel Badré, qui se montra heureux de m'avoir sous sa direction.

X

Le pont Mirabeau

Pour que le téléphone sonne chez moi à huit heures du matin, il faut que ce soit une erreur ou une nouvelle d'importance. La phrase que j'écris reste en suspens, je pose la plume : ma fille m'apprend que sa mère est morte dans la nuit. Elle ajoute : « Elle n'a pas souffert... » Formule consacrée quand on trouve les morts dans leur lit. Qu'en savons-nous ? De surcroît, ma fille entend aussi mal que moi. Si sa mère s'est plainte, si elle a appelé... La mort, quand elle frappe à côté de soi, nous en bouche un coin. On a beau parfois s'y attendre, ça vous souffle. Une bombe saute à côté de vous. Ma page s'arrête au moment où, à l'hôtel Montpensier, rue de Richelieu, à Paris, à peine rentré d'Angleterre, je me demande où j'en suis. Me voilà soudain devenu vieil écrivain mémorialiste. Bouleversé.

Mes beaux-parents voulaient pour leurs filles des noms qui sortent de l'ordinaire. Leur aînée, ils l'avaient appelée Bérengère, un prénom ancien qu'on ne donnait plus en Algérie. Comment avaient-ils déniché celui de Myrrande, avec un y et deux r que je me refuserai toujours à utiliser sous cette forme ? Mirande vient du latin *miranda :* admirable. Hermance aussi, ç'aurait été beau. Mes beaux-parents, de simple condition, étaient dans une mauvaise passe. Le père, asthmatique, ne faisait plus rien. Le docteur, répétait-il, lui avait interdit le moindre effort. Toute la journée assis sur une chaise sur le trottoir devant la porte de l'hôtel, il fumait des cigarettes d'eucalyptus qui empestaient, pendant que sa femme trimait. Le commerce de leur gérance marchait cahin-caha, et soudain leurs deux filles s'étaient mariées à des hommes convenables.

277

L'hôtel Montpensier, troisième ou quatrième ordre, où j'en étais il y a un instant à Paris, était tellement au-dessus de l'hôtel du Nador de Médéa où je m'étais risqué sous-lieutenant. Mon intention dans ces Mémoires est de parler le moins possible de ma vie privée pour me consacrer aux événements et aux hommes que je croise. De là à m'arranger, comme le voulait Flaubert, pour laisser croire à la postérité que je n'ai pas vécu, il y a une marge. Si je me mets à trop parler de moi, ne vais-je pas ennuyer ? C'est pourquoi Mirande, à peine apparue, va disparaître. A peine de retour à Paris, je me prépare à divorcer en me chargeant de tous les torts, oui, mais je ne suis pas Flaubert, je ne raconte pas ma vie comme lui s'est raconté dans ses lettres. Ce sont des Mémoires que j'écris, où je pourrais, si je voulais, en prendre à l'aise avec la vérité. Et voilà que Mirande meurt presque sous mes yeux et interrompt mon travail.

Sa mort m'atteint en plein cœur, que je n'ai pas si dur que certains croient. Je pense à mon ami, mon frère aîné et bien-aimé Jef, Joseph Kessel, moins jeune de dix ans et tellement plus généreux que moi. Son ancienne femme, il l'avait mieux installée que moi la mienne, il allait régulièrement la voir, pleurant avec elle en bon Russe qu'il était et lui glissant tout l'argent qu'elle voulait. Mais les sentiments qu'il éprouvait pour elle n'étaient pas ceux que j'éprouvais pour Mirande. Jef n'était pas riche. Il gagnait beaucoup et dépensait plus encore. Avec son talent, il avait la chance de se jeter dans des sujets qui passionnaient. Tous ses livres, même celui sur les alcooliques anonymes, étaient des triomphes. Ses fortunes, il les distribuait aussitôt à son frère, à ses neveux, à ses anciennes, à sa nouvelle, à des inconnus et, avec le reste, faisait la bombe chez Novy, chez Alexandre ou ailleurs, vidant sa bourse, tonneau des Danaïdes. Je l'ai aimé, il m'a aimé aussi, nous avions été aviateurs tous les deux à vingt ans de distance, et presque alliés un moment par les femmes. Nous avions choisi l'amour des avions et des créatures, lui sans heurter ni blesser personne, applaudi et chéri par tous et toutes, et jetant l'argent par les fenêtres.

J'ai toujours habité de belles maisons et partagé ma vie avec de belles femmes, ce qui explique mes difficultés après mon divorce d'avec Mirande, mon ancienne Vierge de Giotto qui,

me dit-on, meurt sans s'apercevoir de rien, bonheur que je demandais à Dieu pour elle comme je le demande chaque jour pour moi. Et me voilà soudain, ne pouvant plus écrire un mot, partant aussitôt pour Paris, où ma fille me confirme qu'en effet Mirande s'est endormie paisiblement : son cœur a ralenti puis s'est arrêté, elle s'est laissée aller sur son oreiller, les yeux clos, sans souffrance, sans même un soupir, elle a rejoint le pont Mirabeau auquel elle pensait toujours parce qu'elle souhaitait que ses cendres fussent répandues là :

> Sous le pont Mirabeau coule la Seine
> Et nos amours
> Faut-il qu'il m'en souvienne...

S'éteindre ainsi, est-ce possible avec la terrible maladie qui la dévorait ? « Oui, me répond le médecin qu'est mon fils. Il peut y avoir des rémissions, on ne sait pourquoi. C'est merveilleux. » Ce qui ajoute de la violence à cette bombe qui m'a éclaté sous le nez, c'est que la vieille femme que Mirande était devenue dans la vie, mais pas dans mes Mémoires, a été incinérée le jour anniversaire de notre mariage.

*
**

A Alger, ce jour-là, 6 avril 1929, le soleil cognait déjà. Sous son chapeau cloche, Mirande si belle, si fraîche, si ingénue et en même temps si tourmentée, venait de dire oui au sous-lieutenant de réserve en civil que j'étais, nous prenions tous le tram pour gagner l'église Saint-Vincent-de-Paul à l'Esplanade de Bab el-Oued, et mon bon curé au visage si doux, avec qui je faisais les enterrements quand j'étais séminariste, nous bénissait.

Au repas de noces, à la Pêcherie, il y avait Emile, mon nouveau beau-frère, le mari de Bérengère. Si, quand j'ai parlé de mon mariage, je n'ai rien dit d'Emile, c'est qu'il a dû se conduire avec une discrétion voisine de l'effacement. Emile habitait El-Affroun, me semble-t-il, à moins que ce ne soit Marengo, autre village de la Mitidja pas très loin de Rovigo. Par la suite, quand il vint à Médéa, je découvris que j'avais pour beau-frère un rigolo, un homme qui prenait tout à la blague, sauf son métier et la comptabilité : il était percepteur

des contributions. C'était surtout un fantastique tombeur. Sa femme ne le quittait pas d'une semelle car dès que sa surveillance se relâchait, s'il était seul, il fonçait. Beau gosse, élégant, soigneux, discret, et quand il parlait de son travail, sévère. La conversation bifurquait dès qu'une jolie fille passait. Quand Bérengère était là, elle roulait des yeux et menaçait : « Regardez-le. Que je ne l'y prenne pas… » Il avait plaisir à la taquiner. A l'exciter ? Elle avait pu constater plus d'une fois qu'il la trompait. Il niait l'évidence, ce qui amusait le beau-père et assombrissait la belle-mère. Cette femme d'apparence puissante paraissait découragée. Elle connaissait sa fille Bérengère, violente, rancunière, tenaillée par une jalousie féroce. Ma belle-mère imaginait une rupture, un divorce, avec son aînée de nouveau sur les bras, alors qu'il s'agissait d'un enfantillage d'Emile. Emile était un bon mari, un homme intègre, un fonctionnaire d'élite. Porté sur la bagatelle, il avouait qu'il était inspiré irrésistiblement par sa femme deux fois par jour au moins. Quand il se vantait de cela, Bérengère baissait modestement les paupières et se rengorgeait. C'est parce qu'Emile se montrait un amant si ardent qu'elle le voulait à elle seule. Quand nous étions tous deux ensemble, Emile et moi, il me disait que les femmes étaient toutes à conquérir, qu'elles ne demandaient que ça, qu'il suffisait de leur parler et, très vite, de leur montrer qu'on avait envie d'elles. Elles ne résistaient pas. « Jamais ? » demandais-je avec curiosité. « Rarement. Ou alors, c'est qu'elles ne peuvent pas. Toi (car nous nous étions tutoyés d'emblée), tu devrais t'exercer. »

Je ne sais si Emile eut de l'influence sur moi. Je ne lui parlai pas d'une cousine, de qui j'avais été, et étais encore amoureux. Nous n'avions pas la même idée de la chose. Lui, d'après ce que j'entendais, c'était Casanova. Moi, je cherchais la beauté et l'amour. Ma cousine, ulcérée par mon mariage, avait disparu et Mirande me comblait. Dès que je m'absentais pour des manœuvres ou en permission à Alger, Mirande m'écrivait en parfumant son papier à lettres bleu de violette de Parme. J'ai gardé longtemps ses lettres dans des paquets serrés d'une faveur rouge. Si adoratrices, ses lettres, tellement naïves que ça devenait du grand magasin, de la confection : elle n'avait eu pour lectures que les romans à quatre sous que son père lui repassait avec une odeur d'eucalyptus quand il les avait terminés. De mon côté, les mots que j'employais étaient

des mots ordinaires avec un peu de sauce autour, mais pour elle, c'était l'amour, elle y déchirait son cœur, elle en étendait les débris pantelants comme sur une corde à linge. Quand elle écrivait : « mon adoré, mon unique », elle y croyait. Finalement, après notre divorce, gêné de les voir voisiner avec d'autres paquets entourés de faveurs, j'ai brûlé ses lettres. Elle a dû garder les miennes ou peut-être les a-t-elle brûlées aussi puisque pour elle le feu purifie.

Sous-lieutenant à Médéa, les devoirs dont je me sentais alourdi, une épouse, des enfants, m'assombrissaient parfois, mais j'allais bientôt quitter cette vie de garnison étriquée, et ce serait de nouveau l'école de Saint-Maixent, puis Doyon, puis les tentations de Paris. Là, Mirande décida qu'Emile avait eu une mauvaise influence sur moi. Enfin viendra ma seule et tyrannique passion, l'avion, ce qui n'empêchait pas le reste. Emile ne fut jamais lié qu'aux timides débuts de mes relations avec ma belle-famille : inexistantes, incertaines, de plus en plus vagues. Emile montait chaque année un échelon de plus, réussissait à des examens qui le propulsaient vers des grades dans l'administration des finances. Il quitta sa femme, fila d'autres aventures et ascensions, et Bérengère se remaria.

L'amour s'en va comme cette eau courante...

A Paris, quand il eut demandé où j'allais, le chauffeur eut un sursaut : « Moi, monsieur, je n'entre pas dans les cimetières... » Un chauffeur français, même pas un Cambodgien. Il me fallait changer de taxi : le Père-Lachaise était une immense nécropole que je n'aurais pas la force de traverser pour grimper vers le columbarium. Nous parlementâmes, le taxi finit par céder. Il aurait dû savoir qu'il y avait, de l'autre côté du cimetière et à deux pas de l'édifice lugubre, une autre entrée qui aurait pu éviter toute discussion. Finalement, son opposition était qu'on ne roulait pas assez vite là-dedans, comme si les morts avaient besoin de mouvement et de bruit. Bref, avec cet anniversaire de mariage que tout le monde connaissait depuis que ma fille en avait découvert la date à l'intérieur de l'alliance de sa mère, je portais en moi comme une honte mineure et un bonheur étriqué. Petite honte : mon devoir aurait été d'avoir au doigt la même alliance. Petit bonheur : il

s'agissait d'une attention délicate du destin, rappelant à tous que la vie affective de Mirande avait commencé tellement plus tôt. Pourquoi ne s'était-elle pas remariée comme sa sœur Bérengère ? Quand nous avions divorcé, elle était toujours jolie, à trente-huit ans. Elle avait décidé de se sacrifier pour ses enfants puis pour ses petits-enfants. Eut-elle jamais une tentation sérieuse ? Elle savait par moi ce que valent les hommes, même ceux qui ont été élevés chez les lazaristes. Je ne cherche pas d'excuse.

Je reviens à l'hôtel Montpensier, rue de Richelieu, où je pense à la femme que j'ai rencontrée à Londres, qui m'a envoûté et que je n'ai pas encore décidée à recommencer sa vie avec moi. Tout est là. Pour le monde aussi. Le IIIe Reich est détruit, l'Amérique est partout, la France commence à se relever de ses ruines. Mon année de guerre dans la RAF m'a rendu dingo. Nous avons perpétré des choses terribles. Un *intelligence officer* qui était devenu mon ami me disait : « Je suis effrayé de ce qu'on vous oblige à faire... » Sans doute trouva-t-on qu'il se montrait trop sensible, on le muta. Il s'appelait Nelson, comme l'amiral. Je lui ai envoyé certains de mes poèmes qu'il a traduits. A cette époque, nous revenions symboliquement couverts de sang, mes mains qui lâchaient les bombes étaient des mains de massacreur. Oui, oui, je me répète, nous répliquions aux attaques sur Londres, à Coventry rasé par la Luftwaffe en 1940, aux bombes volantes, aux fusées, et même aux camps de concentration dont on commençait à entendre parler, nous devions écraser les usines souterraines où se fabriquait l'arme atomique nazie et donc tout détruire, j'étais un terroriste légal, c'était eux ou nous, j'appelais une miséricorde sur mon front, afin de pouvoir dormir.

Au columbarium, piteuse réplique de la basilique du Sacré-Cœur, je débordais de pitié. Menteur, hypocrite, faux jeton, digne filsque de mon père ! A l'époque de mon retour à Paris après la guerre, j'étais plein de fureur : ne plus vivre avec celle qui m'avait eu puceau, idiot, jeune chien, petit con qui voulait savoir comment les filles étaient tournées, les baiser sans tomber comme un pigeon dans la casserole du mariage. J'entendais Doyon m'exciter. Lui au moins avait, comme Malraux, épousé une femme avec du fric. J'accusais mes beaux-parents, des gens simples et dans la gêne, d'avoir poussé

le nigaud que j'étais dans les bras de Mirande, d'avoir tout agencé et machiné, d'être même venus écouter aux portes et ensuite, la mère du moins, que je n'aimais pas, d'avoir emprunté la mine chafouine, puis l'air soucieux et les traits tirés d'une mamma-la-pudeur. Mon beau-père, non. Lui, c'était un homme, il savait, il regardait sa femme jouer à la vieille renarde. N'empêche que leur fille cadette, pure et passionnée, méritait bien l'appellation de Vierge de Giotto que je lui donnai aussitôt. La victime, c'était elle. Pas moi. Finalement Mirande ne me reprocha rien. C'était à elle qu'elle en voulait. Encore avait-elle des enfants qu'elle adorait. Sa fille avec qui elle vivait.

Vienne la nuit, sonne l'heure
Les jours s'en vont, je demeure...

Sa seule vengeance, son coup de griffe, cet anniversaire qui me mettait dans l'embarras. Je n'avais qu'à bien me conduire, pour une fois.

Peu à peu je me casai dans ma nouvelle vie. Au bureau Etudes et Plans de l'état-major, dans l'immense bâtisse de briques roses du ministère de l'Air, boulevard Victor, j'avais de bons camarades, un surtout, Accart, as de guerre, fidèle de Murtin qu'on avait envoyé en Amérique pour qu'on lui fixe une jambe artificielle. Nous prenions le métro ensemble, les popotes n'étaient pas brillantes, on manquait de tout. Notre cercle, un grand hôtel des Champs-Elysées, le Carlton, occupé et pillé par les Allemands, nous n'avions pu que le transformer en cantine. On ne chantait pas non plus. Ou alors il fallait des occasions, du champagne. Minable. Chez Doyon, au moindre arrivage d'œufs, de jésus de Lyon ou de petit salé, il y avait une fête. Les amis d'avant-guerre voyaient de près un officier qui avait suivi et célébré Pétain et ensuite combattu avec les Rosbifs. Eux, ils avaient seulement supporté les Frizés. Rita apparaissait mais le charme s'était envolé et, d'ailleurs, j'étais tout à ma beauté de Londres qui ne se hâtait pas de rentrer. Amoureux fou, je l'attendais à l'hôtel Montpensier où il s'en passait, à tous les étages, et où j'étais un des clients les plus sérieux. L'hôtel était éclairé à une électricité parcimonieuse.

On croisait des gens bizarres dans une demi-pénombre traversée de cliques louches. Des disputes éclataient souvent. Encore habitais-je un quartier noble. De la chambre voisine dont j'étais séparé par une double porte à moulures dorées et mal ajustée, j'entendais des cris de femmes, mêlés à la voix furieuse d'un homme, parfois de deux, une vraie querelle. Excédé, je tapais contre la cloison. Peine perdue. Ces gens-là se fichaient pas mal des voisins. Je devinais de basses insultes, des ordures, enfin des coups, et alors des sanglots, des gémissements. Quelquefois ça se calmait, ça devenait des murmures, des pâmoisons, des hurlements d'amour. J'imaginais Murtin à ma place. Les outrances de langage ne sont pas mon genre, mais le monde en avait tant vu, on n'en était pas à ça près, pourquoi se gêner ? D'où venaient-ils, ceux-là ? Qu'avaient-ils fait pendant la guerre ?

La solitude me pesait. J'attendais des lettres de Londres, j'en avais parfois. De mon côté, je ne cessais d'en envoyer, j'espérais qu'un jour je trouverais le signe qu'on serait passé à l'hôtel. Parfois, comme un chien qui a perdu son maître, je restais dans ma chambre plus que j'aurais dû, dans la pensée qu'elle viendrait, qui sait ? sans prévenir. J'essayai de savoir qui vivait dans la chambre à côté de moi. On me dit que c'était une chanteuse qui travaillait dans un cabaret : « Edith Piaf, vous ne connaissez pas ? » Je me dis que ce devait être la vie qu'on menait quand on était dans la chanson. Au fond, je sortais à peine du séminaire, l'armée d'Afrique c'était hier, les fureurs de Boum-Boum m'atteignaient encore, je me disais aussi que j'aurais pu aller à la maison des lazaristes, 95 rue de Sèvres, où M. Baligand aurait été heureux de me voir, mais y était-il ? La crainte de rencontrer l'ancien supérieur du séminaire, M. Payen, me retenait. Chaque soir, la guerre déferlait de nouveau sur moi, je décollais en pleines ténèbres à côté de Gronier, sa main droite jouant avec les manettes des gaz, puis c'était la coulée des laves d'or, et, en fin de tout, une collision me fracassait en plein ciel noir. Parfois il arrivait que nous tombions serrés contre la ferraille collante dans un embrassement d'où je sortais avec une clameur. Je devais crier moi aussi, la nuit, cette Edith Piaf et ses compagnons ne protestaient pas, pourquoi me serais-je plaint de leurs scènes à eux qui étaient peut-être leur façon, pourquoi pas ? d'aimer. C'étaient des saltimbanques, au moins ils s'amusaient. On me

cita aussi des noms qui ne me disaient rien : l'un qu'il m'a
semblé reconnaître plus tard, peut-être, et un autre que j'ai
complètement oublié, aussi notoire. J'avais provoqué bien
plus de boucan sur Cologne. N'empêche. Ça me gênait.

Dès le coup de téléphone de ma fille m'annonçant la mort
de sa mère, fini aussi de mon sommeil. Je me demande ce que
les deux femmes peuvent encore se dire, une fois tout
accompli. Ma fille laisse-t-elle ouverte la porte de la chambre
mortuaire ? Sa mère est-elle devenue « le corps » ? Par son
désir exprimé maintes fois d'être incinérée, Mirande rejoint
soudain les flammes qui auraient pu me réduire en cendres, cet
hiver 1944-1945, au-dessus de la Ruhr ou de Leipzig. Dès que
je ferme les yeux, je vois ce qu'une machine va introduire dans
le four, à moins que ce soit la longue pelle du potier quand il a
pétri sa glaise. La porte du four se hisse, ses bras coulissent, un
bras mécanique pousse le cercueil gris-vert foncé feldgrau,
drôle de couleur, dans la ténébreuse entrée, puis tout se
referme comme sur un blockhaus tandis que, n'osant tout de
même pas assister au déchaînement des flammes, nous repar-
tons vers ce qu'on appelle ici le « grand salon ». Nous, c'est-à-
dire les enfants, les petits-enfants, les parents et alliés, de rares
amis et moi. On nous introduit dans quelque chose qui
ressemble à un oratoire lugubre. Vitraux orange sous une
coupole mal éclairée. Il fait froid. Nous nous asseyons sur des
chaises à accoudoirs. Devant nous, ce qui pourrait être une
chapelle en demi-rotonde semée d'étoiles est faiblement éclairé
par des meurtrières bleues. Des marches qu'on devine mènent
peut-être à un autel que nous cache une tenture tendue sur un
filin à hauteur d'homme. De quelle couleur la tenture ? Rouge
foncé peut-être, ou grenat. Peut-être en velours. J'espérais
tout le temps qu'elle serait tirée, que je saurais ce qu'il y avait
derrière. Sur les premières marches qui séparent l'oratoire où
nous sommes de cet autre lieu qui pourrait être l'abside ou le
transept, est couchée la croix de roses roses à quoi nous avons
pensé, ma fille et moi, seul signe religieux visible, posé sur le
corps de Mirande pour traverser Paris, seule pitié, seule
consolation, seul symbole de l'amour qui fut le sien ou qu'elle
fut peut-être tout entière. L'orgue éclate, solennel, puissant,

sur un choral de Bach. On nous a dit que la cérémonie serait longue, mais peut-on appeler cela une cérémonie ?

Rien que du Bach à l'orgue, séparé par des silences inquiétants pendant lesquels on entend un ronflement sourd et lointain. Le ronflement des flammes ? Parfois des coups de talons secs, légers. Quelqu'un qui se déplacerait pour tirer la tenture et finalement renoncerait ? Le froid gagne, le silence étreint. J'entends les cris, les hurlements, les insultes grossières de l'autre côté de la cloison, à l'hôtel Montpensier. Nous sommes dans une immense plaine noire qu'il nous faut traverser derrière l'immobile croix de roses pendant que l'orgue tonne, craque puis s'apaise et se repose, et qu'alors recommencent les sinistres ronflements et claquent les pas légers d'un acolyte qui ne se décide pas à tirer le rideau. Un moment, l'idée me vient que nous participons à une cérémonie socialiste. Pas de luminaire, pas de candélabres ni de torchères, pas de chants, pas de paroles de miséricorde ni d'imploration, pas de prières. Rien qu'une austérité et une sévérité que j'imagine soviétiques comme j'ai pu les mesurer en deux ou trois circonstances, mais je m'aperçois vite que je me trompe. Dans une cérémonie soviétique, il y aurait des drapeaux, des discours, des rappels de ce qui aurait été la créature qui retourne à la cendre. Même les incroyants parlent. Il y aurait au moins, à défaut de l'allocution du chef local du Parti ou du chef de la chorale, l'éloge de la défunte par le chef d'îlot du quartier, et qui sait ? peut-être un hymne célébrant la patrie, l'honneur, la probité, l'amour de la famille. Ici, rien. C'est le pire. Si seulement quelqu'un lisait le poème d'Apollinaire. Nous ne savions pas, personne n'a pensé à quoi que ce soit. Mirande n'a pas voulu de secours de la religion, elle s'est tenue silencieuse et stoïque devant sa propre fatalité, elle a refusé tout prêtre, aussi a-t-elle une cérémonie nue, laïque et polaire sans même la faible flamme d'un cierge, symbole de l'âme qui vit encore tandis que le corps se change en poussière. Une seule croix de roses roses. L'évangile du jour où elle est morte, celui de la résurrection de Lazare, rappelle la parole de Marthe à Marie : « Le maître est là et il t'appelle. » Enfin les pas approchent, on nous fait signe, je monte les quelques marches qui mènent au rideau. Derrière, pas d'autel. Quelque chose qui ressemble, au-dessus de ce qui pourrait être un vague chœur, à une énorme bouche fermée, entourée symbolique-

ment de flammes semblables à des pierres gelées. J'apprends que les ronflements suspects provenaient de la soufflerie de l'orgue, mais personne n'a pu identifier les bruits secs sur le marbre. On me parle de roucoulades des colombes que je n'ai pas entendues, nous nous retrouvons sous le soleil derrière le porteur de l'urne, une coupe où, de Mirande, la mère de mes enfants, il ne reste plus que ça. Nous levons les yeux vers le ciel où naviguent des nuages pareils à des voiliers.

> *Les mains dans les mains restons face à face*
> *Tandis que sous*
> *Le pont de nos bras passe*
> *Des éternels regards l'onde si lasse...*

Nous descendons. Est-ce une crypte ? N'est-ce pas plutôt une salle des pas perdus de gare, ou plutôt, avec toutes ces cases où chacun cache des bagages ou des secrets, et nous le nôtre, une salle de consigne presque déserte, froide encore, seulement habitée plus haut par les gémissements amoureux des tourterelles que j'entends à présent. Parmi tous les noms inconnus que déjà j'ai pu lire par hasard, je découvre celui d'Henri Fiori, « ancien député d'Alger, 1881-1963 ». Un vieux compagnon, pourquoi pas ? Fiori était député de Bab el-Oued quand nous nous sommes mariés, il aurait assisté à la cérémonie si nous l'avions invité. J'ai déjà parlé de lui : on l'appelait Fiori l'Anisette, on prétendait que c'était grâce au flot qui coulait à ses frais dans tous les bars du quartier qu'il était élu. Avec sa célèbre grosse trogne fleurie, il avait fait une guerre courageuse en 14-18 et il était un des rares députés « socialistes » d'une Algérie où triomphaient le capitalisme, l'autorité sur les Arabes, l'ordre et le respect des pouvoirs établis. Il demandait un salaire un peu moins bas pour les ouvriers. Pour les fatmas, je ne suis pas sûr. Jamais un curé n'aurait osé inviter ses ouailles — ne parlons pas des femmes, elles n'avaient pas le droit de vote — à voter pour lui. Mon père non plus, pourtant instituteur laïc à la retraite, ni mon beau-père qui se targuait d'idées avancées. Est-ce qu'on sait ? Peut-être Emile. Moi sûrement pas. En ce temps-là, oserai-je le dire ? Fiori me semblait un suppôt de Satan. Il y avait, non loin du cimetière de Saint-Eugène où dorment mon père, mon frère Robert et sa femme Marie-Louise, un lieu dit « La Consolation ». Les trams s'y arrêtaient. Le mot signifiait peut-

être qu'arrivé là, quand on avait conduit quelqu'un, on devait être consolé. A la sortie du columbarium, rien. Pas un lieu-dit. Pas le moindre signe. La grande porte plus loin ouvre sur les vivants et sur la ville. Seul pâle sourire de la destinée : Mirande n'est pas loin de Fiori. Nous restons découverts, écrasés de tristesse, anéantis en cette consigne de gare pour l'au-delà, nous nous demandons ce que nous faisons, nous n'avons pas l'air de comprendre que, de Mirande, c'est tout ce qui reste, une poignée de cendres que nous aurions dû jeter par-dessus le pont Mirabeau dans le courant qui les aurait fait passer à Rouen, devant Croisset où Flaubert a vécu, et où il n'y a plus rien que le vent qui souffle de la mer. Une de mes petites-filles s'effondre soudain, secouée de sanglots silencieux qui durent, qui durent. Peut-être cherchons-nous des consolations qui ne sont pas de ce monde. Les colombes gémissent si fort que cela devient indécent. Elles n'arrêtent donc jamais ? Et la croix de roses restée sur les marches du « grand salon », où va-t-elle finir ? Nous ne pouvons plus parler, nous dérivons vers la place Gambetta comme des péniches, nous nous coulons dans un tiède rayon de soleil. Je me redis les vers du « Pont Mirabeau » qu'elle aimait tant :

> *L'amour s'en va comme cette eau courante*
> *L'amour s'en va*
> *Comme la vie est lente*
> *Et comme l'Espérance est violente...*

Cahin-caha je me redresse. On me pousse dans un taxi.

XI

Camus

REVENONS à Paris en 1945, à l'hôtel Montpensier où je me consume pour la femme que j'aime, qui n'est plus Mirande. Comment à présent démêler la fiction de la réalité ? J'essaie de me souvenir par des dates, sur des cahiers ou des carnets qui marquent les événements du monde ou les détails de mon existence.

A l'hôtel Montpensier où j'ai du mal à m'endormir parce que mon avion s'abat sans cesse, je revois le visage de cette personne que j'attends, qui ne vient pas, et qui s'obstinera longtemps à ne pas succomber. Je suis un bombardier de nuit avec clameur et foudre, je passe d'un désir brûlant à une descente en flammes suivie d'écrasement. Ce que j'écris sur le Paris de 1945, comment m'en souviendrais-je à présent, sinon à travers un brouillard, si on ne m'avait rendu mes lettres ? Non pas que nous soyons brouillés, celle que j'appelle Marie et moi. Nous avons de l'estime pour nous-mêmes mais aussi parfois un certain étonnement. Comment imaginer par exemple qu'une fois, incident parmi tant d'autres, je sois allé attendre cette femme toute une nuit devant la porte de son immeuble pour la tuer ? Elle ne répondait plus à mes supplications, je la croyais dans les bras d'un autre homme. De longues années après, nous nous regardons avec un sourire et elle me tend un lourd paquet de lettres serrées par année. « Cela pourra vous servir. Vous racontez tout ce qui vous arrive, vous m'aimez encore mais si vous courez beaucoup, la crise est passée, je suis mariée, je vais avoir un enfant. Vos cris de passion, je ne vous les rends pas... »

J'en ai relu quelques-unes où j'emploie un style un peu empesé, mais je me laisse aller à des envolées. C'est cette

289

femme aussi, lorsque je lui ai avoué que j'avais passé huit ans au séminaire, qui m'a dit : « Mon pauvre ami, vous auriez fait un mauvais prêtre. Que vous en soyez parti est une chance pour vous. Vous êtes trop orgueilleux, trop cruel, trop impatient, trop esclave de vos impulsions, un vrai barbare, et, en même temps, vous avez cette fâcheuse manie de cracher à chacun ses vérités, personne ne vous aurait supporté, vous auriez été très malheureux, n'ayez aucun regret ! »

Je n'en ai jamais eu le moindre. J'ai beau dire, je me demande comment une telle démence a pu me posséder à cette époque de l'hôtel Montpensier. D'où je sortais, j'avais un besoin féroce de dévorer. L'objet de ma folle passion revenu de Londres, nos amours d'orage en orage amusaient la galerie mais ne traversaient pas les cloisons. Je la présentai à Doyon, à Camus, à toute l'équipe. Elle témoigna pour Camus une admiration que je soupçonnai vaguement coupable, quelle femme n'était pas amoureuse de Camus ? Elle m'avait enfin cédé, mais la vie était un chemin difficile, souvent accompagné d'éclairs et de tonnerre, où j'allais m'échiner pendant deux ans. Puis la sagesse vint. La sagesse ? Ce mot ne saurait s'appliquer à moi qu'à présent où l'âge a refroidi mon sang. Non, ce fut plutôt l'apparition d'autres beautés, de nouvelles scènes de la chambre d'à côté qui me divertirent. Le nom d'Edith Piaf ne me disait toujours rien, pas plus que ceux de ses compagnons. Ces gens-là n'étaient pas de ma famille. J'étais loin de me douter que la Piaf ferait la carrière que l'on sait. Ses compagnons n'ont pas mal réussi non plus.

Entre Camus et moi, ce fut encore un coup de foudre. Du moins de mon côté. Lui, c'était plutôt pour les femmes. Les hommes, il lui arrivait de les admirer, Sartre, Malraux, Merleau-Ponty, Guilloux, d'autres. Pas au point de s'attacher à eux exagérément, il s'aimait trop lui-même. Nous rencontrâmes-nous au Flore ou aux Deux-Magots ? Et ne pleuvait-il pas ce jour-là, puisqu'il avait son imperméable à la Humphrey Bogart ? L'aura dont il était entouré fit que je le plaçai d'emblée au-dessus d'Amrouche. Je n'étais pas seul avec lui, toute la bande à Charlot était là, Roblès aussi, peut-être Fréminville que nous appelions tous Frémin, qui deviendra

Claude Terrien d'Europe n° 1. Pour le moment, il travaillait à l'hebdomadaire socialiste que personne ne lisait. Il n'y avait que Max-Pol Fouchet et le clan de *Fontaine* qui menaient train à part, par méfiance d'Amrouche et de *l'Arche*.

Ce qui, chez Camus, emballait tout de suite, c'était sa camaraderie, sa générosité. Avec sa tête d'hidalgo, il rayonnait. Un enfant de Belcourt parlait à d'autres enfants de Bab el-Oued ou de Mustapha, des Tagarins, d'Oran ou de Kabylie, tous au-dessus de ceux qu'on appelait les *francaouis* qui tenaient le haut du pavé depuis trop longtemps chez eux et allaient devoir céder la place. Pour lui, il avait sa troupe de fans à *Combat* et chez Gallimard, il était invité partout, on se l'arrachait, il brillait comme un astre.

Je le trouvai beau. Ses yeux pochés sous son grand front ajoutaient à son charme, à ce côté las, désabusé, dont les femmes raffolaient. Elancé, taille mince, il affectait de s'habiller comme quelqu'un qui n'avait que peu de loisir à accorder à l'élégance, et puis il était de santé fragile, son teint le laissait deviner. Ce qu'il disait était plein de naturel, de simplicité, de droiture, il l'exprimait avec tant d'art et d'élévation, il me sembla si accompli dans l'ordre physique et moral que j'eus comme la révélation mystique qu'il était, j'exagère à peine, le prophète annoncé par les Ecritures, pourquoi pas ? le messie.

A peu de chose près, nous, les nouveaux débarqués de la bande à Charlot, pensions de même. Il était le meilleur, le plus fort, le chef, le maître, le gourou, avec ce merveilleux sentiment d'égalité qu'il nous prodiguait : nous étions frères, pas comme dans les familles où on se jalouse, et où, parfois, on n'est pas du même père. Nous avions la même mère, l'Algérie. Nous venions nous jeter dans les bras de la France que nous avions contribué à sauver, nous allions ajouter à sa gloire. Pour lui, c'était déjà fait ou presque. Pour nous, à faire. Le seul à ne douter de rien était Amrouche.

Nous allâmes tous ensemble déjeuner dans un de ces bouis-bouis qui fleurissaient rue des Canettes, ou peut-être déjà à un couscous de la rue Saint-André-des-Arts ou de la rue Saint-Séverin. Camus riait ou s'indignait, rien ne nous séparait, il comprenait tout et se montrait attentionné pour chacun de nous. Nous nous quittâmes avec les embrassades de là-bas. Saint-Germain-des-Prés était devenue la Terre sainte.

Cela, c'est ce que ma mémoire me dicte. Elle me pousse

dans le dos. C'est toujours ainsi que je revois notre première rencontre au Flore ou aux Deux-Magots, un jour de pluie. C'est faux. A l'époque, Camus n'avait pas une seconde à lui. Il était toute la journée au marbre de *Combat,* puis, en passion des événements, il s'enfermait dix minutes pour écrire son éditorial comme il parlait, comme il sentait, avec une rigueur où battait son cœur, ce qui n'était pas fréquent chez les intellectuels, et un peu de solennité, puis Paris l'emportait dans son tourbillon. Quand je revins de Grande-Bretagne, il venait de partir pour Alger embrasser sa mère qu'il avait quittée depuis quatre ans. Si troublé que je suis par mon retour en France et par l'amour, je ne tiens plus de journal. Je couche des notes sur des carnets ou des feuilles volantes. Sur un premier élan, ma mémoire arrange tout à sa façon. Elle présente le passé comme je souhaite le voir. Comme il faut se méfier ! Je manquerais de références aujourd'hui sans ces lettres rendues. A quoi bon inventer puisque la réalité est là ? Le juge d'instruction que je suis pour moi ne veut que du document. Quand je reviens de Grande-Bretagne, Camus n'est pas là.

La veille de la victoire, le 7 mai, j'étais avec des camarades. Il y avait du vent dans les voiles. Ils buvaient beaucoup en souvenir d'York, des pubs où ils allaient les jours de repos. Dans le ciel de Paris un peu brumeux, brillaient Jupiter et un Lion à peine perceptible. Des projecteurs en V étaient plantés dans la nuit comme des épées. Des fusées éclairantes éclataient, les nuages battaient, soulevés par une lumière blanche. Le vent faisait onduler les couleurs sous l'Arc de Triomphe d'où partaient des feux d'étoiles vite éteintes. Les badauds s'exclamaient, nous leur disions qu'à Dortmund et à Cologne, les villes brûlaient et les projecteurs valsaient pour nous épingler. Je ne me souviens plus si Gallois était là. Nous avions grimpé à Montmartre, à la place du Tertre qu'il avait brossée au bar d'Elvington à l'occasion d'une fête. Assise sur les marches du Sacré-Cœur, une foule énorme, qui avait peut-être bu comme nous, chantait *la Marseillaise,* le ventre vide, battait des mains, puis reprenait. Le lendemain, sorti dans les rues comme tout le monde, je remontais l'avenue d'Iéna pour aller à notre cercle

miteux du Carlton quand je me fis renverser par une des rares voitures qui passaient. On me releva, le chauffeur me conduisit lui-même à l'hôpital le plus proche où je passai un sale quart d'heure. Rien de cassé. « Un pas de plus, me dit l'interne, ça y était... » Le lendemain, je regagnai l'hôtel Montpensier dans une fureur noire. Un jour, un camarade que j'aimais bien, Notelle, était rentré de la Ruhr le front ouvert, après avoir été abattu par un chasseur près du camp. Loin d'être défiguré, il était auréolé de gloire. Ici, j'avais seulement l'air d'un éclopé. Je souffrais des braillements que les gens poussaient dans la rue. Je profitai de mon immobilité forcée pour écrire un récit pour *la France libre* et des éditoriaux que Pierre Desgraupes, jeune journaliste de la radio, alerté par Amrouche, m'avait demandés. C'est Amrouche qui vint m'annoncer, le 11 mai, ce qui s'était passé en Algérie trois jours plus tôt et qu'on nous avait caché. Ceux qu'on appelait encore les indigènes avaient attaqué des fermes et des villages dans la région de Sétif. Il y avait quarante et un morts à Périgotville. Des renforts avaient été expédiés, le chef tunisien du Destour s'était enfui en Egypte et réclamait le séparatisme de l'Afrique du Nord, Ferhat Abbas était arrêté une fois de plus. Comme les consignes de silence étaient sévères, les journaux du matin s'étaient contentés de publier le communiqué du conseil des ministres. *Combat,* que je n'avais pas lu, avait sorti sur quatre colonnes une manchette : « Agitation en Algérie. » Amrouche était impressionné par les banderoles que les indigènes avaient brandies avec le mot, non pas de liberté, mais de *freedom.*

Dans *le Monde,* je découvris dans les nouvelles diverses : « Le gouvernement général de l'Algérie communique le 9 mai : Des éléments troubles d'inspiration hitlérienne se sont livrés à Sétif à une agression à main armée contre la population qui célébrait la capitulation de l'Axe. La police aidée de l'armée maintient l'ordre et les autorités prennent toutes les décisions utiles pour assurer la sécurité et réprimer les tentatives de désordre. »

Sétif, c'étaient Mirande et les enfants, il ne leur était rien arrivé, je l'aurais su, mais il fallait que je parte. Mon impression était que nous avions perdu l'Afrique du Nord par sottise et attachement au régime capitaliste. Sur un cahier de

notes de cette époque, je lis : « La France devient là-bas ce que l'Allemagne était en France, mais comment le dire ? » La série de Camus dans *Combat*, « Crise en Algérie », rappelait l'autre série, « Misère en Kabylie », de juin 1939 dans *Alger républicain*. Cette fois, Camus était allé partout où il avait pu, dans les villes et dans les douars reculés. Il concluait : « En Afrique du Nord comme en France, nous avons à inventer de nouvelles formules et à rajeunir nos méthodes si nous voulons que l'avenir ait un sens pour nous. » Pour nous ? Il n'y avait pas que nous, mais aussi les indigènes dont beaucoup étaient morts pour la France. Je griffonnai dans mon cahier : « Courageux article d'Albert Camus dans *Combat* de ce matin. » Seulement courageux, l'article ? Pour moi, oui. Etait-ce l'influence d'Amrouche ? Ou parce que, de retour de Leipzig et de la Ruhr, je me sentais tout à coup proche des tirailleurs algériens de la 1ʳᵉ Armée française qui avaient laissé leurs os à Cassino ? Et encore parce que je me rappelais la façon dont nous les traitions à Médéa où personne ne lisait *Alger républicain* ? Cloué sur mon lit, j'écrivis sur la guerre, sur Saint-Exupéry, sur Hillary des pages dont je ne sais où elles ont pu paraître. Je commençai le plan du récit qu'Amrouche m'avait demandé pour *l'Arche*. J'avais déjà un titre : « Douze cents bombardiers sur Bochum ». A part Amrouche, personne ne me parla de Sétif. Personne ne savait rien, je n'avais pas de téléphone à portée de la main, seulement les gémissements d'amour et les cris de colère de la Piaf, en pleine nuit. Même *Combat* ne lâchait que de vagues informations.

Le 18 mai, à l'aéroport du Bourget en partie détruit, et au milieu des carcasses calcinées, un avion Junker JU 52, prise de guerre, décolla pour Alger, avec des camarades aux commandes. On se traînait, ça puait l'essence, les passagers sombraient dans la torpeur. Un officier de l'armée de terre se mit à jacasser sur la question indigène. Je lui imposai silence brutalement. Après une escale à Marignane et huit heures de vol, l'avion souleva un nuage de sauterelles en se posant à Boufarik. Le port d'Alger était vide, une sorte d'abandon gagnait les rues tristes et sales. Malgré la célébration de la victoire, la ville n'était pas pavoisée, il faisait déjà chaud. Depuis l'Angleterre, ma mère m'attendait. La table de la salle à manger était près de la porte-fenêtre, là où je l'avais poussée en

1943. Pour ma mère, j'avais gagné la guerre à moi seul. Elle sortit tout ce qu'elle avait gardé pour moi : le sucre, le café, les confitures. Je ne lui dis rien des événements du Constantinois. Elle savait vaguement quelque chose : « C'est toujours les Arabes, mon pauvre... »

A Sétif, s'étalait la désolation. Mirande n'avait que des nouvelles rares et incertaines. Les Européens s'étaient barricadés, la troupe était intervenue ; déjà du passé. Mon retour coïncidait avec une invasion de criquets qui montaient à l'assaut de la ville. Nous habitions en lisière, presque au bout, dans la direction de Constantine. J'étais un revenant, mon retour rassurait, tout allait recommencer. Personne ne savait exactement comment les incidents avaient dégénéré ni comment on avait réprimé. Tout le monde disait que c'était fini. On s'occupait des criquets. Le soir, ils se collèrent en grappes sur les murs et sur les troncs des arbres. Le matin, par vagues, ils avançaient, grimpaient aux branches, s'y accrochaient. Hors de la ville, ils dévoraient les trembles et les mûriers, encerclaient des fontaines, butaient contre la voie ferrée, s'y amassaient puis retombaient de l'autre côté. Les indigènes agitaient des lambeaux d'étoffe en criant et creusaient des fossés. De toute part, le flot submergeait les champs de fèves et d'oignons verts, déferlait sur les orges et les blés pas encore moissonnés. A midi, ils recouvraient la rue, grouillaient dans notre cour, dévoraient les lilas, la vigne vierge, les rosiers. Je me souvins de l'invasion de sauterelles dans mon enfance, à la ferme. On avait conquis l'Algérie et on n'était pas encore armé contre les criquets.

Quand ils atteignirent les cinémas, les pouvoirs publics firent vider de l'eau dans les fossés. L'armée fut employée à répandre du son empoisonné. Des indigènes fouettaient les trottoirs avec des branchages, mais les jardins publics étaient détruits. Il fallait attendre. Tout passait. Les criquets comme le reste. Ce qu'on savait des autres événements, c'est que le mouvement de guerre sainte qui s'était étendu un moment dans le Constantinois avait été réprimé. De Gaulle avait autorisé le général Duval à y aller fort. A Sétif, on ne sut jamais combien d'indigènes avaient été tués. Les gens disaient une cinquantaine, peu de chose à côté du malheur des criquets. Dans la montagne, dix-huit avions avaient bombardé les

mechtas, et le croiseur *Duguay-Trouin* les contreforts des Babors.

Plus tard, on sut d'après le général Duval qu'il y aurait eu en tout cinq ou six cents morts, peut-être quinze cents. La Légion, disait-on encore avec précaution, avait brûlé quelques villages. Dans ses jugements, Mirande rejoignait ma mère. Mes enfants avaient grandi. Ils me considéraient un peu comme un étranger : j'avais changé, ils se taisaient. J'avais traversé des contrées sauvages, des ciels encombrés d'épaves, des terres en feu, j'avais servi à détruire l'humanité. Et Mirande ? Elle se doutait, elle savait tout. Je me mis à écrire un conte cruel, *l'Œil de loup du roi de Pharan*, que je fis aussitôt composer dans l'imprimerie où autrefois j'avais sorti mes prières. Dans mon bureau, il y avait l'immense affiche en couleurs de Pétain. Le Maréchal trônait toujours avec son képi à triple couronne d'or, ses yeux pervenche, sa moustache débonnaire. Mirande n'aurait pas osé y toucher. Moi non plus, je n'osai pas, les enfants n'auraient pas compris, je laissai Pétain où il était, la rue portait toujours son nom. Je n'avais à rougir ni de lui ni de moi. D'ailleurs, à Sétif, on croyait toujours en lui. De Gaulle, son ancien disciple, allait le faire passer en jugement au nom de la raison d'Etat.

Il me tardait de partir. J'allai d'abord à Constantine où mes amis Schveitzer avaient été limogés, Gide était passé chez eux, on l'avait mené aux oasis. Puis je regagnai Alger, redevenu une ville de province. On s'y ennuyait. Ma mère pouvait à peine marcher. Mon frère René et sa femme Louise veillaient sur elle mieux que je l'aurais jamais su. Eux, ils étaient ses vrais enfants, moi je n'étais qu'un hasard, m'aurait-elle gardé, autrefois, si elle avait pu ? et surtout je ne l'aimais pas assez. J'avais quitté mon père et ma mère pour m'attacher à des nuées. Je rentrai à Paris comme un bolide avec une escadrille de Marauder. Armand Guibert, tombé du Portugal comme de la lune, avait traduit Pessoa qu'on ne connaissait pas en France. La femme que j'aimais, ma merveille était là.

Dès lors tout me parut facile. L'importance des événements de Sétif semblait avoir été exagérée. Le calme revenu, c'était moins grave qu'on ne pensait. Des bruits couraient cependant que l'aviation et la Légion, employées sauvagement, avaient cassé et massacré aveuglément. Je courus annoncer les nouvelles à Doyon qui m'avait déniché un appartement.

Amrouche intriguait mon petit père au plus haut point. Que le fils d'un Kabyle chrétien fût devenu un intime de Gide et connût tout de Claudel et de Jouhandeau l'épatait. En même temps, Doyon devinait chez Amrouche une ambition démesurée. Charlot et Amrouche allaient-ils réussir où lui avait échoué ? La Libération allait provoquer des règlements de comptes : Gallimard tiendrait, mais la *NRF* semblait en danger. Amrouche allait employer contre elle le bélier Gide qui allait rentrer d'Alger dès que le terrain serait déminé, puis une machine infernale ferait tout sauter. Doyon connaissait bien Paulhan, encore plus éminence grise et directeur de conscience des lettres françaises depuis le rôle qu'il avait joué dans la Résistance. Il mit Amrouche en garde : Paulhan avait plus d'un tour dans son sac et Amrouche, encore inexpérimenté dans la jungle parisienne, avait trop besoin d'argent pour mener combat contre de telles puissances. Charlot en était conscient et usait de modération : Camus représentait à la fois protection et danger. Il dirigeait encore aux éditions Charlot une collection « Poésie et théâtre », mais comment pouvait-il l'animer, pris désormais par tant d'obligations chez Gallimard et à *Combat* ? D'après Doyon qui ne manquait pas de bon sens quand il s'agissait des autres, Camus ne laisserait pas Amrouche, nouveau venu en tout avec un appétit qui effrayait, démolir la *NRF* où brillait l'intelligentsia.

Mon admiration débordante pour Camus fut, pour Amrouche, un désenchantement. Aussitôt nos relations en furent altérées. Charlot avait un programme d'éditeur ambitieux, il avait avec lui une solide équipe de compagnons. Amrouche se mit de lui-même à la tête de tout et les jours suivirent leur cours.

La veille du 14 Juillet, il y eut partout des bals, des projecteurs qui touillaient la nuit, des retraites aux flambeaux. Dans la journée, avec les drapeaux, Paris ressemblait à un avril en fleur. Ma merveille était avec moi, je croyais n'avoir plus rien à envier à cette Edith Piaf qui naviguait âprement dans l'enfer. Pour moi c'était autre chose. On se débattait contre moi, tout en m'aimant. Nulle fête, nulle sortie qui ne tournât

au drame. Deux années de délire vont se déchirer ainsi dans un tourbillon. L'amour, quelle plaie !

Tout à coup, en plein été, éclata le procès du maréchal Pétain. Nous feignîmes d'ignorer ce qui se passait au Palais de justice. Dans son fauteuil d'accusé, triste roi shakespearien de quatre-vint-dix ans, il se taisait. Presque sourd, il somnolait dans la chaleur et les éclats de voix. J'avais honte pour lui et pour ceux qui obligeaient à comparaître l'ancien vainqueur de Verdun devant un tribunal. Oui, mais il avait intrigué pour devenir chef de l'Etat. Il portait à présent les péchés de la France comme il avait jadis porté sa gloire. Etait-ce sa faute si, devenu vieux, il avait cru pouvoir éviter des calamités hors de mesure avec ses forces ? Avait-il vraiment voulu le trône ? N'avait-il pas essayé d'être le père de la nation en douleur ? N'avait-il pas été, partout où il allait, acclamé ? Il avait choisi pour nous le moindre mal, le moindre risque, le moindre déshonneur, et nous avait fait avaler trop de couleuvres.
La vérité était ailleurs. A la place du roi rebelle victorieux, je l'aurais laissé, à l'écart des extrémistes, s'éteindre en paix. Dans l'armée, on se taisait comme devant une tombe. Au mess, jamais un mot, jamais une allusion. Nous lisions fiévreusement le compte rendu des débats dans les journaux.
Le 6 août 1945, en plein procès, explosa la bombe atomique d'Hiroshima. Le Japon écrasé, la guerre était finie. Le monde entier se réjouit qu'une arme d'une telle puissance décidât désormais de la paix. Personne ne pensa qu'elle pouvait aussi provoquer la guerre. Sauf Camus, qui entrevoyait des perspectives terrifiantes. Seul dans toute la presse, il écrivit dans *Combat* du 8 août 1945 : « La civilisation mécanique vient de parvenir à son dernier degré de sauvagerie. Il va falloir choisir, dans un avenir plus ou moins proche, entre le suicide collectif ou l'utilisation intelligente des conquêtes scientifiques. »
Au bureau Etudes et Plans, nous nous agitions. Le colonel Badré approuva l'éditorial de *Combat*. J'avais là un camarade, Jean Accart, qui, après avoir remporté plusieurs victoires au début de la guerre, avait été abattu d'une balle de mitrailleuse dans l'œil. On l'avait sauvé. La balle s'était logée derrière l'orbite et il n'avait pas voulu que le chirurgien l'enlève pour ne pas diminuer une acuité visuelle dont l'intégralité est nécessaire au chasseur, et, en effet, il avait

continué à envoyer des adversaires au tapis. La balle est toujours derrière l'œil gauche, une énorme cicatrice lui scie le front en deux et son regard flotte. Pareil à un grand-duc débonnaire, il semblait toujours se réveiller d'un cauchemar et s'étonner d'être encore en vie, mais son regard avait des reflets d'acier. Ensemble nous allâmes en Allemagne où nous méditâmes sur des ruines.

Gide rentra d'Alger par un transport militaire. Amrouche m'avait demandé d'intervenir. Le chef d'état-major me confia sa voiture, son chauffeur et un mot d'hommage pour l'illustre écrivain. Amrouche et moi allâmes l'attendre à Orly et le déposâmes rue Vaneau. Amrouche porta ses valises jusqu'au cinquième où toute la tribu attendait. Je n'osai pas m'imposer, je m'en fus.

L'appartement que, grâce à Doyon, j'avais obtenu était situé non loin, dans le quartier des Invalides, dans un immeuble cossu. Sans doute mon petit père m'avait-il dépeint à son admirateur comme une des futures étoiles de l'armée et de la littérature. J'achetai des sommiers, des matelas, une bibliothèque d'occasion, une table. Une des chambres ouvrait sur le jardin du ministère des Colonies, je m'y installai avec un poêle de Turpin, ami de Doyon et qu'on appelait l'archevêque, fabricant de poêles en tôle mince, dits « à combustion continue », ce qui n'était qu'à demi vrai, et m'attelai aussitôt au récit que m'avait demandé Amrouche. Psichari m'inspirait, Amrouche me pressait, à ma cadence je tins un long procès-verbal minutieux d'un de nos raids. Il me tardait de quitter mon travail à l'état-major pour courir au métro. Je changeais à la Motte-Picquet-Grenelle, descendais à Duroc, achetais *le Monde*, des tomates, des pâtes, une tranche d' jambon et rentrais chez moi, presque en face de l'hôtel des Jeunes Aveugles. Je mesurais mal l'aubaine que mon petit père m'avait value, j'osais même regretter d'habiter un premier étage un peu sombre, sauf pour les pièces qui ouvraient sur le jardin des Colonies. Quelquefois, ma merveille passait, nous dînions dans un boui-boui de la rue de Babylone. Amrouche disait qu'à mon retour d'Angleterre je ressemblais à un spectre et qu'à présent je rayonnais.

Des commissions d'enquête sur les événements de Sétif, il ressortait que la répression avait été atroce. Les tirailleurs

algériens démobilisés de la 1re Armée ne pardonnaient pas ces abominations à la France, et cependant la presse faisait silence. Il y avait trop de problèmes pour s'embarrasser dans celui-là. On pensait qu'à la longue les choses s'arrangeraient d'elles-mêmes. On oubliait que les indigènes embrigadés dans cette nouvelle guerre ne supportaient plus d'être traités comme avant. Je ne sais pourquoi la conclusion de la série d'articles de Camus dans *Combat* me déçut. Elle était telle que l'opinion du pays, encore peu éclairée, pouvait l'accepter : « Tout ce que nous pouvons faire pour la vérité, française et humaine, écrivait Camus, nous avons à le faire contre la haine. A tout prix, il faut apaiser ces peuples déchirés et tourmentés par de trop longues souffrances. Pour nous, du moins, tâchons de ne rien ajouter aux rancœurs... C'est la force infinie de la justice, et elle seule, qui doit nous aider à reconquérir l'Algérie et ses habitants. » A ses yeux, l'Algérie était sinon perdue, du moins en voie de l'être. Il parlait aussi de « ces peuples » qui n'avaient pas le droit de vote puisque les trois départements d'Algérie n'octroyaient de droits qu'aux Européens. Il demandait du pain, il dénonçait les coupables, et de quelle voix ! Quelque chose s'était passé en moi que je discernais mal, qui me disait que je ne pouvais plus ne pas me souvenir de Meftah, l'ancien serviteur arabe de mon enfance. L'oncle Jules n'était plus, ma mère s'enfonçait dans la pénombre, une autre ère commençait dont j'étais, par hasard, le témoin. Et Meftah ? Et sa descendance ? J'aurais aimé que Camus parlât de fraternité. Puisqu'il s'agissait de reconquête, pourquoi ne pas étendre la citoyenneté à ceux qui avaient laissé leurs os à Cassino, et surtout à ceux qui, de retour chez eux, dans leurs montagnes, butaient sur des ruines encore fumantes ?

Cette question, je n'osai même pas m'en ouvrir à Amrouche. Qu'en pensait Gide ? Un jour qu'avec Jean Denoël j'allais à un dîner de *l'Arche,* près de la rue Vaneau, nous le croisâmes qui rentrait chez lui, cassé, flottant dans un complet à carreaux gris, sa cape sur les épaules, son galurin sur le crâne, le visage terriblement marqué, la poitrine creusée. Il n'avait pourtant que soixante-seize ans.

Ce ne fut qu'en octobre que je rencontrai enfin Camus à un dîner chez Labarthe avec Roger Caillois. Comment

n'aurais-je pas noté cette date-là ? Ce soir-là, je pus l'observer tout à mon aise et m'éprendre pour lui d'un amour qui dure encore. Il était arrivé contracté. « Comme toujours quand je ne vais pas chez des amis », me dira-t-il plus tard. Il se méfiait et croyait qu'on allait l'attaquer. L'intelligentsia parisienne pouvait-elle accepter ce produit de Belcourt né d'un père commis de ferme à Saint-Pierre-Saint-Paul, commune de Mondovi, département de Constantine, et d'une Espagnole illettrée ? Son cheminement : l'école publique puis le lycée Bugeaud et la faculté d'Alger grâce à des bourses, la galère d'*Alger républicain* puis de *Paris-Soir* sous l'Occupation et enfin *Combat*, n'aboutissait pas à des chaires en Sorbonne, où les lumières brillent de tous leurs feux. Sur ses gardes, il ne se livrait d'abord qu'à demi. De moi, il ne redoutait rien, mais d'instinct, avec les autres, il croisait le fer. Sur les problèmes du moment, il relevait à sa façon les idées des maîtres comme un chef cuisinier de génie tire du magique de la vulgaire matière brute. Caillois lui-même ne cacha pas qu'il était ébloui.

Je serais incapable de parler de Camus philosophe philosophant, analyste et critique des philosophes philosophant. C'était quoi, pour lui, la philosophie ? Comme pour Diderot : d'abord douter. Il eût tôt fait de séduire Sartre, Aron, Merleau-Ponty et Gabriel Marcel. Jamais cependant les professeurs et magisters ne le reconnurent comme leur égal et n'eurent pour lui autre chose qu'une condescendance parfois amicale, eux qui ne connaissaient rien à l'amitié. Il ne sortait pas comme eux de la rue d'Ulm, il n'était pas agrégé et n'enseignait pas au Collège de France. Il devait au charme de son esprit et de sa personne le succès populaire qu'un vrai philosophe envie mais ne touche qu'avec des pincettes. La masse peut-elle comprendre les subtilités de l'art ? La masse devait se contenter d'applaudir, le savoir-faire de ces messieurs consistant à transformer le langage raffiné en langage vulgaire, épicé juste ce qu'il faut pour le rendre perceptible aux élèves de l'enseignement supérieur en le laissant fermé aux autres ? Ce soir-là, Caillois joua avec des pierres et des civilisations d'au-delà des mers tropicales. Sa virtuosité séduisait. Il jonglait avec les astéroïdes et les couleurs minérales, il envoûtait, tandis que Camus se tint résolument hors de toute poésie et fit preuve d'une rigueur sans faille.

Nous revînmes à pied, Camus et moi, des jardins du Luxembourg à la rue du Bac. A cette époque, il n'y avait pas de taxis, pas de voitures, on marchait, on parlait, on ouvrait son cœur. Je n'eus pas de peine à ouvrir le mien, déjà conquis. Nous étions du même pays, des mêmes hommes et des mêmes femmes, du même soleil. Sans autre raison que l'élan qui me portait vers lui, je devins son disciple, son ami dévoué, son féal. Le mot de messie que j'ai placé trop tôt plus haut, est exagéré, mais ceux qui ont connu et aimé Camus me comprendront. Il était celui que nous attendions.

Quelques jours plus tard, le numéro 9 de *l'Arche* paraissait sous le patronage de Gide et avec un sommaire imposant : Jean Hytier, Virginia Woolf, Antonio Machado, Ludwig Ullmann, Maurice Blanchot, Jean Grenier, Jacques Lemarchand, René Leibowitz, Pierre Desgraupes, Dominique Aury, Denis Marion, puis mon récit et une étude sur Olivier Messiaen, avec qui il me sembla que je remontais à bicyclette des orgues de Bar-sur-Aube. Presque aussitôt, Amrouche reçut un coup de téléphone de Roger Martin du Gard le félicitant de ce que j'avais écrit et une lettre de Pierre Jean Jouve qui me convoquait chez lui.

Il habitait rue des Plantes, près de la porte de Châtillon, un appartement au plus haut. C'était un jour d'été. Dans son vaste cabinet de travail aux persiennes tirées, des rideaux or pâle diffusaient une lumière glauque. La pièce était nue, meublée seulement d'une longue table luisante au plateau vide. Immense, filiforme, inquiétant, il s'assit sur une chaise à dossier droit et me fit asseoir devant lui. Effilée d'abord, rase comme ses lèvres et ses joues, sa longue tête enflait comme de majesté son crâne. Son regard me terrifia. D'une voix blanche, il me dit que je venais de publier quelque chose dont je ne mesurais peut-être pas l'importance, que la littérature avait besoin de témoignages comme le mien, mais que c'était insuffisant. Il fallait me plonger dans le sujet comme si j'entrais en religion. Je crus entendre un ordre d'En-Haut. Mon style était bon. Il fallait en surveiller le dépouillement, sauf dans les moments de lyrisme stellaire. « Ça se passait bien comme ça ? me demanda-t-il. J'ai bien devant moi un des hommes qui ont vécu ces nuits-là ? » Je crus pouvoir lui répondre oui. « Alors,

c'est vous que j'entendais gronder dans les ténèbres, c'est pour vous que j'ai écrit mes poèmes. J'ai cru. Vous voilà. »

Son regard devint doux et chaleureux. Pour lui, mon récit de *l'Arche* n'était que le début de ce qu'il attendait. J'allais écrire le livre de l'Apocalypse contre l'Antéchrist. « Combien de temps vous faudra-t-il ? » Je ne savais pas. Il me commanda de réfléchir avec minutie à tout ce que j'avais vu et ressenti. Je devais tout dire, absolument tout, ce n'était qu'à ce prix-là que mon livre aurait de la valeur, il m'écrirait une préface pour que tout fût clair, je ne devais me laisser distraire par rien. Il me fixa un nouveau rendez-vous huit jours plus tard et nota la date dans un carnet. « Vous aurez écrit un nouveau chapitre. Nous le lirons ensemble. »

Je sortis de chez lui comme pris de vertige. J'avais des ailes, je ne m'appartenais plus. Je courus chez moi. J'avais tellement hâte à dégorger ce qui m'étouffait que je négligeai pour une fois la plume et le papier. Je me mis à taper furieusement à la machine tout ce qui m'arrivait au cœur et à la mémoire en pulsations serrées.

Le monde sortait de la guerre, de la nuit, pas encore du froid. Les privations duraient, mais pas celle du bonheur. Saint-Germain-des-Prés resplendissait comme le quartier des libertés. Je le jugeais même comme le royaume d'une licence qui me scandalisait souvent. Depuis notre première rencontre, Camus et moi ne nous quittions plus guère. J'exagère en disant « nous ». Il avait un culte pour l'amitié et s'il ne provoquait pas les occasions de nous retrouver, il les saisissait avec empressement. Nous dînions souvent ensemble, la bande à Charlot et lui, une fraternité se nouait, nous nous plongions avec délices dans l'atmosphère qui régnait, les jeunes femmes qu'on rencontrait là étaient belles, vives surtout. Nous n'avions pas le sou, même Camus qui n'aurait jamais, par fierté, osé demander quoi que ce soit à Gallimard. A *Combat*, j'aurais compris, mais chez Gallimard ? Est-ce que l'argent comptait ? Nous avions le meilleur de ce que nous voulions, et nous partagions tout, au besoin les amours qui ne furent jamais un obstacle. Marie se glissait souvent parmi nous. Elle admirait Camus et se méfiait d'Amrouche. Son bonheur était

d'accompagner Camus à la Rose Rouge. Anne-Marie Cazalis et Juliette Gréco y chantaient, et régnaient au Tabou, prêtresses de cette cave où je ne me sentais pas à l'aise parce qu'on ne m'avait jamais appris à me trémousser. Camus, c'était Dionysos, un dieu l'habitait, il dansait, il inventait des mouvements, des figures. Je jalousais son aisance et sa fureur à se contorsionner. Marie l'imitait, parfois face à lui ou dans ses bras. Alors, je me montrais amer. « Allons, Julius, disait-elle, secouez-vous ! » Ça me mettait en rage. Elle rompait avec tout, avec un premier mariage, avec la maladie et des difficultés de toute sorte ; elle explosait avec tant de passion que je croyais qu'elle se libérait aussi de moi. J'avais horreur qu'elle s'exhibât dans cette cohue où la bande à Charlot croyait plonger au cœur de ce qu'on appelait le niou-louque, comme si on distribuait là des passeports pour le succès. Amrouche s'abstenait. La Rose Rouge ou le Tabou, il trouvait que ce n'était pas sa place de directeur de *l'Arche*. Quand j'en avais assez, humilié et jaloux, je rentrais chez moi en croisant des noctambules qui menaient un train bruyant à bord de véhicules excentriques et me mettais au travail avec rage.

J'avais commencé par la collision en vol, tout au début, et j'introduisis d'autres personnages que les membres de mon équipage : Gallois que j'appelais Morin, le Barbu, le colonel pour qui je n'étais pas tendre. Les cadences du Tabou dans la tête, hanté par l'idée que Marie me trompait, je continuais furieusement le chapitre commencé. Depuis le commandement de Pierre Jean Jouve, j'avais scrupule à me montrer digne de l'idée qu'il pouvait avoir de moi. L'ambition m'électrisait. Jouve à qui j'allais montrer ma copie m'éperonnait. Encore, encore ! Il me fallait puiser au plus profond, éviter les clichés, révéler la splendeur des ténèbres en feu. « Et si j'avais eu peur ? » demandai-je. « Eh bien, répondait-il, qui n'aurait peur devant la face de l'Antéchrist ou la face de Dieu ? » Je devais me souvenir de tout ce qui nouait notre gorge, des frayeurs, des silences, des brasiers, des tueries. Je devais, je devais. Quand nous étions perdus, ne nous guidions-nous pas sur les astres ? N'étions-nous pas des explorateurs sidéraux, des compagnons de prophètes à cheval sur des versets de la Bible ? des anges de la colère divine ? Oui, les étoiles avaient été nos compagnes, nous les guettions, que de fois je braquai mon sextant sur la brillante Aldébaran. Plus tard, je me

souviendrai d'elle. Elle jouera un rôle dans *les Chevaux du Soleil* : elle sera l'œil du taureau.

Mon récit avançait, le cours de la vie reprenait, j'aimais Marie à la folie. Mon camarade Accart au crâne fendu et à la balle de mitrailleuse dans l'œil menait une existence familiale retirée, presque pieuse. Nous repartions parfois ensemble vers le Rhin, pour célébrer des héros morts. Je rêvais de recevoir la récompense du guerrier, toujours la même depuis toujours : une belle gretchen à tresses blondes dans mon lit. Hélas, nous avions massacré de haut, nous restions dans les altitudes, sans voir ni le visage de nos ennemis, ni nos amours du lendemain. A Marin La Meslée tombé en Alsace, l'armée de l'air avait élevé un monument en forme d'étoile. Nous nous rassemblâmes comme pour suivre jusqu'au bout un des compagnons du roi Arthur. Marin La Meslée c'était Galaad. Murtin était là, figé sur une jambe de bois qu'il essayait de manœuvrer. Notre cortège funèbre traversa des plaines, puis des forêts. De belles filles en robe rouge et à nœud de velours noir dans les cheveux pleuraient. Le tonnerre nous accompagnait. C'était au moment où le général de Gaulle quittait le gouvernement et se retirait à Colombey. Nous ne l'aimions pas tellement. Nous nous demandions si, le 16 juin 1940, il n'était pas parti pour la Grande-Bretagne sur un mouvement d'humeur personnelle, dans la certitude où il était que le maréchal Pétain ne le prendrait pas dans son gouvernement. Chez nous, ce fut le même silence qu'au procès Pétain. Motus. La France se divisa et se déchira. De Gaulle crut la reconquérir par des discours.

Peut-être parce qu'il ne voulait pas se compromettre aux yeux du nouveau gouvernement ou qu'il estimait qu'il n'avait plus rien à attendre du général de Gaulle, le nouveau chef d'état-major me désigna, moi, simple commandant, pour le représenter. Quelques jours plus tôt, il m'avait demandé d'être son aide de camp : j'avais refusé, par prudence, pour éviter des embarras quand mon livre paraîtrait. Pierre Jean Jouve m'avait ordonné de tout dire et l'armée faisait obligation de lui soumettre tous les textes qui la concernaient. Telle n'était pas mon intention. Je préférai agir par indiscipline en ne sollicitant pas une autorisation qui m'aurait été refusée, que par insubordination en passant outre. Quoi qu'il en soit, ma désignation pour Bayeux fut pour moi l'occasion unique de figurer en

uniforme au pied de la tribune. J'avais emmené Amrouche avec moi. Nous fûmes enfin, moi du moins, à quelques pas du monstre sacré. Il m'apparut comme dans la masse d'un bourgeois de Calais de Rodin, avec un crâne étonnamment petit aux cheveux plaqués, aux tempes à peine argentées et une fine moustache que je vis blonde. Le buste haut et large s'étalait au-dessus de son grand corps filiforme. Il ne savait que faire de ses longs bras maigres ni des poings qu'il serrait. Son discours austère, qui passe pour un de ses meilleurs, s'ennuageait dans l'Histoire et m'ennuya. Peut-être parce qu'il pleuvait? Dans les rues de Bayeux on l'acclama. Il y eut quelques timides cris : « Au pouvoir !... » qu'il apprécia. Trop tard. Il n'y était plus, il devait déjà le regretter, mais aussi pourquoi être parti? J'entendis une femme s'exclamer à l'étonnement de tous : « Qu'il est gracieux... » Imperturbable sous le crachin, il s'arrêta et se courba pour caresser des enfants que le flot humain avait renversés. Malraux devait être là, j'aurais dû le chercher. Le bruit courait qu'avant de quitter sa brigade Alsace-Lorraine, il avait surgi dans la cour de l'hôtel Gallimard avec deux tractions de miliciens et qu'il était reparti avec des valises bourrées de millions de l'époque. C'était le style Malraux, cynique au besoin et sans scrupule. Camus n'aurait jamais fait cela. Il avait de lui-même une idée trop sublime. Un peu janséniste. Plus que la cathédrale de Bayeux, j'admirai un platane gigantesque, arbre de la liberté planté en 1797, intact et solitaire au milieu des carcasses calcinées de chars qui bordaient encore les routes et les forêts hachées. Cet arbre ressemblait à de Gaulle.

Le soir, Amrouche et moi nous arrêtâmes à Verneuil chez Marcel Sauvage tout menu, tout frêle. Amrouche voyait en de Gaulle le recours suprême de la France et cependant, c'était de Gaulle qui avait ordonné la répression de Sétif. « Parce qu'il ignore tout du problème », répondit Amrouche qui nourrissait le dessein de devenir son conseiller pour les affaires algériennes. Nous allâmes visiter Vlaminck, qui possédait là une opulente ferme normande, regorgeant de volailles, de cochons, de vaches, de beurre et de toutes sortes de merveilles qu'il essayait de cacher à un moment où l'on manquait de tout. Il jouait presque au pauvre. Peintre célèbre, il vendait cher ses toiles. Se méfia-t-il de moi? Lui qui ne s'était pas battu, il avait du bien à sauver. C'était l'heure du déjeuner, il ne nous offrit

même pas un verre de vin et nous barba de vues vaseuses sur la vie, le travail, la peine, le talent. On le volait, on le volait, répétait-il. Avec tous les malins de l'époque, il était allé à Berlin où il avait, disait-il, plaidé pour la paix, il plaignait l'humanité. Il était gras, cynique, orgueilleux et inquiet. A mon retour à Paris, je lui envoyai une lettre irritée et arrogante, dont j'ai retrouvé le brouillon et qui se terminait ainsi : « Sur ce, j'ai bien l'honneur de vous saluer, vous, M. de Vlaminck, vos trésors, vos fermes, vos troupeaux et vos chiens. » J'ai précieusement gardé sa réponse à lui, d'une graphie épaisse de plume d'oie. Il était ulcéré. J'étais radieux.

« Ah ! que la victoire demeure avec ceux qui auront fait la guerre sans l'aimer. » Ce cri insolite et presque attendrissant chez lui, pour qui l'attendrissement est une faiblesse, Malraux le pousse à propos de Lawrence d'Arabie. Il pense peut-être aussi à lui, quand il se jetait en imagination dans la révolution chinoise, quand il se voyait déjà gouverneur de l'Espagne en survolant Teruel dans un Potez 540, ou encore quand il se tournait vers l'évangile selon saint Jean au moment des *Antimémoires* où il décrit son simulacre d'exécution. « Etait-ce cette nuit que nous allions mourir ? » Nous nous étions assez posé la question. Nous en sortions, et je passerai une longue partie de ma vie à ressasser tout cela. Dans mon roman *le Désert de Retz*, j'ai tout rassemblé : portant un nom allemand, Krieg, et rescapé de la chute de mon avion abattu, j'échoue, en pleine nuit de neige, chez un hobereau prussien au nom d'exilé français, Doncœur, et nous finissons tous par être écrasés sous un nouveau bombardement de la RAF. La guerre m'a longtemps roulé dans ses pattes comme un lion qui s'apprête à dévorer sa proie et s'en amuse un peu. Il arrive qu'un hasard se produise et que la proie échappe, avec de la chance. Sur ce plan-là, j'en ai eu beaucoup, de la chance.

A présent, j'ai plus de quatre-vingts ans, l'âge où l'on n'est plu capable d'écrire des romans parce que le flux créateur et les forces physiques vous ont quitté, hein pépère ? A des moments, je crains même de n'arriver jamais au bout de ces Mémoires. Devant moi les brumes d'une nouvelle aube se dégagent des vallées et s'enroulent autour des collines et des

forêts. Notre rocher devient une île. Les saisons parfois s'entremêlent ou se bousculent. Les gens disent que c'est la faute de la bombe. Il n'y a pas si longtemps c'était la faute de l'artillerie et de l'aviation. Il arrive qu'une simple centrale nucléaire se détraque et lâche dans le ciel des menaces de cancers et d'agonies. Que serait-ce si, par erreur d'un lampiste, folie d'un homme politique ou d'un général, de vraies fusées chargées de vraies ogives atomiques s'échappaient de chez nous ou d'ailleurs et réduisaient en cendres une ville ou deux pendant que des équipes de télévision enregistreraient de petites femmes nues se trémoussant pour une lessive ? Cela arrivera fatalement, et autrement qu'au cinéma. Le nuage d'une centrale détraquée serait peu de chose à côté du ciel zébré de flammes qui recouvrira le globe terrestre, l'isolera du soleil et répandra la mort et le froid glaciaire, *Apocalypse now* ? *Apocalypse nunc et semper in saecula saeculorum.*

C'est moins cela que je crains à mon âge que de quitter ce à quoi, vieux fripon, je suis attaché, mais il le faut. Si l'homme ne mourait pas, où logerait-on nos multicentenaires et nos amours ? Nos amours ratatinées seraient dans des fauteuils roulants. Fini le temps des cerises ! Continuons. Depuis ma naissance, je n'ai vécu qu'au milieu des forces brutales : la Mitidja avec les colons et les Arabes, le séminaire où, d'une terrasse de terre rouge, je contemplais les morts grimpant à l'assaut de la colline, l'armée où l'on m'a enseigné à imposer l'injustice, parfois par le fer et le feu. A présent, Pierre Jean Jouve, poète et mage au crâne rasé, pointait sur moi un doigt d'où jaillissait la foudre. Me voilà errant des caves du Tabou aux lisières de la Forêt noire, enrageant quand ma belle me fuit.

Est-ce Camus qui me demanda d'envoyer quelque chose à *Combat* ? Un jour, je vis paraître un éditorial de moi sur le prix dont nous avions payé nos bombardements de la Ruhr. Que n'ai-je raconté ma visite à Vlaminck ! Il était admis que seuls les bombardés payaient. Les bombardants devaient casquer : cinq cents tonnes de cellules, de moteurs, d'instruments de précision et une soixantaine de vies humaines en douze équipages pour mille tonnes de TNT et de phosphore lâchées. Entre les bouchers classiques et les petits cochons roses qu'on offrait maintenant après Hiroshima aux expériences de Bikini, nous avions servi d'intermédiaires... Cette

page de moi dans *Combat* me rendit fou d'orgueil, puis *la Vallée heureuse* parut dans *le Monde* en feuilleton. Le journal l'annonçait comme « l'extraordinaire épopée nocturne des bombardiers de la RAF » et publiait un extrait de la préface de Pierre Jean Jouve. Finalement j'avais choisi pour titre le nom que les Anglais donnaient à la Ruhr, *the Happy Valley*. Amrouche avait négocié la publication dans le journal qui remplaçait *le Temps*, interdit pour collaboration. *Le Monde* ne payait pas, ou si peu que rien, mais c'était la notoriété. J'en doutai. C'était vrai. Je fus surpris par les réactions que je suscitai.

Presque aussitôt je fus convoqué par le chef du bureau Etudes et Plans où, en souriant, le colonel Badré me notifia la punition que m'infligeait le nouveau chef d'état-major, un pète-sec : quinze jours d'arrêts de rigueur pour mes articles de *Combat* et du *Monde* parus sans autorisation. « Vous vous y attendiez, j'espère », dit-il. Aussitôt je mis dans la confidence mon camarade Accart. Il tourna vers moi sa face tourmentée et, avec attendrissement : « Allons arroser ça. »

J'en profitai pour rester chez moi comme le règlement l'exigeait. J'avais le téléphone, je n'étais pas puni d'arrêts de forteresse, je pouvais faire mes courses, Charlot m'apporta de grosses fausses moustaches grises. En civil et avec ça, aucun militaire ne pouvait me reconnaître à la terrasse des Deux-Magots. Ces quinze jours furent des vacances, et quand je retournai à l'état-major, je constatai un changement. On s'arrachait *le Monde*, mais certains de mes camarades des autres bureaux m'évitaient. Un ancien bombardier d'Elvington me dit que je l'avais déshonoré. J'en fus bêtement atteint, j'entendrai la même formule toute ma vie. On vient encore de me la jeter à la face récemment à propos de mon livre *Guynemer, l'ange de la mort* ; j'ai lu, dans des bulletins d'anciens pilotes de chasse, des appréciations qui correspondent à une certaine éthique sans quoi il n'y aurait pas, croit-on, d'élite militaire. D'abord je pris la plume pour me justifier, puis j'y renonçai : la mission des chasseurs est bien de détruire l'adversaire et donc de tuer, et le nec plus ultra de la méthode enseignée dans les écoles spécialisées est bien d'attaquer l'ennemi par surprise et par-derrière. Je ne vois donc pas la honte qu'il y a à ça en temps de guerre : les Messerschmitt n'agissaient pas autrement avec nous. A l'état-major, un autre

de mes camarades d'Angleterre refusa de me serrer la main parce que j'avais osé dire que j'avais eu peur : un officier n'a pas peur. Je commençai à me demander si je n'avais pas desservi l'armée et trahi un honneur. Quelqu'un d'aussi chatouilleux sur ce plan que Pierre Jean Jouve me l'aurait dit.

Comme le papier manquait et que les journaux sortaient sur peu de pages, par deux fois le feuilleton ne parut pas, la seconde fois pendant trois jours. On crut que j'avais été interdit. Mais non. Le journal alla jusqu'à la fin de mon récit. Chez mon éditeur, on prétendait que le tirage du *Monde* avait augmenté.

Henri Bosco me parlait souvent de Lourmarin où, depuis son départ du Maroc, il vivait. Charlot avait publié avec succès son roman *le Mas Théotime* dont l'action se passait dans le Lubéron. Bosco insistait pour que je vienne et que j'amène Amrouche et Camus.

Le nom de Lourmarin était déjà magique. Poussé par Marie qui avait là-bas des attaches, Camus accepta, Amrouche aussi. Comme des potaches en vacances, nous partîmes tous les quatre, pleins de joie, à la fin de septembre 1946, par un train du soir, en troisième classe. Le compartiment était bondé. Par excentricité, je me hissai dans le filet à bagages où je ne pus tenir. J'étais trop grand, les tringles m'entraient dans les reins. A l'aube nous étions à Avignon, nous respirions une douceur : les cyprès, les toits de tuiles romaines, c'était l'Algérie. Bosco n'avait envoyé personne nous chercher, et comme les taxis étaient trop chers, nous attendîmes le car. Amrouche voulut savoir ce que Camus pensait de *la Vallée heureuse* qui allait paraître. Pour lui, le livre risquait de provoquer le même bruit que *la Condition humaine,* car je mettais en question la morale et les idées reçues à propos de la guerre. Mon témoignage tirait sa valeur de l'innocence avec laquelle mon héros accomplissait les actes les plus condamnables et les plus horribles de son métier. Marie me considéra, subjuguée. J'étais fier.

Sur la colline devant le village, le château ressemblait au dessin du papier à lettres de Bosco : une façade Renaissance entre des tours puissantes. Sa devise *E cinere phoenix* le

définissait renaissant de ses cendres. Un mécène, l'inventeur du pétrole Hahn, l'avait restauré entre des oliviers au feuillage brillant et un fouillis de géraniums et d'arums. Les pierres avaient la couleur de la lumière, les figues étaient mûres. Bosco habitait le logement des gardiens, et sa femme, que Camus appela tout de suite « la chaisière », nous répéta que le ravitaillement était difficile et qu'on ne trouvait d'aide nulle part. Je ne reconnus pas en Bosco l'homme qui s'était montré si généreux dans ses lettres. Je l'aimais, j'aurais voulu que Camus l'aimât aussi. Sans même songer à nous offrir une tasse de café, il nous distribua dans des chambres merveilleuses et nous mit en garde contre les monstres dont le pays, disait-il, était infesté. Dans le château devenu musée, il nous recommanda de ne rien déranger, de ne toucher à rien. On aurait dit qu'il se méfiait. De qui, de quoi ? Il y avait une telle distance entre le portrait que j'avais brossé de lui et le personnage, que Camus fut outré. « Ton Bosco est un pignouf », me lança-t-il dans un ricanement féroce. Amrouche se régalait de cette brouille. A la façon dont on nous observa, je supposai qu'on se demandait comment un jeune homme comme Camus avait pu avec l'*Etranger,* un livre si mince, conquérir si vite la gloire. Après tant d'années de labeur et au bout d'une œuvre déjà longue, Bosco venait seulement de recevoir le prix Renaudot. Encore le nom de Giono brillait-il d'un éclat plus vif que le sien.

Au village, nous bûmes sans lui du pastis sous les platanes près de la fontaine. A l'hôtel Ollier, les tables, assiégées par les chiens et les chats, ployaient sous les gigots et les omelettes aux truffes. Là, nous apprîmes que des bohémiens, mal reçus jadis au château, avaient jeté un sort à certaines chambres. Lesquelles ? On ne sut pas nous dire, et comme nous prenions cela un peu à la légère, on nous recommanda de nous méfier. Meurtri par le peu d'élan de Bosco, Camus déclara qu'il repartait le lendemain. J'essayai en vain de le retenir. Amrouche l'approuva et l'imita.

A l'aube, nous les accompagnâmes aussi loin que nous pûmes, puis nous revînmes, Marie et moi. Le soir, le château était brûlant. On dormait nus. Un orage tonnait. Il me sembla encore que nous étions au pied du Sinaï où Dieu se faisait entendre. Quel culot ! Dieu, c'était Marie. Nous nous gorgions d'amour, de ragoûts de mouton, de figues gluantes de

miel. Dans le sauvage Lubéron nous visitâmes des abbayes en
ruine transformées en bergeries. On vendangeait, les vignes
étaient toutes rouges, on aurait cru aussi que le vin coulait en
nous, nous nous mîmes à rêver là d'un toit. Jean Grenier, ce
doux philosophe radieux, avait publié une plaquette dans
laquelle il appliquait à la Provence la devise gravée sur les
portes du château de la Tour d'Aigues : *Satiabor cum
apparuerit.* il s'agissait de Marguerite de Valois. « Qu'elle
m'apparaisse seulement et je serai comblé. » Pour moi, je priai
Dieu de ne pas l'être, comblé, sauf après un bon repas.
Comblé d'amour ? Jamais.

Il y avait un secret qui ne se dissipa que peu à peu. Nous
finîmes par savoir que Camus était déjà venu à Lourmarin, en
1936, avec Simone Hié, la belle fille d'Alger qu'il avait enlevée
à Max-Pol Fouchet. Ils ne pouvaient plus vivre ensemble, il
allait rompre avec elle. Pourquoi Lourmarin ? Parce que,
justement, son maître en philosophie Jean Grenier avait parlé
de ce lieu comme d'un paradis. Avec Simone Hié, Camus
voulait essayer une dernière fois. Quand nous y allâmes
ensemble, tous les quatre, Camus ne nous en dit rien. De
même, il ne parla jamais à aucun de nous de Simone Hié, pour
lui une brûlure. Qui sait ? Il était peut-être revenu avec nous
pour retrouver son image et c'était une chaisière qui l'avait
accueilli. Plus tard, il y retourna encore sans nous, toujours en
secret.

Montherlant avait des ennuis. C'était moins Pétain qu'il
avait célébré dans ses ouvrages récents que le nouvel ordre, les
cérémonies avec flambeaux, chants sacrés et pas de l'oie. On
l'excommunia du Comité des écrivains comme un pestiféré.
Au moins avait-il eu le courage de dire à ses compatriotes
qu'ils ne comptaient plus pour grand-chose, que le sang qui
coulait dans leurs veines était du jus de carotte et la France le
pays des midinettes. Tant d'écrivains s'étaient terrés pendant
la guerre. Je lui écrivis. Il me fixa un rendez-vous dans son
nouvel appartement, quai Voltaire, non loin du pont du
Carrousel, un jour de cet hiver précoce. J'étais en battle-dress
d'aviateur.

S'était-il jamais montré chaleureux avec moi ? Il n'aimait

personne que lui, et encore. Contracté, distant, il me fit asseoir dans sa fameuse entrée encombrée de sièges lourds et de masques romains, en pleine lumière, face aux bouquinistes du quai. Il faisait très froid. Il me laissa entendre que le reste de l'appartement était chauffé. J'en conclus qu'il avait hâte de me voir partir.

« Vous êtes allé à Weimar », lui dis-je doucement. Il bondit. Ce n'était pas vrai. Longuement, âprement, il me dit qu'il s'était contenté d'écrire dans les journaux collaborationnistes, puisque écrire était un besoin chez lui comme pour tant d'autres, mais que l'argent qu'il avait reçu « des Boches » (terme qu'il employa), il l'avait versé à la Croix-Rouge de Genève. *Solstice de juin,* un moment interdit, avait été autorisé de nouveau grâce à son traducteur allemand. « Certaines pages des " Nuits de mai " sont un peu ahurissantes. Là, je vous concède que je me demande comment j'ai pu... » A la victoire alliée, il n'avait pas voulu suivre le troupeau, vers le soleil levant et la facilité. C'était beau, ça, je le retrouvais. Je me souvins du monceau de lettres de lui que j'avais lues à Laghouat. Après tout, il avait le droit d'aimer les petits Arabes. Comment aurait-il pu le dire, à l'époque, sans passer pour quelqu'un de méprisable ? Il était peut-être forcé de tromper et de mentir. Il me confia qu'on venait de lui offrir une grosse somme pour des fragments de ses correspondances féminines, et qu'il avait refusé. Ses documents les plus précieux, le manuscrit des *Garçons,* réplique des *Jeunes Filles,* était dans un coffre à la banque Barclays à Londres. Pour lui, la guerre était une déesse barbare qu'il avait célébrée mais devant laquelle il s'était toujours défilé. Avec le *Chant funèbre pour les morts de Verdun,* il m'avait inspiré, et, à présent, nous étions, lui d'un côté, moi de l'autre, presque des ennemis. En pensée, je le revis en photo, quand il avait vingt ans, casqué, alourdi d'un barda et d'un masque à gaz, hésitant entre la frousse et la témérité. Byron raté, tout en dérobades, et cependant l'esprit plein de hauteur et de noblesse. Je m'aperçus que je ne m'étais jamais remis d'avoir découvert qu'il était son contraire en tout. Avec désolation, je pris congé, attristé.

Après avoir écrit cette page, j'ai tiré le *Solstice de juin* de ma bibliothèque et relu les pages des « Nuits de mai » qu'il s'étonnait d'avoir écrites. Il y magnifiait les vertus de la guerre, comparées à l'immense sottise de l'humanité en paix, roucou-

lant, tout entière à des riens ou à des cruautés ; une jument errante échappée à une batterie d'artillerie venait lui flairer le visage pendant qu'il dormait dans un fossé et elle s'enfuyait. C'était le plus pur Montherlant, celui que j'aimais. Je découvris dans le volume une carte interzone de sa main avec un timbre du maréchal Pétain qu'il m'adressait à Fès (Maroc) en date du 5 mars 1942 : il se réjouissait d'avoir de mes nouvelles, me disait qu'il avait été légèrement blessé en mai, dans la Somme, qu'il avait écrit un livre, le *Rêve du guerrier,* et pas du tout le cœur à le publier, enfin qu'il travaillait à une pièce sur Port-Royal... Il me parlait aussi de Guibert. Quelle absurdité nous avait séparés ? Son insolence et son attachement à la grandeur m'avaient toujours séduit, j'aurais dû admirer qu'il refusât la main que je lui tendais comme la main d'un disciple qui désirait lui porter secours. Son aveuglement fut à la fois romain et mesquin. Il s'admirait trop pour avoir besoin de qui que ce soit. L'idée ne me vint pas aussi qu'il pouvait y avoir malentendu, et c'en fut bêtement fini entre nous.

Tous les journaux m'attribuaient d'avance le Goncourt. Finalement, j'eus le Renaudot parce que *la Vallée heureuse* n'était pas, paraît-il, un ouvrage de pure imagination, comme s'il existait des ouvrages où l'auteur ne met rien de lui-même. En tenue d'aviateur, je signai mon livre rue de Verneuil dans les locaux exigus des éditions Charlot. On s'écrasait, Camus était là. Le soir, j'offris un couscous dans un restaurant de la rue des Saints-Pères qui a disparu et s'appelait l'Académie. Pierre Jean Jouve ne vint pas, l'ironie de Doyon put s'exercer à souhait. Il présidait, en face de Marie, à côté de Camus. Il postillonna beaucoup et lâcha beaucoup d'énormités. Camus me glissa à l'oreille : « Ton père est un drôle de lascar. »

Son vrai père à lui aurait pu être Jean Grenier que je ne connaissais pas encore, et qui, jusque dans la tendresse et l'amour, essayait de définir le pourquoi des choses. Je ne crois pas que Camus ait jamais songé à le considérer comme son père. Il l'aimait, il le respectait, il l'honorait, il ne se serait jamais risqué à lui attribuer ce titre-là, il aurait cru manquer à ses devoirs envers sa mère. Son père, commis agricole d'une grosse ferme de Mondovi près de Bône (Algérie), avait été

mortellement blessé au début de la guerre de 1914, un peu avant sa naissance à lui. Moi qui ai dû, dès mon plus jeune âge, éprouver des doutes sur ma filiation et en ai même tiré sujet de boutade et de raillerie, il me semblait qu'un des pères de Camus, au sens où l'entendait Doyon, aurait pu être son oncle le tonnelier qui les avait recueillis, sa mère et lui ; ou encore l'autre oncle Gustave Acault, boucher des quartiers chic d'Alger, qui ne vendait que de la viande de France, et l'installait, vers sa quinzième année où il était si chétif, si malingre, si mal nourri, devant une tranche de viande rouge et un verre de sang de bœuf. Cet oncle-là essayait souvent de le convaincre de devenir boucher à son tour. Ou encore l'instituteur qui intervint pour qu'il ait une bourse et qu'il aille au lycée. Non, non. Pour Camus, on ne plaisantait pas avec ces choses-là, le père était l'homme à qui on devait la vie, sinon on laissait planer sur la mère un doute injurieux. Pour moi, il a bien fallu. Si j'avais pris cette notion au tragique, aurais-je aimé Doyon qui revendiqua son diplôme de père pour m'attribuer le brevet de fils ingrat ?

Doyon voulut éblouir Camus en le couvrant de compliments dans une langue recherchée. Il l'agaça. Il aurait mieux fait de lui dire que son propre père Doyon était boucher à Blida, comme le père de Jouhandeau et de tant d'autres. L'oncle Acault répétait à Camus : « Tu gagneras beaucoup d'argent, ça ne t'empêchera pas d'écrire. » Toute la maison Charlot était à ce dîner, le Tout-Alger de Saint-Germain-des-Prés ! Marcel Sauvage avait été mon supporter chez les Renaudot, Amrouche jouait au magister. Pas de militaires. Gallois m'avait aussi tourné le dos, on se demande pourquoi, Murtin n'était pas en France et je ne me souviens plus si j'avais osé inviter Accart. Quant au chef d'état-major, il avait pris la chose du bon côté : « Il a eu quinze jours d'arrêts de rigueur, il a le prix Renaudot, bravo. » A la place du colonel que j'avais maltraité dans mon livre et qui était maintenant général de brigade, je serais venu flanquer une gifle à l'insulteur. Longtemps après, nous finîmes par nous rencontrer. Les yeux dans les yeux, il me dit ce qu'il pensait, et moi, les yeux dans les yeux, je ne retirai rien de ce que j'avais écrit. Il n'y eut pas d'éclat. Les témoins de la scène en furent pour leurs frais. Aujourd'hui je pense que j'eus tort, j'aurais dû me conduire en gentilhomme.

Pour Charlot, *la Vallée heureuse* fut un succès. La presse fut très élogieuse. Certains libraires commandaient le livre par télégramme et par kilos, mais on manquait de papier. Ma fierté fut immense. Dans l'article qu'il écrivit dans *l'Arche*, Camus parlait de Tolstoï, des écrivains d'aujourd'hui, de l'aventure spirituelle qu'est toute grande œuvre, de l'art qui ne peut se passer de pudeur, et trouvait mon livre exceptionnel parce qu'il apportait un peu de délicatesse dans la tuerie. « Mois après mois, épaule contre épaule, Roy a ainsi poursuivi sa tâche dans la nuit d'une guerre qu'il n'aimait pas, et, plutôt que d'en tirer quelque grande vue sur le destin des hommes, il s'est borné à enregistrer les moments où il avait peur et ceux où il reprenait courage. C'est ainsi qu'il a pu parler pour tous, ne voulant parler pour personne... » Pour Camus, *la Vallée heureuse* ne se plaçait pas parmi les livres d'humanisme mais parmi les œuvres de force et de pudeur. Charlot sortit aussitôt un essai de moi, *Comme un mauvais ange,* où j'avais réuni quelques textes sur la condition des hommes volants. Les voitures étaient rares mais je pus acheter aux domaines une ancienne Peugeot que je fis retaper. J'étais lancé. J'écrivais toujours dans *Combat.* Rentrée de Sétif, ma famille s'installa dans l'appartement que Doyon m'avait procuré et je louai dans la vallée de Chevreuse, presque en pleine forêt, une maison romantique. Elle était vaste, Camus me proposa de la partager avec moi. Un chemin toujours désert menait jusqu'à nous. Marie venait souvent. Comme ma réputation dans l'armée était d'un amateur, d'un paresseux et d'un esprit douteux, on jugea que je n'étais pas digne du bureau Etudes et Plans, et, malgré le colonel Badré, on me muta, par sanction disciplinaire, dans un service. Moi, un combattant, dans un service ? Je refusai. On me désigna alors comme officier de liaison auprès du président de la Commission de défense nationale du Sénat qu'on appelait alors Conseil de la République. La commission se réunissait rarement. Ma voiture me permettait de me déplacer. Je me mis à écrire *le Métier des armes.*

La maison de Choisel était une noble demeure sans autre chauffage que des poêles, sans le moindre luxe, mais harmonieuse et divisée en plusieurs parties. Elle était meublée, il y

avait un billard et un vieux piano avec une montagne de partitions. A l'étage, du balcon, la vue s'étendait sur le parc et un cèdre immense ; Camus avait une belle chambre à côté de la mienne. Nous étions entourés de roseaux et de bois, un ruisseau marécageux nous séparait du hameau. Sur la colline d'en face, se cachait un mignon château de comédie, la chaumière d'un sculpteur hollandais, le professeur Bronner, et quelques résidences dont l'une appartenait à Ingrid Bergman. Plus loin, c'était la campagne, Dampierre et Port-Royal. Des arbres s'échappait le clocher de l'église, les cloches ne sonnaient plus, hélas, qu'à l'occasion d'un enterrement, d'un mariage ou d'un baptême. Camus venait d'habitude en fin de semaine avec sa femme Francine et ses enfants, des jumeaux. Parfois sa secrétaire, Suzanne Labiche, l'accompagnait, pareille à un lis noir. Personne n'avait d'appareil photographique, personne ne songea jamais à prendre le moindre cliché. On se croyait ensemble pour toujours, on avait bien le temps. Camus recevait beaucoup. Ainsi je connus Guilloux qui avait accompagné Malraux et Gide en URSS, ainsi j'admirai la vigueur iconoclaste d'Etiemble, déjà chauve comme un œuf, qui m'apprit que je n'étais pas le seul à ne respecter que le respectable. Avec quelle fureur se lançait-il dans des imprécations à l'égard de tous les faux poètes, de tous ceux qui n'écrivaient pas en français, de tous les profiteurs de situations. Ses dieux étaient Rimbaud et Lawrence d'Arabie. En dehors d'eux, quel jeu de massacre ! Y échappaient seulement Jean Grenier, Raymond Aron, Camus, Aimé Césaire, Alain et Dumézil. Même Gracq était jugé pompeux et vide, mais peut-être l'avait-il mal lu. Quant à Malraux, il sortait de ses mains en lambeaux. Dans cette maison je fus heureux, c'est-à-dire que je n'arrêtai pas de passer d'une extrême exaltation à une extrême tristesse. Cela dépendait de ce que me disait Marie. Francine jouait des fugues de Bach au piano. Parfois nous chantions. Camus connaissait beaucoup d'airs d'opéra, il aimait surtout la *Tosca*, et « Toréador, prends garde... » On riait.

Notre premier été fut brûlant. Nous allions nous baigner à une piscine du voisinage où s'ébattaient des naturistes et où Camus, que Marie appelait Alberto, essayait de retrouver les bains Matarès d'Alger. Il faisait le pitre pour nous amuser, se jetait du plongeoir debout en fermant les yeux et en se pinçant les narines avec les doigts. Un jour, nous revînmes avec

d'effroyables démangeaisons qui devinrent un sujet de plaisanterie. Pour Camus j'aurais dû être un connaisseur puisque j'avais une carrière dans l'armée, et c'est vrai que, chez les tirailleurs, au temps du capitaine Boum-Boum, les soldats étaient couverts de vermine. J'y avais échappé. Ce fut la farce-attrape de cet été-là. Nous passions à la pharmacie de Chevreuse, la pharmacienne était jolie et s'ennuyait beaucoup. Puis Camus fut de plus en plus retenu à Paris, ses séjours s'espacèrent. Je vécus souvent seul avec une femelle de chien-loup que Roger Grenier, qui travaillait alors à *Combat,* et sa femme m avaient confiée. Pas une photo de Camus de ce temps-là, étais-je bête ! Puis, à ma désolation, Marie s'en retourna en Angleterre. Je restai avec la chienne que je gardai des années avec moi, amoureusement.

Marie avait pris une grande place dans mon cœur. Par elle, la femme devenait pour moi sublime, irremplaçable. Elle m'inspirait tant et si hautement, que je me sentais perdu si elle s'éloignait. Je n'étais pas guéri de mes nuits de bombardier. Il me semblait qu'avec Marie je retrouvais la vérité du monde. J'avais besoin d'ordre, de réflexion, et, au lieu de demeurer dans les altitudes, de considérer les choses de la vie avec simplicité et un peu d'ironie. C'est là que Marie m'enseignait. Une nouvelle vie s'ouvrit à moi, je distinguais la route et me distinguais moi-même dans une certaine obscurité. Le seul moyen d'y voir clair était d'écrire sur l'amour. Je voulus d'abord me délivrer de mes fantômes. Je travaillai au *Métier des armes.*

Une fois par semaine, la Commission de défense nationale se réunissait. Je passais à l'état-major où Gallois, avec qui la brouille n'avait pas duré, m'orientait. Alors, j'échangeais quelques idées avec les sénateurs, nous buvions un verre avec les secrétaires et les autres officiers mal en cour comme moi. J'allais beaucoup au théâtre et chez Lipp où l'on se croisait avec moins de hauteur qu'à présent. Un jour Jean Genet vint me voir au palais du Luxembourg pour me demander d'intervenir en faveur d'un de ses amis incorporé dans l'armée et qui risquait Biribi pour une bêtise. Je me méfiais des erreurs que l'armée pouvait commettre car, à Satory, j'avais appartenu un temps à un tribunal militaire. Genet avait une tête de bandit et passait pour une frappe, mais Kanters avait pour lui beaucoup

d'admiration. Je lus *Notre-Dame des fleurs,* cela me suffit. J'agis aussitôt. Genet en fut ému, vint me remercier et m'écrivit une longue lettre que j'ai encore. Par la suite, il m'invita à toutes ses générales, même à celle des *Paravents* où je fus mal à l'aise. J'essayai de le revoir, mais il changeait trop souvent d'hôtel.

Les affaires de Charlot ne résistèrent pas au succès. Faute d'une solide réserve de financement, faute d'assurances, malmené par ses rivaux, en butte à la férocité et à la jalousie des vieilles maisons, il sombra. *L'Arche* s'était déjà écroulée et Paulhan avait ramené Gide au bercail. Parmi les décombres, Amrouche essaya un temps de résister farouchement. Avec lui, je n'arrêtais pas de me fâcher sur des paroles définitives, et de me réconcilier avec des embrassades et des larmes. Camus avait rompu avec lui. Un soir, à un couscous avec Koestler, Amrouche rappela que l'auteur de *la Lie de la terre* avait appartenu au parti communiste. Camus blêmit. Lui aussi s'était inscrit deux ans au parti communiste algérien et ne supportait pas qu'on le lui rappelât, en quelque sorte. Comme Amrouche insistait lourdement, Camus le pria de se taire, puis ne lui adressa plus la parole et le quitta sans lui serrer la main. Camus ne pardonnait pas. Ils ne se réconcilièrent jamais.

Chez Gallimard, Gaston me flatta. Comme aurait dit une petite pute de Maupassant, la NRF devint ma maison, la standardiste me connaissait, j'allais où je voulais, même dans l'hôtel de la rue de l'Université. Aujourd'hui, il y a une réception et des sièges comme chez un grand médecin, on attend qu'on vienne vous chercher, on avance sur de la moquette comme sur un nuage, sans jamais entendre une voix dans les couloirs. A cette époque, on croisait Cioran, Guéhenno, Kanters, Sigaux ou Brice Parain, on se donnait rendez-vous à l'Espérance, le bistrot d'à côté. Jean Dutourd frayait peu ; il errait dans la maison en quête d'auteur qui lui facilitât sa tâche : rédiger le texte de prière d'insérer des ouvrages, et promenait dans les couloirs une hauteur narquoise et des relents de bouffarde. Peu enclin aux confidences, il discernait déjà les bons et les médiocres, ceux qui feraient leur chemin et ceux qui s'enliseraient. Il naviguait en évitant les écueils et en

flattant les puissances jusqu'à ce que, après beaucoup d'obstacles et contre beaucoup d'ennemis, son talent de faux bon sens voisin de la tartufferie finît par s'imposer. Persécuté un temps, victime même de la sottise, il devint puissant à son tour.

A l'étage noble, royaume de lambris et de secret, où de hautes fenêtres ouvraient sur les jardins, était le saint des saints où tout se décidait. On entrait sur la pointe des pieds, on ne respirait qu'à demi, on ne parlait qu'à mi-voix, baissant les yeux et enviant les familiers. Dans une pièce immense, les bureaux Louis XV se faisaient face deux à deux. Tout au fond, Gaston, moins effacé qu'il se voulait, rusé, madré, pareil à un caressant bouddha près d'une bouteille d'Evian, d'un verre et du téléphone, et Claude, le fils aîné, en face de lui, muet, affairé, un peu en dehors. Plus loin, les attachés, les pontes, les ministres du gouvernement des livres, où parfois une conversation s'ébauchait. Le scandale du passage de Malraux avec ses miliciens et ses valises était depuis longtemps éteint. Un hold-up ici ! Du terrorisme en plein dans les chuchotements ! Gaston recevait avec délicatesse. Il cajolait et enjôlait. Il vous priait de vous asseoir, on se disait que le cuir de votre chaise avait été lustré par les fesses pas forcément les plus belles, quoiqu'il y en eût, ni les plus vénérables, même quand elles trempaient parfois dans un bidet d'enfer, mais les plus respectées. J'essayai d'y poser un bout des miennes, de m'assouplir, de m'attendrir, de m'imprégner de style et de gloire à venir. Futilités, agaceries, simagrées qu'un prix Goncourt ou qu'une académie ! Seule ambition, la lumière du Nobel, comme un soleil naissant à l'horizon du nouvel auteur. Gaston bouddha avait un visage lisse et doux, des cheveux presque blancs plaqués, un regard souvent chargé de désir, parfois éraflé de férocité ; il portait un complet gris, clair ou foncé, et un nœud papillon fantaisie. Céline l'a comparé méchamment à un chef de rang de chez Prunier. Non, non. Pour moi, il était le maître, il avait vécu des amours tumultueuses, il avait été longtemps l'esclave de Valentine Tessier, l'impératrice, l'immense actrice, l'étoile de gloire, on disait qu'il avait failli se ruiner pour elle. Qui savait, au juste ? Louise de Vilmorin, c'était sûr, et il avait eu d'autres folies dans sa vie, il en avait peut-être encore. On ne l'imaginait pas amoureux, et cependant je croyais voir danser des flammes derrière lui. Bouddha, évêque de cour, il me séduisit à son

tour, il séduisait tout le monde, personne ne se défendait, on n'espérait qu'être vaincu par lui. Il me chuchota comme à tout le monde qu'il me verserait les mêmes droits qu'à Gide, douze pour cent. Aurais-je jamais osé demander davantage à ce notaire apostolique ? J'étais dans un lieu sacré, dans la plus illustre maison, j'allais dormir avec une couverture blanche à filet rouge, voisiner avec Claudel, Aragon, Malraux depuis 1933, Saint-John Perse et Saint-Exupéry, Camus serait mon protecteur.

La deuxième fois que j'entrai là, après que les problèmes financiers de la succession Charlot eurent été réglés, Gaston me pria de ne plus frapper : j'étais chez moi.

Je me sentais chez moi en effet, comme on peut l'être à l'Elysée. Il me tardait de m'enfuir par un couloir étranglé d'où l'on débouchait sur l'escalier. Camus appartenait au comité de lecture, dirigeait une collection, « l'Espoir », et occupait un bureau au deuxième étage. Parfois rieuse parfois sévère, Suzanne Labiche chuchotait les nouvelles de la santé et de l'humeur du jeune maître. Il était là, si occupé, un peu guindé, un peu gourmé d'abord, puis heureux de renouer avec Alger monté comme lui à l'assaut de Paris, je le quittais heureux. Au box d'à côté, Jacques Lemarchand, critique dramatique du *Figaro littéraire*, long visage mélancolique et glacé, prenait tout au tragique, et, dans l'étroite écurie du *Cheval de Troie*, hennissait le père Bruckberger, en robe blanche de dominicain, fumeur de pipe et familier des princesses. Sa revue, où j'écrivis comme beaucoup, n'allait pas bien. S'il n'était pas trop tôt, s'il n'attendait pas le coup de téléphone d'une dame riche, on descendait aussi boire un verre, lui c'était au bar du Montalembert où il travaillait au *Dialogue des Carmélites* de Bernanos. Bruck était à l'aise dans la littérature, dans la vie, dans les salons, dans la guerre. Lourd, épais, la lèvre exagérément gourmande, la parole prédicante, il préférait aux hommes envieux et sans pitié les femmes belles et miséricordieuses, surtout les comédiennes. Aux regards qu'il posait sur moi, je sentais que j'appartenais maintenant à l'élite de l'élite, à la crème.

Il régnait dans la maison une atmosphère que je n'oserais pas dire religieuse. Bruck n'y était pour rien, ç'aurait été plutôt le contraire. Je ne dirais pas non plus que la maison était un monastère laïc où eussent abouti, en esprit, les frivolités. La

religion ne s'y voyait pas. Elle était partout, derrière ses dignitaires, vicaires généraux ou chanoines, ses prêtres et la foule endiguée des catéchumènes. Je m'y sentais un peu le séminariste que mon archevêque avait serré sur sa poitrine contre sa barbe opulente en lui murmurant quoi ?

Paulhan était ailleurs, avec sa cour, dans l'inatteignable. On l'apercevait parfois glissant dans les couloirs comme un sous-marin en surface. Les jours où il recevait, on célébrait l'office, il allait de l'un à l'autre comme avec une étole brodée, penchant sur nous des yeux de grenouille d'Angkor dans une face de grand prêtre, nous soufflant un mot à l'oreille, puis, comme par doute ou repentir, interrogeant d'un doigt de prélat la nue, la création du monde, le mystère éternel. Lui, c'était l'éminence pas grise du tout, bien qu'il se plaignît à Doyon de n'être rien et même d'exciter les jalousies et les antipathies du comité de lecture ; il osait dire qu'il lui suffisait de souhaiter qu'un manuscrit fût reçu pour que les portes se fermassent. Excuse facile, argument spécieux. Il faisait ce qu'il voulait de ce qu'il aimait ou n'aimait pas. A quelle place aurais-je mis Dominique Aury, son égérie ? Elle, on n'en doutait pas, ressemblait à une moniale subjuguée encore meurtrie des épousailles mystiques. Amrouche avait bien essayé de la débaucher ; avant même que *l'Arche* ait rendu son dernier soupir, elle avait rejoint la nouvelle *NRF*. Etait-elle la Religieuse portugaise ? une sainte laïque ? une simple dévote ? L'œil mi-clos, l'oreille à tout, toute baignée d'onction, d'affection, de liturgie, d'absolu, la plume vive, incisive, piquante et, en même temps, faussement onctueuse, elle accompagnait son maître dans la mesure et la révérence. Je l'aimais beaucoup.

Les personnes du sexe occupaient là des places discrètes, et dans des tenues d'autant plus effacées qu'elles avaient plus d'ambition. Sans compter les sœurs laies du magasin et de l'office, il y avait à la NRF un monde de nonnes et de professes. La secrétaire de Gaston, les secrétaires des pontes, les sublimes assistantes, les adjointes aux grands et petits chefs composaient une communauté que dominait la cheffesse des attachées de direction. Le poste donnait accès au tabernacle, à l'oreille des puissants, à l'intimité, aux confidences, aux découvertes, et il était l'objet de convoitises féroces. Ces dames et demoiselles s'arrachaient les yeux, parfois faisaient intervenir. Des bruits couraient, l'adultère pouvait régner dans

cette cour céleste, et les places se gagnaient comme partout, à l'arraché.

La portion d'espace de la NRF où je me sentais le moins emprunté était moins un coin qu'un recoin, dans un autre département du palais et loin de l'état-major. On l'atteignait, dès l'entrée, en se dirigeant à l'opposé de ce qui comptait. On passait même par ce qui ressemblait à des soutes, on se glissait par le sombre local des empaqueteurs et des distributeurs, à travers une humble population de magasiniers voués à expédier les chefs-d'œuvre dont parfois ils apercevaient l'ombre furtive des auteurs. On traversait ce sombre lieu toujours éclairé au néon, on escaladait une échelle de meunier en fer, on débouchait dans ce qui avait dû être jadis une loge de concierge, basse de plafond, mal aérée, parfois empuantie de tabagie et encombrée de livres neufs, déjà défraîchis. Là, derrière une table et des rayons, sur une discrète estrade, dans une caborgniote se tenait, assise toute droite, une madone, Jacqueline Bour, sœur peut-être en esprit, plus souriante, peut-être plus vulnérable et moins redoutable que Dominique Aury. Même pas redoutable du tout. Prêtresse aussi. Epouse d'un vrai poète. Vestale. Déesse, peut-être Minerve, je ne sais quel mot employer. Personne ne savait montrer pour la littérature plus de considération ni de soin plus délicat. Les auteurs qui, par la tête du roide escalier de fer, arrivaient là, parfois essoufflés s'ils étaient d'un certain âge, ou, comme moi, fringants, surgissaient aux nouvelles. Mme Bour savait, dès l'annonce d'un titre, s'il allait marcher et si les critiques secondaires à qui on n'envoyait pas les ouvrages d'office se précipiteraient ou pas. Les grands auteurs, vieux pontes ou colonnes du lieu, monstres sacrés comme Gide ou Martin du Gard, appelaient souvent à propos d'un texte, et la conversation s'engageait sur tel ou tel. Là, tout à demi-mot, Mme Bour gardait son jugement et ses préférences, qui ne correspondaient pas toujours au critère de la maison. Elle sentait qui allait partir ou rester. Elle ne le disait pas toujours non plus, mais cela se lisait sur son visage baigné d'oraisons et traversé de doutes, parfois de tentations dont elle paraissait rougir. De cette dunette, quel point de vue, quel observatoire sur le passage de presque toute la rue Montalembert qui conduisait à l'abbaye, à la sainte mère, au temple ! Quel poste de guet en demi-lune que ce service de presse, quel mirador ! De là,

Mme Bour voyait qui apparaissait ou s'éclipsait, elle attendait, et si personne ne venait, en tirait pour elle-même postulats ou hypothèses. Si l'on voulait ne pas se montrer, ce n'était pas par là qu'il fallait aborder. Le plus simple était de ne jamais se dérober aux regards et, en passant, d'adresser déjà un geste à la loge. J'y allais souvent. Je repartais parfois hésitant et indécis.

Dans l'anfractuosité d'un recoin, s'insérait le minuscule et gris M. Hirsch, Daniel Hirsch. Dans le site historique depuis ses débuts, M. Hirsch n'avait plus d'âge mais se montrait à l'affût de tout. Courbé en apparence sur études ou devis, attaché à quelles fonctions quand je l'ai connu ? Depuis toujours voûté, fouineur et renifleur, chercheur d'idées, conseiller ou déconseiller, il s'était réfugié là parce qu'on ne voulait plus de lui nulle part. A la retraite depuis des années, il avait refusé de quitter sa place et continuait à travailler pour rien, pour le plaisir et pour la gloire, sinon pour lui ç'aurait été la fin, la nuit, la géhenne. Il s'extirpait lentement de son trou, avançait son bec courbe, son front déplumé, son œil à qui rien n'échappait, et penchait du côté de ce qui commençait à ressembler à une bosse. Surtout, il était fier des quatrièmes pages de couverture qu'il composait seulement pour ceux qu'il chérissait : « Vous avez vu en compagnie de qui je vous ai mis ? » me dira-t-il plus tard avec gourmandise. Devais-je y croire ? Camus, T. E. Lawrence, Saint-Exupéry, Jean Grenier, Louis Martin-Chauffier, Julien Unger... J'avais pour lui un regard de gratitude émue. « Mais oui, c'est votre place, répondait-il. Et maintenant à quoi êtes-vous attelé ? » Je le lui disais. Il était content. En ce temps-là, on savourait l'âpre bonheur de contribuer au lustre de la NRF, d'en tirer gloriole et de montrer un attachement sans mesure à nos maîtres, on n'écrivait que pour le bonheur de Gaston, détenteur des secrets. Une fois le manuscrit accepté, on n'aurait jamais osé, quand on n'était pas Malraux, espérer recevoir un à-valoir quelconque. D'ailleurs Gaston aurait refusé, sinon avec quoi la maison aurait-elle vécu, payé ses cadres, ses imprimeurs et ses employés, avec quoi aurait-on pu propulser les auteurs dans la célébrité, avec quoi aurait-on offert, à la belle saison, des cocktails où tout Paris s'étouffait ?

*⁎
⁎

« Un grand amour vit d'empêchements », murmurait Camus en nous observant, Marie et moi. La phrase figure dans *le Mythe de Sisyphe*. Rien de plus vrai. Lui n'en connaissait aucun, d'empêchement. Les caillettes lui tombaient toutes rôties dans la bouche. Un jour où nous remontions le boulevard Saint-Germain, comme nous parlions des femmes, il me dit : « Il y a chez moi comme chez toi du violeur. Nous aimons ça. » Il ajoutait en riant que ce n'était pas très joli. Il ne violait personne, du moins pouvait-il le croire. Toutes se donnaient à lui avant même qu'il le demande. Marie, je peux parler d'elle puisqu'elle est devenue un personnage des *Flammes de l'été*, sera un temps pour moi ce que Maria Casarès fut toute sa vie pour lui : l'amour partagé qui devenait intelligence et raison une fois la passion éloignée. Je fus pour Marie l'homme qui ne devait pas vivre constamment avec elle pour ne pas l'user et pour qu'elle se croie libre. Camus avait besoin de Maria Casarès, il l'adorait, elle lui pardonnait tout, il la jugeait sublime, elle fut peut-être la seule à qui il ouvrit son cœur. La dernière fois qu'ils se virent, ils avaient tous deux, comme dans un pressentiment, les larmes aux yeux. Grâce à Marie, ma terrifiante fièvre du sortir de la guerre était tombée. Elle m'avait aidé à divorcer et je m'étais montré bêtement dur et froid pour Mirande, mais Marie avait refusé de m'épouser, on n'épouse pas un fou. De moi elle devait plutôt se protéger. Le mariage, même quand il est amoureux, doit reposer sur des rêves communs, un soutien réciproque, l'idée que, sans l'indispensable moitié de soi-même, le monde est vide. La jalousie ne me déchirait plus parce que je m'étais heurté à une décision que je savais irrévocable. Cela ou rien. C'était à ces empêchements que Camus faisait allusion. Marie m'aimait, pas au point de vivre avec moi. Pour le courant de la vie elle préférait quelqu'un d'autre et elle avait raison. Peut-être aimait-elle deux hommes, chacun à sa façon, et, doublement liée, se voulait libre. Elle n'était pas une beauté fatale et il lui restait de son éducation au couvent de la Légion d'honneur comme une certaine gaucherie. Elle voulait aussi être mère, mais pas de mon fait. A-t-on jamais su aussi pourquoi on aime quelqu'un ? J'étais ému par son large regard bleu pâle sous un front bombé, par les cheveux qui lui tombaient sur les épaules. Qu'on ne me demande rien d'autre. Doyon la trouvait à son goût, mais mon petit père avait pour toutes les femmes un

désir violent et fugace qui ne se civilisait que devant les empêchements : toujours Camus. Dans son roman *l'Enfant prodiguée*, il se ruinait, s'usait, se rongeait, se consumait pour le plaisir. Marie le considérait comme un amuseur maladroit qui finirait dans la misère. « Mais il vous aime, me disait-elle. Vous êtes l'homme qu'il aurait voulu être et même quand il se montre féroce, il est bien votre père, vous devez devenir son soutien et sa consolation... »

Dans ma maison au milieu des bois, je retrouvais les embrassades de ma chienne qui avait fait des petits. J'avais gardé un mâle à qui j'avais donné le nom de César en souvenir du chien de la ferme. Il n'était pas très futé. Parfois une pièce avec Kanters, une soirée avec Sigaux ou un hasard galant m'attardait à Paris. L'été torride et flamboyant que nous avions traversé avec Camus s'achevait sur des orages sans fin. Je me couchais, j'essayais de trouver le sommeil. Loin de Marie, je dormais mal. Quand le tonnerre éclatait, je croyais encore qu'un bombardier se fracassait contre moi, je tombais en vrille, je me mettais la tête sous les draps pour ne pas voir la foudre des canons déchirer la nuit. La pharmacienne me gavait de somnifères que j'essayais les uns après les autres. Elle était belle avec un côté « âme perdue », elle se disait fragile et ne désirait qu'être brisée. Un jour où je m'étais montré particulièrement cruel, elle me dit : « Il ne me reste plus qu'à retourner à mes poisons... » Mon ambition avait toujours été de me marier avec une pharmacienne qui n'aurait jamais quitté son office et aurait gagné ma vie pendant que j'aurais galopé ailleurs. J'en avais une, et, par bêtise, je la malmenais. Il est vrai qu'elle était mariée, qu'elle aurait dû divorcer. Je l'écrivis à Marie qui ne m'engagea pas à plus d'aménité. Elle aurait dû. Qui sait ?

C'était de pondération que je manquais. J'aurais dû en acquérir au Sénat quand j'assistais le président de la Commission de la défense nationale. Les commissaires et lui, pleins de bon sens, considéraient les problèmes militaires avec sérénité. Parfois l'armée de l'air me prêtait un avion et je leur fricotais un voyage en Afrique du Nord et en Afrique noire. Ils s'amusaient comme des galopins. Nous étions reçus chez les résidents et les gouverneurs, parfois chez les pachas à diffas, j'envoyais des cartes postales à Marie, je me retrempais dans les plans de vol, je partageais le cockpit avec l'équipage, nous

respirions un air des hauteurs sans chasse ni canonnade, nous revenions guillerets et pleins de confiance. Dans les territoires qu'ils traversaient, mes sénateurs n'approchaient rien qui pût les troubler, de Gaulle se taisait, la paix régnait dans toute l'Union française, sauf en Indochine où nous entretenions un corps expéditionnaire pour rétablir notre souveraineté. Il n'était pas question d'aller si loin et de nous mêler de ce qui, pour l'instant, ne nous regardait pas.

Depuis le prix Renaudot, mes amis étaient moins des militaires que des critiques, des romanciers, des auteurs dramatiques. Un jour, Jean Denoël me transmit une invitation de Florence Gould, la milliardaire américaine qui tenait salon.

Le déjeuner avait lieu le jeudi, avenue Malakoff, dans un riche appartement. S'y pressait ce qui portait un nom dans la littérature tant que brillait le nom. Paulhan, assisté par Dominique Aury, présidait en face de la maîtresse de maison. Les habitués étaient Jouhandeau, Léautaud, souvent Cocteau et Dubuffet, rarement Mauriac, parfois Green. Ensuite il y avait le menu fretin, les nouveaux promus, les familiers comme le banquier Schweiss-Gout, toujours là. On servait une nourriture de palace. Paulhan touchait à tout du bout des lèvres. Jouhandeau ajoutait son grain de sel d'enfer dans la conversation, la discussion roulait souvent sur les célébrités qui s'abstenaient ou refusaient de paraître là, comme Malraux. À la gauche de Florence Gould, superbe lionne, Léautaud bâfrait avec un terrible bruit de gencives, en éructant des exclamations toujours méchantes. Portant la contradiction et l'anathème, il payait ainsi les cabas qu'il emportait pour ses animaux dans la Buick qui le ramenait à Fontenay-aux-Roses après avoir été l'y chercher. Avait-il déjà commencé, avec Robert Mallet, ses entretiens à la radio, où son rire sarcastique était devenu célèbre en quelques jours ? Soudain, sur des ondes officielles, une voix bafouait les valeurs établies, on n'en croyait pas ses oreilles. Il se moquait de tout et prenait plaisir à offusquer. Super-vedette du déjeuner, si Cocteau brillait trop, il ronchonnait. Si Paulhan louait un écrivain illustre, il était furieux. La puissante Florence Gould, que tout le monde appelait Florence, jubilait. Elle avait son vieux singe, ses saltimbanques, ses chiens pékinois brossés et parfumés. Elle assurait la liaison avec l'Occupation où les convives, Colette,

Marie Laurencin, Paul Morand, Vlaminck, Pierre Benoit, Bonnard, Marcel Achard, étaient plus gourmés. Parmi eux, papillotaient le lieutenant Heller qui accordait le papier aux éditeurs et l'énigmatique et glorieux capitaine Ernst Jünger.

Cette nébuleuse, la comète Florence l'avait traversée sans y laisser de plumes. Tout avait changé. Jean Denoël, l'ancien adjudant-chef du service de santé à Casablanca, l'ami de tous, de Gide, de Claudel, d'Amrouche, de Bosco, décidait de tout. On naviguait dans la galaxie d'après-guerre. Dans le cosmos dont j'avais beaucoup entendu parler au bureau Etudes et Plans, le salon de Florence Gould n'était cependant pas une plate-forme à laquelle toutes les nacelles pouvaient s'amarrer. On disait qu'elle était née Florence Lacaze, à San Francisco, d'un père basque émigré et d'une Champenoise, et qu'elle avait voulu d'abord être chanteuse. Elle avait commencé par séduire le directeur du *Gaulois*, Arthur Meyer, qui l'avait conduite en 1920 à un bal en l'honneur d'Alphonse XIII. Là, accompagnée au piano par Reynaldo Hahn, elle avait roucoulé une romance et le milliardaire Franck Jay-Gould, roi des chemins de fer, s'était, paraît-il, jeté à ses pieds. Au fond, elle aimait les vieux, ça lui avait réussi. Quel âge avait-elle ? Certains disaient soixante ans. Plutôt moins. Cinquante peut-être. Comment savoir au juste ? Elle semblait capable encore d'apprécier les choses de l'amour. Forte créature au visage large, hiératique, comme éclairé du dedans par un intense sentiment d'avidité qu'elle cachait sous de grosses lunettes noires, elle portait une crinière fauve, des épaules et une gorge généreuses. Raffinée, établie avec naturel dans la vanité des écrivains, attentive à les flatter, elle leur laissait supposer qu'elle pouvait avoir d'eux l'idée qu'ils avaient eux-mêmes. Si une bagarre éclatait, enlevant ses lunettes et laissant étinceler ses vastes yeux verts pailletés d'or, l'épouse du roi des chemins de fer manœuvrait des trains de fusées et d'astéroïdes parfois encore obscurs. Avec sa face parcheminée, Jean Denoël s'ingéniait à ce que personne ne s'écartât trop des règles du savoir-vivre et de la hiérarchie des valeurs ; il lâchait parfois de sourds grognements ou de furtifs coups de patte. Présidée par Paulhan, grand prêtre crocodile de la NRF, la table, je le vis par la suite, était moins un planétarium qu'une ménagerie avec ses loups, ses tigres, son génie à bec de lièvre Jouhandeau, ses batraciens et ses anguilles, la face triste de Marcel Arland ou la

longue tête de cheval fourbu de Marcel Aymé, la paupière en torpille de Mauriac et une grosse troupe de caniches, dogues, poneys, mulets ou bœufs de labour, parfois caméléons bénis, parfois buses, parfois moutons. Impassible sous son masque, Florence se tournait vers l'un ou l'autre. Elle parlait peu. On entendait rarement les intonations rauques de sa voix. C'était une bête fauve : la lionne que j'ai dit. Beaucoup voyaient plutôt en elle une vache sacrée à gros pis.

Le jour où je fus invité, j'étais placé en face de Léautaud penché sur son assiette, bougon. N'avait-il pas gardé son galurin sur la tête ? Il explosa quand il entendit que j'étais aviateur et que ma notoriété toute récente était due à un livre sur les bombardiers. Il demanda à l'assistance si j'étais militaire de métier, et quand il le sut : « Pour moi, claironna-t-il, les militaires sont des imbéciles et des massacreurs... » et il replongea dans son assiette. On se récria. J'osai lui demander s'il m'avait lu. Il répondit, toujours sans me regarder, par une exclamation de raillerie. Je répliquai que Vauvenargues était un ancien officier, que Psichari avait écrit des livres honorables et que certaines célébrités civiles valaient peut-être moins que ces militaires-là. « Même ici », ajoutai-je. Il me lança enfin un coup d'œil curieux. « En tout cas, dit-il, vous avez dû être occupant, et moi, les occupants, je ne les aime pas, et je préfère encore aux Américains les Allemands. Ils étaient plus polis. » Dans le tollé, son éclat de rire fut superbe. Il répéta en criant : « Oui, oui, les Allemands... » Et il se tourna vers Florence radieuse : « Ça vous embête ? » et se remit à bâfrer sans plus s'occuper de nous. Lui qui n'avait jamais eu de succès ne croyait pas à la renommée fulgurante qui lui amenait des visiteurs jusqu'à son antre de Fontenay-aux-Roses. Entre ses chiens, ses chats, sa guenon et sa lubricité, il se sentait traqué. Robert Mallet me disait qu'il sortait en rasant les murs, ses cabas lui pendant aux mains. Après le café, il s'enfonça dans un fauteuil, fit un petit somme puis s'en alla. Ils avaient tous traficoté. Jouhandeau pour des riens, pour des mots, pour de petits gitons, Léautaud pour moins que rien. Vlaminck pour sa frousse, Paul Morand pour une certaine classe, parce que les Allemands étaient fins. Pas Paulhan. Paulhan se tenait bien. Paulhan ne frayait pas avec l'ennemi.

Epaté, perplexe, j'essayai d'en savoir plus sur Florence. Infirmière au Val-de-Grâce au début de la guerre, on disait

qu'elle s'y faisait conduire dans une Bugatti pleine de foies gras et de champagne. A propos d'elle, on chuchotait plutôt. Ce Chinois de Jean Denoël, le factotum, le confident, ne répondait que par de minuscules exclamations ou des soupirs. Il partageait sa vie entre Gallimard, où il avait de vagues fonctions non payées, et le bazar Florence Gould où il servait, d'un zèle insolite presque louche et jaloux. Intraitable cerbère, il donnait l'impression de garder un trésor et de le protéger des aigrefins et des grossiers personnages. Sur Florence, c'était motus toujours et à jamais, et lui qui ne pensait qu'à faire écrire les autres, s'il écrivait, ne savait que griffonner des banalités sur des bristols de la NRF. Il a fini par s'en aller avec ses secrets. En avait-il ? On ne parlait jamais de la guerre, jamais de Pétain. Toutes les mains avaient été lavées, certaines parmi les innocents, d'autres dans le sang et le feu. Florence ne prononçait plus le nom de son ami Jünger, ancien chef de corps franc à dix-huit ans, tueur tuant s'il ne voulait pas être tué, élevant son destin de zigouilleur à la hauteur d'une religion, portant au cou sa décoration « Pour le mérite » avec feuilles de chêne d'or et brillants, la plus haute de Germanie. Pourquoi n'aurait-elle pas reçu, avec du caviar ce jour-là, Malraux l'aventurier du Cambodge et de la guerre d'Espagne, le héros de la brigade Alsace-Lorraine ? Plus tard, j'appris qu'elle avait convolé une première fois avec un jeune architecte américain, qu'ils étaient venus à Chartres le jour de leur mariage et qu'elle s'était laissé enfermer dans la cathédrale pour contempler les vitraux au clair de lune. Cet imbécile d'architecte n'avait pas apprécié, paraît-il. Ça me plut, cette nuit de noces sacrilège. On me dit aussi qu'un soir où Heller et Jünger lui tenaient compagnie, on sonna alors qu'il était tard. C'était un officier en civil que Florence présenta comme le colonel Patrick et que Jünger prit pour un officier allié parachuté. En réalité, c'était le chef de l'Abwehr, le contre-espionnage allemand.

Je ne me vantai pas de mes nouvelles relations. Pour Camus, fréquenter le salon de Mme Gould, c'était flatter la puissance d'argent qu'il méprisait. A Paris, on lui offrait, pour un article de quatre feuillets, ailleurs qu'à *Combat*, vingt-cinq mille francs, et en Amérique, mille dollars, et il hésitait. En Suisse, cinq cent mille francs pour une édition qu'il refusait

encore. « Je ne veux pas vendre mon âme », me disait-il. Mais un week-end, à cause d'une tuile ou pour payer des arriérés d'impôts, il refit le manuscrit de *l'Etranger* qu'il avait perdu. Jamais il ne mit les pieds avenue Malakoff. En revanche, Amrouche profita de ma percée et se fit inviter. Devant Paulhan, il usa de son verbe avec trop de complaisance et feignit de se croire un peu chez lui. Son dessein était d'intéresser Florence aux éditions Charlot. Il n'y réussit pas. Cependant il figura un temps dans la ménagerie. Comme moi.

Chez les militaires, je me sentais de plus en plus en marge. Amèrement critiquée par eux, *la Vallée heureuse* appartenait désormais à la littérature et était traduite en plusieurs langues. Mes camarades préféraient *le Grand Cirque* de Clostermann qui claquait superbement. Ils étaient surpris qu'avec toutes les questions qu'il posait sur le courage, mon livre soit allé si loin dans la ferveur du public et que, par le tragique plus que par les lieux communs qu'ils chérissaient, j'aie pu contribuer à l'admiration qu'on leur voua. Les militaires, souvent naïfs, sont dupes d'eux-mêmes. Je me dépêtrai comme je pus de l'embrouillamini dans quoi je me trouvais avec eux. Je ne me souviens plus de ce que m'en dit Brohon, qui malgré son esprit hors du commun restait très attaché aux principes. Je ne le voyais plus car il avançait dans la carrière à pas de géant. Un général qui convoitait le poste de chef d'état-major m'embarqua dans son cabinet et m'utilisa à mener campagne dans la presse pour imposer certaines idées de politique aérienne contre la clique au pouvoir. Nous réussîmes. Mon général me récompensa par une promotion au grade supérieur. Du coup, une réputation s'établit. On me craignit. Parfois même on me flattait.

Camus venait de plus en plus rarement à Choisel. A Marie qui s'était mariée en Grande-Bretagne, je racontais mes sorties, mes voyages, mes rencontres. L'amour immortel que je lui avais voué dura quatre ans, après quoi, par la force des choses, j'eus beaucoup de consolatrices, moins qu'on m'en attribua. On fut rarement cruel pour moi, et, de mon côté, je le fus moins que je m'en confessai à Marie. Sait-on pourquoi on est comme on est ? Sait-on pourquoi on hésite parfois à corriger les mauvais côtés de son caractère ? De même qu'on protège des sites et des hommes sauvages, on protège en soi des réflexes que condamnent la raison et le bon sens. On n'en

est pas fier. Au fond de soi, on s'en repent, on peut même s'en accuser. N'empêche : il y a chez moi des colères ou des indignations qui me rappellent, sans que j'y sois pour rien, la férocité du père de mon père que je n'ai pas connu, ou les révoltes de ma mère. Ces mouvements me laissent tout étonné, parfois confus, il me faut du temps pour m'en remettre. Au fond, je ne suis jamais sûr de moi, même de ce qu'on m'attribue généreusement. C'est malgré moi, le plus souvent, qu'il m'arrive de défendre des causes. On dirait qu'alors j'agis comme si quelque chose m'échappait. Je me demande parfois si je suis pour rien dans ce qu'on m'accorde. Qu'y puis-je ?

De plus en plus, pour voir Camus on faisait antichambre. Il avait atteint des hauteurs où je ne suivais plus. Je n'avais ni son brillant ni son goût pour la philosophie. Sa célébrité même l'isolait. J'étais à Paris quand le prix des Critiques fut décerné à *la Peste*. Je courus rue Séguier où il habitait un appartement étroit et très haut de plafond. Francine m'ouvrit. « Qu'est-ce que c'est que ce prix ? » demanda-t-elle. « D'abord, cent mille francs. » Son visage s'éclaira. La « biche », sa secrétaire, arriva confirmer la nouvelle, on déboucha une bouteille, Camus n'était pas là, je m'en fus. L'après-midi, il y eut cocktail chez Gallimard. Gaston paraissait ennuyé parce que Camus n'avait pas l'air si content. D'abord il avait refusé le prix, puis, résigné, avait cédé à Gabriel Marcel, déjeuné avec le jury et reçu les photographes.

Nous allâmes dîner chez Lipp où Camus commanda du champagne. Marie était folle d'orgueil. C'était en 1947, elle hésitait encore à me quitter. *La Peste* se déroulait à Oran où elle était née, comme Francine. Pour moi, il n'y avait pas de quoi être fier d'une ville si morne, un théâtre idéal pour la peste. N'empêche, c'était un grand livre. J'ai retrouvé une note de cette soirée-là qui se termina au Méphisto, la boîte où Camus allait souvent danser. Là, Marie ne se possédait plus. Elle entraîna son Alberto et tous deux se jetèrent avec furie dans les simagrées du rock'n'roll, ce qui me mettait de méchante humeur, quand Sartre arriva, flanqué de Dolorès, sa folie du moment. Je ne sais pourquoi Sartre et Camus étaient fâchés. Oh ! on n'en était pas aux drames qui suivront la

critique de *l'Homme révolté* dans *les Temps modernes*, en 1952. Ce n'était qu'une petite piqûre comme Simone de Beauvoir en évoque dans *les Mandarins*, à cause d'un mot dit ou pas dit, et pas d'une telle gravité puisque l'atmosphère les rapprocha peu à peu et nous rapprocha tous. Sartre se lança dans des histoires sans queue ni tête, Dolorès tutoyait tout le monde et appelait Marie « la gueuse ». Comme je n'étais pas de bon poil, elle me secoua et engueula Marie. « Hé, la souris, tu ne vois pas qu'il souffre ?... » L'équipe de *Combat* surgit en force et la sarabande commença. Je me rapprochai de Sartre : il parlait des Russes, des Américains, du gouvernement d'incapables qu'on avait et de son bonheur de s'être réconcilié avec Camus. « Ça, c'est un mec », répétait Dolorès qui en pinçait pour Camus. Le bonheur de Sartre était si intense qu'il voulut tout payer et sortit de sa poche une poignée de billets qui s'éparpillèrent. De temps en temps, Camus lâchait Marie avec qui il se contorsionnait et revenait s'asseoir à côté de lui. Nous nous en doutions un peu : c'était les deux princes des nuits de Saint-Germain-des-Prés, les deux hommes immenses et discutés qui allaient devenir des supermen et recevraient le Nobel tous les deux, mais l'un l'accepterait et l'autre le refuserait. Je n'avais plus envie de m'en aller. Je crois même que je me risquai sur la piste avec Marie. La piste ? On se faufilait comme on pouvait entre les tables, les tonneaux debout, les couples survoltés par ce qui les emportait, on se laissait rouler, bousculer, renverser les uns sur les autres. « Décidément, vous n'êtes pas doué », me dit Marie. Non, je n'étais pas doué. Je trouvai cela une danse de sauvages ivres, je revins en silence près de Sartre qui parlait de l'avenir du siècle en fumant rageusement sa pipe. Un moment, tourné vers moi, « Vous n'avez pas l'air de vous amuser... » Non, je n'avais pas l'air. Il m'avait fait de grands compliments sur *la Vallée heureuse* et me regardait bizarrement comme s'il ne pouvait croire qu'il y eût des militaires et des guerriers comme moi. Il ne me posa pas la question de Léautaud, si j'étais de carrière. Camus le lui avait dit. A trois heures, il s'en alla avec Dolorès, mais Francine, déchaînée, ne parlait plus de partir. Je bus un peu de whisky que je n'aimais pas alors, et Marie me dit enfin une parole qui m'attendrit. Elle en était avare. Je ne sais plus comment la nuit se termina.

Ce n'était plus ce Camus-là que, plus tard, je retrouvais entre deux portes, dans les couloirs de Gallimard ou dans les coulisses d'un théâtre. Il était devenu autre, et moi je m'enfermais de plus en plus à Choisel où *le Métier des armes* me donnait du fil à retordre. Je recommençais sans cesse cette journée où les émissaires du Führer s'étaient posés sur notre base de Sétif à la nuit tombante, porteurs d'un message de Hitler à l'amiral Darlan, et où personne chez nous ne savait de quel côté la guerre allait tourner, le lendemain : j'en avais assez de Pétain, mais je ne savais pas trahir et je trahissais quand même parce que je n'en pouvais plus, ce n'était pas facile à écrire. J'avançais lentement, âprement, alors que j'avais jeté *la Vallée heureuse* d'un trait.

L'Etat de siège, la pièce de Camus, montée par Jean-Louis Barrault au théâtre Marigny, subit un échec cuisant. Je ne sus quoi dire pour le consoler. C'était mauvais en effet, et pompeux. Tout à coup, cette ville grisante et cruelle de Paris, qui avait prodigué tant de caresses et tant d'éloges au jeune homme qu'il était, se vengeait du succès de *Caligula,* de *l'Etranger* et même de *la Peste* d'où *l'Etat de siège* était tiré. La soirée tourna au lugubre. Les articles du lendemain furent un massacre. L'après-midi, quand je passai rue Séguier, Francine m'ouvrit la porte avec un doigt sur la bouche : il dormait enfin, il se reposait, il croyait à une cabale contre lui. Ceux qui le jalousaient essayaient de transformer le four en cataclysme. Le journal *Arts*, dont Roger Nimier était rédacteur en chef, parut avec une manchette sur quatre colonnes : « Jean-Louis Barrault encore plus mauvais que d'habitude. » L'intelligentsia de droite se déchaînait, celle de gauche était consternée. Jean Denoël me rapporta que Gide venait de dire : « Il va apprendre combien la gloire est difficile à conquérir... »

Il disparut et fila en Bretagne où Guilloux et Jean Grenier le conduisirent sur la tombe de son propre père, mort de ses blessures de guerre en 1914 à Saint-Brieuc.

XII

Florence

PARIS OUBLIE VITE. Le jeudi qui suivit, avenue Malakoff, c'est à peine si quelqu'un évoqua cet échec. D'une voix fluette qui étonnait toujours, Paulhan dit : « Oui, oui, peut-être. Oh ! vous savez... » Et ce fut fini. Paulhan, c'était Socrate. J'étais déjà habitué au cirque, aux fauves, aux macaques, aux pékinois de Florence qui sentaient bon, je m'interrogeais toujours sur elle. J'avais dû lui taper dans l'œil, car invité chaque jeudi, je devenais un singe familier. Pas de femmes à table, sinon Dominique Aury dans le mystère jusqu'au front. Par la suite, je verrai des antiquités de toutes sortes dont la duchesse qui ressemblait à Louis XIV à la fin de son règne, des caricatures comme la Caryatis, épouse Jouhandeau, aux yeux charbonneux de sorcière, d'autres que j'ai oubliées, qui ne risquaient de porter en rien ombrage à Florence, la souveraine. Parfois Mme Tézenas, la riche égérie d'un autre salon, mince, élégante. Entre Florence et elle jouait le pacte de jadis entre augures : on souriait en se croisant, on échangeait des confidences de bestiaire, on partageait peut-être des secrets d'alcôve. Pour être invitée avenue Malakoff quand on était femme, il fallait, d'ordinaire, n'attirer les regards en rien sinon par l'accompli, un peu comme à l'Académie dont on disait que c'était l'antichambre. Florence voulait que Paulhan fût enseveli sous les honneurs de la Coupole et par une sécurité dans la vie. Elle flattait Genevoix et quelques autres pour leur infuser l'illusion qu'ils étaient des écrivains magnifiques et, à condition d'élire Paulhan, leur offrait à brouter dans sa paume. Ainsi, des années après, et bien qu'il s'en défendît mollement, Paulhan fut candidat puis montra sa lourde face de taureau à fleur dans un bel habit doré. Après lui, ce fut Arland.

335

Puis d'autres. Ce qui faisait glapir Léautaud : « Alors, Jouhandeau, ce sera pour quand ? » Et s'esclaffant toujours : « J'oubliais qu'il était d'un sexe à part... » Comme si, pour l'Académie, c'était un obstacle. Léautaud était plus naïf qu'il ne le croyait. C'était à lui qu'Apollinaire avait dédié sa chanson du mal-aimé.

J'y prenais goût, j'étais flatté de voir les gloires de près, de me sentir par elles défrisé, déçu ou consterné parfois. Déjà, grâce à Amrouche, je m'étais frotté de loin à Gide, ce monument. J'approchais Pierre Benoit. Avec leur héroïne dont le nom commençait toujours par A, ses romans, ajustés dans une langue simple, se vendaient à des centaines de milliers d'exemplaires. Rescapé de l'Occupation avec Jouhandeau et Léautaud, il avait payé son erreur de la prison. L'homme était généreux pour ceux qu'il aimait, féroce pour les autres, naïf aussi parfois, alors qu'il se croyait si malin. Grand manitou à l'Académie, il répondait avec humour aux flatteries dont on le couvrait et s'amusait à inquiéter les candidats qui lui léchaient les mains le temps d'un déjeuner. Sa conversation était émaillée de vers de Victor Hugo, il riait beaucoup et il aimait Florence. Lui, ce fut par *le Métier des armes* que je le conquis. J'eus pour ce livre austère une très belle presse, des signatures dans la critique, le feuilleton du *Monde* et un compliment joliment ficelé de Roger Martin du Gard. Seul Doyon ne tarit pas en reproches.

Une fois, tandis qu'on attendait Jouhandeau pour passer à table, Mauriac dit : « Il va falloir que je me défende. » Quand Jouhandeau entra et l'aperçut avec une rougeur subite au visage, les deux hommes se touchèrent la main puis, se détournant aussitôt, Jouhandeau lui tira la langue. Florence mit à sa droite Mauriac confit, et, à l'autre bout de la table et du même côté, Jouhandeau. On faisait silence, Paulhan s'enfouissait derrière la broussaille de ses sourcils, Supervielle ne soufflait mot, il n'y avait que le maître du ciel et le maître des enfers. Jouhandeau commença par lancer des traits perfides, et Mauriac, excité par le silence qui s'était établi pour que rien ne se perdît des chuchotements de sa voix cassée, enveloppa si bien sa louange de Jouhandeau, mêla si bien miel et fiel dans la flatterie que Jouhandeau, d'abord surpris, en sirota la coupe avec toutes sortes de grimaces. A la fin, ils s'embrassaient presque. Jouhandeau debout lui envoyait des

baisers dont Mauriac se protégeait avec effroi quand un formidable ricanement éclata : « Voyez comme ils s'aiment ! » s'écria Léautaud. Mauriac continua sur l'auteur des fameux entretiens, leva une main bénisseuse dont le vieux singe se moqua. Léautaud raconta qu'au chanoine Mugnier qui lui demandait des nouvelles de ses bêtes, il avait répondu : « Comment vont les vôtres ? » D'après le chanoine Mugnier, qui ne daignait s'occuper que des écrivains et des artistes, et se voulait en quelque sorte leur aumônier, on péchait beaucoup à Saint-Philippe-du-Roule, à Saint-Honoré-d'Eylau, on péchait partout. Depuis qu'un soldat lui avait demandé un jour, à la gare de l'Est, de l'entendre en confession, il disait comme une respectueuse : « Je fais les gares. »

De tous ceux qui composaient sa ménagerie, Florence préférait Jouhandeau. Peut-être parce qu'il s'était tellement compromis avec les Allemands et qu'il étalait ses vices. Aux yeux de Florence, il était le plus grand, et comme il n'avait aucun succès de public, elle lui témoignait une indulgence sans borne. Je ne cache pas l'admiration que j'ai pour ce chroniqueur du purgatoire et des enfers, que Doyon m'avait fait lire tôt, et pour son courage d'avouer, non sans élégance, ce qui nous paraissait alors inavouable. Ça me changeait de Montherlant. Jouhandeau, que certains prenaient pour un cabot amateur de soufre, disait souvent ce qu'il pensait sans crainte de choquer et par une sorte de bravade que Florence aimait. On a dit qu'il avait été son amant. Après tout, en passant, pourquoi pas ? Pour l'un et l'autre, tâter de la géhenne, quelle tentation ! De lui émanait une sorte de vérité sauvage, et encore qu'il avouât parfois qu'il se sentait un monstre, je le voyais plutôt comme une abbesse lubrique, femelle diabolique, parfois blasphématoire, parfois adorante, dévorée d'amour de Dieu et se moquant du tiers comme du quart. Je me souviens de l'avoir revu à quatre-vingt-dix ans à la télévision, coiffé d'un bonnet de fourrure de mandarin tibétain, devant un Bernard Pivot plein de délicatesse et subjugué, continuer à dire qu'il avait agencé sa vie comme il lui plaisait. Chez ce « détrousseur d'âmes », selon le mot de Nadeau, il y avait une certaine grandeur. De Caryatis, sa femme, la sorcière qui l'escortait, il exploitait les travers et les méchancetés. Elle lui servait, ils allaient tous deux, unis dans l'horrible, à travers les marécages et les cavernes de leur

malédiction. Ça me changeait aussi de mes années avec les militaires, j'avais l'impression de faire la noce. Je découvrais chez moi une certaine tentation pour ce qui n'était pas la vertu, et même une certaine indulgence pour les faiblesses du temps de l'Occupation. Où Camus ne pardonnait rien, je me montrais moins dur, je ne sais pourquoi. Qui pouvait prévoir ce qui, en d'autres circonstances, aurait pu se passer ? Qui, par exemple, pouvait jeter la pierre aux jeunes gens trompés par le gouvernement de Vichy, qui s'étaient engagés dans la guerre contre les Russes ? Je regrettais de n'avoir pas connu ce fripon de Maurice Sachs qui avait, disait-on, été crucifié sur la porte d'une grange, comme une chouette, par d'imbéciles sanguinaires.

Jouhandeau m'aimait bien. Nous l'appelions souvent M. Godeau, comme il s'appelait lui-même dans ses *Journaliers*. En allusion à la pièce de Beckett où Godot s'écrit autrement, nous attendions Godeau. Avec Florence et Jean Denoël, nous allions quelquefois chez lui. Il m'agaçait quand il se mettait à l'harmonium et me forçait à chanter avec lui le *Salve Regina* ou le *Dies irae*. Un jour, dans la grosse Buick, la voiture royale, nous attendions, quai Voltaire, qu'il descendît de chez Montherlant à qui il avait rendu visite. Je m'étais bien gardé de l'accompagner puisque Montherlant et moi étions brouillés. Tout n'était pas que mensonge chez l'auteur des *Célibataires*. Quand Jouhandeau nous retrouva, il s'assit près de moi en me serrant de près pour me voir m'écarter de lui comme d'un serpent. Cela faisait partie de ses gamineries. Il feignait de ne plus se posséder si, dans la rue, nous croisions un bel éphèbe. Lui, qui avait écrit *De l'abjection*, croyait que sa réputation de Don Juan de pissotière le servait ; c'était sa faiblesse. Au moins ne se prenait-il pas au sérieux comme d'autres qui ne lui arrivaient pas à la cheville, au moins pouvait-on le taquiner. Un jour où Florence lui reprochait de porter des bretelles, il les enleva et me les offrit. Je les gardai un temps, puis on me les déroba. Nous allions tous ensemble au théâtre voir du Genet ou du Claudel, nous allions parfois chez moi, à Choisel où, une fois, il prit fantaisie à Florence de vouloir habiter de temps en temps. Elle ne buvait que son champagne qu'elle battait avec une palette et était saoule très vite. Alors elle naviguait à travers des brouillards. Quelquefois elle me prenait les mains dans les siennes qu'elle avait minces,

courtes et chargées d'énormes émeraudes. Elle n'avait pas d'enfant et il était trop tard pour qu'elle en eût, aussi chérissait-elle ses pékinois et les parfumait-elle au 5 de Chanel. L'amour, si elle l'avait jamais connu, appartenait à l'illusion et elle choisissait ce qui durait. J'admirais son culot, son mépris pour les conventions, sa chance. Un soir où elle ne tenait plus debout, elle s'agrippa à moi, j'eus l'impression d'avoir passé la nuit avec la reine Néfertiti empêtrée dans ses bandelettes, comme Malraux peut-être avec la reine de Saba. Je n'étais pas fier, nous n'étions pas dans la cathédrale de Chartres. Puis ça lui passa.

Comme elle pouvait tout offrir et tout s'offrir, et comme elle s'ennuyait sur son tas d'or, elle avait des foucades et nous emmenait parfois dans le Midi. Elle se croyait peut-être Antinéa, collectionnant les mecs qui lui plaisaient. Son réfrigérateur à elle, sa morgue, c'était « la Vigie », le nom que portait la villa des Gould à Juan-les-Pins. Qui aurait pu m'imaginer en compagnie de ses banquiers, de ses commensaux et de ses duègnes ? Son mari dirigeait ses affaires par câble et téléphone. Parfois, je me demandais ce que je faisais là et je filais. Sans moi, Marie allait devenir mère. Où était la vraie vie ? J'allais, je venais du Conseil de la République à Choisel, je voyais Sigaux, Kanters, mes amis Dreyfus, de moins en moins Camus, mal remis d'un voyage en Amérique. Je lui avais parlé de sa nouvelle pièce chez Hébertot, et il s'était laissé aller à un mouvement d'amertume : Gérard Philipe et Reggiani avaient refusé le rôle, trop mal payé, et Maria Casarès n'avait pas de partenaire digne d'elle. Je passais chez Gallimard pour Minerve et M. Hirsch, je pilotais des avions de liaison, des Nord 1100, je regagnais Juan-les-Pins ou alors j'organisais un nouveau voyage au Maroc et en AOF. J'aurais dû préparer l'école de guerre, mais la littérature s'était emparée de moi. A présent j'écrivais le récit de ce qui avait été ma passion pour Marie, en cet été brûlant sur les hauts de Chevreuse. Marie me disait : « Je n'épouse pas un homme comme vous. » Là s'étendait un plateau balayé par le vent du sud, toutes les mares et les fontaines étaient à sec, je marchais torse nu, derrière mes chiens pareils à des loups.

Mon petit père, plusieurs fois surgi dans la vallée de Chevreuse, répétait que j'étais un fils ingrat et que je

m'égarais. Il avait raison. Mon divorce, mes relations avec l'armée, un premier livre qui avait eu un certain succès, mes amitiés avec des écrivains qu'il ne connaissait pas, Saint-Germain-des-Prés, tout m'excitait. De temps en temps, je sautais dans un courrier pour Alger et j'allais embrasser ma mère. Triste sort des femmes quand elles deviennent veuves et que s'éloignent les enfants qu'elles chérissent, la solitude est leur pain. J'allais dans la vie, ma mère me croyait en pleine gloire et je n'osais pas la détromper. Etait-ce une compagnie recommandable que le bec lubrique de Jouhandeau, ce bonze de Jean Denoël et la belle et puissante Florence agitant un moulinet dans son verre de champagne ?

La Buick allait, venait, nous nous arrêtions à Lourmarin où Marie et moi avions eu envie d'acheter une maison. Giono promettait de m'en trouver une. Oui, mais l'argent ? *La Vallée heureuse* avait sombré dans le naufrage des éditions Charlot. Le rêve m'agita un moment que Florence, qui se voulait mécène, aurait pu fonder là un phalanstère dont l'idée souriait à Denoël. « Il y a en chacun de nous le désir de profiter, disait Doyon, pourquoi n'essaies-tu pas ? » Il venait d'écrire un essai, *Eloge du maquereau*. Ah ! s'il avait été invité, lui, quelle fiesta, quelle providence !

Nous regagnions Juan-les-Pins où le roi des chemins de fer n'apparaissait jamais. Comme Florence lui parlait de moi une fois, il avait dit : « Il est comme vos singes. » C'était l'été, les plages regorgeaient de belles filles bronzées, je m'ennuyais plus encore qu'avenue Malakoff, parce qu'on ne voyait à la Vigie que des mouettes déplumées et des banquiers, parfois quelque vedette décrépite de la littérature dont Florence convoitait la voix pour Paulhan. Nous allions aux îles de Lérins. Quoi, avec un simple canot, même pas un yacht de milliardaire ? Florence, qui se jugeait déjà sur le retour, hésitait à se montrer en maillot. Finalement, comme une baleine, elle faisait trempette dans les rochers. Le soir, on revenait au champagne à moulinette, aux conseillers financiers et aux potins de la Croisette, seule distraction des tristes snobs du lieu. L'amoureuse de Cocteau et de ce vieux clochard persifleur de Léautaud, qu'on ne traînait pas jusqu'ici parce qu'il aurait scandalisé, s'infligeait pénitence pour obéir à son mari, et apparaissait dans les galas de bienfaisance sous une armure étincelante. Moi, les bijoux, les perlouses, les broches, les

breloques, les couronnes, les diadèmes, tout ce qu'on vendra d'elle plus tard à New York pour des centaines de millions de dollars, ça ne m'épatait pas, on ne fait pas l'amour avec des diams. N'empêche, nous la suivions, nous étions sa cour. La voie ferrée passait tout près, sur le rivage, et les Gould entendaient gronder et roucouler leur fortune. Jouhandeau débarquait de Paris, frisé, mielleux, couvert d'écailles d'enfer, Denoël décrochait un nouveau voyage à Lourmarin où le notaire proposait des maisons qui ne convenaient pas : trop petites, trop laides, trop mal situées ou alors trop chères : nous revenions dégrisés. Il en est des maisons comme des femmes. On les imagine telles qu'on les désire, on se hâte, on tremble presque, on frémit, et soudain leur apparition laisse déçu, désolé, presque trompés. Pourquoi Lourmarin ? Parce que tout y était beau et qu'on s'y sentait bien. Jean Grenier, Bosco et Camus avaient fabriqué là un mystère. La mode s'y greffa vite, tout le monde voudra avoir un mas dans le Lubéron. La fureur ira plus loin et s'attaquera aux villages en ruine. Consuelo, la folle petite veuve de Saint-Exupéry, relèvera la citadelle d'Oppède et le Tout-Saint-Germain-des-Prés papotera là un temps. Cependant ce jour-là, en descendant de la Buick : « J'ai donné ordre au notaire que le manoir qui vous plaisait soit à votre nom », me dit-elle. J'en restai cloué sur place, puis vacillant, baba, un peu honteux. Elle exagérait. Qui pourrait croire désormais à rien de ce que j'écrivais ? Le soir même, égarée déjà dans la griserie du champagne, déjà saoule, Florence m'enveloppa de ses bras et, du bout des doigts, m'effleura le visage. Elle avait ce geste pour ce qu'elle avait acheté et qui lui plaisait encore. Elle avait enlevé ses lunettes pour mieux voir, ses yeux brillaient. Qui sait ? Elle se disait peut-être que ce sauvage qui avait grillé l'Allemagne de nuit pendant une année de guerre, elle se l'était payé le prix d'un petit château, qu'elle finirait aussi par le civiliser et le vêtir d'un habit brodé, que ce serait un des fleurons de sa couronne. J'y pense maintenant. Camus m'avait mieux jugé qu'elle. Un jour que Jean Daniel qui ne me connaissait pas encore lui parlait de moi, il avait dit : « Vous verrez bien, ne vous découragez pas. »

Qu'elle, la toute-puissante, la faiseuse d'anges d'Académie, la pourrie d'or et de bank-notes, la protectrice des artistes homosexuels qui n'invitait pas Genet parce qu'il déplaisait à

Jouhandeau et qu'il emportait des babioles, l'ancienne entre-metteuse du temps de l'Occupation, la pharaonne gavée de foie gras et de homards décortiqués, l'idole qui, d'un claque-ment de doigts achetait ou vendait actions, obligations, consciences ou âmes et changeait les cours de la Bourse, elle qui ruinait ce qui lui résistait ou rendait la vie aux ruines, elle à qui les politiciens videurs de pots de chambre baisaient la main avec des courbettes, me prenait pour une tête de chez un antiquaire. Ma main partit comme la foudre. Violente, sèche, imprévisible. Face et revers. Je me souvins du mot que Cioran chez Mme Tézenas lui avait décoché un jour : « Vous, c'est à cause de vos dollars que vous êtes là. » J'ai oublié qui était là, qui nous regardait à ce moment d'avant le dîner. La lumière était douce, grise, un peu verte. Je vois soudain ses yeux humides de larmes. J'entends le sourd rugissement de cette lionne en chaleur, folle d'un ancien massacreur et incendiaire de Leipzig déversant sa charge de phosphore et de tolite sur la ville en feu. Elle se trompait. Rien de moi n'était à elle. Si je me souviens, là ? Ça vous reste, ces choses-là. Vous n'en dormez plus pendant huit jours.

Un instant, je demeurai stupide comme devant un accident, puis brusquement, je m'en allai, filai à ma chambre et fis ma valise. Une goujaterie ? Enfin, un réflexe hono-rable, aurait dit mon petit père, enfin on se retrouve. Le téléphone sonna. Je ne répondis pas. Quelqu'un frappa à la porte. Je ne bougeai pas. Je doublai la dose de somnifère pour éviter l'avion contre lequel chaque nuit je me fracas-sais.

Le lendemain matin, Jean Denoël vint me chercher comme d'habitude, la face lisse, les yeux plissés. Il savait tout et avait tout vu. Ce qu'on ne lui disait pas, il le devinait. Il y avait les mêmes à déjeuner. Jouhandeau, visqueux comme jamais, se répandit en taquineries. Paulhan, descendu avec sa nonne d'un wagon-lit du matin, tout frétillant, récitait avec émerveillement un mot reçu de Ponge. Il aurait aimé saluer Char, et Char allait venir : Florence envoyait la Buick. Florence, quand elle m'aperçut, m'embrassa avec une grande effusion, m'étreignit presque. Elle paraissait sou-lagée.

Denoël m'accompagna au train de nuit. Je me gardai bien de raconter quoi que ce soit à Camus. Il m'aurait dit : « On ne bat pas une femme, même quand elle a de l'oseille. Tu n'es pas un Arabe. » Je l'avais échappé belle.

Au fond, c'était moi que j'avais giflé.

XIII

La mort de ma mère

GIDE mourut. Pour moi, ce qui restait de lui c'était l'homme de courage, sauf au moment de Pétain. Là, il s'était gouré comme nous tous, ou presque. Après, il avait été reçu à Alger à la villa des glycines, et il avait osé demander à de Gaulle : « Quand avez-vous décidé de désobéir ?... » De Gaulle n'avait répondu que par un geste vague. Question naïve. Je fus le premier à signer sur le registre de la rue Vaneau, mais je n'osai pas monter, à cause d'Amrouche peut-être.

A peine Gide était-il inhumé qu'un télégramme m'appela au chevet de ma mère. Le plus grand moment de mon amour pour elle avait été celui où, quelques mois auparavant, à une de mes visites, j'avais tenu étroitement serré contre moi, le protégeant, le portant, le baignant de quelques larmes, son corps presque réduit à rien. Le médecin qui la soignait m'avait dit qu'elle était condamnée. A genoux devant elle, je lui avais demandé pardon de repartir encore. A quatre-vingts ans passés, elle s'éteindrait loin de moi, le front buté, ses mains cherchant les miennes. J'en avais la gorge nouée. Je fixais du regard la peau luisante de ses bras.

Je me hâtai de traverser la mer et de gagner le village où mon frère l'avait recueillie. Louise, ma belle-sœur, fondit en larmes en m'apercevant, et vite je découvris le lit où ma mère était étendue. Le jour tombait. Je m'assis à côté d'elle, comme si elle avait été seulement malade. Trop tard.

Si le vent du sud nous avait moins retardés, j'aurais pu être là plus tôt. Très haut dans le ciel, des nuages ressemblaient à des chevauchées mythiques. M'aurait-elle seulement reconnu ? Elle était devenue une absence, un souvenir. Sa main

345

que je tentai de dénouer pour y glisser mes doigts était de marbre, son front glacé. On me dit que depuis un dernier voyage à Alger pour une consultation, elle s'était emmurée dans le silence. Alors, on m'avait télégraphié. On n'avait pas pu lui lire ma dernière lettre arrivée de la veille, elle n'entendait plus.

Louise l'avait habillée, ses cheveux étaient tirés sur le front et sur la nuque. Il me semblait que sa poitrine se soulevait, que son écharpe bougeait. On me donna son alliance que je glissai à un doigt. Ainsi, pensai-je, je serais fiancé à ma mère. Par moments je me demandais si elle était vraiment morte. Etait-elle désormais du côté où nous avions tellement peur de verser, comme autrefois dans nos voitures à chevaux sur une mauvaise route? A la lueur des bougies qui la veillaient, j'observai son visage. D'un côté, avec la lèvre supérieure rentrée, le nez aux ailes pincées et une orbite profonde meurtrie, déjà noirâtre, une paupière de poupée aux cils collés, il me semblait d'une étrangère, tandis que de l'autre, il reflétait la sérénité. Je la revis à une année de distance, une fois où, dominée par une déchéance physique qu'elle ne pouvait plus cacher, toute droite devant moi, comme soumise enfin à la loi qui nous régit de naître, de vieillir et de nous en aller, elle s'était déjà sentie sur le point de partir. Elle n'était plus et le savait. D'un regard qu'elle eut pour moi, elle me signifia qu'elle ne regrettait rien de rien. Quand elle avait trahi son mari pour l'instituteur, elle cherchait l'amour, et celui qu'elle avait eu pour moi, le dernier, le vrai. C'était une âme cruelle que la fatalité d'épouser d'abord un gendarme, ancien cuirassier à queue de cheval, n'avait pas soumise. Pendant quinze ans, elle avait dissimulé sa déception à ce moment où rien n'était possible pour une femme, sauf si on avait suivi des études et si on pouvait partir, partir, partir, aller ailleurs. Comment suivre des études quand on a des parents illettrés et qu'on est une femme, à la fin du siècle dernier? Seule une Louise Colet pouvait s'en tirer, ou une Florence Lacaze. D'abord ne pas naître dans une petite ferme de la Mitidja, mais en France chez des bourgeois, aller au collège, passer le baccalauréat, être bien tournée, chanter peut-être? Séduire un roi des chemins de fer américains? Devenir la maîtresse d'un homme plus important encore et âgé, fréquenter des gens d'esprit, habiter Paris, se mêler à la société des artistes,

intriguer, et, à la longue, et à condition d'avoir plus de talent que de beauté, se laisser courtiser, ouvrir son lit à ceux qui pouvaient vous aider à vous hisser dans la hiérarchie. Avec Flaubert qui, homme de taille et chaud lapin, se montrait d'une certaine rudesse de caractère, même Louise Colet crut s'être trompée. A son gré, Flaubert n'était pas assez connu. Il lui fallut encore Musset, Vigny, beaucoup d'autres. Elle croyait à ses poèmes à elle, des poèmes de ce temps-là, à la noix. Sa gloire, et elle était loin de s'en douter, devait être les lettres de Flaubert qu'elle avait eu si souvent envie de détruire et sans quoi elle ne serait rien. Ma pauvre mère n'eut qu'un instituteur sans avenir, dans un bled reculé d'Algérie. Sa gloire fut le péché, et sa consolation, son illusion d'avoir donné naissance à un phénix. Je n'avais que mon ardeur à devenir quelqu'un, mais quoi, mais qui ? D'abord elle se vit peut-être mère d'un chanoine. Qui sait ? d'un évêque, d'un prédicateur, puis d'un officier subalterne, sous-lieutenant, qui se compromettait dans un mariage banal, devenait enfin aviateur, et à présent... A chacune de mes visites, âme flottant dans une enveloppe qu'on craignait de percer en la touchant, elle retrouvait un semblant de vie. Née sous le soleil, elle pour qui le soleil était tout, elle se gardait de lui. Je vis là un appel du gouffre. Pourtant, à ses côtés, battait un instant le frêle espoir d'une guérison, et cependant, au médecin qui la soignait, j'avais demandé de ne pas prolonger sa vie si elle endurait de ces souffrances qui, par moments, semblaient atroces.

On me dit qu'à l'hôpital elle avait reçu la visite de l'aumônier. Elle lui avait dit qu'elle se sentait incapable de se confesser mais recevrait volontiers ce qu'on appelait jadis l'extrême-onction et qui portait un nom plus rassurant : le sacrement des malades. Après quoi, une sorte de grâce l'envahit. Comme un lion repu à côté de sa proie à demi dévorée, le mal l'avait laissée en repos. Le lendemain, elle s'affaiblissait encore et mourait. J'aurais voulu une douleur à l'égal de ce que j'éprouvais, et je me sentais le cœur sec.

Cette nuit-là, à côté d'elle, c'était moi qui ne dormais pas. On nous avait laissés seuls pour ce dernier tête-à-tête et une grande part de moi s'en allait. Le vent s'était levé, la mer devait battre les rochers, une chaise craquait et je sursautais, croyant que c'était elle qui avait bougé, que je pouvais encore lui

parler, qu'elle vivait. Je regardais son visage à la lumière des bougies, symbole de nos âmes si faciles à éteindre, il me semblait qu'elle souriait, qu'elle me pardonnait mes infidélités, qu'elle savait enfin, là où elle était, que les fils naissent pour le tourment des mères.

Comme on ne se chauffe jamais en Algérie, même en plein hiver où on allume parfois un réchaud à pétrole, le froid me forçait de temps en temps à me lever. Louise veillait dans la cuisine, avec ses sœurs accourues pour la circonstance, mon frère René nous rejoignait. Je me réchauffais, fumais une cigarette, Louise faisait du café, ouvrait un tiroir sur de misérables trésors : des boucles d'oreilles qu'enfant j'appelais des petites lanternes à cause de leur forme, une boucle de ceinture en argent, des riens. Elle avait demandé qu'on s'épargne la dépense d'un faire-part dans les journaux, pensant qu'elle comptait si peu qu'il n'était pas utile de signaler sa disparition. Je revenais près d'elle, je la regardais. Le premier mort que j'avais vu, ç'avait été sa propre mère, à la ferme de Sidi-Moussa, quand le supérieur du séminaire, M. Payen, m'avait appelé de son doigt crochu, et que Hayek m'avait conduit dans l'auto de louage. Puis mon père, mais aime-t-on un père, surtout quand il est fauteur de péchés ? Puis mon frère Robert, puis des camarades, dans une aviation où il suffisait d'une tempête ou d'une erreur de navigation pour vous tuer. Quant aux morts de la guerre, ils étaient à part, en quelque sorte, les fameux *missing*, les manquants. Que de *missing* dans nos rangs ! Comme si, en ayant assez de nous, ils nous avaient joué une mauvaise farce, à moins qu'ils aient été abattus par des canons ou un chasseur, ou concassés dans une collision ; on ne savait pas non plus si, grâce à leur parachute et à notre fameuse boîte d'évasion, ils n'allaient pas revenir, ça s'était vu, après un petit tour en Hollande. Un espoir planait, les *missing* n'étaient pas forcément morts. Ma mère, je la voyais comme un navire qui prend doucement le large vers des îles, je gardais ses pieds glacés dans mes mains, mon sang battait contre sa funeste présence, elle s'en allait sans que je puisse la retenir, je n'avais plus que le silence pour lui parler.

Les pendules, je n'osais pas les arrêter, comme c'était le rite autrefois quand il y a un défunt. La montre à mon poignet, aurais-je voulu que je n'aurais pas pu. Rien ne peut bloquer ces petites industries qu'en les cassant ou en enlevant leur pile,

pareilles un peu à cette toupie sur laquelle nous tournons au milieu d'un arsenal dont nous savons tout, sauf comment c'est là et ce que ça y fabrique, et nous avec. J'avais dans la bouche le souvenir des gâteaux de patate douce à la cannelle qu'elle me portait au séminaire. J'étais déjà reclus, pour le rachat de son péché, elle s'échinait à monter la côte de Saint-Eugène avec son couffin à provisions, elle trompait le règlement qui n'autorisait le parloir que tous les quinze jours, un dimanche sur deux. Elle, c'était tous les dimanches. Si un professeur avait osé le lui rappeler, elle aurait baissé les yeux, pleuré peut-être. Chez nous, on n'embrassait pas mais on ne pleurait pas non plus. Mon père voulait qu'on soit de vrais barbares. Ce n'était pas son genre à elle, civilisée. Elle prétendait que les enfants ont besoin d'amour. « De coups de pied au cul », disait mon père. Lui-même avait été élevé à la façon des Prussiens et s'en faisait gloire, le pauvre homme, à cause de Hayek élevé en douceur pour ne recevoir de sa femme qu'humiliations, parfois même des baffes.

Ma mère venait tous les dimanches, et plus souvent encore quand on allait chanter à Notre-Dame d'Afrique ou à la cathédrale, elle était là pour voir son Jules adoré, son petit salaud d'ange branleur qui se croyait en faute lui aussi à cause de sa mère. Tout juste si le Supérieur ne nous invitait pas à gronder nos mères ou à les dénoncer. Le dimanche où on ne m'appelait pas au parloir, j'étais tout attrapé, déçu, fait comme un rat. Ma mère, ma mère ! En ce temps-là, je n'avais pas le cœur capable d'éclater pour elle ; les lazaristes nous répétaient que nous devions d'abord aimer Dieu. Dieu ? Mais c'était qui ? Le Christ mort sur la croix était son fils, mais le Père où était-il ? Comment était-il ? Nous étions comme les disciples, un bout de temps après la résurrection, quand le Christ leur apparaît et qu'ils se trouvent tout couillons, ne sachant quoi dire quand il leur parle de la vérité, de la voie à suivre. « Quelle voie ? demandent-ils. Seigneur, montre-nous où nous devons aller ? » Et lui, frappé de leur peu de subtilité, leur répète qu'il est la vie, que là où il va ils seront à leur tour, et ces imbéciles essayent de s'y retrouver et de conclure une sorte de pacte avec lui le Ressuscité, est-ce qu'on ressuscitait sur terre quand on était mort ? On avait bien vu pour Lazare ; il avait fini par mourir pour de vrai. Ils lui disaient : « Bon, bon, n'en parlons plus. Montre-nous le Père, ça nous suffira. »

Ou quelque chose comme ça. Si vous ne me croyez pas, lisez l'évangile selon saint-Jean, chapitre quatorze, versets un à douze.

Ainsi, pendant tout le séminaire, je ne me suis posé aucune question sur Dieu. Dieu, c'était Dieu, fallait pas chercher à savoir. Ça ne me tourmentait pas, ça ne m'intéressait même pas tellement. Le Christ nous ressemblait, ça, je comprenais. Et on aurait voulu que je devienne membre du clergé, que je parle de Dieu à mes chers compatriotes d'Algérie tellement plus concernés par le soleil, les bains de mer, la mouna et les femmes ? Quant aux Arabes qui prétendaient que Dieu, c'était Allah, ils n'avaient qu'un tort : exister, alors qu'on était si heureux sans eux, sauf pour avoir des petits cireurs, des mauresques ou des serviteurs comme Meftah.

En cette nuit qui s'achevait sur les fenêtres brouillées, de quoi ne m'accusais-je pas, près de ma mère endormie ? C'est une nuit qui a compté, j'y suis encore. Je vois briller le baudrier d'Orion, je cherche d'autres étoiles familières, Sirius, Véga, Altaïr, plus resplendissantes qu'au-dessus de l'Europe, on aurait dit que le vent qui soufflait les bousculait. Une faible lumière derrière les persiennes, c'est tout ce qui restait de la réalité de ma mère. Par moments, j'aurais voulu qu'elle me fasse signe, qu'elle me demande d'approcher pour recevoir sa bénédiction comme la fois où je l'avais serrée dans mes bras.

A l'aube, je cueillis quelques fleurs de l'avant-printemps dans le jardin : une jacinthe, un bouton de rose, des œillets que je mis dans ses mains. Quand on monta le cercueil, les femmes nous laissèrent. Mon frère et moi nous enveloppâmes notre mère dans un drap de lin qui avait peut-être servi jadis, il y a bien longtemps, aux impudicités de l'amour, et devenait son linceul. A côté d'elle je glissai ma dernière lettre, qu'elle n'avait pas lue. Mon frère ajouta quelque chose, je ne sais quoi, pour l'aider pendant le terrible passage, un viatique. Par moments encore je me disais : « Avons-nous raison de l'enfermer ? Ne risque-t-elle pas d'être effrayée si elle se réveille maintenant ? » Après quoi, chacun vint l'embrasser sur le front, sauf moi, car cette créature qui changeait à vue d'œil n'était plus ma mère, la femme qui m'avait donné la lumière et à qui, moi son fils, l'enlevais en rabattant le drap sur

son visage. Non, non. Ma vraie mère, c'était sa jeunesse, son visage de péché.

Nous étions en mars, le ciel était clair, le vent de la mer butait sur les talus de la route, et entre les rangs de vigne foisonnait ce qu'on appelle là-bas la vinaigrette, cette verdure qui a un goût aigrelet quand on la mâche. Aux carrefours, des enfants indigènes nous tendaient des bottes d'asperges et de poireaux sauvages, si fins, si délectables. Sur les collines, par la route qu'elle avait prise trois jours plus tôt, les amandiers étaient en fleur, tout roses. Elle avait peut-être vu, en clignant des yeux, l'horizon brillant.

A Sidi-Moussa, on nous attendait. Nous allâmes d'abord à l'église où elle avait fait sa première communion et s'était mariée avec le gendarme. Nous étions peu nombreux : ce qui restait de la famille Paris, ceux qui la connaissaient. Le curé a-t-il chanté le *Requiem* ou le *Libera me* en latin, ou les instructions de Vatican II avaient-elles déjà dévasté les traditions afin qu'il n'y ait plus de mystère pour personne avec les prières en français ? Puis ce fut le cimetière, et presque à l'entrée, presque en face de celui des Pélégri, le tombeau des Paris où dormaient déjà ma grand-mère, mon grand-père, l'oncle Jules, mais pas Meftah, il était où, Meftah ? et avant eux les autres Paris, du côté des hommes, de la Franche-Comté, et, du côté des femmes, de Montségur en Ariège où il y a encore des Bouychou à qui je ressemble, même tête de bois, elle avait raison, Florence. Puis la famille s'égailla chez les uns et les autres. Nous étions en 1951, il ne se passait rien, le drapeau français flottait à la mairie au-dessus de la devise Liberté, Egalité, Fraternité, ce qui faisait ricaner plus d'un ; certaines langues de vipère disaient que les bicots se faufilaient partout, que leurs gosses à l'école envahissaient tout : certains pessimistes ajoutaient que les bicots finiraient par nous flanquer à la porte, ce qui faisait hausser les épaules. Comme je ne connaissais plus personne, depuis le temps où je n'accompagnais plus l'oncle Jules à l'Espérance, je revins au cimetière, près du stade silencieux. Des abeilles butinaient les œillets, les roses et les soucis qui fleurissaient le tombeau en marbre gris surmonté de sa croix en granit, le vent bruissait dans les branches des arbres exotiques plantés là. Dans un mois, par bouffées, ce serait le parfum des vignes pour les colons défunts

qui, autrefois, s'en grisaient. Le lieu n'était pas très beau, mais on voyait par-dessus le mur la montagne de Blida. Je me demandai même si, un jour... Ah! mais, les places étaient chères, il n'y en avait plus tellement dans le caveau, est-ce que ma mère n'avait pas pris la dernière? Et puis, aurais-je eu droit, moi le bâtard, à me pavaner au milieu de ces actes de naissance authentiques?

La source de mes larmes tarie, je me sentis orphelin. On est orphelin dans le secret du cœur, quand c'est un étranger qui vous réveille dans un hôtel et n'ose pas entrer, que vous devez répondre, allumer vous-même la lumière, vous lever. A qui puis-je parler de ma mère, maintenant que mon frère René et Louise sont morts, eux, dans le Midi où, chassés d'Algérie, ils étaient, après un temps passé chez moi, allés mendier un peu de soleil, à Argelès-sur-mer? J'ai encore les cousines dont j'étais amoureux autrefois, je pense à elles et je me dis : « Où sont-elles dans le vaste monde? » Et si je vous disais que je me pose à présent la même question pour ceux à qui je venais de rendre visite dans leur *dormitorium* et même pour ma mère chérie que je venais de déposer au milieu des fleurs, le croiriez-vous? Où sont-ils? Mais nous ne sommes qu'en 1951. Patience. Mal encore remis de mon passage lugubre du Père-Lachaise, où Mirande a une case à côté de Fiori l'Anisette, je me remémore, au moment où j'écris, cette autre visite à venir au cimetière de Sidi-Moussa, et une sorte de vertige me prend. La tête me tourne, je dois m'appuyer au chambranle d'une porte et, si je descends un escalier, tenir solidement la rampe. « Tiens bon! » comme on dit encore là-bas. A Vézelay, il me semble que j'ai peut-être vu pour la dernière fois le soleil se lever dans la brume puis, déjà haut, plaquer sur la basilique une gerbe de violente lumière blonde.

Comme par hasard, hier, je me suis arrêté chez le menuisier. Il était en train d'assembler des planches de chêne qui m'ont paru suspectes. Hé oui, c'était bien ça : il a été débordé cet hiver, il s'en constitue un stock qu'il m'a montré en douce, et, comme une gâterie, m'en a désigné un, superbe, pas trop orné : « Celui-là vous irait très bien, un mètre quatre-vingt-dix... », m'a-t-il lancé avec un clin d'œil. Il a fermé sa porte pour qu'on ne lui dérobe rien et nous sommes allés à l'hôtel du Morvan, tout à côté, pour nous en glisser un

derrière la cravate, façon de parler parce que nous portons rarement la cravate, lui et moi. Lui, c'est toujours un côtes-du-rhône et moi un aligoté pas trop frais, sinon ça casse le bouquet. Après quoi, nous avons parlé de choses et d'autres, de la girouette de la tour Saint-Pierre encore tombée, de l'horloge municipale détraquée, des gens, de notre député, du garagiste qui se débrouille drôlement, et nous nous sommes quittés. C'est un ami. Il porte un nom du pays : Rousseau, il en a vu de toutes les couleurs, il a connu Romain Rolland, mon cher Max-Pol conseiller municipal et tant d'autres. C'est un homme solide, taillé dans le dur, difficile à émouvoir comme à brouiller dans ses idées sur le monde et la façon dont nous sommes gouvernés. Tout cela pour prouver qu'il n'y a pas de hasard, qu'au moment où, au sortir d'un nouveau déjeuner de Florence Gould avec sa bande de génies, de jocrisses et de malins, je recevais un télégramme qui m'appelait au chevet de ma mère, eh bien cette visite au menuisier était dans l'ordre des choses pour conclure. Il suffit de regarder autour de soi, même à Sidi-Moussa, canton de L'Arba, ancien département d'Alger, maintenant dirigé par un préfet arabe, un *ouali* ou un *wali*, comme vous voudrez.

Avant de quitter Alger, je retournai avec mon frère 16, rue Montaigne, où son fils occuperait l'appartement. Dans le bureau de mon père l'instituteur, je fourgonnai dans les tiroirs où il casait ses bricoles, je retrouvai les alènes dont il se servait pour rapetasser ses chaussures et tout son bric-à-brac de vis, clés, verres à lunettes qu'il conservait dans des boîtes. Dire qu'il avait cherché partout sans jamais les trouver les quelques billets de mille de l'héritage de ma grand-mère que ma mère lui cachait : fixés sous le tablier de son bureau, sous ses mains en quelque sorte, ma mère me l'avait dit avec un clin d'œil. Cet argent qui n'était pas à lui et qu'il aurait voulu avoir le tourmentait ; ma mère s'ingéniait à ce qu'il ne le gaspille pas dans des folies, à une industrie nouvelle dont on lui disait monts et merveilles, genre fonds russes. Avant de monter, je m'étais arrêté dans la rue d'épiciers, de droguistes et de matelassiers, que ma mère empruntait pour aller à l'église, et une tendresse que je n'attendais plus me vint aux yeux. De son

353

balcon, ma mère m'avait souvent guetté. Après quoi, je m'aperçus que la rampe de l'escalier, si lisse autrefois quand je la descendais sur le ventre, était devenue rugueuse, rayée et même entamée par des vandales avec des clous ou la pointe d'un couteau. A cela, est-ce bête ? je conclus qu'il ne fallait plus avoir aucun regret d'Alger. Personne ne m'y attendait plus, Louise et René habitaient à soixante kilomètres de là, il n'y avait plus que mon père l'instituteur et son fils Robert au cimetière de Saint-Eugène. Quand une ville ne compte que par le funèbre, on peut lui dire adieu. Eh bien, adieu ! Et les amours ? Mon mariage avec Mirande, d'autres rencontres furtives, il n'y en a pas eu tellement, d'amours, là. Cette fille si frêle, si facile, si discrète, tout de suite après notre arrivée en juin 1940, comme si elle avait voulu me consoler du désastre ? Pétain, de Gaulle, fidélité ou trahison, est-ce qu'on sait toujours où l'on va ? Rue d'Isly, on draguait, comme la drague qui racle éternellement le port de Bougie toujours embarbouillé, emmerdouillé des lies de la Soummam. Je veux bien que les filles d'Alger ne soient pas faciles, qu'elles soient surtout des aguicheuses, des allumeuses, après quoi elles se réfugient derrière leur vertu. Ç'aurait été triste s'il n'y avait eu que le séminaire et l'armée !

Donc, un moment vient où l'on croit en avoir fini avec une ville. Je me fis conduire à l'aérodrome de Maison-Blanche où je quittai mon frère René et Louise. J'avançai vers les terre-pleins du terrain comme si je saluais la naissance du prince qu'est le soleil du matin, si puissant, si royal là-bas. L'avion, encore une vieille ordure du JU 52, était là. Sur la piste gisait une hirondelle morte, un martinet plutôt, déjà raide, que je déposai dans l'herbe. Les moteurs grondaient déjà, l'équipage gagna ses places, le navigateur rectifia ses caps en fonction des forts vents de la météo, le mécanicien contrôla ses pressions, le pilote fit jouer ses commandes : l'avion, un cargo, transportait des caisses de matériel, j'étais le seul passager, j'éprouvai comme le besoin impie de secouer la poussière de mes souliers. Vite, embarquons !

Quand cette pauvre haridelle s'éleva, je m'installai dans le cockpit avec les camarades. La plaine où dormait ma mère s'éloigna dans la lumière. C'était comme si, à cheval, j'avais piqué une fois encore des deux, mais le JU 52, c'était une carne.

XIV

La vie parisienne

Désormais j'espaçai mes déjeuners avenue Malakoff. Gilbert Sigaux, Kanters et moi sortions beaucoup, Moinot, Cayrol et Claude Mauriac nous retrouvaient, le jeudi aussi, aux Deux-Magots puis chez Lipp. Quelquefois Jean-Louis Bory surgissait, quel esprit celui-là, quelle langue de feu ! Avec Kanters, ils n'arrêtaient pas de faire des étincelles. Doyon, chez qui je retournais rarement, vieillissait mal et s'enfonçait dans la débine. Toujours virulent, il souffrait de ce qu'il appelait l'ingratitude de Malraux et l'indifférence de Camus à son égard.

Camus avait quitté *Combat*, on jouait *les Justes*, et cette fois, la critique le ménagea. Dans cette pièce retentissaient les tragiques bêlements de Maria Casarès qui excitaient tellement la verve de Kanters. Camus s'était réfugié dans le théâtre : les comédiens l'aimaient. Avec eux comme avec nous, il formait une famille et n'avait nul besoin de se justifier. Quand il allait embrasser sa mère à Alger, il fréquentait surtout les étudiants. Dans une fringale de vie que la maladie dont il avait souffert aiguisait, il s'entourait de jolies filles, et si une grave question surgissait, il la traitait avec sérieux sans se départir de sa belle humeur. Pour lui, presque tout était évidence ou doute, parfois les deux, et il trouvait dans la justice et la fraternité une solution à tout. A tous les hommes il accordait la même importance, la même attention, la même générosité, le même respect. Il plaçait les événements sur un plan mondial. L'Algérie n'était plus dans l'actualité. Sétif était déjà presque oublié, et cependant nous en parlions avec une certaine inquiétude, on sentait que ce ne serait plus comme du temps des colons et des militaires. Amrouche me rappelait sans cesse le sort misérable de ses frères et le drame qui couvait. Quel

drame ? Je savais à présent que les Arabes avaient une âme, Camus parlait d'eux presque comme s'ils avaient été des siens. A ses yeux, nous avions à leur égard beaucoup de torts que nous devions racheter. Francine, sa femme, se taisait. Elle était d'Oran où l'on est trop proche de l'Espagne pour aimer les Arabes.

Pour son œuvre, on disait que Camus avait établi un plan dès l'âge de vingt ans, par triptyques, et qu'il s'y tiendrait. Il avait déjà écrit *l'Etranger, le Mythe de Sisyphe, le Malentendu.* Il continuait avec *la Peste, l'Homme révolté, les Justes.* Après, il verrait. Jean Grenier, son ancien maître, savait peut-être où il allait mais n'en disait rien. Pour moi, la démarche de Camus révélait une grande pudeur jointe à une grande prudence. Comme il était plus jeune que moi de sept ans, j'avais tendance à le croire immortel. Comment aurait-il pu jamais nous manquer ? Nous le respecions trop pour risquer de l'agacer par notre insistance à l'interroger, nous n'osions même pas le photographier. En littérature, beaucoup le jalousaient parce qu'il plaisait aux femmes. Certains prétendaient qu'il écrivait comme on célèbre la messe, qu'il s'écoutait parler en philo-sophe philosophant, qu'il écrasait tout le monde sous la gravité du ton qu'il employait, et, quand il professait, sous le poids de ses références aux classiques grecs. Certains allaient jusqu'à proclamer qu'il se prenait pour Socrate en personne. Le reproche n'était pas toujours faux. Il y avait chez lui du docteur, mais pas dans les ouvrages qui me touchaient le plus. Pas dans *l'Envers et l'Endroit,* pas dans *l'Etranger,* pas dans *Noces.* Là, son lyrisme se débridait devant la seule terre qu'il aimait à la folie. Quand il abordait un sujet, d'ordinaire c'était avec un peu de solennité et parfois un peu d'ennui ; ainsi avait-il bâti son succès, ainsi l'idolâtrait-on. Etait-il si beau que je l'ai vu ? N'avait-il pas des yeux lourds et globuleux, un regard souvent dur, des joues qui commençaient à tomber, des oreilles mal ourlées ? Peut-être. De sa bouche coulaient des paroles merveilleuses, la lumière baignait son front. Nous l'admirions au point que nous avons tous, à un moment de notre vie, essayé de penser, d'écrire et de regarder le monde comme lui. Dieu merci, je suis resté comme j'étais.

*
**

Un changement d'équipe gouvernementale amena un changement dans l'armée de l'air. Le nouveau chef d'état-major me nomma à la direction de l'information. Ma pénitence militaire était finie. Ma vie fut chamboulée. Je quittai les somnolences du palais du Luxembourg et me laissai emporter dans un tourbillon. Boulevard Victor, tout près de l'aérodrome d'Issy-les-Moulineaux d'où les trapanelles de Louis Blériot et de Santos-Dumont s'étaient élancées au début du siècle, je disposais d'une suite de bureaux en haut d'un des blocs de brique rose du ministère de l'Air. Je devais suivre l'activité de nos escadres et la mettre en valeur. J'avais parfois un discours de ministre à rédiger. Le téléphone sonnait beaucoup, j'avais pour m'assister une équipe d'officiers et quelques jeunes embusqués délurés et intelligents qui firent carrière chez les auteurs dramatiques ou au quai d'Orsay. D'autres disparurent corps et biens. Le caporal Néraud de Boisdeffre me torchait en cinq minutes un feuillet brillant sur n'importe quoi ou n'importe qui de la littérature. Admirateur ébloui de Malraux, boulimique et fouineur du meilleur, avide de tout savoir, il ignorait Doyon. Je devinais dans ses yeux un certain étonnement qu'un individu si mal éduqué que moi ait des relations mondaines si diverses. Il me gardera de l'amitié dans les histoires de la littérature qu'il écrira. Il sera ambassadeur, il finira académicien, il aime trop les habits brodés.

Dans mon service, je disposais de modestes crédits, je devais inspirer des articles, des ouvrages, des affiches, un *digest* pour les cadres subalternes. La télévision n'existait pas encore. De mon passage boulevard Victor il reste peut-être deux courts métrages qui passèrent dans les salles avec de grands films. Au gala des ailes annuel, dans l'immense Gaumont de la place Clichy aujourd'hui détruit, Marie Dubas chantait *Mon légionnaire,* Jeannine Crispin disait une de mes prières pour les pilotes, la *Toccata et fugue en ré* déferlait à l'orgue et l'on repassait à l'écran *Seuls les anges ont des ailes* d'Howard Hughes.

J'allais beaucoup au théâtre, j'avais envie d'écrire une pièce. Je tombai amoureux d'une demoiselle de la Comédie-Française, une pensionnaire, qui me fit travailler sur un sujet à quoi je songeais : les Templiers, le moment de leur condamnation quand on les pourchassait. Un dignitaire de l'ordre, un

homme de mon âge, qui avait combattu à la croisade et nourrissait une solide misogynie, se trouvait face à face avec l'épouse, bien roulée, d'un hobereau.

Le mot de ralliement des Templiers était « Baussant ». Ainsi nommaient-ils leur drapeau noir et blanc. Sur ce terme dont l'orthographe varie, on a discuté à l'infini, jusqu'à se demander s'il ne voulait pas dire « beau séant », ce qui n'aurait pas tellement surpris chez des gaillards mal embouchés, facilement sabreurs, casseurs de bics au nom du Christ, bambocheurs à l'occasion et de mœurs particulières. J'appelai ma pièce *Beau Sang*. Drame de conscience : les Templiers n'avaient pas commis les crimes dont on les accusait. Drame d'amour : mon commandeur, lié par son vœu de chasteté, était sur le point de succomber quand un jeune frère du Temple échappé aux poursuites s'avançait, l'invective aux lèvres et le fouet à la main. Ma comédienne m'avait fait boulonner. *Beau Sang* n'était pas une pièce de patronage à l'eau de rose. On s'y lançait de rudes vérités, la scène de flagellation du commandeur par le jeune frère claquait.

Mon adorable caprice de la Comédie-Française louait un deux-pièces meublé dans une ancienne maison de rendez-vous de l'avenue Carnot. Elle m'offrit de le partager avec elle. Grâce à elle, j'entrai dans un cercle de nouveaux amis où brillait Maurice Druon, fils de Lazare et neveu de Joseph Kessel, auteur avec lui du *Chant des partisans,* à Londres, et qui venait de recevoir le prix Goncourt avec *les Grandes Familles.* Ardent à défendre les déshérités, plein de talent, ambitieux, fastueux, insolent, c'était alors un des princes de Paris. Il avait un train de maison, une Bentley, un chauffeur, Kessel me disait : « Je ne sais pas comment il se débrouille. » Il nous épatait tous, même Kanters. Hé oui, comme on peut changer ! Je ne sus comment expliquer à Marie que ma vie tournait. A la lecture des lettres que je lui écrivais alors, je m'étonne de tant de délicatesse chez moi qui suis plutôt féroce. De tant de vaine hypocrisie aussi, pour ne pas trop me découvrir à ses yeux. Une femme sait bien où va le cœur de l'homme qu'elle a chéri. Marie se demandait ce que j'allais raconter d'elle et à propos de nous. En mal d'inspiration, ne sachant parfois comment apaiser leur fringale d'écrire, les romanciers dévorent tout ce qui flâne à leur portée, heureux encore quand ils ne livrent pas leur vie privée, crue et pantelante, ou qu'ils ne farfouillent pas

dans de vieilles malles. Flaubert, notre père à tous, utilisa tout ce qu'il tira de lui, de ses amis, des femmes qu'il fréquentait. Cette petite fripouille de Maurice Sachs que j'admirais, ne cacha rien de ses amours avec Cocteau. Le seul danger à redouter est le manque de talent, et c'est bien ce qui me faisait peur. J'avais de la peine à passer de la guerre à l'amour, et si dévergondé que parfois je paraisse, j'étais trop pudique, je m'en tirai comme je pus.

Les écrivains ont du goût pour les comédiennes et les comédiennes pour eux. Ils jouent ensemble la comédie de la vie, il en sort parfois quelque chose. Mon maître Vigny avait courtisé Marie Dorval et même Louise Colet ; j'avais peu d'expérience, je crus que mon caprice m'aiderait à découvrir un autre monde et, de son côté, elle crut que je saurais lui écrire un rôle. Dans ce commerce, les actrices courent plus de danger que les écrivains. Le rideau tombé, les feux de la rampe éteints, les écrivains retournent à leur écritoire, et les comédiennes à leurs illusions. Elles ne vivent que de cela, la réalité de l'existence leur est trop souvent un fardeau.

Il m'arrivait, grâce à Kanters et à Sigaux, de dîner à Saint-Germain-des-Prés avec la gloire en personne, François Mauriac, au temps où Juliette Gréco espérait un texte de lui pour une chanson. Nous avions tous un peu la tête tournée, la fin de la guerre n'était pas tellement loin, nous nous grisions de nous-mêmes, de nos espoirs et de nos ambitions, des beaux yeux qui scintillaient. Devant le grand homme nous respirions à peine. A cette époque de l'après-guerre, je devais ressembler à un fauve aux dents pointues, que la faim poussait parfois hors de son territoire. Juliette Gréco n'avait pas encore fait retoucher son nez, ses cheveux noirs tombaient sur ses épaules, elle chantait au nouveau Bœuf sur le toit où nous accompagnions parfois notre maître tout émoustillé. Elle était à la mode, elle avait du talent, elle semait les passions derrière elle, sa voix un peu cassée ravageait les cœurs. Comme tout le monde, j'ai été amoureux d'elle. Je dois l'être encore. Plus tard elle habita avec Michel Piccoli un hôtel particulier rue de Verneuil et je les invitais quand il m'arrivait de donner des dîners. A présent je vis hors de tout.

Mon caprice se mit en tête de présenter *Beau Sang* à la Comédie-Française. Il aurait fallu, pour que la pièce fût reçue, plus d'appuis que nous n'en avions. Victime d'une de ces

cabales qui sévissent là à intervalles réguliers, ma charmante compagne fut écartée de la troupe. Je n'étais dans l'intimité d'aucun sociétaire, et l'administrateur avait d'autres projets en tête. Il m'arriva d'approcher les lambris d'or de cette illustre maison sans jamais voir ses portes s'ouvrir. On ne les force pas, et ceux qui sont déjà dans le sacré ont toutes les raisons d'empêcher les autres d'y entrer : votre pièce traite d'un sujet trop éloigné des préoccupations du moment, il y a trop ou pas assez d'acteurs, le rôle principal est d'un seul tenant ou, au contraire, trop compliqué. « C'est dur à décrocher, écrivait déjà Flaubert à ce propos. Que de canailleries et de canailles ! » Il exagère. La vérité est que vous n'êtes pas en cour et qu'à la Comédie-Française tout est là. N'empêche, l'univers du théâtre est le plus grisant et le plus chimérique qui soit, le plus tentant, le plus cruel aussi. On peut s'y aventurer, si l'on ne craint pas d'y consacrer sa vie pour réussir, si l'on sait essuyer les mots piquants, les rebuffades et les menus mensonges, mais quelle école du langage ! Un mot n'a de signification que suivant la façon dont il est dit, l'intonation qu'on lui prête, le regard qui s'y ajoute, les sous-entendus qui s'y glissent. Le plus subtil dialogue se joue ailleurs que sur scène. Se risquer dans les coulisses d'un théâtre me parut plus dangereux qu'affronter les canons de la Ruhr : on n'y jouait pas la vie mais on pouvait y laisser sa réputation. Nous allâmes montrer notre ours ailleurs car la réussite, en théâtre, en littérature ou en peinture, est souvent le fruit de l'obstination. Jouvet, qui avait eu jadis un sentiment pour mon amie, nous reçut dans sa loge : le rôle de mon templier lui semblait trop viril, trop d'un bloc. Et puis, dès qu'on était de ses proches, ce qui était le cas pour mon amie, on n'avait aucun talent. Il appelait toujours Anouilh, qui avait été son secrétaire, « le miteux » et lui avait refusé *le Voyageur sans bagage* qui avait obtenu le triomphe ailleurs. Il voulait des proches qui l'adoraient et rien de plus. Il disparut peu de temps après, en scène, comme Molière.

Camus aima mon texte et m'aida à obtenir une subvention des Beaux-Arts. Comme le rôle principal ne pouvait être tenu que par un comédien qui avait du coffre, nous cherchâmes. Finalement nous trouvâmes un jeune animateur de troupe ambulante, comme moi affamé de louanges et de succès, un chef de meute toujours en chasse et en rut, efflanqué, poursuivi par les créanciers les plus sordides à qui il

devait trois recettes, une facture d'électricité ou des fripes. Du loup, il avait l'œil luisant, le souffle rauque, la marque d'une blessure à la patte, mais aussi l'humeur méfiante et la rudesse. Il règne à présent dans les Afriques où les espaces sont plus vastes et les publics plus généreux, il s'appelle Raymond Hermantier. Il avait beaucoup joué, beaucoup servi, il n'était pas usé. Parfois, dans les tirades qu'il affectionnait, sa respiration ressemblait à un soufflet de forge. Son style ne manquait pas de majesté ni de violence, c'était un acteur shakespearien. Quand je le rencontrai, il cherchait à jouer la *Marie Stuart* de Schiller en alternance avec autre chose : il sauta à la gorge de ma pièce qu'il jugea romantique et s'empara du rôle du commandeur. Nous conclûmes un accord pour quand il aurait un théâtre.

Le Métier des armes avait paru : de beaux articles, une lettre superbe du général de Gaulle et l'éreintement rituel d'André Rousseaux dans *le Figaro littéraire*. Le charmant Guy Schoeller qui représentait Hachette chez Gallimard m'invita à déjeuner, non dans un restaurant de marché noir, car il craignait peut-être qu'une conscience comme la mienne condamnât le procédé, mais dans une cantine pour écrivains de l'époque, rue des Canettes. C'était encore les vaches maigres, on mangeait des pâtées dont aujourd'hui les chiens ne voudraient pas. Nous parlâmes des uns, des autres, de nos petites amies, de la vie, de l'amour. A une table, je saluai Cioran qui ricanait avec de légers hoquets, toujours en s'écorchant l'âme. Guy Schoeller était un garçon étrange, en quête d'aventure, séduisant. Son frère courait le monde avec des filles, lui roulait à tombeau ouvert dans des Ferrari et allait de foucade en foucade, avec de faramineuses idées d'édition qui inquiétaient les Gallimard. Il trouva que mon livre était un manifeste hautain. Le métier des armes, pensez donc. Pour régler l'addition, il plongea la main dans une poche d'où de gros billets de banque jaillirent de partout jusqu'à terre. A ce moment de mon existence, je tirais le diable par la queue et ce débordement de fric semblait bizarre au milieu des paumés que nous étions. Guy Schoeller représentait le super-éditeur qui assurait la distribution dans les gares, notre rêve à tous. Cioran croyait qu'il n'y serait jamais, dans les gares, et il s'en moquait bien. Il y est maintenant. On n'est jamais sûr de rien.

Il sera peut-être un jour prix Nobel, qu'il refusera comme Sartre.

Une nuit, Sigaux me réveilla pour m'annoncer que Kanters avait tenté de se suicider et qu'on le ranimait. J'accourus. On avait fourré Kanters dans son lit, on essayait de le réchauffer, on le bouchonnait comme un cheval, il avait encore les cheveux mouillés. Il s'était jeté dans la Seine près du pont Royal en fin de soirée, la brigade fluviale l'avait repêché. Il avait bu la tasse et vomissait, on le gavait de grogs brûlants en le traitant de con. Il se taisait, penaud et heureux que nous soyons là. Sigaux me dit que c'était un désespoir d'amour. Ah ! Ah ! Et pour qui ? Pour Jean-Louis Bory, justement. Petit de taille, Bory commençait à se déplumer, il n'était ni un Adonis ni un Apollon, mais tellement vif dans ses reparties. Kanters était tombé amoureux de son intelligence. Nous le quittâmes en emportant tous les tranquillisants et somnifères qu'on dénicha. A l'époque, lecteur chez Julliard et rédacteur en chef de *la Gazette des Lettres*, Kanters ne gagnait rien. J'intriguai auprès de Gaston Gallimard pour qu'il le prenne dans la maison en doublant son salaire. Gaston voulait bien l'avoir mais se fit longtemps tirer l'oreille avant de doubler quoi que ce fût.

Nos relations, à Sigaux et à nous tous, se compliquèrent. Jean-Louis Bory ne vint plus à nos déjeuners. Quel dommage ! On ne l'invitait plus et il nous évitait. Matthieu Galey a noté dans son journal que Bory lui avait avoué, des années après, qu'il rêvait encore à Kanters qui, avant de se jeter à l'eau, aurait écrit à ses amis que Bory était son assassin. Bory le revoyait devant le lavabo plein de bouteilles de whisky vides, Kanters voulait se pendre au tuyau du chauffage central avec sa ceinture. Lui, le merveilleux Bory, se suicidera dix ans après d'un coup de revolver dans la bouche, comme Montherlant, parce qu'il ne supportait pas de vieillir et d'enlaidir. Personne ne put rien pour lui.

Boulevard Victor, je suivais l'aventure des constructeurs qui partaient à la conquête de l'espace, comme René Leduc dont le prototype devait voler à deux fois la vitesse du son

Sans moteur auxiliaire, son engin ne pouvait pas décoller du sol, aussi le lâchait-on d'un puissant porteur, sa tuyère s'allumait dans le piqué, il continuait alors par ses propres moyens et se posait comme un chasseur. Quelques années à peine après la sortie des premiers Messerschmitt à réaction, en avance de vingt ans sur la NASA, Leduc voulait naviguer dans le cosmos avec son avion fusée. Faute de moyens financiers, son expérience ne fut pas poursuivie. Il en mourut de désespoir. A l'époque, la France n'était pas assez riche pour aider un projet en quoi peu croyaient. Moi oui.

En Indochine, on continuait de se battre et de mourir. Le corps expéditionnaire avait à sa tête le général de Lattre de Tassigny, que le gouvernement avait expédié là-bas pour sauver le Tonkin en perdition. Nous avions contre nous des partisans résolus, et nous, nous étions quoi ? Les forces qu'on appelait du monde libre ou les mercenaires de la colonisation ? Le Viêt-minh, solidement organisé, se battait avec férocité. De temps en temps, j'apprenais la mort de quelques anciens camarades. Ah ! si ç'avait été une nouvelle guerre d'Espagne ! Malraux, remarié avec la veuve de son frère, militait dans le parti politique qu'avait fondé le général de Gaulle et écrivait ses livres sur l'art. L'Indochine ne semblait plus l'intéresser du tout, alors qu'avec mon camarade Marchal, le Barbu de *la Vallée heureuse*, nous en parlions comme d'une aventure qui nous menaçait. Marchal n'avait pas plus que moi envie d'y aller, car il rêvait d'une écluse où finir sa vie, mais il croyait qu'une fatalité nous poussait là-bas. « Personne parmi les copains ne comprendrait que nous nous planquions », répétait-il. J'en convenais, la mort dans l'âme. Peut-être n'étions-nous pas tellement sûrs d'avoir acquis la gratitude éternelle des Nations unies ni mérité les faveurs dont nous jouissions. Brohon, à l'Ecole de guerre, escaladait les grades. En stage au Pentagone, il considérait nos problèmes à l'échelle planétaire. « Tu verras, rabâchait le Barbu, nous qui sommes de la petite bière, nous n'y échapperons pas. »

Pourquoi quitter Paris ? J'étais heureux, j'avais de bons amis, le meilleur de tous était Sigaux qui ressemblait à un épagneul triste. Plein de talent, il parlait peu de lui. Il avait reçu le prix Interallié pour un récit déchirant et désabusé au titre prémonitoire, *Fin*. Déçu du peu de succès qu'il avait

363

obtenu, il ne se croyait pas de taille à lutter avec les malins, il préférait servir de nègre à Druon pour ses *Rois maudits* qui faisaient florès, ou à des vedettes de cinéma qui éprouvaient le besoin de raconter leur vie. Je l'éperonnais un peu, je lui reprochais son manque d'ardeur. Dans la littérature, le talent ne suffit pas, il faut que le hasard ou l'ambition s'en mêlent. Il arrive même parfois que ce soit la postérité qui départage les déchets, comme dit Ionesco. Sigaux feignait de se remettre au travail, proposait un manuscrit sur plans à un éditeur, touchait un à-valoir, ne tenait pas ses engagements, sollicitait un autre éditeur qui rachetait sa dette en échange d'un viatique. Nous parlions souvent de Flaubert, notre père vénéré, il répliquait que Flaubert n'avait pas de famille à nourrir. Il habitait en banlieue nord une étrange maison tapissée de livres, avec un enclos où il pratiquait l'élevage des chiens. D'un déjeuner chez lui avec Kanters et Moinot, j'étais revenu épouvanté ; enfermés derrière le grillage, ses chiens en bandes se déchiraient pour des os à la manière des hommes, et il lui fallait les séparer en usant d'une schlague. Je me demandai comment un homme si doux, un intellectuel, pouvait déployer là autant d'autorité. En vérité, détaché de tout sauf des chiens, il errait plutôt à la recherche de son âme sans croire qu'il pourrait bâtir une œuvre. Sa connaissance des classiques et des contemporains l'aidait à se composer une philosophie au milieu de ses amis et donzelles à cuisse légère. Par timidité, il n'avait jamais voulu être invité aux déjeuners de l'avenue Malakoff alors que Kanters n'en manquait pas un. A Paris, si mal logé que j'en avais le cœur serré, il voulait cependant épater ses petites amies par un téléphone couleur crème, à une époque où tous les téléphones étaient noirs. Nous nous retrouvions d'habitude chez Lipp, du temps de Marcelin Cazes, puis de Roger son neveu. Sigaux carburait au Ricard pour noyer le mal dont il souffrait et en commandait toujours un deuxième avant de passer à table. De quelles œuvres complètes Sigaux n'a-t-il pas écrit la préface ? Il allait voir régulièrement Simenon à Genève, tout en livrant sa copie des *Rois maudits*. Comme toujours, nous en revenions à Flaubert. Il préférait *l'Education senti-mentale,* je ne mettais rien au-dessus de *Madame Bovary,* nous nous fâchions un moment puis le passage d'une lettre de Flaubert à Louis Bouilhet ou à ce gros roublard de Maxime Du Camp nous réconciliait. Sigaux m'a toujours aimé au-delà

du raisonnable. Me flattait-il ? Il me conseillait souvent. Il me disait « Méfie-toi de Nourissier ». Chez lui, c'était une ritournelle.

Saint-Germain-des-Prés était notre territoire, notre paradis. Kanters se relevait de son plongeon dans la Seine et renouait avec la vie. Finalement, c'était aux éditions Denoël, satellite des Gallimard, qu'il avait échoué comme conseiller littéraire avec trois sous de plus. Il y avait toujours un ami à saluer sur les banquettes des Deux-Magots, la Rose Rouge avait disparu, les éditeurs emmenaient leurs suites chez Cassel. Sigaux, devenu ma pipelette, me glissait à l'oreille le nom du nouvel heureux élu de Gréco ou me parlait de l'actrice qui venait de recevoir la direction d'un théâtre en cadeau de rupture de Pierre Lazareff. Je voyais souvent un ancien Bat'd'Af', Julien Blanc, qui avait du talent, pour qui j'essayai de décrocher un prix ; je voyais le poète Maurice Fombeure à l'humour féroce, Laurent La Praye, ancien compagnon de Malraux pendant la guerre d'Espagne. Pendant la belle saison, chaque jeudi, tout le gratin des lettres s'écrasait au cocktail Gallimard où Camus n'apparaissait jamais, Malraux non plus, mais des aventures s'ébauchaient, André Maurois disait de nous tous devant Gaston : « Ils seront de l'Académie quand ils voudront. » Druon la guignait déjà. Dutourd aussi. Et pourtant, un jour où nous passions quai Conti, Camus m'avait dit : « Jure-moi que tu n'entreras jamais là-dedans. » J'aurais bien été parjure si je l'avais pu. Comme on est bêtes ! Pour lui, c'était un genre de supermarché de la littérature, les écrivains qui se respectaient n'y allaient pas, mais Gaston m'assurait que j'avais un genre à ça. Je me demande ce qu'il a bien voulu dire. Il ne me voyait pas comme je suis : j'ai bien essayé inconsidérément de frapper à la porte du quai Conti ; on ne m'a pas ouvert, ces sages-là ne sont pas fous. Ils ont eu la bonté de nous céder, à ma femme et à moi, la jouissance d'un appartement à Paris, rue Soufflot, à deux pas du Panthéon et des jardins du Luxembourg. N'est-ce pas mieux qu'un fauteuil, même si le Capoulade, jadis à notre porte, a été remplacé par un fast-food ? Doyon essayait en vain, par Paulhan, de se faire inviter aux cocktails. « Rien que des gens convenables », répétait Gaston qui jouait les cerbères, oh ! là là, un œil sur la tête rase de Genet qu'on aurait dit sorti de taule de la veille. Il n'était pas si radin qu'on prétendait, Gaston. Un jeudi, comme

j'admirais ses escarpins vernis, il me dit : « Allez chez mon bottier, rue Marbeuf, faites-vous tailler les mêmes et demandez qu'on m'envoie la facture. » Je les ai toujours, ils coûtaient une fortune, ils sont inusables, c'est tout ce qui me reste de Gaston.

Le bruit courait que les cocktails disparaîtraient bientôt et que ce serait la fin d'un empire. Claude Gallimard trouvait que cela coûtait cher et ne servait à rien. Cela servait à nous amuser, à rencontrer des poétesses en mal d'amour. Florence non plus ne frayait pas dans des lieux si mêlés et si fiévreux. Avec Jouhandeau nous la retrouvions parfois après. Déjà ivre, elle laissait échapper un long râle en nous apercevant. Plus tard, je remarquai, dans le *Journal* de Jünger, qu'elle avait du goût pour les conversations sur la mort. Ce jeudi-là, nous avions entraîné avec nous un poète américain beau comme un dieu. Nous la trouvâmes en compagnie d'une femme qu'on appelait « la colonelle », toutes deux en train de gratter, étrange détail, un genou de Léautaud, qui s'exclamait gaiement d'une voix bourrue : « Ah ! les Allemands, les Allemands... » A notre apparition, elle abandonna le vieux pantin, se dressa comme elle put devant son compatriote américain, le fixa dans le blanc des yeux, l'enveloppa de passes magnétiques puis se coula sur un divan à côté de lui en le couvrant de caresses qui se voulaient brûlantes. Tout le monde était saoul, même Léautaud, effondré dans un fauteuil, la femme de chambre avait dû, depuis longtemps, coucher les pékinois dans leur lit de cachemire et de soie. Florence repassait péniblement du rouge cerise sur ses lèvres. Jouhandeau tordait son bec-de-lièvre. « Ah ! si Mauriac nous voyait, disait-il. Lui, c'est le prince des prêtres... » Soudain, une crête hérissée sur son front, Léautaud se releva et, dévisageant Florence et la colonelle, s'écria : « Il faut tout de même que j'aille retrouver mes autres guenons... » Le valet chauffeur, une armoire à glace, l'emporta comme un paquet de linge sale tandis que Jouhandeau m'emmenait au piano et me forçait à chanter avec lui le merveilleux motet du moment où le défunt quitte l'église : *In paradisum deducant te angeli...* Ça ne se chante plus. C'est dommage.

Kessel, c'était autre chose. S'il était triste, en vrai Russe, il nous entraînait chez Novy. L'orchestre venait à sa rencontre

et l'escortait jusqu'à sa table. Peu à peu il s'animait, ses yeux brillaient, il se mettait tout entier à scander le rythme des balalaïkas. Brusquement il fourrageait dans sa crinière, avalait sa vodka à grandes goulées rapides, tétait sa cigarette, puis haussant le ton, bramait le refrain : *Iamchtchik nie goni lochadeï...*

> *Cocher ne fouette pas tes chevaux*
> *Plus rien nulle part ne me presse*
> *Personne, plus personne à aimer...*

La sainte Russie, la sienne, si proche de la vraie, semblait surgir. Tout à coup ses ancêtres juifs l'entouraient et célébraient la terre sacrée, le ciel, le vent, la neige qui recouvrait la steppe et la nuit, les étoiles, les yeux de la fiancée bien-aimée,

> *les yeux noirs*
> *les yeux ardents,*
> *les yeux brûlants et merveilleux.*

On croyait voir ce colosse s'engouffrer derrière des tempêtes de songes ; des bourrasques lui arrachaient le cœur et il se retrouvait russe par toutes ses fibres, éclusait des tonneaux d'alcool et rentrait chez lui sans tituber. Le lendemain, il partait pour les Indes ou l'Afrique du Sud. Lazareff lui donnait beaucoup d'argent qu'il répandait aussitôt autour de lui. Quand il fut reçu à l'Académie française, il ressemblait à un général d'Empire après une victoire. Paris tout entier l'acclama. Est-ce ce jour-là que j'aperçus Florence, sans verre de champagne à la main, figée, dignement assise au milieu des immortels en habit brodé ? D'habitude, à ces déjeuners où je n'allais presque plus, Paulhan présidait, un peu pincé. Cette fois, ça y était. Autour d'elle, ils en étaient tous, dans une lumière funèbre, comme une cour. Elle en robe noire de chez Chanel avec son éternelle émeraude au doigt, sur la poitrine un simple rang de perles et le ruban de la Légion d'honneur du même rouge que ses lèvres, encore ne suis-je pas sûr qu'elle ne portait pas une croix de diamants sous le ruban. Il me sembla qu'elle avait pour parrain Julien Green, américain lui aussi, pareil à un sévère dignitaire d'Eglise mais de laquelle ? Ce jour-là, elle reçut à l'hôtel Meurice, et je me demandai dans un élan de malice si son ami Ernst Jünger n'avait jamais songé à lui faire conférer, par Stupnagel, la Croix de fer au titre de leur

attachement commun à la mère des arts, des armes et des lois comme disait Amrouche. Je ne jurerais pas non plus que Jef ne soit pas allé, ce soir-là, casser quelques verres et chanter *Otchi tchiornié* :

> *Comme je vous aime*
> *Comme je vous crains*
> *Vous aurais-je croisés pour mon malheur ?*

Après tout, Florence n'était qu'une riche Américaine amoureuse de la France et de ce qui brillait. J'avais vu des photos de l'Occupation où, sur toute la rue de Rivoli, du Louvre jusqu'à la Concorde, tombaient sur les arcades de longues bannières marquées de la svastika battant au vent, et sous lesquelles on devait passer pour entrer à l'hôtel. J'ignorais encore que Morand allait souvent déjeuner là avec Jünger et avait dit à je ne sais plus qui : « Ça vous gêne, vous ? Moi, pas. » Elles n'y étaient plus, les banderoles noir et rouge, n'empêche : les patries n'ont pas le même sens pour tout le monde.

En janvier 1952, atteint d'une affection maligne de la moelle osseuse, le général de Lattre fut ramené à Paris en toute hâte. Selon le langage médical, c'était un plasmacytosarcome. Le poète Pierre Emmanuel, que je voyais quelquefois, m'appela. Il connaissait un magicien portugais, un certain Ramon, qui lui servait d'intermédiaire avec les puissances célestes quand il s'établissait lui-même en oraison. Pourqui ne pas se fier à l'invisible ? Qu'est-ce que la foi si elle se limite à nos sens ? Pierre Emmanuel voulait sauver de Lattre. J'ai noté dans un carnet que, le 11 janvier 1952, un vendredi, à 13 h 45, sans doute parce que j'avais une voiture et que j'étais dans l'armée avec un grade, Pierre Amado et lui m'envoyèrent chercher Ramon aux Halles où il travaillait comme grossiste en fruits et légumes. C'était un homme effacé qui parlait peu. Il me demanda les prénoms du général et l'adresse de la clinique. « Vous allez le guérir ? » Il ne répondit pas et me promit seulement de venir avec sa femme. Seul d'abord, je parlementai avec un aide de camp qui me conduisit à un médecin. Ramon fut autorisé à approcher de la chambre où agonisait le général et à rester derrière une porte. Il était 16 heures. Ramon entra

en prières. En transe peut-être. Un quart d'heure plus tard, Ramon demanda au docteur de raccompagner sa femme chez lui, puis dans un silence étouffant, disparut tandis que passaient et repassaient des ombres. Un temps plus tard : « Il est sauvé », dit-il. Dans la chambre, j'aperçus des religieuses à genoux. Après quoi, on nous pria de nous en aller. Dans ma voiture où nous attendions, tout à coup la nouvelle fatale nous atteignit : « Le général est mort. »

Quelques jours plus tard dans un bistrot borgne avec Pierre Emmanuel et Pierre Amado nullement découragés, et devant qui personne n'osait formuler de doutes, moi moins que les autres, j'eus l'impression de participer par des voies secrètes au salut de la patrie. Ah! par exemple! Poète et spiritualiste chrétien, Pierre Emmanuel avait conquis une autorité, une aura, un charisme, dirait-on. Pour lui, Ramon était l'incarnation de pouvoirs occultes et souverains. Il fallait croire. Ramon regrettait de n'avoir pu imposer les mains au général. Je me sentais fautif : je n'avais pas su convaincre l'entourage. Cependant ma foi commençait à être ébranlée tandis que, pareil à une statue de cathédrale, Pierre Emmanuel demeurait les yeux perdus dans l'invisible. De Lattre mort, il me sembla que l'Indochine française s'en allait avec lui, tout n'était plus que désolation.

Hermantier avait trouvé rue Fontaine une salle qui s'appelait, comble d'ironie, théâtre de l'Humour. Les répétitions se déroulaient sur une scène bancale, glaciale et ténébreuse, les fauteuils d'orchestre étaient défoncés, des bribes de mon texte : « Il y a la grâce de Dieu, Hamelin... » se mélangeaient avec le jazz du bastringue d'à côté. Hermantier, que ses créanciers venaient traquer dès qu'il apparaissait, ne décolérait pas. Sur scène, on aurait cru qu'il se déchirait la poitrine quand il se déclarait coupable et tombait à genoux devant le jeune templier à étrivière. Tout vibrait de ses coups de gueule, et il faisait si froid qu'il me sembla être revenu au camp de Lossiemouth en Ecosse, quand j'allais voler des boulets en escaladant des grilles. Ici, le seul seau de charbon qu'on jetait dans la chaudière à 5 heures devait durer jusqu'au soir. Un peu hébété, j'entendais mon commandeur s'écrier

dans un décor sordide : « Dis-moi ce que vient faire le salut de mon âme ? Où est mon âme ? Où est la grâce de Dieu ?... »

Sigaux savait que j'allais partir pour l'Extrême-Orient et s'inquiétait du sort de ma pièce et de mon caprice. Ni l'une ni l'autre n'étaient en danger. Après tout, si je m'en allais, c'était peut-être simplement que j'en avais assez de ma vie d'alors. Choisel allait être vendu et je n'avais pas de quoi l'acheter. Mes amis Dreyfus qui habitaient une noble demeure à Saint-Nom-la-Bretèche me trouvèrent une caborgniote dans un hameau voisin, au bord d'une falaise et avec un bout de jardin. Je mis là les trois sous que j'avais. Le hameau s'appelait Rennemoulin, « le moulin aux grenouilles », à quelques kilomètres de Versailles et d'un lieu étrange que mes amis m'avaient fait visiter un jour, au crépuscule : des ruines de tours, de fabriques et de palais que certains gentilshommes du XVIIIe siècle édifiaient pour fuir la cour, peut-être pour sacrifier à la mode, et qu'on appelait des déserts. Celui-là s'appelait le Désert de Retz : enfoui au plus profond de la forêt de Marly, à demi recouvert par la végétation et entrelacé de lianes gigantesques, avec une glacière en forme de pyramide. Un mystère m'y envoûta au point que, des années après, revenu d'Orient, d'Algérie et de beaucoup de choses, j'écrivis un roman violent et étrange, dans ce décor et avec ce nom, *le Désert de Retz*.

La générale de *Beau Sang* eut lieu. Ce ne fut pas, loin de là, le triomphe que nous espérions mais le souper fut gai. Florence, en cure, n'était pas de la partie. Camus y brilla. J'aurais dû convier mon petit père. Je craignis son venin, j'eus tort, il se vengea par une lettre où il tempérait son goût immodéré pour le blâme et la remontrance : c'était un bon début et un succès trop personnel, car il lui semblait que la critique jugeait moins l'œuvre que l'auteur. Pour lui, le soufflet de forge d'Hermantier aurait dû s'exercer dans les mélos. Claude Laydu, qui venait de tenir au cinéma le rôle du curé de campagne de Bernanos, descendait tout droit du ciel ; quant à l'héroïne, il couvrait de fleurs son beau galbe et sa pétillante intelligence pour réclamer plus d'autorité, car c'était moins la bataille qui importait que le conflit, et le templier gisant à terre, flagellé par son jeune frère et en proie à ce qui lui dévorait le cœur, c'était moi.

Le dossier qui m'est resté de la pièce est énorme. Quelle

presse avait-on en ce temps-là ! Avec quel intérêt un jeune auteur était-il accueilli ! Que d'esprits sérieux se penchaient sur lui avec sympathie ! Robert Kemp, critique du *Monde*, eut raison de me reprocher d'avoir écrit trop de tirades et pas assez de dialogues. Je faisais mon apprentissage, le feu de Dieu ne foudroyait pas Hermantier, et des chandelles et une odeur de suie n'évoquaient pas assez le jour de neige.

Le général Bouvard, qui m'aimait, m'emmena en Allemagne visiter Ernst Jünger. Je ne savais pas encore que nous avions, Jünger et moi, une amie commune qui recevait avenue Malakoff. Elle s'était bien gardée de me parler de lui, et son *Journal parisien* n'avait pas encore été édité chez Julliard. Quel dommage ! Même Jouhandeau n'avait pas prononcé le nom de Jünger. Pour moi, il n'était que l'auteur de *Jardins et routes*, des *Falaises de marbre* et de *la Guerre notre mère*. Il m'impressionna par ce qui apparaissait chez lui comme de l'impassibilité et une formidable domination de soi. Entre anciens ennemis, séparés encore par toutes sortes d'obstacles, le dialogue restait difficile. On savait qu'il avait joué un rôle important dans l'opposition politique à Hitler et qu'il ne partageait pas sa folie de destruction, Jünger était un homme d'acier, un esprit goethéen, et n'avait pas encore soixante ans. Petit de taille, il atteignait l'universel et le cosmos, et, dans l'héroïsme, nous avait tous dépassés de très loin. Sans doute n'étions-nous pas sur le même plan et la guerre ne nous avait pas broyés de la même façon, j'éprouvais un immense respect, presque de la vénération pour ce haut dignitaire de la chevalerie teutonique et me sentis un barbare. Peu de temps après, il m'écrivit pour me dire que Speidel, à l'hôtel du Palais d'Orsay, serait heureux d'assister à ma pièce. Je ne sais plus pourquoi cela ne se fit pas.

Trente ans plus tard, je retournai le voir avec François Mitterrand, alors président de la République. Un hélicoptère vint me prendre à Vézelay pour me conduire à Roanne où un Mystère 20 nous emmena avec la suite présidentielle sur le lac de Constance. Le chancelier Kohl nous attendait avec une foule de journalistes. Tous ensemble, dans un fracas de pales, nous escaladâmes les pentes du Jura souabe au ras des brumes, jusqu'à Wilflingen. Là, près d'un château, Jünger occupait une forteresse tout en bibliothèques. Beaucoup de choses avaient

changé depuis 1952. Le monde était en paix, sa femme Perpetua était morte, Liselotte avait pris sa place. Resté jeune et beau à quatre-vingt-douze ans, mince, élégant, il ressemblait, entre les sabliers, les bocaux contenant des insectes rares et des serpents, à un magicien. Dans son cabinet de travail trônait le portrait de Manfred von Richthofen, le baron rouge de l'aviation de chasse allemande. D'abord ce fut le champagne qui pétilla, puis le vin du Rhin coula dans nos flûtes. Nous trinquâmes beaucoup, mais il y avait beaucoup trop de monde pour qu'on pût parler, encore que François Mitterrand, mémorialiste et moraliste, ait la grâce de mettre à l'aise. A Jünger, j'aurais dû parler de Florence. Morte depuis peu, elle avait eu le plus grand mal, paraît-il, à trouver une place dans le tombeau des Gould à New York, plein à craquer. Je n'osai pas. J'étais alors hanté par Guynemer et par le général Udet qui avait appartenu à l'escadrille Richthofen et s'était tiré une balle dans la tête : il aimait trop les femmes et la dolce vita, Jünger l'avait connu et me dit : « Pour ces destins-là, il faut que les astres s'en mêlent. » Pour le sien aussi, il avait fallu. Au fond, je n'avais rien à lui dire, je connaissais son œuvre, J'admirais tout ce qu'il avait bravé comme jeune officier fou de la guerre, j'étais jaloux de ses hauts faits. C'était quelqu'un comme lui, servi comme il l'avait été par les circonstances mais aussi les dominant, que j'aurais voulu être et que je n'étais pas. Rêver en silence à ses côtés me suffisait. Au fond, mon antimilitarisme doit cacher un militarisme forcené. Je n'ose peut-être pas avouer que je suis un farouche traîneur de sabre à l'ambition rentrée et qu'il n'y a pas de quoi être fier. Je demandai à Jünger s'il avait quitté la Wehrmacht avec seulement le grade de major : « J'aurais fait un bon maréchal », me répondit-il. Pendant notre retour sur Paris, quand il fut revenu de sa journée avec le chancelier allemand, François Mitterrand eut ce mot : « Vézelay, c'est tout de même autre chose. » En effet, Wilflingen vit de légende, pas de mystique. Pas d'une ancienne courtisane amoureuse du fils de Dieu.

Avant mon départ pour l'Indochine, Camus et sa femme m'invitèrent à déjeuner dans leur nouvel appartement rue Madame. Camus se demandait ce que j'allais découvrir et en quel état d'esprit j'allais revenir. Nous attendions pour nous mettre à table le jeune poète algérois Jean Sénac qui n'arrivait

pas. Camus téléphona à son hôtel, Sénac dormait encore. Il vint enfin, et Camus le servit. Il avait, pour le bouillant, le pur Sénac, l'affection d'un père pour son fils. Il craignait de le voir s'engager au-delà de son cœur et de sa religion pour la poésie. En vérité, Sénac ira bien plus loin encore, à notre étonnement à tous : il n'était pas de ce monde.

Avec le Barbu et quelques camarades nous achetâmes des tenues de toile et des shorts. On nous piqua contre la fièvre jaune, la fièvre noire, la peste et le choléra, on avait raison, et nous embarquâmes, en civil, à bord d'un vieux DC 4 militaire déguisé en avion de ligne à cause de toutes les escales où nous devions nous ravitailler dans des pays qui condamnaient la guerre d'Indochine. Le premier soir, nous couchâmes à Damas, le deuxième à Calcutta. Nous volions dans le même sens de rotation que la terre, nous avions du mal à avancer. Enfin, le troisième jour, nous débarquâmes à Saigon. Si plat d'abord que me parût le pays, il me sembla que j'étais au pied des *Falaises de marbre*. Je me sentais démuni et très étranger. Déjà, j'étouffais.

XV

La fièvre jaune

LE FILM américain *Apocalypse now*, admirable dans le terrifiant, s'achève en apothéose de la catastrophe. *Platoon*, autre film américain de la guerre du Viêt-nam, laisse l'horreur pénétrer les consciences. On y voit chaque personnage, chaque individu, chaque combattant se décomposer sous nos yeux. C'est presque de l'intimisme, et tellement naturel que rien ne semble surajouté. Quant à *Full Metal Jacket*, cela dépasse tout.

Je me souviens de mon étonnement lorsque j'appris plus tard, à l'époque où les Américains guerroyaient là-bas, que la drogue sévissait dans leur armée au point qu'elle représentait pour eux un ennemi de plus. A cela seul on peut mesurer déjà ce qui séparait les deux méthodes de guerre. Chez nous, le commandant en chef et certains officiers fumaient l'opium plus par plaisir que par besoin. Le reste de la troupe se saoulait au gros rouge de l'intendance ou aux feuilles de coca mâchouillées. Notre guerre n'était qu'une campagne coloniale avec armes perfectionnées, la guerre des Américains fut atroce, et comment supporter l'enfer sans fumer ce qu'il y avait de plus facile à trouver, de l'herbe ? La drogue prit ainsi, de bas en haut, possession de toute l'armée des Etats-Unis et lui permit de résister au quotidien.

Autre remarque : aurais-je supporté, dans l'armée française que j'ai connue en Indochine, le langage qu'on entend dans *Platoon* et dans le film de Kubrick ? Ce langage-là m'aurait paru plus que trivial. Notre langage à nous était un langage de militaires en campagne, du style bat' d'Af' modernisé, ce qui n'est peut-être pas ce qu'on entend dans les salons du boulevard Saint-Germain, encore que cela ait pu changer.

Le dialogue constamment ordurier de *Platoon* ne choque pas : il est naturel et on n'en imagine pas d'autre dans la bouche des personnages, là où ils sont. Un dialogue style Bigeard détonnerait. On peut en conclure que le langage de l'armée française d'Indochine était tout simplement viril avec une forte dose d'hypocrisie, l'hypocrisie du langage n'étant qu'une réplique de la diplomatie politique et gouvernementale. La réalité de la guerre ne s'exprimait qu'à demi-mot : on « traitait ». Restait la façon de traiter, qui appartenait à l'initiative de chacun. Il m'a peut-être fallu *Platoon* pour comprendre le regard à la fois inquiet et attendri que Camus posa sur moi la veille de mon départ pour l'Indochine, à ce dîner où assistait Jean Sénac. Dans la forêt voisine du Cambodge où l'action de *Platoon* se déroule, on tue, on essaie de ne pas être tué soi-même, on résiste à la température, au courrier qui arrive de si loin. Aucune hypocrisie. L'ennemi n'intervient qu'en dernier lieu. S'il n'est pas là, on y supplée, on se tue entre soi. Si nous ne sommes pas en enfer, nous sommes dans son antichambre. L'enfer, c'est peut-être *Full Metal Jacket*. A côté des films américains, les films français sur la guerre d'Indochine, même *Section 317*, réalisés avec les moyens et la bonne conscience d'alors, paraissent des spectacles pour patronage. Quant au court métrage que, sous le titre de *la Bataille du Tonkin*, j'ai moi-même commis, à la fois pour éclairer l'opinion, célébrer la mémoire du général de Lattre et donner un écho à *Beau Sang*, j'en aurais honte aujourd'hui s'il fallait avoir honte de ses illusions. Oui, mes pères, j'ai péché par générosité, j'ai péché par innocence et camusianisme. Quelques années après nous, les GI se drogueront à mort pour échapper à leur condition, ils ne mettront pas de gants pour dire à leurs chefs ce qu'ils pensent, ils cracheront la vérité à tous et massacreront sans discernement pour ne pas être massacrés eux-mêmes. Chose étrange : ils agiront sans révolte et avec un certain fatalisme, comme s'ils avaient tiré le mauvais numéro et que la faute de tout ce mic-mac ne soit imputable qu'au hasard.

Les hommes qui auront l'idée de cette relation de la guerre du Viêt-nam devront lutter pendant des années pour vaincre la résistance des marchands de pellicule qui se demanderont si l'argent dépensé pour dénoncer la vérité ne sera pas perdu, ou encore si l'effroi causé par ce qu'on montrera provoquera le succès commercial qui, à leurs yeux,

justifie le risque. Le courage paie quelquefois. Les réalisateurs ont gagné. On sait, grâce à leurs caméras et grâce à l'Amérique qui les a laissés tourner, ce que fut la guerre du Viêt-nam.

En avril 1952, quand je débarquai à Saigon, je ne savais rien ni de l'Indochine ni de la guerre. L'armée de l'air nous distribua dans des hôtels, pour moi ce fut le *Continental,* en plein centre de la ville, près du théâtre, là où le jeune Malraux et sa femme Clara étaient descendus en 1924-25 au moment du procès de Phnom Penh. Tout ce qui comptait dans la ville se retrouvait là, à midi et le soir, sous les ventilateurs. J'allai me présenter au général Lionel Chassin qui commandait l'air en Extrême-Orient, formule un peu pompeuse pour les modestes forces qui appuyaient le corps expéditionnaire. Ancien marin qui se voulait plus sûr de lui qu'il ne l'était, à l'affût de tout ce qui semblait neuf, souvent bourru, Chassin avait des idées, ce qui n'était pas bien vu. Comme le général Bouvard qui m'aimait et sans liaison avec lui, il pensait, depuis que de Gaulle s'était retiré, qu'un jour on aurait recours à un militaire pour sauver une fois de plus la nation. Ces deux généraux n'étaient pas les seuls à avoir des ambitions politiques. Il y en avait d'autres, ailleurs, que je n'ai pas connus. En 1942, à l'époque où il était colonel d'état-major en Afrique du Nord, Chassin avait grandement aidé Saint-Exupéry à rejoindre son ancienne unité, le groupe II/33, fondu dans l'US Air Force, et qui volait sur Lightning. Saint-Exupéry eut toujours en Chassin un soutien et un défenseur. Il n'est pas impossible que le fait que le général de Gaulle se soit montré hostile à Saint-Exupéry — une des nombreuses fois où il céda à des antipathies personnelles — ait compté dans l'animosité que Chassin éprouvait pour lui. Après tout, Chassin avait déjà trois étoiles, il allait bientôt en coudre une quatrième sur ses manches. A l'annuaire, le général de Gaulle n'en avait que deux. Comme le général qui m'aimait, Chassin avait constitué à tout hasard un réseau plus ou moins occulte, auquel je n'appartenais pas, de connivences et d'intelligences. L'autorité feignait de tout ignorer et se contentait d'éloigner : Chassin avait été dépêché en Extrême-Orient, et le général qui m'aimait en Afrique noire.

Chassin, un faux lion, manquait totalement de prudence et de psychologie. Il avait aidé Saint-Exupéry parce que la

377

célébrité de Saint-Exypéry le flattait. Il ne serait peut-être pas allé jusqu'à compromettre sa carrière pour lui. Il me déclara qu'il était ravi de m'avoir sous son commandement. Je lui demandai de me confier la responsabilité d'une base, comme il venait de le faire pour le Barbu. Il me jugea plutôt apte à célébrer les hauts faits des aviateurs et les mérites de leur chef, et crut m'éviter la confrontation avec les problèmes de notre présence en Extrême-Orient : qui était notre ennemi ? où se tenait-il ? Comment devions-nous le combattre ? Au Tonkin, le général de Lattre avait sacrifié son fils et, finalement, succombé lui-même. L'Indochine était un territoire immense qui s'étendait du nord au sud sur près de deux mille kilomètres et, de l'est à l'ouest, sur plus de mille, du Centre-Viêt-nam au Laos et au Cambodge qu'on appelait « les Etats associés ». Le commandement d'une base m'aurait placé face à face avec des hommes et des réalités. Ma réputation me nuisit. Chassin essaya de me convaincre que c'était avec ma plume que je servirais et me rangea parmi les « propagandistes ». Il avait raison, hélas. Avant de quitter la France, plusieurs journaux m'avaient proposé de leur réserver l'exclusivité de ce que j'écrirais. Comme je préférais m'adresser à un public populaire plutôt qu'à un public déjà averti ou prévenu, Sigaux m'avait conduit à *Radar,* qui avait un fort tirage et était dirigé par Georges Montaron, un journaliste pour qui nous avions beaucoup d'estime.

Saigon, c'était la grande Babylone, la capitale du négoce et du stupre. J'aurais dû renifler de plaisir. Je m'y sentis aussitôt malheureux. Ne sortions-nous pas, même si elle avait été sans croix, d'une croisade contre les nazis ? Eisenhower n'avait-il pas prononcé le mot ? La mort du général de Lattre à qui le gouvernement avait conféré à titre posthume la dignité de maréchal de France avait, paraît-il, tout changé. Lui vivant, on se battait pour une religion, pour la croisade. Reprendre le tombeau du Christ aux Infidèles, c'était s'obliger à présent à malmener les millions d'habitants de cet immense territoire : nous représentions l'Occident, la chrétienté, la liberté d'expression face au dragon socialiste ennemi de Dieu. Pour vaincre, nous avions commencé par donner notre chemise, comme avait dit de Lattre aux Etats-Unis, à présent nous donnions notre peau. De Lattre avait convaincu : d'Amérique

les convois affluaient, les chars, les canons et les lance-flammes s'entassaient sur les quais. Encore à Saigon, n'était-ce pas « Dieu le veut », la parole de saint Bernard, qu'on entendait, mais « Dollar, dollar... ». Saigon était une ville aux larges avenues avec une pseudo-cathédrale, des jardins, de riches hôtels, des cafés, des restaurants, un champ de courses. Le commerce le plus florissant était celui des jeux, des banques et de la prostitution où l'on pouvait faire fortune en deux ans, Cholon n'était qu'un lupanar destiné à pourrir l'Occident. Après venaient les grandes sociétés de transport, de ciment et de caoutchouc. Le flot d'argent et de sang qui coulait de partout aboutissait au port : les capitaux filaient en cabine de luxe, les cercueils bourraient les cales les navires vers Marseille. Loin de m'insuffler les joies de la belle saison, cette fournaise détruisit en moi tout plaisir. De ces jours égaux, de cette nuit qui tombait à la même heure montait une sorte de vapeur d'angoisse. L'éternel et morne été, ses fureurs et ses tornades, tout finissait par lasser. Si seulement il y avait eu, comme pour Jünger à Paris pendant l'Occupation, une Florence Gould ! Chaque soir éclatait un orage qui fondait en pluie torrentielle, la chaleur était accablante, on ne pouvait vivre là sans boire, sans boys et sans ventilateurs, je suffoquais, le bruit des motopousses m'assourdissait, l'humidité de la mousson me couvrit de rougeurs et de démangeaisons. Pour moi, Saigon, c'était Baal, c'était le Veau d'or.

Il fallait remonter aux pirates, aux missionnaires, aux explorateurs, aux planteurs, à l'occupation japonaise, à l'échec des pourparlers avec Hô Chi Minh. Leclerc avait conseillé de négocier, de Gaulle s'était retiré à Colombey. Plus tard, en 1966, il s'écriera : « La France considère que les combats qui ravagent l'Indochine n'apportent par eux-mêmes aucune issue. » Que n'avait-il pensé cela vingt ans plus tôt ! La guerre avait été installée par lui. L'ennemi, formé avec une discipline de fer, occupait tout le pays et se battait contre nous avec acharnement.

Le nouveau haut-commissaire appartenait au MRP. Certains le considéraient un peu comme un gros cul béni, d'autres comme un dignitaire de la franc-maçonnerie. Dans son palais de marbre, il semblait soulagé de n'avoir plus à soumettre ses pouvoirs politiques au général de Lattre, despote à qui rien ne résistait, autocrate amoureux des beaux jeunes gens et des

idées folles, qui me rappelait, en plus grand, Murtin. Je l'aurais adoré. J'arrivais trop tard. Son successeur, Salan, n'était pas n'importe qui. De la suite de De Lattre depuis 1944, il avait couché dans le lit du pape à Castel Gondolfo pendant la marche sur Rome. Il avait beaucoup servi en Indochine, flairant les odeurs subtiles, les pièges, se targuant de percer les intentions de Giap, le tigre qu'il avait en face de lui. Salan visait plus haut et plus loin que son proconsulat, et dressait son plan de bataille en kimono de soie à travers les nuées de l'opium, sous le portrait de l'empereur Bao Dai. Pour la frime, de Lattre avait créé l'armée vietnamienne avec ses généraux, son drapeau rouge et or et ses aventuriers. Elle faisait semblant de se battre, en elle tout était pourriture et concussion. En vérité, elle était un prétexte à draguer les surplus américains et à brandir à la tribune de l'ONU la cause de la France. Au milieu des marchands, des trafiquants, des mercenaires et des putains, le corps expéditionnaire versait généreusement son sang.

Le colonel Clément qui dirigeait le service de propagande jurait facilement, buvait sec, aimait la musique et les jolies filles, prenait de temps en temps une cuite et n'avait pas d'idées préconçues, ce qui est rare chez les militaires. Il me plut. Bel homme, fort en gueule, mal embouché, généreux et intelligent, il avait commandé une place encerclée, connaissait tous les officiers du corps expéditionnaire et toutes les patronnes de bordel. Je lui plus aussi. « Va où tu veux, vois qui tu veux, publie ce que tu voudras où tu voudras », me dit-il.

Je partis aussitôt pour le Tonkin.

J'ai écrit *la Bataille dans la rizière* à chaud, sur des impressions qui me serraient la gorge, un peu comme au sortir du théâtre de l'Humour où, un soir sur deux, Hermantier jouait *Beau Sang.* J'étais encore rue Fontaine, en plein Montmartre, au moment où les mécanismes et les fantasmes de l'amour vénal fusaient et se détraquaient, plus que dans la plaine embrasée du fleuve Rouge. Je me souviens de ce petit poste qui venait d'être attaqué et attendait de l'être encore, car il n'était pas tombé, où j'allai passer quelques jours. La chaleur était torride, on respirait un brasier. Dans la ville de Hanoi,

l'armée vivait comme en occupation, les *nhia-quê* faisaient semblant de ne pas nous voir, personne ne se sentait en sécurité. Le général de Llinarès, qui portait le nom d'un noble hidalgo, avait dans son lit la plus excitante métisse chinoise de tout l'Extrême-Orient. Il ne la montrait pas et il avait raison. Les colonels que l'on appelait les maréchaux emmenaient leurs troupes à travers l'immense plaine du Delta, ils tuaient, razziaient, incendiaient, ripaillaient, et quelquefois subissaient des pertes. Alors ils enterraient leurs morts avec grandeur. Je me souviens de De Castries, qui allait devenir tristement célèbre à Diên Biên Phu, de son calot et de son gilet rouge de spahi, je me souviens du béret vert et du collier de barbe rousse de Van Uxem. Ils ne manquaient de morgue ni les uns ni les autres, et, superbe colosse d'un mètre quatre-vingt-dix, disciple de De Lattre, jouisseur, amoureux du faste, des secrétaires juteuses et de tout ce qui flamboyait, le général Cogny commandait : chic, dignité, discipline, un brin cabot. Je parle de ces messieurs comme si j'étais d'un autre sexe que le mien. Mais non. Je suis sensible aux hommes beaux et aux femmes superbes, qu'y puis-je ? Pas chez les nazis ou quand je m'aperçois qu'il y a de la bêtise ou de la crapule, je m'écarte, parfois trop tard. Bref, c'était la croisade. Il ne manquait que des musiques sonnant de tous leurs cuivres. Les aumôniers célébraient la messe à côté des pagodes où brûlaient des baguettes d'encens pour Bouddha, les paysans labouraient derrière leurs buffles ou fuyaient leurs villages en flammes. « Quel dommage, me disais-je, que Malraux ne soit plus là ! » Remarié avec la veuve de son frère, une pianiste, il habitait Boulogne-sur-Seine. Josette Clotis, morte comme Anna Karénine, les deux jambes coupées par un train, restait la mère de ses deux fils, Clara continuait à voir Doyon et Mme D. et à parler des petits temples abandonnés dans les forêts du Cambodge, ce qui me faisait un peu ricaner à présent : Malraux s'intéressait au RPF, le Rassemblement du peuple français, machinerie sur quoi comptait de Gaulle pour un retour au pouvoir. Sa canadienne en peau de toutou de la brigade Alsace-Lorraine rangée dans la naphtaline, Malraux rêvait de devenir ministre de l'Intérieur, commissaire du peuple, quoi ! mais devait commencer par être prédicateur errant, imprécateur en transe, fustigeant l'état pitoyable de la patrie. Le Tonkin aurait été un cadre pour lui : les canons

tonnaient, les villages flambaient, la soupe au paprika des tirailleurs marocains cuisait sur des feux de brindilles, la plaine était semée de casques percés, de cadavres à demi noyés dans l'eau jaune des rizières et, derrière les montagnes, au nord, il y avait la Chine. La Chine ! Que n'étais-je Malraux quand il volait les statues de dieux khmers ou quand il se prenait pour le délégué politique de la Révolution à Canton, que n'étais-je l'adolescent Jünger quand il partait s'engager à la Légion, que n'avais-je leur génie à tous deux, qu'attendais-je pour changer de style et de façon, moi, ancien sous-lieutenant séminariste sous les ordres du capitaine Boum-Boum à Médéa et amoureux d'une vierge de Giotto. J'aimais l'armée et je n'osais pas dire que celle-là me faisait horreur.

Dans mon livre, *la Bataille dans la rizière*, la discipline est rigide, les combattants supportent bien le climat, les hôpitaux regorgent de blessés qui veulent retourner casser du Viet. Ça se voyait ; les sabreurs, les ivrognes, les baiseurs, les reîtres et les soudards qui avançaient sur leurs claquantes chenilles d'acier m'épataient, et je n'osais pas dire qu'on les employait à une mauvaise besogne. Pourquoi ne pas ajouter aussi qu'aucun de ces gentilshommes ne se posait la moindre question ? Peut-être Bollardière ? Je ne le connus pas là-bas. La guerre était leur mère, leur raison de vivre, la bringue qu'ils déguisaient sous du panache. Clément était comme eux, il avait commandé lui aussi des colonnes de blindés sautant parfois sur des mines et crachant le feu. Tous parlaient du général de Lattre comme d'un dieu disparu. Ils étaient fiers d'avoir été rudoyés et tutoyés par lui. Au moins auraient-ils pu sentir quelque chose les gêner ? Non ? Pas de douleur dans les reins, pas de grosseur, rien qui puisse laisser redouter un cancer ? N'auraient-ils pas pu se dire qu'ils n'avaient peut-être pas le droit de détruire avec ce cynisme ? Que ces pouilleux à face cuite et ridée, que cette marmaille grimpée sur des buffles étaient chez eux, sur leur terre, que la France menait peut-être là, sous de bonnes raisons, une sale et puante guerre ? Ils s'en foutaient, les colonels. Ils étaient heureux d'être des impérialistes et de servir l'Empire. J'aurais pu leur rappeler que Malraux n'avait pas toujours été commandant de la brigade Alsace-Lorraine ou ministre de l'Information du premier gouvernement de Gaulle, et que dans les années 1926 où il fumait le chanvre indien, il luttait à Saigon contre la politique du gouvernement

général et sortait un journal d'opposition qui s'appelait *l'Indochine enchaînée*. J'aurais pu les inviter à visiter l'imprimerie de ce journal à l'existence éphémère. Je n'y avais pas pensé. Si j'avais osé parler de ce Malraux-là, on m'aurait jugé subversif, et puis d'ailleurs, est-ce que les colonels connaissaient Malraux ? Chassin, du geste qu'on a pour chasser les mouches, m'aurait jeté : « C'est vieux tout ça, mon cher, votre Malraux a changé d'avis. Allons, allons, reprenez-vous. Vous croyez peut-être aussi que Malraux irait encore en Espagne ? Au Bangladesh peut-être, plus tard, pour l'épate ! La liberté du monde, c'est nous qui la défendons ici... »

Pour m'éviter au moins d'écrire des dialogues débiles, j'aurais dû penser à la verdeur de Léautaud, à son impudence, à ses maigres débauches. La dernière fois que je l'avais vu, avenue Malakoff, Marie Laurencin vomissait des horreurs sur Apollinaire à qui elle ne pardonnait pas de ne pas l'avoir épousée. Selon elle, il culbutait toutes les bonniches de la maison et se branlait dans son lit, dès le réveil, « pour être tranquille ». Et elle, alors, à quoi servait-elle ? Après quoi, selon elle, il écrivait les quatrains du *Bestiaire* pendant que Picasso dessinait des carpes et des chèvres à côté de lui. Ce jour-là, avenue Malakoff, parmi beaucoup d'autres personnages falots, il y avait une femme étrange, laide et pleine d'esprit qui raconta qu'en 1938, elle était suivie chaque matin au Bois par un homme qui se déculottait à demi derrière un journal pour se masturber. Un jour que son mari l'accompagnait et que l'individu surgit, son mari alla vers lui la main tendue et, se retournant : « Je te présente Pierre Laval... » « Vous fréquentiez du beau monde, grogna Léautaud. Moi j'aurais dénoncé ce salopard. C'est vrai qu'il n'était plus rien à l'époque... » Florence buvait du petit-lait. Léautaud ne se conduisait pas mieux, mais le vieux sagouin ne s'en vantait pas. N'empêche, il savait écrire. Quelle tête ferais-je si, par hasard... « Vous êtes allé à la croisade, mon cher ? me dirait-il. Vous auriez mieux fait de rester chez vous... » Cette personne laide, du nom de qui je ne me souviens plus, nous avait encore dit, tout émoustillée, qu'elle avait retrouvé Pierre Laval à un grand dîner, qu'elle était à sa droite et qu'il n'avait pas arrêté de s'asticoter sous la nappe. Marie Laurencin tordait la bouche de dégoût, ces dames se détestaient, Florence jouissait. Parmi les vieux banquiers au crâne luisant, les diplomates à fesses

plates et les larbins, j'avais l'air d'un enfant de chœur. Caryatis, la monstrueuse femelle de Jouhandeau, ajoutait, pour ne pas être en reste, qu'elle était amoureuse d'un jeune soldat de l'armée de l'air. Un des miens peut-être ? Jünger avait dû entendre ces mêmes horreurs à la même table, au temps de l'Occupation où Florence recevait déjà ces messieurs-dames. Il admirait comme moi Léautaud qui eut le courage de lui offrir asile chez lui, quand l'Allemagne s'effondra et que la Wehrmacht se préparait à quitter Paris.

Dans ses *Antimémoires,* Malraux raconte qu'il annonçait depuis 1933 que les empires coloniaux ne survivraient pas à une guerre européenne. En 1946, à Gaston Palewski, directeur de cabinet du Général, il disait : « Tout ce que nous pouvons sauver, c'est une sorte d'empire culturel, un domaine de valeurs. » Billevesées pour de Gaulle comme je l'ai dit, et depuis, rien n'avait changé. Cogny demandait à l'aviation d'attaquer au napalm, cette gelée de pétrole incandescent qui grillait les buffles et les hommes jusqu'à l'os et réduisait en cendres les bananiers et les bambous comme les paillotes. Tout à coup m'apparaissaient les atrocités que j'avais moi-même commises sur les villes allemandes, quand nos raids terrorisaient les habitants englués dans les caves tandis que les maisons s'écroulaient les unes sur les autres. Eh bien quoi, toujours la même chanson, c'étaient eux qui avaient commencé, nous répliquions. Est-ce que, par hasard, nous nous étions posé des questions ? Un vrai guerrier s'en posait-il, a fortiori un sabreur, un baiseur, un tueur légal et décoré, un général servi par des goumiers en gandoura blanche et ceinture rouge ?

Ici, on anéantissait tout ce qui résistait. Pas le moindre scrupule. Pas de question du genre de celle que poseraient plus tard les GI de *Platoon :* « Qu'est-ce que nous foutons là ? » A Paris, Sartre blâmait, réprouvait, mais qui prêtait l'oreille à Sartre sinon quelques intellectuels décadents ? La France se moquait de Sartre comme elle se moquait de la guerre d'Indochine embrayée par de Gaulle pour restaurer l'Empire. La France se relevait de ses ruines en semant d'autres ruines. La France s'efforçait de retrouver son rang de puissance

coloniale, mais y avait-il encore des colonies ? La France avait besoin de caoutchouc. Bigeard, déjà une vedette, avait déjà sa légende, sa croix de guerre traînait par terre et lui ne manquait ni de ruse ni d'insolence. On lançait son bataillon dans les opérations risquées. Sec, noueux, madré, piaffant, volontiers arrogant, il ne craignait pas d'affronter la mort mais seulement de se réveiller, comme il disait, avec le balancier sur l'épaule. Une retraite épique au pas de course, à un moment où on l'avait cru fichu, et dont il s'était tiré par des marches de quatre-vingts kilomètres par jour. J'évoquais la Retraite des Mille, le récit de Xénophon, Bigeard, héros de *l'Anabase,* pas très malin dans les idées générales, qui se posait encore moins de questions que les autres, et, dans le métier, roublard et tranchant, un poignard.

Camus m'écrivit qu'il m'écouterait à mon retour. Il se méfiait des principes qu'on pouvait tirer dans la tuerie et attendait de moi la lumière. Je cherchais. La polémique Sartre-Camus dans *les Temps modernes* à propos de *l'Homme révolté* me laissa indifférent.

En réplique à l'orage, le canon tonnait, le sol et les vitres tremblaient. Je me disais que ce n'est pas parce qu'on étouffe et qu'on se sent mal à l'aise qu'on doit tout accepter. On peut admirer des acrobates sans approuver ce qu'ils pensent. Je m'étonnais du pharisaïsme des cadres du système en place. Dès que le soir tombait, on s'enfermait car l'ennemi pouvait surgir. Le haut-commissariat regorgeait d'agrégés qui possédaient l'art de transformer les erreurs en succès, et, sur des revers qu'il ne pouvait dissimuler, l'état-major diffusait des instructions laborieuses. Les divisions ennemies se réfugiaient dans des espaces hors d'atteinte, Salan rêvait d'éparpiller une jonchée de places fortes, ravitaillées par air, capables de rayonner et de lancer des traits mortels ; en terme militaire, des hérissons. Ainsi peut-être, un jour de fumerie, imagina-t-il de monter un piège, une force aux moyens importants dans une région où l'ennemi se déplaçait comme chez lui. Il allait attirer le Viet en masse, comme on attire les vautours quand on leur abandonne une charogne, le tenir, et enfin le casser. C'était la formule qu'on entendait partout, le rêve de tous. Le Viet

cassait tellement de postes, de compagnies et parfois de bataillons, qu'on n'avait qu'un désir, le casser à son tour, le faucher à la mitrailleuse, voir ses cadavres pantelants dans les barbelés. Un ample cassage de Viets, un carnage somptueux, une victoire qui se compterait par un chiffre impressionnant de morts, quelle aubaine, quel bonheur ! A Paris, le gouvernement n'attendait que ça, le président du Conseil, un Laniel, un Daniel Mayer, escaladerait la tribune de la Chambre : enfin une victoire ! Enfin magnifiés les sacrifices du corps expéditionnaire ! Le commandant en chef ne pensait qu'à ça, le commandant du Tonkin aussi, et, du Centre-Annam au Laos et au sud, tous les autres ! Finalement, avec minutie et sous des prétextes divers, avait été paré, bricolé et ajusté le piège de Na-San pour barrer la route de l'Ouest. Giap ne pouvait pas revenir dans le Delta en négligeant cet appât. Il allait essayer de l'avaler, et alors...

J'allai voir ça. C'était Verdun à cent vingt kilomètres de Hanoi. Une citadelle formidable. Le soir tombait comme le rideau d'un théâtre, on se sentait loin de tout. Les moustiquaires ressemblaient à des suaires. Salan avait donné à Cogny des renforts énormes, une artillerie qui devait tout broyer. On avait calculé qu'il faudrait à Giap au moins cinquante mille soldats et coolies pour s'attaquer à Na-San. Alors ce serait sa fête.

J'osai exprimer des doutes. Comme aviateur, à première vue, je discernais des dangers. Comment les avions atterriraient-ils sous le feu ? On me répondit que les avions n'auraient pas besoin d'atterrir, qu'ils lâcheraient tout en parachute. En plus, il n'y aurait pas de feu ennemi puisqu'on le jugulerait dans l'instant. Je me tus. Comme j'appartenais au service de propagande et que j'envoyais toutes les semaines un reportage à *Radar*, le général Salan, de passage ce jour-là, m'engagea fort à ne pas mettre une sourdine pour mieux attirer le poisson dans la nasse. Quant à mes objections : « Vous n'y connaissez rien, me dit-il avec une cordiale condescendance. Vous ne connaissez pas Giap non plus. Croyez-moi, il en est encore à digérer son manuel du gradé d'infanterie. » Je l'entends encore, Salan. De l'observatoire qui dominait la citadelle de terre rouge, je le vois, rutilant, pareil à un archange grisonnant, tel qu'il y en a parfois dans les chapiteaux des églises, avec des moignons d'ailes et un regard

perdu dans les songes, mince, mystérieux, imposant, dans sa veste de toile à manches courtes avec son placard de décorations. Plus tard, son aide de camp me rendra mon article : « Le général aimerait que vous laissiez à Giap un véritable espoir pour qu'il s'enferre... »

J'ai fait de mon mieux, j'appartenais à l'armée, j'étais payé pour ça. Pas cher. A ma décharge, je n'ai rien à dire. C'était comme ça. C'était l'époque. La patrie.

Le soleil n'était pas le même qu'à Alger. C'était du plomb. On se gardait de lui comme on pouvait : il tuait. On engloutissait des tonnes de bière ou de perrier. Clément résistait à tout. C'était un type, un gonze, un zigue, un mec de baroud. Bâti à chaux et à sable, il déployait une activité débordante, avait l'œil à tout, était sûr de tout, et parfois, pour nous égayer, jouait un air d'accordéon. « A nous les femmes qui mouillent et qui pètent dans la soie », s'écriait-il. Il m'entraînait dans des soirées où il dansait, flirtait, mangeait, buvait, baisait. Pas moi. Je m'emmerdais. Réaction inattendue, le malaise qui peu à peu m'envahissait du climat, de la cruauté, du Veau d'or, de la tuerie inutile, me rendit à distance amoureux de celle qui m'avait poussé à écrire *Beau Sang*. Elle me parut souverainement belle, ses lettres étaient pleines de tendresse, elle s'occupait d'aménager la masure que j'avais achetée. J'imaginais ma vie là-bas avec elle, tandis que j'écrirais une nouvelle pièce, sur la guerre d'Indochine peut-être, pour Hermantier, et que j'irais parler de mes projets à M. Hirsch. A Saigon, où il était agent général des Messageries maritimes, le poète Louis Brauquier, de qui Guibert avait publié *le Pilote* dans sa collection des Cahiers de Barbarie, écrivait une poésie sensible, pure, fraternelle. C'était un adorateur de la mer, un homme bon et rayonnant. Il comprit tout de suite dans quel pétrin je me débattais : la chevalerie, à quoi je croyais encore au plus noir de la guerre, était morte. En ce temps-là, nous étions les guérilleros du monde libre, nous luttions contre le dragon à petite moustache. En Indochine, je commençais à discerner dans nos rangs des signes de barbarie, je me mettais à douter de cette armée tant aimée. Sans le savoir encore, j'étais dans une situation analogue, avec infiniment moins de danger, à celle de mon maître Jünger, officier de tradition de la Reichswehr quand, à Paris en 1941, il avait mesuré ce qui le

séparait de Hitler. J'avais sous les yeux le spectacle du champ de bataille après le passage de mes chers colonels, et encore étais-je dans la suite de Cogny, au milieu des fumées qui s'élevaient et des canons qui tonnaient, loin derrière l'action. Les villages flambaient, les femmes pleuraient, les hommes, extirpés des galeries où ils se terraient, étaient rassemblés comme des groupes de taupes apeurées. J'étais le seul à être ému, je n'avais jamais vu, sauf en photos à haute altitude, les effets de nos bombardements : les ruines de Cologne ressemblaient à celles de Pompéi. Je me rappelais les railleries du capitaine Boum-Boum. Après mon passage dans la RAF, j'avais droit à considérer le Delta du fleuve Rouge d'un regard différent. Je ne désapprouvais personne, ça me choquait, voilà tout.

Clément vivait sous l'influence de Mars, il avait le cuir plus dur que moi. Il rigolait et m'expliquait que ceux d'en face étaient cruels. Je répliquais qu'ils étaient chez eux, qu'ils résistaient aux envahisseurs que nous étions. « On est toujours envahisseurs ou envahis, répondait-il dans un hoquet de whisky. On ne peut pas rester chez soi comme les bourgeois. » C'était la stratégie du monde libre. J'aurais voulu une guerre juste, une guerre propre, j'étais pourtant officier de métier, j'avais tort de réfléchir, on ne remportait pas de victoire avec de la morale. Comment aurais-je réagi si Chassin m'avait donné un commandement de base ? Je me surpris déclarant à Brauquier que j'avais décidé de ne pas toucher à une arme pendant tout mon séjour.

J'entends dire parfois que c'est à cause de certains hommes comme moi que Saigon s'appelle à présent Hô Chi Minh-Ville. Je pense que non. Dans la lutte des colonisés contre les colonisateurs, ce sont toujours les colonisés qui finissent par vaincre, comme les obstinés sur les forts. Là, je rejoignais Camus, c'était ce que j'allais lui dire à mon retour. De cela nous parlions prudemment avec Brauquier. Lui, il était pour la défense de l'Occident par tous les moyens. Entre nous naquit une amitié qui ne faiblit jamais.

Si le nom d'Ernst Jünger revient souvent sous ma plume, c'est que nos déjeuners avenue Malakoff et ce qui nous avait

unis un temps si court, chacun de nous, avec Florence, devenaient des liens. A le lire, il n'y aurait eu entre Florence et lui qu'une seule vraie conversation, le jour où, par le lieutenant Heller qui contrôlait l'activité des éditeurs français, il fut présenté avenue Malakoff, le 28 mars 1942. Ce jour-là, d'après Jünger, Florence avait parlé de l'expérience de la mort que personne ne pouvait ravir à personne, et d'un papillon qu'elle avait vu, un soir, sous les tropiques, se poser sur le dos d'un gecko. Après quoi, bien qu'il fût devenu un habitué des jeudis de l'avenue Malakoff, il se contenta de noter le nom de Florence. Cependant, Heller dira qu'il était lié à elle « intimement » et nous savons qu'il ne faut accorder qu'un crédit relatif au journal de Jünger. Il arrange beaucoup après coup et ne dit que ce qu'il veut dire. De ses rencontres amoureuses par exemple, il ne laisse de trace que la marque d'une patte d'oiseau ou le souvenir d'un arôme. On reste sur sa faim. Jouhandeau et Léautaud tiennent donc plus de place dans son journal parisien que la belle Florence. En Indochine, j'étais loin de me douter de cela. Je pensais surtout au Jünger de seize ans qui, engagé dans la Légion sous une fausse identité, avait réussi à atteindre Sidi Bel Abbès.

Un jour où je visitais la base de Tourane, mon camarade Marchal me proposa une patrouille dans une région qu'on appelait « les montagnes de marbre », qu'on disait infestées de rebelles. En blindés, nous parcourûmes une trentaine de kilomètres dans le léger vrombissement de nos moteurs vers une haute et abrupte paroi pareille aux buffets d'orgue du Hoggar, puis la piste se rétrécit et devint un sentier. Nous laissâmes nos engins sous la garde des équipages et nous continuâmes à pied pour déboucher sur un théâtre de roc semé de lis rouges où se nichait un monastère de moines bouddhistes. Pour entrer, mes compagnons durent déposer leurs armes. Pas moi qui n'avais rien. Il était près de midi, il faisait une chaleur de paradis, on respirait des fleurs au parfum entêtant. Accroupis parmi les moinillons devant un temple, à côté de cercueils de bois blond, les bonzes nous offrirent le thé. Dans leurs fourreaux étroits, ils ressemblaient à la corolle safran des lis dont l'évangile dit que Salomon dans toute sa gloire n'a pas été vêtu comme l'un d'eux. Au fond des grottes voisines luisaient les statues du dieu gardé par des dragons, le gong devait annoncer notre présence, car il sonnait à un

rythme tantôt lent et tantôt précipité. Comme chaque jour, éclaterait un peu plus tard l'orage qui recouvrait déjà les montagnes de sa masse. Des guerriers de pierre chevauchant des tigres protégeaient les moines du feu du ciel, de larges étoiles tombaient des frangipaniers et les flamboyants plaquaient leurs fleurs pourpres sur l'azur. A Saigon, il y avait aussi des flamboyants, mais l'air y était empuanti par les fumées des motopousses et tout sentait l'étable de Baal. De là, comme au bord d'un brasier, on surplombait la plaine, le cours sinueux de la rivière, semblable à un brillant serpent, et les autres montagnes de la baie. La mer luisait, douce comme une hanche de princesse, et immobile.

Nous dûmes nous arracher à la torpeur qui nous envahissait, et nous prîmes congé en joignant nos mains sur le cœur, puis escortés un moment par des oiseaux aux vives couleurs, nous regagnâmes nos blindés. Comment n'aurais-je pas songé aux *Falaises de marbre* de Jünger ? Comment n'aurais-je pas été tenté, le temps d'un éclair, de rester là pour y finir ma vie ? De cette journée j'ai gardé une vibration pareille à un bonheur brûlant. Un instant, je fus hors de la guerre, dans une sorte de légèreté qui devait ressembler à des vapeurs d'opium.

Après cela, entendre Marchal parler de l'activité de ses avions Marauder me parut dérisoire. Mais comment échapper aux armes et où aller sans armes en Indochine quand on était militaire ? Une fois, je décollai avec un équipage pour une reconnaissance en rase-mottes. Sur ce qui leur paraissait des objectifs, le pilote déclenchait ses mitrailleuses, le bombardier lâchait des crottes un peu au hasard, nous passions comme la flèche d'une tornade, semant la mort dans notre sillage. De cette galopade, je revins avec des nausées pour la vie. A cette époque, j'envoyai au général Chassin une lettre dont, depuis 1952, je garde la copie dans ma Bible. On avait dit devant lui que je n'osais plus me battre et il s'était tu. Il ne m'avait pas défendu. Pourquoi ? M'avait-il quelquefois vu montrer ma peur ? « Si l'armée de l'air et vous en particulier n'avez rien à faire d'un officier comme moi, vous ne tarderez pas d'en être débarrassés. Je souffre de la méchanceté de mes camarades, mais je n'en souffrirai plus longtemps sous vos ordres, et vous, j'aurais tôt fait de vous oublier... »

Je n'ai jamais revu Tourane, son petit port et ses falaises scintillantes sans penser aux moines qui vivaient près de leurs

cercueils au milieu des fleurs. Ils doivent y être encore, à moins que le triste régime socialiste les ait contraints d'aller travailler dans la rizière. C'est à Tourane, sur une plage de sable blanc, qu'un jour j'osai demander à des camarades s'ils croyaient enseigner l'amour de la France en mitraillant des laboureurs. Ils ne me répondirent pas. Ils firent couler du sable dans leurs doigts.

L'armée juge mal ceux des siens qui osent être écrivains et encore plus poètes, ou alors ils doivent mourir à la guerre comme Psichari ou n'écrire que des choses sensibles et douces comme Pierre Loti, ou entrer à l'Académie. L'Académie en impose à ces messieurs qui, pourtant, ne lisent rien. A part quelques esprits cultivés, l'armée ne lit que les règlements, l'annuaire et les journaux, si peu les revues militaires ; rien de ce qu'on écrit à son propos quand on est dans le rang. Cette fausse muette parle souvent sans savoir ce qu'elle dit ou alors avec jalousie. Selon elle, quand on écrit, on ne peut pas se battre : les deux ne vont pas ensemble. Et si on se bat, il faut ne soulever aucun problème. Depuis la publication de mes poèmes à Alger, beaucoup se gaussaient de moi.

A Saigon comme dans toute l'Indochine, chacun se méfiait de son voisin, il était rare qu'on pût dire ce qu'on pensait. On ne fréquentait personne. Lucien Bodard, envoyé spécial permanent de *France-Soir*, fut le seul journaliste à me recevoir. L'œil féroce sous une paupière lourde, à l'affût de tout, il écrivait des articles débordants de vie, de couleur, d'odeur, de mort. Né en Chine où il avait passé sa plus tendre enfance, fils de consul, il était comme un requin dans l'eau, cynique et prêt à tout. Le commandement le redoutait et le gâtait. Mag, sa femme, et lui furent d'une rare gentillesse pour moi. Ils avaient des chats siamois qui savaient ouvrir les portes, et qui se serait douté que Bodard deviendrait un des plus monstrueux écrivains de notre temps, au talent macéré dans le nuoc-mam et le pavot ?

Personne ne connaissait la revue *France-Asie*. Découragé d'avance, j'écrivis à son directeur qui m'invita à dîner. Il habitait un immeuble occupé par des familles vietnamiennes de condition modeste et s'appelait René de Berval, était-ce son

vrai nom ? Venu avec Leclerc, il était tombé amoureux du pays, avait quitté l'armée, vivait à la vietnamienne comme dans une tribu dont il parlait la langue et où il avait femme et famille. Pour rester ici et s'y sentir chez soi, il s'était mis à l'écart de la communauté française, sa revue ne subsistait que des subsides du haut-commissariat et les vastes sujets de civilisation auxquels il se consacrait intéressaient peu un gouvernement en guerre. Le directeur était aussi pauvre que la revue.

Je fus reçus avec un étonnement charmant. Je me sentais, comme chez les moines des montagnes de marbre, sur une autre planète. On ne tarda pas à comprendre que je n'étais pas heureux et que, dans l'armée où je me trouvais, je cherchais éperdument la vérité. Pour moi il n'y en avait qu'une : partir d'ici, mais comment ? Les Vietnamiens sauraient-ils s'opposer à l'arrivée du régime communiste ? Le régime démocratique, si pourri qu'il fût, valait encore mieux que la dictature prolétarienne. Paradoxe : nous étions contraints de rester pour sauvegarder la concussion et la liberté de penser : mieux valait les vices occidentaux que la vertu communiste. Ainsi étais-je forcé de servir le corps expéditionnaire en me berçant de l'illusion qu'il ne défendrait que les justes. C'était la politique du général de Lattre. Naturellement, c'était une politique d'abandon. Les hommes comme moi sont des idéalistes et ils sont dangereux car ils sont irréalistes, ils n'ont de place que dans les lieux retirés.

Dans un film que j'avais composé avec des documents et que j'achevai à Paris, je voulus montrer la férocité des combats et leur enjeu toujours incertain. De Lattre n'était plus, son fils avait été tué dans la bataille, le Tonkin qu'on ne pouvait garder qu'à ce prix était couvert de morts, est-ce que cela valait la peine ? La question ne pouvait échapper à personne et toute l'action se déroulait aux accents wagnériens du *Crépuscule des dieux*. La conclusion me paraissait évidente : on ne pouvait défendre le Tonkin sans qu'il veuille se défendre lui-même des communistes.

Le jour de la présentation à la presse dans un cinéma des Champs-Elysées, Claude Bourdet qui dirigeait *l'Observateur*

me lança, narquois : « Vous avez bien travaillé pour la guerre d'Indochine ! » Il avait raison. Le problème camusien se pose à tous ceux qui ne s'arrogent pas le droit de condamner leurs frères. Je ne vois pas comment j'aurais pu dire que mes camarades étaient des brigands. Ils n'étaient que des soldats. Pouvais-je condamner ceux qui n'étaient pas les promoteurs de cette guerre, de ses raisons et de ses méthodes ? Contre eux il y avait cette évidence qu'on pouvait les confondre avec les nazis, et qu'ils étaient détestés par tous, même par ceux qui profitaient d'eux. En savais-je assez pour porter jugement en profondeur ? Pouvais-je accuser le R.P. Thierry d'Argenlieu, ancien gouverneur général et carme déchaussé, d'être un massacreur quand il avait bombardé Haiphong au nom de Dieu en 1946 ? N'en avait-il pas demandé l'autorisation à de Gaulle ? Il me semblait qu'il n'y eût d'espoir là-bas que pour les agrégés du haut-commissaire, qui seraient, quelle que fût l'issue des événements, promus à un échelon supérieur. Le gouvernement se montrait sûr de lui, nous pensions que nous étions forts, l'armée vietnamienne dont les cadres étaient pourris attendait la suite, le commerce marchait bien, les compagnies de transport faisaient des affaires d'or, les fonctionnaires se laissaient couler dans la séduction du pays, et les militaires dans le vin, l'opium et les femmes. Que pouvais-je, sinon célébrer la vertu des hommes intègres et l'innocence de ceux qui mouraient pour rien ? La guerre d'Indochine continuerait tant qu'un événement d'importance ne secouerait pas l'opinion. Tout désastre était à exclure car personne n'imaginait que Giap pourrait jamais conquérir la supériorité des armes. La logistique ! Chacun avait le mot à la bouche pour dénoncer l'incapacité des Viets. Ils étaient endurants, ils ne mangeaient que du riz qu'ils portaient sur eux en boudin, ils savaient se priver de tout, ils avaient parfois des canons, parfois des camions, mais notre aviation défonçait leurs pistes, labourait leurs routes et détruisait leur armement lourd quand ils réussissaient à en ramener de Chine.

De cela je m'ouvris à Camus. Lui seul comprit que je ne pouvais en dire davantage et sentit de nouvelles menaces monter à l'horizon. Les autres jugèrent que je n'étais pas allé assez loin ou que j'avais montré que les combats de l'Indochine conduisaient au désespoir. Philippe Hériat, prudent et circonspect, et qui avait pour moi un œil à la fois sévère et

cajoleur, me dit que ceux qui étaient pour la guerre trouve-
raient chez moi des arguments, et que le gros public ne verrait
rien de ce que j'avais cru y mettre. Tel fut en effet le résultat.

*
**

Tenté d'avaler Na-San, Giap avait perdu trois mille
soldats dans de furieux assauts. Cependant notre artillerie
n'empêchait pas la sienne de détruire nos avions, et à cause du
crachin d'hiver, l'aviation devait parfois renoncer à ravitailler
la citadelle. J'avais soulevé ces deux objections lors de ma
visite, on avait haussé les épaules, et tout à coup, l'état-major
craignit le pire, un plan d'évacuation du hérisson fut mis sur
pied et heureusement exécuté. Le général Salan paya cet
insuccès d'une disgrâce. Un successeur lui fut désigné.

Revenu dans la gueule même de Baal, je me sentais un
observateur plus subtil. Nous combattions des hommes dont
la force principale était la ruse et je me sentais, comme Jünger à
Paris dans les années 1940, un officier d'armée d'occupation.
Mes camarades semblaient n'y pas prêter attention. La plupart
du temps, à part les putains et les commerçants, les gens
feignaient de ne pas nous voir. Dans les hôtels on nous servait
comme des étrangers. A Hanoi où l'esprit de résistance se
manifestait le plus, la population se détournait de nous dans
les rues, nous allions comme des ombres. Les seuls lieux où
nous pouvions nous croire un peu chez nous était l'immense
caravansérail de l'hôtel Métropole ou la cathédrale qui ressemblait à une minuscule Notre-Dame de Paris en stuc. N'empêche, le dimanche, quand débarquaient sur le parvis les
officiers en uniforme, qu'ils emplissaient la nef et qu'un
aumônier s'adressait à eux comme à l'époque lointaine du
royaume franc de Jérusalem, ça avait de la gueule. L'équivoque s'emparait de nouveau de moi, je me demandais si je ne me
trompais pas, je pensais à ces croisades de la chrétienté où
régnait l'injustice, ce qui n'empêchait pas les migrations de
l'humanité de s'accomplir, les civilisations de se rapprocher et
parfois de s'unir. On nous avait combattus jadis, on nous avait
aussi aimés, le mélange des sangs sur le champ de bataille et
dans les lits n'avait pas été vain. Ici, nos missionnaires avaient
semé la parole du Christ sur des immensités où elle avait levé
et, si barbares qu'on pût nous juger par moments, nous étions

les défenseurs d'un certain ordre mystique face au nihilisme. Dans les travées et la nef, une foule dense, grouillante et miaulante de femmes chargées d'enfants égrenaient leur chapelet, et, à treize mille kilomètres de chez moi, je renouais avec ce qui m'avait conduit à Dieu dans ma jeunesse. Illusion, mirage, leurres fugitifs ! De quel Dieu n'eût-on pas demandé qu'il fût de vérité ? Quand les écailles tombaient de mes yeux, je me redemandais à quoi je servais là, sinon à tromper par ce que j'écrivais et à me tromper moi-même. Le monde avait changé. La guerre dans laquelle j'avais failli être broyé avait été une guerre contre la liberté de l'esprit et voici que, retournés à notre tréfonds d'impérialisme, nous célébrions les causes que nous avions combattues. Après un combat à mort contre Hitler, nous ne pouvions plus nous conduire comme des conquérants. Or, qu'étions-nous ?

Au cours d'une opération dans le delta du Tonkin, une compagnie de Légion passa sous mes yeux tout un village par les armes parce qu'on avait découvert des francs-tireurs cachés dans des galeries. Les hommes, vieux ou jeunes, entassés dans une cour, et hop ! liquidés au pistolet-mitrailleur, devenaient un amas de corps sanglants ; les femmes, poussées dans une pagode avec leur marmaille, se lamentaient à cris aigus, des grenades éclataient dans la fumée, des rafales giclaient et soudain se répandait une abominable odeur de cramé. Comme je m'indignais, on ordonna une enquête : la compagnie tombée dans un guet-apens avait réagi, tout s'était déroulé en un éclair, ces bavures-là étaient monnaie courante. Les aumôniers militaires aspergeaient les troupes de bénédictions et les consciences d'absolutions. Plus tard aux Etats-Unis, les responsables de crimes semblables seront traduits devant des tribunaux civils et condamnés. En France, personne ne s'en offusquait. Si. Moi qui n'y pouvais rien et me reprochais de n'être pas un vrai militaire. Moi non plus, si je me souvenais, je n'avais pas les mains pures.

Sur toutes les bases aériennes, à l'écart des pistes, étaient construites des cahutes qu'on évitait et d'où, la nuit, montaient des hurlements qu'on feignait de ne pas entendre. Sur la base de Tourane de mon camarade Marchal où je disposais d'une certaine liberté de mouvement, on m'avait montré cela de loin avec répugnance : les hommes de main des renseignements

s'exerçaient là, Marchal me disait : « C'est comme ça partout, c'est obligé. » Pourquoi ? Comment ? Un jour, au cours d'une nouvelle opération, comme je parcourais la zone en jeep, j'aperçus devant une pagode un troupeau de paysans accroupis sous la garde de soldats. Je demandai à l'officier qui m'accompagnait ce que c'était. « Rien. Des suspects. » Je demandai qu'on s'arrêtât. J'allai à la pagode, j'entrai : on amenait les files de *nhia-quê* devant des tables où les spécialistes leur brisaient les couilles à la magnéto. Je me fis reconduire à l'hôtel Métropole et restai enfermé deux jours. Quand je sortis, j'avais décidé de quitter l'armée.

Des années après que l'Indochine eut recouvert l'Algérie de son propre linceul : « Alors, padre, ai-je dit à un vieil aumônier qui avait bourlingué partout, les abominations, les massacres, les incendies de villages, les tortures, vous avez tout pardonné ? Vous étiez aussi pour la croisade ? Vous fermiez les yeux ?… » Ainsi ai-je su que, nos bons pères, on les laissait bénir les blessés et les mourants, mais on les écartait de tout, comme à la ferme on éloignait l'enfant que j'étais quand on tuait le cochon. « On nous cachait tout… » Pourquoi pas ? Ames naïves, les aumôniers croient que les omelettes se font sans casser les œufs. L'un d'eux, que le ministre de la Défense de ce temps-là, Pierre de Chevigné, estimait, avait été convoqué un jour à l'état-major. C'était en février 1954 avant la défaite de Diên Biên Phu. Notre révérend attendait le ministre quand le général Navarre surgi sursauta. « Qu'est-ce que vous foutez là ? » Le ministre s'interposa et prit l'aumônier à part : « Que diraient les officiers si on arrêtait cette guerre ? » Là, prenant argument de ce qu'il lui avait semblé apercevoir, de tout ce dont il commençait à se douter, peut-être de ce qu'on avait pu lui confesser, l'aumônier répondit : « L'armée en a assez… »

Sur la misérable écorce terrestre où je ripatonnais, je voyais ce qui se perpétrait là où, autrefois, sur une autre latitude… Ma hantise revenait. Quand je fuyais les lacs d'or qui étincelaient derrière nous, qu'éprouvais-je, sinon la satisfaction d'être arrivé à la minute fixée et d'avoir largué où il fallait notre cargaison de mort ? Une vraie joie. Délivré, je ne pensais pas que nous avions semé derrière nous un amoncellement de ruines, de carcasses de trams et de véhicules dans les

ténèbres où tout brûlait, même les pierres. A la fin de 1944, Jünger avait rejoint sa maison, sa femme et ses chats à Kirchhorst en Basse-Saxe et subi nos bombardements jusqu'à la fin de la guerre. Dans son *Journal*, il parlait des raids de chaque nuit et de chaque jour, du fracas des batteries, des nuages de fumées, des décombres toujours en feu, des meubles brisés amoncelés sur les trottoirs, des visages pleins de larmes, tout comme à Londres dans le brouillard et la perspective du néant. Et il fallait que je sois, même pas dix ans plus tard, dans une rizière du Tonkin pour me soucier des crimes que j'avais, moi aussi, commis ? Alors, comment pouvais-je blâmer les pauvres mecs à moitié saouls de la Légion, et même Cogny ? Parce que j'étais à pied, j'apercevais quelques villages — quelques villages seulement — brûlés par nous, je surprenais un atelier de renseignement en action. Au ras du sol, et non plus à mes hauteurs à poudroiement, je m'indignais alors que j'avais régné un temps dans un empire d'épouvante ?

Dans *Platoon* et *Full Metal Jacket*, les atrocités ne sont pas plus abominables que les nôtres, les villages sont passés au fil de l'épée comme jadis sous Jules César ou Scipion l'Africain, mais, du moins, l'Amérique pouvait-elle savoir de quoi elle et ses boys étaient coupables. Tandis qu'en France, à part les antimilitaristes, tout le monde louait et glorifiait l'armée, tout le monde absolvait ses crimes, et quand il lui arrivait de s'abattre, ivre de vin rouge, de soleil et d'odeur de poudre, nous étendions sur elle un manteau pudique. Surtout ne disons rien, ne dénonçons personne, taisons-nous. Ainsi ai-je fait dans mon livre *la Bataille dans la rizière*, et même dans ce court métrage *la Bataille du Tonkin*, qui dort dans les caves du fort d'Ivry. A l'époque, je n'osais même pas mettre de l'ordre en moi, ni accuser les miens. L'argument qu'on servait dans les sphères politiques que l'Union française se désagrégerait si nous quittions l'Indochine ne valait pas un clou. Pour moi, l'Union française se désagrégerait d'elle-même. Pour moi, ou bien cette guerre n'était pas une croisade contre le communisme et nous n'avions plus de raison de rester au Viêt-nam, ou bien c'en était une, et il fallait la mener autrement. Provoquer un scandale ? Auprès de qui ? Dans les sphères politiques, tout le monde savait, tout le monde trouvait cela

normal, cela se pratiquait dans toutes les armées, il n'y avait que moi à l'avoir ignoré un temps.

Avais-je pensé à inviter Malraux à la présentation de *la Bataille du Tonkin,* ou n'y était-il pas venu ? A mon retour, Clément m'emmena visiter les temples d'Angkor où personne n'allait plus. Un avion nous posa à Sien Reap. De là, par des routes désertes, nous gagnâmes la ville sainte. A cette saison, tout était gorgé d'eau. Notre voiture plongeait dans les fondrières et soulevait des gerbes de boue liquide. Au milieu de leurs vaches, des paysans nous regardaient traverser leurs pâturages forestiers. Le long des étangs, nous dérangions de grands échassiers en train de pêcher. Le conservateur de la cité était à Paris. Son adjoint, un petit homme aux yeux très doux et à la barbiche impériale, affublé d'une veste de pyjama et d'une culotte de cheval et chaussé de pantoufles, vint nous saluer à l'hôtel et nous confia à un guide. Nous traversâmes d'immenses douves pour déboucher sur l'esplanade et l'ensemble des cinq dômes et des sept enceintes. Œuvre des rois, aussi grandiose que les pyramides d'Egypte, mais pas plus majestueux que nos cathédrales, le temple écrasait la cité mystérieuse d'autrefois devenue village de bergers, mais les sanctuaires mineurs s'étendaient à l'infini. Fiévreux, nous allions de trésor en trésor, on nous mena où Malraux avait commis ses rapts historiques, et peu à peu je me sentais une âme de pirate. Moi aussi, si j'avais pu, j'aurais arraché les chefs-d'œuvre qui étouffaient dans les lianes qui les étranglaient et les désarticulaient. Peu à peu les orages les frappaient, les pluies les flagellaient, la terre les ensevelissait. Les arbres bouchaient le ciel, nous suffoquions, nous étions assourdis par le criaillement des perroquets et le glapissement des singes, des couleuvres dorées glissaient sous les Bouddhas.

Le prodige restait Angkor Vat. Les rois qui l'avaient construit n'étaient plus que poussière, les guerres qui avaient battu ses murs, les enfers qui parfois y menaient encore leur sabbat n'avaient pas réussi à le détruire. Nous, au moins, nous le protégions. Les Américains n'étaient pas encore là, Pol Pot non plus. Gigantesque, il résistait depuis plus de mille ans mais s'effritait. Des pierres et des visages avaient éclaté sous les

balles et les obus de mortiers de factions de rebelles. Le bruit des armées disparues ou à venir ne s'entendait pas. De frêles nacelles en forme de gondoles tirées par des cyclistes glissaient sur les routes mouillées, des grenouilles chantaient. A Bayon, que Claudel appelait, en 1921, « un temple maudit », nous allâmes de gradin en gradin, d'enceinte en enceinte, allumant des baguettes d'encens devant chaque dieu. Le premier soir, à travers les galeries et les chaussées dont tant de pas avaient usé les dalles, nous avançâmes vers le bain du roi, puis vers ce qui avait été un monastère où trois mille bonzes priaient et où six cents danseuses dansaient devant Bouddha, tandis qu'errait un grand serpent langoureux. Les danseuses avaient inspiré les sculpteurs au point que, parfois, on pouvait les confondre avec les dieux qu'elles célébraient. Quoi de surprenant ? De retour à l'hôtel, le conservateur adjoint nous dit que la vaisselle des prêtres et des ballerines était d'or pur comme celle du roi Salomon, et que l'odeur d'encens portait jusqu'aux extrémités de la forêt. Nous dormîmes comme si nous avions été sur une autre planète, bercés par d'étranges cris qui ressemblaient à des plaintes. Le lendemain, nous retournâmes à Angkor Vat. De leurs fleurs en forme de cœur, les lotus recouvraient presque toute la surface des lacs. Des camelots locaux nous attendaient pour nous vendre des arcs et des poignards de pacotille.

En hommage à Malraux encore, car si j'admirais Claudel, je ne l'aimais pas, je dérobai, le cœur battant, une humble banderole pareille à une fragile queue de cerf-volant que je dissimulai sous ma chemise, comme un oiseau dont le bec me piquait le cœur. Pour implorer la clémence du dieu et transmettre la prière que j'enlevais, je déposai une aumône. De Sien Reap, c'est tout ce que je ramenai avec une clochette en bois qu'on accroche au cou des vaches pour les retrouver quand elles s'égarent. Le paysan à qui je l'achetai s'étonna qu'un officier étranger pût s'encombrer d'un objet aussi ordinaire. La banderole et la clochette sont toujours chez moi avec un éclat de grès verdi par l'humidité qui gisait au pied d'un génie oiseau. De temps en temps, je touche la banderole, j'agite la clochette, son frêle battant tire d'elle quelques sons aigrelets semblables à ceux des élytres d'un insecte.

Nous étions ivres de soleil et de chaleur. L'orage de l'après-midi menaçait. Le ciel était d'encre noire. Nous allâmes dans une autre cité monastère qui abritait jadis cent

mille âmes et encore mille danseuses dont les visages de pierre nous escortaient. Sans les effigies des génies, des compagnons du dieu et sans ces danseuses tournoyantes toutes proches de notre canon de beauté, on se serait cru en pleine Renaissance italienne avec plafonds ouvragés, colonnades carrées et encadrements effilés dans lesquels passages et portiques se surajoutaient et se prolongeaient. Il y avait aussi la statue d'un cheval nageant seul, sans cavalier. Ses antérieurs levés haut, on aurait cru, car le bassin était vide, qu'il allait escalader les nuées. Nous étions dans le temple de la Sainte-Epée, comparable à notre chapelle des Invalides, mais à quelle échelle ridicule pour nous ! L'épée n'a jamais eu de force que par la flamme qui brûle dans les esprits. Sans cette flamme-là, pas de vaillance. Sans l'encens qui chassait les moustiques, pas de gloire non plus pour les vainqueurs.

Là, Çiva était représenté debout entre deux femmes graciles et de même taille, qui l'encadraient exactement et lui arrivaient aux épaules. L'attachement amoureux prenait une forme admirable : chacune d'elles posait la main sur le haut de la fesse du dieu époux, et le geste, seulement visible des proches, signifiait : « Tu es mon mari et mon amant, je n'appartiens qu'à toi, mais tu es aussi à moi et toutes deux nous te partageons. » Osé, le geste devenait pudeur même. J'ai toujours rêvé de femmes comme celles-là. Sans avoir pensé à Çiva, j'avais toujours, serrés au fond de ma cantine, des chaussons de danse et un exemplaire fatigué de *la Guerre notre mère* de Jünger. Epouser une danseuse, quand on revenait de la guerre une épée au côté, me semblait une sorte d'heureuse fatalité. Pourtant je n'ai jamais été qu'un chevalier errant en quête d'une cause et rarement revenu d'une victoire. D'une bonzerie voisine, peut-être imaginaire, montaient de lourdes psalmodies scandées par des coups de gong. Bientôt, aux coups de gong succéda le tonnerre. Nous courûmes nous réfugier sous une balustrade d'où nous vîmes l'orage galoper par-dessus la ville vers les forêts.

Ma visite au temple de la Sainte-Epée me posait le problème que j'avais à résoudre : comment me délivrer de l'armée et la délivrer de moi ? Une rengaine : j'étais un individu à problèmes, donc dangereux. Puisque nous possédions la prépondérance des armes, il me semblait que nous

devions nous imposer avec justice et magnanimité. Clément jugeait mon sentiment simpliste. Pour lui, c'était le plus fort ou le plus malin qui gagnait ; sans pitié avant la victoire, on devait — là il était d'accord — se montrer miséricordieux après. La guerre était la guerre, il s'agissait de profiter sans faiblesse et sans scrupule de toutes les fautes de l'adversaire. Pour lui, les Viets bannissaient tout ce qui ressemblait au pardon. Ils ne respectaient rien. Je lui demandai encore pourquoi ils auraient respecté quelque chose : nous marchions sur le ventre de leur patrie, c'était nous qu'il fallait exterminer. A quoi Clément répondait par les mêmes balivernes que de Lattre avait transformées en principes supérieurs et qu'à défaut de meilleur argument les fidèles rabâchaient : nous étions là pour imposer l'indépendance à ces peuples et, au besoin, les y contraindre contre eux-mêmes et contre les hors-la-loi qui s'opposaient à Bao Dai, incarnation de la lignée des empereurs d'Annam. Pourquoi se rebellait-on alors ? Parce que le temps des empereurs était accompli, que le vent des révolutions avait soufflé en Russie et en Chine, et que Hô Chi Minh voulait instaurer le gouvernement du peuple. Réplique de nos experts en psychologie et trouvaille du général de Lattre : nous nous battions pour la République, Bao Dai se soumettrait au nouveau régime populaire, mais dans le giron de l'Occident, et tout serait comme avant, sous un monceau d'or et de corruption.

Clément oubliait que des idées de liberté et d'égalité pouvaient encore prévaloir, et que d'indécrottables héritiers de la Révolution comme moi, fils du péché, élevé par l'oncle Jules et par Meftah, pouvaient se sentir plus près des paysans de la rizière que de ceux qui les massacraient. Notre mascarade trompait de bonnes âmes et invitait les dames d'œuvres à prier pour les héros d'une certaine Indochine dont je ne voulais plus du tout, plus du tout ! On m'avait déjà eu. J'avais déjà casqué pour Pétain. De Lattre avait été frappé d'une inspiration lyrique et l'Amérique avait marché. Salan, quand il était convoqué à Paris à un conseil de défense, feignait aussi de croire à la croisade et à la nouvelle république impériale, cette bonne blague ! Et quelle assiette au beurre pour ces messieurs du gouvernement — les Diêm, les Van Tri et toute la clique de ceux qui ont laissé leurs noms à la pourriture et aux désastres.

Bref, puisque pour moi tout était question de morale,

puisque je pensais que, dans une guerre coloniale, on devait se montrer grands seigneurs, il fallait en finir. Je m'assis sur une balustrade. La lumière du couchant dorait les murailles et les dômes. L'orage menaçait depuis l'après-midi, poussait ses colonnes tourbillonnantes sur les hauteurs et, tout à coup, dans un coup de tonnerre majestueux, s'empara du ciel entier et creva. De retour à l'hôtel, je me dis que je ne composerais pas. Comme les règlements de l'armée n'avaient jamais prévu qu'il fût permis de quitter les rangs sur un mouvement d'humeur ou un coup de tête, aucun militaire ne pouvait s'en aller de son plein gré, à moins de déserter, crime sans pardon. Personne ne démissionne de l'armée : on s'en va avec son accord ou elle vous chasse. Le général qui me protégeait de loin voulait que je retourne en France auprès de lui. Ce ne serait qu'une mutation de plus. Je venais d'être promu colonel. Je ne supportais pas de bénéficier d'un traitement de faveur, je devais subir le même sort que mes camarades : un séjour de vingt-sept mois, ou alors le congé du personnel navigant auquel mes états de service me donnaient droit. Ainsi je quitterais définitivement les rangs. C'est à cela que je me décidai.

L'averse frappait le toit de l'hôtel, le ciel flamboyait, j'éprouvai un illusoire sentiment de jouissance.

Nous regagnâmes l'aérodrome en voiture. Un avion venait d'y déposer le frère du roi. L'hymne cambodgien retentit, très doux, vieillot, fané, comme une musique d'orphéon, comme une grappe de fleurs d'oranger de mariée sous un globe. Le frère du roi passa devant la compagnie d'honneur et salua les drapeaux, le nôtre, celui rouge et or du Viêt-nam et celui du Cambodge, rouge noir safran, tandis que je sautais dans l'avion qui repartait pour Saigon. Clément ne voulut pas me suivre : une fille l'attendait dans son lit, à l'hôtel. Une danseuse décrochée de l'éternité? Nous décollâmes sous l'orage qui s'éloignait dans l'assombrissement du crépuscule, et, tels des anges brandisseurs de foudre, les éclairs nous accompagnèrent. Quelquefois nous passions sous la voûte d'une arche de feu et je m'attendais à ce que nous soyons frappés, mais le pilote manœuvrait habilement.

Sous nos ailes, la plaine de Cochinchine glissa enfin, tout inondée aussi, nous nous faufilâmes entre des rideaux de lumières incertaines et des nuages qui se vidaient comme des

outres. Quand nous nous posâmes, un voile violet s'abattit sur Saigon.

*
**

J'étais triste que mon séjour en Indochine fût devenu pour moi une lutte avec l'armée, et comme je souffrais d'être seul, je sentis le besoin d'un maître. Je n'en étais pas à choisir entre mon devoir et un crime, comme Vigny s'exerce à placer ses héros, et je cherchais en vain des camarades qui auraient partagé mes scrupules. Tous me considéraient comme un oiseau rare peu fréquentable et préféraient suivre le gros des consciences et le gros de l'armée. Aurais-je trouvé un frère d'armes dans le colonel Paris de Bollardière qui commandait alors un régiment de parachutistes et se distingua plus tard, général, par un refus d'obéissance en Algérie ? Nous n'étions pas au même endroit au même moment, et cela suffit, en amour comme à la guerre, pour ne jamais se rencontrer. D'ailleurs éprouvait-il ce que j'éprouvais ? J'aurais aimé croiser un poète des armes et du désert, tel Psichari qui avait été tué en 1914. En Afrique la question ne se posait pas comme en Extrême-Orient, même si là-bas on brûlait seulement la plante des pieds aux prisonniers pour savoir où se trouvaient les rezzous. Et puis, pour Psichari comme pour Lawrence d'Arabie, l'amour pour les éphèbes pouvait inspirer des sentiments miséricordieux, équivoques.

J'avais traversé Saigon et l'Indochine sans savoir à qui ni à quoi m'attacher. Ce soir-là, un riche négociant d'import-export rencontré au Continental, un métis qui avait l'or pour patrie, m'entraîna dans une maison de rendez-vous chic protégée par les services de police. Là, on fumait et de belles Laotiennes servaient de geishas. Je ne fumai pas mais je m'abandonnai à l'amour et j'y passai la nuit, je raconte cela dans *les Belles Croisades*. A l'aube, je rentrai chez moi à travers la ville fracassée de soleil neuf, et considérai enfin les choses avec un peu de cynisme. Ce peuple, qui s'était déjà battu deux mille ans avec la Chine et n'avait pas été dévoré, était un peuple silencieux, rusé, qui préférait endormir l'occupant avec de l'opium et des filles avant de l'égorger.

De mon ancien ennemi Jünger, je me sentais de plus en plus proche. Pour lui, tel qu'on le suit à travers ses ouvrages,

tel que je l'avais remarqué dans notre première rencontre en Allemagne, tout avait été tellement plus difficile et dangereux. Mobilisé comme commandant de compagnie dans la Wehrmacht, à peine avait-il traversé la France vaincue en 1940 qu'il était entré dans la résistance contre Hitler. Opposé aux entreprises qu'il appelait les « équarrissoirs » dont, à l'époque, nous n'avions aucune idée, et aux prises d'otages, il avait dû, en esprit, se séparer de l'immense majorité des siens pour ne trouver d'appui précaire qu'auprès de rares généraux, incapables de le protéger comme de se protéger eux-mêmes. A la fin, il avait dû s'isoler d'une meute que la perspective de la défaite rendait furieuse et hagarde. Partout, jusqu'aux derniers moments de la guerre et devant les pires dangers, il avait montré l'âme impavide qu'il s'était forgée depuis sa plus tendre jeunesse.

Parfois on prend le maître que la fatalité vous envoie. Je pouvais saluer celui-là. Je me mis à lire ou à relire son œuvre avec une passion inégale, et c'est alors peu à peu que je découvris qu'il était souvent invité chez Florence.

Si puissante était l'armée que je quittais, que je m'en fus presque sans remords. Comme cadeau de rupture je demandai un ordre de mission pour la Corée où l'Amérique affrontait la Chine. Je gagnai le Japon, j'allai à Nara et à Kyoto parmi les temples, au milieu des biches. De là, ce fut Séoul, puis le champ de bataille et la vaillante unité qui représentait la France en Corée. En plein hiver, on couchait sous des tentes où brûlaient de puants poêles à mazout. Sur la terre couverte de neige et pétrie de cadavres, un déluge d'obus ne cessait de tomber. Les parois des tranchées étaient hérissées de crânes défoncés, de mâchoires, de bouts d'ossements. Les armées s'affrontaient sans manœuvrer : elles avançaient derrière un monstrueux barrage d'artillerie, l'adversaire reculait, l'action s'arrêtait et, quelques jours plus tard, reprenait en sens inverse. C'était une façon comme une autre de tout tuer et de tout broyer ; un ouragan cosmique pulvérisait tout, d'énormes masses de canons tiraient jour et nuit, des nuées de bombardiers lâchaient des bombes au-dessus des lignes chinoises. Loin en arrière du front américain, dans un immense état-

major, un général lisait des bandes dessinées en buvant à la bouteille du Coca-Cola. Les combattants des deux côtés, presque déjà vêtus comme des cosmonautes, s'abritaient comme ils pouvaient dans des casemates. Après les espaces d'Indochine où la guerre s'apparentait à celle de Scipion l'Africain ou d'Hannibal, cela étonnait. Là, je passai aussi vite que je pus et m'en fus, happé par le pont aérien qui tournait sans désemparer entre la Corée et le Japon.

Dans le vertige de Tokyo, je fus frappé par le développement de la ville et la précipitation du rythme de son cœur. Les Japonais semblaient vouloir dévorer le monde pour s'étendre à l'aise. Qu'une telle multitude grouillât sur un si mince territoire m'effraya. De cette horreur comme de l'amour inespéré qui s'y ajouta, mon roman *le Désert de Retz* regorge. Tout ce que j'ai connu de la Corée et du Japon est dans ce livre, odieusement mêlé. Je fus invité chez l'ambassadeur de France, j'allai à Hiroshima, j'en ramenai des affiches, puis je m'ennuyai. En uniforme pour la dernière fois, je revins à Saigon rédiger mon rapport, et, en hâte, me hissai dans un Constellation d'Air France. Je regrettai Clément, Brauquier et Berval, le directeur de *France-Asie*, à qui j'envoyai un article sur mon désenchantement.

Beyrouth fut une longue escale. Des amis de Doyon m'y attendaient et me précipitèrent dans le commerce du poète Georges Schehadé et de Gaëtan Picon. Le Liban était un paradis, personne ne se doutait que les épouvantes et les dévastations le guettaient. Quand je débarquai à Orly, tout me parut hors de saison, comme à mon retour de Grande-Bretagne, quand parfois je flageolais sur mes jambes et que je ne savais plus si c'était le monde ou le temps qui s'était détraqué. Je retournai aux déjeuners du jeudi chez Florence où personne ne s'étonna de me revoir. Le temps avait coulé, je n'apportais plus le même plaisir à ces vanités où l'on ne s'intéressait à rien d'autre qu'à la conversation à table. Florence avait vieilli. Elle me parut plus attachée que jamais à sa ménagerie.

Je me réfugiai dans ma caborgniote que la Comédie-Française avait transformée en cahute vivable, et peu à peu, me remis dans le courant de la vie. Avec l'armée j'en étais arrivé au terminus, comme dans un train dont il faut descendre pour éviter la voie de garage. La prêtresse d'*Histoire d'O*, toujours

à gauche de Paulhan, célébrait l'office avec des regards de chatte ensommeillée.

*

Chez Gallimard, on ne se posait pas mes problèmes, on était pressé de publier *la Bataille dans la rizière*. Ce fut un beau charivari. Camus comprit que j'étais victime de mes illusions. La presse de gauche se scandalisa, *l'Humanité* publia un article de blâme pondéré que je pris très mal, Doyon explosa en sarcasmes, *le Figaro* fut le seul à me couvrir de louanges. Amrouche se tut. J'eus conscience des dangers qu'un écrivain court quand il descend dans l'arène avec un taureau à combattre. J'avais cru éclairer ma position par un dialogue avec un officier prisonnier et que je plaçai tout à la fin du livre, un peu comme si je tendais la clé de ce qui précédait. Ce prisonnier et moi parlions comme des gens de bonne compagnie, du Viêt-nam, de la France et du conflit qui nous opposait, comme dans des nuages. Le prisonnier n'osait pas me dire ce qu'il pensait et j'essayais de le convaincre que mon pays travaillait au salut du sien. Enfin, toutes les sottises d'usage. Un tel aveuglement, c'était fort de café, c'était moi. J'essayais même de justifier la façon dont la guerre était menée par nous sur le terrain. Sans m'en douter, je m'étais fourré dans une situation impossible. Ne pouvant salir ni l'armée ni la France, j'aurais pu laisser échapper quelques-uns des cris que j'avais poussés dans le fond de ma conscience, et sans dénoncer les horreurs dont j'avais été le témoin, j'aurais pu laisser percer un son de vérité. A peine étions-nous arrivés à conclure notre entretien, le prisonnier et moi, sur cet axiome que cette guerre était injuste et cruelle.

Même Frémin, mon ami Claude de Fréminville, le condisciple de Camus, l'ancien de la bande à Charlot devenu Claude Terrien, éditorialiste à Europe n° 1, ne sut comment cacher sa consternation. Je me collai tout le monde à dos, sauf Sigaux, et Claude Mauriac, gaulliste à tous crins. Kanters se montra d'une négligence généreuse, mais je reçus de belles raclées dans les revues. Dans *les Lettres nouvelles*, Maurice Nadeau écrivit qu'on pouvait désormais me ranger parmi les auteurs du communiqué. Quant aux *Temps modernes*, ils m'exécutèrent poliment dans une longue analyse où l'on

comparait *la Bataille dans la rizière* au *Métier des armes*. Dans la *NRF*, la revue de Paulhan, un article de François Nourissier me poignarda. Homme de droite, Nourissier ne jugeait pas la guerre, il jugeait l'écriture d'une manière doucereuse et empoisonnée. Jaloux d'imposer son talent et trouvant là une belle occasion au détriment d'un écrivain qui n'était pas de son bord, il se délectait à me détruire. Paulhan, à qui je m'en ouvris, m'écrivit que la première note de Nourissier lui avait semblé méchante, qu'il lui avait demandé de la reprendre. Pour lui, mon livre l'avait déçu par son côté décoratif, par sa « littérature » sans grande conviction, par ses efforts pour reconstituer *du dehors* une philosophie de la guerre, enfin par tout un côté « journaliste ». Après tout, Nourissier ne disait pas autre chose. N'empêche. Cet article fut longtemps entre lui et moi un sujet d'inimitié et un trouble. Ma seule consolation fut que je dînai avec Mendès France chez Gallois et que je lui vidai mon cœur. J'ai noté le jour dans mes carnets, pas l'entretien. Mendès se contenta de m'écouter. Je l'avais trouvé négligé dans sa mise et surtout mal rasé, mais ses yeux brillaient beaucoup. Avec Pétain, l'Indochine fut la contradiction la plus sournoise de ma vie. Je me sentais tout envahi de honte de moi-même.

Etais-je un imbécile fieffé, un demeuré, un esprit pervers ? J'ai repris avec des pincettes *la Bataille dans la rizière*. Le sujet était pourtant pour moi, le décor tragique, le cas de conscience shakespearien ; hélas, l'auteur écrit les fesses entre deux chaises. Le livre est confus, d'un style lâche, sans rigueur et sans vigueur, sans que j'ose cracher la vérité comme on la crache dans *Platoon*. C'est qu'on ne concilie pas l'inconciliable. J'aurais mieux fait de me taire. Vais-je avoir honte toute ma vie d'un péché de jeunesse ? Au large ! Sigaux ne pouvait pas supporter qu'on m'attaque. « Si tu es ému, troublé pour ça, alors tu es à la merci de n'importe quel mensonge. Il faut couper. Vingt lignes imprimées et tu souffrirais ? Tu n'as pas une larme, pas un mot pour ce qui ne te concerne pas. »

Comme le théâtre me caressait, j'écrivis d'un trait deux pièces : *les Cyclones*, sur des avions fusées qui n'existaient pas encore, et *le Fleuve rouge*, où un capitaine tuait son lieutenant tenté de passer du côté de la rébellion. A Paris, personne ne voulut ni de l'une ni de l'autre. Je n'eus pas plus de réussite

dans *les Belles Croisades,* un roman où je déchirais les équivoques indochinoises. Cela ne servit à rien. Pour être suivi, il vaut mieux illustrer les idées reçues. Aux yeux de l'intelligentsia, sauf pour Sigaux, Kanters et quelques autres, j'étais désormais une vieille baderne, un adjudant en retraite. Je commençais à vivre séparé de l'armée et cependant, au fond de moi, je me sentais inconsolable : on ne change pas de peau du jour au lendemain. Il y avait vingt-cinq ans que j'étais monté sur les hauts d'Alger pour être incorporé au 9e zouaves. Je n'avais que cela de commun avec Paulhan, ancien zouave à Madagascar, qui l'était resté, même en habit brodé, avec Florence à ses côtés.

Soudain ce fut Diên Biên Phu. Avec l'accord du ministre de la Guerre de l'époque et du Veau d'or de Saigon, le président du Conseil, M. René Mayer, avait nommé un autre nouveau commandant en chef du corps expéditionnaire. On voulait un homme neuf et sans complexes. Le général Navarre portait le nom d'un ancien as de la guerre de 1914 que Guynemer considérait comme un voyou. Il n'avait jamais servi en Indochine et, parce qu'il avait passé toute sa carrière dans le renseignement, croyait tout savoir : cavalier d'origine, il allait galoper. Très en dehors, un peu lointain, distant, toujours sur son quant-à-soi, il visita les territoires, inspecta, calcula, réfléchit et bâtit un plan : rester sur une prudente réserve, rendre âme et vigueur au corps expéditionnaire, éviter toute empoignade. L'offensive, on la reprendrait quand Giap bougerait. Cependant la formule de sa première directive était « On ne peut vaincre qu'en attaquant. » Pour défendre le Laos menacé, il versa dans les erreurs de Salan et installa un énorme hérisson qu'il crut offensif à deux cent cinquante kilomètres de Hanoi, en réplique de Na-San qu'on avait été heureux de pouvoir évacuer. Encore à Na-San tenait-on les hauts tandis que Diên Biên Phu était dans une cuvette. « Oui, mais avec quel armement ! » disait Cogny, lui aussi tombé dans le panneau, en novembre 1953.

Le 7 mai 1954, le général de Castries se rendait aux Viets. Des milliers de prisonniers, dont lui et Bigeard, prirent le chemin de la brousse. En France où, depuis des semaines, les

nouvelles étaient alarmantes, les journaux annoncèrent la défaite avec d'énormes manchettes. L'opinion fut atterrée, l'humiliation gigantesque. Une grande tristesse s'empara de moi.

En 1415, à Azincourt, la présomption avait été la même. Nos généraux juraient d'écraser les Anglais et les cadavres de la chevalerie française s'entassèrent par monceaux dans la plaine d'Arras. Au moment de Diên Biên Phu, le tonnerre roula longuement à l'horizon du monde libre. C'était la première fois qu'une ancienne colonie remportait une victoire écrasante sur le colonisateur. Je regrettai d'avoir quitté l'armée quelques mois trop tôt, tant je craignais que mes anciens camarades ne m'accusent d'être sciemment parti à temps. Le 10 mai, le RPF convoqua la foule à l'Arc de Triomphe. De Gaulle fut acclamé. J'y étais, assommé, indigné, avec le pays en deuil. J'écrivis plusieurs *requiem* dans *le Figaro*.

Ce fut vers cette époque-là que de Gaulle me convoqua, comme je l'ai dit au début de ce livre, et je ne lui parlai pas de l'Algérie, qui n'était pas encore une affaire majeure. « Il faut que vous voyiez Malrôôô... » Le Général avait bien saisi tout de suite que l'Indochine avait été pour Malraux et pour moi le contraire de la Terre sainte et bien un lieu de pourriture. Tous deux nous nous étions battus pour une certaine justice, pour le roi de Prusse ou pour la Chine ? Tous deux, nous avions pris là (lui très tôt dans un éclair, moi tard dans l'embarras), conscience de notre condition. Verdict pour lui : de la prison avec sursis, puis la gloire. Malraux avait provoqué le colonialisme omnipotent, et moi rompu avec l'armée, bras du colonialisme. M'écrivant à ce propos, le Général évoquait « les champs de bataille d'Asie ».

Du temps de Doyon, j'aurais dû le voir, Malraux. Il était encore abordable. L'éviter a tenu de l'exploit. A la longue, Doyon avait fini par m'exaspérer aussi. Sa jalousie, sa tyrannie avaient réussi à m'éloigner. J'allais et venais sans plus lui rendre compte, j'écrivais ce qui me plaisait, et je fuyais ses commentaires.

XVI

Les feux de la rampe et le Niger

MA pièce *les Cyclones* reçut un prix d'art dramatique, mais, au théâtre, les choses se font et se défont dix fois par jour, je courais à travers espoirs et déceptions quand Pierre Fresnay me téléphona pour me prier de venir le voir à la Michodière. « Au théâtre d'Yvonne Printemps », précisa-t-il.

Pierre Fresnay fut, avec André Roussin, le seul gentilhomme que j'aie rencontré dans ce milieu de chimères. Peut-être aurait-il aimé pouvoir jouer *Don Juan* et *Hamlet,* et souffrait-il d'une taille moins élevée et d'une apparence moins séduisante qu'il aurait souhaité, mais son œil et sa voix en imposaient. Avec mille précautions, il m'offrit vingt représentations seulement, en attendant son nouveau spectacle. Naturellement j'acceptai. Alors je fus présenté à Yvonne Printemps, devant qui il s'effaçait. Il la plaçait plus haut que tout. Diva inquiète, elle n'apparaissait que le visage caché sous d'épaisses voilettes. Tous deux s'adoraient. Entre eux, les taquineries ne cessaient pas. Pierre Fresnay me laissa entendre que c'était elle qui avait eu l'idée de monter ma pièce, une pièce d'hommes, et je me demandai comment elle avait pu aimer un sujet si éloigné du boulevard, où l'on abordait des problèmes d'avions et de vitesses supersoniques, mais au théâtre tout est miracle.

Nous choisîmes les comédiens et les répétitions commencèrent. Dès lors, nous ne nous occupâmes que d'Yvonne Printemps et elle compta plus que tout. Etait-elle si volage ? Pierre Fresnay voulait toujours savoir où elle était. A la Michodière, il exigeait qu'elle fût dans sa loge de directrice, sous ses yeux, peu importait qu'elle entendît le dialogue pour la centième fois. Sinon, il roulait des regards furieux, puis,

411

brusquement, interrompait tout et courait à sa recherche et la ramenait. « Excusez-moi », disait-il à son retour. Quand la pièce fut jouée, si elle était chez elle à Neuilly, après le dernier acte, il coupait court aux applaudissements et visites en coulisses, et, sans se démaquiller, fonçait la retrouver. Aucune femme ne fut plus chérie qu'elle. Par Sacha d'abord, en vain, jusqu'à ce que Fresnay l'enlevât comme un pirate. Cela, on le savait, on trouvait cela plutôt grand, cela arrive encore ; chez les comédiens, c'est presque de bon aloi. Ce qu'on ne savait pas quand on joua *les Cyclones,* je le découvris seulement trente ans plus tard, par hasard, dans une enquête pour ma biographie de Guynemer.

Pendant la Première Guerre mondiale, les aviateurs faisaient la bringue au Fouquet's et à Montmartre, rossaient les flics et passaient leurs nuits au Moulin Rouge. Le lendemain, ils allaient mourir. Pour Guynemer, né d'une sévère famille bourgeoise, la légende voulait qu'il n'ait rencontré que des Fokker. Un soir de 1916 où il était allé au spectacle, Yvonne Printemps, qui jouait de petits rôles dans des revues, s'était jetée sur lui, l'avait emmené au Maxim's et dansé pour lui sur les banquettes. Eblouissante et effrontée, elle avait le même âge que lui en pleine gloire, qui ressemblait à un jeune aigle sans toutes ses plumes : regard inquiétant et fulgurant, teint gris. Jaloux comme il l'était même du passé, Fresnay avait voulu tout savoir : les rencontres avec Guynemer se passaient à l'hôtel Edouard-VII, pas encore sur l'avenue de l'Opéra mais dans une rue voisine de la Michodière. Ténébreux, vaguement hypocrite, vaguement cafard quand il s'agissait des anciennes liaisons, Fresnay menait des numéros d'équilibriste pour qu'il ne fût jamais question, dans ma pièce et devant nous, des aviateurs d'autrefois, pensez ! Le nom de Guynemer lâché imprudemment eût fait s'écrouler la scène et le décor. Déjà le nom de Sacha Guitry le mettait mal à l'aise. Alors Guynemer ! Car Sacha, elle ne l'avait pas aimé. Comment, avec qui, avec quoi ? Sacha n'avait que le fantastique de ses paroles, les diamants qu'il lui offrait, les pièces qu'il écrivait pour elle en une nuit. Pour le reste, si peu que rien. Elle, chaque nuit, voulait du champagne, une fête et le lit avec un vrai homme. Trop de paroles la bassinait. Tandis que l'autre, l'as des as au bec d'oiseau de proie, le pauvre enfant qui avait encore besoin d'une mère et savait descendre les Fokker... Tapie au fond de

sa loge pendant qu'on jouait *les Cyclones,* il lui revenait, trente ans après, en regardant les acteurs, de rêver au héros adolescent qu'elle avait furieusement idolâtré. Elle promenait sur François Chaumette et Pierre Tabard un œil piquant où se mêlait parfois de l'ironie, et, croisant Pierre Fresnay déguisé en colonel, elle éclatait de rire. Comme il ressemblait peu à Guynemer ! Comme il était sage, comme il manquait de ce regard halluciné qui l'avait foudroyée. Et puis si vieux ! Elle avait parfois pour Fresnay une dureté qui faisait pâlir. Soudain, lui qui savait, pour Guynemer, se demandait : « Est-ce qu'elle ne m'aimerait plus ?... » Il croyait que cela arriverait un jour, qu'il se retrouverait au théâtre et sur terre sans elle, et que la vie s'arrêterait. Alors il l'entourait de dévotions encore plus brûlantes et la servait comme un esclave. Trop. A l'époque où je les connus, ils ne voyaient déjà plus personne. Elle lui suffisait. Elle reportait les démonstrations dont elle raffolait sur son chien Doudou qu'elle ne quittait jamais, un caniche qu'elle mordait férocement à l'oreille et qui ne laissait échapper sa douleur que par de faibles gémissements. Cette manie, c'était gênant. Elle devait mordre Guynemer. A présent, je les imagine ensemble à l'hôtel Edouard-VII. Lui, une rafale ou deux, et il en avait assez, mais elle ! C'est pour cela qu'il ne l'appelait pas toujours quand il venait à Paris, il lui préférait son avion à réviser, et elle croyait le rendre jaloux en lui parlant des avances de Sacha qui le laissaient froid. Ainsi, un jour, avait-elle extorqué un laissez-passer pour la zone des armées, à Fismes en Champagne, où elle avait encore — on se croirait presque à la cour du roi Hérode — dansé pour lui sur la table, à la popote de l'escadrille. Fonck l'avait vue, cette nuit-là. Fonck était mort, je l'avais su par sa veuve, il y avait déjà beaucoup de fantômes autour de Guynemer et d'Yvonne Printemps.

En tournée, en province, quand elle n'accompagnait pas Fresnay au théâtre et que l'hôtel était éloigné, par exemple quand on jouait à Nice et que l'hôtel était à Cannes, il se précipitait dès le rideau tombé, nous poussait dans sa grosse bagnole américaine, et fonçait comme un fou. Inondés de sueur froide, nous nous disions : « Il va nous casser la gueule... » Enfin il stoppait brusquement devant l'hôtel, claquait la portière, nous laissait, bondissait dans les étages et,

413

parfois, elle lui fermait sa porte. Il y grattait d'abord, frappait doucement, insistait, l'appelait, la suppliait. Peine perdue. Son pyjama était déjà sur le canapé de l'entrée. Résigné, il couchait là, heureux d'être son mameluk. On savait cela par les femmes de chambre, ça se voyait aussi à son air de chien battu du lendemain. Pendant des jours, il arrivait à la diva de ne pas paraître. Il disait : « Yvonne Printemps a pris froid. Elle vous prie de l'excuser... » Elle devait approcher de la soixantaine, un âge qui nous paraissait déjà tellement fabuleux, bien qu'elle prétendît à qui voulait l'entendre qu'une femme pouvait, comme Ninon de Lenclos, être désirable jusqu'à soixante-quinze ans, et qu'elle s'y emploierait. « Il a beau se croire, qu'il prenne garde », lui lançait-elle comme un défi.

C'était l'amour fou, pour moi inconcevable : il me fallait des lieux communs d'état civil, des conventions, comme si l'amour et la folie avaient un âge. Au restaurant, quand nous étions assis à leur table, elle relevait sa voilette sur des œillades enflammées, laissait fuser et éclater son rire de rossignol et quelquefois chantait : « *Mon dieu, que c'est bête un homme, un homme...* » Sa voix merveilleuse emplissait le monde, Pierre Fresnay se rengorgeait. « N'allez pas vous fatiguer », disait-il.

Mais elle, se tournant vers nous : « De quoi se mêle-t-il ? Il joue les pères nobles comme Lucien Guitry, comme plus personne ne les joue, la mode en est passée et il ne s'en rend même pas compte... » Il avait l'habitude de ces traits et souriait parce qu'elle était de belle humeur, elle avait incarné Mozart et triomphé sur tant de scènes ! Et après tous ses amants, elle était séquestrée, bouclée, il ne la quittait plus et ne jouait qu'avec elle ou dans des pièces sans rôle de femme, ou presque, comme la mienne. Elle se disait qu'elle ne remonterait plus sur scène et qu'elle n'entendrait plus les applaudissements exploser pour elle, aussi faisait-elle de la vie une scène de théâtre, avec des admirateurs autour d'elle. Elle souffrait du peu de succès de ses disques, la terre changeait, la musique aussi, le jazz et le rock'n'roll triomphaient.

Naturellement à la Michodière, personne ne prononça jamais le nom de Guynemer. Elle non plus. Avec le temps, tout était peut-être oublié. Plus tard, je dus tout réinventer. A présent je sais à qui elle rêvait quand on jouait *les Cyclones* et je ne lui ai jamais parlé de Guynemer, quelle tristesse qu'elle

ne soit plus ! J'aurais osé cette fois, avec le temps, et j'entends Pierre Fresnay : « Laissons les morts où ils sont, cher Julius... » Une fois, un journaliste avait téléphoné chez eux. Fresnay le cerbère gardait la porte des enfers. Il demanda de quel sujet on voulait entretenir Yvonne Printemps. « De Guynemer. » Il faillit s'étrangler, répondit qu'Yvonne Printemps était malade et Guynemer un personnage dont Yvonne Printemps ne parlait jamais. Par Arletty plus tard, je sus qu'elle avait, malgré Sacha, porté le deuil du héros, en 1917, dans les générales, par un foulard ou une écharpe. Quand je les emmenai, Fresnay et elle, sur le terrain d'essais de Brétigny-sur-Orge pour voir de près des bolides et entendre le bruit des réacteurs, elle pensa peut-être que les égards dont elle fut entourée allaient, qui sait ? à ses anciennes amours. Elle dut croire à de la délicatesse de ma part, que sais-je ! Mais non, je ne savais rien, ni moi ni personne, tout était englouti dans les nuées et dans un fleuve de sang. La gloire aussi passait, même celle de Guynemer. Quand Pierre Fresnay mourut et la laissa seule, emmurée dans ses rhumatismes et ses souvenirs, et qu'à son tour elle disparut, elle ne voulut que des amis intimes. Sa fortune et ses brillants allèrent à une vague parentèle, il n'y eut de papiers que ceux de Pierre Fresnay dont hérita l'éditeur Roland Laudenbach, son neveu. Dans leur masse, on découvrit une carte de visite du capitaine Georges Guynemer, avec un tilde sur le n.

Les cent représentations des *Cyclones* firent pleuvoir sur moi un flot d'argent qui épata Amrouche. Je vendis ma bicoque aux grenouilles près de Saint-Nom-la-Bretèche et m'installai dans une garçonnière au-dessus des toits de la villa Montmorency. Les soirs où Yvonne Printemps consentait à nous accompagner, Chaumette et moi, nous les emmenions souper, Fresnay et elle. Fresnay n'aimait pas tellement ces restaurants où l'on vous reconnaît trop vite. Elle, c'était le contraire. Chez Lipp, elle avait l'impression de s'encanailler. Elle relevait sa voilette, on la regardait, et je ne savais pas encore qu'elle avait eu avec Guynemer sa table chez Maxim's. Nous dînions joyeusement, Fresnay ne s'attardait pas, nous nous quittions sous le clocher de Saint-Germain-des-Prés.

La terre tournait. Personne ne croyait que de Gaulle reviendrait au pouvoir, lui-même commençait à désespérer.

Pétain finissait ses jours dans un fort, à l'île d'Yeu, de Gaulle les siens à Colombey, les souvenirs de guerre s'enlisaient. Mendès avait conduit le deuil de l'Indochine, Bigeard était rentré de captivité, j'avais acheté un lit ancien toscan rouge et or qui détonnait un peu dans mon décor plein ciel, un lit de cardinal au temps où les cardinaux recevaient des femmes. J'avais une gouvernante espagnole, Dolorès, qui me faisait la tête à chaque nouvelle invitée. Parfois, sur scène, en face de Fresnay, je tenais le rôle de l'officier d'état-major en civil qui réconfortait l'escadrille éprouvée par des disparitions. Une frénésie d'action, une frénésie d'écrire s'était emparée de moi. J'étais amoureux d'une rencontre à Tokyo la veille de mon départ pour l'équarrissoir de Corée, et cette nouvelle démence que je raconte tout au long, dans le *Désert de Retz* et *la Saison des Za*, me tenait encore dans ses eaux torrentueuses. Des événements continuaient à se produire en Algérie et j'étais scandalisé par la façon dont on employait l'armée, mais les tirailleurs algériens faits prisonniers des Viets par bataillons entiers avaient été instruits par eux. Rentrés, ils ne rapportèrent pas la nouvelle que la France était invincible. Il s'agissait seulement pour nous de ce qu'on appelait la répression, et on grillait les douars pour faire comprendre aux bicots ce que c'était que la force française. Camus n'était pas encore vraiment inquiet.

L'Express qui venait d'être fondé par Jean-Jacques Servan-Schreiber, polytechnicien de choc et ancien pilote de chasse, me demanda de dire ce que je pensais. Je me sentais enfin libre. Sans consulter Camus, et comme pour me vider de ce que je n'avais pas osé exprimer à mon retour d'Indochine, je me laissai aller sur les guerres justes et les autres, sur l'équivoque de nos interventions militaires depuis dix ans, sur la nature des hors-la-loi, sur notre attachement à la terre d'Algérie. « Si j'étais musulman, ce n'est pas de notre côté que je serais. Je refuserais d'égorger des innocents, car cela est de la lâcheté et de la barbarie, mais je serais dans le maquis. » Je terminais ainsi : « Au temps où le capitaine Alfred de Vigny poursuivait les lanciers de Napoléon, les soldats n'étaient pas citoyens. Aujourd'hui, pour combattre en faveur d'une cause, il faut d'abord savoir si elle est juste et si elle vaut la peine qu'on meure pour elle. S'il m'est souvent arrivé de vous

jalouser, mes camarades, cette fois encore, je ne vous envie pas. » Le journal, effaçant l'euphémisme et forçant ma plume, avait titré : « Mes camarades, je vous plains... »

Camus se tut, puis comme je lui demandais ce qu'il en pensait, il me dit : « Ce n'est pas mal, mais c'est noir. Tu ne laisses rien à l'espérance. » C'est vrai. Avec lui vacillait toujours une vague lueur. J'étais son disciple ; plus encore, il m'avait fait. Seulement, je n'étais pas philosophe, je ne savais pas farder la vérité, je croyais même servir de Gaulle en dénonçant des méthodes qu'il se serait peut-être gardé d'employer.

Un peu pour me prouver que ce qui se passait en Algérie n'était pas grave, j'éprouvai le besoin de traverser le Sahara avec une compagnie de Légion. Les officiers ne m'avaient sans doute pas lu et je ne cherchai pas à les troubler. Ils étaient comme ils étaient, ils appartenaient à cette « grande chose que l'on meut et qui tue ». En plein Tassili des Ajars, sur la piste de Djanet, je découvris Fort-Gardel à demi enseveli dans les sables, je m'assis dans les ruines de la citadelle, j'écoutai le vent gémir dans les croix des tombes un peu comme dans le désert des Tartares, puis je rejoignis Tamanrasset, où le général qui m'aimait bien et sa femme, très souveraine, m'attendaient. C'était eux qui m'avaient présenté à Jünger, à peine la guerre finie. A bord d'un bombardier nerveux, ils m'emmenèrent à Gao. Des lionceaux jouaient dans le jardin de l'administrateur devant le miroir du Niger, notre drapeau flottait partout, nous n'étions pas impressionnés par les quelques pétards qui venaient d'éclater en Algérie. L'immense, la profonde, la mystérieuse et redoutable Afrique faisait tourner les tables et les têtes. Je disais au général : « Comme Psichari, on a envie de se coucher par terre et de croire qu'on est dans les étoiles. » Petits ambitieux que nous étions, sans mesure et sans objet avec ce qui n'était qu'une extravagance. Mon général dressait des plans pour conquérir le pouvoir une fois que de Gaulle aurait renoncé à revenir au gouvernement. A Dakar, l'alizé si doux, si large, semblait destiné de toute éternité à gonfler des voiles de navigateurs solitaires. L'Afrique nous cajolait, nous endormait, nous étions des hommes englués dans un songe qui allait se dissiper, après quoi, tout demeurerait comme avant ; les centenaires du Sénégal en boubou et à toison poivre et sel

que nous visitions, devenus sages avec l'âge, laissaient eux aussi couler le sable entre leurs doigts.

Soudain pris de passion pour le Niger qui coulait à Gao, bleu dans une plaine d'or avec ses lionceaux paisibles, je me laissai posséder par le désir de le descendre des sources à l'embouchure. De retour à Paris, je me crus délivré de tout, attaché à rien ni à personne. J'emmenai avec moi Pierre Moinot, alors conseiller à la Cour des comptes et un photographe de *Paris-Match*, Tony Saulnier. A Moinot, son livre *Armes et bagages* me liait beaucoup. Ensemble nous montâmes l'expédition, nous achetâmes un moteur pour notre future pirogue, des filtres à eau, de la pharmacie, des conserves, des moustiquaires, des lits de camp, des lampes d'explorateur, de la verroterie et des tissus pour les chefs de tribu, du sérum contre les piqûres de serpent, des lignes de pêche, des ponchos et des chapeaux de brousse. Camus était en quête d'une garçonnière, je lui laissai la mienne et Dolorès. A ce moment-là, il était fou d'une chanteuse. D'habitude, lui, c'étaient les comédiennes. Maria Casarès, son attitrée, l'aimait d'un amour immense et lui autorisait les autres, comme elle lui passait sa dolente épouse. Je l'enviais de pouvoir, peut-être pas sans drames, butiner ainsi. Il n'en parlait jamais. Il laissa échapper une exclamation devant mon lit rococo rouge et or.

A Conakry, nous fûmes reçus princièrement par Emile Biasini, un administrateur pareil à un rhinocéros avec un oiseau des îles sur son épaule. Par la suite, grâce à Moinot, il deviendra directeur des théâtres sous Malraux, plus tard, directeur de la télévision sous Pompidou, et plus tard encore, maître d'œuvre de la Pyramide du Louvre sous Mitterrand et secrétaire d'Etat aux grands travaux. Il nous aida beaucoup. Nous louâmes des véhicules tout terrain et nous nous lançâmes à l'assaut. Dès le début, à travers la brousse torride, nous fûmes contraints de fréter des porteurs et un guide, souvent de marcher. La sueur coulait à grosses gouttes de nos fronts, ruisselait sur nos reins, nous soufflions comme des bourrins d'artillerie en nous hissant, presque au coupe-coupe, sur des collines comme au temps de Savorgnan de Brazza. Escortés par des singes hurleurs et un nuage de moustiques, nous découvrîmes un vague trou humide et flasque, un marigot grouillant d'araignées d'eau : c'était la source encore

inviolée. A travers les savanes, le sable et les forêts, le fleuve allait couler sur six mille kilomètres, demi-boucle dans l'énorme bosse ouest de l'Afrique. Tout juste si nous ne plantâmes pas un drapeau. Nous avions pensé à tout sauf au drapeau, ce qui fit sourire Moinot, ancien lieutenant des tabors marocains pendant la campagne d'Italie. Notre carte Michelin aux trois millionnièmes de l'Afrique occidentale ne nous assurait pas de fouler la Guinée française. La frontière de la Sierra Leone s'écartait-elle vraiment ? Le guide n'en savait rien non plus et s'en foutait. Le Niger, c'était le soleil tout-puissant, écrasant, suffocant, accablant. Fourmis d'Europe, que faisions-nous ici ? Vite le village le plus proche, les salamalecs, les négrillons, le roi féodal débonnaire, les femmes à leurs mortiers, et pour les étrangers, la hutte, les mouches, la poussière ! Porte-parole dépoitraillé, Moinot traduisait nos mufleries en langage diplomatique. Les voyageurs que nous étions fournissaient l'occasion d'une bamboula avec parapluies d'honneur. Nous rêvions de demis glacés à la terrasse des Deux-Magots, nous y étions un peu, sans demi glacé mais entourés de drôles de cocos pour qui les magots, c'était nous. Moinot s'adaptait à tout, Tony photographiait. Rose écrevisse, je m'habituais mal au poulet filandreux et au couscous de mil. J'étais le plus mauvais ethnologue qui fût, pareil, devant un fleuve à traverser, à un cheval qui ne sait pas qu'il sait nager, et traînant une affligeante lamentation amoureuse hors de propos. Ma belle de Tokyo m'avait quitté pour les dieux de l'Egypte ou pour un pharaon, et le barbare que j'étais lui écrivait des poèmes d'amour. A une extrémité de l'Afrique, dans un village dont j'ai oublié le nom, les tambours nègres battaient, tandis qu'à l'autre extrémité, sur les rives d'un autre fleuve immense, bleu aussi, le Nil, elle gémissait parmi les tombeaux des rois, sous les étoiles, dans les bras d'un archéologue vigoureux. « Le cœur possède plus de chambres qu'un hôtel de putes », dit un héros de Gabriel Garcia Marquez dans *l'Amour au temps du choléra*.

J'évite de parler de ma vie privée qui n'intéresse que moi, mais là ! Ne rien voir, s'ennuyer alors qu'on s'emmêle dans la traîne des siècles parmi les hommes et les femmes qui ne savent pas qui est de Gaulle et qui est Malraux, souffrir parce qu'une femme vous manque, alors là... De Paris, Pierre Fresnay

m'annonça par câble que l'assistance à la Michodière baissait et qu'il serait bientôt contraint d'arrêter mes *Cyclones*; la nuit était une fournaise, nous étouffions sous nos moustiquaires, nous nous gavions de comprimés pour dormir tandis que le village se demandait ce que nous cherchions. Comme si une visite à la source du Niger s'imposait ! A l'aube, nous sirotions un café avec le roi et notre caravane repartait vers les voitures laissées là où la piste était signalée « impraticable par endroits pendant la saison des pluies », en direction de Dabola, à moins que ce ne fût vers Faranah. J'ai retrouvé les dates sur la carte, les 6 et 7 mars 1956. Ce voyage ressemblait à un énorme fantasme. Pierre Moinot a franchi beaucoup de chemin depuis. Il m'a parfois considéré comme quelqu'un qu'il fallait protéger par un garde-fou ; quand, plus tard, il entra au cabinet de Malraux, il nous embringua, Kanters, Sigaux et moi, dans une commission et, sous les lustres et les lambris d'or de la rue de Valois, nous présenta à son ministre sourcilleux, ténébreux, globuleux, grelottant d'émotion, Malraux en personne qu'enfin je croyais tenir ! J'attendais une pause dans le discours, un soupir, un blocage de la suffocation pour lui glisser un mot à propos de Doyon. Impossible. Notre importance à nous, misérables, quant aux crédits à distribuer, prenait chez lui des proportions cosmiques. Après un dernier hoquet, il disparaissait tel un Dieu, suivi de Moinot. Que n'a-t-il, sous Malraux, dirigé ou inspiré, Moinot ? Le théâtre d'abord, puis, après Gaëtan Picon, les arts et lettres ; plus tard, une commission qui porta son nom quand la télévision changea de peau une fois de plus. Auteur de *la Chasse royale*, un grand livre sur l'amour et la forêt, cet homme si bon, si généreux, ne craint ni le gros gibier ni de tuer, et finira chancelier de l'Institut.

Pendant notre voyage, s'en souvient-il encore ? il recevait parfois du courrier qu'il lisait et relisait à l'écart, un peu comme son lieutenant d'*Armes et bagages*. Avant de m'endormir, je me récitais les poèmes que j'écrivais à ma belle en allée. Le fleuve passait aussi, coulait mais demeurait, et cette ligne de vie me hantait de plus en plus. D'où venaient-elles, ces suées de terres arides, de quels orages que nous n'avions pas vu fulminer leurs eaux crevaient-elles ? Comment ne se perdaient-elles pas dans le sable ? Si large par endroits et si peu profond quand les troupeaux de bœufs le traversaient dans un éclaboussement d'écume, le fleuve, miroir du ciel, aveuglait d'un

acier éblouissant dont des lunettes noires ne protégeaient pas ;
à la moindre crue, il emportait tout et, par temps de
sécheresse, devenait un filet avare. Alors pour implorer le
dieu, les tambours appelaient les tornades et battaient sur un
rythme haletant ou menaçant. Comme les propres battements
de mon cœur semblaient futiles soudain ! Comme j'étais loin
de percer les secrets de ces hommes !

Quand nous sortions de chez Lipp avec Yvonne Printemps, la lune apparaissait parfois dans les nuages devant le
clocher de Saint-Germain-des-Prés ; rarement les étoiles, sauf
celles qui m'enorgueillissaient naïvement, des banquettes de la
brasserie. Sur les rives du Niger, ce n'était pas les mêmes.
Couchée bas sur l'horizon, quand toutes les autres étincelaient
d'un éclat de joaillerie, pâle encore, indistincte, scintillait la
Croix du Sud que les Touaregs figuraient sur le pommeau de
leur selle et à la poignée de leur sabre. J'appelais Orion, qui
m'avait escorté toute la guerre, je récitais les noms de ses
composantes, Bételgeuse, Bellatrix, Rigel, et Saïph, les seules
dont je me souvienne encore ; puis il y avait Véga et Altaïr,
Jupiter, Vénus, Arcturus, d'autres que je ne connaissais pas
parce que je n'étais pas un familier du tropique du Cancer, là
où nous cheminions presque. Un peu plus bas, palpitaient
d'énormes flambeaux bleus comme le fleuve, puis le groupe
des Pléiades, qui jouait un si grand rôle dans la vie des
riverains, semblait se détacher pour nous asperger d'un coup
de goupillon. Nous avancions, nous avions dépassé Siguiri, et,
non loin des rives, nous allions visiter ce que la carte appelait
des mines d'or : des trous abandonnés. A Bamako, nous
débouchâmes dans notre pirogue triomphale, nous rendîmes
visite aux autorités pour nous tenir informés des problèmes du
pays. Après quoi, la vraie aventure commença. Nous nous
soumettions au maître des eaux, nous ne fixions jamais notre
moteur à l'arrière d'une nouvelle pirogue sans le sacrifice d'un
poulet et sans la bénédiction du sorcier, forgeron d'habitude,
qui changeait le fer en feu pour lui tourner des formes et
décidait des lieux de chasse ou de pêche. En son honneur
battaient les calebasses et les tambours, frères et sœurs du
tonnerre. Parfois le sorcier recevait des pouvoirs encore plus
étendus : capable de déchaîner les éléments, il devenait le
fleuve lui-même, le *djoliba*. Il pouvait vivre dans l'eau, sous
l'eau, comme ces gros poissons qu'on appelait des capitaines,

se glisser entre les herbes, converser avec les caïmans et les hippopotames qui nous observaient de loin, et c'était l'*issa koï*. Il naissait investi d'un tel pouvoir. Quand il priait, ses paumes aux reflets de bronze s'élevaient au-dessus des eaux.

La chaleur du jour s'apaisait, le miroir en feu s'adoucissait, nous nous arrêtions d'habitude près d'un village, à l'heure où les femmes emplissent leurs calebasses et baignent leurs enfants. Les hommes cueillaient l'eau dans le creux de leur main d'un geste rapide, le fleuve engloutissait le ciel, sa coulée de métal et de flammes dévalait, la nuit venait, les bêtes féroces s'apprêtaient à s'entr'égorger, des feux s'allumaient, le tamtam battait : le spectacle commençait à devenir monotone. De toute part on venait toucher notre pirogue, notre moteur, on interrogeait notre guide, Moinot distribuait la verroterie et les saluts comme des bénédictions, nous faisions réchauffer nos conserves, parfois une choucroute comme chez Lipp, avec des boîtes de bière dans la glace de notre réserve. Une choucroute sur le Niger me ramenait à Sigaux et à Yvonne Printemps. Sur le rivage, nous dressions nos lits de camp, et c'était chaque soir la même chose. A peine bouclé dans sa moustiquaire, Moinot sombrait dans le sommeil sous une coupole de constellations. Des cases voisines s'échappaient des odeurs étranges. Comment me souviendrais-je de toutes ces ombres d'il y a trente ans et qui durèrent si peu, de Ségou, des flottilles de pêcheurs de Mopti, de Bandiagara et des Dogons, de leurs masques, de leurs processions et de toute leur singerie de danses et de défilés ? Une misère de cailloux colorés mettait en branle une vague commémoration magique fabricotée en notre honneur, au gré des chefs et des rois. On avait le sacré pour quatre sous, dont Malraux aurait tiré des fricotées de mystère et de civilisation.

Nous traversâmes Tombouctou au nom merveilleux. On disait qu'un cavalier inconnu rôdait autour des remparts, certaines nuits, mais l'esprit du lieu s'était dissipé depuis que René Caillé déguisé en esclave avait atteint la cité sainte avec une caravane de marchands mandingues, y avait séjourné et en était reparti. Y était-il seulement jamais allé ? Sur ses traces, un ancien père blanc devenu patriarche avait troqué la gandoura pour un boubou ; son rosaire lui servait à dévider les étoiles. Nous allâmes le saluer au milieu de sa troupe de négrillons, il

suait le bonheur à grosses gouttes et s'éventait de lui-même, aurait-on dit.

Chasseur dans l'âme, Moinot était tenté par l'espoir d'un hippopotame. A Conakry, il avait acquis le droit d'en tuer un. Il cherchait son « hippo » comme il disait, et nous arrivâmes, après Goa et Firgoun, avant Niamey, dans la zone où ces énormes bestiaux vivaient en tribus, apparaissaient et disparaissaient dans les eaux en soufflant. Après tout, ils étaient chez eux comme les Dogons, et bien avant eux. Depuis mon équipée sur Leipzig et depuis l'Indochine, j'étais contre toutes les tueries, mais comment désobliger un ami ? Foudroyer des crocodiles pouvait paraître de bonne guerre, Flaubert s'y était amusé quand il remontait le Nil avec l'innénarrable Maxime du Camp. Un innocent hippopotame à qui on ne pouvait reprocher que de saccager parfois des cultures, n'était-ce pas criminel ? « Un seul, disait Moinot, un seul... » Gide, au Congo, avait laissé son petit ami Marc Allégret en tuer, par plaisir. Les Noirs aussi chassaient, une fois ou deux par an, avec des harpons. Pour eux, l'hippo, c'était l'abondance de nourriture, et donc une fête, et Tony voulait aussi ses photos pour les lecteurs de *Paris-Match* qui exigeaient du sang à la une. Moinot organisa tout. On palabra beaucoup par une chaleur terrifiante ; je n'en pouvais plus, j'étais presque aveugle. Je me couchai à l'abri de la lumière et j'attendis, de mauvais poil, dans un ennui profond. Les sauvages, c'était nous, qui tuions sans besoin de tuer, uniquement par plaisir.

La chasse dura plusieurs jours. Moinot l'a racontée dans un reportage qui parut dans *le Figaro littéraire*. Un jour, de ce voyage il fourgonnera un livre fort et savoureux. C'est un lent, un prudent, il avance comme les chasseurs, face au vent, sans laisser traîner son odeur, sans bruit, et soudain...

Le dieu du fleuve se vengea : Moinot fut piqué par une tarentule. Pendant deux jours, il erra dans une sorte de coma. Que pouvions-nous où nous étions, loin de tout ? Veiller sur son repos, éloigner les bruits, sacrifier à l'esprit miséricordieux des hippopotames : Moinot n'en avait tué qu'un. Peu à peu, le venin se résorba, la fièvre tomba, l'ombre s'écarta. Moinot se remit à bouger puis refit brusquement surface, comme un hippo, en soufflant. Il se remit à la barre de notre pirogue et

nous descendîmes les rapides avec une belle inconscience. Dieu sait qu'il y en avait et d'impressionnants. Soudain, au Nigeria, on nous considéra comme des espions et nos difficultés s'aggravèrent, il nous tarda de rentrer. Nous n'avions pas vu grand-chose : le fleuve, les poissons, les étoiles. En Afrique, nous n'étions plus des colonialistes, ou si peu. Les nouveaux négriers étaient noirs et il y avait toujours des esclaves. A bout de résistance, à bout de course aussi, nous vendîmes tout ce que nous pûmes de notre équipement. L'Afrique avait perdu son charme. Du moins pour moi.

Dès mon retour, je courus porter à Verrières, à Louise de Vilmorin, un minuscule et superbe coq rouge, notre mascotte depuis Bandiagara, que j'avais appelé Gaston par dévotion pour les Gallimard. Hautain et arrogant, il s'empara tout de suite de la basse-cour et montra à un rival que le chef c'était lui. Chez moi, Camus organisa une petite bamboula et emmena sa belle à qui je laissai des poèmes avec l'espoir qu'elle les chanterait un jour, mais non. Camus m'apprit que, pendant mon absence, le prix des Bouquinistes avait été décerné à Doyon. « Tu devrais lui téléphoner. C'est ton père, quand même. » Camus me taquinait mais j'aurais dû, je ne le fis pas. Malraux, qui lui avait remis le prix : un franc en argent, apparaissait avec son regard orageux, et faisait un laïus qui doit être dans la Pléiade. Dans *la Saison des Za*, j'ai raconté ce déjeuner à deux pas de la Coupole sous laquelle Malraux refusait de s'asseoir avant qu'on lui ait attribué le Nobel. Après, il voulait bien que ces messieurs l'y conduisent en triomphe, sur un char. Devant Doyon, chaleureusement, Malraux avait évoqué le paradis des bouquinistes où ils se retrouveraient tous plus tard puis chacun s'en était allé de son côté, Malraux à sa pianiste et aux voix du silence, et Doyon à ses puces savantes.

L'événement était que Camus sortait *la Chute* qui d'abord me dérouta. Fréminville publia un article déconcertant sur nos deux livres, car Gallimard avait édité, en même temps que *la Chute*, mon propre récit, *les Flammes de l'été*. Je ne reconnus pas tout de suite que Camus avait écrit là son meilleur ouvrage. La confession de ce juge pénitent me parut lugubre. Ce que Camus écrivait nous ouvrait le cœur,

l'attachement que nous avions pour lui s'enracinait au plus profond de nous et, comme devant le saint sacrement, on se taisait. En présence de notre dieu, on n'osait trop s'exprimer. Ce que disent les disciples est-il si malin ? C'est souvent maladroit, enfantin, débile même. Devant Camus nous nous taisions ou nous posions des questions idiotes. Il nous pardonnait. Il savait qu'on ne peut jamais comprendre quelqu'un près de qui on vit. A présent qu'il nous a quittés, s'il nous arrive de nous rencontrer, certains d'entre nous, nous disons comme les pèlerins d'Emmaüs, pas plus rusés : « Comme notre cœur était chaud tandis qu'il nous parlait... »

J'avais mis près de huit ans à écrire *les Flammes de l'été*, dont l'héroïne était Marie. Le critique redouté du *Figaro littéraire*, André Rousseaux, m'éreinta : à ses yeux, c'était trop sombre, trop léché, cela cachait mon désir d'entrer à l'Académie. Il m'avait déjà reproché dans *le Métier des armes* de singer les maîtres sans arriver à leur cheville. Peut-être ne me pardonnait-il pas de l'avoir croisé en Tunisie, en 1941, alors qu'il faisait une tournée de conférences sur Péguy sous le patronage de la Légion, en un temps où nous étions nombreux à prendre des vessies pour des lanternes ? Il n'arrêta jamais de me poursuivre de je ne sais quelle vindicte. Dans son feuilleton, il me mettait dans le même sac qu'André Chamson, qu'il étrillait aussi. Il n'aimait que Claudel, Mauriac et Char.

A un dernier déjeuner chez Florence d'avant le Niger, Léautaud n'était plus qu'un fantôme. Il ne supportait plus que les grands morts. Chateaubriand, Flaubert, Voltaire, La Rochefoucauld, Diderot et Vauvenargues avaient droit à des compliments, Chamfort aussi. En vérité, il n'acceptait que lui-même, encore avait-il la modestie de ne le dire que si on l'y forçait et, désignant la riche lionne à lunettes noires qui battait son champagne : « Voyez où ça m'a mené. » Aussitôt fusait son ricanement célèbre, trille aigu de vieux rossignol enroué qui devenait plus bref et comme fêlé. Il mastiquait lentement en silence et de temps en temps, haussait les épaules pendant que Marie-Louise Bousquet postillonnait dans nos assiettes. Les jeudis devenaient tristes.

De l'amour, Florence avait fait son deuil, l'argent lui suffisait, elle semblait lasse des chichis. Elle savait comment on conquiert les hommes et comment on les retient, elle en usait et abusait. Elle n'aurait pas fini en converse comme Cécile Sorel, ni porté le cilice sous ses robes de Chanel. Elle avait choisi ce qui brille, et tandis que les thuriféraires entretenaient autour d'elle un nuage d'encens, elle méprisait les flatteurs et les gloires affichées. Reconnaissante au destin de ce qu'il lui avait prodigué, elle fonda des bourses pour les malades et les talents malheureux. Sans être miséricordieuse, elle se bâtissait des titres pour l'au-delà, et, comme la maréchale de Villeroy, décatie mais lucide, qui se lamentait, au moment où une montgolfière s'élevait dans les airs, que les médecins n'aient pas encore découvert le miracle souverain, elle pensait souvent que les hommes deviendraient immortels et que ce serait trop tard pour elle.

XVII

Louise de V.

A VERRIÈRES, j'étais heureux. Belle, intelligente et languoureuse, Louise de Vilmorin ne rêvait que d'amour et de frivolité, c'était son drame. Avec elle et ses frères André, Roger et Olivier, je me croyais en famille. On m'aimait comme j'étais. Je les aimais comme ils étaient.

Chaque dimanche, Louise recevait le gratin. On s'amusait beaucoup. Tout ce qui comptait voulait être allé au moins une fois à Verrières, et, pour Louise, ce qui comptait ne comptait vraiment que par elle. Elle avait connu Saint-Exupéry très jeune. Ils étaient cousins. Elle n'avait jamais pensé qu'un vague pilotaillon de la société Latécoère deviendrait l'auteur de *Vol de nuit*. Passionnément épris d'elle, il lui écrivait du cap Juby de longues pages de pattes de mouche qui la laissaient songeuse. Il se disait son fiancé. Des fiancés, elle en avait dix à l'époque. Ce fut en désespoir de Louise qu'il épousa Consuelo. « Il ne sut jamais comment s'en défaire », concluait Louise. La coxalgie dont elle souffrait la condamnait à boitiller ; pour elle, un charme et comme une grandeur de plus. Elle se plaignait avec le regard et le front d'une reine. Elle avait aussi connu Malraux, avant la guerre, dans les milieux de la NRF où Yvonne de Lestrange, cousine de Saint-Ex, l'entraînait. La crut-il riche ? Il lui fit une cour ardente. Crut-elle qu'il l'entraînerait dans son génie ? Rien ne suivit. Obstacle aussi, le mari de Louise, un comte magyar, car elle était mariée et avait des filles, le comte se montrait jaloux. Louise alla se perdre aux Amériques à Santa Fe où elle jouait de la guitare, peignait et s'ennuyait. Elle l'écrivit à Malraux qui répondit : « Vous feriez mieux d'écrire. » Puis ce fut la guerre

427

et la débâcle. Louise s'abrita en Hongrie chez le comte jusqu'en 1943 et, pour Malraux, ce fut Josette Clotis.

Sa poésie lui ressemblait, fière, altière, et aussi douce et tendre, toujours au bord des larmes et du rire comme elle, pudique et d'une suprême élégance. Ses romans aussi la révélaient, ruisselants d'humour et de peines secrètes, avec une grande économie de mots et une passion toujours à vif. Le dimanche, elle devenait l'héroïne : ses frères, par le panache et l'esprit, ressemblaient à des mousquetaires. A Verrières, c'était la bombance de l'âme et du cœur, sans tape-à-l'œil, on s'y chamaillait sans se haïr, Louise recevait les danseurs en vogue, les peintres, les écrivains, l'or de passage (seulement de passage), les magnats du cinéma, les metteurs en scène illustres, rarement des hommes politiques et seulement le dessus du panier, la crème de la crème, tout ce qui pouvait mettre Louise en vedette, et parfois la servir si elle avait moins vécu de mirages. Tout étincelait et, en réalité, tout pour Louise sombrait dans la désillusion, la fortune fût-elle tombée du ciel, qu'elle eût peut-être fracassé ce fragile édifice. Les fêtes atteignaient d'elles-mêmes leur zénith avec le hasard. Avait-on réellement besoin de richesse ? Oui, disait Louise qui n'en eut jamais qu'en rêve. Elle avait tellement mieux : ses dons, son charme, ses peines, ses frères et leurs femmes qui ne la desservirent jamais, son parc, son château, sa foi dans la gloire et les étoiles. Qui n'était venu ou ne souhaitait venir à Verrières ? J'ai vu là Edmonde Charles-Roux, Maggy Bodard qui, de Saigon, était devenue, grâce à Pierre Lazareff, productrice de films, André Bernheim et la belle Hélène Rochas, l'ancien préfet de Paris André Dubois et Carmen Tessier, Léo Ferré et Guy Béart, Bernard Buffet, Zizi Jeanmaire et Roland Petit, Françoise Sagan, Marcel Aymé, Georges Clouzot, Denise Bourdet, Hervé Mille, Roger Nimier, René Clair et sa femme Brognia qui avait été la maîtresse de Radiguet, tant et tant d'autres en plus des compères habituels comme le producteur de cinéma Jean Lourau, le conservateur en chef de Versailles et moi. André, le frère aîné, veillait à tout avec sa femme Andrée, ainsi que l'autre frère Roger et sa femme Edith. Le troisième frère vivait en Amérique. Le dernier, Olivier, bourru et solitaire, se tua, une nuit de verglas, au volant de sa voiture. Sa mort fut cruelle, mais Verrières continua.

Le champagne coulait à flots, le dîner aux chandelles était drôle, le vin moins généreux et la chère moins savoureuse que l'esprit. Tout se déroulait dans la simplicité même. Après dîner, on jouait au poker menteur, ou, si c'était après déjeuner, aux boules. Parfois, Louise lisait un de ses poèmes étincelants et douloureux, parfois quelqu'un se mettait au piano et chantait, je n'ai jamais assisté à une querelle ou à un esclandre comme cela arrivait avenue Malakoff. Je n'entendis jamais parler politique, sauf le jour où les chars soviétiques entrèrent à Prague et où Druon fut interdit à cause de je ne sais quel article qu'il avait écrit et qui ne fut pas compris. Les femmes de Verrières avaient du charme et du mystère, et d'elles toutes, Louise fut la plus brillante. Verrières n'était pas la demeure de la puissance, mais une gentilhommière au milieu des fleurs et des essences rares. A Verrières on manquait toujours d'argent, mais personne n'aurait commis la grossièreté de le montrer ; seule Louise se plaignait d'être sans le sou et attendait toujours le miracle d'Amérique ou de Grande-Bretagne. Louise et moi fûmes des amis tendres et respectueux. Elle boitait plus qu'elle n'aurait dû, par coquetterie, cela en imposait. Elle exigeait aussi qu'on prît trop soin d'elle, tandis qu'on pouvait traiter Florence comme une duchesse couverte d'or qui cachait on ne savait quels vices sous les bonnes œuvres. Chez Florence, à côté de leurs matous écœurés par l'éternelle sole Dugléré, toutes les chattes étaient engluées dans les mondanités. Pas chez Louise.

Amrouche ne fut jamais invité à Verrières, et ne le fut qu'un temps avenue Malakoff. Il étalait trop son jeu, de prétendre à une trop large part. Etablis chacun sur une étoile de la même galaxie, comme des frères que les histoires de famille ne heurtaient pas, nous ne pouvions plus nous brouiller, lui et moi. L'une des dernières fois où je le rencontrai appartient presque à l'immémorial : c'était près d'un square de Saint-Germain-des-Prés, un merle annonçait la fin de l'hiver, Amrouche avait paru soudain respirer et espérer. Je ne savais pas qu'il allait en Suisse et en Tunisie voir ses amis du FLN. Mon scandaleux article sur l'armée et ma déclaration de foi à propos du parti que j'aurais embrassé si j'avais été algérien l'avaient rassuré. Nous étions sur la même rive. J'avais vainement tenté de le réconcilier avec Camus qui ne vint

jamais non plus à Verrières. Camus tenait Amrouche pour un dangereux sophiste qui envenimait les relations avec la rébellion. En vérité, je l'ai déjà dit, Camus ne pardonnait jamais à qui l'avait offensé. Il n'avait pas oublié la gaffe d'Amrouche, le soir du dîner dont j'ai parlé, où Amrouche avait lourdement rappelé que Koestler avait appartenu au parti communiste. Amrouche sentait que Camus n'irait jamais au-delà de certains interdits et qu'il n'était frère que des siens, qui pourtant l'avaient renié. Sa mère n'était pas de sang espagnol pour rien.

Louise de Vilmorin reçut une invitation pour un spectacle de son et lumière à Vézelay. Nous partîmes un samedi avec son frère André en voiture. Tous à peu près du même âge, débitant beaucoup de gaudrioles, nous nous arrêtâmes pour le thé dans un hôtel d'Auxerre. Nous aurions pu aller saluer Marie Noël, poétesse inspirée, mais Louise la tenait très au-dessous d'elle. Louise racontait une fois de plus avec drôlerie sa quête du mari ou de l'amant fortunés qu'elle avait cru débusquer tant de fois avec l'espoir de mener la seule vie qui comptait pour elle : des châteaux, des amours superbes, des fêtes, et, pour son cœur toujours saignant et toujours enchanté, la poésie. « Tout ça coûte cher, tu comprends. Mais non, tu ne comprends pas, tu as tout pour rien », me lançait-elle. Elle qui connaissait tout ce qui avait un nom dans le monde, avait brisé tant de cœurs et ensorcelé tant d'hommes qu'on s'y perdait. De Gaston Gallimard elle disait : « Celui-là n'était large qu'en promesses, oui, mais de gloire... »

Je ne connaissais pas Vézelay. C'était le soir. Bien qu'on fût en juin, il faisait froid, le vent soufflait, je portais par bonheur une grande cape noire dans laquelle nous nous enveloppâmes tous. Des lambeaux de lumière s'accrochaient à la colline sacrée, il fut question de saint Bernard : Dieu le veut, du roi Saint Louis. Pour les Vilmorin, j'étais né en Algérie, j'avais bombardé l'Allemagne, je rentrais d'Indochine, j'avais tout du croisé. Après le spectacle qui me parut long et ennuyeux, nous aperçûmes entre les bourrasques la basilique dédiée à sainte Marie-Madeleine la pécheresse, comme une brillante fleur de pierre, et nous allâmes coucher chez des amis, les Vilmorin en avaient partout. Je me souviens d'un escalier en colimaçon, de tentures rouges, de flambeaux et du feu qui brûlait dans une cheminée. Louise aimait dîner aux

chandelles avec des candélabres en argent sur la nappe, et boire du vin rouge, du château-margaux de préférence, dans des verres de cristal.

Le lendemain, André, le chef de clan, décida qu'on devait aller saluer Balthus, à qui Louise prêtait tant de talent et que je n'avais jamais vu. Pour travailler, il lui fallait d'immenses ateliers, et on disait que son marchand lui en avait enfin dégoté un dans le Morvan. Le matin était clair, le vent avait tourné, des écharpes de brume s'étiraient dans l'encaissement des vallées. Par une route tout en tournants, dans un pays de bosses et de ravins criblé d'étangs, nous atteignîmes Corbigny où les Vilmorin n'eurent pas un mot pour Jules Renard, si féroce, et que j'admirais tant. Après quoi ce fut, dissimulé au milieu des bois, derrière une haute grille déglinguée et une bourbeuse cour de ferme, un castel biscornu, à demi délabré et à demi branlant, féerique ou diabolique ? Pas très chrétien. Sur toutes les toiles accrochées aux murs, la même jeune fille nue au visage de nonne et à longs cheveux noirs sur les épaules, et, quand elle était vêtue, le corsage dégrafé ou les jambes entrouvertes, endormie, un chat près d'elle. Du feu flambait encore dans les cheminées pour réchauffer modèle et visiteurs. Balthus, tendre géant en costume de velours, vivait là, dieu des forêts et maître des formes, silencieux, énigmatique, une flamme d'enfer au-dessus des oreilles. Vîmes-nous son atelier ? En avait-il un ? C'était tout le château. Sa nièce, son inspiratrice, s'appelait Frédérique Tison, un nom pour l'hiver et le Morvan.

Dans une haute galerie glacée, nous bûmes du vin blanc puis nous partîmes, je ne me souviens pas que nous ayons déjeuné. Fine gueule, sang ardent, esprit raffiné, André de Vilmorin pouvait festoyer de n'importe quoi chez des amis, d'une simple omelette. S'il la tournait, elle devenait succulente car il était un cuisinier inspiré. Sur la route, Louise et lui parlèrent beaucoup de Balthus Balthasar. J'écoutai. J'emportai de notre visite à Vézelay un mortel enchantement. Nous n'étions pas tellement loin de Colette non plus. Il y avait chez Balthus du jouisseur secret et un personnage proche du Heathcliff des *Hauts de Hurlevent*. Sa peinture méritait-elle une telle admiration ? N'y avait-il pas une symbolique littéraire dans trop de tableaux ? Les poses du modèle, le chat, les provocations et la diablerie, tout cela faisait un peu voyeur, un

peu voyou. Aujourd'hui, je me sens dans l'œuvre de Balthus comme un vieillard de la Bible, l'œil fripon sur la belle Suzanne au bain, ému aussi quand je retrouve dans ses toiles de 1950 à 1960 la cour de ferme, les cerisiers et les collines de Chassy. Des années plus tard, quand je chercherai une maison, c'est de ce côté-là que je me dirigerai tout naturellement. Je retournerai à son manoir, où bien des toiles étaient encore, tandis qu'il dirigeait la villa Médicis que Malraux lui avait confiée. L'été, venait Pierre Klossowski, le frère aîné, écrivain précieux et rare, qui dessinait sa propre femme, nue aussi ou à demi, dans des poses ou des toilettes balthusiennes et avec un talent encore plus sulfureux. Tous deux, Balthus et Klossowski, Klossowski de Rola, fils d'un comte polonais ruiné, filleuls de Rilke et de Pierre Jean Jouve. Dans cette atmosphère, on se sentait, sinon en présence, du moins en voisinage de l'absolu et du Malin. A Vézelay aussi, il y avait parenté d'ombre et de lumière, d'encens et de messes noires. Sur le rocher, coulait une lave aux écailles luisantes.

Cette année-là, j'allai en Corse où André de Vilmorin et sa femme possédaient une maison au-dessus de Centuri. Louise y passa comme une étoile endolorie ; sa précieuse chambre, sauvagement protégée du soleil, personne n'avait le droit de l'occuper en son absence. Nous allions en mer dans la barcasse *le Tchiken,* nous pêchions puis nous abordions un îlot désert, nous allumions du feu, André cuisait une fantastique soupe de poissons à la rouille, nous nous baignions, nous déjeunions dans les rochers. Je n'ai jamais tant ri. Louise nous parlait encore de ses donjons et de ses amants, versait une larme et écrivait de nouveaux poèmes. Les événements qui secouaient l'Algérie m'atteignaient moins, et cependant nous en étions au moment où le gouvernement de Guy Mollet mobilisait le contingent.

Depuis *le Métier des armes,* j'avais publié chez Gallimard huit livres dont trois pièces de théâtre. J'attendais ce que tout écrivain attend : le succès qui peut le caresser de l'illusion qu'il est lu, qu'on l'aime, et que ce qu'il écrit sert à quelque chose. Je traitais encore de la guerre, d'hommes de guerre, j'avais beau être en position de congé, j'appartenais toujours à

l'armée. Les articles que j'avais publiés dans *l'Express* m'avaient valu un blâme du ministre de la Défense et quand je rencontrais certains de mes anciens camarades, ils m'évitaient. Dans mon récit j'avais abordé le problème de l'amour avec tant de retenue que cela restait d'une lecture austère. On me considérait comme un écrivain un peu hautain, encore embarrassé dans les fumées des combats. Pourtant la guerre s'éloignait de plus en plus, l'Indochine était engloutie, l'Algérie tabou, et je venais d'achever un nouveau titre, *l'Homme à l'épée*, où il n'était question que de vertu. Un certain désintérêt de l'intelligentsia vis-à-vis de moi m'atteignait. Pour s'obstiner dans cette voie, il fallait me contenter de peu d'argent. Mon succès des *Cyclones* était devenu ma garçonnière, je vivais d'une maigre pension que l'armée me versait au titre des services rendus, que j'écornais pour ma vierge de Giotto et mes enfants. J'espérais un autre succès de théâtre qui ne vint pas, comme j'espérais retourner au Niger pour le cinéma. En vain. Je traversais une mauvaise passe. Sigaux me consolait et m'écrivait qu'il fallait m'armer de patience. Lui boulonnait comme un nègre et vantait la générosité de Druon à qui tout réussissait. La vie me tourmentait, les amours me tourmentaient, j'étais un mauvais père, un méchant amant, et pourtant, depuis ma Pharaonne, je ne rencontrais que des anges. Je ne voyais plus que rarement Doyon. Le peu de crédit que j'avais, il le jugeait même immérité et nous étions de nouveau fâchés, je ne sais plus pourquoi. L'Algérie qu'il détestait et où il prétendait qu'il n'y avait que des imbéciles ou des fripouilles, il se mit soudain à la chérir et vomit sur moi tout un Livret du Mandarin où il dénonçait mes noirceurs et mes hontes. Je le rencontrai un jour sur le seuil de Gallimard, pliant sous le poids de son libelle qu'il distribuait à Paulhan et à Camus pour se venger de moi. J'ai raconté tout cela dans *la Saison des Za*.

Louise prétendait qu'elle poserait la plume si elle n'avait pas la promesse de Gaston Gallimard, obtenue à quel prix ? d'être tirée au moins à cent mille exemplaires. Puisque mes livres se vendaient mal, pourquoi s'obstiner ? Soudain, au Pays basque, je crus avoir trouvé la clé de mes problèmes et le salut. Fini la littérature ! Labourer la terre, semer, récolter, me parurent soudain plus de mon mérite. Lancelot se transforma en chevalier servant de petit trianon et se lança dans l'élevage

des bovidés et le défrichage de landes qu'avec les conseils d'André de Vilmorin je transformai en prairies. On ne devenait pas fermier du jour au lendemain, mais j'avais les mêmes furies opiniâtres que mes ancêtres, et chaque matin je livrais notre production dans les crémeries de Bayonne et de Saint-Jean-de-Luz. Les vaches étaient de délicates usines de fabrication de lait, il leur fallait beaucoup d'herbe tendre et de soins, sujettes comme elles l'étaient à tant de maladies. L'été, l'enchanteresse qui m'hébergeait et moi allions suivre les corridas de Luis Miguel Dominguin, le célèbre matador aux amours de star. A Ciboure où il habitait, je rencontrai Pierre Benoit et me mis à le chérir. Il était plutôt court et rond, cravaté d'un nœud papillon et toujours à l'affût d'un mot, et avait l'œil rusé. A date et heure fixes, il s'attablait face à la mer dans ce qui ressemblait à une cabine de navire, pissait sa copie sans jamais de ratures, terminait selon son plan, et le roman paraissait le jour prévu avec un nom d'héroïne commençant encore par un A. A la belote il trichait. Dès qu'on parlait de ses triomphes, il citait dix vers railleurs de Victor Hugo. Sa femme Marcelle, qu'il adorait, était atteinte d'un cancer et se décomposait sous nos yeux. Elle lui disait souvent qu'il avait une vilaine âme, car il y avait chez lui un brin de cruauté charmante. Farceur mélancolique, il n'arrêtait pas de se gausser des écrivains qui croyaient avoir du génie.

Nous allions parfois dîner au Café de Paris à Biarritz où l'on mangeait les plus délicieuses moules du monde. Il vivait de ses amis morts, de Maurice Ravel qui avait aussi hanté Ciboure, chérissait ses amis vivants et surtout Paul Morand qu'il voulait voir siéger sous la Coupole. Il me fit attribuer le Grand Prix de littérature, puis se dépensa avec fougue pour la candidature de Paul Morand.

Le héros de l'époque était l'homme à la moto d'Edith Piaf, tandis que Guy Mollet était président du Conseil. Bouillant politicien de ce temps-là, gonflé de suffisance, il disait en parlant des rebelles algériens : « Nous avons en face de nous des gens qui ne comprennent pas la situation française. » Si, ils la comprenaient. Ils n'étaient pas français, voilà tout. Pour déranger la bonne conscience nationale, il aurait fallu que Camus devînt le leader d'une première étape dans l'affranchissement de nos sujets. Sartre allait plus loin,

mais Sartre était considéré comme un voyou par la droite, et avec sa face de crapaud baveur d'idées, quelle influence pouvait-il avoir, sauf auprès des intellectuels aux yeux de qui, pour compter, il faut d'abord être laid ? Maintenant qu'il est mort et empaillé, on l'admire de tous les bords.

1956 fut l'année d'une comète. Je reçus une nouvelle lettre du général de Gaulle à propos de mon livre *l'Homme à l'épée*. Je n'étais pas allé le voir à Colombey et je n'osais toujours pas. Je n'avais pas vu Malraux non plus. Camus revint d'Alger où il avait lancé un appel pathétique pour une trêve civile. Les ultras l'avaient hué, on avait essayé de l'abattre, puis ce fut sur Guy Mollet qu'on lança des tomates devant le monument aux morts d'Alger. J'allai voir Camus à Paris. Entre nous, nous évitions de parler du problème, nous allions au parc des Princes assister aux matches du Racing dont nous étions de fervents supporters. Camus avait appartenu dans sa jeunesse au Racing universitaire d'Alger où il était gardien, on disait *goal* en ce temps-là, sous le même maillot à bandes bleu clair. Au stade, il critiquait le jeu d'une voix forte et grinçante et nous nous levions ensemble en hurlant quand le Racing marquait un but. Puis ce fut l'affaire de Suez. L'expédition remettait à sa place Nasser, un des soutiens les plus farouches de la rébellion. Je me souviens de notre joie, ce dimanche-là : nos avions de chasse écrasaient l'aviation égyptienne, nos parachutistes avaient sauté sur le canal. Au bistrot le plus proche, nous commandâmes deux whiskies, pour lui un *baby*, et nous trinquâmes. Une victoire de nos armes allait permettre de s'entendre enfin, les Arabes allaient reconnaître que nous étions les plus forts, et nous, les libéraux, derrière Camus, nous allions exiger du gouvernement la paix dans la fraternité.

Le lendemain, ce fut l'ultimatum de la Russie soviétique et de l'Amérique. L'armée rembarqua la mort dans l'âme. Le nouveau résident à Alger, Robert Lacoste, chargea Massu et Bigeard de faire régner l'ordre et nous entrâmes dans la tragédie. En France, les voitures ne roulaient plus, faute d'essence, le marché immobilier fut bloqué. J'ai raconté dans *la Saison des Za* comment une comtesse russe, entrée dans ma vie avec fracas tandis que je courais le festival de Cannes pour *le Figaro littéraire*, me fit acheter pour quatre sous dans un hameau près de Houdan, au bout d'un chemin de terre, une vieille maison que j'appelai « la Grange » en souvenir de Port-

Royal. J'avais besoin de solitude, et parfois, quittant la ferme, l'enchanteresse et le Pays basque, je me réfugiais là, l'hiver, avec mon chien César, fils de la femelle de chien-loup du temps où je vivais avec Camus dans la vallée de Chevreuse. César n'était pas très intelligent mais je l'aimais. Le roman que j'écrivais me tourmentait. Je marchais à travers les labours, sous la neige, le capuchon de mon duffle-coat rabattu sur mon front, roulant des images d'Indochine et me demandant par quelle aberration amoureuse j'étais allé me fourrer à l'autre bout de la France, au milieu d'un troupeau de vaches frisonnes dont il fallait tirer le lait et le vendre. La littérature m'avait reconquis et me possédait de nouveau, j'errais dans les hasards, le vent me cinglait, je sentais des ombres m'escorter, César me lâchait parfois pour filer sur les traces d'une femelle en chaleur, je passais une mauvaise nuit à l'attendre et il rentrait le lendemain matin, crotté, le poil humide, tout guilleret. J'écrivis là *les Belles Croisades*, un symétrique à *la Vallée heureuse*, et, soulagé, je rentrai au Pays basque où César égorgea quelques brebis avant d'être abattu par un berger.

On avait bombardé Murtin général de brigade et attaché de l'air à Washington où l'on exhibait sa jambe de bois. Il avait une riche résidence, tenue par un couple d'anciens esclaves : un vieux Noir à cheveux blancs et sa femme, une imposante mamma. Porteur d'une immense casquette à l'italienne qui le couronnait d'or, il revenait de temps en temps à Paris en compagnie de gros capitalistes américains qui s'intéressaient aux problèmes de notre aviation. Certains constructeurs le chargeaient parfois de balader leurs clients dans les boîtes de Montmartre et de soudoyer quelques petites femmes. Il me disait : « Je suis une lope. » Il avait raison. Il jouait les entremetteurs d'Etat.

Enfiévré d'une nervosité extrême, il bougeait sans cesse et ne pouvait plus se souffrir. Comme il s'épuisait en démarches pour la sortie d'une voiture achetée là-bas, un douanier avait commis l'imprudence de s'apitoyer : « Vous êtes un mutilé, je crois ? » Il avait failli étouffer de rage. Mutilé, lui ? Il frémissait encore de honte à l'idée qu'on pouvait croire qu'il n'était pas comme tout le monde ! Il fréquentait un camarade de calvaire, le colonel de France qui feignait de tirer gloire de sa propre

jambe de bois et y plantait férocement des punaises. Murtin et lui ne parlaient que de ça, de leur guibolle en moins. De France disait : « Des morts et de nous, ce sont les morts qui sont vivants. » Tous deux appartenaient à une espèce qui n'a plus de place nulle part. Un peu comme moi, dans un autre genre. A la fin de la guerre, on n'imaginait pas un Murtin avec sa patte coupée. Il pilotait encore mais n'aurait pas pu, comme Bader, un as britannique de la bataille d'Angleterre, mener un combat avec deux jambes artificielles. D'ailleurs, il n'y avait plus de combats, et pour Murtin la vie n'avait plus de sens. Plus de lions non plus qu'à la cour du Négus, encore ceux-là étaient-ils apprivoisés. Pour les autres, il ne restait que les zoos.

Finalement, un jour, sans tambour ni trompette, Murtin se maria. Sa femme donna des dîners pour lui faire croire qu'il existait toujours. Une nuit, il se logea une balle dans la tête, comme un autre as allemand, Udet, que Goering avait embringué en 1941 dans la reconstruction de la Luftwaffe. A moins de devenir des saints, ces hommes-là ne peuvent plus vivre, et si, malgré eux, ils survivent, ils s'isolent, tel Heurtaux au soir de sa vie. Imagine-t-on Guynemer gâtouillard ou infirme ? La seule fin du héros est la mort, a fortiori quand c'est un dandy. A Wilflingen, Jünger avait ajouté en parlant de ces hommes-là : « Quand les astres les lâchent, ils se suicident... » Pour Murtin, on en était à un moment où l'Eglise était moins miséricordieuse que Dieu. L'aumônier refusa de célébrer l'office, on l'y contraignit, il n'y eut pas de scandale, Accart était là, le ban et l'arrière-ban de la chevalerie rendirent les honneurs à Murtin qui repose où il est né par hasard : à Bâgé-le-Châtel, dans l'Ain.

Aigle à l'œil un peu triste, Ventré, mon frère des vols sur les Alpes du début de la guerre et à Sétif, disparut aussi. Mécontent de son sort et de lui, il se fit mettre en congé, se retira dans son village des Pyrénées, ne vit plus personne et mourut. Un moment vient où, pour ces hommes-là, rien n'est plus possible. Si l'on me demande pourquoi, je ne sais que répondre. Pour Ventré, parce qu'il avait perdu ses camarades et les avions, parce qu'il s'ennuyait. Pourquoi ne nous sommes-nous pas revus ? On se quitte, ce qui donne du prix à la vie n'est plus et on ne peut plus rien les uns pour les autres.

En amour encore moins. Murtin et Ventré me manquent. Dans l'armée, je n'ai admiré personne plus qu'eux.

Je me mis donc à me partager entre le Pays basque et Paris. Nous étions chez Lipp avec Kanters et Sigaux, quand, le 17 octobre de cette année 1957, un coup de tonnerre retentit : Camus prix Nobel. Le soir même, fier et heureux, je parlai de lui à la radio. Le journal *Arts*, toujours impertinent, publia un article méchant de Jacques Laurent : « Le prix Nobel couronne une œuvre terminée. » Tout le monde se montrait abasourdi que ce ne fût pas Malraux. Devant Pierre Cardinal qui travaillait à un film sur lui, François Mauriac laissa éclater sa déception qu'un homme si jeune reçût **un** honneur que lui-même avait dû attendre jusqu'à près de soixante-dix ans. « Ce n'est pas à lui qu'on l'a décerné, n'est-ce pas ? C'est à l'Algérie ? » s'écria-t-il. Il ne se trompait pas. Comme l'écrivain à qui le Nobel est attribué en reçoit confidence l'avant-veille, Camus m'avoua plus tard qu'il n'avait pas dormi cette nuit-là, se demandant s'il ne devait pas le refuser ; puis, à la pensée que c'était à l'Algérie qu'on l'offrait plus qu'à lui, il accepta. L'académie de Stockholm précisait qu'elle couronnait une œuvre qui éclairait « avec un sérieux pénétrant les problèmes posés de nos jours aux consciences humaines ».

Nous, d'Algérie, devions beaucoup à Camus : il nous avait ouvert les yeux et ce qu'il avait écrit avait un sens universel. Dans tous ses livres, même au théâtre, ses personnages se posaient la même question : « La vie vaut-elle la peine d'être vécue ? » Chez lui, le cœur adoucissait les coups que l'intelligence portait. Nous n'étions pas forcément condamnés, sauf dans *la Chute* peut-être. Partout ailleurs, il laissait une échappatoire, mais à quel prix ! « Il ne suffit pas de dénoncer l'injustice, il faut donner sa vie. » Cette phrase des *Justes* rejoignait le brave, le pur Saint-Ex dans la sainteté laïque et l'idée qu'avait de lui, dans sa jeunesse, Louise de Vilmorin : que ce gentil garçon ne dirait de mal de personne et n'irait pas loin. Pouvait-on porter un jugement sur l'œuvre de Camus quand on était un de ses intimes ? « Oui, oui, rétorquait Kanters, ça fait tout de même un peu prêchi-prêcha. » L'homme Camus, parfois difficile mais toujours chaleureux, ne faisait qu'un avec l'écrivain. Bernard Frank publia dans *la Nef* un article assassin. « On l'a pris pour un penseur et il n'a

que peu d'idées... Quand Camus pense, il met son beau style... » Pour Bernard Frank au talent et aux humeurs féroces, et que nous n'étions pas nombreux à lire à cette époque, Camus n'avait pas les moyens de sa gloire, ses articles politiques ressemblaient aux périodes agacées d'un officier de réserve, on attendait Saint-Just et ce n'était qu'un Prévost-Paradol, son œuvre n'était qu'une « bonne œuvre ». Druon protesta. Il aurait dû être le dernier à s'indigner. Druon, c'était ma conscience bourgeoise et progressiste, mon exemple de succès. Bernard Frank allait jusqu'à reprocher à Camus de n'avoir rien écrit sur un problème algérien qui prenait les allures d'une tragédie. Cela me parut scandaleux, et cependant Frank avait raison. Quant à Malraux à qui allaient toutes les sympathies, s'était-il jamais intéressé à l'Algérie ? Avait-il jamais pris une position quelconque depuis qu'il n'était plus communiste ou anarchiste ? En tout, il s'en remettait à de Gaulle, comme je m'en remettais à Camus. Je sentais déjà, moins bien qu'Amrouche, qu'Alberto imposait à notre zèle de néophytes plus de limites que d'encouragements à aller de l'avant. Aller plus loin, c'était le dépasser, c'était l'aventure. Là, il faisait les gros yeux, et je me soumettais.

L'actualité du temps flambait dans les vitrines des libraires et aux kiosques des journaux. On parlait d'arbitraire, d'exactions, de tortures. Camus avait réagi à l'arrestation de son ami Jean de Maisonseul et en avait profité pour déclarer qu'il n'approuvait rien de ce qui se disait à propos de l'Algérie, à droite comme à gauche. Le Nobel n'était qu'un coup d'épée dans l'eau.

Le 2 décembre, un grand dîner aux chandelles eut lieu à l'ambassade de Suède à Paris. Quinze jours après, c'était Stockholm où seuls les Gallimard furent de la partie. *Paris-Match* publia des photos du wagon-restaurant. Sur le ferry du Danemark à la Suède, à la gare d'arrivée, seule Francine en manteau de ratine laissait éclater sa joie. Au bal d'après le banquet de l'Hôtel de Ville, dansant avec une étudiante en casquette blanche, puis coincé entre deux beautés sur les accoudoirs de son fauteuil, Camus ressuscitait, hilare dans son habit à queue-de-pie loué pour la circonstance. Enfin, il s'amusait avant de s'incliner devant le roi, les feuillets de son remerciement à la main. Plus tard il me dira : « Pour fêter la

Sainte-Lucie, le jour le plus court de l'année, des pépées viennent te chercher dans la nuit en chantant, avec des candélabres, et toi, tu couronnes la plus charmante... » Rien que ça vous donnait la fringale d'avoir le Nobel. Son discours sur l'art à l'université d'Uppsala me parut très ennuyeux, après quoi les étudiants lui demandèrent s'il existait une censure en Algérie. Il le reconnut en le regrettant, et ajouta : « Il n'y a pas de pression gouvernementale en France mais des groupes d'influence, des conformistes de droite et de gauche. Croyez-moi, c'est ma conviction la plus sincère, aucun gouvernement au monde ayant à traiter le problème algérien ne le ferait avec des fautes aussi relativement bénignes que celles du gouvernement français. »

Soudain, le dialogue dégénéra. Un représentant du FLN l'accusa de ne jamais signer de pétitions en faveur des Algériens, essaya de l'empêcher de répondre et l'insulta grossièrement. Dominique Birmann, le correspondant du *Monde,* relata ainsi l'incident : « Camus parvint enfin, non sans peine, à se faire entendre. " Je n'ai jamais parlé à un Arabe ou à l'un de vos militants comme vous venez de me parler publiquement. Vous êtes pour la démocratie en Algérie, soyez donc démocrate tout de suite et laissez-moi parler. Laissez-moi finir mes phrases car souvent les phrases ne prennent tout leur sens qu'avec leur fin. " »

Lui qui, le premier de tous, avait réclamé du pain et de la justice pour ceux qu'on appelait les Arabes, et avait été le premier journaliste expulsé d'Algérie devait en avoir gros sur le cœur. Cette agression souleva l'indignation de l'assistance. Le silence enfin rétabli, Camus, dans une ambiance hachée d'interruptions, se lança dans un long plaidoyer et termina ainsi : « C'est avec une certaine répugnance que je donne ainsi mes raisons au public. J'ai toujours condamné la terreur. Je dois condamner aussi un terrorisme qui s'exerce aveuglément, dans les rues d'Alger, par exemple, et qui un jour peut frapper ma mère, ma famille. Je crois à la justice, mais je défendrai ma mère avant la justice. »

Le mot fit la une de tous les journaux du lendemain : la mère avant la justice. Ce mot-là, une réplique de théâtre, me suffoqua. Pour moi, c'était un mot facile. On ne lui en demandait pas tant. La presse de droite exulta. « Enfin Camus existe », s'écria Jacques Perret dans *la Nation française.* Pour

la droite, la France était la mère. Certains allaient jusqu'à voir en elle « Antigone la vierge mère de l'ordre ». La gauche s'interrogeait. Camus avait le mérite de nous placer devant la vérité. Il rejoignait sa famille, sa tribu, le clan. Albert Memmi, qui aimait Camus, avouait, et je me reconnaissais là, qu'il incarnait « le colonisateur de bonne volonté ». Nous n'étions pas autre chose. Je condamnais cette guerre mais je plaignais aussi mes anciens camarades. J'avais vu la guerre d'Indochine et je n'avais rien dit dans la crainte d'être blâmé par Camus.

La France s'agitait, des complots se tramaient, de Gaulle donnait des conférences de presse. Le bruit courait que Malraux aurait dit à sa fille Florence : « La France, c'est de Gaulle et moi. » Camus passa l'été en Grèce et je retournai dans les prairies du Pays basque. Pierre Benoit avait installé sa femme à Paris dans une clinique où de grands professeurs veillaient sur elle. Il avait beaucoup vieilli et marchait difficilement. Il me disait : « Elle était la doyenne de l'Académie. » Je ne lui répondais pas. Dès son réveil, il sirotait un verre de rhum, attendait midi pour son bordeaux et noyait la journée dans le whisky. On avait beau mettre les bouteilles sous clé, il buvait quand même. Les yeux rougis et larmoyants, il s'obstinait à régler l'ordonnance des obsèques religieuses à Saint-Philippe-du-Roule dont le curé était son obligé. « Marcelle n'est pas morte, répétais-je. Ne vous hâtez pas de l'enterrer. » Il répondait par une rasade de Johnny Walker. Le soir, je l'écoutais vitupérer sa bête noire, de Gaulle revenu au pouvoir, à qui il ne pardonnait pas les six mois de prison qu'il avait passés à Fresnes où Florence Gould s'était beaucoup dépensée en visites auprès de ses amis dans le malheur. Paul Morand s'annonçait quelquefois. Nous allions déjeuner au Bar basque de Saint-Jean-de-Luz. Pierre Benoit me disait : « Surtout pas un mot sur 1940 ni sur de Gaulle. » Je n'allais pas chagriner des hommes dont j'admirais le talent. Avec son visage glacé de riche bouddha, Paul Morand m'intimidait. Il ressemblait aussi au maréchal Juin, ce qui ne me rassurait qu'à demi, et peut-être me prenait-il pour un combattant de la France libre à tous crins. J'imaginais assez la surprise désagréable qu'un de Gaulle rebelle avait pu lui causer en juin 1940 quand il était chef de mission à l'ambassade de France à Londres, que rien ne le prédestinait à ce genre de cas de

conscience. Bref, bien que, par la suite, il m'écrivît des lettres exagérément chaleureuses, il me considéra toujours avec ce que j'appelai une arrière-pensée : je n'étais pas des siens.

L'échec de son élection blessa mortellement Pierre Benoit qui commit alors la légèreté de démissionner de l'Académie, ce dont je le grondai fort. Naïvement, il s'étonna qu'on n'expédiât pas aussitôt une délégation pour le ramener en fanfare quai Conti. Je lui dis qu'on devait y être trop heureux qu'il fût parti. Il ne voulut pas me croire, tant il était généreux et plein d'illusions.

Le 13 mai surgit dans une tempête de cris. Les pieds-noirs s'agitaient, un livre accablant, *la Question* d'Henri Alleg, parut sans que Camus réagît. Il avait acheté sa maison de Lourmarin, il y vivait souvent. Même à Paris, le Nobel l'avait isolé, il ne riait plus, ou alors ricanait d'un humour grinçant, pesait chacune de ses paroles ou ne disait plus rien, sauf à des amis sûrs, sauf quand des ministres sollicitaient son avis, sauf quand il demandait audience en faveur des uns et des autres. Horrifié par le terrorisme des Algériens, il s'étonnait aussi, comme Guy Mollet, qu'on puisse avec une telle obstination refuser la France pour patrie... Pour lui, et je l'approuvais, les Arabes devaient remercier le ciel que leur pays ait été conquis par une puissance aussi libérale que la France. Avec son visage lourd de tourments, il ressemblait de plus en plus à son héros *l'Etranger,* qu'on aurait sorti de prison pour lui annoncer qu'il avait le Nobel. Il ne s'en étonnait pas, puisque tout pouvait arriver, le bien comme le mal, sans raison et à propos de rien.

Sans mon gourou, un peu à la dérive, désespérant de conquérir jamais la notoriété qui permet aux écrivains de vivre de leur métier, je me disais que je serais plus à l'aise ailleurs que chez Gallimard où tant de célébrités se côtoyaient : dans un de leurs satellites, chez Denoël par exemple, où Kanters était directeur littéraire et s'occuperait mieux de moi. Je m'en ouvris à Camus. Il me répondit : « Tant que je serai où je suis, je te protégerai. Nous avons besoin de toi et de ta voix. Quant aux éditeurs, pourquoi quitter l'un pour l'autre ? Ils sont tous les mêmes. » Je m'obstinai cependant car je croyais moins en lui. J'écrivis à Claude Gallimard une longue lettre assez cruelle dans laquelle je lui demandai de me laisser partir. Après quoi,

soulagé, je me remis au milieu des vaches à flotter dans le lait, j'en avais jusqu'au cou.

Les événements se succédèrent. De Gaulle revint au pouvoir grâce à un complot inavoué de l'armée, avec une forte odeur de cuir et un bruit de godillots. Peut-être éprouvai-je alors, plus cuisant, le regret de n'avoir pas su mieux l'approcher. Camus pensait comme moi qu'avec de Gaulle l'affaire algérienne allait avancer. J'espérais que de Gaulle irait du côté des rebelles car il n'aimait pas les pieds-noirs qui l'avaient mal reçu en 1943 et qu'il considérait toujours comme vichystes. A Alger il reçut un accueil triomphal et une vaste coalition politico-militaire transforma la ville en une marmite de sorcière. Là-bas on avait du goût pour la violence et l'insubordination, au moins dans les mots. Depuis toujours, Alger se croyait doté d'un statut à part et refusait de se plier aux lois de la République. On l'avait vu en 1870 après la défaite et quand Alger avait élu Drumont député au moment de *la France juive*. D'ordinaire, Paris capitulait. Lorsque de Gaulle voulut briser la nouvelle fronde et que le dessein qu'il s'attribuait d'une Algérie réintégrée à la France parut douteux, l'armée rechigna et les pieds-noirs hurlèrent à la trahison.

Un lundi de janvier 1960, le 4, j'étais chez Pierre Benoit. Le vieil homme s'enfonçait dans les ténèbres, sa femme était au plus mal, nous étions en train de jouer à la belote, il était 7 heures du soir quand le téléphone sonna. C'était pour moi. Un télégramme de Kanters m'annonçait que Camus venait de se tuer en voiture.

Je rejoignis la table. Pierre Benoit me demanda si ce n'était pas une bonne nouvelle. L'émotion m'empêcha de répondre.

XVIII

La guerre d'Algérie

A LOURMARIN, l'aube naissait, le village sentait le pain chaud. Après la fontaine, je montai vers une maison à gros ventre où des fenêtres brillaient. Je frappai à la porte, on m'ouvrit. Dans la salle à manger luisaient sous la suspension des visages autour d'une table. Francine se leva et se jeta dans mes bras en pleurant. « Il est là. Suzy m'a dit que c'était son étoile. Tu crois à des étoiles comme ça ? »

Je ne répondis pas. Suzy, c'était sa sœur à elle. Suzy devait penser au destin. Dans la pièce à côté, sur deux chaises de paille, reposait le cercueil de chêne clair, et déjà des fleurs s'entassaient à même le carrelage. Assis, la face fermée, un homme à la puissante charpente et une femme. Je mis un genou à terre, puis les deux, j'avais les yeux secs, le cœur sec, la gorge serrée, Dieu devait tous nous accueillir en notre douleur, les prières et les paroles n'étaient pas nécessaires. Voilà que je parle de Dieu tout à coup depuis qu'il a disparu de ma vie, dirait-on, depuis ma rupture avec le séminaire. Non, Dieu n'avait pas disparu. Seul dans le ciel et, pendant la guerre, pendant les secondes de ma collision en vol et quand nous appareillions par centaines et par milliers vers les projecteurs et les canons, où aurais-je été sinon dans ses mains ? Là, tous les gestes étaient soumission, toutes les pensées prière tandis qu'au pied du cercueil de Camus, rien, pas le moindre frémissement. Maintenant, je me souviens qu'un jour, se plaignant qu'on exigeât de lui des monuments d'éternité, il m'avait dit : « C'est peut-être comme une loi que j'ignore, mais qui est déjà établie. » Des fleurs, mais pas une bougie d'allumée, rien qui rappelât l'âme invisible de ce corps broyé.

L'homme à la puissante charpente se leva, vint à moi et

me serra la main. Il avait un visage de navigateur au long cours. C'était René Char. Francine se laissa emmener et je revins à la voiture. A l'hôtel Ollier, on me montra la pièce exiguë où Camus prenait ses repas : déjà le musée. On me raconta que le 3 janvier, alors qu'il avait son billet de train en poche, Michel et Janine Gallimard avaient fait le détour pour le presser de rentrer avec eux dans leur puissante Facel Vega ; qu'ils avaient passé la nuit dans un hôtel près de Mâcon. Le lendemain ils n'avaient sûrement pas déjeuné à Saulieu, à la *Côte d'Or,* où nous nous arrêtions avec Florence quand la grosse Buick nous ramenait de Juan-les-Pins. Dans la Facel Vega, Camus était assis à côté de Michel qui conduisait ; derrière, Janine Gallimard et Annie, dix-sept ans, sa fille. Il n'y avait pas d'autoroute en ce temps-là, on roulait moins vite, on s'arrêtait souvent. Au début de l'après-midi de ce lundi, sur une ligne droite bordée de platanes de la nationale 6, passé Villeblevin et avant Villeneuve-la-Guyard, soudain la Facel Vega fit une embardée à droite, heurta un arbre, se disloqua contre un autre et éjecta ses passagers dans un champ. Après un long moment, un médecin accourut. Il s'appelait aussi Camus, Marcel Camus. Une ambulance transporta les voyageurs à l'hôpital de Montereau. Michel Gallimard, inanimé et couvert de sang, était dans le coma. Camus avait le crâne et la colonne vertébrale brisés : on déposa son corps dans une salle de la mairie de Villeblevin. Les passagers du siège arrière étaient commotionnés. On ne retrouva jamais le teckel. En recevant la nouvelle à Paris, rue Madame, Francine s'évanouit, on l'emmena à Villeblevin d'où elle ne quitta plus son Alberto. On disait que la cause probable de l'accident était l'éclatement du pneu arrière gauche. Le compteur de vitesse était, paraît-il, bloqué sur cent quarante-cinq. Des automobilistes dirent que la Facel Vega les avait dépassés à une « vitesse terrifiante ». Sur une enveloppe où il demandait à l'hôtel Ollier qu'on lui renvoie son courrier, Camus avait écrit : « A bientôt. » En effet, il était là, en quel état ! Il avait horreur des longues routes et de la vitesse en voiture. Pourquoi avait-il cédé à ses amis Gallimard ? Il les aimait. On disait des choses à voix haute, d'autres à voix basse. Advienne ce qui doit arriver. Quelqu'un vous prend la main. On ne résiste pas à qui on aime.

Au petit matin, nous étions presque tous là, les fidèles, décomposés. Les uns à côté des autres, muets, confondus, ne

pouvant nous faire à l'idée qu'il n'était plus, cherchant des formules pour le garder encore un peu. Char fumait avec rage. C'était lui qui avait poussé Camus à s'installer à Lourmarin pour l'avoir près de lui dans le flot mystérieux qui dévale du Lubéron et baigne cette région enchantée. Dans mon journal tous les détails y sont. Des gerbes de fleurs s'amoncelaient, on se passait un article de Sartre, d'une tendresse inattendue. Les Gallimard, Gaston et Claude titubants presque, et la vieille Jeanne comme égarée, apparurent. La nouvelle les avait atteints aux sports d'hiver. Jeanne me chuchota des choses alarmantes : Michel était toujours dans le coma, on ne savait s'il survivrait. Pour Roblès, que Camus ait été tué par la vitesse l'étonnait beaucoup, Roblès n'imaginait pas Camus laissant le conducteur s'emballer. « Quand je l'emmenais parfois, dès que j'accélérais un peu, il me disait : " Tu finiras cul-de-jatte. " Ou alors c'est qu'il s'est assoupi un moment. » Je pensais à ce qu'il m'avait dit, un jour par plaisanterie, à l'idée d'une vieillesse qu'il ne supporterait pas : « Une voiture puissante, tu la pousses à fond, un petit coup de volant et ça y est... »

De la terrasse de sa chambre on touchait presque le temple, et, au-delà, le Lubéron. En fin de matinée, le cortège se forma. Les fleurs d'abord comme pour une noce, pas de clergé, pas de croix, puis le cercueil que les hommes de l'équipe de foot portaient à bras, à ras de terre. Entre Jean Grenier et moi qui la soutenions, Francine, et c'était tout de suite la campagne, les jardins, les cyprès, les vignes, le château où Bosco nous avait distribué les chambres avec leur sort. Est-ce qu'il savait à qui les bonnes et à qui les mauvaises, Bosco ? Le glas sonnait : c'était le pasteur. Il avait dit qu'il ferait un geste. Une cloche est la voix de Dieu et la voix des hommes quand ils en appellent à Dieu. Toutes auraient dû sonner. Celles de l'église restèrent muettes. La fosse sans prière, le discours du maire, tout fut intolérable. « C'est un assassinat », répétions-nous avec Moinot et Roblès. Qui était l'assassin ? Personne. La fatalité. Moi qui connaissais à peine Michel Gallimard, je pensai — dans quel ténébreux subconscient ? que c'était lui. Nous nous regardions les uns les autres, effondrés. Parmi nous, il y avait le parti de celui qui avait été tué et le parti de celui qui était au volant de la voiture meurtrière.

Nous nous enfuîmes pour cuver notre douleur. Je rentrai au Pays basque, inquiet et sombre. Trois jours après, Michel Gallimard mourait. J'envoyai un télégramme de condoléances. Entre-temps, chez Gallimard, on avait lu la lettre, écrite avant tous ces malheurs, où je demandais, chose inconcevable, chose qui ne s'était jamais vue, de quitter la maison. La lettre ne rendait plus le même son. Quand je l'avais écrite, Camus et Michel Gallimard vivaient, et, dans cette lettre prémonitoire, je parlais de tombeau, de morgue, de cruauté, de sentiments posthumes. Alors, tout se précipita. Les Gallimard et moi nous nous fâchâmes. Sur une carte de visite non affranchie, Gaston m'écrivit que s'il lui arrivait de me rencontrer il ne me serrerait pas la main. Nimier publia dans *Arts* un article qui me parut scandaleux. Moinot et Sigaux abondèrent dans le même sens que moi : Nimier avait déposé une crotte sur la tombe de Camus et ils le lui écrivirent. A Moinot, il répondit : « Je savais qu'il y aurait beaucoup d'imbéciles aux obsèques de Camus, mais je ne savais pas qu'on vous y trouverait au premier rang. » J'ai déterré cet article de mes dossiers, l'ai relu et n'y ai rien relevé d'insultant. Insolent comme d'habitude avec les puissances établies, Nimier avait même pour Camus des attentions plutôt attendrissantes. J'aurais dû avoir de l'estime pour le caractère de Nimier qui couvrait d'avanies, en public, la souveraine avec qui il couchait, j'aurais dû avoir de l'admiration pour son talent de provocateur qui soutenait Céline accablé, avec cette impertinence de droite qui flanquait tous les gens de gauche dans le même sac. « Nous ne ferons pas la prochaine guerre avec les épaules de Sartre et les poumons de Camus » était un de ses mots récents. Ma douleur était si forte qu'elle me fit déraisonner, j'écrivis à Claude Gallimard que je ne souhaitais plus rencontrer Nimier dans les couloirs de la NRF. Je n'en eus plus le moyen. Claude Gallimard me répondit que la maison n'avait plus rien de commun avec mes ouvrages passés, présents et futurs. Du jour au lendemain, mon nom fut retiré du fonds de l'éditeur et des librairies. Je me débattis un moment et me heurtai à la puissance offusquée. Ce n'était pas une scène où, entre amants, on se jette les affaires par la fenêtre. C'était pire : j'avais commis un crime de lèse-majesté. J'avais à peu près tout perdu.

A la fin de janvier, après une interview où il déclarait son opposition à la politique du général de Gaulle, Massu fut limogé. Aussitôt des barricades s'élevèrent à Alger dans le quartier des facultés, le Premier ministre Michel Debré traversa la Méditerranée pour adjurer en vain l'armée d'obéir aux ordres, de Gaulle somma les révoltés de se soumettre. Le ton suffit. Les barricades furent démantelées après quelques répliques dignes de l'antique, quand les héros s'injuriaient sous les murs de Troie. L'Assemblée vota les pouvoirs spéciaux et le ministère de la Défense changea de titulaire.

Un numéro spécial de la *NRF* consacré à Camus parut. Personne ne me demanda d'y collaborer. Deux mois encore, j'errai à travers ma tristesse. Enfin n'en pouvant plus, j'allai à Paris où Kanters, bien placé pour entendre ce qui se disait, m'avertit qu'il était conseillé aux éditeurs de l'obédience Gallimard de ne pas m'accueillir. Kanters paya sa confidence d'une défaveur qui ne le lâcha plus jamais, on le vida du *Figaro littéraire* où, après André Rousseaux, il tenait le feuilleton de critique, Nourissier le remplaça et, comme Kanters perdait la vue, on précipita sa retraite. Les forces de ce monde, quand on les brave, essaient de vous réduire en miettes. Je m'aperçus qu'ayant offensé mon souteneur dans le métier — qu'est-ce qu'un écrivain sans éditeur ? — j'étais, telle une prostituée, rejeté dans les ténèbres extérieures. Je relus ma lettre, à l'origine du conflit : elle était dure et féroce mais pas insultante, on y devinait mon désarroi de n'être pas aimé comme je rêvais de l'être. En quelques instants, tout fut réduit à néant : marques d'affection, embrassades, accès direct au sanctuaire : on n'osa cependant pas me réclamer ces merveilleux escarpins que Gaston m'avait offerts et que je mets toujours dans certaines circonstances. J'avais rué dans les brancards, je n'existais plus. Je vécus deux mois d'anxiété quand René d'Uckermann, le tout-puissant directeur littéraire des éditions Flammarion, rivales de Gallimard, m'appela.

Pour René d'Uckermann, je devais reprendre les mancherons de la charrue des mains de Camus. Revenons à l'époque, en mars 1960. J'avais essuyé une tempête, j'étais une épave rejetée par les flots en furie, la tombe de Camus était à peine refermée, je me rappelais ses angoisses, je ne me sentais même pas capable d'être son ombre. Avec sa position fondamentale

pour l'Algérie — Européens et musulmans condamnés à vivre ensemble —, il insistait sur la responsabilité majeure des gouvernements, inclinait vers un certain fédéralisme, mais ne cachait pas que si la violence continuait, chaque communauté se refermerait sur elle-même. Plus tard, Jean Daniel me dit que, recevant un jour des étudiants algériens, Camus les avait mis en garde : « Méfiez-vous. Si tout continue comme à présent, ce sera, même pour un homme comme moi, le devoir de retourner vers les miens. Je ne puis ni rester neutre ni vivre en dehors. »

L'année avait passé, désespérante, haletante. Pour ma part, je ne considérais pas avec horreur l'idée d'une république algérienne associée à la France, mais je n'avais là-bas, en vie, qu'un frère et des cousins, et on a beau dire à son frère : « Frère, mon frère... » cela ne suffit pas. Il faut encore défendre le soleil de son frère, sa patrie, qui est la vôtre, la terre où sont les morts. Je ne m'en sentais pas capable. Je le dis à d'Uckermann. « C'est qu'il y a longtemps que vous n'êtes pas retourné là-bas », répliqua-t-il. Il m'invita à dîner dans son hôtel de petit marquis, rue du Cherche-Midi, avec Pierre Clostermann, l'auteur du *Grand Cirque*.

Clostermann était notre premier chasseur de guerre. Il avait remporté trente-trois victoires sûres et cinq probables. Homme de stature, au visage ferme et impassible, au bec acéré et à la bouche impitoyable, c'était aussi un homme de réflexion et de raison. Sa chevalerie était de courtoisie, d'élégance un peu gourmée. Il ne se battait pas contre des moulins à vent ni contre plus fort que lui. Comme tous les chasseurs, il usait de précaution et de ruse. Prédateur, il fondait sur ses victimes avec fougue. Son livre *le Grand Cirque* avait fait de lui une vedette de l'édition. Rappelé sous les drapeaux dans la réserve, il rentrait d'Algérie avec un nouvel ouvrage, *Appui-feu sur l'oued Allali*.

De cela il parla peu et laissa planer une sorte de mystère. Il avait vu les habitants d'un camp de regroupement accroupis et lapant comme des chiens dans une rigole où l'on vidait l'eau d'une citerne, il avait vu... Il se tut soudain, habité de doutes et d'ombres. Il avait vu là-bas des choses qu'on ne devait pas cacher plus longtemps, mais ce n'était ni son domaine ni la terre où il était né. « Moi, je ne peux pas, dit-il. Vous, vous devez. »

Ce mot me frappa. De quelqu'un d'autre, j'aurais été moins impressionné. Je décidai sans plus réfléchir, car si on réfléchit, on ne fait rien. Il me sembla que c'était une sorte de commandement mystique, comme lorsque Pierre Jean Jouve m'avait imposé d'écrire *la Vallée heureuse.* Je fis mes adieux au Pays basque, d'Uckermann m'aida à régler les nombreuses et délicates formalités auprès de la préfecture de police et, trop prudent pour s'engager, me couvrit de caresses. De mon côté, je ne sollicitai rien de lui, ni contrat ni à-valoir, uniquement la promesse, quand Flammarion publierait ce livre-là, de racheter à Gallimard le fonds de mes livres précédents. Je ne pris contact avec aucun journal, sauf avec Pierre Lazareff qui s'éclipsa. Amrouche me donna une adresse à Alger. Comme tout le territoire là-bas était sous le contrôle de l'armée, j'écrivis au général de Gaulle pour lui demander la faveur d'un ordre de mission sans frais de déplacement qui me permettrait d'aller où je voudrais, et, sans attendre de réponse, je partis. Nikita Khrouchtchev était reçu à Paris et la première explosion atomique française venait d'avoir lieu à Reggane, dans le Sahara. Un de mes anciens compagnons d'Angleterre, Thiry, le capitaine qui volait à tour de rôle avec nous sur notre avion, le F Fox, et avait Gallois comme navigateur, dirigeait l'équipe du tir nucléaire comme général. A ceux qui me demandaient ce que j'allais chercher, je répondais comme Gide sur le point d'embarquer vers le Congo : « J'attends d'être là-bas pour le savoir. »

Dix jours après, j'étais à Alger, à l'hôtel Aletti. J'ai raconté cela dans *la Guerre d'Algérie,* dans *Etranger pour mes frères* et dans la dernière partie des *Chevaux du Soleil.* Ce n'était pas Alger que je retrouvais, mais Oran tel que le décrivait Camus au moment de la peste, jaune de crasse, puant, gluant d'immondices et grouillant de rats, hérissé de chevaux de frise et en état de siège. Les maîtres de la ville étaient les bidasses, les gardes mobiles qu'on employait aux besognes les plus rudes. Les Européens allaient d'un côté, les Arabes de l'autre, sans plus se voir ni se parler, comme Camus avait prévu que ce serait. Lyon, quand j'y étais passé sous l'Occupation en 1942, n'était rien à côté de cela. Cette fois, les

Allemands, c'était nous. Les terrasses des cafés étaient vides partout on s'évitait, les Arabes qu'on croisait semblaient se hâter de rentrer chez eux. Je ne reconnus rien de chez moi : j'étais ailleurs, en pays ennemi.

J'allai d'abord au cimetière de Saint-Eugène sur la tombe de mon père et de mon frère Robert, au pied de Notre-Dame d'Afrique, puis chez Charlot. Sa librairie de la rue Charras, *les Vraies Richesses,* avait été plastiquée parce qu'on y vendait des ouvrages qui ne plaisaient pas. On plastiquait beaucoup, on ne faisait que ça. Il s'était installé dans un passage couvert, en haut de la rue Michelet, non loin du tournant où les trams grinçaient, dans mon enfance, devant l'épicerie de ma tante Marie. Charlot m'ouvrit sa maison et son cœur. S'il y a encore des éditeurs comme lui, ils sont comme lui, ruinés. Il me mit dans les mains d'Himoud Brahimi, un musulman qui avait lu et étudié Camus, et que tout le monde appelait Momo. Etait-ce un marabout, un saint laïque, un illuminé qui jugeait les événements et leurs acteurs d'un œil aigu, un poète ou un prophète des rues et des places publiques, ou encore une sorte de camelot de Dieu qui proclamait des certitudes aveuglantes ? Un emploi dans une administration d'Etat le couvrait auprès des autorités. Quand je lui parlai du choix de Camus pour sa mère, il me dit : « C'est la seule fois où il n'a pas été absurde, la mère est au-dessus de tout. » D'un seul coup, grâce à lui, je découvris à la Casbah un monde et un peuple que j'ignorais, moi, né ici. Après quoi, les jours qui suivirent, j'allai visiter des prêtres, des ultras de tous bords, d'anciens camarades de l'armée, je touchai Clément, mon ancien directeur de la propagande en Indochine : général de brigade, il commandait le territoire des oasis et promit de venir me chercher. Je passai une soirée avec Mouloud Feraoun qui dirigeait une immense école sur les hauts de la ville où Européens et musulmans se côtoyaient, grâce à leurs enfants, puis j'allai chez mon frère René et sa femme Louise. Ils habitaient une agglomération à une soixantaine de kilomètres d'Alger. Mon frère subsistait de sa retraite de cheminot et de ruches, Louise ne se portait pas bien. Ils ne songeaient qu'à vivre en paix avec les Arabes et ne comprenaient rien aux événements ni à la politique du général de Gaulle. Je passai la nuit chez eux. Le lendemain, ils m'emmenèrent dans leur 2 CV sur la tombe de ma mère et des nôtres, à Sidi-Moussa, et à ce qui restait de la ferme de nos

origines. Y ai-je vu mes cousins, les fils de l'oncle Jules, ou est-ce dans *les Chevaux du Soleil* que j'imagine la ferme ressuscitée ? Hélas, ces lieux sacrés n'étaient plus rien. Mes cousins avaient tout vendu. A un Arabe. Ce jour-là, je rencontrai le curé et le maire de Sidi-Moussa ; nous eûmes une conversation digne des enfers. Le curé me dit qu'il n'ouvrait jamais le soir, quand on frappait à sa porte, et ne sortait jamais sans sa mitraillette dans la Volkswagen. C'était vivre ainsi ou la mort. Dans mon livre *la Guerre d'Algérie*, je n'ai pas toujours respecté la chronologie, dans *Etranger pour mes frères*, il s'agit déjà de Mémoires, dans *les Chevaux du Soleil*, l'imagination recrée à sa guise. A présent, j'essaie de reconstituer ce voyage à travers les dévastations, je traque une vérité qui m'échappe en partie, mes personnages errent à travers eux-mêmes dans une plaine déjà à l'abandon, parmi des fermes gérées par des syndics de faillite où flânent des militaires résignés et souvent avachis comme ils le sont loin de chez eux, au milieu de gens qu'ils ne connaissent pas, et quand ils attendent la quille. Où suis-je ? Où suis-je ? Heureusement il m'est resté un agenda où, jour par jour, j'ai consigné les noms de lieux ou de personnes. Ce n'est ni de mon enfance ni de mes morts que je suis en quête, ni même de l'âme de l'oncle Jules, ni des mânes de Meftah (car Meftah n'a toujours pas d'âme, il est né et mort trop pauvre, trop misérable, trop déshérité), c'est de Camus. Je ne l'ai jamais vu à Alger qu'une fois dans une librairie, chez Charlot sans doute, un jour où il signait des livres, et encore je ne suis pas sûr que ce soit à Alger. N'était-ce pas boulevard de l'Opéra, à Paris, au siège de l'Office d'Algérie où, à l'occasion peut-être du prix des Critiques décerné à *la Peste,* je suis photographié à ses côtés avec Gabriel Audisio et la charmante, la généreuse Janine Montupet qui écrivait une saga ? Où était donc ce Camus à qui je devais d'avoir découvert le soleil, les filles ardentes, leurs yeux noirs, les collines de Tipasa, la mer, le vent de Djemila, les approches du désert, l'exil et le royaume ? Après avoir obéi au commandement de Clostermann, je risquais mes premiers pas dans la zone ténébreuse qui avait commencé au moment où l'on descendait Camus dans la tombe. La nuit m'enveloppait, j'étais entouré d'ombres, je cherchais la tombe de Camus, j'errais sans fin dans un cimetière où je ne la trouvais pas. Puis, pareil à un personnage de Bernanos, j'allais sur un chemin de campagne, toujours

dans la nuit, en marche vers quoi ? D'autres périodes de ma vie se bousculaient et me pressaient de prendre parti. Pourquoi ? Pour qui ? Contre qui ? Je me revoyais sous-lieutenant godiche, pas encore ajusté aux manières des officiers, fou d'orgueil à la tête de ma section de tirailleurs, torturé à l'idée que j'avais pu trahir mes maîtres et mes condisciples du séminaire pour les mensonges du monde. Je me revoyais plus tard, le sac du parachute à la main, grimpant avec mon équipage dans la ferraille du quadrimoteur Halifax que nous arrachions au béton pour rejoindre le flot des bombardiers et, plus tard encore, en Indochine, décidant de me séparer de mes camarades pour des questions de conscience, parce que je n'étais pas d'accord avec eux, à cause des crimes qu'on les obligeait à commettre. Il fallait donc toujours se séparer ? Quand, par milliers, on nous avait envoyés raser Cologne et Leipzig, je n'avais pas hésité. C'est que, dans la guerre contre le nazisme, pour la survie des libertés humaines, il s'agissait de vaincre à tout prix, tandis que dans une guerre coloniale déguisée en croisade, nos chars, nos canons, nos avions et notre napalm tuaient et grillaient des misérables *nhia-quê*, hommes et femmes, qui se battaient avec des pétoires et des bambous parce qu'ils ne voulaient pas de nous, chez eux. Clostermann, le brave des braves, le pur, l'as, le héros Clostermann avait déposé en moi un doute épouvantable. Quoi, ce serait donc possible ? La presse de gauche le serinait assez, nous nous conduisions là avec d'autant plus de fureur et de cruauté que nous avions lâché l'Indochine par mollesse, comme disait le général Chassin passé dans la Cagoule, et que la menace des fusées soviétiques nous avait bloqués à Suez, l'avais-je assez entendu dire ? « Plus aucune concession sinon tout sera perdu. » Nous ne voulions pas larguer l'Algérie pour quelques scrupules dans les belles âmes et dans la mienne, l'Algérie c'était la France, mon pays, ma patrie, la terre de mes aïeux, la ferme de l'oncle Jules, les écoles de mon père l'instituteur, apôtre laïque un peu provocateur, les tirailleurs de notre armée, les harkis enrôlés chez nous, Meftah qui me hissait sur ses épaules à travers les labours, la tombe des miens. Ça, pour les tombes, nous étions fortiches, nous n'avions vraiment à nous que des cimetières. Car on ne vivait plus dans les fermes où les hors-la-loi — les fellaghas — coupaient les cerisiers et les vignes, les colons s'étaient réfugiés dans les

villes et, là encore, j'entends les tirades de Momo, l'illuminé de la Casbah, ce fou de Dieu, ce fou d'Allah, et les lamentations des mouquères qui me demandaient où étaient leurs maris emmenés par les parachutistes, est-ce que je savais, moi ?

Non, non, me répétait mon frère, on n'allait pas leur donner ça, ces jardins à perte de vue, ces vignes dans toute la plaine, ces routes droites pour voir venir de loin, ces hôpitaux, ces écoles où il n'y avait plus que leur saloperie de marmaille à eux, et toute cette merveille de civilisation mécanique déversée de France à pleins cargos. Dans les villes, la troupe tenait ses quartiers en force. A la campagne, chaque soir, mon frère collait derrière ses fenêtres des plaques de tôle contre les coups de fusil de chasse. Louise pleurait : « Qu'est-ce qu'on leur a fait, mon pauvre ? » Rien. On ne leur avait rien fait. Que du bien. Sauf que l'armée de M. de Bourmont leur avait volé Alger en 1830, sauf que nous avions mis leur pays en valeur, sauf qu'il y avait deux communautés : les Arabes et les Français, ou comme on disait : les Européens et les musulmans qu'on appelait plutôt les bicots. On en revenait à Camus, au problème de toujours, aux injustices, à la patrie commune, à la trêve civile, au terrorisme, aux tortures, aux fellaghas, aux parachutistes, aux ultras, à de Gaulle qui préparait une nouvelle tournée des popotes avant d'annoncer une paix négociée, la « paix des braves », un mot pour plaire à tous. L'armée qui s'était attribué la mission de garder l'Algérie à la France rechignait et parfois grognait. A la longue, notre présence avait établi le droit et en tenait lieu : nous étions chez nous.

De l'Algérie de l'oncle Jules, j'avais vu quelques tenants enclins à accorder à Meftah les facilités, les salaires, les logements et jusqu'à une intégration dans la société française. On commençait à voir des sous-préfets musulmans, on tolérait même à de Gaulle trois ou quatre préfets ratons et pourquoi pas ? des colonels s'ils étaient capables. J'aurais dû demander audience au général Salan. Il avait remplacé en 1958 le général Lorillot, mon ancien capitaine au camp de Satory, quand j'étais jeune lieutenant d'infanterie. Lorillot était toujours célibataire, moine laïc, jugulaire jugulaire, pas rigolo du tout, mais il avait passé tous les examens, franchi tous les grades, commandé en chef, et s'en était allé tristement après avoir passé ses pouvoirs à Salan de plus en plus décoré, de plus en

plus décidé à casser du bic après avoir cassé du Viet. Salan avait échappé à un attentat au bazooka, où, paraît-il, mon ami Cogny avait joué un rôle. J'aurais dû rencontrer Bigeard, commandant un régiment de paras, j'aurais dû. Je préférai m'abstenir. Ce que j'avais vu déjà me laissait pressentir que le dialogue serait ardu et même impossible.

Clément ne put envoyer un avion me chercher, mais quelle bonne voix il avait, comme il m'aimait ! On en était au moment annoncé par le prophète Camus : les deux peuples d'Algérie étaient rentrés chacun chez soi, l'action des parachutistes avait réussi l'union des plus déshérités, mais Camus n'avait pas prévu que les Arabes, de qui on disait qu'ils n'avaient pas de nation, avaient soudain une patrie.

Je téléphonai à l'adresse qu'Amrouche m'avait fournie. On me demanda si je voulais voir son village natal. Je connaissais mal la Kabylie. Mouloud Ferraoun m'avait dit : « Là-bas vous comprendrez tout. » Quand je commandais une escadrille à Sétif, j'avais souvent survolé cet énorme massif montagneux, âpre et toujours rebelle : Ighil Ali, la terre d'Amrouche, où quelques écailles sur un piton luisaient sur la droite de mon itinéraire. Nous prîmes rendez-vous. M. Belrachid, de qui je peux livrer le nom à présent, me conduisit en voiture. Il avait un titre de conseiller de quelque chose, une carte tricolore ; avec mille ruses et précautions, il passait. Nous contournâmes le massif par le sud, par Bouïra, nous laissâmes à notre gauche les pentes abruptes du Djurdjura au sommet encore enneigé. Le versant nord était le plus peuplé, les routes en lacets devenaient des chemins muletiers, parfois des sentiers vers les villages les plus hauts, là où les vues s'étendaient à travers une immensité de crêtes et de ravins jusqu'à la plaine côtière, jusqu'à la mer. La langue kabyle n'était pas une langue écrite mais le mot « kabyle » signifie « homme libre ». Là, on avait toujours manifesté de la passion pour l'indépendance, même contre les envahisseurs arabes, tout était divisé en familles, en clans, en classes, en castes, en partis qui, d'habitude, luttaient entre eux. En 1845, l'armée française avait dû conquérir la Kabylie village par village ; en 1871, la révolte avait flambé juste dans la Mitidja. Après avoir anéanti les rebelles, on avait rasé les vergers, brûlé les maisons, et expédié les hommes en Nouvelle-Calédonie, où, à présent, là-bas, ils

sont citoyens français et colonisateurs, pas toujours du côté des Canaques.

De l'autre côté d'une vallée qui s'étendait au sud et se dirigeait ensuite vers la ville de Bougie, sur la côte, la petite Kabylie comprenait au nord la chaîne des Babors, la chaîne des Bibans au centre, le défilé des Portes de fer, et, plus au sud, avant le désert, la chaîne du Hodna. En 1945, quand il avait fallu réprimer les troubles de Sétif, la Légion et l'aviation avaient anéanti des villages entiers dans les Babors et la paix ne régnait toujours pas. Des opérations militaires purgeaient les régions de ses rebelles — des meutes de loups. Comme en Indochine, des postes contrôlaient les passages. Par bonheur, avant de quitter Alger, j'avais reçu à l'hôtel Aletti la lettre de l'Elysée qui m'accordait les facilités que j'avais demandées. Devant ce document, les barrages s'ouvrirent. Les ruines nous escortaient, l'armée avait détruit ce que les fellaghas n'avaient pas incendié. Quelquefois nous croisions une automitrailleuse, nous avions l'air honteux de voyageurs qui se glissaient en fraude, des slogans émaillaient notre itinéraire : « le FLN est foutu. FLN = misère, crime. France = paix, prospérité ». A Ighil Ali, on nous reçut avec des embrassades et des saluts à n'en plus finir. Il n'y avait plus de famille Amrouche ni de Pères blancs. Les maisons s'appuyaient les unes sur les autres avec leurs toits de tuiles chargés de pierres pour résister au vent. C'était là qu'Amrouche avait recueilli de la bouche de sa mère Marguerite Fadhma Aït Mansour les poèmes que Guibert a été le premier à publier en 1939, *Chants berbères de Kabylie.* Là aussi naissait la voix étrange, la voix puissante de sa sœur Taos qui n'était qu'un écho de sa mère ; la voix jaillissait des montagnes, emplissait le ciel, faisait trembler la terre et interrogeait Dieu, pareille peut-être à la voix des bergers antiques qui s'appelaient de crête en crête et, seuls face à l'éternité, chantaient leurs amours et se déchiraient aux roches et à eux-mêmes. Un des chefs de la rébellion s'appelait Amirouche. De quel côté aurait pu être l'ami difficile avec qui j'avais franchi tant de caps écumeux et qu'on venait de vider des services de la radio et de la télévision française à Paris ? De mes yeux, des écailles tombaient. La famille de M. Belrachid offrit le couscous, les gens s'étonnaient de voir dans ce coin perdu un Français qui n'était ni soldat ni contrôleur des impôts.

A l'époque où il donna des séries d'articles à *l'Express*, Camus était-il, comme il l'a dit plus d'une fois, malade de l'Algérie comme je le suis encore à grimper dans ma mémoire ? Il avait plu, les rues d'Ighil Ali, si on pouvait appeler rues ces passages pour ânes et chèvres, étaient glissantes et crottées, je me demandais pourquoi j'étais là et ce que je voulais savoir. Il aurait été plus sage de ne pas écouter Clostermann, mais la sagesse m'a toujours manqué et pour le risque j'ai toujours éprouvé un attrait malsain qui doit être aussi le goût de la provocation.

Non loin d'Ighil Ali, dans la chaîne des Bibans, au nord d'un bourg pouilleux vaguement érigé en forteresse, Bordj Boni, il y a, au bout d'un chemin qui longe un ravin presque inaccessible, quelques maisons crénelées en équilibre sur des escarpements. Au sommet de ce piton, l'eau ruisselle de partout. Il y a même une école coranique, et naturellement une djamaa, c'est-à-dire une mosquée avec lieu de palabres d'où l'on voit loin. C'est l'ancien repaire de Mokrani, le chef des Beni Abbès qui leva l'étendard de la révolte contre la France en 1871. La carte d'état-major au cinquante millième n'est pas facile à déchiffrer. Le relief est si tourmenté, les courbes du nivellement sont si serrées, les noms de lieux si difficiles à lire, il y a tant de sources, tant de gourbis, d'oueds, de monts, de marabouts, de rigoles même — car tout est noté —, qu'on s'y perd. C'est le domaine des sangliers, des chèvres, des lièvres, des fouines, du vent, de Dieu aussi. Là, les hommes deviennent des bêtes féroces. Des années après mon voyage, à dos de mulet, j'irai là, je situerai là le cas de conscience d'un capitaine qui me ressemble comme un frère. De retour en Algérie après la débâcle de Sedan, il commande une compagnie du détachement qu'on envoie détruire le fief des Mokrani. Mokrani a déjà été tué, mais sa femme et ses filles vivent là et, contre ses propres chefs, le capitaine refuse de les laisser écrabouiller par l'artillerie. C'est le dernier chapitre du troisième tome des *Chevaux du Soleil*. Dans ce pays sauvage tout en crêtes et en gouffres, si pauvre que la moitié des hommes doivent s'expatrier pour donner du pain aux leurs, et où les femmes, vêtues et peintes comme des idoles, travaillent plus que des mules, il y avait des Kabyles dans les administrations de l'Etat, il y en avait dans l'armée française comme dans les rangs des rebelles,

il y en avait chez les harkis. Amrouche, interlocuteur de Gide, de Claudel, de Mauriac et de Jouhandeau, était un de ceux-là.

Nous gagnâmes Bougie par la vallée de la Soummam, avec une bonne route. Enfin, je respirais.

*
**

Ancienne colonie phénicienne puis romaine, ancienne capitale de souverains hammadides puis almohades, ancien repaire de corsaires, et bâtie sur une énorme roche qui avance dans la mer comme la proue d'un navire, Bougie, quand nous l'avions prise aux Turcs en 1833, n'était riche que de quelques palais mauresques mais offrait toujours ce balcon d'où, de cent mètres de haut, on domine le golfe et l'immensité. Sur la place Foch, qui avait déjà dû s'appeler Jules-César ou Scipion ou peut-être Pétain, on pouvait, au temps de la colonisation, siroter l'anisette en reluquant les filles, provocantes et belles comme dans toute l'Algérie, comme l'était Mirande, ma vierge de Giotto quand je débarquai, en 1927, à Médéa avec ma cantine. A Bougie, il arrivait qu'un ancien président de la République du Portugal, comme Manuel Teixeira-Gomes, autre écrivain révélé par Armand Guibert, soudain frappé de la foudre d'amour, refusât d'aller plus loin et finît ses jours là. C'est à Bougie qu'Isabelle Eberhardt aurait dû débarquer plutôt qu'à Bône, quand elle aborda l'Algérie pour la première fois. Tout à coup, devant Bougie, on croit avoir trouvé la paix, ce qui ne va avec rien, surtout pas avec l'amour. On se dit, je ne sais pourquoi, probablement parce que tout à coup on se sent bien, que le bonheur est là et vous attend. Au sortir de la Kabylie, je me dis que j'allais pouvoir m'arrêter pour contempler la mer et peut-être l'éternité, un mot dont les écrivains abusent volontiers. Sinon l'éternité, du moins quelque chose d'approchant ou encore mieux. Le décor m'aidait. Surtout, j'allais rencontrer un colonel dont on parlait beaucoup.

L'année d'avant, établi sur le plateau entre le massif des Babors et les monts du Hodna, à Bordj-bou-Arreridj, un nom impossible à prononcer quand on n'est pas coutumier de l'arabe, ce colonel avait commandé toute la Petite Kabylie ; il se baladait à travers son territoire avec un hélicoptère comme sur un tapis volant, de la mer au désert, et comme il était, au fond de lui, poète, il se gorgeait de splendeur, de couleurs, là

459

où, plus tard, Isabelle Eberhardt n'avait vu que des rochers déchiquetés, des collines grisâtres, une désolation vaguement dorée par les chaumes. Pour elle, Bordj-bou-Arreridj était un bled morne, triste et désespérant. Pas pour le colonel. Peut-être pour donner à la région de l'éclat, les villages portaient des noms illustres : Tocqueville, Lecourbe, Lavoisier, Colbert, La Fayette. Le colonel tendait des pièges aux rebelles et en tuait beaucoup, mais proprement. On ne trouvait pas chez lui de ces unités infernales que l'armée tolérait, qui m'avaient tant indigné en Indochine et qu'on cachait dans les pavillons d'où s'échappaient parfois des hurlements. Une honte. Pas de ça chez le colonel, compagnon de la Libération et gaulliste. Chez lui, on respectait l'ennemi et les prisonniers avaient droit à des égards. On disait aussi qu'il était d'une intrépidité rare, qu'il ne se baissait jamais et ne hâtait jamais le pas quand les balles claquaient autour de lui. Bref, il avait une légende et son courage physique n'avait d'égal que son courage civique : à ses chefs, que ça leur plaise ou pas, il disait ce qu'il pensait. Il avait eu la chance de recevoir de Gaulle en tournée des popotes, de Gaulle l'avait interrogé sur la situation en Kabylie. Le colonel avait répondu sans détour, le général lui en avait manifesté publiquement de l'estime. Depuis lors, il était le phénomène qui croyait à de Gaulle, l'armée n'en regorgeait pas, et qui cassait du fell. Muté à Bougie, il commandait le secteur. Il transmettait les ordres supérieurs, les exécutait parfois et parfois s'en dictait d'autres à lui-même. Ainsi avait-il débarrassé les alentours des rebelles qui s'y baladaient impunément avant lui. Dans la ville, on n'égorgeait plus, on allait au cinéma, l'ordre régnait. Pour moi, Bougie, c'était surtout connaître le colonel qui commandait là, le colonel Georges Buis. Je lui avais écrit pour lui demander s'il m'autorisait à le rencontrer. Il m'avait répondu : « Venez. » Je sus ensuite que d'Alger, on lui avait téléphoné comme si j'avais été l'ennemi numéro un : « Jules Roy arrive. On vous l'envoie. Débrouillez-vous avec lui. » Ce n'était pas l'état-major qui m'expédiait à lui, c'était moi qui, sans prendre l'avis de l'état-major, souhaitais le voir. Sans m'en douter, j'étais suivi à la piste.

Dans le port, une Marie-Salope raclait les fonds. Elle doit toujours y être, car les courants entraînent là les limons rouges de la Soummam qui se déverse un peu au sud. De sa poitrine épuisée, la drague crachait, éructait, sifflait, grinçait, gémissait,

barrissait. Des boues qu'elle remontait elle chargeait un chaland. Aujourd'hui, à Bougie, tout a changé. Un énorme complexe de réservoirs encombre l'estuaire de la Soummam. Le pétrole a tout pourri. Sur la place qui doit s'appeler maintenant Abd el-Kader, ça sent le gaz et il n'y a plus de cafés. On peut encore regarder la mer, seulement la mer, parce qu'il n'y a plus de filles non plus. Quand j'y passai en avril 1960, on construisait le pipe-line qui partait des puits de Sidi-Messaoud. De Gaulle l'avait survolé.

Du colonel Buis je me souviens d'abord de son képi bleu ciel à galons d'argent. C'était un homme élégant, d'une grande finesse. Des lunettes adoucissaient son visage. Il venait d'Allemagne où il avait commandé le 5e hussards. Buis était un de ces hommes qui ne font pas n'importe quoi et ne se commettent pas avec n'importe qui. Le respect et parfois l'amour du cheval confèrent aux cavaliers une dignité qui les sépare du commun. Même s'il est idiot, un cavalier a au moins pour lui qu'il monte, qu'il voit d'un peu plus haut que les autres. Ainsi n'appartient-il pas tout à fait au reste du monde. S'il est intelligent, alors c'est Lyautey ou peut-être Rommel. Là, c'était Buis. Un gentilhomme, pas n'importe lequel. Quelqu'un de racé, qui ne traitait pas les autres sans façon et qu'on traitait avec honneur. En lui, au-dessus de lui flottait quelque chose comme un rêve. Un chevalier, quand il en existe encore, n'est pas dans la vie : il est à part, ailleurs.

Buis n'était pas non plus quelqu'un de facile. J'appréhendais notre premier contact à cause de mon idée de l'armée, à cause de Murtin tombé en mer pas loin d'ici en 1943, à cause d'Accart, à cause de Brohon, à cause d'hommes que je respectais pour leur intégrité, leur désintéressement et leur ardeur à servir la patrie. Mon vieil article de *l'Express* qu'on se repassait encore dans les popotes était un test. Il ne m'en dit rien. Il me parut vaguement distant, un peu raide et un peu triste, ou peut-être était-ce moi qui l'étais. Comme à un journaliste, il m'exposa la situation militaire qu'il jugeait bonne. Il tenait solidement son secteur et ne circulait pas en automitrailleuse. En parlant des rebelles, il ne disait pas « les fellaghas » mais « les fellouzes », il y avait une certaine aménité dans le mot. La douceur de son langage cachait une grande discrétion. Je lui dis que j'étais là pour essayer de

comprendre, et où aller pour cela ? Est-ce moi qui lui demandai si je pouvais passer quelques jours quelque part avec ses troupes ou lui qui me le proposa ? Il me parla d'une de ses compagnies, pas très loin dans les collines. J'irais où je voudrais.

A peine étais-je rentré à l'hôtel de l'Etoile où Manuel Teixeira-Gomes avait occupé dix ans la chambre 13, que Buis m'appelait : les autorités l'avertissaient que je ne pouvais suivre les opérations que si je disposais d'une carte verte, accordée par les services d'information de la délégation générale. Je téléphonai aussitôt à Alger en tirant argument de la lettre du cabinet de l'Elysée et j'obtins des apaisements. Cette lettre-ordre de mission, c'est tout ce que je dois matériellement à de Gaulle, ce fut la seule attention qu'il m'accorda, puisque je ne fus jamais invité à l'Elysée avec les écrivains. Mais Clostermann non plus, il devait nous considérer comme des gens à part. Il y a deux pages blanches sur mon agenda, deux jours pendant lesquels je ne me souviens plus à quoi on m'employa. Le 12 mai 1960, dans une jeep précédée d'une automitrailleuse, je fus conduit à Toujda.

Pour le lecteur qui n'a rien connu de cette époque, je dirai seulement que je fus reçu par le capitaine de chasseurs à pied qui commandait là, et qu'au poste même où il logeait, il m'attribua une cellule et un lit de camp. Aussitôt je participai aux opérations de la compagnie, j'allai partout où elle allait, je parlai à qui je voulus, j'interrogeai qui je voulus comme je voulus, je me fis montrer les archives de la section administrative spécialisée et les recoupai avec mes propres renseignements.

Toujda était un village tout en longueur à une douzaine de kilomètres au nord de la riche vallée de Soummam, à proximité d'un col et d'une paroi verticale dans les chênes-lièges. De là, au loin vers le sud-est, brillaient les crêtes enneigées du Djurdjura : les oliviers, les figuiers et les caroubiers escaladaient les pentes, les sources abondaient, l'eau ruisselait de partout. En temps de paix, on faisait là quatre récoltes de pommes de terre par an. Depuis, les choses allaient comme elles pouvaient. Au village même, la plupart des boutiques fermées avaient rouvert, un car allait trois fois par semaine à Bougie derrière une automitrailleuse. On disait que, depuis le début des événements, trois mille habitants

avaient fui vers la vallée et vers Bougie où ils grossissaient le nombre des misérables ; neuf cents habitants des villages voisins avaient cherché refuge près du poste militaire dans des logis désertés. De ces gens-là on avait les noms, mais d'autres disparaissaient sans qu'on sût ce qu'ils devenaient. A Toujda, on ne savait plus, à un jour près, qui vivait encore et qui ne vivait plus, ce qui m'étonna, car tout le village était en fiches. On ne connaissait pas le nom des morts des tombes fraîches, sans compter ceux qu'on enterrait par-ci par-là, sous quelques pierres ou branchages. On disait qu'il en était de même dans toute l'Algérie. J'essayai donc de savoir ce qui se passait et quel mécanisme jouait dès que la nuit tombait. J'évitais les harkis. Ils avaient une vie à eux, des chefs à eux, ils dépendaient aussi du capitaine, mais le capitaine ne parlait pas le kabyle et ne pouvait écouter tous les racontars, et puis, entre les fellaghas et les harkis, il avait choisi : il était pour les harkis, rangés sous les plis du drapeau français. Aussi leur accordait-il une certaine liberté d'action.

Les deux premiers jours, la situation me parut inextricable. Puis, avec patience et insistance, observant mille détails et suivant quelques cas à la trace, comparant sur les registres, mois par mois et semaine par semaine, les chiffres des rations alimentaires distribuées par la section administrative, j'obtins des résultats : les manquants étaient bien quelque part. C'est à démêler cela que je m'employai. J'étais jeune, ardent, accrocheur et, à ce moment-là de la guerre, le quadrillage était si serré, avec des forces militaires si bien dénombrées, que pas un mouton n'aurait pu échapper aux contrôles. Il est vrai que pour un mouton, échapper était plus difficile que pour un homme : le mouton se mangeait, il était précieux. Pour un homme, bien des yeux ne voulaient pas voir. Il y avait les harkis, il y avait aussi la pourriture dont Buis n'avait pas voulu chez lui mais qu'il ne pouvait exterminer chez les autres, les DOP, les bourreaux silencieux, les tueurs des ténèbres, les gangsters de l'ombre, massacreurs par idéologie et peut-être, qui sait ? par patriotisme, ces nazis sur qui on m'avait fait déverser des tonnes de bombes au phosphore pendant mes nuits au-dessus de l'Allemagne. Encore la nuit, toujours la nuit. Avec minutie et opiniâtreté, et aussi avec l'aide, parfois involontaire, des services comptables — on ne distribuait plus de semoule ni d'huile aux morts dont on était sûr —, je

découvris ce qu'on me cachait, où allaient ceux qui disparaissaient et surtout combien il y en avait. Le chiffre m'effraya. Le capitaine eut l'air de ne pas s'étonner.

Les fontaines de Toujda avaient été construites par les Romains, une partie de l'aqueduc vers Bougie tenait encore, les pierres avaient pris avec les siècles la couleur de la lumière de midi. Les femmes stériles répandaient de l'huile au pied d'un double phallus sculpté sur la corniche d'un arceau, les soldats relevaient les empreintes de pataugas des rebelles qui venaient aussi puiser de l'eau. Pour moi, cette eau dont nous buvions tous était un symbole. Il faudrait bien finir de s'entretuer, pourquoi attendre ? « C'est eux qui ont commencé », disait le capitaine. Les villages détruits servaient de boîte aux lettres, il y avait d'autres villages que l'armée avait rasés pour créer une zone de misère, et d'autres où l'on avait regroupé la population. De temps en temps, un gradé de la section administrative spéciale posait quelque part un faux billet de dix mille francs sans numéro de la banque d'Algérie et de Tunisie ; derrière était écrit en arabe et en français : « Présente-toi à un berger qui te conduira à un poste français. Tu recevras un vrai billet. » Dix mille francs, c'était une somme en ce temps-là. On disait encore que les fellaghas attendaient les Chinois et les avions égyptiens comme on attend Godot. Nous visitions les familles. Le capitaine autorisait les femmes à récolter les fèves et les pommes de terre. Elles s'en revenaient avec des ânes chargés de fourrage vert et de pauvres trésors : des poêles, des plaques de tôle, des tuiles. Sur leur visage, les larmes avaient creusé des ravinements, on leur arrachait leurs fils ou leur mari ; parfois, quand elles étaient jeunes et belles, il y avait à cause d'elles des ralliements. Les femmes cependant ne cédaient pas au chantage des troupes d'occupation : en chacune d'elles vivait une Antigone.

Nous allions à travers la rocaille, nous visitions les postes voisins. D'autres capitaines discutaient avec moi et parfois se laissaient aller à des confidences : les uns acceptaient les solutions qu'envisageait de Gaulle, d'autres annonçaient qu'ils prendraient le maquis. On a oublié ce que furent pour la France ces années où se jouait le sort de l'Algérie, province française divisée en départements. Entre nous, on se battait, on se tuait pour ça. A côté de Toujda, on reconstruisait, on

entassait des tonnes de tuiles et des rouleaux de barbelés. Quand on interrogeait les enfants sur ce qu'ils deviendraient plus tard, ils montraient sur une crête voisine un camp de détention bourré à craquer et répondaient : « On sera là... »

Comme pour les bêtes sauvages, la nuit était le domaine de la chasse. Les rebelles allaient et venaient comme chez eux, les harkis leur tendaient des pièges, le capitaine sortait aussi. De temps en temps, un coup de feu claquait au loin sous les étoiles. Le capitaine, quand il était là, soufflait dans son micro. Si je demandais quelque chose, il ne répondait pas. Je ne vais pas reprendre en détail tout ce que j'ai vu là. Ça me fait mal encore. Tout est dans ce livre de feu qu'on ne réédite plus parce que la guerre d'Algérie est loin et que les ordinateurs indiquent qu'elle n'intéresse plus personne. Et maintenant que je reparle de tout cela, je dors mal, une fièvre incendie mes veines, je brûle et des frissons courent sur l'échine de ma vieille carcasse.

Quand, deux semaines plus tard, je revins à Bougie, j'avais découvert le chiffre des hommes que l'armée avait fait disparaître à Toujda. A Toujda seulement. Je le dis tout bas à Buis. J'ajoutai que je devais me tromper. « Vous êtes dans la bonne moyenne, me répondit-il. C'est partout pareil. Il y a des endroits où c'est pire. » Quand même, douze cents morts pour une seule commune, douze cents morts dus au DOP, aux bidasses, à mon seul capitaine, un tel monceau de cadavres, c'était un score. Je demandai à Buis si je pouvais en faire état. « Pourquoi pas, puisque c'est la vérité ? » Il me parut comme soulagé, non pas de me voir partir, mais de constater que je n'étais pas venu pour rien, que ce qu'il ne pouvait me dire, lui, je l'avais découvert, que j'étais un bon chien de chasse. A quoi tient parfois le hasard ! Si je n'avais pas rencontré Buis, je ne serais pas allé à Toujda, je n'aurais pas eu les facilités que, grâce à lui, j'obtins. Qui sait ? Peut-être mes conclusions pour la guerre d'Algérie eussent-elles été tout autres.

Notre conversation fut moins tendue qu'à mon arrivée à Bougie. Buis employa devant moi des termes très militaires et même cavaliers, je veux dire un peu lestes, qui me laissèrent penser qu'il était content. Je ne sais pourquoi, quand nous nous connûmes mieux, plus tard, peut-être à cause de son goût pour les femmes d'une certaine classe ou à cause d'une sorte de

comportement passionné qui existe chez lui en toute chose, j'ai pu le comparer à un cardinal portant épée, confesseur de princesses de sang.

A Constantine, je dus saluer le général qui commandait la région. Je m'acquittai de cette corvée sans déplaisir car le général habitait l'ancien palais du bey. Nous ne nous dîmes que des banalités, mais j'obtins l'autorisation de visiter le barrage électrifié qui séparait l'Algérie de la Tunisie. Je m'y rendis aussitôt. Ce n'était pas tout près, on ne facilitait pas mes déplacements, ce qui m'arrangeait plutôt, car je découvrais ainsi beaucoup de détails qui m'auraient échappé. Je mis deux jours pour gagner Bône qui était le lieu de tri, le sas, là où Isabelle Eberhardt, à vingt ans, était arrivée de Genève et de Marseille avec sa mère. Au village de Gambetta, le pont-levis s'abaissa devant moi. Quelque chose aussi commençait à basculer dans mon esprit.

Depuis Constantine, je tirais derrière moi l'image de Lamoricière entraînant ses zouaves à l'assaut. Place de la Brèche, un des lieux les plus importants de la ville, on lui avait élevé une statue monumentale et bravacharde qui m'avait choqué. Lamoricière chargeait, le sabre haut, la bouche ouverte sur un cri qu'on entendait encore. On en était toujours à la prise de Constantine après un siège qu'il avait fallu recommencer en 1837 : une boucherie et le pillage. Là encore, si j'avais été musulman, cette statue m'aurait rappelé de mauvais souvenirs. Par pudeur et simple bon sens, on aurait dû la reléguer au musée de l'armée. Mais non. Des civils patriotes, des préfets, des militaires pensaient qu'ainsi on en imposait.

A Gambetta, on me reçut fraîchement. Les officiers étaient conscients du rôle que jouait cette œuvre gigantesque. Ce n'était pas le mur de l'Atlantique ; c'était, contrôlé par radars, truffé de mines bondissantes, rasé par des tirs de mitrailleuses, le barrage sur la frontière avec mise en valeur de l'organisation DOP. On me promena le long des réseaux, à travers les chicanes, partout où je voulais aller, il ne manquait pas un bouton de guêtre, pas un watt, les groupes électrogènes ronflaient, on se serait cru en mer sur la passerelle d'un croiseur de bataille. C'était une mécanique formidable, un système à tuer qu'il fallait perfectionner sans cesse. Dès qu'un

lièvre touchait un fil, les commandos surgissaient. La nuit, des
projecteurs s'allumaient, des ouragans d'artillerie s'abattaient.
Sur un flanc du barrage se serraient les camps de regroupement
à perpète, les cités de détention avec électrodes et magnéto-
phones pour doux aveux. Comme tout le système de l'armée
en Algérie, cet énorme appareil ne servait à rien. Le problème
était ailleurs. A la popote, les officiers et moi commençâmes à
opposer nos points de vue. Ils obéissaient, je considérais le
problème de plus haut. J'admirais leur abnégation et leur
esprit de sacrifice mais nous n'avions pas la même façon
d'aimer la communauté musulmane. Eux, c'était du Lamoricière amélioré : on soumet, on gagne ; après on concède, on
octroie. Tout en reconnaissant que l'armée française avait des
droits, comme les pieds-noirs, et que la moralité coloniale
n'avait plus cours, chacun restait sur ses positions. Je reconnus
chez les officiers certaines idées camusiennes : justice pour
tous. Pour moi, trop de chances avaient été gâchées. On avait
beau appeler maintenant les Arabes du nom de « Français
musulmans », rien n'avait changé. Mes compatriotes pensaient
que c'étaient des gens en qui on ne pouvait pas avoir confiance
parce qu'ils avaient du monde et de l'au-delà une idée
différente de la nôtre, ce qui est vrai. Quant à mes amis
libéraux, on les plastiquait, quelquefois on les tuait. Puisque
l'armée avait lu Camus, les jeunes officiers tiraient de lui
quelques notions généreuses, au moins ne désignaient-ils pas
les Arabes par les sobriquets courants : bicots, bougnouls,
ratons, troncs de figuier, fromages rouges, melons, pimpins.
On avait semé trop de mépris et il y avait trop de différence
dans l'échelle sociale, trop de crimes avaient été commis par les
DOP, trop de rebelles avaient été jetés dans la mer du haut des
hélicoptères sous le règne de Massu et de Bigeard, trop de
terroristes avaient été torturés par les organisations qui
enfouissaient leurs victimes au bulldozer dans des charniers et,
de l'autre côé, trop de bombes avaient éclaté, trop d'innocents
avaient été massacrés et trop de dévastations commises, bref,
c'était trop tard. Clostermann m'avait poussé à travers la
géhenne qu'était devenue ma terre natale, Camus était dépassé,
et maintenant, lui qui se disait « riche de ses seuls doutes », il
n'était plus. Miséricordieuse en ce sens-là, la mort l'avait
épargné, il n'allait pas être obligé de se ranger du côté des siens
contre les autres. J'avais vu à Tazmalt sur les pentes du

Djurdjura, un vieux colon et sa femme qui m'avaient rappelé mon oncle Jules et les miens. On les avait obligés de s'installer à Alger, et ils étaient revenus, ils ne pouvaient pas vivre ailleurs qu'au milieu de leurs montagnes, dans leur pays. Les militaires avaient coupé des oliviers qui gênaient leur champ de tir ; les fellaghas avaient coupé la vigne. « Quelle sale race », disait la femme sans qu'on sache de qui elle parlait.

L'armée allait jusqu'à envisager pour l'Algérie une certaine indépendance à condition que les pieds-noirs conservent leurs biens. La plupart d'entre eux étaient comme mon frère, de petites gens, d'humbles et courageux travailleurs, mais les autres ? Ceux qui possédaient des milliers d'hectares de vigne, les moulins, les huileries, les transports, les banques ? Là, il faudrait partager. « Nous irons plus loin que vous, les bouchons de champagne sauteront quand nous aurons détruit les cent familles régnantes d'Algérie. » Là, les officiers et moi nous rejoignions.

Long, sec, noueux, élégant, le colonel qui commandait le barrage me retenait parfois le soir après dîner. Une vieille blessure lui rendait la marche difficile et le faisait ressembler à un héros de *Servitude et grandeur militaires*. Il était, comme Buis, compagnon de la Libération et voulait rester sur son barrage jusqu'à la victoire, car il craignait que le FLN ne plonge le pays dans le malheur. Parfois, nous nous heurtions, car il voulait aussi que la France demeure là et je pensais que c'était impossible. L'atmosphère devenait orageuse, des étincelles jaillissaient. Pour moi, il me semblait que j'assistais à la fin de notre puissance militaire, que l'œuvre d'art du barrage était le signe même de notre échec. Quelques fells s'empêtraient dans les barbelés et y grillaient, on les capturait ou ils réussissaient à s'infiltrer. La belle affaire que ce barrage ! On n'arrêtait pas les idées, il fallait discuter, dialoguer. Pire encore que celle d'Indochine, cette guerre était inutile et cruelle, le monde colonial s'était perdu lui-même, nous en étions ses derniers soubresauts, les nations allaient s'articuler autrement, nous assistions à la naissance aux forceps d'une Algérie que nous avions fabriquée avec notre façon de tout nous approprier et d'enseigner en même temps dans les écoles que les hommes naissent libres et égaux en droits.

Nous prolongions nos conversations tard dans la nuit. Parfois je n'en dormais pas. Les dialogues du livre que j'écrivis

468

par la suite contiennent l'essentiel de nos propos. Ensuite, je construisis des répliques qui devinrent classiques et qu'on ne me pardonna pas. Camus n'était plus là pour tempérer ma douleur, je n'en pouvais plus, Clostermann m'avait fourré dans un joli pétrin.

A Bône, je sautai dans l'avion pour Tunis. Quand la police militaire arriva à l'aérodrome pour m'interpeller et me ramener à Alger, l'avion venait de décoller. Bône, c'était là aussi que Malraux, après son expédition de la reine de Saba et au sortir d'une tempête fantastique dans les airs, « dessaoulait du néant », comme il disait. Bône est une ville magique, c'était là encore qu'on avait rassemblé nos équipages après que nous eûmes franchi la mer pour continuer la lutte en juin 1940. Nous nous y étions beaucoup ennuyés avec Ventré. Pour nous consoler de ne plus pouvoir voler, il n'y avait qu'une longue plage de sable et de belles filles, plus farouches qu'il n'y paraissait, pareilles à celles qu'admirait tant, à Bougie, l'ancien président du Portugal.

Dans l'avion qui me ramenait à Orly, j'écrivis aussitôt ce que je pris pour les premières pages de mon livre, et qui furent en réalité les dernières : des réflexions sur la nature de cette guerre et sur la façon dont l'armée s'y comportait. A peine à Paris, je demandai un rendez-vous à Beuve-Méry qui me reçut dans son sévère bureau du *Monde*, m'interrogea sur mon voyage et promit de me dire le lendemain s'il publiait mon texte. L'article parut les 8 et 9 juin 1960, en première page d'abord, sous un titre « Le conflit algérien », puis sous un autre : « L'esprit de révolte ». A la fin du mois de juillet, l'administration du journal me fit parvenir un chèque de vingt nouveaux francs que je fis encadrer dans mon bureau. Je l'ai toujours. En ce temps-là, au *Monde* on travaillait pour la gloire.

Quelques jours plus tard, je courus m'enfermer au Pays basque. Là, bourrelé d'inquiétudes, je devins pareil à une ombre. Un autre avait pris place en moi qui écoutait ce qui m'était dicté. Libéré de tout, j'avançais sans crainte et sans rien ménager à travers ma conscience déchirée, je taillais ma route à coups d'épée, comme au moment de ma rupture avec Pétain, lors de mon passage sur l'autre bord en novembre 1942. L'Indochine n'avait été qu'un moment d'aveuglement. Partagé

entre la colère et la pitié, je racontai mon itinéraire à travers le pays qui autrefois avait été ma patrie. Je n'inventai rien. Pendant son voyage au Congo, Gide dissertait sur *Cinna* et *Iphigénie*, j'étais loin de ces délicatesses de pensée. Parfois, dans la crainte qu'on ne me crût pas, j'hésitais encore à dire ce que j'avais vu et entendu.

A Tunis, où j'étais resté peu de temps, ma rencontre avec les gens du Front ne m'avait pas impressionné. Je me méfiais. Amrouche était-il là ? Je savais vaguement qu'il servait de négociateur plus ou moins accrédité entre de Gaulle et Ferhat Abbas : ainsi expliquait-il les facilités que la police des frontières lui accordait. A Sakhiet Sidi Youssef, le village bombardé par nous en représailles de je ne sais plus quoi, on me conduisit au camp des réfugiés. Là je vis une petite fille, devenue folle après le bombardement aérien et attachée à un piquet par la cheville, comme un ânon, pour l'empêcher de vaguer. Comme je la regardais avec pitié, un vieil Arabe vint à moi et me dit : « C'est ta France à toi qui a fait ça. » Sa voix vibrait d'une sorte de désespoir qui m'atteignit. J'avais vu ce dont nous étions capables en Indochine. Ici, avec la même conscience professionnelle, nous rasions les mechtas. « ... ta France à toi.. » Tout à coup je me détachai de cette France qui n'était pas la mienne. C'était déjà ce que j'avais éprouvé quand on grillait le delta du Tonkin au napalm et qu'on passait les suspects à la gégène, mais là, c'était mon aviation à moi, celle qu'on avait envoyée avec moi sur les usines de la Ruhr, sur Leipzig et sur les îles de la Frise où l'Allemagne construisait des armes secrètes. A présent, les nazis c'était nous, hélas.

Mon Dieu, quelle guerre cruelle
Je trouve deux hommes en moi...

Il y a longtemps que Robert Kanters m'avait appliqué ces vers de Racine que nous chantions au séminaire. De son côté, mon ami le poète Jean Pélégri a identifié ces deux hommes : c'est don Quichotte et Sancho Pança. Sancho occupe souvent la scène, mais dès qu'il cède la parole ou qu'il a le dos tourné, don Quichotte reprend l'avantage avec vigueur et arrogance. Hélas, hélas, je me reconnais sous les traits de ce noble

hidalgo, parfois grotesque, plastronnant, haranguant avec hauteur. Cependant, mes ennemis n'ont pas toujours été des moulins à vent, la dame de mes pensées n'a jamais été Dulcinée et je n'ai pas toujours monté Rossinante. De don Quichotte ou de Sancho, ce n'est pas don Quichotte qui a le mieux combattu, le mieux choisi entre tous les hasards de la vie, Sancho a souvent tenu la plume, et souvent, si don Quichotte agit, c'est Sancho qui parle. Parfois l'inverse. Sancho me répète toujours que si, au lieu de ma petite bédouine, j'étais tombé sur une famille de colons égorgés, j'aurais, à l'inverse, dénoncé ·la sauvagerie de la rébellion, crié vengeance et poussé les miens à prendre les armes pour défendre leurs terres, leurs biens et leurs femmes au lieu de boucler leurs valises. Qui sait ? Digne de mon oncle Jules et des morts qui, à travers les générations, m'auraient béni, j'aurais peut-être fouaillé ceux qui fichaient le camp honteusement. Autour de nous, c'était la débandade, personne n'avait plus foi en rien, même pas l'armée. Don Quichotte apostropha un capitaine avec des mots qu'on a souvent montés en épingle pour me louer ou m'accabler. Au dernier moment, Camus modérait don Quichotte et reprenait le dessus, mais je n'étais plus à ses côtés.

XIX

Adagio

LE DIMANCHE 17 juillet 1960, sautant du train de Bayonne, je déposai, comme il me l'avait demandé, chez René d'Uckermann, rue du Cherche-Midi, mon manuscrit qui n'avait pas encore de titre, puis je filai à Verrières.

Louise me dit que j'avais changé. J'avais maigri, mes yeux étaient brûlés de fièvre. D'un geste vague j'esquivai les questions et me laissai aller à ma joie d'être dans une famille qui m'était chère et où on ne soulevait jamais de problèmes qui pouvaient diviser. Les affaires qui ne marchaient pas et les amours suffisaient. Vite un verre de champagne, vite des nouvelles de Gaston, le coq de Bandiagara. Malgré sa petite taille, c'était encore un rude tombeur de poules, paraît-il. Les invités arrivaient, on s'embrassait. Louise essuyait une larme et jouait son rôle auprès de sa cour, les lustres brillaient, du feu brûlait dans la cheminée du salon bleu. Parfois apparaissaient de vieilles passions ou dévotions de Louise, qu'on examinait jalousement ou cruellement, en se demandant comment les choses avaient pu se nouer, oui, comment ? A Verrières, il y avait du cœur à revendre, de la beauté, de la chaleur, du bonheur. On se mettait à table, les flambeaux donnaient de l'éclat à l'argenterie, aux visages, aux yeux. Parfois surgissait une immense vedette comme Orson Welles que Louise tutoyait, ou Marlène Dietrich qui semblait voguer sur l'aile d'un nuage. Alors, immense folie, le festin durait toute la soirée. Les conversations bourdonnaient, les rires fusaient ; le vin, un petit bordeaux, déliait les langues mieux que des crus orgueilleux servis par des larbins. N'était-ce pas chaque fois un peu, en moins somptueux, le festin de Balthazar, le dernier

roi de Babylone ? Qui pouvait venir, comment ce règne époustouflant à la recherche et à la célébration du bonheur pouvait-il se terminer ? Qui, de nous tous, était Balthazar ? Qui pouvait-on attendre encore ? On aurait dit que Louise se le demandait aussi en regardant par-dessus notre épaule, en écoutant les approches de la nuit, les voix qui s'y perdent, le nouveau poème qu'elle disait déjà, qui lui montait de cette chaleur et qu'elle allait signer de son trèfle à quatre feuilles dont toute sa vie était semée. Je m'étourdissais, je chassais les images et les sombres pressentiments qui me poursuivaient, je n'accordais que la moitié de moi-même à ce raout une fois de plus improvisé. Après le poker menteur où chacun se groupait selon ses affinités, on s'en allait, les voitures s'évanouissaient comme par magie. Je pensais au soir où Olivier de Vilmorin avait dérapé sur le verglas et s'était tué, et pourtant, à chaque retour de Verrières, j'étais apaisé.

Mon manuscrit comptait à peine deux cents pages. René d'Uckermann avait promis de me rappeler. Il me demanda une journée de grâce et eut ce mot : « Evidemment, vous avez un ton bien convaincant. » Le lendemain, il se déclara enthousiasmé et effrayé. « Etes-vous sûr des douze cents morts dans ce village ? » Après quoi, comme je le craignais, il s'éclipsa. Désormais M. d'Uckermann était toujours en conférence. Enfin sa secrétaire m'annonça qu'elle venait de taper un pneu pour moi : le livre allait déclencher de violentes polémiques, le ton trop amer portait atteinte à la politique du général de Gaulle.

J'avais craint ce contretemps, j'avais pensé à proposer mon ours ailleurs. A qui songer maintenant ? Paul Flamand qui dirigeait les éditions du Seuil me fit dire que cela ne l'intéressait pas. Je crus discerner là une manœuvre, mais de qui ? Kanters me suggéra un éditeur peu engagé : Albin Michel. André Sabatier en était le directeur littéraire, je laissai une copie de mon texte rue Huyghens, puis décidai de retourner rue Racine, dans la forteresse Flammarion où je demandai, avec force, d'Uckermann. J'attendis, puis, muette, une secrétaire me rendit mon manuscrit entouré, était-ce un hasard ? d'un mince lien doré. Mes espoirs s'envolaient puisqu'on n'avait signé aucun contrat, et, depuis ma rupture avec la NRF, je savais qu'on ne pratiquait pas la charité dans l'édition. Cela me choqua et, un moment, me fit douter de

tout. N'était-ce pas plutôt parce que mon manuscrit ne valait rien ? Sans doute mon texte était-il un cri de douleur et peut-être un délire d'écrivain plus qu'un travail bien ficelé. Sans doute aussi, à jouer le sort de l'Algérie sur l'apparition d'une petite folle, faisais-je preuve d'une naïveté dangereuse.

J'eus recours à une amie illustre, Annabella, star de cinéma, qui jura de me réconcilier avec les Gallimard et n'imaginait pas d'échouer. Elle fut reçue par Gaston et Claude. Elle leur dit que je venais d'écrire un récit pathétique, si déchirant que ce serait désolation qu'il parût ailleurs que chez eux. On l'écouta. On allait réfléchir, étudier mon cas. Quel cas ? Le lendemain, elle téléphona à Gaston. Elle eut son fils Claude : la réponse était non, je les avais « trop gravement offensés ». Pour Albin Michel, c'était encore non : on ne me croirait pas. Je me vis soudain entouré d'épées de feu. D'un pas mal assuré, je m'en fus aux éditions de Minuit, rue Bernard-Palissy, où je grimpai l'étroit escalier d'un ancien bordel, tout près de celui où Amrouche avait régné aux éditions Charlot. Jérôme Lindon avait la réputation d'un pur. Il l'a toujours. Il me promit de me rendre sa décision le lendemain matin.

Dévoré de doutes sur moi-même, je courus à l'église Saint-Sulpice, miséricorde peut-être disposée là pour les réprouvés comme moi, et m'abîmai dans une sorte de panique, perdu, banni, entravé, ligoté. Même si Jérôme Lindon me publiait, mon livre serait saisi comme la plupart de ceux qu'il éditait. Comme je sortais, je tombai par hasard sur Gaëtan Picon qui traversait la place. Il occupait un poste au cabinet de Malraux. L'avais-je revu depuis Beyrouth ? Je m'entends lui parler, convaincu du pire par mon naturel, le visage sillonné de larmes. Picon me dit : « Tout n'est peut-être pas si noir. Il n'y a pas que Gallimard et Flammarion à Paris. Contactez Julliard. C'est un homme courageux et dans la vague… » René Julliard était à Bayreuth au festival Wagner, il me demanda par télégramme de lui envoyer mon manuscrit. Tout à coup je me remis à espérer. Huit jours après, dans un nouveau télégramme de cinquante mots, il s'engageait à sortir le livre deux mois plus tard.

Mon texte fut aussitôt sous presse. De tous les titres auxquels j'avais songé, un seul était vrai : *la Guerre d'Algérie.*

Mais ce mot-là était tabou et personne encore n'avait osé s'en servir tant le risque était grand. Christian Bourgois, alors conseiller de Julliard, conclut un accord avec *l'Express*, les imprimeurs ne tardèrent pas à recevoir la visite des renseignements généraux et Christian Bourgois se prépara à fabriquer le livre hors des frontières dans le cas où la composition serait détruite en France. Amrouche était en Suisse. Je lui envoyai une copie de mon texte et il me répondit qu'il l'avait lu dans la nuit même, et que c'était ce qu'il attendait de moi. Fin août, je signai mon service de presse rue de l'Université, dans le bureau même de René Julliard, face aux fenêtres de l'hôtel Gallimard. Quelques jours plus tard, *l'Express* paraissait avec le titre sur toute la première page et, dans les librairies, le livre s'arrachait. Le bruit courut qu'il avait été question au conseil des ministres de le saisir. Edmond Michelet, garde des Sceaux, s'y était opposé et le général de Gaulle l'avait approuvé. Dans une déclaration à l'AFP, René Char et Jean Grenier m'accusèrent d'abuser du nom de Camus et dénoncèrent ma mauvaise foi. Excommunié par eux, je n'étais plus de l'Eglise dont ils se disaient les héritiers.

Ma brouille avec les Gallimard dura, je me demande comment. Sur moi qui ne songe qu'à me réconcilier avant le coucher du soleil, comme l'évangile en fait commandement, un rideau de haine tomba. Les gens qui appartenaient à l'illustre maison n'osaient plus m'adresser la parole quand ils me rencontraient. J'existais quand même. Parfois je repassais devant ce qui avait été la loge de Mme Bour et le recoin de M. Hirsch, mais personne ne m'attendait plus. Il m'arrivait de rencontrer Gaston au Montalembert où il déjeunait toujours seul et triste, à la retraite. Les décisions de sa maison ne lui appartenaient plus. On se saluait. Se souvenait-il ?

Une fois de plus, ma vie changea. J'allai provoquer les parachutistes dans leur garnison de Pau avec une conférence sur Camus : l'atmosphère fut tendue, mais rien ne se passa. Le lendemain, à Bayonne, des menaces furent proférées contre moi et le préfet interdit la conférence. Je quittai une fois de plus le Pays basque et mon enchanteresse, et me jetai à corps perdu dans le combat que menait *l'Express*. Cette bourrasque dura deux ans. Quand on lui demandait autrefois comment reviendrait au pouvoir le général de Gaulle, Malraux répon-

dait : « Par un complot de l'armée d'Indochine qui croira se servir de lui et s'en mordra les doigts. » Une fois, dans un meeting du RPF, je l'avais entendu hurler contre les communistes devant un micro, dingue, hoquetant, et annoncer de Gaulle comme le Sauveur des Ecritures. Il ne s'était pas trompé. En 1958, l'armée d'Indochine et d'Algérie avait, dans un énorme bruit de bottes, ramené un souverain, un roi, de Gaulle qu'elle croyait à sa dévotion, et de Gaulle, non sans machiavélisme, avait forcé l'armée à lui obéir. Revenu au pouvoir, il ne reniait pas tout ce qu'il avait dit sur l'Algérie ; il ne l'oubliait pas non plus. Sans cesse, il rejetait le passé comme des lames d'écume et continuait, impavide. Tout devant lui devait céder.

Dès mon arrivée à *l'Express,* je me plongeai dans la mêlée dont Camus m'avait jusqu'alors préservé. J'assistai à une conférence de presse à l'Elysée. Je vis de Gaulle écarter une tenture de damas rouge, le rideau de scène, apparaître sur l'estrade et s'asseoir sur son trône. Devant lui, à ses pieds, ministres et journalistes se serraient sous les lustres rutilants, les caméras tournaient le visage de Malraux crispé dans l'adoration, rejetant une mèche sur son front. Plein d'orgueil, fougueux dans ses répliques, souvent goguenard et parlant par-delà l'éternité, de Gaulle, de qui j'avais toujours admiré le courage civique et le courage physique, n'était plus le même homme qui m'avait convoqué rue de Solférino et m'avait écouté sans m'interrompre. Je m'en voulais encore de n'avoir pas répondu à son invitation. Pas assez intrigant pour cela, je ne l'aimais pas assez non plus, et croyais trop peu en lui à cette époque. La répression atroce qu'il avait déclenchée à Sétif, son jugement abrupt à propos de l'Indochine, l'homme d'Eglise qu'il avait mis là-bas comme responsable de la politique, un Leclerc conciliant qu'il n'avait pas soutenu, tout m'avait déçu, à commencer par le RPF qu'il avait fondé. Un parti ! Qu'avais-je à voir avec un général qui prenait la tête d'un parti ? Quant à Malraux, peut-être aurais-je dû, malgré Doyon, le rencontrer. Echaudé avec Montherlant, j'en étais, j'en suis toujours à vouloir que les écrivains qui manient des héros ne soient pas trop différents d'eux. Saint-Exupéry restait mon exemple. Chez Malraux, il se désignait trop, et par trop de mythomanie, comme l'égal de Lawrence d'Arabie, chez qui personne n'aurait pu démêler le vrai du faux. Je n'ai rien contre

l'imaginaire, mais n'aime pas qu'on se donne pour qui on n'est pas. Malraux tel qu'il était aurait dû se suffire à lui-même.

Rompu, depuis l'Ecole de guerre, à ses auditoires, de Gaulle parlait, avec des gestes lourds, un style d'Etat un peu guindé, enveloppant ses réponses dans des épaisseurs de nuages catégoriques : « Voilà ce que la France attend... La France dit, la France pense... » La France, c'était lui et tout le monde s'en félicitait. Le roi était homme de théâtre, l'homme de théâtre jouait au roi, Malraux se raclait la gorge et, son éternelle mèche sur le front, opinait du bonnet. L'aventurier de génie qu'il était servait à présent le roi de France. Il aurait aussi bien servi Staline si les staliniens avaient triomphé. Il servait qui pouvait le servir.

Resurgi à l'actualité, je renouai du coup avec les déjeuners de Florence. L'hôtel Meurice sur les Tuileries, discret, un peu morne, était moins tape-à-l'œil que le Crillon. Paulhan présidait toujours, de plus en plus lointain et absent, académicien co-auteur de *Histoire d'O*, entouré à présent d'autres académiciens. Parmi les fauves édentés, Jean Denoël ajoutait parfois quelque poète dans cette ménagerie où, depuis près de quinze ans, tout ternissait et jaunissait. Florence était moins belle, plus lourde. Elle se parait davantage, souriait mécaniquement, buvait autant et agitait toujours son bâtonnet dans son champagne. Les secrétaires et dames de compagnie s'affaissaient, flasques, tout s'écroulait sauf Paulhan au cruel sourire de marbre parmi vieillards et candidats vieillards avides d'honneurs et de situations, tous impétrants, soupirants, aspirants ou nouveaux promus. Un célèbre amateur d'art chuchotait que son élection lui avait coûté cent millions de centimes en invitations. Nous profitions mécaniquement de la nôtre : hors-d'œuvres, fameuse sole Dugléré, rôti de bœuf haricots verts et pommes vapeur, fromages, bombe glacée, n'empêche, le cadre était là, le bordeaux aussi. Réplique de son chef-d'œuvre *l'Ordre*, Arland était d'une fragile rondeur et d'une rigueur triste. De ses compagnons, Florence tirait de moins en moins de plaisir. Sans Léautaud, le jeudi était sans risque d'apostrophe et sans éclat. Jouhandeau flanqué de l'éternelle et charbonneuse Caryatis perdait son insolence, il lui fallait Mauriac en face de lui, et Mauriac s'embêtait dans les rares déjeuners où il se traînait encore. Au moment de la sortie de mon livre dont personne n'aurait osé parler là, il avait

hoché la tête et m'avait dit, en se couchant presque sur moi, de sa voix de confessionnal à péchés mortels : « Vous y êtes allé un peu fort. » Le mot de Camus à mon premier article sur l'armée, j'y allais toujours un peu fort. Comment donc fallait-il y aller ? J'avais cependant, selon Jean Schlumberger, l'ami de Gide, le don de convaincre.

En sortant de l'hôtel Meurice nous traversions les Tuileries, je fulminais, ce qui scandalisait un peu la belle Dominique Rollin. « Bof », concluait Kanters. Quinze jours après, nous revenions, nous attendions Godot. Je me demandais si Florence avait encore, au fond de son œil vert, un zeste, un rien de ce qui avait été sa nuit de Chartres avec son premier mari : il n'y paraissait pas et qu'en aurais-je fait ? Elle se complaisait dans l'ennui où elle baignait, comme dans une tombe, elle luisait déjà dans la gloire immobile des cimetières, les sentiments n'avaient jamais compté pour elle. La puissance suffisait, que parfois elle mettait en danger, comme elle s'y était risquée sous l'Occupation : elle méprisait et ignorait la peur. Quand Jünger notait dans son *Journal*, en 1943, qu'elle s'était cassé la jambe, il ne disait pas où. Une lettre de Céline à cette époque fournissait la réponse : la nuit, et ivre, au bas de son escalier, à Montmartre. « J'ai refusé d'aller la voir dans son lit, comme elle m'y conviait, à la soigner ! » Elle arrivait rue Girardon, où habitait alors Céline, en compagnie de Marie Bell et avec leur dîner, Céline à qui elle essayait d'acheter des manuscrits était bien forcé de les recevoir.

J'allai à Metz interroger le colonel Argoud qui accusait le Général de forfaiture, j'allai à Tunis interviewer Ferhat Abbas. A la foire de Francfort, Claude Gallimard demandait au représentant de la maison Julliard si, au moment où on m'avait embauché, on savait que nous étions brouillés, Gallimard et moi. Peut-être un écrivain coupable de mon crime aurait-il dû mourir de misère ? Le général de Gaulle m'écrivit une nouvelle lettre, dans laquelle il approuvait ma position sur l'Algérie. Seuls, à *l'Express*, l'aimaient François Mauriac dans son bloc-notes, et Jean Daniel dans de subtiles analyses des relations entre la rébellion et l'Elysée ; de mon côté, en m'efforçant de tenir tête à l'armée, je pensais le servir. Provocateur froid et obstiné, Roger Stéphane me lança à la télévision comme une torpille dans un « portrait souvenir » de Vigny. Ce fut le moment que choisit le Théâtre en rond pour monter ma pièce

le Fleuve Rouge dont, jusqu'à présent, personne n'avait voulu. L'Indochine devenait prétexte à la guerre d'Algérie : dans un poste attaqué, un capitaine menaçait d'abattre son lieutenant sur le point de trahir. Michel Piccoli, à l'époque comédien peu connu, tint le rôle du capitaine, Eric Le Hung celui de l'officier vietnamien, la répétition générale fut un four, nous n'eûmes qu'un bon papier de Jacques Lemarchand dans *le Figaro littéraire* et, malgré Piccoli, nous ne tînmes pas un mois. A Piccoli je me liai par une fervente amitié. Les amitiés, hélas, sont souvent de clocher, elles vivent quand on partage le pain et le sel, et Koestler écrit qu'il est difficile d'être à l'aise avec quelqu'un qui est promu officier après avoir servi avec vous comme simple soldat. Ce fut le cas lorsque Piccoli devint soudain vedette de cinéma. Je gardai longtemps pour lui un attachement qui, faute d'aliment, dépérit. Dans un livre qui a pour titre son propre nom, il a même oublié qu'il a joué un rôle dans *le Fleuve Rouge* devant des rangées de banquettes vides. Il s'amusa une fois ou deux à faire ronfler sa Porsche jusqu'à Vézelay, puis se laissa ensevelir sous sa charge de gloire. De mon côté, j'étais en butte à beaucoup d'attaques. Un jour, comme *l'Express* avait publié la lettre d'un diplomate français d'Amérique du Sud qui m'insultait, je demandai à ce gentleman de prendre l'avion au plus tôt avec une épée : je l'attendais. Au cocktail annuel du *Figaro*, François Mauriac me reçut en jouant l'épouvante : ce diplomate était l'un de ses gendres. Tant mieux. Je ne désarmai pas. Le duel n'eut pas lieu, ce ne fut pas de ma faute.

Toute l'armée me haïssait. J'en souffrais bêtement. Pour beaucoup d'officiers, j'étais un félon. Certains d'entre eux, je le sus plus tard, voulaient me descendre et suspendre mon cadavre à un croc de boucherie comme ça se pratiquait couramment à la fin de la guerre. « Vous ne serez pas plus insulté par eux que je le fus pendant la guerre d'Espagne », me dit un jour Corniglion-Molinier rencontré par hasard. Il ajouta : « Certains officiers me tournaient le dos, d'autres m'écrivaient : « Ne vous étonnez pas si je ne vous serre pas la main », le mot de Gaston Gallimard pour moi au moment de la mort de Camus. « Malraux et moi, ajouta Corniglion, on nous refusait l'entrée dans les mess d'officiers. » Malraux ne s'est pas vanté de cela dans ses *Antimémoires* et il ne parle de

Corniglion-Molinier que dans son équipée de la reine de Saba. En 1943, à l'époque où Malraux vivait avec Josette Clotis, j'avais croisé Corniglion-Molinier (Edouard, Alfred, Flaminius) à Londres, à l'état-major de nos forces aériennes. Il revenait de Libye et allait être promu général de brigade, il avait une longue tête olivâtre de serpent et brûlait des *Capstain* au bout d'un fume-cigarette en écume de mer. Tiré à quatre épingles, précieux, un peu rasta ou dandy, je l'aurais plutôt vu dans l'armée du prince de Saxe, mercenaire. Quinze ans plus tard, ministre d'Etat, Corniglion m'invitait à dîner avec Gallois. Ce soir-là, nous parlâmes de l'Espagne et de Malraux beaucoup plus que de l'Algérie. « C'est la même chose, disait Corniglion. L'armée est toujours en retard. Elle court toujours après les victoires qu'elle n'a pas eues. Quant aux officiers, ils sont comme nous avons été : pas très malins. »

Puis il en vint à Malraux. Quand Malraux avait eu le Goncourt en 1934, on se l'arrachait dans les dîners en ville. Un soir où Corniglion était là, Malraux, jaloux de Lawrence d'Arabie, le ballon de cognac à la main, parlait du Yémen d'où revenait un ancien pharmacien de Djedda déguisé en marchand et monté sur un âne hermaphrodite. Malraux voulait y aller aussi, déguisé en Persan. C'était dangereux, Corniglion avait lancé : « L'avion existe. » Le lendemain, Malraux lui téléphonait et Corniglion arrangeait tout : Paul-Louis Weiller fournissait l'avion ; *l'Intransigeant* et Hachette l'argent, Corniglion piloterait, Malraux photographierait. La légende datait de trente siècles, il n'y avait plus la moindre trace de la reine de Saba, mais au Caire, le correspondant de *l'Intran* les aida et ils partirent. Sur la côte sud du Yémen, personne n'était capable de situer Mareb, la ville fameuse, Malraux savait-il seulement manier les lourds appareils de prise de vue ? Savait-il changer les magasins de plaques ? Qu'importe ! L'irréel est son domaine, et la vérité ce que les autres ne distinguent pas. En lisière d'un désert jaune et blanc aux rivières taries, le vent tourbillonnait, Malraux revint avec des images de murailles effondrées, d'éboulements, de coulées de sable. Où avait-il trouvé que la reine était ensevelie dans un cercueil de cristal que veillait un serpent immortel ? Où, surtout, avait-il appris que la reine avait des jambes inégales ? Où les avait-il mesurées ? Pour me consoler de l'armée, Corniglion m'assura que les jugements des militaires comptaient peu.

Des bruits de putsch couraient parce que de Gaulle suscitait de terribles haines, des complots se formaient, comme jadis à Rome contre César. Les conjurés étaient des hommes d'honneur qui ne pardonnaient pas d'avoir été trompés par lui, comme si un roi tout-puissant, placé sur le trône par eux et oint par le peuple, pouvait, après son sacre, avoir des intérêts suprêmes de la nation les mêmes vues qu'avant.

Aveugle à tout et, comme à Suez, refusant de mesurer les conséquences de ce qu'elle rêvait de faire, l'armée voulait envahir la Tunisie pour en finir avec la rébellion qu'elle croyait matée. A l'époque où j'écris ces Mémoires, le déchirement des partis ne mène qu'à des oppositions de propos, des joutes oratoires et des élections. Dans les années 1960, l'enjeu de la nation se jouait dans les consciences, et l'homme qui allait en décider était un héros de Shakespeare. La guerre civile menaçait, le corps des parachutistes semblait un fer de lance pointé sur de Gaulle, dont la brigade de blindés de Rambouillet restait le seul soutien, près de Paris.

J'allai à Madrid interroger Salan, chef de la sédition. Salan gardait sa superbe, sa rouerie, et accusait de Gaulle de tous les crimes. Bigeard, qui avait acquis sous Massu une solide réputation, se sentait devenir à son tour « sauveur de la patrie » et n'attendait qu'un signe d'En-Haut. Une nuit, on annonça que les avions d'Alger allaient déverser une division de paras sur nous, le Premier ministre exhorta les patriotes à courir aux aérodromes pour barrer les routes : « *Allez-y à pied, à cheval, en voiture.* » Nous fûmes quelques-uns, sur le conseil d'Edgar Faure qui nous avait réunis dans un café discret, à patrouiller le long de la frontière de Belgique à l'écoute des nouvelles : en cas de dictature, nous voulions continuer à défendre de Gaulle hors de France. Finalement il ne se passa rien. A l'aube, nous étions rentrés. Le ministre des armées expédia Bigeard à N'Djamena, au fin fond de l'Afrique, où son impatience s'épuisa. Plus tard, député après avoir été, sous Giscard, secrétaire d'Etat à la Défense, il proclama son dévouement à la mémoire de De Gaulle et osa claironner que s'il avait été algérien, il aurait été dans le maquis. J'ai dit cela longtemps avant lui, et à un moment où cela signifiait quelque chose ; j'ai même écrit à Bigeard, à l'époque, pour le convaincre de servir là-bas un drapeau tricolore frappé de

l'étoile et du croissant. Les idées ne sont pas son fort et il n'a jamais risqué un blâme pour ce qui ne l'avantage pas.

Le putsch, on s'en souvient, avait une double tête en quatre personnes. La première tête était Salan revenu de Madrid. La deuxième, Maurice Challe, mon ancien chef d'escadrille de Bron en 1935, qui avait mené carrière dans les états-majors et brillamment fini comme commandant en chef en Algérie : gonflé de vent, il ne possédait ni la force d'âme ni le prestige nécessaire. Le troisième membre du complot, un mameluk, était un ancien officier d'aviation, oranais de naissance. Du quatrième j'ai presque oublié le nom, Zeller, jusqu'à me demander à quoi il pouvait servir. Tout cela sentait la caserne et la dictature de fayots. De ce pronunciamiento de plastrons, rien ne pouvait sauver César sinon César lui-même. Il parla à la télévision et son verbe eut raison de tout, le « quarteron de généraux en retraite » s'effondra, Challe se rendit comme on sait, avec dignité, Salan et mon compatriote s'évanouirent dans la nature et crurent qu'ils allaient pouvoir jouer les poissons dans l'eau. Ils n'étaient pas Mao et les pieds-noirs n'étaient pas des Chinois. Le quatrième conjuré disparut corps et biens.

Acheter quoi que ce fût en Algérie à cette époque d'attentats, de vols, de crimes, ne serait venu à l'esprit de personne, surtout pas à l'esprit de Florence Gould. Il y avait chez moi une telle foi en l'avenir, une telle conviction que l'Algérie ne pourrait pas être indépendante sans nous, un tel besoin d'administrer la preuve que nous avions raison, nous les illuminés de la coexistence et de l'amitié entre les peuples, que mon devoir était de montrer combien, dans une situation si hasardeuse, je croyais à une Algérie de bonheur et de paix : j'essayai de racheter la ferme de mes grands-parents déjà vendue aux Arabes. Drôle d'idée au moment où tout s'effondrait, où on tuait par plaisir, où rien ne valait plus rien ! Si encore j'avais combiné une affaire comme d'acheter à la baisse, mais j'ai toujours tout ignoré de la Bourse, sinon en achetant quelques livres sterling en 1940. Moi qui me crois si malin quand il s'agit de juger l'adversaire, comment ai-je pu espérer qu'une fois vainqueurs, les Algériens se montreraient généreux à l'égard de leurs anciens maîtres, les colons ! Par la force des choses, mon projet tomba à l'oued.

J'étais très lié avec un maître des requêtes au Conseil d'Etat, Paul Teitgen, qui avait été un moment, sous Massu, secrétaire général de la préfecture de police à Alger. Il avait connu Bigeard, la sinistre villa Sésini sur les hauts d'El Biar où l'on interrogeait et où l'on tuait, puis on l'avait vidé de son poste quand on s'était aperçu qu'il défendait les droits des suspects. Inflexible, insouciant des dangers qu'il courait, il témoignait en faveur des persécutés, et, dans les prétoires et les meetings, dénonçait d'une terrible voix les abominations qu'il avait vues. Mince, élégant, pétri de fer, noir de poil et de vêture, déjà chauve, l'œil lançant des éclairs derrière des lunettes d'écaille, il ressemblait, malgré son nœud papillon, à un juge de l'inquisition espagnole dénonçant les inquisiteurs. Pour moi, il fut un exemple de droiture, de loyauté, d'intransigeance, soutenant de Gaulle sans l'appui de l'Elysée quand les factieux semblaient triompher, plaçant au-dessus de tout, en tous lieux et à chaque instant, la République. Pétain était diablement loin. Loin aussi le temps où, jeune lieutenant à Satory, je m'indignais qu'on pût utiliser l'armée contre les Croix-de-feu en sédition.

Depuis l'échec du putsch, l'OAS menaçait et frappait. Elle prétendait avoir des réseaux partout et abusait de l'intoxication. Beaucoup d'officiers s'y ralliaient dans l'obsession d'un nouveau putsch qui réussirait. A l'écoute des flashes des radios, et prêts à disparaître chez les uns ou chez les autres, moi à Verrières, nous prêtions attention à tout ce qui pouvait se dissimuler sous le tapis brosse, mais nous ne songeâmes jamais à nous placer sous la protection de quiconque. Trépidante, la vie nous excitait, l'amour et l'amitié aussi, je ne ratais pas un match du Racing, il me semblait retrouver Camus. Là où il reposait, il n'avait plus à déclarer de quel côté il se rangeait.

A *l'Express*, l'alignement des loges de la rédaction ressemblait à des cabines de bain sans la mer, sans l'été. Les amis d'alors, Claude Krief, K.S. Karol, François Erval, Paul-Marie de La Gorce ou Jean Cau se retiraient dans leur case pour gratter leur papier, comme les poules grimpent sur leur nid pour pondre. Lorsque Jean Daniel, souvent en Tunisie ou au Maroc, était de passage, je me rapprochais de lui. Il appartenait à une dynastie de minotiers de Blida et avait été sur les bancs

du lycée Bugeaud à Alger avec Camus. Ensuite, à Paris, il l'avait beaucoup servi et aimé. Pour son article, il s'enfermait, entrait comme en oraison, puis, à sa secrétaire, presque une moniale, dictait son inspiration dans une souffrance qui se voyait. Il n'écrivait jamais. Quelquefois il corrigeait.

Nous étions convoqués rarement dans les bureaux de la direction dont les fenêtres donnaient sur l'avenue triomphale des Champs-Elysées. Là, quand ce n'était pas dans le secret, étincelaient les idées et se combinaient les coups d'éclat : Gaston Defferre quand on le poussa à briguer la présidence de la République contre de Gaulle, Mendès France, Mauriac. D'une grande famille de finance et de presse, J.-J. S.-S. avait sa façon de se hisser vers une ambition qu'il ne cachait pas : la présidence des Etats-Unis d'Europe. Il avait été pilote de chasse pendant la guerre et, comme Clostermann, rappelé en Algérie. Les relations avec lui étaient difficiles. De son côté, ambitieux, inquiet, soucieux de ne pas se voir dépassé, Jean Daniel, qui rencontrait les têtes pensantes des rébellions, souhaitait des responsabilités qu'on rechignait à lui donner. Avec un courage indomptable, car les tendances de sa communauté étaient de plus en plus opposées aux siennes, avec réalisme et un vrai mysticisme politique, il défendait à la fois les droits des pieds-noirs et ceux des rebelles. Nous étions tous deux nés dans la Mitidja, cela créait un lien de sang que j'ai toujours tenu pour sacré.

J'éprouvais le même sentiment pour Jean Pélégri qui venait de publier *les Oliviers de la justice,* un récit poignant des derniers jours de son père, à Sidi-Moussa où, je l'ai dit, les tombeaux de nos familles se touchent presque. Mon livre *la guerre d'Algérie* le secoua. Nous ne nous connaissions pas et il eut, à un moment où j'étais très attaqué, le front, devant les siens, de se ranger à mes côtés, ce qui n'était pas une mince affaire. C'est un homme tranquille, un poète du déluge, un visionnaire. Malgré l'écart de nos âges, nos souvenirs étaient les mêmes : les odeurs, le vent, les chacals, les Arabes. Mon dessein de m'enfoncer dans mes racines, de racheter quelques murs, quelques tuiles et quelques arpents de nuées se rattachait à une réalité où tout allait en empirant et basculait dans la mort. Les officiers et les ultras qui résistaient à de Gaulle prétendaient que l'URSS s'apprêtait à occuper la rade de Mers el-Kébir, l'Algérie devenait un théâtre d'atrocités, je recevais

beaucoup de lettres d'insultes et de menaces, car j'étais du côté de Meftah le déshérité. Des années après, le cœur encore battant mais l'esprit froid, quand je décrirai ce moment, je prendrai tous les torts à ma charge. La tragédie suivra son cours, les hommes n'y pouvaient pas grand-chose. C'est souvent une rencontre qui décide, un hasard, cinq centimètres de plus ou de moins dans une collision en vol, et on se demande parfois s'il n'aurait pas mieux valu ne pas en réchapper.

La guerre d'Algérie était presque finie. Parfois on sombrait dans la rancœur, parfois on essayait de ne plus rien entendre. Le problème que je tentais de résoudre pour ma part existe encore. Il rassemble ce que François Mitterrand appelle les composants du drame colonial, il nous atteint encore sournoisement et placera les hommes, un jour ou l'autre, devant une alternative plus âpre : celle de l'affrontement entre ceux qui possèdent et ceux qui n'ont rien. J'assistai pour l'*Express* au procès des généraux du putsch. Trois d'entre eux étaient en fuite, il n'y eut que Challe à se montrer exemplaire. Il avait échoué parce qu'il ne savait pas parler à la télévision, sinon peut-être aurait-il eu l'armée derrière lui et tout aurait changé. La rédaction de l'*Express* s'enrichit d'une normalienne, puissante, vive, coquette et sûre d'elle-même, qui s'appelait Françoise Verny. Comme elle supportait mal d'être en second, elle ne tarda pas d'entrer en conflit. Vite déçue, elle quitta l'*Express* et fut promue par Pierre Lazareff rédactrice en chef de *Candide* qui reparaissait, où elle me pressa de la rejoindre. Je lui cédai sous prétexte d'un article insultant que J.-J. S.-S. venait de publier sur de Gaulle, et ne tardai pas à regretter mon départ. L'*Express* avait des défauts horripilants, mais il était dirigé ; on savait où on allait et avec qui. Pierre Lazareff n'avait ressuscité *Candide* que pour démolir l'*Express*. Perpétuellement en transe pour ne pas déplaire au gouvernement, soucieux de grimper dans les tirages, de compter davantage, de brouiller les cartes, recevant avec Hélène Lazareff dans son manoir de Vaucresson tout ce qui brillait ou faisait scandale, cet homme délirant, minuscule par la taille, presque un gnome, et sublime par les ambitions, avait besoin d'être rassuré que le roi était toujours sur son trône et lui en faveur. Il avait son cortège de flatteurs et ne savait

résister aux jolies femmes. Elles feignaient de l'adorer, et de ses mains pleuvaient les places, l'argent, les chimères, parfois les rôles ou les théâtres. Je ne pouvais pas être de ses courtisans. A mon premier article, les difficultés surgirent car Pierre Lazareff voulait faire plaisir aux puissants dont je n'étais pas, et ce que j'écrivis sur l'affaire de Bizerte ne lui plut pas. Soudain, tel un coq d'Inde grisé par une invitation à Rambouillet, Bourguiba planta subitement son bec dans les jarrets du Général, sans raison : pour ne pas être en reste avec les Algériens, ou pour montrer qu'il ne se laissait pas impressionner. Aussitôt, sous les murs de Bizerte, les armes entrèrent en action et Jean Daniel fut grièvement blessé par une mitrailleuse française. Par miracle, on put l'évacuer. A la clinique de Neuilly où on l'avait opéré, son courage m'impressionna. Comme on craignait qu'il ne fût découvert et achevé par l'OAS, on lui trouva un refuge et, de mon côté, je me hâtai de revenir à *l'Express*. L'agitation gagnait le monde étudiant, l'affaire de Bizerte s'acheva enfin. Après les généraux, les officiers du putsch comparurent non sans noblesse devant les tribunaux ; ceux-là avaient osé se mouiller. Pendant l'hiver, la police parisienne se livra à un massacre des Algériens, la Seine charria des radeaux de cadavres et de Gaulle laissa faire. Nous réagîmes en termes violents. A la fin de l'été, dans une conférence de presse, de Gaulle lâcha délibérément un mot méprisant : il parla de « dégagement ». On allait dégager d'Algérie comme une armée se retire en ordre, regroupe ses caissons d'artillerie et abandonne le terrain avec les douilles d'obus, sans plus s'occuper de ce qu'elle laisse derrière elle. Je m'indignai dans un article vengeur, une sorte d'oraison funèbre que de Gaulle prit très mal. Il ne pardonnait jamais rien à personne, ce qui fut sa seule petitesse.

Ce fut en Algérie, dans la vallée de la Soummam, que la mort d'Amrouche à Paris me frappa. En Kabylie, les orangers étaient en fleur, les gitans de Lourmarin jetaient leur sort pour la deuxième fois. Amrouche rêvait de devenir ambassadeur de la République algérienne auprès du Saint-Siège comme il rêvait d'écrire une œuvre claudélienne pour montrer aux colonisateurs de quoi est capable un colonisé. J'ai souvent pensé que l'aventure de la France en Algérie avec ses souffrances, ses bonheurs, ses injustices et le gouffre des sommes englouties eût été justifiée par la seule existence d'un colonisé comme lui.

Il est enterré à Sargey-sur-Braye près de Vendôme, dans le Loir-et-Cher, là où il avait acheté une maison de campagne avec un chèque en bois que Florence Gould couvrit et qu'il remboursa. Je n'ai jamais eu le courage d'aller sur sa tombe. Il y a, dans la mort d'un proche, un avertissement : « Pourquoi pas moi ? » Le compagnon qui s'assied, épuisé, au bord du chemin et vous regarde continuer, est une part de vousmême.

Avant la proclamation de l'indépendance, le moment vint de nommer un haut-commissaire en Algérie : le général Billotte, pressenti, me demanda d'entrer dans son cabinet comme directeur de l'information. Billotte et moi avions été officiers de transmissions vingt ans plus tôt, lui au 46e régiment d'infanterie à Paris, moi au 24e à Versailles. Son père avait comandé un groupe d'armées et connu une fin tragique en 1940 ; lui avait rejoint de Gaulle. Avant de s'installer hors d'Alger, dans un ensemble bâti depuis peu, il voulait débarquer par mer devant la ville et gagner en grande pompe le palais d'Eté pour montrer que la France ne s'en allait pas la queue entre les jambes. Billotte avait des idées politiques trop libérales, l'armée le récusa et de Gaulle le lâcha après une entrevue dramatique. Le Premier ministre se hâta de désigner un autre haut-commissaire, et nous nous retrouvâmes, le colonel Buis et moi, comme à Bougie. En un an, beaucoup d'eau avait coulé sous les ponts, beaucoup de sang aussi. Nous en étions au moment de la passation des pouvoirs du gouvernement à l'exécutif algérien, Georges Buis était en train d'écrire *la Grotte*, un des grands livres de mystique militaire. Salan fut arrêté et Mouloud Ferraoun assassiné. A Oran, le port flambait. Là, grâce à Julien Besançon, brillant reporter d'Europe n° 1, j'échappai aux sbires de l'OAS et me réfugiai auprès de mon camarade de Saint-Maixent, Joseph Katz, devenu général, et qui commandait la place. Dans le lycée transformé en forteresse, il vivait au milieu de sa garde, chef de bande plus que chef de guerre, cassant la croûte et faisant le coup de feu avec les CRS. Katz, qui se voulait sorti du peuple, rêvait du pont d'Arcole. Les circonstances lui furent contraires. *Rara avis,* il est un des deux ou trois seuls généraux de gauche que j'aie connus. Les pieds-noirs en panique s'écrasaient dans les paquebots pour Marseille. A mon frère, je conseillai de ne pas bouger ; sa femme et lui restèrent sur place,

chez eux, et ne furent pas inquiétés, seuls ou presque au milieu des Arabes en liesse.

Je ne vais pas raconter le crève-cœur de la fin. J'y étais. Tout est dans mon journal et dans *les Chevaux du Soleil*. Le défilé dura deux jours et deux nuits, des gendarmes français saouls défilaient dans des bagnoles volées. Comme tous ils criaient : « *Djezaïra Yahia !* » Ce fut une fête énorme, toni-truante, formidable, déchirante, d'un autre monde. Des hauts de la ville jusqu'à la mer, les youyous vrillaient le ciel. C'était la nouvelle lune, comme en juillet 1830, lorsque les troupes du général de Bourmont étaient entrées dans Alger. Pour nous qui partions, c'était une lune de deuil, pour les Arabes une lune de miel, une charge de cavaliers fous à travers les vivants et les morts, et vers la mer toujours là.

Ainsi se terminait ce qui m'avait rendu témoin et rebelle.

Avant de regagner Paris, je voulus m'agenouiller devant le tombeau des miens, à Sidi-Moussa. Peut-être m'étais-je trompé en plaçant trop haut la justice ; peut-être, à l'opposé de Camus, avais-je commis un péché contre ma mère en aidant au triomphe des hommes qui s'étaient dressés contre nous, et qu'elle et l'oncle Jules m'avaient pourtant appris à connaître. Je m'en fus, seul, avec un chauffeur de taxi qui m'emmena non sans réticence.

Dans la plaine, il y avait encore de la troupe, parfois des gens de chez nous, parfois des bandes armées de l'autre bord, on s'y reconnaissait mal. Je ne passai pas par la ferme où ne vivait plus personne de chez moi. Le village de Sidi-Moussa était vide, le café de l'Espérance fermé, à peine crus-je apercevoir des ombres ici et là. Le taxi refusa d'aller plus loin et je m'en fus à pied. La porte du cimetière était ouverte, et là, j'eus un haut-le-corps : on aurait dit qu'une tornade était passée ou qu'il y avait eu un bombardement. D'abord figé, j'avançai prudemment puis, avec horreur, je découvris que tout était dévasté. Les tombeaux étaient éventrés, les croix abattues, les entourages et les vases d'ornement renversés ; dans les chapelles funéraires, tout était défoncé, brisé, cassé, autels, plaques de marbre, inscriptions, souvenirs, photogra-phies. Je crus même reconnaître des lambeaux de cercueils,

parfois des choses sans nom, des débris informes qui, je dus en convenir, ressemblaient à des ossements.

Un moment, j'errai à travers cette désolation, le cœur broyé, respirant une odeur atroce, une puanteur sèche et stagnante que le soleil tenait au-dessus de ce théâtre funèbre comme un brouillard. Pas le moindre vent. Bizarrement, comme si on avait voulu marquer là des intentions, certains tombeaux étaient intacts, celui des Pélégri par exemple, d'autres encore. On aurait dit que les dévastateurs ne s'étaient pas acharnés au hasard. Sur les miens par exemple, le tombeau des Paris, je crus déceler une rage qui semblait une paradoxale réponse à ma propre position, en quelque sorte ma récompense sadique, mais de qui ? ou un châtiment infligé par qui ? et j'entendais ma grand-mère dire à une de ses filles qui avait peur de rôdeurs, des bédouins : « Ma fille, chez nous, à la ferme, il n'y a pas une motte de terre qui soit injuste... » Alors je sentis une colère blanche et froide m'envahir, s'emparer de moi violemment, je sentis mes propres os devenir en moi pareils aux ossements répandus, comme si l'ange Gabriel de la vallée de Josaphat avait embouché sa trompette, et cette colère me déchira au couperet comme une carcasse de bête. En même temps, je me demandai ce que j'allais faire, comment j'allais me conduire, de quelle façon je pouvais réagir. Oui, comment ? Au village il n'y avait plus personne que le chauffeur de taxi et ces ombres que j'avais cru apercevoir. Alors, qui appeler au secours ? A qui se plaindre ? Et, surtout, sur qui me venger, puisque je voulais me venger ? Dans un furieux bouillonnement, comme le vin après les vendanges dans les cuves, et avec un bruit que je connais bien, j'entendis mon cœur battre, mon sang se ruer dans mes veines, quand soudain je me dis qu'à la place de ces gens-là, des inconnus, à la place de ces « Français musulmans » qui avaient été traités de bicots toute leur vie, j'aurais peut-être agi de même. Oui, oui, de même. Quand on est à la fois ivre de rage, impie, aveugle ou fou d'Allah, que sais-je ? quand on se découvre en proie à la sauvagerie, quand on est jeune et sans raison, comment retenir ce qui déborde en vous de toute part ? Avec quoi marquer la victoire sur ces roumis débarqués en 1830, qui s'étaient emparés de tout pendant un siècle et rembarquaient enfin ? Oui, sur quoi se jeter ? Sur la mairie ? C'était à eux. Sur les écoles ? Elles allaient servir. Sur les maisons ? Elles leur appartenaient déjà, l'Espé-

rance deviendrait un café maure et l'église une mosquée. Quant aux vivants, ils avaient fui. Alors sur quoi ? Seul signe de légitime saisie et d'appropriation, les morts, le cimetière, qu'on allait violer. A la place de ces salopards, j'aurais peut-être tout jeté aux quatre vents et aux gémonies, tout démoli, tout labouré, tout retourné et anéanti. Debout devant le tombeau des miens et de ma mère, ma seule et dernière patrie, je restai comme lié à un gibet nu, et c'est là que, dans *les Chevaux du Soleil*, je fais abattre Hector, c'est-à-dire moi, à coups de fusil, sans qu'on sache jamais qui, les Arabes, ou les siens, l'auront tué. A la télévision, on me voit doucement m'effondrer, on entend les coups de feu claquer sur moi, tandis que, dans ma main, roule un peu de terre.

Aussi, quand on me demande comment je m'en suis tiré, de tout ça, je réponds que je ne m'en suis pas tiré du tout. Sans le savoir je suis passé de l'autre côté de la montagne, là où l'oncle Jules me répétait qu'il y avait le désert, c'est-à-dire un monde mystérieux, vide et mortel. Pour m'en tirer, il m'aurait fallu être un intellectuel avec des idées sur tout et réponse à tout. Pour Camus, la question ne se posa pas, puisque en 1961 et 1962, il n'eut plus rien à se demander. D'après Simone de Beauvoir et d'après le personnage qui interprète Sartre dans *les Mandarins*, Camus était un type qui « se préférait » et voulait passer pour un intellectuel au grand cœur, d'où leur brouille qui ne pouvait finir qu'à la mort de l'un d'eux. Sur Sartre, Faulkner écrit, dans *Réponse aux étudiants de Virginie*, qu'il n'a pas la grâce, et que Dieu lui a été refusé, ce qui semble la vérité même, l'explication majeure.

A propos de l'Algérie, il ne fallait surtout pas raisonner, mais aller où l'on devait, envers et contre tout, selon sa conscience et un instinct plus fort que tout, comme chez les animaux, quand il s'agit des choses essentielles. Comment rendre leur terre à ceux à qui on l'a prise quand, en plus, ils profanent vos cimetières ? Avec la fatalité et la fin de tout, je n'ai pas eu besoin de signer le manifeste des 121, et, des années après, j'ai écrit un long poème sur ce thème, qu'à chaque fête des morts je relis et retouche, et que je n'ai jamais publié.

XX

L'aventure chinoise

A CHAQUE retour au Pays basque, Pierre Benoit, solitaire et désabusé, m'apprenait que tout passe, nous restions de longs moments sans rien dire. S'il avait lu ce que j'avais ramené d'Algérie, lui qui avait célébré avec tant d'ardeur les bienfaits de la colonisation, peut-être m'aurait-il considéré comme un gogo ou un barbare, peut-être m'aimait-il pour cela, car la candeur et l'ingénuité n'étaient pas ce qu'il fréquentait d'habitude. Il m'aurait pardonné. Paul Morand non, qui me rangea aussitôt parmi les subversifs qu'il valait mieux tenir à distance, tout en les couvrant d'éloges équivoques. Quand Pierre Benoit s'éteignit, ses amis, moins nombreux qu'on ne l'aurait cru, le conduisirent au cimetière de Ciboure, devant la mer, où sa femme l'attendait. Sur leur tombe, l'eau du ciel recueillie, les oiseaux peuvent s'y baigner.

Une nuit, je rêvai de Diên Biên Phu. L'événement était englouti dans les mémoires, mais de sourds grondements de tonnerre roulaient encore. Je revis des images qu'avait laissées la télévision, les fumées, les obus, la boue, les vagues hurlantes des Viets, leurs visages médusés et hérissés comme des divinités d'enfer, tandis que ronronnait le Dakota d'où le général Cogny laissait tomber deux étoiles sur le calot rouge du colonel de Castries. A mon réveil, je décrochai le téléphone et appelai René Julliard qui ne parut pas surpris. C'était un homme du monde subtil, gris de teint, perspicace, audacieux, et un chasseur à l'affût de tout. Il devait croire aux signes car il me répondit : « Vous allez écrire le récit de la bataille de Diên Biên Phu. »

Le général Cogny avait un temps commandé les troupes au Maroc, et le bruit courait qu'il avait été mêlé à l'affaire du

493

coup de bazooka contre Salan. Dégommé, désœuvré, il occupait de vagues fonctions et m'offrit spontanément ses dossiers. En revanche, le général Navarre, au rancart, refusa avec aigreur de me recevoir.

L'aventure de Diên Biên Phu était tragique. Voulant échapper aux marécages où l'on ne pouvait saisir l'ennemi, Navarre était tombé dans le même piège que Salan à Na-San. Il se crut plus fort que les autres et accepta la bataille d'un cœur léger. Cogny aussi. Attaquée le 13 mars, la forteresse était submergée le 4 mai 1954. Les survivants défilèrent en longues colonnes sinistres devant les caméras chinoises, vers les camps.

Je voulus tout savoir. Avec un ancien camarade de l'armée de l'air, Edmond Petit, un historien, nous interrogeâmes des centaines de témoins : ceux qui avaient tenu un rôle dans la citadelle assiégée, les anciens chefs de bataillon, d'anciens commandants de compagnie, d'anciens chefs de section, des aviateurs, des artilleurs, des légionnaires, jusqu'au capitaine Pouget, l'ancien aide de camp de Navarre qui, fou d'honneur comme il y a des fous de Dieu, avait voulu être parachuté quelques jours avant la fin. A pleines pelletées, je remuai l'invraisemblable, j'édifiai une montagne de fiches et reconstituai la bataille sur cartes, sur croquis, surtout sur photos aériennes. Peu à peu pour moi tout s'éclaira. Je connaissais les numéros des unités, leurs emplacements, l'horaire des mouvements, le caractère des hommes, leurs humeurs, les animosités qui se déclaraient. Je notai tout, je récrivais même tout ce que mon collaborateur rapportait, le vrai nègre c'était moi. Personne n'avait cru que les Viets pouvaient posséder de l'artillerie : par quel itinéraire auraient-ils amené leurs pièces et gagné les crêtes sans que notre aviation les ait vues ? Le colonel Piroth qui commandait l'artillerie de la citadelle était si sûr que ses batteries ne risquaient rien qu'il les avait établies à découvert. Quand, le 13 mars, les 105 ennemis ouvrirent le feu et, en quelques minutes, détruisirent ses canons et la piste aérienne, Piroth se fit sauter la cervelle. Dans la citadelle assiégée, l'héroïsme et la lâcheté devinrent le pain quotidien. A l'hôpital souterrain, les médecins opéraient dans l'ébranlement des coups de mortier, de rares avions sanitaires se posaient encore et repartaient sous les obus, puis toute liaison devint impossible. Je pus étudier les ordres et les contrordres, les télégrammes échangés avec Hanoi, le procès-verbal des inci-

dents qu'on avait tus, la correspondance impitoyable des généraux. Napoléon a écrit : « A la guerre, un grand désastre désigne toujours un grand coupable. » Tous les arguments du général Navarre se trouvaient déjà, à quelques nuances près, dans un plaidoyer qu'il avait publié en 1956. Personne ne lui avait imposé quoi que ce soit, mais la responsabilité du gouvernement était immense : la guerre d'Indochine n'avait jamais été conduite.

Les responsabilités de cette bataille, j'ai conscience de les avoir justement traduites. Je crois avoir approché de près la vérité, et si, parfois, de ma plume s'échappe un jugement acéré pour certains politiques et certains militaires, je n'ai mesuré ni mon admiration ni ma pitié pour ceux qui combattirent dans ce lac de boue devenu un charnier. J'en disais de cruelles. Cette bataille aurait pu être évitée, elle aurait pu aussi être gagnée. Il me parut utile et nécessaire de savoir pourquoi et comment, alors que ses conséquences pesèrent si lourd par la suite, elle avait été perdue. Tout l'état-major se trompa et raisonna comme un état-major occidental et archaïque face à des gens qui ne possédaient ni avions ni camions, mais des canons et qui n'avaient pas peur de la mort. Honte, désespoir, stupeur, trahisons et mésentente. Les avions ne pouvaient plus se poser, et la moitié du ravitaillement parachuté tombait chez l'ennemi. Au plus profond de l'inquiétude, il fut envisagé, pour faire lâcher prise à l'ennemi, d'employer une bombe atomique. Le colonel Brohon, alors directeur de cabinet du général Ely, chef d'état-major de la défense nationale, fut chargé de solliciter cette extrémité du Pentagone. Finalement, les Américains et les Britanniques refusèrent, le gouvernement chuta, et Mendès arriva au pouvoir.

Il ne me restait plus qu'à me rendre dans la cuvette de Diên Biên Phu au milieu des montagnes et à interroger les témoins d'en face. Je gagnai Hanoi par Bangkok et Phnom Penh et suivis la filière fastidieuse que tout pays socialiste impose à ses visiteurs. Hanoi ne nous appartenait plus, les anciennes villas de Navarre et de Cogny étaient transformées en musées, on ne vendait dans les magasins que des casseroles, des bananes vertes, de la salade et des limaces. Sans les officiers du corps expéditionnaire, l'hôtel Métropole me parut lugubre. Il l'était. L'armée populaire s'entraînait à souffrir et à mourir

pour le peuple et l'oncle Hô. Déambuler à travers les malheurs de ma patrie me fut insupportable. Jusqu'aux boîtes d'allumettes qui portaient à présent le nom de Diên Biên Phu.

On me conduisit là-bas en jeep en économisant l'essence : à chaque descente de la piste, le conducteur coupait le moteur, la voiture roulait sur sa lancée. Enfin, muet, le kiki serré, j'arrivai. Là aussi, il y avait un musée. Le terrain était resté truffé de mines et d'obus non éclatés, la végétation repoussait, parfois je m'égarais. J'allai dans les anciens points d'appui aux noms de femme : Isabelle, Béatrice, Eliane, Huguette, Claudine, Junon, où la mort avait frappé lourdement. Partout je prenais un peu de terre que je faisais couler dans mes poches. Des chars encore englués dans un béton de boue, des canons qui n'avaient plus de culasse rouillaient sur place, des casques traînaient partout, l'abri du colonel de Castries était resté intact. A l'époque, le général Cogny avait insisté pour que le drapeau blanc ne fût pas hissé. Il l'avait été cependant, j'en étais sûr, je possédais la bande sonore du dernier message de Cogny à la citadelle. Je m'assis au pied de l'épave d'un char, et là, seul au milieu des morts en poussière et d'anciens ennemis, j'écrivis ce qui devint le final de mon livre, un immense requiem. Là, je redevins le disciple de Montherlant qui avait écrit *Chant funèbre pour les morts de Verdun*.

Du combat, je pris note de ce que me dirent les témoins rassemblés à ma demande, qui me fournirent les contre-champs de ma relation. Je restai là plusieurs jours à méditer et à interroger. J'avais à présent sur moi un petit sac de cette terre sacrée où le sang et la mort avaient séché, que je voulais distribuer en France à des héros de cette défaite qui étaient des amis. Quand on me demandait ce que j'avais là, je répondais : « Des graines de témérité, de la poussière de courage et de démence. » Dans un boîtier d'argent, il m'en reste encore une poignée. On y trouverait, si l'on cherchait bien, des éclats d'acier, et si l'on se servait d'un microscope de laboratoire, des traces de fibrine et de tout ce qui compose ce liquide visqueux, de couleur rouge, qui circule dans les vaisseaux des hommes et, parfois, est répandu pour des raisons sublimes et folles.

Auprès de nos anciens ennemis, je marquai mon étonnement qu'il n'y eût pas de cimetière français. On ne me répondit pas. Dans un avion mal équilibré où la main de Dieu dut être le second pilote, car nous échappâmes au brouillard et

à d'autres dangers, je revins à Hanoi où je dus visiter des fermes d'Etat. Enfin le général Giap et ses officiers me reçurent. On se serait cru dans un cirque. Coiffé d'une casquette rouge et or, Giap ressemblait à un tigre vert à crinière grise. Il souriait. Nous bûmes des tasses de thé. Au premier Français qu'on revoyait sur les lieux de notre défaite, Giap se montra chevaleresque. Ancien prix d'excellence au lycée de Hanoi, il ne m'embarrassa pas de trop de lieux communs comme je l'interrogeais sur sa victoire. « Parfois, me dit-il, on me demande mes secrets. Je n'en ai qu'un. Le seul, c'est de vouloir vaincre. » Pas haut de taille, râblé, la face large, et semblant prêt à bondir, il tapotait la table où le thé fadasse blêmissait. « Vouloir, répéta-t-il. Et puis vaincre. » Il me dit aussi quelque chose comme « Ou l'on est vainqueur ou l'on meurt », formule que nos ancêtres de la Convention avaient inventée avant lui : « La victoire ou la mort » et que, depuis, tous les révolutionnaires se passent de bouche à bouche.

Il me promit qu'un cimetière serait creusé à Diên Biên Phu pour nos soldats et ne s'opposa pas à ce qu'un monument y fût même élevé par nos soins. Naturellement, personne au ministère des Anciens Combattants ou ailleurs n'attacha le moindre crédit à ce que pouvait dire ou écrire un illuminé comme moi, un homme que labouraient tant de colères ou de douleurs, et de mes vœux pieux il ne resta rien. Il n'y a toujours pas de cimetière à Diên Biên Phu pour ceux des nôtres qui y ont laissé la vie. Devenus poussière, ils gémissent avec le vent. A leur mémoire j'entendis la messe à la minuscule cathédrale qui avait été le rendez-vous de nos fringants officiers. Mes meilleures rencontres avec Dieu ont souvent lieu à l'étranger, parmi des païens. Face aux idoles ou à l'athéisme triomphant, j'ai la coquetterie de témoigner pour le Christ, fils du Dieu d'Abraham, d'Isaac et de Jacob. La nef était bondée de pauvres chrétiens de là-bas et il n'y eut pas de sermon en français. Nous n'avions pas seulement perdu la guerre : malgré notre puissance, nous avions été battus par plus faibles que nous, et malgré nos canons, nos avions et nos chars, par la bicyclette qui servait aux Viets à tout transporter. C'était Valmy, mais contre nous.

Mon voyage durait depuis plus d'un mois, j'étais malade, il me tardait de rentrer. Quand j'atteignis Phnom Penh, je m'abattis dans la clinique du chevaleresque médecin et chirur-

gien de Diên Biên Phu, Grauwin, qui n'avait pas voulu quitter l'Extrême-Orient et s'était établi là. Il diagnostiqua une crise aiguë d'amibiase, me gorgea de pilules d'opium et me poussa dans l'avion pour Paris. Tel un fantôme, j'arrivai chez moi où mon fils, interne des hôpitaux, me soigna aux piqûres d'émétine et me remit sur pied.

Mon récit sortit avec tambour et trompette. Je vois *l'Express* bondissant sur ses rotatives comme un ruisseau de montagne, je me vois jaillissant en photo en première page. « Finalement, après pas mal d'essais, Navarre, Cogny et Giap, c'est à vous que nous avons abouti », me dit Françoise Giroud, la meilleure journaliste et l'esprit le plus piquant qui soit, inexorablement perfide aussi, et c'est pourquoi je ne sus interpréter ce mot. On m'avait affirmé que, dans la nuit du 6 au 7 mai 1954, veille de la chute, Navarre avait survolé le camp submergé par les Viets et qu'il avait pleuré. C'était faux. De Hanoi, il avait regagné Saigon sans même dérouter son avion. Ça n'aurait pas manqué d'allure pourtant, un général vaincu laissant couler une larme sur sa chevalerie détruite ! Au soir de Crécy, Philippe VI avait lancé son fameux cri aux gardes du château de Broye : « Ouvrez, c'est l'infortuné roi de France ! » Je dus me passer de ça pour Navarre. Je m'attendais à ce qu'il me traduisît en justice. Il se contenta de protester, et *l'Express* publia ma réponse. De toutes les lettres que je reçus, il n'y eut que la sienne d'offensante.

Mon livre *la Bataille de Diên Biên Phu* ne fut jamais contesté. De la Suède aux Etats-Unis et au Japon, on me traduisit. René Julliard aurait pu se réjouir d'avoir accordé créance à un rêve. Hélas, il nous avait quittés. Il laissait une maison en plein essor et son nom brille toujours. Dix ans plus tard, au moment où Saigon tombait et où les Américains subissaient à leur tour un désastre infamant, des journalistes qui suivaient la déroute se passaient une édition de poche à couverture rouge qu'avait publiée Faber and Faber.

En Algérie, l'honneur était sauf, notre armée « dégageait » comme de Gaulle l'ordonnait. Les Français refusaient de prendre à leur charge dix millions de melons et de mouquères à qui nous n'avions pas su infuser, en plus d'un siècle, la dignité de « citoyens à part entière ». En vérité, nous n'étions pas vaincus par les armes mais par la fatalité qui

marquait la fin des colonies. Malraux l'avait assez dit depuis 1933 : les empires coloniaux ne survivraient pas à une guerre européenne. Qui avait entendu ce farfelu d'alors ? Au Viêtnam, pour nous chasser, les hommes avaient enduré les plus amères souffrances ; les Chinois leur avaient envoyé des armes et des conseillers, nous avions subi une défaite humiliante, notre corps d'officiers et nos parachutistes étaient rentrés de captivité minés par la dysenterie et crevant de faim, mais la tête haute.

Françoise Verny appartenait alors à la maison Grasset. Elle me demanda dans quelle arène je comptais me jeter. Je pensais à Suez, qui avait laissé chez nous une impression de victoire avortée. Alors, toujours la guerre ? Nous n'avions pas arrêté depuis 1939 et il n'y avait que cela qui me passionnait. Je me heurtai d'abord à Guy Mollet, ancien président du Conseil, redevenu secrétaire du parti socialiste SFIO. Il me reçut comme un chien dans un jeu de quilles : « Ce que vous direz ne sera ni plus faux ni plus sot que ce qui a déjà été dit. » Glacé, avantageux, il coula sur moi un regard visqueux. « Ni plus sot ? » demandai-je. Il sourit, alluma une cigarette sans m'en offrir une et acquiesça. Je me levai et pris la porte sans le saluer.

Si, à présent, elle l'est un peu devenue, Françoise Verny n'était pas encore, comme l'a écrit malicieusement Bernard Frank, une romanichelle qui tire les cartes aux jeunes écrivains. Elle ne roulait pas non plus dans une carriole démantibulée. C'était une jeune femme brillante, bouillante d'intelligence et d'ambition. Elle me proposa le problème noir aux USA. « Ou la Chine ». La Chine, depuis Marco Polo, était ce rêve que de Gaulle avait été le premier chef d'Etat en Occident à reconnaître, et puis il y avait eu la Longue Marche que j'allais revivre avec Mao. N'aurions-nous pas été par hasard vaincus à Diên Biên Phu par les Chinois ? Il y avait de quoi être emballé. A l'époque, je vivais des amours tumultueuses. Pourquoi cette allusion, alors que j'évite les détails de ma vie privée ? C'est qu'on ne part pas pour la Chine comme pour le Monténégro. La Chine, c'était à l'autre bout du monde, trois fois l'Europe des dynasties d'empereurs, une civilisation immense et mystérieuse, les anciennes concessions coloniales de l'Europe, les canonnières, la révolution, Mao était un superman. Il avait

libéré le peuple chinois de ses oppresseurs, d'abord des mandarins, puis de l'étranger, qui tirait profit de la misère et de la concussion. Nous étions complices une fois de plus dans le péché de la colonisation. Il fallait nous laver de tout cela et célébrer ce petit instituteur devenu le chef d'un milliard d'hommes. Je me vis sur les traces de Mao à travers les montagnes et les défilés de Sseu-tchouan. Comment mes embarras intimes résisteraient-ils à cela ?

D'abord, je les emmenai au Sahara, mes embarras. Il me fallait toujours mêler le Sahara à mes propres déserts : parfois un nuage fondait sur ce néant de sable, et soudain tout fleurissait, ou alors il ne se passait rien et je courais le risque de les perdre, mes embarras chéris ; tout au moins de mesurer leur étroitesse à l'infini. Nous visitâmes les puits de pétrole dont les flammes dans la nuit léchaient les étoiles, nous montâmes sur les cimes de l'Assekrem où vivaient des disciples du père de Foucauld. Là, nous nous brûlâmes : de ces hommes pareils à des prédateurs, Dieu était la proie et ils étaient la proie de Dieu, ils célébraient la messe au milieu de montagnes d'or et de bronze, sous l'azur et le feu du ciel, tandis que des aigles tournaient au-dessus d'eux. Ne valait-il pas mieux renoncer à tout et les imiter ? La même tentation que chez les bonzes de Tourane me becquetait de nouveau, des orages fondaient sur moi, on aurait dit que la terre était toute gonflée d'orages.

Mes désirs de la Chine traînaient derrière moi comme une queue de comète. Cette année-là, je poussai jusqu'en Corse. Louise était de méchante humeur, irritée de lettres qui n'arrivaient pas et d'un roman qui ne marchait pas. Dans un âpre décor balayé de vents tourbillonnants, elle rêvait de fanfreluches, de lits à colonnes, sa cour dispersée lui manquait, elle avait horreur du soleil et encore plus de la mer où cependant elle nous accompagnait. Là, il fallait la descendre dans l'eau froide au milieu des rochers. Nous parlions de Malraux à qui elle pensait de plus en plus, maintenant qu'il brillait au firmament, tout près d'elle mais à de telles hauteurs. Je ne pouvais pas croire qu'elle l'ait revu sans nous le dire, quelque chose devait bien se tramer, je m'attendais à ce qu'il débarquât un jour d'un yatch dans le port de Centuri qui ressemble à un décor de théâtre. Il n'y vint jamais. Sans doute détestait-il la mer et l'univers étroit des bateaux. Une fois je

demandai à Louise si, de son côté, elle avait été amoureuse de lui. « Moi ? Jamais. Tu penses ! » Je lui demandai alors si elle l'admirait. « Il me fascine. » L'attachement du Malraux d'alors au communisme ne lui paraissait pas scandaleux ; elle avait compris qu'il voulait, par tous les moyens, conquérir un pouvoir. Dans son roman sur la révolution chinoise — était-ce un roman ? —, il tenait le rôle du commissaire du peuple. A présent, ministre d'Etat dans les gouvernements du général de Gaulle, il vivait entre son cabinet doré du Palais-Royal et la Lanterne, résidence princière du château de Versailles. Louise complotait de l'affronter de nouveau et redoutait cependant cette rencontre. Elle se regardait sans cesse dans la glace. « Crois-tu qu'il me trouvera encore belle ? » Elle s'accrochait à mon bras pour gagner le quai où le capitaine Bifteck, comme s'appelait lui-même avec humour son frère André, gréait le *Tchiken*. Elle me priait d'enduire ses épaules d'huile solaire et m'avouait qu'elle n'avait jamais rien compris aux livres de Malraux. Et comme je lui demandais pourquoi il avait toujours besoin de s'attacher à plus grand que lui, à Mao, à de Gaulle, aux dieux : « Il est plus fort que les autres et n'en sait rien ! » me lança-t-elle.

La Chine était à la mode. A Paris, je pillai les agences de photos, je suivis les cours accélérés d'un sinologue en renom. Je les repotassai chez moi, je m'imbibai de Chine. Des favorisés en revenaient, chancelants d'enthousiasme. J'intriguai donc pour la Longue Marche, *l'Express* exigea aussi mes impressions de route. On attendait trop de moi. Je pensais aux soucis de mon maître Flaubert avant son départ pour l'Orient. Depuis l'expédition où Bonaparte avait jeté tant de savants sur le Nil, on ne parlait à cette époque que des pyramides, des pharaons, de Louqsor et de la vallée des Rois. Flaubert suivait un Maxime Du Camp tout à fait dans le vent, aventurier en titre et sur ses cartes de visite, et qui transbahutait avec lui un attirail encombrant de photographie, la coqueluche du moment. Pour se venger peut-être que Du Camp n'ait pas aimé *la Tentation de saint Antoine*, Flaubert se moquait des merveilles scientifiques que Du Camp promettait avec son bazar, mais comment savoir que de tout cela allait sortir pour lui, Flaubert, l'idée de Mme Bovary ? Hélas, je ne partais que pour le récit que je pensais ramener de la Longue Marche.

Quand je m'en étais ouvert à l'ambassadeur de Chine à Paris, on s'était, non sans une réserve qui m'avait paru de bon aloi, montré flatté qu'un impérialiste d'Occident eût l'intention de célébrer la révolution chinoise. C'était simple, cela semblait facile. Mon maître vénéré se demandait s'il reverrait sa mère et s'éloignait de Louise Colet non sans un certain soulagement, mais ses habitudes de Normand, la bonne chère, son cher silence, son travail, *la Tentation de saint Antoine* que Maxime Du Camp et son ami Louis Bouilhet lui conseillaient de jeter au panier, que d'incertitudes ! Je n'étais qu'un loup inquiet, je partais aussi pour me colleter avec l'aventure qui me chambardait et me chamboulait. Résisterait-elle à l'épreuve, et moi-même, résisterais-je à tout ? Ce farceur de Flaubert cachait déjà dans un de ses chapeaux l'étiquette que, pour intriguer, il laisserait tomber en haut de la pyramide de Khéops déjà couverte de graffitis. Moi, rien. D'ailleurs, je ne songeais à Flaubert que pour m'encourager. Lui aussi, rêvant de l'Orient, avait rêvé de la Chine. Il l'avait écrit un jour à Louise Colet : « Pensez que jamais sans doute je ne verrai la Chine... »

Nous décollâmes pour Moscou avec une équipe de télévision privée. Tout de suite, au grand hôtel de l'Intourist, je critiquai les salles de bains. Pas d'eau chaude. En principe, j'étais là en attente de connaître les raisons pour lesquelles Staline avait relâché Tchang Kaï-chek, son prisonnier à Siang en 1936. Naturellement, à l'Union des écrivains, on ne me répondit pas, on voulait savoir pourquoi j'attachais tant d'importance à un détail aussi futile. « Parce que je m'intéresse aux fluctuations de la politique soviétique à l'égard de la Chine », répondis-je. On rappela de vacances le directeur de l'Institut des études asiatiques et je passai de longs après-midi à écouter des sinologues russes. On enfonça dans la paperasse jusqu'au cou, je n'en tirai rien. Deux de mes livres, *le Navigateur* et *la Guerre d'Algérie* avaient été traduits en URSS, j'en escomptais des sommes, j'avais écris à ce sujet au conseiller culturel de l'ambassade soviétique. Le responsable des droits d'auteur n'était pas là non plus. Son assistant m'attribua un avoir ridicule de trois cents roubles. Au change, je ne pus acheter qu'une pauvre dépouille de zibeline qu'on

promit de m'expédier à Paris. Rien ne me plaisait, je cherchais la Russie de *Guerre et Paix,* c'était Dostoïevski. Autant chercher les Trois Mousquetaires sous la tour Eiffel. Il y avait le Kremlin, la place Rouge. Si, au moins, j'avais eu l'humour féroce de mon maître Flaubert, si seulement j'avais couru les mauvais lieux qui devaient exister encore ! Les mauvais lieux, je les avais emmenés avec moi, c'était moi-même. Tout voyageur solitaire est un diable, disait Montherlant qui avait déniché le mot dans le Coran, j'allais en troupe mais je voyais tout en noir. Nous étions fin août, il faisait déjà froid, la foule avançait dans les rues comme une armée rangée en bataille. Mon meilleur souvenir fut le poète Evtouchenko, superve-dette de l'Union des écrivains, grand, élégant, et qui se déplaçait, chevelure au vent, au milieu d'une cour de poétesses et de bas-bleus, de critiques et de romanciers, tel un prince. Le moindre de ses recueils tirait à trois ou quatre cent mille exemplaires. Des zibelines, il en avait une pelisse avec traîne.

Nous partîmes, moi gros-jean comme devant. Le brouil-lard nous bloqua à Omsk, où l'aérodrome se transforma en caravansérail. Je me plaignais de tout, des enfants qui chia-laient, des haut-parleurs qui aboyaient, des avions qui faisaient tout trembler en décollant. Mon maître Flaubert aurait fraternisé avec le peuple russe. Je me mis à tout débiner comme un petit-bourgeois, quelle manie stupide ! Même le brouillard. A la suite d'une erreur de jugement de ma part, nos affaires de toilette étaient restées dans les bagages en soute ; pourquoi se plaindre alors de ne pas pouvoir se raser ? Ma compagne traînait, comme Du Camp, un sac d'appareils photographiques et de bobines plus lourd qu'elle, elle ne pouvait pas dormir, elle pleurait de se voir embarquée avec un zèbre comme moi. Quand nous atteignîmes Irkoutsk, ce fut pire, on ne pouvait même pas s'asseoir tellement l'aérodrome était bondé. Simon, le chef de notre équipe de télévision, nous trouva des lits. Il connaissait la ville. Sinistre. Son oncle, jadis, secrétaire général du parti communiste roumain, y avait été déporté par Staline en 1950 et avait disparu. Il lui prit tout à coup la lubie d'aller à sa recherche, je le suivis. Nous marchâmes au hasard dans la foule, nous arpentâmes les magasins d'alimentation déserts et vides. A la porte des cinémas, il lançait à voix haute en russe : « Avez-vous entendu parler d'un certain Simon ? » Je voyais notre avenir funèbre.

Simon disait que j'avais tort, qu'on n'était pas si malheureux que ça. Nous mangions, nous allions où nous voulions. Notre tour arriva enfin. Avec une horde de passagers nous nous jetâmes à l'assaut de notre avion.

Le lendemain à midi, le Tupolev se posa à Pékin dans une lumière éblouissante. Enfin la Chine, enfin des Chinois ! Les premiers que je vis me semblèrent affables, pacifiques, des écoliers agitaient vers nous des drapeaux, de souriantes hôtesses nous conduisirent à la police et à la douane, nous nous crûmes enfin dans un pays civilisé baigné d'un merveilleux soleil socialiste. Pour moi qui, lorsque j'atteins n'importe quel Orient, ai tendance à tout comparer à l'Algérie, mètre-étalon des patries et modèle, quoi que j'en dise, d'antiques souvenirs de félicité, je me figurai dans la Mitidja. Sauf par l'odeur. L'odeur n'était pas la même. Ici, dans l'empire du centre du monde, ça sentait autre chose, mais quoi ? Déjà un fonctionnaire d'un certain grade, gris souris de la tête aux pieds et boutonné jusqu'au col, me tendait un maigre bouquet de glaïeuls dont je fus bien embarrassé. C'était M. Tsaï. Ma compagne et Simon reçurent aussi des fleurs. Sans cravate, la chemise fripée, le veston sur le bras, rayonnant enfin, je posai le pied sur la Terre promise. On nous conduisit au bar, on nous servit des sodas, on nous offrit des cigarettes de paille, ma compagne serrait des roses sur son cœur, on nous rendit nos passeports sans visiter nos valises. Dans le hall trônait une statue monumentale de Mao. En marbre blanc ? En stuc ? Je me retins d'aller cogner du doigt contre son pied. La chaleur nous enveloppait et soudain, comme nous sortions, ce fut le chant des cigales, d'une stridence bête comme tout, qui nous assourdit, même moi qui entends mal. On nous enfourna dans une sorte de grosse jeep qui cornait pour écarter les charrettes à ânes et les cyclo-pousse en sueur sur leur pédalier. Je me dis qu'en Indochine nous avions apporté des moteurs à ces malheureux. Ici on ne ménageait pas l'effort.

Ainsi, par l'avenue de la Paix éternelle, vide, fîmes-nous notre entrée à Pékin. A l'hôtel *Hsin shao*, hôtel de la paix, les chambres étaient étroites, on avait de la peine à s'y tenir à deux, les fenêtres ouvraient sur un vieux quartier. Pékin se

composait de monuments énormes de style soviétique et de maisons basses aux toits de tuiles luisantes. On entendait des chants de scieries, des grincements de rémouleurs comme dans les rues d'Alger de mon enfance, des vendeurs de fromages ou de légumes comme du temps de Segalen. Nous étions béats. Le soir même commencèrent les agapes officielles, copieusement arrosées d'alcool de riz, par petits verres qu'il fallait vider cul sec : « *Kampé!* » Simon s'en mettait jusque-là, on aurait dit que c'était un habitué des voyages en Chine. Moi pas. Pour mon malheur, je ne raffole pas de la cuisine chinoise.

Le lendemain eut lieu une conférence. On me demanda de rédiger le plan du livre que je comptais écrire et le scénario du film qui devait être la doublure du livre. « C'est normal, dit Simon. Ici on juge sur pièces. » Je me mis devant ma machine à écrire, j'en avais pour des jours. Entre-temps, on visitait la ville. Les cigales ou les grillons chantaient, les sept millions d'habitants de Pékin vaquaient à leurs occupations, des charrettes à ânes, parfois à mulets, déambulaient sur l'avenue de la Paix éternelle parmi les cyclistes, les universités s'élevaient au milieu de champs de maïs, il faisait très chaud, d'une chaleur sèche. Nous achetâmes des chapeaux de paille, des éventails, des sandales. La vie ne coûtait rien. Le lendemain de notre arrivée, une note parut dans le bulletin d'information qu'on glissait sous les portes « Roy Jules Désiré, écrivain français, et des hôtes français sont arrivés à Pékin pour effectuer une visite sur l'invitation de l'association du peuple chinois pour les relations culturelles avec les pays étrangers. Ils ont été salués à l'aérodrome par... » Je demandai où résidait le président Mao. On ne savait pas. Ses bustes et ses statues étaient partout. Lui, nulle part. Dans les musées, on ne pouvait pas photographier les agrandissements de sa calligraphie souveraine, on ne photographiait pas le Saint-Sacrement. Sur l'immense place Tian'anmen où auraient lieu, le 1er octobre, les fêtes de la Révolution, des miliciens et des étudiants s'exerçaient déjà à souffler dans des cuivres, à brandir des fusils de bois et à défiler au pas de l'oie.

Les journaux occidentaux n'étaient pas en vente à Pékin. Même pas *l'Humanité*. Nous n'avions d'informations que par le bulletin dont j'ai parlé, qui citait souvent *Alger républicain* ressuscité qui n'avait pas encore pris le titre d'*El Moudjahid*. Cependant il était possible de téléphoner à Paris. Je tapai

505

vaguement ce qu'on m'avait demandé, je me dis que j'aurais dû emmener Sigaux avec nous. Il était souple, il savait s'adapter à tout, il aurait rédigé mieux que moi le plan de mon livre et le scénario du film ; il avait tellement servi de nègre. Lui, si intelligent, il était l'esclave de tellement de besognes et de boulots que je n'avais pas osé, par respect pour lui. Je regrettai bien ma pudeur. Simon disait : « Le démarrage est toujours long. » Je pensais à la somme de notes que j'avais entassées, je me demandais à quoi cela servirait jamais

L'Express attendait l'hymne de mon arrivée. J'expédiai par la poste aérienne un article désabusé, tiède, mollasson. Comme j'étais. D'autres équipes de journalistes visitaient en bandes des musées et la colline du Charbon. Nous nous croisions quelquefois, échangions prudemment nos impressions, il devai v avoir des micros partout et nous pouvions nous trompei

Non sans raillerie à mon égard, je me rappelle encore à présent le voyage en Orient de mon maître Flaubert, en 1849-1851, je songe à ses lettres à Louise Colet, à Louis Bouilhet, à sa mère, aux uns et aux autres pendant les étapes ou en route, parfois sur le pont de l'embarcation qui remontait le Nil, il tenait à sa façon la chronique du voyage, à moins de distance que le nôtre mais, en comparaison du siècle, tellement plus risqué. A leur retour, Maxime Du Camp, chargé de mission par le ministre de l'Instruction publique et par le secrétaire perpétuel de l'académie des inscriptions, fournira un travail sérieux, honnête, documenté. Le résultat, souvent naïf et conformiste, quelquefois ennuyeux, est parfois amusant, car l'auteur ne fait grâce de rien au lecteur. Les anecdotes s'y logent, sans jamais une allusion au compagnon Flaubert qui n'est pas grand-chose encore. Rarement une plaisanterie, jamais d'incongruité, tout se déroule comme dans un rêve pédagogique. Quand il se laisse aller au naturel de la vie, on le suit. Le clou de l'ouvrage reste ses photographies où, par hasard et de loin, on découvre parfois la silhouette de Flaubert au pied d'un monument, les bras ballants, ne sachant que faire.

Je me demande si je n'ai pas été le Maxime Du Camp de mon propre voyage en Chine. Lié comme je l'étais à l'Express, menacé par la mine sévère de J.-J. S.-S. qui risquait sur moi son argent et la réputation de son organe de presse, épié de

loin par le dur visage méfiant de la responsable de la « tenue »
et de la ligne du journal, étais-je aussi libre que je pensais ?
Christian Bourgois avait signé un accord, tous attendaient de
moi une suite à *la Bataille de Diên Biên Phu*. Où était le
rapport ? Mao avait sauvé la Chine du désordre, de la famine,
de l'impérialisme, des mandarins, on le célébrait partout. Chez
nous, les hommes dans le vent arboraient le col mao. La gêne
que j'éprouvais ne pouvait être engendrée que par un esprit
dénigreur, une nostalgie inconsciente de colonialiste, je n'allais
pas me mettre à célébrer l'aide des Chinois aux rebelles
vietnamiens ni à trahir mes anciens camarades. Quel cas de
conscience ! *L'Express* ne souhaitait qu'une chose : combattre
le gouvernement en place, combattre de Gaulle. Mais alors ?

Simon était un exemple de longanimité ; ma compagne,
que beaucoup prenaient pour ma fille, photographiait ; nous
écoutions avec patience les propos qu'on nous tenait, nous
avions visité en coup de vent l'ancien palais impérial et la Cité
interdite où, paraît-il, on se promène maintenant comme au
château de Versailles. Nous aurions aimé nous attarder dans ce
décor de plafonds dorés, de colonnes et de salles d'audience
laquées de rouge, rêver à ce qui avait été le monde de
splendeur et de cruauté d'autrefois. On disait que le dernier
descendant des empereurs, converti à la Révolution, était
jardinier là, tout près. Une pagode dont le gardien ressemblait
à un éléphant abritait une collection d'horloges, leurs cœurs
battaient toujours dans ce désert d'ombres. Simon déambulait
silencieux, l'esprit ailleurs, sa caméra n'avait pas le droit de
tourner là. Des statues gigantesques de Bouddha se dressaient
sur les collines de l'Ouest et ressemblaient à celles de Mao. En
Chine, plus personne n'allait dans les temples, plus personne
ne priait, et, pour ma part, je guettais l'occasion de m'intéresser aux églises et aux évêques qui existaient encore.
« Patience », répétait Simon.

Dans la ville, Simon lésinait sur la pellicule. Nous
attendions tous de nous précipiter vers la Longue Marche : dix
mille kilomètres. J'entendais encore Françoise Verny me
catéchiser d'une lèvre gourmande : « Tu te la retaperas après
Mao, tu nous la raconteras... » Ses yeux brillaient, devenaient
humides. J'allais la décevoir aussi. Déjà nous n'en demandions
plus tant, nous nous contenterions de ce qu'on nous accorde-

rait, car la durée de notre visa n'était que d'un mois, nous commencerions par où on voudrait, par le Kiang-si ou le Chen-si, nous voulions seulement mettre nos humbles pas dans les pas de Mao. Avec consternation, je constatai que la Chine (mais nous n'étions qu'à Pékin) était divisée en deux classes sociales : le tout-venant et les mandarins du parti qui devaient, eux, chaque année, partager pendant un mois la vie d'une commune populaire. Ah ! nous en avons vu, de ces communes-là ! Quand notre interprète M. Shu, qui se curait le nez avec obstination et s'intéressait longuement à ce qu'il extirpait, nous annonçait d'une voix plate que nous allions en visiter une nouvelle, je me faisais porter malade. Simon disait que ce n'était pas de la bonne politique, on pouvait suggérer de négocier un autre emploi du temps dans un autre musée, on ne pouvait pas dire non, il fallait commencer par apprendre la Révolution.

« Existe-t-il en Chine des... ? » fut la question que je posai un jour à M. Shu sans oser prononcer le mot bordel. Il réfléchit, me regarda avec inquiétude. « Enfin, vous voyez ce que je veux dire... » ajoutai-je avec un sourire égrillard. Il rougit et traduisit longuement à M. Tsaï. La Chine avait changé, la Chine ne subissait plus la domination de l'Occident, les femmes chinoises que nous apercevions en ville, dans les usines ou ailleurs, étaient les égales des hommes, telle fut la réponse de M. Tsaï. Il ne serait venu à aucun d'entre nous l'idée d'un commerce indécent avec elles, qui ne semblaient mises au monde seulement pour accroître la démographie vertigineuse de la Chine. Elles portaient toutes des pantalons coupés dans une ample et grossière cotonnade qui noyait les formes, leur veste effaçait les seins, leurs visages sans le moindre fard étaient des lunes. Parmi elles, ma compagne ressemblait à un oiseau tombé d'un vol de migrateurs à vives couleurs, à lèvres roses et aux yeux pareils à des papillons. Chafouins, hypocrites, tartufes, les fonctionnaires de notre escorte coulaient des regards concupiscents sur cette incarnation de l'Occident et me lorgnaient d'un air fripon.

Après les parcs, les lacs, les carpes, les cocktails de sodas, les fabriques de locomotives et même les prisons où l'on rééduquait, il y eut la Grande Muraille, avec la foule habituelle de badauds chinois, sans Mao à qui tâter le pouls, comme Jean Daniel le fera, vingt-cinq ans plus tard, à François Mitterrand

essoufflé. Là, on aurait eu droit à quarante pages de Maxime Du Camp : historique, architecture, description, réflexions poétiques. La durée de notre visa s'écoulait, nous mangions l'argent de *l'Express.* J.-J. S.-S., furieux de mon premier article, me téléphona. Avec le décalage horaire, il devait être six heures du soir à Paris, il était minuit ici, je dormais. D'une voix courroucée J.-J. S.-S. me dit qu'il devait bien y avoir quelque chose d'intéressant à Pékin. Par exemple, comment, là-bas, jugeait-on les événements ? Je fus interloqué. « Quels événements ? répondis-je. D'ici on ne sait rien, on ne voit rien, le monde n'existe pas. Vous pourriez même m'annoncer qu'il se passe quelque chose en Chine, je ne serais pas surpris de l'ignorer, on nous cache tout. » Il me demanda si j'allais voir Mao. J'espérais. Je ne savais pas. Et où en était la Longue Marche ? Toujours en discussion auprès des autorités. Il raccrocha de mauvaise humeur.

Nous allions au cinéma voir des films chinois non sous-titrés où la caméra ne bougeait pas. Simon commençait à douter. A ses yeux j'étais responsable du jugement qu'on devait porter sur nous. Je ne répétais pas assez combien nous admirions la Chine et combien nous nous sentions chargés des crimes que l'Occident y avait commis. Le travail forcené, les communes populaires, les bas salaires, le pouvoir d'achat ridicule, l'immense armée, le catéchisme du parti et, sur les routes et dans les campagnes, les bicyclettes, les ânes et la seule force musculaire pour vaincre une nature cruelle, c'était le prix dont Mao faisait payer aux Chinois leur liberté, leur dignité, le poids de la Chine dans le monde. La Chine construisait la bombe atomique, aussi se montrait-elle encore plus méfiante à l'égard des néo-colonialistes qui pleuvaient de partout pour espionner.

Qu'étions-nous à côté de la Chine ? En Chine, qui savait ce qu'était la France ? La Révolution de 1789, Napoléon, notre Mao Tsé-toung à nous. Abel Gance était là, bonhomme, curieux et vif, en extase devant tout, il venait négocier le tournage d'un Mao sur écran géant avec foules innombrables, il demandait en grand ce que nous implorions en petit, on le rencontrait aux cocktails pour l'entente des peuples et au cirque de Pékin. Il n'habitait pas l'hôtel des journalistes, le *Hsin shao,* il avait droit, à cause de Napoléon, à la classe au-

dessus et avançait au bras d'une assistante jalouse qui ne le lâchait pas d'un pas. Flegmatique, impassible, amateur de vin chinois et de canard laqué, Marcuse, le correspondant de l'AFP, ne concevait pas que les Chinois puissent laisser tripoter leur révolution par des capitalistes. La Chine n'était pas pressée. Inondations, invasions, incendies, famines, tout passait sur elle sans l'entamer, tout s'engloutissait en elle dans l'horizon des siècles et des siècles, amen. Il fallait attendre. Il faudrait revenir. On nous embarbouilla dans des séances de l'assemblée du Peuple, on nous entartouilla d'expositions de tracteurs. N'avais-je pas des questions pour le maréchal Chou-teh qu'on apercevait parfois dans une loge, immobile, l'œil fixe, aux réunions solennelles où nous étions conviés ? Il avait quatre-vingt-six ans, il nous recevrait certainement à condition que les questions fussent posées d'avance par écrit et qu'il eût le temps d'y réfléchir.

Pierre Nora et sa femme Françoise Cachin tombèrent du ciel avec une bouffée d'air frais. Esprit aigu, intelligence vaste, Pierre Nora brassait l'Histoire. Françoise Cachin, sa femme, était à sa taille, vive et belle. Soudain, le teint terreux, il subit une crise néphrétique et dut être hospitalisé ; on l'emmena et le mystère commença. Où était-il ? Nous ne le sûmes que le lendemain. On disait que l'interne de garde lui avait administré une drogue qui l'avait fait sombrer dans un état comateux. On ne voulait pas révéler non plus pour quoi on le traitait, puis, toujours en catimini, on le changea d'hôpital. Quand, finalement, nous réussîmes à le dénicher, il n'avait pas trop mauvaise mine mais ne songeait qu'à regagner la France. Il murmura qu'à ma place, comme à la sienne, nous devrions plutôt écrire un livre qui s'appellerait *Un voyage raté*. Marcuse nous apprit que le pianiste Samson François qui donnait un concert à Shanghai ne savait pas à quel hôtel il était descendu et que le représentant de la maison Rolls Royce, dont les moteurs équipaient quelques avions Viscount, ne bougeait jamais de son hôtel dans la crainte qu'on lui annonçât une panne. Cela me fit songer à Raymond Roussel à Pékin vers 1930. Il n'était même pas sorti de sa chambre, avait écrit un poème et s'était enfui.

Nous fûmes conviés à visiter le musée de la Révolution : c'est ainsi qu'on souhaitait que nous suivions la Longue

Marche. Le directeur reçut mission de nous instruire. Les portraits des héros et des maréchaux entouraient une nouvelle statue géante de Mao sous un drapeau rouge. Ce que j'avais appris de mon sinologue parisien me laissa entendre que le récit qu'on nous servait n'était pas très conforme à la réalité. Dans ce cas, le scénario de mon film ne devait pas plaire non plus. Le Parti voulait que l'Histoire fût ajustée à ses vues. Quant à rencontrer, comme j'en avais exprimé le désir, des dirigeants pour leur poser des questions sur certains épisodes, les dirigeants étaient trop occupés à construire le présent pour s'embarrasser dans le passé. Plutôt que de vouloir écrire à toute force le récit de ce qu'on s'obstinait à nous cacher, il valait mieux, comme l'avait suggéré Pierre Nora, raconter avec drôlerie ce qui nous était montré. Simon se rallia de mauvaise grâce à mon point de vue.

On nous embarqua pour Wou-han, on nous fit naviguer sur le Yang-tseu, on nous coiffa de casques et on nous poussa dans des aciéries, on nous fit visiter une usine d'abattage de porcs. Là, un représentant de l'autorité me dit qu'il regrettait de n'avoir pu utiliser le cri de l'animal foudroyé par le tueur : c'était seulement cela qui manquait à la récupération. Mon maître Flaubert eût répliqué que nous étions plus forts que les Chinois : nous, les écrivains, savions exploiter les cris de douleur. C'était pendant son fameux voyage en Orient qu'il avait été frappé par l'idée : tout ce tintouin n'avait servi qu'à ça, oui, mais quel miracle, quelle réussite dont Maxime Du Camp ne soufflait mot ! Ce n'est pas moi qui l'ai inventé : Flaubert ne courait-il pas comme un fou en criant : « Elle s'appellera Emma Bovary... » ? A présent, je m'étonne que Malraux, partant plus tard pour l'Egypte et pour la Chine en bateau comme ministre d'Etat du général de Gaulle, ait rappelé dans un discours pour la sauvegarde des monuments de Nubie, que c'était dans une hutte de roseaux et de pisé, parmi les rochers noirs d'Assouan, que le jeune Flaubert avait... Il rappela même que la dame s'appelait Kutchek Hanem, nom qui, à travers la suite des relations, a emprunté des formes diverses, que Maxime Du Camp estropie lui-même et traduit par « la petite Rose », alors que Malraux dit « la petite Dame », peut-être parce qu'il pense à Gide et à la sienne, de petite dame. Du Camp a raconté pudiquement cette visite nocturne, la danse du ventre des almées et l'effeuillage

d'une courtisane qui ne se doute pas qu'elle est en train de passer à la postérité et peut-être d'inspirer à Flaubert des pages de *Madame Bovary*. Du Camp laisse entendre que pour sa part il n'a pas consommé. Flaubert oui, et comment ! Et il faut que ce soit Malraux qui rappelle, à plus d'un siècle de distance et presque pudiquement dans les *Antimémoires*, cette syphilis comme une chose qui allait de soi à cette époque sans pénicilline, et que d'autres situent à Beyrouth. Le mot du directeur des abattoirs de Wou-han me rappelait les commentaires de Flaubert touchant ses performances, cette nuit-là, son souvenir du ventre chaud de la danseuse étoile et sa comparaison hardie avec Judith et Holopherne. Ou Malraux imagine-t-il de son côté que Flaubert pensait qu'il avait la reine de Saba dans ses bras ? Peut-être à cause de la proximité de Djibouti où Malraux se souvient de son équipée aérienne avec Corniglion-Molinier, quand, se prenant pour le roi Salomon, il cherchait les traces de la reine de Saba aux jambes inégales... Où la Chine ne nous entraîne-t-elle pas ?

A Shanghai, j'errai longuement sans trouver la maison où mon ami Louis Brauquier, qui représentait là les Messageries maritimes avant la Seconde Guerre mondiale, avait écrit son poème « Neige sur Shanghai ». C'est vrai que j'étais plus attaché au passé de la Chine qu'à son présent, M. Tsaï avait raison de me le reprocher. J'aurais voulu célébrer à la fois la Cité interdite et la Longue Marche et on ne nous permettait ni l'une ni l'autre. Nous étions venus trop tôt. Après nous et après Mao, les voyages seront plus libéraux, mais la Longue Marche restera tabou. Abel Gance mourra sans l'avoir tournée.

Nous allâmes à Shaoshan, le village natal de Mao transformé en musée, nous revînmes assister aux fêtes du 1er octobre et là, Simon eut l'idée de me donner un micro pour décrire le défilé. Des millions de Chinois, agitant des drapeaux et lâchant des nuages de ballons avançaient en acclamant le maître suprême, des musiques avec tambours géants et cymbales se télescopaient parfois entre elles, des masses énormes de Chinois poussaient devant eux des locomotives en carton, des chars fleuris, des tracteurs débordant de légumes et de

fruits ; des bataillons de bonzes trottinaient en agitant des feuilles de lotus, de nouvelles forêts de drapeaux de soie rouge ondulaient, de nouvelles musiques et de nouvelles troupes de choc martelaient le sol au pas de l'oie devant la tribune impériale. Il y eut aussi une horde de poètes et de littérateurs brandissant les œuvres de Mao, puis des danseurs déguisés en tournesols, des moissonneurs, des athlètes olympiques, des nageurs, des aviateurs, des montagnards, on croyait que c'était la fin et tout recommençait : dix mille nouveaux drapeaux rouges déferlaient précédant une statue colossale du dieu debout, en veston, la main derrière le dos, avec l'air pensif et doux d'un génie universel ; il approchait, nous dépassait et disparaissait dans les flonflons, les cris et les acclamations aux accents d'un orchestre fantastique avec chœurs, Wagner et Berlioz réunis pour l' « Hymne à la joie », un peu comme ce fut pour Mitterrand au Panthéon en 1981 sous la pluie, en réduction, à notre échelle de minables Européens, rien à côté de la Chine. A midi tapant, sur son balcon, le dieu vivant à côté d'un roi nègre en visite agita sa casquette, et hop ! s'éclipsa par les souterrains comme par une trappe. Apparitions subites, disparitions subites, tel Zeus en personne.

Mon reportage fut diffusé en France. Je m'exprimais à mi-voix, comme si j'assistais en catimini à un triomphe auquel je n'aurais pas été convié. Parfois, n'en pouvant plus, je perdais mon souffle. Et là, ensevelis parmi les millions de Chinois en liesse, un cycliste mystérieux nous porta un télégramme qui avait pour origine les Champs-Elysées, oui, mais pas les vrais. Le producteur de Simon, impatient, lui intimait l'ordre de louer une voiture et de se lancer à travers les montagnes et les fleuves vers la Longue Marche. L'optique n'était pas la même à Paris qu'à Pékin. Dans le système dont nous dépendions, rien ne bougeait que les nuages et les régiments vert bouteille acclamant Mao. Le soir, le feu d'artifice fut à l'échelle du matin. Prodigieux. Inventeurs de la poudre à canon, les Chinois transformaient les étoiles innombrables en innombrables oiseaux d'or et en comètes. Dans toute la ville les musiques secouèrent la foule du même air obsédant haché de coups de cymbales, sans commencement ni fin. Toute la nuit, des masses, des nuées de femmes et de jeunes hommes dansèrent un ballet pudique et lent, d'un autre âge. Comme possédés par un esprit souverain, ils s'inclinaient, se redres-

saient, indifférents au froid et au crachin. Ce n'était ni l'hystérie africaine ni l'impudeur occidentale, mais quelque chose de barbare, d'inquiétant et de doux, une danse d'esclaves adorateurs dans une survivance de religion morte, de temples en ruine et du mystère de la Chine éternelle. Le portrait de Mao, les statues de Mao flottant dans la soie rouge dominaient tout et dans le ciel noir éclataient des grappes d'or. Frappés de stupeur et d'admiration, nous regardions, sans pouvoir articuler un mot. J'étais baba. Simon aussi. Rien que cela valait le voyage, pensai-je. Nous n'étions peut-être venus que pour la transfiguration de Mao vivant en dieu tout-puissant. Je le dis. Personne ne me le pardonna.

A Shanghai, j'allai à la messe dans une église qu'on ne me désigna qu'au dernier moment. Trois cents fidèles priaient, un jour de semaine. Je n'étais pas sûr que ce fût du latin qui franchissait les bouches chinoises. On distribua la communion. Plus tard, M. Tsaï me demanda pourquoi je n'avais pas participé à ce qu'il appelait « le repas sacré ». Il attendait de moi je ne sais quel signe d'esprit fort. Ce fut tout le contraire, je lui dis que je ne me sentais pas digne de m'approcher de la table sainte, que j'étais un pécheur. Il me jugea primitif. Selon lui, les hommes civilisés n'avaient pas de religion. « Vous avez bien Mao », lui rétorquai-je. Il prit cela pour une méchante plaisanterie. Après quoi on me conduisit à l'évêque gouvernemental, car l'évêque légitime vivait en détention. J'entendis une condamnation du Vatican. Après tout, où est le devoir d'un évêque quand il s'agit de garder son troupeau au milieu des loups ? Avec le temps, l'évêque fidèle est mort et l'infidèle s'est rallié à Rome sans se rallier. Tout est bien.

La nouvelle la plus importante de notre voyage fut que la Chine venait de faire exploser une bombe atomique. La Chine, puissance nucléaire, s'élevait dans la hiérarchie des nations. Elle pouvait se faire respecter et non plus dépendre du bon vouloir des Occidentaux anciens envahisseurs. Le visage illuminé, M. Tsaï, soudain orgueilleux, se laissa aller devant moi à des menaces à l'égard des Etats-Unis d'Amérique. Peut-être avait-il bu. Il voyait des fusées chinoises franchissant le Pacifique. A sa place j'aurais été moins arrogant. Cependant

j'eus tort de me laisser impressionner par ce qui nous semblait un désir de venger les humiliations de jadis. A lui seul, M. Tsaï n'était ni le peuple chinois ni ses dirigeants. N'empêche que la bombe atomique fut une raison de plus pour nous interdire la Longue Marche. On essaya de corriger notre déception en nous promenant dans des villages de pêcheurs, au mausolée de Sun Yat-sen à Nankin, et en essayant de nous convertir au libéralisme de la révolution par les sermons d'une habile pécore profiteuse du régime, romancière rose bonbon. Je protestai à ma façon, en refusant de signer les tickets de repas, les notes d'hôtel, et en exigeant de tout payer. Rien n'y fit.

A un quart de siècle de distance, et quoique la Chine ait tellement changé depuis, je me dis que mon voyage eût été différent si, au lieu de courir là-bas en soupirant transi, tellement désireux d'être pressé sur le cœur de sa Chine, j'avais pris le temps d'être reconnu pour qui j'étais : un citoyen bêtement épris de justice et avide de chanter la nouvelle Anabase et ses héros. Quelqu'un aurait dû tempérer mes ardeurs. Simon essaya au début, je ne crus pas en lui : j'étais une bourrasque pour la Chine, je voulais tout tout de suite, mon ingénuité effrayait, rien ne pouvait modérer mes transports ni mes déceptions, et mon attitude inspirait des soupçons que je devinais et que l'amoureux de la Chine que j'étais ne pouvait pardonner. Les malentendus s'aggravèrent, le traducteur trahit nos propos et personne n'avait d'humour. Nous souffrions des pieux mensonges de nos accompagnateurs. Très vite nous nous méfiâmes les uns des autres. A présent, je me dis que nous aurions pu et que nous aurions dû. Cela ne se fit pas. Cependant ce voyage, tel qu'il fut, nous montra la Chine de l'époque, cachant une misère qu'il nous arrivait, désemparés, de découvrir parfois. Aux cent fleuves, aux mille monts succédaient cent autres fleuves, mille autres monts, on n'en voyait jamais la fin, les Chinois peuplaient tout, partout uniques et partout différents, sous la statue géante du tyran planant, protecteur et bénisseur. Rien en Chine ne permettait de déceler la vérité du mensonge, la raison de la déraison, le règne du souverain ni la tyrannie du despote. On quittait des proportions humaines pour atteindre l'infini que

devenaient là-bas le soleil, les eaux, la famine, l'injustice, la vie, la survie. Rien n'était à notre échelle, le désordre ni la remise en ordre, la cruauté ni l'ascèse, les rivières bleues et le limon, les murailles barraient des continents entiers et on pouvait les voir de la Lune, les révoltes charriaient d'innombrables cadavres. Quand, jadis, un empereur avait son jardin, ce jardin avait les dimensions d'un royaume, le milliard était l'unité d'emploi courant, le double siècle l'unité de temps. Quant à la langue elle-même, une langue d'oiseaux, un lettré passait encore des examens à quatre-vingts ans et faisait des gammes chaque matin sur quelques signes nouveaux qui, chantés sur un autre ton, prenaient un autre sens. Le Parti voulait simplifier tout cela : il y avait encore dans l'Empire céleste trop de têtes enflées, trop de reines pondeuses. Les Anglais avaient interdit les pelouses de Shanghai aux chiens et aux Chinois, à leur tour les Chinois interdisaient tout.

On voulait à toute force que la Chine fût vertueuse et il est vrai que les Chinois qu'on nous montrait avaient tous l'air honnête, sérieux, travailleur, et plus encore les citadins que les campagnards. Et pourtant il devait bien y avoir des fainéants et des crapules parmi eux comme chez nous, des profiteurs, des salopards, de vieux cochons lubriques ? Non, non, me répondait-on, la Révolution avait tout changé, Mao conduisait un peuple de gens respectables. Il n'était pas question non plus de souhaiter rencontrer des artistes ou des écrivains, j'avais pourtant deux ou trois noms intéressants. D'abord, auraient-ils eu le courage de nous recevoir ? Nous auraient-ils dit ce qu'ils pensaient ? Nous visitions la Chine du silence, alors qu'on apprend aujourd'hui qu'elle est, sous sa masse de pharisaïsme, aussi violente et pourrie qu'autrefois et qu'il existe, en Chine autant sinon plus qu'ailleurs, des putains et des maquereaux. De mon temps, on courait après nous pour nous remettre une boîte d'allumettes oubliée, aujourd'hui on sait que le nombre de voleurs est là-bas plus élevé qu'en Russie ou aux Etats-Unis. De mon temps, il ne fallait pas parler de la misère de la Chine, Mao avait apporté sinon la prospérité, réservée aux mandarins, au moins la décence. C'était faux : la Chine vivait dans le dénuement et dans le mensonge, comme du temps de l'impératrice Tseu-hi qui me faisait toujours un peu penser à Florence Gould.

Depuis la fin de la Longue Marche, Mao rêvait d'une

guerre juste dont on avait brandi devant moi l'épouvantail. A présent le rêve devenait cauchemar, la Chine avait sa bombe, personne en Chine ne craignait la guerre nucléaire, on croyait la Chine assez vaste pour l'encaisser, triompher et posséder le reste du monde, c'était ce que m'avaient dit, peut-être avec un verre dans le nez, nos accompagnateurs. Après tout, pourquoi pas ? Le marxisme-léninisme avait détruit le culte des ancêtres, on enseignait partout le catéchisme du Parti aux enfants, on exerçait la jeunesse au tir au fusil, tous les Chinois, même les femmes, étaient prêts à verser leur sang pour la patrie. Nous, on nous baladait en avion et en wagons-lits, nous mangions et buvions aux frais du populo qui, à l'écart des hôtels pour étrangers, se crevait à pousser des charrettes tandis qu'à des hauteurs où on ne les apercevait pas, les avions espions et les satellites américains surveillaient l'avancement des travaux d'armement nucléaire, et déjà, aux Russes comme aux Américains, se posait le problème de tuer la menace dans l'œuf : pour la Chine elle-même, ses villes, ses barrages, cinquante bombes suffiraient à la ramener à l'âge des cavernes. C'était la conclusion de l'état-major soviétique et du Pentagone, je n'ai rien inventé de ce à quoi songeaient nos propres docteurs à tête enflée. Et pourquoi la Chine n'aurait-elle pas voulu devenir la première nation du monde ? « Parce que c'est un colosse aux pieds d'argile », disait-on. C'est vrai. A l'époque, on parlait de sept cents millions de Chinois qui seraient un milliard en 1980, cinq milliards en l'an 2000. Quand je disais aux mandarins qui nous accompagnaient que la Chine ne pourrait pas nourrir ses Chinois, ils répondaient qu'il suffisait de mettre de nouvelles terres en valeur. Rien ne leur faisait peur. Ils goberaient le Tibet et la Sibérie sans un hoquet. Et les Russes alors ? Selon eux, les Russes avaient trop mauvaise conscience à leur égard, ils n'oseraient pas intervenir. La Chine vivait d'illusions et son immense armée se figurait qu'elle partirait bientôt à l'assaut de la planète, rien ne l'en empêcherait, et une espèce de griserie palpitait au pied des statues géantes de Mao. Lui, laissait dire et se taisait. Les délégations allaient visiter le dieu et s'en revenaient frissonnantes. Qu'il était grand, le héros, massif, puissant, et vêtu de gris comme un énorme rat. On demandait : « Qu'a-t-il dit ? » Rien. D'ailleurs, il ne parlait plus. Il laissait quelques bredouillements s'échapper de ses lèvres, il soupirait effondré dans son

fauteuil, trempait ses lèvres dans sa tasse tiédasse. Nul n'aurait osé élever la voix en sa présence, chacun sirotait le thé fadasse, un ambassadeur dévidait un lieu commun, un ministre un autre, le dieu opinait du chef en souriant. Le sphinx ! A côté de moi, M. Tsaï, ivre, entendait déjà siffler les fusées chinoises au-dessus du Pacifique. New York allait être réduit en cendres. L'ai-je inventé ?

J'aurais été heureux de chanter la traversée de la rivière Ta-tu, heureux de survoler en avion militaire les contreforts neigeux qu'avaient escaladés les débris de la légion de Mao et de Chou-teh. Est-ce ma faute si je revois encore, un sombre dimanche de Tchong-king, sur un chemin boueux, le chef de la commune populaire, que précédait notre caravane automobile, écarter brutalement un vieux cul-terreux en loques avec son sac de légumes au bout d'une perche ? Un moment, je pensai qu'on avait dû se renseigner, qu'on savait que quelqu'un dans notre délégation avait mauvais caractère. Qu'allais-je imaginer ! De la France, on connaissait Montesquieu, Diderot, Robespierre, de Gaulle. Des gens comme moi, comme d'autres et même comme le nouveau ministre de la Culture, n'étaient que poussière. Dans les universités chinoises, on étudiait seulement Karl Marx, on en serait à Bernard Shaw en l'an 2000. Mon idée, germée dans le fertile cerveau de Françoise Verny, d'écrire la Longue Marche était pour les Chinois une intention saugrenue de barbare des mers extérieures. Est-ce que les Chinois l'ont écrite, leur Histoire ? Est-ce que le Parti a décidé de ce qu'on pouvait dire ? Tout le malentendu venait de là. N'empêche que des esprits supérieurs de chez nous avaient leur doctrine, n'empêche que j'aurais dû être suspendu à leurs lèvres, n'empêche que j'aurais pu raconter mon voyage en Chine d'une façon moins sauvage. Par exemple, j'aurais pu, comme ces messieurs de Sorbonne, proclamer que le vent qui soufflait de Chine allait renverser les données du monde, que nous devenions bon gré mal gré les serviteurs de cette mutation, que plus rien ne comptait que l'impérialisme populaire. J'aurais dû aussi ne pas contrarier les nouveaux seigneurs chinois et me laisser embabouiner au son des orchestres géants et de la nouvelle grosse caisse atomique. J'aurais menti, j'aurais trompé. Je ne marchai pas. J'admirais les Chinois, mais leur religion n'était pas la mienne. Que Mao

fût célébré par eux comme il l'était, qu'il fallût, comme dans un lieu saint, se recueillir, partout où Mao avait respiré, marché, écrit un poème, bu une gorgée de thé ou changé de femme, me hérissait. De Gaulle suffisait. Je m'ennuyais, j'étouffais, je le disais, je ne cachais pas mes déceptions, j'oubliais que je n'étais pas au pays de la ligne droite et qu'on avançait là-bas par une succession de détours. Je protestais quand quelqu'un tripatouillait dates et documents. L'Histoire était pareille à un fleuve en crue débouchant sur la mer, toutes les eaux s'y mêlaient, une large vomissure de vase et de boue salissait les estuaires. L'un des pères de la révolution chinoise, Sun Yat-sen, répétait que les Chinois ne savaient pas ce qu'est la liberté et que le peu qu'ils pouvaient en goûter était encore de trop, pensez donc, comment forcer à obéir ces millions et millions d'êtres pensants, cette fourmilière en furie ? Chinois, on est esclave de vocation, on a besoin de maître, et si l'on proteste c'est à cause de la nourriture. Parce que le reste de l'univers, qui le connaît et comment sait-on ce qui s'y passe sinon par le seul journal qui paraisse, ou, maintenant, par le seul journal télévisé qui lance les nouvelles ? J'eus beau râler, rien n'y fit. Nous achevâmes notre voyage à Canton où flottait déjà un certain débraillé et où il y avait des boutiques d'antiquaires. J'achetai quelques babioles et enfin le train nous emmena à Hong Kong.

M. Tsaï et moi, nous nous quittâmes presque en pleurant

Non seulement je ne ramenais pas le récit de la Longue Marche que je dus reconstituer de bric et de broc, mais je n'avais pas su entrer dans les bonnes grâces de notre ambassadeur en Chine, je ne m'étais pas confondu en courbettes et en flatteries, je n'avais pas déclamé que Mao était le plus grand roi du monde, je n'avais même pas su profiter de la visite du nouveau ministre de la Culture, Jacques Duhamel, un ancien ami, pour me faufiler derrière lui dans le palais, il y a des choses qu'il vaut mieux ne pas me suggérer. Partagé entre mon admiration pour Mao, son courage et ma réprobation pour sa cruauté et son orgueil, j'avais une immense curiosité de voir le phénomène de près, je n'allais lécher les pieds de personne. Bref, comme je n'avais pas bonne réputation auprès des

autorités, mon nom ne s'inscrivit pas parmi les élus emmenés en secret, une nuit, sur la colline sacrée. Parmi mes confrères en journalisme et même dans l'entourage de l'ambassadeur, beaucoup s'en réjouirent, qui me considéraient comme un prétentieux dont il fallait clouer le bec. Bref, je ne vis pas Mao. Je dus me contenter du bouillant maréchal Chen Yi, ministre des Affaires étrangères, qu'on me livra comme un os que je rongeai tant que je pus, rude gaillard qui m'annonça l'apocalypse pour bientôt. L'interview, à peine améliorée par mes soins, fut expédiée en télex à *l'Express.* Je ne cachai à personne que mon voyage était loupé, je revenais sans la cantate qu'on attendait. Toujours princier, J.-J. S.-S. décida que j'étais à jeter aux chiens et ne voulut plus entendre parler de moi. Si j'avais vu Mao, mon portrait aurait été au vitriol, personne en France ne l'aurait publié.

Des extrêmes de l'Orient, de la Chine lointaine, je rentrai penaud, avec un cachet d'idéogrammes dont je me sers comme ex-libris et un cerf-volant de bazar que j'accrochai dans mon bureau. Ma jeune compagne m'avait quitté. Elle mit de l'ordre dans son trésor d'images, Christian Bourgois composa un album, *les Chinois,* dont j'écrivis la préface un peu mélancolique. Mon chagrin était cuisant. Louise de Vilmorin me dit que c'était la vie, que j'en tirerais du miel après le fiel, qu'elle aimerait aussi se balader en Chine mais comme impératrice ou, à la rigueur, première courtisane d'un prince qui serait reçu avec le faste d'autrefois. Je voyais bien à qui elle songeait. Il allait y aller enfin, en Chine, on ne pourrait plus dire qu'il avait écrit *la Condition humaine* et raconté qu'il avait été commissaire politique à Shanghai et à Canton sans avoir jamais mis les pieds ailleurs qu'à Hong Kong. Cette fois, débarquant à Pékin comme ministre d'Etat, il allait raviver la mémoire de ses vieux copains Mao et Chou En-lai par des conversations sur la politique de la Chine et sur celle du général de Gaulle, tu parles, Charles ! Ils analyseraient ensemble le monde et la stratégie des USA, il leur citerait des paroles prophétiques de son ami Trotsky, il reprendrait aussi le récit de la Longue Marche dans huit pages des *Antimémoires* parus en 1967, deux ans après moi qui lui en consacre le double. Il inventerait questions et réponses, décor, apartés, exclamations, et, touillant dans un mortier un jaune d'œuf, de l'huile

et le génie de Mao, avec le pilon de son propre génie, il écrirait un chapitre posthume de *la Condition humaine*, quelle mayonnaise ! On lui tendrait le texte de la sténographie de l'entretien, un ambassadeur lui dirait : « C'est un peu léger », et il répondrait « Ne vous inquiétez pas, je compléterai ». Et c'est le « Pigeon André Malraux » de chez Lasserre.

Au printemps, j'arrivai à la fin de mon récit, et Christian Bourgois, toujours mince, toujours brûlant d'une fièvre froide, vint me voir, intrigué et habité d'une appréhension. Un éditeur, quand il aime son auteur, est pour lui plein d'espoir et de crainte. Il cherche à lui éviter tous déboires, il voudrait même voir son front couronné. Pierre Nora l'accompagnait. Tous deux me prièrent puis me supplièrent de supprimer toute allusion à des mésaventures : le lecteur ne comprendrait pas qu'un écrivain en route pour la Chine ne fût pas totalement possédé par cette affaire et osât y mêler des sentiments mineurs. Il s'agissait d'un voyage presque officiel, j'étais presque en service commandé, presque chargé de mission pour un sujet qu'il m'avait été impossible d'atteindre. Quel intérêt présentaient mes brouilles sentimentales ? En maints endroits, suivant mes sinologues de près, je me targuais de raconter l'Histoire en historien, mes propres déboires n'étaient de taille ni avec la Longue Marche ni avec rien. Le genre ne permettait pas de biais, il me fallait choisir : je demeurais quelqu'un de sérieux ou je m'égarais, et alors, on ne pourrait plus jamais m'accorder confiance en rien, je brûlais mes vaisseaux. « Ah ! me dis-je, ah ! mon Dieu, ah ! la funeste idée que m'a inspirée la Longue Marche ! » Si encore, retournant mes batteries, j'avais, ailleurs, raconté la Chine comme Flaubert racontait son voyage en Orient, dans des lettres, on aurait pu, d'un autre côté, en tirer argument de scandale. Ce n'était pas mon cas. Quand elle m'en avait maroufflé l'idée, Françoise Verny ne connaissait pas plus la Chine que moi. Elle croyait naïvement que c'était un empire où l'on pouvait aller comme on voulait. J'aurais dû partir dans le seul dessein de m'en remettre à ce que je verrais ou ressentirais, mais qui m'eût parrainé alors ? A *l'Express* comme ailleurs on ne goûtait que ce qui sentait fort, il fallait du fantastique, de l'insolite, du sublime ou du

faisandé, et je me rebellai soudain contre tous les commandements dont je m'étais laissé charger à mon départ. Qu'avais-je
à vouloir être agréable aux uns ou aux autres en ne m'écartant
pas des conventions pour ne pas me priver du succès qui va
avec elles ? En vérité, ce n'était pas la Chine que j'avais essayé
de conquérir sans être un sinologue, mais, à travers la Chine,
tout ce qui semblait s'opposer à ce que je ressentais pour elle.
N'y avait-il pas là chez moi beaucoup d'orgueil et une certaine
simplicité d'esprit ? Et pourquoi n'eût-ce pas été une méthode
comme les autres ? Je craignais qu'on ironisât parce que
j'accordais trop d'importance à ma propre personne alors qu'il
s'agissait, depuis que la Chine avait sa première bombe
nucléaire, du sort du monde.

Aveuglé comme je l'étais, je m'en tins mordicus à ma
version des choses. A mes yeux, tout écrivain restait influencé
par ce qui lui arrivait, et il était honnête et parfois malicieux
d'ajouter à une déception d'ordre politique une déception
intime ou amoureuse qui, entremêlée à l'autre, laissait mieux
découvrir les raisons qui font agir les hommes. Si, au début de
cette relation de mon voyage en Chine, je me demande si je
n'ai pas été le Maxime Du Camp de Flaubert, c'est parce que le
génie de Flaubert m'en impose. Jamais, menteur et flatteur
comme il était, Maxime Du Camp n'aurait osé parler de ses
déboires sentimentaux ou des petitesses qu'il découvrait à
l'étranger, il tenait trop à appartenir un jour à l'Institut. Je
n'étais pas Flaubert non plus, hélas, mais je lui avais peut-être
emprunté le pire, son caractère, et je le dis non pour m'en
vanter mais pour m'en punir.

Le livre parut sous une superbe couverture imaginée par
Christian Bourgois. Aussitôt, de partout s'élevèrent des cris de
bonzes effarouchés : j'avais attenté à la pudeur de la religion
maoïste, je bafouais la sainte doctrine, j'étais un éléphant
saccageant un magasin de porcelaines, une vipère lubrique. Au
lieu d'intituler mon livre *le Voyage en Chine*, j'aurais dû
l'appeler *Voyage d'un écrivain en Chine*, ou d'un jobard.
Non, non, l'éditeur s'y opposa. On ne voulait pas de moi
comme humoriste ou comme gogo.

Quand je me remémore aujourd'hui cette tempête, je
comprends que je fournissais prétexte à ceux qui ne me
voulaient pas du bien. Il y avait la presse de gauche que

j'agaçais et qui dénonçait les erreurs de doctrine que je commettais : j'osais toucher au maître de la révolution chinoise, à l'homme qu'en Occident tout progressiste considérait comme l'exemple, le demi-dieu, le timonier des idées en cour. Qui étais-je pour tout vilipender ? Mon intelligence, somme toute militaire, se limitait à peu de chose. Une dizaine de sinologues qui se déchiraient entre eux avaient seuls le droit de dire ce qu'on pouvait, après eux, répéter de la Chine : deux ou trois d'entre eux étaient seuls autorisés à parler de Mao, des phases de sa vie, de sa conduite et des événements qui changeaient la face du monde. Personne à gauche n'osait se prononcer sans leur caution, tout jugement était suspect qui s'écartait du leur. Quant à la presse de droite, elle se vengea des coups que je lui avais portés pendant la guerre d'Algérie : j'étais un traître, un parjure, rien de bon ne pouvait venir de moi, mes écarts de moralité accusaient le triste sire que j'étais. Tout juste si on ne me dénonçait pas comme un menteur. Et pourtant, il n'y a pas eu grand changement depuis. Les visas durent plus longtemps, les couleurs agrémentent le vêtement des femmes, mais il y a autant de lieux interdits qu'autrefois et quand une nouvelle croisière Citroën lance 140 AX de Canton à Pékin, les incidents avec la police chinoise émaillent tout le parcours. Défense de photographier les paysans et les ânes. Et personne n'a refait la Longue Marche.

Qui veut réussir doit tenir compte de ce qui se dit et ne se dit pas ; il doit surtout flatter ceux qui font les journaux et la mode. Je me croyais au-dessus des lois. J'appris que chaque courant d'idées, chaque système avait sa mafia : il fallait se montrer humble, demander conseil, encenser, faire sa cour et, seulement après, et si l'on savait, manigancer. Je n'étais qu'un homme d'humeurs qui, avec son goût pour la solitude, se croyait capable de servir sa petite vérité sans se douter qu'il bravait les puissants. Il y avait chez moi du provocateur mais aussi une certaine vanité proche de la présomption.

D'accord, d'accord. De mon temps, Pierre Cardin ne servait pas encore des repas aux nouveaux mandarins de Pékin. De mon temps, régnait Mao souverain maître, et on se disait : « Mon Dieu, que se passera-t-il quand il ne sera plus là ? » Et j'osais mettre en doute cet homme-là ? Je subis la désapprobation générale, mon livre fut une catastrophe. N'empêche. Au

réveillon de Noël qui suivit chez une de mes amies du Pays basque qui s'occupait en vain de me remarier, Kessel et moi chantions ensemble des complaintes russes en tapant des mains.

XXI

Une fière chandelle à Doyon

Averrières, Louise buvait beaucoup de whisky pour se mettre en train, puis avec l'aide de Yolé, sa camériste, se plongeait dans un bain très chaud. Deux cachets de Véganine, elle s'habillait et descendait, fraîche comme une rose. Un soir, Léo Ferré débarqua d'une grosse bagnole américaine immatriculée à Monaco, avec une nouvelle femme et deux chiens énormes, des veaux, lents et lourds, pas méchants, qui s'affalaient partout. Il chanta toute la soirée, dîner compris, en s'accompagnant au piano. Louise s'extasiait, nous étions un peu ahuris. Elle parlait rarement de Malraux. L'avait-elle revu depuis 1946 à l'ambassade d'Angleterre où elle avait vécu un temps avec Duff Cooper ? Malraux était toujours ministre, elle s'obstinait à l'inviter, il ne venait pas. Elle continuait à rêver, et il allait entreprendre ce voyage en Chine sans elle, hélas, qui n'aura jamais mangé de canard laqué que chez Maxim's. Gaston, le coq du Niger, vieillissait au milieu de ses poules, je me hâtai de me retirer dans une maison que je venais d'acheter presque en ruine en vue de Vézelay et me mis au travail. L'hiver approchait. Moinot trouva que j'étais trop seul et me conseilla d'acheter un chien

Ce teckel minuscule que je mettais parfois dans la poche de mon manteau, je l'appelai Mao, nous ne nous quittâmes plus. Je me crus son dieu, j'étais son esclave, je ne lui refusais rien, il couchait dans mon lit sous l'édredron. Après avoir supporté les multitudes de la Chine, je vivais dans une douce campagne de Bourgogne où s'étiraient des brouillards mauves. Déjà des frimas s'effilochaient dans les haies. J'avais hâte de me délivrer de la Chine comme d'une passion malheureuse, ce qui m'inspira de me délivrer aussi de tout ce que j'avais

ressenti là-bas. Je le fis avec trop de pudeur, n'osant pas claironner que je ne revenais pas d'un voyage dans l'empire du Milieu, mais d'une expédition à travers les vastes provinces de l'amour.

Quand, d'Avallon, je reviens chez moi par la route qui va à Clamecy, je débouche sur le calvaire de Montjoie, là où, soudain, Vézelay apparaissait aux pèlerins de Compostelle. En ce temps-là, ils tombaient à genoux et versaient une larme. Un instant, devant cette houle et ce long troupeau de collines où la brume s'étire, se love, s'encapuchonne, s'enfouit, cette lumière du soir qui va bientôt incendier l'horizon, cette douce toison des forêts dans les lointains, ces pitons qui se succèdent, un instant je retrouve une harmonie et un mystère qui me rappellent la Chine indéchiffrable et vaporeuse, et jusqu'à l'idée que nous nous faisions d'elle, empire du Milieu, terre méconnue, ennuagée dans une légende que nous n'étions pas sûrs de jamais comprendre. Ici, les tours de Vézelay annoncent la victoire de la vie sur la mort. Je suis là sans savoir pourquoi, j'y suis heureux, je ne me vois pas ailleurs.

Ainsi, quand j'écrivais ce livre sur la Chine dans la maison que je venais d'acheter, seul enfin avec mes problèmes et mon chien Mao, j'allais me promener à travers un désert enchanté, et je pouvais m'imaginer encore en Chine, mais sans d'innombrables Chinois attachés à mes pas, comme je me sentais bien ! Déjà Françoise Verny me harponnait. Elle m'avait trouvé quelque chose, je ne pouvais pas y échapper, c'était un sujet à quoi personne n'avait encore songé, et pas un petit machin de rien du tout : une histoire du commencement à la fin, une saga. Et qui venait de là-bas ? Qui y avait ses morts ? Qui était capable de ressusciter tout cela ? « Pas moi », répondais-je. Je n'étais pas romancier. « Tu le deviendras. » Je répliquais que ma famille n'était pas ce qu'elle croyait. « Ta famille, tu t'en inventeras une, imbécile !... »

On n'en a jamais fini avec ce métier-là. A peine lève-t-on le nez d'un sujet qu'on vous le remet sur un autre. On se croit libéré, on ne l'est jamais. Si ce n'est pas une idée qui vous inspire, c'est une idée qu'on vous impose. Vous devez, il n'y a que vous, vous ne pouvez pas vous dérober. Et pour couronner le tout, l'attrape-nigaud : « Ce sera ta gloire, tu verras... »

Mon bouquin sur la Chine se vendit mal, j'en fus tout empoicré. Naturellement c'était ma faute, puisque je n'avais pas écouté Christian Bourgois. Pour se venger de quoi ? *l'Express* ne daigna pas souffler un mot du livre que, mélancoliquement, je voyais s'éloigner dans le sombre purgatoire des ouvrages mort-nés quand Jean Daniel, qui avait quitté le journal où il se sentait barré et dirigeait le *Nouvel Obs*, eut l'idée d'ouvrir un débat sur le thème : « Est-ce que la Chine fait peur ? » Je fonçai dans un virulent plaidoyer auquel apporta la contradiction Edgar Snow, le répondant classique, l'Occidental qui connaissait le mieux Mao, et K. S. Karol. Parlant de moi, le *Nouvel Obs* écrivait : « Cet homme de caractère et d'humeur suit sa pente, mais comme dit Gide, en montant. Il est à contre-courant sans le vouloir, simplement parce qu'il ignore le courant. Fasciné par l'épopée personnelle de Mao Tsé-toung, il avait entrepris d'écrire l'histoire de la Longue Marche. Les difficultés qu'il connut en Chine rendirent ce projet irréalisable. Il explique d'une manière tumultueuse et polémique, irritée et irritante, dans *le Voyage en Chine* comment ces difficultés même l'autorisèrent à tirer des conclusions qui seront évidemment très controversées. » Plus tard, dans un portrait qu'il brossa pour *Celfan Review* de Philadelphie, Jean Daniel défendit ma démarche : « Dès la première semaine (...), grâce à une sorte d'instinct de rigueur, pour lui universelle, il avait compris l'essentiel en refusant d'admettre (...) pour les Chinois ce qu'il refusait en France pour les Français. Il m'adressa un article sur les signes extérieurs du despotisme. Parfait d'écriture mais complètement contraire au conformisme ambiant. J'ai décidé de le publier mais en l'équilibrant d'un article très maoïste d'un autre ami (...). Je n'entendis autour de moi que plaintes et récriminations sur le manque de sens politique de Jules Roy à qui j'avais eu le tort de faire confiance. Je viens de relire l'article en question : après tant d'années, pas un mot à reprendre... »

Soudain je fus ailleurs. Cette idée d'une saga m'avait à ce point envahi que j'envisageai de changer de vie puisqu'il me faudrait tout accorder au gigantesque, ça allait de soi. C'est

alors qu'on m'offrit une somme rondelette pour un livre sur Pétain, à l'occasion du centenaire de sa naissance. Le sujet ne m'emballait pas, mais la somme oui, en raison du désastre de la Chine. Je proposai de reprendre le procès, atroce, et de l'ajuster comme une dramatique. Jacques Isorni me confia son dossier de presse. Je m'y plongeai, je me jurai de dire toute la vérité, même si elle était gênante, et travaillai comme un forçat pendant six mois. Cela rendait ma vie ardente. J'allais, je venais, Mao sous le bras, de mon perchoir de Paris à la maison qu'avec une grande dépense j'avais transformée. Je n'avais pas résisté à son charme, j'avais besoin d'elle, elle m'avait conquis. Pour une femme, pour des toits, pour une cause, le coup de foudre, si dangereux qu'il soit, est la seule vérité. Le reste est arrangement, compromis, établissement. André de Vilmorin, le frère de Louise, me fit planter des rosiers et des chèvrefeuilles dans la cour que j'avais pavée, il me dessina une allée de tilleuls de Hollande, me commanda de niveler le parc tout en creux et bosses, et logea des noyers en quinconce dans un verger dépeuplé.

De temps à autre, Mao sur les talons, j'allais à pied à Vézelay où un gendarme qui portait le vieux nom français de Mahaut, croyait que je m'étais moqué en appelant mon chien comme lui. J'empoignais Mao par la peau du cou pour l'aider à sauter les ruisseaux, j'aimais cette vue chinoise sur les collines qu'il fallait dévaler puis escalader avant d'atteindre la longue basilique trapue. J'entrais, Mao caché dans ma poitrine, je priais, je repartais songeur et pacifié. Est-ce parce que j'avais établi là sous un toit voisin mon frère et sa femme depuis leur départ d'Algérie, deux ans après l'indépendance ? Il me semblait que j'avais retrouvé une nouvelle terre natale. Peut-être, peut-être. Pas au point d'en baiser le sol et de me dire, déjà un peu toqué, un peu maso, souvent mégalo, que j'étais là pour toujours. Matthieu Galey vint là plus d'une fois, séduit par le lieu qu'il jugeait sublime, et plein de méfiance pour moi qu'il dénonçait « comme animé par l'Esprit-Saint » dans mes ambitions. De mes extravagances il se raillait. J'avais la tête un peu tournée, c'est vrai. Ne l'ai-je pas encore ? Non loin de là, à Bazoches, se dressait l'énorme château où Vauban, monstre d'architecture et d'assise militaires, rare génie que l'âpre Morvan eût engendré, avait installé son bureau d'études, son brain-trust. Matthieu Galey ne se trompait pas, je rêvais moi

aussi d'avoir mes nègres. Pourquoi pas ? « Comme Dumas père », disait Druon, plus mégalo que moi, et Sigaux serait aussi leur chef. Avec un atelier j'irais plus loin, je brasserais plus de pâte, je construirais une œuvre plus vaste.

Pour le procès de Pétain, dont j'avais hâte de me débarrasser, je cueillis dans Shakespeare la description du misérable roi Lear, et citai dans Byron l'indignation du doge Marino Fallero accusé de trahison par un patricien vindicatif, je relus les débats, les témoignages, les plaidoiries, je reconstituai la discussion des jurés de la Haute Cour. Je revécus mes réactions d'ancien enfant de Pétain, comme disait Doyon, et l'éditeur rappellera un mot de Robert Kanters sur les deux hommes qui sont en moi. Pétain n'avait jamais été un traître, mais un vieillard plein d'illusions, et aucun de ceux qui l'avaient servi n'avait démérité, sauf peut-être par les serments de polichinelle à lui prêtés, en ce temps-là, même par ses propres juges. Son drame était celui de la France vaincue. Lui, quand on lui apprendra qu'il est condamné à mort mais que la sentence ne sera pas exécutée, dira à propos de son ancien disciple de Gaulle : « Je l'ai fait condamner à mort. Lui aussi. Nous sommes quittes. » Cette nuit-là, une ambulance avait conduit le pauvre vieux à Villacoublay où on l'avait hissé dans un engin dont il avait horreur : un avion, qui l'emporta vers le fort du Portalet, là où Mandel, ministre juif, avait été jadis enfermé sur son ordre. Faveur royale ou ironie du sort : cet avion était le Dakota personnel du général de Gaulle. Il pleuvait. C'était sinistre.

Un ambassadeur en fonction me somma à plusieurs reprises de rectifier à propos des amours du général Weygand à Beyrouth. Pourquoi aurais-je rectifié puisque c'était vrai ? Je l'envoyai au bain. Il me promit que cela me coûterait cher, ce qui se produisit quand l'ambassadeur occupa de hautes fonctions à l'ensemble de la télévision-radio qu'on appelait alors l'ORTF. J'avais ce que je méritais : j'avais vidé mon cœur à propos du maréchal et du général de Gaulle. J'ai tellement vidé mon cœur que je devrais me sentir à présent avec un muscle plat, ballottant dans ma poitrine. Eh bien, non. Il bat encore quand je m'indigne. Je ne m'en plains pas.

J'étais à peine rentré de Chine, en butte à de nombreuses désillusions et en plein effort pour m'en fabriquer de nouvel-

les, quand une jeune femme vint m'interviewer à Paris pour le journal *Arts*. Elle était russe. Elle aurait pu m'en vouloir à propos de ce que j'avais écrit de Moscou. Elle fut le seul bonheur que me valut mon voyage en Chine, Mao était couché à mes pieds tandis qu'elle m'interrogeait, nous ne nous sommes jamais quittés depuis, elle et moi. Nous nous mariâmes à la campagne, l'hiver qui suivit, et j'ai raconté cela aussi drôlement que j'ai pu dans *la Saison des Za*, où j'imaginai même, à la table de notre gentille noce, mon père René Louis Doyon, l'œil plein de convoitise et la lèvre humide. Désormais, la maison avait ce qui lui manquait, une âme. Moi aussi J'ai beaucoup changé depuis. Je suis resté barbare mais mon caractère s'est adouci. Je le redis parce que c'est vrai. J'ai toujours sur la tête l'oiseau du sud de la Volga qui s'y posa un jour.

Nous nous mîmes aussitôt au travail. Nous visitâmes la Franche-Comté et l'Ariège dont mes aïeux étaient originaires. De temps en temps, un château en ruine me tentait, et comme ma nouvelle femme avait épousé ma folie, nous faillîmes commettre deux ou trois excentricités dans lesquelles, au dernier moment, j'évitai par miracle de tomber. Puis nous allâmes, avec ma fille, en Algérie fureter dans les archives des mairies et dans les bibliothèques. Quand nous revînmes chez nous, Mao fut écrasé par une voiture. J'en éprouvai tellement de chagrin que j'écrivis aussitôt un récit que Christian Bourgois publia sous le titre *la Mort de Mao*. Dans les librairies, des gens s'arrêtaient songeurs : « Tiens, disaient-ils, il a dû mourir sans qu'on l'ait su... » D'autres s'indignaient qu'un auteur pût tromper le lecteur sur un sujet aussi sérieux. Plus tard, quand nous apprîmes qu'enfin le vrai Mao était mort et vitrifié, cent mille travailleurs lui élevèrent en deux jours et deux nuits un mausolée de trente-trois mètres de haut. La place Tian'anmen est à jamais défigurée par ce mastodonte de béton à l'abri des plus forts tremblements de terre. Contrairement aux pronostics alarmistes, tout continua comme de son vivant. A présent les secrétaires du Parti se succèdent, fabricotent leurs bombes, nous visitent, invitent les présidents des Etats-Unis et se préparent à expédier une navette dans l'espace avec des Chinois aux commandes. Nous nous sommes tous trompés, moi le premier, l'Apocalypse ne s'est pas produite. A mes yeux, le vrai Mao n'est pas le grand,

c'est le petit, c'est le mien. Quant à Doyon qui m'avait tant houspillé, je reçus soudain de lui une lettre bouleversante. Je courus impasse Guéménée.

Tout en haut, à l'étage où il habitait, je le découvris dans un fauteuil éventré, au milieu de l'appartement vide. C'était l'heure de sa sieste, il dormait enveloppé dans un pardessus crasseux. Il se réveilla, nous nous jetâmes dans les bras l'un de l'autre, et comme je lui disais que l'odeur était moins forte « Forcément, plus personne ne s'occupe des chats, répondit-il. Ils n'ont plus rien à manger, ils ont fichu le camp... » C'était l'hiver, il faisait froid chez lui, les huissiers de justice avaient enlevé les meubles, sauf un rayonnage déglingué sans livres, et son grabat. Une sorte de fantôme roux hérissé apparut, qu'il refoula : « C'est mon fils, idiote. » Il avait dû donner asile à une clocharde pour se sentir moins seul.

Nous descendîmes dans un bistrot où il commanda un Viandox. Il était vêtu de loques, son dentier tressautait dans sa bouche quand il parlait. A plus de quatre-vingts ans, il avait perdu toute superbe, Mme D. était morte, comme Léonie et tous ses bienfaiteurs, sa dernière cheffesse l'avait quitté, il s'engloutissait. Il m'accompagna jusqu'au métro Saint-Paul. Je lui fis porter aussitôt des sacs de charbon par un bougnat et j'alertai Moinot, toujours au cabinet de Malraux et toujours miséricordieux, qui me promit qu'on s'occuperait de lui en haut lieu. Malraux ministre tout-puissant, l'aiderait, il lui servirait peut-être une pension sur des cassettes d'Etat, on ne pouvait pas laisser un homme comme Doyon dans la misère. Malgré ses travers, ses tares, ses défauts et ses ridicules, il avait été un esprit brillant et mordant comme Diderot, une langue dorée et méchante, et il n'avait pas eu la chance de vendre sa bibliothèque à une impératrice de Russie. Comme Diderot, il savait tout et aurait pu diriger une encyclopédie s'il avait eu un peu plus d'ordre dans ses pensées, dans ses papiers et dans son style, moins d'aigreur dans ses jugements et juste ce qu'il fallait de talent en plus : *l'Enfant prodiguée* et *Géronte aux assises* n'étaient pas *la Religieuse* ni *le Neveu de Rameau* et, surtout, on ne vivait pas à la même époque. Naturellement, au temps de Diderot il aurait été aussi embastillé, ce qui l'aurait servi, et la révolution venue, il aurait fini délégué à la culture. Il avait édité, en super-luxe, *les Oraisons amoureuses de*

Jeanne-Aurélie Grivolin, Lyonnaise, les *Sonnets* de Du Bellay, le *Port-Royal* de Sainte-Beuve, Remy de Gourmont, Barbey d'Aurevilly, Huysmans, tant et tant d'autres princes de la littérature apparentés aux puissances infernales.

Dans *la Saison des Za,* j'ai raconté comment, le jour où une note de Malraux déposée dans sa boîte aux lettres lui apprenait qu'il allait toucher un pécule, puis une rente, Moinot me téléphona pour m'annoncer qu'on l'avait relevé dans la rue, inanimé, et transporté à la Pitié. Je m'y précipitai, il n'était plus, on me pria de revenir le lendemain à la rue d'à côté, à la morgue. Le lendemain après-midi, avec Guibert, je lui portai des roses ; le surlendemain, avec ma belle Russe, nous suivîmes l'office funèbre à l'église Saint-Paul, en bas de chez lui, parmi les vieux amis, et je revis Rita qui avait tant compté pour moi. Elle avait beaucoup changé, moi aussi, son mari était là, on avait l'air de camarades de la guerre de Quatorze. Un article de moi sur lui dans *le Monde* parut comme on le menait au cimetière, à Pantin où, comme pour Amrouche, je n'eus pas le courage d'aller. Dans *la Saison des Za,* je le célèbre comme un héros brillant et lamentable. Il n'est pas de jour où je ne pense à lui, où je ne lui fasse une place dans ma vie. Sacré petit père, sacré gaillard ! Son poster, la photo de 1931 agrandie, reste sous mes yeux, et la borne fontaine sur laquelle il est assis et où nous l'encadrons, Joseph Bollery, le directeur des *Cahiers Léon Bloy* et moi, coule toujours toujours entre ses cuisses. Il avait beau être impossible, il n'est plus gênant. Il savait tant de choses et n'en tira aucun enseignement pour lui : il se croyait immortel et pensait qu'il aurait toujours des amis pour son foyer et ses impôts. Marteau aussi avait, grâce à lui, reçu Céline pendant l'Occupation dans son appartement de Neuilly, et il était mort sans coucher Doyon sur son testament. En fin de compte, avec son air de se fiche de tout, ses belles promesses et son cœur sur la main, Doyon avait fini par devenir sa propre victime. Farouche anticolonialiste, il s'était déclaré pour l'Algérie française contre son fils ingrat et contre de Gaulle, je l'ai déjà dit, et lui, qui ne pouvait supporter le soleil, affirmait dans ses *Livrets du Mandarin* que, sans ses départements de l'autre côté de la Méditerranée, la France n'était plus rien. Il n'y avait que deux principes à quoi il était resté fidèle mordicus : sa méfiance à l'égard du pouvoir établi et, Mgr Bollon mis à part, son anticléricalisme forcené. Qui

sait ? Si je ne l'avais pas eu comme père putatif, comme il disait, c'est-à-dire père supposé, encore qu'il insistât sur le rappel vaguement putassier du mot, s'il n'avait pas été mon vrai père serais-je aussi méfiant que je le suis de l'avenir ? Ai-je été plus malin que lui ? Ai-je moins choqué ? Au séminaire comme lui, comme lui j'en suis sorti mais ensuite nos chemins ont divergé. Malingre et réformé, il n'avait jamais connu l'armée, où d'ailleurs, persifleur comme il était, il n'aurait jamais fait carrière. Il avait préféré s'introduire, sans le sou, dans la littérature comme secrétaire particulier d'un éditeur de Montparnasse plutôt véreux, Figuière, qui avait pour enseigne un figuier et promettait la lune à ses auteurs, moyennant finances. La Première Guerre mondiale éclatait, Figuière en profitait pour disparaître, Doyon traînait misère ici et là, traficotant, parlant, ça pour parler, il s'était même lancé dans des conférences patriotiques qui rapportaient, oh, pas grand-chose, et à Angers, la femme d'un photographe venue, pour son malheur à elle, l'écouter, et enjôlée, folle d'amour, l'avait suivi, je le rappelle, avec cinquante mille francs-or, un pactole avec quoi il s'était installé impasse Guémenée et galerie de la Madeleine. Là, le jeune Malraux apparaissait, chinait sur les quais et poussait mon Doyon à se lancer dans l'érotique. Après tout, comme dit Télémaque à propos d'Ulysse, à quel signe un enfant reconnaît-il son père ? Avec l'instituteur de Rovigo qui enseignait l'orthographe et les droits de l'homme, et fascinait les femmes de gendarmes avec un chapeau melon et des mots, des mots encore, avec lui donc et Doyon comme pères, comment ne serais-je pas devenu écrivain ?

Si, par la suite, j'ai pu être considéré comme subversif, c'est aux leçons de Doyon plus qu'aux amours coupables et à la révolte de ma mère que je le dus. Doyon fut mon Socrate à moi, comme Bernanos est mon théologien avec Ulysse et Paul de Tarse. Je sais quelles railleries ce mot de subversif peut provoquer dans des esprits sensés et dans une intelligentsia qui a ses têtes, ses tabous, et, à sa honte, ne connaît pas Doyon. C'est ainsi, et je ne m'en repens pas. Il avait de la tripe et de la dent, Doyon, il nous aimait, nous l'aimions, et forcément, on s'engueulait. Versatile dans ses attachements, hâbleur, menteur, dépensier, jeteur de poudre aux yeux, pas toujours sûr de ses références, capable d'exaltations et d'approximations, semant la zizanie, colporteur de ragots, jaloux des réussites

d'autrui, ne résistant jamais à détruire une réputation, écrivant souvent avec ses pieds, incapable de mettre un sou de côté ni de penser à son avenir, il était tout cela et bien plus encore, on pourrait accumuler sans fin des charges contre cet homme abominable, ce baiseur en foulard selon Mme D., ce scorpion qui ne rêvait que de piquer les autres, de s'enfermer ensuite dans un cercle de feu pour se piquer à son tour d'un dard mortel. N'empêche, c'était Doyon, René Louis, dit Quéqué, né, répétons-le, un 2 novembre, le jour des Morts, à Blida. Malgré son bagou, ses travers et sa langue de vipère, on le chérissait parce qu'il avait de l'esprit et du cœur, oui, oui, du cœur ! Il ne résistait pas à l'infortune et au malheur, il accueillait tous ceux qui souffraient, les animaux surtout, parce que les hommes ont, d'habitude, si peu que ce soit, le moyen de se défendre encore, tandis que les chiens et les chats... Il les ramenait chez lui, les réchauffait, leur donnait à manger, et si vous étiez un chat, vous confiait à Mme D. qui s'arrangeait avec la SPA, les voisins et ses petites amies du quartier. Si vous étiez un chien, il vous gardait. Voilà pourquoi, si décidé qu'on fût à ne pas l'écouter, à ne prêter aucune attention à ses vacheries ou même à le blâmer, on retournait chez lui malgré l'odeur qui vous prenait à la gorge sur le palier du quatrième de ce numéro 2 de l'impasse Guéménée, dans le quatrième encore. Toujours le fatal chiffre 2. Alors, quand on poussait la porte...

Longtemps, je cherchai un titre pour ma saga. Le vrai, *les Conquérants*, cet animal de Malraux l'avait pris avant moi. A cause du mythe je tournai longtemps autour du thème des chevaux au grand cœur, parfois ailés, ivres de vent. *Les Chevaux de feu* existaient déjà. Un jour où j'allais aux Archives de France par la rue des Francs-Bourgeois, étincela soudain l'enseigne d'un magasin d'antiquités : *les Chevaux du Soleil*. A deux pas de là, à l'hôtel Rohan, sur un haut-relief de Robert Le Lorrain, ils buvaient la lumière qu'Apollon leur tendait.

A cinq heures du matin en hiver, le réveil sonnait. Mon héroïne russe bondissait hors du lit, je la suivais. Elle avait surtout vécu dans les villes, elle ne connaissait pas les animaux,

ni les plantes, ni le nom des étoiles. Avec la chienne qui avait succédé à Mao, elle sortait dans la campagne et assistait à la naissance de l'aube. Au milieu de la matinée, elle tapait à la machine ce que j'avais pondu ; je relisais ma copie dans l'après-midi. Le soir, nous dînions aux chandelles avec mes personnages. Le vin parfois nous emportait, il arrivait que nous nous heurtions, elle montait dans sa chambre, je l'entendais fourgonner toute la nuit au-dessus de moi et, le matin, je me traînais à ses pieds, nous défaisions ses bagages, nous nous remettions au travail. C'étaient les amours russes, ma violence, notre folie. Le samedi, elle lisait à voix haute les feuillets de la semaine. A l'exemple de mon maître Flaubert, j'aurais pu lire moi-même si je n'avais craint de le singer trop. Je corrigeais à l'oreille.

Je désespérais souvent. Mon cher amour, à qui mes personnages féminins ressemblent tous, me rassurait, je reprenais courage. J'avais découvert que l'expédition d'Alger était un acte de brigandage déguisé en croisade avec les bénédictions de l'Eglise. A l'école, au lycée, chez les pères, on ne m'avait jamais parlé que du coup d'éventail au consul de France, une insulte qu'il fallait venger pour l'honneur national, et encore des corsaires en Méditerranée, des captifs qu'on n'appelait pas encore des otages ; pas un mot des millions-or que nous devions au dey pour des fournitures de fourrage et de blé au temps de la Constituante ou de la Convention. Là s'était entremis Jacob Bacri, que Roland Bacri, le poète du *Canard enchaîné*, s'est donné pour aïeul. Aux yeux du monde, comme libérateurs, nous avions fait main basse sur le pays après une longue suite de batailles, de pillages et de dévastations, d'enfumades et de crimes, puis Louis-Philippe et la République avaient fondé une colonie où mes ancêtres avaient vécu et où j'étais né. J'allais raconter l'histoire d'une épopée que traversaient trois guerres auxquelles les indigènes avaient participé, puis ce serait la rébellion et le sombre retour à l'Hexagone. Tel était mon projet. Tel il fut.

De temps en temps, Françoise Verny venait, accompagnée de Bernard Privat, le neveu de Bernard Grasset à la direction de la maison. Il avait une tête rase, un nez qu'il tendait pour humer les odeurs ; c'était aussi un poète, un homme de culture et de passion qui aimait ses auteurs et les gueuletons. Il flairait mon manuscrit, disparaissait un soir

avec, revenait le lendemain : « C'est un fleuve, ça n'arrête pas, ce sera superbe. » A la fin de l'hiver, des oies sauvages se posaient près de chez nous, nous les entendions caqueter. A l'aube, elles battaient des ailes et s'envolaient. Pour Nourissier, dans *les Nouvelles littéraires,* j'étais « un romancier-architecte ». J'aurais voulu tout écrire d'un jet et ne publier qu'à la fin l'œuvre corrigée et remaniée ; l'éditeur préféra sortir les tomes les uns après les autres. Quand j'eus terminé, dix ans plus tard, le dernier, je ressemblais à Léautaud : miné, ravagé, vidé, je tenais à peine debout. De l'hôtel du Pont-Royal où nous descendions à Paris et que fréquentaient tous les littérateurs de vague renom, j'eus du mal à porter mon manuscrit rue des Saints-Pères, à quelques pas de là, au siège des éditions Grasset. A Jean-Claude Fasquelle, je dis ce que dit chaque écrivain qui croit s'être dépossédé de lui-même : « Là-dedans, il y a la guerre, les trahisons, l'éternité, la vie, la mort... » C'était en 1975. Max-Pol Fouchet posa une couronne sur mon front et Nourissier écrivit dans *le Point :* « La grande aventure et mésaventure algérienne, cette affaire d'amour, de mépris et de colère longue de plus d'un siècle possède désormais son roman. Jules Roy termine la plus belle aventure de sa vie d'écrivain... » Nourissier, hein ? Et plus tard, sur mon *Guynemer, ange de la mort,* il se fendra d'un éloge étincelant. Alors, Sigaux, qui me répétait de me méfier ? Il est comme ça, Nourissier. Bon père, bon époux, il a ses crises parfois, il désespère de ne pas atteindre le zénith, il veut voir des académiciens lui lécher les pieds. Les éditeurs, n'en parlons pas. Petit-bourgeois craint et flatté, il règne sur la littérature, place les bons à sa droite, les méchants à sa gauche. N'empêche, il écrit aussi bien que Paul Morand, il aime les chiens plus que les voitures et les chevaux, voilà ce qui me rapproche de lui.

Depuis la Chine dix ans avaient passé, j'étais devenu quelqu'un d'autre. Les sauvageries, ce n'était plus moi qui les commettais. Je les racontais, j'étais le rejeton de personnages, de héros, de femmes au grand cœur qui traversaient la vie comme des comètes. Le roman m'avait civilisé, je devais une fière chandelle à Doyon.

Dans les années 1980, plus de vingt ans après, comme je n'étais plus un barbare, que ma nouvelle femme m'avait changé, et que l'étoile filante de Françoise Verny s'arrêtait un

instant rue Sébastien-Bottin, j'en profitai pour tenter une ouverture que Simone Gallimard facilita. On m'attendait pour notre rendez-vous, je me rendis dans cette maison tant aimée deux minutes avant l'heure, le cœur un peu battant, presque comme un jeune écrivain, mais sans manuscrit sous le bras. A l'heure dite, une secrétaire vint me chercher pour me conduire à l'étage noble. Claude Gallimard se leva lourdement de son bureau, ses cheveux étaient devenus blancs, nous nous embrassâmes et parlâmes un moment. De rien. Surtout pas du passé. D'un pas qui avait de la peine à s'arracher de la terre, il m'emmena chez son assistante puis chez Robert Gallimard, où se gouverne la postérité. Puisque je désirais voir Françoise Verny, on m'indiqua où elle travaillait, je grimpai sous les combles. Je ne l'avais pas avertie de mon passage, elle semblait à l'étroit, son atelier regorgeait de catéchumènes en extase. Elle vint m'ouvrir en chuchotant, et même avec un doigt sur la bouche. J'hésitai et, soudain, en proie à je ne sais quoi, je m'enfuis. A travers ces couloirs où l'on marchait désormais sur du velours, où jamais ne perçait un éclat de voix, une sorte de panique s'empara de moi. Rien ni personne n'était plus à la même place, ceux que j'avais chéris étaient morts ou près de mourir, m'avaient oublié ou osaient à peine se souvenir de moi. Au bar du Pont-Royal, je me fis servir un double scotch. C'était l'heure où il n'y avait personne encore, que des amoureux qui se parlaient à voix basse, sans regarder autour d'eux.

Je ne sais pourquoi je me mis à songer à notre ancienne bande de lurons des Deux-Magots et de chez Lipp à présent dispersée. Sigaux était mort humblement après son édition de Jules Renard dans la Pléiade, Kanters s'était éteint héroïquement dans le noir parce qu'il n'avait jamais, dans ses articles de critique, écrit autre chose que ce qu'il pensait. Claude Mauriac non plus, mais lui, heureusement, vivait, et d'un jour où il avait été question de moi chez les Goncourt, Bernard Clavel m'avait rapporté le cri presque unanime qui s'était élevé chez Drouant : « Pas de cet emmerdeur-là chez nous !... »

Je me sentis bien seul tout à coup. Pour me consoler, je me dis qu'on ne se refaisait pas, je vidai mon verre avec un nouveau regard vers les amoureux et j'eus un élan vers les brillants sujets parmi nous qui avaient réussi, et de qui, à part Moinot, je parle si peu.

XXII

Allegretto ma non troppo

ON CHUCHOTAIT que Malraux était le chevalier servant d'une ancienne étoile à qui il restait de beaux feux et qui habitait près de la Comédie-Française, presque en face de chez lui. Peut-être était-ce à cause d'elle qu'il n'avait pas d'abord répondu à Louise. Peut-être se lassa-t-il ? A l'occasion de la sortie des *Antimémoires* en 1967, un grand déjeuner eut lieu à Versailles dans les appartements du conservateur en chef, familier de Verrières, Gérard Vanderkemp, fidèle ami de Louise. Moinot y était. A peine une vingtaine de convives par tables rondes, de l'argenterie et, dans ce décor, Louise à côté de Malraux. En face de lui à la même table, Moinot découvrit tout à coup un ministre qu'il ne connaissait pas. Le sien était plutôt grave, empesé, exigeant, souvent lointain ; seuls les problèmes majeurs le retenaient. Miracle, ce Malraux-là s'effaçait derrière un autre qui riait, buvait, n'écoutait que Louise, et s'esclaffait quand elle lui parlait à l'oreille. Le champagne pétillait, les cristaux étincelaient, il y avait du soleil, des larbins déguisés en marquis servaient en gants blancs. Durant tout le repas, Malraux épanoui enfin, heureux, subjugué, ne prêta attention à personne d'autre que Louise ; tout dut s'organiser sans lui, absent. « Comme dans un rêve », me dit Moinot qui ne se souvenait plus de ce qui s'était passé ensuite : disparus, envolés, les tourtereaux ! Probablement, Malraux raccompagna Louise à Verrières, s'aperçut enfin qu'elle boitillait et se livra alors à un fatal rapprochement : souveraine d'allure et de jambes inégales, la reine de Saba avait fait un long voyage pour savoir si la richesse, la sagesse, l'intelligence et la beauté du roi Salomon étaient telles que la légende le répandait jusqu'au

fond de l'Arabie. Selon la Bible, le roi Salomon avait des centaines de concubines. Pouvait-il s'éprendre de Louise de Vilmorin, du même âge que lui ? C'est là qu'Yvonne Printemps intervient pour nous apprendre qu'une femme, une courtisane encore plus, et qu'était-ce que Louise ? pouvait jusqu'à soixante-quinze ans rester irrésistible.

L'amour n'aveugla le roi Salomon pour la reine de Saba qu'une seule nuit. Pour Malraux, cela dura. Louise et lui ne se quittèrent plus, il n'y a pas d'autre mot pour l'amour, que ce soit pour eux comme pour nous. Louise vécut dans le parc de Versailles, à la Lanterne, dans une brillance et un éclat de foudre dont personne ne sut grand détail. Quoi d'étonnant ? Un enchantement n'a nul besoin de s'étaler. Le général de Gaulle tomba et quitta l'Elysée, et Malraux déclina l'offre de Pompidou de continuer à habiter la Lanterne. Louise lui dit alors qu'elle pouvait lui offrir un appartement à Verrières, qu'il pouvait y emmener ses deux chats et ses tableaux, qu'il y aurait son petit déjeuner et, selon son expression favorite, « le brouet noir des Spartiates ». Verrières n'était pas n'importe quoi. Louis XIV y avait construit pour Mlle de La Vallière un hôtel qui, par la suite, fut flanqué d'une aile et de diverses constructions. Louise habitait le premier égage. Malraux n'avait pas de meubles, uniquement des trésors d'art, son déménagement fut simple. Au rez-de-chaussée, il occupa le salon bleu où, de notre temps, Louise recevait et un cabinet de travail ; au deuxième, une chambre, au-dessus du parc d'arbres rares, hybrides inconnus ou espèces du Tibet et de l'Himalaya, grâce à quoi il pouvait encore se croire aux Indes. Sur une photo, on voit Malraux et Louise, dans une allée touchée par l'automne. Lui en costume deux-pièces, pochette, vaguement drogué, dégrisé de frais et raide comme s'il avait avalé un parapluie, peut-être parce qu'à sa droite elle lui tient le bras. Presque aussi grande que lui, elle porte une veste bordée de fourrure, des pantalons de chez Dior, et elle lui montre de la main quelque chose qu'il fait semblant de regarder, semblant seulement car il y a un photographe, la scène n'est pas naturelle du tout, il détourne à peine la tête. Au poing qu'il serre sur sa poitrine, on devine qu'il aimerait autant qu'elle ne s'appuie pas sur lui, car elle boitille pour lui être agréable, il promène la reine de Saba dont il entend parfois, au-dessus de lui, le pas inégal. Elle est peut-être de passage en Europe avec

sa suite et son cercueil de cristal au serpent immortel. Là, avec eux dans le parc, il n'y a qu'un petit chien.

Dès lors, à Verrières, le mystère régna. Le grand homme travaillait à la suite des *Antimémoires*. Louise et lui buvaient beaucoup. Tous les soirs, paraît-il, ils étaient ivres. C'est peut-être à cela que pensa Jean Mauriac, mémorialiste, quand il écrivit que les années de la vie de Malraux avec Louise avaient été « tumultueuses ». Sophie de Vilmorin, la nièce, servait de secrétaire à Malraux, Yolé restant à Louise, qui ne savait plus très bien où elle en était : elle qui aimait tant parler et éblouir devait se taire. Comblée de bonheur, elle en ruisselait, il était là, elle l'entendait discourir toute la journée et toute la nuit bouger à l'étage au-dessus ; à peine descendait-il pour une tasse de thé que déjà il parlait, parlait, parlait : de ce qu'il avait écrit dans la nuit ou de ce qui lui était apparu à l'aube, sombre rouleau de pensées grandioses et compliquées qui traversaient le monde comme un roulement d'orage continu. « C'est Chateaubriand, répétait Louise pour se consoler, et moi je suis Mme Récamier. » Le vrai Chateaubriand restait par moments silencieux, accoudé à une cheminée. Malraux parlait, parlait, rejetait sa mèche en arrière, passait une main nerveuse dans ses cheveux, on ne comprenait pas toujours ce qu'il disait car sa voix s'embarrassait dans des suffocations, des halètements, de sourdes aspirations soulignées d'un clin d'œil amusé, n'allait-il pas parfois jusqu'à se singer lui-même ? Près de lui, Louise vivait ce qu'elle avait rêvé : une vie tourneboulée par le génie, et qui la fatiguait. Elle pouvait difficilement supporter Malraux toute la journée, parfois la nuit. Ebahis, on les considérait avec une certaine inquiétude. Il y avait entre le rêve de Louise et son accomplissement une marge d'imprévu qui faisait vaciller la nouvelle Mme Récamier muette et un brin apeurée. Le bonheur qui la brisait n'était-il pas la pire épreuve de sa vie ? Cette présence lourde et si chérie, quelle place prendrait-elle dans chacune de leurs œuvres ?

Le 26 décembre 1969, quinze jours après qu'il était allé déjeuner à Colombey (le fameux déjeuner des *Chênes qu'on abat*), comme il s'apprêtait à partir en voyage avec Louise pour Venise, Louise grippée s'alita et, subitement, mourut. Un immense coup de tonnerre retentit. Nous accourûmes tous, consternés, anéantis. A l'église de Verrières, le Tout-Paris en larmes s'étouffa pour apercevoir Malraux, bouffi de silence et

d'ombre, secoué par une violente tempête de tics. Louise avait si peur de la solitude qu'elle avait voulu être enterrée dans le parc, à deux pas des siens. Elle y est toujours. Sa tombe a disparu sous le gazon, mais si l'on prête l'oreille, on entend encore le cri qu'elle pousse : « Au secours ! » gravé dans la pierre, près d'elle. Elle imaginait qu'elle partagerait encore la vie de la maison, qu'elle entendrait Malraux, son adoration, parler. Françoise Verny et Claude Santelli ont tourné, dans le salon bleu et même dehors, pour la télévision, tout près d'elle, des entretiens avec Malraux qui ont pour titre « La légende du siècle ». Louise a-t-elle perçu son génie fourgonner à travers l'histoire des civilisations ? A-t-elle écouté ? A-t-il évoqué sa mémoire ou sa présence dans un brusque bafouillement ? Sophie, qui était Louise avec trente ans de moins, s'était mise à boitiller pour mieux lui ressembler. De ces années-là, Jean Mauriac écrit qu'elles furent « heureuses, apaisées, pleines de labeur ». « Sait-on tout ce que Malraux lui doit ? » ajoute-t-il en parlant de Sophie.

« Une grande mémoire, a écrit Diderot dans sa *Lettre sur les sourds et les muets,* suppose une grande facilité d'avoir à la fois ou rapidement plusieurs idées différentes. » Ne pas oublier non plus qu'une gloire pour être vraie a besoin de l'absence : le peuple français n'a jamais mieux aimé de Gaulle que mort. Pouvait-il être aimé vivant ? Servi, obéi, suivi tant qu'on voudra. Ne pas oublier encore que les mots déterminent l'action : le décor suffit souvent pour que l'action se déploie à l'aise. Chez Malraux, les masques africains ou thaïlandais étaient coupés en deux, les objets d'art comme les oiseaux représentaient l'âme et la vie, et la vie ne valait qu'en tant qu'expression de l'inconnu. A Verrières, pendant et après Louise, noyades d'abord dans le whisky et le bordeaux, puis quand l'alcool fut interdit, dans le thé et dans quoi ? Pour lui, ce qui comptait n'était pas le combat de l'ange et tout ce que cet imbécile de Lazare ne nous a pas dit au sortir du tombeau, c'était l'empoignade entre la mort et son génie à lui, tout ce qui fut son déchirant *Lazare.* Personne ne pouvait rien pour lui. A Verrières, on s'efforça de nous cacher le superman qui, à présent, illustrait la maison. On faisait le vide devant lui, on le

couvait, on le protégeait et on n'invitait plus. Parfois, si on se trouvait là par hasard, on retenait sa respiration quand la CX attendait devant le perron et qu'il allait sortir, ou quand le dieu mettait le nez dans le parc, à lui réservé désormais. On avait déjà reçu des génies et des monstres sacrés, jamais quelqu'un de cette dimension.

Je travaillais aux *Chevaux du Soleil*, j'en étais au moment où le personnage du Général allait intervenir dans ma saga, et je me demandais comment le prendre, de face, de biais, de l'extérieur, de l'intérieur, en commençant par Colombey où je n'étais jamais allé. J'éprouvai donc le besoin de poser quelques questions essentielles sur de Gaulle. « Il faut que vous voyiez Malrô-ô-ô... » Quand il m'avait dit cela, le Général n'imaginait pas qu'il serait alors pour moi, déjà, dans l'au-delà. André de Vilmorin fut mon intercesseur, j'allais voir enfin Malraux. « Il t'invitera chez Lasserre, me dit Moinot. C'est sa popote. Il y a sa réserve de bordeaux. »

A l'heure précise, sa voiture le déposa, seul ce jour-là. Une armée de maîtres d'hôtel l'escorta jusqu'à sa table où nous l'attendions, au milieu des azalées mauves, ma femme et moi. Sophie ne l'accompagnait pas. Surgit presque en même temps que lui, dans un vaste mouvement, Salvador Dali qu'on installa loin de nous sur une estrade, avec sa canne à pommeau d'or et ses cocottes. Malraux et moi nous nous saluâmes comme si nous nous étions quittés la veille. En toute une vie, nous n'avions jamais fait qu'à peine nous écrire. En quarante ans, il n'avait pas changé. Il avait vieilli comme moi, puisque nous étions presque du même âge, ses traits étaient plus marqués, son regard plus sombre, sa mèche intacte, sans cheveux blancs, son front plus dégagé, olympien, un totem. Des tics plus sauvages, et la façon de parler d'un haltérophile qui vient de soulever le monde et marque un léger essoufflement. Je venais de lire le premier tome des *Antimémoires* que tout le monde admirait. Pour moi, le style en était surchargé, alourdi de trop d'adjectifs chamarrés. Des pans de son œuvre s'y écroulaient parfois confusément avec fracas dans un nuage de poussière. Je sentais frissonner en moi un fond d'émotion devant lui qui avait tout compris avant tout le monde et avait écrit pour les communistes chinois comme pour les hommes qui se battaient contre l'injustice du sort. Quand il s'asseyait à

sa table chez Lasserre, il n'ignorait pas que des millions de déshérités continuaient à crever de faim. Il avait fait pour eux ce qu'il pouvait, il n'allait pas se priver d'un des rares plaisirs qu'il avait. N'était-il pas quand même un tout petit peu charlatan, comme l'en avait accusé Maurice Sachs ? Je n'étais plus au temps où je brûlais tellement de le rencontrer et je me remettais à l'évoquer en termes d'une monnaie fictive dont nous parlions parfois entre officiers, avant la Seconde Guerre mondiale. Au Sphinx, le fameux bordel de Reims, à une époque où la patronne s'appelait Mme Espéron, nous parlions en « espérons », tarifs d'une visite. Quelques espérons faisaient déjà une somme. Espérer Malraux rejoignait là un brin d'impertinence... Il ne manquait que Doyon pour les commentaires.

« Que buvez-vous pour commencer ? » demanda-t-il à ma femme. Ma femme pensait que le champagne s'imposait. Lui, son whisky, et tout de suite il se lança, comme s'il était à la télé, dans la symbolique du jour qui lui rappelait la Perse, n'est-ce pas ? la couleur rose de la Perse. L'entendre avaler les mots à la vitesse où il pensait était d'un soin sévère. Encore pour nous parlait-il simplement, bien qu'il nous plaçât trop haut, pour nous honorer, et nous traitant d'égal à égal, avec des coups d'œil complices. Il déversa sur nous une armée d'Alexandre dévalant en Thrace et à travers la Mésopotamie, où il n'était pas aisé de le suivre. La phrase de Gide : « Je me sens un imbécile à côté de lui », revenait à la mémoire. Et nous, alors ? Seul Doyon ne s'était pas laissé impressionner : c'était à qui, des deux, esbroufait l'autre. Un jour, j'entendis François Mitterrand, qui l'aime peu, évoquer sa fulgurance d'astre mort. Quand il parle des autres, un homme devenu roi prend d'étranges libertés avec, sans s'en douter, un ton ex cathedra. Souvent Malraux parlait ainsi, toujours prêt à entamer une exploration ou à ouvrir une oraison. A l'époque de ce déjeuner, Malraux continuait à vivre à Verrières, « douloureusement » m'assura-t-il. Son train de maison changeait à peine, il n'était plus ministre, et comme nous en venions au premier tome des *Antimémoires,* il me dit d'une voix éteinte que le whisky ragaillardit bientôt, qu'il craignait de n'avoir pas le temps d'achever le second. Mais nous n'étions pas là pour mariner dans le funèbre, il choisit une salade de

cœurs de palmier et un poussin farci, le « pigeon André Malraux » ne figurait pas encore au menu, et nous, un filet de sandre. Nous restâmes au champagne, et de son côté il s'en tint solidement à son château-pétrus. Il travaillait à sa dernière rencontre avec le Général dont le titre, *les Chênes qu'on abat*, courait déjà les salles de rédaction. « Pourquoi Voltaire n'a-t-il pas fait de même avec Frédéric II de Prusse ? Pourquoi Chateaubriand n'est-il pas allé voir Napoléon à Sainte-Hélène ? » Chateaubriand le hantait. Il allait combler ce vide : il y aurait une rencontre de Gaulle-Malraux. Tout le monde l'appelait : « Monsieur le Ministre », je lui disais « vous », je pensais à Doyon, aux rendez-vous que Doyon lui donnait et où, parfois, Doyon n'était pas là quand le jeune Malraux arrivait, et qu'il devait se contenter d'un œuf sur le plat que lui faisait cuire Mme D. « Il ne faut pas que M. Doyon joue à ce petit jeu-là », disait-il en partant. Déjà il lui fallait des dieux, des rois, des héros, des danseuses. Il vivait dans l'orage, au milieu des éclairs et du tonnerre, il n'avait jamais eu peur que de la médiocrité. Pour lui, si on fréquente des médiocres, on tombe dans le même panier. Pas de médiocres autour de lui. Des super-grands, des géants. Je pensais à tous les tours qu'il nous avait joués après, en snobant les banquets de Doyon, sauf celui des bouquinistes, je pensais à Louise, qui ne l'avait jamais présenté qu'à son frère André et à sa femme, et à Sophie qui était devenue sa secrétaire. A la fin de sa vie, Louise, jalouse, gardait pour elle son trésor, puisqu'elle se targuait avec orgueil d'être Mme Récamier. Si quelqu'un pouvait ne pas se poser de questions, c'était bien elle. Qu'importait qu'il soit allé en Chine ou pas, avant qu'il ait écrit *la Condition humaine*, qu'il ait raconté ce qu'il avait voulu de Trotsky, de Staline ou de Mao Tsé-toung ! Qu'importait que M. de Chateaubriand ait mieux servi l'Empereur que le Roi ? Malraux avait combattu en Espagne contre Franco, dans la Résistance il avait failli être fusillé par les Allemands, il avait commandé la brigade Alsace-Lorraine, de Gaulle l'avait pris comme ministre de la Culture, il était comme il était, vrai et faux héros à la fois, prince, avide de gloire, délicat pour les femmes qu'il trouvait tellement plus subtiles que les hommes. Il savait mentir, mais ses mensonges, mieux que la réalité, devenaient la seule vérité, et cela ne s'appelait pas tromper mais inventer ce qui aurait dû être, et s'il confondait parfois la bravoure et la vantardise, son génie

faisait le reste : son génie devenait nécessaire au mythe qui rejoignait un panthéon imaginaire. Il savait tout, il avait tout retenu de ce qui était et n'était pas, pour Gandhi ou Nehru comme pour de Gaulle qui n'était ni un tendre ni un facile, et personne ne pouvait confondre. Malraux était devenu intouchable, tel que le monde entier voulait qu'il fût. Et puis après ? Mon Dieu, pourquoi nous étions-nous rencontrés enfin, moi qui ne pouvais lui être utile en rien ?

. Justement, nous en arrivions au Général au moment où j'en étais de ma saga, au Général lugubre, perdu dans des nuées, sans un sourire. Qu'avait pu se demander de Gaulle au moment du passage en Haute Cour de Salan et du projet d'exécution de Jouhaud alors qu'il tenait les généraux félons dans ses mains ? Pour Malraux, la seule question que de Gaulle avait pu se poser ne pouvait être que : « Où se trouve l'intérêt de l'Etat ? » Là, je laissai percer un doute. Dans ma saga, j'approchais de la fin de la guerre d'Algérie, je m'étais rallié à la conclusion qu'il fallait me jeter à corps perdu dans le mythe du Général. Je devrais camper mon personnage à Colombey, avec tante Yvonne, le chien, le chat, les promenades en forêt, le tourbillon de l'actualité politique, Alger, le palais d'Eté, puis l'Elysée, la nuit où le sort de Salan se jouait. L'intérêt de l'Etat ! Après tout, pourquoi pas ? Malraux connaissait mieux Zorro que moi. Quant aux aventures intimes avec les femmes, Malraux eut seulement un mot : Mme de Gaulle n'avait jamais été qu'un meuble, la comtesse polonaise une légende et « bitte de marbre », son surnom londonien, une boutade. Le Général n'avait jamais aimé que sa fille. Mais sa fille était sa fille. Les seules femmes qui l'avaient troublé, troublé ? étaient la petite reine de Thaïlande et Jackie Kennedy. Là, il avait dû se dire : « Regarde-toi dans la glace... » En guise de plaisanterie, je lançai : « Et s'il s'était marié avec Brigitte Bardot ? » Quant aux généraux félons, mon sentiment était qu'à l'intérêt de l'Etat devaient se mêler des bribes de réflexes militaires, comme fusiller ces cons-là qui avaient osé braver le pouvoir sous prétexte que lui, de Gaulle, avait agi de même à l'égard de Pétain, et aussi sa fureur à l'idée qu'il pouvait à présent, à cause de l'âge, rappeler le vieux maréchal décati. Pas de ressentiments personnels ? Malraux branlait du chef. Non, pas de ressentiments. J'appris à Malraux qu'à Dakar en 1940, de

Gaulle avait eu en face de lui Salan, chef du renseignement des forces pétainistes. De Gaulle avait perdu. Salan l'avait battu à plates coutures. Il parut étonné, mais comme tous les gaullistes, les défaites de son dieu ne l'affectaient pas. Je parlai aussi de sa colère à la nouvelle que Salan avait sauvé sa tête devant le jury de la Haute Cour grâce aux scrupuleux comme Pasteur Vallery-Radot. Malraux assura que le Général avait pris à son compte les suggestions du garde des Sceaux après la campagne où de nombreux naïfs comme moi étaient intervenus en faveur de Jouhaud.

De quoi pouvions-nous parler sinon du Général ? Après un quiproquo mutuel, de Gaulle l'avait choisi comme chroniqueur et mémorialiste capable de magnifier jusqu'au moins magnifiable. Il avait fait Malraux compagnon de la Libération, puis ministre. Non sans une certaine mélancolie, de Gaulle et lui devenaient pour moi comme l'Erythrée lointaine, inaccessible et légendaire. Trop tard. J'avais raté quelque chose parce que j'étais tel que j'étais, pas assez ambitieux ni assez rusé pour combiner des avantages, pas assez audacieux pour forcer la porte de Malraux et lui demander pourquoi il s'était fait passer pour le chef de l'aviation étrangère en Espagne alors qu'il ne l'était pas, et pourquoi il se décrivait plus tard allant au combat avec une brigade de blindés, puisqu'il n'avait jamais mis les pieds dans un char, lui Malraux. Mais qu'importait toujours ! Ce qu'aucun officier de char n'avait su raconter, il l'avait magnifié, et sa fiction dépassait de loin la réalité. Il était aussi l'homme qui avait le mieux compris de Gaulle en profondeur et comme dans un état de sacerdoce. Ses entretiens avec lui étaient apocryphes, sinon inventés, les conversations dans le bureau de la rue Saint-Dominique pareils à ceux des *Chênes qu'on abat*. Le Général avait-il dit tout cela ? Je me le demandais tandis qu'en face de nous Malraux faisait son numéro de barre fixe et retombait sur ses pieds après un double saut périlleux. Et ce discours avec Léon Blum a Neuilly, et les tirades avec Nehru, Chou En-lai et Mao, plus vrais que s'ils avaient été pris en sténo ? Devant nous, destin, génie, vocation, armée, serviteurs qui veillent, coups de vent, avenues nocturnes vides, fleuves qui battaient contre leurs rives, révolte des paysans, écorce des arbres rongée, tout apparaissait et fulminait. « Gorki m'a dit un jour devant

Staline : les paysans sont partout les mêmes. » Phrase pas très compromettante, mais qui situait les personnages. Tout y passait, avec les *Antimémoires* qui resurgissaient avec lui, surtout ce qui ne s'était jamais passé, sauf pour les chats, qui se souviendront de l'amour qu'il a eu pour eux puisque, le jour de sa mort, l'un d'eux, Fourrure ou Lastrée ? se jettera sur son lit, griffera son gilet, léchera ses mains et disparaîtra. Doyon, qui aimait aussi les chats, aurait apprécié cette trouvaille du destin et admiré son propre flair : il ne s'était pas trompé sur la valeur du jeune Malraux quand il lui demandait d'écrire un article pour sa revue *la Connaissance*.

Passons. Salan et Jouhaud ne l'intéressaient pas tellement, l'Algérie non plus. Plus tard, à je ne sais quelle occasion, ni quand, Sophie me consultera pour me demander quels livres il devrait lire qui lui donneraient une idée juste des événements de là-bas. Peu à peu, ce jour-là, il se mit à rouler des yeux avec égarement et son visage se crispa. Je l'entendis soudain me dire que ma chance avait été de ne pas appartenir à un groupe comme la NRF, que Gide n'avait jamais eu aucun sens de l'Histoire et qu'il reprochait à Moinot ce qu'il appelait « son enfantillage ». Pour lui Moinot agissait comme un haut fonctionnaire de la Cour des comptes sans se douter qu'en dehors du cabinet il avait affaire à des crapules. Cela pour me prouver qu'il n'oubliait pas que j'étais un copain de Moinot. « Si droit, si pur, si honnête !... » Il ricana à peine et revint à la NRF : Paulhan était un zouave et un chercheur d'or, et soudain bifurqua sur l'aventure qui figure dans les *Antimémoires*, des chats qui bouffèrent les rats pendant la peste jusqu'au moment où les rats leur laissèrent le champ libre et retournèrent en Chine. Avec Malraux en face de moi, je me disais qu'il était plus facile d'inventer une épopée qu'on n'avait pas vécue et des paysages qu'on n'a jamais qu'entrevus, comme il valait mieux découvrir la ville de la reine de Saba que personne ne connaissait et revenir avec des photographies de dunes et de rivages désolés plutôt que de s'acharner à serrer de près la vérité. Les hommes avaient besoin de rêves. J'avais perdu mon temps à bombarder les usines de la Ruhr.

Il devina la question que je ne lui avais pas posée. « Vous n'y échapperez pas », me dit-il. Nous nous quittâmes. Nous n'allions pas dans la même direction. Sa DS noire se perdit dans les embarras de Paris.

**
**

Quand nous nous retrouvâmes, *les Chênes qu'on abat* avaient paru, et il venait de ressusciter après un passage à la Pitié, où Doyon avait fini. Plus une goutte d'alcool, deux cigarettes par jour seulement. Sophie veillait à ce qu'on ne lui servît plus de château-pétrus. Jus de tomate au commencement du repas, jus d'orange à la fin. *Lazare* allait suivre avec les nuits à la Salpêtrière, les conversations avec les professeurs, les errances dans la chambre quand il quittait le lit, les égarements, sa quête d'un bouton électrique, les visites. Il n'inventerait qu'à demi, comme halluciné, essayant de se souvenir de la nuit du tombeau au milieu de tous les personnages qui lui revenaient à la mémoire à travers les grands romans de l'Histoire, et à travers les siens aussi, dans un marathon d'éternité. Lawrence était un bon sujet de conversation, je comprenais pourquoi Malraux n'avait jamais cousu sur ses manches les étoiles de général espagnol ou de général FFI : il voulait trop ressembler à son modèle d'Arabie et non à tel ou tel. Lawrence s'était tué à moto en 1935, la veille du jour où il fixait rendez-vous au correspondant qui voulait, légende ou vérité ? l'envoyer voir Hitler. Lawrence se considérait peut-être alors comme le porte-parole de l'Angleterre, et en 1939, Malraux essaiera d'entraîner le journaliste André Beucler, qui comprenait le russe, dans une visite à Staline pour devancer la fatalité, renverser la situation et arrêter la guerre : « J'ai l'appareil, le personnel, les fonds, dira-t-il, nous nous envolons à la fin de la semaine dans le plus grand secret... » Après tout, en 1934, à Moscou, il avait pris la parole avec Gide au congrès des écrivains soviétiques, il prétendait avoir vu Goebbels, il avait plaidé en faveur du communiste Thaelmann en prison. Pourquoi n'aurait-il pas rencontré Staline ? Beucler se dérobera. Beucler ajoute qu'en 1944, il retrouva le colonel Malraux au bar du Pont-Royal. « Ce que je voulais proposer à Staline est arrivé quand même », disait Malraux. Et Camus survenant approuvait.

A Verrières, il paraissait rajeuni, débarrassé de ses tics ; sa tentative de légion au Bangladesh avait avorté, il s'en était remis, parlait de la poésie persane et de la philosophie

hindoue, ne buvait plus que du thé que Sophie, crispée, mal à l'aise, lui servait. Elle lui tenait aussi son briquet d'or car il fumait encore, et quand il ne fuma plus, c'est lui qui tendait son briquet aux femmes, ce qui me ramenait au roi Salomon et à la Bible : « Tout ce qu'avait le roi Salomon était d'or pur », au roi Salomon qui avait été perdu par les femmes, ce qui n'était pas le cas de Malraux. Les femmes étaient pour lui des anges, des walkyries aussi, il n'était heureux qu'en leur compagnie : elles ne le jalousaient pas. Le nom de la reine de Saba était : Douceur.

Sans Louise, Verrières était sans âme. Louise avait beau parfois provoquer ou attiser les amours, les chamailleries, les brouilles, les jalousies, les colères ou la compassion, elle rayonnait tellement qu'après sa mort tout devint sombre. On avait beau se dire avec un pincement au cœur qu'elle reposait tout près, à nous entendre si elle tendait l'oreille, son absence faisait mal, Sophie n'était que son reflet muet. Verrières ne vivait plus que dans le tragique, on ne parlait qu'à mi-voix, il recevait beaucoup de journalistes, mais il ne demandait que ça, parler des civilisations disparues, des chefs d'Etat, de la politique planétaire ou alors de Montaigne, de Manet, de Chagall, des guerriers chinois, des empires Han, Tang ou Ming, ou de Mao franchissant la rivière Ta-tu pendant la Longue Marche. Il n'y était pas allé mais on aurait pu l'y conduire s'il l'avait souhaité, son vieux camarade Mao ne pouvait rien lui refuser. Quand il surgissait en complet sombre, chemise claire, cravate noire, pochette, manchettes, on pouvait croire encore au ministre de la Culture en exercice. Il commençait à s'éloigner du Nobel que, chaque automne, on attendait pour lui et que le destin lui refusait. Il l'espérait encore sourdement. Avait-il fait son deuil de la reine de Saba aux jambes inégales ? Il se remettait à parler de la Grèce, de l'Egypte, de New Delhi d'où il rentrait pour rafraîchir ses *Antimémoires,* des nuits de Bénarès où l'on sentait le Gange oattre dans ses veines, de l'Acropole qui flottait dans ses yeux comme un navire. Labouré peut-être par le kif ou le chanvre indien, à moins que ce ne fût par le sublime qui l'habitait, divagant, délirant tout à coup, lui l'agnostique, enseignait le sens caché des prières, des gestes ou des symboles : le sacré était familier à cet homme marqué par la foudre, par le suicide

à la hache de son père, la fin d'*Anna Karénine* pour Josette Clotis et la mort brutale de ses fils.

De Gaulle s'en était allé, Malraux commençait à se traîner. J'écoutais autant que je pouvais, je l'entendis dire une fois qu'il n'avait jamais jugé Camus important, en contradiction flagrante avec son jugement de lecteur de 1940 quand il avait transmis chez Gallimard le manuscrit de *l'Etranger*. Comme j'insistais et que je lui disais ce que je devais à Camus . « Il a toujours tout raté », décida-t-il. Pour lui, même le Nobel, Camus l'avait raté par ses déclarations intempestives sur la justice. Toujours ex cathedra, il levait un œil sur nous, esquissait un sourire, replongeait. Je ne le considérais pas comme mon maître, mais tout de même, à côté de Montherlant ! Je voyais en lui une sorte d'extraterrestre à la remorque du Général après avoir été en quête du colonel d'Arabie. Au-dessus de tous les contemporains, supérieur même à de Gaulle en ce sens qu'il savait à présent, mieux que de Gaulle, tirer le sens de l'action gaullienne. Lui n'avait fait que la rêver, avec parfois une percée qui tenait plus de l'exploit spirituel. Comme son héros, il était devenu à son tour monument historique et on ne pouvait plus toucher à quoi que ce soit, sinon quelle pagaille ! Après les *Oraisons funèbres*, c'étaient *la Tête d'obsidienne, l'Irréel*, puis *Hôtes de passage*, puis *le Miroir des Limbes*, où il brassait l'ensemble de son génie trop chargé de rois, de souverains, ou encombré de types douteux d'import-export. En un éclair, il comparait les incomparables dans une langue sonore et parfois durement contractée qui obligeait, coulée dans un texte, à lire et à relire. Dieu lui-même a besoin d'exégètes. Jusqu'au bout de l'enfer où je ne sais quoi l'avait conduit, dans les moments de lucidité il restait sûr de lui, pétri de ce verbe qui avait obligé Louise, Mme Récamier émerveillée, à se taire Elle savait qu'il était éblouissant, pas à ce point, personne ne l'avait égalé. Il nous en mettait, si j'ose dire, plein la vue. Il nous atomisait. Il était le cosmos à lui seul. Parfois affleurait chez lui une ertaine enflure qui n'était que la distance, énorme, qui se creusait entre lui et le reste des hommes.

Au fond, malgré les mots désinvoltes de lui sur Camus que j'ai rapportés, personne n'était de taille à soutenir une conversation avec lui, sinon Camus justement, et encore par sous-entendus et par ellipses, comme s'expriment entre eux les

esprits éminents. A les voir en photo l'un en face de l'autre, on les croirait muets. Ils s'admirent, ils dialoguent sans dire grand-chose. Quant à Doyon, mandarin à la noix à qui je reviens, il ne se laissa impressionner qu'après que Malraux l'eut quitté. Alors oui, c'est la lumière de ce temps, mais une lumière ingrate. Doyon était né un 2 novembre, le jour des morts, Malraux le 3, ils pouvaient se comprendre mais pas se supporter. Encore une fois, je me revois au moment où Doyon annonce des banquets en l'honneur de Malraux, des banquets où Malraux sera là, Doyon rameute ses copains, des ratés comme lui, Turpin, Pillement, Talvart, Bollery, il m'extirpe de Versailles où je suis en garnison comme lieutenant, et m'excite avec la promesse que mon flirt Rita sera là aussi, il fricasse des dindons, des boudins d'Auvergne, invite des cocottes de la Madeleine où il tient ses assises, et pas de Malraux. Monsieur n'a pas daigné se déranger. Pauvre petit couillon de filsque à Doyon, je n'aurai jamais vu le fameux Malraux parmi les familiers de l'impasse Guéménée que Malraux laissait à leurs fantasmes et à leurs mirages. D'ailleurs, que lui aurais-je dit à ce moment-là, comme en 1955, à l'invite du Général ? Il sculptait sa propre statue depuis longtemps, il l'avait avoué à sa femme, Clara, et plus comme Rude que comme Giacometti, l'ouvrage était bien avancé, il était déjà plus que Gabriele d'Annunzio, son modèle un certain temps, et s'il avouait aussi qu'il arrangeait la vie, la vie se mettait à ressembler à ses fables. Il voulait être le Byron de notre temps, il l'a été et plus encore, même pour nous qui savons que, chez lui, tout n'est pas toujours aussi sûr qu'il le dit. Nous le lui pardonnons et, plus encore, nous nous disons que le monde ne serait pas le même sans lui. Comme il nous manquerait, lui aussi ! Il a fait passer certaines paroles de rois ou de héros qui n'auraient jamais franchi la distance sans lui. Dommage qu'il n'ait pas connu le Che Lasserre peut-être lui était nécessaire. N'empêche. Imaginons un instant que je sois allé voir Malraux au moment où le Général m'y invitait et que, par la suite, hypothèse ridicule, Malraux m'ait pris comme collaborateur. Eh bien, puisque j'aurais suivi le Général et Malraux, je n'aurais écrit ni *la Guerre d'Algérie* ni *les Chevaux du Soleil*. Autrement dit, à sa remorque comme à celle du Général, je serais moins que rien. Si peu que je vaille par moi-même, c'est parce que, vrai

sauvage, j'ai osé défier ceux qui se réclamaient des valeurs admises.

La dernière fois que je l'ai vu, il avançait à petits pas, soudain devenu vieux, cassé, les pieds en dedans, mon Dieu ! le cheveu sale, un chandail sous sa veste, lui, le ministre de la Culture, le compagnon du Général, le tribun des rendez-vous de l'Histoire ! André de Vilmorin cachait mal sa détresse. N'empêche, par moments, il enfourchait sa chimère, piquait des deux, se baissait sur l'encolure et se mettait à galoper une fois de plus, parfois il s'accrochait au poitrail, hoquetait, avalait les mots, les phrases, qu'importe ! Dans son esprit un ordinateur était en marche, il devait prendre garde à ne pas se tromper de touche. Il aurait fallu une grande malignité pour discerner ce qui était détraqué dans cette sublime mélopée. Après son monologue qu'il jeta sans reprendre son souffle, d'un trait, devant nous qui étions abasourdis, ce qui me frappa, ce soir-là, c'est qu'il s'en alla très tôt, comme un automate, raide, le regard ailleurs, sans tâter le vide qu'il aurait dû chercher devant lui, et dans quoi, quelques semaines plus tard, il sombra.

Si je suis à Vézelay, c'est que Louise de Vilmorin m'y a conduit, en passant, à une époque où Malraux s'occupait de son musée imaginaire. Le hasard, du moins l'ai-je cru, m'y a ramené après la guerre d'Algérie et je n'en ai plus bougé, comme si j'avais trouvé ma voie et ma vie. Un long chemin patient et obstiné me tiendra là, au point qu'il n'est plus question pour moi de me dérober, c'est trop tard, et où irais-je ? Je me répète la parole de Pierre que j'ai déjà citée à propos de notre professeur de littérature au séminaire, M. Lesage, quand il nous lisait de la poésie : « Seigneur, dressons là trois tentes… » Une maison m'attendait là, et depuis que j'ai quitté les rangs de vigne de la Mitidja, enfant, quand j'allais derrière l'oncle Jules, à califourchon sur les maigres épaules de Meftah, nulle part je ne me suis senti mieux.

C'est que l'homme n'est pas que hasard et que, parfois, en lui ou hors de lui, surgit le sacré, qui commande. Ici, sur une de ces collines qui me rappellent la Chine du Sseu-tchouan ou encore certaines régions du Laos où l'on cultive le pavot, les hommes, avant même qu'ils aient été gaulois, romains, celtes ou arvernes, ont élevé des autels à leurs dieux, et les ruines de leurs temples, qu'on ne visite plus, existent encore. A Chartres aussi, les druides célébraient, aux temps messianiques, le culte d'une vierge qui allait enfanter. De tout temps, ici, on ne sait pourquoi, des hommes priaient.

L'été s'achève, la nuit déverse sur nous sa charge d'étoiles. La masse de la basilique, illuminée comme tous les soirs, plante sa façade grêlée par la petite vérole des siècles. Des lucioles se jettent dans les lumières, des avions de ligne aux feux clignotants glissent au-dessus de nous comme des figu-

rants de routine. D'Orion vers Arcturus, une véritable étoile filante trace un trait qui se perd, et soudain tout s'éteint. Une cantate de Bach déverse sur nous une vague de joie sautillante, puis large et grandiose, tandis qu'en fulgurance, le laser projette sur le tympan devenu un écran les images des événements de l'abbatiale et les précipite en une suite d'éclairs : guerres, incendies, croisades, invasions, visites de rois. C'est fantastique. Où sommes-nous ? Dans quel au-delà ? Et pourtant je préfère le moment où le soleil se hisse au-dessus des brumes et où les premiers rayons de l'aube atteignent les verrières de l'abside. Une lourde porte, je m'arrête dans le narthex pour dépouiller le vieil homme en moi, et, par les travées encore noyées dans l'ombre, j'avance vers la lumière. Il est trop tôt, il n'y a personne sinon un père franciscain qui se lève plus tôt que moi, en attente lui aussi de célébrer ce qui tourne à l'enchantement. C'est mieux encore l'hiver, quand la neige et le verglas ont rendu les routes désertes, et qu'on peut déambuler comme en catimini du monde extérieur, une capuche sur les yeux.

Qui me rencontrerait ainsi saurait que me voilà coincé. C'est vrai. De Vézelay, si peu que je m'écarte, je ne revois jamais les tours et les remparts sans un battement de cœur, et les rares fois où le courant de la vie m'éloigna d'ici, j'y revenais en pèlerinage, allumant des cierges et tombant à genoux : « S'il vous plaît, Mademoiselle, ramenez-moi près de vous... » Elle m'écoutait. Qui cela, elle ? Marie-Madeleine, l'ancienne courtisane de la cour du roi Hérode soudain attachée à la suite du Christ, et qui, pour moi, ressemble plus au portrait de la danseuse Salomé par Bertolomeo Veneto, qu'à une dame de Saint-Sulpice. Eh quoi, ne serait-il pas bienséant, pour une fois, d'invoquer une personne du sexe qui serait encore agréable à regarder et nous changerait des bonnes femmes qu'on met sur les autels ? Le Christ n'a-t-il pas dit que les dames de mauvaise vie entreraient avant nous dans le royaume des cieux ? Celle-là est notre souveraine. D'ailleurs, on ne dit pas Vézelay, on dit « La Madeleine ». Forêts, villages parfois, tout ici, par redevance de bailliage à l'ancienne abbaye comme par hommage d'appartenance, est dédié à la femme que ce jésuite de Claudel désigne sous le terme de « sainte pécheresse » et que j'appelle irrespectueusement ma tourterelle, ma toute-belle, mon amour. Et l'ensemble, elle, son abbaye et son

église, devient la citadelle céleste, la terre natale. Tout l'été, des milliers et des milliers de pèlerins, les femmes habillées comme des mouquères, les hommes comme des valets de cirque, escaladent l'escarpement de notre haut lieu. Que répondraient-ils si un ange leur demandait, comme à elle, devant le tombeau vide : « Que cherchez-vous ici ? »

A l'origine du chef-d'œuvre de pierre, il y a la démarche irréfléchie, presque inconsidérée, de quelques moines de l'an mil qui vivaient là en communauté au temps où la foi était ce qui compte le plus. Apprenant que les ossements de Marie de Magdala, morte depuis des siècles, gisaient en Provence, dans une grotte de la Sainte-Baume, ces hommes, emportés par une inspiration subite, se précipitent sur les chemins. Ils veulent, disent-ils, protéger ces reliques des incursions des Sarrasins. En vérité, avec une âme de pirates et de gangsters de la grâce, ils les dérobent, ils veulent les avoir à eux, ils les ramènent derrière les remparts de Vézelay. Pour eux, aucun doute : de Marie de Magdala ce sont les longs cheveux blond vénitien, et la voici désormais à l'abri dans une châsse de leur oratoire, et ces exaltés peuvent frôler les restes encore brûlants du témoin essentiel, de la première qui ait vu le Christ ressuscité. Raison sublime de ce brigandage insensé : la femme qui a inondé de parfum les pieds du maître, la folle d'amour frappée d'un coup de foudre, la sœur de Lazare, celle qui, sur le calvaire, a descendu le condamné de la croix, sûrement pas à demi nue comme la représente Rodin, et peut-être sortie des mains de Camille, la sœur de Claudel, et qui soutient le corps du supplicié, mais attention, ce n'est pas *Histoire d'O*, très loin de moi ! La sainte femme a participé aussi à la mise au tombeau et, le surlendemain, portant des aromates pour embaumer le corps, elle trouve le tombeau vide. Effrayée, désespérée, épouvantée, les yeux noyés de larmes, la voix cassée, elle demande à quelqu'un qu'elle prend pour le jardinier où est celui qui reposait là, elle n'ose pas dire le mort, où l'a-t-on mis, celui qui a ressuscité son frère Lazare ? Le jardinier ne répond pas. Il l'appelle seulement par son nom, il lui dit doucement : « Marie... » et elle se jette à ses genoux et déjà tend les bras. « Ne me touche pas », dit le maître. A présent, si l'ange demandait aux âmes altérées des pèlerins : « En quête de quoi ? » Ma réponse je la connais. Mais les autres ?

A la messe de Sainte-Marie-Madeleine, l'Eglise chante le *Credo* comme pour la messe d'un apôtre : c'est à cette femme-là que les moines ont bâti et dédié leur abbatiale vite devenue lieu de miracles, envahie par les foules en route vers Compostelle, vite rendez-vous de croisade. Comment ne pas se laisser prendre à ce souffle-là comme à la traîne d'une comète ? Comment résister ? Comment ne pas vouloir soi-même approcher celle qui a vu l'Homme-Dieu resurgi de la mort ? Je ne vais pas consulter notre âne Ulysse sans une arrière-pensée. C'est assis sur un de ses congénères que le Christ a fait son entrée à Jérusalem, le jour des Rameaux. Je ne demande pas à Ulysse s'il garde dans sa mémoire que son aïeul a pu franchir la mer avec Marie, Marthe, Lazare et leur suite. La tradition veut qu'il ait débarqué lui aussi aux Saintes-Maries-de-la-Mer et que ses ossements soient maintenant dans une apparence d'âne que des chanoines promènent en procession deux fois par an dans une église de Vérone. Ane ou pas, cet aïeul-là est aussi un témoin. Saint Paul, mon théologien, rappelle à ses frères corinthiens que le Christ lui est apparu à lui aussi, à lui « simple avorton » comme il se déclare. Et il ajoute, lui qui a été terrassé par la lumière, que s'il était un faux témoin, toute foi serait vaine. Pour lui, si le Christ n'est pas ressuscité, la mort n'a pas été vaincue et nous ne ressusciterons pas non plus. « Alors, mangeons et buvons, car demain nous mourrons », s'écrie-t-il. Et j'ajoute : « Mentons, volons et forniquons. Profitons tant que nous pouvons. » Tout est clair : les moines de l'expédition en Provence, ces mystiques éperdus ou peut-être à la foi vacillante ont voulu détenir la preuve suprême, et la lumière de Vézelay devient celle du premier matin de la résurrection. Par symbolique, si l'Eglise avait encore le sens des rites et du sacré, ici, l'encens devrait brûler sans cesse. Tout au moins, devrait-on pouvoir y allumer des baguettes odorantes comme dans les pagodes d'Extrême-Orient en souvenir des parfums sur le corps du Christ, et il n'y a que les cierges des pèlerins, parfois un buisson de feu.

On comprend que les rois de France aient voulu se prosterner sur ces dalles et que Saint Louis y soit revenu quatre fois, d'où le nom de basilique (du grec, *basileus*, roi) attribué au sanctuaire. Jusqu'à la reine Elisabeth d'Angleterre qu'un jour d'hiver j'ai vu descendre de sa Rolls, entourée de sbires. Il pleuvait. Le maire l'attendait avec un parapluie, et le

desservant le mieux désigné pour la visite, le père Pascal Seynhaeve, ancien aumônier général du corps expéditionnaire en Indochine, rappela à Sa Majesté Britannique, peut-être pas sans humour, que Thomas Becket, archevêque primat de Canterbury, avait, là même, menacé d'excommunication son propre souverain Henri II Plantagenêt, et fulminé contre quelques puissants seigneurs et prélats d'Angleterre. Et qu'en 1190, Richard Cœur de Lion, lointain ancêtre de la reine, avait rencontré, là encore, notre Philippe Auguste qui l'expédia, sans lui, à la troisième croisade. « Bon voyage, mon cher frère... » Ce haut lieu est donc une terre d'exception. Le Général n'a jamais daigné y venir. Pompidou non plus et Giscard préférait les tirés de Chambord. Seul, François Mitterrand est un familier, et la mystique et la beauté du lieu sont ce qui nous lie, comme je me sens lié à certains archimandrites de Russie. Accompagnés de moines et de séminaristes, au pire moment de l'hiver, alors qu'on craint des tourmentes de neige, ils apparaissent dans une embellie, les cloches sonnent, on expose pour eux les reliques qu'en procession ils vénèrent, tandis que de leurs larges poitrines s'élève l'hymne orthodoxe à la gloire de Marie de Magdala. J'entends vibrer leurs voix de bronze comme j'entends celles des chœurs du Morvan faire trembler les voûtes avec les formidables acclamations du *Requiem* de Brahms, du *Psaume* de Florent Schmitt ou des *Vêpres* de Monteverdi.

On sait que Mitterrand s'arrête souvent sur notre rocher quand il se rend à son fief de Château-Chinon ou quand il en revient. Elu président, c'est-à-dire roi de France, il continue. On le voit parfois seul ou accompagné par ses barbouzes, à une heure où les visiteurs sont rares. S'il trouve les portes de la basilique fermées, de la terrasse ou du parvis il contemple le vaisseau en silence, s'imprègne de l'invisible poids des pierres, de leur couleur suivant le temps. Quelquefois, il entre chez nous. Si je n'y suis pas, il glisse un mot sous la porte. C'est un homme secret qui se livre rarement. De parole rare, sauf s'il est en confiance, il regarde, écoute, il avance lentement, enraciné dans l'amitié comme il peut l'être dans son contraire S'il parle, c'est surtout pour interroger. Il aime les silences, sauf sur les choses sans importance, et va rarement droit au but sauf quand les circonstances l'y contraignent. Il préfère ne pas avertir car il sait qu'on découvre le vrai par surprise. Il ne déteste pas se

surprendre lui-même mais cela ne lui arrive plus : il est obligé de se voir comme il est. La plupart du temps, de biais.

N'empêche, à présent, depuis son livre *Au-dessus de la mêlée* qui fit scandale en 1915, et depuis qu'il a vécu ici, Vézelay c'est un peu Romain Rolland, c'est l'anticroisade, François Mitterrand le sait. Nous sommes les disciples de Romain Rolland, notre maître triomphe et n'est plus là, il n'a pas vu, pour la première fois de notre histoire à nous, le drapeau allemand noir, rouge et jaune flotter sur l'hôtel de ville à côté du drapeau français : il n'aura pas vu Helmut Kohl et François Mitterrand, le colosse et notre loup chef de meute, l'un à côté de l'autre, passer devant chez lui en montant à pied le raidillon vers la basilique éblouissante. C'est notre seul et unique trésor, mais quel joyau, quel chef-d'œuvre que ce lis de pierre bâti par les bénédictins et les architectes de l'an mil ! Sa façade s'élève sur les siècles, les portes s'ouvrent, le cortège se laisse entraîner à travers les travées jusqu'au chœur étincelant. Les princes de nos démocraties foulent les dalles usées par les pas des pélerins, parfois le fer des chevaux, gravissent des marches où tant de rois se sont agenouillés.

Ainsi, l'antique, la vénérable abbatiale et moi sommes-nous accrochés l'un à l'autre. Moi à elle, pas comme une chauve-souris endormie dans des combles, mais, si j'ose la comparaison, comme un loup, tiens, moi aussi ? à la gorge d'un cerf. Plus souvent, le loup c'est Vézelay, car il arrive de conquérir ou de se laisser conquérir par toutes sortes de sentiments, limpides ou troubles, comme un parcours amoureux peut être tempéré de mille soins ou secoué de tempêtes, tel un ciel sous le sabot de charge des nuées. Ainsi pour beaucoup, sur ce rocher battu par les vents, sans qu'on sache comment s'est fait le cheminement : de lui-même et par hasard si l'on veut, ou avec ce fond d'inexorable et de fatal comme cela se passe dans les pièges : la proie a beau se méfier et flairer longuement les approches, elle finit par succomber. Qu'importe ! Après une longue errance, un comportement souvent barbare, un embrigadement dans des batailles et des croisades, il y a là comme une fatalité.

D'où je suis, je n'ai que quelques pas à faire pour tomber

a genoux devant ce qui reste de notre belle, à moins qu'éprouvé par je ne sais quelle nausée, et par-dessus quelque chose qui serait une rambarde (puisque toutes les églises sont des nefs), j'aille vomir un hoquet d'éternité. Guide ou gardien, je pourrais l'être si l'on me confiait les clefs, mais gardien de quoi ? Nous n'avons pas de statues d'époque, sauf celles qui sont prises dans la pierre, pas de trésor, sauf notre châsse, mais de nos jours, on ne vole plus des reliques qui ne sont pas cotées en Bourse. On n'enlèvera pas non plus le tympan intérieur où un artiste anonyme et son atelier ont taillé une merveille de Christ en gloire, impatient, sous le souffle qui fait flotter ses vêtements, d'expédier ses disciples ailleurs. Ici et là, nos contestataires ont infligé quelques mutilations que Viollet-le-Duc a respectées. Qu'importe ces éraflures ! Au navire lui-même elles ne changent rien, ni à la route qu'il suit, immortel vaisseau, ni à la grande sainte capiteuse à qui il est dédié.

Le recteur Gérald Antoine raconte qu'en 1940, Romain Rolland avait invité chez lui, à Vézelay, Paul Claudel, son ancien condisciple à Louis-le-Grand. Ce jour-là, que Claudel date lui-même du 23 avril 1940, il visite la basilique, touche de ses lèvres les reliques, s'extasie sur les cheveux de celle qu'il appelle obstinément la sainte pécheresse et attribue à la basilique leur blondeur. Puis, de son écriture ronde sans rature, il couvre d'un trait dix pages de génie à travers l'Ancien Testament et enfin, baisant une dernière fois la châsse, il sort. Sur l'esplanade, il voit, soulevée de tous les horizons, comme une marée et une houle profonde où la barque de Lazare et de ses sœurs a jeté l'ancre. Accompagné de Romain Rolland, il redescend la colline. Et là... « Dans la rue, écrit à son tour Romain Rolland, il serait près de crier à notre chien (qui vient de découvrir un os à ronger) : " Ali, apporte la côte de saint Andoche ! " » Claudel, homme du Moyen Age et ambassadeur de la République, avait un humour embarrassant, qu'il était souvent seul à comprendre.

Simples mortels arrêtés là un instant comme après un autre déluge, comme l'arche de Noé sur le mont Ararat, nous nous demandons parfois où nous allons. Le soir, nous voguons parmi les nuées et les étoiles, et comme notre système solaire gravite autour de la Voie lactée depuis quelques milliards d'années, notre arche fantôme en a sûrement pour

quelques millénaires, ce qui fait du temps. Alors, comment, d'ici, juger des changements de gouvernement, discuter d'articles dans les journaux ou de quoi que ce soit, à part la vie, l'amour, la mort ? Seul élément digne de réflexion, peut-être, d'anciennes croisades où des armées remportèrent des victoires et subirent des défaites pour la Terre sainte, « Dieu le veut ! » s'écria saint Bernard, au pied de nos remparts, ici même, en 1146. « Dieu le veut », répondirent les croisés. Il y a toujours des ardents, des fous à pousser ce cri qui se termine dans les larmes.

D'où je suis, mon jugement est tempéré de cruels retours sur moi. Non, non, je ne suis plus un barbare. Peut-être l'ai-je encore été quand Jean Lacouture me demanda de répliquer au général Massu qui publiait un livre triomphaliste sur la bataille d'Alger ? On cherchait un mameluk pour lui rabaisser le caquet, à ce général, j'écrivis un pamphlet comme une toccata, puis vaguement, me souvenant de l'ancien aide de camp de Weygand qui m'accusait de salir la mémoire de son chef, me souvenant aussi du gendre de Mauriac qui m'insultait, comme de Malaparte provoquant Francis Ambrière pour un duel dont je devais être le témoin, je m'attendis encore à tout, mais il ne se passa rien. Le silence engloutit peu à peu les colères, les hargnes s'éteignent. On ne sait plus qui a raison ou tort, car chacun de nous croit posséder la vérité.

Près de Vézelay, j'ai écrit *les Chevaux du Soleil,* la télévision leur a donné du retentissement et, à ma mort, quelques irréductibles viendront pisser sur ma tombe parce que j'aurai aidé les peuples humiliés à se révolter. J'ai dû parfois réconforter mon éditeur en écrivant des ouvrages moins engagés, des zakouski comme *l'Amour fauve* sur l'irruption de l'industrie dans les campagnes, comme *Pour un chien* sur l'irruption d'un animal dans notre vie, ou des romans comme *le Désert de Retz* et *la Saison des Za.* Le destin des livres, entre les mains de beaucoup d'indifférents ou d'envieux, de rares partisans ou défenseurs, a tant besoin de miracles pour resplendir que je me demande où sont ceux-là. Max-Pol Fouchet, bien avant Vézelay où il se croyait à Elseneur, m'évita longtemps parce qu'il en voulait à Camus pour la fille dont j'ai parlé, qu'ils convoitaient tous deux. Les années avaient passé, Max-Pol aurait dû mesurer sa chance puisque la fameuse merveille se droguait, qu'elle devint folle,

que Camus dut se séparer d'elle et qu'elle mourut. N'empêche, cette trahison le tint longtemps éloigné de Camus et méfiant jusqu'au jour où, vidant nos sacs l'un l'autre, nous devînmes amis. Pour lui, poète brillant de tout son feuilletis, j'aurais aimé faire sonner les cloches quand il arrivait Alger et le soleil revenaient avec lui. Comme un jour je lui demandai pourquoi il avait pris aussi la défense des Arabes en Algérie, il me raconta comment une jeune Mauresque lui avait enseigné l'amour des colonisés. Quelquefois, dans la nuit, Maurice Clavel frappait à sa porte : « J'ai vu de la lumière, je suis venu. » Ils étaient tous deux des lumières, ils me manquent. Max-Pol Fouchet était un découvreur. Maurice Clavel un perturbateur, les cloches ne sonnèrent pour eux qu'à leur mort. Au chant du *Kyrie* de Mozart, le cercueil de Max-Pol, recouvert d'un drap rouge, entra dans la basilique, notre vaisseau mais aussi notre dernière maison, notre abri, notre toit. J'ai toujours envié ceux qui reposent là, au creux des pierres qu'on imagine imprégnées de riches parfums de chypre, d'ambre, de cinnamome, d'ilang-ilang ? Max-Pol Fouchet m'entraînait souvent plus bas, au cimetière. D'un geste large, il me montrait l'espace : « Tu vois... » C'était là, plus tard, qu'on le visiterait. Il croyait que des foules viendraient, il me disait : « On pourra s'asseoir sur ma tombe... » Il m'avait promis de faire mon oraison funèbre, c'est moi qui fis la sienne. Comme la basilique, ce lieu est notre rendez-vous : Romain Rolland est ailleurs, Claudel aussi. Ysé, l'héroïne de *Partage de midi*, gît près de Georges Bataille, non loin de Clavel, et c'est le seul endroit de Vézelay où l'on entende les rossignols. L'âne Ulysse, gardien avec moi pour l'instant, pousse parfois de puissants braiments qui devancent les coups de trompette de l'ange Gabriel et s'étendent comme à travers des mers sans fin, plus loin que Troie, plus loin que l'île des Lotophages et que l'île des Sirènes, plus loin que Calypso.

Vézelay, terre d'élection, Jérusalem céleste, Vézelay tout ce qu'on voudra, cela peut durer un été, dix étés. Si le soleil couchant transforme l' « être blond » en brasier, c'est une forteresse où le froid vous glace les os, les jours de pluie. Le don Quichotte que je suis par moments lui tourne alors le dos car il sent qu'on l'épie, il pousse une porte et le même paysage

l'assaille. D'un côté, le roc surplombe la vallée, de l'autre la façade et l'une des tours barrent le ciel. D'un côté, le vertige au-dessus des écailles noires de la Cure, de l'autre, une montagne de sacré lui cache le soleil levant. D'un côté, le vide, l'immensité, de l'autre, le gouffre de Dieu si l'on veut, mais Dieu sait où il va, et don Quichotte ne le sait pas. Contradiction qui n'arrête pas : je vais où je dois, où j'ai de la peine à aller, où cela me coûte, encore qu'avec la pratique et l'ancienneté, j'aie tendance à préférer que le chemin descende. Ulysse, quand il s'échappe de son enclos, trottine vers la rivière. Quant à la surveillance que je subis et de trop près, un jour, n'en pouvant plus : « Seigneur, j'en ai assez de vous et de vos saints, je me taille ! » Scène de ménage avec la maison Dieu comme jadis avec la maison Gallimard. Nous échangeons des mots blessants, on jette mes livres par la fenêtre. Chez Gallimard, je figurais dans l'enquête de Raymond Queneau *Pour une bibliothèque idéale*, j'appartenais aux *Poètes de la NRF*, j'ai disparu du saint des saints, et nous voilà fâchés jusqu'à ce qu'on se retrouve. Ici, de même, nous mettons la bicoque en vente, nous achèterons une ancienne ferme en Beauce d'où l'on verra de loin les flèches de la cathédrale, je marcherai enfin sur du plat. Nous nous tournons le dos, Dieu et don Quichotte, puis la colère éteinte, quelque chose en moi se met à fondre, et d'ailleurs rien ne marche : des acquéreurs qui se présentent, aucun ne nous agrée, nous ne sommes pas des margoulins, nous n'allons pas bazarder notre âme pour un plat de petit salé, mais y a-t-il rien de plus assommant qu'un amour insistant ? Sancho Pança se demande si Marie de Magdala n'aurait pas, par moments, agacé le maître par trop d'empressement ? A moins d'être un peu macho, trop d'admiration épuise, trop de parfum soulève le cœur. « Une seule de ses boucles a suffi pour m'enchaîner », dit le Cantique des cantiques. Mais où aller pour que, parmi tant de collines chinoises, don Quichotte et Sancho Pança découvrent à l'horizon les tours bien-aimées et qu'ils entendent leurs cloches ?

On me dira peut-être que je crois à des balivernes. Je m'en retournerai alors à cette nuit où les rayons laser projetaient l'image de la Madeleine, témoin par-delà des siècles, et je reste où je suis. Je me revois dans la tourelle de plexiglas qui

m'emportait jadis, tout à l'avant de l'équipage, parmi une armée d'ombres rugissantes. Au sextant, dans une nuée de galaxies où personne ne sait où il est ni ce qu'il fait, l'astre de la résurrection n'est qu'un mystère de plus. Un petit. En quoi aurais-je besoin de preuves quand il s'agit de mystère ? Braque disait qu'en matière de foi la preuve affaiblit la vérité.

Table

DU MÊME AUTEUR

ROMANS

LES CHEVAUX DU SOLEIL, t. I, Grasset, 1968.
UNE FEMME AU NOM D'ÉTOILE, t. II, Grasset, 1968.
LES CERISES D'ICHERRIDÈNE, t. III, Grasset, 1969.
LE MAÎTRE DE LA MITIDJA, t. IV, Grasset, 1970.
LES AMES INTERDITES, t. V, Grasset, 1972.
LE TONNERRE ET LES ANGES, t. VI, Grasset, 1975.
LES CHEVAUX DU SOLEIL, Grasset, 1980, édition en un volume.
LE DÉSERT DE RETZ, Grasset, 1978.
LA SAISON DES ZA, Grasset, 1982.

RÉCITS

CIEL ET TERRE, Alger, Charlot, 1943 (épuisé).
LA VALLÉE HEUREUSE, Charlot, Gallimard, Julliard, 1946.
LE MÉTIER DES ARMES, Gallimard, Julliard, 1948.
RETOUR DE L'ENFER, Gallimard, Julliard, 1953.
LE NAVIGATEUR, Gallimard, Julliard, 1954.
LA FEMME INFIDÈLE, Gallimard, Julliard, 1955.
LES FLAMMES DE L'ÉTÉ, Gallimard, Julliard, 1956.
LES BELLES CROISADES, Gallimard, Julliard, 1959.
LA GUERRE D'ALGÉRIE, Julliard, 1960.
LA BATAILLE DE DIÊN BIÊN PHU, Julliard, 1963.
LE VOYAGE EN CHINE, Julliard, 1965.
LA MORT DE MAO, Christian Bourgois, 1969.
L'AMOUR FAUVE, Grasset, 1971.
DANSE DU VENTRE AU-DESSUS DES CANONS, Flammarion, 1976.
POUR LE LIEUTENANT KARL, Christian Bourgois, 1977.
POUR UN CHIEN, Grasset, 1979.
UNE AFFAIRE D'HONNEUR, Plon, 1984.
BEYROUTH VIVA LA MUERTE, Grasset, 1984.
GUYNEMER, L'ANGE DE LA MORT, Paris, Albin Michel, 1986.

ESSAIS

COMME UN MAUVAIS ANGE, Paris, Charlot, Gallimard, 1956.
L'HOMME A L'ÉPÉE, Gallimard, Julliard, 1957.
AUTOUR DU DRAME, Julliard, 1961.
PASSION ET MORT DE SAINT-EXUPÉRY, Gallimard, Julliard, 1964.
LE GRAND NAUFRAGE, Julliard, 1966.
TURNAU, Sienne, 1976 (hors commerce).
ÉLOGE DE MAX-POL FOUCHET, Actes Sud, 1980.
ÉTRANGER POUR MES FRÈRES, Stock, 1982.

POÈMES

TROIS PRIÈRES POUR DES PILOTES, Alger, Charlot, 1942.
CHANTS ET PRIÈRES POUR DES PILOTES, Charlot, 1943, Gallimard, Julliard, 1947.
SEPT POÈMES DE TÉNÈBRES, Paris, 1957 (hors commerce).
PRIÈRE À MADEMOISELLE SAINTE-MADELEINE, Charlot, 1984.
CHANT D'AMOUR POUR MARSEILLE, Jeanne Laffitte, 1988.

THÉÂTRE

BEAU SANG, Gallimard, Julliard, 1952.
LES CYCLONES, Gallimard, Julliard, 1953.
LE FLEUVE ROUGE, Gallimard, Julliard, 1957.
LA RUE DES ZOUAVES *suivi de* SA MAJESTÉ MONSIEUR CONSTANTIN, Julliard, 1970.

PAMPHLET

J'ACCUSE LE GÉNÉRAL MASSU, Le Seuil, 1972.

CONTE

L'ŒIL DE LOUP DU ROI DE PHARAN, Sétif, 1945 (hors commerce).

AVEC JEAN AMROUCHE

CORRESPONDANCE (1937-1962).
D'UNE AMITIÉ, Edisud, 1985.

La composition de ce livre
a été effectuée par Bussière à Saint-Amand,
l'impression et le brochage ont été effectués
sur presse CAMERON
dans les ateliers de la S.E.P.C. à Saint-Amand-Montrond (Cher)
pour les Éditions Albin Michel

AM

Achevé d'imprimer en septembre 1989.
N° d'édition : 10876. N° d'impression : 1785.
Dépôt légal : septembre 1989.

CONTENTS

WARNING

The following is a transcript of a digital recording. In certain places, the audio quality was poor, so some words and phrases represent the author's best guesses. Background noises such as scuffling, hitting, and cursing by the two speakers have not been transcribed. The author makes no claims for the authenticity of the recording. It seems impossible that the two young narrators are telling the truth, but you, the reader, must decide for yourself.

1.
A DEATH AT THE NEEDLE

C A R T E R

We only have a few hours, so listen carefully.

If you're hearing this story, you're already in danger. Sadie and I might be your only chance.

Go to the school. Find the locker. I won't tell you which school or which locker, because if you're the right person, you'll find it. The combination is 13/32/33. By the time you finish listening, you'll know what those numbers mean. Just remember the story we're about to tell you isn't complete yet. How it ends will depend on you.

The most important thing: when you open the package and find what's inside, *don't* keep it longer than a week. Sure, it'll be tempting. I mean, it will grant you almost unlimited power. But if you possess it too long, it will consume you. Learn its secrets quickly and pass it on. Hide it for the next person, the way Sadie and I did for you. Then be prepared for your life to get very interesting.

Okay, Sadie is telling me to stop stalling and get on with the story. Fine. I guess it started in London, the night our dad blew up the British Museum.

*　　　*　　　*

My name is Carter Kane. I'm fourteen and my home is a suitcase.

You think I'm kidding? Since I was eight years

1

old, my dad and I have traveled the world. I was born in L.A. but my dad's an archaeologist, so his work takes him all over. Mostly we go to Egypt, since that's his specialty. Go into a bookstore, find a book about Egypt, there's a pretty good chance it was written by Dr. Julius Kane. You want to know how Egyptians pulled the brains out of mummies, or built the pyramids, or cursed King Tut's tomb? My dad is your man. Of course, there are other reasons my dad moved around so much, but I didn't know his secret back then.

I didn't go to school. My dad homeschooled me, if you can call it 'home' schooling when you don't have a home. He sort of taught me whatever he thought was important, so I learned a lot about Egypt and basketball stats and my dad's favorite musicians. I read a lot, too—pretty much anything I could get my hands on, from dad's history books to fantasy novels—because I spent a lot of time sitting around in hotels and airports and dig sites in foreign countries where I didn't know anybody. My dad was always telling me to put the book down and play some ball. You ever try to start a game of pick-up basketball in Aswan, Egypt? It's not easy.

Anyway, my dad trained me early to keep all my possessions in a single suitcase that fits in an airplane's overhead compartment. My dad packed the same way, except he was allowed an extra workbag for his archaeology tools. Rule number one: I was not allowed to look in his workbag. That's a rule I never broke until the day of the explosion.

*   *   *

2

It happened on Christmas Eve. We were in London for visitation day with my sister, Sadie.

See, Dad's only allowed two days a year with her—one in the winter, one in the summer—because our grandparents hate him. After our mom died, her parents (our grandparents) had this big court battle with Dad. After six lawyers, two fistfights, and a near fatal attack with a spatula (don't ask), they won the right to keep Sadie with them in England. She was only six, two years younger than me, and they couldn't keep us both—at least that was their excuse for not taking me. So Sadie was raised as a British schoolkid, and I traveled around with my dad. We only saw Sadie twice a year, which was fine with me.

[Shut up, Sadie. Yes—I'm getting to that part.]

So anyway, my dad and I had just flown into Heathrow after a couple of delays. It was a drizzly, cold afternoon. The whole taxi ride into the city, my dad seemed kind of nervous.

Now, my dad is a big guy. You wouldn't think anything could make him nervous. He has dark brown skin like mine, piercing brown eyes, a bald head, and a goatee, so he looks like a buff evil scientist. That afternoon he wore his cashmere winter coat and his best brown suit, the one he used for public lectures. Usually he exudes so much confidence that he dominates any room he walks into, but sometimes—like that afternoon—I saw another side to him that I didn't really understand. He kept looking over his shoulder like we were being hunted.

'Dad?' I said as we were getting off the A-40. 'What's wrong?'

3

'No sign of them,' he muttered. Then he must've realized he'd spoken aloud, because he looked at me kind of startled. 'Nothing, Carter. Everything's fine.'

Which bothered me because my dad's a terrible liar. I always knew when he was hiding something, but I also knew no amount of pestering would get the truth out of him. He was probably trying to protect me, though from what I didn't know. Sometimes I wondered if he had some dark secret in his past, some old enemy following him, maybe; but the idea seemed ridiculous. Dad was just an archaeologist.

The other thing that troubled me: Dad was clutching his workbag. Usually when he does that, it means we're in danger. Like the time gunmen stormed our hotel in Cairo. I heard shots coming from the lobby and ran downstairs to check on my dad. By the time I got there, he was just calmly zipping up his workbag while three unconscious gunmen hung by their feet from the chandelier, their robes falling over their heads so you could see their boxer shorts. Dad claimed not to have witnessed anything, and in the end the police blamed a freak chandelier malfunction.

Another time, we got caught in a riot in Paris. My dad found the nearest parked car, pushed me into the backseat, and told me to stay down. I pressed myself against the floorboards and kept my eyes shut tight. I could hear Dad in the driver's seat, rummaging in his bag, mumbling something to himself while the mob yelled and destroyed things outside. A few minutes later he told me it was safe to get up. Every other car on the block had been overturned and set on fire. Our car had

4

been freshly washed and polished, and several twenty-euro notes had been tucked under the windshield wipers.

Anyway, I'd come to respect the bag. It was our good luck charm. But when my dad kept it close, it meant we were going to need good luck.

We drove through the city center, heading east toward my grandparents' flat. We passed the golden gates of Buckingham Palace, the big stone column in Trafalgar Square. London is a pretty cool place, but after you've traveled for so long, all cities start to blend together. Other kids I meet sometimes say, 'Wow, you're so lucky you get to travel so much.' But it's not like we spend our time sightseeing or have a lot of money to travel in style. We've stayed in some pretty rough places, and we hardly ever stay anywhere longer than a few days. Most of the time it feels like we're fugitives rather than tourists.

I mean, you wouldn't think my dad's work was dangerous. He does lectures on topics like 'Can Egyptian Magic Really Kill You?' and 'Favorite Punishments in the Egyptian Underworld' and other stuff most people wouldn't care about. But like I said, there's that other side to him. He's always very cautious, checking every hotel room before he lets me walk into it. He'll dart into a museum to see some artifacts, take a few notes, and rush out again like he's afraid to be caught on the security cameras.

One time when I was younger, we raced across the Charles de Gaulle airport to catch a last-minute flight, and Dad didn't relax until the plane was off the ground, I asked him point blank what he was running from, and he looked at me like I'd just pulled the pin out of a grenade. For a second I was scared he might actually tell me the truth. Then he said, 'Carter, it's nothing.' As if 'nothing' were the most terrible thing in the world.

After that, I decided maybe it was better not to ask questions.

*　　*　　*

My grandparents, the Fausts, live in a housing development near Canary Wharf, right on the banks of the River Thames. The taxi let us off at the curb, and my dad asked the driver to wait.

We were halfway up the walk when Dad froze. He turned and looked behind us.

'What?' I asked.

Then I saw the man in the trench coat. He was across the street, leaning against a big dead tree. He was barrel shaped, with skin the color of roasted coffee. His coat and black pinstriped suit looked expensive. He had long braided hair and wore a black fedora pulled down low over his dark round glasses. He reminded me of a jazz musician, the kind my dad would always drag me to see in concert. Even though I couldn't see his eyes, I got the impression he was watching us. He might've been an old friend or colleague of Dad's. No matter where we went, Dad was always running into people he knew. But it did seem strange that the guy was waiting here, outside my grandparents'. And he didn't look happy.

'Carter,' my dad said, 'go on ahead.'

'But—'

'Get your sister. I'll meet you back at the taxi.'

He crossed the street toward the man in the

trench coat, which left me with two choices: follow my dad and see what was going on, or do what I was told.

I decided on the slightly less dangerous path. I went to retrieve my sister.

*   *   *

Before I could even knock, Sadie opened the door.

'Late as usual,' she said.

She was holding her cat, Muffin, who'd been a 'going away' gift from Dad six years before. Muffin never seemed to get older or bigger. She had fuzzy yellow-and-black fur like a miniature leopard, alert yellow eyes, and pointy ears that were too tall for her head. A silver Egyptian pendant dangled from her collar. She didn't look anything like a muffin, but Sadie had been little when she named her, so I guess you have to cut her some slack.

Sadie hadn't changed much either since last summer.

[As I'm recording this, she's standing next to me, glaring, so I'd better be careful how I describe her.]

You would never guess she's my sister. First of all, she'd been living in England so long, she has a British accent. Second, she takes after our mom, who was white, so Sadie's skin is much lighter than mine. She has straight caramel-colored hair, not exactly blond but not brown, which she usually dyes with streaks of bright colors. That day it had red streaks down the left side. Her eyes are blue. I'm serious. *Blue* eyes, just like our mom's. She's only twelve, but she's exactly as tall as me, which is really annoying. She was chewing gum as usual,

7

dressed for her day out with Dad in battered jeans, a leather jacket, and combat boots, like she was going to a concert and was hoping to stomp on some people. She had headphones dangling around her neck in case we bored her.

[Okay, she didn't hit me, so I guess I did an okay job of describing her.]

'Our plane was late,' I told her.

She popped a bubble, rubbed Muffin's head, and tossed the cat inside. 'Gran, going out!'

From somewhere in the house, Grandma Faust said something I couldn't make out, probably 'Don't let them in!'

Sadie closed the door and regarded me as if I were a dead mouse her cat had just dragged in. 'So, here you are again.'

'Yep.'

'Come on, then.' She sighed. 'Let's get on with it.'

That's the way she was. No 'Hi, how you been the last six months? So glad to see you!' or anything. But that was okay with me. When you only see each other twice a year, it's like you're distant cousins rather than siblings. We had absolutely nothing in common except our parents.

We trudged down the steps. I was thinking how she smelled like a combination of old people's house and bubble gum when she stopped so abruptly, I ran into her.

'Who's that?' she asked.

I'd almost forgotten about the dude in the trench coat. He and my dad were standing across the street next to the big tree, having what looked like a serious argument. Dad's back was turned so I couldn't see his face, but he gestured with his hands like he does when he's agitated. The other guy scowled and shook his head.

'Dunno,' I said. 'He was there when we pulled up.'

'He looks familiar.' Sadie frowned like she was trying to remember. 'Come on.'

'Dad wants us to wait in the cab,' I said, even though I knew it was no use. Sadie was already on the move.

Instead of going straight across the street, she dashed up the sidewalk for half a block, ducking behind cars, then crossed to the opposite side and crouched under a low stone wall. She started sneaking toward our dad. I didn't have much choice but to follow her example, even though it made me feel kind of stupid.

'Six years in England,' I muttered, 'and she thinks she's James Bond.'

Sadie swatted me without looking back and kept creeping forward.

A couple more steps and we were right behind the big dead tree. I could hear my dad on the other side, saying, '—have to, Amos. You know it's the right thing.'

'No,' said the other man, who must've been Amos. His voice was deep and even—very insistent. His accent was American. 'If *I* don't stop you, Julius, *they* will. The Per Ankh is shadowing you.'

Sadie turned to me and mouthed the words 'Per *what?*'

I shook my head, just as mystified. 'Let's get out of here,' I whispered, because I figured we'd be spotted any minute and get in serious trouble. Sadie, of course, ignored me.

'They don't know my plan,' my father was saying. 'By the time they figure it out—'

'And the children?' Amos asked. The hairs stood up on the back of my neck. 'What about them?'

'I've made arrangements to protect them,' my dad said. 'Besides, if I don't do this, we're all in danger. Now, back off.'

'I can't, Julius.'

'Then it's a duel you want?' Dad's tone turned deadly serious. 'You never could beat me, Amos.'

I hadn't seen my dad get violent since the Great Spatula Incident, and I wasn't anxious to see a repeat of *that*, but the two men seemed to be edging toward a fight.

Before I could react, Sadie popped up and shouted, 'Dad!'

He looked surprised when she tackle-hugged him, but not nearly as surprised as the other guy, Amos. He backed up so quickly, he tripped over his own trench coat.

He'd taken off his glasses. I couldn't help thinking that Sadie was right. He did look familiar—like a very distant memory.

'I—I must be going,' he said. He straightened his fedora and lumbered down the road.

Our dad watched him go. He kept one arm protectively around Sadie and one hand inside the workbag slung over his shoulder. Finally, when Amos disappeared around the corner, Dad relaxed. He took his hand out of the bag and smiled at Sadie. 'Hello, sweetheart.'

Sadie pushed away from him and crossed her arms. 'Oh, now it's *sweetheart,* is it? You're late. Visitation Day's nearly over! And what was that

10

about? Who's Amos, and what's the Per Ankh?'

Dad stiffened. He glanced at me like he was wondering how much we'd overheard.

'It's nothing,' he said, trying to sound upbeat. 'I have a wonderful evening planned. Who'd like a private tour of the British Museum?'

*   *   *

Sadie slumped in the back of the taxi between Dad and me.

'I can't believe it,' she grumbled. 'One evening together, and you want to do research.'

Dad tried for a smile. 'Sweetheart, it'll be fun. The curator of the Egyptian collection personally invited—'

'Right, big surprise.' Sadie blew a strand of red-streaked hair out of her face. 'Christmas Eve, and we're going to see some moldy old relics from Egypt. Do you ever think about *anything* else?'

Dad didn't get mad. He never gets mad at Sadie. He just stared out the window at the darkening sky and the rain.

'Yes,' he said quietly. 'I do.'

Whenever Dad got quiet like that and stared off into nowhere, I knew he was thinking about our mom. The last few months, it had been happening a lot. I'd walk into our hotel room and find him with his cell phone in his hands, Mom's picture smiling up at him from the screen—her hair tucked under a headscarf, her blue eyes startlingly bright against the desert backdrop.

Or we'd be at some dig site. I'd see Dad staring at the horizon, and I'd know he was remembering how he'd met her—two young scientists in the

11

Valley of the Kings, on a dig to discover a lost tomb. Dad was an Egyptologist. Mom was an anthropologist looking for ancient DNA. He'd told me the story a thousand times.

Our taxi snaked its way along the banks of the Thames. Just past Waterloo Bridge, my dad tensed.

'Driver,' he said. 'Stop here a moment.'

The cabbie pulled over on the Victoria Embankment.

'What is it, Dad?' I asked.

He got out of the cab like he hadn't heard me. When Sadie and I joined him on the sidewalk, he was staring up at Cleopatra's Needle.

In case you've never seen it: the Needle is an obelisk, not a needle, and it doesn't have anything to do with Cleopatra. I guess the British just thought the name sounded cool when they brought it to London. It's about seventy feet tall, which would've been really impressive back in Ancient Egypt, but on the Thames, with all the tall buildings around, it looks small and sad. You could drive right by it and not even realize you'd just passed something that was a thousand years older than the city of London.

'God.' Sadie walked around in a frustrated circle. 'Do we have to stop for *every* monument?'

My dad stared at the top of the obelisk. 'I had to see it again,' he murmured. 'Where it happened . . .'

A freezing wind blew off the river. I wanted to get back in the cab, but my dad was really starting to worry me. I'd never seen him so distracted.

'What, Dad?' I asked. 'What happened here?'

'The last place I saw her.'

Sadie stopped pacing. She scowled at me uncertainly, then back at Dad. 'Hang on. Do you mean Mum?'

Dad brushed Sadie's hair behind her ear, and she was so surprised, she didn't even push him away.

I felt like the rain had frozen me solid. Mom's death had always been a forbidden subject. I knew she'd died in an accident in London. I knew my grandparents blamed my dad. But no one would ever tell us the details. I'd given up asking my dad, partly because it made him so sad, partly because he absolutely refused to tell me anything. 'When you're older' was all he would say, which was the most frustrating response ever.

'You're telling us she died here,' I said. 'At Cleopatra's Needle? What happened?'

He lowered his head.

'Dad!' Sadie protested. 'I go past this *every* day, and you mean to say—all this time—and I didn't even *know*?'

'Do you still have your cat?' Dad asked her, which seemed like a really stupid question.

'Of course I've still got the cat!' she said. 'What does that have to do with anything?'

'And your amulet?'

Sadie's hand went to her neck. When we were little, right before Sadie went to live with our grandparents, Dad had given us both Egyptian amulets. Mine was an Eye of Horus, which was a popular protection symbol in Ancient Egypt.

In fact my dad says the modern pharmacist's symbol, ℞, is a simplified version of the Eye of Horus, because medicine is supposed to protect you.

13

Anyway, I always wore my amulet under my shirt, but I figured Sadie would've lost hers or thrown it away.

To my surprise, she nodded. ' 'Course I have it, Dad, but don't change the subject. Gran's always going on about how you caused Mum's death. That's not true, is it?'

We waited. For once, Sadie and I wanted exactly the same thing—the truth.

'The night your mother died,' my father started, 'here at the Needle—'

A sudden flash illuminated the embankment. I turned, half blind, and just for a moment I glimpsed two figures: a tall pale man with a forked beard and wearing cream-colored robes, and a coppery-skinned girl in dark blue robes and a headscarf—the kind of clothes I'd seen hundreds of times in Egypt. They were just standing there side by side, not twenty feet away, watching us. Then the light faded. The figures melted into a fuzzy afterimage. When my eyes readjusted to the darkness, they were gone.

'Um . . .' Sadie said nervously. 'Did you just see that?'

'Get in the cab,' my dad said, pushing us toward the curb. 'We're out of time.'

From that point on, Dad clammed up.

'This isn't the place to talk,' he said, glancing behind us. He'd promised the cabbie an extra ten pounds if he got us to the museum in under five minutes, and the cabbie was doing his best.

'Dad,' I tried, 'those people at the river—'

'And the other bloke, Amos,' Sadie said. 'Are they Egyptian police or something?'

'Look, both of you,' Dad said, 'I'm going to

14

need your help tonight. I know it's hard, but you have to be patient. I'll explain everything, I promise, after we get to the museum. I'm going to make everything right again.'

'What do you mean?' Sadie insisted. 'Make *what* right?'

Dad's expression was more than sad. It was almost guilty. With a chill, I thought about what Sadie had said: about our grandparents blaming him for Mom's death. That *couldn't* be what he was talking about, could it?

The cabbie swerved onto Great Russell Street and screeched to a halt in front of the museum's main gates.

'Just follow my lead,' Dad told us. 'When we meet the curator, act normal.'

I was thinking that Sadie never acted *normal,* but I decided not to say anything.

We climbed out of the cab. I got our luggage while Dad paid the driver with a big wad of cash. Then he did something strange. He threw a handful of small objects into the backseat—they looked like stones, but it was too dark for me to be sure. 'Keep driving,' he told the cabbie. 'Take us to Chelsea.'

That made no sense since we were already out of the cab, but the driver sped off. I glanced at Dad, then back at the cab, and before it turned the corner and disappeared in the dark, I caught a weird glimpse of three passengers in the backseat: a man and two kids.

I blinked. There was no way the cab could've picked up another fare so fast. 'Dad—'

'London cabs don't stay empty very long,' he said matter-of-factly. 'Come along, kids.'

15

He marched off through the wrought iron gates. For a second, Sadie and I hesitated.

'Carter, *what* is going on?'

I shook my head. 'I'm not sure I want to know.'

'Well, stay out here in the cold if you want, but *I'm* not leaving without an explanation.' She turned and marched after our dad.

Looking back on it, I should've run. I should've dragged Sadie out of there and gotten as far away as possible. Instead I followed her through the gates.

2.
AN EXPLOSION FOR CHRISTMAS

CARTER

I'd been to the British Museum before. In fact I've been in more museums than I like to admit—it makes me sound like a total geek.

[That's Sadie in the background, yelling that I *am* a total geek. Thanks, Sis.]

Anyway, the museum was closed and completely dark, but the curator and two security guards were waiting for us on the front steps.

'Dr. Kane!' The curator was a greasy little dude in a cheap suit. I'd seen mummies with more hair and better teeth. He shook my dad's hand like he was meeting a rock star. 'Your last paper on Imhotep—brilliant! I don't know how you translated those spells!'

'Im-ho-who?' Sadie muttered to me.

'Imhotep,' I said. 'High priest, architect. Some

16

say he was a magician. Designed the first step pyramid. You know.'

'Don't know,' Sadie said. 'Don't care. But thanks.'

Dad expressed his gratitude to the curator for hosting us on a holiday. Then he put his hand on my shoulder. 'Dr. Martin, I'd like you to meet Carter and Sadie.'

'Ah! Your son, obviously, and—' The curator looked hesitantly at Sadie. 'And this young lady?'

'My daughter,' Dad said.

Dr. Martin's stare went temporarily blank. Doesn't matter how open-minded or polite people think they are, there's always that moment of confusion that flashes across their faces when they realize Sadie is part of our family. I hate it, but over the years I've come to expect it.

The curator regained his smile. 'Yes, yes, of course. Right this way, Dr. Kane. We're very honored!'

The security guards locked the doors behind us. They took our luggage, then one of them reached for Dad's workbag.

'Ah, no,' Dad said with a tight smile. 'I'll keep this one.'

The guards stayed in the foyer as we followed the curator into the Great Court. It was ominous at night. Dim light from the glass-domed ceiling cast crosshatched shadows across the walls like a giant spiderweb. Our footsteps clicked on the white marble floor.

'So,' Dad said, 'the stone.'

'Yes!' the curator said. 'Though I can't imagine what new information you could glean from it. It's been studied to death—our most famous artifact,

17

of course.'

'Of course,' Dad said. 'But you may be surprised.'

'What's he on about now?' Sadie whispered to me.

I didn't answer. I had a sneaking suspicion what stone they were talking about, but I couldn't figure out why Dad would drag us out on Christmas Eve to see it.

I wondered what he'd been about to tell us at Cleopatra's Needle—something about our mother and the night she died. And why did he keep glancing around as if he expected those strange people we'd seen at the Needle to pop up again? We were locked in a museum surrounded by guards and high-tech security. Nobody could bother us in here—I hoped.

We turned left into the Egyptian wing. The walls were lined with massive statues of the pharaohs and gods, but my dad bypassed them all and went straight for the main attraction in the middle of the room.

'Beautiful,' my father murmured. 'And it's not a replica?'

'No, no,' the curator promised. 'We don't always keep the actual stone on display, but for you—this is quite real.'

We were staring at a slab of dark gray rock about three feet tall and two feet wide. It sat on a pedestal, encased in a glass box. The flat surface of the stone was chiseled with three distinct bands of writing. The top part was Ancient Egyptian picture writing: hieroglyphics. The middle section . . . I had to rack my brain to remember what my dad called it: *Demotic,* a kind of writing from the

18

period when the Greeks controlled Egypt and a lot of Greek words got mixed into Egyptian. The last lines were in Greek.

'The Rosetta Stone,' I said.

'Isn't that a computer program?' Sadie asked.

I wanted to tell her how stupid she was, but the curator cut me off with a nervous laugh. 'Young lady, the Rosetta Stone was the key to deciphering hieroglyphics! It was discovered by Napoleon's army in 1799 and—'

'Oh, right,' Sadie said. 'I remember now.'

I knew she was just saying that to shut him up, but my dad wouldn't let it go.

'Sadie,' he said, 'until this stone was discovered, regular mortals . . . er, I mean, no one had been able to read hieroglyphics for centuries. The written language of Egypt had been completely forgotten. Then an Englishman named Thomas Young proved that the Rosetta Stone's three languages all conveyed the same message. A Frenchman named Champollion took up the work and cracked the code of hieroglyphics.'

Sadie chewed her gum, unimpressed. 'What's it say, then?'

Dad shrugged. 'Nothing important. It's basically a thank-you letter from some priests to King Ptolemy V. When it was first carved, the stone was no big deal. But over the centuries . . . over the centuries it has become a powerful symbol. Perhaps the most important connection between Ancient Egypt and the modern world. I was a fool not to realize its potential sooner.'

He'd lost me, and apparently the curator too.

'Dr. Kane?' he asked. 'Are you quite all right?'

Dad breathed deeply. 'My apologies, Dr.

19

Martin. I was just . . . thinking aloud. If I could have the glass removed? And if you could bring me the papers I asked for from your archives.'

Dr. Martin nodded. He pressed a code into a small remote control, and the front of the glass box clicked open.

'It will take a few minutes to retrieve the notes,' Dr. Martin said. 'For anyone else, I would hesitate to grant unguarded access to the stone, as you've requested. I trust you'll be careful.'

He glanced at us kids like we were troublemakers.

'We'll be careful,' Dad promised.

As soon as Dr. Martin's steps receded, Dad turned to us with a frantic look in his eyes. 'Children, this is very important. You have to stay out of this room.'

He slipped his workbag off his shoulder and unzipped it just enough to pull out a bike chain and padlock. 'Follow Dr. Martin. You'll find his office at the end of the Great Court on the left. There's only one entrance. Once he's inside, wrap this around the door handles and lock it tight. We need to delay him.'

'You want us to lock him in?' Sadie asked, suddenly interested. 'Brilliant!'

'Dad,' I said, 'what's going on?'

'We don't have time for explanations,' he said. 'This will be our only chance. They're coming.'

'Who's coming?' Sadie asked.

He took Sadie by the shoulders. 'Sweetheart, I love you. And I'm sorry . . . I'm sorry for many things, but there's no time now. If this works, I promise I'll make everything better for all of us. Carter, you're my brave man. You have to trust me. Remember, lock up Dr. Martin. Then stay out of this room!'

*   *   *

Chaining the curator's door was easy. But as soon as we'd finished, we looked back the way we'd come and saw blue light streaming from the Egyptian gallery, as if our dad had installed a giant glowing aquarium.

Sadie locked eyes with me. 'Honestly, do you have *any* idea what he's up to?'

'None,' I said. 'But he's been acting strange lately. Thinking a lot about Mom. He keeps her picture . . .'

I didn't want to say more. Fortunately Sadie nodded like she understood.

'What's in his workbag?' she asked.

'I don't know. He told me never to look.'

Sadie raised an eyebrow. 'And you never did? God, that is so like you, Carter. You're hopeless.'

I wanted to defend myself, but just then a tremor shook the floor.

Startled, Sadie grabbed my arm. 'He told us to stay put. I suppose you're going to follow that order too?'

Actually, that order was sounding pretty good to me, but Sadie sprinted down the hall, and after a moment's hesitation, I ran after her.

*   *   *

When we reached the entrance of the Egyptian gallery, we stopped dead in our tracks. Our dad stood in front of the Rosetta Stone with his back to

21

us. A blue circle glowed on the floor around him, as if someone had switched on hidden neon tubes in the floor.

My dad had thrown off his overcoat. His workbag lay open at his feet, revealing a wooden box about two feet long, painted with Egyptian images.

'What's he holding?' Sadie whispered to me. 'Is that a boomerang?'

Sure enough, when Dad raised his hand, he was brandishing a curved white stick. It did look like a boomerang. But instead of throwing the stick, he touched it to the Rosetta Stone. Sadie caught her breath. Dad was *writing* on the stone. Wherever the boomerang made contact, glowing blue lines appeared on the granite. Hieroglyphs.

It made no sense. How could he write glowing words with a stick? But the image was bright and clear: ram's horns above a box and an X.

'Open,' Sadie murmured. I stared at her, because it sounded like she had just translated the word, but that was impossible. I'd been hanging around Dad for years, and even I could read only a few hieroglyphs. They are seriously hard to learn.

Dad raised his arms. He chanted: *'Wo-seer, i-ei.'* And two more hieroglyphic symbols burned blue against the surface of the Rosetta Stone.

As stunned as I was, I recognized the first symbol. It was the name of the Egyptian god of the dead.

'Wo-seer,' I whispered. I'd never heard it pronounced that way, but I knew what it meant. 'Osiris.'

'Osiris, come,' Sadie said, as if in a trance. Then her eyes widened. 'No!' she shouted. 'Dad, no!'

22

Our father turned in surprise. He started to say, 'Children—' but it was too late. The ground rumbled. The blue light turned to searing white, and the Rosetta Stone exploded.

*   *   *

When I regained consciousness, the first thing I heard was laughter—horrible, gleeful laughter mixed with the blare of the museum's security alarms.

I felt like I'd just been run over by a tractor. I sat up, dazed, and spit a piece of Rosetta Stone out of my mouth. The gallery was in ruins. Waves of fire rippled in pools along the floor. Giant statues had toppled. Sarcophagi had been knocked off their pedestals. Pieces of the Rosetta Stone had exploded outward with such force that they'd embedded themselves in the columns, the walls, the other exhibits.

Sadie was passed out next to me, but she looked unharmed. I shook her shoulder, and she grunted. 'Ugh.'

In front of us, where the Rosetta Stone had been, stood a smoking, sheared-off pedestal. The floor was blackened in a starburst pattern, except for the glowing blue circle around our father.

He was facing our direction, but he didn't seem to be looking at us. A bloody cut ran across his scalp. He gripped the boomerang tightly.

I didn't understand what he was looking at. Then the horrible laughter echoed around the room again, and I realized it was coming from right in front of me.

Something stood between our father and us. At

first, I could barely make it out—just a flicker of heat. But as I concentrated, it took on a vague form—the fiery outline of a man.

He was taller than Dad, and his laugh cut through me like a chainsaw.

'Well done,' he said to my father. 'Very well done, Julius.'

'You were not summoned!' My father's voice trembled. He held up the boomerang, but the fiery man flicked one finger, and the stick flew from Dad's hand, shattering against the wall.

'I am never summoned, Julius,' the man purred. 'But when you open a door, you must be prepared for guests to walk through.'

'Back to the Duat!' my father roared. 'I have the power of the Great King!'

'Oh, scary,' the fiery man said with amusement. 'And even if you knew how to use that power, which you do not, he was never my match. I am the strongest. Now you will share his fate.'

I couldn't make sense of anything, but I knew that I had to help my dad. I tried to pick up the nearest chunk of stone, but I was so terrified my fingers felt frozen and numb. My hands were useless.

Dad shot me a silent look of warning: *Get out.* I realized he was intentionally keeping the fiery man's back to us, hoping Sadie and I would escape unnoticed.

Sadie was still groggy. I managed to drag her behind a column, into the shadows. When she started to protest, I clamped my hand over her mouth. That woke her up. She saw what was happening and stopped fighting.

Alarms blared. Fire circled around the

doorways of the gallery. The guards had to be on their way, but I wasn't sure if that was a good thing for us.

Dad crouched to the floor, keeping his eyes on his enemy, and opened his painted wooden box. He brought out a small rod like a ruler. He muttered something under his breath and the rod elongated into a wooden staff as tall as he was.

Sadie made a squeaking sound. I couldn't believe my eyes either, but things only got weirder.

Dad threw his staff at the fiery man's feet, and it changed into an enormous serpent—ten feet long and as big around as I was—with coppery scales and glowing red eyes. It lunged at the fiery man, who effortlessly grabbed the serpent by its neck. The man's hand burst into white-hot flames, and the snake burned to ashes.

'An old trick, Julius,' the fiery man chided.

My dad glanced at us, silently urging us again to run. Part of me refused to believe any of this was real. Maybe I was unconscious, having a nightmare. Next to me, Sadie picked up a chunk of stone.

'How many?' my dad asked quickly, trying to keep the fiery man's attention. 'How many did I release?'

'Why, all five,' the man said, as if explaining something to a child. 'You should know we're a package deal, Julius. Soon I'll release even more, and they'll be very grateful. I shall be named king again.'

'The Demon Days,' my father said. 'They'll stop you before it's too late.'

The fiery man laughed. 'You think the House can stop me? Those old fools can't even stop arguing among themselves. Now let the story be told anew. And this time you shall *never* rise!'

The fiery man waved his hand. The blue circle at Dad's feet went dark. Dad grabbed for his toolbox, but it skittered across the floor.

'Good-bye, Osiris,' the fiery man said. With another flick of his hand, he conjured a glowing coffin around our dad. At first it was transparent, but as our father struggled and pounded on its sides, the coffin became more and more solid—a golden Egyptian sarcophagus inlaid with jewels. My dad caught my eyes one last time, and mouthed the word *Run!* before the coffin sank into the floor, as if the ground had turned to water.

'Dad!' I screamed.

Sadie threw her stone, but it sailed harmlessly through the fiery man's head.

He turned, and for one terrible moment, his face appeared in the flames. What I saw made no sense. It was as if someone had superimposed two different faces on top of each other—one almost human, with pale skin, cruel, angular features, and glowing red eyes, the other like an animal with dark fur and sharp fangs. Worse than a dog or a wolf or a lion—some animal I'd never seen before. Those red eyes stared at me, and I knew I was going to die.

Behind me, heavy footsteps echoed on the marble floor of the Great Court. Voices were barking orders. The security guards, maybe the police—but they'd never get here in time.

The fiery man lunged at us. A few inches from my face, something shoved him backward. The air sparked with electricity. The amulet around my neck grew uncomfortably hot.

The fiery man hissed, regarding me more carefully. 'So . . . it's *you*.'

The building shook again. At the opposite end of the room, part of the wall exploded in a brilliant flash of light. Two people stepped through the gap—the man and the girl we'd seen at the Needle, their robes swirling around them. Both of them held staffs.

The fiery man snarled. He looked at me one last time and said, 'Soon, boy.'

Then the entire room erupted in flames. A blast of heat sucked all the air of out my lungs and I crumpled to the floor.

The last thing I remember, the man with the forked beard and the girl in blue were standing over me. I heard the security guards running and shouting, getting closer. The girl crouched over me and drew a long curved knife from her belt.

'We must act quickly,' she told the man.

'Not yet,' he said with some reluctance. His thick accent sounded French. 'We must be sure before we destroy them.'

I closed my eyes and drifted into unconsciousness.

3.

IMPRISONED WITH MY CAT

SADIE

[Give me the bloody mic.]

Hullo. Sadie here. My brother's a rubbish storyteller. Sorry about that. But now you've got me, so all is well.

Let's see. The explosion. Rosetta Stone in a billion pieces. Fiery evil bloke. Dad boxed in a coffin. Creepy Frenchman and Arab girl with the knife. Us passing out. Right.

So when I woke up, the police were rushing about as you might expect. They separated me from my brother. I didn't really mind that part. He's a pain anyway. But they locked me in the curator's office for *ages.* And yes, they used *our* bicycle chain to do it. Cretins.

I was shattered, of course. I'd just been knocked out by a fiery whatever-it-was. I'd watched my dad get packed in a sarcophagus and shot through the floor. I tried to tell the police about all that, but did they care? No.

Worst of all: I had a lingering chill, as if someone was pushing ice-cold needles into the back of my neck. It had started when I looked at those blue glowing words Dad had drawn on the Rosetta Stone and I *knew* what they meant. A family disease, perhaps? Can knowledge of boring Egyptian stuff be hereditary? With my luck.

Long after my gum had gone stale, a policewoman finally retrieved me from the curator's office. She asked me no questions. She just trundled me into a police car and took me home. Even then, I wasn't allowed to explain to Gran and Gramps. The policewoman just tossed me into my room and I waited. And waited.

I don't like waiting.

I paced the floor. My room was nothing posh, just an attic space with a window and a bed and a desk. There wasn't much to do. Muffin sniffed my legs and her tail puffed up like a bottlebrush. I suppose she doesn't fancy the smell of museums. She hissed and disappeared under the bed.

'Thanks a lot,' I muttered.

I opened the door, but the policewoman was standing guard.

'The inspector will be with you in a moment,' she told me. 'Please stay inside.'

I could see downstairs—just a glimpse of Gramps pacing the room, wringing his hands, while Carter and a police inspector talked on the sofa. I couldn't make out what they were saying.

'Could I just use the loo?' I asked the nice officer.

'No.' She closed the door in my face. As if I might rig an explosion in the toilet. Honestly.

I dug out my iPod and scrolled through my playlist. Nothing struck me. I threw it on my bed in disgust. When I'm too distracted for music, that is a very sad thing. I wondered why Carter got to talk to the police first. It wasn't fair.

I fiddled with the necklace Dad had given me. I'd never been sure what the symbol meant. Carter's was obviously an eye, but mine looked a bit like an angel, or perhaps a killer alien robot.

Why on earth had Dad asked if I still had it? *Of course* I still had it. It was the only gift he'd ever given me. Well, apart from Muffin, and with the cat's attitude, I'm not sure I would call her a proper gift.

Dad had practically abandoned me at age six, after all. The necklace was my one link to him. On good days I would stare at it and remember him fondly. On bad days (which were much more frequent) I would fling it across the room and stomp on it and curse him for not being around, which I found quite therapeutic. But in the end, I always put it back on.

At any rate, during the weirdness at the museum—and I'm not making this up—the necklace got *hotter.* I nearly took it off, but I couldn't help wondering if it truly was protecting me somehow.

I'll make things right, Dad had said, with that guilty look he often gives me.

Well, colossal fail, Dad.

What had he been thinking? I wanted to believe it had all been a bad dream: the glowing hieroglyphs, the snake staff, the coffin. Things like that simply don't happen. But I knew better. I couldn't dream anything as horrifying as that fiery man's face when he'd turned on us. 'Soon, boy,' he'd told Carter, as if he intended to track us down. Just the idea made my hands tremble. I also couldn't help wondering about our stop at Cleopatra's Needle, how Dad had insisted on seeing it, as if he were steeling his courage, as if what he did at the British Museum had something to do with my mum.

My eyes wandered across my room and fixed on my desk.

No, I thought. *Not going to do it.*

But I walked over and opened the drawer. I shoved aside a few old mags, my stash of sweets, a stack of maths homework I'd forgotten to hand in, and a few pictures of me and my mates Liz and Emma trying on ridiculous hats in Camden Market. And there at the bottom of it all was the picture of Mum.

Gran and Gramps have loads of pictures. They keep a shrine to Ruby in the hall cupboard—

30

Mum's childhood artwork, her O-level results, her graduation picture from university, her favorite jewelry. It's quite mental. I was determined not to be like them, living in the past. I barely remembered Mum, after all, and nothing could change the fact she was dead.

But I did keep the one picture. It was of Mum and me at our house in Los Angeles, just after I was born. She stood out on the balcony, the Pacific Ocean behind her, holding a wrinkled pudgy lump of baby that would some day grow up to be yours truly. Baby me was not much to look at, but Mum was gorgeous, even in shorts and a tattered T-shirt. Her eyes were deep blue. Her blond hair was clipped back. Her skin was perfect. Quite depressing compared to mine. People always say I look like her, but I couldn't even get the spot off my chin much less look so mature and beautiful.

[Stop smirking, Carter.]

The photo fascinated me because I hardly remembered our lives together at all. But the main reason I'd kept the photo was because of the symbol on Mum's T-shirt: one of those life symbols—an ankh.

My dead mother wearing the symbol for life. Nothing could've been sadder. But she smiled at the camera as if she knew a secret. As if my dad and she were sharing a private joke.

Something tugged at the back of my mind. That stocky man in the trench coat who'd been arguing with Dad across the street—he'd said something about the Per Ankh.

Had he meant *ankh* as in the symbol for life, and if so, what was a *per*? I supposed he didn't mean pear as in the fruit.

31

I had an eerie feeling that if I saw the words *Per Ankh* written in hieroglyphics, I would know what they meant.

I put down the picture of Mum. I picked up a pencil and turned over one of my old homework papers. I wondered what would happen if I tried to *draw* the words *Per Ankh*. Would the right design just occur to me?

As I touched pencil to paper, my bedroom door opened. 'Miss Kane?'

I whirled and dropped the pencil.

A police inspector stood frowning in my doorway. 'What are you doing?'

'Maths,' I said.

My ceiling was quite low, so the inspector had to stoop to come in. He wore a lint-colored suit that matched his gray hair and his ashen face. 'Now then, Sadie. I'm Chief Inspector Williams. Let's have a chat, shall we? Sit down.'

I didn't sit, and neither did he, which must've annoyed him. It's hard to look in charge when you're hunched over like Quasimodo.

'Tell me everything, please,' he said, 'from the time your father came round to get you.'

'I already told the police at the museum.'

'Again, if you don't mind.'

So I told him everything. Why not? His left eyebrow crept higher and higher as I told him the strange bits like the glowing letters and serpent staff.

'Well, Sadie,' Inspector Williams said. 'You've got quite an imagination.'

'I'm not lying, Inspector. And I think your eyebrow is trying to escape.'

He tried to look at his own eyebrows, then

scowled. 'Now, Sadie, I'm sure this is very hard on you. I understand you want to protect your father's reputation. But he's gone now—'

'You mean through the floor in a coffin,' I insisted. 'He's *not* dead.'

Inspector Williams spread his hands. 'Sadie, I'm very sorry. But we must find out why he did this act of . . . well . . .'

'Act of *what*?'

He cleared his throat uncomfortably. 'Your father destroyed priceless artifacts and apparently killed himself in the process. We'd very much like to know why.'

I stared at him. 'Are you saying my father's a terrorist? Are you *mad*?'

'We've made calls to some of your father's associates. I understand his behavior had become erratic since your mother's death. He'd become withdrawn and obsessive in his studies, spending more and more time in Egypt—'

'He's a bloody Egyptologist! You should be looking for him, not asking stupid questions!'

'Sadie,' he said, and I could hear in his voice that he was resisting the urge to strangle me. Strangely, I get this a lot from adults. 'There are extremist groups in Egypt that object to Egyptian artifacts being kept in other countries' museums. These people might have approached your father. Perhaps in his state, your father became an easy target for them. If you've heard him mention any names—'

I stormed past him to the window. I was so angry I could hardly think. I refused to believe Dad was dead. No, no, no. And a terrorist? Please. Why did adults have to be so thick? They always

33

say 'tell the truth,' and when you do, they don't believe you. What's the point?

I stared down at the dark street. Suddenly that cold tingly feeling got worse than ever. I focused on the dead tree where I'd met Dad earlier. Standing there now, in the dim light of a streetlamp, looking up at me, was the pudgy bloke in the black trench coat and the round glasses and the fedora—the man Dad had called Amos.

I suppose I should've felt threatened by an odd man staring up at me in the dark of night. But his expression was full of concern. And he looked *so* familiar. It was driving me mad that I couldn't remember why.

Behind me, the inspector cleared his throat. 'Sadie, no one blames you for the attack on the museum. We understand you were dragged into this against your will.'

I turned from the window. 'Against my will? I chained the curator in his office.'

The inspector's eyebrow started to creep up again. 'Be that as it may, surely you didn't understand what your father meant to do. Possibly your brother was involved?'

I snorted. 'Carter? Please.'

'So you are determined to protect him as well. You consider him a proper brother, do you?'

I couldn't believe it. I wanted to smack his face. 'What's that supposed to mean? Because he doesn't *look* like me?'

The inspector blinked. 'I only meant—'

'I *know* what you meant. Of course he's my brother!'

Inspector Williams held up his hands apologetically, but I was still seething. As much as

34

Carter annoyed me, I hated it when people assumed we weren't related, or looked at my father askance when he said the three of us were a family—like we'd done something wrong. Stupid Dr. Martin at the museum. Inspector Williams. It happened every time Dad and Carter and I were together. *Every* bloody time.

'I'm sorry, Sadie,' the inspector said. 'I only want to make sure we separate the innocent from the guilty. It will go much easier for everyone if you cooperate. Any information. Anything your father said. People he might've mentioned.'

'Amos,' I blurted out, just to see his reaction. 'He met a man named Amos.'

Inspector Williams sighed. 'Sadie, he couldn't have done. Surely you know that. We spoke with Amos not one hour ago, on the phone from his home in New York.'

'He isn't in New York!' I insisted. 'He's right—'

I glanced out the window and Amos was gone. Bloody typical.

'That's not possible,' I said.

'Exactly,' the inspector said.

'But he was here!' I exclaimed. 'Who *is* he? One of Dad's colleagues? How did you know to call him?'

'Really, Sadie. This acting must stop.'

'Acting?'

The inspector studied me for a moment, then set his jaw as if he'd made a decision. 'We've already had the truth from Carter. I didn't want to upset you, but he told us everything. He understands there's no point protecting your father now. You might as well help us, and there will be no charges against you.'

35

'You shouldn't lie to children!' I yelled, hoping my voice carried all the way downstairs. 'Carter would never say a word against Dad, and neither will I!'

The inspector didn't even have the decency to look embarrassed.

He crossed his arms. 'I'm sorry you feel that way, Sadie. I'm afraid it's time we went downstairs . . . to discuss consequences with your grandparents.'

4.

KIDNAPPED BY A NOT-SO-STRANGER

SADIE

I just love family meetings. Very cozy, with the Christmas garlands round the fireplace and a nice pot of tea and a detective from Scotland Yard ready to arrest you.

Carter slumped on the sofa, cradling Dad's workbag. I wondered why the police had let him keep it. It should have been evidence or something, but the inspector didn't seem to notice it at all.

Carter looked awful—I mean even worse than usual. Honestly, the boy had never been in a proper school, and he dressed like a junior professor, with his khaki trousers and a button-down shirt and loafers. He's not bad looking, I suppose. He's reasonably tall and fit and his hair isn't hopeless. He's got Dad's eyes, and my mates Liz and Emma have even told me from his picture that he's *hot,* which I must take with a grain of salt because (a) he's my brother, and (b) my mates are a bit crazed. When it came to clothes, Carter wouldn't have known *hot* if it bit him on the bum.

[Oh, don't look at me like that, Carter. You know it's *true.*]

At any rate, I shouldn't have been too hard on him. He was taking Dad's disappearance even worse than I was.

Gran and Gramps sat on either side of him, looking quite nervous. The pot of tea and a plate of biscuits sat on the table, but no one was having any. Chief Inspector Williams ordered me into the only free chair. Then he paced in front of the fireplace importantly. Two more police stood by the front door—the woman from earlier and a big bloke who kept eyeing the biscuits.

'Mr. and Mrs. Faust,' Inspector Williams said, 'I'm afraid we have two uncooperative children.'

Gran fidgeted with the trim of her dress. It's hard to believe she's related to Mum. Gran is frail and colorless, like a stick person really, while Mum in the photos always looked so happy and full of life. 'They're just children,' she managed. 'Surely you can't blame them.'

'*Pah!*' Gramps said. 'This is ridiculous, Inspector. They aren't responsible!'

Gramps is a former rugby player. He has beefy arms, a belly much too big for his shirt, and eyes sunk deep in his face, as if someone had punched them (well, actually Dad *had* punched them years ago, but that's another story). Gramps is quite scary looking. Usually people got out of his way, but Inspector Williams didn't seem impressed.

'Mr. Faust,' he said, 'what do you imagine the

morning headlines will read? "British Museum attacked. Rosetta Stone destroyed." Your son-in-law—'

'*Former* son-in-law,' Gramps corrected.

'—was most likely vaporized in the explosion, or he ran off, in which case—'

'He didn't run off!' I shouted.

'We need to know where he is,' the inspector continued. 'And the only witnesses, your grandchildren, refuse to tell me the truth.'

'We *did* tell you the truth,' Carter said. 'Dad isn't dead. He sank through the floor.'

Inspector Williams glanced at Gramps, as if to say, *There, you see?* Then he turned to Carter. 'Young man, your father has committed a criminal act. He's left you behind to deal with the consequences—'

'That's not true!' I snapped, my voice trembling with rage. I couldn't believe Dad would intentionally leave us at the mercy of police, of course. But the idea of him abandoning me—well, as I might have mentioned, that's a bit of a sore point.

'Dear, please,' Gran told me, 'the inspector is only doing his job.'

'Badly!' I said.

'Let's all have some tea,' Gran suggested.

'No!' Carter and I yelled at once, which made me feel bad for Gran, as she practically wilted into the sofa.

'We *can* charge you,' the inspector warned, turning on me. 'We can and we will—'

He froze. Then he blinked several times, as if he'd forgotten what he was doing.

Gramps frowned. '*Er,* Inspector?'

'Yes . . .' Chief Inspector Williams murmured dreamily. He reached in his pocket and took out a little blue booklet—an American passport. He threw it in Carter's lap.

'You're being deported,' the inspector announced. 'You're to leave the country within twenty-four hours. If we need to question you further, you'll be contacted through the FBI.'

Carter's mouth fell open. He looked at me, and I knew I wasn't imagining how odd this was. The inspector had completely changed direction. He'd been about to arrest us. I was sure of it. And then out of the blue, he was deporting Carter? Even the other police officers looked confused.

'Sir?' the policewoman asked. 'Are you sure—'

'Quiet, Linley. The two of you may go.'

The cops hesitated until Williams made a shooing motion with his hand. Then they left, closing the door behind them.

'Hold on,' Carter said. 'My father's disappeared, and you want me to leave the country?'

'Your father is either dead or a fugitive, son,' the inspector said. 'Deportation is the kindest option. It's already been arranged.'

'With whom?' Gramps demanded. 'Who authorized this?'

'With . . .' The inspector got that funny blank look again. 'With the proper authorities. Believe me, it's better than prison.'

Carter looked too devastated to speak, but before I could feel sorry for him, Inspector Williams turned to me. 'You, too, miss.'

He might as well have hit me with a sledgehammer.

'You're deporting *me*?' I asked. 'I live here!'

39

'You're an American citizen. And under the circumstances, it's best for you to return home.'

I just stared at him. I couldn't remember any home except this flat. My mates at school, my room, *everything* I knew was here. 'Where am I supposed to go?'

'Inspector,' Gran said, her voice trembling. 'This isn't fair. I can't believe—'

'I'll give you some time to say good-bye,' the inspector interrupted. Then he frowned as if baffled by his own actions. 'I—I must be going.'

This made no sense, and the inspector seemed to realize it, but he walked to the front door anyway. When he opened it, I almost jumped out of my chair, because the man in black, Amos, was standing there. He'd lost his trench coat and hat somewhere, but was still wearing the same pinstripe suit and round glasses. His braided hair glittered with gold beads.

I thought the inspector would say something, or express surprise, but he didn't even acknowledge Amos. He walked right past him and into the night.

Amos came inside and closed the door. Gran and Gramps stood up.

'You,' Gramps growled. 'I should've known. If I was younger, I would beat you to a pulp.'

'Hello, Mr. and Mrs. Faust,' Amos said. He looked at Carter and me as if we were problems to be solved. 'It's time we had a talk.'

*   *   *

Amos made himself right at home. He flopped onto the sofa and poured himself tea. He munched on a biscuit, which was quite dangerous, because Gran's biscuits are horrid.

I thought Gramps's head would explode. His face went bright red. He came up behind Amos and raised his hand as if he were about to smack him, but Amos kept munching his biscuit.

'Please, sit down,' he told us.

And we all sat. It was the strangest thing—as if we'd been waiting for his order. Even Gramps dropped his hand and moved round the sofa. He sat next to Amos with a disgusted sigh.

Amos sipped his tea and regarded me with some displeasure. That wasn't fair, I thought. I didn't look *that* bad, considering what we'd been through. Then he looked at Carter and grunted.

'Terrible timing,' he muttered. 'But there's no other way. They'll have to come with me.'

'Excuse me?' I said. 'I'm not going anywhere with some strange man with biscuit on his face!'

He did in fact have biscuit crumbs on his face, but he apparently didn't care, as he didn't bother to check.

'I'm no stranger, Sadie,' he said. 'Don't you remember?'

It was creepy hearing him talk to me in such a familiar way. I felt I *should* know him. I looked at Carter, but he seemed just as mystified as I was.

'No, Amos,' Gran said, trembling. 'You can't take Sadie. We had an agreement.'

'Julius broke that agreement tonight,' Amos said. 'You know you can't care for Sadie anymore—not after what's happened. Their only chance is to come with me.'

'Why should we come anywhere with you?' Carter asked. 'You almost got in a fight with Dad!'

41

Amos looked at the workbag in Carter's lap. 'I see you kept your father's bag. That's good. You'll need it. As for getting into fights, Julius and I did that quite a lot. If you didn't notice, Carter, I was trying to *stop* him from doing something rash. If he'd listened to me, we wouldn't be in this situation.'

I had no idea what he was on about, but Gramps apparently understood.

'You and your superstitions!' he said. 'I told you we want none of it.'

Amos pointed to the back patio. Through the glass doors, you could see the lights shining on the Thames. It was quite a nice view at night, when you couldn't notice how run-down some of the buildings were.

'Superstition, is it?' Amos asked. 'And yet you found a place to live on the *east* bank of the river.'

Gramps turned even redder. 'That was Ruby's idea. Thought it would protect us. But she was wrong about many things, wasn't she? She trusted Julius and you, for one!'

Amos looked unfazed. He smelled interesting—like old-timey spices, copal and amber, like the incense shops in Covent Garden.

He finished his tea and looked straight at Gran. 'Mrs. Faust, you know what's begun. The police are the least of your worries.'

Gran swallowed. 'You . . . *you* changed that inspector's mind. You made him deport Sadie.'

'It was that or see the children arrested,' Amos said.

'Hang on,' I said. 'You *changed* Inspector Williams's mind? How?'

Amos shrugged. 'It's not permanent. In fact we

should get to New York in the next hour or so before Inspector Williams begins to wonder why he let you go.'

Carter laughed incredulously. 'You can't get to New York from London in a hour. Not even the fastest plane—'

'No,' Amos agreed. 'Not a plane.' He turned back to Gran as if everything had been settled. 'Mrs. Faust, Carter and Sadie have only one safe option. You know that. They'll come to the mansion in Brooklyn. I can protect them there.'

'You've got a mansion,' Carter said. 'In Brooklyn.'

Amos gave him an amused smile. 'The family mansion. You'll be safe there.'

'But our dad—'

'Is beyond your help for now,' Amos said sadly. 'I'm sorry, Carter. I'll explain later, but Julius would want you to be safe. For that, we must move quickly. I'm afraid I'm all you've got.'

That was a bit harsh, I thought. Carter glanced at Gran and Gramps. Then he nodded glumly. He knew that they didn't want him around. He'd always reminded them of our dad. And yes, it was a stupid reason not to take in your grandson, but there you are.

'Well, Carter can do what he wants,' I said. 'But *I live here.* And I'm not going off with some stranger, am I?'

I looked at Gran for support, but she was staring at the lace doilies on the table as if they were suddenly quite interesting.

'Gramps, surely . . .'

But he wouldn't meet my eyes either. He turned to Amos. 'You can get them out of the country?'

43

'Hang on!' I protested.

Amos stood and wiped the crumbs off his jacket. He walked to the patio doors and stared out at the river. 'The police will be back soon. Tell them anything you like. They won't find us.'

'You're going to *kidnap* us?' I asked, stunned. I looked at Carter. 'Do you believe this?'

Carter shouldered the workbag. Then he stood like he was ready to go. Possibly he just wanted to be out of Gran and Gramps's flat. 'How do you plan to get to New York in an hour?' he asked Amos. 'You said, not a plane.'

'No,' Amos agreed. He put his finger to the window and traced something in the condensation—another bloody hieroglyph.

'A boat,' I said—then realized I'd translated aloud, which I wasn't supposed to be able to do.

Amos peered at me over the top of his round glasses. 'How did you—'

'I mean that last bit looks like a boat,' I blurted out. 'But that can't be what you mean. That's ridiculous.'

'Look!' Carter cried.

I pressed in next to him at the patio doors. Down at the quayside, a boat was docked. But not a regular boat, mind you. It was an Egyptian reed boat, with two torches burning in the front, and a big rudder in the back. A figure in a black trench coat and hat—possibly Amos's—stood at the tiller.

I'll admit, for once, I was at a loss for words.

'We're going in that,' Carter said. 'To Brooklyn.'

'We'd better get started,' Amos said.

I whirled back to my grandmother. 'Gran, please!'

She brushed a tear from her cheek. 'It's for the

44

best, my dear. You should take Muffin.'

'Ah, yes,' Amos said. 'We can't forget the cat.'

He turned towards the stairs. As if on cue, Muffin raced down in a leopard-spotted streak and leaped into my arms. She *never* does that.

'Who are you?' I asked Amos. It was clear I was running out of options, but I at least wanted answers. 'We can't just go off with some stranger.'

'I'm not a stranger.' Amos smiled at me. 'I'm family.'

And suddenly I remembered his face smiling down at me, saying, 'Happy birthday, Sadie.' A memory so distant, I'd almost forgotten.

'Uncle Amos?' I asked hazily.

'That's right, Sadie,' he said. 'I'm Julius's brother. Now come along. We have a long way to go.'

5.
WE MEET THE MONKEY

CARTER

It's Carter again. Sorry. We had to turn off the tape for a while because we were being followed by—well, we'll get to that later.

Sadie was telling you how we left London, right?

So anyway, we followed Amos down to the weird boat docked at the quayside. I cradled Dad's workbag under my arm. I still couldn't believe he was gone. I felt guilty leaving London without him, but I believed Amos about one thing: right now Dad was beyond our help. I didn't trust Amos, but

I figured if I wanted to find out what had happened to Dad, I was going to have to go along with him. He was the only one who seemed to know anything.

Amos stepped aboard the reed boat. Sadie jumped right on, but I hesitated. I'd seen boats like this on the Nile before, and they never seemed very sturdy.

It was basically woven together from coils of plant fiber—like a giant floating rug. I figured the torches at the front couldn't be a good idea, because if we didn't sink, we'd burn. At the back, the tiller was manned by a little guy wearing Amos's black trench coat and hat. The hat was shoved down on his head so I couldn't see his face. His hands and feet were lost in the folds of the coat.

'How does this thing move?' I asked Amos. 'You've got no sail.'

'Trust me.' Amos offered me a hand.

The night was cold, but when I stepped on board I suddenly felt warmer, as if the torchlight were casting a protective glow over us. In the middle of the boat was a hut made from woven mats. From Sadie's arms, Muffin sniffed at it and growled.

'Take a seat inside,' Amos suggested. 'The trip might be a little rough.'

'I'll stand, thanks.' Sadie nodded at the little guy in back. 'Who's your driver?'

Amos acted as if he hadn't heard the question. 'Hang on, everyone!' He nodded to the steersman, and the boat lurched forward.

The feeling was hard to describe. You know that tingle in the pit of your stomach when you're on a roller coaster and it goes into free fall? It was kind of like that, except we weren't falling, and the feeling didn't go away. The boat moved with astounding speed. The lights of the city blurred, then were swallowed in a thick fog. Strange sounds echoed in the dark: slithering and hissing, distant screams, voices whispering in languages I didn't understand.

The tingling turned to nausea. The sounds got louder, until I was about to scream myself. Then suddenly the boat slowed. The noises stopped, and the fog dissipated. City lights came back, brighter than before.

Above us loomed a bridge, much taller than any bridge in London. My stomach did a slow roll. To the left, I saw a familiar skyline—the Chrysler Building, the Empire State Building.

'Impossible,' I said. 'That's New York.'

Sadie looked as green as I felt. She was still cradling Muffin, whose eyes were closed. The cat seemed to be purring. 'It can't be,' Sadie said. 'We only traveled a few minutes.'

And yet here we were, sailing up the East River, right under the Williamsburg Bridge. We glided to a stop next to a small dock on the Brooklyn side of the river. In front of us was an industrial yard filled with piles of scrap metal and old construction equipment. In the center of it all, right at the water's edge, rose a huge factory warehouse heavily painted with graffiti, the windows boarded up.

'That is not a mansion,' Sadie said. Her powers of perception are really amazing.

'Look again.' Amos pointed to the top of the building.

'How . . . how did you . . .' My voice failed me. I wasn't sure why I hadn't seen it before, but now it was obvious: a five-story mansion perched on the roof of the warehouse, like another layer of a cake. 'You couldn't build a mansion up there!'

'Long story,' Amos said. 'But we needed a private location.'

'And is this the east shore?' Sadie asked. 'You said something about that in London—my grandparents living on the east shore.'

Amos smiled. 'Yes. Very good, Sadie. In ancient times, the east bank of the Nile was always the side of the living, the side where the sun rises. The dead were buried west of the river. It was considered bad luck, even dangerous, to live there. The tradition is still strong among . . . our people.'

'Our people?' I asked, but Sadie muscled in with another question.

'So you can't live in Manhattan?' she asked.

Amos's brow furrowed as he looked across at the Empire State Building. 'Manhattan has other problems. Other gods. It's best we stay separate.'

'Other *what*?' Sadie demanded.

'Nothing.' Amos walked past us to the steersman. He plucked off the man's hat and coat—and there was no one underneath. The steersman simply wasn't there. Amos put on his fedora, folded his coat over his arm, then waved toward a metal staircase that wound all the way up the side of the warehouse to the mansion on the roof.

'All ashore,' he said. 'And welcome to the Twenty-first Nome.'

*   *   *

48

'Gnome?' I asked, as we followed him up the stairs. 'Like those little runty guys?'

'Heavens, no,' Amos said. 'I hate gnomes. They smell horrible.'

'But you said—'

'*Nome,* n-o-m-e. As in a district, a region. The term is from ancient times, when Egypt was divided into forty-two provinces. Today, the system is a little different. We've gone global. The world is divided into three hundred and sixty nomes. Egypt, of course, is the First. Greater New York is the Twenty-first.'

Sadie glanced at me and twirled her finger around her temple.

'No, Sadie,' Amos said without looking back. 'I'm not crazy. There's much you need to learn.'

We reached the top of the stairs. Looking up at the mansion, it was hard to understand what I was seeing. The house was at least fifty feet tall, built of enormous limestone blocks and steel-framed windows. There were hieroglyphs engraved around the windows, and the walls were lit up so the place looked like a cross between a modern museum and an ancient temple. But the weirdest thing was that if I glanced away, the whole building seemed to disappear. I tried it several times just to be sure. If I looked for the mansion from the corner of my eye, it wasn't there. I had to force my eyes to refocus on it, and even that took a lot of willpower.

Amos stopped before the entrance, which was the size of a garage door—a dark heavy square of timber with no visible handle or lock. 'Carter, after you.'

'Um, how do I—'

49

'How do you think?'

Great, another mystery. I was about to suggest we ram Amos's head against it and see if that worked. Then I looked at the door again, and I had the strangest feeling. I stretched out my arm. Slowly, without touching the door, I raised my hand and the door followed my movement—sliding upward until it disappeared into the ceiling.

Sadie looked stunned. 'How . . .'

'I don't know,' I admitted, a little embarrassed. 'Motion sensor, maybe?'

'Interesting.' Amos sounded a little troubled. 'Not the way I would've done it, but very good. Remarkably good.'

'Thanks, I think.'

Sadie tried to go inside first, but as soon as she stepped on the threshold, Muffin wailed and almost clawed her way out of Sadie's arms.

Sadie stumbled backward. 'What was that about, cat?'

'Oh, of course,' Amos said. 'My apologies.' He put his hand on the cat's head and said, very formally, 'You may enter.'

'The cat needs permission?' I asked.

'Special circumstances,' Amos said, which wasn't much of an explanation, but he walked inside without saying another word. We followed, and this time Muffin stayed quiet.

'Oh my god . . .' Sadie's jaw dropped. She craned her neck to look at the ceiling, and I thought the gum might fall out of her mouth.

'Yes,' Amos said. 'This is the Great Room.'

I could see why he called it that. The cedar-beamed ceiling was four stories high, held up by carved stone pillars engraved with hieroglyphs. A

50

weird assortment of musical instruments and Ancient Egyptian weapons decorated the walls. Three levels of balconies ringed the room, with rows of doors all looking out on the main area. The fireplace was big enough to park a car in, with a plasma-screen TV above the mantel and massive leather sofas on either side. On the floor was a snakeskin rug, except it was forty feet long and fifteen feet wide—bigger than any snake. Outside, through glass walls, I could see the terrace that wrapped around the house. It had a swimming pool, a dining area, and a blazing fire pit. And at the far end of the Great Room was a set of double doors marked with the Eye of Horus, and chained with half a dozen padlocks. I wondered what could possibly be behind them.

But the real showstopper was the statue in the center of the Great Room. It was thirty feet tall, made of black marble. I could tell it was of an Egyptian god because the figure had a human body and an animal's head—like a stork or a crane, with a long neck and a really long beak.

The god was dressed ancient-style in a kilt, sash, and neck collar. He held a scribe's stylus in one hand, and an open scroll in the other, as if he had just written the hieroglyphs inscribed there: an ankh—the Egyptian looped cross—with a rectangle traced around its top.

'That's it!' Sadie exclaimed. 'Per Ankh.'

I stared at her in disbelief. 'All right, how can you read that?'

'I don't know,' she said. 'But it's obvious, isn't it? The top one is shaped like the floor plan of a house.'

'How did you get that? It's just a box.' The thing

was, she was right. I recognized the symbol, and it *was* supposed to be a simplified picture of a house with a doorway, but that wouldn't be obvious to most people, especially people named Sadie. Yet she looked absolutely positive.

'It's a house,' she insisted. 'And the bottom picture is the ankh, the symbol for life. Per Ankh—the House of Life.'

'Very good, Sadie.' Amos looked impressed. 'And this is a statue of the only god still allowed in the House of Life—at least, normally. Do you recognize him, Carter?'

Just then it clicked: the bird was an ibis, an Egyptian river bird. 'Thoth,' I said. 'The god of knowledge. He invented writing.'

'Indeed,' Amos said.

'Why the animal heads?' Sadie asked. 'All those Egyptian gods have animal heads. They look so silly.'

'They don't normally appear that way,' Amos said. 'Not in real life.'

'Real life?' I asked. 'Come on. You sound like you've met them in person.'

Amos's expression didn't reassure me. He looked as if he were remembering something unpleasant. 'The gods could appear in many forms—usually fully human or fully animal, but occasionally as a hybrid form like this. They are primal forces, you understand, a sort of bridge between humanity and nature. They are depicted with animal heads to show that they exist in two different worlds at once. Do you understand?'

'Not even a little,' Sadie said.

'*Mmm.*' Amos didn't sound surprised. 'Yes, we have much training to do. At any rate, the god

52

before you, Thoth, founded the House of Life, for which this mansion is the regional headquarters. Or at least . . . it used to be. I'm the only member left in the Twenty-first Nome. Or I *was,* until you two came along.'

'Hang on.' I had so many questions I could hardly think where to start. 'What *is* the House of Life? Why is Thoth the only god allowed here, and why are you—'

'Carter, I understand how you feel.' Amos smiled sympathetically. 'But these things are better discussed in daylight. You need to get some sleep, and I don't want you to have nightmares.'

'You think I can sleep?'

'Mrow.' Muffin stretched in Sadie's arms and let loose a huge yawn.

Amos clapped his hands. 'Khufu!'

I thought he'd sneezed, because Khufu is a weird name, but then a little dude about three feet tall with gold fur and a purple shirt came clambering down the stairs. It took me a second to realize it was a baboon wearing an L.A. Lakers jersey.

The baboon did a flip and landed in front of us. He showed off his fangs and made a sound that was half roar, half belch. His breath smelled like nacho-flavored Doritos.

All I could think to say was, 'The Lakers are my home team!'

The baboon slapped his head with both hands and belched again.

'Oh, Khufu likes you,' Amos said. 'You'll get along famously.'

'Right.' Sadie looked dazed. 'You've got a monkey butler. Why not?'

Muffin purred in Sadie's arms as if the baboon didn't bother her at all.

'*Agh!*' Khufu grunted at me.

Amos chuckled. 'He wants to go one-on-one with you, Carter. To, ah, see your game.'

I shifted from foot to foot. 'Um, yeah. Sure. Maybe tomorrow. But how can you understand—'

'Carter, I'm afraid you'll have a lot to get used to,' Amos said. 'But if you're going to survive and save your father, you have to get some rest.'

'Sorry,' Sadie said, 'did you say "survive and save our father"? Could you expand on that?'

'Tomorrow,' Amos said. 'We'll begin your orientation in the morning. Khufu, show them to their rooms, please.'

'*Agh-uhh!*' the baboon grunted. He turned and waddled up the stairs. Unfortunately, the Lakers jersey didn't completely cover his multicolored rear.

We were about to follow when Amos said, 'Carter, the workbag, please. It's best if I lock it in the library.'

I hesitated. I'd almost forgotten the bag on my shoulder, but it was all I had left of my father. I didn't even have our luggage because it was still locked up at the British Museum. Honestly, I'd been surprised that the police hadn't taken the workbag too, but none of them seemed to notice it.

'You'll get it back,' Amos promised. 'When the time is right.'

He asked nicely enough, but something in his eyes told me that I really didn't have a choice.

I handed over the bag. Amos took it gingerly, as if it were full of explosives.

'See you in the morning.' He turned and strode

toward the chained-up doors. They unlatched themselves and opened just enough for Amos to slip through without showing us anything on the other side. Then the chains locked again behind him.

I looked at Sadie, unsure what to do. Staying by ourselves in the Great Room with the creepy statue of Thoth didn't seem like much fun, so we followed Khufu up the stairs.

*　　　*　　　*

Sadie and I got adjoining rooms on the third floor, and I've got to admit, they were way cooler than any place I'd ever stayed before.

I had my own kitchenette, fully stocked with my favorite snacks: ginger ale—[No, Sadie. It's not an old person's soda! Be quiet!]—Twix, and Skittles. It seemed impossible. How did Amos know what I liked? The TV, computer, and stereo system were totally high-tech. The bathroom was stocked with my regular brand of toothpaste, deodorant, everything. The king-size bed was awesome, too, though the pillow was a little strange. Instead of a cloth pillow, it was an ivory headrest like I'd seen in Egyptian tombs. It was decorated with lions and (of course) more hieroglyphs.

The room even had a deck that looked out on New York Harbor, with views of Manhattan and the Statue of Liberty in the distance, but the sliding glass doors were locked shut somehow. That was my first indication that something was wrong.

I turned to look for Khufu, but he was gone. The door to my room was shut. I tried to open it, but it was locked.

A muffled voice came from the next room. 'Carter?'

'Sadie.' I tried the door to her adjoining room, but it was locked too.

'We're prisoners,' she said. 'Do you think Amos . . . I mean, can we trust him?'

After all I'd seen today, I didn't trust *anything,* but I could hear the fear in Sadie's voice. It triggered an unfamiliar feeling in me, like I needed to reassure her. The idea seemed ridiculous. Sadie had always seemed so much braver than me— doing what she wanted, never caring about the consequences. I was the one who got scared. But right now, I felt like I needed to play a role I hadn't played in a long, long time: big brother.

'It'll be okay.' I tried to sound confident. 'Look, if Amos wanted to hurt us, he could've done it by now. Try to get some sleep.'

'Carter?'

'Yeah?'

'It was magic, wasn't it? What happened to Dad at the museum. Amos's boat. This house. All of it's magic.'

'I think so.'

I could hear her sigh. 'Good. At least I'm not going mad.'

'Don't let the bedbugs bite,' I called. And I realized I hadn't said that to Sadie since we had lived together in Los Angeles, when Mom was still alive.

'I miss Dad,' she said. 'I hardly ever saw him, I know, but . . . I miss him.'

My eyes got a little teary, but I took a deep breath. I was *not* going to go all weak. Sadie

56

needed me. Dad needed us.

'We'll find him,' I told her. 'Pleasant dreams.'

I listened, but the only thing I heard was Muffin meowing and scampering around, exploring her new space. At least *she* didn't seem unhappy.

I got ready for bed and crawled in. The covers were comfortable and warm, but the pillow was just too weird. It gave me neck cramps, so I put it on the floor and went to sleep without it.

My first big mistake.

6.

BREAKFAST WITH A CROCODILE

CARTER

How to describe it? Not a nightmare. It was much more real and frightening.

As I slept, I felt myself go weightless. I drifted up, turned, and saw my own sleeping form below.

I'm dying, I thought. But that wasn't it, either. I wasn't a ghost. I had a new shimmering golden form with wings instead of arms. I was some kind of bird. [No, Sadie, not a chicken. Will you let me tell the story, please?]

I knew I wasn't dreaming, because I don't dream in color. I certainly don't dream in all five senses. The room smelled faintly of jasmine. I could hear the carbonation bubbles pinging in the can of ginger ale I'd opened on my nightstand. I could feel a cold wind ruffling through my feathers, and I realized the windows were open. I didn't want to leave, but a strong current pulled me out of the room like a leaf in a storm.

The lights of the mansion faded below me. The skyline of New York blurred and disappeared. I shot through the mist and darkness, strange voices whispering all around me. My stomach tingled as it had earlier that night on Amos's barge. Then the mist cleared, and I was in a different place.

I floated above a barren mountain. Far below, a grid of city lights stretched across the valley floor. Definitely not New York. It was nighttime, but I could tell I was in the desert. The wind was so dry, the skin on my face was like paper. And I know that doesn't make sense, but my face felt like my normal face, as if that part of me hadn't transformed into a bird. [Fine, Sadie. Call me the Carter-headed chicken. Happy?]

Below me on a ridge stood two figures. They didn't seem to notice me, and I realized I wasn't glowing anymore. In fact I was pretty much invisible, floating in the darkness. I couldn't make out the two figures clearly, except to recognize that they weren't human. Staring harder, I could see that one was short, squat, and hairless, with slimy skin that glistened in the starlight—like an amphibian standing on its hind legs. The other was tall and scarecrow skinny, with rooster claws instead of feet. I couldn't see his face very well, but it looked red and moist and . . . well, let's just say I was glad I couldn't see it better.

'Where is he?' the toadie-looking one croaked nervously.

'Hasn't taken a permanent host yet,' the rooster-footed guy chided. 'He can only appear for a short time.'

'You're sure this is the place?'

58

'Yes, fool! He'll be here as soon—'

A fiery form appeared on the ridge. The two creatures fell to the ground, groveling in the dirt, and I prayed like crazy that I really was invisible.

'My lord!' the toad said.

Even in the dark, the newcomer was hard to see—just the silhouette of a man outlined in flames.

'What do they call this place?' the man asked. And as soon as he spoke, I knew for sure he was the guy who'd attacked my dad at the British Museum. All the fear I'd felt at the museum came rushing back, paralyzing me. I remembered trying to pick up that stupid rock to throw, but I hadn't been able to do even that. I'd completely failed my dad.

'My lord,' Rooster Foot said. 'The mountain is called Camelback. The city is called Phoenix.'

The fiery man laughed—a booming sound like thunder. 'Phoenix. How appropriate! And the desert so much like home. All it needs now is to be scoured of life. The desert should be a sterile place, don't you think?'

'Oh yes, my lord,' the toadie agreed. 'But what of the other four?'

'One is already entombed,' the fiery man said. 'The second is weak. She will be easily manipulated. That leaves only two. And they will be dealt with soon enough.'

'Er . . . how?' the toadie asked.

The fiery man glowed brighter. 'You are an inquisitive little tadpole, aren't you?' He pointed at the toad and the poor creature's skin began to steam.

'No!' the toadie begged. 'No-o-o-o!'

59

I could hardly watch. I don't want to describe it. But if you've heard what happens when cruel kids pour salt on snails, you'll have a pretty good idea of what happened to the toadie. Soon there was nothing left.

Rooster Foot took a nervous step back. I couldn't blame him.

'We will build my temple here,' the fiery man said, as if nothing had happened. 'This mountain shall serve as my place of worship. When it is complete, I will summon the greatest storm ever known. I will cleanse everything. *Everything.*'

'Yes, my lord,' Rooster Foot agreed quickly. 'And, ah, if I may suggest, my lord, to increase your power . . .' The creature bowed and scraped and moved forward, as if he wanted to whisper in the fiery man's ear.

Just when I thought Rooster Foot was going to become fried chicken for sure, he said something to the fiery dude that I couldn't make out, and the fiery dude burned brighter.

'Excellent! If you can do this, you will be rewarded. If not . . .'

'I understand, my lord.'

'Go then,' the fiery man said. 'Unleash our forces. Start with the longnecks. That should soften them up. Collect the younglings and bring them to me. I want them alive, before they have time to learn their powers. Do not fail me.'

'No, lord.'

'Phoenix,' the fiery man mused. 'I like that very much.' He swept his hand across the horizon, as if he were imagining the city in flames. 'Soon I will rise from your ashes. It will be a lovely birthday present.'

*   *   *

I woke with my heart pounding, back in my own body. I felt hot, as if the fiery guy were starting to burn me. Then I realized that there was a cat on my chest.

Muffin stared at me, her eyes half closed. *'Mrow.'*

'How did you get in?' I muttered.

I sat up, and for a second I wasn't sure where I was. Some hotel in another city? I almost called for my dad . . . and then I remembered.

Yesterday. The museum. The sarcophagus.

It all crashed down on me so hard I could barely breathe.

Stop, I told myself. *You don't have time for grief.* And this is going to sound weird, but the voice in my head almost sounded like a different person— older, stronger. Either that was a good sign, or I was going crazy.

Remember what you saw, the voice said. *He's after you. You have to be ready.*

I shivered. I wanted to believe I'd just had a bad dream, but I knew better. I'd been through too much in the last day to doubt what I'd seen. Somehow, I'd actually left my body while I slept. I'd *been* to Phoenix—thousands of miles away. The fiery dude was there. I hadn't understood much of what he'd said, but he'd talked about sending his forces to capture the younglings. Gee, wonder who that could be?

Muffin jumped off the bed and sniffed at the ivory headrest, looking up at me as if she were trying to tell me something.

61

'You can have it,' I told her. 'It's uncomfortable.'

She butted her head against it and stared at me accusingly. *'Mrow.'*

'Whatever, cat.'

I got up and showered. When I tried to get dressed, I found that my old clothes had disappeared in the night. Everything in the closet was my size, but way different than what I was used to—baggy drawstring pants and loose shirts, all plain white linen, and robes for cold weather, kind of what the *fellahin*, the peasants in Egypt, wear. It wasn't exactly my style.

Sadie likes to tell me that I don't *have* a style. She complains that I dress like I'm an old man—button-down shirt, slacks, dress shoes. Okay, maybe. But here's the thing. My dad had always drilled into my head that I had to dress my best.

I remember the first time he explained it to me. I was ten. We were on our way to the airport in Athens, and it was like 112 degrees outside, and I was complaining that I wanted to wear shorts and a T-shirt. Why couldn't I be comfortable? We weren't going anywhere important that day—just traveling.

My dad put his hand on my shoulder. 'Carter, you're getting older. You're an African American man. People will judge you more harshly, and so you must always look impeccable.'

'That isn't fair!' I insisted.

'Fairness does not mean everyone gets the same,' Dad said. 'Fairness means everyone gets what they need. And the only way to get what you need is to make it happen *yourself.* Do you understand?'

I told him I didn't. But still I did what he asked—like caring about Egypt, and basketball, and music. Like traveling with only one suitcase. I dressed the way Dad wanted me to, because Dad was usually right. In fact I'd never known him to be wrong . . . until the night at the British Museum.

Anway, I put on the linen clothes from the closet. The slipper shoes were comfortable, though I doubted they'd be much good to run in.

The door to Sadie's room was open, but she wasn't there.

Thankfully my bedroom door wasn't locked anymore. Muffin joined me and we walked downstairs, passing a lot of unoccupied bedrooms on the way. The mansion could've easily slept a hundred people, but instead it felt empty and sad.

Down in the Great Room, Khufu the baboon sat on the sofa with a basketball between his legs and a chunk of strange-looking meat in his hands. It was covered in pink feathers. ESPN was on the television, and Khufu was watching highlights from the games the night before.

'Hey,' I said, though I felt a little weird talking to him. 'Lakers win?'

Khufu looked at me and patted his basketball like he wanted a game. *'Agh, agh.'*

He had a pink feather hanging from his chin, and the sight made my stomach do a slow roll.

'Um, yeah,' I said. 'We'll play later, okay?'

I could see Sadie and Amos out on the terrace, eating breakfast by the pool. It should've been freezing out there, but the fire pit was blazing, and neither Amos nor Sadie looked cold. I headed their way, then hesitated in front of the statue of Thoth. In the daylight, the bird-headed god didn't

63

look quite so scary. Still, I could swear those beady eyes were watching me expectantly.

What had the fiery guy said last night? Something about catching us before we learned our powers. It sounded ridiculous, but for a moment I felt a surge of strength—like the night before when I'd opened the front door just by raising my hand. I felt like I could lift anything, even this thirty-foot-tall statue if I wanted to. In a kind of trance, I stepped forward.

Muffin meowed impatiently and butted my foot. The feeling dissolved.

'You're right,' I told the cat. 'Stupid idea.'

Besides, I could smell breakfast now—French toast, bacon, hot chocolate—and I couldn't blame Muffin for being in a hurry. I followed her out to the terrace.

'Ah, Carter,' Amos said. 'Merry Christmas, my boy. Join us.'

'About time,' Sadie grumbled. 'I've been up for ages.'

But she held my eyes for a moment, like she was thinking the same thing I was: *Christmas.* We hadn't spent a Christmas morning together since Mom died. I wondered if Sadie remembered how we used to make god's-eye decorations out of yarn and Popsicle sticks.

Amos poured himself a cup of coffee. His clothes were similar to those he'd worn the day before, and I had to admit the guy had style. His tailored suit was made of blue wool, he wore a matching fedora, and his hair was freshly braided with dark blue lapis lazuli, one of the stones the Egyptians often used for jewelry. Even his glasses matched. The round lenses were tinted blue. A

64

tenor sax rested on a stand near the fire pit, and I could totally picture him playing out here, serenading the East River.

As for Sadie, she was dressed in a white linen pajama outfit like me, but somehow she'd managed to keep her combat boots. She'd probably slept with them on. She looked pretty comical with the red-streaked hair and the outfit, but since I wasn't dressed any better, I could hardly make fun of her.

'Um . . . Amos?' I asked. 'You didn't have any pet birds, did you? Khufu's eating something with pink feathers.'

'*Mmm.*' Amos sipped his coffee. 'Sorry if that disturbed you. Khufu's very picky. He only eats foods that end in *-o*. Doritos, burritos, flamingos.'

I blinked. 'Did you say—'

'Carter,' Sadie warned. She looked a little queasy, like she'd already had this conversation. 'Don't ask.'

'Okay,' I said. 'Not asking.'

'Please, Carter, help yourself.' Amos waved toward a buffet table piled high with food. 'Then we can get started with the explanations.'

I didn't see any flamingo on the buffet table, which was fine by me, but there was just about everything else. I snagged some pancakes with butter and syrup, some bacon, and a glass of OJ.

Then I noticed movement in the corner of my eye. I glanced at the swimming pool. Something long and pale was gliding just under the surface of the water.

I almost dropped my plate. 'Is that—'

'A crocodile,' Amos confirmed. 'For good luck. He's albino, but please don't mention that. He's sensitive.'

'His name is Philip of Macedonia,' Sadie informed me.

I wasn't sure how Sadie was taking this all so calmly, but I figured if she wasn't freaking out, I shouldn't either.

'That's a long name,' I said.

'He's a long crocodile,' Sadie said. 'Oh, and he likes bacon.'

To prove her point, she tossed a piece of bacon over her shoulder. Philip lunged out of the water and snapped up the treat. His hide was pure white and his eyes were pink. His mouth was so big, he could've snapped up an entire pig.

'He's quite harmless to my friends,' Amos assured me. 'In the old days, no temple would be complete without a lake full of crocodiles. They are powerful magic creatures.'

'Right,' I said. 'So the baboon, the crocodile . . . any other pets I should know about?'

Amos thought for a moment. 'Visible ones? No, I think that's it.'

I took a seat as far from the pool as possible. Muffin circled my legs and purred. I hoped she had enough sense to stay away from magic crocodiles named Philip.

'So, Amos,' I said between bites of pancake. 'Explanations.'

'Yes,' he agreed. 'Where to start . . .'

'Our dad,' Sadie suggested. 'What happened to him?'

Amos took a deep breath. 'Julius was attempting to summon a god. Unfortunately, it worked.'

It was kind of hard to take Amos seriously, talking about summoning gods while he spread

66

butter on a bagel.

'Any god in particular?' I asked casually. 'Or did he just order a generic god?'

Sadie kicked me under the table. She was scowling, as if she actually believed what Amos was saying.

Amos took a bite of bagel. 'There are many Egyptian gods, Carter. But your dad was after one in particular.'

He looked at me meaningfully.

'Osiris,' I remembered. 'When Dad was standing in front of the Rosetta Stone, he said, "Osiris, come." But Osiris is a legend. He's make-believe.'

'I wish that were true.' Amos stared across the East River at the Manhattan skyline, gleaming in the morning sun. 'The Ancient Egyptians were not fools, Carter. They built the pyramids. They created the first great nation state. Their civilization lasted thousands of years.'

'Yeah,' I said. 'And now they're gone.'

Amos shook his head. 'A legacy that powerful does not disappear. Next to the Egyptians, the Greeks and Romans were babies. Our modern nations like Great Britain and America? Blinks of an eye. The very oldest root of civilization, at least of Western civilization, is Egypt. Look at the pyramid on the dollar bill. Look at the Washington Monument—the world's largest Egyptian obelisk. Egypt is still very much alive. And so, unfortunately, are her gods.'

'Come on,' I argued. 'I mean . . . even if I believe there's a real thing called magic. Believing in ancient gods is totally different. You're joking, right?'

But as I said it, I thought about the fiery guy in the museum, the way his face had shifted between human and animal. And the statue of Thoth—how its eyes had followed me.

'Carter,' Amos said, 'the Egyptians would not have been stupid enough to believe in imaginary gods. The beings they described in their myths are very, very real. In the old days, the priests of Egypt would call upon these gods to channel their power and perform great feats. That is the origin of what we now call magic. Like many things, magic was first invented by the Egyptians. Each temple had a branch of magicians called the House of Life. Their magicians were famed throughout the ancient world.'

'And you're an Egyptian magician.'

Amos nodded. 'So was your father. You saw it for yourself last night.'

I hesitated. It was hard to deny my dad had done some weird stuff at the museum—some stuff that looked like magic.

'But he's an archaeologist,' I said stubbornly.

'That's his cover story. You'll remember that he specialized in translating ancient spells, which are very difficult to understand unless you work magic yourself. Our family, the Kane family, has been part of the House of Life almost since the beginning. And your mother's family is almost as ancient.'

'The Fausts?' I tried to imagine Grandma and Grandpa Faust doing magic, but unless watching rugby on TV and burning cookies was magical, I couldn't see it.

'They had not practiced magic for many generations,' Amos admitted. 'Not until your

68

mother came along. But yes, a very ancient bloodline.'

Sadie shook her head in disbelief. 'So now Mum was magic, too. Are you joking?'

'No jokes,' Amos promised. 'The two of you . . . you combine the blood of two ancient families, both of which have a long, complicated history with the gods. You are the most powerful Kane children to be born in many centuries.'

I tried to let that sink in. At the moment, I didn't feel powerful. I felt queasy. 'You're telling me our parents secretly worshipped animal-headed gods?' I asked.

'Not worshipped,' Amos corrected. 'By the end of the ancient times, Egyptians had learned that their gods were not to be worshipped. They are powerful beings, primeval forces, but they are not divine in the sense one might think of God. They are created entities, like mortals, only much more powerful. We can respect them, fear them, use their power, or even fight them to keep them under control—'

'*Fight* gods?' Sadie interrupted.

'Constantly,' Amos assured her. 'But we don't worship them. Thoth taught us that.'

I looked at Sadie for help. The old guy had to be crazy. But Sadie was looking like she believed every word.

'So . . .' I said. 'Why did Dad break the Rosetta Stone?'

'Oh, I'm sure he didn't mean to break it,' Amos said. 'That would've horrified him. In fact, I imagine my brethren in London have repaired the damage by now. The curators will soon check their vaults and discover that the Rosetta Stone

69

miraculously survived the explosion.'

'But it was blown into a million pieces!' I said. 'How could they repair it?'

Amos picked up a saucer and threw it onto the stone floor. The saucer shattered instantly.

'That was *to destroy*,' Amos said. 'I could've done it by magic—*ha-di*—but it's simpler just to smash it. And now . . .' Amos held out his hand. 'Join. *Hi-nehm.*'

A blue hieroglyphic symbol burned in the air above his palm.

The pieces of the saucer flew into his hand and reassembled like a puzzle, even the smallest bits of dust gluing themselves into place. Amos put the perfect saucer back on the table.

'Some trick,' I managed. I tried to sound calm about it, but I was thinking of all the odd things that had happened to my dad and me over the years, like those gunmen in the Cairo hotel who'd ended up hanging by their feet from a chandelier. Was it possible my dad had made that happen with some kind of spell?

Amos poured milk in the saucer, and put it on the floor. Muffin came padding over. 'At any rate, your father would never intentionally damage a relic. He simply didn't realize how much power the Rosetta Stone contained. You see, as Egypt faded, its magic collected and concentrated into its remaining relics. Most of these, of course, are still in Egypt. But you can find some in almost every major museum. A magician can use these artifacts as focal points to work more powerful spells.'

'I don't get it,' I said.

Amos spread his hands. 'I'm sorry, Carter. It takes years of study to understand magic, and I'm trying to explain it to you in a single morning. The important thing is, for the past six years your father has been looking for a way to summon Osiris, and last night he thought he had found the right artifact to do it.'

'Wait, why did he want Osiris?'

Sadie gave me a troubled look. 'Carter, Osiris was the lord of the dead. Dad was talking about making things right. He was talking about Mum.'

Suddenly the morning seemed colder. The fire pit sputtered in the wind coming off the river.

'He wanted to bring Mom back from the dead?' I said. 'But that's crazy!'

Amos hesitated. 'It would've been dangerous. Inadvisable. Foolish. But not crazy. Your father is a powerful magician. If, in fact, that is what he was after, he might have accomplished it, using the power of Osiris.'

I stared at Sadie. 'You're actually buying this?'

'You saw the magic at the museum. The fiery bloke. Dad summoned something from the stone.'

'Yeah,' I said, thinking of my dream. 'But that wasn't Osiris, was it?'

'No,' Amos said. 'Your father got more than he bargained for. He did release the spirit of Osiris. In fact, I think he successfully joined with the god—'

'Joined with?'

Amos held up his hand. 'Another long conversation. For now, let's just say he drew the power of Osiris into himself. But he never got the chance to use it because, according to what Sadie has told me, it appears that Julius released *five* gods from the Rosetta Stone. Five gods who were all trapped together.'

I glanced at Sadie. 'You told him everything?'

'He's going to help us, Carter.'

I wasn't quite ready to trust this guy, even if he was our uncle, but I decided I didn't have much choice.

'Okay, yeah,' I said. 'The fiery guy said something like "You released all five." What did he mean?'

Amos sipped his coffee. The faraway look on his face reminded me of my dad. 'I don't want to scare you.'

'Too late.'

'The gods of Egypt are very dangerous. For the last two thousand years or so, we magicians have spent much of our time binding and banishing them whenever they appear. In fact, our most important law, issued by Chief Lector Iskandar in Roman times, forbids unleashing the gods or using their power. Your father broke that law once before.'

Sadie's face paled. 'Does this have something to do with Mum's death? Cleopatra's Needle in London?'

'It has *everything* to do with that, Sadie. Your parents . . . well, they thought they were doing something good. They took a terrible risk, and it cost your mother her life. Your father took the blame. He was exiled, I suppose you would say. Banished. He was forced to move around constantly because the House monitored his activities. They feared he would continue his . . . research. As indeed he did.'

I thought about the times Dad would look over his shoulder as he copied some ancient inscriptions, or wake me up at three or four in the morning and insist it was time to change hotels, or warn me not to look in his workbag or copy certain pictures from old temple walls—as if our lives depended on it.

'Is that why you never came round?' Sadie asked Amos. 'Because Dad was banished?'

'The House forbade me to see him. I loved Julius. It hurt me to stay away from my brother, and from you children. But I could not see you—until last night, when I simply had no choice but to try to help. Julius has been obsessed with finding Osiris for years. He was consumed with grief because of what happened to your mother. When I learned that Julius was about to break the law again, to try to set things right, I had to stop him. A second offense would've meant a death sentence. Unfortunately, I failed. I should've known he was too stubborn.'

I looked down at my plate. My food had gotten cold. Muffin leaped onto the table and rubbed against my hand. When I didn't object, she started eating my bacon.

'Last night at the museum,' I said, 'the girl with the knife, the man with the forked beard—they were magicians too? From the House of Life?'

'Yes,' Amos said. 'Keeping an eye on your father. You are fortunate they let you go.'

'The girl wanted to kill us,' I remembered. 'But the guy with the beard said, *not yet.*'

'They don't kill unless it is absolutely necessary,' Amos said. 'They will wait to see if you are a threat.'

'Why would we be a threat?' Sadie demanded. 'We're children! The summoning wasn't our idea.'

Amos pushed away his plate. 'There is a reason

73

you two were raised separately.'

'Because the Fausts took Dad to court,' I said matter-of-factly. 'And Dad lost.'

'It was much more than that,' Amos said. 'The House insisted you two be separated. Your father wanted to keep you both, even though he knew how dangerous it was.'

Sadie looked like she'd been smacked between the eyes. 'He did?'

'Of course. But the House intervened and made sure your grandparents got custody of you, Sadie. If you and Carter were raised together, you could become very powerful. Perhaps you have already sensed changes over the past day.'

I thought about the surges of strength I'd been feeling, and the way Sadie suddenly seemed to know how to read Ancient Egyptian. Then I thought of something even further back.

'Your sixth birthday,' I told Sadie.

'The cake,' she said immediately, the memory passing between us like an electric spark.

At Sadie's sixth birthday party, the last one we'd shared as a family, Sadie and I had a huge argument. I don't remember what it was about. I think I wanted to blow out the candles for her. We started yelling. She grabbed my shirt. I pushed her. I remember Dad rushing toward us, trying to intervene, but before he could, Sadie's birthday cake exploded. Icing splattered the walls, our parents, the faces of Sadie's little six-year-old friends. Dad and Mom separated us. They sent me to my room. Later, they said we must've hit the cake by accident as we were fighting, but I knew we hadn't. Something much weirder had made it explode, as if it had responded to our anger. I remembered Sadie crying with a chunk of cake on her forehead, an upside-down candle stuck to the ceiling with its wick still burning, and an adult visitor, one of my parents' friends, his glasses speckled with white frosting.

I turned to Amos. 'That was you. You were at Sadie's party.'

'Vanilla icing,' he recalled. 'Very tasty. But it was clear even then that you two would be difficult to raise in the same household.'

'And so . . .' I faltered. 'What happens to us now?'

I didn't want to admit it, but I couldn't stand the thought of being separated from Sadie again. She wasn't much, but she was all I had.

'You must be trained properly,' Amos said, 'whether the House approves or not.'

'Why wouldn't they approve?' I asked.

'I will explain everything, don't worry. But we must start your lessons if we are to stand any chance of finding your father and putting things right. Otherwise the entire world is in danger. If we only knew where—'

'Phoenix,' I blurted out.

Amos stared at me. 'What?'

'Last night I had . . . well, not a dream, exactly . . . ' I felt stupid, but I told him what had happened while I slept.

Judging from Amos's expression, the news was even worse than I thought.

'You're *sure* he said "birthday present"?' he asked.

'Yeah, but what does that mean?'

'And a permanent host,' Amos said. 'He didn't have one yet?'

'Well, that's what the rooster-footed guy said—'

'That was a demon,' Amos said. 'A minion of chaos. And if demons are coming through to the mortal world, we don't have much time. This is bad, very bad.'

'If you live in Phoenix,' I said.

'Carter, our enemy won't stop in Phoenix. If he's grown so powerful so fast . . . What did he say about the storm, exactly?'

'He said: "I will summon the greatest storm ever known."'

Amos scowled. 'The last time he said that, he created the Sahara. A storm that large could destroy North America, generating enough chaos energy to give him an almost invincible form.'

'What are you talking about? Who *is* this guy?'

Amos waved away the question. 'More important right now: why didn't you sleep with the headrest?'

I shrugged. 'It was uncomfortable.' I looked at Sadie for support. 'You didn't use it, did you?'

Sadie rolled her eyes. 'Well, of course I did. It was *obviously* there for a reason.'

Sometimes I really hate my sister. [Ow! That's my foot!]

'Carter,' Amos said, 'sleep is dangerous. It's a doorway into the Duat.'

'Lovely,' Sadie grumbled. 'Another strange word.'

'Ah . . . yes, sorry,' Amos said. 'The Duat is the world of spirits and magic. It exists beneath the waking world like a vast ocean, with many layers and regions. We submerged just under its surface last night to reach New York, because travel through the Duat is much faster. Carter, your

76

consciousness also passed through its shallowest currents as you slept, which is how you witnessed what happened in Phoenix. Fortunately, you survived that experience. But the deeper you go into the Duat, the more horrible things you encounter, and the more difficult it is to return. There are entire realms filled with demons, palaces where the gods exist in their pure forms, so powerful their mere presence would burn a human to ashes. There are prisons that hold beings of unspeakable evil, and some chasms so deep and chaotic that not even the gods dare explore them. Now that your powers are stirring, you must not sleep without protection, or you leave yourself open to attacks from the Duat or . . . unintended journeys through it. The headrest is enchanted, to keep your consciousness anchored to your body.'

'You mean I actually *did* . . .' My mouth tasted like metal. 'Could he have killed me?'

Amos's expression was grave. 'The fact that your soul can travel like that means you are progressing faster than I thought. Faster than should be possible. If the Red Lord had noticed you—'

'The Red Lord?' Sadie said. 'That's the fiery bloke?'

Amos rose. 'I must find out more. We can't simply wait for him to find you. And if he releases the storm on his birthday, at the height of his powers—'

'You mean you're going to Phoenix?' I could barely get the words out. 'Amos, that fiery man defeated Dad like his magic was a joke! Now he's got demons, and he's getting stronger, and—you'll be killed!'

Amos gave me a dry smile, like he'd already weighed the dangers and didn't need a reminder. His expression reminded me painfully of Dad's. 'Don't count your uncle out so quickly, Carter. I've got some magic of my own. Besides, I must see what is happening for myself if we're to have any chance at saving your father and stopping the Red Lord. I'll be quick and careful. Just stay here. Muffin will guard you.'

I blinked. 'The cat will guard us? You can't just leave us here! What about our training?'

'When I return,' Amos promised. 'Don't worry, the mansion is protected. Just do not leave. Do not be tricked into opening the door for anyone. And whatever happens, *do not* go into the library. I absolutely forbid it. I will be back by sunset.'

Before we could protest, Amos walked calmly to the edge of the terrace and jumped.

'No!' Sadie screamed. We ran to the railing and looked over. Below was a hundred-foot drop into the East River. There was no sign of Amos. He'd simply vanished.

Philip of Macedonia splashed in his pool. Muffin jumped onto the railing and insisted we pet her.

We were alone in a strange mansion with a baboon, a crocodile, and a weird cat. And apparently, the entire world was in danger.

I looked at Sadie. 'What do we do now?'

She crossed her arms. 'Well, that's obvious, isn't it? We explore the library.'

7.
I DROP A LITTLE MAN ON HIS HEAD

Honestly, Carter is so thick sometimes I can't believe we're related.

I mean when someone says *I forbid it,* that's a good sign it's worth doing. I made for the library straightaway.

'Hold on!' Carter cried. 'You can't just—'

'Brother dear,' I said, 'did your soul leave your body again while Amos was talking, or did you actually *hear* him? Egyptian gods *real.* Red Lord *bad.* Red Lord's birthday: very soon, very bad. House of Life: fussy old magicians who hate our family because Dad was a bit of a rebel, whom by the way you could take a lesson from. Which leaves us—*just* us—with Dad missing, an evil god about to destroy the world, and an uncle who just jumped off the building—and I *can't* actually blame him.' I took a breath. [Yes, Carter, I do have to breathe occasionally.] 'Am I missing anything? Oh, yes, I also have a brother who is supposedly quite powerful from an ancient bloodline, blah, blah, et cetera, but is too afraid to visit a library. Now, coming or not?'

Carter blinked as if I'd just hit him, which I suppose I had in a way.

'I just . . .' He faltered. 'I just think we should be careful.'

I realized the poor boy was quite scared, which I couldn't hold against him, but it did startle me.

Carter was my *big* brother, after all—older, more sophisticated, the one who traveled the world with Dad. Big brothers are the ones who are supposed to pull their punches. Little sisters—well, we should be able to hit as hard as we like, shouldn't we? But I realized that possibly, just possibly, I'd been a bit harsh with him.

'Look,' I said. 'We need to help Dad, yes? There's got to be some powerful stuff in that library, otherwise Amos wouldn't keep it locked up. You do want to help Dad?'

Carter shifted uncomfortably. 'Yeah . . . of course.'

Well, that was one problem sorted, so we headed for the library. But as soon as Khufu saw what we were up to, he scrambled off the sofa with his basketball and jumped in front of the library doors. Who knew baboons were so speedy? He barked at us, and I have to say baboons have *enormous* fangs. And they're not any prettier when they've been chewing up exotic pink birds.

Carter tried to reason with him. 'Khufu, we're not going to steal anything. We just want—'

'*Agh!*' Khufu dribbled his basketball angrily.

'Carter,' I said, 'you're not helping. Look here, Khufu. I have . . . ta-da!' I held up a little yellow box of cereal I'd taken from the buffet table. 'Cheerios! Ends with an -*o*. Yumsies!'

'Aghhh!' Khufu grunted, more excited now than angry.

'Want it?' I coaxed. 'Just take it to the couch and pretend you didn't see us, yes?'

I threw the cereal towards the couch, and the baboon lunged after it. He grabbed the box in midair and was so excited, he ran straight up the wall and sat on the fireplace mantel, where he began gingerly picking out Cheerios and eating them one at a time.

Carter looked at me with grudging admiration. 'How did you—'

'Some of us think ahead. Now, let's open these doors.'

That was not so easily done. They were made of thick wood laced with giant steel chains and padlocked. *Complete* overkill.

Carter stepped forward. He tried to raise the doors by lifting his hand, which had been quite impressive the night before, only now accomplished nothing.

He shook the chains the old-fashioned way, then yanked on the padlocks.

'No good,' he said.

Ice needles tingled on the back of my neck. It was almost as if someone—or something—was whispering an idea in my head. 'What was that word Amos used at breakfast with the saucer?'

'For join?' Carter said. '*Hi-nehm* or something.'

'No, the other one, for destroy.'

'Uh, *ha-di*. But you'd need to know magic and the hieroglyphics, wouldn't you? And even then—'

I raised my hand toward the door. I pointed with two fingers and my thumb—an odd gesture I'd never made before, like a make-believe gun except with the thumb parallel to the ground.

'*Ha-di!*'

Bright gold hieroglyphs burned against the largest padlock.

And the doors exploded. Carter hit the floor as chains shattered and splinters flew all over the Great Room. When the dust cleared, Carter got

81

up, covered in wood shavings. I seemed to be fine. Muffin circled my feet, mewing contentedly, as if this were all very normal.

Carter stared at me. 'How exactly—'

'Don't know,' I admitted. 'But the library's open.'

'Think you overdid it a little? We're going to be in so much trouble—'

'We'll just figure out a way to zap the door back, won't we?'

'No more zapping, please,' Carter said. 'That explosion could've killed us.'

'Oh, do you think if you tried that spell on a person—'

'No!' He stepped back nervously.

I felt gratified that I could make him squirm, but I tried not to smile. 'Let's just explore the library, shall we?'

The truth was, I couldn't have *ha-di*-ed anyone. As soon as I stepped forward, I felt so faint that I almost collapsed.

Carter caught me as I stumbled. 'You okay?'

'Fine,' I managed, though I didn't feel fine. 'I'm tired'—my stomach rumbled—'and famished.'

'You just ate a huge breakfast.'

It was true, but I felt as if I hadn't had food in weeks.

'Never mind,' I told him. 'I'll manage.'

Carter studied me skeptically. 'Those hieroglyphs you created were golden. Dad and Amos both used blue. Why?'

'Maybe everyone has his own color,' I suggested. 'Maybe you'll get hot pink.'

'Very funny.'

'Come on, pink wizard,' I said. 'Inside we go.'

The library was so amazing, I almost forgot my dizziness. It was bigger than I'd imagined, a round chamber sunk deep into solid rock, like a giant well. This didn't make sense, as the mansion was sitting on top of a warehouse, but then again nothing else about the place was exactly normal.

From the platform where we stood, a staircase descended three stories to the bottom floor. The walls, floor, and domed ceiling were all decorated with multicolored pictures of people, gods, and monsters. I'd seen such illustrations in Dad's books (yes, all right, sometimes when I was in the Piccadilly bookshop I'd wander into the Egypt section and sneak a look at Dad's books, just to feel some connection to him, not because I wanted to read them) but the pictures in the books had always been faded and smudged. These in the library looked newly painted, making the entire room a work of art.

'It's beautiful,' I said.

A blue starry sky glittered on the ceiling, but it wasn't a solid field of blue. Rather, the sky was painted in a strange swirling pattern. I realized it was shaped like a woman. She lay curled on her side—her body, arms, and legs dark blue and dotted with stars. Below, the library floor was done in a similar way, the green-and-brown earth shaped into a man's body, dotted with forests and hills and cities. A river snaked across his chest.

The library had no books. Not even bookshelves. Instead, the walls were honeycombed with round cubbyholes, each one holding a sort of

83

plastic cylinder.

At each of the four compass points, a ceramic statue stood on a pedestal. The statues were half-size humans wearing kilts and sandals, with glossy black wedge-shaped haircuts and black eyeliner around their eyes.

[Carter says the eyeliner stuff is called kohl, as if it matters.]

At any rate, one statue held a stylus and scroll. Another held a box. Another held a short, hooked staff. The last was empty-handed.

'Sadie.' Carter pointed to the center of the room. Sitting on a long stone table was Dad's workbag.

Carter started down the stairs, but I grabbed his arm. 'Hang on. What about traps?'

He frowned. 'Traps?'

'Didn't Egyptian tombs have traps?'

'Well . . . sometimes. But this isn't a tomb. Besides, more often they had curses, like the burning curse, the donkey curse—'

'Oh, lovely. That sounds so much better.'

He trotted down the steps, which made me feel quite ridiculous, as I'm usually the one to forge ahead. But I supposed if someone had to get cursed with a burning skin rash or attacked by a magical donkey, it was better Carter than me.

We made it to the middle of the room with no excitement. Carter opened the bag. Still no traps or curses. He brought out the strange box Dad had used in the British Museum.

It was made of wood, and about the right size to hold a loaf of French bread. The lid was decorated much like the library, with gods and monsters and sideways-walking people.

'How did the Egyptians move like that?' I wondered. 'All sideways with their arms and legs out. It seems quite silly.'

Carter gave me one of his *God, you're stupid* looks. 'They didn't walk like that in real life, Sadie.'

'Well, why are they painted like that, then?'

'They thought paintings were like magic. If you painted yourself, you had to show all your arms and legs. Otherwise, in the afterlife you might be reborn without all your pieces.'

'Then why the sideways faces? They never look straight at you. Doesn't that mean they'll lose the other side of their face?'

Carter hesitated. 'I think they were afraid the picture would be *too* human if it was looking right at you. It might try to *become* you.'

'So is there anything they *weren't* afraid of?'

'Little sisters,' Carter said. 'If they talked too much, the Egyptians threw them to the crocodiles.'

He had me for a second. I wasn't used to him displaying a sense of humor. Then I punched him. 'Just open the bloody box.'

The first thing he pulled out was a lump of white gunk.

'Wax,' Carter pronounced.

'Fascinating.' I picked up a wooden stylus and a palette with small indentations in its surface for ink, then a few glass jars of the ink itself—black, red, and gold. 'And a prehistoric painting set.'

Carter pulled out several lengths of brown twine, a small ebony cat statue, and a thick roll of paper. No, not paper. Papyrus. I remembered Dad explaining how the Egyptians made it from a river plant because they never invented paper. The stuff was so thick and rough, it made me wonder if the poor Egyptians had had to use toilet papyrus. If so, no wonder they walked sideways.

Finally I pulled out a wax figurine.

'*Ew,*' I said.

He was a tiny man, crudely fashioned, as if the maker had been in a hurry. His arms were crossed over his chest, his mouth was open, and his legs were cut off at the knees. A lock of human hair was wrapped round his waist.

Muffin jumped on the table and sniffed the little man. She seemed to think him quite interesting.

'There's nothing here,' Carter said.

'What do you want?' I asked. 'We've got wax, some toilet papyrus, an ugly statue—'

'Something to explain what happened to Dad. How do we get him back? Who was that fiery man he summoned?'

I held up the wax man. 'You heard him, warty little troll. Tell us what you know.'

I was just messing about. But the wax man became soft and warm like flesh. He said, 'I answer the call.'

I screamed and dropped him on his tiny head. Well, can you blame me?

'*Ow!*' he said.

Muffin came over to have a sniff, and the little man started cursing in another language, possibly Ancient Egyptian. When that didn't work, he screeched in English: 'Go away! I'm not a mouse!'

I scooped up Muffin and put her on the floor.

Carter's face had gone as soft and waxy as the little man's. 'What *are* you?' he asked.

'I'm a *shabti,* of course!' The figurine rubbed his dented head. He still looked quite lumpish, only now he was a living lump. 'Master calls me Doughboy, though I find the name insulting. You may call me Supreme-Force-Who-Crushes-His-Enemies!'

'All right, Doughboy,' I said.

He scowled at me, I think, though it was hard to tell with his mashed-up face.

'*You* weren't supposed to trigger me! Only the master does that.'

'The master, meaning Dad,' I guessed. '*Er,* Julius Kane?'

'That's him,' Doughboy grumbled. 'Are we done yet? Have I fulfilled my service?'

Carter stared at me blankly, but I thought I was beginning to understand.

'So, Doughboy,' I told the lump. 'You were triggered when I picked you up and gave you a direct order: *Tell us what you know.* Is that correct?'

Doughboy crossed his stubby arms. 'You're just toying with me now. *Of course* that's correct. Only the master is supposed to be able to trigger me, by the way. I don't know how you did it, but he'll blast you to pieces when he finds out.'

Carter cleared his throat. 'Doughboy, the master is our dad, and he's missing. He's been magically sent away somehow and we need your help—'

'Master is gone?' Doughboy smiled so widely, I thought his wax face would split open. 'Free at last! See you, suckers!'

He lunged for the end of the table but forgot he had no feet. He landed on his face, then began crawling toward the edge, dragging himself with his hands. 'Free! Free!'

He fell off the table and onto the floor with a thud, but that didn't seem to discourage him. 'Free! Free!'

He made it another centimeter or two before I picked him up and threw him in Dad's magic box. Doughboy tried to get out, but the box was just tall enough that he couldn't reach the rim. I wondered if it had been designed that way.

'Trapped!' he wailed. 'Trapped!'

'Oh, shut up,' I told him. '*I'm* the mistress now. And you'll answer my questions.'

Carter raised his eyebrow. 'How come *you* get to be in charge?'

'Because I was smart enough to activate him.'

'You were just joking around!'

I ignored my brother, which is one of my many talents. 'Now, Doughboy, first off, what's a *shabti*?'

'Will you let me out of the box if I tell you?'

'You *have* to tell me,' I pointed out. 'And no, I won't.'

He sighed. '*Shabti* means *answerer,* as even the stupidest slave could tell you.'

Carter snapped his fingers. 'I remember now! The Egyptians made models out of wax or clay—servants to do every kind of job they could imagine in the afterlife. They were supposed to come to life when their master called, so the deceased person could, like, kick back and relax and let the *shabti* do all his work for eternity.'

'First,' Doughboy snipped, 'that is typical of humans! Lazing around while we do all the work. Second, afterlife work is only *one* function of *shabti.* We are also used by magicians for a great number of things in *this* life, because magicians would be total incompetents without us. Third, if

88

you know so much, why are you asking me?'

'Why did Dad cut off your legs,' I wondered, 'and leave you with a mouth?'

'I—' Doughboy clapped his little hands over his mouth. 'Oh, very funny. Threaten the wax statue. Big bully! He cut my legs off so I wouldn't run away or come to life in perfect form and try to kill him, naturally. Magicians are very mean. They maim statues to control them. They are afraid of us!'

'Would you come to life and try to kill him, had he made you perfectly?'

'Probably,' Doughboy admitted. 'Are we done?'

'Not by half,' I said. 'What happened to our dad?'

Doughboy shrugged. 'How should I know? But I see his wand and staff aren't in the box.'

'No,' Carter said. 'The staff—the thing that turned into a snake—it got incinerated. And the wand . . . is that the boomerang thing?'

'The *boomerang thing*?' Doughboy said. 'Gods of Eternal Egypt, you're dense. Of course that's his wand.'

'It got shattered,' I said.

'Tell me how,' Doughboy demanded.

Carter told him the story. I wasn't sure that was the best idea, but I supposed a ten-centimeter-tall statue couldn't do us *that* much harm.

'This is wonderful!' Doughboy cried.

'Why?' I asked. 'Is Dad still alive?'

'No!' Doughboy said. 'He's almost certainly dead. The five gods of the Demon Days released? Wonderful! And anyone who duels with the Red Lord—'

'Wait,' I said. 'I order you to tell me what

happened.'

'Ha!' Doughboy said. 'I only have to tell you what I *know*. Making educated guesses is a completely different task. I declare my service fulfilled!'

With that, he turned back to lifeless wax.

'Wait!' I picked him up again and shook him. 'Tell me your educated guesses!'

Nothing happened.

'Maybe he's got a timer,' Carter said. 'Like only once a day. Or maybe you broke him.'

'Carter, make a *helpful* suggestion! What do we do now?'

He looked at the four ceramic statues on their pedestals. 'Maybe—'

'Other *shabti?*'

'Worth a shot.'

*   *   *

If the statues were *answerers*, they weren't very good at it. We tried holding them while giving them orders, though they were quite heavy. We tried pointing at them and shouting. We tried asking nicely. They gave us no answers at all.

I grew so frustrated I wanted to *ha-di* them into a million pieces, but I was still so hungry and tired, I had the feeling that spell would not be good for my health.

Finally we decided to check the cubbyholes round the walls. The plastic cylinders were the kind you might find at a drive-through bank—the kind that shoot up and down the pneumatic tubes. Inside each case was a papyrus scroll. Some looked new. Some looked thousands of years old.

Each canister was labeled in hieroglyphs and (fortunately) in English.

'*The Book of the Heavenly Cow,*' Carter read on one. 'What kind of name is that? What've you got, *The Heavenly Badger?*'

'No,' I said. '*The Book of Slaying Apophis.*'

Muffin meowed in the corner. When I looked over, her tail was puffed up.

'What's wrong with her?' I asked.

'Apophis was a giant snake monster,' Carter muttered. 'He was bad news.'

Muffin turned and raced up the stairs, back into the Great Room. Cats. No accounting for them.

Carter opened another scroll. 'Sadie, look at this.'

He'd found a papyrus that was quite long, and most of the text on it seemed to be lines of hieroglyphs.

'Can you read any of this?' Carter asked.

I frowned at the writing, and the odd thing was, I *couldn't* read it—except for one line at the top. 'Only that bit where the title should be. It says . . . *Blood of the Great House.* What does that mean?'

'Great house,' Carter mused. 'What do the words sound like in Egyptian?'

'Per-roh. Oh, it's *pharaoh,* isn't it? But I thought a pharaoh was a king?'

'It is,' Carter said. 'The word literally means "great house," like the king's mansion. Sort of like referring to the president as "the White House." So here it probably means more like *Blood of the Pharaohs,* all of them, the whole lineage of all the dynasties, not just one guy.'

'So why do I care about the pharaohs' blood, and why can't I read any of the rest?'

Carter stared at the lines. Suddenly his eyes widened. 'They're names. Look, they're all written inside cartouches.'

'Excuse me?' I asked, because *cartouche* sounded like a rather rude word, and I pride myself on knowing those.

'The circles,' Carter explained. 'They symbolize magic ropes. They're supposed to protect the holder of the name from evil magic.' He eyed me. 'And possibly also from other magicians reading their names.'

'Oh, you're mental,' I said. But I looked at the lines, and saw what he meant. All the other words were protected by cartouches, and I couldn't make sense of them.

'Sadie,' Carter said, his voice urgent. He pointed to a cartouche at the very end of the list—the last entry in what looked to be a catalogue of thousands.

Inside the circle were two simple symbols, a basket and a wave.

'KN,' Carter announced. 'I know this one. It's our name, KANE.'

'Missing a few letters, isn't it?'

Carter shook his head. 'Egyptians usually didn't write vowels. Only consonants. You have to figure out the vowel sounds from context.'

'They really *were* nutters. So that could be KON or IKON or KNEE or AKNE.'

'It could be,' Carter agreed. 'But it's our name, Kane. I asked Dad to write it for me in hieroglyphs once, and that's how he did it. But why are we in this list? And what is "blood of the pharaohs"?'

That icy tingle started on the back of my neck. I remembered what Amos had said, about both sides of our family being very ancient. Carter's eyes met mine, and judging from his expression, he was having the same thought.

'There's no way,' I protested.

'Must be some kind of joke,' he agreed. 'Nobody keeps family records that far back.'

I swallowed, my throat suddenly very dry. So many odd things had happened to us in the last day, but it was only when I saw our name in that book that I finally began to believe all this mad Egyptian stuff was real. Gods, magicians, monsters . . . and our family was tied into it.

Ever since breakfast, when it occurred to me that Dad had been trying to bring Mum back from the dead, a horrible emotion had been trying to take hold of me. And it wasn't dread. Yes, the whole idea was creepy, *much* creepier than the shrine my grandparents kept in the hall cupboard to my dead mother. And yes, I told you I try not to live in the past and nothing could change the fact that my mum was gone. But I'm a liar. The truth was, I'd had one dream ever since I was six: to see my mum again. To actually get to know her, talk to her, go shopping, do *anything*. Just be with her once so I could have a better memory to hold on to. The feeling I was trying to shake was *hope*. I knew I was setting myself up for colossal hurt. But if it really *were* possible to bring her back, then I would've blown up any number of Rosetta Stones to make it happen.

'Let's keep looking,' I said.

After a few more minutes, I found a picture of some of the animal-headed gods, five in a row, with a starry woman figure arching over them protectively like an umbrella. Dad had released five gods. *Hmm.*

'Carter,' I called. 'What's this, then?'

He came to have a look and his eyes lit up.

'That's it!' he announced. 'These five . . . and up here, their mother, Nut.'

I laughed. 'A goddess named Nut? Is her last name Case?'

'Very funny,' Carter said. 'She was the goddess of the sky.'

He pointed to the painted ceiling—the lady with the blue star-spangled skin, same as in the scroll.

'So what about her?' I asked.

Carter knit his eyebrows. 'Something about the Demon Days. It had to do with the birth of these five gods, but it's been a long time since Dad told me the story. This whole scroll is written in hieratic, I think. That's like hieroglyph cursive. Can you read it?'

I shook my head. Apparently, my particular brand of insanity only applied to regular hieroglyphs.

'I wish I could find the story in English,' Carter said.

Just then there was a cracking noise behind us. The empty-handed clay statue hopped off his pedestal and marched towards us. Carter and I scrambled to get out of his way, but he walked straight past us, grabbed a cylinder from its cubbyhole and brought it to Carter.

'It's a retrieval *shabti,*' I said. 'A clay librarian!'

Carter swallowed nervously and took the cylinder. '*Um* . . . thanks.'

The statue marched back to his pedestal, jumped on, and hardened again into regular clay.

'I wonder . . .' I faced the *shabti.* 'Sandwich and

94

chips, please!'

Sadly, none of the statues jumped down to serve me. Perhaps food wasn't allowed in the library.

Carter uncapped the cylinder and unrolled the papyrus. He sighed with relief. 'This version is in English.'

As he scanned the text, his frown got deeper.

'You don't look happy,' I noticed.

'Because I remember the story now. The five gods . . . if Dad really released them, it isn't good news.'

'Hang on,' I said. 'Start from the beginning.'

Carter took a shaky breath. 'Okay. So the sky goddess, Nut, was married to the earth god, Geb.'

'That would be this chap on the floor?' I tapped my foot on the big green man with the river and hills and forests all over his body.

'Right,' Carter said. 'Anyway, Geb and Nut wanted to have kids, but the king of the gods, Ra—he was the sun god—heard this bad prophecy that a child of Nut—'

'Child of Nut,' I snickered. 'Sorry, go on.'

'—a child of Geb and Nut would one day replace Ra as king. So when Ra learned that Nut was pregnant, Ra freaked out. He forbade Nut to give birth to her children on any day or night of the year.'

I crossed my arms. 'So what, she had to stay pregnant forever? That's awfully mean.'

Carter shook his head. 'Nut figured out a way. She set up a game of dice with the moon god, Khons. Every time Khons lost, he had to give Nut some of his moonlight. He lost so many times, Nut won enough moonlight to create five *new* days and tag them on to the end of the year.'

'Oh, please,' I said. 'First, how can you gamble moonlight? And if you did, how could you make extra days out of it?'

'It's a story!' Carter protested. 'Anyway, the Egyptian calendar had three hundred and sixty days in the year, just like the three hundred and sixty degrees in a circle. Nut created five days and added them to end of the year—days that were not part of the regular year.'

'The Demon Days,' I guessed. 'So the myth explains why a year has three hundred and sixty-five days. And I suppose she had her children—'

'During those five days,' Carter agreed. 'One kid per day.'

'Again, how do you have five children in a row, each on a different day?'

'They're gods,' Carter said. 'They can do stuff like that.'

'Makes as much sense as the name Nut. But please, go on.'

'So when Ra found out, he was furious, but it was too late. The children were already born. Their names were Osiris—'

'The one Dad was after.'

'Then Horus, Set, Isis, and, um . . .' Carter consulted his scroll. 'Nephthys. I always forget that one.'

'And the fiery man in the museum said, *you have released all five.*'

'Exactly. What if they were imprisoned together and Dad didn't realize it? They were born together, so maybe they had to be summoned back into the world together. The thing is, one of these guys, Set, was a really bad dude. Like, the villain of Egyptian mythology. The god of evil and chaos

96

and desert storms.'

I shivered. 'Did he perhaps have something to do with fire?'

Carter pointed to one of the figures in the picture. The god had an animal head, but I couldn't quite make out which sort of animal: Dog? Anteater? Evil bunny rabbit? Whichever it was, his hair and his clothes were bright red.

'The Red Lord,' I said.

'Sadie, there's more,' Carter said. 'Those five days—the Demon Days—were bad luck in Ancient Egypt. You had to be careful, wear good luck charms, and not do anything important or dangerous on those days. And in the British Museum, Dad told Set: *They'll stop you before the Demon Days are over.*'

'Surely you don't think he meant *us,*' I said. '*We're* supposed to stop this Set character?'

Carter nodded. 'And if the last five days of *our* calendar year still count as the Egyptian Demon Days—they'd start on December 27, the day after tomorrow.'

The *shabti* seemed to be staring at me expectantly, but I had not the slightest idea what to do. Demon Days and evil bunny gods—if I heard *one* more impossible thing, my head would explode.

And the worst of it? The little insistent voice in the back of my head saying: *It's not impossible. To save Dad, we must defeat Set.*

As if that had been on my to-do list for Christmas hols. See Dad—check. Develop strange powers—check. Defeat an evil god of chaos—check. The whole idea was mad!

Suddenly there was a loud crash, as if something

had broken in the Great Room. Khufu began barking in alarm.

Carter and I locked eyes. Then we ran for the stairs.

8.
MUFFIN PLAYS WITH KNIVES

SADIE

Our baboon was going completely sky goddess—which is to say, *nuts.*

He swung from column to column, bouncing along the balconies, overturning pots and statues. Then he ran back to the terrace windows, stared outside for a moment, and proceeded to go berserk again.

Muffin was also at the window. She crouched on all fours with her tail twitching as if she were stalking a bird.

'Perhaps it's just a passing flamingo,' I suggested hopefully, but I'm not sure Carter could hear me over the screaming baboon.

We ran to the glass doors. At first I didn't see any problem. Then water exploded from the pool, and my heart nearly jumped out of my chest. Two enormous creatures, most definitely not flamingos, were thrashing about with our crocodile, Philip of Macedonia.

I couldn't make out what they were, only that they were fighting Philip two against one. They disappeared under the boiling water, and Khufu ran screaming through the Great Room again,

98

bonking himself on the head with his empty Cheerios box, which I must say was not particularly helpful.

'Longnecks,' Carter said incredulously. 'Sadie, did you *see* those things?'

I couldn't find an answer. Then one of the creatures was thrown out of the pool. It slammed into the doors right in front of us, and I jumped back in alarm. On the other side of the glass was the most terrifying animal I'd ever seen. Its body was like a leopard's—lean and sinewy, with golden spotted fur—but its neck was completely wrong. It was green and scaly and at least as long as the rest of its body. It had a cat's head, but no normal cat's. When it turned its glowing red eyes towards us, it howled, showing a forked tongue and fangs dripping with green venom.

I realized my legs were shaking and I was making a very undignified whimpering sound.

The cat-serpent jumped back into the pool to join its companion in beating up Philip, who spun and snapped but seemed unable to hurt his attackers.

'We have to help Philip!' I cried. 'He'll be killed!'

I reached for the door handle, but Muffin growled at me.

Carter said, 'Sadie, no! You heard Amos. We can't open the doors for any reason. The house is protected by magic. Philip will have to beat them on his own.'

'But what if he can't? Philip!'

The old crocodile turned. For a second his pink reptilian eye focused on me as if he could sense my concern. Then the cat-snakes bit at his underbelly and Philip rose up so that only the tip of his tail still touched the water. His body began to glow. A low hum filled the air, like an airplane engine starting up. When Philip came down, he slammed into the terrace with all his might.

The entire house shook. Cracks appeared in the concrete terrace outside, and the swimming pool split right down the middle as the far end crumbled into empty space.

'No!' I cried.

But the edge of the terrace ripped free, plunging Philip and the monsters straight into the East River.

My whole body began to tremble. 'He sacrificed himself. He killed the monsters.'

'Sadie . . .' Carter's voice was faint. 'What if he didn't? What if they come back?'

'Don't say that!'

'I—I recognized them, Sadie. Those creatures. Come on.'

'Where?' I demanded, but he ran straight back to the library.

*   *   *

Carter marched up to the *shabti* who'd helped us before. 'Bring me the . . . *gah,* what's it called?'

'What?' I asked.

'Something Dad showed me. It's a big stone plate or something. Had a picture of the first pharaoh, the guy who united Upper and Lower Egypt into one kingdom. His name . . .' His eyes lit up. 'Narmer! Bring me the Narmer Plate!'

Nothing happened.

'No,' Carter decided. 'Not a plate. It was . . . one

of those things that holds paint. A palette. Bring me the Narmer Palette!'

The empty-handed *shabti* didn't move, but across the room, the statue with the little hook came to life. He jumped off his pedestal and disappeared in a cloud of dust. A heartbeat later, he reappeared on the table. At his feet was a wedge of flat gray stone, shaped like a shield and about as long as my forearm.

'No!' Carter protested. 'I meant a *picture* of it! Oh great, I think this is the *real* artifact. The *shabti* must've stolen it from the Cairo Museum. We've got to return—'

'Hang on,' I said. 'We might as well have a look.'

The surface of the stone was carved with the picture of a man smashing another man in the face with what looked like a spoon.

'That's Narmer with the spoon,' I guessed. 'Angry because the other bloke stole his breakfast cereal?'

Carter shook his head. 'He's conquering his enemies and uniting Egypt. See his hat? That's the crown of Lower Egypt, before the two countries united.'

'The bit that looks like a bowling pin?'

'You're impossible,' Carter grumbled.

'He looks like Dad, doesn't he?'

'Sadie, be serious!'

'I *am* serious. Look at his profile.'

Carter decided to ignore me. He examined the stone like he was afraid to touch it. 'I need to see the back but I don't want to turn it over. We might damage—'

I grabbed the stone and flipped it over.

'Sadie! You could've broken it!'

'That's what mend spells are for, yes?'

We examined the back of the stone, and I had to admit I was impressed by Carter's memory. Two cat-snake monsters stood in the center of the palette, their necks entwined. On either side, Egyptian men with ropes were trying to capture the creatures.

'They're called serpopards,' Carter said. 'Serpent leopards.'

'Fascinating,' I said. 'But what *are* serpopards?'

'No one knows exactly. Dad thought they were creatures of chaos—very bad news, and they've been around forever. This stone is one of the oldest artifacts from Egypt. Those pictures were carved five thousand years ago.'

'So why are five-thousand-year-old monsters attacking our house?'

'Last night, in Phoenix, the fiery man ordered his servants to capture us. He said to send the longnecks first.'

I had a metallic taste in my mouth, and I wished I hadn't chewed my last piece of gum. 'Well . . . good thing they're at the bottom of the East River.'

Just then Khufu rushed into the library, screaming and slapping his head.

'Suppose I shouldn't have said that,' I muttered.

Carter told the *shabti* to return the Narmer Palette, and both statue and stone disappeared. Then we followed the baboon upstairs.

* * *

The serpopards were back, their fur wet and slimy from the river, and they weren't happy. They prowled the broken ledge of the terrace, their snake necks whipping round as they sniffed the doors, looking for a way in. They spit poison that steamed and bubbled on the glass. Their forked tongues darted in and out.

'*Agh, agh!*' Khufu picked up Muffin, who was sitting on the sofa, and offered me the cat.

'I really don't think that will help,' I told him.

'AGH!' Khufu insisted.

Neither *Muffin* nor *cat* ended in *-o,* so I guessed Khufu was not trying to offer me a snack, but I didn't know what he was on about. I took the cat just to shut him up.

'*Mrow?*' Muffin looked up at me.

'It'll be all right,' I promised, trying not to sound scared out of my mind. 'The house is protected by magic.'

'Sadie,' Carter said. 'They've found something.'

The serpopards had converged at the left-hand door and were intently sniffing the handle.

'Isn't it locked?' I asked.

Both monsters smashed their ugly faces against the glass. The door shuddered. Blue hieroglyphs glowed along the doorframe, but their light was faint.

'I don't like this,' Carter murmured.

I prayed that the monsters would give up. Or that perhaps Philip of Macedonia would climb back to the terrace (do crocodiles climb?) and renew the fight.

Instead, the monsters smashed their heads against the glass again. This time a web of cracks appeared. The blue hieroglyphs flickered and died.

'AGH!' Khufu screamed. He waved his hand vaguely at the cat.

'Maybe if I try the *ha-di* spell,' I said.

Carter shook his head. 'You almost fainted after you blew up those doors. I don't want you passing out, or worse.'

Carter once again surprised me. He tugged a strange sword from one of Amos's wall displays. The blade had an odd crescent-moon curve and looked horribly impractical.

'You can't be serious,' I said.

'Unless—unless you've got a better idea,' he stammered, his face beading with perspiration. 'It's me, you, and the baboon against *those* things.'

I'm sure Carter was trying to be brave in his own extremely unbrave way, but he was shaking worse than I was. If anyone was going to pass out, I feared it would be him, and I didn't fancy him doing that while holding a sharp object.

Then the serpopards struck a third time, and the door shattered. We backed up to the foot of Thoth's statue as the creatures stalked into the great room. Khufu threw his basketball, which bounced harmlessly off the first monster's head. Then he launched himself at the serpopard.

'Khufu, don't!' Carter yelled.

But the baboon sank his fangs into the monster's neck. The serpopard lashed around, trying to bite him. Khufu leaped off, but the monster was quick. It used its head like a bat and smacked poor Khufu in midair, sending him straight through the shattered door, over the broken terrace, and into the void.

I wanted to sob, but there wasn't time. The serpopards came toward us. We couldn't outrun them. Carter raised his sword. I pointed my hand at the first monster and tried to speak the *ha-di* spell, but my voice stuck in my throat.

'*Mrow!*' Muffin said, more insistently. Why was the cat still nestled in my arm and not running away in terror?

Then I remembered something Amos had said: *Muffin will protect you.* Was that what Khufu had been trying to remind me? It seemed impossible, but I stammered, 'M-muffin, I order you to protect us.'

I tossed her on the floor. Just for a moment, the silver pendant on her collar seemed to gleam. Then the cat arched her back leisurely, sat down, and began licking a front paw. Well, really, what was I expecting—heroics?

The two red-eyed monsters bared their fangs. They raised their heads and prepared to strike— and an explosion of dry air blasted through the room. It was so powerful, it knocked Carter and me to the floor. The serpopards stumbled and backed away.

I staggered to my feet and realized that the center of the blast had been *Muffin.* My cat was no longer there. In her place was a woman—small and lithe like a gymnast. Her jet-black hair was tied in a ponytail. She wore a skintight leopard-skin jumpsuit and Muffin's pendant around her neck.

She turned and grinned at me, and her eyes were still Muffin's—yellow with black feline pupils. 'About time,' she chided.

The serpopards got over their shock and charged the cat woman. Their heads struck with lightning speed. They should've ripped her in two, but the cat lady leaped straight up, flipping three times, and landed above them, perched on the

105

mantel.

She flexed her wrists, and two enormous knives shot from her sleeves into her hands. '*A-a-ah*, fun!'

The monsters charged. She launched herself between them, dancing and dodging with incredible grace, letting them lash at her futilely while she threaded their necks together. When she stepped away, the serpopards were hopelessly intertwined. The more they struggled, the tighter the knots became. They trampled back and forth, knocking over furniture and roaring in frustration.

'Poor things,' the cat woman purred. 'Let me help.'

Her knives flashed, and the two monsters' heads thudded to the floor at her feet. Their bodies collapsed and dissolved into enormous piles of sand.

'So much for my playthings,' the woman said sadly. 'From sand they come, and to sand they return.'

She turned towards us, and the knives shot back into her sleeves. 'Carter, Sadie, we should leave. Worse will be coming.'

Carter made a choking sound. '*Worse?* Who— how—what—'

'All in good time.' The woman stretched her arms above her head with great satisfaction. 'So good to be in human form again! Now, Sadie, can you open us a door through the Duat, please?'

I blinked. 'Um . . . no. I mean—I don't know how.'

The woman narrowed her eyes, clearly disappointed. 'Shame. We'll need more power, then. An obelisk.'

'But that's in London,' I protested. 'We can't—'

'There's a nearer one in Central Park. I try to avoid Manhattan, but this is an emergency. We'll just pop over and open a portal.'

'A portal to where?' I demanded. 'Who are you, and why are you my cat?'

The woman smiled. 'For now, we just want a portal out of danger. As for my name, it's *not* Muffin, thank you very much. It's—'

'Bast,' Carter interrupted. 'Your pendant—it's the symbol of Bast, goddess of cats. I thought it was just decoration but . . . that's you, isn't it?'

'Very good, Carter,' Bast said. 'Now come, while we can still make it out of here alive.'

9.

WE RUN FROM FOUR GUYS IN SKIRTS

CARTER

So, yeah. Our cat was a goddess.

What else is new?

She didn't give us much time to talk about it. She ordered me to the library to grab my dad's magic kit, and when I came back she was arguing with Sadie about Khufu and Philip.

'We have to search for them!' Sadie insisted.

'They'll be fine,' said Bast. 'However, *we* will not be, unless we leave now.'

I raised my hand. '*Um,* excuse me, Miss Goddess Lady? Amos told us the house was—'

'Safe?' Bast snorted. 'Carter, the defenses were too easily breached. Someone *sabotaged* them.'

'What do you mean? Who—'

'Only a magician of the House could've done it.'

'Another magician?' I asked. 'Why would another magician want to sabotage Amos's house?'

'Oh, Carter,' Bast sighed. 'So young, so innocent. Magicians are devious creatures. Could be a million reasons why one would backstab another, but we don't have time to discuss it. Now, come on!'

She grabbed our arms and led us out the front door. She'd sheathed her knives, but she still had some wicked sharp claws for fingernails that hurt as they dug into my skin. As soon as we stepped outside, the cold wind stung my eyes. We climbed down a long flight of metal stairs into the industrial yard that surrounded the factory.

Dad's workbag was heavy on my shoulder. The curved sword I'd strapped across my back felt cold against my thin linen clothes. I'd started to sweat during the serpopard attack, and now my perspiration felt like it was turning to ice.

I looked around for more monsters, but the yard seemed abandoned. Old construction equipment lay in rusting heaps—a bulldozer, a crane with a wrecking ball, a couple of cement mixers. Piles of sheet metal and stacks of crates made a maze of obstacles between the house and the street a few hundred yards away.

We were about halfway across the yard when an old gray tomcat stepped in our path. One of his ears was torn. His left eye was swollen shut. Judging from his scars, he'd spent most of his life fighting.

Bast crouched and stared at the cat. He looked up at her calmly.

'Thank you,' Bast said.

The old tomcat trotted off toward the river.

'What was that about?' Sadie asked.

'One of my subjects, offering help. He'll spread the news about our predicament. Soon every cat in New York will be on alert.'

'He was so battered,' Sadie said. 'If he's your subject, couldn't you heal him?'

'And take away his marks of honor? A cat's battle scars are part of his identity. I couldn't—' Suddenly Bast tensed. She dragged us behind a stack of crates.

'What is it?' I whispered.

She flexed her wrists and her knives slid into her hands. She peeped over the top of the crates, every muscle in her body trembling. I tried to see what she was looking at, but there was nothing except the old wrecking-ball crane.

Bast's mouth twitched with excitement. Her eyes were fixed on the huge metal ball. I'd seen kittens look like that when they stalked catnip toy mice, or pieces of string, or rubber balls. . . . Balls? No. Bast was an ancient goddess. Surely she wouldn't—

'This could be it.' She shifted her weight. 'Stay very *very* still.'

'There's no one there,' Sadie hissed.

I started to say, '*Um* . . .'

Bast lunged over the crates. She flew thirty feet through the air, knives flashing, and landed on the wrecking ball with such force that she broke the chain. The cat goddess and the huge metal sphere smashed into the dirt and went rolling across the yard.

'*Rowww!*' Bast wailed. The wrecking ball rolled straight over her, but she didn't appear hurt. She

109

leaped off and pounced again. Her knives sliced through the metal like wet clay. Within seconds, the wrecking ball was reduced to a mound of scraps.

Bast sheathed her blades. 'Safe now!'

Sadie and I looked at each other.

'You saved us from a metal ball,' Sadie said.

'You never know,' Bast said. 'It could've been hostile.'

Just then a deep *boom!* shook the ground. I looked back at the mansion. Tendrils of blue fire curled from the top windows.

'Come on,' Bast said. 'Our time is up!'

*　　　*　　　*

I thought maybe she'd whisk us off by magic, or at least hail a taxi. Instead, Bast borrowed a silver Lexus convertible.

'Oh, yes,' she purred. 'I like this one! Come along, children.'

'But this isn't yours,' I pointed out.

'My dear, I'm a cat. Everything I *see* is mine.' She touched the ignition and the keyhole sparked. The engine began to purr. [No, Sadie. Not like a cat, like an engine.]

'Bast,' I said, 'you can't just—'

Sadie elbowed me. 'We'll work out how to return it later, Carter. Right now we've got an emergency.'

She pointed back toward the mansion. Blue flames and smoke now billowed from every window. But that wasn't the scary part—coming down the stairs were four men carrying a large box, like an oversize coffin with long handles sticking out at both ends. The box was covered with a black shroud and looked big enough for at least two bodies. The four men wore only kilts and sandals. Their coppery skin glinted in the sun as if made of metal.

'Oh, that's bad,' Bast said. 'In the car, please.'

I decided not to ask questions. Sadie beat me to the shotgun seat so I climbed in back. The four metallic guys with the box were racing across the yard, coming straight for us at an unbelievable speed. Before I even had my seat belt on, Bast hit the gas.

We tore through the streets of Brooklyn, weaving insanely through traffic, riding over sidewalks, narrowly missing pedestrians.

Bast drove with reflexes that were . . . well, catlike. Any human trying to drive so fast would've had a dozen wrecks, but she got us safely onto the Williamsburg Bridge.

I thought for sure we must've lost our pursuers, but when I looked back, the four copper men with the black box were weaving in and out of traffic. They appeared to be jogging at a normal pace, but they passed cars that were doing fifty. Their bodies blurred like choppy images in an old movie, as if they were out of sync with the regular stream of time.

'What *are* they?' I asked. *'Shabti?'*

'No, carriers.' Bast glanced in the rearview mirror. 'Summoned straight from the Duat. They'll stop at nothing to find their victims, throw them in the sedan—'

'The what?' Sadie interrupted.

'The large box,' Bast said. 'It's a kind of carriage. The carriers capture you, beat you

111

senseless, throw you in, and carry you back to their master. They never lose their prey, and they never give up.'

'But what do they want us for?'

'Trust me,' Bast growled, 'you don't want to know.'

I thought about the fiery man last night in Phoenix—how he'd fried one of his servants into a grease spot. I was pretty sure I didn't want to meet him face-to-face again.

'Bast,' I said, 'if you're a goddess, can't you just snap your fingers and disintegrate those guys? Or wave your hand and teleport us away?'

'Wouldn't that be nice? But my power in this host is limited.'

'You mean Muffin?' Sadie asked. 'But you're not a cat anymore.'

'She's still my host, Sadie, my anchor on this side of the Duat—and a very imperfect one. Your call for help allowed me to assume human shape, but that alone takes a great deal of power. Besides, even when I'm in a *powerful* host, Set's magic is stronger than mine.'

'Could you please say something I actually understand?' I pleaded.

'Carter, we don't have time for a full discussion on gods and hosts and the limits of magic! We have to get you to safety.'

Bast floored the accelerator and shot up the middle of the bridge. The four carriers with the sedan raced after us, blurring the air as they moved, but no cars swerved to avoid them. No one panicked or even looked at them.

'How can people not see them?' I said. 'Don't they notice four copper men in skirts running up the bridge with a weird black box?'

Bast shrugged. 'Cats can hear many sounds you can't. Some animals see things in the ultraviolet spectrum that are invisible to humans. Magic is similar. Did you notice the mansion when you first arrived?'

'Well . . . no.'

'And you are born to magic,' Bast said. 'Imagine how hard it would be for a regular mortal.'

'Born to magic?' I remembered what Amos had said about our family being in the House of Life for a long time. 'If magic, like, runs in the family, why haven't I ever been able to do it before?'

Bast smiled in the mirror. 'Your sister understands.'

Sadie's ears turned red. 'No, I don't! I still can't believe you're a *goddess*. All these years, you've been eating crunchy treats, sleeping on my head—'

'I made a deal with your father,' Bast said. 'He let me remain in the world as long as I assumed a minor form, a normal housecat, so I could protect and watch over you. It was the least I could do after—' She stopped abruptly.

A horrible thought occurred to me. My stomach fluttered, and it had nothing to do with how fast we were going. 'After our mom's death?' I guessed.

Bast stared straight ahead out the windshield.

'That's it, isn't it?' I said. 'Dad and Mom did some kind of magic ritual at Cleopatra's Needle. Something went wrong. Our mom died and . . . and they released you?'

'That's not important right now,' Bast said. 'The point is I agreed to look after Sadie. And I will.'

She was hiding something. I was sure of it, but her tone made it clear that the subject was closed.

'If you gods are so powerful and helpful,' I said, 'why does the House of Life forbid magicians from summoning you?'

Bast swerved into the fast lane. 'Magicians are paranoid. Your best hope is to stay with me. We'll get as far away as possible from New York. Then we'll get help and challenge Set.'

'What help?' Sadie asked.

Bast raised an eyebrow. 'Why, we'll summon more gods, of course.'

10.
BAST GOES GREEN

CARTER

[Sadie, stop it! Yeah, I'm getting to that part.] Sorry, she keeps trying to distract me by setting fire to my—never mind. Where was I?

We barreled off the Williamsburg Bridge into Manhattan and headed north on Clinton Street.

'They're still following,' Sadie warned.

Sure enough, the carriers were only a block behind us, weaving around cars and trampling over sidewalk displays of tourist junk.

'We'll buy some time.' Bast growled deep in her throat—a sound so low and powerful it made my teeth buzz. She yanked the wheel and swerved right onto East Houston.

I looked back. Just as the carriers turned the corner, a horde of cats materialized all around them. Some jumped from windows. Some ran from the sidewalks and alleys. Some crawled from the

114

storm drains. All of them converged on the carriers in a wave of fur and claws—climbing up their copper legs, scratching their backs, clinging to their faces, and weighing down the sedan box. The carriers stumbled, dropping the box. They began blindly swatting at the cats. Two cars swerved to avoid the animals and collided, blocking the entire street, and the carriers went down under the mass of angry felines. We turned onto the FDR Drive, and the scene disappeared from view.

'Nice,' I admitted.

'It won't hold them long,' Bast said. 'Now—Central Park!'

*   *   *

Bast ditched the Lexus at the Metropolitan Museum of Art.

'We'll run from here,' she said. 'It's just behind the museum.'

When she said run, she meant it. Sadie and I had to sprint to keep up, and Bast wasn't even breaking a sweat. She didn't stop for little things like hot dog stands or parked cars. Anything under ten feet tall she leaped over with ease, leaving us to scramble around the obstacles as best we could.

We ran into the park on the East Drive. As soon as we turned north, the obelisk loomed above us. A little over seventy feet tall, it looked like an exact copy of the needle in London. It was tucked away on a grassy hill, so it actually felt isolated, which is hard to achieve in the center of New York. There was no one around except a couple of joggers farther down the path. I could hear the traffic behind us on Fifth Avenue, but even that seemed far away.

We stopped at the obelisk's base. Bast sniffed the air as if smelling for trouble. Once I was standing still, I realized just how cold I was. The sun was directly overhead, but the wind ripped right through my borrowed linen clothes.

'I wish I'd grabbed something warmer,' I muttered. 'A wool coat would be nice.'

'No, it wouldn't,' Bast said, scanning the horizon. 'You're dressed for magic.'

Sadie shivered. 'We have to freeze to be magical?'

'Magicians avoid animal products,' Bast said absently. 'Fur, leather, wool, any of that. The residual life aura can interfere with spells.'

'My boots seem all right,' Sadie noted.

'Leather,' Bast said with distaste. 'You may have a higher tolerance, so a bit of leather won't bother your magic. I don't know. But linen clothing is always best, or cotton—plant material. At any rate, Sadie, I think we're clear for the moment. There's a window of auspicious time starting right now, at eleven thirty, but it won't last long. Get started.'

Sadie blinked. 'Me? Why me? You're the goddess!'

'I'm not good at portals,' Bast said. 'Cats are protectors. Just control your emotions. Panic or fear will kill a spell. We *have* to get out of here before Set summons the other gods to his cause.'

I frowned. 'You mean Set's got, like, other evil gods on speed dial?'

Bast glanced nervously toward the trees. 'Evil and good may not be the best way to think of it, Carter. As a magician, you must think about chaos

116

and order. *Those* are the two forces that control the universe. Set is all about chaos.'

'But what about the other gods Dad released?' I persisted. 'Aren't they good guys? Isis, Osiris, Horus, Nephthys—where are they?'

Bast fixed her eyes on me. 'That's a good question, Carter.'

A Siamese cat broke through the bushes and ran up to Bast. They looked at each other for a moment. Then the Siamese dashed away.

'The carriers are close,' Bast announced. 'And something else . . . something much stronger, closing in from the east. I think the carriers' master has grown impatient.'

My heart did a flip. '*Set* is coming?'

'No,' Bast said. 'Perhaps a minion. Or an ally. My cats are having trouble describing what they're seeing, and I *don't* want to find out. Sadie, now is the time. Just concentrate on opening a gateway to the Duat. I'll keep off the attackers. Combat magic is my specialty.'

'Like what you did in the mansion?' I asked.

Bast showed her pointed teeth. 'No, that was just combat.'

The woods rustled, and the carriers emerged. Their sedan chair's shroud had been shredded by cat claws. The carriers themselves were scratched and dented. One walked with a limp, his leg bent backward at the knee. Another had a car fender wrapped around his neck.

The four metal men carefully set down their sedan chair. They looked at us and drew golden metal clubs from their belts.

'Sadie, get to work,' Bast ordered. 'Carter, you're welcome to help me.'

The cat goddess unsheathed her knives. Her body began to glow with a green hue. An aura surrounded her, growing larger, like a bubble of energy, and lifting her off the ground. The aura took shape until Bast was encased in a holographic projection about four times her normal size. It was an image of the goddess in her ancient form—a twenty-foot-tall woman with the head of a cat. Floating in midair in the center of the hologram, Bast stepped forward. The giant cat goddess moved with her. It didn't seem possible that a see-through image could have substance, but its foot shook the ground. Bast raised her hand. The glowing green warrior did the same, unsheathing claws as long and sharp as rapiers. Bast swiped the sidewalk in front of her and shredded the pavement to concrete ribbons. She turned and smiled at me. The giant cat's head did likewise, baring horrible fangs that could've bitten me in half.

'*This,*' Bast said, 'is combat magic.'

At first I was too stunned to do anything but watch as Bast launched her green war machine into the middle of the carriers.

She slashed one carrier to pieces with a single swipe, then stepped on another and flattened him into a metal pancake. The other two carriers attacked her holographic legs, but their metal clubs bounced harmlessly off the ghostly light with showers of sparks.

Meanwhile Sadie stood in front of the obelisk with her arms raised, shouting: 'Open, you stupid piece of rock!'

Finally I drew my sword. My hands were shaking. I didn't want to charge into battle, but I felt like I should help. And if I *had* to fight, I figured having a twenty-foot-tall glowing cat warrior on my side was the way to do it. 'Sadie, I—I'm going to help Bast. Keep trying!'

'I *am*!'

I ran forward just as Bast sliced the other two carriers apart like loaves of bread. With relief, I thought: *Well, that's it.*

Then all four carriers began to reform. The flat one peeled himself off the pavement. The sliced ones' pieces clicked together like magnets, and the carriers stood up good as new.

'Carter, help me hack them apart!' Bast called. 'They need to be in smaller pieces!'

I tried to stay out of Bast's way as she sliced and stomped. Then as soon as she disabled a carrier, I went to work chopping its remains into smaller pieces. They seemed more like Play-Doh than metal, because my blade mashed them up pretty easily.

Another few minutes and I was surrounded by piles of coppery rubble. Bast made a glowing fist and smashed the sedan into kindling.

'That wasn't so hard,' I said. 'What were we running for?'

Inside her glowing shell, Bast's face was coated with sweat. It hadn't occurred to me that a goddess could get tired, but her magic avatar must've taken a lot of effort.

'We're not safe yet,' she warned. 'Sadie, how's it coming?'

'It's not,' Sadie complained. 'Isn't there another way?'

Before Bast could answer, the bushes rustled with a new sound—like rain, except more *slithery*.

A chill ran up my back. 'What . . . what is that?'

'No,' Bast murmured. 'It can't be. Not her.'

Then the bushes exploded. A thousand brown creepy-crawlies poured from the woods in a carpet of grossness—all pincers and stinging tails.

I wanted to yell, 'Scorpions!' But my voice wouldn't work. My legs started trembling. I *hate* scorpions. They're everywhere in Egypt. Many times I'd found them in my hotel bed or shower. Once I'd even found one in my sock.

'Sadie!' Bast called urgently.

'Nothing!' Sadie moaned.

The scorpions kept coming—thousands upon thousands. Out of the woods a woman appeared, walking fearlessly through the middle of the arachnids. She wore brown robes with gold jewelry glinting around her neck and arms. Her long black hair was cut Ancient Egyptian–style with a strange crown on top. Then I realized it wasn't a crown— she had a live, supersize scorpion nesting on her head. Millions of the little nasties swirled around her like she was the center of their storm.

'Serqet,' Bast growled.

'The scorpion goddess,' I guessed. Maybe that should've terrified me, but I was already pretty much at my maximum. 'Can you take her?'

Bast's expression didn't reassure me.

'Carter, Sadie,' she said, 'this is going to get ugly. Get to the museum. Find the temple. It may protect you.'

'What temple?' I asked.

'And what about you?' Sadie added.

'I'll be fine. I'll catch up.' But when Bast looked at me, I could tell she wasn't sure. She was just buying us time.

'Go!' she ordered. She turned her giant green cat warrior to face the mass of scorpions.

Embarrassing truth? In the face of those scorpions, I didn't even pretend to be brave. I grabbed Sadie's arm and we ran.

11.
WE MEET THE HUMAN FLAMETHROWER

S A D I E

Right, I'm taking the microphone. There is *no chance* Carter would tell this part properly, as it's about Zia. [Shut up, Carter. You know it's true.]

Oh, who is Zia? Sorry, getting ahead of myself.

We raced to the entrance of the museum, and I had no idea why, except that a giant glowing cat woman had told us to. Now, you must realize I was already devastated by everything that had happened. First, I'd lost my father. Second, my loving grandparents had kicked me out of the flat. Then I'd discovered I was apparently 'blood of the pharaohs,' born to a magical family, and all sorts of rubbish that sounded quite impressive but only brought me loads of trouble. And as soon as I'd found a new home—a mansion with proper breakfast and friendly pets and quite a nice room for me, by the way—Uncle Amos disappeared, my lovely new crocodile and baboon friends were tossed in a river, and the mansion was set on fire. And if *that* wasn't enough, my faithful cat Muffin had decided to engage in a hopeless battle with a swarm of scorpions.

Do you call it a 'swarm' for scorpions? A herd? A gaggle? Oh, never mind.

The point is I couldn't believe I'd been asked to open a magic doorway when clearly I had no such skill, and now my brother was dragging me away. I felt like an utter failure. [And no comments from you, Carter. As I recall, *you* weren't much help at the time, either.]

'We can't just leave Bast!' I shouted. 'Look!'

Carter kept running, dragging me along, but I could see quite clearly what was happening back at the obelisk. A mass of scorpions had crawled up Bast's glowing green legs and were wriggling into the hologram like it was gelatin. Bast smashed hundreds of them with her feet and fists, but there were simply too many. Soon they were up to her waist, and her ghostly shell began to flicker. Meanwhile, the brown-robed goddess advanced slowly, and I had a feeling she would be worse than any number of scorpions.

Carter pulled me through a row of bushes and I lost sight of Bast. We burst onto Fifth Avenue, which seemed ridiculously normal after the magic battle. We ran down the sidewalk, shoved through a knot of pedestrians, and climbed the steps of the Met.

A banner above the entrance announced some sort of special Christmas event, which I suppose is why the museum was open on a holiday, but I didn't bother reading the details. We pushed straight inside.

What did it look like? Well, it was a museum: huge entry hall, lots of columns and so on. I can't claim I spent much time admiring the decor. I do remember it had queues for the ticket windows, because we ran right past them. There were also security guards, because they yelled at us as we dashed into the exhibits. By luck, we ended up in the Egyptian area, in front of a reconstructed tomb sort of place with narrow corridors. Carter probably could've told you what the structure was supposed to be, but honestly I didn't care.

'Come on,' I said.

We slipped inside the exhibit, which proved quite enough to lose the security guards, or perhaps they had better things to do than pursue naughty children.

When we popped out again, we sneaked around until we were sure we weren't being followed. The Egypt wing wasn't crowded—just a few clumps of old people and a foreign tour group with a guide explaining a sarcophagus in French. *'Et voici la momie!'*

Strangely, no one seemed to notice the enormous sword on Carter's back, which surely must've been a security issue (and much more interesting than the exhibits). A few old people did give us odd looks, but I suspect that was because we were dressed in linen pajamas, drenched in sweat, and covered in grass and leaves. My hair was probably a nightmare as well.

I found an empty room and pulled Carter aside. The glass cases were full of *shabti*. A few days earlier I wouldn't have given them a second thought. Now, I kept glancing at the statues, sure they'd come to life any minute and try to bash me on the head.

'What now?' I asked Carter. 'Did you see any temple?'

'No.' He knit his eyebrows as if trying hard to

123

remember. 'I think there's a rebuilt temple down that hall . . . or is that in the Brooklyn Museum? Maybe the one in Munich? Sorry, I've been to so many museums with Dad that they all get mixed together.'

I sighed in exasperation. 'Poor boy, forced to travel the world, skip school, and spend time with Dad while I get a whole two days a year with him!'

'Hey!' Carter turned on me with surprising force. 'You get a *home*! You get friends and a normal life and don't wake up each morning wondering what country you're in! You don't—'

The glass case next to us shattered, spraying glass at our feet.

Carter looked at me, bewildered. 'Did we just—'

'Like my exploding birthday cake,' I grumbled, trying not to let on how startled I was. 'You need to control your temper.'

'*Me?*'

Alarms began to blare. Red lights pulsed through the corridor. A garbled voice came on the loudspeaker and said something about proceeding calmly to the exits. The French tour group ran past us, screaming in panic, followed by a crowd of remarkably fast old people with walkers and canes.

'Let's finish arguing later, shall we?' I told Carter. 'Come on!'

We ran down another corridor, and the sirens died as suddenly as they'd started. The blood-red lights kept pulsing in eerie silence. Then I heard it: the slithering, clacking sounds of scorpions.

'What about Bast?' My voice choked up. 'Is she—'

'Don't think about it,' Carter said, though, judging from his face, that's *exactly* what he was

124

thinking about. 'Keep moving!'

*   *   *

Soon we were hopelessly lost. As far as I could tell, the Egyptian part of the museum was designed to be as confusing as possible, with dead ends and halls that doubled back on themselves. We passed hieroglyphic scrolls, gold jewelry, sarcophagi, statues of pharaohs, and huge chunks of limestone. Why would someone display a rock? Aren't there enough of those in the world?

We saw no one, but the slithering sounds grew louder no matter which way we ran. Finally I rounded a corner and smacked straight into someone.

I yelped and scrambled backwards, only to stumble into Carter. We both fell on our bums in a most unflattering way. It's a miracle Carter didn't impale himself on his own sword.

At first I didn't recognize the girl standing in front of us, which seems strange, looking back on it. Perhaps she was using some sort of magic aura, or perhaps I just didn't want to believe it was *her.*

She looked a bit taller than me. Probably older, too, but not by much. Her black hair was trimmed along her jawline and longer in the front so that it swept over her eyes. She had caramel-colored skin and pretty, vaguely Arab features. Her eyes—lined in black kohl, Egyptian style—were a strange amber color that was either quite beautiful or a bit scary; I couldn't decide which. She had a backpack on her shoulder, and wore sandals and loose-fitting linen clothes like ours. She looked as if she were on her way to a martial arts class. God, now that I think of it, we probably looked the same way. How embarrassing.

I slowly began to realize I'd seen her before. She was the girl with the knife from the British Museum. Before I could say anything, Carter sprang to his feet. He moved in front of me and brandished his sword as if trying to *protect* me. Can you believe the nerve?

'Get—get back!' he stammered.

The girl reached into her sleeve and produced a curved white piece of ivory—an Egyptian wand.

She flicked it to one side, and Carter's sword flew out of his hands and clattered to the floor.

'Don't embarrass yourself,' the girl said sternly. 'Where is Amos?'

Carter looked too stunned to speak. The girl turned towards me. Her golden eyes were both beautiful *and* scary, I decided, and I didn't like her a bit.

'Well?' she demanded.

I didn't see why I needed to tell her a bloody thing, but an uncomfortable pressure started building in my chest, like a burp trying to get free. I heard myself say, 'Amos is gone. He left this morning.'

'And the cat demon?'

'That's *my* cat,' I said. 'And she's a goddess, not a demon. She saved us from the scorpions!'

Carter unfroze. He snatched up his sword and pointed it at the girl again. Full credit for persistence, I suppose.

'Who are you?' he demanded. 'What do you want?'

'My name is Zia Rashid.' She tilted her head as if listening.

Right on cue, the entire building rumbled. Dust sprinkled from the ceiling, and the slithering sounds of scorpions doubled in volume behind us.

'And right now,' Zia continued, sounding a bit disappointed, 'I must save your miserable lives. Let's go.'

*　　　*　　　*

I suppose we could've refused, but our choices seemed to be Zia or the scorpions, so we ran after her.

She passed a case full of statues and casually tapped the glass with her wand. Tiny granite pharaohs and limestone gods stirred at her command. They hopped off their pedestals and crashed through the glass. Some wielded weapons. Others simply cracked their stone knuckles. They let us pass, but stared down the corridor behind us as if waiting for the enemy.

'Hurry,' Zia told us. 'These will only—'

'Buy us time,' I guessed. 'Yes, we've heard that before.'

'You talk too much,' Zia said without stopping.

I was about to make a withering retort. Honestly, I would've put her in her place quite properly. But just then we emerged into an enormous room and my voice abandoned me.

'Whoa,' Carter said.

I couldn't help agreeing with him. The place was extremely *whoa*.

The room was the size of a football stadium. One wall was made completely of glass and looked out on the park. In the middle of the room, on a raised platform, an ancient building had been reconstructed. There was a freestanding stone gateway about eight meters tall, and behind that an open courtyard and square structure made of uneven sandstone blocks carved all over on the outside with images of gods and pharaohs and hieroglyphs. Flanking the building's entrance were two columns bathed in eerie light.

'An Egyptian temple,' I guessed.

'The Temple of Dendur,' Zia said. 'Actually it was built by the Romans—'

'When they occupied Egypt,' Carter said, like this was delightful information. 'Augustus commissioned it.'

'Yes,' Zia said.

'Fascinating,' I murmured. 'Would you two like to be left alone with a history textbook?'

Zia scowled at me. 'At any rate, the temple was dedicated to Isis, so it will have enough power to open a gate.'

'To summon more gods?' I asked.

Zia's eyes flashed angrily. 'Accuse me of that again, and I will cut out your tongue. I meant a gateway to get you out of here.'

I felt completely lost, but I was getting used to that. We followed Zia up the steps and through the temple's stone gateway.

The courtyard was empty, abandoned by the fleeing museum visitors, which made it feel quite creepy. Giant carvings of gods stared down at me. Hieroglyphic inscriptions were everywhere, and I was afraid that if I concentrated too hard, I might be able to read them.

Zia stopped at the front steps of the temple. She held up her wand and wrote in the air. A familiar hieroglyph burned between the columns.

Open—the same symbol Dad had used at the Rosetta Stone. I waited for something to blow up, but the hieroglyph simply faded.

Zia opened her backpack. 'We'll make our stand here until the gate can be opened.'

'Why not just open it now?' Carter asked.

'Portals can only appear at auspicious moments,' Zia said. 'Sunrise, sunset, midnight, eclipses, astrological alignments, the exact time of a god's birth—'

'Oh, come on,' I said. 'How can you possibly know all that?'

'It takes years to memorize the complete calendar,' Zia said. 'But the next auspicious moment is easy: high noon. Ten and a half minutes from now.'

She didn't check a watch. I wondered how she knew the time so precisely, but I decided it wasn't the most important question.

'Why should we trust you?' I asked. 'As I recall, at the British Museum, you wanted to gut us with a knife.'

'That would've been simpler.' Zia sighed. 'Unfortunately, my superiors think you might be *innocents*. So for now, I can't kill you. But I also can't allow you to fall into the hands of the Red Lord. And so . . . you can trust me.'

'Well, I'm convinced,' I said. 'I feel all warm and fuzzy inside.'

Zia reached in her bag and took out four little statues—animal-headed men, each about five centimeters tall. She handed them to me. 'Put the Sons of Horus around us at the cardinal points.'

'Excuse me?'

'North, south, east, west.' She spoke slowly, as if

I were an idiot.

'I know compass directions! But—'

'That's north.' Zia pointed out the wall of glass. 'Figure out the rest.'

I did what she asked, though I didn't see how the little men would help. Meanwhile, Zia gave Carter a piece of chalk and told him to draw a circle around us, connecting the statues.

'Magic protection,' Carter said. 'Like what Dad did at the British Museum.'

'Yes,' I grumbled. 'And we saw how well *that* worked.'

Carter ignored me. What else is new? He was so eager to please Zia that he jumped right to the task of drawing his sidewalk art.

Then Zia took something else from her bag—a plain wooden rod like the one our dad had used in London. She spoke a word under her breath, and the rod expanded into a two-meter-long black staff topped with a carved lion's head. She twirled it around single-handedly like a baton—just showing off, I was sure—while holding the wand in her other hand.

Carter finished the chalk circle as the first scorpions appeared at the gallery's entrance.

'How much longer on that gate?' I asked, hoping I didn't sound as terrified as I felt.

'Stay inside the circle no matter what,' Zia said. 'When the gate opens, jump through. And keep behind me!'

She touched her wand to the chalk circle, spoke another word, and the circle began to glow dark red.

Hundreds of scorpions swarmed towards the temple, turning the floor into a living mass of claws

130

and stingers. Then the woman in brown, Serqet, entered the gallery. She smiled at us coldly.

'Zia,' I said, 'that's a goddess. She defeated *Bast.* What chance do *you* have?'

Zia held up her staff and the carved lion's head burst into flames—a small red fireball so bright, it lit the entire room. 'I am a scribe in the House of Life, Sadie Kane. I am trained to fight gods.'

12.

A JUMP THROUGH THE HOURGLASS

S A D I E

Well, that was all very impressive, I suppose. You should've seen Carter's face—he looked like an excited puppy. [Oh, stop shoving me. You did!]

But I felt much less sure of Miss Zia 'I'm-So-Magical' Rashid when the army of scorpions scuttled towards us. I wouldn't have thought it possible so many scorpions existed in the world, much less in midtown Manhattan. The glowing circle round us seemed like insignificant protection against the millions of arachnids crawling over one another, many layers deep, and the woman in brown, who was even more horrible.

From a distance she looked all right, but as she got closer I saw that Serqet's pale skin glistened like an insect shell. Her eyes were beady black. Her long, dark hair was unnaturally thick, as if made from a million bristling bug antennae. And when she opened her mouth, sideways mandibles snapped and retracted outside her regular human teeth.

The goddess stopped about twenty meters away, studying us. Her hateful black eyes fixed on Zia. 'Give me the younglings.'

Her voice was harsh and raspy, as if she hadn't spoken in centuries.

Zia crossed her staff and wand. 'I am mistress of the elements, Scribe of the First Nome. Leave or be destroyed.'

Serqet clicked her mandibles in a gruesome foamy grin. Some of her scorpions advanced, but when the first one touched the glowing lines of our protective circle, it sizzled and turned to ashes. Mark my words, *nothing* smells worse than burned scorpion.

The rest of the horrible things retreated, swirling round the goddess and crawling up her legs. With a shudder, I realized they were wriggling into her robes. After a few seconds, all the scorpions had disappeared into the brown folds of her clothes.

The air seemed to darken behind Serqet, as if she were casting an enormous shadow. Then the darkness rose up and took the form of a massive scorpion tail, arcing over Serqet's head. It lashed down at us at blazing speed, but Zia raised her wand and the sting glanced off the ivory tip with a hissing sound. Steam rolled off Zia's wand, smelling of sulfur.

Zia pointed her staff towards the goddess, engulfing her body in fire. Serqet screamed and staggered backwards, but the fire died almost instantly. It left Serqet's robes seared and smoking, but the goddess looked more enraged than hurt.

'Your days are past, magician. The House is

weak. Lord Set will lay waste to this land.'

Zia threw her wand like a boomerang. It smashed into the shadowy scorpion tail and exploded in a blinding flash of light. Serqet lurched back and averted her eyes, and as she did, Zia reached into her sleeve and brought out something small—something closed inside her fist.

The wand was a diversion, I thought. *A magician's sleight of hand.*

Then Zia did something reckless: she leaped out of the magic circle—the very thing she'd warned us not to do.

'Zia!' Carter called. 'The gate!'

I glanced behind me, and my heart almost stopped. The space between the two columns at the temple's entrance was now a vertical tunnel of sand, as if I were looking into the funnel of an enormous sideways hourglass. I could feel it tugging at me, pulling me towards it with magical gravity.

'I'm not going in *there*,' I insisted, but another flash of light brought my attention back to Zia.

She and the goddess were involved in a dangerous dance. Zia twirled and spun with her fiery staff, and everywhere she passed, she left a trail of flames burning in the air. I had to admit it: Zia was almost as graceful and impressive as Bast.

I had the oddest desire to help. I wanted—very badly, in fact—to step outside the circle and engage in combat. It was a completely mad urge, of course. What could I possibly have done? But still I felt I shouldn't—or *couldn't*—jump through the gate without helping Zia.

'Sadie!' Carter grabbed me and pulled me back. Without my even realizing it, my foot had almost stepped across the line of chalk. 'What are you thinking?'

I didn't have an answer, but I stared at Zia and mumbled in a sort of trance, 'She's going to use ribbons. They won't work.'

'What?' Carter demanded. 'Come on, we've got to go through the gate!'

Just then Zia opened her fist and small red tendrils of cloth fluttered into the air. *Ribbons.* How had I known? They zipped about like living things—like eels in water—and began to grow larger.

Serqet was still concentrating on the fire, trying to keep Zia from caging her. At first she didn't seem to notice the ribbons, which grew until they were several meters long. I counted five, six, seven of them in all. They zipped around, orbiting Serqet, ripping through her shadow scorpion as if it were a harmless illusion. Finally they wrapped around Serqet's body, pinning her arms and legs. She screamed as if the ribbons burned her. She dropped to her knees, and the shadow scorpion disintegrated into an inky haze.

Zia spun to a stop. She pointed her staff at the goddess's face. The ribbons began to glow, and the goddess hissed in pain, cursing in a language I didn't know.

'I bind you with the Seven Ribbons of Hathor,' Zia said. 'Release your host or your essence will burn forever.'

'Your *death* will last forever!' Serqet snarled. 'You have made an enemy of Set!'

Zia twisted her staff, and Serqet fell sideways, writhing and smoking.

'I will . . . not . . .' the goddess hissed. But then

134

her black eyes turned milky white, and she lay still.

'The gate!' Carter warned. 'Zia, come on! I think it's closing!'

He was right. The tunnel of sand seemed to be moving a bit more slowly. The tug of its magic did not feel as strong.

Zia approached the fallen goddess. She touched Serqet's forehead, and black smoke billowed from the goddess's mouth. Serqet transformed and shrank until we were looking at a completely different woman wrapped in red ribbons. She had pale skin and black hair, but otherwise she didn't look anything like Serqet. She looked, well, *human*.

'Who is that?' I asked.

'The host,' Zia said. 'Some poor mortal who—'

She looked up with a start. The black haze was no longer dissipating. It was getting thicker and darker again, swirling into a more solid form.

'Impossible,' Zia said. 'The ribbons are too powerful. Serqet *can't* re-form unless—'

'Well, she *is* re-forming,' Carter yelled, 'and our exit is closing! Let's go!'

I couldn't believe he was willing to jump into a churning wall of sand, but as I watched the black cloud take the shape of a two-story-tall scorpion— a very *angry* scorpion—I made my decision.

'Coming!' I yelled.

'Zia!' Carter yelled. 'Now!'

'Perhaps you're right,' the magician decided. She turned, and together we ran and plunged straight into the swirling vortex.

13.
I FACE THE KILLER TURKEY

CARTER

My turn.

First of all, Sadie's 'puppy dog' comment was totally out of line. I was *not* starry-eyed about Zia. It's just that I don't meet a lot of people who can throw fireballs and battle gods. [Stop making faces at me, Sadie. You look like Khufu.]

Anyway, we plunged into the sand tunnel.

Everything went dark. My stomach tingled with that top-of-the-roller-coaster weightlessness as I hurtled forward. Hot winds whipped around me, and my skin burned.

Then I tumbled out onto a cold tile floor, and Sadie and Zia crashed on top of me.

'Ow!' I grumbled.

The first thing I noticed was the fine layer of sand covering my body like powdered sugar. Then my eyes adjusted to the harsh light. We were in a big building like a shopping mall, with crowds bustling around us.

No . . . not a mall. It was a two-level airport concourse, with shops, lots of windows, and polished steel columns. Outside, it was dark, so I knew we must be in a different time zone. Announcements echoed over the intercom in a language that sounded like Arabic.

Sadie spit sand out of her mouth. 'Yuck!'

'Come on,' Zia said. 'We can't stay here.'

I struggled to my feet. People were streaming past—some in Western clothes, some in robes and headscarves. A family arguing in German rushed by and almost ran over me with their suitcases.

Then I turned and saw something I recognized. In the middle of the concourse stood a life-size replica of an Ancient Egyptian boat made from glowing display cases—a sales counter for perfume and jewelry.

'This is the Cairo airport,' I said.

'Yes,' Zia said. 'Now, let's go!'

'Why the rush? Can Serqet . . . can she follow us through that sand gate?'

Zia shook her head. 'An artifact overheats whenever it creates a gate. It requires a twelve-hour cooldown before it can be used again. But we still have to worry about airport security. Unless you'd like to meet the Egyptian police, you'll come with me *now*.'

She grabbed our arms and steered us through the crowd. We must've looked like beggars in our old-fashioned clothes, covered head-to-toe in sand. People gave us a wide berth, but nobody tried to stop us.

'Why are we here?' Sadie demanded.

'To see the ruins of Heliopolis,' Zia said.

'Inside an *airport*?' Sadie asked.

I remembered something Dad had told me years ago, and my scalp tingled.

'Sadie, the ruins are *under* us.' I looked at Zia. 'That's right, isn't it?'

She nodded. 'The ancient city was pillaged centuries ago. Some of its monuments were carted away, like Cleopatra's two needles. Most of its temples were broken down to make new buildings. What was left disappeared under Cairo's suburbs. The largest section is under this airport.'

'And how does that help us?' Sadie asked.

Zia kicked open a maintenance door. On the other side was a broom closet. Zia muttered a command—'*Sahad*'—and the image of the closet shimmered and disappeared, revealing a set of stone steps leading down.

'Because not *all* Heliopolis is in ruins,' Zia said. 'Follow closely. And *touch nothing.*'

The stairs must've led down about seven million miles, because we descended *forever*. The passage had been made for miniature people, too. We had to crouch and crawl most of the way, and even so, I bonked my head on the ceiling a dozen times. The only light was from a ball of fire in Zia's palm, which made shadows dance across the walls.

I'd been in places like this before—tunnels inside pyramids, tombs my dad had excavated— but I've never liked them. Millions of tons of rock above me seemed to crush the air out of my lungs.

Finally we reached the bottom. The tunnel opened up, and Zia stopped abruptly. After my eyes adjusted, I saw why. We were standing at the edge of a chasm.

A single wooden plank spanned the void. On the opposite ledge, two jackal-headed granite warriors flanked a doorway, their spears crossed over the entrance.

Sadie sighed. 'Please, no more psychotic statues.'

'Do not joke,' Zia warned. 'This is an entrance to the First Nome, the oldest branch of the House of Life, headquarters for all magicians. My job was to bring you here safely, but I cannot help you cross. Each magician must unbar the path for herself, and the challenge is different for each supplicant.'

She looked at Sadie expectantly, which annoyed me. First Bast, now Zia—both of them treated Sadie like she should have some kind of superpowers. I mean, okay, so she'd been able to blast the library doors apart, but why didn't anyone look at *me* to do cool tricks?

Plus, I was still annoyed with Sadie for the comments she'd made at the museum in New York—how I had it so good traveling the world with Dad. She had no idea how often I wanted to complain about the constant traveling, how many days I wished I didn't have to get on a plane and could just be like a normal kid going to school and making friends. But I couldn't complain. *You always have to look impeccable,* Dad had told me. And he didn't just mean my clothes. He meant my attitude. With Mom gone, I was all he had. Dad needed me to be strong. Most days, I didn't mind. I loved my dad. But it was also hard.

Sadie didn't understand that. *She* had it easy. And now she seemed to be getting all the attention, as if *she* were the special one. It wasn't fair.

Then I heard Dad's voice in my head: 'Fairness means everyone gets what they need. And the only way to get what you need is to make it happen yourself.'

I don't know what got into me, but I drew my sword and marched across the plank. It was like my legs were working by themselves, not waiting for my brain. Part of me thought: *This is a really bad idea.* But part of me answered: *No, we do not fear this.* And the voice didn't sound like mine.

'Carter!' Sadie cried.

139

I kept walking. I tried not to look down at the yawning void under my feet, but the sheer size of the chasm made me dizzy. I felt like one of those gyroscope toys, spinning and wobbling as I crossed the narrow plank.

As I got closer to the opposite side, the doorway between the two statues began to glow, like a curtain of red light.

I took a deep breath. Maybe the red light was a portal, like the gate of sand. If I just charged through fast enough . . .

Then the first dagger shot out of the tunnel.

My sword was in motion before I realized it. The dagger should've impaled me in the chest, but somehow I deflected it with my blade and sent it sailing into the abyss. Two more daggers shot out of the tunnel. I'd never had the best reflexes, but now they sped up. I ducked one dagger and hooked the other with the curved blade of my sword, turned the dagger and flung it back into the tunnel. *How the heck did I do that?*

I advanced to the end of the plank and slashed through the red light, which flickered and died. I waited for the statues to come alive, but nothing happened. The only sound was a dagger clattering against the rocks in the chasm far below.

The doorway began to glow again. The red light coalesced into a strange form: a five-foot-tall bird with a man's head. I raised my sword, but Zia yelled, 'Carter, no!'

The bird creature folded his wings. His eyes, lined with kohl, narrowed as they studied me. A black ornamental wig glistened on his head, and his face was etched with wrinkles. One of those fake braided pharaoh beards was stuck on his chin like a backward ponytail. He didn't look hostile, except for the red flickering light all around him, and the fact that from the neck down he was the world's largest killer turkey.

Then a chilling thought occurred to me: This was a bird with a human head, the same form I'd imagined taking when I slept in Amos's house, when my soul left my body and flew to Phoenix. I had no idea what that meant, but it scared me.

The bird creature scratched at the stone floor. Then, unexpectedly, he smiled.

'Pari, niswa nafeer,' he told me, or at least that's what it sounded like.

Zia gasped. She and Sadie were standing behind me now, their faces pale. Apparently they'd managed to cross the chasm without my noticing.

Finally Zia seemed to collect herself. She bowed to the bird creature. Sadie followed her example.

The creature winked at me, as if we'd just shared a joke. Then he vanished. The red light faded. The statues retracted their arms, uncrossing their spears from the entrance.

'That's it?' I asked. 'What did the turkey say?'

Zia looked at me with something like fear. 'That was *not* a turkey, Carter. That was a *ba*.'

I'd heard my dad use that word before, but I couldn't place it. 'Another monster?'

'A human soul,' Zia said. 'In this case, a spirit of the dead. A magician from ancient times, come back to serve as a guardian. They watch the entrances of the House.'

She studied my face as if I'd just developed some terrible rash.

'What?' I demanded. 'Why are you looking at me that way?'

141

'Nothing,' she said. 'We must hurry.'

She squeezed by me on the ledge and disappeared into the tunnel.

Sadie was staring at me too.

'All right,' I said. 'What did the bird guy say? You understood it?'

She nodded uneasily. 'He mistook you for someone else. He must have bad eyesight.'

'Because?'

'Because he said, "Go forth, good king."'

*   *   *

I was in a daze after that. We passed through the tunnel and entered a vast underground city of halls and chambers, but I only remember bits and pieces of it.

The ceilings soared to twenty or thirty feet, so it didn't feel like we were underground. Every chamber was lined with massive stone columns like the ones I'd seen in Egyptian ruins, but these were in perfect condition, brightly painted to resemble palm trees, with carved green fronds at the top, so I felt like I was walking through a petrified forest. Fires burned in copper braziers. They didn't seem to make any smoke, but the air smelled good, like a marketplace for spices—cinnamon, clove, nutmeg, and others I couldn't identify. The city smelled like Zia. I realized that this was her home.

We saw a few other people—mostly older men and women. Some wore linen robes, some modern clothes. One guy in a business suit walked past with a black leopard on a leash, as if that were completely normal. Another guy barked orders to a small army of brooms, mops, and buckets that

142

were scuttling around, cleaning up the city.

'Like that cartoon,' Sadie said. 'Where Mickey Mouse tries to do magic and the brooms keep splitting and toting water.'

'"The Sorcerer's Apprentice,"' Zia said. 'You do know that was based on an Egyptian story, don't you?'

Sadie just stared back. I knew how she felt. It was too much to process.

We walked through a hall of jackal-headed statues, and I could swear their eyes watched us as we passed. A few minutes later, Zia led us through an open-air market—if you can call anything 'open-air' underground—with dozens of stalls selling weird items like boomerang wands, animated clay dolls, parrots, cobras, papyrus scrolls, and hundreds of different glittering amulets.

Next we crossed a path of stones over a dark river teeming with fish. I thought they were perch until I saw their vicious teeth.

'Are those piranhas?' I asked.

'Tiger fish from the Nile,' Zia said. 'Like piranhas, except these can weigh up to sixteen pounds.'

I watched my step more closely after that.

We turned a corner and passed an ornate building carved out of black rock. Seated pharaohs were chiseled into the walls, and the doorway was shaped like a coiled serpent.

'What's in there?' Sadie asked.

We peeked inside and saw rows of children—maybe two dozen in all, about six to ten years old or so—sitting cross-legged on cushions. They were hunched over brass bowls, peering intently into

143

some sort of liquid and speaking under their breath. At first I thought it was a classroom, but there was no sign of a teacher, and the chamber was lit only by a few candles. Judging by the number of empty seats, the room was meant to hold twice as many kids.

'Our initiates,' Zia said, 'learning to scry. The First Nome must keep in contact with our brethren all over the world. We use our youngest as . . . operators, I suppose you would say.'

'So you've got bases like this all over the world?'

'Most are much smaller, but yes.'

I remembered what Amos had told us about the nomes. 'Egypt is the First Nome. New York is the Twenty-first. What's the last one, the Three-hundred-and-sixtieth?'

'That would be Antarctica,' Zia said. 'A punishment assignment. Nothing there but a couple of cold magicians and some magic penguins.'

'Magic penguins?'

'Don't ask.'

Sadie pointed to the children inside. 'How does it work? They see images in the water?'

'It's oil,' Zia said. 'But yes.'

'So few,' Sadie said. 'Are these the only initiates in the whole city?'

'In the whole *world*,' Zia corrected. 'There were more before—' She stopped herself.

'Before what?' I asked.

'Nothing,' Zia said darkly. 'Initiates do our scrying because young minds are most receptive. Magicians begin training no later than the age of ten . . . with a few dangerous exceptions.'

'You mean us,' I said.

144

She glanced at me apprehensively, and I knew she was still thinking about what the bird spirit had called me: a *good king*. It seemed so unreal, like our family name in that *Blood of the Pharaohs* scroll. How could I be related to some ancient kings? And even if I was, *I* certainly wasn't a king. I had no kingdom. I didn't even have my single suitcase anymore.

'They'll be waiting for you,' Zia said. 'Come along.'

We walked so far, my feet began to ache.

Finally we arrived at a crossroads. On the right was a massive set of bronze doors with fires blazing on either side; on the left, a twenty-foot-tall sphinx carved into the wall. A doorway nestled between its paws, but it was bricked in and covered in cobwebs.

'That looks like the Sphinx at Giza,' I said.

'That's because we are directly under the *real* Sphinx,' Zia said. 'That tunnel leads straight up to it. Or it used to, before it was sealed.'

'But . . .' I did some quick calculations in my head. 'The Sphinx is, like, twenty miles from the Cairo Airport.'

'Roughly.'

'No way we've walked that far.'

Zia actually smiled, and I couldn't help noticing how pretty her eyes were. 'Distance changes in magic places, Carter. Surely you've learned that by now.'

Sadie cleared her throat. 'So why is the tunnel closed, then?'

'The Sphinx was too popular with archaeologists,' Zia said. 'They kept digging around. Finally, in the 1980s, they discovered the

145

first part of the tunnel under the Sphinx.'

'Dad told me about that!' I said. 'But he said the tunnel was a dead end.'

'It was when we got through with it. We couldn't let the archaeologists know how much they're missing. Egypt's leading archaeologist recently speculated that they've only discovered thirty percent of the ancient ruins in Egypt. In truth, they've only discovered one tenth, and not even the *interesting* tenth.'

'What about King Tut's tomb?' I protested.

'That boy king?' Zia rolled her eyes. '*Boring.* You should see some of the *good* tombs.'

I felt a little hurt. Dad had named me after Howard Carter, the guy who discovered King Tut's tomb, so I'd always felt a personal attachment to it. If that wasn't a 'good' tomb, I wondered what was.

Zia turned to face the bronze doors.

'This is the Hall of Ages.' She placed her palm against the seal, which bore the symbol of the House of Life.

The hieroglyphs began to glow, and the doors swung open.

Zia turned to us, her expression deadly serious. 'You are about to meet the Chief Lector. Behave yourselves, unless you wish to be turned into insects.'

14.
A FRENCH GUY ALMOST KILLS US

The last couple of days I'd seen a lot of crazy things, but the Hall of Ages took the prize.

Double rows of stone pillars held up a ceiling so high, you could've parked a blimp under it with no trouble. A shimmering blue carpet that looked like water ran down the center of the hall, which was so long, I couldn't see the end even though it was brightly lit. Balls of fire floated around like helium basketballs, changing color whenever they bumped into one another. Millions of tiny hieroglyphic symbols also drifted through the air, randomly combining into words and then breaking apart.

I grabbed a pair of glowing red legs.

They walked across my palm before jumping off and dissolving.

But the weirdest things were the *displays.*

I don't know what else to call them. Between the columns on either side of us, images shifted, coming into focus and then blurring out again like holograms in a sandstorm.

'Come on,' Zia told us. 'And don't spend too much time looking.'

It was impossible not to. The first twenty feet or so, the magical scenes cast a golden light across the hall. A blazing sun rose above an ocean. A mountain emerged from the water, and I had the feeling I was watching the beginning of the world. Giants strode across the Nile Valley: a man with black skin and the head of a jackal, a lioness with bloody fangs, a beautiful woman with wings of light.

Sadie stepped off the rug. In a trance, she reached toward the images.

'Stay on the carpet!' Zia grabbed Sadie's hand and pulled her back toward the center of the hall. 'You are seeing the Age of the Gods. No mortal should dwell on these images.'

'But . . .' Sadie blinked. 'They're only pictures, aren't they?'

'Memories,' Zia said, 'so powerful they could destroy your mind.'

'Oh,' Sadie said in a small voice.

We kept walking. The images changed to silver. I saw armies clashing—Egyptians in kilts and sandals and leather armor, fighting with spears. A tall, dark-skinned man in red-and-white armor placed a double crown on his head: Narmer, the king who united Upper and Lower Egypt. Sadie was right: he did look a bit like Dad.

'This is the Old Kingdom,' I guessed. 'The first great age of Egypt.'

Zia nodded. As we walked down the hall, we saw workers building the first step pyramid out of stone. Another few steps, and the biggest pyramid of all rose from the desert at Giza. Its outer layer of smooth white casing stones gleamed in the sun. Ten thousand workers gathered at its base and knelt before the pharaoh, who raised his hands to the sun, dedicating his own tomb.

'Khufu,' I said.

'The baboon?' Sadie asked, suddenly interested.

'No, the pharaoh who built the Great Pyramid,' I said. 'It was the tallest structure in the world for almost four thousand years.'

Another few steps, and the images turned from silver to coppery.

'The Middle Kingdom,' Zia announced. 'A bloody, chaotic time. And yet this is when the House of Life came to maturity.'

The scenes shifted more rapidly. We watched armies fighting, temples being built, ships sailing on the Nile, and magicians throwing fire. Every step covered hundreds of years, and yet the hall still went on forever. For the first time I understood just how ancient Egypt was.

We crossed another threshold, and the light turned bronze.

'The New Kingdom,' I guessed. 'The last time Egypt was ruled by Egyptians.'

Zia said nothing, but I watched scenes passing that my dad had described to me: Hatshepsut, the greatest female pharaoh, putting on a fake beard and ruling Egypt as a man; Ramesses the Great leading his chariots into battle.

I saw magicians dueling in a palace. A man in tattered robes, with a shaggy black beard and wild eyes, threw down his staff, which turned into a serpent and devoured a dozen other snakes.

I got a lump in my throat. 'Is that—'

'Musa,' Zia said. 'Or Moshe, as his own people knew him. You call him Moses. The only foreigner ever to defeat the House in a magic duel.'

I stared at her. 'You're kidding, right?'

'We would not kid about such a thing.'

The scene shifted again. I saw a man standing over a table of battle figurines: wooden toy ships, soldiers, and chariots. The man was dressed like a pharaoh, but his face looked oddly familiar. He looked up and seemed to smile right at me. With a chill, I realized he had the same face as the *ba,* the bird-faced spirit who'd challenged me on the bridge.

'Who is that?' I asked.

'Nectanebo II,' Zia said. 'The last native Egyptian king, and the last sorcerer pharaoh. He could move entire armies, create or destroy navies by moving pieces on his board, but in the end, it was not enough.'

We stepped over another line and the images shimmered blue. 'These are the Ptolemaic times,' Zia said. 'Alexander the Great conquered the known world, including Egypt. He set up his general Ptolemy as the new pharaoh, and founded a line of Greek kings to rule over Egypt.'

The Ptolemaic section of the hall was shorter, and seemed sad compared to all the others. The temples were smaller. The kings and queens looked desperate, or lazy, or simply apathetic. There were no great battles . . . except toward the end. I saw Romans march into the city of Alexandria. I saw a woman with dark hair and a white dress drop a snake into her blouse.

'Cleopatra,' Zia said, 'the seventh queen of that name. She tried to stand against the might of Rome, and she lost. When she took her life, the last line of pharaohs ended. Egypt, the great nation, faded. Our language was forgotten. The ancient rites were suppressed. The House of Life survived, but we were forced into hiding.'

We passed into an area of red light, and history began to look familiar. I saw Arab armies riding into Egypt, then the Turks. Napoleon marched his army under the shadow of the pyramids. The

British came and built the Suez Canal. Slowly Cairo grew into a modern city. And the old ruins faded farther and farther under the sands of the desert.

'Each year,' Zia said, 'the Hall of Ages grows longer to encompass our history. Up until the present.'

I was so dazed I didn't even realize we'd reached the end of the hall until Sadie grabbed my arm.

In front of us stood a dais and on it an empty throne, a gilded wooden chair with a flail and a shepherd's crook carved in the back—the ancient symbols of the pharaoh.

On the step below the throne sat the oldest man I'd ever seen. His skin was like lunch-bag paper—brown, thin, and crinkled. White linen robes hung loosely off his small frame. A leopard skin was draped around his shoulders, and his hand shakily held a big wooden staff, which I was sure he was going to drop any minute. But weirdest of all, the glowing hieroglyphs in the air seemed to be coming *from him.* Multicolored symbols popped up all around him and floated away as if he were some sort of magic bubble machine.

At first I wasn't sure he was even alive. His milky eyes stared into space. Then he focused on me, and electricity coursed through my body.

He wasn't just looking at me. He was scanning me—reading my entire being.

Hide, something inside me said.

I didn't know where the voice came from, but my stomach clenched. My whole body tensed as if I were bracing for a hit, and the electrical feeling subsided.

151

The old man raised an eyebrow as if I'd surprised him. He glanced behind him and said something in a language I didn't recognize.

A second man stepped out of the shadows. I wanted to yelp. He was the guy who'd been with Zia in the British Museum—the one with the cream-colored robes and the forked beard.

The bearded man glared at Sadie and me.

'I am Desjardins,' he said with a French accent. 'My master, Chief Lector Iskandar, welcomes you to the House of Life.'

I couldn't think what to say to that, so of course I asked a stupid question. 'He's really old. Why isn't he sitting on the throne?'

Desjardins' nostrils flared, but the old dude, Iskandar, just chuckled, and said something else in that other language.

Desjardins translated stiffly: 'The master says thank you for noticing, he is in fact *really* old. But the throne is for the pharaoh. It has been vacant since the fall of Egypt to Rome. It is . . . *comment dit-on?* Symbolic. The Chief Lector's role is to serve and protect the pharaoh. Therefore he sits at the foot of the throne.'

I looked at Iskandar a little nervously. I wondered how many years he'd been sitting on that step. 'If you . . . if he can understand English . . . what language is he speaking?'

Desjardins sniffed. 'The Chief Lector understands many things. But he prefers to speak Alexandrian Greek, his birth tongue.'

Sadie cleared her throat. 'Sorry, his *birth* tongue? Wasn't Alexander the Great way back in the blue section, thousands of years ago? You make it sound like Lord Salamander is—'

152

'Lord *Iskandar,*' Desjardins hissed. 'Show respect!'

Something clicked in my mind: back in Brooklyn, Amos had talked about the magicians' law against summoning gods—a law made in Roman times by the Chief Lector . . . Iskandar. Surely it had to be a different guy. Maybe we were talking to Iskandar the XXVII or something.

The old man looked me in the eyes. He smiled, as if he knew exactly what I was thinking. He said something else in Greek, and Desjardins translated.

'The master says not to worry. You will not be held responsible for the past crimes of your family. At least, not until we have investigated you further.'

'Gee . . . thanks,' I said.

'Do not mock our generosity, boy,' Desjardins warned. 'Your father broke our most important law twice: once at Cleopatra's Needle, when he tried to summon the gods and your mother died assisting him. Then again at the British Museum, when your father was foolish enough to use the Rosetta Stone itself. Now your uncle too is missing—'

'You know what's happened to Amos?' Sadie blurted out.

Desjardins scowled. 'Not yet,' he admitted.

'You have to find him!' Sadie cried. 'Don't you have some sort of GPS magic or—'

'We are searching,' Desjardins said. 'But you cannot worry about Amos. You must stay here. You must be . . . trained.'

I got the impression he was going to say a different word, something not as nice as *trained.*

153

Iskandar spoke directly to me. His tone sounded kindly.

'The master warns that the Demon Days begin tomorrow at sunset,' Desjardins translated. 'You must be kept safe.'

'But we have to find our dad!' I said. 'Dangerous gods are on the loose out there. We saw Serqet. And Set!'

At these names, Iskandar's expression tightened. He turned and gave Desjardins what sounded like an order. Desjardins protested. Iskandar repeated his statement.

Desjardins clearly didn't like it, but he bowed to his master. Then he turned toward me. 'The Chief Lector wishes to hear your story.'

So I told him, with Sadie jumping in whenever I stopped to take a breath. The funny thing was, we both left out certain things without planning to. We didn't mention Sadie's magic abilities, or the encounter with the *ba* who'd called me a king. It was like I literally *couldn't* mention those things. Whenever I tried, the voice inside my head whispered, *Not that part. Be silent.*

When I was done, I glanced at Zia. She said nothing, but she was studying me with a troubled expression.

Iskandar traced a circle on the step with the butt of his staff. More hieroglyphs popped into the air and floated away.

After several seconds, Desjardins seemed to grow impatient. He stepped forward and glared at us. 'You are lying. That could not have been Set. He would need a powerful host to remain in this world. *Very* powerful.'

'Look, you,' Sadie said. 'I don't know what all

154

this rubbish is about hosts, but I saw Set with my own eyes. You were there at the British Museum—you must have done, too. And if Carter saw him in Phoenix, Arizona, then . . .' She looked at me doubtfully. 'Then he's probably not crazy.'

'Thanks, Sis,' I mumbled, but Sadie was just getting started.

'And as for Serqet, she's real too! Our friend, my cat, Bast, died protecting us!'

'So,' Desjardins said coldly, 'you admit to consorting with gods. That makes our investigation much easier. Bast is not your *friend*. The gods caused the downfall of Egypt. It is forbidden to call on their powers. Magicians are sworn to keep the gods from interfering in the mortal world. We must use all our power to fight them.'

'Bast said you were paranoid,' Sadie added.

The magician clenched his fists, and the air tingled with the weird smell of ozone, like during a thunderstorm. The hairs on my neck stood straight up. Before anything bad could happen, Zia stepped in front of us.

'Lord Desjardins,' she pleaded, 'there *was* something strange. When I ensnared the scorpion goddess, she re-formed almost instantly. I could not return her to the Duat, even with the Seven Ribbons. I could only break her hold on the host for a moment. Perhaps the rumors of other escapes—'

'What other escapes?' I asked.

She glanced at me reluctantly. 'Other gods, *many* of them, released since last night from artifacts all over the world. Like a chain reaction—'

'Zia!' Desjardins snapped. 'That information is not for sharing.'

'Look,' I said, 'lord, sir, whatever—Bast warned us this would happen. She said Set would release more gods.'

'Master,' Zia pleaded, 'if Ma'at is weakening, if Set is increasing chaos, perhaps that is why I could not banish Serqet.'

'Ridiculous,' Desjardins said. 'You are skilled, Zia, but perhaps you were not skilled enough for this encounter. And as for these two, the contamination must be contained.'

Zia's face reddened. She turned her attention to Iskandar. 'Master, please. Give me a chance with them.'

'You forget your place,' Desjardins snapped. 'These two are guilty and must be destroyed.'

My throat started closing up. I looked at Sadie. If we had to make a run for it down that long hall, I didn't like our chances . . . .

The old man finally looked up. He smiled at Zia with true affection. For a second I wondered if she were his great-great-great-granddaughter or something. He spoke in Greek, and Zia bowed deeply.

Desjardins looked ready to explode. He swept his robes away from his feet and marched behind the throne.

'The Chief Lector will allow Zia to test you,' he growled. 'Meanwhile, I will seek out the truth—or the lies—in your story. You will be punished for the lies.'

I turned to Iskandar and copied Zia's bow. Sadie did the same.

'Thank you, master,' I said.

The old man studied me for a long time. Again I felt as if he were trying to burn into my soul—not

156

in an angry way. More out of concern. Then he mumbled something, and I understood two words: *Nectanebo* and *ba*.

He opened his hand and a flood of glowing hieroglyphs poured out, swarming around the dais. There was a blinding flash of light, and when I could see again, the dais was empty. The two men were gone.

Zia turned toward us, her expression grim. 'I will show you to your quarters. In the morning, your testing begins. We will see what magic you know, and how you know it.'

I wasn't sure what she meant by that, but I exchanged an uneasy look with Sadie.

'Sounds fun,' Sadie ventured. 'And if we fail this test?'

Zia regarded her coldly. 'This is not the sort of test you fail, Sadie Kane. You pass or you die.'

15.

A GODLY BIRTHDAY PARTY

S A D I E

They took Carter to a different dormitory, so I don't know how he slept. But *I* couldn't get a wink.

It would've been hard enough with Zia's comments about passing our tests or dying, but the girls' dormitory just wasn't as posh as Amos's mansion. The stone walls sweated moisture. Creepy pictures of Egyptian monsters danced across the ceiling in the torchlight. I got a floating cot to sleep in, and the other girls in training—

initiates, Zia had called them—were much younger than me, so when the old dorm matron told them to go to sleep straightaway, they actually *obeyed.* The matron waved her hand and the torches went out. She shut the door behind her, and I could hear the sound of locks clicking.

Lovely. Imprisoned in a nursery school dungeon.

I stared into the dark until I heard the other girls snoring. A single thought kept bothering me: an urge I just couldn't shake. Finally I crept out of bed and tugged on my boots.

I felt my way to the door. I tugged at the handle. Locked, as I suspected. I was tempted to kick it till I remembered what Zia had done in the Cairo Airport broom closet.

I pressed my palm against the door and whispered, *'Sahad.'*

Locks clicked. The door swung open. Handy trick.

Outside, the corridors were dark and empty. Apparently, there wasn't much nightlife in the First Nome. I sneaked through the city back the way we'd come and saw nothing but an occasional cobra slithering across the floor. After the last couple of days, that didn't even faze me. I thought about trying to find Carter, but I wasn't sure where they'd taken him, and honestly, I wanted to do this on my own.

After our last argument in New York, I wasn't sure how I felt about my brother. The idea that he could be jealous of *my* life while he got to travel the world with Dad—please! And he had the nerve to call my life *normal?* All right, I had a few mates at school like Liz and Emma, but my life was hardly easy. If Carter made a social faux pas or met people he didn't like, he could just move on! I had to stay put. I couldn't answer simple questions like 'Where are your parents?' or 'What does your family do?' or even 'Where are you from?' without exposing just how odd my situation was. I was always the *different* girl. The mixed-race girl, the American who wasn't American, the girl whose mother had died, the girl with the absent father, the girl who made trouble in class, the girl who couldn't concentrate on her lessons. After a while one learns that blending in simply doesn't work. If people are going to single me out, I might as well give them something to stare at. Red stripes in my hair? Why not! Combat boots with the school uniform? Absolutely. Headmaster says, 'I'll have to call your parents, young lady.' I say, 'Good luck.' Carter didn't know anything about my life.

But enough of that. The point was, I decided to do this particular bit of exploring alone, and after a few wrong turns, I found my way back to the Hall of Ages.

What was I up to, you may ask? I certainly didn't want to meet Monsieur Evil again or creepy old Lord Salamander.

But I *did* want to see those images—*memories,* Zia had called them.

I pushed open the bronze doors. Inside, the hall seemed deserted. No balls of fire floated around the ceiling. No glowing hieroglyphs. But images still shimmered between the columns, washing the hall with strange, multicolored light.

I took a few nervous steps.

I wanted another look at the Age of the Gods. On our first trip through the hall, something about

159

those images had shaken me. I knew Carter thought I'd gone into a dangerous trance, and Zia had warned that the scenes would melt my brain; but I had a feeling she was just trying to scare me off. I felt a connection to those images, like there was an answer within—a vital piece of information I needed.

I stepped off the carpet and approached the curtain of golden light. I saw sand dunes shifting in the wind, storm clouds brewing, crocodiles sliding down the Nile. I saw a vast hall full of revelers. I touched the image.

*   *   *

And I was in the palace of the gods.

Huge beings swirled around me, changing shape from human to animal to pure energy. On a throne in the center of the room sat a muscular African man in rich black robes. He had a handsome face and warm brown eyes. His hands looked strong enough to crush rocks.

The other gods celebrated round him. Music played—a sound so powerful that the air burned. At the man's side stood a beautiful woman in white, her belly swollen as if she were a few months pregnant. Her form flickered; at times she seemed to have multicolored wings. Then she turned in my direction and I gasped. She had my mother's face.

She didn't seem to notice me. In fact, none of the gods did, until a voice behind me said, 'Are you a ghost?'

I turned and saw a good-looking boy of about sixteen, dressed in black robes. His complexion was pale, but he had lovely brown eyes like the man on the throne. His black hair was long and tousled—rather wild, but it worked for me. He tilted his head, and it finally occurred to me that he'd asked me a question.

I tried to think of something to say. Excuse me? Hello? Marry me? Anything would've done. But all I could manage was a shake of the head.

'Not a ghost, eh?' he mused. 'A *ba* then?' He gestured towards the throne. 'Watch, but do not interfere.'

Somehow I wasn't interested in watching the throne so much, but the boy in black dissolved into a shadow and disappeared, leaving me no further distraction.

'Isis,' said the man on the throne.

The pregnant woman turned towards him and beamed. 'My lord Osiris. Happy birthday.'

'Thank you, my love. And soon we shall mark the birth of our son—Horus, the great one! His new incarnation shall be his greatest yet. He shall bring peace and prosperity to the world.'

Isis took her husband's hand. Music kept playing around them, gods celebrating, the very air swirling in a dance of creation.

Suddenly the palace doors blew open. A hot wind made the torches sputter.

A man strode into the hall. He was tall and strong, almost a twin to Osiris, but with dark red skin, blood-colored robes, and a pointed beard. He looked human, except when he smiled. Then his teeth turned to fangs. His face flickered—sometimes human, sometimes strangely wolflike. I had to stifle a scream, because I'd seen that wolfish face before.

161

The dancing stopped. The music died.

Osiris rose from his throne. 'Set,' he said in a dangerous tone. 'Why have you come?'

Set laughed, and the tension in the room broke. Despite his cruel eyes, he had a wonderful laugh—nothing like the screeching he'd done at the British Museum. It was carefree and friendly, as if he couldn't possibly mean any harm.

'I come to celebrate my brother's birthday, of course!' he exclaimed. 'And I bring entertainment!'

He gestured behind him. Four huge men with the heads of wolves marched into the room, carrying a jewel-encrusted golden coffin.

My heart began to race. It was the same box Set had used to imprison my dad at the British Museum.

No! I wanted to scream. *Don't trust him!*

But the assembled gods oohed and aahed, admiring the box, which was painted with gold and red hieroglyphs, trimmed with jade and opals. The wolf-men set down the box, and I saw it had no lid. The interior was lined with black linen.

'This sleeping casket,' Set announced, 'was made by my finest craftsmen, using the most expensive materials. Its value is beyond measure. The god who lies within, even for a night, will see his powers increase tenfold! His wisdom will never falter. His strength will never fail. It is a gift'—he smiled slyly at Osiris—'for the *one and only* god who fits within perfectly!'

I wouldn't have queued up first, but the gods surged forward. They pushed each other out of the way to get at the golden coffin. Some climbed in but were too short. Others were much too big. Even when they tried to change their shapes, the

162

gods had no luck, as if the magic of the box were thwarting them. No one fit exactly. Gods grumbled and complained as others, anxious to try, pushed them to the floor.

Set turned to Osiris with a good-natured laugh. 'Well, brother, we have no winner yet. Will you try? Only the best of the gods can succeed.'

Osiris's eyes gleamed. Apparently he wasn't the god of brains, because he seemed completely taken in by the box's beauty. All the other gods looked at him expectantly, and I could see what he was thinking: if he fit the box, what a brilliant birthday present. Even Set, his wicked brother, would have to admit that he was the rightful king of the gods.

Only Isis seemed troubled. She laid her hand on her husband's shoulder. 'My lord, do not. Set does not bring presents.'

'I am offended!' Set sounded genuinely hurt. 'Can I not celebrate my brother's birthday? Are we so estranged that I cannot even apologize to the king?'

Osiris smiled at Isis. 'My dear, it is only a game. Fear nothing.'

He rose from his throne. The gods applauded as he approached the box.

'All hail Osiris!' Set cried.

The king of the gods lowered himself into the box, and when he glanced in my direction, just for a moment, he had my father's face.

No! I thought again. *Don't do it!*

But Osiris lay down. The coffin fit him exactly.

A cheer went up from the gods, but before Osiris could rise, Set clapped his hands. A golden lid materialized above the box and slammed down on top of it.

Osiris shouted in rage, but his cries were muffled.

Golden latches fastened around the lid. The other gods surged forward to intervene—even the boy in black I'd seen earlier reappeared—but Set was faster. He stamped his foot so hard, the stone floor trembled. The gods toppled over each other like dominoes. The wolf-men drew their spears, and the gods scrambled away in terror.

Set said a magic word, and a boiling cauldron appeared out of thin air. It poured its contents over the coffin—molten lead, coating the box, sealing it shut, probably heating the interior to a thousand degrees.

'Villain!' Isis wailed. She advanced on Set and began to speak a spell, but Set held up his hand. Isis rose from the floor, clawing at her mouth, her lips pressed as if an invisible force were suffocating her.

'Not today, lovely Isis,' Set purred. 'Today, I am king. And your child shall never be born!'

Suddenly, another goddess—a slender woman in a blue dress—charged out of the crowd. 'Husband, no!'

She tackled Set, who momentarily lost his concentration. Isis fell to the floor, gasping. The other goddess yelled, 'Flee!'

Isis turned and ran.

Set rose. I thought he would hit the goddess in blue, but he only snarled. 'Foolish wife! Whose side are you on?'

He stamped his foot again, and the golden coffin sank into the floor.

Set raced after Isis. At the edge of the palace,

Isis turned into a small bird of prey and soared into the air. Set sprouted demon's wings and launched himself in pursuit.

Then suddenly *I* was the bird. I was Isis, flying desperately over the Nile. I could sense Set behind me—closing. Closing.

You must escape, the voice of Isis said in my mind. *Avenge Osiris. Crown Horus king!*

Just when I thought my heart would burst, I felt a hand on my shoulder. The images evaporated.

The old master, Iskandar, stood next to me, his face pinched with concern. Glowing hieroglyphs danced round him.

'Forgive the interruption,' he said in perfect English. 'But you were almost dead.'

That's when my knees turned to water, and I lost consciousness.

* * *

When I awoke, I was curled at Iskandar's feet on the steps below the empty throne. We were alone in the hall, which was mostly dark except for the light from the hieroglyphs that always seemed to glow around him.

'Welcome back,' he said. 'You're lucky you survived.'

I wasn't so sure. My head felt like it had been boiled in oil.

'I'm sorry,' I said. 'I didn't mean to—'

'Look at the images? And yet you did. Your *ba* left your body and entered the past. Hadn't you been warned?'

'Yes,' I admitted. 'But . . . I was drawn to the pictures.'

'*Mmm.*' Iskandar stared into space, as if remembering something from long ago. 'They *are* hard to resist.'

'You speak perfect English,' I noticed.

Iskandar smiled. 'How do you know I'm speaking English? Perhaps you are speaking Greek.'

I hoped he was kidding, but I couldn't tell. He seemed so frail and warm, and yet . . . it was like sitting next to a nuclear reactor. I had a feeling he was full of more danger than I wanted to know.

'You're not really *that* old, are you?' I asked. 'I mean, old enough to remember Ptolemaic times?'

'I am *exactly* that old, my dear. I was born in the reign of Cleopatra VII.'

'Oh, please.'

'I assure you, it's true. It was my sorrow to behold the last days of Egypt, before that foolhardy queen lost our kingdom to the Romans. I was the last magician to be trained before the House went underground. Many of our most powerful secrets were lost, including the spells my master used to extend my life. Magicians these days still live long—sometimes centuries—but I have been alive for two millennia.'

'So you're immortal?'

His chuckle turned into a racking cough. He doubled over and cupped his hands over his mouth. I wanted to help, but I wasn't sure how. The glowing hieroglyphs flickered and dimmed around him.

Finally the coughing subsided.

He took a shaky breath. 'Hardly immortal, my dear. In fact . . .' His voice trailed off. 'But never mind that. What did you see in your vision?'

I probably should've kept quiet. I didn't want to be turned into a bug for breaking any rules, and the vision had terrified me—especially the moment when I'd changed into the bird of prey. But Iskandar's kindly expression made it hard to hold back. I ended up telling him everything. Well, almost everything. I left out the bit about the good-looking boy, and yes, I know it was silly, but I was *embarrassed.* I reckoned that part could've been my own crazed imagination at work, as Ancient Egyptian gods could *not* have been that gorgeous.

Iskandar sat for a moment, tapping his staff against the steps. 'You saw a very old event, Sadie—Set taking the throne of Egypt by force. He hid Osiris's coffin, you know, and Isis searched the entire world to find it.'

'So she got him back eventually?'

'Not exactly. Osiris was resurrected—but only in the Underworld. He became the king of the dead. When their son, Horus, grew up, Horus challenged Set for the throne of Egypt and won after many hard battles. That is why Horus was called the Avenger. As I said—an old story, but one that the gods have repeated many times in our history.'

'Repeated?'

'The gods follow patterns. In some ways they are quite predictable: acting out the same squabbles, the same jealousies down through the ages. Only the settings change, and the hosts.'

There was that word again: *hosts.* I thought about the poor woman in the New York museum who'd turned into the goddess Serqet.

'In my vision,' I said, 'Isis and Osiris were married. Horus was about to be born as their son.

But in another story Carter told me, all three of them were siblings, children of the sky goddess.'

'Yes,' Iskandar agreed. 'This can be confusing for those who do not know the nature of gods. They cannot walk the earth in their pure form—at least, not for more than a few moments. They must have hosts.'

'Humans, you mean.'

'Or powerful objects, such as statues, amulets, monuments, certain models of cars. But they *prefer* human form. You see gods have great power, but only humans have creativity, the power to change history rather than simply repeat it. Humans can . . . how do you moderns say it . . . think outside the cup.'

'The box,' I suggested.

'Yes. The combination of human creativity and godly power can be quite formidable. At any rate, when Osiris and Isis first walked the earth, their hosts were brother and sister. But mortal hosts are not permanent. They die, they wear out. Later in history, Osiris and Isis took new forms—humans who were husband and wife. Horus, who in one lifetime was their brother, was born into a new life as their son.'

'That's confusing,' I said. 'And a little gross.'

Iskandar shrugged. 'The gods do not think of relationships the way we humans do. Their hosts are merely like changes of clothes. This is why the ancient stories seem so mixed up. Sometimes the gods are described as married, or siblings, or parent and child, depending on their hosts. The pharaoh himself was called a living god, you know. Egyptologists believe this was just a lot of propaganda, but in fact it was often literally true.

168

The greatest of the pharaohs became hosts for gods, usually Horus. He gave them power and wisdom, and let them build Egypt into a mighty empire.'

'But that's good, isn't it? Why is it against the law to host a god?'

Iskandar's face darkened. 'Gods have different agendas than humans do, Sadie. They can overpower their hosts, literally burn them out. That is why so many hosts die young. Tutankhamen, poor boy, died at nineteen. Cleopatra VII was even worse. She tried to host the spirit of Isis without knowing what she was doing, and it shattered her mind. In the old days, the House of Life taught the use of divine magic. Initiates could study the path of Horus, or Isis, or Sekhmet, or any number of gods, learning to channel their powers. We had many more initiates back then.'

Iskandar looked round the empty hall, as if imagining it filled with magicians. 'Some adepts could call upon the gods only from time to time. Others attempted to host their spirits . . . with varying degrees of success. The ultimate goal was to become the "eye" of the god—a perfect union of the two souls, mortal and immortal. Very few achieved this, even among the pharaohs, who were born to the task. Many destroyed themselves trying.' He turned up his palm, which had the most deeply etched lifeline I'd ever seen. 'When Egypt finally fell to the Romans, it became clear to us— to *me*—that mankind, our rulers, even the strongest magicians, no longer had the strength of will to master a god's power. The only ones who could . . .' His voice faltered.

'What?'

'Nothing, my dear. I talk too much. An old man's weakness.'

'It's the blood of the pharaohs, isn't it?'

He fixed me in his gaze. His eyes no longer looked milky. They burned with intensity. 'You are a remarkable young girl. You remind me of your mother.'

My mouth fell open. 'You knew her?'

'Of course. She trained here, as did your father. Your mother . . . well, aside from being a brilliant scientist, she had the gift of divination. One of the most difficult forms of magic, and she was the first in centuries to possess it.'

'Divination?'

'Seeing the future. Tricky business, never perfect, but she saw things that made her seek advice from . . . *unconventional* places, things that made even *this* old man question some long-held beliefs . . .'

He drifted off into Memoryland again, which was infuriating enough when my grandparents did it, but when it's an all-powerful magician who has valuable information, it's enough to drive one mad.

'Iskandar?'

He looked at me with mild surprise, as if he'd forgotten I was there. 'I'm sorry, Sadie. I should come to the point: you have a hard path ahead of you, but I'm convinced now it's a path you must take, for all our sakes. Your brother will need your guidance.'

I was tempted to laugh. 'Carter, need my guidance? For what? What path do you mean?'

'All in good time. Things must take their

course.'

Typical adult answer. I tried to bite back my frustration. 'And what if *I* need guidance?'

'Zia,' he said, without hesitation. 'She is my best pupil, and she is wise. When the time comes, she will know how to help you.'

'Right,' I said, a bit disappointed. 'Zia.'

'For now you should rest, my dear. And it seems I, too, can rest at last.' He sounded sad but relieved. I didn't know what he was talking about, but he didn't give me the chance to ask.

'I am sorry our time together was so brief,' he said. 'Sleep well, Sadie Kane.'

'But—'

Iskandar touched my forehead. And I fell into a deep, dreamless sleep.

16.

HOW ZIA LOST HER EYEBROWS

SADIE

I woke to a bucket of ice water in my face.

'Sadie! Get up,' Zia said.

'God!' I yelled. 'Was that *necessary*?'

'No,' Zia admitted.

I wanted to strangle her, except I was dripping wet, shivering, and still disoriented. How long had I slept? It felt like only a few minutes, but the dormitory was empty. All the other cots were made. The girls must've already gone to their morning lessons.

Zia tossed me a towel and some fresh linen

clothes. 'We'll meet Carter in the cleansing room.'

'I just *got* a bath, thanks very much. What I need is a proper breakfast.'

'The cleansing prepares you for magic.' Zia slung her bag of tricks over her shoulder and unfolded the long black staff she'd used in New York. 'If you survive, we'll see about food.'

I was tired of being reminded that I might die, but I got dressed and followed her out.

After another endless series of tunnels, we came to a chamber with a roaring waterfall. There was no ceiling, just a shaft above us that seemed to go up forever. Water fell from the darkness into a fountain, splashing over a five-meter-tall statue of that bird-headed god. What was his name—Tooth? No, Thoth. The water cascaded over his head, collected in his palms, then spilled out into the pool.

Carter stood beside the fountain. He was dressed in linen with Dad's workbag over one shoulder and his sword strapped to his back. His hair was rumpled, as if he hadn't slept well.At least he hadn't been doused in ice water. Seeing him, I felt a strange sense of relief. I thought about Iskandar's words last night: *Your brother will need your guidance.*

'What?' Carter asked. 'You're staring at me funny.'

'Nothing,' I said quickly. 'How'd you sleep?'

'Badly. I'll . . . I'll tell you about it later.'

Was it my imagination, or did he frown in Zia's direction? *Hmm,* possible romantic trouble between Miss Magic and my brother? I made a mental note to interrogate him next time we were alone.

Zia went to a nearby cabinet. She brought out two ceramic cups, dipped them into the fountain, then offered them to us. 'Drink.'

I glanced at Carter. 'After you.'

'It's only water,' Zia assured me, 'but purified by contact with Thoth. It will focus your mind.'

I didn't see how a statue could purify water. Then I remembered what Iskandar had said, how gods could inhabit anything.

I took a drink. Immediately I felt like I'd had a good strong cup of Gran's tea. My brain buzzed. My eyesight sharpened. I felt so hyperactive, I almost didn't miss my chewing gum—almost.

Carter sipped from his cup. 'Wow.'

'Now the tattoos,' Zia announced.

'Brilliant!' I said.

'On your tongue,' she added.

'Excuse me?'

Zia stuck out her tongue. Right in the middle was a blue hieroglyph.

'Nith ith Naat,' she tried to say with her tongue out. Then she realized her mistake and stuck her tongue back in. 'I mean, this is Ma'at, the symbol of order and harmony. It will help you speak magic clearly. One mistake with a spell—'

'Let me guess,' I said. 'We'll die.'

From her cabinet of horrors, Zia produced a fine-tipped paintbrush and a bowl of blue dye. 'It doesn't hurt. And it's not permanent.'

'How does it taste?' Carter wondered.

Zia smiled. 'Stick out your tongue.'

To answer Carter's question, the tattoo tasted like burning car tires.

'*Ugh.*' I spit a blue gob of 'order and harmony' into the fountain. 'Never mind breakfast. Lost my

173

appetite.'

Zia pulled a leather satchel out of the cabinet. 'Carter will be allowed to keep your father's magic implements, plus a new staff and wand. Generally speaking, the wand is for defense, the staff is for offense, although, Carter, you may prefer to use your *khopesh*.'

'Khopesh?'

'The curved sword,' Zia said. 'A favored weapon of the pharaoh's guard. It can be used in combat magic. As for Sadie, you will need a full kit.'

'How come *he* gets Dad's kit?' I complained.

'He is the eldest,' she said, as if that explained everything. Typical.

Zia tossed me the leather satchel. Inside was an ivory wand, a rod that I supposed turned into a staff, some paper, an ink set, a bit of twine, and a lovely chunk of wax. I was less than thrilled.

'What about a little wax man?' I asked. 'I want a Doughboy.'

'If you mean a figurine, you must make one yourself. You will be taught how, if you have the skill. We will determine your specialty later.'

'Specialty?' Carter asked. 'You mean like Nectanebo specialized in statues?'

Zia nodded. 'Nectanebo was extremely skilled in statuary magic. He could make *shabti* so lifelike, they could pass for human. No one has ever been greater at statuary . . . except perhaps Iskandar. But there are many other disciplines: Healer. Amulet maker. Animal charmer. Elementalist. Combat magician. Necromancer.'

'Diviner?' I asked.

Zia looked at me curiously. 'Yes, although that is quite rare. Why do you—'

I cleared my throat. 'So how do we know our specialty?'

'It will become clear soon enough,' Zia promised, 'but a good magician knows a bit of everything, which is why we start with a basic test. Let us go to the library.'

*   *   *

The First Nome's library was like Amos's, but a hundred times bigger, with circular rooms lined with honeycomb shelves that seemed to go on forever, like the world's largest beehive. Clay *shabti* statues kept popping in and out, retrieving scroll canisters and disappearing, but we saw no other people.

Zia brought us to a wooden table and spread out a long, blank papyrus scroll. She picked up a stylus and dipped it in ink.

'The Egyptian word *shesh* means scribe or writer, but it can also mean magician. This is because magic, at its most basic, turns words into reality. You will create a scroll. Using your own magic, you will send power into the words on paper. When spoken, the words will unleash the magic.'

She handed the stylus to Carter.

'I don't get it,' he protested.

'A simple word,' she suggested. 'It can be anything.'

'In English?'

Zia curled her lip. 'If you must. Any language will work, but hieroglyphics are best. They are the language of creation, of magic, of Ma'at. You must be careful, however.'

175

Before she could explain, Carter drew a simple hieroglyph of a bird.

The picture wriggled, peeled itself off the papyrus, and flew away. It splattered Carter's head with some hieroglyphic droppings on its way out. I couldn't help laughing at Carter's expression.

'A beginner's mistake,' Zia said, scowling at me to be quiet. 'If you use a symbol that stands for something alive, it is wise to write it only partially—leave off a wing, or the legs. Otherwise the magic you channel could make it come alive.'

'And poop on its creator.' Carter sighed, wiping off his hair with a bit of scrap papyrus. 'That's why our father's wax statue, Doughboy, has no legs, right?'

'The same principle,' Zia agreed. 'Now, try again.'

Carter stared at Zia's staff, which was covered in hieroglyphics. He picked the most obvious one and copied it on the papyrus—the symbol for fire.

Uh-oh, I thought. But the word did not come alive, which would've been rather exciting. It simply dissolved.

'Keep trying,' Zia urged.

'Why am I so tired?' Carter wondered.

He definitely looked exhausted. His face was beaded with sweat.

'You're channeling magic from within,' Zia said. 'For me, fire is easy. But it may not be the most natural type of magic for you. Try something else. Summon . . . summon a sword.'

Zia showed him how to form the hieroglyph, and Carter wrote it on the papyrus. Nothing happened.

'Speak it,' Zia said.

'Sword,' Carter said. The word glowed and vanished, and a butter knife lay on the papyrus.

I laughed. 'Terrifying!'

Carter looked like he was about to pass out, but he managed a grin. He picked up the knife and threatened to poke me with it.

'Very good for a first time,' Zia said. 'Remember, you are not creating the knife yourself. You are summoning it from Ma'at—the creative power of the universe. Hieroglyphs are the code we use. That's why they are called Divine Words. The more powerful the magician, the easier it becomes to control the language.'

I caught my breath. 'Those hieroglyphs floating in the Hall of Ages. They seemed to gather around Iskandar. Was he summoning them?'

'Not exactly,' Zia said. 'His presence is so strong, he makes the language of the universe visible simply by being in the room. No matter what our specialty, each magician's greatest hope is to become a speaker of the Divine Words—to know the language of creation so well that we can fashion reality simply by speaking, not even using a scroll.'

'Like saying *shatter*,' I ventured. 'And having a door explode.'

Zia scowled. 'Yes, but such a thing would take years of practice.'

'Really? Well—'

Out of the corner of my eye, I saw Carter shaking his head, silently warning me to shut up.

'*Um*...' I stammered. 'Some day, I'll learn to do that.'

Zia raised an eyebrow. 'First, master the scroll.'

I was getting tired of her attitude, so I picked up

the stylus and wrote *Fire* in English.

Zia leaned forward and frowned. 'You shouldn't—'

Before she could finish, a column of flame erupted in her face. I screamed, sure I'd done something horrible, but when the fire died Zia was still there, looking astonished, her eyebrows singed and her bangs smoldering.

'Oh, god,' I said. 'Sorry, sorry. Do I die now?'

For three heartbeats, Zia stared at me.

'Now,' she announced. 'I think you are ready to duel.'

*   *   *

We used another magic gateway, which Zia summoned right on the library wall. We stepped into a circle of swirling sand and popped out the other side, covered in dust and grit, in the front of some ruins. The harsh sunlight almost blinded me.

'I hate portals,' Carter muttered, brushing the sand out of his hair.

Then he looked around and his eyes widened. 'This is Luxor! That's, like, hundreds of miles south of Cairo.'

I sighed. 'And that amazes you after teleporting from New York?'

He was too busy checking out our surroundings to answer.

I suppose the ruins were all right, though once you've seen one pile of crumbly Egyptian stuff, you've seen them all, I say. We stood on a wide avenue flanked by human-headed beasties, most of which were broken. The road went on behind us as far as I could see, but in front of us it ended at a temple much bigger than the one in the New York museum.

The walls were at least six stories high. Big stone pharaohs stood guard on either side of the entrance, and a single obelisk stood on the left-hand side. It looked as if one used to stand on the right as well, but it was now gone.

'Luxor is a modern name,' Zia said. 'This was once the city of Thebes. This temple was one of the most important in Egypt. It is the best place for us to practice.'

'Because it's already destroyed?' I asked.

Zia gave me one of her famous scowls. 'No, Sadie—because it is still full of magic. And it was sacred to your family.'

'Our family?' Carter asked.

Zia didn't explain, as usual. She just gestured for us to follow.

'I don't like those ugly sphinxes,' I mumbled as we walked down the path.

'Those ugly sphinxes are creatures of law and order,' Zia said, 'protectors of Egypt. They are on *our* side.'

'If you say so.'

Carter nudged me as we passed the obelisk. 'You know the missing one is in Paris.'

I rolled my eyes. 'Thank you, Mr. Wikipedia. I thought they were in New York and London.'

'That's a different pair,' Carter said, like I was supposed to care. 'The other *Luxor* obelisk is in Paris.'

'Wish I was in Paris,' I said. 'Lot better than this place.'

We walked into a dusty courtyard surrounded by crumbling pillars and statues with various missing body parts. Still, I could tell the place had once been quite impressive.

'Where are the people?' I asked. 'Middle of the day, winter holidays. Shouldn't there be loads of tourists?'

Zia made a distasteful expression. 'Usually, yes. I have encouraged them to stay away for a few hours.'

'How?'

'Common minds are easy to manipulate.' She looked pointedly at me, and I remembered how she'd forced me to talk in the New York museum. Oh, yes, she was just *begging* for more scorched eyebrows.

'Now, to the duel.' She summoned her staff and drew two circles in the sand about ten meters apart. She directed me to stand in one of them and Carter in the other.

'I've got to duel *him*?' I asked.

I found the idea preposterous. The only thing Carter had shown aptitude for was summoning butter knives and pooping birds. Well, all right, and that bit on the chasm bridge deflecting the daggers, but still—what if I hurt him? As annoying as Carter might be, I didn't want to accidentally summon that glyph I'd made in Amos's house and explode him to bits.

Perhaps Carter was thinking the same thing, because he'd started to sweat. 'What if we do something wrong?' he asked.

'I will oversee the duel,' Zia promised. 'We will start slowly. The first magician to knock the other out of his or her circle wins.'

'But we haven't been trained!' I protested.

'One learns by doing,' Zia said. 'This is not

180

school, Sadie. You cannot learn magic by sitting at a desk and taking notes. You can only learn magic by doing magic.'

'But—'

'Summon whatever power you can,' Zia said. 'Use whatever you have available. Begin!'

I looked at Carter doubtfully. *Use whatever I have?* I opened the leather satchel and looked inside. A lump of wax? Probably not. I drew the wand and rod. Immediately, the rod expanded until I was holding a two-meter-long white staff.

Carter drew his sword, though I couldn't imagine what he'd do with it. Rather hard to hit me from ten meters away.

I wanted this over, so I raised my staff like I'd seen Zia do. I thought the word *Fire*.

A small flame sputtered to life on the end of the staff. I willed it to get bigger. The fire momentarily brightened, but then my eyesight went fuzzy. The flame died. I fell to my knees, feeling as if I'd run a marathon.

'You okay?' Carter called.

'No,' I complained.

'If she knocks herself out, do I win?' he asked.

'Shut up!' I said.

'Sadie, you must be careful,' Zia called. 'You drew from your own reserves, not from the staff. You can quickly deplete your magic.'

I got shakily to my feet. 'Explain?'

'A magician begins a duel full of magic, the way you might be full after a good meal—'

'Which I never got,' I reminded her.

'Each time you do magic,' Zia continued, 'you expend energy. You can draw energy from *yourself*, but you must know your limits. Otherwise you could exhaust yourself, or worse.'

I swallowed and looked at my smoldering staff. 'How much worse?'

'You could literally burn up.'

I hesitated, thinking how to ask my next question without saying too much. 'But I've done magic before. Sometimes it doesn't exhaust me. Why?'

From around her neck, Zia unclasped an amulet. She threw it into the air, and with a flash it turned into a giant vulture. The massive black bird soared over the ruins. As soon as it was out of sight, Zia extended her hand and the amulet appeared in her palm.

'Magic can be drawn from many sources,' she said. 'It can be stored in scrolls, wands, or staffs. Amulets are especially powerful. Magic can also be drawn straight from Ma'at, using the Divine Words, but this is difficult. Or'—she locked eyes with me—'it can be summoned from the gods.'

'Why are you looking at me?' I demanded. *'I didn't summon any gods. They just seem to find me!'*

She put on her necklace but said nothing.

'Hold on,' Carter said. 'You claimed this place was sacred to our family.'

'It was,' Zia agreed.

'But wasn't this . . .' Carter frowned. 'Didn't the pharaohs have a yearly festival here or something?'

'Indeed,' she said. 'The pharaoh would walk down the processional path all the way from Karnak to Luxor. He would enter the temple and become one with the gods. Sometimes, this was purely ceremonial. Sometimes, with the great pharaohs like Ramesses, here—' Zia pointed to one of the huge crumbling statues.

'They actually hosted the gods,' I interrupted, remembering what Iskandar had said.

Zia narrowed her eyes. 'And yet you claim to know nothing of your family's past.'

'Wait a second,' Carter protested. 'You're saying we're related to—'

'The gods choose their hosts carefully,' Zia said. 'They always prefer the blood of the pharaohs. When a magician has the blood of *two* royal families . . .'

I exchanged looks with Carter. Something Bast said came back to me: 'Your family was born to magic.' And Amos had told us that both sides of our family had a complicated history with the gods, and that Carter and I were the most powerful children to be born in centuries. A bad feeling settled over me, like an itchy blanket prickling against my skin.

'Our parents were from different royal lines,' I said. 'Dad . . . he must've been descended from Narmer, the first pharaoh. I told you he looked like that picture!'

'That's not possible,' Carter said. 'That was five thousand years ago.' But I could see his mind was racing. 'Then the Fausts . . .' He turned to Zia. 'Ramesses the Great built this courtyard. You're telling me our mom's family is descended from him?'

Zia sighed. 'Don't tell me your parents kept this from you. Why do you think you are so dangerous to us?'

'You think we're hosting gods,' I said, absolutely stunned. 'That's what you're worried about—just because of something our great-times-a-thousand grandparents did? That's completely daft.'

'Then prove it!' Zia said. 'Duel, and show me how weak your magic is!'

She turned her back on us, as if we were completely unimportant.

Something inside me snapped. I'd had the worst two days ever. I'd lost my father, my home, and my cat, been attacked by monsters and had ice water dumped on my head. Now this *witch* was turning her back on me. She didn't want to train us. She wanted to see how dangerous we were.

Well, fine.

'Um, Sadie?' Carter called. He must've seen from my expression that I was beyond reason.

I focused on my staff. *Maybe not fire. Cats have always liked me. Maybe . . .*

I threw my staff straight at Zia. It hit the ground at her heels and immediately transformed into a snarling she-lion. Zia whirled in surprise, but then everything went wrong.

The lion turned and charged at Carter, as if she knew I was supposed to be dueling him.

I had a split second to think: *What have I done?*

Then the cat lunged . . . and Carter's form flickered. He rose off the ground, surrounded by a golden holographic shell like the one Bast had used, except that his giant image was a warrior with the head of a falcon. Carter swung his sword, and the falcon warrior did likewise, slicing the lion with a shimmering blade of energy. The cat dissolved in midair, and my staff clattered to the ground, cut neatly in half.

Carter's avatar shimmered, then disappeared. He dropped to the ground and grinned. 'Fun.'

He didn't even look tired. Once I got over my

184

relief that I hadn't killed him, I realized I didn't feel tired either. If anything, I had *more* energy.

I turned defiantly to Zia. 'Well? Better, right?'

Her face was ashen. 'The falcon. He—he summoned—'

Before she could finish, footsteps pounded on the stones. A young initiate raced into the courtyard, looking panicked. Tears streaked his dusty face. He said something to Zia in hurried Arabic. When Zia got his message, she sat down hard in the sand. She covered her face and began to tremble.

Carter and I left our dueling circles and ran to her.

'Zia?' Carter said. 'What's wrong?'

She took a deep breath, trying to gather her composure. When she looked up, her eyes were red. She said something to the adept, who nodded and ran back the way he'd come.

'News from the First Nome,' she said shakily. 'Iskandar . . .' Her voice broke.

I felt as if a giant fist had punched me in the stomach. I thought about Iskandar's strange words last night: *It seems I, too, can rest at last.* 'He's dead, isn't he? That's what he meant.'

Zia stared at me. 'What do you mean: "That's what he meant"?'

'I . . .' I was about to say that I'd spoken with Iskandar the night before. Then I realized this might not be a good thing to mention. 'Nothing. How did it happen?'

'In his sleep,' Zia said. 'He—he had been ailing for years, of course. But still . . .'

'It's okay,' Carter said. 'I know he was important to you.'

She wiped at her tears, then rose unsteadily. 'You don't understand. Desjardins is next in line. As soon as he is named Chief Lector, he will order you executed.'

'But we haven't done anything!' I said.

Zia's eyes flashed with anger. 'You still don't realize how dangerous you are? You are hosting gods.'

'Ridiculous,' I insisted, but an uneasy feeling was building inside me. If it were true . . . no, it couldn't be! Besides, how could anyone, even a poxy old nutter like Desjardins, seriously execute children for something they weren't even aware of?

'He will order me to bring you in,' Zia warned, 'and I will have to obey.'

'You can't!' Carter cried. 'You *saw* what happened in the museum. We're not the problem. Set is. And if Desjardins isn't taking that seriously . . . well, maybe he's part of the problem too.'

Zia gripped her staff. I was sure she was going to fry us with a fireball, but she hesitated.

'Zia.' I decided to take a risk. 'Iskandar talked with me last night. He caught me sneaking around the Hall of Ages.'

She looked at me in shock. I reckoned I had only seconds before that shock turned to anger.

'He said you were his best pupil,' I recalled. 'He said you were wise. He also said Carter and I have a difficult path ahead of us, and you would know how to help us when the time came.'

Her staff smoldered. Her eyes reminded me of glass about to shatter.

'Desjardins will kill us,' I persisted. 'Do you think that's what Iskandar had in mind?'

I counted to five, six, seven. Just when I was sure she was going to blast us, she lowered her staff. 'Use the obelisk.'

'What?' I asked.

'The obelisk at the entrance, fool! You have five minutes, perhaps less, before Desjardins sends orders for your execution. Flee, and destroy Set. The Demon Days begin at sundown. All portals will stop working. You need to get as close as possible to Set before that happens.'

'Hold on,' I said. 'I meant you should come with us and help us! We can't even use an obelisk, much less destroy Set!'

'I cannot betray the House,' she said. 'You have four minutes now. If you can't operate the obelisk, you'll die.'

That was enough incentive for me. I started to drag Carter off, but Zia called: 'Sadie?'

When I looked back, Zia's eyes were full of bitterness.

'Desjardins will order me to hunt you down,' she warned. 'Do you understand?'

Unfortunately, I did. The next time we met, we would be enemies.

I grabbed Carter's hand and ran.

17.
A BAD TRIP TO PARIS

Okay, before I get to the demon fruit bats, I should back up.

The night before we fled Luxor, I didn't get much sleep—first because of an out-of-body experience, then a run-in with Zia. [Stop smirking, Sadie. It wasn't a *good* run-in.]

After lights out, I tried to sleep. Honest. I even used the stupid magic headrest they gave me instead of a pillow, but it didn't help. As soon as I managed to shut my eyes, my *ba* decided to take a little trip.

Just like before, I felt myself floating above my body, taking on a winged form. Then the current of the Duat swept me away at blurring speed. When my vision cleared, I found myself in a dark cavern. Uncle Amos was sneaking through it, finding his way with a faint blue light that flickered on the top of his staff. I wanted to call to him, but my voice didn't work. I'm not sure how he could miss me, floating a few feet away in glowing chicken form, but apparently I was invisible to him.

He stepped forward and the ground at his feet suddenly blazed to life with a red hieroglyph. Amos cried out, but his mouth froze half open. Coils of light wrapped around his legs like vines. Soon red tendrils completely entwined him, and Amos stood petrified, his unblinking eyes staring straight ahead.

I tried to fly to him, but I was stuck in place, floating helplessly, so I could only observe.

Laughter echoed through the cavern. A horde of *things* emerged from the darkness—toad creatures, animal-headed demons, and even stranger monsters half hidden in the gloom. They'd been lying in ambush, I realized—waiting for Amos. In front of them appeared a fiery silhouette—Set, but his form was much clearer now, and this time it wasn't human. His body was emaciated, slimy, and black, and his head was that of a feral beast.

'*Bon soir,* Amos,' Set said. 'How nice of you to come. We're going to have so much fun!'

*   *   *

I sat bolt upright in bed, back in my own body, with my heart pounding.

Amos had been captured. I knew it for certain. And even worse . . . Set had known somehow that Amos was coming. I thought back to something Bast had said, about how the serpopards had broken in to the mansion. She'd said the defenses had been sabotaged, and only a magician of the House could've done it. A horrible suspicion started building inside me.

I stared into the dark for a long time, listening to the little kid next to me mumbling spells in his sleep. When I couldn't stand it any longer, I opened the door with a push of my mind, the way I'd done at Amos's mansion, and I sneaked out.

I was wandering through the empty marketplace, thinking about Dad and Amos, replaying the events over and over, trying to figure out what I could've done differently to save them, when I spotted Zia.

She was hurrying across the courtyard as if she were being chased, but what really caught my attention was the shimmering black cloud around her, as if someone had wrapped her in a glittery shadow. She came to a section of blank wall and waved her hand. Suddenly a doorway appeared. Zia glanced nervously behind her and ducked inside.

Of course I followed.

I moved quietly up to the doorway. I could hear Zia's voice inside, but I couldn't make out what she was saying. Then the doorway began to solidify, turning back into a wall, and I made a split-second decision. I jumped through.

Inside, Zia was alone with her back to me. She was kneeling at a stone altar, chanting something under her breath. The walls were decorated with Ancient Egyptian drawings and modern photographs.

The glittery shadow no longer surrounded Zia, but something even stranger was happening. I'd been planning to tell Zia about my nightmare, but that went completely out of my thoughts when I saw what she was doing. She cupped her palms, the way you might hold a bird, and a glowing blue sphere appeared, about the size of a golf ball. Still chanting, she raised her hands. The sphere flew up, straight through the ceiling, and vanished.

Some instinct told me this was *not* something I was supposed to see.

I thought about backing out of the room. Only problem: the door was gone. No other exits. It was only a matter of time before—*Uh-oh.*

Maybe I'd made a noise. Maybe her magical senses had kicked in. But faster than I could react, Zia pulled her wand and turned on me, flames flickering down the edge of the boomerang.

'Hi,' I said nervously.

Her expression turned from anger to surprise, then back to anger. 'Carter, what are you doing here?'

'Just walking around. I saw you in the courtyard, so—'

'What do you mean you *saw* me?'

'Well . . . you were running, and you had this black shimmery stuff around you, and—'

'You *saw* that? Impossible.'

'Why? What was it?'

She dropped her wand and the fire died. 'I don't appreciate being followed, Carter.'

'Sorry. I thought you might be in trouble.'

She started to say something, but apparently changed her mind. 'In trouble . . . that's true enough.'

She sat down heavily and sighed. In the candlelight, her amber eyes looked dark and sad.

She stared at the photos behind the altar, and I realized she was in some of them. There she was as a little girl, standing barefoot outside a mud-brick house, squinting resentfully at the camera as if she didn't want her picture taken. Next to that, a wider shot showed a whole village on the Nile—the kind of place my dad took me to sometimes, where nothing had changed much in the last two thousand years. A crowd of villagers grinned and waved at the camera as if they were celebrating, and above them little Zia rode on the shoulders of a man who must've been her father. Another

191

photo was a family shot: Zia holding hands with her mother and father. They could've been any *fellahin* family anywhere in Egypt, but her dad had especially kindly, twinkling eyes—I thought he must have a good sense of humor. Her mom's face was unveiled, and she laughed as if her husband had just cracked a joke.

'Your folks look cool,' I said. 'Is that home?'

Zia seemed like she wanted to get angry, but she kept her emotions under control. Or maybe she just didn't have the energy. 'It *was* my home. The village no longer exists.'

I waited, not sure I dared to ask. We locked eyes, and I could tell she was deciding how much to tell me.

'My father was a farmer,' she said, 'but he also worked for archaeologists. In his spare time he'd scour the desert for artifacts and new sites where they might want to dig.'

I nodded. What Zia described was pretty common. Egyptians have been making extra money that way for centuries.

'One night when I was eight, my father found a statue,' she said. 'Small but very rare: a statue of a monster, carved from red stone. It had been buried in a pit with a lot of other statues that were all smashed. But somehow this one survived. He brought it home. He didn't know . . . He didn't realize magicians imprison monsters and spirits inside such statues, and break them to destroy their essence. My father brought the unbroken statue into our village, and . . . and accidentally unleashed . . .'

Her voice faltered. She stared at the picture of her father smiling and holding her hand.

'Zia, I'm sorry.'

She knit her eyebrows. 'Iskandar found me. He and the other magicians destroyed the monster . . . but not in time. They found me curled in a fire pit under some reeds where my mother had hidden me. I was the only survivor.'

I tried to imagine how Zia would've looked when Iskandar found her—a little girl who'd lost everything, alone in the ruins of her village. It was hard to picture her that way.

'So this room is a shrine to your family,' I guessed. 'You come here to remember them.'

Zia looked at me blankly. 'That's the problem, Carter. I *can't* remember. Iskandar tells me about my past. He gave me these pictures, explained what happened. But . . . I have no memory at all.'

I was about to say, 'You were only eight.' Then I realized I'd been the same age when my mom died, when Sadie and I were split up. I remembered all of that so clearly. I could still see our house in Los Angeles and the way the stars looked at night from our back porch overlooking the ocean. My dad would tell us wild stories about the constellations. Then every night before bed, Sadie and I would cuddle up with Mom on the sofa, fighting for her attention, and she'd tell us not to believe a word of Dad's stories. She'd explain the science behind the stars, talk about physics and chemistry as if we were her college students. Looking back on it, I wondered if she'd been trying to warn us: Don't believe in those gods and myths. They're too dangerous.

I remembered our last trip to London as a family, how nervous Mom and Dad seemed on the plane. I remembered our dad coming back to our grandparents' flat after Mom had died, and telling us there had been an accident. Even before he explained, I knew it was bad, because I'd never seen my dad cry before.

The little details that *did* fade drove me crazy— like the smell of Mom's perfume, or the way her voice sounded. The older I got, the harder I held on to those things. I couldn't imagine not remembering anything. How could Zia stand it?

'Maybe . . .' I struggled to find the right words. 'Maybe you just—'

She held up her hand. 'Carter, believe me. I've tried to remember. It's no use. Iskandar is the only family I've ever had.'

'What about friends?'

Zia stared at me as if I'd used a foreign term. I realized I hadn't seen anyone close to our age in the First Nome. Everyone was either much younger or much older.

'I don't have time for friends,' she said. 'Besides, when initiates turn thirteen, they're assigned to other nomes around the world. I am the only one who stayed here. I like being alone. It's fine.'

The hairs stood up on the back of my neck. I'd said almost the same thing, many times, when people asked me what it was like being homeschooled by my dad. Didn't I miss having friends? Didn't I want a normal life? 'I like being alone. It's fine.'

I tried to picture Zia going to a regular public high school, learning a locker combination, hanging out in the cafeteria. I couldn't picture it. I imagined she would be as lost as I would.

'Tell you what,' I said. 'After the testing, after the Demon Days, when things settle down—'

'Things won't settle down.'

'—I'm going to take you to the mall.'

She blinked. 'The mall? For what reason?'

'To hang out,' I said. 'We'll get some hamburgers. See a movie.'

Zia hesitated. 'Is this what you'd call a "date"?'

My expression must've been priceless, because Zia actually cracked a smile. 'You look like a cow hit with a shovel.'

'I didn't mean . . . I just meant . . .'

She laughed, and suddenly it was easier to imagine her as a regular high school kid.

'I will look forward to this *mall,* Carter,' she said. 'You are either a very interesting person . . . or a very dangerous one.'

'Let's go with interesting.'

She waved her hand, and the door reappeared. 'Go now. And be careful. The next time you sneak up on me, you might not be so fortunate.'

At the doorway, I turned. 'Zia, what was that black shimmery stuff?'

Her smile faded. 'An invisibility spell. Only very powerful magicians are able to see through it. *You* should not have.'

She stared at me for answers, but I didn't have any.

'Maybe it was . . . wearing off or something,' I managed. 'And, can I ask, the blue sphere?'

She frowned. 'The what?'

'The thing you released that went into the ceiling.'

She looked mystified. 'I . . . I don't know what you mean. Perhaps the candlelight was playing tricks on your eyes.'

Awkward silence. Either she was lying to me, or

I was going crazy, or . . . I didn't know what. I realized I hadn't told her about my vision of Amos and Set, but I felt that I'd already pushed her as far as I could for one night.

'Okay,' I said. 'Good night.'

I made my way back to the dorm, but I didn't get to sleep again for a long time.

* * *

Fast-forward to Luxor. Maybe now you understand why I didn't want to leave Zia behind, and why I didn't believe Zia would actually hurt us.

On the other hand, I knew she wasn't lying about Desjardins. That guy wouldn't think twice about turning us into escargots. And the fact that Set has spoken French in my dream—'*Bon soir*, Amos.' Was that just a coincidence . . . or was something a *lot* worse going on?

Anyway, when Sadie tugged on my arm, I followed.

We ran out of the temple and headed for the obelisk. But naturally, it wasn't that simple. We're the Kane family. Nothing is *ever* that simple.

Just as we reached the obelisk, I heard the *slish*-ing sound of a magic portal. About a hundred yards down the path, a bald magician in white robes stepped out of a whirling sand vortex.

'Hurry,' I told Sadie. I grabbed the staff-rod from my bag and threw it to her. 'Since I cut yours in half. I'll stick with the sword.'

'But I don't know what I'm doing!' she protested, searching the obelisk's base as if she hoped to find a secret switch.

The magician regained his balance and spit the

196

sand out of his mouth. Then he spotted us. 'Stop!'

'Yeah,' I muttered. 'That's gonna happen.'

'Paris.' Sadie turned to me. 'You said the other obelisk is in Paris, right?'

'Right. *Um,* not to rush you, but . . .'

The magician raised his staff and started chanting.

I fumbled for the hilt of my sword. My legs felt like they were turning to butter. I wondered if I could pull off that hawk warrior thing again. That had been cool, but it had also been just a duel. And the test at the chasm bridge, when I'd deflected those daggers—that hadn't seemed like *me.* Every time I'd drawn this sword so far, I'd had help: Zia had been there, or Bast. I'd never felt completely alone. This time, it was just me. I was crazy to think I could hold off a full-fledged magician. I was no warrior. Everything I knew about swords came from reading books—the history of Alexander the Great, *The Three Musketeers*—as if that could help! With Sadie occupied at the obelisk, I was on my own.

No you're not, said a voice inside me.

Great, I thought. *I'm on my own* and *going crazy.*

At the far end of the avenue, the magician called out: 'Serve the House of Life!'

But I got the feeling he wasn't talking to me.

The air between us began to shimmer. Waves of heat flowed from the double lines of sphinxes, making them look as if they were moving. Then I realized they *were* moving. Each one cracked down the middle, and ghostly apparitions appeared from the stone like locusts breaking out of their shells. Not all of them were in good shape. The spirit creatures from broken statues had missing heads or feet. Some limped along on only three legs. But at least a dozen attack sphinxes were in perfect condition, and they all came toward us—each one the size of a Doberman, made of milky white smoke and hot vapor. So much for the sphinxes being on *our* side.

'Soon!' I warned Sadie.

'Paris!' she called, and raised her staff and wand. 'I want to go there *now*. Two tickets. First-class would be nice!'

The sphinxes advanced. The nearest one launched itself toward me, and with sheer luck I managed to slice it in half. The monster evaporated into smoke, but it let out a blast of heat so intense I thought my face was going to melt right off.

Two more sphinx ghosts loped toward me. A dozen more were only a few steps behind. I could feel my pulse pounding in my neck.

Suddenly the ground shook. The sky darkened, and Sadie yelled, 'Yes!'

The obelisk glowed with purple light, humming with power. Sadie touched the stone and yelped. She was sucked inside and disappeared.

'Sadie!' I yelled.

In my moment of distraction, two of the sphinxes slammed into me, knocking me to the ground. My sword skittered away. My rib cage went *crack!* and my chest erupted in pain. The heat coming off the creatures was unbearable—it was like being crushed under a hot oven.

I stretched out my fingers toward the obelisk. Just a few inches too far. I could hear the other sphinxes coming, the magician chanting, 'Hold him! Hold him!'

With my last bit of strength, I lurched toward the obelisk, every nerve in my body screaming with pain. My fingertips touched the base, and the world went black.

Suddenly I was lying on cold, wet stone. I was in the middle of a huge public plaza. Rain was pouring down, and the chilly air told me I was no longer in Egypt. Sadie was somewhere close by, yelling in alarm.

The bad news: I'd brought the two sphinxes with me. One jumped off me and bounded after Sadie. The other was still on my chest, glaring down at me, its back steaming in the rain, its smoky white eyes inches from my face.

I tried to remember the Egyptian word for *fire*. Maybe if I could set the monster ablaze . . . but my mind was too full of panic. I heard an explosion off to my right, in the direction Sadie had run. I hoped she'd gotten away, but I couldn't be sure.

The sphinx opened its mouth and formed smoky fangs that had no business on an Ancient Egyptian king. It was about to chomp my face when a dark form loomed up behind it and shouted, *'Mange des muffins!'*

Slice!

The sphinx dissolved into smoke.

I tried to rise but couldn't. Sadie stumbled over. 'Carter! Oh god, are you okay?'

I blinked at the other person—the one who had saved me: a tall, thin figure in a black, hooded raincoat. What had she yelled: *Eat muffins?* What kind of battle cry was that?

She threw off her coat, and a woman in a leopard-skin acrobatic suit grinned down at me, showing off her fangs and her lamplike yellow eyes.

'Miss me?' asked Bast.

18.

WHEN FRUIT BATS GO BAD

CARTER

We huddled under the eaves of a big white government building and watched the rain pour down on the Place de la Concorde. It was a miserable day to be in Paris. The winter skies were heavy and low, and the cold, wet air soaked right into my bones. There were no tourists, no foot traffic. Everyone with any sense was inside by a fire enjoying a hot drink.

To our right, the River Seine wound sluggishly through the city. Across the enormous plaza, the gardens of the Tuileries were shrouded in a soupy haze.

The Egyptian obelisk rose up lonely and dark in the middle of the square. We waited for more enemies to pop out of it, but none came. I remembered what Zia had said about artifacts needing a twelve-hour cooldown before they could be used again. I hoped she was right.

'Hold still,' Bast told me.

I winced as she pressed her hand against my chest. She whispered something in Egyptian, and the pain slowly subsided.

'Broken rib,' she announced. 'Better now, but you should rest for at least a few minutes.'

'What about the magicians?'

'I wouldn't worry about them just yet. The House will assume you teleported somewhere else.'

'Why?'

'Paris is the Fourteenth Nome—Desjardins' headquarters. You would be insane trying to hide in his home territory.'

'Great.' I sighed.

'And your amulets *do* shield you,' Bast added. 'I could find Sadie anywhere because of my promise to protect her. But the amulets will keep you veiled from the eyes of Set and from other magicians.'

I thought about the dark room in the First Nome with all the children looking into bowls of oil. Were they looking for us right now? The thought was creepy.

I tried to sit up and winced again.

'Stay still,' Bast ordered. 'Really, Carter, you should learn to fall like a cat.'

'I'll work on that,' I promised. 'How are you even alive? Is it that "nine lives' thing?'

'Oh, that's just a silly legend. I'm *immortal.*'

'But the scorpions!' Sadie scrunched in closer, shivering and drawing Bast's raincoat around her shoulders. 'We saw them overwhelm you!'

Bast made a purring sound. 'Dear Sadie, you do care! I must say I've worked for *many* children of the pharaohs, but you two—' She looked genuinely touched. 'Well, I'm sorry if I worried you. It's true the scorpions reduced my power to almost nothing. I held them off as long as I could. Then I had just enough energy to revert to Muffin's form and slip into the Duat.'

'I thought you weren't good at portals,' I said.

'Well, first off, Carter, there are many ways in

and out of the Duat. It has many different regions and layers—the Abyss, the River of Night, the Land of the Dead, the Land of Demons—'

'Sounds lovely,' Sadie muttered.

'Anyway, portals are like doors. They pass through the Duat to connect one part of the mortal world to another. And yes, I'm not good at those. But I *am* a creature of the Duat. If I'm on my own, slipping into the nearest layer for a quick escape is relatively easy.'

'And if they'd killed you?' I asked. 'I mean, killed Muffin?'

'That would've banished me deep into the Duat. It would've been rather like putting my feet in concrete and dropping me into the middle of the sea. It would've taken years, perhaps centuries, before I would've been strong enough to return to the mortal world. Fortunately, that didn't happen. I came back straightaway, but by the time I got to the museum, the magicians had already captured you.'

'We weren't exactly *captured*,' I said.

'Really, Carter? How long were you in the First Nome before they decided to kill you?'

'Um, about twenty-four hours.'

Bast whistled. 'They've gotten friendlier! They used to blast godlings to dust in the first few minutes.'

'We're *not*—wait, what did you call us?'

Sadie answered, sounding as if in a trance: ' "Godlings." That's what we are, aren't we? That's why Zia was so frightened of us, why Desjardins wants to kill us.'

Bast patted Sadie's knee. 'You always were bright, dear.'

202

'Hold on,' I said. 'You mean hosts for *gods*? That's not possible. I think I'd know if . . .'

Then I thought about the voice in my head, warning me to hide when I met Iskandar. I thought about all the things I was suddenly able to do—like fight with a sword and summon a magical shell of armor. Those were not things I'd covered in home school.

'Carter,' Sadie said. 'When the Rosetta Stone shattered, it let out five gods, right? Dad joined with Osiris. Amos told us that. Set . . . I don't know. He got away somehow. But you and I—'

'The amulets protected us.' I clutched the Eye of Horus around my neck. 'Dad said they would.'

'*If* we had stayed out of the room, as Dad told us to,' Sadie recalled. 'But we were there, watching. We wanted to help him. We practically *asked* for power, Carter.'

Bast nodded. 'That makes all the difference. An invitation.'

'And since then . . .' Sadie looked at me tentatively, almost daring me to make fun of her. 'I've had this feeling. Like a voice inside me . . .'

By now the cold rain had soaked right through my clothes. If Sadie hadn't said something, maybe I could've denied what was happening a little longer. But I thought about what Amos had said about our family having a long history with the gods. I thought about what Zia had told us about our lineage: 'The gods choose their hosts carefully. They always prefer the blood of the pharaohs.'

'Okay,' I admitted. 'I've been hearing a voice too. So either we're both going crazy—'

'The amulet.' Sadie pulled it from her shirt collar and held it for Bast to see. 'It's the symbol of a goddess, isn't it?'

I hadn't seen her amulet in a long time. It was different from mine. It reminded me of an ankh, or maybe some kind of fancy tie.

'That is a *tyet*,' Bast said. 'A magic knot. And yes, it is often called—'

'The Knot of Isis,' Sadie said. I didn't see how she could know that, but she looked absolutely certain. 'In the Hall of Ages, I saw an image of Isis, and then I *was* Isis, trying to get away from Set, and—oh, god. That's it, isn't it? I'm her.'

She grabbed her shirt like she physically wanted to pull the goddess away from her. All I could do was stare. My sister, with her ratty red-highlighted hair and her linen pajamas and her combat boots—how could she possibly worry about being possessed by a *goddess*? What goddess would want her, except maybe the goddess of chewing gum?

But then . . . I'd been hearing a voice inside me too. A voice that was definitely not mine. I looked at my amulet, the Eye of Horus. I thought about the myths I knew—how Horus, the son of Osiris, had to avenge his father by defeating Set. And at Luxor I'd summoned an avatar with the head of a falcon.

I was afraid to try it, but I thought: *Horus?*

Well it's about time, the other voice said. *Hello, Carter.*

'Oh, no,' I said, panic rising in my chest. 'No, no, no. Somebody get a can opener. I've got a god stuck in my head.'

Bast's eyes lit up. 'You communicated with Horus directly? That's excellent progress!'

'Progress?' I banged my palms against my head. 'Get him out!'

204

Calm down, Horus said.

'Don't tell me to calm down!'

Bast frowned. 'I didn't.'

'Talking to him!' I pointed at my forehead.

'This is awful,' Sadie wailed. 'How do I get rid of her?'

Bast sniffed. 'First off, Sadie, you don't have *all* of her. Gods are very powerful. We can exist in many places at once. But yes, part of Isis's spirit now resides inside you. Just as Carter now carries the spirit of Horus. And frankly, you both should feel honored.'

'Right, very honored,' I said. 'Always wanted to be possessed!'

Bast rolled her eyes. 'Please, Carter, it's *not* possession. Besides, you and Horus want the same thing—to defeat Set, just as Horus did millennia ago, when Set first killed Osiris. If you don't, your father is doomed, and Set will become king of the earth.'

I glanced at Sadie, but she was no help. She ripped the amulet off her neck and threw it down. 'Isis got in through the amulet, didn't she? Well, I'll just—'

'I really wouldn't do that,' Bast warned.

But Sadie pulled out her wand and smashed the amulet. Blue sparks shot up from the ivory boomerang. Sadie yelped and dropped her wand, which was now smoking. Her hand was covered in black scorch marks. The amulet was fine. *'Ow!'* she said.

Bast sighed. She put her hand on Sadie's, and the burn marks faded. 'I *did* tell you. Isis channeled her power through the amulet, yes, but she's not there now. She's in *you*. And even so, magical amulets are practically indestructible.'

'So what are we supposed to do?' Sadie said.

'Well, for starters,' Bast said, 'Carter must use the power of Horus to defeat Set.'

'Oh, is that all?' I said. 'All by myself?'

'No, no. Sadie can help.'

'Oh, super.'

'I'll guide you as much as possible,' Bast promised, 'but in the end, the two of you must fight. Only Horus and Isis can defeat Set and avenge the death of Osiris. That's the way it was before. That's the way it must be now.'

'Then we get our dad back?' I asked.

Bast's smile wavered. 'If all goes well.'

She wasn't telling us everything. No surprise. But my brain was too fuzzy to figure out what I was missing.

I looked down at my hands. They didn't seem any different—no stronger, no godlier. 'If I've got the powers of a god, then why am I so . . .'

'Lame?' Sadie offered.

'Shut up,' I said. 'Why can't I use my powers better?'

'Takes practice,' Bast said. 'Unless you wish to give over control to Horus. Then he would use your form, and you would not have to worry.'

I could, a voice said inside me. *Let me fight Set. You can trust me.*

Yeah, right, I told him. *How can I be sure you wouldn't get me killed and just move on to some other host? How can I be sure you're not influencing my thoughts right now?*

I would not do that, the voice said. *I chose you because of your potential, Carter, and because we have the same goal. Upon my honor, if you let me control—*

'No,' I said.

I realized I'd spokn aloud; Sadie and Bast were both looking at me.

'I mean I'm not giving up control,' I said. 'This is *our* fight. Our dad's locked in a coffin. Our uncle's been captured.'

'Captured?' Sadie asked. I realized with a shock that I hadn't told her about my last little *ba* trip. There just hadn't been time.

When I gave her the details, she looked stricken. 'God, no.'

'Yeah,' I agreed. 'And Set spoke in French— *"Bon soir."* Sadie, what you said about Set getting away—maybe he didn't. If he was looking for a powerful host—'

'Desjardins,' Sadie finished.

Bast growled deep in her throat. 'Desjardins was in London the night your father broke the Rosetta Stone, wasn't he? Desjardins has always been full of anger, full of ambition. In many ways, he would be the perfect host for Set. If Set managed to possess Desjardins' body, that would mean the Red Lord now controls the man who is Chief Lector of the House . . . By Ra's throne, Carter, I hope you're wrong. The two of you will have to learn to use the power of the gods quickly. Whatever Set is planning, he'll do it on his birthday, when he's strongest. That's the third Demon Day—three days from now.'

'But I've already used Isis's powers, haven't I?' Sadie asked. 'I've summoned hieroglyphs. I activated the obelisk at Luxor. Was that her or me?'

'Both, dear,' Bast said. 'You and Carter have

207

great abilities on your own, but the power of the gods has hastened your development, and given you an extra reservoir to draw on. What would've taken you years to learn, you've accomplished in days. The more you channel the power of the gods, the more powerful you will become.'

'And the more dangerous it gets,' I guessed. 'The magicians told us hosting the gods can burn you out, kill you, drive you crazy.'

Bast fixed her eyes on me. Just for a second they were the eyes of a predator—ancient, powerful, dangerous. 'Not everyone can host a god, Carter. That's true. But *you* two are *both* blood of the pharaohs. You combine *two* ancient bloodlines. That's very rare, very powerful. And besides, if you think you can survive *without* the power of the gods, think again. Don't repeat your mother's—' She stopped herself.

'What?' Sadie demanded. 'What about our mother?'

'I shouldn't have said that.'

'Tell us, cat!' Sadie said.

I was afraid Bast might unsheathe her knives. Instead she leaned against the wall and stared out at the rain. 'When your parents released me from Cleopatra's Needle . . . there was much more energy than they expected. Your father spoke the actual summoning spell, and the blast would've killed him instantly, but your mother threw up a shield. In that split second, I offered her my help. I offered to merge our spirits and help protect them. But she would not accept my help. She chose to tap her own reservoir . . .'

'Her own magic,' Sadie murmured.

Bast nodded sadly. 'When a magician commits

herself to a spell, there is no turning back. If she overreaches her power . . . well, your mother used her last bit of energy protecting your father. To save him, she sacrificed herself. She literally—'

'Burned up,' I said. 'That's what Zia warned us about.'

The rain kept pouring down. I realized I was shivering.

Sadie wiped a tear from her cheek. She picked up her amulet and glared at it resentfully. 'We've got to save Dad. If he's really got the spirit of Osiris . . .'

She didn't finish, but I knew what she was thinking. I thought about Mom when I was little, her arm around my shoulders as we stood on the back deck of our house in L.A. She'd pointed out the stars to me: Polaris, Orion's Belt, Sirius. Then she'd smile at me, and I'd feel like I was more important than any constellation in the sky. My mom had sacrificed herself to save Dad's life. She'd used so much magic, she literally burned up. How could I ever be that brave? Yet I had to try to save Dad. Otherwise I'd feel like Mom's sacrifice had been for nothing. And maybe if we could rescue Dad, he could set things right, even bring back our mom.

Is that possible? I asked Horus, but his voice was silent.

'All right,' I decided. 'So how do we stop Set?'

Bast thought for a moment, then smiled. I got the feeling that whatever she was about to suggest, I wasn't going to like it. 'There *might* be a way without completely giving yourself over to the gods. There's a book by Thoth—one of the rare spell books written by the god of wisdom himself.

The one I'm thinking of details a way to overcome Set. It is the prized possession of a certain magician. All we need to do is sneak into his fortress, steal it, and leave before sunset, while we can still create a portal to the United States.'

'Perfect,' Sadie said.

'Hold up,' I said. 'Which magician? And where's the fortress?'

Bast stared at me as if I were a bit slow. 'Why, I think we already discussed him. Desjardins. His house is right here in Paris.'

*   *   *

Once I saw Desjardins' house, I hated him even more. It was a huge mansion on the other side of the Tuileries, on the rue des Pyramides.

'Pyramids Road?' Sadie said. 'Obvious, much?'

'Maybe he couldn't find a place on Stupid Evil Magician Street,' I suggested.

The house was spectacular. The spikes atop its wrought iron fence were gilded. Even in the winter rain, the front garden was bursting with flowers. Five stories of white marble walls and black-shuttered windows loomed before us, the whole thing topped off by a roof garden. I'd seen royal palaces smaller than this place.

I pointed to the front door, which was painted bright red. 'Isn't red a bad color in Egypt? The color of Set?'

Bast scratched her chin. 'Now that you mention it, yes. It's the color of chaos and destruction.'

'I thought black was the evil color,' Sadie said.

'No, dear. As usual, modern folk have it backward. Black is the color of good soil, like the

210

soil of the Nile. You can grow food in black soil. Food is good. Therefore black is good. Red is the color of desert sand. Nothing grows in the desert. Therefore red is evil.' She frowned. 'It *is* strange that Desjardins has a red door.'

'Well, I'm excited,' Sadie grumbled. 'Let's go knock.'

'There will be guards,' Bast said. 'And traps. And alarms. You can bet the house is heavily charmed to keep out gods.'

'Magicians can do that?' I asked. I imagined a big can of pesticide labeled *God-Away*.

'Alas, yes,' Bast said. 'I will not be able to cross the threshold uninvited. You, however—'

'I thought we're gods too,' Sadie said.

'That's the beauty of it,' Bast said. 'As hosts, you are still quite human. I have taken full possession of Muffin, so I am pretty much *me*—a goddess. But you are still—well, yourselves. Clear?'

'No,' I said.

'I suggest you turn into birds,' Bast said. 'You can fly to the roof garden and make your way in. Plus, I like birds.'

'First problem,' I said, 'we don't know how to turn into birds.'

'Easily fixed! And a good test at channeling godly power. Both Isis and Horus have bird forms. Simply imagine yourselves as birds, and birds you shall become.'

'Just like that,' Sadie said. 'You won't pounce on us?'

Bast looked offended. 'Perish the thought!'

I wished she hadn't used the word *perish*.

'Okay,' I said. 'Here goes.'

I thought: *You in there, Horus?*

211

What? he said testily.

Bird form, please.

Oh, I see. You don't trust me. But now you need my help.

Man, come on. Just do the falcon thing.

Would you settle for an emu?

I decided talking wasn't going to help, so I closed my eyes and imagined I was a falcon. Right away, my skin began to burn. I had trouble breathing. I opened my eyes and gasped.

I was really, really short—eye-level with Bast's shins. I was covered in feathers, and my feet had turned into wicked claws, kind of like my *ba* form, but this was real flesh and blood. My clothes and bag were gone, as if they'd melted into my feathers. My eyesight had completely changed, too. I could see a hundred and eighty degrees around, and the detail was incredible. Every leaf on every tree popped out. I spotted a cockroach a hundred yards away, scurrying into a sewer drain. I could see every pore on Bast's face, now looming above me and grinning.

'Better late than never,' she said. 'Took you almost ten minutes.'

Huh? The change had seemed instantaneous. Then I looked next to me and saw a beautiful gray bird of prey, a little bit smaller than me, with black-tipped wings and golden eyes. I'm not sure how, but I knew it was a kite—like the *bird* kite, not the kind with a string.

The kite let out a chirping sound—*'Ha, ha, ha.'* Sadie was laughing at me.

I opened my own beak, but no sound came out.

'Oh, you two look delicious,' Bast said, licking her lips. 'No, no—*er,* I mean wonderful. Now, off

212

you go!'

I spread my majestic wings. I had really done it! I was a noble falcon, lord of the sky. I launched myself off the sidewalk and flew straight into the fence.

'*Ha—ha—ha,*' Sadie chirped behind me.

Bast crouched down and began making weird chittering noises. *Uh-oh.* She was imitating birds. I'd seen enough cats do this when they were stalking. Suddenly my own obituary flashed in my head: *Carter Kane, 14, died tragically in Paris when he was eaten by his sister's cat, Muffin.*

I spread my wings, kicked off with my feet, and with three strong flaps, I was soaring through the rain. Sadie was right behind me. Together we spiraled up into the air.

I have to admit: it felt amazing. Ever since I was a little kid, I'd had dreams in which I was flying, and I always hated waking up. Now it wasn't a dream or even a *ba* trip. It was one hundred percent real. I sailed on the cold air currents above the rooftops of Paris. I could see the river, the Louvre Museum, the gardens and palaces. And a mouse—yum.

Hang on, Carter, I thought. *Not hunting mice.* I zeroed in on Desjardins' mansion, tucked in my wings, and shot downward.

I saw the rooftop garden, the double glass doors leading inside, and the voice inside me said: *Don't stop. It's an illusion. You've got to punch through their magic barriers.*

It was a crazy thought. I was plummeting so fast I would smack against the glass and become a feathery pancake, but I didn't slow down.

I rammed straight into the doors—and sailed

213

through them as if they didn't exist. I spread my wings and landed on a table. Sadie sailed in right behind me.

We were alone in the middle of a library. So far, so good.

I closed my eyes and thought about returning to my normal form. When I opened my eyes again, I was regular old Carter, sitting on a table in my regular clothes, my workbag back on my shoulder.

Sadie was still a kite.

'You can turn back now,' I told her.

She tilted her head and regarded me quizzically. She let out a frustrated croak.

I cracked a smile. 'You can't, can you? You're stuck?'

She pecked my hand with her extremely sharp beak.

'Ow!' I complained. 'It's not my fault. Keep trying.'

She closed her eyes and ruffled her feathers until she looked like she was going to explode, but she stayed a kite.

'Don't worry,' I said, trying to keep a straight face. 'Bast will help once we get out of here.'

'Ha—ha—ha.'

'Just keep watch. I'm going to look around.'

The room was huge—more like a traditional library than a magician's lair. The furniture was dark mahogany. Every wall was covered with floor-to-ceiling bookcases. Books overflowed onto the floor. Some were stacked on tables or stuffed into smaller shelves. A big easy chair by the window looked like the kind of place Sherlock Holmes would sit smoking a pipe.

Every step I took, the floorboards creaked,

which made me wince. I couldn't hear anyone else in the house, but I didn't want to take any chances.

Aside from the glass doors to the rooftop, the only other exit was a solid wooden door that locked from the inside. I turned the deadbolt. Then I wedged a chair up under the handle. I doubted that would keep magicians out for very long, but it might buy me a few seconds if things went bad.

I searched the bookshelves for what seemed like ages. All different types of books were jammed together—nothing alphabetized, nothing numbered. Most of the titles weren't in English. None were in hieroglyphics. I was hoping for something with big gold lettering that said *The Book of Thoth*, but no such luck.

'What would a *Book of Thoth* even look like?' I wondered.

Sadie turned her head and glared at me. I was pretty sure she was telling me to hurry up.

I wished there were *shabti* to fetch things, like the ones in Amos's library, but I didn't see any. Or maybe . . .

I slung Dad's bag off my shoulder. I set his magic box on the table and slid open the top. The little wax figure was still there, right where I'd left him. I picked him up and said, 'Doughboy, help me find *The Book of Thoth* in this library.'

His waxy eyes opened immediately. 'And why should I help you?'

'Because you have no choice.'

'I hate that argument! Fine—hold me up. I can't see the shelves.'

I walked him around the room, showing him the books. I felt pretty stupid giving the wax doll a

215

tour, but probably not as stupid as Sadie felt. She was still in bird form, scuttling back and forth on the table and snapping her beak in frustration as she tried to change back.

'Hold it!' Doughboy announced. 'This one is ancient—right here.'

I pulled down a thin volume bound in linen. It was so tiny, I would've missed it, but sure enough, the front cover was inscribed in hieroglyphics. I brought it over to the table and carefully opened it. It was more like a map than a book, unfolding into four parts until I was looking at a wide, long papyrus scroll with writing so old I could barely make out the characters.

I glanced at Sadie. 'I bet you could read this to me if you weren't a bird.'

She tried to peck me again, but I moved my hand.

'Doughboy,' I said. 'What is this scroll?'

'A spell lost in time!' he pronounced. 'Ancient words of tremendous power!'

'Well?' I demanded. 'Does it tell how to defeat Set?'

'Better! The title reads: *The Book of Summoning Fruit Bats*!'

I stared at him. 'Are you serious?'

'Would I joke about such a thing?'

'Who would want to summon fruit bats?'

'*Ha—ha—ha,*' Sadie croaked.

I pushed the scroll away and we went back to searching.

After about ten minutes, Doughboy squealed with delight. 'Oh, look! I remember this painting.'

It was a small oil portrait in a gilded frame, hanging on the end of a bookshelf. It must've been

216

important, because it was bordered by little silk curtains. A light shone upon the portrait dude's face so he seemed about to tell a ghost story.

'Isn't that the guy who plays Wolverine?' I asked, because he had some serious jowl hair going on.

'You disgust me!' Doughboy said. 'That is Jean-François Champollion.'

It took me a second, but I remembered the name. 'The guy who deciphered hieroglyphics from the Rosetta Stone.'

'Of course. Desjardins' great uncle.'

I looked at Champollion's picture again, and I could see the resemblance. They had the same fierce black eyes. 'Great uncle? But wouldn't that make Desjardins—'

'About two hundred years old,' Doughboy confirmed. 'Still a youngster. You know that when Champollion first deciphered hieroglyphics, he fell into a coma for five days? He became the first man outside the House of Life to ever unleash their magic, and it almost killed him. Naturally, that got the attention of the First Nome. Champollion died before he could join the House of Life, but the Chief Lector accepted his descendants for training. Desjardins is very proud of his family . . . but a little sensitive too, because he's such a newcomer.'

'That's why he didn't get along with our family,' I guessed. 'We're like . . . ancient.'

Doughboy cackled. 'And your father breaking the Rosetta Stone? Desjardins would've viewed that as an insult to his family honor! Oh, you should've seen the arguments Master Julius and Desjardins had in this room.'

'You've been here before?'

'Many times! I've been everywhere. I'm all-knowing.'

I tried to imagine Dad and Desjardins having an argument in here. It wasn't hard. If Desjardins hated our family, and if gods tended to find hosts who shared their goals, then it made total sense that Set would try to merge with him. Both wanted power, both were resentful and angry, both wanted to smash Sadie and me to a pulp. And if Set was now secretly controlling the Chief Lector . . . A drop of sweat trickled down the side of my face. I wanted to get out of this mansion.

Suddenly there was a banging sound below us, like someone closing a door downstairs.

'Show me where *The Book of Thoth* is,' I ordered Doughboy. 'Quick!'

As we moved down the shelves, Doughboy grew so warm in my hands, I was afraid he would melt. He kept a running commentary on the books.

'Ah, *Mastery of the Five Elements*!'

'Is that the one we want?' I asked.

'No, but a good one. How to tame the five essential elements of the universe—earth, air, water, fire, and cheese!'

'Cheese?'

He scratched his wax head. 'I'm pretty sure that's the fifth, yes. But moving right along!'

We turned to the next shelf. 'No,' he announced. 'No. Boring. Boring. Oh, Clive Cussler! No. No.'

I was about to give up hope when he said, 'There.'

I froze. 'Where—here?'

'The blue book with the gold trim,' he said. 'The one that's—'

I pulled it out, and the entire room began to

shake.

'—trapped,' Doughboy continued.

Sadie squawked urgently. I turned and saw her take flight. Something small and black swooped down from the ceiling. Sadie clashed with it in midair, and the black thing disappeared down her throat.

Before I could even register how gross that was, alarms blared downstairs. More black forms dropped from the ceiling and seemed to multiply in the air, swirling into a funnel cloud of fur and wings.

'There's your answer,' Doughboy told me. '*Desjardins* would want to summon fruit bats. You mess with the wrong books, you trigger a plague of fruit bats. That's the trap!'

The things were on me like I was a ripe mango—diving at my face, clawing at my arms. I clutched the book and ran to the table, but I could hardly see. 'Sadie, get out of here!' I yelled.

'*SAW!*' she cried, which I hoped meant yes.

I found Dad's workbag and shoved the book and Doughboy inside. The library door rattled. Voices yelled in French.

Horus, bird time! I thought desperately. *And no emu, please!*

I ran for the glass doors. At the last second, I found myself flying—once again a falcon, bursting into the cold rain. I knew with the senses of a predator that I was being followed by approximately four thousand angry fruit bats.

But falcons are wicked fast. Once outside, I raced north, hoping to draw the bats away from Sadie and Bast. I outdistanced the bats easily but let them keep close enough that they wouldn't give up. Then, with a burst of speed, I turned in a tight circle and shot back toward Sadie and Bast in a hundred-mile-an-hour dive.

Bast looked up in surprise as I plummeted to the sidewalk, tumbling over myself as I turned back into a human. Sadie caught my arm, and only then did I realize she was back to normal as well.

'That was awful!' she announced.

'Exit strategy, quick!' I pointed at the sky, where an angry black cloud of fruit bats was getting closer and closer.

'The Louvre.' Bast grabbed our hands. 'It's got the closest portal.'

Three blocks away. We'd never make it.

Then the red door of Desjardins' house blasted open, but we didn't wait to see what came out of it. We ran for our lives down the rue des Pyramides.

19.
A PICNIC IN THE SKY

SADIE

[Right, Carter. Give me the mic.]

So I'd been to the Louvre once before on holiday, but I hadn't been chased by vicious fruit bats. I would've been terrified, except I was too busy being angry with Carter. I couldn't believe the way he'd treated my bird problem. Honestly, I thought I would be a kite *forever,* suffocating inside a little feathery prison. And he had the nerve to make fun!

I promised myself I'd get revenge, but for the

time being we had enough worries staying alive.

We raced along in the cold rain. It was all I could do to avoid slipping on the slick pavements. I glanced back and saw two figures chasing us—men with shaved heads and goatees and black raincoats. They might've passed for normal mortals except they each carried a glowing staff. Not a good sign.

The bats were literally at our heels. One nipped my leg. Another buzzed my hair. I had to force myself to keep running. My stomach still felt queasy from eating one of the little pests when I was a kite—and no, that had *not* been my idea. Totally a defensive instinct!

'Sadie,' Bast called as we ran. 'You'll have only seconds to open the portal.'

'Where is it?' I yelled.

We dashed across the rue de Rivoli into a wide plaza surrounded by the wings of the Louvre. Bast made straight for the glass pyramid at the entrance, glowing in the dusk.

'You can't be serious,' I said. 'That isn't a *real* pyramid.'

'Of course it's real,' Bast said. 'The *shape* gives a pyramid its power. It is a ramp to the heavens.'

The bats were all around us now—biting our arms, flying around our feet. As their numbers increased, it got harder to see or move.

Carter reached for his sword then apparently remembered it wasn't there anymore. He'd lost it at Luxor. He swore and rummaged around in his workbag.

'Don't slow down!' Bast warned.

Carter pulled out his wand. In total frustration, he threw it at a bat. I thought this a pointless gesture, but the wand glowed white-hot and thumped the bat solidly on the head, knocking it out of the air. The wand ricocheted through the swarm, thumping six, seven, eight of the little monsters before returning to Carter's hand.

'Not bad,' I said. 'Keep it up!'

We arrived at the base of the pyramid. The plaza was thankfully empty. The last thing I wanted was my embarrassing death by fruit bats posted on YouTube.

'One minute until sundown,' Bast warned. 'Our last chance for summoning is *now.*'

She unsheathed her knives and started slicing bats out of the air, trying to keep them away from me. Carter's wand flew wildly, knocking fruit bats every which way. I faced the pyramid and tried to think of a portal, the way I'd done at Luxor, but it was almost impossible to concentrate.

Where do you wish to go? Isis said in my mind.

God, I don't care! America!

I realized I was crying. I hated to, but shock and fear were starting to overwhelm me. Where did I want to go? Home, of course! Back to my flat in London—back to my own room, my grandparents, my mates at school and my *old life.* But I couldn't. I had to think about my father and our mission. We had to get to Set.

America, I thought. *Now!*

My burst of emotion must've had some effect. The pyramid trembled. Its glass walls shimmered and the top of the structure began to glow.

A swirling sand vortex appeared, all right. Only one problem: it was hovering above the very top of the pyramid.

'Climb!' Bast said. Easy for her—she was a cat.

'The side is too steep!' Carter objected.

He'd done a good job with the bats. Dazed heaps littered the pavement, but more still flew round us, biting every bit of exposed skin, and the magicians were closing in.

'I'll toss you,' Bast said.

'Excuse me?' Carter protested, but she picked him up by his collar and pants and tossed him up the side of the pyramid. He skittered to the top in a very undignified manner and slipped straight through the portal.

'Now you, Sadie,' Bast said. 'Come on!'

Before I could move, a man's voice yelled, 'Stop!'

Stupidly, I froze. The voice was so powerful, it was hard not to.

The two magicians were approaching. The taller one spoke in perfect English: 'Surrender, Miss Kane, and return our master's property.'

'Sadie, don't listen,' Bast warned. 'Come here.'

'The cat goddess deceives you,' the magician said. 'She abandoned her post. She endangered us all. She will lead you to ruin.'

I could tell he meant it. He was absolutely convinced of what he said.

I turned to Bast. Her expression had changed. She looked wounded, even grief-stricken.

'What does he mean?' I said. 'What did you do wrong?'

'We have to leave,' she warned. 'Or they will kill us.'

I looked at the portal. Carter was already through. That decided it. I wasn't going to be separated from him. As annoying as he was, Carter was the only person I had left. (How is that for depressing?)

'Toss me,' I said.

Bast grabbed me. 'See you in America.' Then she chucked me up the side of the pyramid.

I heard the magician roar, 'Surrender!' And an explosion rattled the glass next to my head. Then I plunged into the hot vortex of sand.

*   *   *

I woke in a small room with industrial carpeting, gray walls, and metal-framed windows. I felt as if I were inside a high-tech refrigerator. I sat up groggily and discovered I was coated in cold, wet sand.

'*Ugh,*' I said. 'Where are we?'

Carter and Bast stood by the window. Apparently they'd been conscious for a while, because they'd both brushed themselves off.

'You've got to see this view,' Carter said.

I got shakily to my feet and nearly fell down again when I saw how high we were.

An entire city spread out below us—I mean *far* below, well over a hundred meters. I could almost believe we were still in Paris, because a river curved off to our left, and the land was mostly flat. There were white government buildings clustered around networks of parks and circular roads, all spread out under a winter sky. But the light was wrong. It was still afternoon here, so we must've traveled west. And as my eyes made their way to the other end of a long rectangular green space, I found myself staring at a mansion that looked oddly familiar.

'Is that . . . the White House?'

Carter nodded. 'You got us to America, all right.

Washington, D.C.'

'But we're sky high!'

Bast chuckled. 'You didn't specify any particular American city, did you?'

'Well . . . no.'

'So you got the default portal for the U.S.—the largest single source of Egyptian power in North America.'

I stared at her uncomprehendingly.

'The biggest obelisk ever constructed,' she said. 'The Washington Monument.'

I had another moment of vertigo and moved away from the window. Carter grabbed my shoulder and helped me sit down.

'You should rest,' he said. 'You passed out for . . . how long, Bast?'

'Two hours and thirty-two minutes,' she said. 'I'm sorry, Sadie. Opening more than one portal a day *is* extremely taxing, even with Isis helping.'

Carter frowned. 'But we need her to do it again, right? It's not sunset here yet. We can still use portals. Let's open one and get to Arizona. That's where Set is.'

Bast pursed her lips. 'Sadie can't summon another portal. It would overextend her powers. I don't have the talent. And you, Carter . . . well, your abilities lie elsewhere. No offense.'

'Oh, no,' he grumbled. 'I'm sure you'll call me next time you need to boomerang some fruit bats.'

'Besides,' Bast said, 'when a portal is used, it needs time to cool down. No one will be able to use the Washington Monument—'

'For another twelve hours.' Carter cursed. 'I forgot about that.'

Bast nodded. 'And by then, the Demon Days will

225

have begun.'

'So we need another way to Arizona,' Carter said.

I suppose he didn't mean to make me feel guilty, but I did. I hadn't thought things through, and now we were stuck in Washington.

I glanced at Bast out the corner of my eye. I wanted to ask her what the men at the Louvre had meant about her leading us to ruin, but I was afraid to. I wanted to believe she was on our side. Perhaps if I gave her a chance, she'd volunteer the information.

'At least those magicians can't follow us,' I prompted.

Bast hesitated. 'Not through the portal, no. But there are other magicians in America. And worse . . . Set's minions.'

My heart climbed into my throat. The House of Life was scary enough, but when I remembered Set, and what his minions had done to Amos's house . . .

'What about Thoth's spellbook?' I said. 'Did we at least find a way to fight Set?'

Carter pointed to the corner of the room. Spread out on Bast's raincoat was Dad's magic toolbox and the blue book we'd stolen from Desjardins.

'Maybe you can make sense of it,' Carter said. 'Bast and I couldn't read it. Even Doughboy was stumped.'

I picked up the book, which was actually a scroll folded into sections. The papyrus was so brittle, I was afraid to touch it. Hieroglyphs and illustrations crowded the page, but I couldn't make sense of them. My ability to read the language

226

seemed to be switched off.

Isis? I asked. *A little help?*

Her voice was silent. Maybe I'd worn her out. Or maybe she was cross with me for not letting her take over my body, the way Horus had asked Carter to do. Selfish of me, I know.

I closed the book in frustration. 'All that work for nothing.'

'Now, now,' Bast said. 'It's not so bad.'

'Right,' I said. 'We're stuck in Washington, D.C. We have two days to make it to Arizona and stop a god we don't know how to stop. And if we can't, we'll never see our dad or Amos again, and the world might end.'

'That's the spirit!' Bast said brightly. 'Now, let's have a picnic.'

She snapped her fingers. The air shimmered, and a pile of Friskies cans and two jugs of milk appeared on the carpet.

'*Um,*' Carter said, 'can you conjure any people food?'

Bast blinked. 'Well, no accounting for taste.'

The air shimmered again. A plate of grilled cheese sandwiches and crisps appeared, along with a six-pack of Coke.

'Yum,' I said.

Carter muttered something under his breath. I suppose grilled cheese wasn't his favorite, but he picked up a sandwich.

'We should leave soon,' he said between bites. 'I mean . . . tourists and all.'

Bast shook her head. 'The Washington Monument closes at six o'clock. The tourists are gone now. We might as well stay the night. If we must travel during the Demon Days, best to do it in daylight hours.'

We all must've been exhausted, because we didn't talk again until we'd finished our food. I ate three sandwiches and drank two Cokes. Bast made the whole place smell like fish Friskies, then started licking her hand as if preparing for a cat bath.

'Could you not do that?' I asked. 'It's disturbing.'

'Oh.' She smiled. 'Sorry.'

I closed my eyes and leaned against the wall. It felt good to rest, but I realized the room wasn't actually quiet. The entire building seemed to be humming ever so slightly, sending a tremble through my skull that made my teeth buzz. I opened my eyes and sat up. I could still feel it.

'What is that?' I asked. 'The wind?'

'Magic energy,' Bast said. 'I told you, this is a powerful monument.'

'But it's modern. Like the Louvre pyramid. Why is it magic?'

'The Ancient Egyptians were excellent builders, Sadie. They picked shapes—obelisks, pyramids—that were charged with symbolic magic. An obelisk represents a sunbeam frozen in stone—a life-giving ray from the original king of the gods, Ra. It doesn't matter *when* the structure was built: it is still Egyptian. That's why any obelisk can be used for opening gates to the Duat, or releasing great beings of power—'

'Or trapping them,' I said. 'The way you were trapped in Cleopatra's Needle.'

Her expression darkened. 'I wasn't actually trapped *in* the obelisk. My prison was a magically created abyss deep in the Duat, and the obelisk was the door your parents used to release me. But, yes. All symbols of Egypt are concentrated nodes of magic power. So an obelisk can definitely be used to imprison gods.'

An idea was nagging at the back of my mind, but I couldn't quite pin it down. Something about my mother, and Cleopatra's Needle, and my father's last promise in the British Museum: *I'll put things right.*

Then I thought back to the Louvre, and the comment the magician had made. Bast looked so cross at the moment I was almost afraid to ask, but it was the only way I'd get an answer. 'The magician said you abandoned your post. What did he mean?'

Carter frowned. 'When was this?'

I told him what had happened after Bast chucked him through the portal.

Bast stacked her empty Friskies cans. She didn't look eager to reply.

'When I was imprisoned,' she said at last, 'I—I wasn't alone. I was locked inside with a . . . creature of chaos.'

'Is that bad?' I asked.

Judging from Bast's expression, the answer was yes. 'Magicians often do this—lock a god up together with a monster so we have no time to try escaping our prison. For eons, I fought this monster. When your parents released me—'

'The monster got out?'

Bast hesitated a little too long for my taste.

'No. My enemy couldn't have escaped.' She took a deep breath. 'Your mother's final act of magic sealed that gate. The enemy was still inside. But that's what the magician meant. As far as he was concerned, my "post" was battling that monster forever.'

It had the ring of truth, as if she were sharing a painful memory, but it didn't explain the other bit the magician had said: *She endangered us all.* I was getting up the nerve to ask exactly what the monster had been, when Bast stood up.

'I should go scout,' she said abruptly. 'I'll be back.'

We listened to her footsteps echo down the stairwell.

'She's hiding something,' Carter said.

'Work that out yourself, did you?' I asked.

He looked away, and immediately I felt bad.

'I'm sorry,' I said. 'It's just . . . what are we going to do?'

'Rescue Dad. What else can we do?' He picked up his wand and turned it in his fingers. 'Do you think he really meant to . . . you know, bring Mom back?'

I wanted to say yes. More than anything, I wanted to believe that was possible. But I found myself shaking my head. Something about it didn't seem right. 'Iskandar told me something about Mum,' I said. 'She was a diviner. She could see the future. He said she made him rethink some old ideas.'

It was my first chance to tell Carter about my conversation with the old magician, so I gave him the details.

Carter knit his eyebrows. 'You think that has something to do with why Mom died—she saw something in the future?'

'I don't know.' I tried to think back to when I was six, but my memory was frustratingly fuzzy.

'When they took us to England the last time, did she and Dad seemed like they were in a hurry—like they were doing something really important?'

'Definitely.'

'Would you say freeing Bast was really important? I mean—I love her, of course—but *worth dying for* important?'

Carter hesitated. 'Probably not.'

'Well, there you are. I think Dad and Mum were up to something bigger, something they didn't complete. Possibly that's what Dad was after at the British Museum—completing the task, whatever it was. *Making things right.* And this whole business about our family going back a billion years to some god-hosting pharaohs—why didn't anyone *tell* us? Why didn't Dad?'

Carter didn't answer for a long time.

'Maybe Dad was protecting us,' he said. 'The House of Life doesn't trust our family, especially after what Dad and Mom did. Amos said we were raised apart for a reason, so we wouldn't, like, trigger each other's magic.'

'Bloody awful reason to keep us apart,' I muttered.

Carter looked at me strangely, and I realized what I'd said might have been construed as a compliment.

'I just mean they should've been honest,' I rushed on. 'Not that I *wanted* more time with my annoying brother, of course.'

He nodded seriously. 'Of course.'

We sat listening to the magic hum of the obelisk. I tried to remember the last time Carter and I had simply spent time like this together, talking.

'Is your, *um* . . .' I tapped the side of my head.

'Your *friend* being any help?'

'Not much,' he admitted. 'Yours?'

I shook my head. 'Carter, are you scared?'

'A little.' He dug his wand into the carpet. 'No, a lot.'

I looked at the blue book we'd stolen—pages full of wonderful secrets I couldn't read. 'What if we can't do it?'

'I don't know,' he said. 'That book about mastering the element of cheese would've been more helpful.'

'Or summoning fruit bats.'

'Please, not the fruit bats.'

We shared a weary smile, and it felt rather good. But it changed nothing. We were still in serious trouble with no clear plan.

'Why don't you sleep on it?' he suggested. 'You used a lot of energy today. I'll keep watch until Bast gets back.'

He actually sounded concerned for me. How cute.

I didn't want to sleep. I didn't want to miss anything. But I realized my eyelids *were* incredibly heavy.

'All right, then,' I said. 'Don't let the bedbugs bite.'

I lay down to sleep, but my soul—my *ba*—had other ideas.

20.
I VISIT THE STAR-SPANGLED GODDESS

SADIE

I hadn't realized how unsettling it would be. Carter had explained how his *ba* left his body while he slept, but having it happen to me was another thing altogether. It was much worse than my vision in the Hall of Ages.

There I was, floating in the air as a glowing birdlike spirit. And there was my body below me, fast asleep. Just trying to describe it gives me a headache.

My first thought as I gazed down on my sleeping form: *God, I look awful.* Bad enough looking in a mirror or seeing pictures of myself on my friends' Web pages. Seeing myself in person was simply *wrong.* My hair was a rat's nest, the linen pajamas were not in the least flattering, and the spot on my chin was *enormous.*

My second thought as I examined the strange shimmering form of my *ba*: *This won't do at all.* I didn't care if I was invisible to the mortal eye or not. After my bad experience as a kite, I simply refused to go about as a glowing Sadie-headed chicken. That's fine for Carter, but I have standards.

I could feel the currents of the Duat tugging at me, trying to pull my *ba* to wherever souls go when they have visions, but I wasn't ready. I concentrated hard, and imagined my normal appearance (well, all right, perhaps my appearance as I'd *like* it to be, a bit better than normal). And *voilà,* my *ba* morphed into a human form, still see-through and glowing, mind you, but more like a proper ghost.

Well, at least that's sorted, I thought. And I allowed the currents to sweep me away. The world melted to black.

At first, I was nowhere—just a dark void. Then a young man stepped out of the shadows.

'You again,' he said.

I stammered. '*Uh* . . .'

Honestly, you know me well enough by now. That's *not* like me. But this was the boy I'd seen in my Hall of Ages vision—the very handsome boy with the black robes and tousled hair. His dark brown eyes had the most unnerving effect on me, and I was *very* glad I'd changed out of my glowing chicken outfit.

I tried again, and managed three entire words. 'What are you . . .'

'Doing here?' he said, gallantly finishing my sentence. 'Spirit travel and death are very similar.'

'Not sure what that means,' I said. 'Should I be worried?'

He tilted his head as if considering the question. 'Not this trip. She only wants to talk to you. Go ahead.'

He waved his hand and a doorway opened in the darkness. I was pulled towards it.

'See you again?' I asked.

But the boy was gone.

I found myself standing in a luxury flat in the middle of the sky. It had no walls, no ceiling, and a see-through floor looking straight down at city lights from the height of an airplane. Clouds

234

drifted below my feet. The air should've been freezing cold and too thin to breathe, but I felt warm and comfortable.

Black leather sofas made a U round a glass coffee table on a blood-red rug. A fire burned in a slate fireplace. Bookshelves and paintings hovered in the air where the walls should've been. A black granite bar stood in the corner, and in the shadows behind it, a woman was making tea.

'Hello, my child,' she said.

She stepped into the light, and I gasped. She wore an Egyptian kilt from the waist down. From the waist up, she wore only a bikini top, and her skin . . . her skin was dark blue, covered with stars. I don't mean *painted* stars. She had the entire cosmos living on her skin: gleaming constellations, galaxies too bright to look at, glowing nebulae of pink and blue dust. Her features seemed to disappear into the stars that shifted across her face. Her hair was long and as black as midnight.

'You're the Nut,' I said. Then I realized maybe that had come out wrong. 'I mean . . . the sky goddess.'

The goddess smiled. Her bright white teeth were like a new galaxy bursting into existence. 'Nut is fine. And believe me, I've heard all the jokes about my name.'

She poured a second cup from her teapot. 'Let's sit and talk. Care for some *sahlab*?'

'Uh, it's not tea?'

'No, an Egyptian drink. You've heard of hot chocolate? This is rather like hot vanilla.'

I would've preferred tea, as I hadn't had a proper cup in ages. But I supposed one didn't turn down a goddess. '*Um* . . . yeah. Thanks.'

235

We sat together on the sofa. To my surprise, my glowing spirity hands had no trouble holding a teacup, and I could drink quite easily. The *sahlab* was sweet and tasty, with just a hint of cinnamon and coconut. It warmed me up nicely and filled the air with the smell of vanilla. For the first time in days I felt safe. Then I remembered I was only here in spirit.

Nut set down her cup. 'I suppose you're wondering why I've brought you here.'

'Where exactly is "here"? And, ah, who's your doorman?'

I hoped she'd drop some information about the boy in black, but she only smiled. 'I must keep my secrets, dear. I can't have the House of Life trying to find me. Let's just say I've built this home with a nice city view.'

'Is that . . .' I gestured to her starry blue skin. '*Um* . . . are you inside a human host?'

'No, dear. The sky itself is my body. This is merely a manifestation.'

'But I thought—'

'Gods need a physical host outside the Duat? It's somewhat easier for me, being a spirit of the air. I was one of the few gods who was never imprisoned, because the House of Life could never catch me. I'm used to being . . . *free-form.*' Suddenly Nut and the entire apartment flickered. I felt like I would drop through the floor. Then the sofa became stable again.

'Please don't do that again,' I begged.

'My apologies,' Nut said. 'The point is, each god is different. But all my brethren are free now, all finding places in this modern world of yours. They won't be imprisoned again.'

236

'The magicians won't like that.'

'No,' Nut agreed. 'That's the first reason you are here. A battle between the gods and the House of Life would serve only chaos. You must make the magicians understand this.'

'They won't listen to me. They think I'm a godling.'

'You *are* a godling, dear.' She touched my hair gently, and I felt Isis stirring within me, struggling to speak using my voice.

'I'm Sadie Kane,' I said. 'I didn't ask for Isis to hitch a ride.'

'The gods have known your family for generations, Sadie. In the olden days, we worked together for the benefit of Egypt.'

'The magicians said that gods caused the fall of the empire.'

'That is a long and pointless debate,' Nut said, and I could hear an edge of anger in her voice. 'All empires fall. But *the idea* of Egypt is eternal—the triumph of civilization, the forces of Ma'at overcoming the forces of chaos. That battle is fought generation after generation. Now it's your turn.'

'I know, I know,' I said. 'We have to defeat Set.'

'But is it that simple, Sadie? Set is my son, too. In the old days, he was Ra's strongest lieutenant. He protected the sun god's boat from the serpent Apophis. Now *there* was evil. Apophis was the embodiment of chaos. He hated Creation from the moment the first mountain appeared out of the sea. He hated the gods, mortals, and everything they built. And yet Set fought against him. Set was one of us.'

'Then he turned evil?'

237

Nut shrugged. 'Set has always been Set, for better or worse. But he is still part of our family. It is difficult to lose any member of your family . . . is it not?'

My throat tightened. 'That's hardly fair.'

'Don't speak to me of fairness,' Nut said. 'For five thousand years, I have been kept apart from my husband, Geb.'

I vaguely remembered Carter saying something about this, but it seemed different listening to her now, hearing the pain in her voice.

'What happened?' I asked.

'Punishment for bearing my children,' she said bitterly. 'I disobeyed Ra's wishes, and so he ordered my own father, Shu—'

'Hang on,' I said. 'Shoe?'

'S-h-u,' she said. 'The god of the wind.'

'Oh.' I wished these gods had names that weren't common household objects. 'Go on, please.'

'Ra ordered my father, Shu, to keep us apart, forever. I am exiled to the sky, while my beloved Geb cannot leave the ground.'

'What happens if you try?'

Nut closed her eyes and spread her hands. A hole opened where she was sitting, and she fell through the air. Instantly, the clouds below us flickered with lightning. Winds raged across the flat, throwing books off the shelves, ripping away paintings and flinging them into the void. My teacup leaped out of my hand. I grabbed the sofa to avoid getting blown away myself.

Below me, lightning struck Nut's form. The wind pushed her violently upward, shooting past me. Then the winds died. Nut settled back onto the couch. She waved her hand and the flat repaired itself. Everything returned to normal.

'*That* happens,' she said sadly.

'Oh.'

She gazed at the city lights far below. 'It has given me appreciation for my children, even Set. He has done horrible things, yes. It is his nature. But he is still my son, and still one of the gods. He acts his part. Perhaps the way to defeat him is not the way you would imagine.'

'Hints, please?'

'Seek out Thoth. He has found a new home in Memphis.'

'Memphis . . . Egypt?'

Nut smiled. 'Memphis, Tennessee. Although the old bird probably *thinks* it is Egypt. He so rarely takes his beak out of his books, I doubt he would know the difference. You will find him there. He can advise you. Be wary, though: Thoth often asks for favors. He is sometimes hard to predict.'

'Getting used to that,' I said. 'How are we supposed to get there?'

'I am goddess of the sky. I can guarantee you safe travel as far as Memphis.' She waved her hand, and a folder appeared in my lap. Inside were three plane tickets—Washington to Memphis, first-class.

I raised my eyebrow. 'I suppose you get a lot of frequent flyer miles?'

'Something like that,' Nut agreed. 'But as you get closer to Set, you will be beyond my help. And I cannot protect you on the ground. Which reminds me: You need to wake up soon. Set's minion is closing in on your hideout.'

I sat up straight. 'How soon?'

'Minutes.'

'Send my spirit back, then!' I pinched my ghostly arm, which hurt just like it would on my normal arm, but nothing happened.

'Soon, Sadie,' Nut promised. 'But two more things you must know. I had five children during the Demon Days. If your father released all of them, you should consider: Where is the fifth?'

I racked my brain trying to remember the names of all of Nut's five children. Bit difficult without my brother, the Human Wikipedia, around to keep track of such trivia for me. There was Osiris, the king, and Isis, his queen; Set, the evil god, and Horus, the avenger. But the fifth child of Nut, the one Carter said he could never remember . . . Then I recalled my vision in the Hall of Ages—Osiris's birthday and the woman in blue who'd helped Isis escape Set. 'You mean Nephthys, Set's wife?'

'Consider it,' Nut said again. 'And lastly . . . a favor.'

She opened her hand and produced an envelope sealed with red wax. 'If you see Geb . . . will you give him this?'

I'd been asked to pass notes before, but never between gods. Honestly, Nut's anguished expression was no different than those of my love-struck friends back at school. I wondered if she'd ever written on her notebook: GEB + NUT = TRUE LOVE or MRS. GEB.

'Least I can do,' I promised. 'Now, about sending me back . . .'

'Safe travels, Sadie,' the goddess said. 'And Isis, restrain yourself.'

The spirit of Isis rumbled inside me, as if I'd

eaten a bad curry.

'Wait,' I said, 'what do you mean restrain—'

Before I could finish, my vision went black.

* * *

I snapped awake, back in my own body at the Washington Monument. 'Leave now!'

Carter and Bast jumped in surprise. They were already awake, packing their things.

'What's wrong?' Carter asked.

I told them about my vision while I frantically searched my pockets. Nothing. I checked my magician's bag. Tucked inside with my wand and rod were three plane tickets and a sealed envelope.

Bast examined the tickets. 'Excellent! First class serves salmon.'

'But what about Set's minion?' I asked.

Carter glanced out the window. His eyes widened. 'Yeah, *um* . . . it's here.'

21.
AUNT KITTY TO THE RESCUE

CARTER

I'd seen pictures of the creature before, but pictures didn't come close to capturing how horrible it was in real life.

'The Set animal,' Bast said, confirming my fear.

Far below, the creature prowled the base of the monument, leaving tracks in the new-fallen snow. I had trouble judging its size, but it must've been at least as big as a horse, with legs just as long. It had an unnaturally lean, muscled body with shiny reddish gray fur. You could almost mistake it for a huge greyhound—except for the tail and the head. The tail was reptilian, forked at the end with triangular points, like squid tentacles. It lashed around as if it had a mind of its own.

The creature's head was the strangest part. Its oversize ears stuck straight up like rabbit ears, but they were shaped more like ice cream cones, curled inward and wider on the top than the bottom. They could rotate almost three hundred and sixty degrees, so they could hear anything. The creature's snout was long and curved like an anteater's—only anteaters don't have razor-sharp teeth.

'Its eyes are glowing,' I said. 'That can't be good.'

'How can you see that far?' Sadie demanded.

She stood next to me, squinting at the tiny figure in the snow, and I realized she had a point. The animal was at least five hundred feet below us. How was I able to see its eyes?

'You still have the sight of the falcon,' Bast guessed. 'And you're right, Carter. The glowing eyes mean the creature has caught our scent.'

I looked at her and almost jumped out of my skin. Her hair was sticking straight up all over her head, like she'd stuck her finger in a light socket.

'*Um,* Bast?' I asked.

'What?'

Sadie and I exchanged looks. She mouthed the word *scared.* Then I remembered how Muffin's tail would always poof up when something startled her.

'Nothing,' I said, though if the Set animal was so dangerous that it gave our goddess light-socket hair, that had to be a very bad sign. 'How do we get out of here?'

'You don't understand,' Bast said. 'The Set animal is the perfect hunter. If it has our scent, there is no stopping it.'

'Why is it called the "Set animal"?' Sadie asked nervously. 'Doesn't it have a name?'

'If it did,' Bast said, 'you would not want to speak it. It is merely known as the Set animal—the Red Lord's symbolic creature. It shares his strength, cunning . . . and his evil nature.'

'Lovely,' Sadie said.

The animal sniffed at the monument and recoiled, snarling.

'It doesn't seem to like the obelisk,' I noticed.

'No,' Bast said. 'Too much Ma'at energy. But that won't hold it back for long.'

As if on cue, the Set animal leaped onto the side of the monument. It began climbing like a lion scaling a tree, digging its claws into the stone.

'That's messed up,' I said. 'Elevator or stairs?'

'Both are too slow,' Bast said. 'Back away from the window.'

She unsheathed her knives and sliced through the glass. She punched out the window, setting off alarm bells. Freezing air blasted into the observation room.

'You'll need to fly,' Bast yelled over the wind. 'It's the only way.'

'No!' Sadie's face went pale. 'Not the kite again.'

'Sadie, it's okay,' I said.

She shook her head, terrified.

I grabbed her hand. 'I'll stay with you. I'll make

243

sure you turn back.'

'The Set animal is halfway up,' Bast warned. 'We're running out of time.'

Sadie glanced at Bast. 'What about you? You can't fly.'

'I'll jump,' she said. 'Cats always land on their feet.'

'It's over a hundred meters!' Sadie cried.

'A hundred and seventy,' Bast said. 'I'll distract the Set animal, buy you some time.'

'You'll be killed.' Sadie's voice sounded close to breaking. 'Please, I can't lose you too.'

Bast looked a little surprised. Then she smiled and put her hand on Sadie's shoulder. 'I'll be fine, dear. Meet me at Reagan National, terminal A. Be ready to run.'

Before I could argue, Bast jumped out the window. My heart just about stopped. She plummeted straight toward the pavement. I was sure she'd die, but as she fell she spread her arms and legs and seemed to relax.

She hurtled straight past the Set animal, which let out a horrible scream like a wounded man on a battlefield, then turned and leaped after her.

Bast hit the ground with both feet and took off running. She must've been doing sixty miles an hour, easy. The Set animal wasn't as agile. It crashed so hard, the pavement cracked. It stumbled for a few steps but didn't appear hurt. Then it loped after Bast and was soon gaining on her.

'She won't make it,' Sadie fretted.

'Never bet against a cat,' I said. 'We've got to do our part. Ready?'

She took a deep breath. 'All right. Before I

change my mind.'

Instantly, a black-winged kite appeared in front of me, flapping its wings to keep its balance in the intense wind. I willed myself to become a falcon. It was even easier than before.

A moment later, we soared into the cold morning air over Washington, D.C.

*   *   *

Finding the airport was easy. Reagan National was so close, I could see the planes landing across the Potomac.

The hard part was remembering what I was doing. Every time I saw a mouse or a squirrel, I instinctively veered toward it. A couple of times I caught myself about to dive, and I had to fight the urge. Once I looked over and realized I was a mile away from Sadie, who was off doing her own hunting. I had to force myself to fly next to her and get her attention.

It takes willpower to stay human, the voice of Horus warned. *The more time you spend as a bird of prey, the more you think like one.*

Now you tell me, I thought.

I could help, he urged. *Give me control.*

Not today, bird-head.

Finally, I steered Sadie toward the airport, and we started hunting for a place to change back to human form. We landed at the top of a parking garage.

I willed myself to turn human. Nothing happened.

Panic started building in my throat. I closed my eyes and pictured my dad's face. I thought about

245

how much I missed him, how much I needed to find him.

When I opened my eyes, I was back to normal. Unfortunately, Sadie was still a kite. She flapped around me and cawed frantically. *'Ha—ha—ha!'* There was a wild look in her eyes, and this time I understood how scared she was. Bird form had been hard enough for her to break out of the first time. If the second time took even more energy, she could be in serious trouble.

'It's all right.' I crouched down, careful to move slowly. 'Sadie, don't force it. You have to relax.'

'Ha!' She tucked in her wings. Her chest was heaving.

'Listen, it helped me to focus on Dad. Remember what's important to you. Close your eyes and think about your human life.'

She closed her eyes, but almost instantly cried out in frustration and flapped her wings.

'Stop,' I said. 'Don't fly away!'

She tilted her head and gurgled in a pleading way. I started talking to her the way I would to a scared animal. I wasn't really paying attention to the words. I was just trying to keep my tone calm. But after a minute I realized I was telling her about my travels with Dad, and the memories that had helped me get out of bird form. I told her about the time Dad and I got stuck in the Venice airport and I ate so many cannoli, I got sick. I told her about the time in Egypt when I found the scorpion in my sock, and Dad managed to kill it with a TV remote control. I told her how we'd gotten separated once in the London Underground and how scared I was until Dad finally found me. I told her some pretty

246

embarrassing stories that I'd never shared with anyone, because who could I share them with? And it seemed to me that Sadie listened. At least she stopped flapping her wings. Her breathing slowed. She became very still, and her eyes didn't look so panicked.

'Okay, Sadie,' I said at last. 'I've got an idea. Here's what we're going to do.'

I took Dad's magic box out of its leather bag. I wrapped the bag around my forearm and tied it with the straps as best I could. 'Hop on.'

Sadie flew up and perched at my wrist. Even with my makeshift armguard, her sharp talons dug into my skin.

'We'll get you out of this,' I said. 'Keep trying. Relax, and focus on your human life. You'll figure it out, Sadie. I know you will. I'll carry you until then.'

'*Ha.*'

'Come on,' I said. 'Let's find Bast.'

With my sister perched on my arm, I walked to the elevator. A businessman with a rolling suitcase was waiting by the doors. His eyes widened when he saw me. I must've looked pretty strange—a tall black kid in dirty, ragged Egyptian clothes, with a weird box tucked under one arm and a bird of prey perched on the other.

'How's it going?' I said.

'I'll take the stairs.' He hurried off.

The elevator took me to the ground level. Sadie and I crossed to the departures curb. I looked around desperately, hoping to see Bast, but instead I caught the attention of a curbside policeman. The guy frowned and started lumbering in my direction.

247

'Stay calm,' I told Sadie. Resisting the urge to run, I turned and walked through the revolving doors.

Here's the thing—I always get a little edgy around police. I remember when I was like seven or eight and still a cute little kid, it wasn't a problem; but as soon as I hit eleven, I started to get the Look, like *What's that kid doing here? Is he going to steal something?* I mean it's ridiculous, but it's a fact. I'm not saying it happens with *every* police officer, but when it doesn't happen—let's just say it's a pleasant surprise.

This was not one of the pleasant times. I knew the cop was going to follow me, and I knew I had to act calm and walk like I had a purpose . . . which is not easy with a kite on your arm.

Christmas vacation, so the airport was pretty full—mostly families standing in line at the ticket counters, kids arguing and parents labeling luggage. I wondered what that would be like: a normal family trip, no magic problems or monsters chasing you.

Stop it, I told myself. *You've got work to do.*

But I didn't know where to go. Would Bast be inside security? Outside? The crowds parted as I walked through the terminal. People stared at Sadie. I knew I couldn't wander around looking lost. It was only a matter of time before the cops—

'Young man.'

I turned. It was the police officer from outside. Sadie squawked, and the cop backed up, resting his hand on his nightstick.

'You can't have pets in here,' he told me.

'I have tickets . . .' I tried to reach my pockets. Then I remembered that Bast had our tickets.

The cop scowled. 'You'd better come with me.'

Suddenly a woman's voice called: 'There you are, Carter!'

Bast was hurrying over, pushing her way through the crowd. I'd never been happier to see an Egyptian god in my life.

Somehow she'd managed to change clothes. She wore a rose-colored pantsuit, lots of gold jewelry, and a cashmere coat, so she looked like a wealthy businesswoman. Ignoring the cop, she sized up my appearance and wrinkled her nose. 'Carter, I *told* you not to wear those horrible falconry clothes. Honestly, you look like you've been sleeping in the wild!'

She took out a handkerchief and made a big production of wiping my face, while the policeman stared.

'*Uh,* ma'am,' he finally managed. 'Is this your—'

'Nephew,' Bast lied. 'I'm so sorry, officer. We're heading to Memphis for a falconry competition. I hope he hasn't caused any problems. We're going to miss our flight!'

'*Um,* the falcon can't fly . . .'

Bast giggled. 'Well, of course it can fly, officer. It's a bird!'

His face reddened. 'I mean on a plane.'

'Oh! We have the paperwork.' To my amazement, she pulled out an envelope and handed it to the cop, along with our tickets.

'I see,' the cop said. He looked our tickets over. 'You bought . . . a first class ticket for your falcon.'

'It's a black kite, actually,' Bast said. 'But yes, it's a very temperamental bird. A prizewinner, you know. Give it a coach seat and try to offer it pretzels, and I won't be held responsible for the consequences. No, we *always* fly first class, don't we, Carter?'

'*Um*, yeah . . . Aunt Kitty.'

She flashed me a look that said: *I'll get you for that.* Then she went back to smiling at the cop, who handed back our tickets and Sadie's 'paperwork.'

'Well, if you'll excuse us, officer. That's a very handsome uniform, by the way. Do you work out?' Before he could respond, Bast grabbed my arm and hurried me toward the security checkpoint. 'Don't look back,' she said under her breath.

As soon as we turned the corner, Bast pulled me aside by the vending machines.

'The Set animal is close,' she said. 'We've got a few minutes at best. What's wrong with Sadie?'

'She can't . . .' I stammered. 'I don't know exactly.'

'Well, we'll have to figure it out on the plane.'

'How did you change clothes?' I asked. 'And the document for the bird . . .'

She waved her hand dismissively. 'Oh, mortal minds are weak. That "document" is an empty ticket sleeve. And my clothes haven't really changed. It's just a glamour.'

I looked at her more closely, and I saw she was right. Her new clothes flickered like a mirage over her usual leopard-skin bodysuit. As soon as she pointed it out, the magic seemed flimsy and obvious.

'We'll try to make it to the gate before the Set animal,' she said. 'It will be easier if you stow your things in the Duat.'

'What?'

'You don't really want to tote that box around

under your arm, do you? Use the Duat as a storage bin.'

'How?'

Bast rolled her eyes. 'Honestly, what do they teach magicians these days?'

'We had about twenty seconds of training!'

'Just imagine a space in the air, like a shelf or a treasure chest—'

'A locker?' I asked. 'I've never had a school locker.'

'Fine. Give it a combination lock—anything you want. Imagine opening the locker with your combination. Then shove the box inside. When you need it again, just call it to mind, and it will appear.'

I was skeptical, but I imagined a locker. I gave it a combination: 13/32/33—retired numbers for the Lakers, obviously: Chamberlain, Johnson, Abdul-Jabbar. I held out my dad's magic box and let it go, sure it would smash to the floor. Instead, the box disappeared.

'Cool,' I said. 'Are you sure I can get it back?'

'No,' Bast said. 'Now, come on!'

22.

LEROY MEETS THE LOCKER OF DOOM

CARTER

I'd never gone through security with a live bird of prey before. I thought it would cause a holdup, but instead the guards moved us into a special line. They checked our paperwork. Bast smiled a lot, flirted with the guards and told them they must be working out, and they waved us through. Bast's knives didn't set off the alarms, so maybe she'd stored them in the Duat. The guards didn't even try to put Sadie through the X-ray machine.

I was retrieving my shoes when I heard a scream from the other side of security.

Bast cursed in Egyptian. 'We were too slow.'

I looked back and saw the Set animal charging through the terminal, knocking passengers out of its way. Its weird rabbit ears swiveled back and forth. Foam dripped from its curved, toothy snout, and its forked tail lashed around, looking for something to sting.

'Moose!' a lady screamed. 'Rabid moose!'

Everyone started screaming, running in different directions and blocking the Set animal's path.

'Moose?' I wondered.

Bast shrugged. 'No telling what mortals will perceive. Now the idea will spread by power of suggestion.'

Sure enough, more passengers started yelling 'Moose!' and running around as the Set animal plowed through the lines and got tangled up in the stanchions. TSA officers surged forward, but the Set animal tossed them aside like rag dolls.

'Come on!' Bast told me.

'I can't just let it hurt these people.'

'We can't stop it!'

But I didn't move. I wanted to believe Horus was giving me courage, or that maybe the past few days had finally woken up some dormant bravery gene I'd inherited from my parents. But the truth was scarier. This time, nobody was making me take a stand. I *wanted* to do it.

People were in trouble because of us. I *had* to fix it. I felt the same kind of instinct I felt when Sadie needed my help, like it was time for me to step up. And yes, it terrified me. But it also felt *right*.

'Go to the gate,' I told Bast. 'Take Sadie. I'll meet you there.'

'What? Carter—'

'Go!' I imagined opening my invisible locker: 13/32/33. I reached out my hand, but not for my dad's magic box. I concentrated on something I'd lost in Luxor. It *had* to be there. For a moment, I felt nothing. Then my hand closed around a hard leather grip, and I pulled my sword out of nowhere.

Bast's eyes widened. 'Impressive.'

'Get moving,' I said. 'It's my turn to run interference.'

'You realize it'll kill you.'

'Thanks for the vote of confidence. Now, scat!'

Bast took off at top speed, Sadie flapping to stay balanced on her arm.

A shot rang out. I turned and saw the Set animal

plow into a cop who'd just fired at its head to no effect. The poor cop flew backward and toppled over the metal detector gate.

'Hey, moose!' I screamed.

The Set animal locked its glowing eyes on me.

Well done! Horus said. *We will die with honor!*

Shut up, I thought.

I glanced behind me to make sure Bast and Sadie were out of sight. Then I approached the creature.

'So you've got no name?' I asked. 'They couldn't think of one ugly enough?'

The creature snarled, stepping over the unconscious policeman.

'*Set animal* is too hard to say,' I decided. 'I'll call you Leroy.'

Apparently, Leroy didn't like his name. He lunged.

I dodged his claws and managed to smack him in the snout with the flat of my blade, but that barely fazed him. Leroy backed up and charged again, slavering, baring his fangs. I slashed at his neck, but Leroy was too smart. He darted to the left and sank his teeth into my free arm. If it hadn't been for my makeshift leather armguard, I would've been minus one arm. As it was, Leroy's fangs still bit clear through the leather. Red-hot pain shot up my arm.

I yelled, and a primal surge of power coursed through my body. I felt myself rising off the ground and the golden aura of the hawk warrior forming around me. The Set animal's jaws were pried open so fast that it yelped and let go of my arm. I stood, now encased in a magical barrier twice my normal size, and kicked Leroy into the wall.

Good! said Horus. *Now dispatch the beast to the netherworld!*

Quiet, man. I'm doing all the work.

I was vaguely aware of security guards trying to regroup, yelling into their walkie-talkies and calling for help. Travelers were still screaming and running around. I heard a little girl shout: 'Chicken man, get the moose!'

You know how hard it is to feel like an extreme falcon-headed combat machine when somebody calls you 'chicken man'?

I raised my sword, which was now at the center of a ten-foot-long energy blade.

Leroy shook the dust off his cone-shaped ears, and came at me again. My armored form might've been powerful, but it was also clumsy and slow; moving it around felt like moving through Jell-O. Leroy dodged my sword strike and landed on my chest, knocking me down. He was a lot heavier than he looked. His tail and claws raked against my armor. I caught his neck in my glowing fists and tried to keep his fangs away from my face, but everywhere he drooled, my magical shield hissed and steamed. I could feel my wounded arm going numb.

Alarms blared. More passengers crowded toward the checkpoint to see what was happening. I had to end this soon—before I passed out from pain or more mortals got hurt.

I felt my strength fading, my shield flickering. Leroy's fangs were an inch from my face, and Horus was offering no words of encouragement.

Then I thought about my invisible locker in the Duat. I wondered if other things could be put in there too . . . large, evil things.

I closed my hands around Leroy's throat and wedged my knee against his rib cage. Then I imagined an opening in the Duat—in the air right above me: 13/32/33. I imagined my locker opening as wide as it could go.

With my last bit of strength, I pushed Leroy straight up. He flew toward the ceiling, his eyes widening with surprise as he passed through an unseen rift and disappeared.

'Where'd it go?' someone yelled.

'Hey, kid!' another guy called. 'You okay?'

My energy shield was gone. I wanted to pass out, but I had to leave before the security guys came out of their shock and arrested me for moose fighting. I got to my feet and threw my sword at the ceiling. It disappeared into the Duat. Then I wrapped the torn leather around my bleeding arm as best I could and ran for the gates.

I reached our flight just as they were closing the door.

Apparently, word of the chicken man incident hadn't spread quite yet. The gate agent gestured back toward the checkpoint as she took my ticket. 'What's all the noise up there?'

'A moose got through security,' I said. 'It's under control now.' Before she could ask questions, I raced down the jetway.

I collapsed into my seat across the aisle from Bast. Sadie, still in kite form, was pacing in the window seat next to me.

Bast let out a huge sigh of relief. 'Carter, you made it! But you're hurt. What happened?'

I told her.

Bast's eyes widened. 'You put the Set animal in your locker? Do you know how much strength that

256

requires?'

'Yeah,' I said. 'I was there.'

The flight attendant started making her announcements. Apparently, the security incident hadn't affected our flight. The plane pushed back from the gate on time.

I doubled forward in pain, and only then did Bast notice how bad my arm was. Her expression turned grim.

'Hold still.' She whispered something in Egyptian, and my eyes began to feel heavy.

'You'll need sleep to heal that wound,' she said.

'But if Leroy comes back—'

'Who?'

'Nothing.'

Bast studied me as if seeing me for the first time. 'That was extraordinarily brave, Carter. Facing the Set monster—you have more tomcat in you than I realized.'

'*Um*—thanks?'

She smiled and touched my forehead. 'We'll be in the air soon, my tomcat. Sleep.'

I couldn't really object. Exhaustion washed over me, and I closed my eyes.

*   *   *

Naturally my soul decided to take a trip.

I was in *ba* form, circling above Phoenix. It was a brilliant winter morning. The cool desert air felt good under my wings. The city looked different in the daylight—a vast grid of beige and green squares dotted with palm trees and swimming pools. Stark mountains rose up here and there like chunks of the moon. The most prominent mountain was right below me—a long ridge with two distinct peaks. What had Set's minion called it on my first soul visit? Camelback Mountain.

Its foothills were crowded with luxury homes, but the top was barren. Something caught my attention: a crevice between two large boulders, and a shimmer of heat coming from deep within the mountain—something that no human eye would've noticed.

I folded my wings and dove toward the crevice.

Hot air vented out with such force that I had to push my way through. About fifty feet down, the crevice opened up, and I found myself in a place that simply couldn't exist.

The entire inside of the mountain had been hollowed out. In the middle of the cavern, a giant pyramid was under construction. The air rang with the sound of pickaxes. Hordes of demons cut blood-red limestone into blocks and hauled it to the middle of the cave, where more swarms of demons used ropes and ramps to hoist the blocks into place, the way my dad said the Giza pyramids were built. But the Giza pyramids had taken, like, twenty years each to complete. This pyramid was already halfway done.

There was something odd about it, too—and not just the blood-red color. When I looked at it I felt a familiar tingle, as if the whole structure were humming with a tone . . . no, a *voice* I almost recognized.

I spotted a smaller shape floating in the air above the pyramid—a reed barge like Uncle Amos's riverboat. On it stood two figures. One was a tall demon in leather armor. The other was a burly man in red combat fatigues.

I circled closer, trying to stay in the shadows because I wasn't sure I was really invisible. I landed on the top of the mast. It was a tricky maneuver, but neither of the boat's occupants looked up.

'How much longer?' asked the man in red.

He had Set's voice, but he looked completely different than he had in my last vision. He wasn't a slimy black thing, and he wasn't on fire—except for the scary mixture of hatred and amusement burning in his eyes. He had a big thick body like a linebacker's, with meaty hands and a brutish face. His short bristly hair and trimmed goatee were as red as his combat fatigues. I'd never seen camouflage that color before. Maybe he was planning on hiding out in a volcano.

Next to him, the demon bowed and scraped. It was the weird rooster-footed guy I'd seen before. He was at least seven feet tall and scarecrow thin, with bird talons for feet. And unfortunately, this time I could see his face. It was almost too hideous to describe. You know those anatomy exhibits where they show dead bodies without skin? Imagine one of those faces alive, only with solid black eyes and fangs.

'We're making excellent progress, master!' the demon promised. 'We conjured a hundred more demons today. With luck, we will be done at sunset on your birthday!'

'That is unacceptable, Face of Horror,' Set said calmly.

The servant flinched. I guessed his name was Face of Horror. I wondered how long it had taken his mom to think of that. *Bob? No. Sam? No. How about Face of Horror?*

'B-but, master,' Face stammered. 'I thought—'

'Do not think, demon. Our enemies are more resourceful than I imagined. They have temporarily disabled my favorite pet and are now speeding toward us. We must finish before they arrive. *Sunrise* on my birthday, Face of Horror. No later. It will be the dawn of my new kingdom. I will scour all life from this continent, and this pyramid shall stand as a monument to my power—the final and eternal tomb of Osiris!'

My heart almost stopped. I looked down at the pyramid again, and I realized why it felt so familiar. It had an energy to it—*my father's* energy. I can't explain how, but I knew his sarcophagus lay hidden somewhere inside that pyramid.

Set smiled cruelly, as if he would be just as happy to have Face obey him or to rip Face to pieces. 'You understand my order?'

'Yes, lord!' Face of Horror shifted his bird feet, as if building up his courage. 'But may I ask, lord . . . why stop there?'

Set's nostrils flared. 'You are one sentence away from destruction, Face of Horror. Choose your next words carefully.'

The demon ran his black tongue across his teeth. 'Well, my lord, is the annihilation of only one god worthy of your glorious self? What if we could create even more chaos energy—to feed your pyramid for all time and make you the eternal lord of all worlds?'

A hungry light danced in Set's eyes. ' "Lord of all worlds" . . . that has a nice ring to it. And how would you accomplish this, puny demon?'

'Oh, not I, my lord. I am an insignificant worm. But if we were to capture the others: Nephthys—'

260

Set kicked Face in the chest, and the demon collapsed, wheezing. 'I told you never to speak her name.'

'Yes, master,' Face panted. 'Sorry, master. But if we were to capture her, and the others . . . think on the power you could consume. With the right plan . . .'

Set began nodding, warming to the idea. 'I think it's time we put Amos Kane to use.'

I tensed. Was Amos here?

'Brilliant, master. A brilliant plan.'

'Yes, I'm glad I thought of it. Soon, Face of Horror, *very* soon, Horus, Isis, and my treacherous wife will bow at my feet—and Amos will help. We'll have a nice little family reunion.'

Set looked up—straight at me, as if he'd known I was there all along, and gave me that rip-you-to-pieces smile. 'Isn't that right, boy?'

I wanted to spread my wings and fly. I had to get out of the cavern and warn Sadie. But my wings wouldn't work. I sat there paralyzed as Set reached out to grab me.

23.
PROFESSOR THOTH'S FINAL EXAM

SADIE

Sadie here. Sorry for the delay, though I don't suppose you'd notice on a recording. My nimble-fingered brother dropped the microphone into a pit full of . . . oh, never mind. Back to the story.

Carter woke with such a start, he banged his

knees against the drinks tray, which was quite funny.

'Sleep well?' I asked.

He blinked at me in confusion. 'You're human.'

'How kind of you to notice.'

I took another bite of my pizza. I'd never eaten pizza from a china plate or had a Coke in a glass (with ice no less—Americans are so odd) but I was enjoying first class.

'I changed back an hour ago.' I cleared my throat. 'It—ah—was helpful, what you said, about focusing on what's important.'

Awkward saying even that much, as I remembered everything he'd told me while I was in kite form about his travels with Dad—how he'd gotten lost in the Underground, gotten sick in Venice, squealed like a baby when he'd found a scorpion in his sock. So much ammunition to tease him with, but oddly I wasn't tempted. The way he'd poured out his soul . . . Perhaps he thought I didn't understand him in kite form—but he'd been so honest, so unguarded, and he'd done it all to calm me down. If he hadn't given me something to focus on, I'd probably still be hunting field mice over the Potomac.

Carter had spoken about Dad as if their travels together had been a great thing, yes, but also quite a chore, with Carter always struggling to please and be on his best behavior, with no one to relax with, or talk to. Dad *was,* I had to admit, quite a presence. You'd be hard-pressed *not* to want his approval. (No doubt that's where I get my own stunningly charismatic personality.) I saw him only twice a year, and even so I had to prepare myself mentally for the experience. For the first time, I

262

began to wonder if Carter really had the better end of the bargain. Would I trade my life for his?

I also decided not to tell him what had finally changed me back to human. I hadn't focused on Dad at all. I'd imagined Mum alive, imagined us walking down Oxford Street together, gazing in the shop windows and talking and laughing—the kind of ordinary day we'd never gotten to share. An impossible wish, I know. But it had been powerful enough to remind me of who I was.

Didn't say any of that, but Carter studied my face, and I sensed that he picked up my thoughts a little too well.

I took a sip of Coke. 'You missed lunch, by the way.'

'You didn't try to wake me?'

On the other side of the aisle, Bast burped. She'd just finished off her plate of salmon and was looking quite satisfied. 'I could summon more Friskies,' she offered. 'Or cheese sandwiches.'

'No thanks,' Carter muttered. He looked devastated.

'God, Carter,' I said. 'If it's that important to you, I've got some pizza left—'

'It's not that,' he said. And he told us how his *ba* had almost been captured by Set.

The news gave me trouble breathing. I felt as if I were stuck in kite form again, unable to think clearly. Dad trapped in a red pyramid? Poor Amos used as some sort of pawn? I looked at Bast for some kind of reassurance. 'Isn't there anything we can do?'

Her expression was grim. 'Sadie, I don't know. Set will be most powerful on his birthday, and sunrise is the most auspicious moment for magic.

263

If he's able to generate one great explosion of storm energy at sunrise on that day—using not only his own magic, but augmenting it with the power of other gods he's managed to enslave . . . the amount of chaos he could unleash is almost unimaginable.' She shuddered. 'Carter, you say a simple demon gave him this idea?'

'Sounded like it,' Carter said. 'Or he tweaked the original plan, anyway.'

She shook her head. 'This is not like Set.'

I coughed. 'What do you mean? It's *exactly* like him.'

'No,' Bast insisted. 'This is horrendous, even for him. Set wishes to be king, but such an explosion might leave him nothing to rule. It's almost as if . . .' She stopped herself, the thought seemingly too disturbing. 'I don't understand it, but we'll be landing soon. You'll have to ask Thoth.'

'You make it sound like you're not coming,' I said.

'Thoth and I don't get along very well. Your chances of surviving might be better—'

The seat belt light came on. The captain announced we'd started our descent into Memphis. I peered out the window and saw a vast brown river cutting across the landscape—a river larger than any I'd ever seen. It reminded me uncomfortably of a giant snake.

The flight attendant came by and pointed to my lunch plate. 'Finished, dear?'

'It seems so,' I told her gloomily.

*   *   *

Memphis hadn't gotten word that it was winter.

264

The trees were green and the sky was a brilliant blue.

We'd insisted Bast not 'borrow' a car this time, so she agreed to rent one as long as she got a convertible. I didn't ask where she got the money, but soon we were cruising through the mostly deserted streets of Memphis with our BMW's top down.

I remember only snapshots of the city. We passed through one neighborhood that might've been a set from *Gone with the Wind*—big white mansions on enormous lawns shaded by cypress trees, although the plastic Santa Claus displays on the rooftops rather ruined the effect. On the next block, we almost got killed by an old woman driving a Cadillac out of a church parking lot. Bast swerved and honked her horn, and the woman just smiled and waved. Southern hospitality, I suppose.

After a few more blocks, the houses turned to rundown shacks. I spotted two African American boys wearing jeans and muscle shirts, sitting on their front porch, strumming acoustic guitars and singing. They sounded so good, I was tempted to stop.

On the next corner stood a cinder block restaurant with a hand-painted sign that read CHICKEN & WAFFLES. There was a queue of twenty people outside.

'You Americans have the strangest taste. What planet is this?' I asked.

Carter shook his head. 'And where would Thoth be?'

Bast sniffed the air and turned left onto a street called Poplar. 'We're getting close. If I know Thoth, he'll find a center of learning. A library, perhaps, or a cache of books in a magician's tomb.'

'Don't have a lot of those in Tennessee,' Carter guessed.

Then I spotted a sign and grinned broadly. 'The University of Memphis, perhaps?'

'Well done, Sadie!' Bast purred.

Carter scowled at me. The poor boy gets jealous, you know.

A few minutes later, we were strolling through the campus of a small college: red brick buildings and wide courtyards. It was eerily quiet, except for the sound of a ball echoing on concrete.

As soon as Carter heard it, he perked up. 'Basketball.'

'Oh, please,' I said. 'We need to find Thoth.'

But Carter followed the sound of the ball, and we followed him. He rounded the corner of a building and froze. 'Let's ask them.'

I didn't understand what he was on about. Then I turned the corner and yelped. On the basketball court, five players were in the middle of an intense game. They wore an assortment of jerseys from different American teams, and they all seemed keen to win—grunting and snarling at each other, stealing the ball and pushing.

Oh . . . and the players were all baboons.

'The sacred animal of Thoth,' Bast said. 'We must be in the right place.'

One of the baboons had lustrous golden hair much lighter than the others, and a more, er, colorful bottom. He wore a purple jersey that seemed oddly familiar.

'Is that . . . a Lakers jersey?' I asked, hesitant to even name Carter's silly obsession.

He nodded, and we both grinned.

266

'Khufu!' we yelled.

True, we hardly knew the baboon. We'd spent less than a day with him, and our time at Amos's mansion seemed like ages ago, but still I felt like we'd recovered a long-lost friend.

Khufu jumped into my arms and barked at me. *Agh! Agh!'* He picked through my hair, looking for bugs, I suppose [No comments from you, Carter!], and dropped to the ground, slapping the pavement to show how pleased he was.

Bast laughed. 'He says you smell like flamingos.'

'You speak Baboon?' Carter asked.

The goddess shrugged. 'He also wants to know where you've been.'

'Where *we've* been?' I said. 'Well, first off, tell him I've spent the better part of the day as a kite, which is *not* a flamingo and does not end in *-o,* so it shouldn't be on his diet. Secondly—'

'Hold on.' Bast turned to Khufu and said, *'Agh!'* Then she looked back at me. 'All right, go ahead.'

I blinked. 'Okay . . . *um,* and secondly, where has *he* been?'

She relayed this in a single grunt.

Khufu snorted and grabbed the basketball, which sent his baboon friends into a frenzy of barking and scratching and snarling.

'He dove into the river and swam back,' Bast translated, 'but when he returned, the house was destroyed and we were gone. He waited a day for Amos to return, but he never did. So Khufu made his way to Thoth. Baboons are under his protection, after all.'

'Why is that?' Carter asked. 'I mean, no offense, but Thoth is the god of knowledge, right?'

'Baboons are very wise animals,' Bast said.

'Agh!' Khufu picked his nose, then turned his Technicolor bum our direction. He threw his friends the ball. They began to fight over it, showing one another their fangs and slapping their heads.

'Wise?' I asked.

'Well, they're not *cats,* mind you,' Bast added. 'But, yes, wise. Khufu says that as soon as Carter keeps his promise, he'll take you to the professor.'

I blinked. 'The prof— Oh, you mean . . . right.'

'What promise?' Carter asked.

The corner of Bast's mouth twitched. 'Apparently, you promised to show him your basketball skills.'

Carter's eyes widened in alarm. 'We don't have time!'

'Oh, it's fine,' Bast promised. 'It's best that I go now.'

'But where, Bast?' I asked, as I wasn't anxious to be separated from her again. 'How will we find you?'

The look in her eyes changed to something like guilt, as if she'd just caused a horrible accident. 'I'll find you when you get out, if you get out . . .'

'What do you mean *if*?' Carter asked, but Bast had already turned into Muffin and raced off.

Khufu barked at Carter most insistently. He tugged his hand, pulling him onto the court. The baboons immediately broke into two teams. Half took off their jerseys. Half left them on. Carter, sadly, was on the no-jersey team, and Khufu helped him pull his shirt off, exposing his bony chest. The teams began to play.

Now, I know nothing about basketball. But I'm fairly sure one isn't supposed to trip over one's shoes, or catch a pass with one's forehead, or dribble (is that the word?) with both hands as if petting a possibly rabid dog. But that is exactly the way Carter played. The baboons simply ran him over, quite literally. They scored basket after basket as Carter staggered back and forth, getting hit with the ball whenever it came close to him, tripping over monkey limbs until he was so dizzy he turned in a circle and fell over. The baboons stopped playing and watched him in disbelief. Carter lay in the middle of the court, covered in sweat and panting. The other baboons looked at Khufu. It was quite obvious what they were thinking: *Who invited this human?* Khufu covered his eyes in shame.

'Carter,' I said with glee, 'all that talk about basketball and the Lakers, and you're absolute *rubbish*! Beaten by monkeys!'

He groaned miserably. 'It was . . . it was Dad's favorite game.'

I stared at him. Dad's favorite game. God, why hadn't that occurred to me?

Apparently he took my gobsmacked expression as further criticism.

'I . . . I can tell you any NBA stat you want,' he said a bit desperately. 'Rebounds, assists, free throw percentages.'

The other baboons went back to their game, ignoring Carter and Khufu both. Khufu let out a disgusted noise, half gag and half bark.

I understood the sentiment, but I came forward and offered Carter my hand. 'Come on, then. It doesn't matter.'

'If I had better shoes,' he suggested. 'Or if I wasn't so tired—'

269

'Carter,' I said with a smirk. 'It *doesn't* matter. And I'll not breathe a word to Dad when we save him.'

He looked at me with obvious gratitude. (Well, I am rather wonderful, after all.) Then he took my hand, and I hoisted him up.

'Now for god's sake, put on your shirt,' I said. 'And Khufu, it's time you took us to the professor.'

Khufu led us into a deserted science building. The air in the hallways smelled of vinegar, and the empty classroom labs looked like something from an American high school, not the sort of place a god would hang out. We climbed the stairs and found a row of professors' offices. Most of the doors were closed. One had been left open, revealing a space no bigger than a broom closet stuffed with books, a tiny desk, and one chair. I wondered if that professor had done something bad to get such a small office.

'*Agh!*' Khufu stopped in front of a polished mahogany door, much nicer than the others. A newly stenciled name glistened on the glass: DR. THOTH.

Without knocking, Khufu opened the door and waddled inside.

'After you, chicken man,' I said to Carter. (And yes, I'm sure he was regretting telling me about that particular incident. After all, I couldn't *completely* stop teasing him. I have a reputation to maintain.)

I expected another broom closet. Instead, the office was impossibly big.

The ceiling rose at least ten meters, with one side of the office all windows, looking out over the Memphis skyline. Metal stairs led up to a loft

270

dominated by an enormous telescope, and from somewhere up there came the sound of an electric guitar being strummed quite badly. The other walls of the office were crammed with bookshelves. Worktables overflowed with weird bits and bobs—chemistry sets, half-assembled computers, stuffed animals with electrical wires sticking out of their heads. The room smelled strongly of cooked beef, but with a smokier, tangier scent than I'd ever smelled.

Strangest of all, right in front of us, half a dozen longnecked birds—ibises—sat behind desks like receptionists, typing on laptop computers with their beaks.

Carter and I looked at each other. For once I was at a loss for words.

'*Agh!*' Khufu called out.

Up in the loft, the strumming stopped. A lanky man in his twenties stood up, electric guitar in hand. He had an unruly mane of blond hair like Khufu's, and he wore a stained white lab coat over faded jeans and a black T-shirt. At first I thought blood was trickling from the corner of his mouth. Then I realized it was some sort of meat sauce.

'Fascinating.' He broke into a wide grin. 'I've discovered something, Khufu. This is *not* Memphis, Egypt.'

Khufu gave me a sideways look, and I could swear his expression meant, *Duh.*

'I've also discovered a new form of magic called blues music,' the man continued. 'And barbecue. Yes, you must try barbecue.'

Khufu looked unimpressed. He climbed to the top of a bookshelf, grabbed a box of Cheerios, and began to munch.

The guitar man slid down the banister with perfect balance and landed in front of us. 'Isis and Horus,' he said. 'I see you've found new bodies.'

His eyes were a dozen colors, shifting like a kaleidoscope, with hypnotic effect.

I managed to stutter, '*Um*, we're not—'

'Oh, I see,' he said. 'Trying to share the body, eh? Don't think I'm fooled for a minute, Isis. I know you're in charge.'

'But she's not!' I protested. 'My name is Sadie Kane. I assume you're Thoth?'

He raised an eyebrow. 'You claim not to know me? Of course I'm Thoth. Also called Djehuti. Also called—'

I stifled a laugh. 'Ja-hooty?'

Thoth looked offended. 'In Ancient Egyptian, it's a perfectly fine name. The Greeks called me Thoth. Then later they confused me with their god Hermes. Even had the nerve to rename my sacred city Hermopolis, though we're nothing alike. Believe me, if you've ever met Hermes—'

'*Agh!*' Khufu yelled through a mouthful of Cheerios.

'You're right,' Thoth agreed. 'I'm getting off track. So you claim to be Sadie Kane. And . . .' He swung a finger toward Carter, who was watching the ibises type on their laptops. 'I suppose you're not Horus.'

'Carter Kane,' said Carter, still distracted by the ibises' screens. 'What *is* that?'

Thoth brightened. 'Yes, they're called computers. Marvelous, aren't they? Apparently—'

'No, I mean what are the birds typing?' Carter squinted and read from the screen. '"A Short Treatise on the Evolution of Yaks"?'

'My scholarly essays,' Thoth explained. 'I try to keep several projects going at once. For instance, did you know this university does not offer majors in astrology or leechcraft? Shocking! I intend to change that. I'm renovating new headquarters right now down by the river. Soon Memphis will be a true center of learning!'

'That's brilliant,' I said halfheartedly. 'We need help defeating Set.'

The ibises stopped typing and stared at me.

Thoth wiped the barbecue sauce off his mouth. 'You have the nerve to ask this after last time?'

'Last time?' I repeated.

'I have the account here somewhere . . .' Thoth patted the pockets of his lab coat. He pulled out a rumpled piece of paper and read it. 'No, grocery list.'

He tossed it over his shoulder. As soon as the paper hit the floor, it became a loaf of wheat bread, a jug of milk, and a six-pack of Mountain Dew.

Thoth checked his sleeves. I realized the stains on his coat were smeared words, printed in every language. The stains moved and changed, forming hieroglyphs, English letters, Demotic symbols. He brushed a stain off his lapel and seven letters fluttered to the floor, forming a word: *crawdad*. The word morphed into a slimy crustacean, like a shrimp, which wiggled its legs for only a moment before an ibis snapped it up.

'Ah, never mind,' Thoth said at last. 'I'll just tell you the short version: To avenge his father, Osiris, Horus challenged Set to a duel. The winner would become king of the gods.'

'Horus won,' Carter said.

'You do remember!'

'No, I read about it.'

'And do you remember that without my help, Isis and you both would've died? Oh, I tried to mediate a solution to prevent the battle. That is one of my jobs, you know: to keep balance between order and chaos. But no-o-o, Isis convinced me to help your side because Set was getting too powerful. And the battle almost destroyed the world.'

He complains too much, Isis said inside my head. *It wasn't so bad.*

'No?' Thoth demanded, and I got the feeling he could hear her voice as well as I could. 'Set stabbed out Horus's eye.'

'Ouch.' Carter blinked.

'Yes, and I replaced it with a new eye made of moonlight. The Eye of Horus—your famous symbol. That was *me,* thank you very much. And when you cut off Isis's head—'

'Hold up.' Carter glanced at me. 'I cut off her *head?*'

I got better, Isis assured me.

'Only because I healed you, Isis!' Thoth said. 'And yes, Carter, Horus, whatever you call yourself, you were so mad, you cut off her head. You were reckless, you see—about to charge Set while you were still weak, and Isis tried to stop you. That made you so angry you took your sword— Well, the point is, you almost destroyed each other before you could defeat Set. If you start another fight with the Red Lord, beware. He will use chaos to turn you against each other.'

We'll defeat him again, Isis promised. *Thoth is just jealous.*

'Shut up,' Thoth and I said at the same time.

He looked at me with surprise. 'So, Sadie . . . you *are* trying to stay in control. It won't last. You may be blood of the pharaohs, but Isis is a deceptive, power-hungry—'

'I can contain her,' I said, and I had to use all my will to keep Isis from blurting out a string of insults.

Thoth fingered the frets of his guitar. 'Don't be so sure. Isis probably told you she helped defeat Set. Did she also tell you she was the reason Set got out of control in the first place? She exiled our first king.'

'You mean Ra?' Carter said. 'Didn't he get old and decide to leave the earth?'

Thoth snorted. 'He was old, yes, but he was *forced* to leave. Isis got tired of waiting for him to retire. She wanted her husband, Osiris, to become king. She also wanted more power. So one day, while Ra was napping, Isis secretly collected a bit of the sun god's drool.'

'*Eww,*' I said. 'Since when does drool make you powerful?'

Thoth scowled at me accusingly. 'You mixed the spit with clay to create a poisonous snake. That night, the serpent slipped into Ra's bedroom and bit him on the ankle. No amount of magic, even mine, could heal him. He would've died—'

'Gods can die?' Carter asked.

'Oh, yes,' Thoth said. 'Of course most of the time we rise again from the Duat—eventually. But this poison ate away at Ra's very being. Isis, of course, acted innocent. She cried to see Ra in pain. She tried to help with her magic. Finally she told Ra there was only one way to save him: Ra must tell her his secret name.'

'Secret name?' I asked. 'Like Bruce Wayne?'

'Everything in Creation has a secret name,' Thoth said. 'Even gods. To know a being's secret name is to have power over that creature. Isis promised that with Ra's secret name, she could heal him. Ra was in so much pain, he agreed. And Isis healed him.'

'But it gave her power over him,' Carter guessed.

'Extreme power,' Thoth agreed. 'She forced Ra to retreat into the heavens, opening the way for her beloved, Osiris, to become the new king of the gods. Set had been an important lieutenant to Ra, but he could not bear to see his brother Osiris become king. This made Set and Osiris enemies, and here we are five millennia later, still fighting that war, all because of Isis.'

'But that's not my fault!' I said. 'I would never do something like that.'

'Wouldn't you?' Thoth asked. 'Wouldn't you do anything to save your family, even if it upset the balance of the cosmos?'

His kaleidoscope eyes locked on mine, and I felt a surge of defiance. Well, why shouldn't I help my family? Who was this nutter in a lab coat telling me what I could and couldn't do?

Then I realized I didn't know who was thinking that: Isis or me. Panic started building in my chest. If I couldn't tell my own thoughts from those of Isis, how long before I went completely mad?

'No, Thoth,' I croaked. 'You have to believe me. I'm in control—me, Sadie—and I need your help. Set has our father.'

I let it spill out, then—everything from the

British Museum to Carter's vision of the red pyramid. Thoth listened without comment, but I could swear new stains developed on his lab coat as I talked, as if some of my words were being added to the mix.

'Just look at something for us,' I finished. 'Carter, hand him the book.'

Carter rummaged through his bag and brought out the book we'd stolen from Paris. 'You wrote this, right?' he said. 'It tells how to defeat Set.'

Thoth unfolded the papyrus pages. 'Oh, dear. I hate reading my old work. Look at this sentence. I'd never write it that way now.' He patted his lab coat pockets. 'Red pen—does anyone have one?'

Isis chafed against my willpower, insisting that we blast some sense into Thoth. *One fireball,* she pleaded. *Just one enormous magical fireball, please?*

I can't say I wasn't tempted, but I kept her under control.

'Look, Thoth,' I said. 'Ja-hooty, whatever. Set is about to destroy North America at the very least, possibly the world. Millions of people will die. You said you care about balance. Will you help us or not?'

For a moment, the only sounds were ibis beaks tapping on keyboards.

'You *are* in trouble,' Thoth agreed. 'So let me ask, why do you think your father put you in this position? Why did he release the gods?'

I almost said, *To bring back Mum.* But I didn't believe that anymore.

'My mum saw the future,' I guessed. 'Something bad was coming. I think she and Dad were trying to stop it. They thought the only way was to release the gods.'

277

'Even though using the power of the gods is incredibly dangerous for mortals,' Thoth pressed, 'and against the law of the House of Life—a law that I convinced Iskandar to make, by the way.'

I remembered something the old Chief Lector had told me in the Hall of Ages. 'Gods have great power, but only humans have creativity.' 'I think my mum convinced Iskandar that the rule was wrong. Maybe he couldn't admit it publicly, but she made him change his mind. Whatever is coming—it's so bad, gods and mortals are going to need each other.'

'And what is coming?' Thoth asked. 'The rise of Set?' His tone was coy, like a teacher trying a trick question.

'Maybe,' I said carefully, 'but I don't know.'

Up on the bookshelf, Khufu belched. He bared his fangs in a messy grin.

'You have a point, Khufu,' Thoth mused. 'She does not sound like Isis. Isis would never admit she doesn't know something.'

I had to clamp a mental hand over Isis's mouth.

Thoth tossed the book back to Carter. 'Let's see if you act as well as you talk. I will explain the spell book, provided you prove to me that you truly have control of your gods, that you're not simply repeating the same old patterns.'

'A test?' Carter said. 'We accept.'

'Now, hang on,' I protested. Maybe being homeschooled, Carter didn't realize that 'test' is normally a bad thing.

'Wonderful,' Thoth said. 'There is an item of power I require from a magician's tomb. Bring it to me.'

'Which magician's tomb?' I asked.

But Thoth took a piece of chalk from his lab coat and scribbled something in the air. A doorway opened in front of him.

'How did you do that?' I asked. 'Bast said we can't summon portals during the Demon Days.'

'Mortals can't,' Thoth agreed. 'But a god of magic can. If you succeed, we'll have barbecue.'

The doorway pulled us into a black void, and Thoth's office disappeared.

24.
I BLOW UP SOME BLUE SUEDE SHOES

SADIE

'Where are we?' I asked.

We stood on a deserted avenue outside the gates of a large estate. We still seemed to be in Memphis—at least the trees, the weather, the afternoon light were all the same.

The estate must've been several acres at least. The white metal gates were done in fancy designs of silhouetted guitar players and musical notes. Beyond them, the driveway curved through the trees up to a two-story house with a white-columned portico.

'Oh, no,' Carter said. 'I recognize those gates.'

'What? Why?'

'Dad brought me here once. A great magician's tomb . . . Thoth has got to be kidding.'

'Carter, what are you talking about? Is someone buried here?'

He nodded. 'This is Graceland. Home to the

most famous musician in the world.'

'Michael Jackson lived here?'

'No, dummy,' Carter said. 'Elvis Presley.'

I wasn't sure whether to laugh or curse. 'Elvis Presley. You mean white suits with rhinestones, big slick hair, Gran's record collection—*that* Elvis?'

Carter looked around nervously. He drew his sword, even though we seemed to be totally alone. 'This is where he lived and died. He's buried in back of the mansion.'

I stared up at the house. 'You're telling me Elvis was a magician?'

'Don't know.' Carter gripped his sword. 'Thoth did say something about music being a kind of magic. But something's not right. Why are we the only ones here? There's usually a mob of tourists.'

'Christmas holidays?'

'But no security?'

I shrugged. 'Maybe it's like what Zia did at Luxor. Maybe Thoth cleared everyone out.'

'Maybe.' But I could tell Carter was still uneasy. He pushed the gates, and they opened easily. 'Not right,' he muttered.

'No,' I agreed. 'But let's go pay our respects.'

As we walked up the drive, I couldn't help thinking that the home of 'the King' wasn't very impressive. Compared to some of the rich and famous homes I'd seen on TV, Elvis's place looked awfully small. It was just two stories high, with that white-columned portico and brick walls. Ridiculous plaster lions flanked the steps. Perhaps things were simpler back in Elvis's day, or maybe he spent all his money on rhinestone suits.

We stopped at the foot of the steps.

'So Dad brought you here?' I asked.

'Yeah.' Carter eyed the lions as if expecting them to attack. 'Dad loves blues and jazz, mostly, but he said Elvis was important because he took African American music and made it popular for white people. He helped invent rock and roll. Anyway, Dad and I were in town for a symposium or something. I don't remember. Dad insisted I come here.'

'Lucky you.' And yes, perhaps I was beginning to understand that Carter's life with Dad hadn't been all glamour and holiday, but still I couldn't help being a bit jealous. Not that I'd ever wanted to see Graceland, of course, but Dad had never insisted on taking me anywhere—at least until the British Museum trip when he disappeared. I hadn't even known Dad was an Elvis fan, which was rather horrifying.

We walked up the steps. The front door swung open all by itself.

'I don't like that,' Carter said.

I turned to look behind us, and my blood went ice cold. I grabbed my brother's arm. '*Um,* Carter, speaking of things we don't like . . .'

Coming up the driveway were two magicians brandishing staffs and wands.

'Inside,' Carter said. 'Quick!'

I didn't have much time to admire the house. There was a dining room to our left and a living room–music room to our right, with a piano and a stained glass archway decorated with peacocks. All the furniture was roped off. The house smelled like old people.

'Item of power,' I said. 'Where?'

'I don't know,' Carter snapped. 'They didn't have "items of power" listed on the tour!'

281

I glanced out the window. Our enemies were getting close. The bloke in front wore jeans, a black sleeveless shirt, boots, and a battered cowboy hat. He looked more like an outlaw than a magician. His friend was similarly dressed but much heftier, with tattooed arms, a bald head, and a scraggly beard. When they were ten meters away, the man with the cowboy hat lowered his staff, which morphed into a shotgun.

'Oh, please!' I yelled, and pushed Carter into the living room.

The blast shattered Elvis's front door and set my ears ringing. We scrambled to our feet and ran deeper into the house. We passed through an old-fashioned kitchen, then into the strangest den I'd ever seen. The back wall was made of vine-covered bricks, with a waterfall trickling down the side. The carpet was green shag (floor *and* ceiling, mind you) and the furniture was carved with creepy animal shapes. Just in case all that wasn't dreadful enough, plaster monkeys and stuffed lions had been strategically placed around the room. Despite the danger we were in, the place was so horrid, I just had to stop and marvel.

'God,' I said. 'Did Elvis have *no* taste?'

'The Jungle Room,' Carter said. 'He decorated it like this to annoy his dad.'

'I can respect that.'

Another shotgun blast roared through the house.

'Split up,' Carter said.

'Bad idea!' I could hear the magicians tromping through the rooms, smashing things as they came closer.

'I'll distract them,' Carter said. 'You search. The

trophy room is through there.'

'Carter!'

But the fool ran off to protect me. I *hate* it when he does that. I should have followed him, or run the other way, but I stood frozen in shock as he turned the corner with his sword raised, his body beginning to glow with a golden light . . . and everything went wrong.

Blam! An emerald flash brought Carter to his knees. For a heartbeat, I thought he'd been hit with the shotgun, and I had to stifle a scream. But immediately, Carter collapsed and began to shrink, clothes, sword and all—melting into a tiny sliver of green.

The lizard that used to be my brother raced toward me, climbed up my leg and into my palm, where it looked at me desperately.

From around the corner, a gruff voice said, 'Split up and find the sister. She'll be somewhere close.'

'Oh, Carter,' I whispered fondly to the lizard. 'I will *so* kill you for this.'

I stuffed him in my pocket and ran.

The two magicians continued to smash and crash their way through Graceland, knocking over furniture and blasting things to bits. Apparently they were not Elvis fans.

I ducked under some ropes, crept through a hallway, and found the trophy room. Amazingly, it was full of trophies. Gold records crowded the walls. Rhinestone Elvis jumpsuits glittered in four glass cases. The room was dimly lit, probably to keep the jumpsuits from blinding visitors, and music played softly from overhead speakers: Elvis warning everyone not to step on his blue suede shoes.

I scanned the room but found nothing that looked magical. The suits? I hoped Thoth did not expect me to wear one. The gold records? Lovely Frisbees, but no.

'Jerrod!' a voice called to my right. A magician was coming down the hallway. I darted toward the other exit, but a voice just outside it called back, 'Yeah, I'm over here.'

I was surrounded.

'Carter,' I whispered. 'Curse your lizard brain.'

He fluttered nervously in my pocket but was no help.

I fumbled through my magician's bag and grasped my wand. Should I try drawing a magic circle? No time, and I didn't want to duel toe-to-toe with two older magicians. I had to stay mobile. I took out my rod and willed it into a full-length staff. I could set it on fire, or turn it into a lion, but what good would that do? My hands started to tremble. I wanted to crawl into a ball and hide beneath Elvis's gold record collection.

Let me take over, Isis said. *I can turn our enemies to dust.*

No, I told her.

You will get us both killed.

I could feel her pressing against my will, trying to bust out. I could taste her anger with these magicians. How dare they challenge us? With a word, we could destroy them.

No, I thought again. Then I remembered something Zia had said: *Use whatever you have available.* The room was dimly lit . . . perhaps if I could make it darker.

'Darkness,' I whispered. I felt a tugging

sensation in my stomach, and the lights flickered off. The music stopped. The light continued to dim—even the sunlight faded from the windows until the entire room went black.

Somewhere to my left, the first magician sighed in exasperation. 'Jerrod!'

'Wasn't me, Wayne!' Jerrod insisted. 'You always blame me!'

Wayne muttered something in Egyptian, still moving towards me. I needed a distraction.

I closed my eyes and imagined my surroundings. Although it was pitch-black, I could still sense Jerrod in the hallway to my left, stumbling through the darkness. I sensed Wayne on the other side of the wall to the right, only a few steps from the doorway. And I could visualize the four glass display cases with Elvis's suits.

They're tossing your house, I thought. *Defend it!*

A stronger pull in my gut, as if I were lifting a heavy weight—then the display cases blew open. I heard the shuffling of stiff cloth, like sails in the wind, and was dimly aware of four pale white shapes in motion—two heading to either door.

Wayne yelled first as the empty Elvis suits tackled him. His shotgun lit up the dark. Then to my left, Jerrod shouted in surprise. A heavy *clump!* told me he'd been knocked over. I decided to go in Jerrod's direction—better an off-balance bloke than one with a shotgun. I slipped through the doorway and down a hall, leaving Jerrod scuffling behind me and yelling, 'Get off! Get off!'

Take him while he's down, Isis urged. *Burn him to ashes!*

Part of me knew she had a point: if I left Jerrod in one piece, he would be up in no time and after me again; but it didn't seem right to hurt him, especially while he was being tackled by Elvis suits. I found a door and burst outside into the afternoon sunlight.

I was in the backyard of Graceland. A large fountain gurgled nearby, ringed by grave markers. One had a glass-encased flame at the top and was heaped with flowers. I took a wild guess: it must be Elvis's.

A magician's tomb.

Of course. We'd been searching the house, but the item of power would be at his gravesite. But what exactly *was* the item?

Before I could approach the grave, the door burst open. The big bald man with the straggly beard stumbled out. A tattered Elvis suit had its sleeves wrapped around his neck like it was getting a piggyback ride.

'Well, well.' The magician threw off the jumpsuit. His voice confirmed for me that he was the one called Jerrod. 'You're just a little girl. You've caused us a lot of trouble, missy.'

He lowered his staff and fired a shot of green light. I raised my wand and deflected the bolt of energy straight up. I heard a surprised coo—the cry of a pigeon—and a newly made lizard fell out of the sky at my feet.

'Sorry,' I told it.

Jerrod snarled and threw down his staff. Apparently, he specialized in lizards, because the staff morphed into a komodo dragon the size of a London taxicab.

The monster charged me with unnatural speed. It opened its jaws and would've bitten me in half, but I just had time to wedge my staff in its mouth.

Jerrod laughed. 'Nice try, girl!'

I felt the dragon's jaws pressing on the staff. It was only a matter of seconds before the wood snapped, and then I'd be a komodo dragon's snack. *A little help,* I told Isis. Carefully, very carefully, I tapped in to her strength. Doing so without letting her take over was like riding a surfboard over a tidal wave, trying desperately to stay on my feet. I felt five thousand years of experience, knowledge, and power course through me. She offered me options, and I selected the simplest. I channeled power through my staff and felt it grow hot in my hands, glowing white. The dragon hissed and gurgled as my staff elongated, forcing the creature's jaws open wider, wider, and then: *boom!*

The dragon shattered into kindling and sent the splintered remains of Jerrod's staff raining down around me.

Jerrod had only a moment to look stunned before I threw my wand and whapped him solidly on the forehead. His eyes crossed, and he collapsed on the pavement. My wand returned to my hand.

That would've been a lovely happy ending . . . except I'd forgotten about Wayne. The cowboy-hatted magician stumbled out the door, almost tripping over his friend, but he recovered with lightning speed.

He shouted, 'Wind!' and my staff flew out of my hands and into his.

He smiled cruelly. 'Well fought, darlin'. But elemental magic is always quickest.'

He struck the ends of both staffs, his and mine, against the pavement. A wave rippled over the dirt and pavement as if the ground had become liquid, knocking me off my feet and sending my wand flying. I scrambled backwards on hands and knees, but I could hear Wayne chanting, summoning fire from the staffs.

Rope, Isis said. *Every magician carries rope.*

Panic had made my mind go blank, but my hand instinctively went for my magic bag. I pulled out a small bit of twine. Hardly a rope, but it triggered a memory—something Zia had done in the New York museum. I threw the twine at Wayne and yelled a word Isis suggested: *'Tas!'*

A golden hieroglyph burned in the air over Wayne's head.

The twine whipped toward him like an angry snake, growing longer and thicker as it flew. Wayne's eyes widened. He stumbled back and sent jets of flame shooting from both staffs, but the rope was too quick. It lashed round his ankles and toppled him sideways, wrapping round his whole body until he was encased in a twine cocoon from chin to toes. He struggled and screamed and called me quite a few unflattering names.

I got up unsteadily. Jerrod was still out cold. I retrieved my staff, which had fallen next to Wayne. He continued straining against the twine and cursing in Egyptian, which sounded strange with an American Southern accent.

Finish him, Isis warned. *He can still speak. He will not rest until he destroys you.*

'Fire!' Wayne screamed. 'Water! Cheese!'

Even the cheese command did not work. I reckoned his rage was throwing his magic off balance, making it impossible to focus, but I knew he would recover soon.

'Silence,' I said.

Wayne's voice abruptly stopped working. He kept screaming, but no sound came out.

'I'm not your enemy,' I told him. 'But I can't have you killing me, either.'

Something wriggled in my pocket, and I remembered Carter. I took him out. He looked okay, except of course for the fact he was still a lizard.

'I'll try to change you back,' I told him. 'Hopefully I don't make things worse.'

He made a little croak that didn't convey much confidence.

I closed my eyes and imagined Carter as he should be: a tall boy of fourteen, badly dressed, very human, very annoying. Carter began to feel heavy in my hands. I put him down and watched as the lizard grew into a vaguely human blob. By the count of three, my brother was lying on his stomach, his sword and pack next to him on the lawn.

He spit grass out of his mouth. 'How'd you do that?'

'I don't know,' I admitted. 'You just seemed . . . wrong.'

'Thanks a lot.' He got up and checked to make sure he had all his fingers. Then he saw the two magicians and his mouth fell open. 'What did you do to them?'

'Just tied one up. Knocked one out. Magic.'

'No, I mean . . .' He faltered, searching for words, then gave up and pointed.

I looked at the magicians and yelped. Wayne wasn't moving. His eyes and mouth were open, but he wasn't blinking or breathing. Next to him,

Jerrod looked just as frozen. As we watched, their mouths began to glow as if they'd swallowed matches. Two tiny yellow orbs of fire popped out from between their lips and shot into the air, disappearing in the sunlight.

'What—what was that?' I asked. 'Are they dead?'

Carter approached them cautiously and put his hand on Wayne's neck. 'It doesn't even feel like skin. More like rock.'

'No, they were human! I didn't turn them to rock!'

Carter felt Jerrod's forehead where I'd whacked him with my wand. 'It's cracked.'

'What?'

Carter picked up his sword. Before I could even scream, he brought the hilt down on Jerrod's face and the magician's head cracked into shards like a flowerpot.

'They're made of clay,' Carter said. 'They're both *shabti.*'

He kicked Wayne's arm and I heard it crunch under the twine.

'But they were casting spells,' I said. 'And talking. They were *real.*'

As we watched, the *shabti* crumbled to dust, leaving nothing behind but my bit of twine, two staffs, and some grungy clothes.

'Thoth was testing us,' Carter guessed. 'Those balls of fire, though . . .' He frowned as if trying to recall something important.

'Probably the magic that animated them,' I guessed. 'Flying back to their master—like a recording of what they did?'

It sounded like a solid theory to me, but Carter

seemed awfully troubled. He pointed to the blasted back door of Graceland. 'Is the whole house like that?'

'Worse.' I looked at the ruined Elvis jumpsuit under Jerrod's clothes and scattered rhinestones. Maybe Elvis had no taste, but I still felt bad about trashing the King's palace. If the place had been important to Dad . . . Suddenly an idea perked me up. 'What was it Amos said, when he repaired that saucer?'

Carter frowned. 'This is a whole house, Sadie. Not a saucer.'

'Got it,' I said. *Hi-nehm!*'

A gold hieroglyphic symbol flickered to life in my palm.

I held it up and blew it towards the house. The entire outline of Graceland began to glow. The pieces of the door flew back into place and mended themselves. The tattered bits of Elvis clothing disappeared.

'Wow,' Carter said. 'Do you think the inside is fixed too?'

'I—' My vision blurred, and my knees buckled. I would've knocked my head on the pavement if Carter hadn't caught me.

'It's okay,' he said. 'You did a lot of magic, Sadie. That was amazing.'

'But we haven't even found the item Thoth sent us for.'

'Yeah,' Carter said. 'Maybe we have.'

He pointed to Elvis's grave, and I saw it clearly: a memento left behind by some adoring fan—a necklace with a silver loop-topped cross, just like the one on Mum's T-shirt in my old photograph.

'An ankh,' I said. 'The Egyptian symbol for

eternal life.'

Carter picked it up. There was a small papyrus scroll attached to the chain.

'What's this?' he murmured, and unrolled the sheet. He stared at it so hard I thought he'd burn a hole in it.

'What?' I looked over his shoulder.

The painting looked quite ancient. It showed a golden, spotted cat holding a knife in one paw and chopping the head off a snake.

Beneath it, in black marker, someone had written: *Keep up the fight!*

'That's vandalism, isn't it?' I asked. 'Marking up an ancient drawing like that? Rather an odd thing to leave for Elvis.'

Carter didn't seem to hear. 'I've seen this picture before. It's in a lot of tombs. Don't know why it never occurred to me . . .'

I studied the picture more closely. Something about it did seem rather familiar.

'You know what it means?' I asked.

'It's the Cat of Ra, fighting the sun god's main enemy, Apophis.'

'The snake,' I said.

'Yeah, Apophis was—'

'The embodiment of chaos,' I said, remembering what Nut had said.

Carter looked impressed, as well he should have. 'Exactly. Apophis was even worse than Set. The Egyptians thought Doomsday would come when Apophis ate the sun and destroyed all of Creation.'

'But . . . the cat killed it,' I said hopefully.

'The cat had to kill it over and over again,' Carter said. 'Like what Thoth said about repeating

292

patterns. The thing is . . . I asked Dad one time if the cat had a name. And he said nobody knows for sure, but most people assume it's Sekhmet, this fierce lion goddess. She was called the Eye of Ra because she did his dirty work. He saw an enemy; she killed it.'

'Fine. So?'

'So the cat doesn't look like Sekhmet. It just occurred to me . . .'

I finally saw it, and a shiver went down my back. 'The Cat of Ra looks exactly like Muffin. It's Bast.'

Just then the ground rumbled. The memorial fountain began to glow, and a dark doorway opened.

'Come on,' I said. 'I've got some questions for Thoth. And then I'm going to punch him in the beak.'

25.
WE WIN AN ALL-EXPENSES-PAID TRIP
TO DEATH

CARTER

Being turned into a lizard can really mess up your day. As we stepped through the doorway, I tried to hide it, but I was feeling pretty bad.

You're probably thinking: *Hey, you already turned into a falcon. What's the big deal?* But someone else *forcing* you into another form— that's totally different. Imagine yourself in a trash compactor, your entire body smashed into a shape smaller than your hand. It's painful and it's

293

humiliating. Your enemy pictures you as a stupid harmless lizard, then imposes their will on you, overpowering your thoughts until you have to be what *they* want you to be. I guess it could've been worse. He could've pictured me as a fruit bat, but still . . .

Of course I felt grateful to Sadie for saving me, but I also felt like a complete loser. It was bad enough that I'd embarrassed myself on the basketball court with a troop of baboons. But I'd also totally failed in battle. Maybe I'd done okay with Leroy, the airport monster, but faced with a couple of magicians (even clay ones), I got turned into a reptile in the first two seconds. How would I stand a chance against Set?

I was shaken out of those thoughts when we emerged from the portal, because we were definitely not in Thoth's office.

In front of us loomed a life-size glass-and-metal pyramid, almost as big as the ones at Giza. The skyline of downtown Memphis rose up in the distance. At our backs were the banks of the Mississippi River.

The sun was setting, turning the river and the pyramid to gold. On the pyramid's front steps, next to a twenty-foot-tall pharaoh statue labeled RAMESSES THE GREAT, Thoth had set out a picnic with barbecued ribs and brisket, bread and pickles, the works. He was playing his guitar with a portable amp. Khufu stood nearby, covering his ears.

'Oh, good.' Thoth strummed a chord that sounded like the death cry of a sick donkey. 'You lived.'

I stared up at the pyramid in amazement.

294

'Where did this come from? You didn't just . . . build it, did you?' I remembered my *ba* trip to Set's red pyramid, and suddenly pictured gods building monuments all over the U.S.

Thoth chuckled. 'I didn't have to build it. The people of Memphis did that. Humans never really forget Egypt, you know. Every time they build a city on the banks of a river, they remember their heritage, buried deep in their subconscious. This is the Pyramid Arena—sixth largest pyramid in the world. It used to be a sports arena for . . . what is that game you like, Khufu?'

'*Agh!*' Khufu said indignantly. And I swear he gave me a dirty look.

'Yes, basketball,' Thoth said. 'But the arena fell on hard times. It's been abandoned for years. Well, no longer. I'm moving in. You do have the ankh?'

For a moment, I wondered if it had been such a good idea helping Thoth, but we needed him. I tossed him the necklace.

'Excellent,' he said. 'An ankh from the tomb of Elvis. Powerful magic!'

Sadie clenched her fists. 'We almost died getting that. You tricked us.'

'Not a trick,' he insisted. 'A test.'

'Those *things*,' Sadie said, 'the *shabti*—'

'Yes, my best work in centuries. A shame to break them, but I couldn't have you beating up on *real* magicians, could I? *Shabti* make excellent stunt doubles.'

'So you saw the whole thing,' I muttered.

'Oh, yes.' Thoth held out his hand. Two little fires danced across his palm—the magic essences we'd seen escape from the *shabti*'s mouths. 'These are . . . recording devices, I suppose you'd say. I got a full report. You defeated the *shabti* without killing. I must admit I'm impressed, Sadie. You controlled your magic and controlled Isis. And you, Carter, did well turning into a lizard.'

I thought he was teasing me. Then I realized there was genuine sympathy in his eyes, as if my failure had also been some kind of test.

'You will find worse enemies ahead, Carter,' he warned. 'Even now, the House of Life sends its best against you. But you will also find friends where you least expect them.'

I didn't know why, but I got the feeling he was talking about Zia . . . or maybe that was just wishful thinking.

Thoth stood and handed Khufu his guitar. He tossed the ankh at the statue of Ramesses, and the necklace fastened itself around the pharaoh's neck.

'There you are, Ramesses,' Thoth said to the statue. 'Here's to our new life.'

The statue glowed faintly, as if the sunset had just gotten ten times brighter. Then the glow spread to the entire pyramid before slowly fading.

'Oh, yes,' Thoth mused. 'I think I'll be happy here. Next time you children visit me, I'll have a much bigger laboratory.'

Scary thought, but I tried to stay focused.

'That's not all we found,' I said. 'You need to explain *this.*'

I held out the painting of the cat and the snake.

'It's a cat and a snake,' Thoth said.

'Thank you, god of wisdom. You placed it for us to find, didn't you? You're trying to give us some kind of clue.'

'Who, me?'

Just kill him, Horus said.

Shut up, I said.

At least kill the guitar.

'The cat is Bast,' I said, trying to ignore my inner psycho falcon. 'Does this have something to do with why our parents released the gods?'

Thoth gestured toward the picnic plates. 'Did I mention we have barbecue?'

Sadie stomped her foot. 'We had a deal, Jahooty!'

'You know . . . I like that name,' Thoth mused, 'but not so much when *you* say it. I believe our deal was that I would explain how to use the spell book. May I?'

He held out his hand. Reluctantly I dug the magic book out of my bag and handed it over.

Thoth unfolded the pages. 'Ah, this takes me back. So many formulae. In the old days, we believed in ritual. A good spell might take weeks to prepare, with exotic ingredients from all over the world.'

'We don't have weeks,' I said.

'Rush, rush, rush.' Thoth sighed.

'Agh,' Khufu agreed, sniffing the guitar.

Thoth closed the book and handed it back to me. 'Well, it's an incantation for destroying Set.'

'We *know* that,' Sadie said. 'Will it destroy him forever?'

'No, no. But it will destroy his form in this world, banishing him deep into the Duat and reducing his power so he will not be able to appear again for a long, long time. Centuries, most likely.'

'Sounds good,' I said. 'How do we read it?'

Thoth stared at me like the answer should be obvious. 'You cannot read it now because the words can only be spoken in Set's presence. Once before him, Sadie should open the book and recite the incantation. She'll know what to do when the time comes.'

'Right,' Sadie said. 'And Set will just stand there calmly while I read him to death.'

Thoth shrugged. 'I did not say it would be easy. You'll also require two ingredients for the spell to work—a verbal ingredient, Set's secret name—'

'*What?*' I protested. 'How are we supposed to get that?'

'With difficulty, I'd imagine. You can't simply read a secret name from a book. The name must come from the owner's own lips, in his own pronunciation, to give you power over him.'

'Great,' I said. 'So we just force Set to tell us.'

'Or trick him,' Thoth said. 'Or convince him.'

'Isn't there any other way?' Sadie asked.

Thoth brushed an ink splotch off his lab coat. A hieroglyph turned into a moth and fluttered away. 'I suppose . . . yes. You could ask the person closest to Set's heart—the person who loves him most. She would also have the ability to speak the name.'

'But nobody loves Set!' Sadie said.

'His wife,' I guessed. 'That other goddess, Nephthys.'

Thoth nodded. 'She's a river goddess. Perhaps you could find her in a river.'

'This just gets better and better,' I muttered.

Sadie frowned at Thoth. 'You said there was another ingredient?'

'A physical ingredient,' Thoth agreed, 'a feather of truth.'

'A what?' Sadie asked.

But I knew what he was talking about, and my

298

heart sank. 'You mean from the Land of the Dead.'

Thoth beamed. 'Exactly.'

'Wait,' Sadie said. 'What is he talking about?'

I tried to conceal my fear. 'When you died in Ancient Egypt, you had to take a journey to the Land of the Dead,' I explained. 'A really *dangerous* journey. Finally, you made it to the Hall of Judgment, where your life was weighed on the Scales of Anubis: your heart on one side, the feather of truth on the other. If you passed the test, you were blessed with eternal happiness. If you failed, a monster ate your heart and you ceased to exist.'

'Ammit the Devourer,' Thoth said wistfully. 'Cute little thing.'

Sadie blinked. 'So we're supposed to get a feather from this Hall of Judgment *how*, exactly?'

'Perhaps Anubis will be in a good mood,' Thoth suggested. 'It happens every thousand years or so.'

'But how do we even get to the Land of the Dead?' I asked. 'I mean . . . without dying.'

Thoth gazed at the western horizon, where the sunset was turning blood-red. 'Down the river at night, I should think. That's how most people pass into the Land of the Dead. I would take a boat. You'll find Anubis at the end of the river—' He pointed north, then changed his mind and pointed south. 'Forgot, rivers flow south here. Everything is backward.'

'Agh!' Khufu ran his fingers down the frets of the guitar and ripped out a massive rock 'n' roll riff. Then he belched as if nothing had happened and set down the guitar. Sadie and I just stared at him, but Thoth nodded as if the baboon had said

299

something profound.

'Are you sure, Khufu?' Thoth asked.

Khufu grunted.

'Very well.' Thoth sighed. 'Khufu says he would like to go with you. I told him he could stay here and type my doctoral thesis on quantum physics, but he's not interested.'

'Can't imagine why,' Sadie said. 'Glad to have Khufu along, but where do we find a boat?'

'You are the blood of pharaohs,' Thoth said. 'Pharaohs always have access to a boat. Just make sure you use it wisely.'

He nodded toward the river. Churning toward the shore was an old-fashioned paddlewheel steamboat with smoke billowing from its stacks.

'I wish you a good journey,' Thoth said. 'Until we meet again.'

'We're supposed to take *that*?' I asked. But when I turned to look at Thoth, he was gone, and he'd taken the barbecue with him.

'Wonderful,' Sadie muttered.

'*Agh!*' Khufu agreed. He took our hands and led us down to the shore.

26.
ABOARD THE *EGYPTIAN QUEEN*

CARTER

As far as rides to the Land of Death go, the boat was pretty cool. It had multiple decks with ornate railings painted black and green. The side paddlewheels churned the river into froth, and along the paddlewheel housings the name of the boat glittered in gold letters: *Egyptian Queen*.

At first glance, you'd think the boat was just a tourist attraction: one of those floating casinos or cruise boats for old people. But if you looked closer you started noticing strange little details. The boat's name was written in Demotic and in hieroglyphics underneath the English. Sparkly smoke billowed from the stacks as if the engines were burning gold. Orbs of multicolored fire flitted around the decks. And on the prow of the ship, two painted eyes moved and blinked, scanning the river for trouble.

'That's odd,' Sadie remarked.

I nodded. 'I've seen eyes painted on boats before. They still do that all over the Mediterranean. But usually they don't move.'

'What? No, not the stupid eyes. That lady on the highest deck. Isn't that . . .' Sadie broke into a grin. 'Bast!'

Sure enough, our favorite feline was leaning out the window of the pilot's house. I was about to wave to her, when I noticed the creature standing next to Bast, gripping the wheel. He had a human body and was dressed in the white uniform of a boat captain. But instead of a head, a double-bladed axe sprouted from his collar. And I'm not talking about a *small* axe for chopping wood. I'm talking *battle*-axe: twin crescent-shaped iron blades, one in front where his face should be, one in the back, the edges splattered with suspicious-looking dried red splotches.

The ship pulled up to the dock. Balls of fire began zipping around—lowering the gangplank, tying off ropes, and basically doing crew-type stuff.

How they did it without hands, and without setting everything on fire, I don't know, but it wasn't the strangest thing I'd seen that week.

Bast climbed down from the wheelhouse. She hugged us as we came aboard—even Khufu, who tried to return the favor by grooming her for lice.

'I'm glad you survived!' Bast told us. 'What happened?'

We gave her the basics and her hair poofed out again. 'Elvis? *Gah!* Thoth is getting cruel in his old age. Well, I can't say I'm glad to be on this boat again. I *hate* the water, but I suppose—'

'You've been on this boat before?' I asked.

Bast's smile wavered. 'A million questions as usual, but let's eat first. The captain is waiting.'

I wasn't anxious to meet a giant axe, and I wasn't enthusiastic about another one of Bast's grilled-cheese-and-Friskies dinners, but we followed her inside the boat.

The dining parlor was lavishly decorated in Egyptian style. Colorful murals depicting the gods covered the walls. Gilded columns supported the ceiling. A long dining table was laden with every kind of food you could want—sandwiches, pizzas, hamburgers, Mexican food, you name it. It *way* made up for missing Thoth's barbecue. On a side table stood an ice chest, a line of golden goblets, and a soda dispenser with about twenty different choices. The mahogany chairs were carved to look like baboons, which reminded me a little too much of Graceland's Jungle Room, but Khufu thought they were okay. He barked at his chair just to show it who was top monkey, then sat on its lap. He picked an avocado from a basket of fruit and started peeling it.

Across the room, a door opened, and the axe dude came in. He had to duck to avoid cleaving the doorframe.

'Lord and Lady Kane,' the captain said, bowing. His voice was a quivery hum that resonated along his front blade. I saw a video one time of a guy playing music by hitting a saw with a hammer, and that's sort of the way the captain sounded. 'It is an honor to have you aboard.'

' "Lady Kane," ' Sadie mused. 'I like that.'

'I am Bloodstained Blade,' the captain said. 'What are your orders?'

Sadie raised an eyebrow at Bast. 'He takes orders from us?'

'Within reason,' Bast said. 'He is bound to your family. Your father . . .' She cleared her throat. 'Well, he and your mother summoned this boat.'

The axe demon made a disapproving hum. 'You haven't told them, goddess?'

'I'm getting to it,' Bast grumbled.

'Told us what?' I asked.

'Just details.' She rushed on. 'The boat can be summoned once a year, and only in times of great need. You'll need to give the captain your orders now. He must have clear directions if we're to proceed, ah, *safely*.'

I wondered what was bothering Bast, but the axe dude was waiting for orders, and the flecks of dried blood on his blades told me I'd better not keep him in suspense.

'We need to visit the Hall of Judgment,' I told him. 'Take us to the Land of the Dead.'

Bloodstained Blade hummed thoughtfully. 'I will make the arrangements, Lord Kane, but it will take time.'

'We don't have a lot of that.' I turned to Sadie. 'It's . . . what, the evening of the twenty-seventh?'

She nodded in agreement. 'Day after tomorrow, at sunrise, Set completes his pyramid and destroys the world unless we stop him. So, yes, Captain Very Large Blade, or whatever it is, I'd say we're in a bit of a rush.'

'We will, of course, do our best,' said Bloodstained Blade, though his voice sounded a little, well, sharp. 'The crew will prepare your staterooms. Will you dine while you wait?'

I looked at the table laden with food and realized how hungry I was. I hadn't eaten since we were in the Washington Monument. 'Yeah. *Um,* thanks, BSB.'

The captain bowed again, which made him look a little too much like a guillotine. Then he left us to our dinner.

At first, I was too busy eating to talk. I inhaled a roast beef sandwich, a couple of pieces of cherry pie with ice cream, and three glasses of ginger ale before I finally came up for air.

Sadie didn't eat as much. Then again she'd had lunch on the plane. She settled for a cheese-and-cucumber sandwich and one of those weird British drinks she likes—a Ribena. Khufu carefully picked out everything that ended with -*o*—Doritos, Oreos, and some chunks of meat. Buffalo? Armadillo? I was scared to even guess.

The balls of fire floated attentively around the room, refilling our goblets and clearing away our plates as we finished.

After so many days spent running for our lives, it felt good to just sit at a dinner table and relax. The captain's informing us that he couldn't transport us instantly to the Land of the Dead was the best news I'd had in a long time.

'*Agh!*' Khufu wiped his mouth and grabbed one of the balls of fire. He fashioned it into a glowing basketball and snorted at me.

For once I was pretty sure what he'd said in Baboon. It wasn't an invitation. It meant something like: 'I'm going to play basketball by myself now. I will not invite you because your lack of skill would make me throw up.'

'No problem, man,' I said, though my face felt hot with embarrassment. 'Have fun.'

Khufu snorted again, then loped off with the ball under his arm. I wondered if he'd find a court somewhere on board.

At the far end of the table, Bast pushed her plate away. She'd hardly touched her tuna Friskies.

'Not hungry?' I asked.

'*Hmm?* Oh . . . I suppose not.' She turned her goblet listlessly. She was wearing an expression I didn't associate with cats: guilt.

Sadie and I locked eyes. We had a brief, silent exchange, something like:

You ask her.

No, you.

Of course Sadie's better at giving dirty looks, so I lost the contest.

'Bast?' I said. 'What did the captain want you to tell us?'

She hesitated. 'Oh, that? You shouldn't listen to demons. Bloodstained Blade is bound by magic to serve, but if he ever got loose, he'd use that axe on all of us, believe me.'

'You're changing the subject,' I said.

Bast traced her finger across the table, drawing

305

hieroglyphs in the condensation ring from her goblet. 'The truth? I haven't been on board since the night your mother died. Your parents had docked this boat on the Thames. After the . . . accident, your father brought me here. This is where we made our deal.'

I realized she meant *right* here, at this table. My father had sat here in despair after Mom's death—with no one to console him except the cat goddess, an axe demon, and a bunch of floating lights.

I studied Bast's face in the dim light. I thought about the painting we'd found at Graceland. Even in human form, Bast looked so much like that cat—a cat drawn by some artist thousands of years ago.

'It wasn't just a chaos monster, was it?' I asked.

Bast eyed me. 'What do you mean?'

'The thing you were fighting when our parents released you from the obelisk. It wasn't just a chaos monster. You were fighting Apophis.'

All around the parlor, the servant fires dimmed. One dropped a plate and fluttered nervously.

'Don't say the Serpent's name,' Bast warned. 'Especially as we head into the night. Night is his realm.'

'It's true, then.' Sadie shook her head in dismay. 'Why didn't you say anything? Why did you lie to us?'

Bast dropped her gaze. Sitting in the shadows, she looked weary and frail. Her face was etched with the traces of old battle scars.

'I was the Eye of Ra.' She spoke quietly. 'The sun god's champion, the instrument of his will. Do you have any idea what an honor it was?'

She extended her claws and studied them.

'When people see pictures of Ra's warrior cat, they assume it's Sekhmet, the lioness. And she *was* his first champion, it's true. But she was too violent, too out of control. Eventually Sekhmet was forced to step down, and Ra chose *me* as his fighter: little Bast.'

'Why do you sound ashamed?' Sadie asked. 'You said it's an honor.'

'At first I was proud, Sadie. I fought the Serpent for ages. Cats and snakes are mortal enemies. I did my job well. But then Ra withdrew to the heavens. He bound me to the Serpent with his last spell. He cast us both into that abyss, where I was charged to fight the Serpent and keep it down forever.'

A realization crept over me. 'So you *weren't* a minor prisoner. You were imprisoned longer than any of the other gods.'

She closed her eyes. 'I still remember Ra's words: "My loyal cat. This is your greatest duty." And I was proud to do it . . . for centuries. Then millennia. Can you imagine what it was like? Knives against fangs, slashing and thrashing, a never-ending war in the darkness. Our life forces grew weaker, my enemy's and mine, and I began to realize that was Ra's plan. The Serpent and I would rip each other to nothingness, and the world would be safe. Only in this way could Ra withdraw in peace of mind, knowing chaos would not overcome Ma'at. I would have done my duty, too. I had no choice. Until your parents—'

'Gave you an escape route,' I said. 'And you took it.'

Bast looked up miserably. 'I am the queen of cats. I have many strengths. But to be honest, Carter . . . cats are not very brave.'

307

'And Ap—your enemy?'

'He stayed trapped in the abyss. Your father and I were sure of it. The Serpent was already greatly weakened from eons of fighting with me, and when your mother used her own life force to close the abyss, well . . . she worked a powerful feat of magic. There should've been no way for the Serpent to break through that kind of seal. But as the years have gone by . . . we became less and less sure the prison would hold him. If somehow he managed to escape and regain his strength, I cannot imagine what would happen. And it would be my fault.'

I tried to imagine the serpent, Apophis—a creature of chaos even worse than Set. I pictured Bast with her knives, locked in combat with that monster for eons. Maybe I should've been angry at Bast for not telling us the truth earlier. Instead, I felt sorry for her. She'd been put in the same position we were now in—forced to do a job that was way too big for her.

'So why did my parents release you?' I asked. 'Did they say?'

She nodded slowly. 'I was losing my fight. Your father told me that your mother had foreseen . . . horrible things if the Serpent overcame me. They had to free me, give me time to heal. They said it was the first step in restoring the gods. I don't pretend to understand their whole plan. I was relieved to take your father's offer. I convinced myself I was doing the right thing for the gods. But it does not change the fact that I was a coward. I failed in my duty.'

'It isn't your fault,' I told her. 'It wasn't fair of Ra to ask of you.'

308

'Carter's right,' Sadie said. 'That's too much sacrifice for one person—one cat goddess, whatever.'

'It was my king's will,' Bast said. 'The pharaoh can command his subjects for the good of the kingdom—even to lay down their lives—and they must obey. Horus knows this. He was the pharaoh many times.'

She speaks truly, Horus said.

'Then you had a stupid king,' I said.

The boat shuddered as if we'd ground the keel over a sandbar.

'Be careful, Carter,' Bast warned. 'Ma'at, the order of creation, hinges on loyalty to the rightful king. If you question it, you'll fall under the influence of chaos.'

I felt so frustrated, I wanted to break something. I wanted to yell that order didn't seem much better than chaos if you had to get yourself killed for it.

You are being childish, Horus scolded. *You are a servant of Ma'at. These thoughts are unworthy.*

My eyes stung. 'Then maybe *I'm* unworthy.'

'Carter?' Sadie asked.

'Nothing,' I said. 'I'm going to bed.'

I stormed off. One of the flickering lights joined me, guiding me upstairs to my quarters. The stateroom was probably very nice. I didn't pay attention. I just fell on the bed and passed out.

* * *

I seriously needed an extra-strength magic pillow, because my *ba* refused to stay put. [And no, Sadie, I don't think wrapping my head in duct tape would've worked either.]

309

My spirit floated up to the steamboat's wheelhouse, but it wasn't Bloodstained Blade at the wheel. Instead, a young man in leather armor navigated the boat. His eyes were outlined with kohl, and his head was bald except for a braided ponytail. The guy definitely worked out, because his arms were ripped. A sword like mine was strapped to his belt.

'The river is treacherous,' he told me in a familiar voice. 'A pilot cannot get distracted. He must always be alert for sandbars and hidden snags. That's why boats are painted with my eyes, you know—to see the dangers.'

'The Eyes of Horus,' I said. 'You.'

The falcon god glanced at me, and I saw that his eyes were two different colors—one blazing yellow like the sun, the other reflective silver like the moon. The effect was so disorienting, I had to look away. And when I did, I noticed that Horus's shadow didn't match his form. Stretched across the wheelhouse was the silhouette of a giant falcon.

'You wonder if order is better than chaos,' he said. 'You become distracted from our real enemy: Set. You should be taught a lesson.'

I was about to say, *No really, that's okay.*

But immediately my *ba* was whisked away. Suddenly, I was on board an airplane—a big international aircraft like planes my dad and I had taken a million times. Zia Rashid, Desjardins, and two other magicians were scrunched up in a middle row, surrounded by families with screaming children. Zia didn't seem to mind. She meditated calmly with her eyes closed, while Desjardins and the other two men looked so uncomfortable, I almost wanted to laugh.

310

The plane rocked back and forth. Desjardins spilled wine all over his lap. The seat belt light blinked on, and a voice crackled over the intercom: 'This is the captain. It looks like we'll be experiencing some minor turbulence as we make our descent into Dallas, so I'm going to ask the flight attendants—'

Boom! A blast rattled the windows—lightning followed immediately by thunder.

Zia's eyes snapped open. 'The Red Lord.'

The passengers screamed as the plane plummeted several hundred feet.

'Il commence!' Desjardins shouted over the noise. 'Quickly!'

As the plane shook, passengers shrieked and grabbed their seats. Desjardins got up and opened the overhead compartment.

'Sir!' a flight attendant yelled. 'Sir, sit down!'

Desjardins ignored the attendant. He grabbed four familiar bags—magical tool kits—and threw them to his colleagues.

Then things really went wrong. A horrible shudder passed through the cabin and the plane lurched sideways. Outside the right-hand windows, I saw the plane's wing get sheared off by a five-hundred-mile-an-hour wind.

The cabin devolved into chaos—drinks, books, and shoes flying everywhere, oxygen masks dropping and tangling, people screaming for their lives.

'Protect the innocents!' Desjardins ordered.

The plane began to shake and cracks appeared in the windows and walls. The passengers went silent, slumping into unconsciousness as the air pressure dropped. The four magicians raised their wands as the airplane broke to pieces.

For a moment, the magicians floated in a maelstrom of storm clouds, chunks of fuselage, luggage, and spinning passengers still strapped to their seats. Then a white glow expanded around them, a bubble of power that slowed the breakup of the plane and kept the pieces swirling in a tight orbit. Desjardins reached out his hand and the edge of a cloud stretched toward him—a tendril of cottony white mist, like a safety line. The other magicians did likewise, and the storm bent to their will. White vapor wrapped around them and began to send out more tendrils, like funnel clouds, which snatched pieces of the plane and pulled them back together.

A child fell past Zia, but she pointed her staff and murmured a spell. A cloud enveloped the little girl and brought her back. Soon the four magicians were reassembling the plane around them, sealing the breaches with cloudy cobwebs until the entire cabin was encased in a glowing cocoon of vapor. Outside, the storm raged and thunder boomed, but the passengers slept soundly in their seats.

'Zia!' Desjardins shouted. 'We can't hold this for long.'

Zia ran past him up the aisle to the flight deck. Somehow the front of the plane had survived the breakup intact. The door was armored and locked, but Zia's staff flared, and the door melted like wax. She stepped through and found three unconscious pilots. The view through the window was enough to make me sick. Through the spiraling clouds, the ground was coming up fast—*very* fast.

Zia slammed her wand against the controls. Red energy surged through the displays. Dials spun, meters blinked, and the altimeter leveled out. The plane's nose came up, its speed dropping. As I watched, Zia glided the plane toward a cow pasture and landed it without even a bump. Then her eyes rolled back in her head, and she collapsed.

Desjardins found her and gathered her in his arms. 'Quickly,' he told his colleagues, 'the mortals will wake soon.'

They dragged Zia out of the cockpit, and my *ba* was swept away through a blur of images.

I saw Phoenix again—or at least *some* of the city. A massive red sandstorm churned across the valley, swallowing buildings and mountains. In the harsh, hot wind, I heard Set laughing, reveling in his power.

Then I saw Brooklyn: Amos's ruined house on the East River and a winter storm raging overhead, howling winds slamming the city with sleet and hail.

And then I saw a place I didn't recognize: a river winding through a desert canyon. The sky was a blanket of pitch-black clouds, and the river's surface seemed to boil. Something was moving under the water, something huge, evil, and powerful—and I knew it was waiting for me.

This is only the beginning, Horus warned me. *Set will destroy everyone you care about. Believe me, I know.*

The river became a marsh of tall reeds. The sun blazed overhead. Snakes and crocodiles slid through the water. At the water's edge sat a thatched hut. Outside it, a woman and a child of about ten stood examining a battered sarcophagus. I could tell the coffin had once been a work of art—gold encrusted with gems—but now it was dented and black with grime.

The woman ran her hands over the coffin's lid.

'Finally.' She had my mother's face—blue eyes and caramel-colored hair—but she glowed with magical radiance, and I knew I was looking at the goddess Isis.

She turned to the boy. 'We have searched so long, my son. Finally we have retrieved him. I will use my magic and give him life again!'

'Papa?' The boy gazed wide-eyed at the box. 'He's really inside?'

'Yes, Horus. And now—'

Suddenly their hut erupted into flames. The god Set stepped from the inferno—a mighty red-skinned warrior with smoldering black eyes. He wore the double crown of Egypt and the robes of a pharaoh. In his hands, an iron staff smoldered.

'Found the coffin, did you?' he said. 'Good for you!'

Isis reached toward the sky. She summoned lightning against the god of chaos, but Set's rod absorbed the attack and reflected it back at her. Arcs of electricity blasted the goddess and sent her sprawling.

'Mother!' The boy drew a knife and charged Set. 'I'll kill you!'

Set bellowed with laughter. He easily sidestepped the boy and kicked him into the dirt.

'You have spirit, nephew,' Set admitted. 'But you won't live long enough to challenge me. As for your father, I'll just have to dispose of him more permanently.'

Set slammed his iron staff against the coffin's lid.

Isis screamed as the coffin shattered like ice.

'Make a wish.' Set blew with all his might, and the shards of coffin flew into the sky, scattering in all directions. 'Poor Osiris—he's gone to pieces, scattered all over Egypt now. And as for you, sister Isis—run! That's what you do best!'

Set lunged forward. Isis grabbed her son's hand and they both turned into birds, flying for their lives.

The scene faded, and I was back in the steamboat's wheelhouse. The sun rose in fast-forward as towns and barges sped past and the banks of the Mississippi blurred into a play of light and shadow.

'He destroyed my father,' Horus told me. 'He will do the same to yours.'

'No,' I said.

Horus fixed me with those strange eyes—one blazing gold, one full-moon silver. 'My mother and Aunt Nephthys spent years searching for the pieces of the coffin and Father's body. When they collected all fourteen, my cousin Anubis helped bind my father back together with mummy wrappings, but still Mother's magic could not bring him back to life fully. Osiris became an undead god, a half-living shadow of my father, fit to rule only in the Duat. But his loss gave me anger. Anger gave me the strength to defeat Set and take the throne for myself. You must do the same.'

'I don't want a throne,' I said. 'I want my dad.'

'Don't deceive yourself. Set is merely toying with you. He will bring you to despair, and your sorrow will make you weak.'

'I have to save my dad!'

'That is not your mission,' Horus chided. 'The

315

world is at stake. Now, wake!'

*   *   *

Sadie was shaking my arm. She and Bast stood over me, looking concerned.

'What?' I asked.

'We're here,' Sadie said nervously. She'd changed into a fresh linen outfit, black this time, which matched her combat boots. She'd even managed to redye her hair so the streaks were blue.

I sat up and realized I felt rested for the first time in a week. My soul may have been traveling, but at least my body had gotten some sleep. I glanced out the stateroom window. It was pitch-black outside.

'How long was I out?' I demanded.

'We've sailed down most of the Mississippi and into the Duat,' Bast said. 'Now we approach the First Cataract.'

'The First Cataract?' I asked.

'The entrance,' Bast said grimly, 'to the Land of the Dead.'

27.
A DEMON WITH FREE SAMPLES

SADIE

Me? I slept like the dead, which I hoped wasn't a sign of things to come.

I could tell Carter's soul had been wandering

316

through some frightening places, but he wouldn't talk about them.

'Did you see Zia?' I asked. He looked so rattled I thought his face would fall off. 'Knew it,' I said.

We followed Bast up to the wheelhouse, where Bloodstained Blade was studying a map while Khufu manned—*er*, babooned—the wheel.

'The baboon is driving,' I noted. 'Should I be worried?'

'Quiet, please, Lady Kane.' Bloodstained Blade ran his fingers over a long stretch of papyrus map. 'This is delicate work. Two degrees to starboard, Khufu.'

'*Agh!*' Khufu said.

The sky was already dark, but as we chugged along, the stars disappeared. The river turned the color of blood. Darkness swallowed the horizon, and along the riverbanks, the lights of towns changed to flickering fires, then winked out completely.

Now our only lights were the multicolored servant fires and the glittering smoke that bloomed from the smokestacks, washing us all in a weird metallic glow.

'Should be just ahead,' the captain announced. In the dim light, his red-flecked axe blade looked scarier than ever.

'What's that map?' I asked.

'*Spells of Coming Forth by Day,*' he said. 'Don't worry. It's a good copy.'

I looked at Carter for a translation.

'Most people call it *The Book of the Dead,*' he told me. 'Rich Egyptians were always buried with a copy, so they could have directions through the Duat to the Land of the Dead. It's like an *Idiot's*

Guide to the Afterlife.'

The captain hummed indignantly. 'I am no idiot, Lord Kane.'

'No, no, I just meant . . .' Carter's voice faltered. *'Uh,* what is *that?'*

Ahead of us, crags of rock jutted from the river like fangs, turning the water into a boiling mass of rapids.

'The First Cataract,' Bloodstained Blade announced. 'Hold on.'

Khufu pushed the wheel to the left, and the steamboat skidded sideways, shooting between two rocky spires with only centimeters to spare. I'm not much of a screamer, but I'll readily admit that I screamed my head off. [And don't look at me like that, Carter. You weren't much better.]

We dropped over a stretch of white water—or red water—and swerved to avoid a rock the size of Paddington Station. The steamboat made two more suicidal turns between boulders, did a three-sixty spin round a swirling vortex, launched over a ten-meter waterfall, and came crashing down so hard, my ears popped like a gunshot.

We continued downstream as if nothing had happened, the roar of the rapids fading behind us.

'I don't like cataracts,' I decided. 'Are there more?'

'Not as large, thankfully,' said Bast, who was also looking seasick. 'We've crossed over into—'

'The Land of the Dead,' Carter finished.

He pointed to the shore, which was shrouded in mist. Strange things lurked in the darkness: flickering ghost lights, giant faces made of fog, hulking shadows that seemed unconnected to anything physical. Along the riverbanks, old bones

318

dragged themselves through the mud, linking with other bones in random patterns.

'I'm guessing this isn't the Mississippi,' I said.

'The River of Night,' Bloodstained Blade hummed. 'It is every river and no river—the shadow of the Mississippi, the Nile, the Thames. It flows throughout the Duat, with many branches and tributaries.'

'Clears that right up,' I muttered.

The scenes got stranger. We saw ghost villages from ancient times—little clusters of reed huts made of flickering smoke. We saw vast temples crumbling and reconstructing themselves over and over again like a looped video. And everywhere, ghosts turned their faces towards our boat as we passed. Smoky hands reached out. Shades silently called to us, then turned away in despair as we passed.

'The lost and confused,' Bast said. 'Spirits who never found their way to the Hall of Judgment.'

'Why are they so sad?' I asked.

'Well, they're dead,' Carter speculated.

'No, it's more than that,' I said. 'It's like they're . . . expecting someone.'

'Ra,' Bast said. 'For eons, Ra's glorious sun boat would travel this route each night, fighting off the forces of Apophis.' She looked round nervously as if remembering old ambushes. 'It was dangerous: every night, a fight for existence. But as he passed, Ra would bring sunlight and warmth to the Duat, and these lost spirits would rejoice, remembering the world of the living.'

'But that's a legend,' Carter said. 'The earth revolves around the sun. The sun never actually descends under the earth.'

'Have you learned nothing of Egypt?' Bast asked. 'Conflicting stories can be equally true. The sun is a ball of fire in space, yes. But its image you see as it crosses the sky, the life-giving warmth and light it brings to the earth—that was embodied by Ra. The sun was his throne, his source of power, his very spirit. But now Ra has retreated into the heavens. He sleeps, and the sun is just the sun. Ra's boat no longer travels on its cycle through the Duat. He no longer lights the dark, and the dead feel his absence most keenly.'

'Indeed,' Bloodstained Blade said, though he didn't sound very upset about it. 'Legend says the world will end when Ra gets too tired to continue living in his weakened state. Apophis will swallow the sun. Darkness will reign. Chaos will overcome Ma'at, and the Serpent will reign forever.'

Part of me thought this was absurd. The planets would not simply stop spinning. The sun would not cease to rise.

On the other hand, here I was riding a boat through the Land of the Dead with a demon and a god. If Apophis was real too, I didn't fancy meeting him.

And to be honest, I felt guilty. If the story Thoth told me was true, Isis had *caused* Ra to retreat into the heavens with that secret name business. Which meant, in a ridiculous, maddening way, the end of the world would be my fault. Bloody typical. I wanted to punch myself to get even with Isis, but I suspected it would hurt.

'Ra should wake up and smell the *sahlab,*' I said. 'He should come back.'

Bast laughed without humor. 'And the world should be young again, Sadie. I wish it could be so . . .'

Khufu grunted and gestured ahead. He gave the captain back the wheel and ran out of the wheelhouse and down the stairs.

'The baboon is right,' said Bloodstained Blade. 'You should get to the prow. A challenge will be coming soon.'

'What sort of challenge?' I asked.

'It's hard to tell,' Bloodstained Blade said, and I thought I detected smug satisfaction in his voice. 'I wish you luck, Lady Kane.'

*　　*　　*

'Why me?' I grumbled.

Bast, Carter, and I stood at the prow of the boat, watching the river appear out of the darkness. Below us, the boat's painted eyes glowed faintly in the dark, sweeping beams of light across the red water. Khufu had climbed to the top of the gangplank, which stood straight up when retracted, and cupped his hand over his eyes like a sailor in a crow's-nest.

But all that vigilance didn't do much good. With the dark and the mist, our visibility was nil. Massive rocks, broken pillars, and crumbling statues of pharaohs loomed out of nowhere, and Bloodstained Blade yanked the wheel to avoid them, forcing us to grab hold of the rails. Occasionally we'd see long slimy lines cutting through the surface of the water, like tentacles, or the backs of submerged creatures—I really didn't want to know.

'Mortal souls are always challenged,' Bast told me. 'You must prove your worth to enter the Land of the Dead.'

'Like it's such a big treat?'

I'm not sure how long I stared into the darkness, but after a good while a reddish smudge appeared in the distance, as if the sky were becoming lighter.

'Is that my imagination, or—'

'Our destination,' Bast said. 'Strange, we really should've been challenged by now—'

The boat shuddered, and the water began to boil. A giant figure erupted from the river. I could see him only from the waist up, but he towered several meters over the boat. His body was humanoid—bare-chested and hairy with purplish skin. A rope belt was tied around his waist, festooned with leather pouches, severed demon heads, and other charming bits and bobs. His head was a strange combination of lion and human, with gold eyes and a black mane done in dreadlocks. His blood-splattered mouth was feline, with bristly whiskers and razor-sharp fangs. He roared, scaring Khufu right off the gangplank. The poor baboon did a flying leap into Carter's arms, which knocked them both to the deck.

'You *had* to say something,' I told Bast weakly. 'This a relative of yours, I hope?'

Bast shook her head. 'I cannot help you with this, Sadie. *You* are the mortals. You must deal with the challenge.'

'Oh, thanks for that.'

'I am Shezmu!' the bloody lion man said.

I wanted to say, 'Yes, you certainly are.' But I decided to keep my mouth shut.

He turned his golden eyes on Carter and tilted his head. His nostrils quivered. 'I smell the blood of pharaohs. A tasty treat . . . or do you dare to

322

name me?'

'N-name you?' Carter sputtered. 'Do you mean your secret name?'

The demon laughed. He grabbed a nearby spire of rock, which crumpled like old plaster in his fist.

I looked desperately at Carter. 'You don't happen to have his secret name lying around somewhere?'

'It may be in *The Book of the Dead,*' Carter said. 'I forgot to check.'

'Well?' I said.

'Keep him busy,' Carter replied, and scrambled off to the wheelhouse.

Keep a demon busy, I thought. *Right. Maybe he fancies a game of tiddlywinks.*

'Do you give up?' Shezmu bellowed.

'No!' I yelled. 'No, we don't give up. We will name you. Just . . . Gosh, you're quite well muscled, aren't you? Do you work out?'

I glanced at Bast, who nodded approval.

Shezmu rumbled with pride and flexed his mighty arms. Never fails with men, does it? Even if they're twenty meters tall and lion-headed.

'I am Shezmu!' he bellowed.

'Yes, you might've mentioned that already,' I said. 'I'm wondering, *um,* what sort of titles you've earned over the years, eh? Lord of this and that?'

'I am Osiris's royal executioner!' he yelled, smashing a fist into the water and rocking our boat. 'I am the Lord of Blood and Wine!'

'Brilliant,' I said, trying not to get sick. 'Er, how are blood and wine connected, exactly?'

'*Garrr!*' He leaned forward and bared his fangs, which were not any prettier up close. His mane was matted with nasty bits of dead fish and river moss. 'Lord Osiris lets me behead the wicked! I crush them in my wine press, and make wine for the dead!'

I made a mental note never to drink the wine of the dead.

You're doing well. Isis's voice gave me a start. She'd been quiet so long, I'd almost forgotten her. *Ask him about his other duties.*

'And what are your other duties . . . O powerful wine demon guy?'

'I am Lord of . . .' He flexed his muscles for maximum effect. 'Perfume!'

He grinned at me, apparently waiting for terror to set it.

'Oh, my!' I said. 'That must make your enemies tremble.'

'Ha, ha, ha! Yes! Would you like to try a free sample?' He ripped a slimy leather pouch off his belt, and brought out a clay pot filled with sweet-smelling yellow powder. 'I call this . . . Eternity!'

'Lovely,' I gagged. I glanced behind me, wondering where Carter had gone to, but there was no sign of him.

Keep him talking, Isis urged.

'And, *um* . . . perfume is part of your job because . . . wait, I've got it, you squeeze it out of plants, like you squeeze wine . . .'

'Or blood!' Shezmu added.

'Well, naturally,' I said. 'The blood goes without saying.'

'Blood!' he said.

Khufu yelped and covered his eyes.

'So you serve Osiris?' I asked the demon.

'Yes! At least . . .' He hesitated, snarling in doubt. 'I did. Osiris's throne is empty. But he will

324

return. He will!'

'Of course,' I said. 'And so your friends call you what . . . Shezzy? Bloodsiekins?'

'I have no friends! But if I did, they would call me Slaughterer of Souls, Fierce of Face! But I don't have any friends, so my name is not in danger. Ha, ha, ha!'

I looked at Bast, wondering if I'd just gotten as lucky as I thought. Bast beamed at me.

Carter came stumbling down the stairs, holding *The Book of the Dead*. 'I've got it! Somewhere here. Can't read this part, but—'

'Name me or be eaten!' Shezmu bellowed.

'I name you!' I shouted back. 'Shezmu, Slaughterer of Souls, Fierce of Face!'

'*GAAAAHHHHH!*' He writhed in pain. 'How do they always know?'

'Let us pass!' I commanded. 'Oh, and one more thing . . . my brother wants a free sample.'

I just had time to step away, and Carter just had time to look confused before the demon blew yellow dust all over him. Then Shezmu sank under the waves.

'What a nice fellow,' I said.

'*Pah!*' Carter spit perfume. He looked like a piece of breaded fish. 'What was *that* for?'

'You smell lovely,' I assured him. 'What's next, then?'

I was feeling very pleased with myself until our boat rounded a bend in the river. Suddenly the reddish glow on the horizon became a blaze of light. Up in the wheelhouse, the captain rang the alarm bell.

Ahead of us, the river was on fire, rushing through a steaming stretch of rapids towards what looked like a bubbling volcanic crater.

'The Lake of Fire,' Bast said. 'This is where it gets interesting.'

28.
I HAVE A DATE WITH THE GOD OF TOILET PAPER

S A D I E

Bast had an interesting definition of *interesting*: a boiling lake several miles wide that smelled like burning petrol and rotten meat. Our steamboat stopped short where the river met the lake, because a giant metal gate blocked our path. It was a bronze disk like a shield, easily as wide as our boat, half submerged in the river. I wasn't sure how it avoided melting in the heat, but it made going forward impossible. On either bank of the river, facing the disk, was a giant bronze baboon with its arms raised.

'What is this?' I asked.

'The Gates of the West,' Bast said. 'Ra's sunboat would pass through and be renewed in the fires of the lake, then pass through to the other side and rise through the Gates of the East for a new day.'

Looking up at the huge baboons, I wondered if Khufu had some sort of secret baboon code that would get us in. But instead he barked at the statues and cowered heroically behind my legs.

'How do we get past?' I wondered.

'Perhaps,' a new voice said, 'you should ask me.'

The air shimmered. Carter backed up quickly, and Bast hissed.

In front of me appeared a glowing bird spirit: a *ba*. It had the usual combination of human head and killer turkey body, with its wings tucked back and its entire form glowing, but something about this *ba* was different. I realized I knew the spirit's face—an old bald man with brown, papery skin, milky eyes, and a kindly smile.

'Iskandar?' I managed.

'Hello, my dear.' The old magician's voice echoed as if from the bottom of a well.

'But . . .' I found myself tearing up. 'You're really dead, then?'

He chuckled. 'Last I checked.'

'But *why?* I didn't make you—'

'No, my dear. It wasn't your fault. It was simply the right time.'

'It was horrible timing!' My surprise and sadness abruptly turned to anger. 'You *left* us before we got trained or anything, and now Desjardins is after us and—'

'My dear, look how far you've come. Look how well you have done. You didn't need me, nor would more training have helped. My brethren would have found out the truth about you soon enough. They are excellent at sniffing out godlings, I fear, and they would not have understood.'

'You knew, didn't you? You knew we were possessed by gods.'

'*Hosts* of the gods.'

'Whatever! You knew.'

'After our second meeting, yes. My only regret is that I did not realize it sooner. I could not protect you and your brother as much as—'

327

'As much as who?'

Iskandar's eyes became sad and distant. 'I made choices, Sadie. Some seemed wise at the time. Some, in retrospect . . .'

'Your decision to forbid the gods. My mum convinced you it was a bad idea, didn't she?'

His spectral wings fluttered. 'You must understand, Sadie. When Egypt fell to the Romans, my spirit was crushed. Thousands of years of Egyptian power and tradition toppled by that foolish Queen Cleopatra, who thought she could host a goddess. The blood of the pharaohs seemed weak and diluted—lost forever. At the time I blamed everyone—the gods who used men to act out their petty quarrels, the Ptolemaic rulers who had driven Egypt into the ground, my own brethren in the House for becoming weak and greedy and corrupt. I communed with Thoth, and we agreed: the gods must be put away, banished. The magicians must find their way without them. The new rules kept the House of Life intact for another two thousand years. At the time, it was the right choice.'

'And now?' I asked.

Iskandar's glow dimmed. 'Your mother foresaw a great imbalance. She foresaw the day—very soon—when Ma'at would be destroyed, and chaos would reclaim all of Creation. She insisted that only the gods and the House together could prevail. The old way—the path of the gods—would have to be reestablished. I was a foolish old man. I knew in my heart she was right, but I refused to believe . . . and your parents took it upon themselves to act. They sacrificed themselves trying to put things right, because I was too stubborn to change. For that, I am truly sorry.'

As much as I tried, I found it hard to stay angry at the old turkey. It's a rare thing when an adult admits they are wrong to a child—especially a wise, two-thousand-year-old adult. You rather have to cherish those moments.

'I forgive you, Iskandar,' I said. 'Honestly. But Set is about to destroy North America with a giant red pyramid. What do I *do* about it?'

'That, my dear, I can't answer. Your choice . . .' He tilted his head back toward the lake, as if hearing a voice. 'Our time is at an end. I must do my job as gatekeeper, and decide whether or not to grant you access to the Lake of Fire.'

'But I've got more questions!'

'And I wish we had more time,' Iskandar said. 'You have a strong spirit, Sadie Kane. Someday, you will make an excellent guardian *ba.*'

'Thanks,' I muttered. 'Can't wait to be poultry forever.'

'I can only tell you this: your choice approaches. Don't let your feelings blind you to what is best, as I did.'

'What choice? Best for whom?'

'That's the key, isn't it? Your father—your family—the gods—the world. Ma'at and Isfet, order and chaos, are about to collide more violently than they have in eons. You and your brother will be instrumental in balancing those forces, or destroying everything. That, also, your mother foresaw.'

'Hang on. What do you—'

'Until we meet again, Sadie. Perhaps some day, we will have a chance to talk further. But for now, pass through! My job is to assess your courage—

and you have that in abundance.'

I wanted to argue that no, in fact, I didn't. I wanted Iskandar to stay and tell me exactly what my mother had foreseen in my future. But his spirit faded, leaving the deck quiet and still. Only then did I realize that no one else on board had said a thing.

I turned to face Carter. 'Leave everything to me, eh?'

He was staring into space, not even blinking. Khufu still clung to my legs, absolutely petrified. Bast's face was frozen in mid-hiss.

'*Um,* guys?' I snapped my fingers, and they all unfroze.

'*Ba!*' Bast hissed. Then she looked around and scowled. 'Wait, I thought I saw . . . what just happened?'

I wondered how powerful a magician had to be to stop time, to freeze even a goddess. Some day, Iskandar was going to teach me that trick, dead or no.

'Yeah,' I said. 'I reckon there was a *ba*. Gone now.'

The baboon statues began to rumble and grind as their arms lowered. The bronze sun disk in the middle of the river sank below the surface, clearing the way into the lake. The boat shot forward, straight into the flames and the boiling red waves. Through the shimmering heat, I could just make out an island in the middle of the lake. On it rose a glittering black temple that looked not at all friendly.

'The Hall of Judgment,' I guessed.

Bast nodded. 'Times like this, I'm glad I don't have a mortal soul.'

As we docked at the island, Bloodstained Blade came down to say good-bye.

'I hope to see you again, Lord and Lady Kane,' he hummed. 'Your rooms will be waiting aboard the *Egyptian Queen*. Unless, of course, you see fit to release me from service.'

Behind his back, Bast shook her head adamantly.

'*Um*, we'll keep you around,' I told the captain. 'Thanks for everything.'

'As you wish,' the captain said. If axes could frown, I'm sure he would have.

'Stay sharp,' Carter told him, and with Bast and Khufu, we walked down the gangplank. Instead of pulling away, the ship simply sank into the boiling lava and disappeared.

I scowled at Carter. ' "Stay sharp?" '

'I thought it was funny.'

'You're hopeless.'

We walked up the steps of the black temple. A forest of stone pillars held up the ceiling. Every surface was carved with hieroglyphs and images, but there was no color—just black on black. Haze from the lake drifted through the temple, and despite reed torches that burned on each pillar, it was impossible to see very far through the gloom.

'Stay alert,' Bast warned, sniffing the air. 'He's close.'

'Who?' I asked.

'The Dog,' Bast said with disdain.

There was a snarling noise, and a huge black shape leaped out of the mist. It tackled Bast, who

331

rolled over and wailed in feline outrage, then raced off, leaving us alone with the beast. I suppose she had warned us that she wasn't brave.

The new animal was sleek and black, like the Set animal we'd seen in Washington, D.C., but more obviously canine, graceful and rather cute, actually. A jackal, I realized, with a golden collar around its neck.

Then it morphed into a young man, and my heart almost stopped. He was the boy from my dreams, quite literally—the guy in black I'd seen twice before in my *ba* visions.

In person, if possible, Anubis was even more drop-dead gorgeous. [Oh . . . ha, ha. I didn't catch the pun, but thank you, Carter. God of the dead, drop-dead gorgeous. Yes, hilarious. Now, may I continue?]

He had a pale complexion, tousled black hair, and rich brown eyes like melted chocolate. He was dressed in black jeans, combat boots (like mine!), a ripped T-shirt, and a black leather jacket that suited him quite nicely. He was long and lean like a jackal. His ears, like a jackal's, stuck out a bit (which I found cute), and he wore a gold chain around his neck.

Now, please understand, I am *not* boy crazy. I'm not! I'd spent most of the school term making fun of Liz and Emma, who were, and I was very glad they weren't with me just then, because they would've teased me to no end.

The boy in black stood and brushed off his jacket. 'I'm *not* a dog,' he grumbled.

'No,' I agreed. 'You're . . .'

No doubt I would've said *delicious* or something equally embarrassing, but Carter saved me.

332

'You're Anubis?' he asked. 'We've come for the feather of truth.'

Anubis frowned. He locked his very nice eyes with mine. 'You're not dead.'

'No,' I said. 'Though we're trying awfully hard.'

'I don't deal with the living,' he said firmly. Then he looked at Khufu and Carter. 'However, you travel with a baboon. That shows good taste. I won't kill you until you've had a chance to explain. Why did Bast bring you here?'

'Actually,' Carter said, 'Thoth sent us.'

Carter started to tell him the story, but Khufu broke in impatiently. *'Agh! Agh!'*

Baboon-speak must have been quite efficient, because Anubis nodded as if he'd just gotten the whole tale. 'I see.'

He scowled at Carter. 'So you're Horus. And you're . . .' His finger drifted towards me.

'I'm—I'm, *um*—' I stammered. Quite unlike me to be tongue-tied, I'll admit, but looking at Anubis, I felt as if I'd just gotten a large shot of Novocain from the dentist. Carter looked at me as if I'd gone daft.

'I'm not Isis,' I managed. 'I mean, Isis is milling about inside, but I'm not her. She's just . . . visiting.'

Anubis tilted his head. 'And the two of you intend to challenge Set?'

'That's the general idea,' Carter agreed. 'Will you help?'

Anubis glowered. I remembered Thoth saying Anubis was only in a good mood once an eon or so. I had the feeling this was not one of those days.

'No,' he said flatly. 'I'll show you why.'

He turned into a jackal and sped back the way

333

he'd come. Carter and I exchanged looks. Not knowing what else to do, we ran after Anubis, deeper into the gloom.

*   *   *

In the center of the temple was a large circular chamber that seemed to be two places at once. On the one hand, it was a great hall with blazing braziers and an empty throne at the far end. The center of the room was dominated by a set of scales—a black iron T with ropes linked to two golden dishes, each big enough to hold a person— but the scales were broken. One of the golden dishes was bent into a V, as if something very heavy had jumped up and down on it. The other dish was hanging by a single rope.

Curled at the base of the scales, fast asleep, was the oddest monster I'd seen yet. It had the head of crocodile with a lion's mane. The front half of its body was lion, but the back end was sleek, brown, and fat—a hippo, I decided. The odd bit was, the animal was tiny—I mean, no larger than an average poodle, which I suppose made him a hippodoodle.

So that was the hall, at least *one* layer of it. But at the same time, I seemed to be standing in a ghostly graveyard—like a three-dimensional projection superimposed on the room. In some places, the marble floor gave way to patches of mud and moss-covered paving stones. Lines of aboveground tombs like miniature row houses radiated from the center of the chamber in a wheel-spokes pattern. Many of the tombs had cracked open. Some were bricked up, others ringed with iron fences. Around the edges of the chamber, the black pillars shifted form, sometimes changing into ancient cypress trees. I felt as if I were stepping between two different worlds, and I couldn't tell which one was real.

Khufu loped straight over to the broken scales and climbed to the top, making himself right at home. He paid no attention to the hippodoodle.

The jackal trotted to the steps of the throne and changed back into Anubis.

'Welcome,' he said, 'to the last room you will ever see.'

Carter looked around in awe. 'The Hall of Judgment.' He focused on the hippodoodle and frowned. 'Is that . . .'

'Ammit the Devourer,' Anubis said. 'Look upon him and tremble.'

Ammit apparently heard his name in his sleep. He made a yipping sound and turned on his back. His lion and hippo legs twitched. I wondered if netherworld monsters dreamed of chasing rabbits.

'I always pictured him . . . bigger,' Carter admitted.

Anubis gave Carter a harsh look. 'Ammit only has to be big enough to eat the hearts of the wicked. Trust me, he does his job well. Or . . . he *did* it well, anyway.'

Up on the scales, Khufu grunted. He almost lost his balance on the central beam, and the dented saucer clanged against the floor.

'Why are the scales broken?' I asked.

Anubis frowned. 'Ma'at is weakening. I've tried to fix them, but . . .' He spread his hands helplessly.

I pointed to the ghostly rows of tombs. 'Is that why the, ah, graveyard is butting in?'

Carter looked at me strangely. 'What graveyard?'

'The tombs,' I said. 'The trees.'

'What are you talking about?'

'He can't see them,' Anubis said. 'But you, Sadie—you're perceptive. What do you hear?'

At first I didn't know what he meant. All I heard was the blood rushing through my ears, and the distant rumble and crackle of the Lake of Fire. (And Khufu scratching himself and grunting, but that was nothing new.)

Then I closed my eyes, and I heard another distant sound—music that triggered my earliest memories, my father smiling as he danced me round our house in Los Angeles.

'Jazz,' I said.

I opened my eyes, and the Hall of Judgment was gone. Or not *gone,* but faded. I could still see the broken scales and the empty throne. But no black columns, no roar of fire. Even Carter, Khufu, and Ammit had disappeared.

The cemetery was *very* real. Cracked paving stones wobbled under my feet. The humid night air smelled of spices and fish stew and old mildewed places. I might've been back in England—a churchyard in some corner of London, perhaps—but the writing on the graves was in French, and the air was much too mild for an English winter. The trees hung low and lush, covered with Spanish moss.

And there was music. Just outside the cemetery's fence, a jazz band paraded down the street in somber black suits and brightly colored party hats. Saxophonists bobbed up and down. Cornets and clarinets wailed. Drummers grinned and swayed, their sticks flashing. And behind them, carrying flowers and torches, a crowd of revelers in funeral clothes danced round an old-fashioned black hearse as it drove along.

'Where *are* we?' I said, marveling.

Anubis jumped from the top of a tomb and landed next to me. He breathed in the graveyard air, and his features relaxed. I found myself studying his mouth, the curve of his lower lip.

'New Orleans,' he said.

'Sorry?'

'The Drowned City,' he said. 'In the French Quarter, on the west side of the river—the shore of the dead. I love it here. That's why the Hall of Judgment often connects to this part of the mortal world.'

The jazz procession made its way down the street, drawing more onlookers into the party.

'What are they celebrating?'

'A funeral,' Anubis said. 'They've just put the deceased in his tomb. Now they're "cutting the body loose." The mourners celebrate the dead one's life with song and dance as they escort the empty hearse away from the cemetery. Very Egyptian, this ritual.'

'How do you know so much?'

'I'm the god of funerals. I know every death custom in the world—how to die properly, how to prepare the body and soul for the afterlife. I live for death.'

'You must be fun at parties,' I said. 'Why have you brought me here?'

'To talk.' He spread his hands, and the nearest tomb rumbled. A long white ribbon shot out of a crack in the wall. The ribbon just kept coming, weaving itself into some kind of shape next to Anubis, and my first thought was, *My god, he's got a magic roll of toilet paper.*

Then I realized it was cloth, a length of white linen wrappings—*mummy* wrappings. The cloth twisted itself into the form of a bench, and Anubis sat down.

'I don't like Horus.' He gestured for me to join him. 'He's loud and arrogant and thinks he's better than me. But Isis always treated me like a son.'

I crossed my arms. 'You're *not* my son. And I told you I'm *not* Isis.'

Anubis tilted his head. 'No. You don't act like a godling. You remind me of your mother.'

That hit me like a bucket of cold water (and sadly, I knew exactly what *that* felt like, thanks to Zia). 'You've met my mother?'

Anubis blinked, as if realizing he'd done something wrong. 'I—I know all the dead, but each spirit's path is secret. I should not have spoken.'

'You can't just say something like that and then clam up! Is she in the Egyptian afterlife? Did she pass your little Hall of Judgment?'

Anubis glanced uneasily at the golden scales, which shimmered like a mirage in the graveyard. 'It is not *my* hall. I merely oversee it until Lord Osiris returns. I'm sorry if I upset you, but I can't say anything more. I don't know why I said anything at all. It's just . . . your soul has a similar glow. A strong glow.'

'How flattering,' I grumbled. 'My soul glows.'

'I'm sorry,' he said again. 'Please, sit.'

I had no interest in letting the matter drop, or sitting with him on a bunch of mummy wrappings, but my direct approach to information gathering didn't seem to be working. I plopped down on the bench and tried to look as annoyed as possible.

'So.' I gave him a sulky glare. 'What's *that* form, then? Are you a godling?'

He frowned and put his hand to his chest. 'You mean, am I inhabiting a human body? No, I can inhabit any graveyard, any place of death or mourning. This is my natural appearance.'

'Oh.' Part of me had hoped there was an actual boy sitting next to me—someone who just happened to be hosting a god. But I should've known that was too good to be true. I felt disappointed. Then I felt angry with myself for feeling disappointed.

It's not like there was any potential, Sadie, I chided myself. *He's the bloody god of funerals. He's like five thousand years old.*

'So,' I said, 'if you can't tell me anything useful, at least help me. We need a feather of truth.'

He shook his head. 'You don't know what you're asking. The feather of truth is too dangerous. Giving it to a mortal would be against the rules of Osiris.'

'But Osiris isn't here.' I pointed at the empty throne. 'That's his seat, isn't it? Do you see Osiris?'

Anubis eyed the throne. He ran his fingers along his gold chain as if it were getting tighter. 'It's true that I've waited here for ages, keeping my station. I was not imprisoned like the rest. I don't know why . . . but I did the best I could. When I heard the five had been released, I hoped Lord Osiris would return, but . . .' He shook his head dejectedly. 'Why would he neglect his duties?'

'Probably because he's trapped inside my dad.'

Anubis stared at me. 'The baboon did not explain this.'

'Well, I can't explain as well as a baboon. But basically my dad wanted to release some gods for reasons I don't quite . . . Maybe he thought, *I'll just pop down to the British Museum and blow up the Rosetta Stone!* And he released Osiris, but he also got Set and the rest of that lot.'

'So Set imprisoned your father while he was hosting Osiris,' Anubis said, 'which means Osiris has also been trapped by my—' He stopped himself. 'By Set.'

Interesting, I thought.

'You understand, then,' I said. 'You've got to help us.'

Anubis hesitated, then shook his head. 'I can't. I'll get in trouble.'

I just stared at him and laughed. I couldn't help it, he sounded so ridiculous. 'You'll get in *trouble*? How old are you, sixteen? You're a god!'

It was hard to tell in the dark, but I could swear he blushed. 'You don't understand. The feather cannot abide the smallest lie. If I gave it to you, and you spoke a single untruth while you carried it, or acted in a way that was not truthful, you would burn to ashes.'

'You're assuming I'm a liar.'

He blinked. 'No, I simply—'

'You've never told a lie? What were you about to say just now—about Set? He's your father, I'm guessing. Is that it?'

Anubis closed his mouth, then opened it again. He looked as if he wanted to get angry but couldn't quite remember how. 'Are you always this infuriating?'

'Usually more,' I admitted.

'Why hasn't your family married you off to someone far, far away?'

He asked as if it were an honest question, and now it was my turn to be flabbergasted. 'Excuse me, death boy! But I'm twelve! Well . . . almost thirteen, and a very mature almost thirteen, but that's *not* the point. We don't "marry off" girls in my family, and you may know everything about funerals, but apparently you aren't very up to speed on courtship rituals!'

Anubis looked mystified. 'Apparently not.'

'Right! Wait—what were we talking about? Oh, thought you could distract me, eh? I remember. Set's your father, yes? Tell the truth.'

Anubis gazed across the graveyard. The sound of the jazz funeral was fading into the streets of the French Quarter.

'Yes,' he said. 'At least, that's what the legends say. I've never met him. My mother, Nephthys, gave me to Osiris when I was a child.'

'She . . . gave you away?'

'She said she didn't want me to know my father. But in truth, I'm not sure she knew what to do with me. I wasn't like my cousin Horus. I wasn't a warrior. I was a . . . *different* child.'

He sounded so bitter, I didn't know what to say. I mean, I'd asked for the truth, but usually you don't actually *get* it, especially from guys. I also knew something about being the different child—and feeling like my parents had given me away.

'Maybe your mum was trying to protect you,' I said. 'Your dad being Lord of Evil, and all.'

'Maybe,' he said halfheartedly. 'Osiris took me under his wing. He made me the Lord of Funerals, the Keeper of the Ways of Death. It's a good job, but . . . you asked how old I am. The truth is I don't know. Years don't pass in the Land of the Dead. I still feel quite young, but the world has gotten old around me. And Osiris has been gone so long . . . He's the only family I had.'

Looking at Anubis in the dim light of the graveyard, I saw a lonely teenage guy. I tried to remind myself that he was a god, thousands of years old, probably able to control vast powers *well* beyond magic toilet paper, but I still felt sorry for him.

'Help us rescue my dad,' I said. 'We'll send Set back to the Duat, and Osiris will be free. We'll all be happy.'

Anubis shook his head again. 'I told you—'

'Your scales are broken,' I noticed. 'That's because Osiris isn't here, I'm guessing. What happens to all the souls that come for judgment?'

I knew I'd hit a nerve. Anubis shifted uncomfortably on the bench. 'It increases chaos. The souls become confused. Some cannot go to the afterlife. Some manage, but they must find other ways. I try to help, but . . . the Hall of Judgment is also called the Hall of Ma'at. It is meant to be the center of order, a stable foundation. Without Osiris, it is falling into disrepair, crumbling.'

'Then what are you waiting for? Give us the feather. Unless you're afraid your dad will ground you.'

His eyes flashed with irritation. For a moment I thought he was planning *my* funeral, but he simply sighed in exasperation. 'I do a ceremony called the opening of the mouth. It lets the soul of the dead person come forth. For you, Sadie Kane, I would invent a new ceremony: the closing of the mouth.'

'Ha, ha. Are you going to give me the feather or not?'

He opened his hand. There was a burst of light, and a glowing feather floated above his palm—a snowy plume like a writing quill. 'For Osiris's sake—but I will insist on several conditions. First, only you may handle it.'

'Well, of course. You don't think I'd let Carter—'

'Also, you must listen to my mother, Nephthys. Khufu told me you were looking for her. If you manage to find her, listen to her.'

'Easy,' I said, though the request did leave me strangely uncomfortable. Why would Anubis ask something like that?

'And before you go,' Anubis continued, 'you must answer three questions for me as you hold the feather of truth, to prove that you are honest.'

My mouth suddenly felt dry. 'Um . . . what sort of questions?'

'Any that I want. And remember, the slightest lie will destroy you.'

'Give me the bloody feather.'

As he handed it to me, the feather stopped glowing, but it felt warmer and heavier than a feather should.

'It's the tail feather from a *bennu*,' Anubis explained, 'what you'd call a phoenix. It weighs exactly the same as a human soul. Are you ready?'

'No,' I said, which must've been truthful, as I didn't burn up. 'Does that count as one question?'

Anubis actually smiled, which was quite dazzling. 'I suppose it does. You bargain like a Phoenician sea trader, Sadie Kane. Second question, then: Would you give your life for your brother?'

'Yes,' I said immediately.

(I know. It surprised me too. But holding the feather forced me to be truthful. Obviously it didn't make me any wiser.)

Anubis nodded, apparently not surprised. 'Final question: If it means saving the world, are you prepared to lose your father?'

'That's not a fair question!'

'Answer it honestly.'

How could I answer something like that? It wasn't a simple yes/no.

Of course I knew the 'right' answer. The heroine is supposed to refuse to sacrifice her father. Then she boldly goes off and saves her dad *and* the world, right? But what if it really *was* one or the other? The whole world was an awfully large place: Gran and Gramps, Carter, Uncle Amos, Bast, Khufu, Liz and Emma, everyone I'd ever known. What would my dad say if I chose him instead?

'If . . . if there really was no other way,' I said, 'no other way *at all*— Oh, come off. It's a ridiculous question.'

The feather began to glow.

'All right,' I relented. 'If I had to, then I suppose . . . I suppose I would save the world.'

Horrible guilt crushed down on me. What kind of daughter was I? I clutched the *tyet* amulet on my necklace—my one remembrance of Dad. I know some of you lot will be thinking: *You hardly ever saw your dad. You barely knew him. Why would you care so much?*

But that didn't make him any less my dad, did

it? Or the thought of losing him forever any less horrible. And the thought of failing him, of *willingly* choosing to let him die even to save the world—what sort of awful person was I?

I could barely meet Anubis's eyes, but when I did, his expression softened.

'I believe you, Sadie.'

'Oh, really. I'm holding the bloody feather of truth, and you believe me. Well, thanks.'

'The truth is harsh,' Anubis said. 'Spirits come to the Hall of Judgment all the time, and they *cannot* let go of their lies. They deny their faults, their true feelings, their mistakes . . . right up until Ammit devours their souls for eternity. It takes strength and courage to admit the truth.'

'Yeah. I feel so strong and courageous. Thanks.'

Anubis stood. 'I should leave you now. You're running out of time. In just over twenty-four hours, the sun will rise on Set's birthday, and he will complete his pyramid—unless you stop him. Perhaps when next we meet—'

'You'll be just as annoying?' I guessed.

He fixed me with those warm brown eyes. 'Or perhaps you could bring me up to speed on modern courtship rituals.'

I sat there stunned until he gave me a glimpse of a smile—just enough to let me know he was teasing. Then he disappeared.

'Oh, very funny!' I yelled. The scales and the throne vanished. The linen bench unraveled and dumped me in the middle of the graveyard. Carter and Khufu appeared next to me, but I just kept yelling at the spot where Anubis had stood, calling him some choice names.

'What's going on?' Carter demanded. 'Where

are we?'

'He's horrible!' I growled. 'Self-important, sarcastic, incredibly hot, insufferable—'

'*Agh!*' Khufu complained.

'Yeah,' Carter agreed. 'Did you get the feather or not?'

I held out my hand, and there it was—a glowing white plume floating above my fingers. I closed my fist and it disappeared again.

'Whoa,' Carter said. 'But what about Anubis? How did you—'

'Let's find Bast and get out of here,' I interrupted. 'We've got work to do.'

And I marched out of the graveyard before he could ask me more questions, because I was in *no* mood to tell the truth.

29.
ZIA SETS A RENDEZVOUS

CARTER

[Yeah, thanks a lot, Sadie. You get to tell the part about the Land of the Dead. I get to describe Interstate 10 through Texas.]

Long story short: It took forever and was totally boring, unless your idea of fun is watching cows graze.

We left New Orleans about 1 A.M. on December twenty-eighth, the day before Set planned to destroy the world. Bast had 'borrowed' an RV—a FEMA leftover from Hurricane Katrina. At first Bast suggested taking a plane, but after I told her about my dream of the magicians on the exploding flight, we agreed planes might not be a good idea. The sky goddess Nut had promised us safe air travel as far as Memphis, but I didn't want to press our luck the closer we got to Set.

'Set is not our only problem,' Bast said. 'If your vision is correct, the magicians are closing in on us. And not just *any* magicians—Desjardins himself.'

'And Zia,' Sadie put in, just to annoy me.

In the end, we decided it was safer to drive, even though it was slower. With luck, we'd make Phoenix just in time to challenge Set. As for the House of Life, all we could do was hope to avoid them while we did our job. Maybe once we dealt with Set, the magicians would decide we were cool. Maybe . . .

I kept thinking about Desjardins, wondering if he really could be a host for Set. A day ago, it had made perfect sense. Desjardins wanted to crush the Kane family. He'd hated our dad, and he hated us. He'd probably been waiting for decades, even centuries, for Iskandar to die, so he could become Chief Lector. Power, anger, arrogance, ambition: Desjardins had it all. If Set was looking for a soulmate, literally, he couldn't do much better. And if Set could start a war between the gods and magicians by controlling the Chief Lector, the only winner would be the forces of chaos. Besides, Desjardins was an easy guy to hate. *Somebody* had sabotaged Amos's house and alerted Set that Amos was coming.

But the way Desjardins saved all those people on the plane—that just didn't seem like something the Lord of Evil would do.

Bast and Khufu took turns driving while Sadie

and I dozed off and on. I didn't know baboons could drive recreational vehicles, but Khufu did okay. When I woke up around dawn, he was navigating through early morning rush hour in Houston, baring his fangs and barking a lot, and none of the other drivers seemed to notice anything out of the ordinary.

For breakfast, Sadie, Bast, and I sat in the RV's kitchen while the cabinets banged open and the dishes clinked and miles and miles of nothing went by outside. Bast had snagged us some snacks and drinks (and Friskies, of course) from a New Orleans all-night convenience store before we left, but nobody seemed very hungry. I could tell Bast was anxious. She'd already shredded most of the RV's upholstery, and was now using the kitchen table as a scratching post.

As for Sadie, she kept opening and closing her hand, staring at the feather of truth as if it were a phone she wished would ring. Ever since her disappearance in the Hall of Judgment, she'd been acting all distant and quiet. Not that I'm complaining, but it wasn't like her.

'What happened with Anubis?' I asked her for the millionth time.

She glared at me, ready to bite my head off. Then she apparently decided I wasn't worth the effort. She fixed her eyes on the glowing feather that hovered over her palm.

'We talked,' she said carefully. 'He asked me some questions.'

'What kind of questions?'

'Carter, don't ask. Please.'

Please? Okay, that really wasn't like Sadie.

I looked at Bast, but she wasn't any help. She

was slowly gouging the Formica to bits with her claws.

'What's wrong?' I asked her.

She kept her eyes on the table. 'In the Land of the Dead, I abandoned you. *Again.*'

'Anubis startled you,' I said. 'It's no big deal.'

Bast gave me the big yellow eyes, and I got the feeling I'd only made things worse.

'I made a promise to your father, Carter. In exchange for my freedom, he gave me a job even more important than fighting the Serpent: protecting Sadie—and if it ever became necessary, protecting *both* of you.'

Sadie flushed. 'Bast, that's . . . I mean, thank you and all, but we're hardly more important than fighting . . . you know, *him.*'

'You don't understand,' Bast said. 'The two of you are not just blood of the pharaohs. You're the most powerful royal children to be born in centuries. You're the only chance we have of reconciling the gods and the House of Life, of relearning the old ways before it's too late. If you could learn the path of the gods, you could find others with royal blood and teach *them.* You could revitalize the House of Life. What your parents did—*everything* they did, was to prepare the way for you.'

Sadie and I were silent. I mean, what do you say to something like that? I guessed I'd always felt like my parents loved me, but willing to *die* for me? Believing it was necessary so Sadie and I could do some amazing world-saving stuff? I didn't ask for that.

'They didn't want to leave you alone,' Bast said, reading my expression. 'They didn't plan on it, but they knew releasing the gods would be dangerous. Believe me, they understood how special you are. At first I was protecting you two because I promised. Now even if I hadn't promised, I would. You two are like kittens to me. I won't fail you again.'

I'll admit I got a lump in my throat. I'd never been called someone's kitten before.

Sadie sniffled. She brushed something from under her eye. 'You're not going to wash us, are you?'

It was good to see Bast smile again. 'I'll try to resist. And by the way, Sadie, I'm proud of you. Dealing with Anubis on your own—those death gods can be nasty customers.'

Sadie shrugged. She seemed strangely uncomfortable. 'Well, I wouldn't call him *nasty*. I mean, he looked hardly more than a teenager.'

'What are you talking about?' I said. 'He had the head of a jackal.'

'No, when he turned human.'

'Sadie . . .' I was starting to get worried about her now. 'When Anubis turned human he *still* had the head of a jackal. He was huge and terrifying and, yeah, pretty nasty. Why, what did he look like to you?'

Her cheeks reddened. 'He looked . . . like a mortal guy.'

'Probably a glamour,' Bast said.

'No,' Sadie insisted. 'It couldn't have been.'

'Well, it's not important,' I said. 'We got the feather.'

Sadie fidgeted, as if it was *very* important. But then she closed her fist, and the feather of truth disappeared. 'It won't do us any good without the secret name of Set.'

'I'm working on that.' Bast's gaze shifted around the room—she seemed afraid of being overheard. 'I've got a plan. But it's dangerous.'

I sat forward. 'What is it?'

'We'll have to make a stop. I'd rather not jinx us until we get closer, but it's on our way. Shouldn't cause much of a delay.'

I tried to calculate. 'This is the morning of the second Demon Day?'

Bast nodded. 'The day Horus was born.'

'And Set's birthday is tomorrow, the third Demon Day. That means we have about twenty-four hours until he destroys North America.'

'And if he gets his hands on us,' Sadie added, 'he'll ramp up his power even more.'

'It'll be enough time,' Bast said. 'It's roughly twenty-four hours driving from New Orleans to Phoenix, and we've already been on the road over five hours. If we don't have any more nasty surprises—'

'Like the kind we have every day?'

'Yes,' Bast admitted. 'Like those.'

I took a shaky breath. Twenty-four hours and it would be over, one way or the other. We'd save Dad and stop Set, or everything would've been for nothing—not just what Sadie and I had done, but all our parents' sacrifices too. Suddenly I felt like I was underground again, in one of those tunnels in the First Nome, with a million tons of rock over my head. One little shift in the ground, and everything would come crashing down.

'Well,' I said. 'If you need me, I'll be outside, playing with sharp objects.'

I grabbed my sword and headed for the back of

351

the RV.

*   *   *

I'd never seen a mobile home with a porch before. The sign on the back door warned me not to use it while the vehicle was in motion, but I did anyway.

It wasn't the best place to practice swordplay. It was too small, and two chairs took up most of the space. The cold wind whipped around me, and every bump in the road threw me off balance. But it was the only place I could go to be alone. I needed to clear my thoughts.

I practiced summoning my sword from the Duat and putting it back. Soon I could do it almost every time, as long as I kept my focus. Then I practiced some moves—blocks, jabs, and strikes—until Horus couldn't resist offering his advice.

Lift the blade higher, he coached. *More of an arc, Carter. The blade is designed to hook an enemy's weapon.*

Shut up, I grumbled. *Where were you when I needed help on the basketball court?* But I tried holding the sword his way and found he was right.

The highway wound through long stretches of empty scrubland. Once in a while we'd pass a rancher's truck or a family SUV, and the driver would get wide-eyed when he saw me: a black kid swinging a sword on the back of an RV. I'd just smile and wave, and Khufu's driving soon left them in the dust.

After an hour of practice, my shirt was stuck to my chest with cold sweat. My breathing was heavy. I decided to sit and take a break.

'It approaches,' Horus told me. His voice

sounded more substantial, no longer in my head. I looked next to me and saw him shimmering in a golden aura, sitting back in the other deck chair in his leather armor with his sandaled feet up on the railing. His sword, a ghostly copy of *my* sword, was propped next to him.

'What's approaching?' I asked. 'The fight with Set?'

'That, of course,' Horus said. 'But there is another challenge before that, Carter. Be prepared.'

'Great. As if I didn't have enough challenges already.'

Horus's silver and gold eyes glittered. 'When I was growing up, Set tried to kill me many times. My mother and I fled from place to place, hiding from him until I was old enough to face him. The Red Lord will send the same forces against you. The next will come—'

'At a river,' I guessed, remembering my last soul trip. 'Something bad is going is happen at a river. But what's the challenge?'

'You must beware—' Horus's image began to fade, and the god frowned. 'What's this? Someone is trying to—a different force—'

He was replaced by the glowing image of Zia Rashid.

'Zia!' I stood up, suddenly conscious of the fact that I was sweaty and gross and looked like I'd just been dragged through the Land of the Dead.

'Carter?' Her image flickered. She was clutching her staff, and wore a gray coat wrapped over her robes as if she were standing somewhere cold. Her short black hair danced around her face. 'Thank Thoth I found you.'

'How did you get here?'

'No time! Listen: we're coming after you. Desjardins, me, and two others. We don't know exactly where you are. Desjardins' tracking spells are having trouble finding you, but he knows we're getting close. And he knows where you're going—Phoenix.'

My mind started racing. 'So he finally believes Set is free? You're coming to help us?'

Zia shook her head. 'He's coming to stop you.'

'*Stop* us? Zia, Set's about to blow up the continent! My dad—' My voice cracked. I hated how scared and powerless I sounded. 'My dad's in trouble.'

Zia reached out a shimmering hand, but it was just an image. Our fingers couldn't touch. 'Carter, I'm sorry. You have to see Desjardins' point of view. The House of Life has been trying to keep the gods locked up for centuries to prevent something like *this* from happening. Now that you've unleashed them—'

'It wasn't *my* idea!'

'I know, but you're trying to fight Set with divine magic. Gods can't be controlled. You could end up doing even more damage. If you let the House of Life handle this—'

'Set is too strong,' I said. 'And I *can* control Horus. I can do this.'

Zia shook her head. 'It will get harder as you get closer to Set. You have no idea.'

'And you do?'

Zia glanced nervously to her left. Her image turned fuzzy, like a bad television signal. 'We don't have much time. Mel will be out of the restroom soon.'

'You've got a magician named Mel?'

'Just listen. Desjardins is splitting us into two teams. The plan is for us to cut you off on either side and intercept you. If *my* team reaches you first, I think I can keep Mel from attacking long enough for us all to talk. Then maybe we can figure out how to approach Desjardins, to convince him we have to cooperate.'

'Don't take this the wrong way, but why should I trust you?'

She pursed her lips, looking genuinely hurt. Part of me felt guilty, while part of me worried this was some kind of trick.

'Carter . . . I have something to tell you. Something that might help, but it has to be said in person.'

'Tell me now.'

'Thoth's beak! You are impossibly stubborn.'

'Yeah, it's a gift.'

We locked eyes. Her image was fading, but I didn't want her to go. I wanted to talk longer.

'If you won't trust me, I'll have to trust you,' Zia said. 'I will arrange to be in Las Cruces, New Mexico, tonight. If you choose to meet me, perhaps we can convince Mel. Then together, we'll convince Desjardins. Will you come?'

I wanted to promise, just to see her, but I imagined myself trying to convince Sadie or Bast that this was a good idea. 'I don't know, Zia.'

'Just think about it,' she pleaded. 'And Carter, don't trust Amos. If you see him—' Her eyes widened. 'Mel's here!' she whispered.

Zia slashed her staff in front of her, and her image vanished.

30.
BAST KEEPS A PROMISE

CARTER

Hours later, I woke up on the RV's couch with Bast shaking my arm.

'We're here,' she announced.

I had no idea how long I'd been asleep. At some point, the flat landscape and complete boredom had zonked me out, and I'd started having bad dreams about tiny magicians flying around in my hair, trying to shave me bald. Somewhere in there, I'd had a nightmare about Amos too, but it was fuzzy. I still didn't understand why Zia would mention him.

I blinked the sleep out of my eyes and realized my head was in Khufu's lap. The baboon was foraging my scalp for munchies.

'Dude.' I sat up groggily. 'Not cool.'

'But he gave you a lovely hairdo,' Sadie said.

'Agh-agh!' Khufu agreed.

Bast opened the door of the trailer. 'Come on,' she said. 'We'll have to walk from here.'

When I got to the door I almost had a heart attack. We were parked on a mountain road so narrow, the RV would've toppled over if I'd sneezed wrong.

For a second, I was afraid we were already in Phoenix, because the landscape looked similar. The sun was just setting on the horizon. Rugged mountain ranges stretched out on either side, and the desert floor between them seemed to go on forever. In a valley to our left lay a colorless city—hardly any trees or grass, just sand, gravel, and buildings. The city was much smaller than Phoenix, though, and a large river traced its southern edge, glinting red in the fading light. The river curved around the base of the mountains below us before snaking off to the north.

'We're on the moon,' Sadie murmured.

'El Paso, Texas,' Bast corrected. 'And that's the Rio Grande.' She took a big breath of the cool dry air. 'A river civilization in the desert. Very much like Egypt, actually! *Er,* except for the fact that Mexico is next door. I think this is the best spot to summon Nephthys.'

'You really think she'll tell us Set's secret name?' Sadie asked.

Bast considered. 'Nephthys is unpredictable, but she has sided against her husband before. We can hope.'

That didn't sound very promising. I stared at the river far below. 'Why did you park us on the mountain? Why not closer?'

Bast shrugged, as if this hadn't occurred to her. 'Cats like to get as high up as possible. In case we have to pounce on something.'

'Great,' I said. 'So if we have to pounce, we're all set.'

'It's not so bad,' Bast said. 'We just climb our way down to the river through a few miles of sand, cacti, and rattlesnakes, looking out for the Border Patrol, human traffickers, magicians, and demons—and summon Nephthys.'

Sadie whistled. 'Well, I'm excited!'

'Agh,' Khufu agreed miserably. He sniffed the air and snarled.

357

'He smells trouble,' Bast translated. 'Something bad is about to happen.'

'Even *I* could smell that,' I grumbled, and we followed Bast down the mountain.

*   *   *

Yes, Horus said. *I remember this place.*

It's El Paso, I told him. *Unless you went out for Mexican food, you've never been here.*

I remember it well, he insisted. *The marsh, the desert.*

I stopped and looked around. Suddenly I remembered this place, too. About fifty yards in front of us, the river spread out into a swampy area—a web of slow-moving tributaries cutting a shallow depression through the desert. Marsh grass grew tall along the banks. There must've been some kind of surveillance, its being an international border and all, but I couldn't spot any.

I'd been here in *ba* form. I could picture a hut right there in the marsh, Isis and young Horus hiding from Set. And just downriver—that's where I'd sensed something dark moving under the water, waiting for me.

I caught Bast's arm when she was a few steps from the bank. 'Stay away from the water.'

She frowned. 'Carter, I'm a *cat.* I'm not going for a swim. But if you want to summon a river goddess, you really need to do it at the riverbank.'

She made it sound so logical that I felt stupid, but I couldn't help it. Something bad was about to happen.

What is it? I asked Horus. *What's the challenge?*

358

But my ride-along god was unnervingly silent, as if waiting.

Sadie tossed a rock into the murky brown water. It sank with a loud *ker-plunk!*

'Seems quite safe to me,' she said, and trudged down to the banks.

Khufu followed hesitantly. When he reached the water, he sniffed at it and snarled.

'See?' I said. 'Even Khufu doesn't like it.'

'It's probably ancestral memory,' Bast said. 'The river was a dangerous place in Egypt. Snakes, hippos, all kinds of problems.'

'Hippos?'

'Don't take it lightly,' Bast warned. 'Hippos can be *deadly.*'

'Was that what attacked Horus?' I asked. 'I mean in the old days, when Set was looking for him?'

'Haven't heard that story,' Bast said. 'Usually you hear that Set used scorpions first. Then later, crocodiles.'

'Crocodiles,' I said, and a chill went down my back.

Is that it? I asked Horus. But again he didn't answer. 'Bast, does the Rio Grande have crocodiles?'

'I very much doubt it.' She knelt by the water. 'Now, Sadie, if you'd do the honors?'

'How?'

'Just ask for Nephthys to appear. She was Isis's sister. If she's anywhere on this side of the Duat, she should hear your voice.'

Sadie looked doubtful, but she knelt next to Bast and touched the water. Her fingertips caused ripples that seemed much too large, rings of force

359

emanating all the way across the river.

'Hullo, Nephthys?' she said. 'Anyone home?'

I heard a splash downriver, and turned to see a family of immigrants crossing midstream. I'd heard stories about how thousands of people cross the border from Mexico illegally each year, looking for work and a better life, but it was startling to actually see them in front of me—a man and a woman hurrying along, carrying a little girl between them. They were dressed in ragged clothes and looked poorer than the poorest Egyptian peasants I'd ever seen. I stared at them for a few seconds, but they didn't appear to be any kind of supernatural threat. The man gave me a wary look and we seemed to come to a silent understanding: we both had enough problems without bothering each other.

Meanwhile Bast and Sadie stayed focused on the water, watching the ripples spread out from Sadie's fingers.

Bast tilted her head, listening intently. 'What's she saying?'

'I can't make it out,' Sadie whispered. 'Very faint.'

'You can actually hear something?' I asked.

'*Shhh,*' they both said at once.

'*"Caged"* . . .' Sadie said. 'No, what is that word in English?'

'Sheltered,' Bast suggested. 'She is sheltered far away. *A sleeping host.* What is *that* supposed to mean?'

I didn't know what they were talking about. I couldn't hear a thing.

Khufu tugged at my hand and pointed downriver. *'Agh.'*

The immigrant family had disappeared. It seemed impossible they could cross the river so quickly. I scanned both banks—no sign of them—but the water was more turbulent where they'd been standing, as if someone had stirred it with a giant spoon. My throat tightened.

'*Um,* Bast—'

'Carter, we can barely hear Nephthys,' she said. 'Please.'

I gritted my teeth. 'Fine. Khufu and I are going to check something—'

'*Shh!*' Sadie said again.

I nodded to Khufu, and we started down the riverbank. Khufu hid behind my legs and growled at the river.

I looked back, but Bast and Sadie seemed fine. They were still staring at the water as if it were some amazing Internet video.

Finally we got to the place where I'd seen the family, but the water had calmed. Khufu slapped the ground and did a handstand, which meant he was either break dancing or really nervous.

'What is it?' I asked, my heart pounding.

'*Agh, agh, agh!*' he complained. That was probably an entire lecture in Baboon, but I had no idea what he was saying.

'Well, I don't see any other way,' I said. 'If that family got pulled into the water or something . . . I have to find them. I'm going in.'

'*Agh!*' He backed away from the water.

'Khufu, those people had a little girl. If they need help, I can't just walk away. Stay here and watch my back.'

Khufu grunted and slapped his own face in protest as I stepped into the water. It was colder and swifter than I'd imagined. I concentrated, and summoned my sword and wand out of the Duat. Maybe it was my imagination, but that seemed to make the river run even faster.

I was midstream when Khufu barked urgently. He was jumping around on the riverbank, pointing frantically at a nearby clump of reeds.

The family was huddled inside, trembling with fear, their eyes wide. My first thought: *Why are they hiding from me?*

'I won't hurt you,' I promised. They stared at me blankly, and I wished I could speak Spanish.

Then the water churned around me, and I realized they weren't scared of me. My next thought: *Man, I'm stupid.*

Horus's voice yelled: *Jump!*

I sprang out of the water as if shot from a cannon—twenty, thirty feet into the air. No way I should've been able to do that, but it was a good thing, because a monster erupted from the river beneath me.

At first all I saw were hundreds of teeth—a pink maw three times as big as me. Somehow I managed to flip and land on my feet in the shallows. I was facing a crocodile as long as our RV—and that was just the half sticking out of the water. Its gray-green skin was ridged with thick plates like a camouflage suit of armor, and its eyes were the color of moldy milk.

The family screamed and started scrambling up the banks. That caught the crocodile's attention. He instinctively turned toward the louder, more interesting prey. I'd always thought of crocodiles as slow animals, but when it charged the immigrants, I'd never seen anything move so fast.

Use the distraction, Horus urged. *Get behind it and strike.*

Instead I yelled, 'Sadie, Bast, help!' and I threw my wand.

Bad throw. The wand hit the river right in front of the croc, then skipped off the water like a stone, smacked the croc between the eyes, and shot back into my hand.

I doubt I did any damage, but the croc glanced over at me, annoyed.

Or you can smack it with a stick, Horus muttered.

I charged forward, yelling to keep the croc's attention. Out of the corner of my eye, I could see the family scrambling to safety. Khufu ran along behind them, waving his arms and barking to herd them out of harm's way. I wasn't sure if they were running from the croc or the crazy monkey, but as long as they kept running, I didn't care.

I couldn't see what was happening with Bast and Sadie. I heard shouting and splashing behind me, but before I could look, the crocodile lunged.

I ducked to the left, slashing with my sword. The blade just bounced off the croc's hide. The monster thrashed sideways, and its snout would've bashed my head in; but I instinctively raised my wand and the croc slammed into a wall of force, bouncing off as if I were protected by a giant invisible energy bubble.

I tried to summon the falcon warrior, but it was too hard to concentrate with a six-ton reptile trying to bite me in half.

Then I heard Bast scream, 'NO!' and I knew immediately, without even looking, that something was wrong with Sadie.

Desperation and rage turned my nerves to steel. I thrust out my wand and the wall of energy surged outward, slamming into the crocodile so hard, it went flying through the air, tumbling out of the river and onto the Mexican shore. While it was on its back, flailing and off balance, I leaped, raising my sword, which was now glowing in my hands, and drove the blade into the monster's belly. I held on while the crocodile thrashed, slowly disintegrating from its snout to the tip of its tail, until I stood in the middle of a giant pile of wet sand.

I turned and saw Bast battling a crocodile just as big as mine. The crocodile lunged, and Bast dropped beneath it, raking her knives across its throat. The croc melted into the river until it was only a smoky cloud of sand, but the damage had been done: Sadie lay in a crumpled heap on the riverbank.

By the time I got there, Khufu and Bast were already at her side. Blood trickled from Sadie's scalp. Her face was a nasty shade of yellow.

'What happened?' I asked.

'It came out of nowhere,' Bast said miserably. 'Its tail hit Sadie and sent her flying. She never had a chance. Is she . . .'

Khufu put his hand on Sadie's forehead and made popping noises with his mouth.

Bast sighed with relief. 'Khufu says she'll live, but we have to get her out of here. Those crocodiles could mean . . .'

Her voice trailed off. In the middle of the river, the water was boiling. Rising from it was a figure so horrible, I knew we were doomed.

'Could mean *that*,' Bast said grimly.

364

To start with, the guy was twenty feet tall—and I don't mean with a glowing avatar. He was all flesh and blood. His chest and arms were human, but he had light green skin, and his waist was wrapped in a green armored kilt like reptile hide. He had the head of a crocodile, a massive mouth filled with white crooked teeth, and eyes that glistened with green mucus (yeah, I know—real attractive). His black hair hung in plaits down to his shoulders, and bull's horns curved from his head. If that wasn't weird enough, he appeared to be sweating at an unbelievable rate—oily water poured off him in torrents and pooled in the river.

He raised his staff—a length of green wood as big as a telephone pole.

Bast yelled, 'Move!' and pulled me back as the crocodile man smashed a five-foot-deep trench in the riverbank where I'd been standing.

He bellowed: 'Horus!'

The last thing I wanted to do was say, *Here!* But Horus spoke urgently in my mind: *Face him down. Sobek only understands strength. Do not let him grasp you, or he will pull you down and drown you.*

I swallowed my fear and yelled, 'Sobek! You, uh, weakling! How the heck are ya?'

Sobek bared his teeth. Maybe it was his version of a friendly smile. Probably not.

'That form does not serve you, falcon god,' he said. 'I will snap you in half.'

Next to me, Bast slipped her knives from her sleeves. 'Don't let him grasp you,' she warned.

'Already got the memo,' I told her. I was conscious of Khufu off to my right, slowly lugging Sadie uphill. I had to keep this green guy distracted, at least until they were safe. 'Sobek,

365

god of . . . I'm guessing crocodiles! Leave us in peace or we'll destroy you!'

Good, Horus said. *'Destroy' is good.*

Sobek roared with laughter. 'Your sense of humor has improved, Horus. You and your kitty will destroy me?' He turned his mucus-filmed eyes on Bast. 'What brings you to my realm, cat goddess? I thought you didn't like the *water!*'

On the last word, he aimed his staff and shot forth a torrent of green water. Bast was too quick. She jumped and came down behind Sobek with her avatar fully formed—a massive, glowing cat-headed warrior. 'Traitor!' Bast yelled. 'Why do you side with chaos? Your duty is to the king!'

'What king?' Sobek roared. 'Ra? Ra is gone. Osiris is dead *again,* the weakling! And this boy child cannot restore the empire. There was a time I supported Horus, yes. But he has no strength in this form. He has no followers. Set offers power. Set offers fresh meat. I think I will start with godling flesh!'

He turned on me and swung his staff. I rolled away from his strike, but his free hand shot out and grabbed me around the waist. I just wasn't quick enough. Bast tensed, preparing to launch herself at the enemy, but before she could, Sobek dropped his staff, grasped me with both massive hands, and dragged me into the water. The next thing I knew I was drowning in the cold green murk. I couldn't see or breathe. I sank into the depths as Sobek's hands crushed the air out of my lungs.

Now or never! Horus said. *Let me take control.*

No, I replied. *I'll die first.*

I found the thought strangely calming. If I was

366

already dead, there was no point in being afraid. I might as well go down fighting.

I focused my power and felt strength coursing through my body. I flexed my arms and felt Sobek's grip weaken. I summoned the avatar of the hawk warrior and was instantly encased in a glowing golden form as large as Sobek. I could just see him in the dark water, his slimy eyes wide with surprise.

I broke his grip and head-butted him, breaking off a few of his teeth. Then I shot out of the water and landed on the riverbank next to Bast, who was so startled, she almost slashed me.

'Thank Ra!' she exclaimed.

'Yeah, I'm alive.'

'No, I almost jumped in after you. I hate the water!'

Then Sobek exploded out of the river, roaring in rage. Green blood oozed from one of his nostrils.

'You cannot defeat me!' He held out his arms, which were raining perspiration. 'I am lord of the water! My sweat creates the rivers of the world!'

Eww. I decided not to swim in rivers anymore. I glanced back, looking for Khufu and Sadie, but they were nowhere in sight. Hopefully Khufu had gotten Sadie to safety, or at least found a good place to hide.

Sobek charged, and he brought the river with him. A massive wave smashed into me, toppling me to the ground, but Bast jumped and came down on Sobek's back in full avatar form. The weight hardly seemed to bother him. He tried to grab her without any luck. She slashed repeatedly at his arms, back and neck, but his green skin seemed to heal as quickly as she could cut him.

I struggled to my feet, which in avatar form is like trying to get up with a mattress strapped to your chest. Sobek finally managed to grab Bast and throw her off. She tumbled to a stop without getting hurt, but her blue aura was flickering. She was losing power.

We played tag team with the crocodile god—stabbing and slashing—but the more we wounded him, the more enraged and powerful he seemed to get.

'More minions!' he shouted. 'Come to me!'

That couldn't be good. Another round of giant crocs and we'd be dead.

Why don't we get minions? I complained to Horus, but he didn't answer. I could feel him struggling to channel his power through me, trying to keep up our combat magic.

Sobek's fist smashed into Bast, and she went flying again. This time when she hit the ground, her avatar flickered off completely.

I charged, trying to draw Sobek's attention. Unfortunately, it worked. Sobek turned and blasted me with water. While I was blind, he slapped me so hard I flew across the riverbank, tumbling through the reeds.

My avatar collapsed. I sat up groggily and found Khufu and Sadie right next to me, Sadie still passed out and bleeding, Khufu desperately murmuring in Baboon and stroking her forehead.

Sobek stepped out of the water and grinned at me. Far downstream in the dim evening light, about a quarter of a mile away, I could see two wake lines in the river, coming toward us fast—Sobek's reinforcements.

From the river, Bast yelled, 'Carter, hurry! Get

Sadie out of here!'

Her face went pale with strain, and her cat warrior avatar appeared around her one more time. It was weak, though—barely substantial.

'Don't!' I called. 'You'll die!'

I tried to summon the falcon warrior, but the effort made my insides burn with pain. I was out of power, and Horus's spirit was slumbering, completely spent.

'Go!' Bast yelled. 'And tell your father I kept my promise.'

'NO!'

She leaped at Sobek. The two grappled—Bast slashing furiously across his face while Sobek howled in pain. The two gods toppled into the water, and down they went.

I ran to the riverbank. The river bubbled and frothed. Then a green explosion lit the entire length of the Rio Grande, and a small black-and-gold creature shot out of the river as if it had been tossed. It landed on the grass at my feet—a wet, unconscious, half-dead cat.

'Bast?' I picked up the cat gingerly. It wore Bast's collar, but as I watched, the talisman of the goddess crumbled to dust. It wasn't Bast anymore. Only Muffin.

Tears stung my eyes. Sobek had been defeated, forced back to the Duat or something, but there were still two wake lines coming toward us in the river, close enough now that I could see the monsters' green backs and beady eyes.

I cradled the cat against my chest and turned toward Khufu. 'Come on, we have to—'

I froze, because standing right behind Khufu and my sister, glaring at me, was a different crocodile—one that was pure white.

We're dead, I thought. And then, *Wait . . . a* white *crocodile?*

It opened its mouth and lunged—straight over me. I turned and saw it slam into the two other crocodiles—the giant green ones that had been about to kill me.

'Philip?' I said in amazement, as the crocodiles thrashed and fought.

'Yes,' said a man's voice.

I turned again and saw the impossible. Uncle Amos was kneeling next to Sadie, frowning as he examined her head wound. He looked up at me urgently. 'Philip will keep Sobek's minions busy, but not for long. Follow me now, and we have a slim chance of surviving!'

31.
I DELIVER A LOVE NOTE

SADIE

I'm glad Carter told that last bit—partly because I was unconscious when it happened, partly because I can't talk about what Bast did without going to pieces.

Ah, but more on that later.

I woke feeling as if someone had overinflated my head. My eyes weren't seeing the same things. Out my left, I saw a baboon bum, out my right, my long-lost uncle Amos. Naturally, I decided to focus on the right.

'Amos?'

He laid a cool cloth on my forehead. 'Rest, child. You had quite a concussion.'

That at least I could believe.

As my eyes began to focus, I saw we were outside under a starry night sky. I was lying on a blanket on what felt like soft sand. Khufu stood next to me, his colorful side a bit too close to my face. He was stirring a pot over a small fire, and whatever he was cooking smelled like burning tar. Carter sat nearby at the top of a sand dune, looking despondent and holding . . . was that Muffin in his lap?

Amos appeared much as he had when we last saw him, ages ago. He wore his blue suit with matching coat and fedora. His long hair was neatly braided, and his round glasses glinted in the sun. He appeared fresh and rested—not like someone who'd been the prisoner of Set.

'How did you—'

'Get away from Set?' His expression darkened. 'I was a fool to go looking for him, Sadie. I had no idea how powerful he'd become. His spirit is tied to the red pyramid.'

'So . . . he doesn't *have* a human host?'

Amos shook his head. 'He doesn't need one as long as he has the pyramid. As it gets closer to completion, he gets stronger and stronger. I sneaked into his lair under the mountain and walked right into a trap. I'm ashamed to say he took me without a fight.'

He gestured at his suit, showing off how perfectly fine he was. 'Not a scratch. Just—*bam*. I was frozen like a statue. Set stood me outside his pyramid like a trophy and let his demons laugh and mock me as they passed by.'

'Did you see Dad?' I asked.

His shoulders slumped. 'I heard the demons talking. The coffin is inside the pyramid. They're planning to use Osiris's power to augment the storm. When Set unleashes it at sunrise—and it will be *quite* an explosion—Osiris and your father will be obliterated. Osiris will be exiled so deep into the Duat he may never rise again.'

My head began to throb. I couldn't believe we had so little time, and if Amos couldn't save Dad, how could Carter and I?

'But you got away,' I said, grasping for any good news. 'So there must be weaknesses in his defenses or—'

'The magic that froze me eventually began to weaken. I concentrated my energy and worked my way out of the binding. It took many hours, but finally I broke free. I sneaked out at midday, when the demons were sleeping. It was much too easy.'

'It doesn't sound easy,' I said.

Amos shook his head, obviously troubled. 'Set allowed me to escape. I don't know why, but I shouldn't be alive. It's a trick of some sort. I'm afraid . . .' Whatever he was going to say, he changed his mind. 'At any rate, my first thought was to find you, so I summoned my boat.'

He gestured behind him. I managed to lift my head and saw we were in a strange desert of white dunes that stretched as far as I could see in the starlight. The sand under my fingers was so fine and white, it might've been sugar. Amos's boat, the same one that had carried us from the Thames to Brooklyn, was beached at the top of a nearby dune, canted at a precarious angle as if it had been thrown there.

'There's a supply locker aboard,' Amos offered, 'if you'd like fresh clothes.'

'But where are we?'

'White Sands,' Carter told me. 'In New Mexico. It's a government range for testing missiles. Amos said no one would look for us here, so we gave you some time to heal. It's about seven in the evening, still the twenty-eighth. Twelve hours or so until Set . . . you know.'

'But . . .' Too many questions swam round in my mind. The last thing I remembered, I'd been at the river talking to Nephthys. Her voice had seemed to come from the other side of the world. She'd spoken faintly through the current—so hard to understand, yet quite insistent. She'd told me she was sheltered far away in a sleeping host, which I couldn't make sense of. She'd said she could not appear in person, but that she would send a message. Then the water had started to boil.

'We were attacked.' Carter stroked Muffin's head, and I finally noticed that the amulet—*Bast's* amulet—was missing. 'Sadie, I've got some bad news.'

He told me what had happened, and I closed my eyes. I started to weep. Embarrassing, yes, but I couldn't help it. Over the last few days, I'd lost everything—my home, my ordinary life, my father. I'd been almost killed half a dozen times. My mother's death, which I'd never gotten over to begin with, hurt like a reopened wound. And now Bast was gone too?

When Anubis had questioned me in the Underworld, he'd wanted to know what I would sacrifice to save the world.

What haven't I sacrificed already? I wanted to

scream. *What have I got left?*

Carter came over and gave me Muffin, who purred in my arms, but it wasn't the same. It wasn't Bast.

'She'll come back, won't she?' I looked at Amos imploringly. 'I mean she's immortal, isn't she?'

Amos tugged at the rim of his hat. 'Sadie . . . I just don't know. It seems she sacrificed herself to defeat Sobek. Bast forced him back to the Duat at the expense of her own life force. She even spared Muffin, her host, probably with the last shred of her power. If that's true, it would be very difficult for Bast to come back. Perhaps some day, in a few hundred years—'

'No, not a few hundred years! I can't—' My voice broke.

Carter put his hand on my shoulder, and I knew he understood. We *couldn't* lose anyone else. We just couldn't.

'Rest now,' Amos said. 'We can spare another hour, but then we'll have to get moving.'

Khufu offered me a bowl of his concoction. The chunky liquid looked like soup that had died long ago. I glanced at Amos, hoping he'd give me a pass, but he nodded encouragingly.

Just my luck, on top of everything else I had to take baboon medicine.

I sipped the brew, which tasted almost as bad as it smelled, and immediately my eyelids felt heavy. I closed my eyes and slept.

*   *   *

And just when I thought I had this soul-leaving-the-body business sorted, my soul decided to break the rules. Well, it is *my* soul after all, so I suppose that makes sense.

As my *ba* left my body, it kept its human form, which was better than the winged poultry look, but it kept growing and growing until I towered above White Sands. I'd been told many times that I have a lot of spirit (usually not as a compliment), but this was absurd. My *ba* was as tall as the Washington Monument.

To the south, past miles and miles of desert, steam rose from the Rio Grande—the battle site where Bast and Sobek had perished. Even as tall as I was, I shouldn't have been able to see all the way to Texas, especially at night, but somehow I could. To the north, even farther away, I saw a distant red glow and I knew it was the aura of Set. His power was growing as his pyramid neared completion.

I looked down. Next to my foot was a tiny cluster of specks—our camp. Miniature Carter, Amos, and Khufu sat talking round the cooking fire. Amos's boat was no larger than my little toe. My own sleeping form lay curled in a blanket, so small I could've crushed myself with one misstep.

I was enormous, and the world was small.

'That's how gods see things,' a voice told me.

I looked around but saw nothing, just the vast expanse of rolling white dunes. Then, in front of me, the dunes shifted. I thought it was the wind, until an entire dune rolled sideways like a wave. Another moved, and another. I realized I was looking at a human form—an enormous man lying in the fetal position. He got up, shaking white sand everywhere. I knelt down and cupped my hands over my companions to keep them from getting buried. Oddly, they didn't seem to notice, as if the disruption were no more than a sprinkle of rain.

The man rose to his full height—at least a head taller than my own giant form. His body was made of sand that curtained off his arms and chest like waterfalls of sugar. The sand shifted across his face until he formed a vague smile.

'Sadie Kane,' he said. 'I have been waiting for you.'

'Geb.' Don't ask me how, but I knew instantly that this was the god of the earth. Maybe the sand body was a giveaway. 'I have something for you.'

It didn't make sense that my *ba* would have the envelope, but I reached into my shimmering ghostly pocket and pulled out the note from Nut.

'Your wife misses you,' I said.

Geb took the note gingerly. He held it to his face and seemed to sniff it. Then he opened the envelope. Instead of a letter, fireworks burst out. A new constellation blazed in the night sky above us—the face of Nut, formed by a thousand stars. The wind rose quickly and ripped the image apart, but Geb sighed contentedly. He closed the envelope and tucked it inside his sandy chest as if there were a pocket right where his heart should be.

'I owe you thanks, Sadie Kane,' Geb said. 'It has been many millennia since I saw the face of my beloved. Ask me a favor that the earth can grant, and it shall be yours.'

'Save my father,' I said immediately.

Geb's face rippled with surprise. '*Hmm,* what a loyal daughter! Isis could learn a thing from you. Alas, I cannot. Your father's path is twined with that of Osiris, and matters between the gods cannot be solved by the earth.'

'Then I don't suppose you could collapse Set's mountain and destroy his pyramid?' I asked.

Geb's laughter was like the world's largest sand shaker. 'I cannot intervene so directly between my children. Set is my son too.'

I almost stamped my foot in frustration. Then I remembered I was giant and might smash the whole camp. Could a *ba* do that? Better not to find out. 'Well, your favors aren't very useful, then.'

Geb shrugged, sloughing off a few tons of sand from his shoulders. 'Perhaps some advice to help you achieve what you desire. Go to the place of the crosses.'

'And where is that?'

'Close,' he promised. 'And, Sadie Kane, you are right. You have lost too much. Your family has suffered. I know what that is like. Just remember, a parent would do anything to save his children. I gave up my happiness, my wife—I took on the curse of Ra so that my children could be born.' He looked up at the sky wistfully. 'And while I miss my beloved more each millennium, I know neither of us would change our choice. I have five children whom I love.'

'Even Set?' I asked incredulously. 'He's about to destroy millions of people.'

'Set is more than he appears,' Geb said. 'He is our flesh and blood.'

'Not mine.'

'No?' Geb shifted, lowering himself. I thought he was crouching, until I realized he was melting into the dunes. 'Think on it, Sadie Kane, and proceed with care. Danger awaits you at the place of crosses, but you will also find what you need

377

most.'

'Could you be a little more vague?' I grumbled.

But Geb was gone, leaving only a taller than normal dune in the sands; and my *ba* sank back into my body.

32.
THE PLACE OF CROSSES

SADIE

I woke with Muffin snuggled on my head, purring and chewing my hair. For a moment, I thought I was home. I used to wake with Muffin on my head all the time. Then I remembered I *had* no home, and Bast was gone. My eyes started tearing up again.

No, Isis's voice chided. *We must stay focused.*

For once, the goddess was right. I sat up and brushed the white sand off my face. Muffin meowed in protest, then waddled two steps and decided she could settle for my warm place on the blanket.

'Good, you're up,' Amos said. 'We were about to wake you.'

It was still dark. Carter stood on the deck of the boat, pulling on a new linen coat from Amos's supply locker. Khufu loped over to me and made a purring sound at the cat. To my surprise, Muffin leaped into his arms.

'I've asked Khufu to take the cat back to Brooklyn,' Amos said. 'This is no place for her.'

Khufu grunted, clearly unhappy with his

assignment.

'I know, my old friend,' Amos said. His voice had a hard edge; he seemed to be asserting himself as the alpha baboon. 'It is for the best.'

'*Agh,*' Khufu said, not meeting Amos's eyes.

Unease crept over me. I remembered what Amos said: that his release might have been a trick of Set's. And Carter's vision: Set was *hoping* that Amos would lead us to the mountain so we could be captured. What if Set was influencing Amos somehow? I didn't like the idea of sending Khufu away.

On the other hand, I didn't see much choice but to accept Amos's help. And seeing Khufu there, holding Muffin, I couldn't bear the idea of putting either of them in danger. Maybe Amos had a point.

'Can he travel safely?' I asked. 'Out here all by himself?'

'Oh, yes,' Amos promised. 'Khufu—and all baboons—have their own brand of magic. He'll be fine. And just in case . . .'

He brought out a wax figurine of a crocodile. 'This will help if the need arises.'

I coughed. 'A crocodile? After what we just—'

'It's Philip of Macedonia,' Amos explained.

'Philip is wax?'

'Of course,' Amos said. 'Real crocodiles are much too difficult to keep. And I *did* tell you he's magic.'

Amos tossed the figurine to Khufu, who sniffed it, then stuffed it into a pouch with his cooking supplies. Khufu gave me one last nervous look, glanced fearfully at Amos, then ambled over the dune with his bag in one arm and Muffin in the other.

I didn't see how they would survive out here, magic or no. I waited for Khufu to appear on the crest of the next dune, but he never did. He simply vanished.

'Now, then,' Amos said. 'From what Carter has told me, Set means to unleash his destruction tomorrow at sunrise. That gives us very little time. What Carter would *not* explain is how you plan to destroy Set.'

I glanced at Carter and saw warning in his eyes. I understood immediately, and felt a flush of gratitude. Perhaps the boy wasn't completely thick. He shared my concerns about Amos.

'It's best we keep that to ourselves,' I told Amos flatly. 'You said so yourself. What if Set attached a magic listening device to you or something?'

Amos's jaw tightened. 'You're right,' he said grudgingly. 'I can't trust myself. It's just . . . so frustrating.'

He sounded truly anguished, which made me feel guilty. I was tempted to change my mind and tell him our plan, but one look at Carter and I kept my resolve.

'We should head to Phoenix,' I said. 'Perhaps along the way . . .'

I slipped my hand into my pocket. Nut's letter was gone. I wanted to tell Carter about my talk with the earth god, Geb, but I didn't know if it was safe in front of Amos. Carter and I had been a team for so many days now, I realized that I resented Amos's presence a little. I didn't want to confide in anyone else. God, I can't believe I just said that.

Carter spoke up. 'We should stop in Las

Cruces.'

I'm not sure who was more surprised: Amos or me.

'That's near here,' Amos said slowly. 'But . . .' He picked up a handful of sand, murmured a spell, and threw the sand into the air. Instead of scattering, the grains floated and formed a wavering arrow, pointing southwest toward a line of rugged mountains that made a dark silhouette against the horizon.

'As I thought,' Amos said, and the sand fell to the earth. 'Las Cruces is out of our way by forty miles—over those mountains. Phoenix is northwest.'

'Forty miles isn't so bad,' I said. 'Las Cruces . . .' The name seemed strangely familiar to me, but I couldn't decide why. 'Carter, why there?'

'I just . . .' He looked so uncomfortable I knew it must have something to do with Zia. 'I had a vision.'

'A vision of loveliness?' I ventured.

He looked like he was trying to swallow a golf ball, which confirmed my suspicions. 'I just think we should go there,' he said. 'We might find something important.'

'Too risky,' Amos said. 'I can't allow it with the House of Life on your trail. We should stay in the wilderness, away from cities.'

Then suddenly: *click.* My brain had one of those amazing moments when it actually works correctly.

'No, Carter's right,' I said. 'We have to go there.'

It was my brother's turn to look surprised. 'I am? We do?'

'Yes.' I took the plunge and told them about my talk with Geb.

Amos brushed some sand off his jacket. 'That's interesting, Sadie. But I don't see how Las Cruces comes into play.'

'Because it's Spanish, isn't it?' I said. 'Las Cruces. *The crosses.* Just as Geb told me.'

Amos hesitated, then nodded reluctantly. 'Get in the boat.'

'A bit short on water for a boat ride, aren't we?' I asked.

But I followed him on board. Amos took off his coat and uttered a magic word. Instantly, the coat came to life, drifted to the stern and grasped the tiller.

Amos smiled at me, and some of that old twinkle came back into his eyes. 'Who needs water?'

The boat shuddered and lifted into the sky.

*   *   *

If Amos ever got tired of being a magician, he could've gotten a job as a sky boat tour operator. The vista coming over the mountains was quite stunning.

At first, the desert had seemed barren and ugly to me compared to the lush greens of England, but I was starting to appreciate that the desert had its own stark beauty, especially at night. The mountains rose like dark islands in a sea of lights. I'd never seen so many stars above us, and the dry wind smelled of sage and pine. Las Cruces spread out in the valley below—a glowing patchwork of streets and neighborhoods.

As we got closer, I saw that most of the town was nothing very remarkable. It might've been

Manchester or Swindon or any place, really, but Amos aimed our ship toward the south of the city, to an area that was obviously much older—with adobe buildings and tree-lined streets.

As we descended, I began to get nervous.

'Won't they notice us in a flying boat?' I asked. 'I mean, I know magic is hard to see, but—'

'This is New Mexico,' Amos said. 'They see UFOs here all the time.'

And with that, we landed on the roof of a small church.

It was like dropping back in time, or onto a Wild West film set. The town square was lined with stucco buildings like an Indian pueblo. The streets were brightly lit and crowded—it looked like a festival—with stall vendors selling strings of red peppers, Indian blankets, and other curios. An old stagecoach was parked next to a clump of cacti. In the plaza's bandstand, men with large guitars and loud voices played mariachi music.

'This is the historic area,' Amos said. 'I believe they call it Mesilla.'

'Have a lot of Egyptian stuff here, do they?' I asked dubiously.

'Oh, the ancient cultures of Mexico have a lot in common with Egypt,' Amos said, retrieving his coat from the stern rudder. 'But that's a talk for another day.'

'Thank god,' I muttered. Then I sniffed the air and smelled something strange but wonderful— like baking bread and melting butter, only spicier, yummier. 'I—am—*starving.*'

It didn't take long, walking the plaza, to discover handmade tortillas. God, they were good. I suppose London has Mexican restaurants. We've got everything else. But I'd never been to one, and I doubt the tortillas would've tasted this heavenly. A large woman in a white dress rolled out balls of dough in her flour-caked hands, flattened and baked the tortillas on a hot skillet, and handed them to us on paper napkins. They didn't need butter or jam or anything. They were so delicate, they just melted in my mouth. I made Amos pay for about a dozen, just for me.

Carter was enjoying himself too until he tried the red-chili tamales at another booth. I thought his face would explode. 'Hot!' he announced. 'Drink!'

'Eat more tortilla,' Amos advised, trying not to laugh. 'Bread cuts the heat better than water.'

I tried the tamales myself and found they were excellent, not nearly as hot as a good curry, so Carter was just being a wimp, as usual.

Soon we'd eaten our fill and began wandering the streets, looking for . . . well, I wasn't sure, exactly. Time was a-wasting. The sun was going down, and I knew this would be the last night for all of us unless we stopped Set, but I had no idea why Geb had sent me here. *You will also find what you need most.* What did that mean?

I scanned the crowds and caught a glimpse of a tall young guy with dark hair. A thrill went up my spine—*Anubis?* What if he was following me, making sure I was safe? What if *he* was what I needed most?

Wonderful thought, except it wasn't Anubis. I scolded myself for thinking I could have luck that good. Besides, Carter had seen Anubis as a jackal-headed monster. Perhaps Anubis's appearance with me was just a trick to befuddle my brain—a trick that worked *quite* well.

I was daydreaming about that, and about whether or not they had tortillas in the Land of the Dead, when I locked eyes with a girl across the plaza.

'Carter.' I grabbed his arm and nodded in the direction of Zia Rashid. 'Someone's here to see you.'

Zia was ready for battle in her loose black linen clothes, staff and wand in hand. Her dark choppy hair was blown to one side like she'd flown here on a strong wind. Her amber eyes looked about as friendly as a jaguar's.

Behind her was a vendor's table full of tourist souvenirs, and a poster that read: NEW MEXICO: LAND OF ENCHANTMENT. I doubted the vendor knew just how much enchantment was standing right in front of his merchandise.

'You came,' Zia said, which seemed a bit on the obvious side. Was it my imagination, or was she looking at Amos with apprehension—even fear?

'Yeah,' Carter said nervously. 'You, uh, remember Sadie. And this is—'

'Amos,' Zia said uneasily.

Amos bowed. 'Zia Rashid, it's been several years. I see Iskandar sent his best.'

Zia looked as if he'd smacked her in the face, and I realized Amos hadn't heard the news.

'*Um*, Amos,' I said. 'Iskandar is dead.'

He stared at us in disbelief as we told him the story.

'I see,' he said at last. 'Then the new Chief Lector is—'

'Desjardins,' I said.

'Ah. Bad news.'

Zia frowned. Instead of addressing Amos, she turned to me. 'Do not dismiss Desjardins. He's very powerful. You'll need his help—*our* help—to challenge Set.'

'Has it ever occurred to you,' I said, 'that Desjardins might be *helping* Set?'

Zia glared at me. 'Never. *Others* might. But not Desjardins.'

Clearly she meant Amos. I suppose that should've made me even more suspicious of him, but instead I got angry.

'You're blind,' I told Zia. 'Desjardins' first order as Chief Lector was to have us killed. He's trying to stop us, even though he *knows* Set is about to destroy the continent. And Desjardins was there that night at the British Museum. If Set needed a body—'

The top of Zia's staff burst into flame.

Carter quickly moved between us. 'Whoa, both of you just calm down. We're here to talk.'

'I *am* talking,' Zia said. 'You need the House of Life on your side. You have to convince Desjardins you're not a threat.'

'By surrendering?' I asked. 'No, thank you. I'd rather not be turned into a bug and squashed.'

Amos cleared his throat. 'I'm afraid Sadie is right. Unless Desjardins has changed since I last saw him, he is not a man who will listen to reason.'

Zia fumed. 'Carter, could we speak in *private?*'

He shifted from foot to foot. 'Look, Zia, I—I agree we need to work together. But if you're going to try to convince me to surrender to the House—'

'There's something I must tell you,' she insisted. 'Something you *need* to know.'

The way she said that made the hairs stand up on the back of my neck. Could this be what Geb meant? Was it possible that Zia held the key to defeating Set?

Suddenly Amos tensed. He pulled his staff out of thin air and said, 'It's a trap.'

Zia looked stunned. 'What? No!'

Then we all saw what Amos had sensed. Marching towards us from the east end of the plaza was Desjardins himself. He wore cream-colored robes with the Chief Lector's leopard-skin cape tied across his shoulders. His staff glowed purple. Tourists and pedestrians veered out of his way, confused and nervous, as if they weren't sure what was going on but they knew enough to clear off.

'Other way,' I urged.

I turned and saw two more magicians in black robes marching in from the west.

I pulled my wand and pointed it at Zia. 'You set us up!'

'No! I swear—' Her face fell. 'Mel. Mel must've told him.'

'Right,' I grumbled. 'Blame Mel.'

'No time for explanations,' Amos said, and he blasted Zia with a bolt of lightning. She crashed into the souvenir table.

'Hey!' Carter protested.

'She's the enemy,' Amos said. 'And we have enough enemies.'

Carter rushed to Zia's side (naturally) while more pedestrians panicked and scattered for the edges of the square.

'Sadie, Carter,' Amos said, 'if things go bad, get to the boat and flee.'

'Amos, we're not leaving you,' I said.

'You're more important,' he insisted. 'I can hold off Desjardins for— Look out!'

Amos spun his staff towards the two magicians in black. They'd been muttering spells, but Amos's gust of wind swept them off their feet, sending them swirling out of control at the center of a dust devil. They churned along the street, picking up trash, leaves, and tamales, until the miniature tornado tossed the screaming magicians over the top of a building and out of sight.

On the other side of the plaza, Desjardins roared in anger: 'Kane!'

The Chief Lector slammed his staff into the ground. A crack opened in the pavement and began snaking towards us. As the crevice grew wider, the buildings trembled. Stucco flaked off the walls. The fissure would've swallowed us, but Isis's voice spoke in my mind, telling me the word I needed.

I raised my wand. 'Quiet. *Hah-ri*.'

Hieroglyphs blazed to life in front of us.

The fissure stopped just short of my feet. The earthquake died.

Amos sucked in a breath. 'Sadie, how did you—'

'Divine Words, Kane!' Desjardins stepped forward, his face livid. 'The child dares speak the Divine Words. She is corrupted by Isis, and you are guilty of assisting the gods.'

'Step off, Michel,' Amos warned.

Part of me found it amusing that Desjardins' first name was Michel, but I was too scared to enjoy the moment.

Amos held out his wand, ready to defend us. 'We must stop Set. If you're wise—'

'I would what?' Desjardins said. 'Join you? Collaborate? The gods bring nothing but destruction.'

'No!' Zia's voice. With Carter's help, she'd somehow managed to struggle to her feet. 'Master, we can't fight each other. That's not what Iskandar wanted.'

'Iskandar is dead!' Desjardins bellowed. 'Now, step away from them, Zia, or be destroyed with them.'

Zia looked at Carter. Then she set her jaw and faced Desjardins. 'No. We must work together.'

I regarded Zia with a new respect. 'You really didn't lead him here?'

'I do not lie,' she said.

Desjardins raised his staff, and huge cracks appeared in the buildings all around him. Chunks of cement and adobe brick flew at us, but Amos summoned the wind and deflected them.

'Children, get out of here!' Amos yelled. 'The other magicians won't stay gone forever.'

'For once, he's right,' Zia warned. 'But we can't make a portal—'

'We've got a flying boat,' Carter offered.

Zia nodded appreciatively. 'Where?'

We pointed towards the church, but unfortunately Desjardins was between it and us.

Desjardins hurled another volley of stones. Amos deflected them with wind and lightning.

'Storm magic!' Desjardins sneered. 'Since when is Amos Kane an expert in the powers of chaos? Do you see this, children? How can he be your protector?'

'Shut up,' Amos growled, and with a sweep of his staff he raised a sandstorm so huge that it

389

blanketed the entire square.

'Now,' Zia said. We made a wide arc around Desjardins, then ran blindly towards the church. The sandstorm bit my skin and stung my eyes, but we found the stairs and climbed to the roof. The wind subsided, and across the plaza I could see Desjardins and Amos still facing each other, encased in shields of force. Amos was staggering; the effort was clearly taking too much out of him.

'I have to help,' Zia said reluctantly, 'or Desjardins will kill Amos.'

'I thought you didn't trust Amos,' Carter said.

'I don't,' she agreed. 'But if Desjardins wins this duel, we're all dead. We'll never escape.' She clenched her teeth as if she were preparing for something really painful.

She held out her staff and murmured an incantation. The air became warm. The staff glowed. She released it and it burst into flame, growing into a column of fire a full meter thick and four meters tall.

'Hunt Desjardins,' she intoned.

Immediately, the fiery column floated off the roof and began moving slowly but deliberately towards the Chief Lector.

Zia crumpled. Carter and I had to grab her arms to keep her from falling on her face.

Desjardins looked up. When he saw the fire, his eyes widened with fear. 'Zia!' he cursed. 'You *dare* attack me?'

The column descended, passing through the branches of a tree and burning a hole straight through them. It landed in the street, hovering just a few centimeters above the pavement. The heat was so intense that it scorched the concrete curb and melted the tarmac. The fire came to a parked car, and instead of going round, it burned its way straight through the metal chassis, sawing the car in two.

'Good!' Amos yelled from the street. 'Well done, Zia!'

In desperation, Desjardins staggered to his left. The column adjusted course. He blasted it with water, but the liquid evaporated into steam. He summoned boulders, but they just passed through the fire and dropped into melted, smoking lumps on the opposite side.

'What *is* that thing?' I asked.

Zia was unconscious, and Carter shook his head in wonder. But Isis spoke in my mind. *A pillar of fire,* she said with admiration. *It is the most powerful spell a master of fire can summon. It is impossible to defeat, impossible to escape. It can be used to lead the summoner toward a goal. Or it can be used to pursue any enemy, forcing him to run. If Desjardins tries to focus on anything else, it will overtake him and consume him. It will not leave him alone until it dissipates.*

How long? I asked.

Depends on the strength of the caster. Between six and twelve hours.

I laughed aloud. Brilliant! Of course Zia had passed out creating it, but it was still brilliant.

Such a spell has depleted her energy, Isis said. *She will not be able to work any magic until the pillar is gone. In order to help you, she has left herself completely powerless.*

'She'll be all right,' I told Carter. Then I shouted down to the plaza: 'Amos, come on! We've got to go!'

Desjardins kept backing up. I could tell he was scared of the fire, but he wasn't quite done with us. 'You will be sorry for this! You wish to play gods? Then you leave me no choice.' Out of the Duat, he pulled a cluster of sticks. No, they were arrows—about seven of them.

Amos looked at the arrows in horror. 'You wouldn't! No Chief Lector would ever—'

'I summon Sekhmet!' Desjardins bellowed. He threw the arrows into the air and they began to twirl, orbiting Amos.

Desjardins allowed himself a satisfied smile. He looked straight at me. 'You choose to place your faith in the gods?' he called. 'Then die by the hands of a god.'

He turned and ran. The pillar of fire picked up speed and followed.

'Children, get out of here!' Amos yelled, encircled by the arrows. 'I'll try to distract her!'

'Who?' I demanded. I knew I'd heard the name Sekhmet before, but I'd heard *a lot* of Egyptian names. 'Which one is Sekhmet?'

Carter turned to me, and even with all we'd been through over the last week, I had never seen him look so scared. 'We need to leave,' he said. *'Now.'*

33.
WE GO INTO THE SALSA BUSINESS

CARTER

You're forgetting something, Horus told me.

A little busy here! I thought back.

You might think it's easy steering a magic boat through the sky. You'd be wrong. I didn't have Amos's animated coat, so I stood in the back trying to shift the tiller myself, which was like stirring cement. I couldn't see where we were going. We kept tilting back and forth while Sadie tried her best to keep an unconscious Zia from flopping over the side.

It's my birthday, Horus insisted. *Wish me happy birthday!*

'Happy birthday!' I yelled. 'Now, shut up!'

'Carter, what are you on about?' Sadie screamed, grabbing the railing with one hand and Zia with the other as the boat tipped sideways. 'Have you lost your mind?'

'No, I was talking to—Oh, forget it.'

I glanced behind us. *Something* was approaching—a blazing figure that lit up the night. Vaguely humanoid, definitely bad news. I urged the boat to go faster.

Did you get me anything? Horus urged.

Will you please do something helpful? I demanded. *That thing following us—is that what I think it is?*

Oh. Horus sounded bored. *That's Sekhmet. The Eye of Ra, destroyer of the wicked, the great huntress,*

393

lady of flame, et cetera.

Great, I thought. *And she's following us because . . .*

The Chief Lector has the power to summon her once during his lifetime, Horus explained. *It's an old, old gift—goes back to the days when Ra first blessed man with magic.*

Once during his lifetime, I thought. *And Desjardins chooses now?*

He never was very good at being patient.

I thought that the magicians don't like gods!

They don't, Horus agreed. *Just shows you what a hypocrite he is. But I suppose killing you was more important than standing on principle. I can appreciate that.*

I looked back again. The figure was definitely getting closer—a giant golden woman in glowing red armor, with a bow in one hand and a quiver of arrows slung across her back—and she was hurtling toward us like a rocket.

How do we beat her? I asked.

You pretty much don't, Horus said. *She is the incarnation of the sun's wrath. Back in the days when Ra was active, she would've been much more impressive, but still. . . . She's unstoppable. A born killer. A slaying machine—*

'Okay, I get it!' I yelled.

'What?' Sadie demanded, so loud that Zia stirred.

'Wha—what?' Her eyes fluttered open.

'Nothing,' I shouted. 'We're being followed by a slaying machine. Go back to sleep.'

Zia sat up woozily. 'A slaying machine? You don't mean—'

'Carter, veer right!' Sadie yelled.

I did, and a flaming arrow the size of a predator drone grazed our port side. It exploded above us, setting the roof of our boathouse on fire.

I steered the boat into a dive, and Sekhmet shot past but then pirouetted in the air with irritating agility and dove after us.

'We're burning,' Sadie pointed out helpfully.

'Noticed!' I yelled back.

I scanned the landscape below us, but there was nowhere safe to land—just subdivisions and office parks.

'Die, enemies of Ra!' Sekhmet yelled. 'Perish in agony!'

She's almost as annoying as you, I told Horus.

Impossible, Horus said. *No one bests Horus.*

I took another evasive turn, and Zia yelled, 'There!'

She pointed toward a well-lit factory complex with trucks, warehouses, and silos. A giant chili pepper was painted on the side of the biggest warehouse, and a floodlit sign read: MAGIC SALSA, INC.

'Oh, please,' Sadie said. 'It's not really magic! That's just a name.'

'No,' Zia insisted. 'I've got an idea.'

'Those Seven Ribbons?' I guessed. 'The ones you used on Serqet?'

Zia shook her head. 'They can only be summoned once a year. But my plan—'

Another arrow blazed past us, only inches from our starboard side.

'Hang on!' I yanked at the tiller and spun the boat upside down just before the arrow exploded. The hull shielded us from the brunt of the blast, but the entire bottom of the ship was now on fire, and we were going down.

With my last bit of control, I aimed the boat toward the roof of the warehouse, and we crashed through, slamming into a huge mound of . . . something crunchy.

I clawed my way clear of the boat and sat up in a daze. Fortunately, the stuff we'd crashed into was soft. Unfortunately, it was a twenty-foot pile of dried chili peppers, and the boat had set them on fire. My eyes began to sting, but I knew better than to rub them, because my hands were now covered in chili oil.

'Sadie?' I called. 'Zia?'

'Help!' Sadie yelled. She was on the other side of the boat, dragging Zia out from under the flaming hull. We managed to pull her free and slide down the pile onto the floor.

The warehouse seemed to be a massive facility for drying peppers, with thirty or forty mountains of chilis and rows of wooden drying racks. The wreckage of our boat filled the air with spicy smoke, and through the hole we'd made in the roof, I could see the blazing figure of Sekhmet descending.

We ran, plowing through another pile of peppers. [No, I didn't pick a peck of them, Sadie— just shut up.] We hid behind a drying rack, where shelves of peppers made the air burn like hydrochloric acid.

Sekhmet landed, and the warehouse floor shuddered. Up close, she was even more terrifying. Her skin glowed like liquid gold, and her chest armor and skirt seemed to be woven of tiles made from molten lava. Her hair was like a thick lion's mane. Her eyes were feline, but they didn't sparkle like Bast's or betray any kindness or humor. Sekhmet's eyes blazed like her arrows, designed only to seek and destroy. She was beautiful the way an atomic explosion is beautiful.

'I smell blood!' she roared. 'I will feast on enemies of Ra until my belly is full!'

'Charming,' Sadie whispered. 'So Zia . . . this plan?'

Zia didn't look so well. She was shivering and pale, and seemed to have trouble focusing on us. 'When Ra . . . when he first called Sekhmet to punish humans because they were rebelling against him . . . she got out of hand.'

'Hard to imagine,' I whispered, as Sekhmet ripped through the burning wreckage of our boat.

'She started killing *everyone,'* Zia said, 'not just the -wicked. None of the other gods could stop her. She would just kill all day until she was gorged on blood. Then she'd leave until the next day. So the people begged the magicians to come up with a plan, and—'

'You dare hide?' Flames roared as Sekhmet's arrows destroyed pile after pile of dried peppers. 'I will roast you alive!'

'Run now,' I decided. 'Talk later.'

Sadie and I dragged Zia between us. We managed to get out of the warehouse just before the whole place imploded from the heat, billowing a spicy-hot mushroom cloud into the sky. We ran through a parking lot filled with semitrailers and hid behind a sixteen-wheeler.

I peeked out, expecting to see Sekhmet walk through the flames of the warehouse. Instead, she leaped out in the form of a giant lion. Her eyes blazed, and floating over her head was a disk of fire like a miniature sun.

'The symbol of Ra,' Zia whispered.

Sekhmet roared: 'Where are you, my tasty morsels?' She opened her maw and breathed a blast of hot air across the parking lot. Wherever her breath touched, the asphalt melted, cars disintegrated into sand, and the parking lot turned into barren desert.

'How did she do that?' Sadie hissed.

'Her breath creates the deserts,' Zia said. 'That is the legend.'

'Better and better.' Fear was closing up my throat, but I knew we couldn't hide much longer. I summoned my sword. 'I'll distract her. You two run—'

'No,' Zia insisted. 'There is another way.' She pointed at a row of silos on the other side of the lot. Each one was three stories tall and maybe twenty feet in diameter, with a giant chili pepper painted on the side.

'Petrol tanks?' Sadie asked.

'No,' I said. 'Must be salsa, right?'

Sadie stared at me blankly. 'Isn't that a type of music?'

'It's a hot sauce,' I said. 'That's what they make here.'

Sekhmet breathed in our direction, and the three trailers next to us melted into sand. We scuttled sideways and jumped behind a cinder block wall.

'Listen,' Zia gasped, her face beading with sweat. 'When the people needed to stop Sekhmet, they got huge vats of beer and colored them bright red with pomegranate juice.'

'Yeah, I remember now,' I interrupted. 'They

told Sekhmet it was blood, and she drank until she passed out. Then Ra was able to recall her into the heavens. They transformed her into something gentler. A cow goddess or something.'

'Hathor,' Zia said. 'That is Sekhmet's other form. The flip side of her personality.'

Sadie shook her head in disbelief. 'So you're saying we offer to buy Sekhmet a few pints, and she'll turn into a cow.'

'Not exactly,' Zia said. 'But salsa is red, is it not?'

*   *   *

We skirted the factory grounds as Sekhmet chewed up trucks and blasted huge swathes of the parking lot to sand.

'I hate this plan,' Sadie grumbled.

'Just keep her occupied for a few seconds,' I said. 'And don't die.'

'Yeah, that's the hard bit, isn't it?'

'One . . .' I counted. 'Two . . . three!'

Sadie burst into the open and used her favorite spell: *'Ha-di!'*

The glyphs blazed over Sekhmet's head.

And everything around her exploded. Trucks burst to pieces. The air shimmered with energy. The ground heaved upward, creating a crater fifty feet deep into which the lioness tumbled.

It was pretty impressive, but I didn't have time to admire Sadie's work. I turned into a falcon and launched myself toward the salsa tanks.

'RRAAAARR!' Sekhmet leaped out of the crater and breathed desert wind in Sadie's direction, but Sadie was long gone. She ran sideways, ducking

behind trailers and releasing a few lengths of magical rope as she fled. The ropes whipped through the air and tried to tie themselves around the lioness's mouth. They failed, of course, but they did annoy the Destroyer.

'Show yourself!' Sekhmet bellowed. 'I will feast on your flesh!'

Perched on a silo, I concentrated all my power and turned straight from falcon to avatar. My glowing form was so heavy, its feet sank into the top of the tank.

'Sekhmet!' I yelled.

The lioness whirled and snarled, trying to locate my voice.

'Up here, kitty!' I called.

She spotted me and her ears went back. 'Horus?'

'Unless you know another guy with a falcon head.'

She padded back and forth uncertainly, then roared in challenge. 'Why do you speak to me when I am in my raging form? You know I must destroy everything in my path, even you!'

'If you must,' I said. 'But first, you might like to feast on the blood of your enemies!'

I drove my sword into the tank and salsa gushed out in a chunky red waterfall. I leaped to the next tank and sliced it open. And again, and again, until six silofuls of Magic Salsa were spewing into the parking lot.

'Ha, ha!' Sekhmet loved it. She leaped into the red sauce torrent, rolling in it, lapping it up. 'Blood. Lovely blood!'

Yeah, apparently lions aren't too bright, or their taste buds aren't very developed, because Sekhmet didn't stop until her belly was bulging and her mouth literally began to smoke.

'Tangy,' she said, stumbling and blinking. 'But my eyes hurt. What kind of blood is this? Nubian? Persian?'

'Jalapeño,' I said. 'Try some more. It gets better.'

Her ears were smoking too now as she tried to drink more. Her eyes watered, and she began to stagger.

'I . . .' Steam curled from her mouth. 'Hot . . . hot mouth . . .'

'Milk is good for that,' I suggested. 'Maybe if you were a cow.'

'Trick,' Sekhmet groaned. 'You . . . you tricked . . .'

But her eyes were too heavy. She turned in a circle and collapsed, curling into a ball. Her form twitched and shimmered as her red armor melted into spots on her golden skin, until I was looking down at an enormous sleeping cow.

I dropped off the silo and stepped carefully around the sleeping goddess. She was making cow snoring sounds, like *Moo-zzz, moo-zzz.*' I waved my hand in front of her face, and when I was convinced she was out cold, I dispelled my avatar. Sadie and Zia emerged from behind a trailer.

'Well,' said Sadie, 'that was different.'

'I will never eat salsa again,' I decided.

'You both did wonderfully,' Zia said. 'But your boat is burned. How do we get to Phoenix?'

'*We?*' Sadie said. 'I don't recall inviting you.'

Zia's face turned salsa red. 'Surely you don't *still* think I led you into a trap?'

'I don't know,' Sadie said. 'Did you?'

401

I couldn't believe I was hearing this.

'Sadie.' My voice sounded dangerously angry, even to myself. '*Lay off.* Zia summoned that pillar-of-fire thing. She sacrificed her magic to save us. *And* she told us how to beat the lioness. We need her.'

Sadie stared at me. She glanced back and forth between Zia and me, probably trying to judge how far she could push things.

'Fine.' She crossed her arms and pouted. 'But we need to find Amos first.'

'No!' Zia said. 'That would be a very bad idea.'

'Oh, so we can trust you, but not Amos?'

Zia hesitated. I got the feeling that was *exactly* what she meant, but she decided to try a different approach. 'Amos would not want you to wait. He said to keep going, didn't he? If he survived Sekhmet, he will find us on the road. If not . . .'

Sadie huffed. 'So how do we get to Phoenix? Walk?'

I gazed across the parking lot, where one sixteen-wheeler was still intact. 'Maybe we don't have to.' I took off the linen coat I'd borrowed from Amos's supply locker. 'Zia, Amos had a way of animating his coat so it could steer his boat. Do you know the spell?'

She nodded. 'It's fairly simple with the right ingredients. I could do it if I had my magic.'

'Can you teach me?'

She pursed her lips. 'The hardest part is the figurine. The first time you enchant the piece of clothing, you'd need to smash a *shabti* into the fabric and speak a binding charm to meld them together. It would require a clay or wax figure that has already been imbued with a spirit.'

Sadie and I looked at each other, and simultaneously said, 'Doughboy!'

34.
DOUGHBOY GIVES US A RIDE

CARTER

I summoned Dad's magic toolkit out of the Duat and grabbed our little legless friend. 'Doughboy, we need to talk.'

Doughboy opened his wax eyes. "Finally! You realize how stuffy it is in there? At last you've remembered that you need my brilliant guidance.'

'Actually we need you to become a coat. Just for a while.'

His tiny mouth fell open. 'Do I look like an article of clothing? I am the lord of all knowledge! The mighty—'

I smashed him into my jacket, wadded it up, threw it on the pavement and stepped on it. 'Zia, what's that spell?'

She told me the words, and I repeated the chant. The coat inflated and hovered in front of me. It brushed itself off and ruffled its collar. If coats can look indignant, this one did.

Sadie eyed it suspiciously. 'Can it drive a lorry with no feet for the pedals?'

'Shouldn't be a problem,' Zia said. 'It's a nice long coat.'

I sighed with relief. For a moment, I'd imagined myself having to animate my pants, too. That could get awkward.

403

'Drive us to Phoenix,' I told the coat.

The coat made a rude gesture at me—or at least, it would've been rude if the coat had hands. Then it floated into the driver's seat.

The cab was bigger than I'd thought. Behind the seat was a curtained area with a full-size bed, which Sadie claimed immediately.

'I'll let you and Zia have some quality time,' she told me. 'Just the two of you and your coat.'

She ducked behind the curtains before I could smack her.

The coat drove us west on I-10 as a bank of dark clouds swallowed the stars. The air smelled like rain.

After a long time, Zia cleared her throat. 'Carter, I'm sorry about . . . I mean, I wish the circumstances were better.'

'Yeah,' I said. 'I guess you'll get in a lot of trouble with the House.'

'I will be shunned,' she said. 'My staff broken. My name blotted from the books. I'll be cast into exile, assuming they don't kill me.'

I thought about Zia's little shrine in the First Nome—all those pictures of her village and her family that she didn't remember. As she talked about getting exiled, she had the same expression on her face that she had worn then: not regret or sadness, more like confusion, as if she herself couldn't figure out why she was rebelling, or what the First Nome had meant to her. She'd said Iskandar was like her only family. Now she had no one.

'You could come with us,' I said.

She glanced over. We were sitting close together, and I was very aware of her shoulder pressing against mine. Even with the reek of burned peppers on both of us, I could smell her Egyptian perfume. She had a dried chili stuck in her hair, and somehow that made her look even cuter.

Sadie says my brain was just addled. [Seriously, Sadie, I don't interrupt this much when *you're* telling the story.]

Anyway, Zia looked at me sadly. 'Where would we go, Carter? Even if you defeat Set and save this continent, what will you do? The House will hunt you down. The gods will make your life miserable.'

'We'll figure it out,' I promised. 'I'm used to traveling. I'm good at improvising, and Sadie's not *all* bad.'

'I heard that!' Sadie's muffled voice came through the curtain.

'And with you,' I continued, 'I mean, you know, with your magic, things would be easier.'

Zia squeezed my hand, which sent a tingle up my arm. 'You're kind, Carter. But you don't know me. Not really. I suppose Iskandar saw this coming.'

'What do you mean?'

Zia took her hand away, which kind of bummed me out. 'When Desjardins and I came back from the British Museum, Iskandar spoke to me privately. He said I was in danger. He said he would take me somewhere safe and . . .' Her eyebrows knit together. 'That's odd. I don't remember.'

A cold feeling started gnawing at me. 'Wait, *did* he take you somewhere safe?'

'I . . . I think so.' She shook her head. 'No, he couldn't have, obviously. I'm still here. Perhaps he didn't have time. He sent me to find you in New York almost immediately.'

Outside, a light rain began to fall. The coat turned on our windshield wipers.

I didn't understand what Zia had told me. Perhaps Iskandar had sensed a change in Desjardins, and he was trying to protect his favorite student. But something else about the story bothered me—something I couldn't quite put my finger on.

Zia stared into the rain as if she saw bad things out there in the night.

'We're running out of time,' she said. 'He's coming back.'

'Who's coming back?'

She looked at me urgently. 'The thing I needed to tell you—the thing you need. It's Set's secret name.'

The storm surged. Thunder crackled and the truck shuddered in the wind.

'H-hold on,' I stammered. 'How could you know Set's name? How did you even know we needed it?'

'You stole Desjardins' book. Desjardins told us about it. He said it didn't matter. He said you could not use the spell without Set's secret name, which is impossible to get.'

'So how do *you* know it? Thoth said it could only come from Set himself, or from the person . . .' My voice trailed off as a horrible thought occurred to me. 'Or from the person closest to him.'

Zia shut her eyes as if in pain. 'I—I can't explain it, Carter. I just have this voice telling me the name—'

'The fifth goddess,' I said, 'Nephthys. You were there too at the British Museum.'

Zia looked completely stunned. 'No. That's impossible.'

'Iskandar said you were in danger. He wanted to take you somewhere safe. That's what he meant. You're a godling.'

She shook her head stubbornly. 'But he *didn't* take me away. I'm right here. If I were hosting a god, the other magicians of the House would've figured it out days ago. They know me too well. They would've noticed the changes in my magic. Desjardins would've destroyed me.'

She had a point—but then another terrible thought occurred to me. 'Unless Set is controlling him,' I said.

'Carter, are you really so blind? Desjardins is not Set.'

'Because you think it's Amos,' I said. 'Amos who risked his life to save us, who told us to keep going without him. Besides, Set doesn't need a human form. He's using the pyramid.'

'Which you know because . . .'

I hesitated. 'Amos told us.'

'This is getting us nowhere,' Zia said. 'I know Set's secret name, and I can tell you. But you must promise you will not tell Amos.'

'Oh, come on. Besides, if you know the name, why can't you just use it yourself?'

She shook her head, looking almost as frustrated as I felt. 'I don't know why. . . . I just know it's not my role to play. It must be you or Sadie—blood of the pharaohs. If you don't—'

The truck slowed abruptly. Out the front windshield, about twenty yards ahead, a man in a blue coat was standing in our headlights. It was Amos. His clothes were tattered like he'd been sprayed with a shotgun, but otherwise he looked okay. Before the truck had even stopped completely, I jumped out of the cab and ran to meet him.

'Amos!' I cried. 'What happened?'

'I distracted Sekhmet,' he said, putting a finger through one of the holes in his coat. 'For about eleven seconds. I'm glad to see you survived.'

'There was a salsa factory,' I started to explain, but Amos held up his hand.

'Time for explanations later,' he said. 'Right now we have to get going.'

He pointed northwest, and I saw what he meant. The storm was worse up ahead. A *lot* worse. A wall of black blotted out the night sky, the mountains, the highway, as if it would swallow the whole world.

'Set's storm is gathering,' Amos said with a twinkle in his eyes. 'Shall we drive into it?'

35.
MEN ASK FOR DIRECTIONS (AND OTHER SIGNS OF THE APOCALYPSE)

S A D I E

I don't know how I managed it with Carter and Zia yammering, but I got some sleep in the back of the truck. Even after the excitement of seeing Amos alive, as soon as we got going again I was back in the bunk and drifting off. I suppose a good *ha-di*

408

spell can really take it out of you.

Naturally, my *ba* took this as an opportunity to travel. Heaven forbid I get some *peaceful* rest.

I found myself back in London, on the banks of the Thames. Cleopatra's Needle rose up in front of me. It was a gray day, cool and calm, and even the smell of the low-tide muck made me feel homesick.

Isis stood next to me in a cloud-white dress, her dark hair braided with diamonds. Her multicolored wings faded in and out behind her like the Northern Lights.

'Your parents had the right idea,' she said. 'Bast was failing.'

'She was my friend,' I said.

'Yes. A good and loyal servant. But chaos cannot be kept down forever. It grows. It seeps into the cracks of civilization, breaks down the edges. It cannot be kept in balance. That is simply its nature.'

The obelisk rumbled, glowing faintly.

'Today it is the American continent,' Isis mused. 'But unless the gods are rallied, unless we achieve our full strength, chaos will soon destroy the entire human world.'

'We're doing our best,' I insisted. 'We'll beat Set.'

Isis looked at me sadly. 'You know that's not what I mean. Set is only the beginning.'

The image changed, and I saw London in ruins. I'd seen some horrific photos of the Blitz in World War II, but that was nothing compared to this. The city was leveled: rubble and dust for miles, the Thames choked with flotsam. The only thing standing was the obelisk, and as I watched, it

409

began to crack open, all four sides peeling away like some ghastly flower unfolding.

'Don't show me this,' I pleaded.

'It will happen soon enough,' Isis said, 'as your mother foresaw. But if you cannot face it . . .'

The scene changed again. We stood in the throne room of a palace—the same one I'd seen before, where Set had entombed Osiris. The gods were gathering, materializing as streams of light that shot through the throne room, curled round the pillars, and took on human form. One became Thoth with his stained lab coat, his wire-rimmed glasses, and his hair standing out all over his head. Another became Horus, the proud young warrior with silver and gold eyes. Sobek, the crocodile god, gripped his watery staff and snarled at me. A mass of scorpions scuttled behind a column and emerged on the other side as Serqet, the brown-robed arachnid goddess. Then my heart leaped, because I noticed a boy in black standing in the shadows behind the throne: Anubis, his dark eyes studying me with regret.

He pointed at the throne, and I saw it was empty. The palace was missing its heart. The room was cold and dark, and it was impossible to believe this had once been a place of celebrations.

Isis turned to me. 'We need a ruler. Horus must become pharaoh. He must unite the gods and the House of Life. It is the only way.'

'You can't mean Carter,' I said. 'My mess of a brother—pharaoh? Are you joking?'

'We have to help him. You and I.'

The idea was so ridiculous I would have laughed had the gods not been staring at me so gravely.

'Help him?' I said. 'Why doesn't he help *me*

become pharaoh?'

'There have been strong women pharaohs,' Isis admitted. 'Hatshepsut ruled well for many years. Nefertiti's power was equal to her husband's. But you have a different path, Sadie. Your power will not come from sitting on a throne. I think you know this.'

I looked at the throne, and I realized Isis had a point. The idea of sitting there with a crown on my head, trying to rule this lot of bad-tempered gods, did not appeal to me in the slightest. Still . . . Carter?

'You've grown strong, Sadie,' Isis said. 'I don't think you realize *how* strong. Soon, we will face the test together. We will prevail, if you maintain your courage and faith.'

'Courage and faith,' I said. 'Not my two strong suits.'

'Your moment comes,' Isis said. 'We depend on you.'

The gods gathered round, staring at me expectantly. They began to crowd in, pressing so close I couldn't breathe, grabbing my arms, shaking me . . . .

*   *   *

I woke to find Zia poking my shoulder. 'Sadie, we've stopped.'

I instinctively reached for my wand. 'What? Where?'

Zia pushed aside the curtains of the sleeping berth and leaned over me from the front seat, unnervingly like a vulture. 'Amos and Carter are in the gas station. You need to be prepared to move.'

411

'Why?' I sat up and looked out the windshield, straight into a raging sandstorm. 'Oh . . .'

The sky was black, so it was impossible to tell if it was day or night. Through the gale of wind and sand, I could see we were parked in front of a lighted petrol station.

'We're in Phoenix,' Zia said, 'but most of the city is shut down. People are evacuating.'

'Time?'

'Half past four in the morning,' Zia said. 'Magic isn't working very well. The closer we get to the mountain, the worse it is. And the truck's GPS system is down. Amos and Carter went inside to ask directions.'

That didn't sound promising. If two male magicians were desperate enough to stop for directions, we were in dire straits.

The truck's cab shook in the howling wind. After all we'd been through, I felt silly being scared of a storm, but I climbed over the seat so I could sit next to Zia and have some company.

'How long have they been in there?' I asked.

'Not long,' Zia said. 'I wanted to talk to you before they come back.'

I raised an eyebrow. 'About Carter? Well, if you're wondering whether he likes you, the way he stammers might be an indication.'

Zia frowned. 'No, I'm—'

'Asking if I mind? Very considerate. I must say at first I had my doubts, what with you threatening to kill us and all, but I've decided you're not a bad sort, and Carter's mad about you, so—'

'It's not about Carter.'

I wrinkled my nose. 'Oops. Could you just forget what I said, then?'

'It's about Set.'

'God,' I sighed. 'Not this again. Still suspicious of Amos?'

'You're blind not to see it,' Zia said. 'Set loves deception and traps. It is his favorite way to kill.'

Part of me knew she had a point. No doubt you'll think I was foolish not to listen. But have you ever sat by while someone talks badly about a member of your family? Even if it's not your favorite relative, the natural reaction is to defend them—at least it was for me, possibly because I didn't have that much family to begin with. 'Look, Zia, I can't believe Amos would—'

'*Amos* wouldn't,' Zia agreed. 'But Set can bend the mind and control the body. I'm not a specialist on possession, but it was a very common problem in ancient times. Minor demons are difficult enough to dislodge. A major god—'

'He's *not* possessed. He *can't* be.' I winced. A sharp pain was burning in my palm, in the spot where I'd last held the feather of truth. But I wasn't telling a lie! I *did* believe Amos was innocent . . . didn't I?

Zia studied my expression. 'You need Amos to be all right. He is your uncle. You've lost too many members of your family. I understand that.'

I wanted to snap back that she didn't understand anything, but her tone made me suspect she had known grief—possibly even more than I.

'We've got no choice,' I said. 'There's what, three hours till sunrise? Amos knows the best way into the mountain. Trap or no, we have to go there and try to stop Set.'

I could almost see the gears spinning in her

413

head as she searched for some way, *any* way to convince me.

'All right,' she said at last. 'I wanted to tell Carter something but I never got the opportunity. I'll tell you instead. The last thing you need to stop Set—'

'You couldn't possibly know his secret name.'

Zia held my gaze. Maybe it was the feather of truth, but I was certain she wasn't bluffing. She *did* have the name of Set. Or at least, she *believed* she did.

And honestly, I'd overheard bits of her conversation with Carter while I was in the back of the cab. I hadn't meant to eavesdrop, but it was hard not to. I looked at Zia, and tried to believe she was hosting Nephthys, but it didn't make any sense. I'd spoken with Nephthys. She'd told me she was far away in some sort of sleeping host. And Zia was right here in front of me.

'It will work,' Zia insisted. 'But I can't do it. It must be *you*.'

'Why not use it yourself?' I demanded. 'Because you spent all your magic?'

She waved away the question. 'Just promise me you will use it *now,* on Amos, before we reach the mountain. It may be your only chance.'

'And if you're wrong, we waste the only chance we have. The book disappears once it's used, right?'

Grudgingly, Zia nodded. 'Once read, the book will dissolve and appear somewhere else in the world. But if you wait any longer, we're doomed. If Set lures you into his base of power, you'll never have the strength to confront him. Sadie, please—'

'Tell me the name,' I said. 'I promise I'll use it at

414

the right time.'

'*Now* is the right time.'

I hesitated, hoping Isis would drop some words of wisdom, but the goddess was silent. I don't know if I would've relented. Perhaps things would've turned out differently if I'd agreed to Zia's plan. But before I could make that choice, the truck's doors opened, and Amos and Carter climbed in with a gust of sand.

'We're close.' Amos smiled as if this were good news. 'Very, very close.'

36.
OUR FAMILY IS VAPORIZED

SADIE

Less than a mile from Camelback Mountain, we broke through into a circle of perfect calm.

'Eye of the storm,' Carter guessed.

It was eerie. All around the mountain swirled a cylinder of black clouds. Traces of smoke drifted back and forth from Camelback's peak to the edges of the maelstrom like the spokes of a wheel, but directly above us, the sky was clear and starry, beginning to turn gray. Sunrise wasn't far off.

The streets were empty. Mansions and hotels clustered round the mountain's base, completely dark; but the mountain itself glowed. Ever hold your hand over a torch (sorry, a *flashlight* for you Americans) and watch the way your skin glows red? That's the way the mountain looked: something very bright and hot was trying to burn through the rock.

'Nothing's moving on the streets,' Zia said. 'If we try to drive up to the mountain—'

'We'll be seen,' I said.

'What about that spell?' Carter looked at Zia. 'You know . . . the one you used in the First Nome.'

'What spell?' I asked.

Zia shook her head. 'Carter is referring to an invisibility spell. But I have no magic. And unless you have the proper components, it can't be done on a whim.'

'Amos?' I asked.

He pondered the question. 'No invisibility, I'm afraid. But I have another idea.'

*   *   *

I thought turning into a bird was bad, until Amos turned us into storm clouds.

He explained what he was going to do in advance, but it didn't make me any less nervous.

'No one will notice a few wisps of black cloud in the midst of a storm,' he reasoned.

'But this is impossible,' Zia said. 'This is storm magic, *chaos* magic. We should not—'

Amos raised his wand, and Zia disintegrated.

'No!' Carter yelled, but then he too was gone, replaced by a swirl of black dust.

Amos turned to me.

'Oh, no,' I said. 'Thanks, but—'

Poof. I was a storm cloud. Now, that may sound amazing to you, but imagine your hands and feet disappearing, turning into wisps of wind. Imagine your body replaced by dust and vapor, and having

416

a tingly feeling in your stomach without even *having* a stomach. Imagine having to concentrate just to keep yourself from dispersing to nothing.

I got so angry, a flash of lightning crackled inside me.

'Don't be that way,' Amos chided. 'It's only for a few minutes. Follow me.'

He melted into a heavier, darker bit of storm and raced towards the mountain. Following wasn't easy. At first I could only float. Every wind threatened to take some part of me away. I tried swirling and found it helped keep my particles together. Then I imagined myself filling with helium, and suddenly I was off.

I couldn't be sure if Carter and Zia were following or not. When you're a storm, your vision isn't human. I could vaguely sense what was around me, but what I 'saw' was scattered and fuzzy, as if through heavy static.

I headed towards the mountain, which was an almost irresistible beacon to my storm self. It glowed with heat, pressure, and turbulence—everything a little dust devil like me could want.

I followed Amos to a ridge on the side of the mountain, but I returned to human form a little too soon. I tumbled out of the sky and knocked Carter to the ground.

'Ouch,' he groaned.

'Sorry,' I offered, though mostly I was concentrating on not getting sick. My stomach still felt like it was mostly storm.

Zia and Amos stood next to us, peeping into a crevice between two large sandstone boulders. Red light seeped from within and made their faces look devilish.

Zia turned to us. Judging from her expression, what she'd seen wasn't good. 'Only the pyramidion left.'

'The what?' I looked through the crevice, and the view was almost as disorienting as being a storm cloud. The entire mountain was hollowed out, just as Carter had described. The cavern floor was about six hundred meters below us. Fires blazed everywhere, bathing the rock walls in blood-colored light. A giant crimson pyramid dominated the cave, and at its base, masses of demons milled about like a rock concert crowd waiting for the show to begin. High above them, eye-level to us, two magic barges manned by crews of demons floated slowly, ceremoniously towards the pyramid. Suspended in a mesh of ropes between the boats was the only piece of the pyramid not yet installed—a golden capstone to top off the structure.

'They know they've won,' Carter guessed. 'They're making a show of it.'

'Yes,' Amos said.

'Well, let's blow up the boats or something!' I said.

Amos looked at me. 'Is *that* your strategy, honestly?'

His tone made me feel completely stupid. Looking down on the demon army, the enormous pyramid . . . what had I been thinking? I couldn't battle this. I was a bloody twelve-year-old.

'We have to try,' Carter said. 'Dad's in there.'

That shook me out of my self-pity. If we were going to die, at least we would do it trying to rescue my father (oh, and North America, too, I suppose).

418

'Right,' I said. 'We fly to those boats. We stop them from placing the capstone—'

'Pyramidion,' Zia corrected.

'Whatever. Then we fly into the pyramid and find Dad.'

'And when Set tries to stop you?' Amos asked.

I glanced at Zia, who was silently warning me not to say more.

'First things first,' I said. 'How do we fly to the boats?'

'As a storm,' Amos suggested.

'No!' the rest of us said.

'I will not be part of more chaos magic,' Zia insisted. 'It is *not* natural.'

Amos waved at the spectacle below us. 'Tell me *this* is natural. You have another plan?'

'Birds,' I said, hating myself for even considering it. 'I'll become a kite. Carter can do a falcon.'

'Sadie,' Carter warned, 'what if—'

'I have to try.' I looked away before I could lose my resolve. 'Zia, it's been almost ten hours since your pillar of fire, hasn't it? Still no magic?'

Zia held out her hand and concentrated. At first, nothing happened. Then red light flickered along her fingers, and her staff appeared in her grip, still smoking.

'Good timing,' Carter said.

'Also bad timing,' Amos observed. 'It means Desjardins is no longer pursued by the pillar of fire. He'll be here soon, and I'm sure he'll bring backup. More enemies for us.'

'My magic will still be weak,' Zia warned. 'I won't be much help in a fight, but I can perhaps manage to summon a ride.' She brought out the vulture pendant she'd used at Luxor.

'Which leaves me,' Amos said. 'No worries there. Let's meet on the left boat. We'll take that one out, then deal with the right. And let's hope for surprise.'

I wasn't in the mood to let Amos set our plans, but I couldn't find any fault with his logic. 'Right. We'll have to finish the boats off quickly, then head into the pyramid itself. Perhaps we can seal off the entrance or something.'

Carter nodded. 'Ready.'

At first, the plan seemed to go well. Turning into a kite was no problem, and to my surprise, once I reached the prow of the ship, I managed to turn back into a human on the first try, with my staff and wand ready. The only person more surprised was the demon right in front of me, whose switchblade head popped straight up in alarm.

Before he could slice me or even cry out, I summoned wind from my staff and blew him off the side of the boat. Two of his brethren charged forward, but Carter appeared behind them, sword drawn, and sliced them into piles of sand.

Unfortunately, Zia was a bit less stealthy. A giant vulture with a girl hanging from its feet tends to attract attention. As she flew towards the boat, demons below pointed and yelled. Some threw spears that fell short of their mark.

Zia's grand entrance did manage to distract the remaining two demons on our boat, however, which allowed Amos to appear behind them. He'd taken the form of a fruit bat, which brought back bad memories; but he quickly returned to human form and body-slammed the demons, sending them tumbling into the air.

'Hold on!' he told us. Zia landed just in time to grab the tiller. Carter and I grabbed the sides of the boat. I had no idea what Amos was planning, but after my last flying boat ride, I wasn't taking chances. Amos began to chant, pointing his staff towards the other boat, where the demons were just beginning to shout and point at us.

One of them was tall and very thin, with black eyes and a disgusting face, like muscle with the skin peeled away.

'That's Set's lieutenant,' Carter warned. 'Face of Horror.'

'You!' the demon screamed. 'Get them!'

Amos finished his spell. 'Smoke,' he intoned.

Instantly, the second boat evaporated into gray mist. The demons fell screaming. The golden capstone plummeted until the lines attached to it from our side yanked taut, and our boat nearly flipped over. Canted sideways, we began to sink towards the cavern floor.

'Carter, cut the lines!' I screamed.

He sliced them with his sword, and the boat leveled out, rising several meters in an instant and leaving my stomach behind.

The pyramidion crashed to the cavern floor with much crunching and squishing. I had the feeling we'd just made a nice stack of demon griddlecakes.

'So far so good,' Carter noted, but as usual, he'd spoken too soon.

Zia pointed below us. 'Look.'

All those demons who had wings—a small percentage, but still a good forty or fifty—had launched themselves towards us, filling the air like a swarm of angry wasps.

'Fly to the pyramid,' Amos said. 'I'll distract the demons.'

The pyramid's entrance, a simple doorway between two columns at the base of the structure, was not far from us. It was guarded by a few demons, but most of Set's forces were running towards our boat, screaming and throwing rocks (which tended to fall back down and hit them, but no one says demons are bright).

'They're too many,' I argued. 'Amos, they'll kill you.'

'Don't worry about me,' he said grimly. 'Seal the entrance behind you.'

He pushed me over the side, giving me no choice but to turn into a kite. Carter in falcon form was already spiraling towards the entrance, and I could hear Zia's vulture flapping its great wings behind us.

I heard Amos yell, 'For Brooklyn!'

It was an odd battle cry. I glanced back, and the boat burst into flames. It began drifting away from the pyramid and down towards the army of monsters. Fireballs shot from the boat in all directions as pieces of the hull crumbled away. I didn't have time to marvel at Amos's magic, or worry what had happened to him. He distracted many of the demons with his pyrotechnics, but some noticed us.

Carter and I landed just inside the pyramid's entrance and returned to human form. Zia tumbled in next to us and turned her vulture back into an amulet. The demons were only a few steps behind—a dozen massive blokes with the heads of insects, dragons, and assorted Swiss Army knife attachments.

Carter thrust out his hand. A giant shimmering fist appeared and mimicked his move—pushing right between Zia and me and slamming the doors shut. Carter closed his eyes in concentration, and a burning golden symbol etched itself across the doors like a seal: the Eye of Horus. The lines glowed faintly as demons hammered against the barrier, trying to get in.

'It won't hold them long,' Carter said.

I was duly impressed, though of course I didn't say that. Looking at the sealed doors, all I could think about was Amos, out there on a burning boat, surrounded by an evil army.

'Amos knew what he was doing,' Carter said, though he didn't sound very convinced. 'He's probably fine.'

'Come on,' Zia prodded us. 'No time for second guessing.'

*   *   *

The tunnel was narrow, red, and humid, so I felt like I was crawling through an artery of some enormous beast. We made our way down single file, as the tunnel sloped at about forty degrees—which would've made a lovely waterslide but wasn't so good for stepping carefully. The walls were decorated with intricate carvings, like most Egyptian walls we'd seen, but Carter obviously didn't like them. He kept stopping, scowling at the pictures.

'What?' I demanded, after the fifth or sixth time.

'These aren't normal tomb drawings,' he said. 'No afterlife pictures, no pictures of the gods.'

Zia nodded. 'This pyramid is not a tomb. It is a platform, a body to contain the power of Set. All these pictures are to increase chaos, and make it reign forever.'

As we kept walking, I paid more attention to the carvings, and I saw what Zia meant. The pictures showed horrible monsters, scenes of war, cities such as Paris and London in flames, full-color portraits of Set and the Set animal tearing into modern armies—scenes so gruesome, no Egyptian would ever commit them to stone. The farther we went, the weirder and more vivid the pictures became, and the queasier I felt.

Finally we reached the heart of the pyramid.

Where the burial chamber should've been in a regular pyramid, Set had designed a throne room for himself. It was about the size of a tennis court, but around the edges, the floor dropped off into a deep trench like a moat. Far, far below, red liquid bubbled. Blood? Lava? Evil ketchup? None of the possibilities were good.

The trench looked easy enough to jump, but I wasn't anxious to do so because inside the room, the entire floor was carved with red hieroglyphs—all spells invoking the power of Isfet, chaos. Far above in the center of the ceiling, a single square hole let in blood-red light. Otherwise, there seemed to be no exits. Along either wall crouched four obsidian statues of the Set animal, their faces turned towards us with pearl teeth bared and emerald eyes glittering.

But the worst part was the throne itself. It was a horrid misshapen thing, like a red stalagmite that had grown haphazardly from centuries of dripping sediment. And it had formed itself around a gold coffin—*Dad's* coffin—which was buried in the throne's base, with just enough of it sticking out to form a kind of footrest.

'How do we get him out?' I said, my voice trembling.

Next to me, Carter caught his breath. 'Amos?'

I followed his gaze up to the glowing red vent in the middle of the ceiling. A pair of legs dangled from the opening. Then Amos dropped down, opening his cloak like a parachute so that he floated to the floor. His clothes were still smoking, his hair dusted with ash. He pointed his staff towards the ceiling and spoke a command. The shaft he'd come through rumbled, spilling dust and rubble, and the light was abruptly cut off.

Amos dusted off his clothes and smiled at us. 'That should hold them for a while.'

'How did you do that?' I asked.

He gestured for us to join him in the room.

Carter jumped the trench without hesitation. I didn't like it, but I wasn't going to let him go without me, so I hopped the trench too. Immediately I felt even queasier than before, as if the room were tilting, throwing my senses off balance.

Zia came over last, eyeing Amos carefully.

'You should not be alive,' she said.

Amos chuckled. 'Oh, I've heard that before. Now, let's get to business.'

'Yes.' I stared at the throne. 'How do we get the coffin out?'

'Cut it?' Carter drew his sword, but Amos held up his hand.

'No, children. That's not the business I mean. I've made sure no one will interrupt us. Now it's time we talked.'

A cold tingle started up my spine. 'Talked?'

Suddenly Amos fell to his knees and began to convulse. I ran towards him, but he looked up at me, his face racked with pain. His eyes were molten red.

'*Run!*' he groaned.

He collapsed, and red steam issued from his body.

'We have to go!' Zia grabbed my arm. '*Now!*'

But I watched, frozen in horror, as the steam rose from Amos's unconscious form and drifted towards the throne, slowly taking the shape of a seated man—a red warrior in fiery armor, with an iron staff in his hand and the head of a canine monster.

'Oh, dear,' Set laughed. 'I suppose Zia gets to say "I told you so."'

37.
LEROY GETS HIS REVENGE

Maybe I'm a slow learner, okay?

Because it wasn't until that moment, facing the god Set in the middle of his throne room, in the heart of an evil pyramid, with an army of demons outside and the world about to explode, that I thought, *Coming here was a really* bad *idea.*

Set rose from his throne. He was red skinned and muscular, with fiery armor and a black iron staff. His head shifted from bestial to human. One moment he had the hungry stare and slavering jaws of my old friend Leroy, the monster from the

426

D.C. airport. The next he had sandy hair and a handsome but harsh face, with intelligent eyes that sparkled with humor and a cruel, crooked smile. He kicked our uncle out of the way and Amos groaned, which at least meant he was alive.

I was clenching my sword so tight, the blade trembled.

'Zia was right,' I said. 'You possessed Amos.'

Set spread his hands, trying to look modest. 'Well, you know . . . It wasn't a *full* possession. Gods can exist in many places at once, Carter. Horus could tell you that if he was being honest. I'm sure Horus has been looking for a nice war monument to occupy, or a military academy somewhere—anything but that scrawny little form of yours. Most of my being has now transferred to this magnificent structure.'

He swept his arm proudly around the throne room. 'But a sliver of my soul was quite enough to control Amos Kane.'

He held out his pinky, and a wisp of red smoke snaked toward Amos, sinking into his clothes. Amos arched his back like he'd been hit by lightning.

'Stop it!' I yelled.

I ran toward Amos, but the red mist had already dissipated. Our uncle's body went slack.

Set dropped his hand as if bored with the attack. 'Not much left, I'm afraid. Amos fought well. He was very entertaining, demanding much more of my energy than I had anticipated. That chaos magic—that was *his* idea. He tried his best to warn you, to make it obvious I was controlling him. The funny thing is, I forced him to use his own magic reserves to pull off those spells. He almost burned

427

out his soul trying to send you those warning flares. Turn you into a storm? Please. Who does that anymore?'

'You're a beast!' Sadie shouted.

Set gasped in mock surprise. 'Really? Me?'

Then he roared with laughter as Sadie tried to drag Amos out of harm's way.

'Amos was in London that night,' I said, hoping to keep his attention on me. 'He must've followed us to the British Museum, and you've been controlling him ever since. Desjardins was never your host.'

'Oh, that commoner? Please,' Set sneered. 'We always prefer blood of the pharaohs, as I'm sure you've heard. But I did love fooling you. I thought the *bon soir* was an especially nice touch.'

'You knew my *ba* was there, watching. You forced Amos to sabotage his own house so your monsters could get in. You made him walk into an ambush. Why didn't you just have him kidnap us?'

Set spread his hands. 'As I said, Amos put up a good fight. There were certain things I could not make him do without destroying him completely, and I didn't want to ruin my new plaything quite so soon.'

Anger burned inside me. Amos's odd behavior finally made sense. Yes, he had been controlled by Set, but he'd been fighting it all the way. The conflict I'd felt in him had been his attempts to warn us. He'd almost destroyed himself trying to save us, and Set had thrown him aside like a broken toy.

Give me control, Horus urged. *We will avenge him.*

I've got this, I said.

428

No! Horus said. *You must let me. You are not ready.*

Set laughed as if he could sense our struggle. 'Oh, poor Horus. Your host needs training wheels. You seriously expect to challenge me with *that*?'

For the first time, Horus and I had the same feeling at exactly the same moment: *rage*.

Without thinking, we raised our hand, extending our energy toward Set. A glowing fist slammed into him, and the Red God flew backward with such force, he cracked a column, which tumbled down on top of him.

For a heartbeat, the only sound was the trickle of dust and debris. Then out of the rubble came a deep howl of laughter. Set rose from the ruins, tossing aside a huge chunk of stone.

'Nice!' he roared. 'Completely ineffective, but nice! It will be a pleasure chopping you to bits, Horus, as I did your father before you. I will entomb you all in this chamber to increase my storm—all four of my precious siblings, and the storm will be large enough to envelop the world!'

I blinked, momentarily losing my focus. 'Four?'

'Oh, yes.' Set's eyes drifted to Zia, who had quietly retreated to one side of the room. 'I haven't forgotten you, my dear.'

Zia glanced at me in desperation. 'Carter, don't worry about me. He's trying to distract you.'

'Lovely goddess,' Set purred. 'The form does not do you justice, but your choices were limited, weren't they?'

Set moved toward her, his staff beginning to glow.

'No!' I shouted. I advanced, but Set was just as good at magical shoving as I was. He pointed at me, and I slammed against the wall, pinned as if an entire football team were holding me down.

'Carter!' Sadie cried. 'She's Nephthys. She can take care of herself!'

'No.' All my instincts told me Zia couldn't be Nephthys. At first I'd thought so, but the more I considered, the more it seemed wrong. I felt no divine magic from her, and something told me I would have if she were really hosting a goddess.

Set would crush her unless I helped. But if Set was trying to distract me, it was working. As he stalked toward Zia, I struggled against his magic, but I couldn't free myself. The more I tried to combine my power with Horus's, the way I'd done before, the more my fear and panic got in the way.

You must yield to me! Horus insisted, and the two of us wrestled for control of my mind, which gave me a splitting headache.

Set took another step toward Zia.

'Ah, Nephthys,' he crooned. 'At the beginning of time, you were my treacherous sister. In another incarnation, in another age, you were my treacherous wife. Now, I think you'll make a nice appetizer. True, you're the weakest of us all, but you're still one of the five, and there *is* power in collecting the complete set.'

He paused, then grinned. 'The complete Set! That's funny! Now let's consume your energy and entomb your soul, shall we?'

Zia thrust out her wand. A red sphere of defensive energy glowed around her, but even I could tell it was weak. Set shot a blast of sand from his staff and the sphere collapsed. Zia stumbled backward, the sand ripping at her hair and clothes. I struggled to move, but Zia yelled, 'Carter, I'm

430

not important! Stay focused! Don't resist!'

She raised her staff and shouted, 'The House of Life!'

She launched a bolt of fire at Set—an attack that must have cost all of her remaining energy. Set batted the flames aside, straight at Sadie, who had to raise her wand quickly to protect herself and Amos from getting fried. Set tugged at the air as if pulling an invisible rope, and Zia flew toward him like a rag doll, straight into his hand.

Don't resist. How could Zia say that? I resisted like crazy, but it didn't do me any good. All I could do was stare helplessly as Set lowered his face to Zia's and examined her.

At first Set seemed triumphant, gleeful, but his expression quickly turned to confusion. He scowled, his eyes flaring.

'What trick is this?' he growled. 'Where have you hidden her?'

'You will not possess her,' Zia managed, her breath choked off by his grip.

'Where *is* she?' He threw Zia aside.

She slammed against the wall and would've slid into the moat, but Sadie yelled 'Wind!' and a gust of air lifted Zia's body just enough for her to tumble onto the floor.

Sadie ran over and dragged her away from the glowing trench.

Set roared, 'Is this your trickery, Isis?' He sent another blast of sandstorm against them, but Sadie held up her wand. The storm met a shield of force that deflected the wind around it—the sand pitted the walls behind Sadie, making a halo-shaped scar in the rock.

I didn't understand what Set was so angry about,

431

but I couldn't allow him to hurt Sadie.

Seeing her alone, protecting Zia from the wrath of a god, something inside me clicked, like an engine shifting into higher gear. My thinking suddenly became faster and clearer. The anger and fear didn't go away, but I realized they weren't important. They weren't going help me save my sister.

Don't resist, Zia had told me.

She didn't mean resisting Set. She meant Horus. The falcon god and I had been wrestling with each other for days as he tried to take control of my body.

But *neither* of us could be in control. That was the answer. We had to act in unison, trust each other completely, or we were both dead.

Yes, Horus thought, and he stopped pushing. I stopped resisting, letting our thoughts flow together. I understood his power, his memories, and his fears. I saw every host he had ever been over a thousand lifetimes. And he saw my mind—everything, even the stuff I wasn't proud of.

It's hard to describe the feeling. And I knew from Horus's memory that this kind of union was *very* rare—like the one time when the coin doesn't land heads *or* tails, but stands on its edge, perfectly balanced. He did not control me. I did not use him for power. We acted as one.

Our voices spoke in harmony: 'Now.'

And the magic bonds that held us shattered.

My combat avatar formed around me, lifting me off the floor and encasing me with golden energy. I stepped forward and raised my sword. The falcon warrior mimicked the movement, perfectly attuned to my wishes.

Set turned and regarded me with cold eyes.

'So, Horus,' he said. 'You managed to find the pedals of your little bike, eh? That does not mean you can ride.'

'I am Carter Kane,' I said. 'Blood of the Pharaohs, Eye of Horus. And now, Set—brother, uncle, traitor—I'm going to crush you like a gnat.'

38.

THE HOUSE IS IN THE HOUSE

CARTER

It was a fight to the death, and I felt great.

Every move was perfect. Every strike was so much fun I wanted to laugh out loud. Set grew in size until he was larger than me, and his iron staff the size of a boat's mast. His face would flicker, sometimes human, sometimes the feral maw of the Set animal.

We clashed sword against staff and sparks flew. He pushed me off balance, and I smashed into one of his animal statues, which toppled to the floor and broke. I regained my balance and charged, my blade biting into a chink of Set's shoulder guard. He howled as black blood seeped from the wound.

He swung his staff, and I rolled before the strike could split my head. His staff cracked the floor instead. We fought back and forth, smashing pillars and walls, with chunks of the ceiling falling around us, until I realized Sadie was yelling to get my attention.

Out of the corner of my eye, I saw her trying to

shield Zia and Amos from the destruction. She'd drawn a hasty protective circle on the floor, and her shields were deflecting the falling debris, but I understood why she was worried: much more of this, and the entire throne room would collapse, crushing all of us. I doubted it would hurt Set much. He was probably counting on that. He *wanted* to entomb us here.

I had to get him into the open. Maybe if I gave Sadie time, she could free Dad's coffin from that throne.

Then I remembered how Bast had described her fight with Apophis: grappling with the enemy for eternity.

Yes, Horus agreed.

I raised my fist and channeled a burst of energy toward the air vent above us, blasting it open until red light once again poured through. Then I dropped my sword and launched myself at Set. I grabbed his shoulders with my bare hands, trying to get him in a wrestler's hold. He attempted to pummel me, but his staff was useless at close range. He growled and dropped the weapon, then grabbed my arms. He was much stronger than I was, but Horus knew some good moves. I twisted and got behind Set, my forearm slipping under his arm and grabbing his neck in a vise. We stumbled forward, almost stepping on Sadie's protective shields.

Now we've got him, I thought. *What do we do with him?*

Ironically, it was Amos who gave me the answer. I remembered how he'd turned me into a storm, overcoming my sense of self by sheer mental force. Our minds had had a brief battle, but he had

434

imposed his will with absolute confidence, imagining me as a storm cloud, and that's what I'd become.

You're a fruit bat, I told Set.

No! his mind yelled, but I had surprised him. I could feel his confusion, and I used it against him. It was easy to imagine him as a bat, since I'd seen Amos become one when he was possessed by Set. I pictured my enemy shrinking, growing leathery wings and an even uglier face. I shrank too, until I was a falcon with a fruit bat in my claws. No time to waste; I shot toward the air vent, wrestling with the bat as we spun in circles up the shaft, slashing and biting. Finally we burst into the open, reverting to our warrior forms on the side of the red pyramid.

I stood uneasily on the slope. My avatar shimmered with damage along the right arm, and my own arm was cut and bleeding in the same spot. Set rose, wiping black blood from his mouth.

He grinned at me, and his face flickered with the snarl of a predator. 'You can die knowing you made a good effort, Horus. But it's much too late. Look.'

I gazed out over the cavern, and my heart crawled into my throat. The army of demons had engaged a new enemy in battle. Magicians—dozens of them—had appeared in a loose circle around the pyramid and were fighting their way forward. The House of Life must have gathered all its available forces, but they were pathetically few against Set's legions. Each magician stood inside a moving protective circle, like a spotlight beam, wading through the enemy with staff and wand glowing. Flames, lightning, and tornadoes ripped

435

through the demon host. I spotted all kinds of summoned beasts—lions, serpents, sphinxes, and even some hippos charging through the enemy like tanks. Here and there, hieroglyphs glowed in the air, causing explosions and earthquakes that destroyed Set's forces. But more demons just kept coming, surrounding the magicians in deeper and deeper ranks. I watched as one magician was completely overwhelmed, his circle broken in a flash of green light, and he went down under the enemy wave.

'This is the end of the House,' Set said with satisfaction. 'They cannot prevail as long as my pyramid stands.'

The magicians seemed to know this. As they got closer, they sent fiery comets and bolts of lightning toward the pyramid; but each blast dissipated harmlessly against its stone slopes, consumed in the red haze of Set's power.

Then I spotted the golden capstone. Four snake-headed giants had retrieved it and were carrying it slowly but steadily through the melee. Set's lieutenant Face of Horror shouted orders to them, lashing them with a whip to keep them moving. They pressed forward until they reached the pyramid's base and began to climb.

I charged toward them, but Set intervened in an instant, placing himself in my path.

'I don't think so, Horus,' he laughed. 'You won't ruin this party.'

We both summoned our weapons to our hands and fought with renewed ferocity, slicing and dodging. I brought my sword down in a deadly arc, but Set ducked aside and my blade hit stone, sending a shock wave through my whole body.

Before I could recover, Set spoke a word: *'Ha-wi!'*
Strike.

The hieroglyphs exploded in my face and sent me tumbling down the side of the pyramid.

When my vision cleared, I saw Face of Horror and the snake-headed giants far above me, lugging their golden load up the side of the monument, only a few steps from the top.

'No,' I muttered. I tried to rise, but my avatar form was sluggish.

Then out of nowhere a magician catapulted into the midst of the demons and unleashed a gale of wind. Demons went flying, dropping the capstone, and the magician struck it with his staff, stopping it from sliding. The magician was Desjardins. His forked beard and robes and leopard-skin cape were singed with fire, and his eyes were full of rage. He pressed his staff against the capstone, and its golden shape began to glow; but before Desjardins could destroy it, Set rose up behind him and swung his iron rod like a baseball bat.

Desjardins tumbled, broken and unconscious, all the way down the pyramid, disappearing into the mob of demons. My heart twisted. I'd never liked Desjardins, but no one deserved a fate like that.

'Annoying,' Set said. 'But not effective. This is what the House of Life has reduced itself to, eh, Horus?'

I charged up the slope, and again our weapons clanged together. We fought back and forth as gray light began to seep through the cracks in the mountain above us.

Horus's keen senses told me we had about two minutes until sunrise, maybe less.

437

Horus's energy kept surging through me. My avatar was only mildly damaged, my attacks still swift and strong. But it wasn't enough to defeat Set, and Set knew it. He was in no hurry. With every minute, another magician went down on the battlefield, and chaos got closer to winning.

Patience, Horus urged. *We fought him for seven years the first time.*

But I knew we didn't have seven minutes, much less seven years. I wished Sadie were here, but I could only hope she'd managed to free Dad and keep Zia and Amos safe.

That thought distracted me. Set swept his staff at my feet, and instead of jumping, I tried to back up. The blow cracked against my right ankle, knocking me off balance and sending me somersaulting down the pyramid's side.

Set laughed. 'Have a nice trip!' Then he picked up the capstone.

I rose, groaning, but my feet were like lead. I staggered up the slope, but before I'd closed even half the distance, Set placed the capstone and completed the structure. Red light flowed down the sides of the pyramid with a sound like the world's largest bass guitar, shaking the entire mountain and making my whole body go numb.

'Thirty seconds to sunrise!' Set yelled with glee. 'And this land will be mine forever. You can't stop me alone, Horus—especially not in the desert, the source of my strength!'

'You're right,' said a nearby voice.

I glanced over and saw Sadie rising from the air vent—radiant with multicolored light, her staff and wand glowing.

'Except Horus is *not* alone,' she said. 'And we're

not going to fight you in the desert.'

She struck her staff against the pyramid and shouted a name: the last words I'd ever expect her to utter as a battle cry.

39.
ZIA TELLS ME A SECRET

SADIE

Cheers, Carter, for making me look dramatic and all that.

The truth was a bit less glamorous.

Back up, shall we? When my brother, the crazy chicken warrior, turned into a falcon and went up the pyramid's chimney with his new friend, the fruit bat, he left me playing nurse to two very wounded people—which I didn't appreciate, and which I wasn't particularly good at.

Poor Amos's wounds seemed more magical than physical. He didn't have a mark on him, but his eyes were rolled up in his head, and he was barely breathing. Steam curled from his skin when I touched his forehead, so I decided I'd best leave him for the moment.

Zia was another story. Her face was deathly pale, and she was bleeding from several nasty cuts on her leg. One of her arms was twisted at a bad angle. Her breath rattled with a sound like wet sand.

'Hold still.' I ripped some cloth from the hem of my pants and tried to bind her leg. 'Maybe there's some healing magic or—'

'Sadie.' She gripped my wrist feebly. 'No time. Listen.'

'If we can stop the bleeding—'

'His name. You need his name.'

'But you're not Nephthys! Set said so.'

She shook her head. 'A message . . . I speak with her voice. The name—Evil Day. Set was born, and it was an *Evil Day.*'

True enough, I thought, but could that really be Set's secret name? What Zia was talking about, not being Nephthys but speaking with her voice— it made no sense. Then I remembered the voice at the river. Nephthys had said she would send a message. And Anubis had made me promise I would listen to Nephthys.

I shifted uncomfortably. 'Look, Zia—'

Then the truth hit me in face. Some things Iskandar had said, some things Thoth had said— they all clicked together. Iskandar had wanted to protect Zia. He'd told me if he'd realized Carter and I were godlings sooner, he could've protected us as well as . . . someone. As well as *Zia.* Now I understood how he'd tried to protect her.

'Oh, god.' I stared at her. 'That's it, isn't it?'

She seemed to understand, and she nodded. Her face contorted with pain, but her eyes remained as fierce and insistent as ever. 'Use the name. Bend Set to your will. Make him help.'

'*Help?* He just tried to kill you, Zia. He's not the *helping* type.'

'Go.' She tried to push me away. Flames sputtered weakly from her fingers. 'Carter needs you.'

That was the one thing she might've said to spur me on. Carter was in trouble.

440

'I'll be back, then,' I promised. 'Don't . . . *um*, go anywhere.'

I stood and stared at the hole in the ceiling, dreading the idea of turning into a kite again. Then my eyes fixed on Dad's coffin, buried in the red throne. The sarcophagus was glowing like something radioactive, heading for meltdown. If I could only break the throne . . .

Set must be dealt with first, Isis warned.

But if I can free Dad . . . I stepped towards the throne.

No, Isis warned. *What you might see is too dangerous.*

What are you talking about? I thought irritably. I put my hand on the golden coffin. Instantly I was ripped from the throne room and into a vision.

I was back in the Land of the Dead, in the Hall of Judgment. The crumbling monuments of a New Orleans graveyard shimmered around me. Spirits of the dead stirred restlessly in the mist. At the base of the broken scales, a tiny monster slept—Ammit the Devourer. He opened one glowing yellow eye to study me, then went back to sleep.

Anubis stepped out of the shadows. He was dressed in a black silk suit with his tie unknotted, like he'd just come back from a funeral or possibly a convention for really gorgeous undertakers. 'Sadie, you shouldn't be here.'

'Tell me about it,' I said, but I was so glad to see him, I wanted to sob with relief.

He took my hand and led me towards the empty black throne. 'We have lost all balance. The throne cannot be empty. The restoration of Ma'at must begin here, in this hall.'

He sounded sad, as if he were asking me to

accept something terrible. I didn't understand, but a profound sense of loss crept over me.

'It's not fair,' I said.

'No, it's not.' He squeezed my hand. 'I'll be here, waiting. I'm sorry, Sadie. I truly am . . .'

He started to fade.

'Wait!' I tried to hold on to his hand, but he melted into mist along with the graveyard.

I found myself back in the throne room of the gods, except it looked like it had been abandoned for centuries. The roof had fallen in, along with half of the columns. The braziers were cold and rusty. The beautiful marble floor was as cracked as a dry lakebed.

Bast stood alone next to the empty throne of Osiris. She gave me a mischievous smile, but seeing her again was almost too painful to bear.

'Oh, don't be sad,' she chided. 'Cats don't do regret.'

'But aren't you—aren't you dead?'

'That all depends.' She gestured around her. 'The Duat is in turmoil. The gods have gone too long without a king. If Set doesn't take over, someone else must. The enemy is coming. Don't let me die in vain.'

'But will you come back?' I asked, my voice breaking. 'Please, I never even got to say good-bye to you. I can't—'

'Good luck, Sadie. Keep your claws sharp.' Bast vanished, and the scenery changed again.

I stood in the Hall of Ages, in the First Nome—another empty throne—and Iskandar sat at its feet, waiting for a pharaoh who hadn't existed for two thousand years.

'A leader, my dear,' he said. 'Ma'at demands a

leader.'

'It's too much,' I said. 'Too many thrones. You can't expect Carter—'

'Not alone,' Iskandar agreed. 'But this is your family's burden. You started the process. The Kanes alone will heal us or destroy us.'

'I don't know what you mean!'

Iskandar opened his hand, and in a flash of light, the scene changed one more time.

I was back at the Thames. It must've been the dead of the night, three o'clock in the morning, because the Embankment was empty. Mist obscured the lights of the city, and the air was wintry.

Two people, a man and a woman, stood bundled against the cold, holding hands in front of Cleopatra's Needle. At first I thought they were a random couple on a date. Then, with a shock, I realized I was looking at my parents.

My dad lifted his face and scowled at the obelisk. In the dim glow of the streetlamps, his features looked like chiseled marble—like the pharaoh statues he loved to study. He *did* have the face of a king, I thought—proud and handsome.

'You're sure?' he asked my mother. 'Absolutely sure?'

Mum brushed her blond hair out of her face. She was even more beautiful than her pictures, but she looked worried—eyebrows furrowed, lips pressed together. Like *me* when I was upset, when I looked in the mirror and tried to convince myself things weren't so bad. I wanted to call to her, to let her know I was there, but my voice wouldn't work.

'She told me this is where it begins,' my mother said. She pulled her black coat around her, and I

443

caught a glimpse of her necklace—the amulet of Isis, *my* amulet. I stared at it, stunned, but then she pulled her collar closed, and the amulet disappeared. 'If we want to defeat the enemy, we must start with the obelisk. We must find out the truth.'

My father frowned uneasily. He'd drawn a protective circle around them—blue chalk lines on the pavement. When he touched the base of the obelisk, the circle began to glow.

'I don't like it,' he said. 'Won't you call on her help?'

'No,' my mother insisted. 'I know my limits, Julius. If I tried it again . . .'

My heart skipped a beat. Iskandar's words came back to me: *She saw things that made her seek advice from unconventional places.* I recognized the look in my mother's eyes, and I knew: my mother had communed with Isis.

Why didn't you tell me? I wanted to scream.

My father summoned his staff and wand. 'Ruby, if we fail—'

'We can't fail,' she insisted. 'The world depends on it.'

They kissed one last time, as if they sensed they were saying good-bye. Then they raised their staffs and wands and began to chant. Cleopatra's Needle glowed with power.

*   *   *

I yanked my hand away from the sarcophagus. My eyes stung with tears.

You knew my mother, I shouted at Isis. *You encouraged her to open that obelisk. You got her*

444

killed!

I waited for her to answer. Instead, a ghostly image appeared in front me—a projection of my father, shimmering in the light of the golden coffin.

'Sadie.' He smiled. His voice sounded tinny and hollow, the way it used to on the phone when he'd call me from far away—from Egypt or Australia or god knows where. 'Don't blame Isis for your mother's fate. None of us understood exactly what would happen. Even your mother could only see bits and pieces of the future. But when the time came, your mother accepted her role. It was her decision.'

'To *die?*' I demanded. 'Isis should've helped her. *You* should've helped her. I *hate* you!'

As soon as I said it, something broke inside me. I started to cry. I realized I'd wanted to say that to my dad for years. I blamed him for Mum's death, blamed him for leaving me. But now that I'd said it, all the anger drained out me, leaving me nothing but guilt.

'I'm sorry,' I sputtered. 'I didn't—'

'Don't apologize, my brave girl. You have every right to feel that way. You had to get it out. What you're about to do—you have to believe it's for the right reasons, not because you resent me.'

'I don't know what you mean.'

He reached out to brush a tear from my cheek, but his hand was just a shimmer of light. 'Your mother was the first in many centuries to commune with Isis. It was dangerous, against the teachings of the House, but your mother was a diviner. She had a premonition that chaos was rising. The House was failing. We *needed* the gods.

Isis could not cross the Duat. She could barely manage a whisper, but she told us what she could about their imprisonment. She counseled Ruby on what must be done. The gods could rise again, she said, but it would take many *hard* sacrifices. We thought the obelisk would release all the gods, but that was only the beginning.'

'Isis could've given Mum more power. Or at least Bast! Bast *offered*—'

'No, Sadie. Your mother knew her limits. If she had tried to host a god, *fully* use divine power, she would have been consumed or worse. She freed Bast, and used her own power to seal the breach. With her life, she bought you some time.'

'Me? But . . .'

'You and your brother have the strongest blood of any Kane in three thousand years. Your mother studied the lineage of the pharaohs—she knew this to be true. You have the best chance at relearning the old ways, and healing the breach between magicians and gods. Your mother began the stirring. I unleashed the gods from the Rosetta Stone. But it will be your job to restore Ma'at.'

'You can help,' I insisted. 'Once we free you.'

'Sadie,' he said forlornly, 'when you become a parent, you may understand this. One of my hardest jobs as a father, one of my greatest duties, was to realize that my own dreams, my own goals and wishes, are secondary to my children's. Your mother and I have set the stage. But it is *your* stage. This pyramid is designed to feed chaos. It consumes the power of other gods and makes Set stronger.'

'I know. If I break the throne, maybe open the coffin . . .'

'You might save me,' Dad conceded. 'But the power of Osiris, the power inside me, would be consumed by the pyramid. It would only hasten the destruction and make Set stronger. The pyramid must be destroyed, *all* of it. And you know how that must be done.'

I was about to protest that I *didn't* know, but the feather of truth kept me honest. The way was inside me—I'd seen it in Isis's thoughts. I'd known what was coming ever since Anubis asked me that impossible question: 'To save the world, would you sacrifice your father?'

'I don't want to,' I said. 'Please.'

'Osiris must take his throne,' my father said. 'Through death, life. It is the only way. May Ma'at guide you, Sadie. I love you.'

And with that, his image dissipated.

Someone was calling my name.

I looked back and saw Zia trying to sit up, clutching weakly at her wand. 'Sadie, what are you doing?'

All around us, the room was shaking. Cracks split the walls, as if a giant were using the pyramid as a punching bag.

How long had I been in a trance? I wasn't sure, but I was out of time.

I closed my eyes and concentrated. The voice of Isis spoke almost immediately: *Do you see now? Do you understand why I could not say more?*

Anger built inside me, but I forced it down. *We'll talk about that later. Right now, we have a god to defeat.*

I pictured myself stepping forward, merging with the soul of the goddess.

I'd shared power with Isis before, but this was

447

different. My resolve, my anger, even my grief gave me confidence. I looked Isis straight in the eye (spiritually speaking), and we understood one another.

I saw her entire history—her early days grasping for power, using tricks and schemes to find the name of Ra. I saw her wedding with Osiris, her hopes and dreams for a new empire. Then I saw those dreams shattered by Set. I felt her anger and bitterness, her fierce pride and protectiveness for her young son, Horus. And I saw the pattern of her life repeating itself over and over again through the ages, through a thousand different hosts.

Gods have great power, Iskandar had said. *But only humans have creativity, the power to change history.*

I also felt my mother's thoughts, like an imprint on the goddess's memory: Ruby's final moments and the choice she'd made. She'd given her life to start a chain of events. And the next move was mine.

'Sadie!' Zia called again, her voice weakening.

'I'm fine,' I said. 'I'm going now.'

Zia studied my face, and obviously didn't like what she saw. 'You're not fine. You've been badly shaken. Fighting Set in your condition would be suicide.'

'Don't worry,' I said. 'We have a plan.'

With that, I turned into a kite and flew up the airshaft towards the top of the pyramid.

40.
I RUIN A RATHER IMPORTANT SPELL

S A D I E

I found that things weren't going well upstairs.

Carter was a crumpled heap of chicken warrior on the slope of the pyramid. Set had just placed the capstone and was shouting, 'Thirty seconds to sunrise!' In the cavern below, magicians from the House of Life waded through an army of demons, fighting a hopeless fight.

The scene would've been frightening enough, but now I saw it as Isis did. Like a crocodile with eyes at water level—seeing both below and above the surface—I saw the Duat entwined with the regular world. The demons had fiery souls in the Duat that made them look like an army of birthday candles. Where Carter stood in the mortal world, a falcon warrior stood in the Duat—not an avatar, but the real thing, with feathered head, sharp bloodstained beak, and gleaming black eyes. His sword rippled with golden light. As for Set— imagine a mountain of sand, doused with petrol, set on fire, spinning in the world's largest blender. That's what he looked like in the Duat—a column of destructive force so powerful that the stones at his feet bubbled and blistered.

I'm not sure what I looked like, but I felt powerful. The force of Ma'at coursed through me; the Divine Words were at my command. I was Sadie Kane, blood of the pharaohs. And I was Isis, goddess of magic, holder of the secret names.

As Carter struggled his way up the pyramid, Set gloated: 'You can't stop me by yourself, Horus—especially not in the desert, the source of my strength!'

'You're right!' I called.

Set turned, and the look on his face was priceless. I raised my staff and wand, gathering my magic.

'Except that Horus is *not* alone,' I said. 'And we're *not* going to fight you in the desert.'

I slammed my staff against the stones and shouted, 'Washington, D.C.!'

The pyramid shook. For a moment, nothing else happened.

Set seemed to realize what I was doing. He let out a nervous laugh. 'Magic one-oh-one, Sadie Kane. You can't open a portal during the Demon Days!'

'A mortal can't,' I agreed. 'But a goddess of magic can.'

Above us, the air crackled with lightning. The top of the cavern dissolved into a churning vortex of sand as large as the pyramid.

Demons stopped fighting and looked up in horror. Magicians stammered midspell, their faces slack with awe.

The vortex was so powerful that it ripped blocks off the pyramid and sucked them into the sand. And then, like a giant lid, the portal began to descend.

'No!' Set roared. He blasted the portal with flames, then turned on me and hurled stones and lightning, but it was too late. The portal swallowed us all.

The world seemed to flip upside down. For a

heartbeat, I wondered if I'd made a terrible miscalculation—if Set's pyramid would explode in the portal, and I'd spend eternity floating through the Duat as a billion little particles of Sadie sand. Then, with a sonic boom, we appeared in the cold morning air with a brilliant blue sky above us. Spread out below us were the snow-covered fields of the National Mall in Washington, D.C.

The red pyramid was still intact, but cracks had appeared on its surface. The gold capstone glowed, trying to maintain its magic, but we weren't in Phoenix anymore. The pyramid had been ripped from its source of power, the desert, and in front us loomed the default gateway for North America, the tall white obelisk that was the most powerful focal point of Ma'at on the continent: the Washington Monument.

Set screamed something at me in Ancient Egyptian. I was fairly sure it wasn't a compliment.

'I will rend your limbs from their sockets!' he shouted. 'I will—'

'Die?' Carter suggested. He rose behind Set and swung his sword. The blade cut into Set's armor at the ribs—not a killing blow, but enough to knock the Red God off balance and send him tumbling down the side of his pyramid. Carter bounded after him, and in the Duat I could see arcs of white energy pulsing from the Washington Monument to the Horus avatar, charging it with new power.

'The book, Sadie!' Carter shouted as he ran. 'Do it now!'

I must've been dazed from summoning the portal, because Set understood what Carter was saying a lot faster than I did.

'No!' the Red God shouted. He charged towards

me, but Carter intercepted him halfway up the slope.

He grappled with Set, holding him back. The stones of the pyramid cracked and crumbled under the weight of their godly forms. All around the base of the pyramid, demons and magicians who'd been pulled through the portal and knocked momentarily unconscious were starting to stir.

The book, Sadie . . . Sometimes it's helpful to have someone other than yourself inside your head, because one can slap the other. *Duh, the book!*

I held out my hand and summoned the little blue tome we'd stolen from Paris: *The Book of Overcoming Set.* I unfolded the papyrus; the hieroglyphs were as clear as a nursery school primer. I called for the feather of truth, and instantly it appeared, glowing above the pages.

I began the spell, speaking the Divine Words, and my body rose into the air, hovering a few centimeters above the pyramid. I chanted the story of creation: the first mountain rising above the waters of chaos, the birth of the gods Ra, Geb, and Nut, the rise of Ma'at, and the first great empire of men, Egypt.

The Washington Monument began to glow as hieroglyphs appeared along its sides. The capstone gleamed silver.

Set tried to lash out at me, but Carter intercepted him. And the red pyramid began to break apart.

I thought about Amos and Zia, trapped inside under tons of stone, and I almost faltered, but my mother's voice spoke in my mind: *Stay focused, dearest. Watch for your enemy.*

Yes, Isis said. *Destroy him!*

But somehow I knew that wasn't what my mother meant. She was telling me to watch. Something important was about to happen.

Through the Duat, I saw magic forming around me, weaving a white sheen over the world, reinforcing Ma'at and expelling chaos. Carter and Set wrestled back and forth as huge chunks of the pyramid collapsed.

The feather of truth glowed, shining like a spotlight on the Red God. As I neared the end of the spell, my words began tearing Set's form to shreds.

In the Duat, his fiery whirlwind was being stripped away, revealing a black-skinned, slimy thing like an emaciated Set animal—the evil essence of the god. But in the mortal world, occupying the same space, there stood a proud warrior in red armor, blazing with power and determined to fight to the death.

'I name you Set,' I chanted. 'I name you Evil Day.'

With a thunderous roar, the pyramid imploded. Set fell crashing into the ruins. He tried to rise, but Carter swung his sword. Set barely had time to raise his staff. Their weapons crossed, and Horus slowly forced Set to one knee.

'Now, Sadie!' Carter yelled.

'You have been my enemy,' I chanted, 'and a curse on the land.'

A line of white light shot down the length of the Washington Monument. It widened into a rift—a doorway between this world and the brilliant white abyss that would lock Set away, trapping his life force. Maybe not forever, but for a long, long time.

453

To complete the spell, I only had to speak one more line: 'Deserving no mercy, an enemy of Ma'at, you are exiled beyond the earth.'

The line had to be spoken with absolute conviction. The feather of truth required it. And why shouldn't I believe it? It was the truth. Set deserved no mercy. He *was* an enemy of Ma'at.

But I hesitated.

'Watch for your enemy,' my mother had said.

I looked towards the top of the monument, and in the Duat I saw chunks of pyramid flying skyward and the souls of demons lifting off like fireworks. As Set's chaos magic dispersed, all the force that had been charging up, ready to destroy a continent, was being sucked into the clouds. And as I watched, the chaos tried to form a shape. It was like a red reflection of the Potomac—an enormous crimson river at least a mile long and a hundred meters wide. It writhed in the air, trying to become solid, and I felt its rage and bitterness. This was not what it had wanted. There was not enough power or chaos for its purpose. To form properly, it needed the death of millions, the wasting of an entire continent.

It was not a river. It was a snake.

'Sadie!' Carter yelled. 'What are you waiting for?'

He couldn't see it, I realized. No one could but me.

Set was on his knees, writhing and cursing as white energy encircled him, pulling him towards the rift. 'Lost your stomach, witch?' he bellowed. Then he glared at Carter. 'You see, Horus? Isis was always a coward. She could never complete the deed!'

Carter looked at me, and for a moment I saw the doubt on his face. Horus would be urging him towards bloody vengeance. I was hesitating. This is what had turned Isis and Horus against each other before. I couldn't let it happen now.

But more than that, in Carter's wary expression I saw the way he used to look at me on our visiting days—when we were practically strangers, forced to spend time together, pretending we were a happy family because Dad expected it of us. I didn't want to go back to that. I wasn't pretending anymore. We *were* a family, and we had to work together.

'Carter, look.' I threw the feather of truth into the sky, breaking the spell.

'No!' Carter screamed.

But the feather exploded into silver dust that clung to the form of the serpent, forcing it to become visible, just for an instant.

Carter's mouth fell open as the serpent writhed in the air above Washington, slowly losing power.

Next to me, a voice screamed: 'Wretched gods!'

I turned to see Set's minion, Face of Horror, with his fangs bared and his grotesque face only inches from mine, a jagged knife raised above my head. I only had time to think: *I'm dead,* before a flash of metal registered in the corner of my eye. There was a sickening thud, and the demon froze.

Carter had thrown his sword with deadly accuracy. The demon dropped his knife, fell to his knees, and stared down at the blade that was now sheathed in his side.

He crumpled to his back, exhaling with an angry hiss. His black eyes fixed on me, and he spoke in a completely different voice—a rasping, dry sound, like a reptile's belly scraping over sand. 'This is not over, godling. All this I have wrought with a wisp of my voice, the merest bit of my essence wriggling from my weakened cage. Imagine what I shall do when fully formed.'

He gave me a ghastly smile, and then his face went slack. A tiny line of red mist curled from his mouth—like a worm or a fresh-hatched snake—and writhed upward into the sky to join its source. The demon's body disintegrated into sand.

I looked up once more at the giant red serpent slowly dissolving in the sky. Then I summoned a good strong wind and dispersed it completely.

The Washington Monument stopped glowing. The rift closed, and the little spellbook disappeared from my hand.

I moved towards Set, who was still ensnared in ropes of white energy. I'd spoken his true name. He wasn't going anywhere just yet.

'You both saw the serpent in the clouds,' I said. 'Apophis.'

Carter nodded, stunned. 'He was trying to break into the mortal world, using the Red Pyramid as a gateway. If its power had been unleashed . . .' He looked down in revulsion at the pile of sand that had once been a demon. 'Set's lieutenant—Face of Horror—he was possessed by Apophis all along, using Set to get what he wanted.'

'Ridiculous!' Set glared at me and struggled against his bonds. 'The snake in the clouds was one of your tricks, Isis. An illusion.'

'You know it wasn't,' I said. 'I could've sent you into the abyss, Set, but you saw the real enemy. Apophis was trying to break out of his prison in the Duat. His voice possessed Face of Horror. He was using you.'

'No one uses me!'

Carter let his warrior form disperse. He floated to the ground and summoned his sword back to his hand. 'Apophis wanted your explosion to feed *his* power, Set. As soon as he came through the Duat and found us dead, I'm betting *you* would've been his first meal. Chaos would've won.'

'I *am* chaos!' Set insisted.

'Partially,' I said. 'But you're still one of the gods. True, you're evil, faithless, ruthless, vile—'

'You make me blush, sister.'

'But you're also the strongest god. In the ancient times, you were Ra's faithful lieutenant, defending his boat against Apophis. Ra couldn't have defeated the Serpent without you.'

'I am pretty great,' Set admitted. 'But Ra is gone forever, thanks to you.'

'Maybe not forever,' I said. 'We'll have to find him. Apophis is rising, which means we'll need all the gods to battle him. Even you.'

Set tested his bonds of white energy. When he found he couldn't break them, he gave me a crooked smile. 'You suggest an alliance? You'd trust me?'

Carter laughed. 'You've got to be kidding. But we've got your number, now. Your secret name. Right, Sadie?'

I closed my fingers, and the bonds tightened around Set. He cried out in pain. It took a great deal of energy, and I knew I couldn't hold him like this for long, but there was no point telling that to Set.

'The House of Life tried banishing the gods,' I said. 'It didn't work. If we lock you away, we're no

457

better than they are. It doesn't solve anything.'

'I couldn't agree more,' Set groaned. 'So if you'll just loosen these bonds—'

'You're still a villainous piece of scum,' I said. 'But you have a role to play, and you'll need controlling. I'll agree to release you—*if* you swear to behave, to return to the Duat, and not cause trouble until we call you. And then you'll make trouble only for us, fighting against Apophis.'

'Or I could chop off your head,' Carter suggested. 'That would probably exile you for a good long while.'

Set glanced back and forth between us. 'Make trouble for you, eh? That *is* my specialty.'

'Swear by your own name and the throne of Ra,' I said. 'You will leave now and not reappear until you are called.'

'Oh, I swear,' he said, much too quickly. 'By my name and Ra's throne and our mother's starry elbows.'

'If you betray us,' I warned, 'I have your name. I won't show you mercy a second time.'

'You always were my favorite sister.'

I gave him one last shock, just to remind him of my power, and then let the bindings dissolve.

Set stood up and flexed his arms. He appeared as a warrior with red armor and red skin, a black, forked beard, and twinkling, cruel eyes; but in the Duat, I saw his other side, a raging inferno just barely contained, waiting to be unleashed and burn everything in its path. He winked at Horus, then pretended to shoot me with a finger gun. 'Oh, this will be *good*. We're going to have so much fun.'

'Begone, Evil Day,' I said.

He turned into a pillar of salt and dissolved.

*   *   *

The snow in the National Mall had melted in a perfect square, the exact size of Set's pyramid. Around the edges, a dozen magicians still lay passed out. The poor dears had started to stir when our portal closed, but the explosion of the pyramid had knocked them all out again. Other mortals in the area had also been affected. An early-morning jogger was slumped on the sidewalk. On nearby streets, cars idled while the drivers took naps over the steering wheels.

Not everyone was asleep, though. Police sirens wailed in the distance, and seeing as how we'd teleported practically into the president's backyard, I knew it wouldn't be long before we had a great deal of heavily armed company.

Carter and I ran to the center of the melted square, where Amos and Zia lay crumpled in the grass. There was no sign of Set's throne or the golden coffin, but I tried to push those thoughts out of my mind.

Amos groaned. 'What . . .' His eyes clouded over with terror. 'Set . . . he . . . he . . .'

'Rest.' I put my hand on his forehead. He was burning with fever. The pain in his mind was so sharp, it cut me like a razor. I remembered a spell Isis had taught me in New Mexico.

'Quiet,' I whispered. *'Hah-ri.'*

Faint hieroglyphs glowed over his face.

Amos drifted back to sleep but I knew it was only a temporary fix.

Zia was even worse off. Carter cradled her head and spoke reassuringly about how she would be

459

fine, but she looked bad. Her skin was a strange reddish color, dry and brittle, as if she'd suffered a horrible sunburn. In the grass around her, hieroglyphs were fading—the remains of a protective circle—and I thought I understood what had happened. She'd used her last bit of energy to shield herself and Amos when the pyramid imploded.

'Set?' she asked weakly. 'Is he gone?'

'Yes.' Carter glanced at me, and I knew we'd be keeping the details to ourselves. 'Everything's fine, thanks to you. The secret name worked.'

She nodded, satisfied, and her eyes began to close.

'Hey.' Carter's voice quavered. 'Stay awake. You're not going to leave me alone with Sadie, are you? She's bad company.'

Zia tried to smile, but the effort made her wince. 'I was . . . never here, Carter. Just a message—a placeholder.'

'Come on. No. That's no way to talk.'

'Find her, will you?' Zia said. A tear traced its way down her nose. 'She'd . . . like that . . . a date at the mall.' Her eyes drifted away from him and stared blankly into the sky.

'Zia!' Carter clutched her hand. 'Stop that. You can't . . . You can't just . . .'

I knelt next to him and touched Zia's face. It was cold as stone. And even though I understood what had happened, I couldn't think of anything to say, or any way to console my brother. He shut his eyes tight and lowered his head.

Then it happened. Along the path of Zia's tear, from the corner of her eye to the base of her nose, Zia's face cracked. Smaller fractures appeared, webbing her skin. Her flesh dried out, hardening . . . turning to clay.

'Carter,' I said.

'What?' he said miserably.

He looked up just as a small blue light drifted out of Zia's mouth and flew into the sky. Carter backed away in shock. 'What—what did you do?'

'Nothing,' I said. 'She's a *shabti*. She said she wasn't really here. She was just a placeholder.'

Carter looked bewildered. But then a small light started to burn in his eyes—a tiny bit of hope. 'Then . . . the real Zia is alive?'

'Iskandar was protecting her,' I said. 'When the spirit of Nephthys joined with the real Zia in London, Iskandar knew she was in danger. Iskandar hid her away and replaced her with a *shabti*. Remember what Thoth said: "Shabti make excellent stunt doubles?" That's what she was. And Nephthys told me she was sheltered somewhere, inside a sleeping host.'

'But where—'

'I don't know,' I said. And in Carter's present state, I was too afraid to raise the *real* question: If Zia had been a *shabti* all this time, had we ever known her at all? The real Zia had never gotten close to us. She'd never discovered what an incredibly amazing person I was. God forbid, she might not even like Carter.

Carter touched her face and it crumbled to dust. He picked up her wand, which remained solid ivory, but he held it gingerly as if he were afraid it too would dissolve. 'That blue light,' he began to ramble, 'I saw Zia release one in the First Nome, too. Just like the *shabti* in Memphis—they sent their thoughts back to Thoth. So Zia must've been

461

in contact with her *shabti*. That's what the light was. They must've been, like, sharing memories, right? She must *know* what the *shabti*'s been through. If the real Zia is alive somewhere, she might be locked up or in some kind of magic sleep or— We have to find her!'

I wasn't sure it would be so simple, but I didn't want to argue. I could see the desperation on his face.

Then a familiar voice sent a cold shiver down my back: 'What have you done?'

Desjardins was literally fuming. His tattered robes still smoked from battle. (Carter says I shouldn't mention that his pink boxer shorts were showing, but they were!) His staff was aglow, and the whiskers in his beard smoldered. Behind him stood three equally battered magicians, who all looked as if they'd just regained consciousness.

'Oh, good,' I muttered. 'You're alive.'

'You bargained with Set?' Desjardins demanded. 'You let him *go*?'

'We don't answer to you,' Carter growled. He stepped forward, hand on his sword, but I put out my arm to hold him back.

'Desjardins,' I said as calmly as I could, 'Apophis is rising, in case you missed that part. We need the gods. The House of Life has to relearn the old ways.'

'The old ways destroyed us!' he yelled.

A week ago, the look in his eyes would've made me tremble. He fairly glowed with rage, and hieroglyphs blazed in the air around him. He was the Chief Lector, and I'd just undone everything the House had worked for since the fall of Egypt. Desjardins was a heartbeat away from turning me into an insect, and the thought should've terrified me.

Instead, I looked him in the eye. Right now, I was more powerful than he was. *Much* more powerful. And I let him know it.

'Pride destroyed you,' I said. 'Greed and selfishness and all of that. It's hard to follow the path of the gods. But it is part of magic. You can't just shut it down.'

'You are drunk with power,' he snarled. 'The gods have possessed you, as they always do. Soon you will forget you are even human. We will fight you and destroy you.' Then he glared at Carter. 'And *you*—I know what Horus would demand. You will never reclaim the throne. With my last breath—'

'Save it,' I said. Then I faced my brother. 'You know what we have to do?'

Understanding passed between us. I was surprised how easily I could read him. I thought it might be the influence of the gods, but then I realized it was because we were both Kanes, brother and sister. And Carter, god help me, was also my friend.

'Are you sure?' he asked. 'We're leaving ourselves open.' He glared at Desjardins. 'Just one more good smack with the sword?'

'I'm sure, Carter.'

I closed my eyes and focused.

Consider carefully, Isis said. *What we've done so far is only the beginning of the power we could wield together.*

That's the problem, I said. *I'm not ready for that. I've got to get there on my own, the hard way.*

You are wise for a mortal, Isis said. *Very well.*

463

Imagine giving up a fortune in cash. Imagine throwing away the most beautiful diamond necklace in the world. Separating myself from Isis was harder than that, *much* harder.

But it wasn't impossible. *I know my limits,* my mother had said, and now I understood how wise she'd been.

I felt the spirit of the goddess leave me. Part of her flowed into my necklace, but most of her streamed into the Washington Monument, back into the Duat, where Isis would go . . . somewhere else. Another host? I wasn't sure.

When I opened my eyes, Carter stood next to me looking grief-stricken, holding his Eye of Horus amulet.

Desjardins was so stunned, he momentarily forgot how to speak English. *'Ce n'est pas possible. On ne pourrait pas—'*

'Yes, we could,' I said. 'We've given up the gods of our own free will. And you've got a lot to learn about what's possible.'

Carter threw down his sword. 'Desjardins, I'm not after the throne. Not unless I earn it by myself, and that's going to take time. We're going to learn the path of the gods. We're going to teach others. You can waste time trying to destroy us, or you can help.'

The sirens were much closer now. I could see the lights of emergency vehicles coming from several directions, slowly cordoning off the National Mall. We had only minutes before we were surrounded.

Desjardins looked at the magicians behind him, probably gauging how much support he could rally. His brethren looked in awe. One even started to

464

bow to me, then caught himself.

Alone, Desjardins might've been able to destroy us. We were just magicians now—very tired magicians, with hardly any formal training.

Desjardins' nostrils flared. Then he surprised me by lowering his staff. 'There has been too much destruction today. But the path of the gods shall remain closed. If you cross the House of Life again . . .'

He let the threat hang in the air. He slammed his staff down, and with a final burst of energy, the four magicians dissolved into wind and gusted away.

Suddenly I felt exhausted. The terror of what I'd been through began to sink in. We'd survived, but that was little consolation. I missed my parents. I missed them terribly. I wasn't a goddess anymore. I was just a regular girl, alone with only my brother.

Then Amos groaned and started sitting up. Police cars and sinister-looking black vans blocked the curbs all around us. Sirens blared. A helicopter sliced through the air over the Potomac, closing fast. God only knew what the mortals thought had happened at the Washington Monument, but I didn't want my face on the nightly news.

'Carter, we have to get out of here,' I said. 'Can you summon enough magic to change Amos into something small—a mouse maybe? We can fly him out.'

He nodded, still in a daze. 'But Dad . . . we didn't . . .'

He looked around helplessly. I knew how he felt. The pyramid, the throne, the golden coffin— all of it was gone. We'd come so far to rescue our father, only to lose him. And Carter's first girlfriend lay at his feet in a pile of pottery shards. That probably didn't help either. (Carter protests that she wasn't really his girlfriend. Oh, please!)

I couldn't dwell on it, though. I had to be strong for both of us or we'd end up in prison.

'First things first,' I said. 'We have to get Amos to safety.'

'Where?' Carter asked.

There was only one place I could think of.

41.
WE STOP THE RECORDING, FOR NOW

I can't believe Sadie's going to let me have the last word. Our experience together must've really taught her something. Ow, she just hit me. Never mind.

Anyway, I'm glad she told that last part. I think she understood it better than I did. And the whole thing about Zia not being Zia and Dad not getting rescued . . . that was pretty hard to deal with.

If anybody felt worse than I did, it was Amos. I had just enough magic to turn myself into a falcon and him into a hamster (hey, I was rushed!), but a few miles from the National Mall, he started struggling to change back. Sadie and I were forced to land outside a train station, where Amos turned back into a human and curled into a shivering ball. We tried to talk to him, but he could barely complete a sentence.

Finally we got him into the station. We let him sleep on a bench while Sadie and I warmed up and watched the news.

According to Channel 5, the whole city of Washington was under lockdown. There'd been reports of explosions and weird lights at the Washington Monument, but all the cameras could show us was a big square of melted snow on the mall, which kind of made for boring video. Experts came on and talked about terrorism, but eventually it became clear that there'd been no permanent damage—just a bunch of scary lights. After a while, the media started speculating about freak storm activity or a rare southern appearance of the Northern Lights. Within an hour, the authorities opened up the city.

I wished we had Bast with us, because Amos was in no shape to be our chaperone; but we managed to buy tickets for our 'sick' uncle and ourselves as far as New York.

I slept on the way, the amulet of Horus clutched in my hand.

*   *   *

We got back to Brooklyn at sunset.

We found the mansion burned out, which we'd expected, but we had nowhere else to go. I knew we'd made the right choice when we guided Amos through the doorway and heard a familiar, *'Agh! Agh!'*

'Khufu!' Sadie cried.

The baboon tackled her in a hug and climbed onto her shoulders. He picked at her hair, seeing if she'd brought him any good bugs to eat. Then he jumped off and grabbed a half-melted basketball. He grunted at me insistently, pointing to a makeshift basket he'd made out of some burned

467

beams and a laundry basket. It was a gesture of forgiveness, I realized. He had forgiven me for sucking at his favorite game, and he was offering lessons. Looking around, I realized that he'd tried to clean up in his own baboon way, too. He'd dusted off the one surviving sofa, stacked Cheerios boxes in the fireplace, and even put a dish of water and fresh food out for Muffin, who was curled up asleep on a little pillow. In the clearest part of the living room, under an intact section of roof, Khufu had made three separate mounds of pillows and sheets—sleeping places for us.

I got a lump in my throat. Seeing the care that he'd taken getting ready for us, I couldn't imagine a better welcome home present.

'Khufu,' I said, 'you are one freaking awesome baboon.'

'Agh!' he said, pointing to the basketball.

'You want to school me?' I said. 'Yeah, I deserve it. Just give us a second to . . .'

My smile melted when I saw Amos.

He'd drifted over to the ruined statue of Thoth. The god's cracked ibis head lay at his feet. His hands had broken off, and his tablet and stylus lay shattered on the ground. Amos stared at the headless god—the patron of magicians—and I could guess what he was thinking. *A bad omen for a homecoming.*

'It's okay,' I told him. 'We're going to make it right.'

If Amos heard me, he gave no sign. He drifted over to the couch and plopped down, putting his head in his hands.

Sadie glanced at me uneasily. Then she looked around at the blackened walls, the crumbling ceilings, the charred remains of the furniture.

'Well,' she said, trying to sound upbeat. 'How about *I* play basketball with Khufu, and you can clean the house?'

*   *   *

Even with magic, it took us several weeks to put the house back in order. That was just to make it livable. It was hard without Isis and Horus helping, but we could still do magic. It just took a lot more concentration and a lot more time. Every day, I went to sleep feeling as if I'd done twelve hours of hard labor; but eventually we got the walls and ceilings repaired, and cleaned up the debris until the house no longer smelled of smoke. We even managed to fix the terrace and the pool. We brought Amos out to watch as we released the wax crocodile figurine into the water, and Philip of Macedonia sprang to life.

Amos almost smiled when he saw that. Then he sank into a chair on the terrace and stared desolately at the Manhattan skyline.

I began to wonder if he would ever be the same. He'd lost too much weight. His face looked haggard. Most days he wore his bathrobe and didn't even bother to comb his hair.

'He was taken over by Set,' Sadie told me one morning, when I mentioned how worried I was. 'Do you have any idea how *violating* that is? His will was broken. He doubts himself and . . . Well, it may be a long time . . .'

We tried to lose ourselves in work. We repaired the statue of Thoth, and fixed the broken *shabti* in the library. I was better at grunt work—moving

469

blocks of stone or heaving ceiling beams into place. Sadie was better at fine details, like repairing the hieroglyphic seals on the doors. Once, she really impressed me by imagining her bedroom just as it had been and speaking the joining spell, *hi-nehm*. Pieces of furniture flew together out of the debris, and *boom!*: instant repair job. Of course, Sadie passed out for twelve hours afterward, but still . . . pretty cool. Slowly but surely, the mansion began to feel like home.

At night I would sleep with my head on a charmed headrest, which mostly kept my *ba* from drifting off; but sometimes I still had strange visions—the red pyramid, the serpent in the sky, or the face of my father as he was trapped in Set's coffin. Once I thought I heard Zia's voice trying to tell me something from far away, but I couldn't make out the words.

Sadie and I kept our amulets locked in a box in the library. Every morning I would sneak down to make sure they were still there. I would find them glowing, warm to the touch, and I would be tempted—*very* tempted—to put on the Eye of Horus. But I knew I couldn't. The power was too addictive, too dangerous. I'd achieved a balance with Horus once, under extreme circumstances, but I knew it would be too easy to get overwhelmed if I tried it again. I had to train first, become a more powerful magician, before I would be ready to tap that much power.

*　　　*　　　*

One night at dinner, we had a visitor.

Amos had gone to bed early, as he usually did.

Khufu was inside watching ESPN with Muffin on his lap. Sadie and I sat exhausted on the deck overlooking the river. Philip of Macedonia floated silently in his pool. Except for the hum of the city, the night was quiet.

I'm not sure how it happened, but one minute we were alone, and the next there was a guy standing at the railing. He was lean and tall, with messed-up hair and pale skin, and his clothes were all black, as if he'd mugged a priest or something. He was probably around sixteen, and even though I'd never seen his face before, I had the weirdest feeling that I knew him.

Sadie stood up so quickly she knocked over her split-pea soup—which is gross enough in the bowl, but running all over the table? Yuck.

'Anubis!' she blurted.

Anubis? I thought she was kidding, because this guy did not look anything like the slavering jackal-headed god I'd seen in the Land of the Dead. He stepped forward, and my hand crept for my wand.

'Sadie,' he said. 'Carter. Would you come with me, please?'

'Sure,' Sadie said, her voice a little strangled.

'Hold on,' I said. 'Where are we going?'

Anubis gestured behind him, and a door opened in the air—a pure black rectangle. 'Someone wants to see you.'

Sadie took his hand and stepped through into the darkness, which left me no choice but to follow.

*　　*　　*

The Hall of Judgment had gotten a makeover. The

471

golden scales still dominated the room, but they had been fixed. The black pillars still marched off into the gloom on all four sides. But now I could see the overlay—the strange holographic image of the real world—and it was no longer a graveyard, as Sadie had described. It was a white living room with tall ceilings and huge picture windows. Double doors led to a terrace that looked out over the ocean.

I was struck speechless. I looked at Sadie, and judging from the shock on her face, I guessed she recognized the place too: our house in Los Angeles, in the hills overlooking the Pacific—the last place we'd lived as a family.

'The Hall of Judgment is intuitive,' a familiar voice said. 'It responds to strong memories.'

Only then did I notice the throne wasn't empty anymore. Sitting there, with Ammit the Devourer curled at his feet, was our father.

I almost ran to him, but something held me back. He looked the same in many ways—the long brown coat, the rumpled suit and dusty boots, his head freshly shaven and his beard trimmed. His eyes gleamed they way they did whenever I made him proud.

But his form shimmered with a strange light. Like the room itself, I realized, he existed in two worlds. I concentrated hard, and my eyes opened to a deeper level of the Duat.

Dad was still there, but taller and stronger, dressed in the robes and jewels of an Egyptian pharaoh. His skin was a dark shade of blue like the deep ocean.

Anubis walked over and stood at his side, but Sadie and I were a little more cautious.

'Well, come on,' Dad said. 'I won't bite.'

Ammit the Devourer growled as we came close, but Dad stroked his crocodile head and shushed him. 'These are my children, Ammit. Behave.'

'D-Dad?' I stammered.

Now I want to be clear: even though weeks had passed since the battle with Set, and even though I'd been busy rebuilding the mansion the whole time, I hadn't stopped thinking about my dad for a minute. Every time I saw a picture in the library, I thought of the stories he used to tell me. I kept my clothes in a suitcase in my bedroom closet, because I couldn't bear the idea that our life traveling together was over. I missed him so much I would sometimes turn to tell him something before I forgot that he was gone. In spite of all that, and all the emotion boiling around inside me, all I could think of to say was: 'You're blue.'

My dad's laugh was so normal, so *him,* that it broke the tension. The sound echoed through the hall, and even Anubis cracked a smile.

'Goes with the territory,' Dad said. 'I'm sorry I didn't bring you here sooner, but things have been . . .' He looked at Anubis for the right word.

'Complicated,' Anubis suggested.

'Complicated. I have meant to tell you both how proud I am of you, how much the gods are in your debt—'

'Hang on,' Sadie said. She stomped right up to the throne. Ammit growled at her, but Sadie growled back, which confused the monster into silence.

'What *are* you?' she demanded. 'My dad? Osiris? Are you even alive?'

Dad looked at Anubis. 'What did I tell you

about her? Fiercer than Ammit, I said.'

'You didn't need to tell me.' Anubis's face was grave. 'I've learned to fear that sharp tongue.'

Sadie looked outraged. 'Excuse me?'

'To answer your question,' Dad said, 'I am both Osiris and Julius Kane. I am alive *and* dead, though the term *recycled* might be closer to the truth. Osiris is the god of the dead, and the god of new life. To return him to his throne—'

'You had to die,' I said. 'You knew this going into it. You *intentionally* hosted Osiris, knowing you would die.'

I was shaking with anger. I didn't realize how strongly I'd felt about it, but I couldn't believe what my dad had done. 'This is what you meant by "making things right"?'

My dad's expression didn't change. He was still looking at me with pride and downright *joy*, as if everything I did delighted him—even my shouting. It was infuriating.

'I missed you, Carter,' he said. 'I can't tell you how much. But we made the right choice. We *all* did. If you had saved me in the world above, we would have lost everything. For the first time in millennia, we have a chance at rebirth, and a chance to stop chaos because of you.'

'There had to be another way,' I said. 'You could've fought as a mortal, without . . . without—'

'Carter, when Osiris was alive, he was a great king. But when he died—'

'He became a thousand times more powerful,' I said, remembering the story Dad used to tell me.

My father nodded. 'The Duat is the foundation for the real world. If there is chaos here, it reverberates in the upper world. Helping Osiris to

474

his throne was a first step, a thousand times more important than anything I could've done in the world above—except being your father. And I am still your father.'

My eyes stung. I guess I understood what he was saying, but I didn't like it. Sadie looked even angrier than me, but she was glaring at Anubis.

'Sharp tongue?' she demanded.

Dad cleared his throat. 'Children, there is another reason I made my choice, as you can probably guess.' He held out his hand, and a woman in a black dress appeared next to him. She had golden hair, intelligent blue eyes, and a face that looked familiar. She looked like Sadie.

'Mom,' I said.

She gazed back and forth from Sadie to me in amazement, as if *we* were the ghosts. 'Julius told me how much you'd grown, but I couldn't believe it. Carter, I bet you're shaving—'

'Mom.'

'—and dating girls—'

'Mom!' Have you ever noticed how parents can go from the most wonderful people in the world to totally embarrassing in three seconds?

She smiled at me, and I had to fight with about twenty different feelings at once. I'd spent years dreaming of being back with my parents, together in our house in L.A. But not like this: not with the house just an afterimage, and my mom a spirit, and my dad . . . recycled. I felt like the world was shifting under my feet, turning into sand.

'We can't go back, Carter,' Mom said, as if reading my mind. 'But nothing is lost, even in death. Do you remember the law of conservation?'

It had been six years since we'd sat together in

the living room—*this* living room, and she'd read me the laws of physics the way most parents read bedtime stories. But I still remembered. 'Energy and matter can't be created or destroyed.'

'Only changed,' my mother agreed. 'And sometimes changed for the better.'

She took Dad's hand, and I had to admit—blue and ghostly or not—they kind of looked happy.

'Mum.' Sadie swallowed. For once, her attention wasn't on Anubis. 'Did you really . . . was that—'

'Yes, my brave girl. My thoughts mixed with yours. I'm so proud of you. And thanks to Isis, I feel like I know you as well.' She leaned forward and smiled conspiratorially. 'I like chocolate caramels, too, though your grandmum never approved of keeping sweets in the flat.'

Sadie broke into a relieved grin. 'I know! She's impossible!'

I got the feeling they were going to start chatting for hours, but just then the Hall of Judgment rumbled. Dad checked his watch, which made me wonder what time zone the Land of the Dead was in.

'We should wrap things up,' he said. 'The others are expecting you.'

'Others?' I asked.

'A gift before you go.' Dad nodded to Mom.

She stepped forward and handed me a palm-size package of folded black linen. Sadie helped me unwrap it, and inside was a new amulet—one that looked like a column or a tree trunk or . . .

'Is that a spine?' Sadie demanded.

'It is called a *djed,*' Dad said. 'My symbol—the spine of Osiris.'

'Yuck,' Sadie muttered.

476

Mom laughed. 'It is a bit yuck, but honestly, it's a powerful symbol. Stands for stability, strength—'

'Backbone?' I asked.

'Literally.' Mom gave me an approving look, and again I had that surreal shifting feeling. I couldn't believe I was standing here, having a chat with my somewhat dead parents.

Mom closed the amulet into my hands. Her touch was warm, like a living person's. '*Djed* also stands for the power of Osiris—renewed life from the ashes of death. This is exactly what you will need if you are to stir the blood of the pharaohs in others and rebuild the House of Life.'

'The House won't like that,' Sadie put in.

'No,' Mom said cheerfully. 'They certainly won't.'

The Hall of Judgment rumbled again.

'It is time,' Dad said. 'We'll meet again, children. But until then, take care.'

'Be mindful of your enemies,' Mom added.

'And tell Amos . . .' Dad's voice trailed off thoughtfully. 'Remind my brother that Egyptians believe in the power of the sunrise. They believe each morning begins not just a new day, but a new world.'

Before I could figure out what that meant, the Hall of Judgment faded, and we stood with Anubis in a field of darkness.

'I'll show you the way,' Anubis said. 'It is my job.'

He ushered us to a space in the darkness that looked no different from any other. But when he pushed with his hand, a door swung open. The entrance blazed with daylight.

Anubis bowed formally to me. Then he looked

at Sadie with a glint of mischief in his eyes. 'It's been . . . stimulating.'

Sadie flushed and pointed at him accusingly. 'We're not done, mister. I expect you to look after my parents. And next time I'm in the Land of the Dead, you and I will have words.'

A smile tugged at the corner of his mouth. 'I'll look forward to that.'

We stepped through the doorway and into the palace of the gods.

It looked just like Sadie had described from her visions: soaring stone columns, fiery braziers, a polished marble floor, and in the middle of the room, a gold-and-red throne. All around us, gods had gathered. Many were just flashes of light and fire. Some were shadowy images that shifted from animal to human. I recognized a few: Thoth flickered into view as a wild-haired guy in a lab coat before turning into a cloud of green gas; Hathor, the cow-headed goddess, gave me a puzzled look, as if she vaguely recognized me from the Magic Salsa incident. I looked for Bast, but my heart fell. She didn't seem to be in the crowd. In fact, most of the gods I didn't recognize.

'What have we started?' Sadie murmured.

I understood what she meant. The throne room was full of hundreds of gods, major and minor, all darting through the palace, forming new shapes, glowing with power. An entire supernatural army . . . and they all seemed to be staring at us.

Thankfully, two old friends stood next to the throne. Horus wore full battle armor and a *khopesh* sword at his side. His kohl-lined eyes—one gold, one silver—were as piercing as ever. At his side stood Isis in a shimmering white gown,

478

with wings of light.

'Welcome,' Horus said.

'*Um,* hi,' I said.

'He has a way with words,' Isis muttered, which made Sadie snort.

Horus gestured to the throne. 'I know your thoughts, Carter, so I think I know what you will say. But I have to ask you one more time. Will you join me? We could rule the earth and the heavens. Ma'at demands a leader.'

'Yeah, so I've heard.'

'I would be stronger with you as my host. You've only touched the surface of what combat magic can do. We could accomplish great things, and it *is* your destiny to lead the House of Life. You could be the king of two thrones.'

I glanced at Sadie, but she just shrugged. 'Don't look at me. I find the idea horrifying.'

Horus scowled at her, but the truth was, I agreed with Sadie. All those gods waiting for direction, all those magicians who hated us—the idea of trying to lead them made my knees turn to water.

'Maybe some day,' I said. 'Much later.'

Horus sighed. 'Five thousand years, and I still do not understand mortals. But—very well.'

He stepped up to the throne and looked around at the assembled gods.

'I, Horus, son of Osiris, claim the throne of the heavens as my birthright!' he shouted. 'What was once mine shall be mine again. Is there any who would challenge me?'

The gods flickered and glowed. A few scowled. One muttered something that sounded like 'Cheese,' although that could've been my imagination. I caught a glimpse of Sobek, or possibly another crocodile god, snarling in the shadows. But no one raised a challenge.

Horus took his seat on the throne. Isis brought him a crook and flail—the twin scepters of the pharaohs. He crossed them over his chest and all the gods bowed before him.

When they'd risen again, Isis stepped toward us. 'Carter and Sadie Kane, you have done much to restore Ma'at. The gods must gather their strength, and you have bought us time, though we do not know how much. Apophis will not stay locked away forever.'

'I'd settle for a few hundred years,' Sadie said.

Isis smiled. 'However that may be, today you are heroes. The gods owe you a debt, and we take our debts seriously.'

Horus rose from the throne. With a wink at me, he knelt before us. The other gods shifted uncomfortably, but then followed his example. Even the gods in fire form dimmed their flames.

I probably looked pretty stunned, because when Horus got up again he laughed. 'You look like that time when Zia told you—'

'Yeah, could we skip that?' I said quickly. Letting a god into your head has serious disadvantages.

'Go in peace, Carter and Sadie,' Horus said. 'You will find our gift in the morning.'

'Gift?' I asked nervously, because if I got one more magic amulet, I was going to break out in a cold sweat.

'You'll see,' Isis promised. 'We will be watching you, and waiting.'

'That's what scares me,' Sadie said.

Isis waved her hand, and suddenly we were back on the mansion's terrace as if nothing had happened.

Sadie turned toward me wistfully. ' "Stimulating." '

I held out my hand. The *djed* amulet was glowing and warm in its linen wrapping. 'Any idea what this thing does?'

She blinked. '*Hmm?* Oh, don't care. What did Anubis look like to you?'

'What did . . . he looked like a guy. So?'

'A good-looking guy, or a slobbering dog-headed guy?'

'I guess . . . not the dog-headed guy.'

'I knew it!' Sadie pointed at me as if she'd won an argument. 'Good-looking. I knew it!'

And with a ridiculous grin, she spun around and skipped into the house.

My sister, as I may have mentioned, is a little strange.

*   *   *

The next day, we got the gods' gift.

We woke to find that the mansion had been completely repaired down to the smallest detail. Everything we hadn't finished yet—probably another month's worth of work—was done.

The first thing I found were new clothes in my closet, and after a moment's hesitation, I put them on. I went downstairs and found Khufu and Sadie dancing around the restored Great Room. Khufu had a new Lakers jersey and a brand-new basketball. The magical brooms and mops were busy doing their cleaning routine. Sadie looked up

481

at me and grinned—and then her expression changed to shock.

'Carter, what—what are you *wearing*?'

I came down the stairs, feeling even more self-conscious. The closet had offered me several choices this morning, not just my linen robes. My old clothes had been there, freshly cleaned—a button-down shirt, starched khaki slacks, loafers. But there had also been a third choice, and I'd taken it: some Reeboks, blue jeans, a T-shirt, and a hoodie.

'It's, *um,* all cotton,' I said. 'Okay for magic. Dad would probably think I look like a gangster . . .'

I thought for sure Sadie would tease me about that, and I was trying to beat her to the punch. She scrutinized every detail of my outfit.

Then she laughed with absolute delight. 'It's brilliant, Carter. You look almost like a regular teenager! And *Dad* would think . . .' She pulled my hoodie over my head. 'Dad would think you look like an impeccable magician, because that's what you are. Now, come on. Breakfast is waiting on the patio.'

We were just digging in when Amos came outside, and his change of clothes was even more surprising than mine. He wore a crisp new chocolate-colored suit with matching coat and fedora. His shoes were shined, his round glasses polished, his hair freshly braided with amber beads. Sadie and I both stared at him.

'What?' he demanded.

'Nothing,' we said in unison. Sadie looked at me and mouthed *O-M-G,* then went back to her bangers and eggs. I attacked my pancakes. Philip thrashed around happily in his swimming pool.

Amos joined us at the table. He flicked his fingers and coffee magically filled his cup. I raised my eyebrows. He hadn't used magic since the Demon Days.

'I thought I'd go away for a while,' he announced. 'To the First Nome.'

Sadie and I exchanged glances.

'Are you sure that's a good idea?' I asked.

Amos sipped his coffee. He stared across the East River as if he could see all the way to Washington, D.C. 'They have the best magic healers there. They will not turn away a petitioner seeking aid—even me. I think . . . I think I should try.'

His voice was fragile, like it would crack apart any moment. But still, it was the most he'd said in weeks.

'I think that's brilliant,' Sadie offered. 'We'll watch after the place, won't we, Carter?'

'Yeah,' I said. 'Absolutely.'

'I may be gone for a while,' Amos said. 'Treat this as your home. It *is* your home.' He hesitated, as if choosing his next words carefully. 'And I think, perhaps, you should start recruiting. There are many children around the world with the blood of the pharaohs. Most do not know what they are. What you two said in Washington—about rediscovering the path of the gods—it may be our only chance.'

Sadie got up and kissed Amos on the forehead. 'Leave it to us, Uncle. I've got a plan.'

'That,' I said, 'sounds like very bad news.'

Amos managed a smile. He squeezed Sadie's hand, then got up and ruffled my hair as he headed inside.

I took another bite of my pancakes and wondered why—on such a great morning—I still felt sad, and a little incomplete. I suppose with so many things suddenly getting better, the things that were still missing hurt even worse.

Sadie picked at her scrambled eggs. 'I suppose it would be selfish to ask for more.'

I stared at her, and I realized we were thinking the same thing. When the gods had said a gift . . . Well, you can hope for things, but as Sadie said, I guess you can't get greedy.

'It's going to be hard to travel if we need to go recruiting,' I said cautiously. 'Two unaccompanied minors.'

Sadie nodded. 'No Amos. No responsible adult. I don't think Khufu counts.'

And that's when the gods completed their gift.

A voice from the doorway said, 'Sounds like you have a job opening.'

I turned and felt a thousand pounds of grief drop from my shoulders. Leaning against the door in a leopard-spotted jumpsuit was a dark-haired lady with golden eyes and two very large knives.

'Bast!' Sadie cried.

The cat goddess gave us a playful smile, as if she had all kinds of trouble in mind. 'Someone call for a chaperone?'

*   *   *

A few days later, Sadie had a long phone conversation with Gran and Grandpa Faust in London. They didn't ask to talk to me, and I didn't listen in. When Sadie came back down to the

Great Room, she had a faraway look in her eyes. I was afraid—*very* afraid—that she was missing London.

'Well?' I asked reluctantly.

'I told them we were all right,' she said. 'They told me the police have stopped bothering them about the explosion at the British Museum. Apparently the Rosetta Stone turned up unharmed.'

'Like magic,' I said.

Sadie smirked. 'The police decided it might've been a gas explosion, some sort of accident. Dad's off the hook, as are we. I could go home to London, they said. Spring term starts in a few weeks. My mates Liz and Emma have been asking about me.'

The only sound was the crackle of fire in the hearth. The Great Room suddenly seemed bigger to me, emptier.

At last I said, 'What did you tell them?'

Sadie raised an eyebrow. 'God, you're thick sometimes. What do you think?'

'Oh.' My mouth felt like sandpaper. 'I guess it'll be good to see your friends and get back your old room, and—'

Sadie punched my arm. 'Carter! I told them I couldn't very well go home, because I already *was* home. This is where I belong. Thanks to the Duat, I can see my friends whenever I want. And besides, you'd be lost without me.'

I must've grinned like a fool, because Sadie told me to wipe the silly look off my face—but she sounded pleased about it. I suppose she knew she was right, for once. I would've been lost without her. [And no, Sadie, I can't believe I just said that either.]

*　　　*　　　*

Just when things were settling down to a nice safe routine, Sadie and I embarked on our new mission. Our destination was a school that Sadie had seen in a dream. I won't tell you which school, but Bast drove us a long way to get there. We recorded this tape along the way. Several times the forces of chaos tried to stop us. Several times we heard rumors that our enemies were starting to hunt down other descendants of the pharaohs, trying to thwart our plans.

We got to the school the day before the spring term started. The hallways were empty, and it was easy to slip inside. Sadie and I picked a locker at random, and she told me to set the combination. I summoned some magic and mixed around the numbers: 13/32/33. Hey, why mess with a good formula?

Sadie said a spell and the locker began to glow. Then she put the package inside and closed the door.

'Are you sure about this?' I asked.

She nodded. 'The locker is partially in the Duat. It'll store the amulet until the right person opens it.'

'But if the *djed* falls into the wrong hands—'

'It won't,' she promised. 'The blood of the pharaohs is strong. The right kids will find the amulet. If they figure out how to use it, their powers should awaken. We have to trust that the gods will guide them to Brooklyn.'

'We won't know how to train them,' I argued.

486

'No one has studied the path of the gods for two thousand years.'

'We'll figure it out,' Sadie said. 'We have to.'

'Unless Apophis gets us first,' I said. 'Or Desjardins and the House of Life. Or unless Set breaks his word. Or a thousand other things go wrong.'

'Yes,' Sadie said with a smile. 'Be fun, eh?'

We locked the locker and walked away.

Now we're back at the Twenty-first Nome in Brooklyn.

We're going to send out this tape to a few carefully chosen people and see if it gets published. Sadie believes in fate. If the story falls into your hands, there's probably a reason. Look for the *djed*. It won't take much to awaken your power. Then the trick is learning to use that power without dying.

As I said at the beginning: the whole story hasn't happened yet. Our parents promised to see us again, so I know we'll have to go back to the Land of the Dead eventually, which I think is fine with Sadie, as long as Anubis is there.

Zia is out there somewhere—the real Zia. I intend to find her.

Most of all, chaos is rising. Apophis is gaining strength. Which means we have to gain strength too—gods and men, united like in olden times. It's the only way the world won't be destroyed.

So the Kane family has a lot of work to do. And so do you.

Maybe you'll want to follow the path of Horus or Isis, Thoth or Anubis, or even Bast. I don't know. But whatever you decide, the House of Life needs new blood if we're going to survive.

So this is Carter and Sadie Kane signing off.
Come to Brooklyn. We'll be waiting.

AUTHOR'S NOTE

Much of this story is based on fact, which makes me think that either the two narrators, Sadie and Carter, did a great deal of research . . . or they are telling the truth.

The House of Life did exist, and was an important part of Egyptian society for several millennia. Whether or not it still exists today—that is something I cannot answer. But it is undeniable that Egyptian magicians were famed throughout the ancient world, and many of the spells they could supposedly cast are exactly as described in this story.

The way the narrators portray Egyptian magic is also supported by archaeological evidence. Shabti, curved wands, and magicians' boxes have survived, and can be viewed in many museums. All of the artifacts and monuments Sadie and Carter mention actually exist—with the possible exception of the red pyramid. There is a 'Red Pyramid' at Giza, but it is only called that because the original white casing stones were stripped away, revealing the pink granite blocks underneath. In fact the pyramid's owner, Senefru, would be horrified to learn his pyramid is now red, the color of Set. As for the magical red pyramid mentioned in the story, we can only hope that it has been destroyed.

Should further recordings fall into my hands, I will relay the information. Until then, we can only hope that Carter and Sadie are wrong in their predictions about the rise of chaos . . . .